For Ann

Acknowledgments

Thanks to Phil Athans, my editor,
and to Bob Salvatore for overseeing this project.

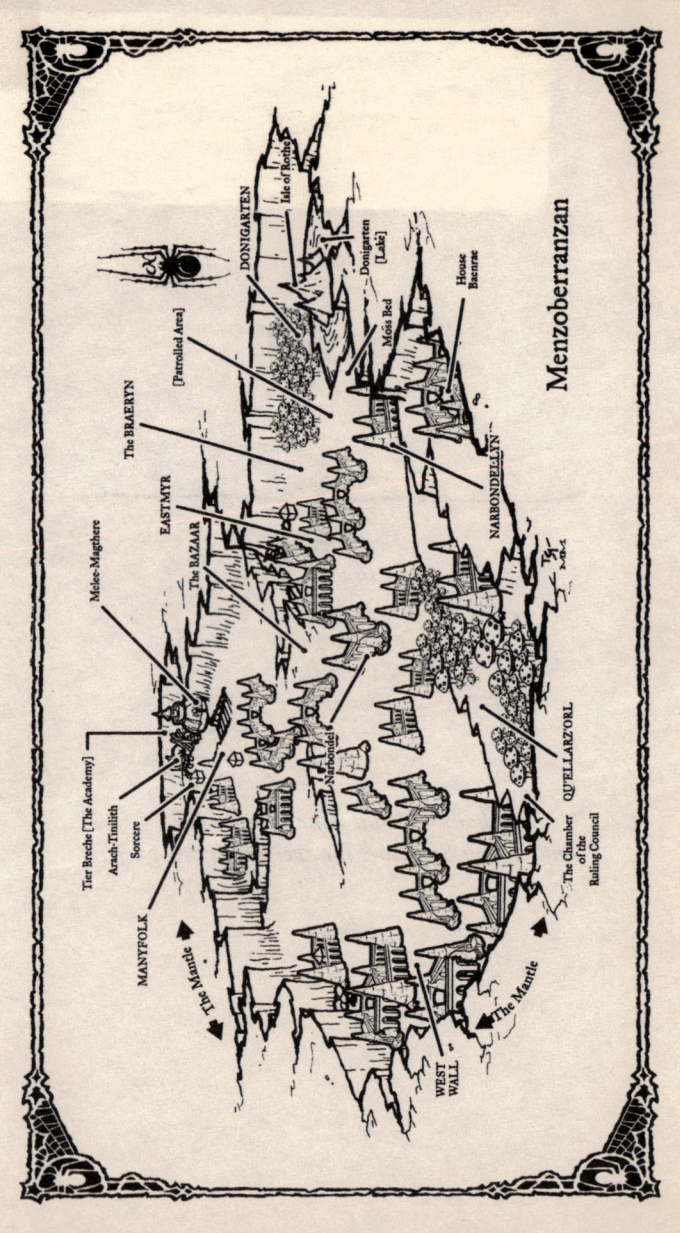

Menzoberranzan

DONIGARTEN

Isle of Rothé

Donigarten [Lake]

Móis Bed

House Baenre

[Patrolled Area]

The BRAERYN

NARBONDELLYN

EASTMYR

The BAZAAR

Melee-Magthere

Narbondel

Q'XELLARZORL

Tier Breche [The Academy]

Arach-Tinilith

Sorcere

The Chamber of the Ruling Council

MANYFOLK

The Mantle

WEST WALL

The Mantle

In the Mind of a Dark Elf

Evil, like chaos, is one of the fundamental forces of Creation, manifest in both the macrocosm of the wide world and the microcosm of the individual soul. As chaos gives rise to possibility and imagination, so evil engenders strength and will. It makes sentient beings aspire to wealth and power. It enables them to subjugate, kill, rob, and deceive. It allows them to do whatever is required to better themselves with never a crippling flicker of remorse.

And They're Turning on Each Other

❦   ❦   ❦

R.A. Salvatore's
WAR OF THE SPIDER QUEEN

R.A. Salvatore's
WAR OF THE SPIDER QUEEN BOOK 1

Dissolution

RICHARD LEE BYERS

R. A. SALVATORE'S

War of the Spider Queen Book 1: Dissolution

Distributed in the United States by Holtzbrinck Publishing. Distributed in Canada by Fenn Ltd.

Distributed to the hobby, toy, and comic trade in the United States and Canada by regional distributors.

Distributed worldwide by Wizards of the Coast, Inc. and regional distributors.

Cover art by Brom
First Printing: July 2002
First Paperback Edition: August 2003
Library of Congress Catalog Card Number: 2002114366

9 8 7 6 5 4

US ISBN: 0-7869-2944-8
UK ISBN: 0-7869-2945-6
620-17879-001-EN

U.S., CANADA,
ASIA, PACIFIC, & LATIN AMERICA
Wizards of the Coast, Inc.
P.O. Box 707
Renton, WA 98057-0707
+1-800-324-6496

EUROPEAN HEADQUARTERS
Wizards of the Coast, Belgium
T Hofveld 6d
1702 Groot-Bijgaarden
Belgium
+322 467 3360

Visit our website at **www.wizards.com**

It was a flicker of clarity in the foggy realm of shadowy chaos, where nothing was quite what it seemed, and everything was inevitably more treacherous and dangerous. But this, the crystalline glimmer of a single silken strand, shone brightly, caught her eye, and showed her all that it was and all that would soon be, and all that she was and all that she would soon be.

The glimmer of light in the dark Abyss promised renewal and greater glory and made that promise all the sweeter with its hints of danger, mortal danger for a creature immortal by nature. That, too, was the allure, was, in truth, the greatest joy of the growth. The mother of chaos was fear, not evil, and the enjoyment of chaos was the continual fear of the unknown, the shifting foundation of everything, the knowledge that every twist and turn could lead to disaster.

It was something the drow had never come to fully understand and appreciate, and she preferred that ignorance. To the drow, the chaos was a means for personal gain; there were no straight ladders in the tumult of drow life for one to climb. But the beauty was not the ascent, she knew, if they did not. The beauty was the moment, every moment, of living in the swirl of the unknown, the whirlpool of true chaos.

So this, then, was a movement forward, but within that movement, it was a gamble, a risk that could launch the chaos of her world to greater heights and surprises. She wished she could remain more fully conscious to witness it all, to bask in it all.

But no matter. Even within, she would feel the pleasure of their fear, the hunger of their ambition.

That glimmer of the silk edge, cutting the gray perpetual fog of the swirling plane, brought a singular purpose to this creature of shifting whims and reminded her that it was time, was past time.

Never taking her gaze off that glimmer, the creature turned slowly, winding herself in the single strand. The first strand of millions.

The start of the metamorphosis, the promise.

chapter

O N E

Gromph Baenre, Archmage of Menzoberranzan, flicked a long, obsidian-skinned finger. His office door, a black marble rectangle incised all over with lines of tiny runes, swung noiselessly shut and locked itself.

At least certain that no one could see him, the drow wizard rose from the white bone desk, faced the back wall, and swirled his hands in a complex pattern. A second doorway opened in the stippled calcite surface.

His dark elf vision unimpaired by the lack of light, Gromph stepped into the blackness beyond the new exit. There was no floor there to receive his tread, and for a moment he fell, then he invoked the power of levitation granted by the House Baenre insignia brooch that he was never without. He began to rise, floating up a featureless shaft. The cool air tingled and prickled against his skin as it always did, and it also carried a rank, unpleasant smell. Evidently one of the creatures native to this peculiar pseudoplane of existence had been nosing around the conduit.

Sure enough, something rattled above his head. The rank smell was suddenly stronger, pungent enough to make his scarlet eyes water and sting his nose.

Gromph looked up. At first he saw nothing, but then he discerned a vague ovoid shape in the darkness.

The archmage wondered how the beast had gotten inside the shaft. Nothing ever had before. Had it torn a hole in the wall, oozed through like a ghost, or done something stranger still? Perhaps—

It plummeted at him, putting an end to his speculations.

Gromph could have effortlessly blasted the creature with one of his wands, but he preferred to conserve their power for genuine threats. Instead, he coolly dismissed the force of levitation lifting his body and allowed himself to drop back down the shaft. The fall would keep him away from the beast for long enough to cast a spell, and he didn't have to worry about hitting the ground. In this reality, there was no ground.

The bejeweled and sigil-adorned Robes of the Archmage flapping around him, he snatched a vial of venom from his pocket, set it alight with a spurt of flame from his fingertip, and recited an incantation. On the final syllable, he thrust his arm at the creature, and a glob of black, burning liquid erupted from his fingertips.

Propelled by magic, the blazing fluid hurtled straight up the shaft to splash against the descending predator. The creature emitted a piercing buzz that was likely a cry of pain. It floundered in the air, bouncing back and forth against the walls as it fell. Its body sizzled and bubbled as the spattered acid ate into it, but it resumed diving in a controlled manner.

Gromph was mildly impressed. A venom bolt would kill most creatures, certainly most of the petty vermin one encountered in the empty places between the worlds.

Manipulating an empty cocoon, he cast another spell. The beast's body crumpled and folded into itself, and for a heartbeat, it was a helplessly tumbling mouse—then it swelled and rippled back into its natural form.

All right, thought Gromph, then I'll cut you up.

He prepared to conjure a hail of blades, but at that moment, the creature accelerated.

Gromph had no idea the creature could descend any faster than it had hitherto, and he wasn't prepared for the sudden burst of speed. The creature closed the distance between them in an instant, until it was hovering right in his face.

It had the melted or unfinished look common to many such beings. Rows of blank little eyes and a writhing proboscis sat off center in its bump of a head, only vaguely differentiated from its rubbery blob of a body. The monster possessed no wings, but it was flying—the goddess only knew how. Its legs were the most articulate part of it. Ten thin, segmented members terminated in barbed hooks, which lashed at Gromph again and again and again.

As he expected, the frenzied scratching failed to harm him. The enchantments woven into Gromph's *piwafwi*—not to mention a ring and an amulet—armored him at least as well as a suit of plate. Still, it irked him that he had allowed the beast to get so close, and he felt more irritated still when he noticed that the creature's exertions were flinging tiny smoking droplets of his own conjured acid onto his person.

He growled a final spell and snatched hold of the malodorous predator, seizing handfuls of the blubber on its torso. Instantly the magic began its work. Strength and vitality flowed into him, and he cried out at the shocking pleasure of it.

He was drinking his adversary's very life, much as a vampire might have done. The flying creature buzzed, thrashed, and became still. It withered, cracked, and rotted in his grasp. Finally, when he was certain he'd sucked out every vestige of life, he shoved it away.

Focusing his will, he arrested his fall and drifted upward again. After a few minutes, he spied the opening at the top of the shaft. He floated through, grabbed a convenient handrail, pulled himself over onto the floor of the workroom, then allowed his weight to return. His vestments rustled as they settled around him.

The large circular chamber was in most respects a part of the tower of Sorcere—the school of wizardry over which the Archmage presided—but Gromph was reasonably certain that none of the masters of Sorcere suspected its existence, accustomed to secret and magical architecture though they were. The place, lit by everlasting candles like the office below, was well nigh undetectable, even unguessable, because its tenant had set it a little apart from normal space and conventional time. In some subtle respects it existed in the distant past, in the days of Menzoberra the Kinless, founder of the city, and in another way, in the remote and unknowable future. Yet on the level of gross mortal existence, it sat firmly in the present, and Gromph could work his most clandestine magic there secure in the knowledge that it would affect the Menzoberranzan of today. It was a neat trick, and sometimes he almost regretted killing the seven prisoners, master mages all, who had helped him build the place in exchange, they imagined, for their freedom. They had been genuine artists, but there was no point in creating a hidden refuge unless one ensured it would remain hidden.

Dusting a few specks and smears of the flying vermin from his nimble hands, Gromph moved to the section of the room containing an extensive collection of wizard's tools. Humming, he selected a spiral-carved ebony staff from a wyvern's-foot stand, an onyx-studded iron amulet from its velvet-lined box, and a wickedly curved athame from a rack of similar ritual knives. He sniffed several ceramic pots of incense before finally selecting, as he often did, the essence of black lotus.

As he murmured a invocation to the Abyssal powers and lit a brazen censor with the tame little flame he could conjure at will, he hesitated. To his surprise, he found himself wondering if he truly wanted to proceed.

Menzoberranzan was in desperate straits, even though most of her citizens hadn't yet realized it. In Gromph's place, many another wizard would embrace the situation as an unparalleled opportunity to enhance his own power, but the archmage saw deeper. The city had experienced too many shocks and setbacks in recent years. Another upheaval could cripple or even destroy it, and he didn't fancy life in a Menzoberranzan that was merely a broken mockery of its former glory. Nor did he see himself as a homeless wanderer begging sanctuary and employment from the indifferent rulers of some foreign realm. He had resolved to correct the current problem, not exploit it.

Except I am about to exploit it in at least a limited way, aren't I? he thought. *Give in to temptation and seize the advantage, even if so doing further destabilizes the already precarious status quo.*

Gromph snorted his momentary and uncharacteristic misgivings away. The drow were children of chaos—of paradox, contradiction, and perhaps even perversity. It was the source of their strength. So yes, curse it, why not walk in two opposite directions at the same time? When would he get another chance to so alter his circumstances?

He moved to one of the complex pentacles inlaid in gold on the marble floor and traced the tip of the black staff along its curves and angles, sealing it. That done, he swept the athame in ritual passes and chanted a rhyme that returned to its own beginning like a serpent swallowing its tail. The cloying sweetness of black lotus hung in the air, and he could feel the narcotic vapors lifting his consciousness into a state of almost painful concentration and lucidity.

He lost all track of time, had no idea whether he'd been reciting for ten minutes or an hour, but the moment finally came when he'd recited long enough. The netherspirit Beradax appeared in the center of the pentacle, seeming to jerk up out of the floor like a fish at the end of an angler's line.

His centuries of wizardry had rendered Gromph about as indifferent to ugliness and grotesquerie as a member of his callous race could get, yet even he found Beradax an unpleasant spectacle. The creature wore the approximate shape of a dark elf female or perhaps a human woman, but her body was made of soft, wet, glistening eyeballs adhering together. About half of them had the crimson irises characteristic of the drow, while the rest were blue, brown, green, gray—a miscellany of the colors commonly found in lesser races.

Her body flowing, her shape warping, Beradax flung herself at her summoner. Fortunately, she couldn't pass beyond the edge of the pentacle. She slammed into an unseen barrier with a wet, slapping sound, then rebounded.

Undeterred, she lunged a second time with the same lack of success. Her resentment and malice infinite, she would spring a million times if left to her own devices. Gromph had caught her, trapped her, but something more was needed if they were to converse. He shoved the ritual dagger into his belly.

Beradax reeled. The eyeballs comprising her own stomach churned and shuddered. A few fell away from the central mass to fade and vanish in the air.

"*Kill you!*" she screamed, her shrill voice unnaturally loud, her gaping mouth affording a shadowy glimpse of the eyeball bumps lining the interior. "I'll kill you, wizard!"

"No, slave, you will not," Gromph said. He realized the chanting and incense had parched his throat, and he swallowed the dryness away. "You'll serve me. You'll calm yourself and submit, unless you want another taste of the blade."

"Kill you!"

Beradax sprang at him again and kept springing while he pulled the athame back and forth through her abdomen. Finally she collapsed to her knees.

"I submit," she growled

"Good." Gromph extracted the athame. It didn't leave a tear in his robes or in his flesh, which was to say, the knife's enchantments had worked precisely as expected, hurting the demon rather than him.

Beradax's belly stopped heaving and shaking.

"What do you want, drow?" the creature asked. "Information? Tell me, so I can discharge my errand and depart."

"Not information," the dark elf said. He'd summoned scores of netherspirits over the past month, and none had been able to tell him what he wished to know. He was certain Beradax was no wiser than the rest. "I want you to kill my sister Quenthel."

Gromph had hated Quenthel for a long time. She always treated him like some retainer, even though he too was a Baenre, a noble of the First House of Menzoberranzan, and the city's greatest wizard besides. In her eyes, he thought, only high priestesses deserved respect.

His antipathy only intensified as the two of them attempted to advise their mother, Matron Mother Baenre, the uncrowned queen of Menzoberranzan. Predictably, they'd disagreed on every matter of policy from trade to war to mining and had vexed one another no end.

Gromph's animus intensified still further when Quenthel became Mistress of Arach-Tinilith, the school for priestesses. The mistress governed the entire Academy, Sorcere included, and thus Gromph had found himself obliged to contend with her—indeed, to suffer her oversight—in this one-time haven as well.

Still, he might have endured Quenthel's arrogance and meddling indefinitely, if not for their mother's sudden and unexpected death.

Counseling the former matron mother had been more an honor than a treat. She generally ignored advice, and her deputies were lucky if she let it go at that. Often enough, she responded to their suggestions with a torrent of abuse.

But Triel, Gromph's other sister and the new head of House Baenre, had, over time, proved to be a different sort of sovereign. Indecisive, overwhelmed by the responsibilities of her new office, she relied heavily on the opinions of her siblings.

That meant the archmage, though a "mere male," could theoretically rule Menzoberranzan from behind the throne, and at long last order all things to please himself. But only if he disposed of the matron's other counselor, the damnably persuasive Quenthel, who continued to oppose him on virtually every matter. He'd been contemplating her assassination for a long time, until the present situation afforded him an irresistible opportunity.

"You send me to my death!" Beradax protested.

"Your life or death are of no importance," Gromph replied, "only my will matters. Still, you may survive. Arach-Tinilith has changed, as you know very well."

"Even now, the Academy is warded by all the old enchantments."

"I'll dissolve the barriers for you."

"I won't go!"

"Nonsense. You've submitted and must obey. Stop blathering before I lose my patience."

He hefted the athame, and Beradax seemed to slump.

"Very well, wizard, send me and be damned. I'll kill her as I will one day butcher you."

"You can't go quite yet. For all your bluster, you're the lowliest kind of netherspirit, a grub crawling on the floor of Hell, but tonight you'll wear the form of a genuine demon, to make the proper impression on the residents of the temple."

"*No!*"

Gromph lifted his staff in both hands and shouted words of power. Beradax howled in agony as her mass of eyeballs flowed and humped into something quite different.

Afterward, Gromph descended to his office. He had an appointment with a different kind of agent.

🕷   🕷   🕷

As Pharaun Mizzrym and Ryld Argith strolled through the cool air, fresher than that pent up in Melee-Magthere, the latter looked about Tier Breche, realized he hadn't bothered to set foot outside in days, and rather wondered why, for the view was as spectacular as ever.

Tier Breche, home to the Academy since that institution's founding, was a large cavern where the labor of countless spellcasters, artisans, and slaves had turned enormous stalagmites and other masses of rocks into three extraordinary citadels. To the east rose pyramidal Melee-Magthere, where Ryld and others like him turned callow young drow into warriors. By the western wall stood the many-spired tower of Sorcere, where Pharaun and his colleagues taught wizardry, while to the north crouched the largest and most imposing school of all, Arach-Tinilith, a temple built in the eight-limbed shape of a spider. Inside, the priestesses of Lolth, goddess of arachnids, chaos, assassins, and the drow race, trained dark elf maidens to serve the deity in their turn.

And yet, magnificent as was Tier Breche, considered in the proper context, it was only a detail in a scene of far greater splendor. The Academy sat in a side cavern, a mere nook opening partway up the wall of a truly prodigious vault. The primary chamber was two miles wide and a thousand feet high, and filling all that space was Menzoberranzan.

On the cavern floor, castles, hewn like the Academy from natural protrusions of calcite, shone blue, green, and violet amid the darkness. The phosphorescent mansions served to delineate the plateau of Qu'ellarz'orl, where the Baenre and those Houses nearly as powerful made their homes; the West Wall district, where lesser but still well-established noble families schemed how to supplant the dwellers on Qu'ellarz'orl; and Narbondellyn, where parvenus plotted to replace the inhabitants of West Wall. Still other palaces, cut from stalactites, hung from the lofty ceiling.

The nobles of Menzoberranzan had set their homes glowing to display their immensity, their graceful lines, and the ornamentation sculpted about their walls. Most of the carvings featured spiders and webs, scarcely surprising, Ryld supposed, in a realm where Lolth was the only deity anyone worshiped, and her clergy ruled in the temporal sense as well as the spiritual one.

For some reason, Ryld found the persistence of the motif vaguely oppressive, so he shifted his attention to other details. If a drow had good eyes, he could make out the frigid depths of the lake called Donigarten at the narrow eastern end of the vault. Cattle-like beasts called rothé and the goblin slaves who herded them lived on an island in the center of the lake.

And there was Narbondel itself, of course. It was the only piece of unworked stone remaining on the cavern floor, a thick, irregular column extending all the way to the ceiling. At the start of every day, the Archmage of Menzoberranzan cast a spell into the base of it, heating it until the rock glowed. Since the radiance rose through the stone at a constant rate, its progress enabled the residents of the city to tell the time.

In their way, the Master of Melee-Magthere supposed, he and Pharaun were, if nowhere near as grand a sight as the vista before them, at least a peculiar one by virtue of the contrasts between them. With his slender build, graceful manner, foppish, elegant attire, and intricate coiffure, the Mizzrym mage epitomized what a sophisticated noble and wizard should be. Ryld, on the other hand was an oddity. He was huge for a member of his sex, bigger than many females, with a burly, broad-shouldered frame better suited to a brutish human than a dark elf. He compounded his strangeness by wearing a dwarven breastplate and vambraces in preference to light, supple mail. The armor sometimes caused others to eye him askance, but he'd found that it maximized his effectiveness as a warrior, and that, he'd always believed, was what really mattered.

Ryld and Pharaun walked to the edge of Tier Breche and sat down with their legs dangling over the sheer drop-off. They were only a few yards from the head of the staircase that connected the Academy with the city below, and at the top of those steps, beside the twin pillars, a pair of sentries—last-year students of Melee-Magthere—stood watch. Ryld thought that he and Pharaun were distant enough for privacy if they kept their voices low.

Low, but not silent, curse it. Ever the sensualist, the mage sat savoring the panorama below him, obviously prolonging his contemplation well past the point where Ryld's mouth had begun to tighten with impatience, and never mind that on the walk up, he'd admired the view himself.

"We drow don't love one another, except in the carnal sense," Pharaun remarked at last, "but I think one could almost love Menzoberranzan itself, don't you? Or at least take a profound pride in it."

Ryld shrugged. "If you say so."

"You sound less than rhapsodic. Feeling morose again today?"

"I'm all right. Better, at least, now that I see you still alive."

"You assumed Gromph had executed me? Does my offense seem so grievous, then? Have you never annihilated a single specimen of our tender young cadets?"

"That depends on how you look at it," Ryld replied. "Combat training is inherently dangerous. Accidents happen, but no one has ever questioned that they *were* accidents occurring during the course of Melee-Magthere's legitimate business. The goddess knows, I never lost seven in a single hour, two of them from Houses with seats on the Council. How does such a thing happen?"

"I needed seven assistants with a degree of magical expertise to help me perform the summoning ritual. Had I called upon full-fledged wizards, they would have joined the experiment as equal partners. They would have emerged from the ritual possessed of the same newly discovered secrets as myself, equally able to conjure and control the Sarthos demon. Naturally I wished to avoid such a sharing, so I opted to use apprentices instead."

Pharaun grinned and continued, "In retrospect, I must admit that it may not have been a good idea. The fiend didn't even require seven heartbeats to smash them all."

An updraft wafted past Ryld's face, carrying the constant murmur of the metropolis below. He caught its scent as well, a complex odor made of cooking smoke, incense, perfume, the stink of unwashed thralls, and a thousand other things.

"Why perform such a dangerous ritual in the first place?" he asked.

Pharaun smiled as if it was a silly question. Perhaps it was.

"To become more powerful, of course," the wizard answered. "At present, I'm one of the thirty most puissant mages in the city. If I controlled the Sarthos demon, I'd be one of the five. Perhaps even the first, mightier than dreary old Gromph himself."

"I see."

Ambition was an essential part of the drow character, and Ryld sometimes envied Pharaun his still-passionate investment in the struggle for status. The warrior supposed that he himself had achieved the pinnacle of his ambitions when he became one of the lesser masters of Melee-Magthere, for certainly he, born a commoner, could never climb any higher. From that day forward, he'd stopped peering hungrily upward and concentrated on looking down, to guard against all those who wished to kill him in hopes of ascending to his position.

Pharaun was a Master of Sorcere as Ryld was a Master of Melee-Magthere, but perhaps, being of noble blood, Pharaun really did aspire to assassinate the formidable Gromph Baenre and seize his office. Even if he didn't, wizards, by the nature of their intricate and clandestine art, maintained a rivalry that encompassed more than who was a master, who was chief wizard in a great House, and who was neither. They also cared about such things as who could know the most esoteric secrets, could conjure the deadliest specter, or see most clearly into the future. In fact, they cared so deeply that they occasionally sought to murder each other and plunder one another's spellbooks even when such hostilities ran counter to the interests of their Houses, severing an alliance or disrupting a negotiation.

"Now," Pharaun said, reaching inside the elegant folds of his *piwafwi* and producing a silver flask, "I'll have to turn my back on the Sarthos demon for a while. I hope the poor behemoth won't be lonely without me."

He unscrewed the bottle, took a sip, and passed the container to Ryld.

Ryld hoped the flask didn't contain wine or an exotic liqueur. Pharaun was forever pressing such libations on him and insisting that he try to recognize all the elements that allegedly blended together to create the taste, even though Ryld had demonstrated time and again that his palate was incapable of such a dissection.

He drank and was pleased to find that for a change, the flask contained simple brandy, probably imported at some expense from the inhospitable world that lay like a rind atop the Underdark, baking in the excruciating sunlight. The liquor burned his mouth and kindled a warm glow in his stomach.

He handed the brandy back to Pharaun and said, "I assume Gromph told you to leave the entity alone."

"In effect. He assigned me another task to occupy my time. Should I succeed, the archmage will forgive me my transgressions. Should I fail . . . well, I'll hope for a nice beheading or garroting, but I'm not so unrealistic as to expect anything that quick."

"What task?"

"A number of males have eloped from their families, and not to a merchant clan or Bregan D'aerthe either but to an unknown destination. I'm supposed to find them."

Pharaun took another sip, then offered the flask again.

"What did they steal?" asked Ryld, waving off the drink.

Pharaun smiled and said, "That's a good guess, but you're wrong. As far as I know, no one walked off with anything important. You see, it isn't just a few fellows from one particular House. It's a bunch of them from any number of homes, noble and common alike."

"All right, but so what? Why does the Archmage of Menzoberranzan care?"

"I don't know. He offered some vague excuse of an explanation, but there's something—several somethings, belike—that he's not telling me."

"That's not going to make your job any easier."

"How true. The old tyrant did condescend to say that he isn't the only one interested in the fugitives' whereabouts. The priestesses are equally concerned, but that emphatically did not make them want to join forces with Gromph. Matron Mother Baenre herself ordered him to drop the matter."

"Matron Baenre," said Ryld. "I like this less with every word you speak."

"Oh, I don't know. Just because Triel Baenre rules all Menzoberranzan, and I'm about to flout her express wishes . . . Anyway, the archmage says he can no longer investigate the disappearances himself. Seems the ladies have their eyes on him, but, lucky me, I am not so burdened."

"That doesn't mean you're going to find the missing males. If they fled the city, they could be anywhere in the Underdark by now."

"Please," said Pharaun with a grin, "you don't have to try to cheer me up. Actually, I'm going to start looking in Eastmyr and the Braeryn. Apparently some of the runaways were last sighted in those déclassé vicinities, and perhaps they linger there still. Even if they do intend to depart Menzoberranzan, they may still be making preparations for the journey."

"If they've already decamped," Ryld said, "you might at least find a witness who can tell you what tunnel they took. It's a sensible plan, but I can think of another. It's reckless to gamble your life when you don't even understand the game. You could flee Menzoberranzan yourself. With your wizardry, you're one of the few people capable of undertaking such a dangerous trek alone."

"I could try," Pharaun said, "but I suspect Gromph would track me down. Even if he didn't, I would have lost my home and forfeited the rank I worked my whole life to earn. Would you give up being a master just to avoid a spot of danger?"

"No."

"Then you understand my predicament. I imagine you've also figured out why I called on you today."

"I think so."

"Of course you have. Whatever it is that's truly transpiring, my chances of survival improve if I have a comrade to watch my back."

Ryld scowled. "You mean, a comrade willing to defy the express will of Matron Mother Baenre and risk running afoul of the Archmage of Menzoberranzan as well."

"Quite, and by a happy coincidence you have the look of a drow in need of a break from his daily routine. You know you're bored to death. It's painful to watch you grouch your way through the day."

Ryld pondered for a moment, then said, "All right. Maybe we'll find out something we can turn to our advantage."

"Thank you, my friend. I owe you." Pharaun took a drink and held out the flask again. "Have the rest. There's only a swallow left. We seem to have guzzled the whole pint in just a few minutes, though that scarcely seems possible, refined, genteel fellows that we—"

Something crackled and sizzled above their heads. Waves of pressure beat down on them. Ryld looked up, cursed, scrambled to his feet, and drew a dagger, meanwhile wishing he'd strapped on his weapons before stepping outside Melee-Magthere.

Pharaun rose in a more leisurely fashion.

"Well," he said, "this is interesting."

c h a p t e r

T W O

Scourge of vipers writhing in her hand, soft, thin gown whispering, Quenthel Baenre, Mistress of Arach-Tinilith, prowled about, glaring at the younger females standing huddled in the center of the candlelit, marble-paneled room. She always had a knack for striking fear into the hearts of those who displeased her, and these students were no exception. Some trembled or appeared to be biting back tears, and even the sullen, fractious ones refused to look her in the eye.

Enjoying their apprehension, Quenthel prolonged her silent inspection until it was surely on the verge of becoming unbearable, then she cracked the whip. Some of her startled pupils gasped and jumped.

As the five long black- and crimson-banded vipers that comprised the lashes of the whip rose twisting and probing from the adamantine handle, Quenthel said, "All your lives, your mothers have told you that when a student ascends to Tier Breche, she remains here, sequestered from the city below, for ten years. On the day you entered the Academy, I told you the same thing."

She stalked up to one of the students trapped at the front of the group, Gaussra Kenafin, slightly plump and round-faced, with teeth as black as her skin. Responding to Quenthel's unspoken will, the whip snakes explored the novice's body, gliding over its contours, tongues flickering. The Mistress of Arach-Tinilith could see Gaussra straining mightily not to recoil for fear that it would provoke the reptiles into striking.

"So you did know," Quenthel purred, "didn't you?"

"Yes," Gaussra gasped. "I'm sorry. Please, take the snakes away!"

"How impertinent of you. You and these others have forfeited the right to ask me for anything. You may kiss her."

The last statement was addressed to the serpents, and they responded instantly, driving their long fangs into cheek, throat, shoulder, and breast. Gaussra collapsed—fully expecting to fall into a seizure, mouth foaming, her own blackened incisors chewing her purple tongue.

Shaking from the sting of the bites, Gaussra sat on the floor, very much alive; her terror was apparent, her humiliation complete.

"You will return to your House," Quenthel said, relishing the look on Gaussra's face as the true meaning of that statement sank in. "If you come that close to my scourge again, the vipers will allow their venom to flow."

Quenthel stepped away from Gaussra, who scrambled to her feet and ran from the chamber.

"You all knew what was expected of you," she said to the rest of the novices, "but you tried to sneak home anyway. In so doing, you have offered an affront to the Academy, to your own families, to Menzoberranzan, and to Lolth herself!"

"We just wanted to go for a little while," said Halavin Symryvvin, who seemed to carry half of her insignificant House's paltry wealth in the form of the gaudy, gold ornaments hanging about her person. "We would have come back."

"Liar!" shouted Quenthel, eliciting a flinch.

Rearing, the whip vipers echoed the cry.

"Liar!"

"Liar!"

"Liar!"

In other circumstances, Quenthel might have smiled, for she was proud of her weapon. Many priestesses possessed a whip of fangs, but hers was something special. The snakes were venomous and likewise possessed a demonic intelligence and the power of speech. It was the last magical tool she'd crafted before everything turned to dung.

"Oh, you would have returned," she continued, "but only because your mothers would have sent you back or else killed you for shaming them. They have sense enough to cleave to the sacred traditions of Menzoberranzan even if their degenerate offspring do not.

"Your mothers wouldn't mind if I slaughtered you, either. They'd thank me for wiping clean the honor of their Houses. But Lolth desires new priestesses, and, despite all appearances to the contrary, it is remotely possible that one or two of you are worthy to serve. Therefore I will give you one more chance. You won't die today. Instead you will sever a finger from each of your hands and burn them before the altar of the goddess to beg her forgiveness. I'll ring for a cleaver and a chopping block."

Quenthel surveyed their stricken faces, enjoying the sickly, shrinking fear. She would enjoy watching the actual mutilations as well. The most amusing part might be when a novice had already cut one hand, and had to employ it, throbbing and streaming blood, to maim the other. . . .

"No!"

Surprised by the outburst, Quenthel peered to see who had spoken. The mass of would-be truants obliged her by dividing in the center, opening a lane to the willowy female standing in the back. It was Drisinil Barrison Del'Armgo, she of the sharp nose and green eyes, whom Quenthel had from the first suspected of instigating the mass elopement. Somehow the long-legged novice had smuggled a sizable dagger, more of a short sword really, into the disciplinary session. She held it ready in a low guard.

Quenthel reacted as would any dark elf in the same situation. She yearned to accept the challenge and kill the other female, felt the need like a sensual tension pressing for an explosive release. Either responding to her surge of emotion or else themselves vexed by Drisinil's temerity, the whip vipers reared and hissed.

The problem was that, despite Quenthel's assertions to the contrary, the students were not altogether devoid of importance. They were the raw but valuable ore sent to the Academy to be refined and hammered into useful implements. No one would fret over a few amputated pinkies, but the matron mothers did expect that, for the most part, their children would survive their education, an assumption the idiot Mizzrym renegade had already called into question. True, Pharaun had only lost males, but still, by any sensible reckoning, he had used up the school's quota of allowable deaths for several years to come.

At this juncture it would be a poor idea for Quenthel to kill any student, certainly a scion of the powerful Barrison Del'Armgo. Quenthel didn't want to stir up discord between the Academy and the noble Houses when Menzoberranzan already perched on the brink of dissolution.

Besides, she was a bit concerned that the other failed runaways might take it into their heads to jump into the fight on their ringleader's side.

Quenthel quieted the vipers with a thought, fixed Drisinil with her steeliest stare, and said, "Think."

"I have thought," Drisinil retorted. "I've thought, why should we spend ten years of our lives cooped up on Tier Breche when there's nothing for us here?"

"There is everything for you here," said Quenthel, maintaining the pressure of her gaze. "This is where you learn to be all that a lady of Menzoberranzan must be."

"What? What am I learning?"

"At the moment, patience and submission."

"That's not what I came for."

"Evidently not. Consider this, then. All the priestesses of Menzoberranzan are currently playing a game, and the object of the game is to convince others that nothing is amiss. If a student leaves Arach-Tinilith prematurely, as none has ever done since the founding of the city, that will seem peculiar, a hint that all is not as it ought to be."

"Perhaps I don't care about the game."

"Your mother does. She plays as diligently as the rest of us. Do you think she will welcome you home if you jeopardize her efforts?"

Drisinil's emerald eyes blinked, the first sign that Quenthel's stare was unsettling her. "I . . . yes, certainly she would!"

"You, a traitor to your House, your city, your sex, and the goddess herself?"

"The goddess—"

"Don't say it!" Quenthel snapped. "Or your life ends, and your soul is bound to torment forevermore. I speak not only as Mistress of Arach-Tinilith, but as a Baenre. You remember Baenre, Barrison Del'Armgo? We are the First House, and you, merely the Second. Even if you should succeed in departing Arach-Tinilith, even if your gross and uncouth dam should be so unwise as to accept you back into that hovel you Del'Armgo call a home, you will not survive the month. My sister Triel, Matron Mother Baenre, will personally attend to your destruction."

It was no less than the truth. There was no love lost between the two Baenre sisters, but when it came to maintaining the supremacy of their House, they supported one another absolutely.

Drisinil swallowed and lowered her eyes a hair. "Mistress, I mean no disrespect. I just don't want to mutilate myself."

"But you will, novice, and without any further delay. You really have no other option . . . and isn't it convenient, you already have a knife in your grasp."

Drisinil swallowed again, and, her dagger hand shaking a little, brought the blade into position to saw at her little finger. Quenthel thought the procedure might go easier if the novice walked a few steps and braced her pinkie atop the nearby table, but apparently she was taking "without any further delay" quite literally, and that was fine with the high priestess. In her imagination, she was already savoring the first slice when a blare like a sour note blasted from a hundred glaur horns split the air.

For an instant, Quenthel faltered, not frightened but disoriented. She had been told what this ugly noise was but had expected never to actually hear it. To the best of her knowledge, no one ever had.

The priestesses of Menzoberranzan enjoyed a complex relationship with the inhabitants of the Abyss. Some infernal entities were the knights or handmaidens of Lolth, and during worship were venerated as such, but on other occasions the clerics did not scruple to snare spirits with their summoning spells and compel them to do their bidding. Sometimes the creatures stalked the physical plane of their own volition, slaughtering any mortal who crossed their path, not excepting the drow, who were by some accounts their kindred.

The founders of the Academy had shielded Tier Breche in general and Arach-Tinilith in particular with enchantments devised to keep out any spirit save those the occupants saw fit to welcome. Countless generations of priestesses had deemed those wards impregnable, but if the ear-splitting alarm told true, the barriers were falling one by one.

The blare seemed to be coming from the south. The pleasures of chastisement forgotten, Quenthel ran in that direction past countless chapels, altars, and icons of Lolth in both her dark elf and spider forms; past the classrooms where the faculty gave instruction in dogma, ritual, divine magic, torture, sacrifice, and all the other arts the novices needed to learn. Their books, chalkboards, and whimpering, half-dissected slave victims forgotten, some of the teachers and students appeared on the brink of venturing out to investigate the alarm, while others still looked startled and confused.

The blaring stopped. Either the demon had given up attempting to force its way in, or else it had breached every single ward. Quenthel suspected the latter was the case, and when the screaming started, she knew she was right.

"Do you know what's breaking through?" she panted.

"No," hissed Yngoth, perhaps the wisest of the whip vipers. "The intruder has shielded itself from the Sight."

"Wonderful."

The echoing cries led Quenthel into a spacious candlelit hall filled with towering black marble sculptures of spiders, set there to make the temple's entryway as impressive as possible. The battered valves of the great adamantine double door in the curved south wall gaped crookedly, half off their hinges, affording a glimpse of the plateau outside. Several priestesses lay battered and insensible on the floor. For a moment, Quenthel couldn't make out what had caused the mess, then the culprit scuttled across her field of vision toward another hapless servant of Lolth.

The intruder was a gigantic spider bearing a close resemblance to the gleaming black effigies around it, and upon seeing it, Quenthel scowled at an unfamiliar and unwelcome pang of doubt.

On the one hand, the demon, if that was what it truly was, was attacking her pupils and staff, but on the other, it was a kind of spider, sacred to Lolth. Perhaps it was even her emissary, sent to punish the weak and heretical. Maybe Quenthel should simply step aside and permit it to continue its rampage.

It sensed her somehow, turned, and rushed toward her as if it had been looking for her all along.

Though many spiders possessed several eyes, this one, she observed, was exceptional beyond the point of deformity. The head behind the jagged mandibles was virtually nothing but a mass of bulging eyes, and a scatter of others opened here and there about the creature's shiny black bulb of a body.

Its peculiarities notwithstanding, the spider's manifest hostile intent resolved Quenthel's uncertainty in an instant. She would kill the freakish thing.

The question was, how? She did not feel weak—she never had and never would—but she knew it was scarcely the optimal time for her to fight such a battle. On top of any other disadvantages, she wasn't even wearing her mail tunic or *piwafwi*. She rarely did within the walls of Arach-Tinilith. For the most part, her minions feared her too much to attempt an assassination, and she had always been confident that she wouldn't need armor to disappoint any who did not.

As she backed away from the charging spider, her slim, gleaming obsidian hands opened the pouch at her belt, extracted a roll of vellum, and unrolled it for her scrutiny, all with practiced ease and likewise with a certain annoyance, for the magical scroll was a treasure, and she was about to use it up. But it was necessary, and the parchment was scarcely the only magical implement hoarded within those walls.

Rapidly, but with perfect rhythm and pronunciation, she read the verses, the golden characters vanishing from the page as she spoke the words. Dark, heatless flame leaped from the vellum to the floor and shot across that polished surface faster than a wildfire propagating itself across a stand of dead, dry fungus, defining a path that led from herself to the demon.

The black conflagration washed over the demon's dainty bladed feet. It should also have driven the many-eyed creature helplessly backward, but it didn't. The arachnid kept coming nimbly as before, which was to say, considerably faster than the best effort of a drow.

"The spirit has defenses against the magic!" cried K'Sothra, perhaps the least intelligent of the whip vipers and certainly the one most inclined to belabor the obvious.

Quenthel wouldn't have time to attempt another spell before the spider reached her, nor could she outrun it. She would have to outmaneuver it instead. Dropping the useless sheet of parchment, she turned and dived beneath the belly of one of the statues. Unless it had the power to shrink or shapeshift, the invader wouldn't be able to negotiate the same low space.

She slid on the floor, rubbing her elbows hot. One of the snakes cursed foully when its scaly, wedge-shaped head rapped against the stone. She rolled over and saw that she had only bought herself a moment. No, the demon couldn't slip under the statue but, clustered eyes glaring, it was rapidly clambering over the top of it. Up close, it had a foul, carrion smell.

Quenthel knew that if she permitted the spider to pounce down on her, the monster would hold her down and snip her apart with its mandibles. She sprang to her feet and swung her whip.

The vipers twisted in flight to bring their fangs to bear. Those poisonous spikes plunged deep and ripped downward, tearing gashes in some of the demon's bulging, clustered eyes before yanking free. The organs gushed fluid and collapsed, and the serpents thrashed in joy.

Quenthel could feel their exultation through the psionic link they shared, but she knew it was premature. The spider had plenty of other eyes, and the stroke had only balked it for an instant. It was still going to spring.

Though caught without certain of her protections, Quenthel was at least wearing the necklace of dull black pearls. She reached up, slipped one of the enchanted beads from the specially crafted fine gold chain, and threw it at the spider.

White light blazed around her, seemingly emanating from all directions at once. Thanks be to Lolth, this time her magic had an effect. The spider slipped and floundered. Encased in an invisible sphere of magical force it thrashed about in panic. The explosion had opened horrid sores that speckled the creature's body. Unfortunately, it seemed able to ignore whatever pain those wounds caused it and continued scratching at the restraining sphere. Blue-white sparks flashed at the tips of its feet, and Quenthel knew it was using more than brute force and panic to break free.

Speak to me, Quenthel thought, sure the words would be heard in the spider's mind. She felt a connection, but a tenuous one, perhaps attenuated by the sphere of force.

The sphere faded as Quenthel swung the whip again, trying to smash through the creature's hideous visage and into the brain that presumably lay behind it.

The spider sprang away as explosively as one of its tiny jumping cousins, arcing high and landing at the far end of the chamber behind a rank of sculptures. The spirit scuttled through the shadows, and even though Quenthel was watching intently, in another second she lost track of it.

Where are you? she sent.

The reply was a burst of anger from the creature no mere words could convey. Quenthel gave up trying to communicate with it, though if it was a servant of Lolth, it should respond to her.

"You could get out now, Mistress," said Hsiv, the first imp Quenthel had bound inside a whip viper. "From over there, it couldn't reach you before you run out the door."

"Nonsense!" she snapped. "The brute disrupted my Academy, threatened my person, and I will have my vengeance."

Infected with her anger, the banded vipers reared and hissed until she silenced them with a mental command.

One of the priestesses sprawled on the floor was moaning in pain. Quenthel stalked over to the spider's victim and kicked her in the head, silencing her instantly.

The drow high priestess had eliminated all extraneous sounds, but it didn't help her locate the spider. Save for the soft hiss of her own breathing, the chamber was silent.

Turning slowly, heart pounding, she inspected the arachnid effigies all around her. Did that jointed spindle of a leg just twitch? Did that head, coyly turned just enough that she couldn't quite get an adequate look at it, possess too many eyes? Had the figure on the right shifted a hair closer when she wasn't looking?

No, no, and no. It was just her imagination, trying to supply what observation had not.

She sniffed repeatedly, but that was no help, either. The spider's stink hung in the air, but it seemed no stronger in one direction than another.

Curse it, the demon had to be somewhere!

Yes, she realized, but it didn't have to still be on the floor, not if it could skitter up vertical surfaces like its smaller kindred.

Assuming the demon was clinging to the upper walls or ceiling it might have taken it a moment to shake off the shock of the flare and its ugly wounds, but surely it was creeping into the best position from which to leap down on its adversary.

Quenthel peered upward. The artists had decorated the shadowy highest reaches of the chamber as well. The ceiling was an octagonal web acrawl with painted spiders, providing splendid camouflage for the creature. If it was in fact crouching in their midst, she couldn't see it.

Still scanning the ceiling, the whip vipers keeping watch as well, she backed to one of the wall sconces and read the trigger phrase from another scroll, whereupon the candle flame leaped up and turned a roiling black. She put her arm into the darkfire, and her flowing gossamer sleeve caught instantly.

Though they were at the end of what was, thus far, the non-burning arm, the serpents hissed and coiled in alarm. Quenthel brought them to heel with a brutal thrust of her will. Feeling naught but a pleasant warmth, she silently commanded the darkfire. A portion of the magical stuff flowed down her arm and congealed into a soft, semisolid ball in her palm. She threw it, and her magic shot it up like a sling bullet to strike the ceiling fresco where it splashed into a great gout of murky flame.

Quenthel followed that first missile with a steady barrage. Where the darkfire had kissed it, the fresco began to burn with ordinary yellow flame, suffusing the air with eye-stinging smoke and a vile stink that was also a sickening, throat-clenching taste at the back of her mouth.

She was throwing blindly, but with the blaze above spreading, it shouldn't matter. Surely the spider wouldn't simply sit still and allow itself to burn. The fire ought to spur it into motion and thus into visibility.

Unless, of course, the spider wasn't really on the ceiling, which was a real possibility. Maybe it was actually hiding elsewhere. It might even be creeping up on her while she stared at the burning painting and the nervous vipers worried more about their proximity to a darkfire than about keeping watch.

No, her intuition had pointed her in the right direction. She spotted the spider as it gathered itself to spring down at her, and having flushed it out, she need only survive its renewed attack.

She dived from beneath its plummeting form and rolled, leaving a trail of black, burning scraps of cloth behind on the floor. The creature with its tattered, oozing eyes landed with a thump, its eight legs flexing to absorb the impact.

Quenthel scrambled up and backed away from it. Her whole gown was aflame, nearly her entire body shrouded in darkfire. She threw another ball of the stuff, which spattered on the demon's back and streamed down its flanks. To her delight, her magic affected it again. The spider too wore a mantle of shadowy flame, the heat rippling the air above it.

That meant it ought to drop, didn't it, or at least flounder about in helpless agony? The fire was surely damaging it, for Quenthel could smell its flesh charring even through the omnipresent reek of burning paint, but the demon turned and scuttled after her.

She aimed the next burning missile at the cluster of eyes that seemed in some indefinable way to constitute the very core of the thing. The spider did lurch and falter when the burning darkness splashed over the orbs, but only for a second, and it kept coming.

Unable to outrun it, hoping she'd at least softened it up a little, Quenthel shouted her goddess's name and lunged to meet it. Sheathed in darkfire, her whole body was a weapon and would burn the spider wherever it touched. Where the black flame on the monster's limbs was giving way to yellow, it could burn her, too, but not if she didn't let it. Their natural savagery overcoming their fear of fire, the whip vipers lashed and struck in a frenzy of bloodlust.

At first, swinging the whip, ducking and dodging, she kept herself clear of the spider's mandibles. She shifted left when she should have jumped right, and the razor-sharp pincers snapped shut around her.

They stopped short of piercing her flesh. Loath to clasp her blazing body and be seared thereby, the spider faltered for just an instant. Before it could muster the will to proceed, Quenthel struck a final blow.

The ophidian lashes crashed through the demon's charred and tattered visage and bit into what lay beneath. The spider jerked, froze, twitched two of its legs in a purposeless way, and the burning hulk of it slowly sank to the floor, just as Quenthel's spell elapsed and all the darkfire still crackling in the chamber winked out of existence.

She shouted in exultation. Equally ecstatic, only a little singed, the vipers danced at the end of the scourge. Everyone's good mood lasted just as long as it took for the Baenre priestess, clad primarily in smoke and ash, to turn toward the door.

Though she'd been far too busy to notice hitherto, at some point a number of teachers and students had evidently crowded into the space to watch the battle. They were watching Quenthel still, eyes wide, faces uncertain.

"It was a desecration," said Quenthel. "A mockery."

She stared at them with haughty expectation.

They peered back at her for a moment, then folded their hands and bowed their heads in obeisance.

Tall and lithe, the left side of her otherwise handsome face creased with an old battle scar of which, she recognized, she was rather foolishly proud, Greyanna Mizzrym entered her mother's presence dirty, sweaty, and still clad in her mail shirt. Greyanna knew Mother didn't like for her daughters and other chattels to come to meet with her fully armed, but she had an excuse. She'd just returned from an inspection tour of Mizzrym operations in Bauthwaf—"around-cloak," as the dangerous network of tunnels immediately surrounding Menzoberranzan was called—only to hear from a frantic functionary bearing the fresh marks of a whip of fangs that the matron mother wished to see her as soon as possible.

Actually, even knowing the articles likely wouldn't save her if things went horribly wrong, Greyanna rather liked having a justification to walk in on her parent with her mace in her hand and her shield on her arm. She couldn't think of any reason why Mother would have decided to kill her at this particular point in time, but one could never be altogether sure, could one?

Certainly not with Miz'ri Mizzrym, a female regarded even by other dark elves as excessively and capriciously cruel. She sat enthroned in her temple with all of *her* weapons and protections ready to hand, the six-headed whip and the purple rod of tentacles, the enchanted rings gleaming on her fingers. She might have been considered comely even by the exacting standards of her exquisite race, except that her mouth drew down in an ugly and all but perpetual scowl. She regarded her daughter's martial appointments coldly but without comment.

Greyanna lowered her head and spread her hands, offering the proper obeisance, and said, "Matron Mother. You wished to see me?"

"I wished to see you yesterday."

"I was off conducting family business." Of course, Mother knew that as well as she did. "We have to keep up with our duties even now. Especially now—as you yourself have observed on more than one occasion."

"Watch your insolent tongue!"

Greyanna sighed. "Yes, Mother. I apologize. I didn't mean to speak out of turn."

"See that you refrain from doing so again."

Miz'ri fell silent, perhaps to gather her thoughts, perhaps simply in an effort to rattle her daughter's nerves. Such petty, pointless attempts at intimidation were virtually a reflex with her.

Greyanna wondered if a servant had been instructed to fetch her a chair for the remainder of the interview. It didn't look like it. That was typical of her mother as well.

"Your brother Pharaun . . ." Miz'ri said at last.

Greyanna's eyes opened wide. "Yes?"

"I think it might finally be time for the two of you to get reacquainted."

The younger female held her scarred features calm and composed. It was rarely a good idea to show strong emotion to anyone, particularly Mother. If you showed her that something mattered to you, she would find a way to hurt you with it. Even so, Greyanna couldn't quite suppress a shiver of anticipation.

She and her twin sister Sabal had loathed one another from the cradle onward. Of course, in the noble Houses of Menzoberranzan, rivalry between sisters was expected and encouraged. Certainly Miz'ri encouraged it, perhaps simply for her own amusement. But for some reason—perhaps it had something to do with the fact that outwardly, they were identical—her daughters' enmity far transcended even her expectations. It was more bitter and more personal. Each yearned to injure and thwart the other for its own sake at least as much as to improve her own relative standing in the family.

All but choking on their loathing of one another, they fought a duel that lasted decades and encompassed every facet of their existence, and gradually, on every battlefield, Greyanna began to prevail. She sabotaged many of Sabal's plans to enhance the fortunes of House Mizzrym and found ways to take credit for those that succeeded. By secretly tainting some of the sacred articles in this very shrine, she ensured that her twin's public rituals would fail to produce even the feeblest sign that the Spider Queen found her worship acceptable. She sowed doubt about Sabal's competence and loyalty in the ears of everyone who would listen.

Over time, Greyanna rose to become her mother's most valued aide, while Sabal was seen as a dolt fit only for the simplest of tasks. She was forbidden the use of her family's more powerful magical artifacts, lest she break them or turn them to some ill-conceived purpose. From kin to slave warriors, any member of the household who might once have supported her aspirations shunned her as if she were diseased. At that point, Greyanna could have killed her easily, and she expected she'd get around to it eventually, but Sabal's misery was so satisfying that she put it off.

Put if off until Pharaun came home from Sorcere.

Before her little brother departed to Tier Breche, Greyanna had barely noticed him. Of course, you didn't pay attention to young males unless you were unlucky enough to be put in charge of them. They were the silent little shadows creeping about the house, cleaning, ever cleaning, straining to master their inherent magical abilities, and learning their subordinate place in the world, all under the impatient eyes—and whips—of their minders. As far as she could remember, Pharaun had been as cowed and pathetic as the rest.

The Academy transformed him into something considerably more interesting, though, to say nothing of dangerous. Perhaps it was mastering the formidable powers of wizardry, or maybe it was immersion in an enclave comprised entirely of males, but somehow he emerged from his schooling polished, clever, and bold, possessed of a sharp wit and glib tongue that frequently danced him up to the brink of chastisement and safely back again.

Amazingly, he threw in with Sabal, who had all but abandoned hope of ever climbing higher than her current degraded estate. To this day, Greyanna could only explain his decision by positing a perverse and unnatural bond between them, but whatever his reasons, with the help of Pharaun's ideas, advocacy, and magic, Sabal essayed new ventures, succeeded brilliantly, and began to scale the ladder of status once more. She did so more quickly than Greyanna could have imagined, and the family came once more to regard the twins as peers, equal in merit and promise. Accordingly, their private war resumed, even more vicious and murderous than before, but this time Sabal—say Pharaun, rather—proved a match for her.

Greyanna tried to break the stalemate by convincing Pharaun to change sides. She expected it to work, for after all, she and Sabal looked exactly alike and shared precisely the same prospects. Why, then, should the wizard not throw in with the stronger, shrewder sister who had risen to the top of House Mizzrym without his help? Think of the triumphs they could accomplish together! Though inwardly sickened by the prospect, she even smiled lasciviously and offered him the inducement she believed Sabal had given him.

Her brother laughed at her. It was at that instant that Greyanna came to hate him just as savagely as she did her sister.

Perhaps she owed him a debt for his cutting mockery. Conceivably, it goaded her to new heights of ingenuity, for it was shortly afterward that she hit on the stratagem that would destroy Sabal.

A band of gray dwarves had been raiding in the tunnels southeast of the city, and Sabal was leading the force endeavoring to hunt the bandits down. Taking extraordinary measures, driving her agents, whether mortal, elemental, or demonic, relentlessly, Greyanna located the duergar in advance of her twin. Then came the hard part. She and her helpers had to abduct one of the slate-colored little males without the knowledge of his fellows, equip him with a platinum amulet that her subordinate clerics, mages, and her personal jeweler had created in an amazingly brief time, bind the marauder with spells of forgetfulness and persuasion, and slip him back among his friends.

Sabal found the duergar two days later. After her troops exterminated the brigands, they looted the bodies and found the brooch, which was valuable, beautiful, and, as those wizards who were present soon discovered, conferred several useful magical abilities. It never occurred to Sabal that a treasure plundered from a dead dwarf might constitute a trap laid by a sister dark elf, and she happily laid claim to that portion of the spoils.

From that day forward, Sabal slowly, subtly sickened in body, mind, and spirit, meanwhile struggling pathetically to hide any appearance of weakness from all who might discern it and decide to exploit it to kill her, torment her, or strip her of her rank. Which, of course, was pretty much everyone in Menzoberranzan.

Pharaun probably recognized her deterioration, but he was unable to arrest it. Perhaps he didn't even know she was constantly carrying an unusual new magical device about her person. The curse that was poisoning her, that lay insidiously threaded among all the benign enchantments, made her cling to the amulet with an obsessive fascination and fear that others would steal it if she didn't keep it hidden.

During the several months of Sabal's malaise, Greyanna sometimes wondered if Pharaun would ally himself with her if asked again. She didn't. She just watched and waited for her chance to finish Sabal off. She'd learned her lesson. No matter how unlikely the possibility seemed, she would not leave her twin alive to recoup her fortunes yet again.

One night, Pharaun left the castle, either on some errand or simply because he was finding the situation inside oppressive. Later on, the suspicious, insomniac Sabal somehow slipped away from her guards and servants and began aimlessly wandering the citadel on her own.

Greyanna and half a dozen of her minions confronted Sabal in the fungus garden, where the topiarist had trimmed the phosphorescent growths into fanciful shapes, fertilized in some cases with the ripe, diced remains of expired slaves. Sabal's final moments might have seemed pitiful, had Greyanna been susceptible to that crippling emotion. Her addled, desperate twin tried to use the platinum amulet against its maker, but Greyanna dispelled its powers with a thought. Then Sabal endeavored to cast a spell, but she couldn't recite the lines with the proper cadence or execute the gestures with the necessary precision.

Laughing, Greyanna and the other waylayers closed in on their victim, and they didn't even have to strike a blow. Their mere proximity made Sabal wail, clutch at her heart, and fall over dead as a stone. Weak to the last.

For a second, Greyanna felt a bit cheated, but she shook the feeling off. Sabal was dead, that was the main thing, and with a bit of luck, she would still have Pharaun to torture.

Chanting words that sent a cold, charnel breeze moaning through the garden, she reanimated Sabal's corpse. She had use for it, first as a lure then as an instrument of humiliation. She hoped that before his extermination, her brother might be induced to spend one more tender interlude with it.

When Pharaun returned to House Mizzrym an hour later, his hair and garments were as immaculate as ever, but he reeked of wine and walked with a slightly weaving and excessively careful tread. Evidently he'd been drinking his troubles away. Perfect.

As it had been instructed, the zombie stepped out of a doorway at the other end of the hall. Its arms were extended in a beseeching gesture.

Pharaun took a few steps toward it and faltered. Drunk or not, he had finally noticed that, despite Greyanna's efforts to keep it warm, it was moving stiffly, awkwardly, as Sabal, even in the throes of her illness, never had. But he'd spotted the anomaly too late. He'd already advanced to the very center of the trap.

Greyanna whispered a spell of paralysis. Pharaun staggered as his muscles all clenched at once. The fighters swarmed out of their hiding places, surrounded him, clubbed him repeatedly, and threw him down beneath them.

She laughed with delight. Then her henchmen, more or less clumped in a pile on the floor, cried out in surprise and consternation. They started to stand up, and she saw that Pharaun did not lie crushed, bloody, and helpless on the floor beneath them. Impossible as it seemed, somehow he'd resisted the paralysis, then used his wizardry to extricate himself from the midst of his attackers.

Knowing that Sabal was dead, Pharaun must likewise assume that without the aegis of a high priestess he could no longer survive in House Mizzrym. Certainly he couldn't count on his vicious mother, who hadn't bestirred herself to save one daughter from another, to do more for a paltry son. He was surely running back toward the exit.

"That way! Fast!" Greyanna shouted, pointing, goading her agents into motion.

When they rounded a corner, they saw Pharaun sprinting along ahead of them, his *piwafwi* billowing out behind him. He wasn't weaving or stumbling—evidently desperation had cured his intoxication—but he was clutching his head, and leaving a trail of bloody drops on the polished floor. Evidently all the bludgeoning had done at least a little good.

Greyanna's minions shot their hand crossbows, but the darts bounced off the wizard's cloak, which had obviously been enchanted to serve as armor. She stopped running long enough to conjure a blaze of fire under Pharaun's feet. Her assassins cried out and shielded their eyes against the glare. Though surely burned, her brother stayed on his feet and kept going. The flames winked out behind him as suddenly as they'd appeared.

The chase rounded another corner. Ahead of Pharaun was an adamantine double door, which swung open seemingly of its own accord. In reality, Greyanna knew, the wizard had used his silver-

and-jet Mizzrym House token to open it. She tried to use her own insignia to slam it shut again, but she was just out of range.

Pharaun plunged through the exit. He was on the landing, a sort of balcony from which the occupants of the stalactite castle that was House Mizzrym could look down on the city. As was the custom, a company of guards stood watch there, and Greyanna screamed for them to stop the mage.

They no doubt intended to be obey. She was a high priestess and he, a mere male, and manifestly trying to run away to boot. But alas, since their primary function was to look for miscreants trying to *enter* the castle, Pharaun had taken them by surprise. He had time to conjure some sort of hindering spell and dash on.

When Greyanna made it to the door, she saw what manner of hindrance the fugitive had chosen. The guards were all bewildered, some standing stupefied or milling aimlessly, a couple fighting with each other.

A clattering, followed a split second later by grunts and cries of pain, snapped her head around to the right. At the far end of the landing, a second contingent of sentries also looked at least temporarily incapacitated, these because Pharaun had pelted them with a conjured barrage of ice. He disappeared down the exit they'd been guarding, the winding crystal staircase, gorgeous with magical luminescence, which connected House Mizzrym with the cave floor below.

Greyanna felt a twinge of annoyance, but only that. Apparently she wasn't going to get a chance to torture Pharaun, but he was unquestionably going to die. He really had nowhere to run, and if the wretch weren't mired in a blind panic, he'd know it.

At least she could deliver the stroke that would seal his doom. She hurried to the edge of the landing, saw that the blistered, bloody-headed fool was better than halfway down the radiant diamond steps, and pronounced, as quickly as possible, the long, awkward arcane word that would make the staircase vanish. That alone wouldn't kill him unless he lost his head. The ability to levitate granted by the same brooch that allowed him to pass through the

House's doors would keep him from falling. Limited to strictly vertical movement, however, he ought to make an easy mark for spells and arrows.

She spoke the final syllable. Just as the steps seemed to pop like a bubble, Pharaun leaped, his long legs making him look like a pair of scissors spread to the maximum possible width. He barely made it onto the flattened apex of the gigantic stalagmite that served as the stair's lower terminus.

Greyanna was impressed. That jump was an impressive display of athleticism for a battered scholar of hedonistic habits. Not that it would do him any good. He really had run to the end of his race. She leaned out and shouted for the foulwings to kill him. Winded, still stumbling off-balance from hurdling across the empty space, Pharaun surely couldn't fend off both of them at once.

Grotesque winged predators that commonly reeked of their caustic ammonia breath, the foulwings bespoke the Mizzrym's power and magical prowess and lent the first step on the path to their citadel a certain style that mere soldiers could not match They also made terrifying watchbeasts. With a snap of their clawed, batlike wings, in no wise hindered by their lack of legs, they spun their long-necked bodies around to loom over Pharaun. Forked snouts with fanged jaws at the end of either branch came questing hungrily down. From her perch, Greyanna looked on with a rapacity no less keen than theirs, albeit a rapacity of the soul.

Pharaun shouted something. Greyanna couldn't quite make it out, but it didn't seem to be a magical word, just a cry of fear or a desperate plea for mercy—a plea the giant beasts would not heed.

Except that they did. They hesitated, and he lifted his hands. Their deadly jaws played delicately about his fingers, taking in his scent.

She cried again for the brutes to kill him. They twisted their heads around to look at her, but he spoke to them once more, and they ignored her command.

Greyanna stared in amazement. Pharaun had no doubt had some limited contact with the foulwings, for after all, he lived in the same castle with them, but she knew he'd never ridden one.

Only the females of House Mizzrym enjoyed that privilege, and it was only by riding that you established genuine mastery over the creatures. How, then, could he possibly enjoy a rapport with them deeper than her own?

Pharaun scrambled onto a foulwing's back, and both it and its fellow sprang into the air. Obviously her brother had managed to dissolve the enchantment that made the beasts want to sit contentedly at their post.

The wizard managed his mount more deftly than Greyanna herself could have done without benefit of saddle, bridle, and goad. He shot her a mocking grin as he turned to flee. The other, riderless foulwing soared and swooped aimlessly, enjoying its liberty.

Greyanna shook off her stunned disbelief. She still desperately wanted to know how Pharaun had learned to ride the creatures—probably Sabal had taught him, but how had they managed it without anyone else finding out?—but she wasn't going to stand there pondering the question. The answer was less important than the kill.

She turned and looked around. Those guards whom Pharaun had addled were disoriented still, but some of the soldiers he'd battered with hailstones appeared to have regained their composure.

"Shoot him!" she shouted, pointing at the rapidly receding target. "Shoot!"

With commendable haste, they obeyed. They took up their crossbows, aimed, and the bolts leaped forth in a ragged clatter.

Pharaun's foulwing lurched, then plummeted down and down and down, crashing to earth somewhere amid the hollowed stalagmite edifices of the city.

"Got him," said the captain of the guard.

Bigger and stronger than he, Greyanna had no difficulty knocking the male to the floor.

"You got the foulwing," she said. "We don't know that you hit Pharaun at all. We don't know that he didn't use his wizardry or his levitation to cushion his fall. We don't know that he isn't down there alive and well laughing at us. I need to see his corpse, and one way or the other, you will fetch it for me. Turn out every available priestess, wizard, and warrior—drow or slave. *Jump!*"

Jump he did. It was the last bit of satisfaction that was to come her way.

Her mortal agents flooded the streets, while she remained in her personal sanctum in House Mizzrym, summoning spirits and casting divinations to aid the search. Astonishingly, maddeningly, it was all to no avail. When light flowered in the base of Narbondel, signaling the advent of the new day, she was forced to admit that at least for the time being, Pharaun had eluded her.

A month later, she learned that her brother had somehow made his way all the way up to Tier Breche and begged the Archmage of Menzoberranzan himself for a place in Sorcere, and, remembering the wizardly talent the younger male had demonstrated throughout his training, Gromph had seen fit to take him in.

The news came as a considerable relief. She'd feared her brother had fled Menzoberranzan and placed himself permanently beyond her reach. Instead, he'd simply hopped up on a shelf above the city. He was bound to hop down again eventually, and she would have him.

Or so she thought, until her mother sent for her. Possessed of the same intelligence concerning her fugitive son's whereabouts, Miz'ri had formed a very different idea of what ought to be done about it: Nothing.

Even though they were only males, the Masters of Sorcere possessed both a degree of practical autonomy and an abundance of mystical power, and, always weaving her labyrinthine schemes to elevate the status of House Mizzrym, Mother had decided not to unnecessarily provoke the wizards. Which was to say, as Pharaun had obtained a place in that cloistered, many-spired tower, he was more significant in exile than he had ever been at home, and Greyanna would have to let him live. She had achieved what ought to have been her primary goal, preeminence among her sisters and cousins, but her vengeance would remain unfinished.

Through all the decades that followed, it galled her. A hundred times she planned to defy her mother's command and kill Pharaun anyway, only to abandon her stratagems just short of implementation. As fiercely as she hated him, she feared Miz'ri's displeasure even more.

Was it possible that at long last the matron mother had changed her mind? Or was this some new cruelty, was Miz'ri perhaps going to somehow force Greyanna into an odious proximity with a brother who was still untouchable?

"It might be nice to see Pharaun again," the younger female said in the blandest tone she could muster.

Miz'ri laughed. "Oh, I daresay it would, to see him and kill him, isn't that the way of it?"

"If you say so. You know our history. We played out the whole *sava* game under your nose." I imagine you relished every minute of it, she thought.

"Yes, you did, and so I know this will interest you. Sadly, a problem has arisen that even supercedes my desire to get along with the mages of the Academy. While you were away, males continued to desert—"

"Pharaun ran off from Sorcere?" Greyanna interrupted, her eyes narrowed. "Were they finally going to punish him for getting those novices killed?"

"No, and no! Shut your mouth, let me tell the tale, and we'll come to your little obsession in a moment."

"Yes, Mother."

"Males continue to elope, and despite our warning him off, Gromph still intends to investigate the matter. Hoping to escape our notice and displeasure, he decided to do so by proxy, and summoned a suitable agent to his office to discuss the matter. Happily, we members of the Council possess a scrying crystal with which we recently managed to pierce the obscuring enchantments shrouding the room. Some of them, anyway. We still can't see in, but we can hear what goes on, and that sufficed to reveal the archmage's plan as well as the identity of his minion. Now, if you must, you may excitedly babble your brother's name."

"I imagine Gromph told him this is his one big chance to redeem himself."

"Exactly. The question is, how shall we priestesses respond?"

"I gather there's a reason you don't just tell Gromph you're on to his plan."

"Of course, several. For one, our first confrontation with him was courteous and mild, but who knows, a second might be less so. As things stand, we hesitate to push him very hard. For another, we don't want him to know we can eavesdrop on him. He'd either block us out or hatch his plots elsewhere. It's better all around simply to take his pawn out of play. Given that Pharaun is a *secret* operative, whatever may befall him, the archmage can hardly take exception to it. The catch being that dealing with your brother is a formidable undertaking, arguably on any occasion but certainly at the moment."

Greyanna nodded. "Because he's a wizard, and we are . . . what we are."

"So where, the Council wondered, can we find a priestess so bold, so motivated, that even now she'll be eager to hunt the male when he descends to the city. I told the others I thought I knew of a candidate."

"You were right."

"The beauty of it is that you do have a personal score to settle. If people see you do something unpleasant to Pharaun, they won't have to wonder what the reason is."

"Yes, I see that. May I draw on all the resources of our House to aid me in my efforts?"

"I can only give you a few helpers. If people saw you descend on the city with House Mizzrym's entire army at your back, they wouldn't assume it's a personal matter. You can have your pick of magic weapons from the armory. Don't waste them, though. Expend only what you need."

Greyanna inclined her head. "I'll start preparing right away."

Miz'ri finally smiled, and somehow, in defiance of any reasonable expectation, it made her face more threatening, not less.

The Silken Rack was not, as visitors to Menzoberranzan sometimes assumed, a fine cloth emporium. It was, technically, a massage parlor, but only a vulgarian would call it that. Rather, it was a palace of delight, where the most skilled body servants in the Underdark provided what many dark elves considered to be most exquisite of all pleasures.

Waerva Baenre was herself of that opinion. She had already soaked her pampered, voluptuous form in warm, scented oil, and she would have liked nothing better to lose herself utterly in the touch of her masseur.

But that, alas, was not possible. She'd come to this shrine of the senses on business, business that could be conducted far more safely and discreetly there than in the Baenre citadel or the ambassador's residence in West Wall. That was why she, by nature gregarious, had hired a cozy private room containing only two contoured couches and a pair of hulking deaf-mute human masseurs in preference to her supremely gifted Tluth.

Happily, the tongueless slave she'd chosen for herself was also highly competent. He kneaded her neck muscles in a way that was pain and bliss at the same time, wringing a groan of sweet release out of her. Naturally, it was at this somewhat undignified moment that Umrae came though the door.

Not that Waerva's momentary discomposure made Umrae smile. The Baenre couldn't imagine what it would take to accomplish that. A rather gaunt, homely female, her skin the unhealthy dull gray-black color of charcoal, the cut of her nondescript garments subtly divergent from the styles of Menzoberranzan, Umrae always arrived at these clandestine meetings stiff and awkward with nervous tension. Waerva supposed that was the difference between commoners and nobles. No matter how perilous the situation, an aristocrat always managed a certain grace.

"She's looking at maps!" declared Umrae. Her voice matched her appearance. There was no music in it.

"I'm not surprised," Waerva replied. "Your mistress is reasonably clever. I never thought she would remain complacent forever." The body servant dug his fingertips into Waerva's upper back, and she shivered. "We'll talk about it, but first, please, set my mind at ease. Tell me that no one who matters saw you enter this particular room."

Umrae scowled, apparently irked by the very suggestion. "No, of course not."

"Then for pity's sake, take off your clothes. You supposedly came here for a deepstroke, and you want to look as if you've had one when you get back home. Besides, these fellows are worth the rent."

Still frowning as if she suspected Waerva was perpetrating some sort of joke at her expense, Umrae gestured brusquely to the human, slightly smaller and less muscular than his compatriot, whom the Baenre had left for her use. Careful not to make eye contact, the slave began to undress her and hang her garments on the hooks set in the wall.

"So what are we going to do?" the commoner asked. "She's guarded. Even with the resource you gave me, I'm not sure I could kill her and escape, but surely you have skilled assassins at your disposal."

"Of course." Waerva had to close her slanted ruby eyes as her body servant squeezed and rubbed another clenched muscle into warm, limp submission. It was remarkable how she didn't even realize they were tight until the masseur got his hands on them. "Murder would have its advantages. It would take her off the *sava* board for good and all."

"Then we're agreed?" Umrae asked as she lay down on her couch. Her body servant gently spread her mane of coarse white hair to expose the flesh beneath.

Waerva grinned. "You sound so eager."

"I admit I'm not fond of her." Umrae's human opened a white porcelain bottle of unguent, and a sweet scent tinged the air. "That's not the point. The point is to shield us all for as long as we need it."

"I quite agree," said Waerva, "and my concern is that an assassination could prove counterproductive. Might it not call attention to your mistress's suspicions? Might it not lend weight to them? Does she not have a deputy of like mind ready to take over in the event of her demise?"

Umrae scowled, pondering the questions, plainly not enjoying it much. Her slave spread a thin coat of amber oil onto her back.

From elsewhere in the building echoed the faint, distorted sounds of shouting, laughter, and splashing. Waerva guessed it must be males amusing themselves in one of the bathing pools. The females of the city were scarcely in the mood for boisterous horseplay.

At last Umrae said, "All right, what do you want to do?"

"Counter the threat in a subtler way. She can't injure us if she's never afforded the chance to confirm her suspicions."

"How will you ensure that?" Umrae's voice quavered as her thrall began to lightly pummel her gleaming back with the bottoms of his fists.

Good luck loosening up those petrified limbs, Waerva thought. "I am a priestess of the Baenre, am I not?"

"The least of them."

"How insolent of you to say so." Waerva tensed with annoyance until her masseur's hands rebuked her.

45

"I only meant—"

"I know what you meant, and I don't deny it. It's why I'm here, after all. Yet consider this: My aunt Triel has always depended on the advice of two people, Gromph and Quenthel. She can't really talk to Gromph anymore because she's keeping him in the dark with the rest of the males. I doubt she'll see much of Quenthel for a while, either. The tiny she-demon will stay busy contending with her own problems. She's endured some sort of mishap up on Tier Breche."

Umrae twisted her head around to look at her sister conspirator and said, "I've heard rumors about that. What actually happened?"

"I don't know—" Though I wish to the goddess I did, she thought—"but whatever it was, it works to our advantage. We want Triel to suffer a dearth of counselors."

"What about her magical new son? They say he accompanies her everywhere."

Waerva smiled. "Jeggred's not a factor. He's a magnificent specimen but scarcely a font of sage advice. I assure you poor, uncertain Triel will be absolutely frantic for plausible insights from other Baenre priestesses, even the lowlier ones like me. I will buy our friends the time they need to work free of outside interference."

"You will if Triel trusts you."

"In this, she will. We Baenre are proud. It will be inconceivable to Triel that one of our females would wish to abandon the First House in favor of a new life elsewhere. Of course, she wasn't born at the absolute bottom of the internal hierarchy, was she, with dozens of older sisters and cousins taking precedence over her and holding all the important offices. Even if I started recklessly trying to pick them off whenever one lowers her guard even slightly, it could still take me centuries to ascend to a position of genuine power within the family."

"All right, that makes sense. What will you tell her?"

"The obvious." Waerva sighed shakily as her human went to work on her sacroiliac. "For all we know, it may even be the truth."

"I suppose."

46

Umrae lapsed into a sullen silence. Her body servant's hands made slapping and sucking sounds as they played about her slick, moist, bony back.

"By the six hundred and sixty-six layers of the Abyss," said Waerva, "what ails you? If you're having seconds thoughts, the time for that is well past."

"I'm not. I want to be something better than milady's secretary. I want a surname. I want to be a high priestess and a noble."

"And you will. When your cabal crushes the established order, they'll reward me for my help by making me matron mother of a new but exalted House, whereupon I will adopt you as my daughter. Why, then, do you appear so morose?"

"I just wonder. This silence . . . is it really a boon for us, or a calamity? Are we seizing a great opportunity or madly rushing to our doom?"

How much better I'd rest if only I knew, thought Waerva.

"Let me ask a question," the Baenre priestess said. "Deep down in your heart of hearts, did you serve out of reverence or fear?"

"I served for power."

"Come to think of it," said Waerva, "I did, too. So let us seize the power that still sparkles within our reach."

"I—" Umrae moaned and curled her toes as her human finally managed to send a thrill of pleasure singing along her nerves.

Waerva thought it was a good sign.

Pharaun drank in the spectacle of the Bazaar. Born and raised a Menzoberranyr, he had of course visited this bustling place countless times before, but after several tendays of house arrest spent wondering if his life was at an end, it seemed rather wonderful to him.

Many of the stalls shone with light, be it phosphorescent fungus positioned to flatter the vendor's wares, magical illumination cast for the same purpose, or merely the incidental fallout of some other enchantment. The gleaming was never so fierce as to offend a dark elf's eyes, though. The citizens of the city wended their way through the aisles in the nurturing darkness that was their natural habitat, and what an interesting lot those citizens were.

A high priestess, from House Fey-Branche judging from the livery of her retainers, emerged from her curtained litter to inspect riding lizards with an eye as knowledgeable and a hand as steady as any groom's. A somewhat seedy looking boy, perhaps a disfavored son from one of the lesser Houses, engaged a cobbler in conversation while a confederate opened his voluminous mantle to slip an expensive pair of snakeskin boots inside. Male commoners, obliged to lower their eyes to every female and step aside for every noble of either gender, compensated by sneering and swaggering their way among the creatures less exalted than any drow. These latter were a motley assortment of beings—gray dwarves, the goggle-eyed fish-men called kuo-toas, and even a huge, horned ogre mage from the World Above—bold enough to trade or even dwell in a dark elf city. Lowliest of all, at least as numerous as the free but in their utter insignificance far easier to overlook, were the slaves. Orc, gnoll, and bugbear warriors guarded their masters and mistresses, harried, starveling goblins fetched and carried for the merchants, and little reptilian kobolds collected litter and hauled it away.

Pharaun knew from occasional errands there that if this hub of commerce had existed in one of the lands that saw the sky, it would have been exceptionally noisy. But the Menzoberranyr, to keep their cavern from roaring with a constant echoing clamor, had laid subtle enchantments about the smooth stone floor. Sounds close at hand were as audible as was natural, but those farther away faded and blended to the faint drone he and Ryld had heard while sitting on the brink of Tier Breche.

In the Bazaar, several of the magical buffers operated in close proximity to one another. To newcomers, the effect could be a little disconcerting as a single step sufficed to carry them from whispering quiet to raucous noise, the full volume of an auctioneer's shout or a piper's skirling.

Happily, no such enchantments existed to suppress the smells of the marketplace, a glorious olfactory tapestry redolent of spice, exotic produce imported from the surface world and, alas, a little past its prime, mulled wine, leather, burned frying oil, rothé dung, freshly spilled blood, and a thousand other things. Pharaun closed his eyes and breathed in the scent.

"This is always grand, isn't it?"

"I suppose," answered Ryld.

For his excursion away from Tier Breche, Ryld had tossed a *piwafwi* around his burly shoulders. The cloak covered his dwarf-made armor and short sword, and its cowl obscured his features, but no garment could have hidden the enormous weapon sheathed across his back. Ryld called the greatsword Splitter, and while Pharaun deplored the name as ugly and prosaic, he had to admit that it was apt. In his friend's capable hands, the enchanted weapon could with a single swing cleave almost anything in two.

Ryld looked entirely relaxed, but the wizard knew the appearance was in one sense deceptive. The Master of Melee-Magthere was reflexively scrutinizing their surroundings for signs of danger with a facility that even Pharaun, who regarded himself as considerably more observant than most, could never match.

"You suppose," Pharaun repeated. "Is that just your usual glumness speaking, or do you find something lacking?"

"I do," said Ryld. He waved his hand in a gesture that took in the diverse throng, the stalls, and the maze of paths snaking among them. "I think the Bazaar could use some order."

Pharaun grinned and said, "Careful, or I'll have to report you for blasphemy. It's chaos that made us, and made us what we are."

"Right. Chaos is life. Chaos is creativity. Chaos makes us strong. I remember the creed, but as a practical matter, don't you see that all this confusion could serve as a mask for the city's enemies? They could use it to smuggle their spies and assassins in and to smuggle stolen secrets and treasure out."

"I'm sure they do. That's certainly the way our agents operate in marketplaces elsewhere in the Underdark."

An orc female came scurrying through the crowd with her head down and a parchment clutched in her hand. Perhaps her master had threatened her with a whipping if she didn't deliver a message quickly. She tried to dodge through the narrow space between Pharaun and another pedestrian, misstepped, and bumped into the wizard.

The pig-faced slave looked up and saw that she'd just jostled an elegantly and expensively dressed dark elf. Her mouth with its prominent lower canines fell open in terror. With a flick of his fingers, Pharaun bade her begone. She turned and ran.

"Then the Council should control the Bazaar properly," said Ryld. "Don't just send the occasional patrol marching through to discourage thievery. License the merchants. Conduct routine searches of their pack animals, tents, and kiosks."

"From what I understand," said Pharaun, "it's been tried, and every time it was, the Bazaar became less profitable and wound up pouring fewer coins into the coffers of the matron mothers. I daresay the same thing would happen today. Regulation would also inconvenience all the Houses who are themselves running illicit operations hereabouts. I assure you, a goodly number of them do."

Pharaun should know. Before his exile from his own family, he and Sabal had played a substantial role in House Mizzrym's covert and highly illegal trade with the deep gnomes, or svirfneblin, arguably the deadliest of the dark elves' many foes.

"If you say so," said Ryld. "Not being a noble, I wouldn't know about things like that."

The wizard sighed. It was true, his friend was about as humbly born as a dark elf could be, but during his climb to his present eminence, he had perforce become fully acquainted with the ways of the aristocracy. It was just that at odd moments he took an obscure satisfaction in pretending to a peasantlike ignorance.

"Well, I rejoice that you remain so close to your roots," Pharaun said. "I'm counting on your familiarity with the slums to see me safely through my encounters with the lower orders."

"I've been wondering when that's going to happen. Shouldn't we have gone to Eastmyr or the Braeryn straightaway?"

"No point going there blind if we can acquire some intelligence first."

Pharaun supposed that in fact, they'd better collect it quickly, but it was a pity. He could have used some idle time drifting through emporia like, for instance, Daelein Shimmerdark's Decanter with its astonishing collection of wines, liquors, and, for those who knew how to ask, potions and poisons from all over the world. Perhaps it would clear his head.

Or maybe it would only give him another enigma to ponder, for though there was still plenty to buy, it seemed to him the Bazaar as a whole was offering fewer goods than usual. Why was that? Could it possibly have anything to do with the runaway males?

And what about the demon spider that had materialized above him and Ryld on the plateau and proceeded to break into Arach-Tinilith? Did that tie in, or was it simply a gambit in one of Menzoberranzan's innumerable secret feuds that had nothing at all to do with his concerns?

He had to grin. He knew so little, and what little he had gleaned was scarcely a source of reassurance.

"There it is," said Ryld.

"Indeed."

Carved from a long, relatively low protrusion of stone, the Jewel Box sat just inches beyond what custom decreed to be the limits of the Bazaar, where all traders were required to shift their stalls to a different spot every sixty-six days. Despite its lack of a signboard or other external advertisement, the establishment had always attracted a steady trickle of shoppers and merchants, and when the two masters descended the stair that ran from street level to the limestone door, Pharaun could hear considerably more sounds of revelry that usual. There was laughter, animated conversation, and a longhorn, yarting, and hand-drum trio playing a lively tune. The third string of the yarting was a little flat.

Ryld knocked with the brass knocker, whereupon a little panel slid open in the center of the door. A pair of eyes peered out, then disappeared. The portal swung open.

Pharaun grinned. In all his visits there, he had never seen anyone turned away, and he suspected the business with the peephole was just an agreeable bit of nonsense intended to make a visit to the Jewel Box seem even more piquantly criminal. Perhaps the doorman actually would attempt to dissuade a female if one had sought admittance.

The low-ceilinged room beyond the threshold smelled of a sweet and mildly intoxicating incense. The three musicians had crowded themselves onto a tiny platform against the west wall. A few of the patrons were attending to the performance, but most had elected to focus on other pleasures. At one table, half a dozen disheveled fellows tossed back their liquor simultaneously in what appeared to be a drinking contest. Other males threw daggers at the target on the wall with a blithe disregard for the safety of those standing in the immediate vicinity of their mark. Dice clattered, cards rustled and slapped, and coins scraped across tabletops as the luckier gamblers raked in their winnings.

Ryld studied his surroundings with his customary unobtrusive vigilance, surreptitiously cataloging every potential threat. Still, Pharaun was amused to see that his friend's eyes lingered on the web-shaped *sava* boards for an instant, which was likely all the time he required to analyze the four contests in progress.

Sava was an intricate game representing a war between two noble Houses—at least that was what it currently represented. Pharaun had seen an antique set that recapitulated in miniature the drow's eternal struggle with another race, but such pieces had gone out of fashion long before his birth, probably because no player had wanted to be the dwarves.

With its gridlike board regulating movement and its playing pieces of varying capacities, *sava* resembled games devised by many cultures, but celebrating the chaos in their blood the drow had found a way to introduce an element of randomness into what would otherwise unfold with a mechanical precision. Once per game, each player could forgo his normal move to throw the *sava* dice. If the spider came up on each, he could move one of his opponent's pieces to eliminate any man of its own color within its normal reach, a rule that acknowledged the dark elves' propensity for doing down their kin even in the face of a serious external threat.

Pharaun, who privately considered himself cleverer than Ryld, had always been a little chagrined that he couldn't defeat the weapons master at *sava*, but alas, his friend wielded mother, priestess, wizard, warrior, orc slave soldier, and dice as brilliantly as he did a sword. Indeed, he claimed that fighting and *sava* were the same thing, though Pharaun had never quite understood what the assertion meant.

The wizard clapped Ryld on the shoulder and said, "Play. Amuse yourself. Win their gold. Just remember to make conversation while you're at it. See what you can learn. Meanwhile, I'll try my luck in the cellar."

Ryld nodded.

Pharaun navigated his way across the crowded room to the bar. Behind it on a stool sat wizened, one-legged Nym, an elderly male who for sheer surly, unwavering misanthropy rivaled any demon the Master of Sorcere had ever conjured. The old retired battle mage was happily engaged in snarling threats, obscenities, and orders at the goblin thralls pouring drinks, but he grudgingly suspended the harassment long enough to accept a handful of gold. In return, he tendered a worn, numbered leather tab with several keys attached.

Thus equipped, Pharaun walked through the arch beside the bar and down another flight of steps. At the bottom waited the real business of the Jewel Box and the reason Nym had not seen fit to hang a placard outside.

In Menzoberranzan, where a goddess and her priestesses reigned supreme, few female dark elves ever found it necessary to sell their bodies. Only a handful of the sick and infirm, dwelling in the most abject need, had ever stooped to such a degradation. Accordingly, one might assume that any male wishing to purchase intimate companionship would find his choice limited to these rare unappealing specimens or the females of one of the inferior species.

But that wasn't quite the case, at least not if a male had a heavy purse. The reason was that, while they generally devoted their military efforts to fighting cloakers, svirfneblin, and other competing civilizations of the Underdark, drow cities on rare occasions waged war on one another. Once in a while, such conflicts yielded female prisoners.

The prudent, legitimate thing to do with such potentially dangerous captives was interrogate, torture, and kill them. That fact notwithstanding, Nym had on several occasions managed to bribe officers to give him their prisoners, whom he then smuggled into Menzoberranzan and down to the cellar of the Jewel Box.

Nym had gone to all this trouble based on the shrewd and well-proven assumption that a goodly number of Menzoberranyr males would pay handsomely for the privilege of dominating a female, and in his establishment, one could do anything one wanted with a captive. Nym would even provide a customer with a bastinado, a brazier of coals, thumbscrews . . . his only stipulation being that one must pay a surcharge if one left a permanent mark.

Since the brothel's existence was an open secret, Pharaun wasn't sure why the matron mothers hadn't shut it down. On the face of it, it certainly seemed to encourage disrespect for the ruling gender. Perhaps they felt that if a male had a refuge in which to act out his resentments, it would make him all the more deferential to the females in his home. More likely, Nym was slipping them a substantial portion of the take.

At any rate, the Jewel Box seemed a reasonable place to seek information concerning rogue males, especially if one had a spy in place. Pharaun wasn't confident that he did anymore, but one never knew.

The stairs emptied into a hallway of numbered doors. Moans of passions and grunts of pain sounded faintly from behind several of them. It was busier than usual.

The mage strolled down the passage until he found number fourteen. He hesitated for an instant, then scowled and turned the largest of his keys in the lock. The door swung open.

Seated on the bed, shackles clutching her wrists and ankles, Pellanistra looked much as he remembered, the same powerful, shapely limbs and heart-shaped face, with only a few more scars where one or another of her visitors had pressed down two hard, as well as a split lip and closed, puffy eye where a more recent caller had beaten her.

She lifted her face, saw him, and charged with her long-nailed hands outstretched. Then she staggered as one of her governing enchantments riddled her body with pain, and an instant later hit the end of the chains securing her to the wall. She lost her balance and fell on her rump.

"Hello, Pellanistra," Pharaun said.

She spat at him, then screwed up her face at another flare of punishment. The gobbet of saliva fell well short of the wizard's soft, high boots.

"Much as I dislike descending to the obvious," Pharaun said, "I feel compelled to observe that you're only hurting yourself." He stepped forward and extended his hand. "Come on, let's sit and have a talk, just like in the old days. I'll even remove the shackles if you wish."

"We had a bargain!" she said.

"I refuse to have an extended conversation with someone sitting on the floor. It compromises my dignity as much as it does yours. Come on, be sensible. Take my hand."

She didn't do that, but, chains clinking, she did clamber to her bare feet unassisted. He caught a whiff of some flowery scent that Nym had forced her to wear.

"Now, isn't that better?" he asked. "Do you want the manacles off?"

"We had a compact, and I was holding up my end."

"I wish you'd invite me to sit down."

"You abandoned me!"

Pharaun spread his slender, long-fingered hands and said, "All right, priestess. If you think it necessary, we'll belabor the self-evident a bit longer. Yes, I recruited you into my service. Yes, you were doing splendidly—well on your way to earning your liberation—but my circumstances changed. Surely you heard something about it."

"Yes. You backed the wrong sister, and Greyanna made a fool of you. She killed her twin, and you were powerless to stop it. If you hadn't turned tail and run away to Sorcere, she would have slain you, too."

Pharaun smiled crookedly. "I don't think I'll encourage the bards to put it quite that way when they compose the epic story of my life."

"But after you established yourself up on Tier Breche, after you were free to come and go as you pleased, you could have returned here."

"I have, on occasion, just not to call on you. I thought it might be a little awkward."

"I could have helped you the same as before."

"Alas, no. After my withdrawal from House Mizzrym, I no longer had a stake in the power struggles within my family or among the noble Houses, either. I no longer needed intelligence about such matters. The only rivalry that concerned me was the one among wizards, and even if you number the foremost practitioners of my art among your guests, I doubt they whisper the esoterica of their newly invented spells in your ears. When it comes to our discoveries, we wizards are a closemouthed breed."

"You don't know what it was like for me . . . *is* like for me, abused and degraded by my inferiors, constrained in body, mind, and soul, unable to commune with Lolth. . . ."

Pharaun raised his hand. "Please, you're embarrassing yourself. You sound like a whining human, or one of our foul cousins in the World Above. Cease this tirade, take a breath, and think, then you will realize, enemy of Menzoberranzan, that my concern for your well-being has always been, at best, limited. How could it be otherwise? Sentiment certainly wasn't strong enough to make me spend a fortune buying you free of Nym, or, if he and I couldn't strike a deal, break you out of here. Not when you hadn't fulfilled the terms of our covenant. As you no doubt recall, you were supposed to provide me useful information over the full course of twenty years. I admit it wasn't your fault that you couldn't, but still, that's just the way things fell out."

"Fine," she gritted. "You're right, I'm being ridiculous. In forsaking me, you simply behaved as any sensible drow would. Now what in the name of the Demonweb do you want?"

He nodded at the other end of the room and said, "May we . . . ?"

She gave a curt nod, and they seated themselves, she on the mattress of her wide octagonal bed and he on a cushioned granite chair.

"This is much nicer," he said. "Would you like me to send for some wine?"

"Just get on with it."

"Very well. I imagine my plight will amuse you. After the goddess knows how many years breathing the rarefied and dispassionate air of scholarship, imparting knowledge to eager young minds, advancing the frontiers of the mystic arts—"

"Murdering other wizards for their talismans and grimoires."

He grinned. "Well, that was implied, of course. Anyway, after all that, I find myself again embroiled in the more mundane aspects of life in our noble metropolis. There's a puzzle I must solve on pain of the archmage's severe displeasure, and I will be grateful unto death and beyond if you help me unravel it."

"How would I do that?"

"Don't be disingenuous. It doesn't suit you. The same way as always. I assume foolish boys still sometimes gossip and boast to their hired females, even though if they stopped to think about it, they'd remember you loathe them and wish them only ill. I likewise imagine that you still sometimes find yourself obliged to entertain at gatherings where such idiots, unmindful of your presence, discuss their most secret affairs with one another."

"In other words, you wish to resume our old arrangement. Which still had four years to run. If I assist you with your current problem, will you continue to concern yourself with 'mundane' affairs, or will you lock yourself away in your tower once more?"

He considered lying, but his instincts told him she'd see through it.

"I'm not entirely sure what will become of me," he said. "As far as I know, if I'm successful, I ought to wind up reestablished in Sorcere with all my transgressions forgiven, but for some murky reason, I wonder. I'm caught up in something I don't yet understand, and only the dark powers know where it will lead."

"Then if you want my help, you'll have to set me free . . . *today*."

"Impossible, I don't have the requisite funds on my person, nor the leisure to dicker with Nym, for that matter. You know he'd stretch any negotiation out for days, just to be annoying. Nor do I have time to arrange an escape."

She only stared at him, and he understood.

"Ah," he said.

"Is it a bargain?"

"It is if you actually give me some help. My problem is this: An unusual number of males have run away from home of late."

"That's your errand? To find some rogues? What makes it important enough to send a Master of Sorcere?"

He smiled. "I have no idea. Do you know anything about it?"

She shook her head. "Not much."

"Frankly, any crumb of genuine information will put me ahead of where I am now."

"Well, I've heard only the vaguest hints, but they suggest this isn't just a case of an unusual number of males deciding independently to elope. They all ran to the same place for the same reason, whatever that reason may be."

"I thought as much," said Pharaun. "Otherwise, why would Gromph be interested? But it's reassuring to hear that your own agile mind has arrived at the same conclusion."

She sneered.

Pharaun absently ran his fingertip along one of the swirling lines woven into his robe.

"I doubt a threat would suffice to draw so many boys away from home," he said. "Some would have the courage to defy the threatener or the sense to appeal to their kin for protection. Nor would a hypnotic charm do the trick. Aside from the natural resistance to such effects that all we dark elves possess, some of the males would have carried wards in the form of amulets and such. No, I think we have to assume the rogues sneaked away of their own volition to accomplish some positive end. But what?"

"They're organizing a new merchant clan?"

"I thought of that, but Gromph says no, and I'm sure he's correct. For if that were the case, then why the secrecy? Since trade is important to all Menzoberranzan, people don't generally object when a male becomes a merchant. It's one of the two or three legitimate ways to distance oneself from Mother's harsh and arbitrary hand." He grinned. "No offense. I'm sure that in happier times, the males under your authority had no reason to complain of you."

"You can bet I would give them reason now."

"Given your more recent experiences, that's understandable. So, if the rogues aren't putting together a caravan, what are they doing? Preparing to flee Menzoberranzan for good and all? Or, goddess forbid, have they slipped away already?"

"I don't think so. I can't tell you precisely where they are, but I believe they're still somewhere in the city proper, the Mantle, or conceivably out in the Bauthwaf."

"Now that truly is good news. I wasn't keen on a hunt through the wilds of the Underdark. Not only is there a general lack of amenities, the winemakers are uncorking the new vintages the tenday after next."

Pellanistra shook her head. "You haven't changed."

"Thank you, I'll take that as a compliment. Now, let's get down to the crux of the matter, shall we? I require names. Which of your visitors dropped these 'vaguest hints' which you have so sagaciously interpreted?"

She gave him a smile radiant with spite. "Alton Vandree and Vuzlyn Freth."

"Who themselves subsequently disappeared and are thus unavailable for questioning. It makes sense, I suppose, but it's unfortunate all the same."

"I've given you everything I have," she said. "Now fulfill your end of the deal."

The wizard frowned and said, "My dear collaborator, it would devastate me to disappoint you. Yet I stipulated that you'd have to offer me information of some significance, and frankly, I'm not sure you've delivered. I really know little more than I did before."

"Do it, or I'll tell every soul who comes into this cell that you're looking for the runaways. Perhaps that will have some 'significance' for your mission. I assume it is supposed to be a secret. Things usually are where you're involved, and you haven't mentioned a legion of assistants following you about."

Pharaun laughed. "Well played. I surrender. How shall we do this?"

"I don't care. Burn me with your magic. Stick a dagger in me. Break my neck with those long, clever fingers."

"Interesting suggestions all, but I'd just as soon that Nym didn't bill me for your demise. If we can make it look as if your heart just stopped of its own accord sometime after I look my leave, I'll have a chance."

He cast about, noticed the thick, fluffy pillow on the bed, picked it up, and experimentally gripped it at both ends. It felt good in his hands.

"This ought to work," he said. "Perhaps you could oblige me by lying down?"

Ryld sipped his chilled, tart wine with a sense of satisfaction, secure in the knowledge that the game, though technically still in progress, was already won. In three more moves, his onyx wizard and orc would trap and mate his opponent's carnelian mother.

As usual, he had accomplished his victory without recourse to the dice. Truth to tell, those clattering ivory cubes with the magically warmed images incised on the faces were the one aspect of *sava* he didn't like. They interjected blind luck into what should be a contest of pure cunning.

Ryld's adversary, a scrawny young merchant clansman with an uncouth habit of letting drops of liquor slide from the corners of his mouth as he guzzled, had thrown the dice early on and gloated when chance allowed him to eliminate one of the older male's priestesses.

Shoulders hunched, brow sweaty, he stared at the board as if the fate of his soul were being decided thereupon. A truly competent player would have recognized almost instantly that there was only one move he could make. Indeed, he would have foreseen the inevitable mate just three moves hence and resigned.

Mindful of his true purpose for visiting the Jewel Box, Ryld, doing his best to sound only casually interested, took up the thread of the conversation that he and the slightly tipsy trader had been carrying on in fits and starts.

"Did your cousin give you any warning that he was going to run away?"

"No," the clansman answered curtly. "Why would he? We despised each other. Now shut up! You're trying to break my concentration."

Ryld sighed and settled back in his spindly, flimsy-looking limestone chair. From the corner of his eye he glimpsed something that made him sit up straighter, double-check the precise position of Splitter leaning against the wall, and stealthily loosen his short sword in its oiled sheath on his belt.

He himself didn't quite know what had alerted him. These weren't the first circle of revelers he'd watched rise from their seats and draw their weapons, either to play at fencing or to settle a quarrel that had nothing at all to do with the hooded male defeating all comers at *sava*. Indeed, within the confines of the Jewel Box, blades rasped from their scabbards with a certain regularity. Superficially, this new quartet was no different, but somehow Ryld knew that they were. Sure enough, they stalked straight toward him and his oblivious opponent through the fragrant haze of incense. Other patrons, likewise sensing the swordsmen's intent, made haste to clear the way.

A blade with a glowing redness—an imprisoned spirit perhaps—oozing inside the adamantine, flicked in a horizontal sweep at the tabletop. Ryld caught the weapon and pushed it away before it could upset the *sava* pieces or his neatly stacked winnings. The long sword was as sharp as only an enchanted weapon could be, but he managed the grab without cutting his hand. Finally startled from his reverie, the scrawny boy looked wildly about.

"May we help you?" asked Ryld.

"We've been listening to you," said the owner of the long sword.

Though not so big as Ryld, he was nonetheless husky and tall for a drow male, and the points of his prominent ears seemed to reach above the top of his head like a bat's. He was the best dressed and plainly the leader of the foursome, even though his broad, sullen face bore the mottled bruises of a beating. The weapons master assumed that some noble female must have seen fit to give the male a pummeling. His companions would think none the less of him for that.

Especially since, Ryld noted, two of them were hurt as well, moving a trifle stiffly or slightly favoring one leg. Perhaps they were all kinsmen, and one of the priestesses in their House had gone on a regular tear.

"You've been asking a lot of questions about runaways," the swordsman continued in a threatening drawl.

"Have I?" Ryld replied.

He reflected that it was too bad the three musicians had left the stage a few minutes back. He doubted that anyone had managed to eavesdrop on his conversations while the longhorn was shrilling away.

The other male scowled and asked, "Why?"

"Just making conversation. Do you know something about the rogues?"

"No, but I know that in the Jewel Box we don't like it when people are too curious. We don't like them hunting runaways. We don't like them listening to every private thing we say and reporting back to the Mothers."

"I'm not a spy."

Maybe he was, but he had no intention of confessing it to this fool.

"Ha!" the swordsman scoffed. "If you were, you wouldn't admit it."

"Be that as it may, I suggest you and your friends return to your table and let this boy and I finish our game."

The male with the red sword swelled like an inflated bladder on the verge of bursting. "You're trying to dismiss me like a servant? Do you have any idea who I am?"

"Of course, Tathlyn Godeep. I trained you. Do you remember me?"

Ryld pushed back his cowl, exposing his hitherto shadowed features.

Tathlyn and his friends goggled at their former teacher as if he had just revealed himself to be some ancient and legendary dragon.

"I see you do. So I'll bid you good day."

Tathlyn looked as if he was groping for a comment that would allow him to terminate this confrontation with his dignity intact, but the onlookers started to laugh. His fear less compelling than his pride, he screwed the sneer back onto his face.

"Yes," he said, his voice raised to cut through the laughter, "I know you, Master Argith, but you don't know me, not the person I have become. Today I am the weapons master of House Godeep."

House Godeep was one of the petty Houses of Narbondellyn, whose frantic rivalries on the very bottom rungs of the ladder of status were almost beneath the notice of the nobles farther up. Ryld doubted the Godeeps would rise much higher with Tathlyn leading their warriors. During his training, the boy had learned to swing a sword with reasonable skill, but he had always demonstrated extraordinary recklessness and general poor judgment when placed in command of a squad.

"Congratulations," said Ryld.

"Perhaps if you'd known I would rise to such an eminence, you wouldn't have taken such delight in smashing my knuckles and beating my shoulder to pulp."

"I didn't do it for sport. It was to teach you to close the outside line and to stand up straight. I tried simply telling you to make the adjustments, but you didn't heed me.

"Now," Ryld continued, "I've explained I have no intention of tattling to the matrons about anything I might happen to learn in this place. Is my word good enough for you? If so, we should have no quarrel."

"That's what you say."

"Lad—excuse me . . . Weapons Master, pause, breathe, and reflect. I sense you're feeling angry over your aches and bruises. Perhaps you want to take it out on someone, but I'm not the person who administered the beating."

Tathlyn stood silent for an instant, then he said, "No, you're not, and I suppose all the punishment during training was for my own good. No hard feelings, Weapons Master. Enjoy your match."

He started to turn away, then whirled back around. The point of the red long sword streaked at Ryld's neck.

Before the four companions had even reached the *sava* table, Ryld had inconspicuously centered his weight and planted his feet in a manner that would allow him to get out of his chair quickly. He simultaneously sprang up and brushed the blade aside with a sweep of his arm, but he didn't strike it at quite the proper angle. The wicked edge of the red sword drew a little blood.

Ryld realized that this was his first real fight in the better part of a year. He'd intended to go out with one of the companies patrolling Bauthwaf, slaughter himself a few of the predators that were always wandering in from the caverns farther out, but somehow he had never bestirred himself to do it.

That was no problem. He had no fear that he was rusty. It was just that, looking back, he was surprised at his lack of motivation.

All these thoughts flashed through his mind in an instant and without slowing his reactions in the slightest.

Tathlyn jumped back out of reach, but one of his companions was lunging at Ryld. It looked like they all intended to fight, which probably meant they were all the weapons master's kin and subordinates. Otherwise, one or more of them might have stayed out of the quarrel.

Ryld twitched himself out of the way of his attacker's wild head cut, drew his leaf-bladed short sword, and thrust. The onrushing Godeep's momentum, Ryld's strength and skill, and the magical keenness of his point served to bury the weapon deep in the crook of his assailant's fighting arm. Though not his favored weapon, the short sword—enchanted to wound even incorporeal spirits—was a fine blade. Blood started from the puncture, and, staggering, the Godeep dropped his falchion. It would actually have been easier to kill the dolt than merely incapacitate him, but Ryld was on a secret mission, and outright homicide was far more likely to attract attention than a simple tavern brawl.

Tathlyn and his other two friends saw their chance and rushed in. Ryld knew that he didn't have time to pull the embedded short sword out of his victim's flesh. If he tried, his other enemies would have him. He cloaked the wounded Godeep in a ragged bulb of darkness and shoved him at the others.

Ryld couldn't see through the obscuring field any more than his adversaries could, but, peering around the edges of it, he saw the wounded Godeep reel into his fellows and stagger them, startle them, too, with the sudden, unexpected impediment to their sight. That gave the weapons master the time he needed to whirl, take in the obstructive clutter of furniture and gawking *sava* players before him, and leap up onto the table where his own game sat waiting. His racing feet annihilated the snare he'd so cunningly laid for the merchant, hurling the pieces rattling across the board and onto the floor.

He jumped down on the other side, grabbed Splitter, and spun back around to face his enemies. In one smooth blur of motion, he yanked this most trusted of all his weapons from its scabbard and came on guard. Despite its hugeness, the greatsword was so perfectly balanced that it felt as light as a dagger in his grasp.

He noticed that the noncombatants in the taproom had begun shouting encouragement and insults at the fighters. A couple quick-thinking gamblers were giving odds.

Ryld's three remaining adversaries manhandled their shadow-shrouded kinsman out of their way and stalked forward, manifestly hoping to pin the fencing teacher against the wall. The one on the left hung back a bit, none too eager, but he didn't look as if he'd actually turn and run unless Tathlyn told him to, or else he saw the weapons master himself go down under Splitter's razor edge.

Ryld had no intention of letting himself be trapped. He moved away from the wall the same way he'd moved up to it, springing onto the table and charging across.

When he reached the far edge, he discovered a rapier poised to skewer him in the vitals when he plunged off. The Godeep on the other end of the blade—the bolder of Tathlyn's two kinsmen—was quick, and he'd conceived a pretty good tactic. Ryld's impetus was such that he probably wouldn't have been able to stop himself from hurtling right onto the Godeep's point.

But he could whirl Splitter through a sweeping low-line parry. The greatsword clanked into the other male's lighter blade and snapped the last six inches off.

Ryld jumped down almost on top of the rapier fighter, so close it would require a moment to bring Splitter's blade to bear, a moment that the other Godeeps might turn to good advantage. Instead, the weapons master bashed the greatsword's heavy steel ball of a pommel into the center of the rapier-wielder's forehead. The impact thudded, and the male fell backward.

Something clacked hard but harmlessly against Ryld's breastplate. He glanced down and saw that one of the spectators, someone who'd bet on his opponents, perhaps, had shot a hand crossbow at him— but the weapons master didn't have time to look for the culprit. He had to pivot to fend off his fellow swordsmen.

Predictably, Tathlyn was in the lead. Ryld cut at the weapons master's head, and his erstwhile student instantly backpedaled, retreating just far enough to avoid the stroke. He'd learned good footwork somewhere along the way, better than Ryld remembered.

Slipping in and out of the distance, Tathlyn feinted and invited, putting on a show. Meanwhile, the other Godeep, the wary one, circled, trying to get behind Ryld.

The weapons master allowed the boy to creep part way round to his flank, then he sprang at Tathlyn and cut wildly, seemingly off-balance and overcommitted to the attack.

The other Godeep had Ryld's back, at a moment when the teacher looked entirely incapable of turning and defending. Reluctant or not, the boy couldn't pass up such an opportunity. He charged.

Ryld whirled, bringing Splitter around in a sweeping horizontal stroke. The greatsword with its superior length struck one step before the Godeep would have initiated his own attack. Thanks to Ryld's deftness, the huge, preternaturally sharp blade merely gashed the boy's wrist instead of lopping off his hand. The petty noble dropped his broadsword, then had the bad judgment to reach for his dagger. The weapons master slashed his leg, tumbling him to the floor.

Ryld knew that by spinning to attack the one Godeep, he had given his back to Tathlyn, who was surely driving in to kill him. The teacher whirled back around. Sure enough, Tathlyn had rushed into the distance and was cutting at his head. Ryld parried with Splitter's edge, hoping to snap the Godeep weapons master's long sword as he had the rapier. The crimson blade struck the greatsword on the forte, just above the parrying hook, rang, and rebounded, still in one piece. It was made of good metal, Ryld thought, well forged, with strengthening enchantments woven in.

But its virtues alone couldn't save its master. Ryld feinted low to draw the red sword down, then cut high. Splitter sliced Tathlyn's brow, and blood poured into the Godeep weapons master's eyes. He reeled backward.

Ryld could tell that none of his adversaries had any fight left in them. He turned once more, surveying the room. Whoever had shot him, the fellow had prudently put his hand crossbow away.

"Nicely done," said Pharaun, lounging, goblet in hand, by the bar.

"How long have you been there?" Ryld replied, walking to retrieve his short sword. Its victim had pulled it free and left it on the floor. "You could have helped me."

"I was too busy wagering on you." The wizard held out his purse, and grumbling losers dropped coins into it. "I knew you wouldn't need help against a couple drunks."

Ryld grunted, wiped his weapons on a handy bar rag, and asked, "Do you want that red sword? It's a good weapon. Maybe a Godeep family heirloom."

Pharaun grinned. "Which would mean they acquired it when, last tenday? No, thank you anyway, but what would a spellcaster do with it? Besides, I wouldn't want the weight to stretch and chafe my clothes."

"Suit yourself."

The Master of Sorcere sauntered up to Ryld, then spoke far more softly. "Are you about ready to go? I'd just as soon take my leave before Nym wanders downstairs."

Ryld wondered what mischief his friend had committed. "Almost," he said. "Give Nym something to pay for the cleanup."

The warrior walked to the *sava* tables, retrieved Splitter's scabbard and his own winnings, then looked around for the trader. The boy had made a hasty withdrawal from the table the instant the fight began, but he hadn't gone far. Most every drow had a taste for blood sport.

Ryld tossed him a gold coin with the Baenre emblem stamped on it. "Here are your winnings."

The young merchant looked puzzled. Perhaps the drink was to blame.

"If a player disturbs the arrangement of the board, he loses," Ryld explained. "It's in the rules."

🕷   🕷   🕷

"It was gratifying to come upstairs and observe you handling our confidential inquiries with your usual light touch," Pharaun said.

He paused to let a floatchest, attended by a dark elf merchant and six hulking bugbear slaves, drift across the lane. The stone box looked like a sarcophagus. Maybe it was. In the Bazaar, a shopper could purchase nearly anything, including cadavers and mummies once embalmed with strange spices and laid to rest with mystic rites. Indeed, such wares were available either whole or by the desiccated piece.

"It wasn't my fault," Ryld replied. "I did nothing to provoke that fight." He hesitated. "Well, perhaps I was a bit brusque when the Godeeps first stalked up to the table."

"You? Never!"

"Spare me your japes. Why do we have to question people anyway?" The Master of Melee-Magthere ducked beneath the corner of a low-hanging rothé-hide awning and added, "You ought to be able to look in a scrying pool and find the runaways."

Pharaun smiled. "Where would be the fun in that? Now seriously, why did the Godeeps take exception to your no doubt impeccably subtle questions in the first place? Were they in league with the rogues?"

"I don't think they knew anything. I think they were merely sympathetic to the idea of eloping and generally in a foul mood. It looked as if one of the females in House Godeep had disciplined them with her fists or a cudgel, and they only needed an excuse to try and take their resentment out on someone."

"This hypothetical priestess beat the House *weapons master* as if he were a thrall, or at best, the least useful of her male kin? Doesn't that strike you as odd?"

"Now that you mention it, somewhat."

"The Jewel Box was unusually crowded today as well."

Pharaun noticed a blindfolded orc juggling daggers for the amusement of the crowd and paused for a moment to watch the show. Ryld heaved a sigh, signaling his impatience at the interruption in their deliberations.

The wizard counted five sharp knives, which the slave's scarred hands caught and tossed with flawless accuracy. A laudable performance, even if it lacked a certain elan. Pharaun tossed a coin to the orc's owner, then strolled on. Ryld tramped along beside him.

"So," said the weapons master, "Tathlyn gets a thrashing, the brothel enjoys a glut of patrons, and you see a connection. What?"

"What if all those boys endured a beating, or at least some sort of unpleasantness, at the hands of their female relations? What if that's the reason they flocked to their sad little sanctuary, to lie low, lick their wounds, and kick around one of Nym's captives in their turn?"

Ryld frowned, pondering the notion. "You're guessing that priestesses in a diversity of Houses have grown more harsh and unreasonable. Obviously, that could provoke a spate of runaway males, but what could make the dispositions of all those priestesses curdle in unison?"

"I have a hunch that when we figure that out, we'll be getting somewhere."

The two masters circled around a colossal snail pulling a dozen-wheeled cart. The creature's mouth opened into an O and Pharaun—who had once only narrowly survived an encounter with such a giant mollusk in the wild—nearly sacrificed his dignity by flinching, even though he knew this particular specimen had undoubtedly been divested of its ability to spew a caustic sludge. Sure enough, nothing flew from the draft creature's maw except a few clear, harmless droplets. The wagoner lashed the hostile snail with his long-handled whip.

"What did you learn downstairs?" asked Ryld.

"Nothing, really," said Pharaun, "nothing we hadn't already inferred. Still, I was able to oblige an old comrade. That was pleasant in its own way."

"If neither of us discovered anything substantial, our visit to the Jewel Box was a waste of time."

"Not a bit of it. The bloodshed perked you up, didn't it? You've pretty much been smiling ever since."

"Don't be ridiculous. I admit it was an interesting little scuffle . . ."

Ryld began to recount the battle one action at a time, with comprehensive analysis of the alternative options and underlying strategy. Pharaun nodded and did his best to look interested.

Triel, Matron Mother of House Baenre and a diminutive ebony doll of a dark elf, marched briskly down the corridor, covering ground rapidly despite her short stride. Eight feet tall, his two goatlike legs more nimble even than most drow's, Jeggred had no difficulty keeping up with his mother. The scurrying, frazzled drow secretary, though, looked as if she was in imminent danger of dropping her armload of parchment.

When Triel heard voices conversing a few yards ahead, she wanted to move faster still. Only a sense that a female in her august position ought not to compromise her dignity by running held the impulse in check.

"I think it's a test," said one soft female voice.

"I worry it's a sign of disfavor," answered the other, a hair deeper and a bit nasal. "Perhaps we've done something to offend—"

Triel and her companions rounded a corner. There before them loitered a pair of her cousins. Their mouths fell open when they saw her.

Triel looked up at her son's face, which, with its slightly elongated muzzle, mouthful of long, pointed fangs, slanted eyes, and pointed ears, seemed a blend of drow and wolf. That wordless glance sufficed to convey her will.

Jeggred pounced, his long, coarse mane streaming out behind him. With each of his huge, clawed fighting hands, he grabbed a cousin by the throat and hoisted her up against the calcite wall. His two smaller, drowlike hands flexed as if they too wished to get in on the violence.

Perhaps they did.

Triel had conceived a child in a ritual coupling with the glabrezu demon Belshazu. The result was Jeggred, a half-fiend known as a draegloth, a precious gift of the Spider Queen. His mother was quite prepared to believe that cruelty and bloodlust burned in every mote and particle of his being. Only his reflexive subservience, tendered not because Triel had borne him but because she was first among the priestesses of Lolth, kept him from immediately slaughtering his prisoners, or, indeed, pretty much anyone else with whom he came in contact.

Occasionally Triel's lack of height was an advantage. It didn't feel awkward or claustrophobic to step inside the circle of Jeggred's two longer arms and stand before the cousins. Up close, she could smell the sweat of their fear just as easily as she could hear the little choking sounds they were making or the thuds as their heels bumped against the carved surface behind them.

"I forbade you to speak of the situation in public," she snarled.

The cousin on the left started making more noise, a tortured gargling. Perhaps she was trying to say that she and the other one had been alone.

"This is a public part of the castle," Triel said. "Anyone, any *male* might have come along and overheard you."

She swung her whip of fangs, aiming low to ensure she didn't accidentally lash Jeggred's hands or arms. The five writhing adders gashed their targets but not enough to satisfy their mistress. She struck again and again. Her anger rose and rose until it became a kind of rapture, a sweet simplicity in which nothing existed but the cousins' thrashing, the smell and feel of their blood spattering her face, and the pleasant exertion of her snapping arm.

She never knew what brought her out of that joyous condition. Perhaps it was simply that she was winded, but when she came to her senses, the two babblers were dangling limp and silent in Jeggred's grip.

Both the draegloth and the scribe were smiling. They'd thoroughly enjoyed the cousins' excruciating torture, but there were things still to be done, and she'd wasted time losing her temper.

Which was bad. Matron Mother Baenre, de facto ruler of the entire city of Menzoberranzan, should be able to govern herself as well.

Triel's emotional volatility was of comparatively recent origin. She'd been calm and competent all the while she served as Mistress of Arach-Tinilith. That role, arguably second only to her mother's in prestige, had suited her well, and she'd never aspired to anything more.

Nor had she truly believed that more was even possible. Her mother seemed immortal. Indestructible. But then, suddenly, she was gone, and the ambition that at one time or another goaded every dark elf awoke in Triel's breast. How could she *not* strive to ascend to her mother's throne? How could she let Quenthel or one of her other kin climb over her head to order her about forever after?

She managed to claim the title of Matron Mother, and though she soon came to feel somewhat overwhelmed by the scope and intricacies of the position, at first it wasn't so bad. Things were relatively normal and didn't require some dramatic intervention from on high to set them right.

Moreover, she had Quenthel and Gromph to advise her. True, her sister and brother invariably disagreed, but Triel could review their competing proposals and pick the one that suited her. It was considerably easier than having to come up with the ideas herself.

But she had a crisis to manage, perhaps the greatest crisis in the long history of the dark elves, and apparently she would have to do it alone. She obviously couldn't confide in Gromph, and insolent Quenthel claimed she had to attend to the security of Tier Breche before she could focus on anything else.

Triel gave her head a shake, trying to dislodge her doubts and worries.

"Let them down."

Jeggred obeyed, and she turned to the secretary.

"When you get a chance," she said, raising her voice over the choking gasps of the two cousins, "have somebody haul them out to Arach-Tinilith to be patched back together, and have someone wash away the blood. But for now, we'd best get moving. I think we're late."

The trio moved on. A final turn brought them to the door. Behind it was the dais overlooking the largest audience chamber in House Baenre. A pair of sentries guarded the entry to ensure that no one would sneak through to stab the matron mother in the back. They snapped to attention when they saw her coming.

Triel swept on through the entry with Jeggred and the clerk in tow. The hall on the other side glowed with soft magical light to facilitate the examination of documents. A sweet perfume scented the air, and a fresco of Lolth adorned the ceiling. The guards along the walls—dark elves near the dais, ogre and minotaur slaves farther down—saluted, while the supplicants and petitioners made the obeisance proper to their stations, anything from a dignified inclination of the head and spreading of the hands to an abject grovel flat on the floor.

Looking down on them from the elevated platform, Triel reflected that it was astonishing just how many such folk turned up each and every tenday. She'd thought people were always demanding her attention when she ruled the Academy, but she'd had no conception of the hordes of idiots who constantly sought Matron Baenre's ear, often to resolve trivial if not nonsensical concerns.

She sat down on her mother's throne, an empress's ransom in gold with a flaring back shaped to resemble an arc of spiderweb. Her predecessor had been a relatively large female, and her successor always felt a bit childlike and lost in the chair. She had enough of a sense of irony to comprehend the accidental symbolism.

She surveyed the waiting throng and discovered Faeryl Zauvirr at the very front with some long, bulky rolled papers tucked under her arm. The matron mother smiled, for at least she knew how to deal with this one particular petitioner. For a blessed change, Waerva, one of the lesser females of her House, had made herself useful. She'd come up with some significant information and a sensible idea of what to do about it.

Triel decided she might as well start out feeling dominant and shrewd. Perhaps it would set the tone for the rest of the session. She waited for the herald to conclude the ceremonials and the crowd to rise. Then, still spattered with blood, and with Jeggred looming reassuringly behind her throne, she motioned for Faeryl to step forward.

Faeryl was pleased to be chosen first. In retrospect, she thought the same thing would have occurred even if she hadn't made sure of a position immediately in front of the dais. The haughty Menzoberranyr often feigned disinterest in their client city, but she knew they understood the importance of Ched Nasad.

It was hard not to hurry, but she forced herself to approach the throne with a stately tread consonant with the dignity of her position, the stature of her House, and the grandeur of her homeland. It was also difficult to offer a second graceful obeisance without dropping her roll of maps, but she accomplished that as well.

"Ambassador," said Triel without any extraordinary warmth. Perhaps she considered Faeryl's presence inappropriate.

"Matron Mother," Faeryl replied. Tall, broad-shouldered and thick-waisted by the standards of her slender race, she would have dwarfed the Baenre had the two of them been standing side by side. "I know we sometimes meet in private, but after tendays of deliberation I arrived at a conclusion, one that compelled me to confer with you at the earliest opportunity."

"What conclusion?" Triel asked.

She still seemed unconcerned if not downright cold. Perhaps she was preoccupied with her affliction.

Faeryl had of course fallen prey to the same malaise, but to her own surprise, she'd discovered she was at least as worried about something else: the well-being of House Zauvirr and the magnificent city in which it amassed its wealth, fought its covert battles, and worked its magic.

"I keep track of the caravans arriving from Ched Nasad," the ambassador said. "For the past six tendays, none has. None. As the Matron Mother is undoubtedly aware, several major trade routes converge in the City of Shimmering Webs, which then funnels the merchants on to Menzoberranzan. At least half the goods that reach your cavern come through us. Except that now, they aren't reaching you. The steady flow has dried up. Except in time of war, that's unprecedented."

"It's an odd coincidence, certainly, all the merchant clansmen choosing other destinations, but I'm sure they'll decide to head for Menzoberranzan next trip, or the trip after that."

Faeryl had to make a conscious effort to compose her features. Otherwise she would have scowled. If she hadn't known better, she would have thought Triel was being deliberately obtuse.

"I suspect it may be more than a coincidence," the ambassador said. "A thousand thousand dangers haunt the Underdark, and the philosophers tell us new ones are spawning all the time. What if something has cut the route between Menzoberranzan and Ched Nasad? What if it's killing everyone who tries to pass through?"

"More than one tunnel connects the cities," rumbled the drae-gloth unexpectedly, and despite the perfume wafting through the air, Faeryl caught a whiff of the creature's putrid breath. "Is that not so?"

"Exactly!" Triel reached back around the edge of her golden chair and gave the half-fiend an approving pat on the leg. "Your theory doesn't stand up, Ambassador."

Not for the first time, Faeryl wished that Triel's mother was still leading House Baenre. The greedy, vicious old autocrat could be hard to contend with, but though she would have cherished a drae-gloth as a mark of Lolth's approval and delighted in the demidemon's gift for slaughter, she wouldn't have tolerated it speaking unbidden at a formal conference, any more than she would have borne such disrespect from anyone else.

"If the threat consists of more than one beast," the emissary said, "or more than one manifestation of a phenomenon, it could cut more than one passage."

Triel shrugged. "If you say so."

"I hesitate to mention it," said Faeryl, "lest I be thought an alarmist, but it's even possible that some misfortune has befallen Ched Nasad itself."

"A misfortune so abrupt and all-encompassing that your folk never even had a chance to dispatch a messenger to Menzoberran-zan?" Triel replied. "Nonsense. Even Golothaer, home of our ances-tors, didn't perish in an hour. Besides, I am personally aware of several communiqués having reached here from Ched Nasad in only the past few days."

"I have received some of those sendings myself, Matron Mother, and find their excuses suspicious at best. In any case, the dearth of traffic from Ched Nasad warrants investigation, and as my city's rep-resentative in Menzoberranzan, the task is my responsibility."

"No one has charged you with it."

"Then I take it upon myself. Yet I'm reluctant to venture across the Underdark with merely my own little entourage for protection. Traders guard their caravans very well. Anything that could destroy all those merchant trains would likely put a quick end to me, too, in which case, Matron Mother, the priestesses of Menzoberranzan would know no more about the new menace beyond their borders than they do now. Accordingly, I ask you to provide me with a siz-able escort. I'll march it to Ched Nasad and back again and see what befalls me along the way."

"You have an enterprising nature," said Triel "It does you credit.

Alas, Menzoberranzan can't spare any troops. Not at this time. Our forces are engaged in training exercises."

Faeryl fancied she knew the real reason the Baenre was at present reluctant to divest herself of any portion of her military strength. Her caution made perfect sense on its own terms, but surely it must yield to the gravity of the envoy's concerns!

"Matron Mother, if trade with Ched Nasad does not resume, the people of Menzoberranzan will find themselves bereft of countless amenities. Some of your craftsmen will lack the raw materials they need for their work. Your own merchant clans will endeavor to send caravans to my city, and those expeditions will probably not return."

"I imagine some clever male will import the same goods via a different route if he can reap a profit thereby."

Faeryl was beginning to feel as if she were mired in some lunatic dream.

"Matron, you can't be serious. Ched Nasad is the single greatest source of wealth your people possess."

Demons of the Web, it was in fact half again as populous as Menzoberranzan itself. The two realms had long been equals, and it was only a comparatively recent happenstance that had reduced the once independent City of Shimmering Webs to vassalage.

Triel spread her dainty, obsidian hands in a gesture of helpless resignation and said, "Wealth that is as much ours when stored in our trading costers in Ched Nasad as in our own vaults here."

Faeryl didn't know what else to say. No argument, however cogent, seemed capable of piercing Triel's shield of bland, almost mocking complacency.

"Very well," the ambassador said through gritted teeth, struggling to keep a grip on her temper. "If I must, I'll manage without your help. It will exhaust my purse, but perhaps I can hire some of the sellswords of Bregan D'aerthe."

Triel smiled. "No, my dear, that won't be necessary."

"I don't understand."

"I cannot give you leave to depart so precipitously. Who then would speak on behalf of your people? Even more importantly, I believe you may be right. Some new peril may be lurking in the Underdark and massacring drow left and right. I don't want it to kill you as well. I hold you in too high an esteem, and I certainly wouldn't want the other nobles of Ched Nasad to think that I blithely sent you to your doom. They might infer that I have little regard for even the most exalted officers of your splendid city, when of course, nothing could be farther from the truth."

"You honor me. Yet considering what's at stake—"

"Nothing is more important than your safety. *Anything* could happen if you attempt to traverse the tunnels at this unsettled time. You might not even make it out of Bauthwaf. Why, one of Menzoberranzan's own patrols, weary from too much duty, imagining a dwarf crouched behind every stalagmite, might mistake your band for a hostile force and loose a volley of poison darts at you. You might die an agonizing death at the hands of your own friends, in which case I would never forgive myself."

A chill crept up Faeryl's spine, because she understood what Triel had really said. The matron mother had just forbidden her to leave the city, on pain of death.

But why? What accounted for Matron Baenre's sudden hostility? Faeryl had no idea until she happened to glance up at the draegloth's face. Somehow the half-fiend's leer suggested an explanation.

Triel had decided Faeryl was less diplomat than spy, an agent for some power inimical to Menzoberranzan, who'd concocted this business of missing traders to provide herself with a good excuse to leave the city and report to her superiors.

Matron Baenre couldn't allow it, couldn't permit a spy to pass along the tale of Menzoberranzan's newfound weakness. She didn't dare, because it was entirely possible that not all dark elf enclaves had suffered the same calamity, and even if they had, perhaps the dwarves, duergar, deep gnomes, and illithids had not.

What remained unclear was why Triel believed as she did. Who had put the idea in her head, and what did that person have to gain by holding Faeryl in the city?

Jaw tight, the emissary stifled the impulse to confront Triel about the latter's true concerns. She knew she wouldn't be able to draw the

Baenre into an genuine consideration of the allegations against her. Taking a malicious pleasure in the play-acting, Triel would simply feign shock that Faeryl doubted her trust and good will.

Indeed, if Faeryl wanted to avoid further humiliation, all she could do was go along with the pretense.

She smiled and said, "As I said before, Matron Mother, your concern honors me, and I will of course obey you. I'll remain in the City of Spiders and savor its many delights."

"Good," said Triel, and Faeryl imagined the words that remained unspoken: We'll know where to find you when it's time for your arrest.

"May I have your permission to withdraw? I see there are many others seeking the benefit of your wisdom."

"Go, with my blessing."

Faeryl offered her obeisance, exited the hall, and walked through the great mound that was the Baenre citadel until she found herself alone and unobserved in a short connecting passageway. She took the rolled maps of the Underdark, the charts she had imagined that she and Triel might consult together, from beneath her arm. Teeth bared in a snarl, she smashed them repeatedly against the wall until the stiff parchment cylinder flopped limp and battered in her hands.

⚜ ⚜ ⚜

Gromph and Quenthel strolled about the plateau watching the apprentices and masters of Sorcere perform the rituals. The sound of chanting and the pungent scent of incense filled the air, along with various conjured phenomena: flashes of light, dancing shadows, demonic faces appearing and disappearing, moaning and crackling. All to lay a new set of wards about Tier Breche.

Gromph was mildly impressed. By and large, his minions were doing a good job of it, though they weren't laying any enchantments he couldn't pierce. In fact, since he was supervising them at their labors, getting past the wards would be easy.

"I wonder if all this will actually protect us," said Quenthel, scowling, her long skirt rippling in the stray breeze kicked up by someone's incantation.

Gromph was surprised that even after Beradax's attack, she hadn't donned a suit of mail. Perhaps she thought her frightened novices and priestesses required a show of confidence.

"It didn't protect us before," hissed one of the annoyingly vocal snakes comprising the whip on her belt.

Four of them were twisting this way and that, watching for danger. The fifth kept its cold eyes staring at Gromph, not, the archmage was convinced, because his sister suspected him of trying to murder her. Or rather she did, but not specifically. She simply had too many viable suspects. There were subordinates who aspired to be Mistress of Arach-Tinilith, and the myriad foes of House Baenre. Perhaps it was even Triel seeking to forestall the all but inevitable day when Quenthel would challenge her for preeminence.

"Enchantments can attenuate with time," said Gromph, honestly enough. "The new ones will be stronger. Strong enough, I trust, to keep you safe in Arach-Tinilith."

"It isn't just the temple at risk," Quenthel snapped. "Next time, a demon could attack Sorcere or Melee-Magthere."

Don't count on it, Gromph thought, but he said, "I understand."

"I've seen enough for now," said the mistress, her scowl deepening. "Don't let your males slack off. I want the defenses complete before you leave to cast your spell into Narbondel."

"Consider it done."

Quenthel turned and walked back toward Arach-Tinilith. The primary entrance to the imposing spider-shaped temple had become merely an odd-looking hole. The artisans hadn't yet finished repairing the crumpled adamantine leaves of the gate. Gromph smiled to think how that must annoy his sister. Knowing her as he did, he was fairly certain the unfortunate metalworkers had already felt the weight of her displeasure.

Well, perhaps they wouldn't have to bear it for much longer. He fingered a small ornament, a black stone clasped in a silver claw dangling over his heart.

Quenthel hadn't asked about the trinket, nor had Gromph expected her to. He always wore his amulet of eternal youth and the brooch that helped him imbue Narbondel with radiant warmth. Beyond those two staples, he tended to adorn the Robes of the Archmage with a constantly changing array of charms and talismans, depending on his whim and the particular magical tasks he expected to perform that day. His sister had had no reason to suspect that this particular trinket was of any particular significance, certainly not to herself.

If she had noticed it at all, she probably assumed the stone was onyx, ebony, or jet. In actuality, it was polished ivory cut from a unicorn's horn after Gromph slew the magical equine—sacred to the despicable elves of the World Above—in a necromantic rite. The orb was only black because of the entity he had placed inside it only two hours before.

"That was her," he murmured, too softly for any of the spellcasters bustling about him to overhear. "Did you take her scent?"

Yes, the demon answered, its silent voice like a nail scratching the inside of Gromph's head. *Though it was unnecessary. I may not possess the power of sight, but that has never hindered me as I sought my prey.*

"I was just making sure. Now, can you succeed where Beradax failed?"

Of course. No one of your world has ever escaped me. Afterward, I will feast on Quenthel's soul, one tiny morsel at a time.

Most likely the netherspirit would do exactly that, and if it failed, Gromph had six more waiting in line to pick up where it left off. Perhaps it wouldn't even come to that. He had, after all, manipulated events in such a way as to inspire more mundane assassins.

A third-year student came scurrying up with a stubby chalcedony wand in his hand. Recalled to more immediate concerns, Gromph sighed and prepared to teach the youth how the device worked.

Pretending to take an interest in an itinerant vendor's rack of cheaply forged and poorly balanced daggers, Ryld turned and surreptitiously surveyed the intersection.

A fellow with what the weapons master suspected were self-inflicted sores on his legs chanted for alms and shook a ceramic bowl. Since it was a rare if not demented dark elf who ever felt the tug of pity, the beggar sat near the entrance to a shabby boarding house catering to non-drow.

A female hurried by with a hooked and pointed pole—virtually a pike, when one really looked at it—on her shoulder and a giant weasel on a leash. She was plainly an exterminator headed out to rid a household of some substantial infestation.

A snarling noble from House Hunzrin drew his rapier and lashed a commoner with the flat, evidently because the latter had been a trifle slow stepping out of his way. The Hunzrins were notorious for their virulent arrogance. Perhaps it stemmed from the fact that they controlled the greater part of Menzoberranzan's agriculture. Or maybe they were compensating for the fact that, for all their wealth, they were stuck living in "mere East."

Any number of other rather drab and hungry-looking souls rushed on about their business.

"Reliving childhood memories?" the wizard asked.

"You forget," Ryld replied, "I was born in the Braeryn. I had to work my way up to get to Eastmyr."

"I daresay you took one look around, then kept right on climbing."

"You're right. Just now, I was checking to see if someone's tailing us. No one is."

"What a pity. I was hoping that if we asked enough questions in diverse male gatherings, some more friends of the runaways would try to murder us, or at least seek to learn what we're about. Perhaps the rogues are too canny for that."

"What do we do now?"

"Visit the next vile tavern, I suppose."

They started walking, and Pharaun continued, "Say, did I ever tell you how, two days into my first mission to the World Above, I wound up having to tail a human mage while the sun was blazing in the sky? I was blind with the glare, my eyes—"

"Enough," Ryld said. "You've told this a thousand times."

"Well, it's a good story. I know you'll enjoy hearing it again. There I was, blind with the glare . . ."

As the two masters strolled on, they passed a doorway sealed with a curtain of spiderweb. Forbidden by sacred law to disturb the silken trap until such time as its builder ceased to occupy it, the luckless occupant of the house had placed a box beneath his front window to serve as a makeshift step.

Across the way, a ragged half-breed child, part dark elf, part human by the look of her, brushed past a drunken laborer, then quickened her pace a trifle. Ryld hadn't actually seen her lift the tosspot's purse, but he was fairly certain she had.

Pharaun came to a sudden halt. "Look at this," he said.

Ryld turned, the long, comfortable weight of Splitter shifting ever so slightly across his back. On a wall at the mouth of an alley, someone had clumsily daubed a rudimentary picture of a clawed hand surrounded by flames. Though it was small and smeared in paint that barely contrasted with the stone behind it, Ryld was slightly chagrined that Pharaun had noticed it and he hadn't, but he supposed wizards had a nose for glyphs.

"Do you know what this is?" asked Pharaun.

"An emblem of the Skortchclaw horde, one of the larger tribes of orcs. I've been to the Realms that See the Sun a time or two myself, remember?"

"Good, I'm glad you confirm my identification. Now, what is it doing here?"

Ryld took a reflexive glance around, searching for potential threats, and said, "I assume some orc painted it."

"That would be my supposition, too, but have you ever known a thrall to do such a thing?"

"No."

"Of course not. What slave would dare deface the city, knowing that each and every drow takes pride in its perfection?"

"A crazy one. We've all seen them go mad under the lash."

"Whereupon they attack their handlers. They don't creep about scrawling on walls. I'd like to questions the people in these houses on either side. Perhaps someone can shed some light on this occurrence."

"You get curious about the strangest things," Ryld said, shaking his head. "Sometimes I think you're a little mad yourself."

"Genius is so often misperceived."

"Look, I know this puzzle is going to nag at you, but we're right in the middle of trying to find the runaways and so save your life. Let's stick to that."

The tall, thin wizard smiled and said, "Yes, of course."

They walked on.

"But eventually," Pharaun said after a moment, "when we've located the rogues and covered ourselves in glory—or at least convinced Gromph to let me continue breathing—I am going to inquire into this."

They traveled another block, then a column of roaring yellow fire fell from the sky, engulfing Pharaun's body. Wings beat the air, and an arrow streaked at Ryld.

The netherspirit couldn't see the new enchantments surrounding Tier Breche, but as the uttermost attenuated projection of its substance washed over them, it could feel them.

Metaphorically speaking, the wards were not unlike a castle. There was the motte, the steep slopes of which would slow an enemy's approach while the defenders rained missiles down on him. Atop that loomed the thick, high walls, virtually unbreachable and unclimbable. Amid those was the recessed gate, defensible by spears and arrows loosed from three directions. Within the passage itself, murder holes gaped in the ceiling to rain burning oil on the invaders' heads, while beyond it rose a gatehouse with battlements at the top, another barrier to enclose the first section of the courtyard and turn it into a killing pit.

Gromph's first countermagic, the one that had admitted the late and unlamented Beradax to the temple, had stormed the fortress like a rampaging army equipped with catapults, rams, and siege towers. The archmage's second effort resembled a mine sappers had excavated to pass unobtrusively beneath the walls. Except that this hole ran though extradimensional space.

As the netherspirit understood it, this method of egress was arranged by the Baenre eldermale so that the occupants of Arach-Tinilith would experience another kind of terror. They had already discovered the dread of a screaming alarm, and they would learn the fear that came when death slipped into their midst without any warning at all.

Pulling in the longer tendrils of its ectoplasmic substance, the entity—it and its kind had no names, an advantage in that most wizards therefore lacked the ability to summon them—poured its formless form into the tunnel, albeit not without a measure of trepidation. If Gromph's magic was unable to neutralize the conjurations of his minions, this was where the spirit would discover it in some unpleasant way.

As it crept down the mine, it sensed the wards poised above and around it, enchantments like hanging axes, precariously balanced and eager to fall, or taut tripwires attached to crossbows, or caltrops strewn lavishly underfoot. The constructs of mystical force fairly quivered like living things with their compulsion to slay, but none of them detected the intruder.

The other end of the tunnel, which would not exist for mortal eyes unless they were magically augmented, opened on a corridor. The netherspirit climbed out and took its bearings. It was inside one of the spider leg annexes of Arach-Tinilith, some distance from Quenthel's suite, but that was all right. It was confident that nothing could bar its path to its target.

The intruder hunched and drifted around a corner and saw a novice standing watch. Happily, the dark elf female didn't notice it, though that was scarcely a surprise. For some reason it didn't fully understand, Gromph had given it the guise of a demon of darkness, and it was all but indistinguishable from the ordinary, empty gloom behind it.

The netherspirit yearned to kill the mortal, but Gromph had forbidden it to do harm to anyone but Quenthel unless she was fool enough to stand between it and its appointed prey. With a pang of regret, it slipped past the sentry and on down the corridor. Soon it came upon a row of cells. Within the square little rooms, students recited their devotions.

So eager for bloodshed was the entity that the hall seemed to last forever. Soon enough, though, the spirit reached the spider's cephalothorax. This was the round, firelit heart of the temple, home to the grandest chapels, the holiest of altars, and the quarters of the temple's senior priestesses.

The intruder flowed into a spacious and largely empty octagonal chamber, where the air was perceptibly cooler than in the surrounding rooms and hallways. Statues of Lolth stood between the eight open rectangular doorways, and inlaid lines and curves of gold defined a complex magical sigil on the floor, a pentacle seemingly focused on a nexus of power at the exact center of the room. The same figure adorned the lofty ceiling, reinforcing the enchantment.

The netherspirit had no particular desire to discover what that enchantment was. It crawled along the walls, making sure not to touch the edge of the design.

Waves of power beat from the middle of the figure as something woke or became more real in the center of the chamber. A sharpness tore into the top of the spirit's vaporlike body, stunning it for an instant with a burst of unexpected pain.

Something jerked the living darkness toward the middle of the chamber. It realized that despite its lack of solidity, something had caught it with the equivalent of a hook and line. It also understood that simply avoiding the pentacle hadn't been good enough. Apparently when one entered the room, one was supposed to say a password or something.

The pulling ended abruptly, and the pain diminished. Shaking off its shock and disorientation, the darkness cast about and discerned the being crouching over it. The attacker was nearly as amorphous as itself, but the essence of it was fixed, hard, a mass of knobs and angles.

The attacker extruded additional lengths of itself to transfix the darkness. The piercings burned, made the spirit shake uncontrollably, and seemed to be leeching out its strength.

This, Gromph's agent realized with a kind of wonder, was the cold that could extinguish a mortal life in a heartbeat. The intruder had never felt the sensation before—not in a painful way—and shouldn't have been feeling it at all, but the prisoner of the pentacle wasn't just cold. It was the *essence* of cold, the pure *idea* of cold given life, just as the netherspirit to some degree embodied the concept of darkness.

Bits of the assassin began to clot, to gum, and to harden to a brittle rigidity, at which point they broke away. It wasn't truly injured as yet, but if it wanted to keep it that way, it knew it had better strike back at its assailant.

It washed its leading edge over the spirit of cold and discovered stress points, hairline cracks, imperfect junctures. Of course—the prisoner's structure resembled a mass of ice.

Gromph's agent materialized members like hammers, which pounded at the weak spots. It slid thin planes of itself into the fissures, then thickened them, forcing the edges apart.

The cold spirit snatched its frigid claws out of its foe. Its mind babbled a psionic offer of surrender. The cloud of darkness ignored it and continued the attack.

The freezing prisoner of the sigil exploded into motes of frost. They peppered the spirit of darkness for a second then they were gone.

Pleased with itself, the victor turned, inspecting each of the doorways in turn, trying to see if the battle had attracted anyone's attention. Apparently not, and actually, that made sense. The struggle had been relatively quiet, conducted largely on another level of existence.

The darkness reached the entrance to Quenthel's suite without further incident. Another sentry waited there, a spiked mace all but crackling with mystic force in her hand. Left to her own devices, she might hear her superior's distress and try to intervene, and the spirit decided to prevent such an occurrence. It rose around the priestess, blinding her, thickened a length of itself, and whipped it around her neck.

The female thrashed a little, then passed out for want of air. Her assailant laid her down and slid beneath the door.

Scores of costly icons decorated Quenthel's private rooms, so many that the place seemed a temple of Lolth in its own right. Beyond that, however, the suite was sparsely furnished, albeit with exquisite pieces, as if the Mistress of Arach-Tinilith practiced an asceticism at odds with the habits of the average sybaritic Menzoberranyr.

The darkness sent an intangible ripple of itself probing ahead. At once it discovered an element of Quenthel's personal defenses. It was not, as the spirit might have expected, a hidden mantrap woven of potent divine magic but a simple set of crystal wind chimes rendered invisible and hung at a point where any oblivious intruder would be sure to bump his head on them. Apparently the Baenre priestess believed that so long as an assassin gave her a second's warning, she would be able to handle the threat herself.

Maybe she could. The netherspirit would never know, because it had no intention of informing her of its coming. It took a certain ironic amusement in sliding its smokelike form directly through the dangling crystals without disturbing them in the slightest.

Eyes closed, in Reverie no doubt, Quenthel sat straight-backed and cross-legged on a rug. Along the back wall, pulses of mystical force throbbed from a pair of iron chests and from behind a theoretically secret door. The high priestess had invoked some formidable magic to protect her valuables. It was too bad she wasn't similarly careful with her life.

Gromph's agent flowed forward, and something reared hissing atop a round little table. It was the five vipers comprising an enchanted whip. Distracted by the magical power blazing at the back of the chamber, the netherspirit had missed feeling the lesser emanations of the vipers.

Fortunately, it didn't matter. The animate darkness had skulked too close to its prey for anything to balk it. It solidified a twisting strand of itself and slapped the table over, sending the whip flying. At the same time it darted, stretching, to pounce on Quenthel.

Her slanted eyes opened but of course saw only blackness. She opened her mouth to speak or shout, and the demon shoved a tendril inside.

For an instant, the world blazed bright and hot, searing Pharaun's skin. However, when the flame was gone it left little more than a tactile memory of pain. Gasping, the wizard took stock of himself. Except for a blister or two, he was all right. Some combination of the protective enchantments woven into both his vest and *piwafwi*, his innate drow resistance to hostile magic, and the silver ring he wore bearing the insignia of Sorcere, had saved him from fatal burns.

Ryld had drawn Splitter. An arrow whizzed down from a rooftop across the street, and the burly swordsman batted it out of the air. A huge flying mount wheeled overhead, vanishing from view before Pharaun could get a good look at it.

"Are you all right?" Ryld asked.

"Just singed a little," Pharaun replied.

"Here are your rogues, not so canny after all. We'll either have to rise into the air after them or pull them down to the street."

"We'll do neither. Follow me."

"Run?" the weapons master asked, swatting away another arrow. "I thought we wanted to catch one of them."

"Just follow."

Pharaun began moving down the street, meanwhile peering upward, looking for his attackers. Ryld scowled but trailed along behind him.

The Master of Sorcere glimpsed a swirling motion from the corner of his eye. He pivoted. Crouched on the edge of a roof, a spellcaster spun his hands in fluid mystic passes.

Gesturing, speaking rapidly, Pharaun rattled off his own incantation. He was racing the other mage, and he finished his magic first. Five darts of azure light leaped from his fingertips, shot at the spellcaster, and plunged into his chest. From that distance, he couldn't tell how badly he'd hurt his colleague, but at the least his foe flailed his arms in pain. The Academician's attack had disrupted his spell.

Ryld knocked another arrow away, and only then did Pharaun realize that this time, the shaft had been hurtling at him. An instant later, a studded mace seemingly made of shadow flew out of nowhere and swung itself at his head. Splitter flicked over and tapped that manifestation. As conjured objects often did, the war club vanished at the greatsword's touch.

"In here," Pharaun said.

The two masters ran to the arched sandstone door of one of the modest houses on the street. Pharaun suspected that the tenants had locked it at the first sign of trouble, and evidently Ryld agreed, because he didn't bother trying the handle. He simply booted the door and broke the latch. The weapons master scrambled inside.

The front room of the home was crowded. Pharaun might have expected that. The population of the city had grown considerably since its founding but the number of stalagmite buildings was of necessity fixed. The poor had to squeeze in wherever they could.

Thus, an abundance of paupers lived in the hovel, and a goodly number of them had gathered in this common space, either to relax or to dip rothé stew from the iron caldron on the trestle table. Surprisingly, the simple meal actually smelled appetizing. The aroma made Pharaun's mouth water and reminded him that he hadn't dined in several hours.

Ryld brandished Splitter at the occupants of the house with a flashy facility calculated to quell aggressive impulses.

"We apologize for the intrusion," Pharaun said.

The weapons master glowered at him. "*Why* are we running?"

"That pillar of fire was divine magic, not arcane." Pharaun lifted his hand, displaying the silver Sorcere ring and reminding his friend of its power to identify, not just protect him from, magic. "It's priestesses attacking us. Killing them would call attention to us, make the Council even more eager to put a stop to our inquiry. It might even make them want to kill us irrespective of how our mission turns out or of what Gromph decides."

Pharaun grinned and added, "I know I promised you glorious mayhem, but that will have to wait."

Ryld replied, "It's a difficult thing to sneak away from foes who hold the high ground."

"I'm an inexhaustible font of tricks, haven't you noticed?" Pharaun beamed at the assembled paupers and said, "How would you all like to assist two masters of the Academy engaged in a mission of vital importance? I assure you, Archmage Baenre himself will wax giddy with gratitude when I inform him of your aid."

His audience stared back at him, fear in their eyes. One of the female commoners produced a bone-handled, granite-headed mallet and threw it. Ryld caught it and hurled it back. The makeshift weapon thudded into the center of the laborer's forehead, and she collapsed.

"Would anyone else care to express a reservation of any sort?" Pharaun asked. He waited a beat. "Splendid, then just stand still. I assure you, this won't hurt."

The Master of Sorcere pulled a wisp of fleece from a pocket and recited an incantation. With a soft hissing, a wave of magical force shimmered through the room. When it touched the paupers, they changed, each into a facsimile of Ryld or Pharaun himself. Only a single child remained unaffected.

"Excellent," said Pharaun. "Now all you have to do is go outside, at which point, I recommend you scatter. With luck, many, if not all of you, will survive."

"No!" cried one of Ryld's doubles in a high, agitated voice. "You can't make us—"

"But we can," said Pharaun. "I can fill the house with a poisonous vapor, my friend can start chopping you to pieces. . . . So please, be sensible, go now. If the enemy breaks in here, your chances will be significantly worse."

They looked sullenly back at him. He smiled and shrugged, and Ryld hefted Splitter. The commoners began to scurry toward the door.

The two masters fell in at the back of the crowd, prepared to chivvy folk along as necessary.

"Shadows of the Pit," murmured Pharaun, "I wasn't at all sure they would actually do it. I am a persuasive devil, aren't I? It must be my honest face."

"Decoys aren't a bad idea," said Ryld, "but now that I think of it, why not just turn us invisible?"

Pharaun snorted. "Do I tell you which end of the sword to grip? Invisibility's too common a trick. I'm sure our foes are prepared to counter it. Whereas the illusion may work. It's one of my personal, private spells, and we Mizzrym are famously deft with phantasmata. Now, when we get outside, don't lose track of me. You don't want to go skipping off with the wrong Pharaun."

Most of the commoners had vacated the house. Pharaun drew a deep breath, steadying himself, and he and Ryld plunged out into the open.

The commoners were scattering as directed. As far as Pharaun could tell, no one had attacked any of them. Perhaps, as he'd hoped, the enemy was entirely flummoxed.

The masters, fleeing like the rest, turned one corner and another. Pharaun was beginning to feel the smugness that comes from outwitting an adversary when something rattled and rustled above his head. He looked up in time for it to slam him in the face and knock him down. Dropped from a fair height, the thick, coarse strands of rope comprising the net struck with the force of a club.

Also trapped, Ryld cursed, the language vulgar enough to make the Braeryn proud.

Pharaun needed a second to shake off the shock of the impact, and he realized his current situation was even more unfortunate than he'd initially thought. The net, woven in a spiderweb pattern, was animate. Scraping his skin, striving to render him completely immobile, the heavy mesh shifted and tightened around him.

A foulwing landed on the street. In the saddle sat an otherwise handsome priestess with a scarred face—a Mizzrym face, lean, intelligent, and sardonic. Strangely, she wore a domino mask, and Pharaun suspected he knew why.

Grinning, the female said, "I knew you'd try to trick me with illusions, Pharaun. That's why I brought a talisman of true seeing."

Though he wasn't sure she could see it from outside the net, Pharaun made it a point to smile back when he said, "And you were correct. Hello, Greyanna."

❈   ❈   ❈

Quenthel was immune to fear. She did not, could not, panic. Or so she had always believed, and in fact, she wasn't panicking, but she was as desperate and bewildered as any ill-wisher could desire.

She wasn't certain, but she believed the vipers' hissing and a bump and clatter had roused her from her trancelike state of repose. She'd opened her eyes and seen nothing. Evidently someone had conjured a patch of darkness around her, or worse, cursed her with a blindness spell. She opened her mouth to speak to the whip snakes, and something cold and thick jammed itself inside.

Her throat clogged, she was suffocating. Meanwhile, something else, something that felt like the cool, dexterous tip of a demon's tentacle, slid around her wrist.

She yanked her hand away just before the unseen member could lock around it and thrashed to keep her limbs free of the other tendrils that began to grope after them. None of it helped her breathe.

She battered furiously at the space around her. Logic told her that her attacker had to be there, but her fists merely swept through empty space. Her chest ached with the need for air, and she felt unconsciousness nibbling at her mind.

She did the only thing left. She bit down.

At first, she couldn't penetrate the mass, but she strained, snarled in her throat with effort, and her teeth sank into something leathery and oily.

In an instant, it vanished. It didn't yank itself free, it just melted away. Quenthel's teeth snapped together with a clack.

Scrambling to her knees, she sucked in a couple deep breaths, then called, "Whip!"

"Here!" Yngoth cried from somewhere on the floor. "We didn't see the demon until the last second. It *is* the darkness!"

"I understand."

At least she wasn't blind. She'd heard of demons made of darkness itself, though she had never had occasion to summon one. They were said to be hard to catch and even harder to bind.

"Guard!" she called.

This time she didn't hear an answer and wasn't surprised. The invader's presence suggested the sentry was either a traitor or dead.

Quenthel sensed something rushing at her. She flung herself sideways, and something crashed against the patch of wall immediately behind the space she'd just vacated. The stone floor chilled her through her gauzy wisp of a chemise.

As planned, she fetched up against the stand where she kept certain small pieces of her regalia. She leaped up and groped about the rectangular stone tabletop. To her disgust, a couple items rattled to the floor, but then her fingers closed on a medallion of beautifully cut glass.

Squinting, she invoked the trinket's power. A dazzling glare blazed through the room. Quenthel had to shield her own eyes, hoping the terrible light would destroy a living darkness altogether.

The magic light and the equally supernatural darkness made for a split second when the lighting in the room was as it was before the creature had entered. At least Quenthel could open her eyes.

Her assailant, seemingly unaffected by the light, was a ragged central blot with long, tattered arms snaking throughout the room, ubiquitous as smoke. Drinking in all the glow, reflecting none, it was dead black and deceptively flat-looking. It thrust a long, thin probe at the medallion and Quenthel jerked the token aside. The shaft of blackness veered, compensating, and struck the medallion hard enough to knock it out of her hand. The light died instantly when the glass medallion shattered on the floor.

Fortunately, the illumination had lasted long enough for her to note the locations of several other objects on the stand. She instinctively ducked, the tentacle swept over her head and tousled her hair, and she grabbed a scroll. As before, she would regret expending any of the spells contained therein, but she'd regret dying even more.

Conversant with the contents of the parchment, she didn't need to see the trigger phrase to "read" it. She recited the words, and a shaft of yellow flame roared down from the ceiling through the spot where the core of the demon had been floating. The firelight showed that it was still there. The blaze passed right through it, and all its arms and streamers of murk convulsed.

The column of flame vanished after a moment, leaving, despite the care the drow had taken to shield her eyes, a haze of afterimage bisecting her vision. It took her a second to realize that dull, wavering stripe was the only thing she could see. The darkness had survived. It had clotted its essence around her to seal her eyes once more.

You're a tough one, she thought, sending the unspoken words to the mind of the demon as she, a divine emissary of Lolth, was trained to do.

There was no response, and Quenthel felt no connection made between her mind and the consciousness of the demon. This was no servant of Lolth's.

Alive and impossible to command, it would surely grab or strike at her, and this time intuition was failing her. She had no idea from where the attack would come, so she didn't know which way to dodge to evade it. She simply had to guess, jump somewhere and not let blindness and indecision delay her. She pivoted, and something struck her shoulder.

At first it was just a startling jolt, then pain burned at the point of impact, and wet blood flowed. Either the darkness could harden its members into claws or else it had picked up a blade from somewhere in the chamber.

Quenthel was glad her teachers had taught her to suffer a wound without the shock of it freezing her in her tracks, helpless to avert her adversary's follow-up attack. She kept moving, making herself, she hoped, a more difficult target.

Something hissed. The source of the sound was almost under her feet. Evidently, dragging the whip handle behind them, her vipers had been slithering about endeavoring to locate her in the dark. She stooped, fumbled about their cool, sinuous lengths for a moment, achieved the proper grip, and lifted the weapon.

The serpents reared, hissed, and peered, each in a different direction. Quenthel realized they could see what she could not. The darkness was preparing to attack.

The priestess deepened her psionic link with her snake-demon servants. She still couldn't see where her adversary's tentacles were poised, but she had a sense of them. That would have to do.

The darkness reached for her, and, turning and turning, she swung the whip repeatedly. Her aim was inexact, but the vipers twisted in the air to correct it.

Toward the end, she was breathing harder, and her actions were getting bigger, slower, and wilder, as any combatant's will if she performs too many without a pause. Then something long and pointed plunged into the back of her thigh.

Quenthel knew at once from the flare of pain and the gush of blood that this puncture wound was worse than the gash in her shoulder. She staggered a step, and her leg began to fold. The whip vipers hissed in alarm.

She shouted to focus her will and quell the agony, to force the limb to obey. Throbbing, it straightened.

She spun and struck at the tentacle that had stabbed her, lashing it to pieces before it could do the same again. At that same instant, her serpent familiars detected hands reaching for her neck. She spun, destroyed those as well, and at last the shadow stopped attacking.

Feeling the blood stream down her leg to pool on the floor, her mind racing, Quenthel considered her situation. She must be causing the demon pain—if not it would attack relentlessly, never faltering until she fell—but that didn't necessarily mean she was well on her way to killing it. From what she knew of such entities, it seemed entirely possible that she would have to do more harm to the nucleus at the end of the tendrils to accomplish that. Assuming she could reach or even locate it amid the obfuscating gloom.

It might be better not to try, to take advantage of this momentary respite and make a run for it, but she knew that if she moved the demon would move with her, which would mean she'd still be scurrying sightlessly along. In her suite, that wasn't an enormous problem—she knew every inch of the space by heart—but outside, she could easily take a hard, incapacitating fall. If that happened or if her leg gave out before she found help, her foe would have little difficulty finishing her off.

No, she would kill the cursed thing by herself, quickly, while she was still on her feet. The only question was, how?

One of the weapons in her hidden closet might do the trick, but she had no way of reaching them. The demon would slay her while she fumbled in the dark to manipulate the hidden lock. She would have to make do with the resources in her hands, which meant using another scroll spell and taking a gamble as well.

The demon renewed the attack. Quenthel struck and deflected a tentacle with sawlike teeth on the edge. Next came an arm terminating in a studded bulb like the head of a mace. Poised to beat her skull in, that one was no use either. She sidestepped the blow, the vipers tore into the limb, and the living darkness snatched it back.

A simple tentacle, with no blades or bludgeons sprouting from its end, snaked toward her. It seemed as if it was going to try to grab and restrain her weapon arm. She pretended she didn't notice.

The strand of shadow dipped to the floor, hooked around Quenthel's ankle, and jerked her good leg out from under her. The change of target caught her by surprise, and she fell hard on her back, banging her head and shooting pain through her wounded limbs.

It took her an instant to shake off the shock. When she did, she sensed the fiend's other limbs poised to slash and pound. She was almost out of time to recite the trigger phrase.

But not quite.

She rattled off the three words, and power seethed and tingled inside her flesh. She discharged it into the living darkness, an easy task since the demon was holding onto her. She held her breath, waiting to see what would happen.

Like allowing her adversary to seize her, this too was a part of the gamble. The magic she had just unleashed would weaken a dark elf or pretty much any other mortal being to the point of death. However, depending on its precise nature, the demon—or whatever it was—might simply shrug it off. It might even feed on the blast of force and grow stronger than before.

The ploy worked. The fiend was susceptible, at least to some degree. She knew it when the entity's limbs flailed and thrashed in spasms, the one on her ankle releasing her to twist and flop about. The ambient darkness blinked out of existence for a second as the creature's grip on its surroundings wavered.

One instant of vision was all Quenthel needed to mark where her enemy's ragged core was floating. She scrambled up, charged it, and found that she was hobbling, every other stride triggering a jolt of pain. She didn't let the discomfort slow her down.

The creature of darkness was recovering. Two tendrils squirmed at Quenthel. She ducked one and lashed the other, which flinched back.

After two more steps, she judged, hoped, that she'd limped within striking distance of the entity's formless heart. She swung the whip, and shouted in satisfaction when she felt the vipers' fangs rip something more resistant than empty air.

She struck as hard and as fast as she could, grunting with every stroke. Her snakes warned her of tendrils looping around behind her, and she ignored the threat. If she left off attacking the center of the darkness, she might not get another chance.

The darkness obscuring the room started rapidly oscillating between presence and absence. Quenthel's motions looked oddly jerky in the disjointed moments of vision.

Tentacles grabbed and dragged her backward. She shouted in rage and frustration. As if responding to her cry, the arms dissolved, dumping her back on the floor.

Quenthel raised her head and peered about. There was no longer any impediment to sight. The murderous darkness was gone. Her last blow must have been mortal. It had just taken the creature another second or two to succumb.

"It's dead!" hissed Hsiv. "What now, Mistress?"

"First . . . I'm going to sit . . . and tend my wounds, then we're going to look . . . for my sentry," panted Quenthel, attenuating her rapport with the vipers. In too deep and prolonged a communion, shades of identity could bleed in one direction or the other. "If she's lucky, she's already dead."

She wished she were as undaunted as she was trying to sound, but it appeared that demonic assassins were going to keep coming for her. She'd hoped that the appearance of the spider demon might be an isolated incident. She'd thought that if any more such fiends did appear, the renewed wards would keep them out. Plainly, she'd been too optimistic.

At least Arach-Tinilith was the seat of her power. There, she could deploy a small army of retainers and a hoard of magical devices in her own defense, but those resources hadn't helped her against the darkness, and she couldn't help wondering how many hostile visitations a priestess in her condition could hope to survive.

Greyanna's henchmen came floating down around her. Two were warriors, one a wizard, and the third was another priestess. All wore the half masks of true seeing, giving them the deceptively foolish look of actors in a pantomime.

Pharaun tried to levitate, but the net was too heavy. He willed his animate rapier into existence. The steel ring vanished from his finger, and the long, slim sword materialized outside the net. The blade started slicing at the thick ropes, but to little effect. A rapier was a thrusting weapon and not suited to sawing. Tensing his muscles against the remorseless pressure of the tightening web, he turned the floating sword around to threaten his fellow representatives of House Mizzrym.

Greyanna laughed. "Is that one little bodkin supposed to hold us all at bay?"

"Possibly not," said Pharaun, straining to work his fingers closer to one of his pockets. "That's why I instructed it to kill you first."

"Did you, now?"

His sister motioned her warriors forward. Twin brothers possessed of the same slightly yellowish hair and deeply cleft chin, they carried pale bone longbows slung over their backs in preference to the more common crossbows.

Greyanna herself remained on her mount and produced a scroll from within her *piwafwi*. Thanks to his remaining ring, Pharaun could see from the complex corona of magical force shining around the rolled parchment that it contained, among others, a spell to disrupt the other fellow's magic. Perhaps she intended to use it to render the dancing rapier inert long enough for her minions to break or immobilize it.

The wretched ropes were digging into the wizard's flesh like knives. He would hardly have been surprised if they drew blood. They were certainly cutting off his circulation and numbing his extremities. Trembling with effort, he shifted his fingers another inch.

"My companion is Ryld Argith," he said, "a Master of Melee-Magthere. He's never done anything to you, and you will place yourself in debt to the warriors of the pyramid by killing him."

Entangled as he was, Pharaun couldn't even turn his head to look at his friend anymore, but he could hear Ryld grunting and swearing and feel him shaking the net. The swordsman was plainly trying to free himself, but it seemed unlikely that even his extraordinary strength would be enough if he was unable to bring one of his blades to bear, and apparently such was the case.

"I've kept tabs on you through the years." Greyanna said. "I know Master Argith is your most valued comrade. I don't need him trying to liberate or avenge you. Our mother will handle Melee-Magthere."

On further inspection, Pharaun observed that the subordinate priestess had readied a scroll as well. That struck him as vaguely odd, but he supposed this was hardly the time to ponder the possible significance.

The warriors were approaching steadily but warily, and not merely, he suspected, because of the hovering rapier. Greyanna could neutralize the weapon, but they feared that Pharaun would work some terrible magic that only required speech, not gestures or a focal object. He was sorry to disappoint them. He did have one or two such spells in his memory but none that could annihilate all five of these unpleasant folk at a single stroke, and he knew that once he conjured some devastating attack, they would abandon any intention of taking him alive for a demise by torture. They would strike back as fast and murderously as possible, and immobilized in the mesh, he would have little hope of defending against their efforts.

"Actually, you ought to think twice about harming either of us," he said, hoping that further conversation would slow the fighters' advance, even if only for a second.

Greyanna chuckled. "Be assured, I've thought of it a thousand thousand times."

"The archmage won't like it."

"I'm acting on behalf of the Council. I doubt he'll deem it politic to retaliate . . . any more than Melee-Magthere will."

"Well, Gromph won't sign his name to your cadaver, but someday . . ."

Pharaun's fingers finally jerked into the pocket and closed around a small but sturdy leather glove. With the net still tightening every second, it was just as hard to withdraw the article as it had been to reach it. He experimented to see if he could possibly fumble it through the proper mystical pass.

Such a cramped, tiny motion was neither easy nor natural for him. He was accustomed to conjure with a certain flair, making sweeping, dramatic gestures. Yet he had on occasion practiced making the signs as small as possible. It was good for his control and had a few times allowed him to cast a spell without an adversary realizing what he was about. So he had some hope of properly manipulating the glove. If only the web wasn't so constrictive or his hand so dead and awkward.

"Excuse me," Greyanna said, then suspended the conversation to read from her scroll.

It was of course divine magic, not arcane, and Pharaun didn't recognize all the words. The effect, however, was unmistakable. The rapier jerked and fell to the ground with a clank. The masked wizard stepped forward and scooped it up. Pharaun was content at least with the fact that the rapier's peculiar enchantment would make it impossible for Greyanna's henchman to turn the weapon on him— at least not for an hour or so.

Pharaun recognized the mage, whose high, wide forehead and small, pointed chin were unmistakable. Pharaun had always thought they made the other mage's head look like an egg. He was Relonor Vrinn, an able wizard and longtime Mizzrym retainer. He was still wearing his silk sash with the spell foci tucked inside and an eight-pointed gold brooch securing it.

Scimitars in hand, the warriors approached the net. Judging from their smiles, they'd decided there was nothing to fear and were looking forward to beating the two prisoners unconscious.

Pharaun was not yet satisfied with his employment of the glove, but he was rather clearly out of time. He would just have to try the pass and see if it worked. He shifted the focus one more time, meanwhile reciting an incantation under his breath.

A giant hand, radiant and translucent, appeared beneath the net. The instantaneous addition of another object lodged inside jerked the mesh even tighter. Pharaun knew the jolt was coming, but he cried out anyway.

The pain only intensified when, responding to the wizard's unspoken command, the hand hurtled twenty-five feet into the air, carrying the net and its prisoners along. For a moment, Pharaun feared he would black out, but the pressure eased. As he'd hoped, and despite the best sliding, bunching efforts of the web of ropes, his own weight was dragging him free. He shoved and thrashed to speed the process along.

When he was able, he looked over at Ryld. The hulking warrior was wrestling free of the net as well, though he lost hold of Splitter doing it. The greatsword fell point first, narrowly missed plunging through one of the Mizzrym warriors, and stuck pommel up in the smooth stone surface of the street.

"We have to fall," said Ryld. "If we just float here, they'll shoot and magic us to pieces."

"Let's go," Pharaun replied.

The masters released their holds and plummeted. One of the soldiers hit Ryld with an arrow, but the missile failed to penetrate his armor. A ball of flame exploded in the air, but Relonor had aimed too high, and the blast only made his targets flinch. Pharaun used his House insignia to slow his descent just a little. He thought that otherwise he'd break his legs.

As a result, he saw Ryld—who possessed a similar levitating talisman, his bearing the sigil of Melee-Magthere—reach the ground a moment ahead of him. The Master of Melee-Magthere tucked into a ball, rolled, sprang up with short sword in hand, and lunged at the soldier who'd loosed the arrow. The masked male leaped backward, dropped his bow, and whipped his scimitar out of its scabbard again. While he was so engaged, Ryld yanked Splitter out of the ground.

Pharaun landed. Despite his attempt to cushion the impact, it slammed up his legs and sent him staggering. As he fought to recover his balance, he noticed Relonor swirling his hands in a star-shaped pattern.

As the Master of Sorcere lurched upright, the other mage completed his incantation. A long, angular reptilian thing sprang from the palms of the older drow's outstretched hands as if they were the doorway to another world. Wreathed in flowing blue flame, the monster charged Pharaun.

Relonor was a gifted mage but no marvel as a tactician. In the excitement of the moment, he'd reflexively cast his favorite spell, and characteristically for a Mizzrym retainer, it was an illusion. He'd forgotten that his foe, born in the same House, might well recognize the sequence of mystic passes. Of course, even if Pharaun hadn't, his silver ring would have shown him what sort of magic the other male was creating.

He ignored the phantasm and reached into a pocket to snatch a tiny crystal and commence a spell. He ignored the apparition even when it lunged so close he felt the imaginary but searing heat of its halo of flame.

An intense coldness, visible in the fan of drifting ice crystals it instantly created, exploded from his hand. It passed right through the reptile, dissipating the illusion in the process, and washed over Relonor. It painted him with rime, and he fell backward.

Pharaun grinned. Greyanna was a fool to accost him with so few retainers in her train. Didn't she realize that two masters of Tier Breche were more than equal to the worst that she and her four dolts could do?

The foulwing flapped its batlike wings and hopped closer to the melee. As its legless body pounded down on the ground, Greyanna opened a leather bag and flung a handful of its contents into the air.

The falling motes flared with greenish light when they struck the ground. Each seethed and sparkled upward like a spore instantaneously growing into a fungus. In an instant, a number of animate skeletons stood upon the street. They carried a miscellany of weapons and shields but shared a common purpose. As one, they oriented on the masters and advanced.

Shifting back and forth, Ryld cut the undead creatures down. Pharaun took momentary shelter behind his friend, then the swordsman cried out, staggered, and dropped his guard. The skeletons surged forward, and the twins, who'd been hovering at the periphery of the fight, darted in as well.

Caught by surprise, Pharaun only just had time to conjure a dazzling, crackling fork of lightning. The power held the enemy back for a moment, and Ryld recovered his balance.

"All right?" asked the Master of Sorcere.

"Yes." Ryld chopped a spear-wielding skeleton's legs out from under it. "Something was trying to tamper with my mind, but it's gone now."

"It won't stay gone unless I confront the spellcasters."

Pharaun floated up into the air, beyond the skeletons' reach, making sure he would have a clear shot at Greyanna and the others. In his absence, the creatures would likely be able to surround Ryld, but that couldn't be helped.

Surveying the scene, he saw that Relonor was still lying motionless on his back. Positioned beyond the melee, Greyanna and her sister priestess were reading from scrolls.

For a moment, Pharaun's thoughts exploded into a terrifying madness, but reason quickly reasserted itself. He sucked in a deep breath, trying to quell the residual fear, and a second assault wracked his body. He cried out, and the agony passed. Somehow he'd weathered both spells.

He threw a seething ball of lighting at Greyanna, but it winked out of existence halfway to the target, unmade by the priestess's defenses. She and the other cleric employed their scrolls again.

A dazzling, searing beam of light erupted from Greyanna's hand. It slashed across Pharaun's face, and he closed his eyes just in time to keep it from blinding him. It was painful nonetheless, but his own defenses kept it from burning his face off.

The other priestess flailed at him with a sizzling bolt of lightning. As it was one of his own favorite forces to command, it hardly seemed fair. He stiffened with the shock for a moment or two, and the magic lost its grip on him.

He feared the spasm had cost him precious time. By the time it passed, he thought the priestesses were surely in the process of casting new spells, but when he looked at the lesser of the two she wasn't creating any magic. She'd dropped her suddenly blank scroll on the ground and was rooting in her leather pouch, presumably for another means of magical attack.

Clasping a bit of coal and a tiny dried eyeball held in a little vial, Pharaun created an effect. Power sighed and rippled through the air, and a mass of darkness appeared around the female's head, blinding her.

The wizard's thoughts flew apart once more, then reassembled themselves. He rounded on Greyanna. She was still clutching her scroll, evidently still casting from it. He began to conjure, and she, evidently uncertain of the parchment's power to protect her, tore open the bag.

It had occurred to Pharaun that the sack might have more spores in it, but he'd assumed they would produce more skeletons. This time, though, the glittering motes burst in midair, swelling into ugly little beasts resembling a cross between a bat and a mosquito.

The stirges swirled around him, jabbing at him with their proboscises, striving to drink his blood. They interfered with the motion of his hands and so spoiled his conjuration. He restored his weight and fell back to the ground, where Ryld, beset by clinking skeletons on all sides, beheaded one with a sudden cut. One of the twins edged toward him but balked when the big male pivoted in his direction.

Pharaun slammed down on the street. Trailing chattering stirges, he sprinted toward the fallen Relonor. A couple skeletons turned to hack at him, but most of them were too intent on killing Ryld to notice him. Up close, the things stank. Pharaun thought they must still have some scraps of rotting flesh about them somewhere.

Just as he reached the unconscious wizard, Greyanna's foulwing landed on the other side of the body with a ground-shaking thump. Pharaun roared out a painfully loud magical shout, and the beast recoiled, carrying its rider with it.

Pharaun stooped, ripped the brooch off Relonor's sash, turned, and ran. Greyanna screamed in rage. The foulwing roared its strange double roar, and two sets of jaws clashed shut behind the fleeing male.

A stirge's proboscis jabbed him in the back, staggering him, but was unable to penetrate his *piwafwi*. Another spell rattled his mind but with no permanent ill effects. A skeleton appeared on his flank, swinging a notched, rusty axe at his head. Splitter flashed in an arc and smashed the undead thing into tiny pieces.

Pharaun caught hold of the hem of Ryld's *piwafwi* and glanced around at Greyanna.

Her face a mask of fury, she tossed away her scroll, which was likely blank, and held her hands high to receive the long staff materializing from some extradimensional storage. He could see why she wanted the instrument. It blazed with mystic power, but it was also slow in attaining tangibility. Some chance interaction of the magical energies playing about the battleground was retarding its transition to the physical plane.

Why, then, didn't she leave off summoning it and attack in some other manner? Why—

In a flash of inspiration, the answer came to him, and it was astonishing.

But he was scarcely in a place conducive to contemplation of his discovery, and it was time to remedy that. He peered at the brooch he'd taken from Relonor, found the trigger word implicit in the kaleidoscopic pattern shining around it, and spoke.

🕷   🕷   🕷

Greyanna regarded the open space in the middle of the ring of aimlessly milling skeletons, and the stirges swooping and wheeling above. A moment before, Pharaun and his hulking accomplice had been standing there, but they were gone. If her eyes had not deceived her, her brother had flashed her that old familiar mocking grin as he vanished. How dare he smirk at her like that when it was she who had driven him from House Mizzrym!

She regarded her iron staff, taller than she was, square in cross-section, graven with hundreds of tiny runes, and warm as blood to the touch. The weapon had failed her. She trembled with the impulse to swing it over her head and smash it against the stone beneath her feet until it was defaced, deformed, and useless.

She didn't, because she knew Pharaun's escape was really her fault, not the staff's. She should have summoned the weapon sooner. She should have been more aggressive with the sack. Damn this degrading and inexplicable season! Because of its vicissitudes, her mother had instructed her to play the miser with every personal resource, even though she was fighting for the welfare of House Mizzrym and all Menzoberranzan.

Well, she wouldn't make the same mistake next time. It was her responsibility to look after her troops and return them to the castle.

She dismounted, squared her shoulders, put on a calm, commanding expression, and proceeded with the business at hand.

Neither of the twins were hurt, and her cousin Aunrae merely needed the ball of darkness around her head dispelled. It was Relonor who concerned Greyanna, but fortunately the mage was still alive. A healing potion mended him sufficiently to stand, clutching his sash so it wouldn't slip off and shrugging out of his ice-encrusted cloak.

While the twins helped Relonor hobble about and so restore his circulation, Aunrae came sidling up to Greyanna. To her cousin's admittedly jaundiced eye, in Aunrae the usual Mizzrym tendency to leanness had run to a grotesque extreme. The younger female resembled a stick insect.

"My commiseration on your failure," Aunrae said.

Her expression was grave, but she wasn't really trying to hide the smile lurking underneath.

"I didn't realize just how powerful Pharaun has become," Greyanna admitted. "Before his exile, he was quite competent but nothing extraordinary. It was his cunning that made him so dangerous. I see that all the decades in Tier Breche have turned him into one of the most formidable wizards in the city. That complicates things, but I'll manage."

"I hope the matron will forgive you your ignorance," Aunrae said. "You've wasted so much magic to no effect."

The conjured skeletons and stirges began to wink out of existence, leaving a residue of magic energy. The air seemed to tingle and buzz, though if a person stopped and listened, it really wasn't.

"Is that how you see it?" Greyanna asked.

Aunrae shrugged. "I'm just worried she'll feel you bungled things, that your hatred of Pharaun made you blind and clumsy. She might even decide someone else is more deserving of the preeminence you currently possess. Of course, I hope not! You know I wish you well. My plan for my future has always been to support you and prosper as your aide."

"Cousin, your words move me," Greyanna said as she lifted the staff.

No one could heave such a long, heavy implement into a fighting position without giving the opponent an instant's warning, so Aunrae was able to come on guard. It didn't matter. Not bothering to unleash any of the magic within her weapon, wielding it like an ordinary quarterstaff, Greyanna bashed the mace from the younger priestess's fingers, knocked her flat with a ringing blow to her armored shoulder, and dug the tip of the iron rod into her throat.

"I'd like to confer on one or two matters," said Greyanna. "Do you have a moment?"

Aunrae made a liquid, strangling sound.

"Excellent. Listen and grow wise. Today's little fracas was not in vain. It proved that Relonor can locate Pharaun with his divinations. Even more importantly, the battle enabled me to take our brother's measure. When we track him down again, we'll crush him. Now, do you see that I have this venture well in hand?"

Deprived of her voice, Aunrae nodded enthusiastically. Her chin bumped against the butt of the staff.

"What a sensible girl you are. You must also bear in mind that we aren't hunting Pharaun simply for my own personal gratification. It's for the benefit of all, including yourself. Therefore, this isn't an ideal time to seek to discredit and supplant one of your betters. It's a time for us to swallow our mutual distaste and work together until the threat is gone. Do you think you can remember that?"

Aunrae kept nodding. She was shaking, too, and her eyes were wide with terror. Small wonder; she must have been running short of breath. Still, she had the sense not to try to grab the staff and jerk it away from her neck. She knew what would happen if she tried.

Greyanna was tempted to make it happen anyway. Aunrae's submission was a small pleasure beside the fierce satisfaction that would come from ramming the staff into the helpless female's windpipe. The urge was a hot tightness in her hands and a throbbing in the scar across her face.

But she needed minions to catch the relative she truly hated, and, annoying as she was, Aunrae was game, and wielded magic with a certain facility. It would be more practical to murder her another day.

Greyanna was sure she could manage it whenever she chose. Despite her ambitions, Aunrae was no threat. She lacked the intelligence.

Feeling a strange pang of nostalgia for Sabal, who had at least been a rival worth destroying, Greyanna lifted the staff away from her cousin's throat.

"You will whisper no poison words in Mother's ears," the First Daughter of House Mizzrym said. "For the time being, you will leave off plotting against me or anyone else. You will devote your every thought to finding our truant brother. Otherwise, I'll put an end to you."

🕷   🕷   🕷

Ryld had never experienced instantaneous travel before. To his surprise, he was conscious of the split second of teleportation, and he found it rather unpleasant. It didn't feel as if he were speeding through the world but as if the world were hurtling at and through him, albeit painlessly.

Then it was over. He'd unconsciously braced himself to compensate for the jolt of a sudden stop, and the absence of any such sensation rocked him on his feet.

By the time he recovered his balance, he knew more or less where he was. A whiff of dung told him. He looked around and confirmed the suspicion.

Pharaun had dropped the two of them in a disused sentry post on a natural balcony. The ledge overlooked Donigarten with its moss fields, grove of giant mushrooms, and fungus farms fertilized with night soil from the city. Hordes of orc and goblin slaves either tended the malodorous croplands or speared fish from rafts on the lake, while rothé lowed from the island in the center of the water. Overseers and an armed patrol wandered the fields to keep the thralls in line. Additional guards looked down from other high perches about the cavern wall.

Ryld knew Pharaun had transported them about as far as was possible. In the Realms that See the Sun, teleportation could carry folk around the world, but in the Underdark, the disruptive radiance of certain elements present in the rock limited the range to about half a mile—far enough to throw Greyanna and her pack off the scent.

Pharaun held the pilfered golden ornament up, inspecting it.

"It only holds one teleportation at a time," he said after a moment. Even after all his exertions, he wasn't panting as hard as he might have been; not bad for such a sybarite, thought Ryld as he set down his bloody greatsword. "It's useless now, and I lost my dancing rapier, curse it, but I'm not too disconsol—"

Ryld grabbed Pharaun by the arm and flipped him, laying him down hard.

The wizard blinked, sat up, and brushed a strand of his sculpted hair back into place.

"If you'd told me you craved more fighting," Pharaun said, "I could have left you behind with my kin."

"The hunters, you mean," Ryld growled, "who found us quickly."

"Well, we asked a fair number of questions in a fair number of places. We even *wanted* someone to find us, just not that lot." Pharaun stood back up and brushed at his garments, adding, "Now, I have something extraordinary to tell you."

"Save it," Ryld replied. "Back there in the net, when you and Greyanna were chatting, I got the strong impression that the priestesses weren't just hunting some faceless agent. They knew from the start their target was you, and you knew they knew."

Pharaun sighed. "I didn't know the matrons would choose Greyanna to discourage our efforts. That was a somewhat disconcerting surprise. But the rest of it? Yes."

"How?"

"Gromph has invisible glyphs scribed on the walls of his office. Invisible to most people, anyway. They protect him in various ways. One, a black sigil shaped a little like a bat, is supposed to keep scryers and spellcasters from eavesdropping on his private conversations, but when he and I spoke, it was drawn imperfectly. It still would have balked many a spy, but not someone with the resources and expertise of, oh, say, his sisters . . . or the Council."

Ryld frowned. "Gromph botched it?"

"Of course not," Pharaun snorted. "Do you think the Archmage of Menzoberranzan incompetent? He drew it precisely as he wanted it. He knew the high priestesses were trying to spy on him——they surely always have and doubtless always will——and he intended them to overhear."

"He was setting you up."

"Now you're getting it. While the clerics stay busy seeking me, the decoy, my illustrious chief will undertake another, more discreet inquiry undisturbed, by performing divinations and interrogating demons, probably."

"You knew, and you undertook the mission anyway."

"Because knowing doesn't change my fundamental circumstances. If I want to retain my rank and quite possibly my life, I still have to complete the task the archwizard set me, even though he was playing me for a fool, even with Greyanna striving to hinder the process." Pharaun grinned and added, "Besides, where *did* all those runaways go, and why do the greatest folk in Menzoberranzan care? It's a fascinating puzzle, even more so now that I've inferred a portion of the answer. Did I leave it unsolved, it would haunt me forevermore."

"You played me for a fool," said Ryld. "Granted, you warned me the priestesses might interfere with us, but you greatly understated the danger. You didn't tell me you were marked before we even descended from Tier Breche. Why not? Did you think I'd refuse to accompany you?"

Most uncharacteristically, the glib wizard hesitated. Far below the shelf, a whip snapped and a goblin screamed.

"No," said Pharaun eventually, "not really. I suppose it's just that dark elves are jealous of their secrets. So are the nobly born. So are wizards. And I'm all three! Will you pardon me? It isn't as if you've never kept a secret from me."

"When?"

"During the first three years of our acquaintance, whenever we fraternized, you kept a dagger specially charmed for the killing of mages ever close to your hand. You suspected I was only seeking your company because one of your rivals in Melee-Magthere had engaged me to murder you as soon as the opportunity arose."

"How did you discover that? Never mind, I suppose it was your silver ring. I didn't know what it was back then. Anyway, that's not the same kind of secret."

"You're right, it isn't, and I regret my reticence but I do propose to make up for it by sharing the most astonishing confidence you've ever heard."

Ryld stared into Pharaun's eyes. "I'll pardon you. With the understanding that if you withhold any other pertinent information, I'll knock you over the head and deliver you to your bitch sister myself."

"Point taken. Shall we sit?" Pharaun pointed to a bench hewn from the limestone wall at the back of the ledge. "My discourse may take a little time, and I daresay we could use a rest after our exertions."

As he turned away from the molded rock rampart, Ryld noticed that the cracking of the whip had stopped. When he glanced down, two goblins were carrying the corpse of a third, hauling it somewhere to be chopped apart and the pieces turned to some useful purpose. Possibly chow for other thralls.

The fencing teacher sat down and removed a cloth, a whetstone, and a vial of oil from the pockets of his garments. He unfastened his short sword from his belt, pulled on the hilt, and made a little spitting sound of displeasure when the blade, which he had been forced to put away bloody, stuck in the scabbard. He yanked more forcefully, and it came free.

He looked over at Pharaun, who was regarding with him with a sort of quizzical exasperation.

"Talk," the warrior said. "I can care for my gear and listen at the same time."

"Is this how you attend to mind-boggling revelations? I suppose I'm lucky you don't have to use the jakes. All right, here it is . . . Lolth is gone. Well, maybe not *gone*, but unavailable at least in the sense that it's no longer possible for her Menzoberranyr clerics to receive spells from her."

For a moment, Ryld thought he'd misheard the words. "I guess that's a joke?" he asked. "I'm glad you didn't make it while we were in the middle of a crowd. There's no point compounding our crimes with blasphemy."

"Blasphemy or not, it's the truth."

Rag in hand, Ryld scrubbed tacky blood off the short sword.

"What are you suggesting," the weapons master asked, "another Time of Troubles? Could there be two such upheavals?"

Pharaun grinned and said, "Possibly, but I think not. When the gods were forced to inhabit the mortal world, the arcane forces we wizards command fluctuated unpredictably. One day, we could mold the world like clay. The next, we couldn't turn ice to water. That isn't happening now. My powers remain constant as ever, from which I tentatively infer this is not the Time of Troubles come again but a different sort of occurrence."

"What sort?"

"Oh, am I supposed to know that already? I thought I was doing rather well to detect the occurrence at all."

"Only if it's really happening."

Ryld inspected the point of the short stabbing blade, then took the hone to it. Bemused by Pharaun's contention, he wondered how his canny friend could credit such a ludicrous idea.

"I want you to think back over the confrontation from which we just emerged," said the Master of Sorcere. "Did you even once see Greyanna or the other priestess cast divine magic from her own mind and inner strength as opposed to off a scroll or out of some device?"

"I was fighting the skeletons."

"You keep track of every foe on the battleground. I know you do. So, did you see them casting spells out of their own innate power?"

Ryld thought that of course he had . . . then realized he hadn't.

"What does that suggest?" Pharaun asked. "They have no spells left in their heads, or only a few, which they're hoarding desperately because they can't solicit new ones from their goddess. Lolth has withdrawn her favor from Menzoberranzan, or . . . something."

"Why would she do that?"

"Would she need a reason—or at any rate, one her mortal children can comprehend? She is a deity of chaos. Perhaps she's testing us somehow, or else she's angry and deems us unworthy of her patronage.

"Or, as I suggested before, the cause of her silence, if in fact she is mute when her clerics pray to her and not just uncooperative, may be something else altogether. Perhaps even another happenstance involving all the gods. Since we have only one faith and clergy in Menzoberranzan, it's difficult to judge."

"Wait," Ryld said. He unstoppered his little bottle of oil. The sharp smell provided a welcome counterpoint to the moist stink of the dung fields. "I admit, I didn't see Greyanna or any of the lesser priestesses working magic, but didn't you yourself once tell me that in the turmoil of battle, it's often easier and more reliable to cast your effects from a wand or parchment?"

"I suppose I did. Still, under normal circumstances, would you expect a pair of spellcasters to conjure every single manifestation that way? Just before our exit, I saw Greyanna groping in the ether for a weapon that was slow in coming to her hand. The sister I remember would have said to the Hells with it and dumped some other magic on our heads. That is, unless something had circumscribed her options."

"I see what you mean," Ryld conceded, "but when the clerics lost their powers in the Time of Troubles, it destabilized the balance of power among the noble Houses. Those who believed the change made them stronger in relative terms struck hard to supplant their rivals. As far as I can see, that isn't happening now, just the usual level of controlled enmity."

He laid the short sword aside and picked up Splitter.

Pharaun nodded and said, "You'll recall that none of the Houses attempting to exploit the Time of Troubles ultimately profited thereby. To the contrary, the Baenre and others punished them for their temerity. Perhaps the matron mothers took the lesson to heart."

"So instead of hatching schemes to topple one another, they . . . what? Enlisted every single priestess in a grand conspiracy to conceal their fall from grace? If your mad idea is right, that's what they must have done."

"Why is that implausible? Picture the day—a few tendays past?—when they lost the ability to draw power from their goddess. Clerics of Lolth routinely collaborate in magical rituals, so they would have discovered fairly quickly that they were all similarly afflicted. Apprised of the scope of the situation, Triel Baenre, possibly in hurried consultation with our esteemed Mistress Quenthel and the matrons of the Council, might well have decided to conceal the priesthood's debility and sent the word round in time to keep anyone from blabbing."

"The word would have to pass pretty damn quickly," said Ryld, examining Splitter's edge. As he'd expected, despite all the bone it had just bitten through, it was as preternaturally keen and free of notches and chips as ever.

"Oh, I don't know," the wizard said. "If you lost the strength of your arms, would you be eager to announce it, knowing the news would find its way to everyone who'd ever taken a dislike to you? Anyway, since this is the first we've learned of the problem, the deception obviously did organize in time."

"Or else everything is as it always was, and the plot exists only in your imagination."

"Oh, it's real. I'm sure Triel deemed the ruse necessary to make sure no visitor would discern Menzoberranzan's sudden weakness." He grinned and added, "And to fix it so we poor males wouldn't swoon with terror upon learning that our betters had lost a measure of their ability to guide and protect us."

"Well, it's an amusing fancy."

"Fire and glare, you're a hard boy to convince, and I'll be cursed if I know why. You've already lived through the Time of Troubles, the previous Matron Baenre's death, and the defeat of Menzoberranzan by a gaggle of wretched dwarves. Why do you assume our world cannot have altered in some fundamental way when you've watched it change so many times before? Open your mind, and you'll see my hypothesis makes sense of all that has puzzled us."

"What do you mean?"

"Whatever they're up to, how is it that for the past month an unusual number of males have dared to elope from their families?

Because they somehow tumbled to the fact that a priestess's wrath now constitutes less of a threat."

"While the clerics," said Ryld, catching the thread of the argument, "are eager to catch them because they want to know how the males know about the Silence, if we're going to call it that. Hells, if all those males had the nerve to run away, maybe they even know more about the problem than the females do."

"Conceivably," said Pharaun. "The priestesses can't rule it out until they strap a few of them to torture racks, can they? But they don't want Gromph involved with capturing the rogues because . . . ?"

"They don't want him to find out what the runaways know."

"Very good, apprentice. We'll make a logician of you yet."

"Do you think the archmage already knows the divines have lost their magic?"

"I'd bet your left eye on it, but he's in the same cart as the high priestesses. He posits that the fugitives might know even more."

Ryld nodded. "In a war, or any crisis, you have to cover every possibility."

"The notion of the Silence even explains why the Jewel Box was so crowded, and why some of the patrons were in a belligerent humor or even bruised and battered. Females divested of their magic might well feel weak and vulnerable. Consciously or otherwise, they'd worry about losing control of the folk in their household and compensate by instituting a harsher discipline than usual."

"I see that," said Ryld.

"Of course you do. As I said, the one hypothesis accounts for every anomaly. That's why we can be confident the idea is valid."

"How does it account for the relative paucity of goods in the Bazaar?"

Pharaun blinked, narrowed his eyes in thought, and finally laughed. "You know, it's difficult for genius to soar in the face of these carping little irrelevancies. Actually, you're right. At first glance, the Silence doesn't explain the marketplace, but it explains so much else that I still believe the idea correct. Have I persuaded you?"

"I . . . maybe. You do make a kind of twisted sense. It's just that it's a hard idea to take in. The one truth our people have never questioned is that Menzoberranzan belongs to Lolth. Everything in the cavern is as it is because she willed it so, and the might of her priestesses is the primary force maintaining all that we have and are. If she's turned her face from the entire city, or is lost to us in some other way. . . ." Ryld spread his hands.

"It is unsettling, but perhaps, just perhaps, it affords us an opportunity as well."

Ryld extended a telescoping metal probe, attached a cloth to the hook on the end, and started swamping out the blood-clogged scabbard.

The warrior asked, "What do you mean?"

"Just for fun, let's make the same leap of faith—or fear—that Gromph and the Council did. Assume the rogue males can explain the cessation of Lolth's beneficence. Assume you and I will find them and extract the information. Finally, assume we can somehow employ it to restore the status quo."

"That's a lot of assuming."

"It is. Obviously, I'm letting my imagination run amok. Yet I have a hunch—only a hunch, but still—that if two masters of the Academy could accomplish such a triumph, they might thereby win enough power to make my friend the Sarthos demon look like small beer. You wanted to find something to our advantage, as I recall."

"Your sister may find us first. She tracked us once. Do you still think we shouldn't kill her, or her vassals either?"

"That's a good question," Pharaun sighed. "They're attacking us with potent magic. I suspect that leather bag holds nine sets of servant creatures, each deadlier than the one before."

"In that case, why didn't she chuck them all at us?"

"Perhaps, in the absence of her innate powers, she was trying to conserve her other resources. Alas, she may not be so parsimonious next time."

"So what do we do?"

"Well, you know, I truly do want to kill Greyanna. I always have, but I suppose the prudent course is to avoid our hunters if possible. If not, we'll do what we must to survive. I may at least make a point of disposing of Relonor. I suspect he located us with divinatory magic. He was always good at that."

"Can you shield us?"

"Perhaps. I intend to try. Stay right where you are, and don't speak."

Pharaun rose and reached into one of his pockets. Out in the lake, something big jumped. Noticing the splash, an orc on a raft grunted to his fellows, and they readied their barb-headed lances.

As Drisinil took hold of the door handle, the stump of her little finger throbbed beneath its dressing. The novice still found it difficult to believe that, after fighting for her life against the demon spider, Mistress Quenthel had immediately returned to the matter of the would-be truants and their self-inflicted punishment. It bespoke a calm and meticulous nature. Drisinil admired those qualities, but it didn't make her hate their exemplar any less.

She took a final glance around the deserted corridor. No one was about, and no one was supposed to be, not in that length of that particular wing of Arach-Tinilith at that hour of the night.

She slipped through the sandstone door and pulled it shut behind her. Unlike much of the temple, no lamps, torches, or candles burned in the room beyond the threshold. That was by design, to keep a telltale gleam from leaking out under the door.

Drisinil's sister conspirators awaited her. Some were novices with bandaged hands, just like herself. Others were instructors. Those high priestesses, hampered by their dignity, were having some difficulty making themselves comfortable among the haphazardly stacked boxes and tangles of furniture littering the half-forgotten storeroom. Of course, it didn't help that they hesitated to clear away the shrouds of filthy cobwebs dangling everywhere for fear a living spider remained within.

Drisinil wondered if that particular prohibition made sense any longer. Perhaps spiders were no longer sacred.

Then, angry at herself, she pushed the blasphemous thought away. Lolth abided, beyond any question, and was likely to chastise those who even for a moment imagined otherwise.

Once she wrenched her mind back to immediate concerns, Drisinil was momentarily nonplussed to find the company regarding her expectantly. Did they expect her to preside over the meeting?

But then again, why not? She might be a novice, but she was Barrison Del'Armgo as well, and breeding mattered, perhaps more than ever when even the most powerful priestesses were running out of magic. Besides, the secret gathering had been her idea.

"Good evening," she said. "Thank you all for attending,"—she smiled wryly—"and for not reporting me to Quenthel Baenre."

"We still could," said Vlondril Tuin'Tarl, a strange smile on her wrinkled lips. "Your task is to convince us we shouldn't."

The teacher was so old that she had begun to wither like a human crone. Most folk believed her mystical contemplations of ultimate chaos had left her a little mad. No one, not even another instructor, had opted to sit in her immediate vicinity.

"With respect, Holy Mother," Drisinil said, "isn't that self-evident? The goddess, who nurtured and exalted our city since its founding, has turned her back on us."

Once again, Drisinil couldn't help thinking of other possibilities, but even if she'd seen a point to it, she wouldn't have dared to mention them. No one would, not in her present company.

"And Quenthel is to blame," added Molvayas Barrison Del'Armgo.

Though stockier and shorter than Drisinil, her aunt had the same sort of sharp nose and uncommon green eyes. Richly clad, the elder scion of the House carried an enemy's soul imprisoned in a jade ring, and at quiet moments one could occasionally hear the spirit weeping and pleading for release. Second to Quenthel as Barrison Del'Armgo was ever second to Baenre, Molvayas had helped her niece pass word of the meeting, and her support lent it a certain credibility.

"How do you know that?" asked T'risstree T'orgh.

Deceptively slender, a fully trained warrior as well as a priestess, she was notorious for carrying a naked falchion about in preference to the usual mace or whip of fangs, and gashing the exposed flesh of any student who displeased her with a fast but precisely controlled cut to the face. The short, curved blade lay across her knees.

Drisinil waited a beat to make sure Molvayas intended her to answer the question. Apparently she did, and rightly so, since it was the younger female who had actually conceived the argument.

"When Triel was mistress here," said the novice, "all was well. Shortly after Quenthel assumed the office, Lolth rejected us."

" 'Shortly' being a relative term," said a sardonic voice from somewhere in the back of the room.

"Shortly enough," Drisinil retorted. "Perhaps the goddess gave us time to rectify the error. We failed to do so, so now she's punishing us."

"She's afflicting all Menzoberranzan," T'risstree said, "not just Tier Breche."

"Surely," said Drisinil, "you didn't expect her to be *fair*. I hope a priestess knows Lolth's ways better than that. Her wrath is as boundless as her might. Besides which, Arach-Tinilith is the repository of the deepest mysteries and thus the mystic heart of Menzoberranzan. It makes perfect sense that whatever befalls us here should touch the city as a whole.

"In any case," the novice continued, "Lolth has shown us her intent. Despite our safeguards, two spirits invaded the temple, the first in the guise of a spider, the second a living darkness. Spider and darkness, reflections of the essence of the goddess. The demons injured those who got in their way. They bruised them and broke their bones, but they didn't try to kill any of us, did they? They were plainly seeking Quenthel, and they sought to kill her and her alone."

Some of the other priestesses frowned or nodded thoughtfully.

"It did seem that way," said Vlondril, "but what do you think is unacceptable about Quenthel? Isn't she doing all the same things Triel did?"

"We don't know everything she does," said Drisinil, "and we don't know what she thinks. Lolth does."

"But you don't know she sent the demons," T'risstree said. Born a commoner but risen to a level of power and prestige, she had evidently shed the habit of deference to the aristocracy. "Perhaps one of Quenthel's mortal enemies sent them."

"What mortal possesses a magic potent and cunning enough to penetrate the temple wards?" Drisinil replied.

"The archmage?" Vlondril offered, picking at the skin on the back of her hand. Her tone was light, as if she spoke in jest.

"Even if he does," Drisinil said, "Gromph is a Baenre, too, and Quenthel serving as mistress strengthens his House. He has no reason to kill her, and if it isn't he, then who? Who but the goddess?"

"Quenthel is still alive," said a priestess from House Xorlarrin. She'd worn a long veil to the conclave, apparently so anyone who noticed her walking the halls would assume she was engaged in a certain necromantic meditation. "Do we think Lolth tried to kill her and failed?"

"Perhaps," Drisinil said. Some of her audience scowled or stiffened at what could be construed as blasphemy. "She is all-powerful, but her agents are not. However, I think she intended the first two assassins to fail. She's giving her priestesses a chance to ponder what's happening. To comprehend her will, perform our appointed task, and earn her favor once more."

Vlondril smiled. "And we do that by murdering Quenthel ourselves? Oh, good, child, very good."

"We kill her ourselves," Drisinil agreed, "or, if that isn't feasible, we at least assist the next demonic assassin in whatever way we can."

T'risstree shook her head. "This is sheer speculation. You don't know the mistress's death will bring Lolth back."

"It's worth a chance," Drisinil said. "At the very least, if we give the demons what they want, they'll stop invading Arach-Tinilith.

They haven't slain any of us yet, but if we don't help them, and Quenthel lives on, they may decide to eliminate us, too, for after all, it's a demon's nature to kill."

"The demons may be less dangerous than House Baenre," T'risstree said.

"The Baenre won't know who facilitated Quenthel's demise," Drisinil said. "So what will they do, wreak their vengeance on every priestess in Arach-Tinilith? They can't. They need us to educate their daughters and perform the secret rites."

"If Quenthel dies," said a priestess leaning against the wall, "Molvayas has a fair chance of becoming Mistress of Arach-Tinilith—but how do the rest of us stand to gain?"

"My niece has explained," said Molvayas, "that we'll all renew our bond with the goddess and replenish our magic. Beyond that, I promise that if I become mistress, I'll remember those who lifted me up. High priestesses, you will be my lieutenants, ranking higher than any other instructor. Novices, your time at Arach-Tinilith will be spent far more pleasantly than is the rule. You, too, will exercise authority over your peers. You'll enjoy luxuries. I'll excuse you from the more onerous ordeals and teach you secrets most pupils never learn."

"We'll hold you to that," said another voice from the back, "and expose you if you renege."

"Exactly," said Molvayas. "You'll always be in a position to inform House Baenre of my guilt. Your numbers are too great for me to murder all of you, and so you know you can trust me to keep my pledge. Even if it were otherwise, I'd be stupid to play you false, considering that I'll always need loyal supporters."

"It's tempting," the veiled Xorlarrin said. "I'd take almost any chance to win my magic back. Still, we're talking about the Baenre."

"Damn the Baenre!" Drisinil spat. "Perhaps killing Quenthel is the first rumble of the cave-in that will bury the entire clan."

"What cave-in?" T'risstree asked.

"I don't know, exactly," Drisinil admitted. "Still, consider this: Houses rise and fall. It's the way of Menzoberranzan and the will of

Lolth. Thus far, House Baenre has been the exception, perching on the top of the heap for century after century. Perhaps, with the old matron mother's death, the family has finally forfeited the goddess's regard. Why not . . . everyone knows Triel is out of her depth. Perhaps it's time at last for House Baenre to honor the universal law. If so, wouldn't it be glorious to commence the decline in their fortunes here, now, this very minute in this very room?"

"Yes," T'risstree declared.

Surprised, Drisinil turned to face her. "You agree?"

Setting her razor-edged falchion aside, T'risstree rose and said, "I was dubious, but you convinced me." For an instant, she grinned. "I don't like Quenthel anyway. So yes, we'll usher her into her tomb, regain the goddess's approval, and run the academy as we please."

She extended her hands. Drisinil smiled and clasped them despite the twin shooting pains the pressure produced, then she turned to the other females and said, "What about the rest of you? Are you with us?"

They tendered a ragged chorus of assent. She guessed that those who doubted she had hit on the way to propitiate Lolth were nonetheless eager to move up in the temple hierarchy, or at least disliked Quenthel. Maybe they were simply indulging the innate dark elf taste for bloodshed and betrayal.

Drisinil herself truly did believe she'd contrived the proper metaphysical remedy for their woes but deep down, she was even more excited at the prospect of avenging herself on her torturer. How could it be otherwise? For the rest of her life, her self-mutilated hands would announce to any who looked that someone had once defeated and humiliated her.

"I thank you," she said to the other clerics. "Now, let's put our heads together. We have much to plan and only a little time before others will start to miss us."

And plan they did, whispering, bickering, occasionally grinning at some particularly inventive and vicious suggestion. Drisinil knew that some if not all of the scheming would come to nothing—it was too contingent on Quenthel's doing precisely what the plotters wanted exactly when and where they wanted it done—but the effort served to cement their commitment to the conspiracy and to limn at least the bare bones of a strategy.

Finally it was done. The priestesses started to slip out the way they'd come, one and two at a time. The more restless stood in a clump around the exit, awaiting their turns. T'risstree was among them.

Drisinil crossed the floor in as relaxed and casual a manner as she could affect. She didn't want someone to realize her intent, and, surprised, react in some audible way.

No one did. All dark elves were actors in that they were liars, and perhaps she was a better dissembler than most. She sauntered within arm's reach of T'risstree, took hold of the dirk concealed inside her long, fringed shawl, and drove the blade into the high priestess's spine. This time, for whatever reason, the stumps of her severed pinkies didn't hurt a bit.

T'risstree's back arched in a spasm of agony, and, to Drisinil's surprise, her teacher tried to flounder around to face her. Her arm shaking, T'risstree lifted the falchion.

Drisinil turned along with the high priestess, keeping behind her. She grabbed hold of T'risstree's hair, jerked her head back, and sliced open her throat. The instructor collapsed. The sword slipped from her fingers and clanked on the floor.

The onlookers gawked.

"T'risstree T'orgh meant to betray us," Drisinil said. "I saw it in her eyes when I took her hands. We can leave the carcass here for the time being. With luck, no one will discover it until after Quenthel's death."

Either the other conspirators believed her explanation, or, more likely, didn't care that she'd murdered the teacher. A few congratulated her on her finesse, and, utterly indifferent to the corpse sprawled in their midst, resumed their departures.

Drisinil picked up and examined the fallen falchion. Once Quenthel was slain, it ought to look nice on her wall.

Faeryl prowled the rounded, treacherous surfaces at the apex of the ambassadorial residence. She was trying to monitor all four sides of her home, which entailed clambering about with a certain celerity. Yet she was also trying to hide from anyone who might be peering from the window of a neighboring mansion or up from one of the quiet residential boulevards of prosperous West Wall, and the faster she moved, the more problematic stealth became. She'd sneaked up there two hours ago, when everyone else thought she was bundling or burning documents, and she still wasn't sure she'd struck the proper balance between the two necessities.

She wished she could have ordered a retainer or two up there to help her keep her vigil, but it would have been ill-advised, considering that any of her minions might be the object of her hunt.

She also wished she had more cover. Except for a few token walkways and crenellations so small as to be essentially ornamental, the apex of the stalagmite keep was bare of fortifications or even level places to stand. If Faeryl looked closely, she could see subtle signs that at one time, when the keep had served another purpose, such defenses had existed in abundance, but subsequently, a wizard had melted the ramparts back into the rest of the calcite. It made sense. The Menzoberranyr would see no reason to gift an outsider with any notable capacity to resist a siege.

Faeryl perched on the northeast side of the roof. Outlined in blue, green, or violent phosphorescence, the homes of her wealthier neighbors glowed all around her. Had she looked from a distance, she would have observed her own residence shining in the same way. Fortunately, the luminescence only defined the silhouette of the tower and picked out several spiders sculpted in bas-relief. As long as she stayed away from the images, kept silent, and enjoyed a measure of luck, it shouldn't reveal her presence.

A soft, indefinable sound rose from the northwest. Grateful that she at least still had the brooch that would make her weightless, she scuttled quickly along the sloping pitch of the roof, fearless in the knowledge that even if she lost her footing, she needn't fall.

In a few seconds, she reached the northwest aspect. She peered over the drop and discovered the source of the sound in the plaza below.

Bare to the waist, rapiers in one hand and parrying daggers in the other, two males circled one another. They stood straight and stepped lightly in the manner of well-trained fencers. Their discarded *piwafwis*, mail, and shirts lay where they'd tossed them on the ground along with a pair of empty wineskins. A third male looked on from beneath an overhanging balcony some distance away, where the combatants quite possibly hadn't noticed him.

Faeryl sighed. This little tableau was mildly intriguing, but it clearly had nothing to do with her own situation.

After her frustrating interview with Matron Mother Baenre, she'd realized she had an opponent. Someone who'd traduced her, possibly to keep her from departing Menzoberranzan, though she couldn't imagine why. From that inference, it was a small step to the suspicion that the enemy had an agent inside her household. It was what any intelligent foe would try to arrange, and it arguably explained how Faeryl's intention to go home had been discerned and countered with a word in Triel's ear.

Seething with the need to outwit those who had made a fool of her, Faeryl devised a ruse to unmask the spy. She surprised her retainers with the order to pack. They were slipping out of Menzoberranzan that very night. She thought her loyal vassals would obey, but the traitor would try to sneak away to report the household's imminent flight. Crouched on the roof, Faeryl would spot her when she did.

That was the plan, anyway. The ambassador could think of several reasons why it might fail. The residence had means of egress on all four sides, but she couldn't survey all four at once, not unless she floated well above the roof, and that option presented problems of its own. Most dark elf boots possessed a virtue of silence, and their mantles, one of obscuration. The traitor might even have some more potent means of escaping notice, such as a talisman of invisibility. Were she any higher above the ground, Faeryl might have no hope at all of detecting the spy's surreptitious exit.

Of course, the traitor might also have a means of communicating with her confederates via clairaudience, or a charm of instantaneous transit, in which case the envoy's scheme was doomed no matter what. She'd cling to the roof until someone in authority, a company of Baenre guards, perhaps, showed up to take her and her entourage into custody, but she'd had to try something.

She crawled on. Below and behind her, one of the duelists groaned as his foe's blade plunged through his torso. Magic flickered and sizzled, and the victor dropped as well. The wizard who'd been watching from a distance strolled forward to inspect the steaming corpses.

Faeryl wondered if the three had been siblings, and the wizard was the clever one. She'd had a brother like that once, until an even trickier male turned him to dust and absconded with his wands and grimoires. A minor setback for her House, but interesting to watch.

Overhead, something snapped. She glanced up. Four or five riders on wyvern-back were winging their way east. Above them, projecting from the cavern ceiling, the stalactite castles shone with their own enchantments, a far lovelier sight, in her opinion, than the miniscule monochromatic stars that speckled the night sky of the so-called Lands of Light.

Then, so faintly that she wondered if she'd imagined it, something brushed against something else. The sound had issued from the southwest.

Faeryl scurried over to that part of the roof and peered down. At first glance, nothing appeared changed since the last time she'd checked that way. Perhaps her nerves were playing tricks on her, but she kept on looking anyway.

Octagonal steel grilles protected the round windows cut in the wall below her, but if a drow knew the trick, she could unlatch one and swing it aside for an entrance or exit via levitation. Apparently, someone had, for after a few more moments, Faeryl noticed that one of the web-pattern shields hung ever so slightly ajar. With that sign to guide her, she spotted the shrouded figure skulking toward the mouth of an alleyway.

The noble of Ched Nasad was a fair hand with a crossbow. She might have been able to shoot down the traitor from behind, but that would gain her few answers. She didn't happen to possess a scroll with the spell for interrogating the dead. She needed to catch up with the spy and take the wretch alive.

She read from a scroll she did have, then she stepped away from the top of the tower into empty space.

Except that it wasn't empty for her. The air was as firm as stone beneath her soles. For two paces, she strode on a level surface, and, because she willed it so, the unseen platform dipped into an equally invisible ramp. She sprinted down with no fear of blundering off the edge. Wherever she set her foot, the incline would be there to meet it. That was how the magic worked.

Her progress entirely silent, she dashed unnoticed above the traitor's head, then with a thought dissolved the support beneath her boots. Her crossbow ready, she dropped the last few feet to the ground and landed in front of the spy.

Started, the traitor jumped. Faeryl felt her own pang of surprise, for though she liked to think she maintained a proper suspicion of everyone, in truth, she never could have guessed the pinched, sour face she saw half hidden inside the close-drawn cowl could be the spy's.

"Umrae," the ambassador said, aiming her hand crossbow.

"My lady," the secretary answered, bending with her usual stiffness into an obeisance.

"I know all about it, traitor. I'm not actually planning to leave tonight. My pretending so was a trick to see who would slip away to play informer."

"I don't know what you mean. I just wanted to buy some items for the journey. I thought that if I hurried over to the Bazaar, I could find one of those merchants who stays open late and be back before anyone missed me."

"Do you think I haven't realized I have an enemy here in Menzoberranzan, someone with access to Matron Baenre? Two tendays ago, Triel considered me loyal. She approved of me. She granted a good deal of what I asked on behalf of our people. Now, she doubts me, because someone has persuaded her to question my true intentions. What did my foe offer to lure you to her side? Don't you realize that in betraying me, you betray Ched Nasad itself?"

The scribe hesitated, then said, "Matron Baenre has people watching the residence. Someone is watching us right now."

"Perhaps," Faeryl replied.

Umrae swallowed. "So you can't harm me. Or they'll harm you."

Faeryl laughed. "Rubbish. Triel's agents won't reveal their presence just to keep me from disciplining one of my own retainers. They won't see anything odd or detrimental to Menzoberranzan's interests in that. Now, be sensible and surrender."

After another pause, Umrae said, "Give me your word you won't hurt me. That you'll set me free and help me flee the city."

"I promise you nothing except that your insolence is making me angrier by the second, and a quick capitulation is your only hope. Tell me, who turned you, and why? What does anyone hereabouts have to gain by persecuting an envoy, one who stands apart from the feuds and rivalries among the Menzoberranyr Houses?"

"You must understand, I fear to betray them and remain. They'll kill me if I do."

"They won't get the chance. I'm the one pointing a poisoned dart at you. Who are your employers?"

"I won't say, not without your pledge."

"Your friend didn't slander me to Triel until after I started contemplating a return to Ched Nasad. Was that the point of the lie? To keep me from venturing out into the Underdark? Why?"

Umrae shook her head.

"You're mad," Faeryl said. "Why would you condemn yourself to perpetuate someone else's existence? Ah well, you're plainly unfit to live, so I suppose it's for the best."

She made a show of sighting down the length of the crossbow.

"No!" Umrae cried. "Don't! You're right, why should I die?"

"If you answer my questions, perhaps you won't."

"Yes."

Trembling a little, her nerve having been broken, the clerk raised her hand to her face, perhaps to massage her brow. No—to lift a tiny vial to her lips!

Faeryl pulled the trigger and her aim was true, but by the time the quarrel pierced Umrae's stomach, the secretary's form was changing. She grew even thinner, shriveling, but taller as well. Her flesh cooled and stank of corruption, leathery wings sprouted from her shoulder blades, and her eyes sank into her head. Even her garments altered, blurring and splitting into moldering rags. No blood flowed from the wound the poisoned dart had made, and it didn't seem to inconvenience her in the slightest. She didn't even bother to pull the missile out.

Faeryl was furious at herself for allowing Umrae to trick her. Next time, she'd remember that even a dark elf devoid of beauty, grace, and facile wit, seemingly undone by fear, was yet a drow, born to guile and deception.

The potion had temporarily transformed Umrae into some sort of undead, in which form she likely wouldn't suffer at all from her usual clumsiness. Had Lolth not forsaken her priestesses, Faeryl might have controlled the cadaverous thing with her clerical powers, but that was no longer an option. Nor were any of her other retainers likely to notice her plight and dash to her rescue. She had them all too busy packing up the house.

It was unfortunate, because like most undead, except for the lowly corpses and skeletons spellcasters reanimated to serve as mindless thralls, Umrae in winged-ghoul form could probably do grievous harm with any strike that so much as grazed the skin, and Faeryl didn't even have a shield to fend her off. How was she to know the spy would possess such a potent means of defense?

Umrae took a shambling step, then, with a clap of her wings, bounded forward. Faeryl hastily retreated, dropped the useless cross-bow, and opened the clasp of her cloak. Pulling the garment off her shoulders with one hand, she unsheathed a little adamantine rod with the other. At a snap of her wrist, the harmless-looking object swelled into Mother's Kiss, the long-hafted, basalt-headed warhammer the females of House Zauvirr had borne since the founding of their line.

Perhaps an enchanted weapon would slay Umrae where the enven-omed quarrel had failed.

Faeryl would have to hope so. Even if she were willing to stand meekly aside and let the traitor fly away, Umrae, her thoughts perhaps colored by the predatory guise she'd assumed, plainly wanted a fight, and the envoy could see no way to evade her. It would be stupid to evoke darkness and run. In undead form, Umrae would likely manage better in the murk than its maker did. It would be even more pointless to try to levitate or ascend through the use of the air-walking charm when the shapeshifter could simply spread her ragged wings and follow.

Faeryl waved her *piwafwi* back and forth at the end of her extended arm, to confuse Umrae and serve as some semblance of a shield. No one had ever taught Faeryl to fight thusly, but she'd observed warriors practicing the technique, and she tried to believe that if mere males could do it, it would surely present no difficulty to a high priestess.

Umrae lunged, Faeryl lashed the cloak in a horizontal arc. Possi-bly thanks to luck as much as skill, the garment blocked Umrae's hands. Her talons snagged in the weave.

Surprised, Umrae faltered in the attack and struggled to free her hands. Faeryl stepped through and smashed the pointed stone head of her hammer into the center of the servant's carious brow. Bone crunched, and Umrae's head snapped backward. A goodly portion of her left profile fell off her skull.

Certain the fight was over, Faeryl relaxed, and that was nearly the end of her. Transformed, Umrae could evidently endure more damage than almost any creature with warm flesh and a beating heart. She opened her mouth, exposing long, thin fangs, and what was left of her head shot forward over the top of the cape. The ambassador only barely managed to fling herself back out of the way in time.

The *piwafwi* was stretched taut between the two combatants, as if they were playing tug-of-war. Both yanked on it simultaneously, and Faeryl was the luckier. The cloak tore free of Umrae's grasp, but despite the garment's reinforcing enchantments, it returned to the ambassador with long rips the ghoul's claws had cut. A few more such rendings and it would be useless.

The cape's sudden release also sent Faeryl stumbling backward. With another beat of her festering wings, Umrae hopped and closed the distance. Her clawed hands shot forward.

Crying out in desperation, Faeryl managed to plant her feet and arrest her helpless stagger. She lashed out with the hammer and clipped one of Umrae's hands. The imitation ghoul snatched it back and gave up the attack. Instead, she began to circle. Just as a living creature would, she shook her battered extremity several times as if to dislodge the pain, then lifted it back on guard.

Faeryl turned to keep the foe with her crushed, half-flayed head in view. What is it going to take to stop this thing? the ambassador wondered. *Can* I stop it?

Yes, curse it!

When she was a child, her cousin Merinid, weapons master of House Zauvirr, dead these many years since her mother tired of him, had told her that any opponent could be destroyed. It was just a matter of finding the vulnerable spot.

Umrae lunged. Once again, the ambassador snapped out the folds of her frail, flapping shield. The cloak entangled one of the servant's hands. The other raked, rasping and snagging, across Faeryl's coat of fine adamantine links. The winged ghoul's touch sowed cramping sickness in its wake, but the claws hadn't quite sheared through the sturdy mail, and the sensation only lasted an instant.

Faeryl swung at Umrae's withered chest in its covering of filthy, crumbling cloth. If she couldn't slay the ghoul-thing with a strike to the head, then the heart must be the vulnerable spot, just as with a vampire. Or at least she hoped so.

To her surprise, Umrae denied her the chance to find out one way or the other. It looked as if the traitor had so committed to her attack that she would find it impossible to defend against a riposte. Yet she interposed her withered arm to take the shock of the warhammer, then stooped to claw at Faeryl's unarmored knee.

The envoy avoided that potentially crippling attack with a fast retreat, meanwhile ripping the cloak away from her foul-smelling adversary. The garment was starting to look more like a bunch of ribbons than one coherent piece of silk.

The duelists resumed circling, each looking for an opening. Occasionally Faeryl let the tattered *piwafwi* slip or droop out of line, offering an invitation, but Umrae proved too canny to attack when and how her opponent wished her to.

Faeryl realized she was panting and did the best to control her breathing. She wasn't afraid—she *wasn't*—but she was impressed with her servant's potion-induced prowess. Formidable from the moment she imbibed it, Umrae was truly getting the hang of her borrowed capabilities as the battle progressed.

While still maneuvering and keeping an eye on Umrae, Faeryl nevertheless entered a light trance. With a sense that was neither sight, hearing, nor any faculty comprehensible to those who'd never pledged her service to a deity, she reached into that formless yet somehow jagged place where she had once been accustomed to touch the shadow of the goddess.

The presence of Lolth had absented itself from the meeting ground, leaving a vacancy that somehow throbbed like a diseased tooth. Still, it seemed an appropriate domain in which to pray.

Dread Queen of Spiders, Faeryl silently began, I beg you, reveal yourself to me. Restore my powers, even if only for a moment. Has Menzoberranzan offended you? So be it, but I'm not one of her daughters. I'm from Ched Nasad. Make me as I was, and I'll give you many lives—a slave every day for a year.

Nothing happened.

Umrae sprang in, clawing. Faeryl jerked the part of her spirit that had groped in the void back into her body. Retreating, she blocked the undead creature's claws with her cloak and struck a couple blows with the warhammer. She didn't withdraw quickly enough to take herself completely out of harm's way, nor did she settle into a strong stance and swing as hard as she could have. She wanted the ghoul to feel on the brink of overwhelming her opponent and keep coming. If Umrae grew too eager, she might open herself up for an effective counterattack.

Umrae's talons whizzed through the air, tearing scraps from the sheltering cloak until it was the size of a ragged hand towel. Unexpectedly, the spy beat her riddled wings, hopped in close, and struck at Faeryl's face. The noble recoiled, but even so the claws streaked past a fraction of an inch before her eyes, so close she could feel the malignancy inside them as a pulse of headache.

Still, it was all right, because she thought Umrae was finally open. She sidestepped and swung her stone-headed hammer at the ghoul's rib cage—

—to no avail, even though Faeryl had been correct, Umrae couldn't swing her hands around in time to block the blow. Instead, she took another stride, slapped the ambassador with a flick of her wing, and sent her reeling.

Faeryl's head rang, and the world blurred. As she struggled to throw off the stunning effects of the blow, she thought fleetingly how unfair it was that Umrae, who had long ago forsaken combat training as a humiliating exercise in futility, was demolishing a female who still doggedly reported to her captain-of-the-guard for practice once a tenday.

After what seemed a long time, her head cleared. She whirled, certain that Umrae was about to attack her from behind. She wasn't. In fact, the animate corpse was nowhere to be seen.

Plainly, Umrae had taken to the air. Had she finally done the sensible thing and fled? Faeryl couldn't believe it. Umrae hated her. The envoy didn't know why, but she'd seen it in the traitor's eyes. Such being the case, Umrae wouldn't break off when she had every reason to believe she was winning and close to making the kill. No drow would, which meant she was still hovering somewhere overhead, poised to swoop down and, she undoubtedly hoped, catch her mistress by surprise and smash her to the ground.

Her heart pounding, Faeryl peered upward and saw nothing. She listened for the beat of the creature's wings but heard only the eternal muffled whisper of the city as a whole. She wasn't entirely surprised. The undead were famously stealthy when stalking their prey.

A black sliver momentarily cut the line of violet luminescence adorning a spire of the castle of House Vandree. The obstruction had surely been the tip of one of Umrae's wings.

Faeryl stared for another moment, then jumped when she finally spotted Umrae. Her tattered cloak flapping between her wings, the transformed secretary was already hurtling down like a raptor from the World Above diving to plunge its talons into a rodent.

Hoping Umrae hadn't seen her react to the sight of her, Faeryl kept turning and peering. When she felt the disturbance in the air, or perhaps simply the urgent prompting of her instincts, she jumped aside, pivoted, and swung the warhammer in an overhand blow.

Under those circumstances, she had little chance of smashing the thing's heart, but she'd seen that Umrae could suffer pain. Perhaps the initial blow would freeze the undead thing in place for an instant, affording Faeryl the opportunity for what she prayed would be the finishing stroke.

The ambassador had timed the move properly, and the weapon's basalt head smashed into Umrae's flank. Deprived of her victim, unexpectedly battered, the ghoul slammed into the smooth stone surface of the street with a satisfying crash. Scraps of flesh broke away from her raddled body, releasing a fresh puff of stench.

Faeryl marked her target, the place on Umrae's chest beneath which her heart ought to lie, and swung Mother's Kiss back for the follow-up attack. The traitor rolled and scrambled to her knees. Faeryl struck, and Umrae lashed out with a taloned hand. The ghoul caught the warhammer in mid-flight, tore it out of the ambassador's grip, and sent it spinning to clack down on the ground ten feet away.

Faeryl felt a crazy impulse to turn and go after the thing, but she knew Umrae would rip her apart if she tried. She backstepped instead. The inhumanly gaunt spy leaped to her feet—she looked like a pile of sticks spontaneously assembling themselves into a crude facsimile of a person—and pursued.

While retreating, Faeryl started edging around in a looping course that might ultimately bring her to the spot where the hammer lay. Leering, Umrae moved sideways right along with her in a way that demonstrated she knew exactly what her mistress had in mind and would never permit it.

Well, the aristocrat still had one weapon—pitifully inadequate to the situation though it was—a knife hidden in the belt that gathered her light, supple coat of mail at the waist. The gold buckle was the hilt, and when she pulled on it, the stubby adamantine blade would slide free. She started to reach for it, then hesitated.

Against Umrae's talons, long reach, and resistance to harm, the dagger really would be useless . . . unless Faeryl could get in close enough to use it, and unless she attacked by surprise.

But how in the name of the Demonweb was she to accomplish that? Umrae was rapidly closing the distance, snapping her wings every few steps to lengthen a stride, and for three unnerving backward paces, Faeryl's mind was blank.

Then she remembered the cloak, or rather, the remnants of it, still clutched in her off hand. Perhaps she could employ it to conceal her drawing of the knife. The *piwafwi* was just a sad little mass of tatters, and she was no juggler adept at sleight-of-hand, but curse it, if clumsy Umrae had palmed a potion vial without her mistress noticing until it was too late, surely the mistress could do as well.

Faeryl had been reflexively moving the cloak around the whole time, so it shouldn't look suspicious for her to cover her waist with it. At the same time, she hooked the fingers of her weapon hand in the oval hollow at the center of the buckle and pulled. She had never before had occasion to employ this last desperate means of defense, but in the sixteen years since an artisan had made it to her specifications, she had always kept the knife and scabbard oiled, and the blade easily slid free.

She studied Umrae. As far as the envoy could tell, the imitation ghoul hadn't seen her bare the dagger, but she doubted she could keep it hidden for more than a second or two. She had to manufacture a chance for herself quickly if she was to have one at all.

She pretended to stumble. She hoped her unsteadiness looked genuine. Umrae had touched her, after all, so it might seem credible that her strength was failing.

The ghoul took the bait. She leaped forward and seized Faeryl by the forearms. This time, her claws punched through the envoy's layer of mail and jabbed their tips into her flesh. At once, a surge of nausea wracked Faeryl, then another. Retching, she wasn't sure she could still use the knife in any sort of controlled manner. Perhaps she'd just served herself up to her foe like a plate of mushrooms.

Umrae grinned at Faeryl's seeming—or genuine—helplessness. The envoy felt the clerk's fingers tense, preparing to flense the meat from her bones, even as she pulled the noble closer and opened her jaws to bite down on her head.

Fighting the sickness and weakness, Faeryl tried to thrust her hand forward. The effort strained her flesh against the ghoul's talons, tearing her wounds larger and bringing a burst of pain—but then her arm jerked free. The blade rammed into Umrae's withered chest, slipping cleanly between two ribs and plunging in all the way up to Faeryl's knuckles.

Umrae convulsed and threw back her head for a silent scream. The spasms jerked her hands and threatened to rip Faeryl apart even without the traitor's conscious intent. Umrae froze, and toppled backward, carrying her assailant with her.

In contradiction of every tale Faeryl had ever heard, the shape-shifter didn't revert to her original form when true death claimed her. Still horribly sick, the envoy lay for some time in the ghoul's fetid embrace. Eventually, however, she mustered the trembling strength to pull free of the claws embedded in her bleeding limbs, after which she crawled a few feet away from the winged corpse.

Gradually, despite the sting of her punctures and bruises, she started to feel a little better. Physically, anyway. Inside her mind, she was berating herself for an outcome that wasn't really a victory at all.

Given that she needed to learn what Umrae knew, not kill her, she'd bungled their encounter from the beginning. She supposed she should have agreed to the traitor's terms, but she'd been too angry and too proud. She should also have spotted the vial and fought more skillfully. If not for luck, it would be she and not her erstwhile scribe lying dead on the stone.

She wondered if her sojourn in Menzoberranzan had diminished her. Back in Ched Nasad, she had enemies in- and outside House Zauvirr to keep her strong and sharp, but in the City of Spiders none had wished her ill. Had she forgotten the habits that protected her for her first two hundred years of life? If so, she knew she'd better remember them quickly.

The enemy hadn't finished with her. She wasn't so dull and rusty that she didn't recall how these covert wars unfolded. It was like a *sava* game, progressing a step at a time, gradually escalating in ferocity. Her unknown adversary's first move, though she hadn't known it at the time, had been to turn Umrae and lie to Triel. Faeryl's countermove was to capture the spy and remove her from the board. As soon as Umrae missed some prearranged rendezvous, the foe would know her pawn had been taken and advance another piece. Perhaps it would be the mother. Perhaps the foe would suggest to Matron Baenre that the time had come to throw Faeryl in a dungeon.

But life wasn't really a *sava* game. Faeryl could cheat and make two moves in a row, which in this instance meant truly fleeing Menzoberranzan as soon as possible, before the enemy learned of her agent's demise.

Light-headed and sour-mouthed from her exertions, Faeryl dragged herself to her feet, trudged in search of Mother's Kiss, and wondered just how she would accomplish that little miracle.

chapter

T E N

Cloaked in the semblance of a squat, leathery-skinned orc, whose
twisted leg manifestly made him unfit for service in a noble or even
merchant House, Pharaun took an experimental bite of his sausage
and roll. The unidentifiable ground meat inside the casing tasted
rank and was gristly, as well as cold at the core.

"By the Demonweb!" he exclaimed.

"What?" Ryld replied.

The weapons master too appeared to be a scurvy, broken-down
orc in grubby rags. Unbelievably, he was devouring his vile repast
without any overt show of repugnance.

"What?" The Master of Sorcere brandished his sausage. "This
travesty. This abomination."

He headed for the culprit's kiosk, a sad little construction of
bone poles and sheets of hide, taking care not to walk too quickly.
His veil of illusion would make it look as if he were limping, but it
wouldn't conceal the anomaly of a lame orc covering ground as

145

quickly as one with two good legs.

The long-armed, flat-faced goblin proprietor produced a cudgel from beneath the counter. Perhaps he was used to complaints.

Pharaun raised a hand and said, "I mean no harm. In fact, I want to help."

The goblin's eyes narrowed. "Help?"

"Yes. I'll even pay another penny for the privilege." he said as he extracted a copper coin from his purse. "I just want to show you something."

The cook hesitated, then held out a dirty-nailed hand and said, "Give. No tricks."

"No tricks."

Pharaun surrendered the coins and to the goblin's surprise, squirmed around the end of the counter and crowded into the miniature kitchen. He wrapped his hand in a fold of his cloak, slid the hot iron grill with its load of meat from its brackets, and set it aside.

"First," Pharaun said, "you spread the coals evenly at the bottom of the brazier." He picked up a poker and demonstrated. "Next, though we don't have time to start from scratch right now, you let them burn to gray. Only then do you start cooking, with the grill positioned here."

He replaced the utensil in a higher set of brackets.

"Sausage take longer to fry," the goblin said.

"Do you have somewhere to go? Now, I'm going to assume you buy these questionable delicacies elsewhere and thus can do nothing about the quality, but you can at least tenderize them with a few whacks from that mallet, poke a few holes with the fork to help them cook on the inside, and sprinkle some of these spices on them." Pharaun grinned. "You've never so much as touched a lot of this stuff, have you? What did you do, murder the real chef and take possession of his enterprise?"

The smaller creature smirked and said, "Don't matter now, do it?"

"I suppose not. One last thing: Roast the sausage when the customer orders it, not hours beforehand. It isn't nearly as appetizing if it's cooked, allowed to cool, then warmed again. Good fortune to you."

He clapped the goblin on the shoulder, then exited the stand.

At some point, Ryld had wandered up to observe the lesson.

"What was the point of that?" the warrior asked.

"I was performing a public service," answered the wizard, "preserving the Braeryn from a plague of dyspepsia."

Pharaun fell in beside his friend, and the two dark elves walked on.

"You were amusing yourself, and it was idiotic. You take the trouble to disguise us, then risk revealing your true identity by playing the gourmet."

"I doubt one small lapse will prove our undoing. It's unlikely that any of our ill-wishers will interview that particular street vendor any time soon or ask the right questions if they do. Remember, we're *well* disguised. Who would imagine this lurching, misshapen creature could possibly be my handsome, elegant self? Though I must admit, your metamorphosis wasn't quite so much of a stretch."

Ryld scowled, then wolfed down his last bite of sausage and bread.

"Why didn't you disguise us from the moment we left Tier Breche?" he asked. "Never mind, I think I know. A fencer doesn't reveal all his capabilities in the initial moments of the bout."

"Something like that. Greyanna and her minions have seen us looking like ourselves, so if we're lucky they won't expect to find us appearing radically different. The trick won't befuddle them forever, but perhaps long enough for us to complete our business and return to our sedate, cloistered lives."

"Does that mean you've figured out something else?"

"Not as such, but you know I'm prone to sudden bursts of inspiration."

The masters entered a crowded section of street outside of what was evidently a popular tavern, with a howling, barking gnoll song shaking the calcite walls. Pharaun had never had occasion to walk incognito among the lower orders. It felt odd weaving, pausing, and twisting to avoid bumps and jostles. Had they known his true identity, his fellow pedestrians would have scurried out of his way.

As the two drow reached the periphery of the crowd, Ryld pivoted and struck a short straight blow with his fist. A hunchbacked, piebald creature—the product of a mating of goblin and orc perhaps—stumbled backward and fell on his rump.

"Cutpurse," the warrior explained. "I hate this place."

"No pangs of nostalgia?"

Ryld glowered. "That isn't funny."

"No? Then I beg your pardon," Pharaun said with a smirk. "I wonder why this precinct always seems so sordid, even on those rare occasions when one finds oneself alone in a plaza or boulevard. Well, the smell, of course. We don't call them the Stenchstreets for nothing, but the buildings, though generally more modest than those encountered elsewhere in the city, still wear the same graceful shapes our ancestors cut from the living rock."

The teachers paused to let a spider with legs as long as broadswords scuttle across the street. The Braeryn notoriously harbored hordes of the sacred creatures. Sacred or not, Pharaun reviewed his mental list of ready spells, but the arachnid ignored the disguised dark elves

"That's a foolish question," said Ryld. "Why does the Braeryn seem foul? The inhabitants!"

"Ah, but did the living refuse of our society generate the atmosphere of the district, or did that malignant spirit exist from the beginning and lure the wretched to its domain?"

"I'm no metaphysician," said Ryld. "All I know is that somebody should clear the scavengers out of here."

Pharaun chuckled. "What if said clearing had occurred when you were a tyke?"

"I don't mean exterminate them—except for the hopeless cases—but why just let them squat here in their dirt like a festering chancre on the city? Why not find something useful for them to do?"

"Ah, but they're already useful. Status is all, is it not? Does it not follow, then, that no Menzoberranyr can find contentment without someone upon whom she can look down."

"We have slaves."

"They won't do. Predicate your claim to self-respect on their existence and you tacitly acknowledge you're only slightly better than a thrall yourself. Happily, here in the Stenchstreets, we find a populace starving, filthy, penniless, riddled with disease, living twenty or thirty to a room, yet nominally free. The humblest commoner in Manyfolk or even Eastmyr can turn up his nose at them and feel smug."

"You really think that's the reason Matron Baenre hasn't ordered the slum scoured clean?"

"Well, if that conjecture seems implausible, here's another: Rumor has it that from time to time, someone meets the goddess herself in the Braeryn. Supposedly she likes to visit here in mortal guise. The matrons may feel that the neighborhood is, in some sense, under her protection." The wizard hesitated. "Though if Lolth has gone away for good, perhaps they don't need to worry about it anymore."

Ryld shook his head. "It's still so hard to belie—"

Pharaun pointed. "Look."

Ryld turned.

On a curving wall below a dark elf's eye level was a sketch, this time smeared in blue. It consisted of three overlapping ovals, conceivably representing the links of a chain.

"It's a different mark," said Ryld. "Hobgoblin maybe, though I couldn't tell you the tribe."

"Don't be intentionally dim. It's the same peculiar, reckless, pointless crime."

"Fair enough, and it's still irrelevant to our endeavors."

"It's a dull mind that never transcends pragmatics. Two signs, representing two races, implying two specimens of the lesser races demented in precisely the same way? Unlikely, yet why would a single artist daub an emblem not his own?"

"Coincidence?"

"I doubt it, but as yet I can't provide a better answer."

"It's a puzzle for another day, remember?"

"Indeed."

The masters walked on.

"Still," pressed Pharaun, "don't you wonder how many scrawled signs we passed without noticing and exactly what form they took?"

Ignoring the question, Ryld pointed and said, "That's our destination."

The house's limestone door stood open, most likely for ventilation, for the interior radiated a perceptible warmth, the product of a multitude of tenants crammed in together. It also emitted a muddled drone and a thick stink considerably fouler than the unpleasant smell that clung to the Braeryn as a whole.

Ryld had been born in a similar warren, had fought like a demon to escape it, and he felt a strange reluctance to venture in, as if squalor wouldn't let him escape a second time. Unwilling to appear timid and foolish in the eyes of his friend, he hid the feeling behind an impassive warrior's countenance.

Pharaun, however, freely demonstrated his own distaste. The porcine eyes in his illusory orc face watered, and he swallowed, no doubt trying to quell a surge of queasiness.

"Get used to it," said Ryld.

"I'll be all right. I've visited the Braeryn frequently enough to have some notion of what these little hells are like, though I confess I never entered one."

"Then stick close and let me do the talking. Don't stare at anybody, or look anyone in the eye. They're likely to take it as an insult or challenge. Don't touch anyone or anything if you can avoid it. Half the residents are sick and probably contagious."

"Really? And their palace gives off such a salubrious air! Ah, well, lead on."

Ryld did as his friend had asked. Beyond the threshold was the claustrophobic nightmare he remembered. Kobolds, goblins, orcs, gnolls, bugbears, hobgoblins, and a sprinkling of less common creatures squeezed into every available space. Some, the warrior knew, were runaway slaves. Others had entered the service of Menzoberranyr travelers who picked them up in far corners of the world, took them back to the city, and dismissed them without any means of making their way home. The rest were descendants of unfortunate souls in the first two categories.

Wherever they came from, the paupers were trapped in the Braeryn, begging, stealing, scavenging, preying on one another—often in the most literal sense—and hiring on for any dangerous, filthy job anyone cared to give them. It was the only way they could survive.

This particular lot had likewise learned to live packed into the common space without the slightest vestige of privacy. Undercreatures babbled, cooked, ate, drank, tended a still, brawled, twitched and moaned in the throes of sickness, shook and cuffed their shrieking infants, threw dice, fornicated, relieved themselves, and, amazingly, slept, all in plain view of anyone with the ill luck to look in their direction.

As Ryld had expected, within moments of their entrance, a pair of toughs—in this instance bugbears—slouched forward to accost them. With their coarse, shaggy manes and square, prominent jaws, bugbears were the largest and strongest of the goblin peoples, towering over the rest—and dark elves, too, for that matter. This pair was, by the standards of their destitute household, relatively well-fed and adequately dressed. They likely bullied tribute out of the rest.

"You don't live here," rumbled the taller of the two.

He wore what appeared to be a severed goblin hand strung around his burly neck. Drow occasionally affected similar ornaments, usually mementos of hated enemies, but they sent them to a taxidermist first. It was too bad the bugbear hadn't done the same. It would have prevented the rot and the carrion smell.

"No," Ryld said, tossing the bugbear a shaved coin, paying the toll to pass in and out of the house. "We came to see Smylla Nathos."

The hulking goblinoids just looked at him, as did several others creatures. A scaly, naked little kobold tittered crazily.

Something was wrong, and the Master of Melee-Magthere didn't know what. He felt a sudden tension and exhaled it away. Looking nervous was a bad idea.

"Isn't this Smylla's house?" he asked.

The shorter bugbear, who still loomed nearly as huge as an ogre, laughed and said, "No, not no more, but she still live here . . . kind of."

"Can we see her?" said Ryld.

"What for?" asked the bugbear with the severed goblin hand.

The weapons master hesitated. He'd intended to say that he and Pharaun wished to consult Smylla in her professional capacity as a trader in information. It was essentially the truth, though that didn't matter. What did was that he hadn't expected it to provoke a hostile response.

Pharaun stepped up beside him.

"Smylla sold our sister Iggra the secret of how to break into a merchant's strongroom," the wizard said in a creditably surly Orcish rasp. "How to get around all the traps. . . . Only she left one out, see? It squirted acid on Sis and burned her to death. Slow. Almost got us too. It's Smylla's fault, and we come to 'talk' to her about it."

The smaller bugbear nodded. "You ain't the only ones wantin' that kind of talk. Us, too, but we can't get at the bitch."

Pharaun cocked his head. "How come?"

"A couple tendays ago," said the bugbear with the severed hand necklace, "we decided we was tired of her bossing us and her lamps hurting our eyes. We jumped her, hit her, but she chucked one of those stones that makes a flash of light. It blinded us, and she run up to her room." He nodded toward the head of a twisting staircase. "We can't get through the door. She locked it with magic or somethin'."

Pharaun snorted. "Ain't no door my brother and me can't bust through."

The bugbears exchanged glances. The smaller one, who, Ryld noticed, was missing several of his lower teeth, shrugged.

"You can try," the larger one said. "Only, Smylla belongs to us, too. Hit her, bleed her, slice off a piece of her and eat it, but you can't keep her all to yourself."

"It's a deal," Pharaun said.

"Come on, then."

The bugbears led them through the crowded room and onto the stairs, where they still had to pick their way through lounging paupers. Partway up, the brute wearing the decaying hand put it in his mouth and began slurping and sucking on it.

At the top of the steps were a small landing and a limestone door with a rounded top. Two sentries, an orc and a canine-faced gnoll with sores on his muzzle, sat on the floor looking bored.

The disguised teachers made a show of examining the door.

"Can you knock it down?" Pharaun whispered.

"When the bugbears couldn't? Don't count on it. Can you open it with magic?"

"Probably. It's magically sealed, so a counterspell should suffice, but I don't want our friends to observe me casting it. That really would compromise my disguise. Stand where you obstruct their view and do something distracting."

"Right." Ryld positioned himself in the appropriate spot and glowered up at the two bugbears. "We can open it. What loot is inside?"

The larger bugbear scowled and, the odious object in his mouth garbling his speech a little, said, "We made a deal. It didn't say nothing about no loot."

"Smylla took Sis's treasure," Ryld replied. "We want it back, and extra too, for wergild."

"Hell with that."

The bugbear with the missing teeth reached for the knife tucked through his belt. Ryld could see it was a butcher's tool, not a proper fighting blade, but no doubt it served in the latter capacity well enough.

Ryld rested his hand on the hilt of his short sword, the weapon of choice for these tight quarters, and said, "You want to fight, we'll fight. I'll slice your face off your skull and wear it like a breechcloth, but my brother and I came to kill Smylla, not you. Let's talk. If you never get the door—"

"Open," Pharaun said.

White light shone at Ryld's back, making the bugbears wince. Squinting, the warrior whirled and scrambled for the opening.

"Hey!" yelped the smaller bugbear.

Ryld felt a big hand fumble at his shoulder, trying to grab him, but it was an instant too slow. He followed Pharaun over the threshold and slammed the door.

"You need to hold it shut," the wizard said.

"I can't do it for long."

Leaning forward, Ryld planted his hands on the limestone slab and braced himself.

The door bucked inward. For a split second, the dark elf's feet slid on the calcite floor, then they caught, and he held the barrier in place. Barely.

Meanwhile, Pharaun was peering about. He gave a little cry of satisfaction, picked up a small iron bar, and set it so it overlapped the edge of the door and the jamb about halfway up. When he took his hand away, the charm remained in place.

"This is quite a clever little device," the wizard said. "Oh, and you can let go now."

🕷 🕷 🕷

Pharaun turned the mechanical locks his spell of opening had disengaged, snapping each shut in its turn. It was actually the enchanted length of iron that had up to then kept the goblinoids out, but he thought he and Ryld might as well be as secure as possible. It also seemed the courteous thing to do.

His hostess, however, didn't seem to appreciate the gesture.

"Get out!" she croaked. "Get out, or I'll slay you with my sorcery!"

The masters turned. Smylla Nathos had lit her sparsely furnished room with a pair of slender brass rods, the tips of which emitted a steady magical glow. They protruded from the necks of wax-encrusted wine bottles like tapers sitting in candelabra, which they perhaps were meant to resemble. Maybe Smylla missed the spellcaster's traditional mode of illumination but couldn't obtain it anymore.

She herself lay at the limit of the light, on a cot in the shadows at the far end of the room. Pharaun could just barely make her out.

154

"Good afternoon, my lady," the wizard said, bowing. "It shames me beyond measure to ignore your request. Yet should this gentleman and I pass through your door a second time, the bugbears and their ilk will rush in, and that, I think, is the very eventuality you sought to forestall."

"Who are you? You don't talk like an orc."

"My lady is a marvel of perspicacity. We are in fact drow lords come to consult you on a matter of some importance."

"Why are you disguised?"

"The usual reason: To confound our enemies. May we approach? It's tedious trying to converse across the length of the room."

Smylla hesitated, then said, "Come."

Pharaun and Ryld started forward. Behind them, the bugbears were cursing, shouting threats and questions, and pounding on the far side of the door.

After four paces, the wizard's stomach turned at yet another stench, this one humid and gangrenous. He'd half expected something of the sort, but that didn't make it any easier to bear. Even the phlegmatic Ryld looked discomfited for an instant.

"Close enough," Smylla said, and Pharaun supposed it was.

He had no desire to come any nearer to that wasted form with its boils and pustules, even though the enchantments bound into his mantle and Ryld's cloak and dwarven armor would probably protect them from infection.

"Can you help us?" asked Ryld.

The sick woman leered. "Will you pay me with the magnificent greatsword you wear across your back?"

Pharaun was somewhat impressed. The illusion of pig-faced orcishness shrouding his friend made Splitter look like a battle-axe, but Smylla's rheumy, sunken eyes had pierced that aspect of the deception.

When he recovered from his surprise, Ryld shook his head. "No, I won't give you the sword. I worked too hard to get it, and I need it to stay alive, but if you want I can use it to clear away the goblinoids outside. My comrade and I are also carrying a fair amount of gold."

Her dry white hair spread about her head, Smylla lay propped against a mound of stained, musty pillows. She struggled to hitch herself up straighter, then abandoned the effort. Apparently it was beyond her strength.

"Gold?" she said. "Do you know who I am, swordsman? Do you know my history?"

"I do," Pharaun said. "The gist of it, anyway. It happened after I more or less withdrew from participation in the affairs of the great Houses."

"What do you know?" she asked.

"An expedition from House Faen Tlabbar," the wizard replied, "ventured up into the Lands of Light to hunt and plunder. When they returned, a lovely human sorceress and clairvoyant accompanied them, not as a newly captured slave but as their guest.

"Why did you want to come? Perhaps you were fleeing some implacable enemy, or were fascinated by the grace and sophistication of my people and the idea of living in the exotic Underdark. My hunch is that you wanted to learn drow magic, but it's pure speculation. No outsider ever knew.

"For that matter, why did the Faen Tlabbar oblige you? That's an even greater mystery. Conceivably someone harbored amorous feelings for you, or you, too, had secrets to teach."

"I had a way of persuading them," Smylla said.

"Obviously. Once you reached Menzoberranzan, you made yourself useful to House Faen Tlabbar as countless minions from the lesser races had done before you. The difference being that you were accorded a certain status, even a degree of familiarity. Matron Ghenni let you dine with the family and attend social functions, where you reportedly acquitted yourself with a drowlike poise and charm."

"I was their pet," said Smylla, sneering at the memory, "a dog dressed in a gown and trained to dance on its hind legs. I just didn't know it at the time."

"I'm sure many saw you that way. Perhaps some saw something else. From all accounts, Matron Ghenni behaved as if she regarded you as a ward, just one notch down from a daughter, and with the mistress of the Fourth House indulging you, few would dare challenge your right to comport yourself like a Menzoberranyr noble. Indeed, no one did, until she turned against you."

"Until I fell ill," said the sorceress.

"Quite. Was it a natural disease, bred, perhaps, by the lack of the searing sunlight that is a natural condition for your kind? Or did an enemy infect you with poison or magic? If so, was the culprit someone inside House Faen Tlabbar, who saw you as a rival for Ghenni's favor, or the agent of an enemy family, depriving their foes of a resource?"

"I was never able to find out. That's funny coming from me, isn't it?"

"Ironic, perhaps. At any rate, several priestesses tried to cure you, but for some reason, the magic failed, whereupon Ghenni summarily expelled you from her citadel."

"Actually," Smylla said, "she sent a couple trolls, slave soldiers, to murder me. I escaped them and the castle, too. Afterward, I tried to offer my services to other Houses, noble and merchant alike, but no door would open to a human who'd lost the favor of Faen Tlabbar."

"My lady," said Pharaun, "if it's any consolation, you were still receiving precisely the same treatment we would have given a member of our own race. No dark elf would abide the presence of anyone afflicted with an incurable malady. The Spider Queen taught us the weak must die, and in any case, what if the sickness was contagious?"

"It's not a consolation."

"Fair enough. To continue the tale: Unwelcome anywhere else, you made your way to the Braeryn. Despite your infirmity, some magic remained within your grasp, and you employed it to cow the residents of this particular warren into providing you with a private space in which to live. I daresay that wasn't easy. Then, using divinatory rituals, your natural psionic gifts, and whatever secrets you'd discovered during your time with House Faen Tlabbar, you set up shop as a broker of knowledge. At first, only the lower orders availed themselves of your services, then gradually, as your reputation grew, even a few of my people started consulting you. We wouldn't let you dwell among us, but some were willing to risk a brief contact if they anticipated sufficient advantage from it."

"I never heard of you," said Ryld, "but within the district, your reputation seems to be considerable. We've been asking questions all day, and more than one suggested we seek you out."

The door banged particularly loudly, and he glanced back to make sure the bugbears weren't breaching it.

"That's all I know of your saga," said Pharaun, "but I infer from the hostility of your cohabitants that a new stanza has begun."

"I suppose I couldn't bluff them forever," Smylla said. "My powers, sorcerous and psionic alike, are all but gone, devoured by my malady. Once I acquired my stock in trade primarily through scrying, divinations, and such. In recent years, I've cajoled my secrets from a web of informers, whom I betray one to the other."

The withered creature smirked.

"Well," said Ryld, "I hope you teased out the one we need."

She coughed. No, it was a laugh. "Even if I did, why would I share it with you, dark elf?"

"I told you," the warrior said, "we can protect you from the bugbears and goblins."

"So can my little iron trinket."

"But eventually, if you simply remain in here, you'll die of hunger and thirst."

"I'm dying anyway. Can't you tell? I'm not an old woman——I'm a baby as you drow measure time!——but I look like an ancient hag. I just don't want to perish at the hands of those miserable undercreatures. I've ruled here for fifteen years, and if I die beyond their reach, I win. Do you see?"

"Well, then, my lady," said Pharaun, "your wish suggests the terms of a bargain. Oblige us, and we'll refrain from admitting the bugbears."

She made a spitting sound and said, "Admit them if you must. I loathe the brutes, but I hate you dark elves more. It was you who made me as I am. I bartered information with you for as long as I had something to gain, but now that the disease is finally killing me, you can all go to the Abyss where your goddess lives, and burn."

Pharaun might have replied that as far as he could tell, Smylla had sealed her own fate on the day she decided to descend into the Underdark, but he doubted it would soften her resolve.

"I don't blame you," he said, making a show of sympathy. It wouldn't have deceived any drow, but even though she'd trafficked with his race for decades, perhaps she still had human instincts. "Sometimes I hate other dark elves myself. I'd certainly despise them if they served me as they've treated you."

She eyed him skeptically. "But you're the one who's different from all the others?"

"I doubt it. I'm a child of the goddess. I follow her ways. But I've visited the Realms that See the Sun, where I learned that other races think and live differently. I understand that by the standards of your own people, we've treated you abominably."

For a moment, she looked up at him as if no one had commiserated with her about anything since that long-lost season when she was the belle, or at least the coveted curiosity, of the revels and balls.

She said, "Do you think a few gentle words will make me want to help you?"

"Of course not. I just don't want your bitterness to get in the way of your good sense. It would be a pity if you turned your back on your salvation."

"What are you saying?"

"I can take away your sickness."

"You're lying. How could you do what the priestesses cannot?"

"Because I'm a wizard." Pharaun snapped his fingers and dissolved his mask of illusion. "My name is Pharaun Mizzrym. You may have heard of me. If not, you've surely heard of the Masters of Sorcere."

She was impressed, though trying not to show it.

"Who aren't healers," she said.

"Who *are* transmuters. I can change you into a drow, or, if you prefer, a member of another race. Whatever we choose, the transformation will purge the sickness from your new body."

"If that's true," she said, "then why do your people fear illness?"

"Because this remedy is inappropriate for them. It's unthinkable for a drow, one of the goddess's chosen people, to permanently assume the form of a lesser creature except as a punishment. Also, most wizards can't cast the spell deftly enough to purge a disease. It requires a certain facility, which happily, I possess."

He grinned.

"And you'll use it to help me?"

"Well, to aid myself, really."

The soothsayer scowled, pondering the offer.

Eventually she said, "What do I have to lose?"

"Exactly."

"But you have to change me first."

"No, first of all, we must establish that you do indeed possess the information my colleague and I require. We're seeking a number of runaway males hailing from noble and humble residences alike."

"We have a handful of drow hiding out in the Braeryn. Some are sick like me. Some are outcast for some other offense. A couple are just taking a long illicit holiday from their responsibilities and female relations. I can tell you where to find most of them."

"I'm sure," said Pharaun, "but I imagine they've resided here for a while, have they not? We're seeking rogues of more recent vintage. Menzoberranzan has suffered a mass migration in recent tendays."

Smylla frowned. From a subtle shift of expression, the mage knew she was deciding whether or not to lie.

"More drow males than usual have visited the Braeryn," she said. "Indulging their most sordid impulses, I assumed, but as far as I know they didn't stay here. If they did, I don't know where."

Ryld sighed. Pharaun knew how he felt. Generally speaking, the wizard relished a baffling, brain-cramping puzzle, but even he was growing impatient at their lack of progress.

Given the lack of any sensible leads, he resolved to follow where intuition led. Still caught up in his role of sympathizer, he dared to step to the cot and pat Smylla on her bony shoulder. She gasped. In all likelihood, no one had touched her for a long while, either.

"Don't abandon hope," Pharaun said. "Perhaps we can still make a trade. Fortunately, my comrade and I are interested in other matters as well. Has anything peculiar occurred in the Braeryn of late?"

The clairvoyant rasped out another painful-sounding laugh.

"You mean aside from the fact that last tenday, the animals rose up against me?"

"I do find that interesting. As you confessed, your magical talents withered away some time ago. Since then, you've dominated the goblins through bluff and force of personality, and it worked until a few days ago. What changed? Where did the undercreatures find the courage to turn against you? Have you noticed anything that might account for it?"

"Well," said Smylla, "it could just be they saw me failing physically, but—" Her cracked lips stretched into a grin. "You're good, Master Mizzrym. You give me a smile, friendly conversation, a soft touch on the arm, and my tongue starts to flap. That's loneliness for you. But I will have my cure before I give up anything of importance."

"Very sensible." Pharaun extracted an empty cocoon from one of his pockets. "What do you wish to become?"

"One of you," she said, leering. "I once heard a philosopher say that everyone becomes the thing he hates."

"He must have been a cheery fellow to have about. Now, brace yourself. This will only take a moment, but it may hurt a little."

Employing greater care than usual, he recited the incantation and used the ridged silken case to write a symbol on the air.

Magic shrilled through the air, and the temperature plummeted. For a moment, the whole room rippled and shimmered, then the distortion concentrated itself on Smylla's shriveled body. Tendons standing out in her neck, she screamed.

Beyond the door, one of the bugbears shouted, "We want to get even, too! We had a bargain!"

Smylla's sores faded away, and her emaciated form filled out into a healthy slimness. Her ashen skin darkened to a gleaming black, her blue eyes turned red, and her ears grew points. Her features became more delicate. Her snowy hair thickened, changing from brittle and lusterless to wavy and glossy.

"The pain went away," she breathed. "I feel stronger."

"Of course," Pharaun said.

She stared at her hands, then sat up, rose from the cot, and tried to walk. At first she moved with an invalid's caution, but gradually, as she proved to herself that she wouldn't fall, that hesitancy passed. After a few seconds, she was striding, jumping, and spinning like an exuberant little girl testing her strength, her grimy nightshirt flapping about her.

"You did it!" she said, and the pure, uncalculated gratitude in her crimson eyes showed that even wearing the flesh of a dark elf maiden, she was still human at the core.

Though it was foreign to his own nature, Pharaun found her appreciation rather gratifying. Still, he hadn't transformed her to bask in her naïve sentimentality but to elicit some answers.

"Now," he said, "please, tell us."

"Right." She took a deep breath to compose herself and said, "I do believe something emboldened the undercreatures in this house. What's more, I think it's affected goblinoids throughout the Braeryn."

"What is it?" asked Ryld.

"I don't know."

The warrior grimaced.

"What led you to infer this agency?" Pharaun asked. "I assume you were housebound even before you barricaded yourself in your room."

"I saw a change in the brutes who live here. They were surly, insolent, and foul-tempered, ready to maim and kill one another at the slightest provocation."

Ryld hitched his shoulders, working stiffness out or shifting Splitter to lie more comfortably across his back.

"How is that different than normal?" asked the weapons master.

Smylla scowled at him and said, "All things are relative. The creatures exhibited those qualities to a greater extent than before, and whenever I heard tidings from beyond these walls, they suggested the entire precinct shared the same truculent humor."

Pharaun nodded. "Did you hear about tribal emblems appearing in the streets?"

"Yes," she said. "That bespeaks a kind of madness, don't you think?"

"Maybe in one or two thralls," said Ryld. "What of it? You promised my friend information. Tell us something we don't already know, and I mean facts, not your impressions."

The clairvoyant smiled. "All right. I was building up to it. Every few nights a drum beats somewhere in the Braeryn, calling the lower orders to some sort of gathering. Many of the occupants of this house clear out. With what little remains of my clairvoyance, I've sensed many others skulking through the streets, all converging on a common destination."

"Nonsense," said Ryld. "Why has no drow patrol heard the signal and come to investigate?"

"Because," said Pharaun, "the city possesses enchantments to mute sound."

"Well, maybe." Ryld turned back to Smylla. "Where do the creatures go, and why?"

"I don't know," she said, "but perhaps, with my health and occult talents restored, I could find out." She beamed at Pharaun. "I'd be happy to try. I fulfilled the letter of our bargain, but I do realize I haven't provided you with all that much in exchange for the priceless gift you gave me."

"That remark touches on the question of your future," the wizard said. "You'd have no difficulty reestablishing your dominion here in the Stenchstreets, but why live so meanly? I could use an aide of your caliber. Or, if you prefer, I can arrange your safe repatriation to the World Above."

As he spoke, he surreptitiously contorted the fingers of his left hand, expressing himself in the silent language of the dark elves, a system of gestures as efficient and comprehensive as the spoken word.

"I think—" Smylla began, then her eyes opened wide.

She whimpered. Ryld pulled his short sword out of her back, and she collapsed. Pharaun skipped back to keep her from toppling against him.

"Despite her previous experiences," the lanky wizard said, "she couldn't quite leave off trusting drow. I suppose it shows you can take the human out of the sunshine, but not the sunshine out of the human." He shook his head. "This is the second female I've slain or murdered by proxy in the brief time since our adventure began, and I didn't particularly want to kill either one of them. Do you suspect an underlying metaphysical significance?"

"How would I know? I take it you bade me kill the snitch because she was feeding us lies."

"Oh, no. I'm convinced she was telling the truth. The problem was that I deceived her. Her metamorphosis didn't really purge her disease. It was a bit tricky just suppressing it for a few minutes."

Pharaun stepped back again to keep the spreading pool of blood from staining his boots, and Ryld cleaned the short sword on the dead human's bedding.

"You didn't want to leave her alive and angry to carry tales to Greyanna," the weapons master said.

"It's unlikely they would have found one another, but why take the chance?"

"And you asked Smylla about the marks on the walls. You're just too cursed curious to let the subject go."

Pharaun grinned. "Don't be silly. I'm the very model of single-minded determination, and I was asking to further our mission."

Ryld glanced at the door and the iron bar. They were still holding.

"What does the strange behavior of goblins have to do with the rogue males?" he asked.

"I don't know yet," Pharaun answered, "but we have two oddities occurring at the same time and in the same precinct. Doesn't it make sense to infer a relationship?"

"Not necessarily. Menzoberranzan has scores of plots and conspiracies going on at any given time. They aren't all connected."

"Granted. However, if these two situations are linked, then by inquiring into one, we likewise probe the other. You and I have experienced a depressing lack of success picking up the trail of our runaways. Therefore, we'll investigate the lower orders and see where that path takes us."

"How will we do that?"

"Follow the drum, of course."

The door banged.

"First," said Ryld, "we have to get out of here."

"Easily managed. I'll remove the locking talisman from the door, then use illusion to make us blend with the walls. In a minute or two, the residents will break the door down. When they're busy abusing Smylla's corpse and ransacking her possessions, we'll put on goblin faces and slip out in the confusion."

c h a p t e r

E L E V E N

Quenthel's patrol had stalked the shadowy, candlelit passages of Arach-Tinilith for hours, until spaces she knew intimately began to seem strange and subtly unreal, and her subordinates' nerves visibly frayed with the waiting. She called a halt to let the underlings rest and collect themselves. They stopped in a small chapel with the images of skulls, daggers, and spiders worked in bas-relief on the walls and the bones of long-dead priestesses interred beneath the floor. Rumor whispered that a cleric had cut her own throat in this sanctuary and her ghost sometimes haunted it, but the Baenre had never seen the apparition, and it wasn't in evidence then.

The priestesses and novices settled on the pews. For a while, no one spoke.

Eventually Jyslin, a second-year student with a heart-shaped face and silver studs in her earlobes, said, "Perhaps nothing will happen."

Quenthel stared coldly at the novice. Like the rest of the party, the younger female cut a warlike figure with her mace, mail, and shield, but her dread showed in her troubled maroon eyes and shiny, sweaty brow.

"We will face another demon tonight," Quenthel said. "I feel it, so it's pointless to hope otherwise. Instead I suggest you concentrate on staying alert and remembering what you've learned."

Jyslin lowered her eyes and whispered, "Yes, Mistress."

"Wishful thinking is for cowards," Quenthel said, "and if you fools are lapsing into it, we've lingered here too long. Up with you."

Reluctantly, someone's links of supple black mail chiming ever so faintly, Quenthel's minions rose. She led them onward.

In light of the two previous intrusions and the obvious uselessness of the wards the mages of Sorcere had created, Quenthel had placed Arach-Tinilith on alert and organized her staff and students into squads of eight. Most of the units would stand watch at set locations, but several would patrol the entire building. The Baenre princess had opted to lead one of the latter.

She'd also decided to throw open the storerooms and armories and dispense all the potent enchanted tools and weapons still deposited there. Even the first-year students bore enchanted arms and talismans worthy of a high priestess.

Not that the gear had done much to bolster Jyslin's morale, nor that of many another novice. Had Quenthel not been suffering her own carefully masked anxieties, their glumness might have amused her. The girls had seen demons throughout their childhoods. They'd even achieved a certain intimacy with them in Arach-Tinilith, but this was the first time such entities had posed a threat to them, and they'd realized they hadn't truly known the ferocious beings at all.

No doubt some of the females had also been perceptive enough to recognize that they themselves had been in comparatively little danger until Quenthel mustered them in what was more or less her personal defense. If so, their resentment, like their uneasiness, was irrelevant. They were her underlings, and it was their duty to serve her.

"It's the wrath of Lolth herself," whispered Minolin Fey-Branche, a fifth-year student who wore her hair in three long braids. Obviously, she didn't intend for her voice to carry to the front of the procession. "First she strips us of our magic, then sends her fiends to kill us."

Quenthel whirled. Sensing her anger, her whip vipers rose, weaving and hissing.

"Shut up!" she snapped. "The Spider Queen may be testing us, eliminating the unfit, but she has not condemned her entire temple. She would not."

Minolin lowered her eyes. "Yes, Mistress," she said tonelessly.

Quenthel noticed that no one else looked reassured, either.

"You disgust me," the Baenre said. "All of you."

"We apologize, Mistress," said Jyslin.

"I remember my training," Quenthel said. "If a novice showed a hint of cowardice or disobedience, my sister Triel would make her fast for a tenday, and eat rancid filth for another after that. I should do the same, but unfortunately, with Arach-Tinilith under siege, I need my people strong. So all right, though it should shame you take it, you can have another rest. You'll fill your bellies, and it had better stiffen your spines. Otherwise, we'll see how many of you I have to flog before the rest cease their cringing and whining. Come."

She led them on to a classroom where the kitchen staff had set a table. She'd ordered them to prepare a cold supper and leave it at various points around the temple, so that the weary sentinels could at least refresh themselves with food, and the cooks had done a decent job of it. On a silver salver lay pink and brown slices of rothé steak steeped in a tawny marinade, their aroma competing with Arach-Tinilith's omnipresent scent of incense. Other trays and bowls held raw mushroom pieces with a creamy dipping sauce and a salad of black, white, and red diced fungus, while the pitchers presumably contained wine, watered as per her command. Quenthel hoped the alcohol would hearten those residents whom Lolth's absence and the incursions of the past two nights had terrified, but she didn't want any of the temple's defenders sloppy drunk and incapacitated.

Some of Quenthel's minions fell to as if they expected this to be their last meal. Others, likely as certain of their fate, seemed too tense to do more than pick at the viands.

The mistress of the Academy supposed that, though she intended to survive the night, in a sense, she belonged to the latter party. Her stomach was somewhat queasy, and the long hours of edgy anticipation had killed her appetite.

Come on, demon, she thought, *let's get this over with. . . .*

The entity failed to respond to her silent plea.

She decided her throat was a little parched, caught Jyslin's eye, and said, "Pour me a cup."

"Yes, Mistress."

The second-year novice performed the service with commendable alacrity. She filled the silver goblet too high for gentility's sake, but Quenthel expected no better from a commoner. The Baenre accepted the cup with a nod and raised it to her lips.

Her whip of fangs hung from her wrist by the wyvern-hide loop that pierced its handle. She felt a thrill of alarm surge across the psionic link she shared with the vipers. At the same instant, the snakes reared and dashed the goblet from her grasp. She stared at them in amazement.

"Poison," Yngoth said, his slit-pupiled eyes glinting in their scaly sockets. "We smelled it."

Quenthel looked around. Her followers had heard the serpent's declaration and were gawking at her and the reptiles in consternation. They appeared to be in perfectly good health, but she trusted the vipers and knew it wouldn't last.

"Purge yourselves," she said. "Now!"

They never got the chance. Almost as one, they succumbed to the toxin, swaying, staggering, and collapsing. Some retched involuntarily as the sickness hit them, but it didn't help. They passed out like the rest.

Quenthel shifted the whip back to her hand, peered in all directions, and bade the vipers do the same. She'd realized her demonic assailants were supposed to suggest the several dominions of the goddess, and therefore an "assassin" of some sort would turn up sooner or later. Still, she foolishly assumed that being would attack in some obvious way just as the "spider" and "darkness" had. She hadn't expected it to employ stealth and attempt to poison her, though in retrospect, that tactic made perfect sense.

The question was, had the demon done all it planned to do, or, since its first ploy had failed, would it strike at her in some other way?

Off to the west, someone screamed, the sound echoing down the stone halls. Quenthel had her answer, and it was the one she'd expected.

Her heart beat faster, her mouth felt drier still, and she realized she wasn't eager to confront this new intruder, certainly not without the support of her personal guards. Yet she was mistress in these halls, and it was unthinkable to turn tail and let an invader make free with her domain.

Besides, if she fled, the cursed thing would probably track her anyway.

Leaving her fallen patrol with their useless magical treasures strewn about them on the floor, she strode toward the noise. She shouted for other underlings to attend her, but no one responded.

In a minute or so, she entered a long gallery, where wall carvings told the history of Lolth as it had occurred and as it was prophesied: her seduction of Corellon Larethian, chief deity of the contemptible elves of the World Above, their union and her first attempt to overthrow him, her discovery of her spider form and her descent into the Abyss, her conquest of the Demonweb and her adoption of the drow as her chosen people, and her future triumph over all other gods and ascendancy over all creation.

A silhouette appeared in the arched entry at the far end of the hall. It changed color and shape—humanoid, quadruped, blob, worm, cluster of spikes—from one instant to the next. Somehow perceiving Quenthel, it let out a cry. Its voice sounded like a wavering, cacophonous jumble of every noise she'd ever heard and some she hadn't. Within the first discordant howl she caught the shrill note of a flute, the grunt of a rothé, a baby crying, water splashing, and fire crackling.

Quenthel recognized the demon for the profound threat it was, but for a moment, she was less concerned for her safety or fired with a fighter's rage than she was surprised. Poison surely suggested an assassin, yet the demon before her was plainly an embodiment of chaos.

The spirit started down the gallery, and the walls bulged, flowed, and changed color around it. Quenthel reached into the leather bag hanging from her belt and brought out a scroll, then something hit her hard in the back of the neck.

※　　※　　※

Ryld peered about the room. Judging from the sunken arena in the center of the floor, the ruinous place had, in another era, served as a drinking pit—one of those rude establishments where dark elves of every station went to forget about caste and grace for a few hours, guzzle raw spirit, and watch undercreatures slaughter one another in contests that were often set up in such a way as to give them a comical aspect.

In other words, it would have been a crude sort of place by the standards of elegant Menzoberranzan, but it had grown cruder since the goblinoids had taken it over. Scores if not hundreds of them packed into the space, and the mingled stink of their unwashed bodies, each race malodorous in its own particular fashion, was sickening. The loud gabbling in their various harsh and guttural languages was nearly as unpleasant. It all but drowned out the rhythmic thuds that filtered through the ceiling, but of course the shaggy gnoll drummer on the roof wasn't playing for the folk already inside but to guide others still in transit.

To Ryld's surprise, a fair number of the creatures assembling there hailed from outside the Braeryn. He observed plain but relatively clean and intact garments suggestive of Eastmyr, and even liveries, steel collars, shackles, whip marks, and brands—the stigmata of thralls who'd sneaked away from their mistresses' affluent households. Obviously, those who'd come from beyond the district couldn't have heard the drum through the magical buffers. Some runner must have carried word to them.

Still magically disguised as orcs, though not the same ones who'd tricked the two bugbears, the masters of Tier Breche had squeezed into a corner to watch whatever would transpire.

Certain no one would hear him over the ambient din, Ryld leaned his head close to Pharaun's and said, "I think it's just a party."

"Do you see them celebrating?" Pharaun replied. His new porcine face had a broken nose and tusk. "No, not as such. They'd be considerably more boisterous. They're waiting for something, and eagerly, too. Observe those female goblins chattering and passing their bottle back and forth." Pharaun nodded toward a trio of filthy, bandy-legged creatures with flat faces and sloping brows. "They're aquiver with anticipation. If they're still as giddy after the gathering breaks up, we may want to seek solace for our frustrations in their hairy, misshapen arms."

Certain his friend was joking, Ryld snorted . . . then realized he wasn't quite sure after all.

"You'd have relations with a *goblin*?"

"A true scholar always seeks new experiences. Besides, what's the point of being a dark elf, a lord of the Underdark, if you don't exploit the slave races to the utmost?"

"Hmm. I admit they might be no worse than one of those priestesses who demand you grovel and do exactly as you're—"

"Hush!"

The drum had stopped.

"Something's happening," Pharaun added.

Ryld saw that his friend was correct. A stir ran through the crowd and they started to shout, "Prophet! Prophet! Prophet!"

The master of Melee-Magthere didn't know what he expected to see next, but it certainly wasn't the figure in the nondescript cloak and hood whose upper body appeared above the heads of the crowd. Perhaps he'd climbed up on a bench or table, or maybe he'd simply levitated, for this "Prophet," plainly beloved of the lower orders, appeared to be a handsome drow male.

The Prophet let his followers chant and shout for a minute or so, then he raised his slender hands and gradually they subsided. Pharaun leaned close to Ryld again.

"It's possible the fellow's not really one of us," the wizard said. "He's wrapped in a glamour somewhat like ours, but his spell makes every observer perceive him in a favorable light. I imagine the goblins see him as a goblin, the gnolls, as one of their own, and so forth."

"What's inside the illusion?"

"I don't know. The enchantment is peculiar. I've never encountered anything quite like it. I can't see through it, but I suspect we're about to learn his intentions."

"My brothers and sisters," the Prophet said.

His voice sparked another round of cheering, and he waited for it to run its course.

"My brothers and sisters," he repeated. "Since the founding of this city, the Menzoberranyr have held our peoples in bondage or in conditions equally degraded. They work us until we die of exhaustion. They torture and kill us on a whim. They condemn us to starve, sicken, and live in squalor."

The audience growled its agreement.

"You witness our misery everywhere you look," the hooded orator continued. "Yesterday, I walked through Manyfolk. I saw a hobgoblin girl-child, surely no older than five or six, trying to pick up a scrap of mushroom from the street. With her teeth! Her hands wouldn't serve. Some drow had magically fused them together behind her back so she would live and die a cripple and a freak."

The crowd snarled in outrage, even though their races commonly engaged in tortures equally cruel, albeit far less varied and imaginative.

"I walked through Narbondellyn," the Prophet said. "I saw an orc, paralyzed in some manner, lying on the ground. A dark elf slit his chest, spread the flaps of skin, cut some ribs with a saw, and whistled his riding lizard over to feed on the still-living thrall's organs. The drow told a companion that he gave the reptile one such meal every tenday to make it a faster racer."

The audience howled its wrath. One female orc, transported with fury, gashed her cheeks and brow with a piece of broken glass.

The Prophet's litany of atrocities ran on and on, and Ryld gradually felt a strange emotion overtaking him. He knew it couldn't be guilt—no dark elf experienced that ridiculous condition—but perhaps it was a kind of shame, a disgust at the sheer waste and childishness manifest in Menzoberranzan's abuse of its undercreatures and a desire to rectify the situation if he could.

The feeling was irrational, of course. The goblins and their kin existed only to serve the pleasure of the drow, and if you ruined one, you just caught or bought another. The weapons master gave his head a shake, clearing it, then turned to Pharaun.

Even through his orc mask, the wizard's amusement was apparent.

"Resolved to mend your wicked ways?"

"I gather you feel the influence, too," said Ryld. "What's happening?"

"The Prophet has magic buttressing his oratory, again, in a sort of configuration I don't quite understand."

"Right, but what's the point of all this bellyaching?"

"I assume he'll get around to telling us."

The speaker continued in the same vein a while longer, goading the crowd to the brink of hysteria.

At last he cried, "But it does not have to be that way!"

The undercreatures howled, and for a moment, until he pushed the feelings away, Ryld felt his magically induced disgust blaze up into savage bloodlust.

"We can be avenged! Repay every injury a thousandfold! Cast down the drow to be *our* slaves! We'll wrap ourselves in silks and cloth-of-gold and make them run naked, feast on succulent viands and feed them garbage! We'll sack Menzoberranzan, and afterward those of us who wish it will return to our own peoples laden with treasure, while the rest of us rule the cavern as our own!"

Not likely, thought Ryld. He turned to say as much to Pharaun, then blinked in surprise. The wizard looked as if he was taking this diatribe seriously.

"They're just venting their resentment in the form of a fantasy," the warrior whispered. "They'd never dare, and we'd crush them in a matter of minutes if they did."

"So one would assume," Pharaun replied. "Come on, I want a closer look."

They started working their way forward through the agitated throng. Some of their fellow spectators plainly resented their shoving. Ryld had to toss one hobgoblin down onto the floor of the sunken arena, but no one seemed to think it odd that they wanted to get closer to the charismatic leader. Others were doing the same.

The Prophet continued his oration.

"I thank you for your work and your patience, which soon will reap their reward. Word of our revolt has reached every street and alley. We have warriors everywhere, and each understands what he is to do when he hears the Call. Meanwhile, the drow suspect nothing. Their arrogance makes them complacent. They won't suspect until it's too late, until the Call comes and we rise as one—until we burn them."

Ryld and Pharaun had forced their way close enough to see the Prophet pick up a sandstone rod and anoint the end with an oil from a ceramic bottle. The rod burst into yellow, crackling flame as if it were made of dry wood, that exotic combustible product of the World Above. The master of Melee-Magthere squinted at the sudden flare of light.

"Eyes of the Goddess!" Pharaun exclaimed.

"It's a neat trick," Ryld said, "but surely nothing special by your standards."

"Not the fire, those two bugbears standing behind the Prophet."

"His bodyguards, I imagine. What of them?"

"They're Tluth Melarn and one Alton the cobbler, two of our runaways. They're wearing veils of illusion, too, but of a simpler nature. I can see past theirs."

"Are you serious? What are drow, even rogues, doing aiding the instigator of a slave revolt?"

"Perhaps we'll find out when we tail the Prophet and his entourage away from here."

"I taught you how to use the fire pots," the orator continued, "and my friends and I have brought plenty of them." He gestured toward several hovering floatchests. "Take them and hide them until the day of reckoning."

The bright notes of a brazen glaur horn blared through the air. For a moment, confused, Ryld thought "the Call"—whatever that was—had arrived, then a thrill of panic, or at least the memory of it, reminded him what the trumpet truly portended. Judging by the goblins' babbling and frantic peering about, they knew, too.

"What is it?" Pharaun asked.

"You're nobly born," said Ryld, hearing a trace of an old bitterness in his voice. "Didn't you ever go hunting through the Braeryn, slaying every wretch you could catch?"

The wizard smiled and said, "Now that you mention it, but it's been a long time. It occurs to me that this is probably Greyanna's doing. Not a bad tactic, really, even though it involves a lot of waste motion. Once I shielded us our hunters couldn't pinpoint our location, but they knew our mission would bring us to the Braeryn so they organized a hunt for a party of nobles. The idea is that all the turmoil is likely to flush us out and send us scrambling frantically through the streets, at which point they'll have a better chance of spotting us."

"What's more," said Ryld, making sure his swords were loose in their scabbards, "your sister gives us the choice of retaining our veils of illusion and being harried by our own kind, or casting them off and facing the wrath of the undercreatures. Either way, someone might do her killing for her."

The Prophet raised his hands for calm, and the undercreatures quieted a little.

"My friends, in a moment we will scatter as we must, for a little while longer, but before you go, take the fire pots. Once the danger is past, share the weapons and news of our gathering with all those who were unable to attend. Remember your part in the plan and wait for the Call. Now, go!"

Some of the rebels bolted without further delay, but at least half lingered long enough to take a jug or two from the hovering boxes.

One orc lost his footing in the press, then screamed as other goblinoids trampled him in their haste. Meanwhile, the Prophet and his bodyguards slipped out a door in the back wall.

"Shall we?" said Pharaun, striding after them.

"What of Greyanna and all the hunters?" asked Ryld.

"We'll contend with them as necessary, but I'll be damned if I hide in a hole while two of the boys we worked so hard to find vanish into the night."

The masters stalked out onto the street. The Braeryn already echoed with more trumpeting, the sporting cries of dark elves, and the screams of undercreatures.

The teachers shadowed the Prophet and the rogues for half a block. The trio moved briskly but without any trace of panic. Evidently they were confident of their ability to elude the hunters. Ryld wondered why.

Then the night gave him other things to think about.

He and Pharaun skulked by a house where several shouting goblins pounded on the granite front door. As was the common practice during a hunt, the inhabitants refused to admit them. They wouldn't let in anyone but folk who actually lived there. Otherwise, a rush of terrified refugees flooding into the already crowded warren might trample or crush some of the residents—or the influx might make the house a more provocative target. It had happened before.

Finally Ryld heard the small, long-armed creatures turn away from the structure. They cried out, then broke into a run, their rapid footsteps drumming on the ground.

Ryld had no idea why the goblins were charging him and Pharaun. Perhaps the creatures had mistaken them for tenants of the house that had denied them entry and thus appropriate targets for revenge. Maybe they simply wanted to take their frustrations out on someone.

Not that it mattered. The brutes were no match for masters of Tier Breche. The dark elves would kill them in a trice.

Ryld drew Splitter from its scabbard and came on guard, meanwhile taking in his assailants' pitiful makeshift weaponry and lack of armor. It was pathetic, really, so much so that the next few seconds would almost be a bore.

Two goblins spread out, trying to flank him. He stepped in and swung Splitter left, then right. The undercreatures fell, one dropping its crowbar to clang against the ground and the other keeping hold of its mallet.

The next two bat-eared creatures hesitated. They should have turned and run, because Ryld couldn't stand and wait for them to ponder whether they still wanted to fight. The Prophet and the rogues were getting farther away by the second.

He stepped in and cut downward. A goblin, this one possessed of a short sword—a proper warrior's weapon, and some martial training to go with it—lifted the weapon to parry. It didn't matter. Splitter sheared right through its blade and streaked on into its torso.

Knife in hand, the fourth goblin dodged behind its foe. Sensing its location, Ryld kicked backward. His boot connected solidly, snapping bone, and when he turned the creature lay motionless on the ground, likely dead of a broken back.

Ryld turned to survey the battlefield. His eyes widened in shock and dismay.

Pharaun too was on the ground. Three goblins crouched over him on their bandy legs. One scabrous creature had blood on the iron spike that served it as a poniard.

Ryld bellowed a war cry, sprang at them, and struck them down before they could do any more damage. He kneeled beside his friend. Beneath the elegant *piwafwi*, Pharaun's equally gorgeous robe had two punctures in it, and was dark and wet from breastbone to thighs.

"I heard them coming a moment after you did," the wizard wheezed. "I didn't turn around fast enough."

"Don't worry," said Ryld. "It's going to be all right."

In reality, he wasn't at all sure of that.

"The goblin thrust through the gap between the wings of my cloak. The little bastard hurt me when Greyanna and her followers couldn't. Isn't that silly?"

c h a p t e r

<h1 style="text-align: center;">T W E L V E</h1>

When Quenthel had decided she must don armor, she had performed the task as methodically as she did everything else. She'd put on a cunningly crafted adamantine gorget, a Baenre heirloom, beneath her chain mail and *piwafwi*, and it was likely that protective collar that saved her life.

Still, the unexpected impact on the nape of her neck knocked her forward and down onto one knee, and the edge of her enchanted buckler clanked against the floor.

For a moment, she was dazed. The whip vipers hissed and clamored to rouse her, their outburst clashing with the jumbled howling of the advancing chaos demon.

She felt something hanging down her back and bade the serpents pull it off. Hsiv reared over her shoulder, tugged the article out of the mail links and cloth with his jaws, and displayed it for her inspection. She recognized it from the armory. It was an enchanted quarrel sized for a two-hand arbalest, and if it, or one

179

like it, so much as pricked a dark elf's skin, it would almost certainly kill.

Quenthel thought her assailant had had just about enough time to reload. If so, the Baenre obviously couldn't trust her cloak and mail to protect her—the first bolt had pierced them easily enough.

Though it meant turning her back on the demon, she wrenched herself around, remaining on one knee to make a smaller target, and did her best to cover herself with her tiny shield.

Just in time. A second quarrel cracked against the armor. A shadowy but recognizably female figure ducked back into an arched doorway, no doubt to ready her weapon again.

Trapped between two foes, Quenthel thought that if she didn't eliminate one of them quickly, they were almost certainly going to kill her. Judging her sister dark elf the easier mark, she leveled a long, thin rod at her.

A glob of seething green vitriol materialized in the air before her, then shot toward her enemy. Quenthel could just see the edge of her opponent's body in the recessed space, and that was what she aimed for. Even if she missed, the magic ought to slow the assassin down.

The green mass clipped her foe's shoulder. It exploded, and the dark figure jumped. The stonework around her was covered in a sticky mass of something like glue. Quenthel smiled, but her foe, apparently unhindered by the entrapping magic, returned to the task of cocking the crossbow. Something, her innate drow resistance to hostile magic, perhaps, had shielded her from harm.

Quenthel glanced over her shoulder as she slipped the rod back into her belt. Though moving at a leisurely pace, the chaos demon had already traversed more than half of the lengthy gallery, and of course its speed could increase at any moment, just as every other aspect of its being altered unpredictably from one second to the next.

But if the Spider Queen favored Quenthel and the entity didn't accelerate, she might have time for another strike at her foe of flesh and blood. Silently directing the vipers to keep an eye on the demon, she turned back, and read from a precious scroll.

When Quenthel pronounced the last syllable, the scroll disappeared in a puff of dust and a brilliant light filled the chamber. The dark elf in the doorway reeled and clutched blindly at the door frame. She touched the slowly-dripping mass of glue and snatched her fingers away, leaving skin behind.

Quenthel started to read another scroll as the air around her stirred, blowing one direction then another. Hot one second and cold the next, the gusts wafted countless smells, pleasant and foul alike. She took it for a sign that the demon had drawn very close, and the vipers' warning confirmed it.

Still, she wanted to finish her lesser adversary off before the girl recovered her sight. She completed the spell, the exquisitely inked characters burning through the parchment like hot coals.

From the elbow down, the enemy female's left arm rippled and swelled, becoming an enormous black spider with green markings on its bristling back. Still attached to the rest of her body, it lunged at her throat and plunged its mandibles in.

Quenthel spun around. Mauve with golden spots, then white, then half red and half blue, the demon loomed over her. Most of the time it looked flat, like a hole into some other luminous, turbulent universe, and an observer had only its inconstant outline from which to infer its shape. Over the course of a couple seconds, it seemed to become an enormous crab claw, a wagon complete with driver, and a whirling dust devil. The length of gallery behind it resembled a tunnel carved from melting rainbow-colored slush except for one little stretch. That section appeared unchanged until Quenthel noticed that the carvings had flipped upside down.

The high priestess scrambled to her feet. As she rooted in her bag for another scroll, her scourge dangled from her wrist. The vipers writhed and twisted.

The chaos demon blinked from ochre to a pattern of black and white stripes, and from the form of a simple isosceles triangle to that of an ogre. Its cry currently a mix of roaring and cawing, it swung its newly acquired club.

Quenthel caught the blow on her buckler. To her surprise, she didn't feel the slightest shock, but the shield turned blue, changed from round to rectangular, and became many times heavier than it had been before.

The unexpected weight dragged her down to the floor again. Resembling a cresting wave, the intruder flowed toward her. She yanked, but her shield arm was caught somehow and wouldn't pull free of the straps.

Rippling from magenta to brown stippled with scarlet, the demon advanced to within inches of her foot. Quenthel's boot evaporated into wisps of vapor, and pain stabbed through the extremity.

Finally her hand jerked out of its restraints, and she flung herself backward, rolling, her mail whispering against the floor.

When she'd put sufficient distance between herself and her foe, she rose, then faltered. For an instant, she couldn't locate the fiend, and her mind struggled to make sense of the scene before her. Green and blue, shaped like an hourglass, the demon was gliding along the ceiling, not the floor. It was still pursuing her. The cursed thing was random in every respect save its doggedly murderous intent.

The entity's howl ceased for a moment, then resumed with a peal of childish laughter. Quenthel snatched and unrolled a scroll, which abruptly turned into a rothé's jawbone. The air took on a sooty tinge, and her next breath seared her lungs.

Choking, she stumbled back out of the cloud. She could breathe, though the stinging heat in her throat and chest persisted. She suspected that, had she inhaled any more of it, the taint might well have killed her. As it was, it had incapacitated and possibly slain the vipers, who hung inert from the butt of the whip.

She tossed away the jawbone, grabbed another scroll, and started reading the powerful spell contained therein. Shaped like some hybrid of dragon and wolf, the demon, back on the floor again, advanced without moving its legs. Though colored the blue and gold of flame, it threw off a bitter chill that threatened to freeze the skin on her face and spoil her recitation with a stammer.

Quenthel thanked the goddess that her own education in Arach-Tinilith had taught her to transcend discomfort. She forced out the words in the proper manner, and a black blade, like a greatsword without a guard, hilt, or tang, shimmered into existence in front of her.

She smiled. The floating weapon was a devastating magic known only to the priestesses of Lolth. Quenthel had never seen any creature resist it. Though the stone floor was still chilly against the sole of her bare foot, the ghastly cold had passed, and she stood her ground, the blade interposed between her and her pursuer.

"Do you know what this is?" she asked it. "It can kill you. It can kill anything."

Certain the demon could hear her thoughts, she sent it the words, *Surrender and tell me who sent you, or I'll slice you to pieces.*

Emitting a sweet scent she'd never encountered before, looking like a giant frog crudely chiseled from mica with rows of wicked fangs in its sparkling jaws, the chaos demon waddled forward.

Fine, the Baenre thought, *be stupid.*

Controlling the black blade with her thoughts, she bade it attack. It hacked a long gash in the top of the frog head and knocked the demon down on its belly. The edges of the wound burned with scarlet fire.

The intruder turned inky black while flowing into a shape that resembled two dozen hands growing on long, leafy stalks. The stems stretching and twisting, the creature grabbed for the sword.

Quenthel let the hands seize hold of it, and as she'd expected, the magically keen double edge cut them to pieces, which dropped away onto the floor. The demon gave a particularly loud cry, which sounded in part like the rhythmic clanging of a hammer beating metal in a forge. Wincing at the noise, the priestess didn't know if the extreme volume equated to a scream of pain, but she hoped so.

The demon turned into a miniature green tower shaped according to the uncouth architectural notions of some inferior race. A force surrounding it tugged at the sword as if the keep were a magnet and the conjured weapon, forged of steel. Quenthel found it easy to compensate for the pull. She slashed away chunks of masonry.

The tower opened lengthwise like a sarcophagus. It lurched forward, swallowed the sword, and closed up again.

The entity had caught Quenthel by surprise, but she didn't see why it should matter. It might even be more effective to cut and stab her foe from the inside. She used the blade to thrust, felt the point bite, and her psionic link with the weapon snapped.

Startled, she nonetheless reflexively reached for another scroll. The demon spread out into a low, squirming red and yellow mass. A hole dilated in the midst of it, and it spat the sword out. The weapon retained its shape but rippled with shifting colors just as the intruder did, and Quenthel still couldn't feel it with her mind.

She backed away, the blade followed, and, rattling and growling, the demon brought up the rear. The sword swept back and forth, up and down, while she ducked and dodged. So far, she was evading it, but it hampered and hurt her simply by being near. Her mail turned to moss and crumbled away. Her flesh throbbed with sudden pains as the demon's power sought to transform it. One leg turned numb and immobile for a second, and she nearly fell. Itchy scales grew on her skin then faded away. Her eyes ached, the world blurred to black, white, and gray, and the colors exploded back into view. Her identity itself was in flux. For one instant, she thought the thoughts and felt the soft, alien emotions of an arthritic human seamstress dwelling somewhere in the World Above.

Somehow, despite all such disconcerting phenomena, she managed to read the spell on the scroll and avoid the radiant blade at the same time.

She wasn't sure how this particular parchment had found its way to Arach-Tinilith. She questioned that a dark elf had scribed it, for it contained a spell that few drow ever cast. Indeed, some priestesses would disdain to cast it, because it invoked a force regarded as anathema to their faith. But Quenthel knew the goddess would want her to use any weapon necessary to vanquish her foe, and it was remotely possible that this magic would prevail where even the supposedly invincible black blade had failed.

Bright, intricate harmonies sang from the empty air. A field of bluish phosphorescence sprang up around her. Within it, she could make out intangible geometric forms revolving around one another in complex symmetrical patterns.

The cool radiance expressed the power of order, of law, the antithesis of chaos. The sword that had become an extension of the demon's will froze inside it like an insect in amber—and the demon was equally still. For a moment, at least. The creature began hitching ever so slightly forward, working itself loose of the restricting magic.

The Mistress of Arach-Tinilith was essentially a creature of chaos as well, but mortal and native to the material plane, and thus the spell had no power over her. She wheeled and dashed to the body lying in the doorway. Only the spider part of it was moving, chewing and slurping on the rest.

The dead girl turned out to be Halavin Symryvvin, who'd had the surprisingly good sense to remove all that gaudy, clinking jewelry before attempting to attack by surprise. The novice had managed the arbalest rather deftly, considering her sore, mutilated hands.

Quenthel stooped to pick up the weapon and the quiver containing the rest of the enchanted quarrels. She moved warily, but the feasting arachnid paid her no mind.

She turned, laid a dart in the channel, and shot. When the shaft hit it, the demon shuddered in its nearly immobile form, but didn't die.

It occurred to her that she could get away from it while it was trapped, muster any loyal minions who hadn't partaken of the poisoned supper, and fight the thing at the head of a company, just as she'd originally intended. After the harrowing events of the past minutes, the idea had a certain appeal.

But after what she'd endured, she wanted to be the one to teach this vermin a lesson about molesting the clergy of Lolth. Besides, the appearance of strength was vital. So she kept shooting as fast as the cocking action of the weapon would allow. The demon inched its way toward her as if it was made of half-cooled magma.

Four bolts left, then three. She pulled the trigger, the dart struck the demon in the middle of its horned, triangular head, and it winked out of existence.

She could still hear its voice, but knew that was just because it had shrieked so long and loudly. She gave her head a shake, trying to quell the phantom sound, then glimpsed yet another shadow watching her from some distance away.

"You!" she shouted, cocking the arbalest to receive the penultimate quarrel. "Come here!"

The other dark elf bolted. Quenthel gave chase, but she was still a little winded from the struggle with the demon, and her quarry outdistanced her and disappeared.

The Baenre stalked on through the labyrinthine chambers and corridors until she rounded a bend and came face to face with three of her minions. The goddess only knew what their true sentiments were, but confronted with her leveled arbalest and the obvious fact that, while her gear was much the worse for wear, she herself was unscathed, they hastily saluted.

"I killed tonight's intruder," she said, "and a homegrown enemy as well. What do you know of our situation? Is anyone else dead?"

"No, Mistress," said a priestess. The lowered visor of her spider-crested helmet completely concealed her features, but from her voice, Quenthel recognized Quave, one of the senior instructors. "Most of those who ate and drank the tainted meal are waking. I think the poisoner only wanted to render us unconscious, not kill us."

"Apparently," said Quenthel, "she was willing to let the demon administer the coup de grâce to me. What of those who encountered the entity before I did?"

Quave hesitated, then said, "When they tried to hinder it, it hurt them, but not to the point of death. They should recover as well."

"Good," Quenthel said, though she took no joy in knowing she was the unknown enemy's sole target.

"What are your orders, Mistress?" asked Quave.

"We'll have to sort out the living from the dead, and deal with each accordingly. We'll also look for the place where the demon got in, and seal it."

These were tasks that would doubtless keep her occupied for the rest of the night, but she knew she had to find a way to stop the intrusions, and pull the fangs of another crisis as well.

It would all for make an arduous day's labor, with the outcome uncertain enough to depress even a high priestess. Still, her mood lifted slightly when her vipers began to stir.

☙   ☙   ☙

"I have a healing potion," said Ryld. He took a small pewter vial from his pouch, unstoppered it, and held it to Pharaun's lips. The wizard drank the liquid down.

"That might be a little better," Pharaun said after a moment. "But it's still bad. I'm still bleeding. On the inside, too, I think. Do you have any more?"

"No."

"Pity. A wretched little goblin did this. I can't believe it."

"Can you walk?" asked Ryld.

Pharaun would have to move or be moved, somehow. He couldn't just lie in the street, not in the Braeryn, not on a night when the hunt was out. It was far too dangerous.

"Possibly." The mage strained to lift himself up with his hands, then slumped back down. "But apparently not."

"I'll carry you," said Ryld.

He gathered the mage in his arms, and bidding Pharaun do the same, called upon the magic of his House insignia. They floated slowly upward, and swung onto a rooftop.

The view from that vantage point was far from encouraging. Screaming undercreatures ran through the streets and alleys of the Braeryn with whooping riders in pursuit. The dark elves killed the goblins with the thrust of a lance, the slash of a sword, or simply by trampling them under the clawed feet of their lizards. They tended to find intimate mayhem more amusing. Some, however, had no qualms about loosing a quarrel or conjuring a blast of magic.

187

Still other drow wheeled above the scene on foulwings, wyverns, and other winged mounts. Ryld saw danger on every side.

He hauled Pharaun up against a sort of gable in the hope that it would provide cover against the scrutiny of the flyers.

"It's bad," the swordsman said. "A lot of drow are hunting. There's no clear path out of the district."

The wizard didn't reply.

"Pharaun!"

"Yes," sighed his friend, "I'm still conscious. Barely."

"We'll hide here until the hunt ends. I'll cover us with a patch of darkness."

"That might w—"

Pharaun gasped and thrashed. Ryld held on to him for fear that he'd roll off the roof.

When the seizure ended, the Mizzrym's face seemed gaunt and drawn in a way it hadn't been before. More blood seeped from his wounded stomach.

"This isn't going to work," said Ryld, "not by itself. Unless you have some more healing, you're going to die."

"That would be . . . a profound tragedy . . . but . . ."

"We have plenty of dark elves in the Braeryn tonight. One of them surely brought some restorative magic along. I'll just have to take it from him, or her. Here's that darkness."

Ryld touched the roof and conjured a shadow that covered the Master of Sorcere and not much else. With luck, the effect was localized enough that no one would notice the obscuration itself.

The weapons master rose and raced away. Whenever possible, he ran along the rooftops, bounding from one to the next. Often enough, however, the houses were far enough apart that he had to jump down to the ground and skulk his way through the slaughter.

It was at such a time that he saw another hunting party. Unfortunately, the group was too large to tackle. He had to hide from it instead. Crouched low, he watched a mage on lizard-back lob a yellow spark through the window of one of the houses. Booming, yellow flame exploded through the room beyond. A moment after it died, the screaming began. Ryld winced. As a child of six, he'd survived precisely such a massacre, and, severely blistered, lain trapped for hours beneath a weight of charred, stinking bodies, the luckier ones dead, the live ones whimpering and twitching in their helpless agony.

But it wasn't him burned nor buried tonight, and he spat the unpleasant memory away. He glanced about, checking to see if anyone was looking at him, then broke from cover and floated upward.

He dashed on along a steeply sloping roof engraved with web patterns and defaced, he noticed, with another slave race emblem. He sensed something above and behind him, and pivoted. His boots slipped, and he levitated for an instant while he found his footing amid the carvings.

He looked up and spied a huge black horse galloping through the air as easily as the common equines of the World Above could run across a field. Fire crackled around its hooves and pulsed from its nostrils. The dark elf male on its back held a scimitar, but wasn't making any extraordinary effort to lift it into position for a cut. Apparently he was counting on his demonic steed to make the kill, and why not? What goblinoid could withstand a nightmare?

Ryld froze as if he were such a hapless undercreature paralyzed with fear. Meanwhile, he timed the speed of the nightmare's approach. At the last possible moment, hoping to take the phantom horse and its master by surprise, he whipped Splitter out of its scabbard and cut.

And missed. Somehow the demon arrested its charge, and the blade fell short.

Its fiery hooves churning eighteen inches above the rooftop, the nightmare snorted. Thick, hot, sulfurous smoke streamed from its nostrils, enveloping Ryld, stinging and half blinding him. He heard more than saw the black creature lunging, striking with its reptilian fangs, and he retreated a step. The move saved him, but when he counterattacked, the nightmare too had taken itself out of range.

Through the stinking vapor, he glimpsed the infernal horse circling. It sprang at him again, this time rearing to batter him with its front hooves. He crouched and lifted Splitter. The point took the steed in the chest, and for a moment, he thought he'd disposed of it, but, its legs working frantically, it flew upward, lifting itself off the blade before it could penetrate too deeply.

The next few seconds were difficult. Ryld could barely make out his foes, while the nightmare could apparently see through its own smoke perfectly well. He stood and turned precariously on the crest of the roof, in constant danger of losing his balance, whereas the flying horse could maneuver wherever it pleased. Just to make life even more interesting, the rider started swinging his curved sword. Fortunately, like most denizens of the Underdark, he had little notion of how to fight on horseback, but his clumsy strokes still posed a danger.

Ryld wanted to end the confrontation quickly, before someone discovered Pharaun's hiding place. Unfortunately, in light of all his disadvantages, the weapons master thought the only way of doing that was to take a risk. The next time the demon reared, he let one of the blazing hooves slam him in the chest.

His dwarven breastplate rang but held. The blow hurt cruelly but didn't break any ribs or otherwise incapacitate him. He fell backward, banged down on the east pitch of the roof, and started to tumble. Kicking and scrabbling, negating his weight, he managed to catch himself and twist around into a low fighting stance.

The nightmare was rushing in to finish him off. He swung Splitter, and this time the demon was too committed to the attack to halt its forward momentum. The greatsword slashed through its neck, nearly severing the head with its luminous scarlet eyes. The steed toppled sideways and rolled, leaving a trail of embers. The rider tried to jump free, but he was too slow. The nightmare crushed him on its way to the ground.

Ryld tore open the dead male's purse, then floated down to the demon horse and checked the saddlebags. There were no potions or any other means of mending a wound.

Why, he wondered, should he expect to find such a thing among the noble's effects? The noble had come to the Braeryn for some lighthearted sport. He hadn't believed the goblins couldn't hurt him or that he was in any other danger, so why bring a remedy for grievous harm to the festivities, even if he was lucky enough to possess one?

There were only five hunters who'd come there with a deadly serious purpose, prepared to cross swords with formidable foes: Greyanna and her retainers. They were far more likely to carry healing magic than any other drow whom Ryld might opt to waylay.

Alas, they were likely to prove more trouble as well, but if he wanted to save Pharaun, he'd just have to cope. Pharaun was a useful ally, and Ryld was unwilling to let that carefully nurtured relationship expire easily. He skulked on, ignoring the hunters who obliviously crossed his path, until he finally spied a familiar figure on a rooftop just ahead of him.

Still masked, one of Greyanna's twin warriors was stalking along that eminence. An arrow nocked, he peered down into the street below.

Ryld threw himself down behind a stubby little false minaret on his roof. He peered around it, looking for the rest of the would-be murderers.

He didn't see them. Maybe the band had split up, the better to look for their quarry. They'd have to, wouldn't they, to oversee the entire district.

He ducked back, cocked his hand crossbow and laid a poisoned dart in the channel. He and Pharaun had been reluctant to kill their pursuers, but with the wizard dying, Ryld was no longer overly concerned with a petty retainer's life.

He leaned back around, his finger already tightening on the trigger—and the space where the archer had stood was empty. Ryld cast about, and after a moment spotted the male atop a round, flat-roofed little tower adhering to the main body of the building.

That posed two problems. One was that the warrior was farther away and ten feet higher up, at or beyond the limit of the little crossbow's range. The other was that the male happened to be looking in Ryld's direction. His eyes flew open wide when he spotted his quarry.

Ryld shot, and his dart fell short of the tower. A split second later, the twin pulled back his bowstring and loosed his arrow in one fluid motion. The shaft looked like a gradually swelling dot, which meant it was speeding straight at its target.

Ryld dodged back. The arrow whizzed past, and the archer shouted, "Here! I've got him here!"

The weapons master scowled, feeling the pressure of passing time even more acutely than before. He didn't want to be there when the rest of the enemy arrived, and the only hope of avoiding it was to dispose of his present opponent quickly. The longbow simply had his hand crossbow outclassed. He needed to get in close.

He drew Splitter, sprang out into the open, and strode toward his foe. The archer sent one arrow after another winging his way, and he knocked them out of the air. The defense was considerably more difficult advancing across the irregular surface of the roof than it would have been standing still on the ground.

Ryld began to sweat, and his heart beat faster, but he was managing. There came another shaft, this one aglitter with some form of enchantment, and he swatted it down. Rattling, it rolled on down the pitch of the roof.

He took another step, slapped aside another missile, then heard something—he didn't know what, just an indefinable change in the sounds around him. He remembered that some enchanters created magical weapons capable of more than flying truer and hitting harder.

He spun around. The sparkling arrow had launched itself back into the air and circled around behind him. It was streaking toward its target and was only a few feet from his body.

Ryld wrenched Splitter across in a desperate parry. The edge caught the arrow and split it in two. Spinning through the air, the piece with the point hit his shoulder, but, thanks to his armor, did him no harm.

He lurched back around with barely enough time to deflect the next shaft, then marched on. Four more paces brought him to the end of the roof.

The gap between this house and the next was five yards across. He took a running start, made himself nearly weightless, and jumped. The twin tried to hit when he was in the air, but for a blessed change, his arrow flew wild. Ryld thumped down atop the same structure his opponent occupied. It felt as if it had taken forever to get this far, even though he knew it had really been less than a minute.

Not that he was done running the gauntlet. The arrows kept hurtling at him, including one that gave an eerie scream, filling him with an unnatural fear until he quashed the feeling, and another that turned into a miniature harpy in flight. Yet another struck two paces in front him and exploded into a curtain of fire. Squinting at the glare, he wrapped his *piwafwi* around him and dived through, emerging singed but essentially unscathed.

After that, he was close enough to the tower to cancel most of his weight and leap up to the top. He sprang into the air like a jumping spider and alit on the platform. The twin hastily set down his bow and drew his scimitar.

"Do you have any healing magic?" Ryld asked. "If so, give it to me, and I'll let you go."

The other warrior smiled unpleasantly and said, "My comrades will start arriving any second. Surrender now, tell me where Pharaun is, and perhaps Princess Greyanna will let you live."

"No."

Ryld cut at the warrior's head. The other male jumped back out of range, sidestepped, and slashed at the weapons master's arm. Ryld parried, beat the scimitar aside, and the fight was on.

Over the course of the next few seconds, the Mizzrym warrior gave ground consistently. Twice, he nearly stepped off the flat, round tabletop that was the apex of the tower but on both occasions spun himself away from the edge in time. He was a good duelist, and he was fighting defensively while he waited for reinforcements to arrive. That made him hard to hit. Hard, but not impossible.

Pressing, Ryld feinted high on the inside to draw the parry, swung his greatsword down and around, and cut low on the outside. Splitter sheared into the Mizzrym's torso just below the ribs, and he collapsed in a gush of blood.

Magic trilled and flickered through the air. When Ryld spun around, the other twin and Relonor popped into being on the rooftop below. Obviously, House Mizzrym's mage could teleport on his own, without the aid of the brooch Pharaun had pilfered.

His voluminous sleeves sliding down to his elbows, Relonor lifted his arms and started to cast a spell. The newly arrived twin nocked an arrow and drew back the string of his pale bone bow.

Ryld threw himself down on his stomach. He was ten feet above his adversaries, and he hoped that they couldn't see him. Sure enough, no magic or arrow flew in his direction. He scuttled across the platform—enchantments in his armor deadening the sound of his footfalls—and grabbed his previous opponent's bow and quiver, then scrambled to his knees.

The twin and the wizard rose above the platform, the former levitating, the latter soaring in an arc that revealed some magical capacity for actual flight. The archer loosed an arrow, and mystical energy flashed from Relonor's fingertips.

The Mizzrym's magic reached its target first. A ghastly shriek stabbed through Ryld's ears and into his brain. He cried out and flailed in agony. The warrior's arrow plunged into his thigh, and the razor-edged point burst from the other side.

After a moment, the screaming stopped. Ryld could feel that it had hurt him, perhaps worse than the arrow had, but had no time or inclination to fret about it. Quickly as few folk save a master of Melee-Magthere could manage, he loosed two shafts of his own.

The first took Relonor in the chest, and the second stabbed into the warrior's belly. They both dropped down out of sight.

Ryld looked at the twin with the sword cut in his flank. The male appeared to be unconscious, which would facilitate searching him. Ryld hobbled over to him to rifle his pockets and the leather satchel he wore on his belt.

Blessedly, he found four silver vials, each marked with the rune for healing. Greyanna had indeed outfitted her agents properly for a martial expedition. It was the twin's misfortune that he hadn't had time to drink of her bounty before going into shock.

His brother and Relonor no doubt carried healing draughts as well, and Ryld had no guarantee that they'd be unable to use them. They might come after him again any second, and he'd just as soon avoid a second round. He needed to beat a hasty—

Enormous wings beat the air. A long-necked, legless beast passed overhead with Greyanna and the other priestess, the skinny one, astride its back. Glaring down at Ryld, Pharaun's sister pulled at the laces securing the mouth of her bag of monsters.

Ryld dumped the remaining arrows out of the quiver, the better to examine them. One was fletched with red feathers while the rest had black.

He'd already seen his first foe shoot one fire arrow. Praying that the red-fletched arrow was another, he drew back his bowstring and sent it hurtling into the air.

The arrow plunged into the sack, and burst into flame. The scarred high priestess reflexively dropped the bag, and it fell, burning as it went. The magic spores combusting inside turned the fire green, then blue, then violet.

Greyanna screamed in fury and sent the foulwing swooping lower. Ryld looked for another magic arrow and found that none were left. He nocked an ordinary one, and his hands began to shake, no doubt an aftereffect of the punishment he'd taken.

For a moment, it seemed to him that he was finished. If he couldn't shoot accurately, he couldn't hit one of the foulwing's vital spots, or the riders on its back, for that matter. Nor was he in any shape to fight them hand to hand.

Then he realized he still had a chance. He surrounded his arrow with a cloud of murky darkness, then shot it upward.

The descending beast was a huge target. Even shooting blind with trembling hands, he had a fair chance of hitting in somewhere, and the foulwing gave a double shriek that told him he'd succeeded.

He watched the mass of darkness he'd created tumble and zig-zag drunkenly through the air. Stung, suddenly and inexplicably sightless, the winged mount inside had panicked, and Greyanna was evidently unable to control it. She quite possibly could have dissolved the darkness with some scroll or talisman, but she couldn't see either or lay hands on her equipment easily with the foulwing lurching and swooping about beneath her.

Ryld snapped the head off the arrow in his leg and pulled the offending object out. He gathered up the healing potions, and quickly as he was able, activated the magic in his talisman, floated down off the roof, and limped away.

T H I R T E E N

As Quenthel skulked down the corridor, it occurred to her that at the same time, Gromph was casting his radiant heat into the base of Narbondel. Even revelers and necromancers were settling in for a rest. She, however, was too busy to do the same. She wouldn't have a chance to relax until late the next night, unless, of course, she wound up resting forever.

Fortunately, one of the Baenre alchemists brewed a stimulant to delay the onset of the aching eyes, fuzzy head, and leaden limbs that lack of rest produced. Quenthel extracted a silver vial of the stuff from one of the pouches on her belt and took a sip of it. She gasped, and her shoulder muscles jumped. Jolted back to alertness, she continued on her way.

In another minute, she reached the door to Drisinil's quarters. In deference to the status of her family, the novice resided in one of Arach-Tinilith's most comfortable student habitations. Quenthel regretted not sticking her in a dank little hole. Perhaps then the girl would have learned her place.

The high priestess inspected the arched limestone panel that was the door. She couldn't see any magical wards.

"Is it safe?" she whispered to the vipers.

"We believe so," Yngoth replied.

How reassuring, Quenthel thought, but it was either trust them or use another precious, irreplaceable scroll to wipe away protections that probably didn't exist.

She activated the power of her brooch. When a novice came to Arach-Tinilith, the enchantments on certain doors were keyed to allow her to enter, based on the unique magical signature of her House insignia, rooms the high priestesses deemed it necessary for her to pass into. Only Quenthel's brooch could unlock them all.

She unlocked Drisinil's door and warily cracked it open. No magic sparked, nor did any mechanical trap jab a blade at her. As quietly as she could, Quenthel crept on into the suite. Sensing her desire for quiet, the snakes hung mute and limp.

She found Drisinil sitting motionless in a chair, her bandaged, mutilated hands in her lap. For a moment, Quenthel, thinking the other female must have a dauntless spirit to enter the Reverie at such a perilous time, rather admired her—then she caught the smell of brandy, and noticed the bottle lying in a puddle of liquor on the floor.

Quenthel stalked toward the novice. It occurred to her that she was doing to Drisinil as the living darkness had done to her. The thought vaguely amused her, perhaps simply because she was finally the predator, not the prey. Smiling, she gently laid the vipers across the other drow's face and upper torso. The snakes hissed and writhed.

Drisinil roused with a cry and a start. She started to rear up, and Quenthel pushed her back down in her chair.

"Sit!" the Baenre snapped, "or the serpents will bite."

Her wide eyes framed by the cool, scaly loops of the vipers, Drisinil stopped struggling.

"Mistress, what's wrong?"

Quenthel smiled and said, "Very good, child, you sound sincere.

After your first ploy failed, you should at the very least have rested elsewhere."

"I don't know what you mean."

Drisinil's hand shifted stealthily, no doubt toward a hidden weapon or charm. The vipers struck at the student's face, their fangs missing her sharp-nosed features by a fraction of an inch. She froze.

"Please," Quenthel said. "This will go easier if you don't insult my intelligence. You have spirit, you believe I punished you too harshly, and you're Barrison Del'Armgo, eager to bring down the one House standing between your family and supremacy. Of course you're involved in the plot against me. You're also an idiot if you didn't think I'd realize it."

"Plot?"

Quenthel sighed. "Halavin tried to kill me last night, and she didn't act alone. A single traitor couldn't have drugged all the food and drink set out at various points around the temple. It would have required abandoning her station for long enough that someone would have marked her absence."

"Halavin could have tainted the meal while it was still in the kitchen."

"She was never there."

"Then perhaps the demon poisoned the viands with its magic."

"No. As I'm sure you noted, each spirit represents *one* of the facets of reality over which the goddess holds special dominion. Poison is the weapon of an assassin, while with its continually fluctuating form, last night's assailant was plainly a manifestation of chaos.

"The conspirators," Quenthel continued, "had to contaminate each and every table because they didn't know where I would stop and eat. Many fell unconscious, but you and the other plotters knew not to sample the repast."

Drisinil said, "I had no part in it."

"Novice, you're beginning to irritate me. Admit your guilt, or I'll give you to the vipers and interrogate someone else." The serpents hissed and flicked their tongues.

"All right," said Drisinil, "I was involved. A little. The others talked me into it. Don't kill me."

"I know what your little cabal has done, but I want to understand how you *dared*."

Drisinil swallowed and said, "You . . . you said it yourself. Each demon seeks to kill only you, and each in its own particular way reflects the divine majesty of Lolth. We thought she sent them. We thought we were doing what the goddess wanted."

"Because you're imbeciles. Has no one taught you to look beyond appearances? If Lolth wanted me dead, I couldn't survive her displeasure for a heartbeat, let alone three nights. The attacks resemble her doing because some blasphemous mortal arranged it so, to manipulate you into doing her killing for her. I'd hoped you conspirators knew the trickster's identity, but I see it isn't so."

"No."

"*Curse you all!*" Quenthel exploded. "The goddess favors *me*. How could you possibly doubt it? I'm a Baenre, the Mistress of Arach-Tinilith, and I rose to the rank of high priestess more quickly that any Menzoberranyr ever has!"

"I know . . ." The novice hesitated, then said, "The Mother of Lusts must have some reason for distancing herself from the city, and we . . . speculated."

"Some of you did, I'm sure. Others simply liked the idea of eliminating me. I imagine your Aunt Molvayas would relish seeing me dead. She'd have an excellent chance of becoming mistress in her turn. We Baenre don't have another princess seasoned enough to assume the role."

"It *was* my aunt!" Drisinil exclaimed. "She came up with the idea of helping the demons kill you. I didn't even want to help. I thought it was a stupid idea, but within our family, she holds authority over me."

Quenthel smiled. "It's too bad you weren't more impressed with my authority."

"I'm sorry."

"No doubt that. Now, I need the names of all the conspirators."

Drisinil didn't hesitate an instant. "My aunt, Vlondril Tuin'-Tarl . . ."

As ever, Quenthel maintained a calm, knowing expression, but inwardly she was surprised at the number of conspirators. An eighth of the temple! It was unprecedented, but then she was living in unprecedented times.

When Drisinil finished, the Baenre said, "Thank you. Where did you gather to hatch your schemes?"

"One of the unused storerooms in the fifth leg," Drisinil said.

Quenthel shook her head. "That won't do. It's not big enough. Convene the group in Lirdnolu's old classroom. Nobody's used it since she had her throat slit, so it will seem a safe meeting place."

Drisinil blinked. "Convene?"

"Yes. Last night's plot failed, so obviously you must hatch a new one. You've chosen a new chamber for the conference because you suspect the storeroom is no longer safe. Say whatever you need to say to assemble your cabal in four hours' time."

"If I do, will you spare me?"

"Why not? As you've explained, you only participated reluctantly. But you know, it suddenly occurs to me that we have a problem. If I send you forth to perform this task, how do I know you won't simply flee Tier Breche and take refuge in your mother's castle?"

"Mistress, you already explained that such a course could only lead to my death."

"But did you believe me? Do you still? How can I be sure?"

"Mistress . . . I . . ."

"If I had my magic, I could compel you to do as you're told, but in its absence, I must take other measures."

Quenthel raised the whip, sweeping the vipers off Drisinil's face in the process, and slammed the metal butt of the weapon down in the middle of her forehead.

The mistress then took out the silver vial. She pinched the dazed, feebly struggling girl's nostrils closed, poured the stimulant into her open mouth, and forced her to swallow.

The effect was immediate. The younger female bucked and thrashed until her eyes flew open.

The high priestess hopped back down to the floor. "How does it feel? I imagine your heart is hammering."

Drisinil trembled like the string of a viol. Sweat seeped from her pores.

"What did you do to me?"

"That should be obvious to an accomplished poisoner like yourself."

"You've poisoned me?"

"It's a slow toxin. Do as I ordered, and I'll give you the antidote."

"I can't cozen the others like this. They'll see something's wrong with me."

"The external signs should ease in a minute or two, though you'll still feel the poison speeding your heart and gnawing at your nerves. You'll just have to put up with that."

"All right," Drisinil said. "Just bring the antidote with you when you come to Lirdnolu's room."

The mistress arched an eyebrow, and Drisinil added, "Please."

Quenthel smiled. Catching her mood, the whip vipers sighed with pleasure.

"How did you know your darkness would madden the beast?" asked Pharaun, lathering his narrow chest.

The night before, after he made way back to Pharaun, the two of them had found they had enough healing potions to cure all the wounds that either had sustained. Still, despite their restoration to full vitality, the next few hours proved exhausting, as they struggled to survive the madness of the hunt and watch out for Greyanna at the same time. At last they'd escaped the Braeryn.

Claiming that while Greyanna was seeking them in the Stench-streets, they'd be safe in pleasant, prosperous Narbondellyn, Pharaun had insisted that he and Ryld dispense with disguises and celebrate their sundry discoveries and escapes with a visit to one of

Menzoberranzan's finest public baths. The warrior had objected to what he saw as reckless bravado, but not too vehemently. Ryld supposed that he and Pharaun would climb beyond their foes' reach soon enough. The prospect made him feel rather wistful.

Over the course of the past few minutes, he'd been enjoying the luxury of scrubbing off the sweat and grime that had accumulated on his person, sitting down, and thinking about nothing in particular. He should have known the peace and quiet couldn't last for long. Pharaun couldn't go long without craving conversation.

"How did you know that, shrouded in darkness or no, the foulwing wouldn't just keep descending, guided by its other senses?" the wizard persisted.

The warrior shrugged and said, "I didn't know, but it seemed like a good guess. The thing's an animal, isn't it?"

Pharaun grinned. "Not really. It's a creature from another plane. Still, your instincts were sound."

Ryld shrugged and replied, "I was lucky to get away from there with my life. Very lucky."

"Fire and glare, you're a master of Tier Breche. You're not supposed to be modest. Are you ready to move?"

They rose from an octagonal pool set in the black marble floor, and, having completed the quotidian business of cleaning themselves, headed for a larger basin where they would luxuriate in steaming, scented mineral water. Later in the day, it would be packed, but it wasn't fashionable to visit the baths so early in the morning. They had it to themselves, which was convenient. They could converse without fear of eavesdroppers.

Ryld walked straight down the steps and sat on the underwater ledge. The warmth felt good on his leg, mended but still a little sore, and he sighed with contentment. Pharaun made a production of immersing himself in stages, an inch at a time, as if the heat were almost more than he could bear.

"I've been thinking about your malaise," the wizard said, once everything but his head was finally submerged. "I have a solution."

"What do you mean?"

"Resign from Melee-Magthere and become the weapons master of a noble House. It will have to be one of the lesser ones, of course, you being a commoner, but that's all right. You may see more excitement that way."

"Why would I do that? It's not a move up. It might not be a loss of rank, depending on the House, but still, what would be the point?"

"You're bored, and it would be a change."

"One that would put me under the thumb of any number of high priestesses. I'd have less autonomy than I do as an instructor.".

"I managed to pursue my own objectives while under my mother's supervision. Still, you make a legitimate point. You might find yourself abhorring the tug of the reins. What's the answer, then?"

"Who says there is one? Except, perhaps, further lunatic holidays with you. I admit, this one broke the tedium."

A diminutive female gnome carried a pile of freshly laundered and folded towels out of a doorway on the far wall. Ryld wondered if she was one of the Prophet's followers, and if she had any of the rabble-rouser's duergar firepots stashed somewhere in the bathhouse. It felt strange to think of a humble undercreature that way—wielding stone-burning bombs against its betters.

"You speak of our errand in the past tense," the wizard said.

"Well, once you tell the archmage the runaways are in the Braeryn fomenting a pitiful little goblin uprising, it'll be over, won't it? Gromph will pardon your transgressions. The Council, having failed to stop our inquiries, will, I trust, see no point in continuing to try to kill us. It'll be more to their advantage to let us go on training wizards and soldiers to serve them."

"You're very certain the insurrection will be pitiful. Is it because Greyanna's followers exterminated so many undercreatures last night?"

Ryld scooped up a handful of hot water and splashed it on his neck, which had gotten a little stiff from his exertions.

"No," he said. "The hunters killed plenty of goblins, but they were only a fraction of a fraction of the creatures jammed into every nook and cranny of the district—you saw the interior of Smylla's home. Trust me, you still don't really understand."

"I understand that many other such specimens inhabit the rest of the city as well. Why, then, do you doubt their ability to do some appreciable damage? It can't be for want of spirit. The underfolk are in an excellent humor, enflamed by their Prophet's oratory, painting their racial emblems hither and yon, and murdering potential informers and unbelievers."

"They still lack martial training and proper weapons."

"Some were warriors before the slavers captured them. Some are thrall soldiers still. As for the arms, well, when visiting the World Above, did you ever see a city burn? I did. I had to torch one myself to complete a mission. The destruction and loss of life were impressive, even though the inhabitants knew their buildings could catch fire and had procedures for dealing with it."

"Whereas we don't? Surely you wizards . . . ?"

Pharaun shrugged. "Not really. Why would it occur to us? Perhaps we could improvise something, but if we didn't catch the conflagration early, it might not be entirely effective."

"But you would catch it early. The undercreatures won't rebel all at once, and that will make it possible to quash each little uprising as it begins."

"You're assuming 'the Call,' whatever it is, will pass by word of mouth, or at any rate, that it won't be disseminated rapidly. You could be right. The noise baffles may hinder it, but what if the Prophet has some arcane means of rousing every goblin and bugbear at the exact same instant?"

"Do you know of such a magic?"

"No."

"And you're a Master of Sorcere. So it's reasonable to assume no such power exists."

Pharaun arched an eyebrow. "Indeed? Thank you for your expert opinion."

Ryld made a spitting sound and said, "Look. You think a rebellion could amount to something. I disagree, but say you're right. Isn't that all the more reason to report to Gromph immediately?"

The wizard waved to a goblin slave who was sauntering by. "The difficulty is that I have yet to succeed."

"What?"

"My assignment is to find the runaways. I glimpsed two of them for a matter of minutes, then lost them. Do you think the Baenre will deem that satisfactory?"

Frowning, Ryld said, "Considering that we did uncover something of interest . . ."

"Remember, our great and glorious archmage doesn't hold me in high esteem. He sent me out as a decoy, a target for the priestesses to harass. Knowing him as I do, I'm sure that if I fulfill the letter of our agreement, he'll swallow his dislike and keep his end, but should I fall the least bit short, it will be a different matter."

"You can at least tell him the rogues are in the Braeryn."

"Can I? We sifted through the Stenchstreets as well as any outsiders could. We didn't find the house where the runaways hang their cloaks, and we actually have only the flimsiest of reasons for assuming it's in the Braeryn at all."

"I suppose you're right."

"Of course. When am I not? Now, here's what I intend to do: Find the rogues' hiding place. Discover who the Prophet is and how his wizardry—or whatever it is—works. Learn where the firepots came from, where they're cached around the city, and the master plan for the rebellion. And most importantly of all, determine what the fugitives know about the clergy losing its magic."

"In hopes of coming out of this affair more powerful than you ever were before."

Pharaun grinned. "More powerful than *we* ever were before. That might dispel your boredom for good and all."

"And those are the real reasons you aren't ready to go back to Tier Breche."

"All my motives are genuine, including my wariness of Gromph. I take it you *are* in a frantic hurry to return?"

Ryld sighed. "I'm in no rush. Our excursion has been interesting, and I like to finish what I start, but what if the orcs rebel before we get around to warning our fellow drow?"

"Then we'll make sure never to tell anyone we knew it was coming." The wizard grinned and added, "Actually, the awareness that we race to avert a calamity will make our exploits all the more stimulating."

"And should we lose the race, maybe the rebellion won't kill anyone who matters to the two of us. I suppose I agree. We'll keep on searching."

"Excellent!"

Bearing a silver tray, the goblin bustled to the side of the pool. Bending the knees of his splayed, bristly legs, he brought the salver low enough for the dark elves to take the goblets on top of it.

Pharaun gave the thrall a smile and a wave, dismissing him, then lifted his cup.

"To mystery and glory!"

Ryld sipped from his own cup, acknowledging the toast. The drink was red morel juice, sweet and very cold, a pleasant contrast to the heat of the water.

"So I guess it's back to looking like orcs," said the weapons master.

"I grieve to disappoint you, but the time for that sort of deception has passed."

"What do you mean? If we don't look like undercreatures, how are we going to get into another one of those secret meetings?"

"We don't know that the Prophet will hold another assembly. He's already explained his strategy and distributed his secret weapon. Even if he does, it might not be for several days, during which we'll have Greyanna seeking us relentlessly. We've evaded her so far, but we must acknowledge the possibility that our luck could sour eventually."

"You're right about that."

"Therefore, we need to find the rogues quickly, which means a change of tactics is in order. Why are the boys trying to instigate a goblin revolt?"

"I don't know."

"Nor do I, really. It doesn't appear to make sense. Still, would you agree that the intent, like the act of eloping itself, reflects an antipathy to the established order?"

"Possibly."

"Then let's assume the Prophet or some other ringleader lured the males away from their homes because he knew they were more than ordinarily resentful of their places in the world."

"It's possible. Where does the notion lead?"

The wizard grinned and said, "If we demonstrate that we share their distemper, the rogues may recruit us as well."

"How can we do that? We may not be clerics, but we're Masters of the Academy. We're pillars of the hierarchy, and more to the point, we have a pleasanter lot and thus less reason for discontent than most."

"That doesn't seem to slow you down."

"Even so."

"Here's what you're overlooking. Thanks to my misadventure with the Sarthos demon, I'm a *disgraced* master, likely in line for some ghastly punishment. Whereas you with your dour demeanor and dwarven armor are clearly an iconoclast and malcontent. Moreover, we've been asking everywhere for news of the runaways. They must know of it, even though they didn't see fit to make contact. During that same time, a high priestess from House Mizzrym has tried to murder us. They surely have some cognizance of that as well."

"Yet they still didn't approach us. Why would they do it now?"

Pharaun smiled. "Because we'll provide proof that we do in fact share their perspective."

"How?"

"The priestesses lead regular patrols through the Bazaar. We'll destroy one, repair to the Braeryn, boast of the deed, and await developments. The rogues will seek us out. How can they not? Whatever their ultimate objective, I'm sure they can use the services of two such talented fellows."

"No doubt, but back up. You want to murder a patrol?"

"In as showy a manner as possible. With a bit of planning, it should be easy enough. They won't be as numerous as Greyanna's hunters and they won't be expecting that sort of trouble."

"What happened to not killing anybody, especially clerics, unless we absolutely have to?"

"We do absolutely have to. We're in a race against time, remember, and this is the speediest route to our objective."

"Maybe, but what happens afterward? Won't any number of folk want to punish us for our impudence?"

"We won't confide our involvement to those likely to prove unsympathetic."

"The priestesses will figure it out."

"Ah, but snug and safe in the lair of our friend the Prophet, we won't care. Besides, the Council has already authorized our annihilation, so we really have nothing to lose."

"Perhaps the crime can't worsen our current situation, but what about the long term?"

"In the long term," Pharaun said, "it won't matter. As you yourself observed mere moments ago, we Menzoberranyr are a pragmatic lot. People forgive whatever outrages I committed yesterday if I make myself useful today."

"Greyanna didn't."

The wizard laughed and replied, "Well, of course, we're likewise prone to grudges, vendettas, and blood feuds. It's one of the paradoxes central to our natures. With luck, though, no one of importance will take our little massacre personally. I doubt we'll be murdering any princesses, or anyone of genuine significance to her family."

"I think it's crazy," Ryld said, shaking his head. "You don't know that the rogues will contact us, or if they'll like what they see if they do."

"Then we'll simply hatch another scheme."

Ryld scowled and shook his head again.

"You're mad," the weapons master said, "but I'm with you."

"Splendid! We must toast our homicidal designs with something stronger than juice." Pharaun looked about and spotted the goblin. "May we see the wine list, please?"

Ryld said, "It's the very beginning of the morning."

"Don't be misled by superficial appearances," Pharaun replied. "As neither of us has enjoyed a moment of repose, it must still be night. Do you think they have any of that '53 Barrison Del'Armgo heartwine?"

chapter

FOURTEEN

Until someone murdered her, Lirdnolu had taught her classes in a sort of indoor amphitheater, one of many architectural oddities scattered through Arach-Tinilith, and as the conspirators slunk in, they seated themselves on the C-shaped tiers.

Drisinil wondered what to say to them, how to stall until Quenthel arrived to confront them. The novice's mind was a blank, but she knew she'd have to think of something. Her mouth was dry and tasted of metal. Her armpits were clammy with sweat, and her accelerated pulse pounded in the stumps of her severed fingers. The poison was obviously well on its way to killing her, and she had to please Quenthel Baenre sufficiently to earn the antidote.

Wrinkled old Vlondril Tuin'Tarl leered at Drisinil as if she knew of the student's distress, but all she said was, "I believe most everyone's here. Let's get this done before our colleagues start missing us."

"Uh, yes," Drisinil said, gazing up at the rows of faces staring back down at her. "Well, mothers, sisters, we all know what happened last night. The vipers in the mistress's whip detected the drugs—"

"So they did," said Quenthel.

Startled, Drisinil spun around. A figure shrouded in a cowled *piwafwi* rose from the first row. She lifted her head, pushed the hood back, and stood revealed as the Mistress of Arach-Tinilith. Somehow she'd entered the room without her enemies realizing her identity.

Quenthel pushed back one wing of her cloak, freeing the arm that held her whip. She sauntered to the center of the room. It occurred to Drisinil that at that moment the plotters could have fallen on their target en masse, but they didn't. The mistress cowed them with her unexpected appearance, her contemptuous demeanor, and the simple fact that she was a Baenre princess.

The mistress smiled at Drisinil and said, "You've done well, novice, except for one detail. It's traditional for priestesses to conduct their affairs by candlelight. That's all right, I've taken care of it." She turned toward the door. "Come."

Two teachers marched in carrying silver candelabra. After a moment, Drisinil, squinting, saw they weren't alone. Many of the residents of Arach-Tinilith filed in after them, all well armed and wearing mail.

Quenthel beckoned to the plotters.

"Move down to the lower seats, why don't you? The latecomers won't mind climbing to the top." She waited a beat, then said, "That wasn't a suggestion."

The conspirators hesitated a moment longer, and the show of force convinced them to obey.

"Thank you," Quenthel said, then waited until everyone had taken a seat and the plotters all had armed loyalists at their backs. "Now, let's discuss the matter that concerns you so."

"I don't know what my niece told you about this gathering," said Drisinil's Aunt Molvayas, clad in a gown of a dark and shimmering green that matched her eyes, "but I assure you, its purpose is entirely innocent."

"Its purpose is to contrive your death, Mistress," Vlondril called out. "I know. I've been in on it from the start."

Quenthel nodded to the mad priestess.

"Thank you, Holy Mother. Your candor helps move things along." The Baenre surveyed her enemies and said, "I understand that your excuse for seeking to depose me was the supposition that the goddess desires it. You postulate that she so abhors my rule of Arach-Tinilith that she renounces all Menzoberranzan."

Molvayas drew a deep breath, evidently screwing up her courage. "We do. Do you deny it's possible?"

"Of course," Quenthel replied. "It's a ludicrous notion unsupported by a single shred of evidence . . . though I'm sure it seems plausible to the lieutenant who covets my position."

Drisinil noticed that while the Baenre appeared perfectly at ease, the twisting whip serpents were keeping watch in all directions.

"What of the demons? They reflect the attributes of Lolth—"

"And they come for me. Because one of my mortal enemies sends them in guises intended to stimulate your imaginations."

"What enemy?" Molvayas demanded.

"That has yet to be determined."

"In other words," said Quenthel's second-in-command, "you don't know what's going on any more than we do."

"At least I know what *isn't* happening."

"Do you? What makes your one opinion superior to all of ours?"

"The answer to that is readily apparent to those with some smattering of intelligence."

"Insults won't resolve this matter, Mistress, but I can think of a test that might. Step down for a year, and we'll see what happens."

Quenthel laughed.

"Meekly surrender the Academy to you, Barrison Del'Armgo? Not likely. As it happens, I too have conceived a test to determine who truly enjoys Lolth's favor, your sad little cabal or me."

"What do you mean?" Molvayas asked, wariness in her eyes.

"My test is simplicity itself. We simply ask Lolth whom she prefers, and await her answer."

"That's insane. The Spider Queen no longer speaks to us."

"Perhaps if we petition, she will at least condescend to give us a sign. Are you willing to try?"

"Perhaps," Molvayas said, no doubt aware that with blades at her back, she actually had little choice. "Do you propose to perform some sort of ritual?"

"As we've lost our magic, what would that accomplish? My idea is simpler. We all bide in this room, engaged in silent prayer and meditation, until the Dark Mother reveals her will."

Vlondril snorted. "What if she chooses to ignore us?"

Quenthel shrugged. "I don't believe she's truly abandoned her chosen people or her chosen ministers. My faith is too strong to credit such a calamity. How strong is yours, Barrison Del'Armgo?"

"Strong enough that I have no fear of the goddess preferring you to me," Molvayas spat back. "I just don't see the point of your scheme. Lolth will speak when she wishes, not when we desire it."

"It's not a waste of time if it's keeping you alive. I could have had my loyal followers kill you the moment they entered the chamber. Instead, I'm proposing an honest inquiry into your concerns, for the sake of all the temple. Under the circumstances, what could be more magnanimous than that?"

"All right," Molvayas said. "We'll remain for a time, but if nothing happens, my comrades and I go free. You can't chastise us if the results of the test are inconclusive. That wouldn't be an honest inquiry."

"Agreed," the mistress said.

Drisinil was bewildered and appalled. This strange, passive procedure sounded as if it could take hours. She needed the antidote before her thundering heart tore itself apart, but she could do nothing to speed things along.

Though plainly just as puzzled as she, the company obediently fell quiet. Meditation was a familiar practice to all of them, though frustrating and futile since Lolth had receded beyond their ken.

For what seemed a long while, nothing happened, except that a muscle under Drisinil's eye twitched uncontrollably, and some of those whom she'd betrayed surreptitiously glared at her, wordlessly vowing revenge. A tiny something scurried across the floor. Or perhaps it did. By the time she tried to focus on it, it was gone.

More minutes crawled by. Cloth whispered as someone shifted position. Later, somebody else smothered a little sneeze. Drisinil realized she could just barely smell the ghost of the funereal incense Lirdnolu had burned when teaching necromancy.

Another mite scuttled along. Drisinil saw that this one was a spider. Nothing unusual in that. Arach-Tinilith was full of the sacred creatures. Still, something about this particular specimen tugged at her despite her sickness and terror. She stared until she discerned that it had a blue shell with red markings.

That was a little odd. This particular species generally spent its time lurking in webs, not roaming about. Still, she didn't see why the anomaly should trigger a twinge of alarm. It must be the poison clawing at her nerves.

Time dragged on. A priestess on the lowest tier sang a hymn under her breath. She was flat. Another novice with mutilated hands surreptitiously checked the knife strapped under her sleeve, making sure the weapon was loose in the sheath. And, Drisinil noticed, more black dots were creeping on the walls and floor. More than were normal for a disused part of the temple? She thought so, and she glanced over at Quenthel, seeking some sign to confirm her formless suspicions. The Baenre stood motionless with head bowed, the very picture of a mystic absorbed in her devotions.

A novice with a gold earring cried out in pain. She dragged on her shirt, baring her right shoulder, and found the spider that was biting her. Her frantic efforts to remove the arachnid without hurting it should have been comical but Drisinil couldn't laugh. Frazzled, addled by the poison, she could only stare at the dark flecks swarming thickly on every side. Some of the other conspirators had started to notice as well. They whispered to one another, and their eyes grew wide.

Something brushed Drisinil's arm. She cried out and spun around. It was one of the Quenthel's vipers that had touched her.

"Stay close," the mistress said.

Once again, the spiders increased in number. Somehow hordes of them were scuttling over the bodies of the conspirators, biting, crawling under their clothing, freckling their skins like the sores of some hideous plague. Shrieking, no longer caring that the creatures were sacrosanct, their victims struggled to crush them and brush them off, but they couldn't get them all. A few of the traitors retained the presence of mind to activate protective talismans, only to discover that the magic didn't help, either.

The one place free of spiders was the upper tiers. Once they realized the creatures weren't going climb up and attack them, the loyalists mocked and jeered at the plight of the traitors. Whenever one of the plotters tried to grope her way into their safe space, a loyalist would knock her back with a casual swat from a mace or whip. Some even shot down with hand crossbows any conspirator who attempted to stagger for the door.

Drisinil did remain at Quenthel's side, and the spiders crawled over her feet but otherwise took no notice of her. They didn't avoid the Baenre, however. They climbed all over her body without biting, and, laughing, she stooped, picked up more, and poured them over her head until the creatures virtually encrusted her. Her bright red eyes shone from a pebbled, squirming mask.

Finally the shrieking stopped, uncovering the sound of Vlondril ecstatically chanting one of the litanies as the spiders destroyed her. After another moment, that noise ceased as well. Drisinil noticed her aunt's corpse slumped among the carnage, though she only recognized it by the jade gown. Molvayas's face was swollen and bloodied beyond recognition.

Quenthel gazed up at the living and called, "We asked Lolth for a sign, and she gave us one. My foes are dead and I remain, robed in the goddess's sacred spiders. I am the Mistress of Arach-Tinilith, and my minions will question my leadership no more or else die in agony for their effrontery."

The surviving priestesses and novices hastily paid her obeisance.

"Good," the Baenre said. "You are wise, and so I make you a vow. We will put an end to these nightly attacks. We will regain our magic.

We will hear Lolth's voice again. We will make our order and our temple greater than ever before. Now, clear away this mess."

The spiders began to disappear, from the room and Quenthel's person as well. Drisinil couldn't quite tell if they were simply scuttling away or teleporting out.

"I did it," the student said. "I brought the traitors together for you. Now, please give me the antidote."

Quenthel smiled and said, "There is none."

"What?"

"I didn't poison you. The liquid was simply a stimulant to combat drowsiness. I gave you enough to make the effect alarming, but it'll wear off."

"You're lying! Playing with me!"

"I would have administered a slow poison had I been carrying one, but as I was not, I had to improvise."

Drisinil felt a surge of bitter humiliation and a need to demonstrate she wasn't entirely a fool.

"Well," she blurted, "then, you've tricked everyone all the way around. I know Lolth didn't control those spiders. You did. You read a scroll or used some sort of charm before you entered the room."

"If so, does it matter?" A yellow arachnid crawled out of Quenthel's snowy hair and onto her shoulder. She paid it no mind. "Lolth teaches that the cunning and strong must master the foolish and weak. However you look at it, this outcome is in accordance with her will. Now, let's talk about your future."

Drisinil swallowed. "You promised to spare me."

"I did, didn't I?" a smiling Quenthel replied. "Unlike some, we Baenre generally keep our word. A reputation for fair dealing facilitates certain transactions. However, I never promised not to punish you."

"I understand. Of course I'll take a flogging or whatever you think appropriate."

"That's quite agreeable of you. How about this, then? We'll nip off the other eight fingers and cut out your tongue as well."

For a moment, Drisinil thought she hadn't heard correctly.

"Now you're joking."

"Oh, no. I firmly believe you engineered the plot against me, and I intend to make sure you don't get up to any more mischief. Ever. If you can't communicate, work magic, or grip a weapon, that should take care of it. Obviously, it won't be possible for you to continue at Arach-Tinilith, and I wouldn't count on the warmest of welcomes when you return home. I doubt Mez'Barris Armgo will have much interest in a grotesquely crippled and thoroughly useless daughter. She may even consider you an embarrassment to be killed or locked away."

Enraged, panicked, Drisinil lunged, but never landed a blow. Powerful hands grabbed her from behind, hauled her back, and something hard and heavy bashed her over the head. Her legs folded beneath her. She would have fallen if not for her captors holding her up.

Quave's voice sounded over Drisinil's shoulder. "We've got her, Mistress."

"Thank you," Quenthel said. "Take her to the penance chamber and secure her."

"Yes, Mistress," said Quave. "I assume you'll do the cutting yourself."

"I'd like to," said the Baenre, "but there's another matter demanding my attention. You can do it. Enjoy yourself. Just mind she doesn't die of it. They can drown in their own blood when you take the tongue."

※　　※　　※

Pharaun relaxed in the chair, enjoying the feel of the barber's fingers kneading tonic into his scalp. It wasn't as relaxing as a full-body massage, but soothing nonetheless.

The barber chattered away, and the wizard periodically responded with a noncommittal, "Indeed," or a grunt. Like, he suspected, tonsorial customers of all races in all ages of the world, he wasn't actually listening.

The barber's stall, a little box redolent of unguents and pomades, was open at the front, and it was more interesting to gaze out at the sights of the Bazaar. A commoner strode by carrying a clucking chicken, imported from the Lands of Light, in a box. A merchant had probably promised the fellow the fowl would lay for years to come, though in reality, such birds rarely thrived in the Underdark. A portrait painter rendered his subject, the enchantments in the brush enabling him to fill the canvas with astonishing speed. An armorer drove a rapier through a bound, gagged kobold to demonstrate the sharpness of the point.

Cowl up, mantle drawn close around him, and Splitter hidden by the charm of concealment Pharaun had cast on it, Ryld loitered across the way in a tent with the sides folded up. There, games of all sorts were on display. The hulking swordsman stood pondering a *sava* board, where he'd set up a problem with the onyx and carnelian pieces.

A change came over the scene beyond the doorway, and people looked to the north. Some started to squeeze up against the stalls, clearing the center of the lane. A ragged, furtive-looking commoner hurried away in the opposite direction.

Ryld sauntered to the near edge of the tent, glanced where everyone else was peering, then gave Pharaun a subtle nod, confirming what the wizard had already guessed. A patrol was headed their way.

Pharaun wished the guards could have waited just five more minutes, but alas, he would have to go to work before the barber finished with him. A tragedy, but it couldn't be helped.

A moment later the patrol marched by, casting stern glances hither and yon, their tread silent thanks to their enchanted boots. In at least nominal command was a priestess of Arach-Tinilith armed with a polished wooden wand. Assisting her were a teacher from Melee-Magthere and Gelroos Zaphresz, one of Pharaun's junior colleagues in Sorcere. It was unfortunate. Possessed of a store of jokes and comical ditties, Gelroos was congenial company. At least if Pharaun murdered the other mage today, he wouldn't have to worry about Gelroos trying to assassinate him tomorrow.

In addition to its officers, the patrol consisted of a number of warriors-in-training, boys whom Ryld had almost certainly instructed at one time or another. Pharaun wasn't particularly worried about them. His fellow teachers were the real threat.

The Master of Sorcere waited until the guards had marched past then, surprising the barber, he tossed aside the hair-sprinkled cloth covering his chest, stood up, and handed the craftsman a gold coin, a princely overpayment for his services. He touched a finger to his lips in wordless explanation of what he actually wanted to buy. He picked up his *piwafwi*, whose elegance he'd obscured with a minor illusion, swirled it around his shoulders, walked to the doorway of the stall, and peeked out.

The patrol had tramped about twenty yards down the lane. Any farther and they'd turn a corner, so Pharaun had attained as much separation from the enemy as he was going to get. He draped a fold of silk across the lower half of his face, then stepped out into the open, brandished a glass marble and a pinch of rust, and recited an incantation. His half-barbered hair stood on end, and the air around him smelled of ozone. A crackling blue-white spark appeared in the air before him, then shot down the aisle.

When it reached the patrol, the flickering point of radiance exploded, shooting flares of lightning in all directions. Many of the callow young soldiers danced, burned, and fell, as they possessed neither the spiritual strength nor the protective talismans that might have minimized their injuries and kept them on their feet. Unfortunately, the sizzling, jumping arcs of power struck a handful of vendors and shoppers as well. Pharaun hadn't particularly wanted to harm noncombatants, but the aisle was simply too cramped.

The rest of the patrol began to pivot. The captain from Melee-Magthere was smoking, blackened, and blistered, but if he was anything like Ryld, his burns weren't likely to slow him down. Gelroos and the priestess looked as if the lightning hadn't even touched them. The female was spinning around a hair faster than the other two, raising her baton. Thanks to his silver ring, Pharaun could tell it was a spider wand, a weapon capable of entangling him in sticky webbing.

He had no intention of enduring that kind of humiliation. He rattled off a string of magic words and thrust his arm out. Five slivers of arcane force leaped from his fingertips, hurtled across the intervening space, and slammed into the cleric's torso. She stumbled backward and collapsed.

A wiry male with deep-set eyes, and a trace of a scholar's stoop, Gelroos peered up the street and called, "Master Mizzrym!"

"So much for my ability to manufacture a nonmagical disguise," Pharaun answered, grinning, "but then we do know one another fairly well."

"You're allowed to try to kill another Master of Sorcere," said Gelroos. "That's entirely proper. But you overstepped when you struck down these youths. It was pointless and sloppy, and their mothers won't appreciate the waste. They'll reward me for taking you down."

"Does it help if I explain that all I do, I do to deliver Menzoberranzan from twin calamities?" Pharaun asked.

Gelroos raised his hands, preparing to conjure, and the remaining warriors charged.

"Ah. I thought not."

He too began to cast.

Gelroos completed his spell a moment before Pharaun finished his. Crashing and crunching, the surface of the lane spat stone in the air. It was like a geyser, save for the fact that the chunks of rock didn't fall back to earth. Instead, they shifted around one another and fitted together, forming a towering, massive, and vaguely drowlike form, like a heroic statue abandoned when the sculptor had barely begun. Its footsteps shaking the ground, the creature lurched up the corridor between the stalls.

Pharaun was mildly impressed. It wasn't easy to summon and control an essential spirit of the earth—nor easy to fend one off, either—but the manifestation didn't shake his concentration. He continued his recitation without a flub, meanwhile floating up into the air to avoid, if only momentarily, the swords of the onrushing warriors.

He spoke the final syllable of the conjuration. A dagger made of ice flew from his hand. Gelroos dodged it, but the conjured blade exploded, peppering its target with frozen shards. One slashed open the mage's cheek and he stumbled, but Pharaun could tell he wasn't seriously hurt.

Below the Mizzrym, some of the warriors were readying their crossbows. Others began to levitate. By rushing him, they'd drawn even with the game merchant's tent, and Ryld burst from underneath it. Half an hour earlier, he'd purchased a scimitar to use in this particular battle, but it was Splitter, rendered visible by his touch, that he currently clasped in his hands. He must have decided that, since Gelroos had already called out Pharaun's name, it would be pointless to try to conceal his own identity.

The greatsword leaped back and forth, each stroke dropping a foe to the ground. Bellowing for his minions to turn and face the new threat, Ryld's fellow instructor tried to shove his way toward him.

Stone, liquid as magma, flowed upward from the ground into the elemental's body. Most of the rock served to grow the creature bigger and taller, but some of it accumulated in the palm of its hand, forming a spiky sphere that it no doubt intended to hurl at Pharaun.

The wizard snatched a tiny vial of water from one of his pockets. Brandishing it, he chanted. He felt the walls of the cosmos attenuating, and for a moment, sensed an infinite number of Pharauns conjuring in adjacent realities, receding away from him like reflections in a mirror, growing subtly less and less like himself with each step.

A pulse of scarlet light struck him in the chest. Gelroos must have conjured it. The blaze of pain was extraordinary. Pharaun strained to complete the last word of power and final mystic pass without a fumble.

He wasn't sure he'd succeeded until a vacancy, a gap not in matter but in the medium that underlies it, opened under the elemental's feet. The creature cocked back its arm to throw, and the animating force fell out of the body it had created for itself and down the hole. The wound in the fabric of the world contracted and sealed itself. Rumbling and thudding, the huge stone form fell apart.

Pharaun took stock of himself. It didn't look as if the red light had done more than scrape and prick his skin. He grinned down at Gelroos.

"Not quite, colleague."

"This time," the younger wizard said through gritted teeth.

He started casting, and Pharaun did the same.

Force crackled around the outcast Mizzrym but failed to bite into his flesh. His own magic, launched from the same round little mirror he used to check his appearance, made the air surrounding Gelroos tinkle like chiming crystals. The junior wizard screamed, and in the blink of an eye he was transformed into an inert figure made of cool, smooth glass.

Metal rang below Pharaun's feet. He looked down. Ryld appeared as if he might be having a difficult time of it, but a conjured barrage of ice, flung into the midst of the surviving students, turned the tide. Ryld cut down his fellow Master of Melee-Magthere, whirled to do the same to a young spearman, and the fight was over.

Pharaun surveyed the battlefield. Though burned and incapacitated, some of the warriors-in-training were still alive, but that was all right. The important thing had always been to murder his fellow instructors. That was what would impress the rogues.

He floated back down to earth. "That wasn't too difficult. Looking back, it's a pity we didn't slaughter Greyanna and her allies in the same fashion."

Ryld grunted, pulled up the hem of a fallen fighter's cloak, and wiped the blood from Splitter.

"Can you shatter Gelroos before we decamp?" Pharaun asked. "Otherwise, he'll eventually revert to flesh and blood."

"If you like."

Ryld hefted his blade.

F I F T E E N

Wrapped in a plain, dark *piwafwi*, the cowl drawn over her head, Quenthel tramped south across the city. The experience was strange, unique in her personal experience. She was on foot, not mounted on a lizard or enthroned on a floating stone disk. She was alone, not accompanied by a column of guards and servants, and most strangely of all, no one paid her any real attention. Oh, slaves scurried out of her path, and males offered her a cursory show of respect, but no one feared her or cringed in awe of her. Indeed, she herself had to offer obeisance to the noble females she encountered along the way, lest their soldiers chastise her for insolence.

It was galling, unsettling, and somehow tempting as well. In her most private thoughts, she'd imagined herself simply running away from the implacable foe who worked so assiduously to kill her. It might be the only way she could survive. If she opted to flee this minute, she was already off to a good start. She'd managed to slip away from Tier Breche with no one, she hoped, the wiser.

Flight was a cowardly notion, though, unworthy of a Baenre, and it angered her when she entertained it even for a moment. Until the attacks began, she never had before. She turned a corner, and Qu'ellarz'orl came into view. Her destination was nigh, and she focused her thoughts on the task at hand.

Sneaking away from the Academy had been a little complicated. First, she'd had to surreptitiously lay hands on nondescript outerwear that would allow her to pass for a commoner. Such a *piwafwi* certainly hadn't existed among her own garments, all of which were costly and bejeweled, but she'd found it among the effects of one of the kitchen staff. After disposing of the cook lest the missing garment be reported, she had to exit Arach-Tinilith without anyone realizing it was her, including her own watchful sentries. Finally, she needed to skulk to the edge of the plateau and float down to the cavern floor below without the guards at the top of the staircase noticing.

She'd managed it, though, and she was confident of her ability to sneak back into the Academy, even after the plateau had been put on a state of heightened security.

A road ran up the eminence that was Qu'ellarz'orl to the castles of Menzoberranzan's greatest families. It wasn't off limits to commoners. Merchants and supplicants used it all the time, but they were subject to search and interrogation by House Baenre patrols.

Quenthel started up the twisting road and made it better than halfway to the top before she heard the distinctive grunt and hiss of a riding lizard. She scurried off the path into the forest of giant, phosphorescent mushrooms, where she crouched behind a particularly massive specimen.

The patrol, a mounted officer and a dozen foot soldiers, marched by without so much as glancing her way. Hiding from her own troops was another bizarre, almost surreal experience.

When the warriors passed, she hurried on up the slope. In another minute, she reached the top of the rise. Before her rose the most opulent fortresses in the city. At the easternmost end of the expanse, House Baenre towered on the highest ground of all, dwarfing every other structure.

RICHARD LEE BYERS

She turned her steps toward the tall, slender spire known as Spelltower Xorlarrin, residence of the Fifth House. Bands of shimmering faerie fire striped the iron walls.

She climbed the steep steps to the gate under the watchful eyes of the sentries on the battlements. Had she not already known it, their vigilance would have shown that she could maintain complete anonymity no longer.

Still, she'd do the best she could.

When a sentry armed with spear and long sword strode over to ask her business, she said, "I'm going to show you something remarkable. Don't let your amazement show."

He looked skeptical. He lived in the Spelltower, after all, and had seen his share of marvels.

"All right, ma'am. Show me, if you will."

She twitched open her *piwafwi*, giving him a glimpse of the Baenre House insignia hanging at her throat.

His eyes widened, but otherwise, he did a fair job of doing as she'd bade him.

"How may I serve you?" he asked softly, the slightest quaver in his voice.

"I want to enter the tower without anyone paying the least attention to me, and I want to talk to your matron alone."

"Please, come with me."

The guard led her through the gate and into a confusion of service passages such as every castle possessed. The corridors eventually brought them into a nicely appointed room with comfortable-looking sandstone chairs, a carnelian-and-obsidian *sava* set awaiting a pair of players, and frescos of some of Lolth's attendant demons adorning the walls.

Her escort departed in search of his mistress, leaving Quenthel to prowl restlessly about the room. Finally the door opened, and Zeerith Q'Zorlarrin slipped through. Her features were plain and nondescript, but she was notable for a dignified bearing and composure that rarely failed her even in the most extreme situations. For a matron, her costume was rather plain and austere.

The two princesses saluted one another, then Zeerith ushered her guest to a seat.

"When Antatlab told me you'd come without a single guard, I wondered if he'd gone mad," the matron remarked.

"Can I trust him not to gossip about my visit?"

"He's discreet enough. Now, may I ask why I'm so unexpectedly enjoying the honor of your company?"

Quenthel related the events of the past three nights.

"If I still possessed my magic," she concluded. "I could deal with this matter easily, but as things stand . . . I need help."

The words galled her, but they had to be said.

"Why have you sought it here?" Zeerith asked.

"The Xorlarrins have always supported the Baenre and profited thereby. Try as I might, I can't think of a compelling reason you'd want me dead, and your House boasts many of the best wizards in Menzoberranzan. So, if I must trust someone, you're a good chance. Will you aid me, Matron?"

Zeerith took her time replying. Quenthel knew the other female was cold-bloodedly pondering whether to help, deny, or betray her. Where did the greatest advantage lie?

"Your plight is an outrage," the Xorlarrin said at last, "an affront to all priestesses. Of course I'll aid you. For ten thousand talents of gold, and your support when my clan's dispute with House Agrach Dyrr becomes public knowledge."

"What dispute?"

"The one I'll be stirring up in a tenday or two. Do we have a bargain?"

Quenthel's mouth tightened. If she'd come to the Spelltower in the full panoply of a Baenre princess, Zeerith would have thought twice about making conditions, but by arriving incognito the mistress had shown her desperation and in so doing, shifted the transaction to another level.

"Yes," she growled, "I agree."

"I thank you for your generosity. What do you require?"

"Every night," said Quenthel, "a new demon comes to kill me, and I fend it off as best I can. If this goes on, a night will come when the entity kills me instead. I need to do more. I need to end the siege, and it's my hope your mages know a way. I confess I don't. I've ransacked every vault, chest, and drawer in Arach-Tinilith and found nothing that will serve."

"So that's why you came in secret. You want a weapon, and you don't want your foe to know about it. Otherwise, he might take countermeasures."

"Correct."

Zeerith rose. "We'll ask Horroodissomoth. He can do it if anyone can, and he'll keep his mouth shut after."

She opened the door and directed Antatlab, who'd been standing watch outside, to go and fetch her patron and House wizard.

Horroodissomoth arrived shortly thereafter. Quenthel felt a little twinge of disgust, for the mage was the antithesis of the typical vital dark elf male. His features were lined and wrinkled, and his posture, bent. Rumor had it that his appearance of decrepitude had resulted not from extreme age but rather some dangerous magical experimentation.

Moving stiffly, all but creaking audibly, Horroodissomoth tendered obeisance then, at Zeerith's invitation, settled in a chair to listen to a reprise of Quenthel's story. At first the wizard's demeanor was impassive, perhaps even utterly disinterested, but a light came into his rheumy eyes when he realized she was asking him to solve a magical problem.

"Hmm," he said, "hmm. I think I might have something that will help. In a way, I regret giving it to you, because as far as I know, it's unique. Even we Xorlarrins don't know how to make another. But on the other hand, I've always been curious to see if it actually works."

Gossip whispered that at some point in the distant past, the females of House Ousstyl had interbred with humans. Naturally the contemporary Ousstyls denied it and would do their meager best to punish anyone they suspected of passing the rumor. Still, as Faeryl gazed across the table at Talindra Ousstyl, Matron Mother of the

Fifty-second House, she could readily believe it. Talindra was tall and, for a dark elf, extraordinarily rawboned. Her jaw was too square, and her ears, insufficiently pointed. Most telling of all was the scatter of empty plates before her. She'd annihilated every morsel of her seven-course supper with a lesser being's insatiable voracity.

Talindra finished with a juicy belch.

"Excuse me."

"Of course," Faeryl said. She thought she heard a thump issuing from elsewhere in the ambassadorial residence. Inwardly, she flinched but Talindra didn't seem to notice the sound.

"Well," the matron said, "that was tasty, but I believe you invited my brood to supper and spirited me away to this private room, because you wanted to talk of something more important than cuisine."

Faeryl smiled and said, "You've found me out, and I have a confession to make. I don't always devote myself to the interests of Ched Nasad as a whole. Occasionally I work solely to advance the fortunes of House Zauvirr."

"How could it be otherwise?" Talindra said, raising her golden cup. "Family, always. Family over all."

Faeryl joined the other noble in the toast. She'd always enjoyed the sweet dessert wine, but this time it tasted too sweet, almost sickeningly so. She supposed her nerves were to blame.

The envoy set down her drink and said, "Let us discuss how our two families might be of service to one another. In Ched Nasad, we Zauvirr are allied with House Mylyl. For the immediate future, we must remain so. Yet it's also time for the Mylyls to begin their decline, for their wealth and influence to start passing into our hands. You see the problem."

Talindra grinned and said, "You want to attack the Mylyls without them realizing who's to blame."

"So why not do it through an intermediary?"

Elsewhere, someone let out a thin, little wail. Faeryl tensed, but once again, her guest failed to react. Fortunately, the sounds of pain were reasonably common in dark elf dwellings.

"You want me to lend you some of my males," the matron said, "to make the long, dangerous journey to Ched Nasad to raid and kill for you. It makes sense. The Mylyls would have no idea who they are, nor that they're working for you. But what do I get out of it? Why—?"

A warrior threw open the door, strode to Talindra's side, and raised a steel baton.

The matron was too quick for him. Surging up in her chair, she knocked him cold with a punch to the jaw, drew a long knife from her belt, and pivoted toward Faeryl.

The ambassador snatched up Mother's Kiss, which had been lying under the table all the while. She sprang up, swung the basalt-headed warhammer in an arc and balked the oncoming Talindra for an instant.

For the next few seconds, the two nobles battled, neither able to score; then Talindra used her free hand to clasp a round medallion pinned to her bodice. Red light shone from between her fingers.

If the matron had the capacity to throw a spell, that changed the complexion of the fight considerably. Faeryl needed to end it quickly, perhaps before the first magical effect manifested. She charged her opponent, striking at her head in an all-out attack.

It was a reckless move, and she suffered the consequences. The knife point jabbed painfully into her ribs. Luckily, it failed to penetrate the mail she wore beneath her silken gown. Mother's Kiss slammed into the Menzoberranyr's head and dashed her to the ground. Her hand slipped away from the amulet, and the glow faded.

An instant later, a second guard burst into the room.

"We've secured them all, my lady."

The warrior was a rugged-looking male with a chipped incisor and a broken nose, whom she had on occasion summoned to her bed.

"Good," Faeryl replied. "How many did you have to kill?"

"Only one, but we could slaughter the rest. If I may say so, it seems more sensible and less bother than tying them up."

"It does, but I came here to promote good relations between Menzoberranzan and Ched Nasad. Even though some schemer has rendered my efforts futile, I won't exacerbate the situation by committing any more outrages than necessary. You soldiers will do as I bade you. Strip the Ousstyls, gag them, and tie them up."

Talindra groaned and groped feebly for her knife. Impressed that the matron was still conscious to any degree at all after the blow she'd suffered, Faeryl kicked the blade out of her reach.

"You can't do this," Talindra croaked, "not to House Ousstyl. We are mighty and never forget at affront."

Tense as she was, Faeryl smiled. The matron's arrogance was woefully misplaced. The Ousstyls were so insignificant they hadn't even known the ambassador had lost the good will of Triel Baenre. Otherwise, they would never have accepted an invitation to feast with such a pariah.

Faeryl bashed Talindra again, this time rendering her entirely insensible, then she roamed through the castle, exhorting her minions to make haste. Soon all were wearing the clothing of the Ousstyls. For the first time, Faeryl was grateful that her household was relatively small. Otherwise, they wouldn't have had enough pilfered garments to go around.

She and her lieutenants sported the finery of the Ousstyl dignitaries, while the common soldiers had donned *piwafwis* and mail, and carried the arms of Talindra's bodyguards.

The outlanders stowed provisions beneath their mantles. The quantity was insufficient, for they couldn't conceal all that much. With luck, they'd be able to hunt and forage on the trail. They headed for the mansion's enclosed stable, where Talindra had left her driftdisc.

Faeryl noticed that some of her retainers were sweaty and wide-eyed. Though she was careful not to show it, she still felt just as apprehensive herself. Was she mad to flout Triel Baenre's express command, especially when she and her subordinate priestesses had virtually no magic implements left?

Well, no. It would be lunacy to sit on her rump and do nothing, knowing that Triel would eventually get around to ordering her arrest. Even if Faeryl weren't concerned about her own fate, with every passing hour she grew more anxious to learn what had halted all traffic from Ched Nasad, and not just because the trade was important in its own right. Absurd as it seemed, she couldn't shake the irrational fear that some misfortune had befallen the City of Shimmering Webs itself.

She had to know. Any great event affecting Ched Nasad could conceivably injure House Zauvirr and diminish her own status. Moreover, though she would never admit it to another, she cared about her homeland for its own sake. Not, she assured herself, that she suffered from love, loyalty, or any other soft, un-drowlike emotion. Yet Ched Nasad had shaped her into the person she was. It was a part of her, and anything that harmed the city would trouble her as well.

In any case, having assaulted and robbed her dinner guests, the die was cast.

The pack and riding lizards hissed and grunted when the party entered the stable. Faeryl dearly wished she could take some of the reptiles with her, but since Talindra hadn't brought any such beasts along with her, it was out of the question.

The matron's driftdisc was a round, flat stone with an ivory throne fastened on top, the whole floating about a foot above the floor. The device glowed with a soft white light tinged ever so faintly with green.

Since it was Faeryl who'd appropriated Talindra's attire, she hopped up on the driftdisc, sat in the ornate cushioned chair, and mentally commanded the apparatus to levitate up to the proper dignified height. She endured a bad moment during which nothing happened, and she was sure the Ousstyl had rigged the vehicle in such a way as to keep anyone else from riding it, then the circular platform rose. It was just sluggish, about what you'd expected of the equipment of the Fifty-second House.

Two of Faeryl's soldiers threw open the gates, and the party ventured out into the open, her retainers forming a proper column around her as soon as they had the room.

They marched away from the luminous keep that had been their home for fourteen years, past the alleyway where Umrae had died, and onward. Faeryl couldn't see Triel's watchers, but she could feel their eyes on her. She felt all but certain they would recognize her.

But maybe not. Most people saw what they expected to see. The spies had watched the Ousstyls enter the residence, and just as anticipated, the petty nobles were departing. Why would anyone bother to peer closely when he was sure he already knew what was going on?

That was the theory, anyway. At the moment, it seemed a dubious notion on which to gamble her life.

Her company left the immediate vicinity of the residence without anyone trying to hinder them, which proved nothing. The watchers wouldn't pop out of hiding and confront the fugitives themselves, They'd scurry away to rouse a company of warriors, who'd intercept the daughters and sons of Ched Nasad in the street.

Thus, while her expression conveyed the proper mix of serenity and haughtiness, her muscles were stiff, and her mouth dry as she floated down the avenues. For the moment, she was heading for Narbondellyn, site of the Ousstyls' modest citadel. It was where the spies would expect her to go.

Drow did their best to clear the way for the matron of even a minor House. She was grateful for that. Still, heavily laden carts and the like could only pull aside so quickly. The impostors' progress was necessarily and nerve-rackingly sedate.

Finally, though, they passed Narbondel itself, where the magical glow had climbed three quarters of the way to the top of the great stone column. Faeryl spotted Talindra's fortress and turned her company aside. If they actually approached the place, some guard peering down from the ramparts was bound to penetrate their disguises.

They marched south, still without interference. If someone was chasing them, the ambassador was sure it would have become apparent by then. Faeryl took a deep breath, told herself her ruse had succeeded, and tried to relax. She couldn't, quite. Perhaps when she reached the Bauthwaf, or better still, escaped Menzoberranyr territory altogether . . .

The outlanders' route carried them to the west of the elevation that was Qu'ellarz'orl, its slopes thick with enormous mushrooms. Then, at last, they reached one of the city's hundred gates to the tunnels beyond. The Menzoberranyr defended all of them, but this one at least was a minor exit. It boasted fewer guards than most.

The fugitives approached boldly, as if they had every legitimate expectation of the sentries ushering them through. The guards must have wondered why a high priestess would wear an elegant cloak and gown and ride her ceremonial transport for an excursion into the dirty, dangerous caves beyond the city, but a matron's whim was law in Menzoberranzan. They offered her obeisance, then set about the cumbersome process of unbarring the granite-and-adamantine valves—or most of them did.

One officer eyed Faeryl thoughtfully. He had a foxy, humorous face and was smaller than most males, which apparently didn't hinder him when wielding the heavy broadsword hanging from his baldric. Though he carried the blade of a warrior, he'd eschewed mail—which could disrupt arcane spells—for a cloak and jerkin possessed of the countless telltale pockets of a wizard. Evidently he was fighter and wizard both. When she gazed directly at him, he respectfully lowered his head but resumed his scrutiny as soon as she turned her head.

She pivoted around to face him and asked, "Captain, is it?"

The small male gave her a smart salute.

"Captain Filifar, my lady, at your service."

"Please, come here."

Filifar obeyed. If he betrayed any wariness, it was only in his eyes. The two gigantic spiders graven in the leaves of the gate stirred ever so slightly. Faeryl realized they would emerge from the carving and fight for him if commanded.

"You have the look of an intelligent male," she said, gazing down at him from atop the driftdisc.

"Thank you, my lady."

"Perhaps you received orders," she continued, "to refuse passage to the delegation from Ched Nasad."

"No, my lady."

Filifar's hand twitched ever so slightly. It wanted to reach for either the hilt of his sword or the spell components in one of his pockets.

"Your subordinates were content to receive their instructions and let it go at that, but not a sharp boy like you. Somehow you contrived to find out what the ambassador looks like, thus making sure you'd be able to recognize her if she came this way."

Filifar's mouth tightened. "My lady," he said, "my company is well armed and well trained. You may also have observed the spiders graven—"

She raised her hand. "Don't agitate yourself, Captain. I mean you no harm. We're just two Menzoberranyr idly chatting, passing the time it takes your fellows to open the gate."

"I regret, my lady, that now that I've seen you up close, I can't allow them to do that."

He took two careful steps back, retreating beyond her reach, then pivoted to shout the order.

Faeryl stopped him dead by displaying a gaudy ruby brooch, formerly Talindra's property.

"I said you were an intelligent lad, Captain Filifar, but I don't believe you're a prosperous one. You wear no jewelry, and your clothing is made of common stuff."

"You're right, milady. Fortune hasn't favored me."

"It can."

Faeryl brought out one ornament after another, the jewels her retainers had stolen from the Ousstyls and her own legitimate treasure as well. She filled her lap with them and laid the surplus on the pale, luminous rim of the driftdisc.

"Here's enough wealth to improve your luck and that of your minions as well."

Filifar hesitated before saying, "My lady, I was told that Matron Triel herself wishes you detained. It's no light matter to cross the Baenre."

"Just say the Zauvirr didn't pass through *this* gate, or if they did, you didn't recognize them. No one will know any different."

He jerked his head in a nod. "Right. Why not, curse it?"

He removed his *piwafwi* to use as a makeshift bag and swept the jewelry in. Some of the soldiers noticed what their captain was doing and scurried over to investigate.

Once the gate was well behind her, Faeryl abandoned the drift-disc. The stately conveyance was just too slow. She and her party quick-marched on through the mostly unimproved passages at the fringe of Menzoberranyr territory, past hunters' outposts and adamantine mines, making for the genuine wilderness beyond.

Faeryl realized she was grinning. It was absurd, really. She'd just surrendered a queen's ransom in gems, Triel would send troops after her, and she was all but certain some dire peril lay ahead, but somehow, for the moment, none of it mattered. Faeryl had outwitted her foes and finally, after fourteen years, she was going home.

The fugitives rounded a bend, and dark figures seemed to flow from the tunnel walls just ahead. The Zauvirr turned to run. Somehow, the shadows were behind them as well.

🕷   🕷   🕷

On the fringe of Menzoberranyr territory, Valas Hune could sense the genuine wilderness beyond. He could feel its vast and labyrinthine spaces and hear its pregnant silences. He could smell and taste its variations of rock and imagined himself simply slipping away into that limitless world.

As fancies went, his wasn't entirely absurd. Most dark elves feared to travel the Underdark except in armed convoys, and with good reason. They, however, lacked the abilities he'd spent decades developing, survival skills that made him one of the finest scouts in Menzoberranzan.

Indeed, the small, wiry male in the rugged outdoorsman's garb liked traversing the subterranean world alone. He relished the wonders, the quiet, and the freedom. Sometimes, when he'd idled in camp too long, he felt he preferred it to the striving, conniving existence of his fellow drow, the luxuries of Menzoberranzan notwithstanding. He yearned for an errand that would take him out into the wilderness, and played with the notion of simply running away.

He heard the Zauvirr coming and put the dream aside. Like it or not, his mission this day wasn't to explore the wild. It was to direct his company, fellow mercenaries of Bregan D'aerthe, in the taking of Faeryl Zauvirr and her retainers.

That was the theory, anyway. In point of fact, he didn't have to give any more orders. No doubt the warriors of Ched Nasad were competent fighters in their own right, but when the sellswords swarmed out of hiding, they caught them entirely by surprise, then proceeded to cut them down with murderous efficiency.

Once Valas was certain his band would be victorious, he started searching for Faeryl herself. His smallness and natural agility enabled him to thread his way through the fury of battle without harm.

He found the princess at the center of the carnage. She'd just finished killing one of his command. The dead male's brains and bloody hair adhered to one end of her basalt-headed warhammer.

"Ambassador," Valas called. "I have orders to take you alive, if possible."

She answered with a curse. He didn't blame her for that. In her place, he wouldn't want to be delivered alive to Matron Baenre, either.

He hefted one of his matched pair of kukris—vicious curved daggers—and fingered a little brass ovoid, one of many trinkets adorning his tunic and cloak.

He'd collected the amulets and brooches from races and civilizations across the Underdark. Fashioned according to alien aesthetics, most of the ornaments were ugly and uncouth to dark elf eyes, but he hadn't acquired them for their appearance, nor were they merely souvenirs. Each contained a different enchantment.

Three images, exact facsimiles of himself, flickered into existence around him. He edged toward Faeryl, and the phantoms came with him.

She stared fiercely, obviously trying to pick out the real Valas from the false. It didn't help. When she swung, she struck at the image on his left.

The illusion vanished on contact, and at the same instant, he sprang. She couldn't come back on guard in time to fend him off. He hooked a leg behind her and threw her to the ground, then kicked her repeatedly in the head until she went limp.

S I X T E E N

Laughter echoed through the candlelit corridors of Arach-Tinilith. Quenthel frowned. She'd been expecting something to happen, eagerly anticipating it, in fact. What she wasn't expecting was an explosion of mirth, and she couldn't guess what it meant.

She strode forward, and her patrol followed behind. They seemed edgy, but not quite as reluctant as they had the night before. The fate of Drisinil, Molvayas, and the rest of the plotters had convinced the survivors that Quenthel still enjoyed the favor of Lolth, at least to the same dubious extent as the rest of the stricken clergy.

The laughter rang on and on until at last the searchers found the source. Hunched over, her shoulders shaking, a novice knelt before one of the smaller altars of the goddess. Steady despite the paroxysms of glee, her index finger painted lines of graceful calligraphy on the floor. Quenthel couldn't make out what the girl was using for pigment until she lifted her hand to her face like an artist dipping a brush in a paint pot. She'd gouged her eyes out, another seeming handicap that didn't impair her writing.

The mistress stepped close enough to inspect the lines of blood. For all her erudition, she couldn't read the characters, but she could feel the power in them. They pulled at her and repelled her at the same time, as if they might yank her spirit, or a piece of it, out of her body.

She wrenched her eyes away from the symbols and swung her whip. The vipers cracked into the eyeless female's back, their venomous fangs tore into her, and she collapsed, dead or merely insensible. Quenthel didn't particularly care which.

"What was she writing, Mistress?" Jyslin asked.

"I don't know," Quenthel admitted, smearing the glyphs with her toe, "something in one of the secret tongues of the Abyss. Scribing it may have been a way of casting a spell, so I made sure she wouldn't finish."

"What was wrong with her?" Minolin asked.

Quenthel was still surprised that the Fey-Branche had not, as expected, turned out to be one of the traitors.

"I don't know that, either," said the Mistress of Arach-Tinilith. She actually did have an idea, but wasn't sure of it yet. "Let's move on."

Fifteen minutes later, a runner, dispatched from a squad stationed in the third leg of the spider, found Quenthel to report that one of her comrades had gone mad. Quenthel went to see for herself, half expecting more gouged eyes and bloody writing.

But the new dementia took a somewhat different form. The victim had taken shelter, if that was the right word for it, in a small library devoted, for the most part, to musty treatises on warfare in all its aspects. She sat on the floor in the corner defined by two tall sandstone bookshelves, rocking and whimpering to herself.

Quenthel stooped, jammed her fist under the girl's chin and forced up her head.

"Rilrae Zolond! What ails you? What happened?"

Rilrae's face was blank and seemingly devoid of comprehension. Tears flowed down her cheeks. She smelled of mucus, and the breath snuffled in her nose. She didn't answer Quenthel's question, just made a feeble, ineffectual effort to turn her face away.

The mistress sighed and let her go. She'd seen cases like Rilrae before, generally in some dungeon or torture chamber. The junior priestess had experienced something sufficiently unpleasant to drive her deep inside her own mind. Had Quenthel still possessed her Lolth-granted powers, or been carrying the proper equipment, she might have been able to shake Rilrae out of her delirium, but as matters stood, the useless creature wouldn't be providing any information. Annoyed, the mistress nearly vented her frustration by giving Rilrae a stroke from her whip, but she didn't want to appear rattled or upset in the eyes of her followers.

She led the patrol on and eventually found a suicide sprawled in the corridor with froth on her lips and an empty poison bottle still clutched in her hand.

One of the second-year students reeled from a doorway a few yards farther down. Glaring and twitching, she unrolled a parchment, possibly one Quenthel herself had dispensed from the temple armory, and began shouting the words. The Baenre recognized the trigger phrase of a spell intended to summon a certain type of plague demon.

She snatched out her hand crossbow and pulled the trigger. Others did the same. The flurry of poisoned darts punctured the scroll and the novice as well. She fell onto her back, cracking her head against the calcite floor. The spell, still a syllable or two from activation, dissipated its power in a harmless sizzle of red light.

Quenthel reflected that a pattern was becoming clear. Some power struck a female and more or less drove her mad. She then separated herself from her companions, either making an excuse or just running off, the better to manifest her lunacy in one bizarre behavior or another.

It was odd that the girls' companions never even noticed the attack occurring, odd, too, that the demon assaulted only one member of a group and not all—or that it attacked any, given that the previous intruders had only attacked those lesser priestesses who attempted to hinder them.

The unseen demon's search pattern was equally peculiar. The location and sequences of its attacks seemed to indicate that the being was bouncing erratically around from one end of the temple to the other.

"Mistress," said Yngoth, "I know what's happening."

"As do I," Quenthel said. "I've merely been confirming it." She turned to Minolin. "Fey-Branche."

"Yes?" Minolin asked.

"You're in command of these others. You will all evacuate the temple. Get the sane people out, and the mad ones, too, but only if you can do it quickly."

The Fey-Branche princess blinked. "Mistress, we believe in your authority," she said. "We're not afraid to stand with you."

"I'm touched," Quenthel sneered, "but this isn't a test. I want you to go."

"Exalted Mother," Jyslin said, "what's happening? Which demon invaded the temple tonight? The assassin? Did it poison our sisters to make them go insane?"

"No," the Baenre said, "not in the way you mean."

"Then—"

"Go!" Quenthel raged. "Minolin, I told you to take them out of here."

"Yes, Mistress!"

The Fey-Branche hastily formed them up and led them away. The corridor seemed very quiet once they'd disappeared.

"Mistress," said Hsiv, "was it wise to send them away?"

"You question my judgment?" Quenthel asked.

The viper flinched. "No!"

"You sought to protect me, so I'll let it go. This time. I dismissed the girls because they can't help me, and I'd like to have some underlings left when this nonsense is over."

"They might have guarded you from another would-be mortal killer."

"We can hope that if Minolin gets everyone out, there won't be any more. Besides, why in the name of the Demonweb did I create *you*?"

Greenish candlelight rippling on black scales, Yngoth reared and twisted around to look Quenthel in the face.

"Mistress," the viper hissed, "we are rebuked. We'll keep watch. What will you do?"

"Wait, and prepare myself."

She found a classroom possessed of a reasonably comfortable instructor's chair, the high limestone back carved into the stylized shape of a stubby-legged spider. She sat down, laid the whip at her feet, removed a thin shaft of polished white bone from her pouch, and set it in her lap, holding it at either end.

Closing her eyes, she commenced a breathing exercise. Within a heartbeat or two, she slipped into a meditative trance. She thought she would need the utmost clarity to contend with the night's demon, because Jyslin had guessed wrong. The intruder didn't encapsulate the art of the assassin, nor the spirit of the drow race, for that matter. It embodied the concept of evil.

The traitor elves of the World Above professed to hate evil. In reality, Quenthel thought, they feared what they didn't understand. Thanks to the tutelage of Lolth, the drow did, and having understood it, they embraced it.

For evil, like chaos, was one of the fundamental forces of Creation, manifest in both the macrocosm of the wide world and the microcosm of the individual soul. As chaos gave rise to possibility and imagination, so evil engendered strength and will. It made sentient beings aspire to wealth and power. It enabled them to subjugate, kill, rob, and deceive. It allowed them to do whatever was required to better themselves with never a crippling flicker of remorse.

Thus, evil was responsible for the existence of civilization and for every great deed any hero had ever performed. Without it, the peoples of the world would live like animals. It was amazing that so many races, blinded by false religions and philosophies, had lost sight of this self-evident truth. In contrast, the dark elves had based a society on it, and that was one of the points of superiority that served to exalt them above all other races.

Paradoxically, though, a touch of the pure black heart of this darkest of all powers could be deadly, just as the highest expression of comforting warmth was the fire that consumed. Even folk who spent their lives in the adoration of evil generally had no real comprehension of the endless burning sea of it raging below and beyond the material world, and that was just as well. Even a fleeting glimpse could convey secrets too huge and fearsome for the average mind. Its touch could annihilate sanity and even identity. The threat was sufficiently grave that the majority of spellcasters hesitated to regard the force directly. They preferred to treat with evil at one remove, by dealing with the devils and undead that embodied it.

But it appeared that Quenthel's unknown enemy was the exception. He'd dipped right into the virulent fountainhead and drawn forth a power that dwelled therein.

That demon was presently intangible, a creature of pure mind. That was why it seemed to move and act so erratically; it was passing not through physical space, a medium in which it didn't exist, but from consciousness to consciousness, head to head. And simply through that intimate contact it poisoned its hosts, even if it didn't particularly intend to. It suffused them with a darkness too big and too powerful for their little minds to sustain

It was searching for Quenthel all the while, to show her the most profound malevolence of all.

She prayed she could endure the venom for just a second, until she worked the Xorlarrin's magic. She'd have to. Since the demon was invisible and insubstantial, she wouldn't know it hadn't come close enough for the talisman to affect until she felt it infesting herself.

To make sure she would indeed detect it, she sank ever deeper into her trance. She became acutely conscious of the rise and fall of her chest and the air hissing in and out of her lungs. The steady thud of her heartbeat and the surge of blood through her arteries. The pressure of her buttocks and spine against the chair. The feeblest of drafts caressing and cooling her left profile. The vipers shifting restlessly, brushing her feet and ankles, the touch perceptible even through her boots.

Yet none of the sensations was of any particular significance. They presented themselves so vividly only because she'd entered a state of utter dispassionate quietude, and thus receptivity. A condition in which she would be equally cognizant of events within her mind and soul.

She recalled acquiring this capacity when she herself was a novice in Arach-Tinilith. She'd learned every divine art easily. It had been one of the signs that Lolth had chosen her for greatness. But relatively speaking, this particular mastery had come harder than most. According to Vlondril, unwrinkled but showing signs of madness even then, it had been because Quenthel was of too dynamic a character. She had no instinct for passivity.

Abruptly the Baenre realized her thoughts were nudging her out of the desired state. Vlondril had also said that was always the way. The mind didn't like to hush. It wanted to babble. Quenthel took another deep, slow breath, exhaled it through her mouth, and expelled that importunate inner voice along with it.

Time passed. She had no idea how much time, nor, immersed in the meditation, did she care. The temple was utterly silent, which surely meant that most everyone had exited, or perhaps, in one or two instances, perished.

Gradually it dawned on Quenthel that her trance wasn't quite perfect. The dead quiet, proof that all instruction, prayers, and rituals had ceased, irked her just a little, and she doubted she could purge that final hint of emotion. She cared too much about her role of Mistress of Arach-Tinilith. She'd come to the Academy intent on making it grander and more effective than ever before. Thus would she honor Lolth and demonstrate her fitness to one day rule the entire city. Instead, she'd presided over an extended disaster, regular functions disrupted, residents battered or even dead.

It galled her to think how many of her sister nobles would blame her, but she knew it wasn't her fault. It was in large measure the fault of the teachers and students themselves. Most who had perished earned their destruction by dint of their idiotic little mutiny, and actually, that was as it should be. The traitors had violated the precepts of Lolth.

Indeed, when Quenthel thought about it, the real misfortune might be that weaklings like Jyslin and Minolin were still alive. They were cowards and whiners, unfit, but they'd survive merely because the manifestation of evil hadn't passed their way, and because the Baenre herself had sent them to safety. Perhaps that had been a mistake.

Quenthel realized she was ruminating once more. With an effort of will she arrested the internal monologue. For a few seconds.

But as Vlondril had taught her, it was devilishly hard to attain passivity by straining for it. Besides, Quenthel was pondering important matters, new insights that would guide her steps in the days to come.

If preserving even the most worthless specimens of her flock constituted an error, at least it was one she could rectify. She'd already slaughtered the mutineers. How easy, then, it would be to butcher those who lacked even the spirit to rebel. She imagined herself stalking among her underlings, peering into their eyes, swinging the whip whenever she discerned inadequacy. The trance state facilitated visualization, and the fantasy was as vivid as life. She smelled the blood and felt it splatter her face. The muscles of her whip arm clenched and relaxed.

Quenthel could kill *everyone* if necessary. She'd enjoy it, and perhaps when the clergy was pure and strong again, Lolth would condescend to speak.

If not, that might mean that all Menzoberranzan required cleansing, beginning with the First House. Quenthel would usurp pathetic, indecisive Triel's throne—not in a hundred years but *now*, and preparation be damned. Then, the very next day, she and her kin would wage a war of extermination on the thousands who served the goddess and her chosen prophet with false hearts or insufficient zeal.

How glorious it would be, and it could begin as soon as she ferreted out the first weakling. Her fingers closed on the haft of her whip, or rather they tried and in so doing reminded her that she was in reality holding the thin bone wand.

She'd forgotten all about the magical artifact and the demon as well, and she could only think of one explanation. Despite her vigilance, the spirit had managed to possess her without her realizing it.

For without its influence, those thoughts would never have occurred to her. Destroy her own followers? Try to murder Triel without the vaguest semblance of a strategy, and fight virtually every other House in the city at once?

It wasn't the prospect of wholesale bloodshed that dismayed her—war and torture were her birthright and often her delight—but this was evil without sense, a delirium that would surely destroy her and conceivably even House Baenre along with her.

Yet did it matter? She sensed the ecstasy implicit in letting go. If she permitted it, the demon would exalt her, and even if she perished an hour later, what difference would it make? She'd find more joy in that brief span that in centuries of mundane life.

For what seemed a long while, she wavered, uncertain whether to manipulate the wand or cast it aside, take up her whip, and go hunting. In the end, one consideration enabled her to choose the former. No matter how sweet the temptation to become a pure and transcendent being, doing so would be to surrender to the will of her phantom enemy, allowing the faceless spellcaster to dominate, transform, and ultimately destroy her. Quenthel Baenre could not embrace defeat.

Instead, she snapped the length of bone in two.

An instant later, she felt an extraordinary lightness and clarity in her head, a sign that the demon had departed, as, in fact, her eyes confirmed. Vaguely visible at last, a misshapen shadow without a source, the entity floated in front of her, then, without turning or shifting any of its amorphous limbs, receded quick as a bow shot. It was tiny, a dot, and gone.

Quenthel felt a pang of loss, but it only lasted a moment. Then she smiled.

Gromph sat before one of the enchanted windows in his hidden chamber. He'd crossed his feet atop a hassock and held a crystal goblet of black wine in his hand. He'd thrown the strangely carved ivory casements wide and supposed he must look like the soul of ease awaiting some pleasant entertainment.

Well, that was the hope, but despite himself the Archmage of Menzoberranzan was growing used to disappointment.

He hadn't made any progress in finding the runaway males. His divinations were so oblique and contradictory as to be useless. Apparently some able spellcaster had forestalled his efforts. His genuine spies had turned up nothing, indeed, had managed to get themselves strangled in Eastmyr by parties unknown. The only satisfaction, if one could call it that, was that his decoy was still on the loose, still occupying the priestesses' attention. Why Pharaun Mizzrym had deemed it expedient to slaughter a patrol from the Academy, though, was more than Gromph could comprehend.

The Baenre wizard hadn't yet managed to kill Quenthel, either. For the past few nights, he'd dispatched his conjured minions, then settled before the window to watch them do his bidding. Impossibly, even stripped of her magic, his sister had disposed of the first three spirits and the traitors he'd inspired as well. Like some bungler in a farce, Gromph had only managed to account for a few lesser clerics with whom he had no quarrel, who would otherwise have gone on to contribute to the strength of Menzoberranzan and the House that controlled it. It was maddening!

This night, he prayed, would be different. Quenthel had turned out to be competent at disposing of spirits wearing some semblance of material form, but surely she would prove more vulnerable to an assailant that slipped imperceptibly into her mind.

The enchanted window afforded Gromph a view of the interior of Arach-Tinilith as if he were but a few feet away. He watched his sister and her squad encounter wretches whom the spirit had already overwhelmed with the infusion of an evil more profound than any mortal, even a dark elf, could readily bear. He looked for some sign that Quenthel was growing afraid. The indication would be subtle if she let it slip at all, but perhaps a brother would spot it.

He didn't, and eventually Quenthel ordered her minions to evacuate the building and sat down to meditate.

The archmage frowned. Evidently the imperious bitch had figured out what was going on and had in a sense responded appropriately. But it shouldn't matter. *He'd* withstood contact with the ultimate essence of evil, but he was the greatest wizard in the world and had taken precautions. Quenthel enjoyed neither advantage.

In time, a sublime cruelty twisted her features. Gromph exclaimed in triumph, for the netherspirit plainly had her in its grasp. Evidently she wasn't going to drop dead of an aneurysm or commit suicide, but no matter: she was doomed. Her personality erased, consumed by the compulsion to degrade and destroy, she was bound to provoke someone into killing her.

Then she broke the skinny white wand in two, unleashing a magic that thrust the netherspirit out of her. Gromph, for all his knowledge, had never seen anything quite like it. Taking on just a hint of palpable form, his agent fled the scene.

The Baenre wizard bolted up in his chair and threw his goblet, smashing it against the wall. He cursed foully, and the malignancy in his words, hammering through the black lotus-scented air, made the greenish flames of the everlasting candles gutter.

Struggling for composure, he told himself it didn't matter. He'd get her eventually. He'd throw entity after entity at her until . . .

But what had happened to the netherspirit? Constrained by Gromph's command, it should have kept attacking until either it toppled the pillars of Quenthel's reason or she destroyed it. Instead, it had run away.

The mistress's unfamiliar magic had broken the binding—so much was clear—but where had the creature gone? Back to its own world? Probably, but something—a slight acceleration of his heartbeat or a subtle prickling on the back of his neck, perhaps—made Gromph want to check.

The casement responded to his will. Framed in that rectangular space, the netherspirit, still visible, perhaps as tangible as smoke, half flew, half bounded down one of the labyrinthine corridors of

Sorcere. A defensive ward activated, piercing the intruder with criss-crossing shafts of yellow light, but it tore itself free and charged on. A blue-gowned master peered out the door of his sanctum, spotted the wraith, started to conjure, and the intruder stopped him with a sweep of a shadowy paw. The blow didn't rock the wizard backward or leave a mark, but he fell like a block of stone.

Gromph surmised his erstwhile agent was coming after him. Either it was angry over its forced servitude, or Quenthel had done more than merely dissolve his control. She'd wrested it away from him and turned the entity into her own assassin.

Either way, the spirit represented a threat, and unfortunately, Gromph himself didn't know its full capabilities. Still, he had no real reason for concern. His magic was more than a match for any such entity, especially in his stronghold.

He watched the netherspirit flow through the black marble door of his office like water through a sieve. It scrambled over the white bone desk and headed straight for the hidden access to his sanctum. Magic crackled purple and blue around it, but it burst through. It hurtled up the shaft.

Gromph smiled. He had the creature where he wanted it, for he'd created the passage with defense in mind. Simply by focusing his will, he destroyed it.

The shaft wasn't made of matter. Still, a metallic crashing and grinding sounded through the hole in the middle of the floor as the artificial space folded in on itself. If the rebellious spirit screamed, its voice was lost among the din.

Gromph would have enjoyed hearing it squeal, but the important thing was that it was gone. Most likely, the collapse had crushed it to nothing, but even if not, it had surely ejected it, maimed and dis-oriented, in some remote halfworld. The crisis was over, and the archmage was left only with the annoyance of transporting himself in and out of his hideaway via spell until such time as he invested the six hours necessary to recreate the passage.

However, just to maintain the habit of caution that had balked a thousand enemies, he turned back to the window, then scowled.

The space still framed the spirit, and as far as Gromph could see, the shadowy thing was unharmed. Darting and wheeling through curtains of pale phosphorescence, it was casting about in the bent spaces surrounding the stronghold.

Gromph didn't see how the creature could find him. Nothing could locate a refuge hidden in a haze of scrambled time, not without the tenant in some way guiding it in. Nonetheless, the wizard hurried into one of the protective golden pentacles adorning the marble floor.

An instant later, a different window burst inward, the casements flying from their hinges. The spirit flowed through, in the process resuming the form it had worn before Gromph transformed it into the semblance of a kind of demon. It somewhat resembled a wingless dragon with long, taurine horns sweeping from its head, which also possessed a single globular eye. The archmage couldn't actually see the orb—it was one with the inky shadow of the spirit's body—but he could feel its baleful regard.

Slightly anxious and uncertain, and all the angrier for it, Gromph shouted, "K'rarza'q! I named, summoned, and bound you, and I am your master. By the Prince Who Dreams in the Heart of the Void and by the Word of Naratyr, I command you to kneel!"

The netherspirit released a humid stink that somehow conveyed the essence of scornful laughter, then it bounded forward.

Very well, Gromph thought, have it your way.

He thrust the curved blade of his ritual dagger into his belly.

As he'd expected, the creature floundered in agony, but only for an instant. Anguish erupted in the archmage's own stomach. He yanked the athame out of his flesh an instant before it would have dealt him an actual wound.

K'rarza'q lunged. Ignoring the residual pain in his gut, Gromph recited a brief incantation and thrust out his arm. The air rang like a bell, and a little red ball of fire shot from his hand. It struck the creature and . . . nothing. The missile winked out of existence.

The entity reached the edge of the pentacle. A barrier of azure light sprang up and vanished with a tortured whine as the spirit drove though. The creature dipped its head and jerked it upward, ramming the tip of one of its horns into Gromph's chest.

The spirit was entirely solid. If not for the Robes of the Archmage and his other protections, the long blade of shadow stuff would surely have impaled Gromph. As it was, it picked him up and tossed him across the room. In midair, he strained to throw off the numbing shock and activate the powers of levitation in his House insignia.

The power woke with a sort of sickening pang, but wake it did. He floated down as light as a wisp of spider silk, avoiding what might have been a bone-shattering fall.

As soon as he got his feet under him, he snatched a polished wooden wand from its sheath on his left hip, pointed it, and murmured the trigger word. A bubble of pungent brown acid swelled on the end, then hurtled at the spirit. It plunged into the being's cyclopean mask, but apparently without inflicting any harm.

The spirit charged. Gromph stood in place until his foe was nearly on top of him, then he spoke a single word. A minor teleportation shifted him instantaneously to the other end of the circular room, behind his attacker's back.

K'rarza'q skidded to a halt and cast about in confusion. Gromph had bought himself a second, no more. He quickly dropped the wand of acid, snatched a spiral-cut staff of polished carnelian from its place on a rack of wizard's tools, lifted it over his head, and began to chant. The rod possessed special virtues against beings from other levels of reality. Perhaps with it in his hand, he could finally drive a spell through his foe's defenses.

The netherspirit heard his voice, turned, and hurtled toward him. This time it charged without moving its limbs, simply shifting over the distance with terrifying speed. Preserving the cadence and intonation as only a master wizard could, Gromph picked up the pace of his incantation. He very much wanted to finish before the creature closed with him again.

He succeeded, though only barely. K'rarza'q was nearly within arm's reach when the magic blazed into existence. A lance of dazzling glare plunged into the netherspirit's eye.

The reeking creature dropped to the floor, its substance unraveling into shapeless clumps and tatters. Gromph smiled, and a dozen strands of spirit-stuff reared up at him like the vipers in his cursed sister's whip.

The archmage gripped the scarlet staff with both hands, just as a Master of Melee-Magthere had taught him centuries before, during the six months every student mage was obliged to spend in the warriors' pyramid. Wielding the implement like a common spear, he thrust one end of it into what seemed to be K'rarza'q's ragged, squirming core.

The netherspirit burst into inert flecks of gray-black slime. Gromph's protective enchantments prevented any of the splatter from fouling his own person.

He felt a certain satisfaction at his victory, but it withered quickly because he hadn't killed the object of his hatred, merely preserved himself from the result of another failed attempt, and in the process discovered he'd utterly failed to comprehend Quenthel's resources and capacities.

What was that bone wand? Where had it come from, and how did it work? Had it merely broken his own control, or had it summarily placed his minion under his enemy's dominance?

He glumly concluded that until he knew more, it would be foolish to continue attacking a foe seemingly capable of turning his own potent wizardry against him.

So he'd break off hostilities.

And, he thought, with a sudden pang of uneasiness, hope his sister didn't guess who'd engineered her recent perils.

c h a p t e r

S E V E N T E E N

All the undercreatures gawked when Pharaun and Ryld strolled into the cellar, and why not? The mage doubted this foul little drinking pit had ever seen such an elegant figure as himself, an aristocrat of graceful carriage, exquisite ornaments, dress, and coiffure . . . well, he hoped that, after some emergency adjustments, his hair was at least passable.

In any case, it was plain the goblins, orcs, and whatevers had little interest in aesthetic appreciation. They whispered, glowered, and fingered their weapons whenever they thought the two dark elves weren't looking at them, and the fear and hate in the sweltering, low-ceilinged room were palpable. Pharaun supposed that considering what Greyanna and her hunters had wrought in the Braeryn the previous night, a measure of surliness was, if not good form, at least understandable.

He wondered how they'd react if they discovered his sister had slaughtered their fellows by the score merely to create an opportunity to kill him. Perhaps it was a question best left in the realm of the hypothetical.

Knowing that Ryld was watching his back, the Master of Sorcere sauntered to the bar and, with a sweep of his arm, scattered clattering coins across it. The currency was the usual miscellany encountered in Menzoberranzan—rounds, squares, triangles, rings, spiders, and octagons—half of it minted by the dozen or so greatest noble Houses and the rest imported from other lands in the Underdark and even the World Above. It was all silver, platinum, or gold, though, more precious metal than this squalid hole probably saw in a decade.

"Tonight," Pharaun announced, "this company of boon companions drinks at my expense!"

The taverner, a squat orc with a twisted, oozing mouth and a mangy scalp, stared for a heartbeat or two, scooped up the coins, and began dipping some foul-smelling brew from a filthy tub. Cursing and threatening one another, the rest of the undercreatures shoved forward to get it. The wizard noted that no one thanked him.

After looking around for another moment, Pharaun spotted another dark elf slouched in a corner, evidently one of the wretches who'd sunk so low the goblinoids accepted him as one of their own.

"Come here, my friend," the wizard beckoned.

The outcast flinched. "Me?"

"Yes. What's your name?"

The fellow hesitated, then said, "Bruherd, once of House Duskryn."

"Indeed, until your noble kin kicked you out. We have much in common, Bruherd, for I myself am outcast twice over. Now come advise me on a matter of vital importance."

"I'm, uh, all right where I am."

"I know you don't mean to be unsociable," said Pharaun, setting blue sparks dancing on his fingertips.

The Duskryn sighed, and, limping in a manner that betrayed some chronic pain, did as Pharaun had bade him. He was gaunt, and half a dozen boils studded his neck and jaw. He'd evidently parted with his *piwafwi* at some point during his decline, but he still wore a filthy robe that, the Mizzrym noted with mild surprise, had once been a wizard's. With the aid of the silver ring, he could see that the dozens of pockets no longer held the slightest trace of magic.

"They may kill me for this," Bruherd said, subtly indicating the goblins. "They only tolerate me because they believe me cut off from my own race."

"I'll pray for your welfare," Pharaun said. "Meanwhile, what I need to know is this: Of all the libations laid up in our host's no doubt vast and well-stocked cellar, which is the least vile?"

"Vile?" Bruherd's lip twitched. "You get used to them."

"One hopes not."

Pharaun handed the other drow a gold, hammer-shaped coin minted in some dwarf enclave.

"Tell the barkeep you want the stuff that bubbles," Bruherd advised.

" 'The stuff that bubbles.' Charming. Clearly, I've fallen among connoisseurs."

"It'll do," said Ryld, still unobtrusively studying the crowd. "The important thing is that we toast our victory."

Pharaun waited a beat, then chuckled. "You're supposed to ask him what he's talking about," he said to Bruherd, "thus affording us a graceful way to commence boasting of our triumph."

The lip twitched again. "I don't think much about victories or triumphs anymore."

Pharaun shook his head. "So much bitterness in the world! It weighs on the heart. Would it cheer you to learn I've avenged us in some small measure?"

"Us?" Bruherd grunted.

Across the room, a scuffle erupted between a shaggy hobgoblin and a wolf-faced gnoll. As the combatants rolled about the floor, somebody tossed them a knife, apparently just out of curiosity as to which would manage to grab it first.

"Hark to the glad tidings," said the Master of Sorcere. "I'm Pharaun Mizzrym, expelled first from the Seventh House and now Tier

Breche, neither time for any rational cause. Incensed, I chose to take vengeance on the Academy. With the aid of my similarly disgruntled friend Master Argith, I destroyed a patrol in the Bazaar earlier today. You may have heard something about it."

Bruherd stared. The kobold and goblins within earshot did the same.

"It's true," said Ryld.

"That was you?" Bruherd said. "And you're bragging about it? Are you insane? They'll hunt you down!"

Pharaun said, "They were trying anyway." The entire cellar was falling quiet. "I've heard rumors of an agency that will spirit a drow boy away if he's well and truly discontent with his lot in life, as I trust Ryld and I have shown we are."

Bruherd said, "I don't know what you're talking about."

"Well," Pharaun said, "they probably have to think you can be of some use to them, and if you'll forgive my saying so . . ."

He caught a flash of movement from the corner of his eye, and turned just in time to see the taverner fall back in two pieces. Evidently he'd been in the process of climbing silently over the bar with a short sword in hand, and Ryld, sensing him, had pivoted and cut him. The drow warrior spun smoothly back around, Splitter at the ready.

Pharaun turned back as well, just in time to see a mass of under-creatures rushing him. He snatched three smooth gray stones from a pocket and started to recite a spell. Ryld's greatsword flicked across the wizard's field of vision, killing two gnolls that sought to engage him, allowing him to finish the incantation unmolested.

A cloud of vapor boiled into existence in front of him. Those orcs and goblins caught in the fumes collapsed. Others recoiled to avoid their touch.

The fog blinked out of existence a heartbeat later.

"I'm afraid I can't permit you to kill us and sell the corpses to the authorities," Pharaun told the crowd, "and I'm shocked— shocked!—you would even try. Aren't you pleased we massacred a patrol?"

"They don't want the priestesses to find you here," said Bruherd. He hadn't made a move during the skirmish. Perhaps he'd frozen, or maybe he'd figured his best hope of survival lay in passivity. "I don't, either. They're liable to kill us, too."

"How disappointing," Pharaun said. "And here I thought Ryld and I had found a cozy enclave of kindred spirits. But of course we won't force our company on those who lack the rarified sensibility to appreciate it. Neither, however, will we quit this place before we slake our thirst. You goblins and whatnot will have to withdraw. Good evening."

The undercreatures glowered. The mage could tell what they were thinking. They were many, and the intruders only two. Yet they'd seen what those two could do, and after a few seconds, they started trudging out, leaving their unconscious comrades sprawled on the floor.

"You're crazy," Bruherd told the masters. "You need to keep your heads down very low for a few years. Give the matrons and the Academy time to forget."

"Alas," Pharaun said, "I suspect I'm unforgettable. You too may depart if you can bear to tear yourself away."

"Crazy," the outcast repeated.

He limped for the stairs and in a moment was gone like the rest.

Pharaun walked behind the bar. "Now," he said, "to begin drow's eternal search for *the stuff that bubbles.*"

Ryld surveyed the slumbering goblins as if pondering whether to stick his sword in them.

"I still think this is a bad idea," the weapons master said.

Careful not to soil his boots, Pharaun stepped around the two bloody pieces of the barkeep and inspected a rack of jugs and bottles.

"You always say that, and you're always mistaken. The goblinoids will carry word of our whereabouts far and wide. The rogues are bound to hear."

"As will your sister and everyone else we've managed to annoy."

Pharaun uncorked a jug. The pungent liquid inside didn't seem to be fizzing, so he moved on.

"Care to make a wager on who'll arrive first?"

"Either way," Ryld snorted, "we wind up dead."

"Had I wished to hear the dreary voice of pessimism, I would have detained our friend Bruherd," the wizard said as he inspected a jar full of cloudy liquid. "Here's a jar of pickled sausages if you care to break your fast, but I won't vouch for the ingredients. I think I see a kobold's horn floating in the brine."

He opened a glass bottle with a long, double-curved neck, and the contents hissed.

"Aha! I've found the draught the Duskryn recommended."

"Someone's here," said Ryld.

The mage turned. Two figures were descending the stairs. They looked like orcs, with coarse, tangled manes and lupine ears, but Pharaun's silver ring revealed that the appearance was an illusion, disguising dark elf males. The wizard saw the masks as translucent veils lying atop the reality.

He conveyed the truth of the situation to Ryld with a rapid flexing and crooking of his fingers.

"Gentlemen," said the mage, "well met! My comrade and I have been looking everywhere for you."

"We know," said the taller of the newcomers, evidently not surprised that a Master of Sorcere had instantly penetrated his disguise. He was Houndaer Tuin'Tarl, one of the highest ranked of the missing males, likewise one of the first to elope, and thus almost certainly one of the ringleaders. Certainly he looked like a princely commander of lesser folk. His rich silk and velvet garments, the magical auras of many of his possessions, and strutting demeanor all proclaimed it. He wore crystals in his thick, flowing hair—a nice effect—had close-set eyes and a prominent jaw, and looked as if he knew how to manage the scimitar hanging at his side. He also looked rather tense

"We've known for a while," said the other stranger, whom Pharaun didn't recognize.

At first glance, he appeared to be a nondescript commoner, with the squint and small hands of a craftsman proficient at fine work.

However, the dagger tucked in his sash fairly blazed with potent enchantments, as did an object concealed within his jerkin. Evidently he'd layered one disguise on another.

"Well," said Ryld, "you took your time contacting us. I guess that's understandable."

"I think so," said Houndaer as he and his comrade advanced. A goblin moaned, and the noble kicked the creature silent. "Why were you seeking us?"

"It's our understanding," said Pharaun, stepping from behind the bar, "that you offer a haven for males who find existence under the thumbs of their female relatives uncongenial and who, for whatever reason, aspire neither to the Academy, a merchant clan, nor Bregan D'aerthe. If so, then we wish to join your company."

"But you two already did aspire to the Academy," the aristocrat said. "You rose to high rank there. Some might say that gives my associates and I cause for concern."

The orc mask's tusked mouth perfectly copied the motions of his actual lips. Pharaun couldn't have created a better illusion himself.

"You speak of the dead past," Pharaun said. "You've no doubt heard I'm in disgrace, and Master Argith finds Melee-Magthere stale and tedious." The dark powers knew, his discontented friend shouldn't have much trouble convincing them of that. "We require an alternative way of life."

Houndaer nodded and replied, "I'm glad to hear it, but what assurances can you give that you aren't an agent the matrons sent to find us?"

Pharaun grinned. "My solemn oath?"

Everyone chuckled, even Ryld and the boy with the dagger, who were both quietly, thoughtfully watching their more loquacious companions palaver.

"Seriously," the wizard continued, "if our escapade in the Bazaar failed to convince you of our bona fides, I have no idea what other persuasion we can offer. But it didn't fail, did it? Otherwise, you wouldn't be here. So unless you perceive something in our manner that screams spy . . ."

The faux commoner smiled. "You're right." He turned to Houndaer and added, "They smell all right to me, and if they're not, I doubt a little quizzing in this stinking goblin hole will prove otherwise. Let's get them home before some servant of the clergy comes sniffing for them and finds us. Either way, it'll all get sorted out in the end."

For a moment, as the power of Pharaun's silver ring wavered, the drow's mild, civilized tone became an orc's growl. He even smelled like a dirty undercreature.

The Tuin'Tarl's mouth tightened. Pharaun suspected he didn't much like taking advice from anyone, his companion included.

"I'm just being careful—as should you—but you may have a point." He turned back to the masters and said, "If we take you to our stronghold, there's no going back. You'll aid our cause or die."

Pharaun grinned. "Well spoken, and quite in the spirit of a thousand thousand conspiracies before you. Whisk us away."

"Gladly," the noble said with a mean little smile of his own, "as soon as the two of you surrender your weapons and that cloak of pockets."

The wizard crooked an eyebrow and said, "I thought you'd decided to trust us."

"It's time for you to show a little trust," Houndaer replied.

Pharaun surrendered his *piwafwi*, hand crossbow, and dagger. He was a little worried about Ryld's willingness to do the same. He could easily imagine the warrior deciding that, in preference to entering the dragon's cave unarmed, he'd subdue Houndaer and his companion there and then and wring what information out of them he could.

The problem with that strategy was that the Tuin'Tarl and his nameless companion might not be privy to all the mystic secrets held by the cabal as a whole, and those who were might flee when the two emissaries failed to return. Thus, while the masters would likely succeed in forestalling a goblin revolt, they'd miss acquiring the extraordinary power they sought.

Besides, it would be much more fun to join, and undo the rogues from within.

Apparently Ryld shared Pharaun's perspective, or else he was simply content to follow the wizard's lead, for he handed over Splitter and his other weapons to Houndaer without demur.

The Tuin'Tarl reached into his pouch, extracted a stone, and tossed it. It exploded in a strange, lopsided way, tearing a wound in the air, a gash the size and shape of a sarcophagus standing on end and the color of the light that swims inside closed eyelids.

He gestured to the portal and said, "After you."

Pharaun smiled.

"Thank you."

As easy as that? Pharaun thought. He was experiencing a certain sense of anticlimax, which was absurd, really. It had been astonishingly difficult to get this far.

He stepped into the portal, and experienced none of the spinning vertigo of ordinary teleportation. Save for a split second of blindness, it was just like striding from one room to the next. The only problem was the drider waiting on the other side.

The wizard struggled not to make a sound. Still, the huge creature, half spider, half drow, a bow in its hand and a quiver of arrows slung across its naked back, turned toward him. Pharaun had no fear of a single such aberration, but the goddess only knew just how elaborate this trap actually was. He whirled back toward the magical doorway just as Ryld came through.

❀   ❀   ❀

Ryld, who'd slain his share of driders in the caverns surrounding Menzoberranzan, knew that this one—a hybrid creature with the head, arms, and torso of a dark elf male married to the body and segmented legs of a colossal spider—was larger than average; a robust example of its species, if species was the proper term. Nature didn't make them, magic did. Sometimes, when the goddess deemed one of her worshipers insufficiently reverent, the punishment was transformation at the hands of a circle of priestesses and a demon called a yochlol.

The Master of Melee-Magthere naturally focused on the venomous aberration as soon as he stepped through the portal, but like every competent warrior—and unlike Pharaun, evidently—he also took in the disposition of the entire area.

The portal had deposited them in a large, unfurnished hall with a number of openings along the wall. It was the sort of central hub used in castles to link the various wings. A couple males were wandering through, and while neither had ventured into the drider's immediate vicinity, they weren't preparing to attack him or flee from him, either. Nor did the creature himself appear on the verge of assaulting anyone, though he regarded the newcomers with a scowl.

Somewhat pleased to be ahead of his clever friend for once, Ryld gripped Pharaun by the shoulder.

"Steady," the swordsman said. "Don't embarrass yourself."

The wizard looked around, then grinned and said, "Right. Our friends didn't trick us into entering a trap. The drider's magically constrained."

"No."

Ryld glanced back to see that the two bogus orcs had stepped through the portal, which dwindled to nothing behind them. It was the bigger and more talkative of the duo who was speaking.

"The driders help us of their own free will."

"Interesting," said Pharaun.

In the blink of an eye, the goblinoids turned into an aristocratic warrior—Houndaer Tuin'Tarl, specifically, whom Ryld had trained—and a craftsman of one sort or another. The prince closed the portal with a wave of his arm.

"Do you still use that second-intention indirect attack?" Ryld asked. "That was a nice move."

For the first time, Houndaer smiled a smile that had neither malice nor suspicion in it.

"You remember that, Master? It's been so long, I'm surprised you even remember me."

"I always remember the ones who truly learn."

"Well, thank you. It's good to have you with us, and you're going to be glad you are. Great things are in store." the noble said. The drider scuttled toward them. "Ah, here comes Tsabrak. You'll see his mind isn't sluggish or otherwise crippled, yet he's on our side nonetheless."

In point of fact, the drider didn't look especially congenial. The length of his legs lifted his head above those of the four dark elves, and he glared down at them with eyes full of madness and hate. Ryld inferred that Tsabrak had entered into a typical Menzoberranyr alliance. He'd thrown in with the runaways to secure some practical advantage, but he still loathed *all* the drow who'd deformed him and cast him out.

"What is this?" the drider snarled, exposing his fangs. They seemed to impede his speech a trifle. "Syrzan said no!"

Syrzan wasn't a typical drow name, but Ryld had no idea to which other race it might belong. He glanced over at Pharaun, who conveyed with a subtle shrug that he didn't know, either.

"Syrzan is my ally, not my superior," said Houndaer, glaring back at the spider-thing. "I make my own decisions, and I've decided these gentlemen can help us. They're masters of Tier Breche—"

"I know who they are!" Tsabrak screamed, flecks of foam, perhaps mixed with venom, flying from his lips. "Do you think me a mindless beast? I studied on Tier Breche the same as anyone!"

"Then you know how useful their talents could be," said the craftsman, "and how unlikely it is they can do us any harm, particularly now that the prince has disarmed them."

"Just point us to Syrzan," Houndaer said. "It will allay your fears." It? Ryld wondered.

"I can't," the drider said. "It's gone off somewhere."

"Where?" Houndaer asked

"Agitating slaves? Acquiring more magic fire from its secret source? How do I know? You'll just have to sit on these two until it gets back."

"That's all right," the noble said. "Master Argith and I can reminisce about old times. We'll all wait in the room where Syrzan interviewed the other recruits."

"Perhaps you'd care to tag along," the craftsman said, "to make absolutely sure the masters don't cause any trouble."

Pharaun beamed up at the bloodthirsty aberration and asked, "Please? There are half a dozen questions concerning drider existence that have perplexed me for years."

Tsabrak ignored him, instead glowering at Houndaer and the artisan as if he suspected them of playing a trick on him.

Finally, he said, "Yes. I'll go. Somebody with sense needs to be there."

"Fine." Houndaer nodded to Ryld and Pharaun and said, "Come this way."

The masters and their hosts, or captors, set off through a maze of passageways. As promised, Pharaun treated Tsabrak to a barrage of questions, and, when the drider failed to respond, cheerfully answered himself with a gush of scholarly speculation.

Ryld paid little attention. He was too busy studying the rogues' citadel, a forlorn and dusty place where Pharaun's monologue echoed away into the quiet. No servants were in evidence, merely runaway males and driders, who often recognized their former instructors and curiously peered after them. The marks of magical attacks, bursts of lightning and sprays of acid, scarred the walls.

By all appearances, the conspirators were hiding in the seat of a House extinguished by its enemies. No one was supposed to take possession of such a fortress without the Baenre's permission, and few would dare. The vacant castles were supposedly cursed and haunted places, breeding grounds for sickness, insanity, and bad luck. As if to compound the potential for ill fortune, the squatters had broken the copious shrouds of spiderweb wherever they impeded traffic and even in corners where they didn't.

At one point, the masters and their warders passed a row of small octagonal windows. The glass was gone but the molded calcite cames remained. Ryld glanced out and saw mansions shining green and violet far below. The rogues had taken a stalactite castle, hanging from the cavern ceiling, for their hiding place. No doubt the isolation had attracted them.

A minute later, the little procession reached its destination, a chapel with rows of benches, a crooked aisle snaking up the middle to an asymmetrical basalt altar, and murals, agleam with silvery phosphorescence, carved in bas-relief on the walls and ceiling. To Ryld's surprise, these last depicted not the Demonweb but other hells entirely devoid of spiders, yochlols, or the goddess Lolth herself. Apparently the House that once abode here had sacrificed to forbidden deities. Perhaps that transgression had contributed to its downfall.

The dark elves settled themselves in the pews. While Houndaer and the commoner seemed convinced of the masters' claim of estrangement from Tier Breche, they nonetheless retained possession of the newcomers' gear. Tsabrak crouched just inside the door, his legs splayed out on either side of the entrance.

"I admire the decor," Pharaun said. "Without even trying, I noticed images of Cyric, Orcus, Bane, Ghaunadaur, and Vhaeraun. Quite a nice selection of patron powers for the discriminating worshiper."

"We're not looking for a new god," Houndaer spat.

"I'm sure," the wizard said. "Perhaps you'd be kind enough to tell Master Argith and me what your grand and glorious scheme *is* all about. And why now?"

"Why now?" the noble asked.

"Our fellowship has existed for decades," the craftsman cut in, "though it's only recently that we all eloped and took up residence here full time. Formerly we merely gathered for an hour or two every fortnight or so."

"If you're a male," Houndaer said, "and utterly dissatisfied with your place in Menzoberranzan, you need some sort of a refuge, don't you?"

"I quite agree," the wizard said. "Of course, others have opted for a merchant House, the Academy, or Bregan D'aerthe."

Houndaer made a spitting sound. "Those are just places to hide from the matrons. This is a fortress for males who want to turn Menzoberranzan upside down and put ourselves on top. Why not? Aren't our mages and even our warriors as powerful as the clergy?"

Pharaun grinned and said, "They certainly are now that the priestesses have mislaid their magic."

Houndaer blinked. "You know about that?"

"I've inferred it. You obviously know as well. Otherwise, you wouldn't run about breaking spiderwebs simply for the fun of it, to say nothing of putting your master plan into motion. I'd be curious to hear how you found out and if you know why."

"We don't know why," Houndaer said, shaking his head. "We started to figure it out after a couple of us saw priestesses die fighting gricks out in the Bauthwaf. The bitches should've used spells to save themselves, but they didn't, and we guessed it was because they couldn't. After that, we kept our eyes open and waylaid a few clerics to see what they'd do to defend themselves. Everything we learned supported our theory."

Pharaun sighed and said, "Then you aren't in touch with some chatty informant in the realms of the divine. Like me, you merely observed and deduced. What a pity. Aren't you, in your ignorance, apprehensive that Lolth will rekindle the priestesses' magic just when it's least convenient?"

"Maybe the goddess turned against the clergy because it's our turn to rule," said the commoner. "Who's to say? In any case, this is our chance, and we're taking it."

"Your chance to do what?" asked Ryld. "You talk as if you intend to revolt, but instead you're inciting the slaves into an uprising."

Houndaer cursed. "You know that, too?"

"We stumbled on it while looking for you," Pharaun explained. He brushed a stray strand of his coiffure back into place. His white hair shone like ghost flesh in the soft light shining from the carvings. "As Master Argith noted, on first inspection, whipping the undercreatures into a lather would seem irrelevant to your objective."

"Look deeper," the noble said. "We're canny enough to know we can't topple the matriarchy all at once. Even without their spells, our mothers and sisters are too powerful. They have too many talismans, fortresses, and, most importantly, troops and vassals serving out of fear."

"I begin to comprehend, and I apologize for not giving you sufficient credit," Pharaun said. "This is merely the opening gambit in a *sava* game that will last a number of years."

"When fighting engulfs Menzoberranzan," Houndaer said, "and the clerics cast no spells to put down the revolt, their weakness will become apparent to everyone. Meanwhile, our brotherhood will take advantage of the chaos to assassinate those females who pose the greatest obstacles to our ambitions. With luck, the orcs will account for a few more. At the end of the day, our gender's position in the scheme of things will be considerably stronger, and every male in the city will start aspiring to supremacy.

"In the years to come, our cabal will do whatever we can to diminish the females and put ourselves in their place. One day soon, we'll see a noble House commanded by a male and eventually, a master in every House."

He smiled and added, "Needless to say, a master who belongs to this fraternity. I'll enjoy ruling over House Tuin'Tarl, and I imagine that you, Brother of Sorcere, wouldn't say no to primacy over your own family."

Pharaun nodded and said, "You're far too canny to have forgotten we've all gone rogue. . . ."

"Our kin will welcome us back once we've weakened them to the point where they're desperate for reinforcements. We'll concoct tales of travels to the far ends of the Underdark, or something. It won't matter to them when they're desperate enough."

"Indeed, you've plotted everything out so shrewdly that I only see one potential pitfall, Pharaun said. "What if the goblins and gnolls should actually *succeed* in slaughtering us all, or at least inflicting such damage on our city that the devastation breaks our hearts?"

Houndaer stared at the mage for a moment, then laughed. "For a moment, I almost thought you serious."

Pharaun grinned. "Forgive me. I have a perverse fondness for japes at inappropriate moments, as Master Argith will attest."

Houndaer smiled at Ryld and said, "I'd just as soon hear him attest that I mastered all those lessons on strategy he pounded into my skull."

"You did," said Ryld, and perhaps it was true. His instincts told him that this scheme, outlandish as it seemed, might work, and he abruptly realized he didn't know how he felt about the possibility.

He and Pharaun had infiltrated the rogues to betray them, to placate the archmage, and because the Mizzrym wizard had some vague notion that they'd achieve greater status and power and thus a permanent cure for Ryld's formless dissatisfaction, thereby. Yet now the conspirators were offering high rank and a role in a grand adventure. Perhaps, then, the teachers should become in truth the rebels they were pretending to be.

The warrior glanced over at Pharaun. With a flick of his fingers so subtle that no one else would notice, the wizard signed one word in the silent language: *Persevere.*

Ryld took it to mean that his friend, with his usual acuity, had divined what he was thinking and was urging him to hold to their original intent. He gave a tiny nod of assent. He didn't know if Pharaun was making a wise choice, but he did realize he wouldn't even be here listening to this apocalyptic talk if his friend hadn't asked for his aid. When all was said and done, Ryld had descended from Melee-Magthere to help the wizard achieve *his* ends, and that was what he was going to do.

Pharaun turned to Tsabrak and said, "I assume the driders have allied themselves with the conspiracy because the boys promised you a place of honor in the splendid Menzoberranzan to come. Perhaps they even pledged to find a way to transform you back into a drow."

"Something like that," Tsabrak sneered. "Mainly, though, those of us who joined did it for the chance to kill lots and lots of priestesses."

"I can't say I blame you," Pharaun said. "Well, gentlemen, your plans are inspiring to say the least. I'm glad we sought you out."

"So am I," said Ryld.

"The only things I'm still hazy on," the mage continued, "are Syrzan and the Prophet. One and the same? I see by your expressions that they are. Who is . . . *it* really, and what power does it use to so enthrall the goblins?"

"I think you're about to find out," Houndaer said.

An instant later, something droned through the air, almost like a noise, but not. Actually, the sensation existed solely within the mind. Pharaun turned, and Tsabrak scuttled aside to reveal the robed figure in the doorway. Ryld felt a jolt of dismay. Afraid it was already too late, he sprang up from the bench.

E I G H T E E N

Off to Faeryl's left stood an iron maiden cast in the form of a tubby jester in cap and bells. The bells looked real, and would evidently jingle while a victim writhed inside. The device was open just a crack, not enough to expose the spikes inside.

Straight ahead, a chain and hook dangled from their pulley, fishing for a prisoner to hoist, and a rack waited to stretch one. To the left, a brazier of coals threw off dazzling heat, and a collection of probes, knives, pincers, and pears hung on their pegs. Her nemesis, the small male with all the ugly baubles, lounged in that vicinity in an iron chair with shackles attached to the armrests.

That was about as much as the envoy could see while roped naked to a molded calcite post.

She was hungry, thirsty, and sore from standing for hours in one position. Her bonds chafed her, and her head ached. However, she had yet to endure one of the genuine agonies this stuffy cellar provided, and she thought she knew why. Some messenger had instructed the torturers to wait for Triel to arrive before commencing the festivities.

Faeryl had already attempted to converse with the little male and her jailers and failed to elicit a response from either. She had nothing else to do but struggle to govern her thoughts. She didn't want to imagine all the things the Baenre might do to her, but she herself had presided over enough excruciations that it was difficult not to envision the possibilities. She didn't want to dwell on the massacre of her followers, either, but the memories kept welling up inside her.

Surrounded and outnumbered, the daughters and sons of Ched Nasad had perished one by one. As Faeryl watched the slaughter, her eyes ached with the tears she refused to shed. Naturally, she didn't "love" her minions, but she was used to them, even fond of a few, and she knew that without a retinue she was nothing, just a fallen priestess in a land of enemies, bereft of goddess and home alike.

Then the small male confronted her and used his magic to confound her and knock her out. She woke tied to the stone stake.

A door creaked, and voices murmured. Faeryl's instincts warned her that Triel had come at last. The ambassador closed her eyes, took a deep breath, and let it out slowly, composing herself. She wouldn't show fear. Dignity was all she had left—for a little while longer anyway, until her captors lashed and burned it out of her.

Sure enough, Triel and her draegloth son emerged from the doorway that apparently led to more salubrious precincts of the Great Mound. The Baenre matron was smiling. Fangs bared in a grin, Jeggred bounded along on his caprine legs.

The little male rose and offered obeisance.

"Valas," said Triel. "Well done. Did the Zauvirr give you any trouble?"

"They tried to sneak away in disguise," the male replied. "It almost fooled the lookout, but once he figured out what was what, everything went as planned."

The Baenre proffered a fat pouch that looked too big and heavy for her tiny hand.

"I'll send word when I need Bregan D'aerthe again," she said.

Valas took the pouch, then bowed low. He withdrew, and Triel and her monstrous son turned toward the prisoner.

"Good evening, Matron," Faeryl said, "or is it morning now?"

Fighting hands outstretched, talons at the ready, jaws agape, Jeggred lunged at the prisoner. Despite herself, Faeryl flinched. Both the claws and the pointed teeth stopped less than an inch from her flesh. The draegloth loomed over her, pressing close, almost seeming to embrace her like a lover. He ran a pointed nail across her cheek, then lifted it to his bestial muzzle. He sucked, and a bit of warm, viscous drool, mixed, perhaps, with a trace of her blood, dripped onto her forehead.

"Have a care," the ambassador said with as much nonchalance as she could muster. "If your son kills me quickly, won't that spoil the fun?"

Jeggred made a low, grinding sound. Faeryl couldn't tell if he was growling or laughing.

Triel said, "You underestimate him. True, I've watched him butcher eight prisoners in as many seconds, but I've also seen him spend days picking one little faerie child apart a mote of flesh at a time. It depends on his humor, and, needless to say, my instructions."

"Of course," Faeryl said. The shallow gash in her cheek began to sting. Jeggred traced the edges of her lips with his claw, not quite cutting, not yet. "I hope the traitor whelp appreciated the honor."

"It was hard to tell," she said. "What about you? Will you savor it?"

"Alas, Exalted Mother," Faeryl said, "your daughter can take no pleasure in an honor she didn't earn."

Still stroking the prisoner's features with the claw, Jeggred lifted one of the smaller hands that, save for their dusting of fine hair, looked no different than those of an ordinary dark elf. He caught hold of Faeryl's ear and twisted it, and she gasped at the brutal stab of pain. When he finally let go, the organ kept on throbbing and ringing. She wondered if the draegloth had inflicted permanent damage, though it really didn't matter. In the hours to come, deafness would be the least of her problems.

"I wish you wouldn't deny your guilt," sighed the dainty little Baenre matriarch. "I always find that dull."

"Even when it's true?" Faeryl felt a fresh cut bleeding under her eye. Apparently, when Jeggred had abused her ear, she'd bucked against his claw.

"Don't be tiresome," Triel said. "You were fleeing, and that confirms your guilt."

"All it confirms is my certainty that someone has poisoned your mind against me," Faeryl retorted. Jeggred caught hold of a lock of her hair and gave it a vicious tug. "My aversion to being condemned unjustly."

"Did you think to escape by running back to Ched Nasad?" Triel asked. "My word is law there, too."

"How do you know?" Faeryl asked.

Jeggred slapped her with one of his enormous fighting hands, bashing her head sideways. For a moment, the shock froze her mind. When her senses returned, she tasted blood in her mouth.

The draegloth crouched, placing his bestial face directly in front of her own, and growled, "Respect the chosen of Lolth."

"I mean no disrespect," Faeryl said. "I'm just saying that for all we know, anything could be happening in Ched Nasad. Cloakers could have overrun the city, or it may have drowned in tides of lava. I doubt it, I pray not, but we don't *know*. We need to find out, and that's why I was sneaking away. Not to betray the weakness of Menzoberranzan's clergy to some enemy or other. Mother of Lusts, it's my weakness too! To gather intelligence, to reestablish communication—"

"I told you I have been in communication with Ched Nasad," Triel said.

"To reestablish *trustworthy* communication . . ." Faeryl persisted, "to make myself useful and so demonstrate I'm your loyal vassal, never a traitor."

Triel made a spitting sound, then said, "My loyal servants obey me."

Faeryl wanted to weep, not from fear, though she was experiencing plenty of that, but from sheer frustration. Jeggred ran his claw along her carotid artery.

"Matron," the Zauvirr said, "I beg you. Let me confront the person who traduced me. Give me that one chance to prove my fidelity. Is it so hard to imagine someone telling you a lie? Don't your courtiers slander one another all the time as a means of vying for your favor? Is it impossible that someone or something in Ched Nasad is lying to you even now—telling you all is well while days, then tendays, then months go by without a single caravan?"

Triel hesitated, and Faeryl felt a thrill of hope. Then the ruler of Menzoberranzan said, "You're the liar, and it will do you no good. If you want me to show any mercy at all, tell me whose creature you are. The svirfneblin? The aboleths? Another drow city?"

"I serve only you, Sacred Mother."

Faeryl said the words without hope, for she saw that she would never convince the Baenre of her innocence. It was too hard for Triel to measure up to her predecessor, too hard to rule in these desperate times, too hard to make decisions. She wasn't about to rethink one of the few she'd managed to squeeze out, no matter how foolish it was.

Jeggred slapped Faeryl and kept on slapping until she lost count of the blows. Finally time seemed to skip somehow, and he wasn't hitting her anymore. Why should he bother? He'd already battered all the strength out of her. She would have fallen if not for the ropes holding her up. A broken tooth had lodged under her tongue, and it was all she could do just to spit it out.

"I told you," the draegloth snarled, "*respect!*"

"I am respectful," Faeryl wheezed. "That's why I give the truth even when it might be easier to lie."

Triel peered up at her son and said, "Princess Zauvirr will not distract you from your duties."

Jeggred inclined his head. "No, Mother."

"But at such times as I do not require you," the matron continued, "you may use the spy as you see fit. If she tells you anything of interest, pass it along, but the point of your efforts is chastisement, not interrogation. I doubt she has anything all that important to confide. We already know who our enemies are."

"Yes, Mother." The half-demon crouched, leered into Faeryl's face, and said, "I can make the fun last. You'll see."

He stuck out his long, pointed tongue and licked blood from her face. The member was as rough as a beast's.

🕷 🕷 🕷

The figure in the chapel doorway had a bulbous head with huge, protruding eyes, dry, wrinkled hide, and four wriggling tentacles surrounding and obscuring the mouth. It had gnarled three-fingered hands, a body with contours and proportions different than those of a drow, and an assortment of talismans and amulets burning with strange enchantments.

Syrzan, Pharaun had no doubt, was a member of the psionically gifted species called illithids. Specifically, it was one of the few such creatures to follow the path of wizardry and ultimately transform itself into an undead entity known as an alhoon. The thing was surely prodigiously powerful, immune to the ravages of time, and still entirely capable of reading the masters' minds and discerning the treachery therein.

Like Pharaun, Ryld had sprung up from his bench. The hulking warrior flung himself at Houndaer, no doubt in an attempt to get his weapons back. Pharaun, who thought he needed his spell components just as badly, scrambled after his friend.

The weapons master threw a punch, knocked Houndaer backward off his bench, and snatched up Splitter. He whirled, looking for the next threat, and almost whacked his fellow teacher with the blade.

Pharaun reached for his cloak, then realized Houndaer's unassuming companion was singing a wordless arpeggio.

Had Pharaun already been wearing the *piwafwi* with all its protective enchantments, he might have resisted the song, but instead its power stabbed into his mind. He laughed convulsively, uncontrollably, and staggered backward. Finally, he fell to his knees, his stomach muscles clenching and aching.

He'd suspected the nondescript little male was more than he'd seemed, a formidable combatant employing a bland appearance to throw his adversaries off guard, and he'd been right. The "craftsman" was in reality a bard, a spellcaster who worked his wonders through the medium of music.

Teeth gritted, Pharaun shook off the compulsion to laugh. Gasping, he lifted his head and looked around. The bard was simultaneously drawing his enchanted dagger and starting another song, this time pitched falsetto. Houndaer was on his feet battling Ryld, their swords ringing. At the end of the room, Tsabrak, shifting his eight legs in agitation, aimed an arrow at Pharaun, while in the doorway the alhoon simply stood with only its mouth tentacles moving, seemingly content to let its compatriots do the fighting.

Pharaun threw himself sideways. The arrow missed him and clacked and skipped across the floor. The mage slapped the stone, and a wall of sheltering darkness sprang up between him and the foe. Moving with a practiced, silent grace, he scrambled on.

Something clamped down on Pharaun's mind, smothering his will and robbing him of the ability to move. The undead mind flayer hadn't been idle after all. Syrzan had simply utilized its psionic strength in preference to its wizardry and thus hadn't needed to whirl its three-fingered hands in arcane passes. The wall of shadow no impediment, the Prophet had reached out, found Pharaun's intellect, and struck a crippling blow.

The barricade of darkness disappeared. Syrzan must have employed a bit of countermagic to dispel it and in so doing, afforded Pharaun a view of the space beyond. Rather to his surprise, Houndaer was still alive, perhaps because Tsabrak had discarded his bow, drawn a broadsword, and come to fight alongside him. The two conspirators were trying to catch Ryld between them, generally an effective tactic, but thus far the teacher's *piwafwi*, dwarven armor, and prowess had preserved him from harm.

The Tuin'Tarl made a halfhearted slash, and Ryld, recognizing the feint for what it was, didn't react. The pale phosphorescence of the carvings gleaming on his naked limbs, Tsabrak spat venom onto his blade. The bard brought his shrill singing to a crescendo, crossed his legs, and wrapped his arms tightly around his torso, all but tying himself in knots.

With the aid of his ring, Pharaun saw a glittering pulse of magic fly from the singer to Ryld. He could even tell what it was intended to do. His friend was supposed to contort his own body in helpless imitation of the bard's constrictive posture. But, strong of spirit, Ryld resisted the compulsion without even realizing he was doing it.

The weapons master faked a cut at Houndaer's head, then whirled and dived. He slid between Tsabrak's legs, breaking away from the drider and Houndaer, too, leaped up, and charged Syrzan. He recognized the alhoon as the most dangerous of his foes, even though the illithilich hadn't attacked him yet.

Syrzan reached into a pocket and produced a small ceramic vial. When it swung the bottle from right to left, a dozen orbs of bright flame materialized in its wake. They shot at Ryld in one straight line and exploded one after the other, banging rapidly like some hellish drum roll.

The glare was dazzling. For a moment, Pharaun couldn't see anything, and he made out Ryld through floating blobs of afterimage. His friend appeared unscathed. He was still charging and almost in sword's reach of the alhoon.

Syrzan used its mind flayer talents. Even though the lich hadn't directed the attack at him, Pharaun felt the fringe of it. It was like a sprinkle of hot ash burning his brain. Ryld dropped.

Syrzan gazed down at the warrior for a moment, evidently making sure he was truly incapacitated, then walked over to Pharaun. Despite the long skirt of its robe, there was something noticeably strange about its gait, as if its legs bent in too many places. Up close, it exuded a faint stink not unlike rotten fish. Its garments, once of princely quality, were frayed and stained.

It touched a finger to Pharaun's brow, and they were elsewhere.

The Underdark was boundless, its mysteries infinite, and despite centuries of following wherever his curiosity led, Pharaun had never seen an illithid city. Save for a dearth of inhabitants, he thought he'd just stepped into one.

Artisans had carved the walls and columns of the vault into spongiform masses like brain tissue, then covered the convolutions with lines of graven runes. Pools of warm fluid dotted the floor. Redolent of salt, the ponds crawled and throbbed with a mental force that even a non-psionic intelligence dimly sensed as a whisper of alien, incomprehensible thought at the back of the mind.

Pharaun recognized that the cavern was in some sense an illusion, but that didn't make it any less interesting. He would have liked nothing better than to explore every nook and cranny. It was an inclination rooted in a profound sense of well-being, a blithe unconcern no more genuine than the landscape, but seductive all the same. He would have to fight it.

He turned, saw Syrzan standing a few feet away, and cast darts of force, a spell requiring only words of power and a flourish of the hands. Halfway to their target, the streaking shafts of azure radiance stopped dead in the air, fell to the ground, and turned into limbless things like leeches or tadpoles, which, squealing telepathically, slithered toward the nearest pool.

"Your spells won't work here," said Syrzan in the Prophet's rich, compelling tones.

"I suspected as much, but I had to try. Are we inside your mind?"

"More or less."

Syrzan strolled closer. Off to the side, liquid splashed and plopped as the tadpoles wallowed.

"We're conversing in my special haven," the undead mind flayer said, "but we're also still in the heretic's chapel. In that reality I'm rebuking Houndaer for fetching you after I told him it was dangerous, and you're insensible."

"Fascinating," Pharaun said, "and I suppose you spirited me into the dream for a private tête-à-tête."

"Essentially," the alhoon said. Even in this phantasmal domain, it smelled faintly of decaying fish. "This is actually a form of mind-reading. You won't be able to lie."

The Master of Sorcere chuckled. "Some people would say that so handicapped, I won't be able to speak at all."

The mages began stroll along side by side. The atmosphere felt quite congenial.

"How is it," Syrzan asked, "that you came looking for my associates and me?"

Pharaun explained. He didn't see how it could do any harm.

When he was finished, the illithilich said, "You couldn't wield my particular sort of power."

"I understand that now. You enthrall the undercreatures through a deft combination of wizardry and mind flayer arts, and I lack the innate capacity to master the latter. What's more, you conspirators know nothing about the priestesses' difficulties." Pharaun cocked his head. "Or perhaps you do, Master Lich."

"No," said Syrzan, its mouth tentacles coiling and twisting. "Like the others, I know what's happened but not why."

"So none of what I sought was ever here for the finding." Pharaun laughed and said, "My sister Sabal once told me that a clever drow's wits can lead him into follies no dunce would dare to undertake . . . but that's blood down the gutter. What of you? What in the wide world prompted a creature such as yourself to throw in with a band of Menzoberranyr malcontents?"

"You seek information you can use against me."

"Well, partly . . ." Pharaun had to pause for a second when a wave of psionic force from one of the larger pools dizzied him and threatened to wash his own thoughts away. "In the unlikely event I'm ever afforded the chance. Mostly, though, I'm just curious. You're a mage. Surely we share that trait even if little else."

Syrzan shrugged, the narrow shoulders beneath its faded robes hitching higher than would a drow's.

"Well," the alhoon said, "I suppose it can do no harm to enlighten you, and it's been a long while since I've had the opportunity to converse with a colleague of genuine ability. Not that you're my equal— no elf or dwarf could ever be—but you're several cuts above any of Houndaer's allies."

"Your kind words overwhelm me."

The two wizards stepped onto a bridge, a crooked limestone span arching over one of the briny pools.

"Dark elves will abide a lich," the alhoon said, a brooding note entering its musical and almost certainly artificial voice. "Illithids won't. By and large, they hate the idea of sorcery, a foreign discipline as potent as the psionic skills that constitute our birthright. Still, they'll tolerate a limited number of *mortal* mages, those of us drawn to wizardry despite the stigma, for the advantages we bring. But the thought of undying wizards enduring for millennia, amassing arcane power the while, terrifies them."

"So on the day you achieved your immortality," Pharaun said, "you forsook your homeland forever, or at least until the day when you could conquer it."

The two mages stopped at the highest point on the bridge and looked out over an expanse of warm, briny fluid. Pharaun noticed that the stuff rippled and flowed sluggishly, as if it was thicker than water.

"Indeed," Syrzan said. "I hoped to manage my departure circumspectly, but somehow the folk of Oryndoll sensed my metamorphosis. For decades, they hunted me like an animal, and I existed like one in the wilds of the Underdark. Those times were hard. Even the undead crave the comforts of civilization. Finally Oryndoll forgot me or gave up on me. That was an improvement, but still I had no home."

"I've heard," said Pharaun, "that one or two secret enclaves of illithiliches exist. Didn't you search for one?"

"I searched for ninety years and found one," Syrzan replied, sounding slightly miffed that its prisoner had jumped ahead in the story. "For a time, I dwelled therein but I quarreled with the eldest alhoons, who considered themselves the leaders of the rest. I conducted certain investigations they had, in their ignorance and timidity, forbidden."

The Master of Sorcere laughed and said, "If you can't find it in your heart—assuming an illithilich retains the organ—to consider us equals, you must at least concede we're kindred spirits. You weren't angling for the Sarthos demon, were you?"

"No," said Syrzan curtly. "Suffice it to say that if not for some bad luck, I would have usurped the place of the eldest lich of all, but as matters fell out, I had to flee into the wilderness, a solitary wanderer once more."

"Surely you found someone to enslave."

Pharaun noticed the air in the dream cavern had grown cooler. Perhaps it was responding to its maker's somber reflections.

"I found small encampments," Syrzan said. "A family of goblins here, a dozen troglodytes there. I used them, used them up, each in its turn, but no little hole infested with a handful of brutes could give me what I truly craved. I yearned for a teeming city, full of splendors and luxuries, over which I would rule, and from which I could conquer an empire. But the taking of such exceeded even my powers."

"Or mine," Pharaun said, "hard as that is to credit. So, lusting for what you couldn't have, you spied on the cities of the Underdark, didn't you, or one of them, anyway. You kept your eye on Menzoberranzan."

"Yes," Syrzan said, "I've watched your people for a long while. I discovered the cabal of renegade males some forty years ago. More recently, I observed the priestesses' debility; no mere dark elves could hide such an enormous change from an observer with my talents. I remembered the would-be rebels and arranged for them to make the same discovery, then I emerged from the shadows and offered them my services."

"Why?" Pharaun asked. "Your collaborators are drow, and you're, if you'll pardon my bluntness, a member of an inferior species. Jumped up vermin, really. You don't expect Houndaer and the boys to honor a pact with you once the prize is won? Dark elves don't even keep faith with one another."

"Fortunately, the prize won't be won for decades, and during those years, I'll be subtly working to impose my will on my associates. Long before they assume the rulership of the city, I'll be ruling them."

"I see. The fools have given you your opening, and now that which you could never conquer from the outside you'll subjugate from within, extending the web of compulsion farther and farther, one assumes, until all Menzoberranyr are mind-slaves marching to your drum."

"Obviously, you understand the fundamentals of illithid society," said Syrzan. "You probably also know that we prefer to dine on the brains of lesser sentients and that we share your own race's fondness for torture. Still, some of your folk will fare all right. I can't eat or flay *everyone*, can I?"

"Not unless you want to wind up a king of ghosts and silence. And where, may I ask, do these stone-burning fire bombs come from?"

"Menzoberranzan isn't the only drow city possessed of ambitious males," the illithilich said.

Pharaun was momentarily speechless. Another drow city—

"Now, it's your turn to satisfy my curiosity," Syrzan said, interrupting the drow's reverie.

"I live for the opportunity."

"When Houndaer and the others explained our scheme, did you sincerely consider joining us?"

Pharaun grinned and said, "For about a quarter of a second."

"Why did you reject the idea? You're no more faithful or less ambitious than any other drow."

"Or illithid, I'll hazard. Why then did I remain firm in my resolve to betray you to Gromph?" The slender dark elf spread his hands. "So many reasons. For one, I'm a notable wizard, if I do say so myself, and in Menzoberranzan we mages have our own tacit hierarchy. In recent years, I've channeled my aspirations into that. Should I rise to the top, it will make me a personage nearly as exalted as a high priestess."

Syrzan flipped its tentacles, a gesture that conveyed impatience, and a flake of skin fell off. Unlike the slimy hide of living mind flayers, the lich's flesh was cracked and dry.

"The renegades are trying to place themselves *above* the females," the undead creature said.

"I understand that, but I doubt it'll work out the way they plan, or even the way *you* plan."

"You believe the priestesses are too formidable, even divested of their spells?"

"Oh, they're powerful. They may well extinguish this little cabal. Yet for the moment, I'm more concerned about the undercreatures. Do you realize how many goblins there are, how fervently they hated us even before you maddened them, or how dangerous your stone-consuming fire is? It could be that after they riot, we won't have a Menzoberranzan left for anyone to rule."

"Nonsense. The orcs will have their hour, and your people will butcher them."

Pharaun sighed. "That's what folk keep telling me. I wish your consensus comforted me, but it doesn't. That's one of the drawbacks of knowing yourself shrewder than everybody else."

"I assure you, the orcs cannot prevail."

"At the very least, they'll destroy some of the lovely architecture the founders sculpted from the living rock, and they'll set a defiant example for future generations of thralls. Your scheme will harm not merely the priestesses but Menzoberranzan itself, and I disapprove of that. It's sloppy and inept. Only a fool mars the very treasure he's striving to acquire."

A sneer in its tone, Syrzan said, "I wouldn't have taken you for a patriot."

"Odd, isn't it? I'll tell you something even stranger. In my way, I'm also a devout child of Lolth. Oh, it's never kept me from pursuing my own ends—even past the point of murdering a priestess or two—but though I strive for personal preeminence, I would never seek to topple the entire social order she established. I certainly wouldn't conspire to place her chosen people and city under the rule of a lesser creature."

"Even gods die, drow. Perhaps Lolth is no more. If Menzoberranzan is indeed the mortal realm she loves best, why else would she abandon you?"

"A test? A punishment? A whim? Who can say? But I doubt the Spider Queen is dead. I saw her once, and I don't just mean the manifestation who visited Menzoberranzan during the Time of Troubles. I've gazed upon the Dark Mother in the full majesty of her divinity, and I can't imagine that anything could ever lay her low."

"You have looked upon the Spider Queen?"

"I thought you might be interested in that," said the mage. "It wasn't long after I graduated from Sorcere, returned home to serve my mother, and sided with my sister Sabal against her twin Greyanna. One night, a delegation of priestesses came to our stalactite castle. Triel Baenre herself led the expedition—she was Mistress of Arach-Tinilith in those days—and she'd brought along dignitaries from Houses Xorlarrin, Agrach Dyrr, Barrison Del'Armgo, and other families of note. It was a momentous occasion, especially for me, because all these great ladies had come to arrest me.

"I never did find out if Greyanna instigated the affair. It was the kind of thing she would have done, but it needn't have been her. You'll scarcely credit it, but in those days, I was considered an insolent, uppity scapegrace, a far cry from the meek and modest gentleman you see before you today. A good many clerics may have suspected me of irreverence."

"This is what happened to Tsabrak," Syrzan said. "The priestesses arrested him, turned him into a drider, and drove him forth."

"Sometimes they mete out punishments even fouler," Pharaun said, "but first they examine you to determine your true sentiments. I hoped my mother would intervene. She was one of the great Matrons of Menzoberranzan, and I'd scored a number of coups for House Mizzrym, but she never said a word. Perhaps she believed me a traitor in the making or was reluctant to disagree with the Baenre. Maybe she simply found my predicament amusing. Miz'ri's like that.

"Be that as it may, the priestesses threw me in a dungeon and put me to the question, employing whips and other toys. Somehow I managed to resist the urge to make a spurious confession merely to stop the pain. A fellow wizard cast a mind-reading spell, only to slap up against the defenses most mages erect to protect their thoughts. I imagine an illithid would have smashed right through, but he was unequal to the challenge."

"Then you passed the test?" Syrzan asked.

"Alas, no," Pharaun laughed. "The examiners deemed the results inconclusive and accordingly asked a higher power to make the determination. They laid me on an obsidian altar, performed a dancing, keening, self-mutilating ritual together, and the torture chamber faded away. You'd think I would have been glad of it, wouldn't you, but my new surroundings were no less ominous."

Pharaun's captors had ignored his silver ring, obviously thinking it mere jewelry, if they noticed it at all. As soon as he'd looked at Syrzan, he'd discovered its magic operated even within the confines of the lich's phantasmal creation. He forced an idea into his subconscious and continued to prattle.

"The priestesses had drugged me to prevent my resisting their attentions, then used me with considerable brutality. It took me a while just to lift my battered head and look around. When I did, I perceived that I lay atop an enormous object with the shape of a staff or length of cord made of a substance that gave ever so slightly but was as strong as adamantine nonetheless. Otherwise, it would have disintegrated under its own weight. Far ahead, my perch fused at right angles with another such object, which connected with still others, the pattern spreading out to form, I suddenly realized, a spiderweb of insane complexity, huge enough to make a world. If it was attached to anything, the anchor points were too distant for me to see. Perhaps it just went on and on forever."

"The Demonweb," Syrzan said.

Pharaun surreptitiously examined his captor's talismans, using the magic in the silver ring, trying to figure out which one would allow an illithid to send a psionic "Call" to every orc and goblin in Menzoberranzan.

"Very good," the mage said. "I see you were paying attention when your teachers discoursed on the sundry planes of existence. I was indeed exiled to that layer of the Abyss where Lolth holds sway. I remembered hearing that the strands of the web were hollow and that much of the life of the place existed inside. Well, I certainly couldn't see any source of food or water on the outside, let alone a portal to take me home, so, still dazed and sick from the clerics' attentions, I started crawling and searching for a means of entry.

"Eventually, I might have found one, but I ran out of time. The strand I was traversing began to tremble. I peered about and saw her scuttling toward me."

"Lolth?" Syrzan asked.

"Who else? Her priestesses say she travels her domain in a mobile iron fortress, but she must have left it behind that day. I beheld the goddess herself in the guise of a spider as huge as the Great Mound of the Baenre. She's appeared to others in the same shape only smaller, but she was colossal when she came for me.

"I was terrified, but what was one to do about it? Run? Fight? Either effort would have been equally absurd. I exercised the only sensible option. I huddled atop the thread and covered my eyes.

"Alas, she denied me the comforts of blindness. Her will took hold of me and forced me to look up. She was looming over me, staring down with a circle of luminous ruby orbs.

"I felt as if her gaze was not merely piercing but dissolving me. The sensation was intolerable, I wanted to die, and in a way, she granted my wish.

"Her legs were immense, but they tapered to points at the ends, and, moving with a dainty precision, she used the two front-most members to dissect me. Did the process kill me? I don't know. By all rights, it should have, but if I lost my life, my spirit lingered in my divided flesh, still suffering the horror and pain.

"My soul was conscious, too, of its own destruction. Somehow, as the Spider Queen picked apart my flesh and bones, she was filleting my mind and spirit as well. It irks me that I can't describe how it felt. I hail from a race of torturers and spellcasters, but I still lack the vocabulary. Suffice it to say, it wasn't pleasant.

"In the end, every aspect of my self lay in pieces before her—for inspection, I realize now, though I was in too much agony and dread to work it out at the time. When she'd looked her fill, she put me back together."

Still careful not to betray himself, keeping his mind focused on the story, Pharaun decided it was the triangle that would power the alhoon's Call. The question then was what to do about it. The real brooch hung on the chest of Syrzan's physical body, back in the material world. The one inside his mind was a sort of echo. An analogue. Would depriving Syrzan of it accomplish anything?

Pharaun continued, "Do you think she reconnected every subtle juncture of my intellect and spirit exactly as they'd been before? Over the course of the next few years, I invested a fair amount of time brooding over that particular question, but it's unanswerable, so let it not detain us.

"After the Mother of Lusts cobbled me together, she tossed me back to my native reality, back onto the altar, in fact, thus indicating she found me acceptable. I imagine the clerics were disappointed. I've never known an inquisitor to rejoice in a suspect's acquittal.

"Perhaps they took a bit of solace in the discovery that I'd gone altogether mad. They carted me back to my family, who strapped me to a bed and debated whether it wouldn't be more convenient all around to smother me with a pillow. Sabal was my advocate and guard. She couldn't afford to lose her staunchest ally.

"Let's skip over all the raving and hallucinations, shall we? Eventually my wits returned, and as I reflected on my experiences in the Abyss, I realized that while Lolth was infinitely dreadful and malign, she was transcendently beautiful as well. I'd simply been too distraught to recognize it at the time."

The magic of both the ring and the brooch had accompanied the dreamers into the dream. Otherwise, Pharaun wouldn't be able to see the triangle glowing. So perhaps if he disposed of the talisman in this place, its counterpart in mundane reality would lose its enchantments.

Possibly not, also, but the Master of Sorcere felt he had to take a chance. He doubted he'd get another.

"Certainly she exemplified that supreme power to which all dark elves, particularly we wizards, aspire," the drow rambled on. "I felt inspired that she was our patron. She's worthy of us, as we are worthy of her."

"She impressed you," Syrzan said, its mouth tentacles wriggling, "as even the pettiest deity can overawe a mortal. Still, you're a scholar of the mysteries. You should know there are powers greater than Lolth, entities who, if they saw fit—"

Pharaun snatched the triangular ivory brooch off the undead mind flayer's soiled and shabby robe and slammed it down on the convoluted parapet at the edge of the bridge. The ornament didn't break. In desperation, he pulled back his arm to throw it. Perhaps the illithilich would have difficulty retrieving it from the murky pool below.

A cold, rough hand grabbed him by the collar and wrenched him down. He was powerless to resist. In the reality Syrzan had created for itself, it was as strong as a titan.

The lich ripped the brooch from Pharaun's grasp and thrust it into a pocket. It clutched the dark elf with both hands, leaned its head close, and wrapped its dry, flaking mouth tentacles over the mage's skull. Pharaun knew this was how mind flayers fed. They wormed their members into whatever orifices were most convenient and yanked out their victim's brain.

He wondered what would happen when Syrzan subjected his dream self to such treatment. Would his physical body perish, or would it survive as a living but mindless shell?

"Didn't you like my story?" Pharaun gasped. The lich's grip was squeezing the breath out of him. "You seemed quite engrossed. That was why I dared to hope I could catch you by surprise."

"You put your hands on me! I do not permit that!"

The mellifluous voice of the Prophet was roughening into an ugly combination of hisses and buzzes. The tentacles squeezed tighter

"Technically, these aren't my hands," Pharaun said. Goddess, it felt as if his skull was going to shatter! "Since this is all imaginary."

"You will tell me how you knew which charm to grab."

"My ring. It allows me to see and interpret patterns of magical force. No wizard should be without one."

"You were a fool to try to thwart me here in my private world. Don't you understand that inside this construct, I'm a *god*."

"I'm dead regardless," replied Pharaun, "and when a drow knows his life is forfeit, he bends his thoughts to revenge."

"But you're mistaken." Syrzan loosened the grip of the tentacles and said, "I'm not going to kill you. That would be wasteful. As you observed, my objective is to enslave all Menzoberranzan. Certainly you, with all your talents, will make a useful thrall. Had you not manhandled me, your bondage might have been relatively light, for I enjoy the society of other mages. Now I'm afraid you aren't going to enjoy it in the slightest."

Pain ripped through Pharaun's head. He screamed.

"Let me do it," Houndaer growled.

His scimitar at the ready, he stalked toward Ryld.

The Master of Melee-Magthere tried and failed to rise. As a student at the Academy and in all the years since, he'd studied techniques for transcending pain, but he'd never felt anything comparable to the invisible blow the undead illithid had struck him. It had been like a spear driving through his mind.

Syrzan emerged from its momentary trance and said, "No."

Houndaer turned. "No?" he asked. "You were right about them. Obviously."

"And I trust," said the lich, its mouth tentacles wriggling, "that you'll remember whose judgment is superior. Now that they're here, however, they might as well serve our cause as you hoped they would. It's just a matter of reshaping their minds."

The bard lifted an eyebrow and asked, "Can you do that?"

"Yes," said Syrzan, "but not instantaneously, and not now. I need my strength to give the Call."

It pulled Pharaun's silver ring off the unconscious drow's finger.

"Lock them up for the time being," the alhoon ordered.

"All right," said Tsabrak. "I hope you're going to fix it so we can all control them."

He too advanced on Ryld.

The weapons master struggled once again to rise. Someone lashed him over the head with the flat of a blade, and all the strength spilled out of him like wine from an overturned cup.

The next few minutes were a blur. Houndaer, Tsabrak, the bard, and another renegade carried their captives to a cell. It had the same grime and air of desolation as much of the rest of the castle, but someone, exhibiting a proper dark elf's sense of priorities, had gone to the trouble to refurbish the locks and restraints.

The rogues divested Ryld of his cloak and armor, then chained him to the wall. As he'd expected, the conspirators took more elaborate precautions with the wizard, even though Pharaun had suffered a violent seizure shortly after Syrzan stunned him, had apparently passed from that into complete unconsciousness, and showed no sign of rousing any time soon. In addition to shackling him, the rogues locked a steel bridle around his head, forcing the bit into his mouth to keep him from enunciating words of power or anything else. They inserted his forearms into the two ends of a hinged metal tube, a sort of muff or double glove that would make it impossible for him to gesture or crook his fingers into a cabalistic sign.

By the time they finished, Ryld's strength had begun to return, enough, at least, to permit him to speak.

"It'll get you, too," he croaked.

Houndaer turned, scowling. "What?"

"The lich. It doesn't want to share power. It's planning to turn every Menzoberranyr, including you, into its mind-slave. That's what illithids do."

"Do you think we trust the beast?" the Tuin'Tarl sneered. "We're not idiots. It'll serve its purpose, and we'll dispose of it."

"So you intend, but what if Syrzan's already working on subjugating you, so subtly you don't even know it? What if, when the time comes—"

Houndaer punched his former teacher in the mouth, dashing his head against the calcite wall.

"Shut up," the noble said. "You fooled me once and made me look like an imbecile. It's not going to happen again."

The rogues made their departure. With his spidery lower body, Tsabrak had to squeeze through the door. The last one out, the bard gave Ryld a wry smile and a shrug. The door slammed shut.

Ryld licked the salty taste of blood from his gashed lower lip.

"Pharaun," he said in a low tone. "Are you truly unconscious, or is it a trick?"

Slumped with the steel harness clamped around his head, the Master of Sorcere didn't respond. If not for the rise and fall of his chest, Ryld would have feared him dead.

The swordsman tried to go to Pharaun, but his chains were too short. He undertook an examination of the shackles. The cuffs fit tightly, and the locks were strong. The links were heavy, well forged, and anchored securely in the wall. Ryld had broken free of bonds a time or two in his turbulent early years, but without tools or a miracle, he wouldn't be sundering these.

Nor, denied the use of his voice and hands, was Pharaun likely to fare any better. Still, Ryld suspected the mage was his only hope. Pharaun was clever. Perhaps he could think of a workable ploy, if only he was conscious.

"*Wake up!*" Ryld roared. "Wake up, curse it. You've got to get us out of here!"

To add to the din, he beat a length of chain against the wall.

To no avail. He shouted until his throat was raw, but Pharaun didn't stir.

"Bleed it!" the weapons master swore.

He hunkered down on the floor and tried to work up some saliva to wash away the dryness in his mouth. As the renegades hadn't bothered to provide a water jug, spit was the best he could do.

"You have to wake up," he said in a softer voice. "Otherwise, they've beaten us, and we've never let anyone do that. Do you remember when we hunted that cloaker lord? We found out too late that it had *sixty-seven* other chasm rays in its raiding party, many more than our little band of third-year students was prepared to confront. But you said, 'It's all right, it just takes the proper spells to even the odds.' First you conjured a wall of fire . . ."

Ryld rambled on for hours, talking his throat raw, recounting their shared experiences as they occurred to him. Perhaps the stories would strike a spark in Pharaun's unconscious mind, and in any case, it was better than just sitting and wondering what life would be like after Syrzan corrupted his mind.

Finally the wizard's chin jerked up off his chest. His eyes were wild, and he tried to cry out. The bit turned the sound into a strangled gurgle even as it cut into the corners of his mouth. Beads of blood blossomed from the wounds.

"It's all right," Ryld said. "Whatever the lich did to you, it's over."

Pharaun took a deep breath and let it out slowly. Rationality returned to his eyes. Ryld got the feeling that if not for the harness, the wizard would have smiled his usual cheery smile. He nodded to the weapons master, thanking him for the reassurance, then he inspected the sheath constraining his hands. He bashed it on the floor a few times to see if he could jolt the catches open. They held with nary a rattle. He shook his head, sat still for several seconds, then closed his eyes and settled back against the wall, no doubt pondering their plight.

After several minutes, the wizard straightened up. He started scraping the heel of one boot against the side of the other.

Ryld felt a stir of excitement. He could only assume his fellow master had a talisman hidden inside the footwear. It was odd the wizard hadn't remembered until then, but perhaps it was a result of the seizure.

Like all drow boots, Pharaun's were high and fit snugly. By the time it slid off the mage's foot, Ryld was avid with curiosity to see . . . nothing. Nothing but trews and a stocking.

Pharaun set to work shoving off the other boot. Ryld wished he knew what his friend had in mind, but knew it would be pointless to ask. With his hands concealed, the spellcaster couldn't answer even in the silent drow sign language.

Eventually the second boot slipped free, whereupon Pharaun pushed off his socks. His bare feet were of a piece with his hands, slender and long, the digits included.

The wizard lifted his right foot, stared at it intently, and started curling and crossing the toes. He fumbled through a sequence of moves, then repeated it. It took Ryld another few moments to comprehend, and he didn't know whether to laugh or cry.

In point of fact, the Underdark abounded in creatures, Syrzan included, whose extremities differed notably from a dark elf's, yet who worked magic nonetheless. So maybe Pharaun had a chance. Maybe he could cast one of those spells that only required movement, not an incantation or material components.

But only if he could shift his feet and toes through the proper patterns, those precise and intricate passes he'd spent years learning to execute with his hands.

When the toes of his right foot grew tired, he started working with those of his left. After that, he shifted his weight back, lifted his legs, and practiced twining them together. Ryld might have found it quite a comical spectacle had his life not depended on the mage's success.

Soon Pharaun began to sweat and occasionally to tremble, which always forced him to stop and rest for a bit. After an hour, he moved on to the next phase of his experiment: putting the elements of the spell together, moving everything at the same time with the proper sequence and timing.

Ryld watched the process intently. He was no wizard, but to his untutored eye, it appeared that after a while, Pharaun was producing exactly the same pattern two times out of three. The rest he fumbled in one way or another.

Finally, breathing hard, he looked at the weapons master and shrugged.

"That's all right," the swordsman replied. "Two out of three is good odds."

Pharaun slumped back and spent the next few minutes resting. When he sat up and, heedless of the fresh blood that started from the corners of his mouth, he growled through the mask. He banged the box encasing his hands twice against the floor, then looked at Ryld.

"I understand," the warrior said. "Make noise. Bring someone."

Pharaun nodded. The cage around his head clinked.

"Ho!" Ryld shouted. "Somebody, come here! I'm a Master of Melee-Magthere. I know secrets about the defenses of the great Houses, secrets you must know for your plans to succeed. I'll trade them for my freedom!"

He continued in the same vein for several minutes, clashing his chains against the wall for emphasis. Meanwhile Pharaun lay motionless, as if he were still unconscious.

Finally, eyes appeared at the little barred window in the door.

"What?" the newcomer snarled. It wasn't a voice Ryld had heard before.

"I need to talk to you," the weapons master said.

"I heard," said the other drow. "You have secrets. The alhoon will rip them out of you, no bargain required."

"Syrzan said it would take time to turn us into mind-slaves," Ryld replied. "I have information you need before you unleash the under-creatures. Their rebellion will do you no good if the weapons masters strike them all dead before they even get started."

"How could the masters-of-arms do that?" asked the rogue.

"A secret," said Ryld, "that we brothers of the pyramid teach to a chosen few."

"I don't believe you."

"We've been studying war for millennia. Do you think we impart all we know to every young dullard who enrolls in the Academy, or is it likely we hold greater, deadlier mysteries in reserve?"

The rogue hesitated.

"All right, tell me. If there's anything to it, I'll set you free."

Ryld shrugged, rattling his fetters. They were already rubbing his wrists raw.

"Shout it through a closed door?" the weapons master asked. "Is that what you really want?"

"Wait."

The contempt in the prisoner's tone had reminded the rogue of a basic principle. It was best to keep information to yourself, at least until you figured out how to reap a benefit from sharing it. This rogue didn't want anyone overhearing what Ryld had to say.

The door clacked as a key turned in the lock. It creaked open, and the renegade stepped through. He was stocky, with a broken nose squashed across an angular face. He'd decorated rather nondescript clothing with gaudy ornaments, including a silver fillet set with garnets. His rapier hung from a baldric, the hilt of a dagger protruded from the top of either boot, and a hand crossbow dangled from his belt.

He stopped just inside the doorway, where he had every right to think himself safe. The cell was large enough, and the prisoners' shackles short enough, that he was beyond their reach. He swung the door shut behind him but didn't permit it to latch.

"All right," he said, "now you can tell me."

"First," said Ryld, "unchain me."

He thought he had to keep the renegade occupied for just a few more seconds, long enough for Pharaun to cast his spell.

The guard just laughed and said, "Don't be absurd."

"Why not?"

"You know why not."

"But you might just listen to the secrets and leave me imprisoned," said Ryld, watching Pharaun from the corner of his eye.

To his dismay, the wizard wasn't conjuring. He wasn't moving at all. Had he passed out again?

"You're caged," said the renegade, "and I'm not. Therefore, *you* will have to trust *me*, not the other way around."

Ryld scowled, meanwhile racking his brains for inspiration. With Pharaun inert, he was going to have to improvise a story to detain the rogue and pray the wizard would make a move before much longer.

"All right, I suppose I have no choice. Not far beyond Bauthwaf lies the entrance to a tunnel leading to the deepest reaches of the Underdark, where even our people do not—"

"What's this got to do with weapons masters killing slaves?" the guard demanded.

"Listen, and you'll find out. At the lower end of the passage is a mineral I've never seen anywhere else . . ." At last Pharaun moved his feet. Now, if only the renegade didn't notice. "When you crush the rock to powder . . ."

"Hey!"

Evidently the guard's peripheral vision was almost as good as Ryld's, for he pivoted toward Pharaun, but not in time. A disembodied hand made of pale yellow light appeared beside his shoulder and gave him a push.

The impetus sent him staggering closer to Ryld. The weapons master grabbed him and smashed his head against the wall until it left a sticky mess on the stone, then he searched the corpse and found a ring of keys clipped to its belt.

He discovered the one that opened his own restraints, and Pharaun's. The wizard flexed his fingers, restoring circulation, produced a silken handkerchief from his sleeve, and dabbed at the blood on the sides of his mouth.

"I think I'll establish a new school of magic," the wizard said. "Pedomancy—the sorcery of the feet."

"Why did you wait so long to throw the spell?" Ryld asked.

"I was looking for our friend's keys. It wouldn't have done any good to attack him had he not been carrying the means to release us from our fetters. His cape was hanging over them, and it took me a minute to spot them."

"I was certain something had gone wrong. Are you ready to get us out of here?"

"Momentarily," Pharaun said as he pulled on his socks and boots. "I think everything's going splendidly, don't you? We've acquired the knowledge we came for, and now we'll escape, just as planned."

"We didn't plan on having to do it without our gear."

"Please, don't harp on the obvious. It makes for a dreary conversation. Where exactly are we, by the way? Where's the nearest exit?"

"I don't know. They gave me a knock on the head before they carried us here. I think we're up inside the cavern ceiling."

"So we won't encounter a window or balcony unless we descend a ways, but we might find a door opening on a tunnel."

Ryld scavenged the dead rogue's weapons and *piwafwi*. The cloak was much too small for him, but would provide some protection nonetheless. The mail shirt, alas, he simply couldn't wear.

"No gear for me?" Pharaun asked.

"I'm the fighter, and I'll be standing in front."

"Well, when you put it that way . . ."

"Let's go."

The masters stood up. Ryld felt dizzy, swayed, but then recovered his balance. They started for the door, and something happened. It was like the blare of a trumpet and a white light, too, but it was neither. The weapons master didn't know what it was, only that it froze him in place until it faded away.

"What just happened?" he asked.

"The Call," Pharaun replied. "This close to the source, one can vaguely sense it even if one isn't a goblin. The slaves are rising."

T W E N T Y - O N E

When the instructors rounded the corner, Pharaun saw a rogue about five yards away. Well armed, the conspirator was striding purposefully along, perhaps to join one of the assassination squads that would descend on the city once the goblin rebellion plunged it into chaos.

He had good reflexes. As soon as he spotted the fugitives, he reached for the wall, no doubt to conceal himself behind a curtain of darkness.

Pharaun lifted his hands to cast darts of force—he had two such spells remaining, neither requiring a focal object—but Ryld was quicker. He shot his hand crossbow. The quarrel plunged into the renegade's eye, and he fell.

The masters skulked up to the corpse and crouched down to examine it. Pharaun was hardly surprised yet disappointed to find that the dead warrior hadn't been carrying any spell ingredients.

The Master of Sorcere hadn't lost faith in himself, but he realized that overconfidence coupled with ambition had lured him and Ryld into a desperate situation. They were stuck in the midst of their enemies. Without the proper triggers, most of the wizard's magic was unavailable to him, and the weapons master was feeling the effects of the blow on the head and Syrzan's psionic assault. Most people wouldn't have noticed, but Pharaun, who knew him well, could see subtle indications in the way he moved.

Well, at least Ryld wasn't bored.

Pharaun stole the dead male's hand crossbow, dirk, and *piwafwi*—including the insignia of a lesser House Pharaun assumed was enchanted in the same way as all the others. The mantle wasn't a bad fit but felt strange without the weight of the hidden pockets to which he was accustomed. At least, he hoped, he'd be able to levitate. Ryld exchanged the rapier he'd been wearing for the fallen drow's broadsword.

The Master of Melee-Magthere cocked his crossbow and loaded a fresh shaft in the channel. The fugitives stalked on down the hallway, and the walls screamed. Pharaun and Ryld screwed up their faces at the painful loudness. Blue sparks of discharged magic showered from the walls and ceiling, and a hot, raw stink of power fouled the air.

The screech stopped as suddenly as it had started, though it left echoes sobbing through the citadel.

"Alarm spell?" said Ryld, trotting onward.

"Yes," Pharaun said, racing to catch up. His ears were ringing. "Had I seen it, I would have dispelled it, but—"

"But as it stands, the rogues will be coming for us." Pharaun frowned. "Unless they're too busy getting ready to murder priestesses."

"No, they'll realize they have to catch us at any cost. If a spy slipped away from here and reported their plans to the Council, it would ruin everything for them."

"You're right, curse it."

The masters had been moving stealthily and therefore slowly ever since departing their cell, and they would have to sneak along even more warily, backtracking and detouring whenever they sensed their enemies were near. That would make it easier to get lost. The long-dead nobles had built their fortress according to a defensive strategy still occasionally employed in Menzoberranzan. The place was something of a maze. If a person had grown up there, that wouldn't pose a problem. He'd know every turn and dead end, but outsiders had a difficult time moving about. Outsiders like Pharaun and Ryld, who had yet to find an exit.

Perhaps, the wizard thought, the renegades will have trouble navigating as well.

Though they'd squatted in the castle, they might not know it as well as the original occupants had. It was possible they'd simply familiarized themselves with a few key areas and primary passageways and left the rest of the allegedly cursed and haunted keep pretty much alone.

Still, Pharaun knew it was only a matter of time until the hunters stumbled onto their prey, and he was correct. He and Ryld were traversing a gallery hung with musty phosphorescent tapestries when something rustled behind them. The masters pivoted. Silent in their drow boots, half a dozen warriors had appeared behind them and were leveling their crossbows.

Ryld crouched and lifted a fold of his cloak in front of his face. Pharaun copied the move. Two arrowheads plunged through his makeshift shield, which apparently wasn't as powerfully enchanted as the *piwafwi* Houndaer had taken from him. One quarrel hung up in the weave. The other hurtled right through and grazed the mage's shoulder, stinging him and slicing a shallow cut. He prayed it wasn't poisoned.

Hearing a ragged clatter, Pharaun uncovered his eyes. The rogues had dropped their crossbows and were charging. They'd already dashed too close for him to employ the incantation he would have preferred. Instead he cast darts of light and dropped two renegades. He discharged his crossbow and missed a third.

Ryld bellowed a war cry and sprang forward to meet the foes remaining. The broadsword flashed back and forth, thrusting, cutting, and parrying with the small, precise movements that characterized true mastery. Pharaun edged forward with his dirk in hand but never got a chance to use it. The rogues all died before he could advance into range.

Pharaun took stock of himself and decided he didn't have any venom in his system, but Ryld groaned, made a face, and clutched at his temple.

"What is it?" the wizard asked.

It seemed likely that one of the enemy had scored, but he didn't see any blood slipping between his friend's fingers, and head wounds bled copiously.

"A throbbing headache," said the swordsman. "Left over from Houndaer and Syrzan, I suppose, made worse when my heart started beating harder. I'm all right now."

"I rejoice to hear it." Pharaun turned, right into a second volley of quarrels.

He had no time to raise his cloak, dodge, or do anything else but gawk at the second band of renegades who'd crept up from the other direction. Miraculously, every shaft missed.

One of the newcomers shouted, "They're here!"

The guards charged, and Pharaun brandished a bit of spiderweb, the one spell focus he'd had no difficulty replacing. A mesh of taut, luminous cables appeared around the onrushing renegades. Anchored to the wall, the cables were as strong as rope and as sticky as glue. They snared and held the rogues.

All but the two in front. Either they'd been nimble enough to jump clear before the effect fully materialized, or their innate dark elf resistance to magic had protected them.

Undeterred by the loss of their comrades, the warriors drove onward into sword range. The one who focused on Pharaun had a birthmark staining his left profile.

Pharaun shot. The shaft hit the male square in the chest but glanced off his mail. The ugly male swung his sword in a flank cut. Pharaun twisted aside and commenced an incantation.

He had to dodge two more attacks before he finished. Shafts of light sprang from his fingertips.

Only one such spell left, he thought, and only one more chance to conjure a trap of webbing, too.

The missiles passed through the renegade's mail and sent him reeling backward. Wounded but still alive, the rogue gave his head a shake. Pharaun yanked his new dirk out of his belt and flung himself at the guard. The wizard rammed his point up under the ugly male's chin before the latter had quite recovered his wits.

Pharaun turned. Feinting low and striking high, Ryld whipped his broadsword through his opponent's neck. The renegade fell, his severed head tumbling away. For a moment, Pharaun felt a touch of relief, then he noticed his friend's grimace and the blood on his thigh, and heard the calls of other pursuers drawing near.

"It sounds as if *all* the rogues are hunting us," the wizard said. "What a gracious compliment."

"They heard the fight," Ryld replied. "They have some idea where we are, and thanks to you, this passage has become a cul-de-sac. We have to move—*now*."

"Perhaps you would have preferred me to let the rest of our attackers swarm all over us."

"Just move."

They did, with the prisoners in the web shouting imprecations after them. Pharaun soon discerned that Ryld was making an effort not to limp nor show any sort of distress but couldn't mask his pain completely.

The wizard considered leaving patches of darkness behind to hinder pursuit, but had he done so, he would have been marking his trail. He could only think of one trick he could use to evade the renegades, and hoped it wouldn't be necessary.

Twice, the masters sensed a band of rogues was near and hid in a room until they passed. Finally they found a staircase leading downward. Pharaun hoped their descent to the lower level would throw off the pursuit but soon realized it hadn't. Perhaps it was because the fugitives were leaving a trail of blood. Pharaun's little cut had stopped bleeding, but Ryld's gashed leg had not.

Despite himself, the burly swordsman began taking uneven strides, one shorter than the other. Pharaun heard a murmur of voices coming from behind and out of a side passage as well.

He said, "Stay where you are. I have an idea."

Ryld shrugged.

The wizard advanced a few paces down the corridor. He lifted his wisp of cobweb and chanted. Power groaned through the air, and crisscrossing cables sealed the corridor. The rogues he'd heard were on the other side. So was Ryld.

The swordsman looked at his friend through the interstices and said, "I don't understand."

"And you a master tactician. Truly, I regret this, but I could either stick with you and let your injuries retard my progress or else leave you behind as a rear guard to slow my pursuers. Considering how vulnerable I currently am, the choice was reasonably obvious."

"Damn you! How many times have I saved your life?"

"I've lost count. At any rate, this will make one more, in the course of which you'll finally be rid of your melancholy. Good-bye, old friend."

Pharaun turned and strode away.

He heard a crossbow clack, and flung himself to the side. The quarrel flew past him. Ryld had needed commendable accuracy to avoid snagging the missile in the adhesive mesh.

Pharaun glanced back and said, "Nice shot, but you might want to save your quarrels for the renegades."

He skulked on, and quickened his pace when someone shouted behind him, and metal clashed on metal.

🦂　　🦂　　🦂

Ryld quickly learned that one of the rogues was a wizard, and a deft one at that. He had no difficulty lobbing spells through the line his comrades had formed across the hall, leaving them unscathed but battering the weapons master with one attack after another.

So far the flares of power had seared and chilled the Master of Melee-Magthere but done no serious harm. He doubted that would last. He needed to put a stop to the magic before the mage slipped an attack through his natural resistance, and that meant breaking through the line

He faked a sidestep to the left, then dodged right. His wounded leg throbbed, and a soreness, the residue of Syrzan's attack, twisted through his mind. The pain slowed him just enough to render the deception ineffective. Urlryn, the long-armed, gap-toothed renegade on the right, another of Ryld's former students and a good one, met him with a wicked thrust to the belly.

As every warrior knows, you can't retreat at the same instant you're advancing. Ryld had no choice but to defend with the blade. He swept his broadsword across his body in a lateral parry. Urlryn tried to dip his point beneath the block, but moved just a hair too slowly. Ryld smashed his adversary's blade aside, loosening his grip in the bargain.

The weapons master started to riposte with a chest cut, then sensed movement on his flank. He pivoted. Hoping to take him unawares, the rogue next to Urlryn was swinging an axe at his knee. It was how warriors fought in a line. You killed the male who was focused on your neighbor.

Ryld leaped over the attack. When he landed, his leg screamed with pain and threatened to buckle beneath him. Shouting, he made it hold and cut at the axeman's belly. The broadsword crunched through mail, and the rogue toppled.

Ryld's blade was still buried in the axeman's guts when Urlryn and the other surviving warrior rushed him. The master floundered backward, dragging the broadsword free. Swords flashed at him, and somehow, even off-balance, he dodged them, but in so doing, fell on his rump.

The rogues scrambled forward to finish him. He surprised the other stranger with a bone-shattering kick to the ankle, knocking him reeling backward, then reared up on one knee, his sword raised in a high guard for what he knew was coming.

Urlryn's blade crashed down on his own, and he felt the jolt all the way to his shoulder. With both feet planted beneath him, the renegade could bring all his strength to bear. Ryld couldn't.

But he was bigger and more powerful than his adversary and was nicely positioned to hamstring other drow. Teeth gritted, he maintained his defense until his enemy faltered, then whipped the broadsword behind the rogue's leg for a drawing cut.

Urlryn let out a shrill cry and staggered sideways. Ryld heaved himself up and turned toward the wizard, only to discover he could no longer see him. Deprived of his wall of warriors, the spellcaster had conjured another defender, a vaguely bearish thing with folded bat wings and luminous crimson eyes, so huge it nearly filled the corridor.

Ryld had watched Pharaun exercise the famous Mizzrym talent for illusion on numerous occasions, and his experiences stood him in good stead. He sensed, though he couldn't say how, that the demon bear was just a phantasm. He limped forward, flicked the broadsword at it, and it popped like a fungus discharging a cloud of spores. It was strange to think that, had he believed in it, it could have torn him to shreds.

The rogue mage turned tail. Ryld didn't want the bastard to reappear and try to kill him again later, so he gave chase. His head and wounded leg seemed to scream in unison, and he had to stop. The sorcerer scuttled round a corner and disappeared.

As Ryld waited for the pain to subside, he realized he couldn't survive many more fights in his present condition. He either had to escape his foes posthaste or shed his disabilities.

Sadly, he had just about come to the conclusion that he was fated to wander through the castle, ducking his enemies the while, until pure luck led him to an exit. That could take hours.

He had reason to hope he wouldn't need nearly as long to revitalize himself, but he'd leave himself vulnerable during the process. He wouldn't be able to sneak in the opposite direction whenever he detected a party of hunters. He'd have to stay in one place. Still, it seemed the better option.

He skulked along the corridor, peering into doorways. One led to a desolate training hall. The target mannequins looked like ghosts in their shrouds of spiderweb.

Near the right-hand wall were tiers of seats, from which spectators could watch the warriors train. If Ryld crouched down behind the structure, no one would see him without making a careful search of the entire room.

Besides, the master thought, going to ground in a salle might bring him luck. The dark powers knew, he needed it.

He limped behind the sculpted seats and sat down on the floor with his legs crossed. He rested his hands on his thighs, closed his eyes, and commenced a breathing exercise.

Spellcasters smugly imagined they were the only folk who truly knew how to meditate. They were mistaken. The brothers of Melee-Magthere had mastered the practice as well. It helped them reach the highest level of martial proficiency.

Spellcasters. The thought reminded him of Pharaun. It brought the shock and anger flooding back.

But at the moment, those feelings were an impediment. He had to relax and empty his mind.

He could heal the wound Syrzan had left inside his head. He could stop his leg bleeding. He could banish pain and fatigue and tap his body's deepest reservoirs of strength.

If only the enemy gave him time.

$$\text{\Large\&} \qquad \text{\Large\&} \qquad \text{\Large\&}$$

Pharaun groped his way onward for just a few more minutes, then found another staircase, this one a narrow spiral leading downward. It was almost as if the mysteriously silent Lolth had returned long enough to reward him for his treachery.

If so, he soon had cause to recall that she was a fickle and treacherous entity herself. He reached the bottom of the steps, headed down a hallway with a high, arched ceiling, and heard another band of hunters. It sounded as if they were just about to round the corner dead ahead. Pharaun looked around at the blank walls. The corridor lacked any doorways into which a fugitive might duck.

The wizard could run, but he didn't want to retreat back the way he'd come. He could evoke a curtain of darkness, but that would alert the rogues that someone was hiding behind it. He could throw darts of force, but it would exhaust his offensive magic. He decided to take a chance.

Concentrating on the stolen House insignia, he shed his weight and floated upward to stretch out horizontally, his spine pressed against the crest of the rounded ceiling.

The hunters passed below him, oblivious to his presence. He stared down, looking for a fellow mage. If there was a chance he could obtain new spell foci, he might attack and the odds be damned, but the males were all warriors.

Once they'd gone by, he drifted back down to the ground and skulked onward. He got turned around once more, then unexpectedly found himself before a small service entrance to a stable much like the one in his family's castle. Moldy stone troughs, casks, mounting blocks, and rusty iron-ring hitches defined regular patterns across the floor, while musty, rotting tack hung along the walls. The aerial steeds were long gone, stolen by the conquerors, evidently, as he didn't see any bones. Two rogues stood watch, guarding the huge sliding doors.

Pharaun smiled, threw his last darts of light, and, without waiting to see how much damage they did, broke from cover and sprinted toward the sentries.

One renegade coughed blood and fell. The other appeared unaffected. A nice-looking fellow with a single elegant tendril dangling beside each cheek, he turned, spotted Pharaun, and calmly lifted his crossbow.

The wizard threw himself flat, and the bolt whizzed over his head. Still prone, he shot his own crossbow. The shaft plunged into the renegade's chest.

The rogue snarled, drew his scimitar, and advanced, but only for three steps. He stopped, and his arm fell, his sword clattering against the floor. An astonished look on his face, he dropped to his knees.

Rising, Pharaun noticed that the dying male's garments were as tasteful as his coiffure.

"Who's your tailor?" Pharaun asked, but the renegade merely fell facedown. "Ah, well."

The wizard strode on to one of the outside doors, unbolted it, and shoved it open. Perhaps the casters were magical, for they worked as well as ever. The panel rolled easily and quietly aside.

On the other side was a sheer drop to the glowing palaces a thousand feet below. Silently thanking the dead guard's House, he touched the stolen brooch and sprang over the edge.

chapter

T W E N T Y - T W O

Pharaun could float down a thousand feet, or he could fall, relying on levitation to slow his descent at the end. The latter course was dangerous. If he waited too long to counteract the pull of gravity, he would break bones or even pulp himself when he landed.

Still, he chose to plummet, because of what he saw beneath him.

He'd lost track of time inside the rogues' citadel, but it was plain that the Call had gone forth around the black death of Narbondel, when most dark elves had gone home for the night. With few drow about to contest them for possession of the streets, the undercreatures had erupted from their kennels to kill, loot, and destroy. Pharaun couldn't make out individuals, but he could see the mobs as great surging, formless masses like the living jellies that infested certain caverns, and he could certainly see the fires they were setting. He could smell the strange, foul smoke of burning stone, and he could hear the goblins shouting.

Perhaps the embattled commoners looked to the noble Houses for succor. If so, they waited in vain. Sorcerous power flashed white and red from the windows and baileys of the stalactite castles as the nobles struggled with their own rebellious slave soldiers. For the time being, at least, the drow were pinned down, unable to brace the marauders outside their own walls.

A house was growing larger and larger beneath Pharaun's boots. He made himself lighter than air but still slammed down hard. The impact knocked the wind and the sense out of him, and when his wits returned, he was bouncing upward again.

Restoring a portion of his weight, he achieved a more graceful landing, flattened himself against the roof, and peered about. The goblins weren't running amok in his immediate vicinity—not yet— so he jumped down onto the street. Glad the Bazaar was just three blocks away, he dashed in that direction.

He'd almost reached his destination when a motley assortment of scaly little kobolds, pig-faced orcs, and shaggy, hulking bugbears surged from an alley. So far, the revolt was going well for them. They'd manage to lay their hands on spears, swords, and axes, and bloody them, too.

Pharaun ran even faster. A javelin flew past him, but the thralls didn't chase him. Evidently they were more interested in other prey.

When the wizard reached the marketplace, he cursed, for the riot had arrived there ahead of him. Undercreatures were looting and burning the stalls, creating patches of dazzling glare. Some of the merchants had fled. Others attempted to defend their wares, unsuccessfully if they relied on goblin underlings for assistance.

Pharaun skirted the edge of the Bazaar, witnessing scenes of carnage as he skulked along. Laughing, a goblin flogged his master's corpse with a scourge. A bugbear used her manacles to strangle a merchant. Trapped in a blazing stone pen, riding lizards hissed and scuttled back and forth in fear.

The first stall Pharaun had hoped to find intact was burning merrily, and the second was crawling with gnolls, growling, whining, and barking as they pawed through the vendor's goods. The Master of Sorcere knew of only one more possibility on the perimeter of the

Bazaar. Should that one be lost to him as well, he would either have to venture deeper into the burning, orc-infested maze of stalls or conceive another plan.

Warty, bearded ogres overturned a twelve-wheeled wagon, dumping out the dark elves who'd been making a stand inside. A walking mushroom, taller than any of the brutes, and, with its slender, fluted stem, far more graceful, swung wide to avoid the little massacre.

Pharaun slipped around the slaughter as well. A few more strides brought him to a scene that, after the carnage he'd just witnessed, seemed almost unreal. The westernmost portion of the marketplace was quiet. Some of the merchants had armed themselves and taken up positions outside their tents and kiosks, but they seemed calm and unafraid.

Over the course of an adventurous life, Pharaun had witnessed the same phenomenon before. Under the proper circumstances, it was possible for folk to remain essentially oblivious to a pitched battle raging just a few yards away.

The wizard ran on. Ahead, a luminous green circle scribed on the ground surrounded a commodious stall built of hardened fungus. A heavyset male stood in the doorway with an arbalest in his hand and a toad, his familiar, squatting on his shoulder. He wore a nightshirt, and his feet were bare. The merchant scowled when he spotted Pharaun.

"Stay back," he said, his throaty voice even deeper than Ryld's.

Pharaun halted, took a breath, and wound up coughing, thanks to the smoke fouling the air.

"My dear master Blundyth, is that any way to greet a faithful customer?"

"It's the way to greet the madman who attacked a patrol only yesterday."

That was right, Pharaun thought, it had been only yesterday. So much had happened since, it felt like a year.

"My past indiscretions no longer matter," the Mizzrym said. "Do you have any notion what's going on?"

"You mean the smoke and commotion over yonder?" Blundyth nodded to the east. "I guess a merchant's eliminating the competition. It's nothing to do with me, though I'm ready if trouble spills this way."

"Would that were true," said Pharaun. "Alas, none of us is truly ready for tonight. Have you glanced up over the roof of your shop?"

He pointed to the orange light presently flickering in the east.

"The nobles are up to something," Blundyth said. "Maybe some of the Houses have joined forces to wipe out a common rival. Again, it's nothing to do with me."

"You're mistaken. All across the city, the undercreatures are rebelling."

Blundyth snorted, "You *are* mad."

"Don't you or your neighbors own thralls?"

"Of course. They're off somewhere."

"Indeed. Off preparing to cut your throats."

"Just go away, Master Mizzrym." Blundyth shifted his grip on the staff and added, "We always got along. Don't make me hurt you."

"The orcs pose a considerable threat. I know how to oppose it, but I need your help. I still have credit here, don't I?"

"I don't sell to outlaws. I don't want any trouble with the priestesses."

Pharaun looked into the merchant's eyes and saw that he'd never convince him.

"Too bad. You'll regret this decision. In just a few minutes, most likely, but by then it will be too late."

The master turned and strode away, but once he was out of Blundyth's sight, he circled back around. Creeping through the cramped spaces between the booths, he approached the burly drow's stall from the side. As he skulked along, he listened to hear if the undercreatures were coming closer, but he couldn't tell. He suspected that one of the cursed sound baffles was muffling the noise.

At any rate, he reached the dimpled fungal structure without any orcs attacking him. He swept his hands through a mystic pass and whispered an incantation. The protective circle of light winked out of existence.

Pharaun ran to the stall, floated upward, and swung himself onto the roof. The petrified fungus supported him like stone. Blundyth cursed and came stalking around the side of the stand, his crossbow at the ready. Pharaun thought he'd better make sure the merchant didn't get a chance to use it.

The wizard jumped off the roof onto Blundyth's back. He knew he hadn't executed the move as nimbly as poor Ryld would have, but it worked. It slammed the merchant to his knees. The toad hopped away.

Clinging to his victim, the master drove his dirk repeatedly into the big male's side. Sometimes the blade plunged deep, and sometimes it caught on a rib. Blundyth flailed and bucked for a while, couldn't break free, then tried to aim the arbalest back over his shoulder. Pharaun ducked away from it. Finally the merchant fell sideways, pinning his attacker's knife and hand beneath him.

Pharaun dragged his hand free, but didn't bother with the dirk. He was about to procure a set of vastly superior weapons. He wiped his bloody fingers on Blundyth's clothing, then rose and headed for the entrance to the stall.

Blundyth's neighbors watched him, but didn't interfere. As the dead male might have observed, his murder was nothing to do with them.

The wizard's supply shop was as well-stocked as usual. Jars, bottles, and boxes stood on limestone shelves, and a greenish mirror glowed on a wooden stand in the corner. The air smelled of spices, herbs, bitter incense, and decay.

Blundyth's *piwafwi* lay carelessly draped across a chest, and it was the first item Pharaun appropriated. The cloak fit him like a tent, but it had the customary row upon row of hidden pockets. Next he examined the vials and drawers, finding the magical components that corresponded to the spells he had prepared. With every one he filched, he felt a little better, almost like a cripple regaining the use of his legs.

As he worked his way across the room, he spotted a pair of boots sitting atop a little cupboard. They were plainly special in some way, for the maker had tooled runes into the leather. Without his silver ring, Pharaun lacked the ability to instantly discern what virtues they possessed, but playing a hunch, he decided to take the time to try them on.

The boots squirmed, molding themselves to his feet, then quivered against his flesh like an animal eager to run. He took an experimental step, and the magical footwear kicked off on its own, augmenting the strength of his legs and propelling him all the way across the shop in a single bound.

Not bad, he thought. Not as good as a flying carpet, but helpful nonetheless.

He took a few more strides, getting the feel of the boots, then headed out. Just as he exited the shop, a howling, shrieking cacophony exploded out of the air. An instant later, a horde of undercreatures—orcs, mostly, with a sprinkling of long-armed goblins—came charging out of the stands of stalls and kiosks to the east.

Blundyth's neighbors gaped in utter astonishment. For some, the instant of consternation was fatal. The undercreatures swarmed over them like ants harvesting the carcass of a mouse.

Some of the remaining merchants bolted. Others shot their hand crossbows, or conjured flashes of magic. One optimist sought to cow the rebels with threats, invective, and commands until a scrofulous orc, slopping the liquid out of a tin bucket, threw some of Syrzan's liquid fire on him. The incendiary ignited flesh as easily as stone.

His great blanket of a *piwafwi* flapping around him, Pharaun ran. Each amplified stride bounced him off the ground, but thanks to the virtues of the magic boots, he always landed softly.

A pair of orcs glared at him and hefted their spears. He whispered an incantation, and a ragged blackness, the essence of death itself, danced among the undercreatures. They collapsed, already rotting.

For the moment at least, Pharaun was in the clear. He raced on, while all around him, his city went down in blood and fire.

"You must know some song, some magic, to track an enemy," Houndaer said.

"If I did, I'd be singing it," Omraeth said curtly. "Now be quiet. If the masters hear us coming, they'll do their best to evade us."

"He's right," said Tsabrak, scuttling along on his eight segmented legs. "Shut up, or we'll never get this done."

Houndaer was wearing Ryld Argith's greatsword strapped across his back, and for an instant he fairly quivered with the urge to try it out on his companions. He wasn't used to such insolence, not from other males, and certainly not from a degraded creature like a drider.

Yet he restrained himself, because he needed them. He prayed he'd be the one to catch up with the fugitives, who'd made him look a fool in the eyes of the other renegades, but he knew he couldn't kill both of them by himself.

Tsabrak raised his hand and whispered, "Wait!"

"What is it?" Houndaer asked.

Instead of replying, the half-spider started taking deep breaths. His nostrils flared. He turned this way and that, then crouched down to sniff along the floor. His front legs bent, and his arachnid lower body tilted like a tray to bring his dark elf head down.

"Did you pick up the scent?" Houndaer asked.

He felt an upswelling of excitement, and made a conscious effort to quell it. He didn't doubt that Tsabrak smelled something pertinent, but over the course of the last hour, the brute, whose metamorphosis had evidently altered his perceptions, had picked up the trail several times only to lose it again.

"Follow me," said Tsabrak, nocking an arrow.

The drider led his companions to the arched entrance to a training hall, where target mannequins stood in shrouds of spiderweb and a tally board hung on the left-hand wall. Over the years, the chalk had lost most of its phosphorescence, but Houndaer could still read the score of a fencing bout in faintly gleaming ciphers.

Peer as he might, however, he could see no sign of Masters Argith and Mizzrym. He gave Tsabrak a questioning and somewhat impatient glance. The drider responded by pointing at the floor.

When a proud noble family had held the castle, a workman in their employ had painted the floor with pistes and dueling circles. Like the chalk, the magical enamel still radiated a trace of light. At one spot, a spatter of blood was occluding it.

Houndaer's pulse ticked faster. He looked up at the drider and mouthed, "Where?"

Tsabrak led them toward the tiers of seats on the right. The noble noticed for the first time that a space separated the sculpted calcite risers and the wall.

Elsewhere in the castle, one hunter shouted to another.

Relax, thought Houndaer. It's *my* kill.

He held his breath as he and his underlings—for that they were, even if they, by virtue of belonging to the conspiracy, imagined otherwise—peeked around the edge of the steps. Master Argith was sitting cross-legged a few yards down the aisle.

The Tuin'Tarl instantly pointed his crossbow. Indeed, he nearly pulled the trigger before he took in all the details of the scene. His former teacher sat motionless, his eyes shut. To all appearances, he was unconscious, or in any case oblivious to the advent of his foes. Master Mizzrym was nowhere to be seen.

Ryld's passivity left Houndaer unsure as to the best course of action. Should he and his minions summarily dispatch the spy or seize the opportunity to take him prisoner? If the weapons master was dead, he couldn't tell them what had become of his partner.

Then the noble realized that while he'd stood pondering the matter, Tsabrak had drawn back his bow string and sighted down the arrow. Houndaer lifted a hand to signal him to desist, then thought better of it. Master Argith was a superb warrior even by the standards of Melee-Magthere. That was why, when a student, the Tuin'Tarl had admired him so, and had been so eager to recruit him. Perhaps it would be wiser to kill him while they had the chance.

Besides, Houndaer was reluctant to risk the vexation of giving Tsabrak an order and having it ignored.

He lifted his hand crossbow. He and the drider took their time aiming, and why not? Ryld was still unaware of them.

Tsabrak released the string, and Houndaer pulled the trigger. The shafts leaped at the still-motionless weapons master. The noble had no doubt the two missiles would suffice. They were flying true, and the heads were poisoned. It was strange and vaguely unsatisfying to dispatch a master of war so easily, as if it was vengeance on the cheap.

Then, when surely it was too late to react, Ryld moved. He twitched himself out of the way of the crossbow quarrel and caught the hurtling arrow in his hand.

Swiftly, yet somehow without the appearance of haste, the weapons master flowed to his feet and advanced. His bloody thigh didn't hinder him in the slightest. His face and eyes were empty, like those of a medium awaiting communion with the dead.

His voice pitched deep, Omraeth sang a quick rhymed couplet. Power glittered through the air. Evidently the spell was supposed to afflict Ryld, but as far as Houndaer could observe, it didn't. The huge male just kept coming. Tsabrak loosed another arrow, and the teacher slapped it out of the air with his broadsword.

Tsabrak and Houndaer dropped their bows and drew their swords. The drider spat poison on his blade. They'd engage Ryld while he was still in the cramped space behind the seats with no room to maneuver. Omraeth took up a position behind his comrades, where he could augment their efforts with bardic magic.

Houndaer felt a pang of fright and willed the feeling away. He had nothing to fear. It was three against one, wasn't it, and the one had no mail. Indeed, by the look of him, he might not even have any wits.

Except that then he proved he did. Ryld touched the vertical surface that was the back of the steps. He summoned darkness, blinding his foes.

Houndaer hacked madly, and sensed Tsabrak doing the same. Darkness or no, when the spy lunged forward, they'd cut him to pieces. Their swords split nothing but air.

After a few seconds, Omraeth shouted, "Come back this way! Now!"

Houndaer and Tsabrak turned and blundered their way toward the sound of their comrade's voice. The drider's envenomed sword bumped the Tuin'Tarl's arm, but fortunately without sufficient force to penetrate his armor and *piwafwi*.

When Houndaer stumbled out of the murk, Master Argith was in the center of the salle. Under the cover of darkness, he'd made it to the top of the steps and bounded down the other side. He had a good chance of reaching the exit unchecked.

He didn't take it, though. Standing in the center of one of the faintly luminous circles, he settled into a fighting stance. He hadn't scrambled over the steps to flee, rather to reach a battleground more to his liking.

Houndaer swallowed away a dryness in his mouth. Ryld hadn't the sense to run? Well, good. Then they'd kill him.

The noble and drider fanned out to come at the Master of Melee-Magthere from opposite sides. Omraeth hung back and commenced another song.

Advancing to meet his adversaries, Master Argith glided through the first of three moves—parry, feint high, slash low—of one of the broadsword katas he'd taught Houndaer back on Tier Breche. The noble discerned an instant too late that the purpose was to distract attention from the crossbow in the weapons master's other hand. The dart plunged into Omraeth's throat, ending his song in an ugly gurgle and dissipating the charged heaviness of arcane force accumulating in the air. The spellsinger fell backward, and it was two to one.

Houndaer told himself it didn't matter. Not when he was wielding Ryld's own greatsword, a weapon that could supposedly shear through anything, and Tsabrak's blade was dripping poison. They only needed to land one light little cut to incapacitate their foe.

Ryld gave ground before them. Houndaer assumed he wanted to put his back against the wall, so neither of his opponents could get behind him, but with an agility astonishing in so massive a fighter, Ryld changed direction. In the blink of an eye, he was driving forward instead of back, plunging at the half-spider on his left.

Startled, Houndaer faltered, then scrambled toward Ryld and the drider. It would take him a few heartbeats to close the distance.

In that time, Ryld charged in on Tsabrak's right, the side opposite the creature's sword arm. A drider's spidery lower half was sufficiently massive that, like a mounted warrior, he had difficulty striking or parrying across his torso.

Tsabrak slashed at the weapons master's head. The stroke was poorly aimed, and Ryld didn't bother to duck or parry, simply concentrated on his own attack.

Tsabrak made a desperate effort to heave himself aside. Still, Ryld's broadsword crunched through the top of one of the drider's chitinous legs. Tsabrak cried out and lurched off-balance.

Stepping, Ryld whirled his weapon around for what would surely be the coup de grâce. Houndaer shouted a war cry, ran a final stride, and swung the greatsword. He wasn't in a proper stance, and the stroke was a clumsy one, but it sufficed to drive the weapons master back. Ryld knew better than anyone how deadly was that enormous blade.

As soon as the stroke whizzed past, the master advanced with a thrust to the chest. Houndaer wrenched the greatsword around for a parry. It should have been impossible to bring such a huge weapon about so quickly, but it seemed to grow as light as a roll of parchment in his hands. Ryld's broadsword caught on one of the hooks just above the leather-girt ricasso.

Ryld retreated, snatching his weapon free. Houndaer shifted the greatsword into a middle guard, and Tsabrak hobbled up beside him. The drider's face twisted in pain, and pungent fluid spattered rhythmically from his wound.

Ryld continued to back away. The rogues spread out again, though not so widely as before. Tsabrak began to make a soft whining sound in the back of his throat.

Then, seemingly without any windup, just a sudden extension of his arm, Ryld threw his sword. Though the weapon wasn't intended for such an action, it streaked through the air as straight and sure as an arrow. The point plunged into Tsabrak's chest.

The drider's eyes widened. He coughed blood, then flopped forward at the waist, dropping his sword. His spider half, slower to die than the upper portion, continued to limp forward.

It was all right, though, because Ryld had no melee weapon save for a dagger, which would surely be of little use against a blade as long as the greatsword. Houndaer rushed in to deliver the finishing stroke.

"*Tuin'Tarl!*" he screamed.

His face still as blank as a zombie's, the weapons master dodged to the side.

Houndaer turned, following the target, and saw that Ryld had ducked behind one of a row of wooden mannequins. Up close, the crudely carved dummies were oddly disquieting figures, smirking identical smiles despite their countless stigmata of dents and gashes.

Ryld stood poised, waiting, and Houndaer discerned the spy's intent. When his adversary lunged around one side of the dummy, the master would circle in the opposite direction, thus maintaining a barrier between them.

Houndaer saw no reason to play that game, not if his new sword was as keen as it was supposed to be. He brought the blade around in a low arc. It tore away the mannequin with scarcely a jolt, depriving Ryld of his pitiful protection.

Unfortunately, the weapons master sprang forward at the very same instant, before Houndaer could pull the greatsword back for another cut. Ryld slashed at the noble's throat.

Houndaer frantically wrenched himself back, interposing his weapon between himself and the spy, before recognizing that the cut had been more of a feint than anything else. Ryld had tricked him into assuming a completely defensive attitude, then seized the opportunity to dash past him. Houndaer cut at the master's back but only managed to tear his billowing cloak.

The Tuin'Tarl gave chase, and Tsabrak, dying or dead but still mindlessly ambulatory, staggered into his path. Houndaer shouted in frustration and cut the drider down.

When the hybrid fell, the noble could see what was happening behind him. Ryld had reached Tsabrak's fallen sword. Heedless of the venom drying on the blade, the teacher slipped his toe under the weapon, flipped it into the air, and caught it neatly by the hilt. His expression as unfathomable as ever, he came on guard and advanced.

I can still kill him, Houndaer thought, I still have the reach on him.

Aloud, he shouted, "Here! I've got one of the masters here!"

Ryld stepped to the verge of the distance, then hovered there. Confident in his ability to defend, he wanted Houndaer to strike at him. A fencer couldn't attack without opening himself up.

At first, the noble declined to oblige. He intended to wait his opponent out. Ryld beat his blade.

The clanging impact startled a response out of him, but at least it was a composed attack. Feint to the chest, feint to the flank, cut low and hack the opponent's legs out from underneath him.

Even as he flowed into the final count, he remembered Ryld teaching him the sequence, and sure enough, the instructor wasn't fooled. He parried the genuine low-line attack, then riposted to Houndaer's wrist. The broadsword bit through his gauntlet and into the flesh beneath.

Ryld pulled his weapon free in a spatter of gore. He drove deeper, cutting at Houndaer's torso. The Tuin'Tarl floundered backward out of the distance, meanwhile heaving the greatsword back into a threatening position.

His bloody wrist throbbed, and the huge blade trembled. It was brutally hard to hold it up, its enchantments notwithstanding. He choked up on it, his weakened hand clutching the ricasso, but that only helped a little. He listened for the sound of another party of rogues rushing to his aid. He didn't hear it.

"Well done, Master Argith!" Houndaer declared. "I declare myself beaten. I yield."

Ryld stalked forward, broadsword at the ready.

"Please!" said the Tuin'Tarl. "We always got along, didn't we? I was one of your most dutiful students, and I can help you get out of here."

The teacher kept coming, and Houndaer saw that his face wasn't empty or expressionless after all. It might be devoid of emotion, but it revealed a preternatural, almost demonic concentration, focused entirely on slaughter.

Houndaer saw his own inescapable death there, and, suffused with a strange calm, he lowered the greatsword. Ryld's blade sheared into his chest an instant later.

🕷 🕷 🕷

The echoing metallic crash startled Quenthel. It was well that she'd spent a lifetime learning self control, for otherwise, she might have cried out in dismay.

She and her squad were patrolling the temple. After the events of the past four nights it would have been mad to relax their vigilance, but as the hours had crept uneventfully by, her troops began to speculate that the siege was over. After all, it was supposed to be. The bone wand had supposedly turned the malignancy of the past night's sending back on she who cast the curse.

Yet Quenthel had found she wasn't quite ready to share in the general optimism. Yes, she'd turned an attack back on its source, but that didn't necessarily mean her faceless enemy had succumbed to the demon's attentions. The spellcaster could have survived, and if so, she could keep right on dispatching her unearthly assassins.

From the sound of it, another such had just broken in, and Quenthel didn't have another little bone wand.

For a moment, the Baenre felt a surge of fear, perhaps even despair, and she swallowed it down.

"Follow me," she snapped.

Perhaps her subordinates would prove of some use for a change.

Their tread silent in their enchanted boots, the priestesses trotted in the direction of the noise. Greenish torchlight splashed their shadows on the walls. Parchment rattled as one novice fumbled open a scroll. Female voices began to shout. Power reddened the air

324

for an instant and brushed a gritty, pricking feeling across the priestesses' skin.

"It's not a demon," said Yngoth, twisting up from the whip handle to place his eyes on a level with Quenthel's own. Her stride made his scaly wedge of a head bob up and down.

"No?" she asked. "Has my enemy come to continue our duel in person?"

She hoped so. With her minions at her back, Quenthel would have a good chance of crushing the arrogant fool.

But alas, it wasn't so. Her course led her to the entry hall with the spider statues. The poor battered valves hung breached and crooked once again. This time the culprit was a huge, disembodied, luminous hand, floating open with fingers up as if signaling someone to halt. A lanky male in a baggy cloak had taken shelter behind the translucent manifestation from the spears and arrows that several priestesses were sending his way.

Quenthel sighed, because she knew the lunatic, and he couldn't possibly be her unknown foe. By all accounts, he'd been too busy down in the city the past few days.

She gestured with the whip, terminating the barrage of missiles.

"Master Mizzrym," she called. "You compound your crimes by breaking in where no male may come unbidden."

Pharaun bent low in obeisance. He looked winded, and, most peculiarly for such a notorious dandy, disheveled.

"Mistress, I beg your pardon, but I must confer with you. Time is of the essence."

"I have little to say to you except to condemn you as the archmage should have done."

"Kill me if you must." The giant hand winked out of existence and he continued, "Given my recent peccadilloes, I half expected it. But hear my message first. The undercreatures are rebelling."

Quenthel narrowed her eyes and asked, "The archmage sent you here with this news?"

"Alas," the mage replied, "I was unable to locate him but knew this was something that must be brought to the attention of the most senior members of the Academy. I realize no one ever dreamed it could happen, but it has. Walk to the verge of the plateau with me, and you'll see."

The Baenre frowned. Pharaun's manner was too presumptuous by half, yet something in it commanded attention.

"Very well," she said, "but if this is some sort of demented jest, you'll suffer for it."

"Mistress," Minolin said, "he may want to lead you into—"

Quenthel silenced the fool with a cold stare, then turned back to Pharaun.

"Lead on, Master of Sorcere."

In point of fact, the high priestess didn't have to walk all the way to the drop-off to tell that something was badly wrong in the city below. The wavering yellow glare of firelight and a foul smoky tang in the air alerted her as soon as she stepped outside the spider-shaped temple. Heedless of her dignity, she sprinted for the edge, and Pharaun scrambled to keep up with her.

Below her, portions of Menzoberranzan—portions of the *stone*, how could that be?—were in flames. Impossibly, even the Great Mound of the Baenre sprouted a tuft of flame at its highest point, like a tassel on a hat. Once Quenthel's eyes adjusted to the dazzling brightness, she could vaguely make out the mobs rampaging through the streets and plazas.

"You see," said Pharaun, "that's why I ran halfway across the city, dodging marauders at every turn, to reach you, my lady. If I may say so, the situation's even worse than it may look. By and large, the nobles haven't even begun reclaiming the streets. They're bogged down on their estates fighting their own household goblins. Therefore, I suggest you—"

The mage was smart enough to stop talking at the sight of Quenthel's glare.

"We will mobilize Tier Breche," she said. "Melee-Magthere and Arach-Tinilith can fight. Sorcere will divide its efforts between supporting us and extinguishing the fires. You will either find my brother Gromph or act in his stead."

Pharaun bowed low.

Quenthel turned and saw that her priestesses and novices had followed her out onto the plateau. Something in their manner brought her up short.

"Mistress," said long-eared Viconia Agrach Dyrr, one of the senior instructors, rather diffidently, "it makes perfect sense for Melee-Magthere and Sorcere to descend the stairs, but . . ."

"But you ladies have lost your magic," Pharaun said.

The sisters of the temple gaped at him.

"You know?" Quenthel asked.

"A good many males know," the mage replied, just a hint of impatience peeking through, "so there's no point in killing me for it. I'll explain it all later." He turned back toward the rest of the clerics. "Holy Mothers and Sisters, while you may have lost your spells, you have scrolls, talismans, and the rest of the divine implements your order hoards. You can swing maces, if it comes to that. You can fight."

"But we've lost too many sisters," Viconia said to Quenthel. "The demons killed a couple, and you, Mistress, by summoning the spiders, slew more. We don't dare risk the rest. Someone must endure to preserve the lore and perform the rituals."

"That's far too optimistic," Pharaun said.

Viconia scowled. "What is, boy?"

"The assumption that, should you remain up here, annihilation will pass you by," the wizard replied. "It's more plausible to assume that if the orcs triumph below, they'll climb the stairs to continue their depredations up here. You profess devotion to Arach-Tinilith. Surely it would be more reverent to engage the undercreatures in the vault below and thus deny them the slightest opportunity to profane your shrines and altars. Similarly, it would be better strategy to fight alongside allies than to wait till they perish and you're left to struggle alone."

"You're glib, wizard," the Agrach Dyrr priestess sneered, "but you don't know our efforts are needed. Flame and glare, they're only goblins! I think you're just a scareling."

"Perhaps he is," Quenthel said, "but how dare we seek the Dark Mother's favor if we decline to defend her chosen city in its hour of need? Surely, then, we never would hear her voice again."

"Mistress," said Viconia, spreading her hands, "I know we can find a better way to please her than brawling with vermin in the street."

Quenthel lifted her hand crossbow and shot her lieutenant in the face. Viconia made a choking sound and stumbled backward. The poison was already blackening her face as she collapsed.

"I thought I'd already demonstrated that *I* rule here," the Baenre said. "Does anyone else wish to contest my orders?"

"If so," Pharaun said, "she should be aware that I stand with the mistress, and I have the power to scour the lot of you from the face of the plateau."

Ignoring the boastful wizard, Quenthel surveyed her minions. It appeared that no one else had anything much to say.

"Good," the Baenre said. "Let us rouse the tower and the pyramid."

chapter

TWENTY-THREE

With Quenthel in the lead, the Academy descended from Tier Breche like a great waterfall. Some scholars tramped after her on the staircase, while others floated down the cliff face. A few, possessed of magic that enabled them to fly, flitted about like bats.

"Perhaps Mistress would care to bide a moment," said Pharaun. At some point he had slipped off to his personal quarters long enough to wash his face, comb his hair, and throw on a new set of handsome clothes. He returned alone, still claiming ignorance of Gromph's whereabouts. "This is as good a spot as any to spy out the lay of the land. We're below some of the smoke but still high enough for an aerial inspection."

Since Gromph was still either unavailable or uninterested, the Mizzrym was—with obvious relish—acting in the archmage's stead. It was arguably an affront to House Baenre as much as the archmage, but Quenthel had given the order anyway. Until her brother returned or the crisis abated, she needed someone to speak for Sorcere, and she was sure it would upset Gromph in an amusing way to have this dandy taking his place for so important a task.

She halted, and her minions came to a ragged, jostling stop behind her. The whip vipers reared to survey the cityscape along with her. From the corner of her eye, she saw Pharaun smile briefly as if he found the serpents' behavior comical.

"There," said Quenthel, pointing, "in Manyfolk. It looks as if House Auvryndar may have finished exterminating their own slaves, but a mob keeps them penned within their walls."

"I see it, Blessed Mother," said Malaggar Faen Tlabbar from the step behind her. The First Sword of Melee-Magthere was a merry-looking, round-faced boy with a fondness for green attire and emeralds. "With your permission, that might be a good place to start. We'll lift the siege and add the Auvryndar to our own army."

"So be it," Quenthel said

The residents of the Academy reached the floor of the lower cavern, whereupon the instructors, particularly the warriors of the pyramid, set about the business of forming the scholars into squads, with swordsmen and spearman protecting the spellcasters. Then they had to arrange the units into some semblance of a marching order.

Like every princess of a great House, Quenthel had a working knowledge of military matters, and she watched the attempt to create order with a jaundiced eye.

"I could wish for a proper army," she muttered.

She hadn't meant for anyone to hear, but Pharaun nodded.

"I understand your sentiments, Mistress, but they're all we have, and I'm sure that if we've trained them properly, we have a chance." He coughed. "Against the thralls, anyway."

"Your meaning?"

"The greatest danger of all is this pall of smoke. I think Syrzan, for all its cunning, miscalculated. If the mages we left upstairs don't extinguish the flames, we'll all suffocate, female and male, elf and orc alike, leaving the alhoon a necropolis to rule. Still, I suppose we must concentrate on our task and not fret about the rest."

"What alhoon?" she demanded.

He hesitated. "It really is a long story, Mistress, and not crucial at this moment."

"I will decide what is crucial, mage," she said. "Speak."

Before Pharaun could begin she saw the First Sword approaching, presumably to inform her that the company was ready to set forth.

As they started to march, she listened to the mage's tale of the undead mind flayer and its designs for Menzoberranzan. There was more, she was sure, that he was holding back, but she could always torture it out of him later.

Along the way, the teachers and students found their way littered with mangled dark elf corpses, some headless, some partially devoured, firelight gilding their sightless eyes. The rich smell of blood competed with the acrid foulness of the smoke.

Or course, no drow objected to the spectacle of violent death, but the ubiquity of the ravaged shapes, combined with the glare of the flames and the uncanny sight of burning stone, made it seem as if Menzoberranzan itself had become a sort of hell, and that was, for Quenthel at least, unsettling.

The Mistress of Arach-Tinilith thought that were she a weaker person, she might have felt as if she were moving through a nightmare, or interpreted the carnage as proof positive that Lolth had turned her back on Menzoberranzan for good and all. She consoled herself with the thought that at least this time she was marching against an enemy she could see and smite.

Periodically the scholars saw small groups of undercreatures looting, slaughtering hapless commoners, or even flinging stones and arrows at the column. The younger students sought to attack the thralls, and the teachers bellowed at them to desist. The Academy had to act as a unit and stick to a plan if it hoped to win the day.

Malaggar raised his hand, signaling a stop.

We're close, I think, he reported in the silent drow sign language.

They stood in place until a flying scout, a brother of the pyramid possessed of a cloak that converted into batlike wings, swooped down and gave his report.

Mistress, Malaggar signed, *may I suggest that ten squads keep on straight, and the rest of us circle around that block of houses. We'll take the orcs from two sides.*

Very well, Quenthel replied as she surveyed her army. *All of you from the head of the column to the mouth of that alley, follow me. The rest of you, go with Master Faen Tlabbar. Everyone, quietly as you can.*

Hands lifted at intervals down the column to relay the orders to those who couldn't see her.

The company divided, then Quenthel's troops crept on, toward a clamoring mob that quite possibly outnumbered them. Fortunately, the slaves hadn't noticed the Academy's arrival, and she meant to take full advantage of their ignorance. She quickly arranged her troops in a ragged but serviceable formation, then bade them attack as one.

Power howled and flashed, burning, blasting, and devouring masses of goblins. Darts leaped through the air to pierce orcs and bugbears. Undercreatures fell by the score.

Yet after that first volley, scores remained, and they flung themselves at the scholars in a yammering frenzy. The drow hastily abandoned their crossbows for swords and spears. Hidden behind lines of warriors, mages and priestesses peered, trying to see what was going on in the midst of the savage melee so they could target their spells without harming their own comrades.

Quenthel could have cowered behind her own rank of protectors—perhaps, as high priestess and leader, she should have—but she thought it might stiffen the spines of the first- and second-year students if she led from the front, and in any case, she wanted to kill up close and see the pain and fear in her victims' faces. Her vipers rearing and hissing, she shoved her way to the front.

She slew several goblinoids, and dazzling yellow light flashed and crackled around her. The fire magic did her no harm—her mystical defenses held—but several of the folk around her, drow and undercreature alike, shrieked and fell.

For a moment, everyone, every survivor in the immediate vicinity, was stunned. Then orcs scrambled forward at the gaps the blaze had created in the drow line, and scholars darted forward to fill them. No one paid any heed to the burned comrades beneath their feet, save to curse them if she tripped.

Quenthel stepped back, letting a student warrior from House Despana take her place, then cast about, seeking the source of the burst of flame. She had a vague sense that the magic had plunged down from above, so she looked there first, at the upper stories of the buildings to either side.

She blinked in surprise. Like true arachnids, driders were scuttling about the walls and rooflines. Many such debased creatures retained their spellcasting abilities, and one of them must have conjured the fire.

Quenthel had no idea how the thralls and outcasts could have conspired together, nor did she have time to stop and ponder the question. She had to stop the driders before they destroyed her company from above. She levitated upward through the smoky air, meanwhile looking about for the mage who'd created the flame.

Barbed arrows and bolts of light streaked at her from all directions. She shielded her face with a fold of her *piwafwi*, and the missiles rebounded or dissolved when they encountered her layers of enchanted protection. The impacts stung but did no serious damage.

When she'd ascended to their level, she recognized certain snarling faces even with the fangs, driders whom she herself had helped to make. Perhaps it explained why they'd throw magic at her despite the inevitable damage to the mob of orcs.

She quickly unrolled another scroll and read the trigger phrase therein. Blades appeared, floating among the driders in front of her, then began to revolve around a central point. The razor-sharp slivers of metal sped along so fast they were invisible, and their orbits curved through the bodies of their foes. The blades sliced and pierced the half-spiders without even slowing down, reducing the brutes to scraps of meat and splashes of blood.

Quenthel laughed and started to twist around to face the driders atop the stalagmite buildings on the opposite side of the street. A length of something sticky lashed her and looped tightly about her torso, binding her free hand to her chest.

It was webbing. She knew that some driders could spin the stuff. As they sought to reel her in, she levitated once more, resisting the pull like a fish on a line. Meanwhile, she struggled to reach another scroll despite the constriction of her arm. The vipers bit and chewed at the cable.

Pharaun levitated into view, and sizzling white lightning leaped from his fingertips. It stabbed one drider, then leaped to the next, then another, until the twisting, dazzling power linked all the half-spiders like beads on a chain. They danced spasmodically until the magic ended, then instantly collapsed. Stinking smoke rose from the remains.

Pharaun smiled at Quenthel and said, "I've often wondered why the goddess doesn't transform our misfits into something harmless," he said. "I suppose driders are another tool for culling the weak."

Ignoring his blather, Quenthel peered down to see what was transpiring on the battlefield.

Malaggar's contingent had arrived and was tearing into the enemy's flank. At virtually the same instant, the Auvryndar threw open their gates, and, mounted on their lizards, charged forth in a sortie.

Teeth gritted, Quenthel pulled the gummy web off her person and floated down to rejoin her troops on the ground. Contemptuous of the enemies' arrows, Pharaun continued to hang above the warriors' heads from which point it was no doubt easier to aim his magic.

The scholars only had to fight for a few more minutes then, hammered on three sides, the mass of goblins collapsed in on itself, the implosion laying a carpet of corpses in its wake.

Quenthel allowed her troops only a few minutes to collect themselves, then she formed them up and marched them on toward the next of the goddess only knew how many battles.

🕷 🕷 🕷

"Out!" Greyanna shouted. "*Now!*"

The canoe maker gawked at her and sputtered, "Wh-what about my stock?"

The items in question sat about the floor of the workroom or hung cradled in straps hooked to the ceiling.

"The goblins will destroy them," the scar-faced princess said. "Like this." She smashed a half-finished kayak, a fragile-looking construction of curved bone ribs and hide, with a sweep of her mace. "Afterward, you'll make more, but only if you live. Now get moving, or I'll kill you myself."

The craftsman scrambled off his stool, and she chivvied him out the door. Up and down the street, her half dozen minions were rousting out the occupants of other manufactories and shops.

A mob of hairy hobgoblins, all well-armed and many a head taller than the average dark elf, slouched around a corner onto the thoroughfare. They spotted the drow, bellowed their uncouth battle cries, and charged.

After the disastrous encounter with Ryld Argith, one of the twins was dead. The other, and Relonor, lay grievously wounded, as they still did in House Mizzrym. There they would live or die without recourse to further doses of healing magic, since Miz'ri declined to squander the House's limited resources on such incompetents. Greyanna had entirely agreed.

After taking the wounded home, Greyanna, with the questionable aid of Aunrae, had selected five new males to join her in the hunt. This time, they'd stalk Pharaun on foot, Greyanna having belatedly realized that foulwings weren't lucky for her.

She and her band had been wandering the streets seeking word of their quarry when the rebellion erupted. Once she'd grasped the magnitude of the disturbance, she wondered if it was the raid on the Braeryn that she had engineered, that brutal attempt to flush her brother out of hiding, that had inspired the thralls to revolt. In a mad, dark way, the possibility pleased her, but she decided not to share her hypothesis. Few would see the humor.

Most of her thinking, however, was given over to practical considerations. She thought her hunting party could help put down the undercreatures, but only if it could combine forces with a bona fide army. Otherwise, the larger mobs would overwhelm it.

In those first minutes of slaughter and destruction, she watched for some noble clan to ride forth from their castle and drive the goblins before them. To her consternation, none did, at least not in her immediate vicinity. Her little troop was on its own.

Life then became an infuriating business of running and hiding from orcs of all things, of watching beasts no better than rothé destroy beauty and sophistication they couldn't even perceive. Occasionally, she and her companions slew a small group of goblinoids wandering on their own, but it meant nothing, would do nothing to arrest the dissolution of all that was finest in the world.

Where was the Spider Queen? Perhaps she was bored with her toy Menzoberranzan, magnificent though it was. Perhaps she intended to break it to make space for a new one.

In time, Greyanna's dodging and backtracking brought her to a street she recognized, a double row of prosperous shops—to be precise, establishments owned by tradesmen under the patronage of House Mizzrym. She herself had called hereabouts, collecting rents and fees, occasionally chastising a fool who was late paying on a loan or had otherwise displeased Matron Mother Miz'ri.

It occurred to Greyanna that if the merchants perished, they'd contribute no more gold to Mizzrym coffers. Whereas if she conducted them to safety, she might curry some favor with her mother. Miz'ri had grown impatient with her continuing failure to kill Pharaun and had even hinted that another might carry the mantle of First Daughter with more grace.

At the very least, preserving Mizzrym assets would feel more constructive and less frustrating than simply skulking about, and so Greyanna instructed her followers to extract the frightened traders and artisans from their homes.

She loosed a crossbow bolt at the hobgoblins, and her soldiers did the same. Her wizard conjured a cold, towering shadow like the silhouette of a mantis, which mangled several thralls in its oversized pincers before melting out of existence. In all, at least a dozen brutes fell, but others shambled forth from the smoke and fiery glare to take their place.

Voices of torment, she thought, how many undercreatures were there in Menzoberranzan?

Until that day, Greyanna had never really noticed. She guessed no one else had, either.

The hobgoblins charged.

The Mizzrym princess shouted, "Dark wall!"

Three of her retainers, those closest to the onrushing thralls, stooped and touched the ground, conjuring a curtain of shadow between themselves and the undercreatures, then fell back.

One of the Mizzrym warriors herded the shopkeepers farther from the threat. The rest, Greyanna included, scrambled to form a line at a narrow place three yards behind the intangible barrier. The princess pulled a little silver vial from her belt pouch and guzzled the bitter, lukewarm contents down. She shuddered and doubled over as her muscles cramped, and the discomfort gave way to a tingling warmth.

Hobgoblins strode from the darkness. They'd dwelled among dark elves too long for the trick to deter them more than a few seconds.

At least the blinding veil precluded their advancing in anything resembling a coherent formation. They screamed and charged in a gapped and formless wave, which looked murderous even so.

The first hobgoblin to lunge at Greyanna was particularly large and, in marked contrast to his fellows, hairless from the shoulders up. A mistress or master had depilated the slave to prepare the canvas for a work of art, hundreds of tiny round burn scars arranged in a complex swirling pattern.

The thrall cut at Greyanna's head. Under other circumstances, she would have retreated out of range, but that would break the line. Wishing she'd brought a shield to the revel, she lifted her mace in a high parry. The hobgoblin's broadsword rang against the stone haft of the war club and skipped off.

At once she riposted with a strike to the flank, and the undercreature whipped his targe around to block. The blow bashed a dent in the round steel shield and knocked the hobgoblin reeling back, his slanted eyes wide with surprise. He didn't know about the potion that had lent her an ogre's strength.

Greyanna struck to the side, slaying the slave who was menacing her neighbor, then her own bald adversary came edging back. He hovered a second, then feinted to the flank and finished with a cut to the chest. Discerning the true threat, she half-stepped inside the arc of the attack and swung at his jaw. The blow crunched home, and he toppled backward with a shattered, bloody chin and a broken neck.

She killed two more hobgoblins, then something prodded her shin, a thrust that failed to penetrate her boot. She looked down, and it was a kobold, armed with a fireplace poker, who had apparently been scurrying about the feet of the larger slaves. Greyanna killed the reptilian imp with a roundhouse kick.

She cast about for her next adversary. She didn't seem to have one. The fight was over, and the few surviving hobgoblins were running away.

"Form up!" she shouted. "I want a column with the traders in the middle. Fast!"

Once the procession was under way, Aunrae, striding along at Greyanna's side, asked, "May I know where we're going? An ally's castle?"

"No," Greyanna replied. "I suspect we couldn't get in. We're going to hide our charges in Bauthwaf."

The column crept past corpses and burning stone, and as they made their way to the cavern wall, other commoners came running out of their homes to join the procession. Greyanna's first impulse was to turn away those without ties to House Mizzrym, but she thought better of it. Many of the newcomers carried swords, and she could press the dolts into martial service if needed.

Occasionally someone collapsed, coughing feebly, poisoned by the stinging smoke. The rest stepped over her and pressed on.

Someone gave a thin, high cry, as if at an unexpected pain. Greyanna spun around. The goblins weren't attacking. Her client the canoe maker had simply seized his opportunity to knife another male in the back.

"A competitor," the craftsman explained.

🕷 🕷 🕷

The labyrinthine fortress known as the Great Mound contained a number of magically sealed areas. Unbelievably, the rebellious slave troops penetrated everywhere else. The Baenre fought the goblinoids in the stalagmite towers, across the aerial bridges that connected them, and through the tunnels beneath them, even along the balconies and skywalks of the stalactite bastions, reclaiming their domain a bloody inch at a time.

The thralls made their final stand in the courtyard, a spacious area surrounded by a weblike iron fence. The barrier was a potent magical defense, and, as the Baenre had just discovered, of no use whatsoever if one's foe was already inside the compound.

Triel floated down from the battlements above to take a hand in the last of the fighting. Jeggred, who'd stood beside her since the battle commenced, drifted down as well. Both mother and demidemon son wore a copious spattering of blood, none of it their own.

In truth, Triel could have left the task of clearing the yard to her warriors, but she was enjoying herself. Partly, it was simple drow bloodlust, but she'd also found a directness, a simplicity, in slaughtering goblins that was sadly lacking in the complex task of ruling the city. For the first time since ascending to her mother's throne, she felt she knew what she was doing.

Half a dozen minotaurs, formidable brutes she had often employed as her own personal guards, chanted, "Freedom! Freedom!" as they swung their axes or crouched to gore an enemy with their horns. Triel read the last line of runes from a scroll that, when the rebellion commenced, had contained seven spells.

Dazzling flame blazed up from the ground beneath the minotaurs' hooves. Four of the huge beasts fell down screaming and thrashing. The other two leaped clear of the conflagration. They didn't escape harm entirely. The fire burned away patches of their shaggy fur and seared the flesh beneath, but the injuries didn't slow them down. They bellowed and charged.

A minotaur towered over a drow of normal stature, and made Triel look like a tiny sprite. Still, she smiled as she stepped forward to meet the foe. One of the slaves focused on her and the other, on Jeggred.

The matron mother knew a minotaur liked to overwhelm an opponent with the momentum of its initial rush. She waited until the creature was nearly on top of her, then sidestepped. He was lumbering too fast to stop or compensate, and she smashed his knee with her mace as he plunged by.

The slave fell on his face, and she robbed him of the use of his limbs with a bone-breaking strike to the spine. Meanwhile, Jeggred simultaneously chewed on his own opponent's neck and ripped at the brute's torso, hooking the guts out.

After that, Triel and the draegloth killed several gnolls before running out of foes. Panting, the Baenre strode to the foot of a wall and floated upward again, high enough to peer beyond the eminence of Qu'ellarz'orl to the burning city beyond. Jeggred followed.

Earlier, when she'd first discerned that slaves throughout Menzoberranzan were rebelling, she'd used a certain magical diamond to call the males of Bregan D'aerthe from their secret lair. The sellswords were at their work.

One neighborhood in the south of the city was thick with goblins. Even from the Great Mound, she could make out the boil of motion in the streets. Then, over the course of just a few seconds, that agitation ceased, as the creatures apparently fell dead all at once.

It was an extraordinary feat of mass assassination, but the mercenaries had only cleared one small part of Menzoberranzan. They couldn't reclaim the entire city by themselves, if, in fact, the job could be done at all.

Triel shouted down into the yard, to any officer within earshot, "Assemble my troops. We're marching out."

Jeggred couldn't speak for joy. This had already been the best night of his admittedly young life, and he was drunk on slaughter. He'd killed and killed and killed and killed again, an ecstasy that put his sport with Faeryl Zauvirr to shame.

And his mother said it wasn't over! They were going to descend into the city to gorge on murder, and Jeggred would know a fiend's transcendent bliss. The only hard part would be remembering not to kill dark elves, just everyone else.

He squeezed Triel's shoulder with a quivering hand, one of the smaller ones.

🕷   🕷   🕷

Valas Hune skulked around the corner, then blinked. A keep blocked the street, where no bastion should be—then the huge thing moved.

No, not a keep after all, but the biggest stone giant he'd ever seen. The scout knew that some Houses kept giant slaves as well as the more common goblinoids and ogres, and, gray in the firelight, with a long head and black, sunken eyes, this specimen still wore iron bracelets dangling lengths of broken chain. From somewhere it had procured a greataxe sized for a creature of its immensity, and was using it to pulp any drow it noticed scurrying about.

Valas had gotten separated from his comrades sometime back. That was all right. He was used to traversing wild places by himself, though in truth, he'd never explored any tunnel as perilous and unpredictable as Menzoberranzan had become this night.

He'd been killing orcs and gnolls, first with his shortbow, and, after the arrows ran out, close in with his kukris. He'd thought he was making some genuine progress until he encountered this.

It was a daunting sight, but someone would have to kill the big undercreatures as well as the little ones, if Menzoberranzan was to survive and Bregan D'aerthe was to be paid for its services.

Valas touched a fingertip to a nine-pointed tin star pinned to his shirt, and murmured a word in a language of a race few Menzoberranyr had ever even heard of. In the blink of an eye he was crouched on the stone giant's shoulder.

The surface was smooth and rounded. He started to slip off, but, reacting like the accomplished rock climber he was, negated his weight and caught himself. He clambered within reach of the giant's neck and started hacking at the arteries within the behemoth's neck with both kukris.

To no avail. Perched somewhat precariously, Valas couldn't use his strength and weight to full advantage, and his first stroke skipped harmlessly off the giant's rocklike hide.

The behemoth did feel the impact, though. Its head snapped around, the chin nearly brushing Valas away. The giant glared down at him, and he struck, this time with greater success. With a crackle of lightning, the enchanted weapon split the slave's lower lip.

Crying out in pain and anger, a deep sound Valas felt in his bones, the stone giant flinched its head away. A huge gray hand rose up to catch the drow, who scrambled forward and cut at the colossus's neck.

Dark, thick blood leaped forth and washed Valas into space. He fell hard onto a rooftop and watched the giant stumble about, clutching at its throat. After a few steps, the huge thrall fell backward, crushing some unlucky hobgoblins that were wandering by.

Gromph was in a vile humor as he floated up the cliff face. He'd cast light into the foot of Narbondel the same as always, and the world exploded into madness. Orcs lunged out of nowhere and attacked his guards. His own ogre litter-bearers summarily dumped his luxurious conveyance on the ground and joined in the uprising.

The archmage had sought to strike the undercreatures dead with a spell, but nothing happened. Someone had conjured a magical dead zone around him. Either one of the orcs was a shaman powerful enough to create such an effect, or, more likely, one of the brutes had stolen a talisman from his owner.

However they'd managed it, the beasts were charging, and the spells in Gromph's memory were just odd little rhymes, his robe and cloak, mere flimsy cloth, and his weapons, inert sticks and ornaments. Well, probably not all of them, but he wasn't reckless enough to stand and experiment while the orcs assailed him with their pilfered blades. Forfeiting his dignity, he turned and ran. The exertion made his chest throb where K'rarza'q had gored him.

When he reached the edge of the plaza, he thought he must have exited the dead zone. He'd better have, because he could hear the grunting ogres with their long legs catching up behind him. He turned, pointed a wand, and snarled the trigger word.

A drop of liquid shot from the tip of the rod. It struck the belly of the lead ogre and burst into a copious splash of acid.

With his magic restored, Gromph obliterated every attacker who lacked the sense to run away. His dark elf attendants were already dead, leaving him to make his way back to Tier Breche alone.

As it turned out, the slave rebellion was pandemic, and the trek wasn't altogether easy. He considered going to ground in some castle or house, but when he saw the flames gnawing stone, he knew he had to get back.

Dirty, sore, and coughing, he eventually made it home, and when he rose to the top of the limestone wall, he saw something that lifted his spirits, albeit only a little.

Eight Masters of Sorcere stood in the open air, chanting, gesturing, attempting a ritual, while an equal number of apprentices looked on. The wizards had fetched much of the proper equipment out of the tower. That was something, Gromph supposed, but the incantation was a useless mess.

The Baenre reached out and hauled himself onto solid ground and his hands and knees, another irksome affront to his dignity.

He rose and shouted, "Enough!"

The teachers and students twisted around to gawk at him. The chanting died.

"Archmage!" cried Guldor Melarn. He was supposedly without peer in the realm of elemental magic, though it couldn't be proved by his performance thus far that night. "We were worried about you!"

"I'm sure," said Gromph, striding closer. "I noticed all the search parties you sent out looking for me."

Guldor hesitated. "Sir, the mistress of the Academy commanded—"

"Shut up," said Gromph. He'd come close enough to see that the teachers were standing in a complex pentacle, written in red phosphorescence on the ground. "Pitiful."

He extended his index finger and wrote on the air. The magic words and sigils reshaped themselves.

"My lord Archmage," said Master Godeep. "We drew this circle to extinguish the fires below. If you break it—"

"I'm not breaking it," said Gromph, "I'm fixing it." He turned his gaze on one of the apprentices, some commoner youth, and the dolt flinched. "Fetch me a bit of fur, an amber rod, and one of the little bronze gongs the cooks use to summon us to supper. *Run!*"

"Archmage," said Guldor, "you see we already have all the necessary foci for fire magic." He gestured to a brazier of ruddy coals. "I'm whispering to the flames below, commanding them to dwindle."

"And making more smoke in the process. That's just what we need." Gromph kicked the brazier over, scattering embers across the rock. "Your approach isn't working, elementalist. I should exile you to the Realms that See the Sun for a few decades, then you might figure out what it takes to extinguish a fire of this magnitude."

The male came sprinting back with the articles Gromph had requested. The Baenre whispered a word of power, and the pentacle changed from red to blue.

"Right, then," he said to the wizards. "I assume you can tell where you're meant to stand, so do it and we'll begin. I'll say a line, you repeat it. Copy my passes if you're up to it."

For a properly schooled wizard, magic was generally easy. He relied on an armamentarium of spells, many devised by his predecessors, a few, perhaps, invented by himself. In either case, they were perfected spells that he thoroughly understood. He knew he could cast them properly, and what would happen when he did.

An extemporaneous ritual was a different matter. Relying on their arcane knowledge and natural ability, a circle of mages tried to generate a new effect on the fly. Often, nothing happened. When it did, the power often turned on those who had raised it or discharged itself in some other manner contrary to their intent. Yet occasionally such a ceremony worked, and with his station, his wealth, and his homeland at stake, Gromph was resolved to make this one of those times.

After the mages chanted for fifteen minutes, power began to whisper and sting through the air. The archmage tapped the beater to the gong, sounding a clashing, shivering tone. At once a vaster note answered and obscured the first, a booming, grinding, deafening roar. Gromph's subordinates flinched, but the Baenre smiled in satisfaction, because the noise was thunder.

Perched high in the side cavern, the residents of Sorcere had an excellent view of what transpired next. The air at the top of the great vault, already thick with smoke, grew denser still as masses of vapor materialized. The shapeless shadows flickered like great translucent dragons with fire leaping in their bellies. Following each flash, they bellowed that godlike hammering blast, as if the flames pained them.

Gromph knew that many of the folk in the city below had no idea what was occurring—it was possible that even some of his erudite colleagues didn't know—but whether they understood or not, clouds, lightning, and weather were paying a call on the hitherto changeless depths of the Underdark.

As one, the clouds dropped torrents of water to fall in frigid veils. The Baenre could hear the sizzling sound as it pounded the cavern wall.

"That's impressive," said Guldor, "but are you sure it will put out the flames? The fire's magical, after all."

Gromph's bruise gave him a twinge.

"Yes, instructor," he growled, "because I'm not an incompetent from a House of no account. I'm a Baenre and the Archmage of Menzoberranzan . . . and I'm *sure*."

❊ ❊ ❊

Before it was over, Pharaun lost track of how many battles he and his comrades had fought. He only knew they kept winning them, through superior tactics more than anything else, and that despite their losses, their numbers kept growing, swelled by garrisons that had fought their way out of their castles.

Occasionally the ragtag army came upon a section of the city that had already been pacified, and though he never caught so much of a glimpse of them, Pharaun knew Bregan D'aerthe was fighting in concert with his own company. It was as much a comfort as anything could be on this fierce and desperate night.

Finally the army from Tier Breche encountered an equally impressive force under Matron Baenre's command. The two companies united and marched on Narbondellyn, where several bugbears with some degree of martial experience had striven to organize thousands of their fellow undercreatures into a force capable of withstanding their masters' wrath.

The great stone pillar of Narbondel shone above fighting that was wild and chaotic. Miraculously, partway through, the upper reaches of the cavern began to storm, allaying Pharaun's greatest fear. An hour later, the drow swept in and annihilated the opposing force, and thus they took their homeland back.

In the aftermath, the wizard walked through the downpour, looking this way and that. Strands of wet hair clung to his forehead, and his boots squelched. As a mage, he had to concede the storm was a glorious achievement, to say nothing of the salvation of Menzoberranzan, but it was a pity his colleagues couldn't have accomplished the same thing without wreaking havoc on everyone's appearance and chilling them to the bone.

The Mizzrym grinned. Neither Quenthel nor Triel was anywhere around. He'd taken direction from them all night, willingly enough, but he wanted to command the finale of this extraordinary affair himself, and their absence gave him an excuse to proceed without consulting them.

He cast about once more and spied Welverin Freth. The capable weapons master of the Nineteenth House, Welverin excelled at combat despite the seeming impediment of a prosthetic silver leg, and had fought in tandem with Pharaun several times during the night. Currently he was huddled in a doorway conferring with two of his lieutenants.

"Weapons Master!" Pharaun called.

Welverin looked up and gave him a nod. "How can I help you, Master Mizzrym?"

"How would you like to help me kill the creature responsible for this insurrection?"

The warrior's eyes narrowed and he said, "Is this another of your jokes?"

"By no means. But if we're going to do this, we'd better do it quickly, before our quarry slinks away into the Underdark. I trust that you and your troops can ride aerial mounts?"

Pharaun gestured to the giant bats, created by some enchanter, penned in a nearby latticework dome. It seemed a petty miracle they'd survived the rebellion unsuffocated and unburned.

"Where do they keep the tack?" Welverin asked, peering at the cage.

TWENTY - FOUR

Water dripping from the hem of his cloak, Pharaun found that the layout of the renegades' fortress wasn't quite so perplexing when he wasn't dodging hunters and suffering the brain-jangling aftereffects of a psionic assault. The empty, echoing rooms and corridors still seemed just as ominous, however, just as fitting an abode for wraiths and maledictions.

The Mizzrym watched Welverin and the other warriors of House Freth to see if the place was unsettling them. It didn't look like it. Perhaps they were too brave. Or perhaps the fresh, butchered corpses littering the floor turned their thoughts from shadowy terrors to the commonplace violence that was their profession.

They found the bodies, often cut in two or more pieces, lying here and there about the castle. Pharaun was astonished at the quantity. Apparently poor wounded Ryld had had a nice long homicidal run of it before the conspirators slew him. Perhaps it had even required Syrzan to do the job.

In retrospect, Pharaun wondered why the alhoon hadn't joined the search for the escaped prisoners right from the start. Maybe giving the Call had temporarily depleted its strength.

The Master of Sorcere led the soldiers into a long, spacious hall with a large dais at the far end. there, no doubt, a matron mother had held court and also dined, judging by the benches and trestle tables stacked in an alcove. Carved and painted spiders crawled everywhere, a sort of mask, Pharaun supposed, given that the former tenants of the keep had petitioned other deities in private. Sheets of genuine spiderweb veiled the artwork.

Welverin said, "Look."

Pharaun turned his head, then caught his breath in surprise. Ryld Argith had just stepped from the mouth of a servants' passage midway up the left-hand wall.

The weapons master's strides were even and sure despite his wounded leg. He was noticeably thinner, as if his body was burning fuel at a prodigious rate, and somehow he'd recovered Splitter.

The soldiers aimed their crossbows.

"No!" Pharaun said. Not yet, anyway.

Ryld pivoted toward the newcomers and stalked forward. His eyes were intent yet somehow empty, his face, expressionless, and he seemed indifferent to the weapons leveled at his burly frame. One warrior muttered uneasily, as if he'd mistaken the Master of Melee-Magthere for a ghost. Pharaun knew better; he recognized a deep trance when he saw one. Evidently his friend had utilized some esoteric martial discipline to keep himself alive.

"Ryld!" Pharaun said. "Well met! I knew you could defeat Houndaer and the rest of those buffoons. Otherwise I never would have left you."

The lie sounded thin even to the liar.

Certainly it didn't impress Ryld. Perhaps in his altered statue of consciousness, he hadn't even heard it or recognized his fellow master, either. He just kept coming.

"Wake up!" the wizard said. "It's me, Pharaun, your friend. I came back to rescue you. These boys hail from House Freth, and they're our allies."

Ryld took another gliding swordsman's advance, still directly toward the Master of Sorcere.

I'm sorry, Pharaun thought, but this time you bring it on yourself. He drew breath to give the order to shoot, and shapes surged through the three tall arched doorways at the rear of the dais.

In the lead capered several human-sized creatures wrapped in lengths of clattering chain. They were kytons, malign spirits whom mages could summon and control. Behind the devils strode the surviving conspirators, and Syrzan in its decaying robes.

Ryld wheeled and oriented on the conspirators. The rogues shot a flight of whistling quarrels, and the Freth warriors responded in kind. The renegades had the advantage of their elevated platform, and the soldiers, of numerical superiority, but neither volley dropped more than a smattering of its targets. The combatants were too well armored, by metal, magic, or both.

Eager to see if swords would serve where the darts had failed, the Freth soldiers howled a battle cry and charged. Most of them, anyway. In his deep, booming voice, Welverin ordered some of the troops back outside to find their way around to the entrances the traitors had used and attack them from the rear. Not a bad idea, but Pharaun thought the warriors had a good chance of getting lost instead

Whirling loose lengths of chain, eight kytons, each a match for a dozen ordinary fighters, leaped down off the stage to meet the oncoming foe. The rogues remained on the platform with Syrzan, where they started reloading their crossbows with the obvious intention of shooting down into the melee.

Pharaun decided he wouldn't allow that. He levitated above his comrades, thus obtaining a clear shot at the dais.

He felt a twinge in the center of his forehead, but only for a second. As he'd expected, Syrzan had attacked first with a psionic thrust, not realizing its foe had warded himself against such effects with apposite talismans and spells.

This time, the Mizzrym thought, you'll have to fight me charm to charm and spell to spell.

To his surprise, he received an answer, a telepathic voice grating and buzzing inside his mind.

So be it, mammal, the alhoon said. *Either way, I'll have revenge on the wretch who condemned me to exile yet again.*

Even as he attended to Syrzan's threat, Pharaun was murmuring an incantation and manipulating a little steel tube. A bright pellet of flame hurtled from the open end, expanding into a skull-sized orb as it flew. It smashed into one of the renegades on the dais, rebounded, and struck another. It bounced and slashed back and forth across the platform, sowing a zigzag trail of sparks and afterimage in its wake, striking everyone. Before it winked out of existence, it killed a good many of the rogues or turned them into reeling, flailing living torches, whom their own allies had to slay lest they ignite them as well. Syrzan, however, was unaffected.

Below his feet, Pharaun glimpsed the clash of stabbing, cutting blades and spinning chains. As they flailed at their adversaries, the kytons, who resembled oozing, festering corpses within their coiled armor of chains, altered their features. The devils had the capacity to take on the appearance of a deceased intimate from an enemy's past. Supposedly svirfneblin and their ilk found this deeply distressing, but it was only slightly discomfiting to representatives of a race that did not love.

Ryld was at the forefront of the fighting, sweeping Splitter about with all his accustomed strength and skill. Pharaun was glad to see that his friend was only striking at the demons.

Mouth tentacles writhing, bulbous eyes glaring, Syrzan lifted its three-fingered hands to conjure. Around it, many of the rogues who still survived jumped off the dais. Evidently they'd rather fight the Freth warriors on the floor than stand near the alhoon while Pharaun threw spells at it.

The Master of Sorcere was surprised that so few of the traitors simply tried to run away. Certainly loyalty—that alien conceit—didn't hold them there. They must have known that with their schemes thwarted, their conspiracy revealed, they were outlaws, outcast from all they coveted and cherished. Perhaps their plight filled them with such rage that they prized vengeance above survival.

As Syrzan wove magic, its dark elf counterpart was hastily doing the same. The lich finished first. A blaze of lightning, kin to those still twisting and forking through the open air outside, leaped from its parched, scaling hand, crackled entirely through Pharaun's torso, and burned a black spot on the ceiling.

Pharaun's muscles clenched, and his hair lifted away from his head, but his protections averted any real harm. Indeed, the attack didn't even disrupt his own conjuring. On the final word, he thrust out his hand, releasing a wave of cold, fluttering shadows like ghostly bats.

Screeching and chattering, the phantoms swooped and whirled about the alhoon, slashing at it with their claws. The mind flayer growled a word in some infernal tongue, and a jagged crack snaked up one of the walls. Pharaun's illusory minions vanished.

The Mizzrym extracted five glass marbles from one of his pockets, rolled them dexterously in his palm, and rattled off a brief tercet. A quintet of luminous spheres appeared in the air and shot toward Syrzan, attacking it with fire, sound, cold, acid, and lightning simultaneously. Surely at least one of those forces would pierce its defenses.

Syrzan gave a rasping, clacking shriek and swept its hand through the air. In an instant, the orbs reversed their courses, streaking back at their source as fast as they'd sped away.

Caught by surprise, Pharaun nonetheless attempted to dodge in the only manner possible. He restored his weight and dropped toward the floor like a stone. Two of the radiant projectiles streaked past him to explode against the ceiling. Two more simply vanished when they came into contact with his *piwafwi*. The fifth ghosted into his chest.

The loudest scream he'd ever heard shook his bones, jabbed agony through his ears, and smashed his thoughts to pieces. Stunned, he kept plummeting until he smashed down in the midst of the melee.

For a moment he simply lay amidst scores of shifting, stamping feet, then his mind focused, and he realized he needed to get off the floor before somebody trampled him. He started to scramble up, and a swinging length of chain struck him on the temple.

It was just a glancing blow, but it knocked him back down. A kyton loomed over him, whirling its flexible weapons around for another attack. The spirit had Sabal's face.

Pharaun pointed his finger and rattled off a spell, realizing partway through that he couldn't hear himself—or anything else. Seconds before, the battle had been a hammering cacophony, but it had fallen silent.

Luckily he didn't need to hear his voice to recite a spell. Power blazed from his fingertip into the devil's body. In a heartbeat, the kyton's flesh shriveled within its wrapping of chain. The links sliding and flopping around it, the fiend collapsed.

A hand gripped Pharaun's shoulder and hauled him up. He turned and saw Welverin. The officer's mouth moved, but the wizard had no idea what he was saying. He shook his head and pointed to his ears, which, though useless, were far from numb. They throbbed and bled. His insides hurt as well, and the pain made him want to destroy Syrzan all the more.

Pharaun levitated, only to find himself mere feet from something the illithilich must have conjured while its fellow mage was floundering about below. It was a huge, phosphorescent, disembodied illithid head, with mouth tentacles longer than the drow was tall. The members writhing, the squidlike construct flew forward. Up close, it smelled fishy.

Pharaun snatched a white leather glove and a chip of clear crystal from his cloak and commenced a spell. A tapered tentacle tip whipped around his forearm, tugged, and nearly spoiled the final manipulation, but he pulled free and completed the pass successfully.

An immense hand made of ice appeared beside the mind flayer's head. It wrapped its fingers around it, dug its talons in, and held the thing immobile.

The only problem was that the phantom illithid head was still blocking Pharaun's view. He simultaneously wove a spell and bobbed lower until he saw Syrzan.

On the final word of the incantation, white fire erupted from the alhoon's desiccated flesh . . . fire that died a second later. The magic should have transformed the undead wizard into an inanimate corpse, but the only effect had been to singe its shabby robe a little. Pharaun reflected that despite several attempts, he had yet to injure or even jostle his adversary. If the dark elf hadn't known better, he might have wondered if Syrzan was not in fact the better arcanist.

Much as the Mizzrym disliked hand-to-hand combat, perhaps a change of tactics was in order. He snatched a delicate little bone, dissected from a petty demon he'd killed in a classroom demonstration, and started to conjure.

Syrzan swung its arm and hurled a dozen flaming arrows. They missed, bumped off course by their target's protective enchantments. Pharaun completed his incantation and so inflicted a hundred stabbing pains upon himself.

His body grew as large as an ogre's, and his hide thickened into scaly armor. His teeth lengthened into tusks, and his nails into talons, while long, curved horns erupted from his brow. A hairless tail sprouted from the base of his spine, and a whip appeared in his hand.

The transformation only took a moment, and the discomfort was gone. With a beat of his leathery new wings, Pharaun hurled himself at his foe.

The wizard raised his monstrous arms high and bellowed an incantation. Pharaun felt a surge of churning vertigo. The scene before him seemed to spin and twist, and despite himself, he veered off course. He smashed down on the dais, and time skipped. When he came to his senses, he'd reverted to his natural form and felt as weak and sick as Smylla Nathos.

The lich was staring down at him.

"What an idiot you were to return," Syrzan said. "You knew you were no match for me."

Pharaun realized he could hear again, albeit through a jangling in his ears. He wouldn't die deaf, for whatever that was worth.

"Stop preening," said the Master of Sorcere. "You look ridiculous. This isn't your pathetic dream world. This is reality, where I'm a prince of a great city and you're just a sort of mollusk, and a dead, putrid one at that."

As he taunted the creature, he groped for the strength to cast a final spell. No doubt the attack would fail like all the others.

So why, he thought, bother to attack? Try something else instead. Shaking with effort, he cast a spell off the side of the platform. Blue scintilla of power glittered briefly in the air.

"You call *me* pathetic?" Syrzan sneered. "What was that supposed to be?"

If you were wearing the ring you stole, Pharaun thought, you'd know, but I doubt it would fit on your bloated fingers.

The alhoon hoisted him off the ground, then wrapped dry, flaking tentacles around his head.

You're still going to serve me, Syrzan said directly into the mage's mind, holding up one gnarled finger to reveal the silver ring. *When I devour your brain, I'll learn all your secrets.*

"Perhaps the infusion would even cure your stupidity," Pharaun wheezed, "but I fear we'll never know. Look around."

The lich turned, and he felt it jerk with surprise.

The lens of illusion he'd formed in front of the dais made Syrzan look exactly like a certain witty Master of Sorcere, and Pharaun himself resemble yet another humble orc. Once the Mizzrym created it, he'd willed the hand of ice to release the illithid's head, and there came the construct, swooping straight at its originator.

Syrzan threw Pharaun down and faced its creation. No doubt if left unmolested, it could have averted the construct somehow, but Pharaun found the strength for one more spell. His labored incantation shattered the floor of the dais, staggering the alhoon and breaking its concentration.

The huge tentacles scooped Syrzan up and conveyed it to the maw behind them, whereupon the strangely shaped mouth began to suck and chew. The alhoon's own magic mangled him as Pharaun's never had. The lich faded for a moment, then became opaque and solid again. It was trying to shift to another plane of existence but couldn't focus past the agony.

After a time, the enormous head blinked out of existence. Its passing dumped inert chunks of mummified mind flayer on the floor.

Pharaun's strength began to trickle back. He rummaged through the alhoon's stinking remains until he found his silver ring, then turned his magic on the renegades, though it wasn't really necessary. Ryld, Welverin, and their cohorts already had the upper hand.

When the last rogue lay dead, the entranced Master of Melee-Magthere sat down cross-legged on the floor. His chin drooped down onto his chest, and he started to snore. Silver leg rattling as if a blow had loosened the components, Welverin limped over to check him and, Pharaun supposed, tend him as needed.

The Mizzrym thought he ought to take a look as well but when he tried to stand, his head spun, and he had to flop back down.

Triel stood on the balcony gazing down at the city below. It was virtually the same view she'd surveyed on the night of the slave uprising, the burning spectacle that showed her all Menzoberranzan was in turmoil.

The fires were gone. In their place, cold pools of standing water dotted the streets and hindered traffic. The rain had flooded cellars and dungeons as well, and it would take time to get rid of it. No one had anticipated a downpour, not with miles of rock between the City of Spiders and the open sky, and in consequence, no builder had made much provision for drainage.

Someone coughed a discreet little cough. Triel turned. Standing in the doorway, Gromph inclined his head.

"Matron."

She felt a thrill of pleasure—relief, actually—at the sight of her brother, who'd come to her so quickly once she'd given him leave. She took care to mask the feeling.

"Archmage," she said. "Join me."

"Of course."

Gromph walked somewhat stiffly toward the balustrade.

In one corner of the terrace, Jeggred slouched on a chair too small for him and gnawed a raw haunch of rothé. He looked entirely engrossed in his snack, but Triel was confident he was watching her sibling's progress. That was his task, after all, to ward her from all potential enemies, including her own kin. *Especially* her own kin.

Gromph looked out at the city's domes and spires. Some had lost their luminescence, as if his rain had washed it away, and many had flowed and twisted in the fire's embrace, warping the spider carvings into crippled shapes or effacing them entirely. The wizard's mouth twisted.

"It could have been worse," Triel said. "The stoneworkers can repair the damage."

"They have their work cut out for them, especially without slaves to help."

"We have some. A few undercreatures declined to revolt or were captured instead of slain. We'll drive them hard and buy and capture more."

"Still, does anyone remember precisely how every rampart and sculpture looked? Can anyone recreate Menzoberranzan exactly as it was? No. We're changed, scarred, and—"

He winced and rubbed his chest.

"Forgive me," the archmage continued. "I didn't come to lament but to perform my function as your advisor, to share my thoughts on how to meet the challenges to come."

Triel rested her hand atop the cool, polished stone of the rail and asked, "How do you see those challenges?"

"It's obvious, isn't it? We've just experienced what promises to be the first in a series of calamities. By dint of observing you in combat, every Menzoberranyr with half a brain now knows you priestesses have lost your power. Rest assured, no matter what measures the Council takes, the word will spread beyond our borders. Perhaps some escaped thrall is proclaiming it even now. Soon, one or another

357

enemy will march on us, or, if our luck is really bad, they might all unite in a grand alliance."

Triel swallowed. "None of our foes dares even to dream of taking Menzoberranzan."

"This Syrzan did. When its kin, and others, find out we've lost our divine magic, a significant fraction of our drow warriors, and virtually all our slave troops, it may inspire them to optimism. And they're not even the greatest threat."

"We ourselves are," Triel sighed.

"Exactly. We always have our share of feuds and assassinations. Occasionally one House exterminates another outright, and that's as it should be. It's our way, it makes us strong. But we can't endure constant, flagrant warfare. That would be too much . . . chaos. It would tear Menzoberranzan to shreds. Up to now, fear of the Spider Queen and her clergy has kept the lid on, but it won't anymore." He spat. "It's a pity our new heroes didn't die heroic deaths in their homeland's defense."

"You refer to Quenthel and the outcast Mizzrym?"

"Who else? Do you imagine them any less ambitious than the rest of us? They championed the established order yesterday, but, inspired by the knowledge that many would rally to their banners, may themselves seek to topple it tomorrow. Quenthel may try to seize your throne, not in a hundred years but now. Pharaun may strike for the Robes of the Archmage—by the Six Hundred and Sixty-six Layers, he all but did, having spent no effort in finding me before scurrying to your side. What a disaster that would be! Aside from any personal inconvenience to you and me, the city in its weakened state can't withstand that sort of disruption."

"I suppose they could be planning just that," Triel said, frowning. "Perhaps we should have followed through and at least killed Master Pharaun."

"If we execute one of the saviors of Menzoberranzan—damn his miserable little hide—it would have made House Baenre look frightened and weak." The archmage smiled a crooked smile. "Which we are, at the moment, but we don't dare give the appearance."

"What, then, do you recommend?"

Below the balcony, a lizard hissed and wheels creaked as a cart rolled by.

"Use them in a way that simultaneously benefits us and neutralizes the threat they represent," said Gromph. "Surely you and I agree that the present situation can't continue. We must find a way to restore the priesthood's magic."

Triel nodded, looking away from her battered city.

"I propose that as a first step," the archmage continued, "we send agents to another city—likely Ched Nasad—to find out if their divines are similarly afflicted, and if so, whether they know why. You can assign Quenthel to lead the expedition. After all, it concerns Arach-Tinilith perhaps most of all. I'll be delighted to loan you the services of Master Pharaun. If the story I heard was correct, that weapons master friend of his should go as well, if for no other reason than it'll make Pharaun squirm."

"Ched Nasad . . ." Triel whispered.

"The three of them ought to be more than capable of surviving a trek as far as Ched Nasad," continued Gromph, "and they can't very well try to overthrow us while they're leagues away from the city, can they? Who knows, perhaps Lolth will return before they do, and in any case, with time, their notoriety will fade."

His suggestion left Triel feeling a little sheepish. She hid it as best she could by pretending to consider his plan.

"Faeryl Zauvirr proposed an expedition to Ched Nasad. She claimed to be concerned because the caravans have stopped."

Gromph cocked his head. "Really? Well, our representatives can sort that out as well. You know, it's good that the ambassador is already keen to go. She'll make a valuable addition and a more than adequate cover for the whole enterprise."

"Waerva told me Faeryl was a spy," said Triel, "and sought to depart the city in order to report our weakness to her confederates. So I forbade her to leave."

"What proof did Waerva offer?"

"She told me she learned of Faeryl's treachery from one of her informants."

Gromph waited a moment as if expecting something more.

"And that's it?" he asked at length. "With respect, Matron, may I point out that if you haven't spoken with the informer yourself, if you haven't probed the matter any further, then you really only have Waerva's word for it that the envoy is a traitor."

"I can't handle everything personally," Triel scowled. "That's why we have retainers in the first place. I have not entirely lost touch with my—*our* interests in Ched Nasad, though their explanations and excuses do wear thin."

"Of course, Matron," Gromph said quickly. "I quite understand. I have the same problem with my own retainers, and I only have Menzoberranzan's wizards to oversee, not an entire city."

"Why would Waerva lie?"

"I don't know, but I've had some dealings with Faeryl Zauvirr. She never struck me as stupid enough to cross the Baenre. Waerva, on the other hand, is reckless and discontented enough for any game. Accordingly, I think it might be worthwhile to inquire into this matter ourselves."

Triel hesitated before saying, "That could prove difficult. Despite my orders, the Zauvirr tried to flee Menzoberranzan. I hired some agents of Bregan D'aerthe, led by Valas Hune—do you know him?"

"I've heard the name mentioned," Gromph replied.

"He would make a fair addition to your little band of explorers," Triel said. "He's known to be more than passingly familiar with the wilds of the Underdark—a guide of some accomplishment, in fact."

Gromph bowed his agreement.

"Be that as it may, it was Valas Hune I hired to fetch Faeryl back. He completed his task well, and I gave the ambassador to Jeggred."

The wizard rounded on the draegloth.

"What's the prisoner's condition?" he asked the creature. "Is she alive?"

"Yes," said Jeggred through a mouthful of bloody meat. "I was taking my time, to prove I can. But you can't have her. Mother gave her to me. She just told you."

Gromph stared up into the half-demon's eyes.

"Nephew," he said, "I'm sore, frustrated, and in a foul mood generally. Right now I don't give a leaky sack of rat droppings whether you're a sacred being or not. Show some respect, lead me to this prisoner forthwith, or I'll blight you where you sit."

Clutching the rothé bone like a club, Jeggred sprang upward from his seat.

Triel said, "Do as the archmage bade you. I wish it as well."

The draegloth lowered his makeshift weapon.

"Yes, Mother," he sighed.

chapter

TWENTY-FIVE

Her pack weighting her shoulders, her heart pounding, Waerva turned and peered about. The cave stretched out before her and behind, with stalactites stabbing down from the ceiling and stalagmites jutting up from the uneven floor. Nothing moved.

What, then, had she heard? As if in response to her unspoken question, a drop of falling water plopped somewhere in the passages ahead. It was one of the most common sounds of the Underdark, and scarcely a harbinger of peril.

Waerva wiped sweat from her brow and scowled at her own jumpiness. She had good reason to be edgy, though. Everyone said it was suicide to travel the subterranean wilderness alone.

Sadly, thanks to the cursed goblin rebellion, she had little choice. Because of the desperate fighting all across the city, the clergy's incapacity was no great secret anymore. Certainly Gromph had discerned it, which meant Triel no longer had anything to hide from him. Surely, then, she would seek his counsel once more.

Waerva had been confident she could manipulate the frazzled matron mother, but she very much doubted she could fool the canny archmage. Accordingly, she'd cleared out of the Great Mound and Menzoberranzan itself before her kinsman could start asking questions, and there she was, a solitary wayfarer hiking through a perilous wilderness.

But she was strong and cunning, and she'd survive. She'd make her way to her secret allies, and everything would be all right.

She took four more strides, then heard another little sound, and this one wasn't falling water. It sounded more like a stealthy footstep brushing stone, and it came from behind her.

She whirled and saw no one, then something stung her arm. She pivoted. At her feet lay the pebble someone had thrown. Soft, sibilant laughter rippled through the air. From the sound of it, the merrymakers were all around her.

Why, then, couldn't she see them?

Adamantine mace at the ready, one wing of her *piwafwi* tossed back to facilitate the action of her weapon arm, Waerva advanced in the direction from which the rock had come. Weaving her way through the stalagmites, she reached the cavern wall without so much as glimpsing her attacker. She caught a whiff of a familiar reptilian musk, though, and she knew.

Kobolds. The horned, scaly undercreatures were small enough that it was relatively easy for them to hide amid the calcite bumps and spikes.

She turned once more, and despite herself, gave a start. Evidently the kobolds lacked the patience to play their skulking game for very long, because they were done hiding. While her back was turned, they'd crept out into the open and there formed a ragged **C**-shaped line to pen her against the wall.

The brutes were Menzoberranyr thralls. House brands and whip scars gave that fact away. Indeed, a couple still wore broken shackles. Waerva plainly wasn't the only one who'd fled the city.

She glared at the kobolds and said, "I'm a Baenre. You know what that means. Make way, or I'll strike you dead."

The undercreatures stared back at her for a moment, then lowered their eyes. The line broke in the middle, making an exit.

Sneering, head held high, Waerva started for the opening. For a moment, all was silent, then the reptiles laughed, screeched, and rushed her.

Bellowing a battle cry, she swung her mace, and every stroke smashed the life from a thrall. But for every one she killed, there were dozens more hacking and beating at her legs.

Her knee screamed with pain, and she fell. The kobolds swarmed over her and pounded her until she just couldn't struggle any more.

With some difficulty, they divested her of her armor and clothing, and went to work on her. Amazingly for such a bestial race, they seemed to understand anatomy as thoroughly as her dear Tluth, but their ministrations were nothing like massage.

※ ※ ※

Faeryl had learned to court unconsciousness. It brought surcease from the lingering pains of past tortures. Unfortunately, it couldn't avert new ones. When Jeggred found her so, he simply waved a bottle of pungent smelling salts beneath her nose until it jolted her awake.

She could hear him coming. So could the jailers, who scurried to the back of the dungeon to give him privacy. Shivering, she struggled to compose herself. Perhaps she could deny him the satisfaction of a scream—at least for a while—or even provoke him into killing her. That would be wonderful.

The draegloth appeared in the doorway, stooping to pass through. Despite herself, Faeryl flinched, then saw he was not alone. Dainty little Triel accompanied him. So did her harsh-featured brother, clad as usual in the Robes of the Archmage.

"My . . . salutations, Matron," the Zauvirr croaked.

"Hush," said Gromph, "and all will be well." He looked up at the glowering half-demon. "Free her, and be gentle about it."

Jeggred strode to Faeryl. This time, she managed not to cringe. The draegloth supported her weight with his smaller hands while cutting her bonds with the claws of the larger ones, then scooped her up in his arms. She passed out.

Next came a blur of hours or days, during which she would wake for a few muddled seconds, then lapse into unconsciousness again. She lay on a soft divan, where servants salved and bandaged her wounds and sometimes spooned broth into her mouth. Priestesses read scrolls of healing, and Gromph appeared periodically to cast his own spells over her. She noticed Mother's Kiss lying on a little table beside her, and when she felt strong enough, stretched out her trembling arm and touched it.

Finally she opened her eyes to find her thoughts clear and vitality tingling in her limbs. The servants helped her don new raiment. They said it was for a meeting with Triel.

Faeryl considered taking her warhammer along, then thought better of it. If her rehabilitation was an elaborate prank, if the Baenre was summoning her to further torment, the weapon wouldn't save her.

Her legs still the least bit unsteady, she followed a male through the endless corridors of the Great Mound. Eventually he opened the door to a small but lavishly decorated room.

Triel sat at the table in the center of the space, with two bodyguards standing against the wall behind her. Faeryl inferred that this was a chamber the matron used when she wished to palaver away from the formal trappings of her court.

The Baenre rose and took her prisoner's hands.

"My child," Triel said, "I rejoice to see you. Some folk said you wouldn't recover, but I never doubted it. I knew you were strong, a true drow princess favored of Lolth."

"Thank you, Matron," said Faeryl, thoroughly perplexed.

Triel conducted her a chair.

"You'll be glad to know we caught them," the matron said.

"Them?"

"The brigands who waylaid you and murdered your followers, who left you for dead in that place where my servant Valas found you. I supervised the executions myself."

Faeryl was beginning to comprehend her situation. For some reason, Triel had forgiven her her disobedience. The Zauvirr could go free, her honor and rank restored, but there was a catch. Henceforth, she would have to endorse the fiction that Triel was in no way responsible for any of her misfortunes. For after all, the sovereign of Menzoberranzan was a perfect being, whom the Spider Queen herself had exalted above all others. How, then, could she possibly make a mistake?

It rankled a little, but Faeryl was more than willing to embrace the lie to avoid a return to the dungeon.

"Thank you, Matron," she said. "Thank you with all my heart."

Triel waved her hand, and a servant brought wine.

"Do you still want to go home?" the Baenre asked.

Pharaun had been summoned to a good many audiences in the course of his checkered career, and it had been his experience that no matter how urgent the occasion, one generally wound up parked in an antechamber for a while. Matron Baenre's waiting area was considerably more lavish than most, and in ordinary circumstances, he would have amused himself by passing esthetic judgment on the décor. Instead he had to address another matter, for when he arrived, Ryld was sitting on a chair in the corner, half hidden behind a marble statue.

The carving depicted a beautiful female doing something unpleasant to a deep gnome, for the greater glory of the Dread Queen of Spiders, one assumed.

The Mizzrym hadn't spoken to his friend since the slaughter of the renegades. He supposed the time had come. But first he paid his respects to Quenthel, who, much to her annoyance, was being kept waiting as well. The mage then bowed to a stern-faced drow male, looking ill at ease and out of place in rough outdoorsman's clothes and ugly trinkets. Pharaun didn't know him.

"Valas Hune," the warrior said, "of Bregan D'aerthe."

Pharaun introduced himself, then strolled toward the Master of Melee-Magthere.

"Ryld!" the wizard said. "Good afternoon! Have you any idea why the Council summoned us?"

The burly swordsman rose and said, "No."

"To shower us with honors, one assumes. How are you?"

"Alive."

"I rejoice to hear it. I was concerned because I could tell that warrior's trance strained even your constitution."

For a moment, the two masters regarded one another in silence.

"My friend," Pharaun said, having lowered his voice. "I truly regret what happened."

"What you did was tactically sound," said Ryld. "It was what any sensible drow would have done. I hold no grudge."

The wizard looked into weapons master's eyes and realized that for the first time, he couldn't read him.

Perhaps Ryld meant what he was saying, but it was just as likely he was lying, lulling his betrayer's suspicions to facilitate some eventual revenge. Thus, while Pharaun might continue to observe the forms of their long friendship, he could never trust his fellow master again.

For a moment he felt a pang of loss, but he quashed the sensation. Friendship and trust were for lesser races. They weakened a dark elf, and he was better off without them.

Pharaun gave Ryld an affectionate clap on the shoulder, just as he had a thousand times before.

🕷 🕷 🕷

When the tall doors opened, all eight Matrons of the Council sat enthroned and illuminated on an eight-tiered pyramid of a dais, with Triel of course set higher than the others, and a span of radiant marble webbing arching overhead. Quenthel stalked in proudly, ahead of Pharaun and the other males, and why not? She was Mistress of Arach-Tinilith and a Baenre.

Truth to tell, a miniscule part of her, a part she loathed and repudiated, hadn't wanted to come in, because her unknown enemy was very likely in the room

The matriarchs weren't the only folk in the vicinity of the platform. A symbol of the goddess's favor and a source of practical protection, Jeggred loomed behind Triel's chair. Servants scurried about the steps to do the great ladies' bidding. Gromph stood on the highest riser, a place of ultimate honor for a male.

When she, the mage, the weapons master, and the mercenary reached the foot of the dais, Triel began to praise them for their efforts against the illithilich and its pawns. At first the oration was pretty much what Quenthel had expected, but soon it took an unexpected turn.

She herself would lead an expedition to Ched Nasad to find out why no travelers came from that direction, and what the priestesses of the vassal city might know concerning the silence of Lolth. Ryld Argith, Pharaun Mizzrym, and Valas Hune would serve as her lieutenants, accompanying the ambassador, Faeryl Zauvirr.

Upon hearing the news, the hulking warrior in the dwarven breastplate simply inclined his head in acquiescence. The wizard grinned, and the scout smiled. At first the envoy, who was standing nearby, looked equally pleased.

Then Triel said, "Finally, dear sister, I lend you my own son Jeggred for your journey. A draegloth carries the blessing of the Dark Mother, and you may need his strength."

For an instant, it looked as if Faeryl would protest, and Jeggred leered down at her. Plainly, something had once transpired between them, an unpleasantness that made the ambassador loathe and mistrust him.

Gromph shifted his weight as well and Quenthel thought he looked surprised, even a bit put out. Perhaps he hadn't thought Triel had sense enough to want her own special agent on the mission, a minion devoted to her particular interests alone.

A thousand arguments against her being sent away at so uncertain a time for Menzoberranzan, the faith, House Baenre . . . came to Quenthel in a rush. Ultimately, however, she said nothing.

The assembly discussed the practicalities of their scheme for an hour or so, and Triel dismissed her newly appointed emissaries. Pharaun caught up with Quenthel in the antechamber. He bowed to her, and she waved her hand, giving him permission to speak.

"I assume, Mistress, that you know why they picked us?" he murmured.

"I understand better than you," she said.

Pharaun arched an eyebrow and asked, "Indeed. Will you elucidate?"

She hesitated, but why not state at least the obvious? He had come to her, after all, when the slave revolt began. He was a true drow—ambitious and ruthless enough that she could always trust him to do what was to his advantage. Gromph had made him a decoy and a target, perhaps someday she would make him Archmage of Menzoberranzan.

"My brother and sister send us both forth because they fear our ambitions."

"I daresay that's very sensible of them," Pharaun said. "Does this mean you undertake our errand reluctantly?"

"By no means. Whatever my siblings' motives, the plan has merit, and I would go anywhere and do anything to restore my bond with Lolth and save Menzoberranzan; it is of course the same thing."

In fact, she was eager to distance herself from them until such time as she recovered her magic, provided she could do it without a loss of status, and surprisingly, it seemed she could. The matter of the demonic assassins had still not been settled, too, and she wondered if her leaving the city would bring her unknown assailant into the open.

She looked her foppish companion up and down.

"What of you?" she asked the wizard. "You're brave enough—I've seen the proof—but still, are you eager to march across the Underdark?"

"You mean, can an exquisite specimen such as myself bear to dispense with warm, scented baths, succulent meals, and delicate, freshly laundered attire?" Pharaun asked with a grin. "It will be excruciating, but under the circumstances, I'll manage. I enjoy unraveling mysteries, particularly when I suspect I might enhance my personal power thereby."

"Perhaps you will," Quenthel said, "but I recommend you keep your hands off any prize your leader covets for herself."

"Of course, Mistress, of course."

The Master of Sorcere bowed low.

Pharaun cast a spell, then slipped through the closed door like a ghost. On the other side was a drab, stale-smelling little room. Wrapped in a blanket like an invalid, her scarred face a mask of bitterness, Greyanna sat in the only chair.

For an instant, she stared at him stupidly, then started to throw off the cover, presumably with the intent of jumping up. He lifted his hands as if to cast a spell, and the threat froze her in place.

"What a dreary habitation," he said. "It was Sabal's, wasn't it, when her fortunes were at their nadir. Mother has a good memory and a charming sense of irony as well."

"And she'll kill you, outcast, for breaking into the castle."

"I always assumed so. That's one reason I never paid you a visit hitherto. But our circumstances have changed. The Council needs me to help determine what's become of the Spider Queen, and you, dear sib, are no longer a person of any importance. As Miz'ri's demoted you for your repeated failures to kill me, I doubt she'll make an issue of your extinction, even if she's certain I'm responsible. She *smiled* at me this afternoon when I saw her in House Baenre, can you believe it? She must have decided she'd like me to resign from Sorcere and rejoin the family someday. Evidently she's just realizing how powerful I've become in the decades since you chased me out the door."

"I'm surprised you still want to kill me," Greyanna said. "You've already defeated and ruined me. Death may prove a mercy."

"I considered that, but I'm going on a journey into the unknown, a quest fraught with peril and adversity to be sure, and I need something special to hearten me, a memory fraught with spectacle and drama to cheer me on the trail."

"I suppose I understand," the priestess said, "but I wonder why it's come to this. All these years, I've never truly understood the basis for our feud. If I'm to die, will you at least tell me why you chose Sabal over me? Was it fondness? Was it lust?"

"Neither," Pharaun chuckled. "My choice had nothing whatever to do with personalities. How could it, when you twins were so alike? I threw in with Sabal simply because she was dangling from the bottom rung of the Mizzrym ladder. I thought it would be an amusing challenge to lift her to the top."

"Thank you for explaining," Greyanna said. "Now die."

Pharaun's own living rapier leaped from beneath the blanket. Obviously Greyanna had not only claimed the fallen weapon but figured out how to control it. No doubt she'd been wearing it in its steel-ring form when he entered the room. Knowing how he loved to talk, she'd lulled him with conversation and took him by surprise.

The long, thin-bladed sword hurtled across the room toward Pharaun's chest. He frantically shifted to the side, and the point plunged into his left forearm instead. For a second, he couldn't feel the puncture, and it flared with pain.

He had to immobilize the weapon or it would pull itself free and attack again. He grabbed hold of the blade with his right hand, and it sliced into his palm. A rapier was made for thrusting, but it had sharp edges even so. Sharp enough, anyway.

At the same instant, Greyanna cast off the blanket and snatched a mace from behind her chair. She jumped up and charged.

Pharaun narrowly dodged her first swing, then threw himself against her, ramming her with his shoulder. The impact knocked her stumbling backward.

It didn't hurt her, though. She laughed and advanced on him again.

He knew why she was so exhilarated. She thought that with his left hand dangling at the end of a spastic arm and the right busy gripping the rapier, he wouldn't be able to cast any appropriate spells to fend her off.

And she was right.

Edging away from Greyanna, his hand dripping blood, he let go of the living sword and started to conjure, rapidly as only a master could.

His sister rushed him. The rapier jerked itself out of his wound, hurting him anew. It pivoted in the air and aimed itself at his heart.

Five darts of azure force shot from his right hand into Greyanna's body. She made a sighing sound and collapsed, her mace clanking against the floor.

At once the rapier became inert, and fell clattering to the floor.

He studied Greyanna, making sure she was truly dead, then examined his own wounds. They were unpleasant, but a healing potion or two would mend them.

"Thank you, sister," he said, "for a most inspiring interlude. When I sally forth to save our beloved Menzoberranzan, it will be with a heart full of joy."

The New York Times bestselling author
R.A. Salvatore
brings you a new series!

The Sellswords

SERVANT OF THE SHARD
Book I

Powerful assassin Artemis Entreri tightens his grip on the streets of Calimport, but his sponsor Jarlaxle grows ever more ambitious. Soon the power of the malevolent Crystal Shard grows greater than them both, threatening to draw them into a vast web of treachery from which there will be no escape.

VOLUME TWO OF THE SELLSWORDS WILL BE AVAILABLE IN 2005!

ALSO BY R.A. SALVATORE

STREAMS OF SILVER
The Legend of Drizzt, Book V

The fifth installment in the deluxe hardcover editions of Salvatore's classic Dark Elf novels, *Streams of Silver* continues the epic saga of Drizzt Do'Urden™.

THE HALFLING'S GEM
The Legend of Drizzt, Book VI

The New York Times best-selling classic for the first time in a deluxe hardcover edition that includes bonus material found nowhere else.

HOMELAND
The Legend of Drizzt, Book I

Now in paperback, the *New York Times* best-selling classic that began the tale of one of fantasy's most beloved characters. Experience the Legend of Drizzt from the beginning!

ED GREENWOOD

THE CREATOR OF THE FORGOTTEN REALMS WORLD

BRINGS YOU THE STORY OF
SHANDRIL OF HIGHMOON

SHANDRIL'S SAGA

SPELLFIRE
Book I

Powerful enough to lay low a dragon or heal a wounded warrior, spellfire
is the most sought after power in all of Faerûn. And it is in the reluctant
hand of Shandril of Highmoon, a young, orphaned kitchen-lass.

CROWN OF FIRE
Book II

Shandril has grown to become one of the most powerful magic-users in
the land. The powerful Cult of the Dragon and the evil Zhentarim want
her spellfire, and they will kill whoever they must to possess it.

HAND OF FIRE
Book III

Shandril has spellfire, a weapon capable of destroying the world, and
now she's fleeing for her life across Faerûn, searching for somewhere to
hide. Her last desperate hope is to take refuge in the sheltered city of
Silverymoon. If she can make it.

www.wizards.com

STARLIGHT AND SHADOWS IS FINALLY GATHERED INTO A CLASSIC GIFT SET!

BY ELAINE CUNNINGHAM

"I have been a fan of Elaine Cunningham's since I read *Elfshadow*, because of her lyrical writing style."
– R.A. Salvatore

DAUGHTER OF THE DROW
Book I

Beautiful and deadly, Liriel Baenre flits through the darkness of Menzoberranzan where treachery and murder are the daily fare. Seeking something beyond the Underdark, she is pursued by enemies as she ventures towards the lands of light.

TANGLED WEBS
Book II

Exiled from Menzoberranzan, the beautiful dark elf Liriel Baenre wanders the surface world with her companion Fyodor. But even as they sail the dangerous seas of the Sword Coast, a drow priestess plots a terrible fate for them.

WINDWALKER
Book III

Liriel and Fyodor travel across the wide realms of Faerun in search of adventure and reach the homeland of Rashemen. But they cannot wander far enough to escape the vengeance of the drow, and from the deep tunnels of the Underdark, glittering eyes are watching their every move.

THE TWILIGHT GIANTS TRILOGY
Written by *New York Times* bestselling author
TROY DENNING

THE OGRE'S PACT
Book I

This attractive new re-release by multiple *New York Times* best-selling author Troy Denning, features all new cover art that will re-introduce Forgotten Realms fans to this excellent series. A thousand years of peace between giants and men is shattered when a human princess is stolen by ogres, and the only man brave enough to go after her is a firbolg, who must first discover the human king's greatest secret.

THE GIANT AMONG US
Book II

A scout's attempts to unmask a spy in his beloved queen's inner circle is her only hope against the forces of evil that rise against her from without and from within.

THE TITAN OF TWILIGHT
Book III

The queen's consort is torn between love for his son and the dark prophesy that predicts his child will unleash a cataclysmic war. But before he can take action, a dark thief steals both the boy and the choice away from him.

In the City of Shimmering Webs

Behind them, the crowd that had gathered around the confrontation stirred, and grew rowdy. Several other drow in the throng found themselves pushed and prodded as they tried to extricate themselves from the roiling multitudes. The other races were growing bold after witnessing the murder of a dark elf. Shouts rose up, curses to drow and their missing goddess. Finally, the handful of dark elves scrambled free, either rising up above the aggressors around them, or pushing through to more open streets. The mood was turning ugly in Ched Nasad.

And Things Will Only Get Worse

🕷   🕷   🕷

Featuring a
Prologue by
New York Times
Best-Selling Author
R. A. Salvatore

FORGOTTEN REALMS®

R.A. Salvatore's
WAR OF THE SPIDER QUEEN

R.A. Salvatore's
WAR OF THE SPIDER QUEEN BOOK II

Insurrection

THOMAS M. REID

R. A. SALVATORE'S

War of the Spider Queen Book II: Insurrection

Cover art by Brom
First Printing: December 2002
Library of Congress Catalog Card Number: 2003100847

9 8 7 6

ISBN: 978-0-7869-3033-3
620-17993-001-EN

U.S., CANADA,   EUROPEAN HEADQUARTERS
ASIA, PACIFIC, & LATIN AMERICA   Hasbro UK Ltd.
Wizards of the Coast, Inc.   Caswell Way
P.O. Box 707   Newport, Gwent NP9 0YH
Renton, WA 98057-0707   GREAT BRITAIN
+1-800-324-6496   Save this address for your records.

Visit our web site at **www.wizards.com**

To Quinton Riley

*you, like a good book,
are a wondrous treasure
in a small package.*

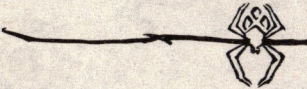

Acknowledgments

*A very special thanks to my editors, Philip Athans
and R.A. Salvatore; this book is so much better
for your tireless efforts.
also, thanks to Richard Lee Byers and Richard Baker;
One's a new friendship and one's an old one,
but both of you were there "guarding my flanks."*

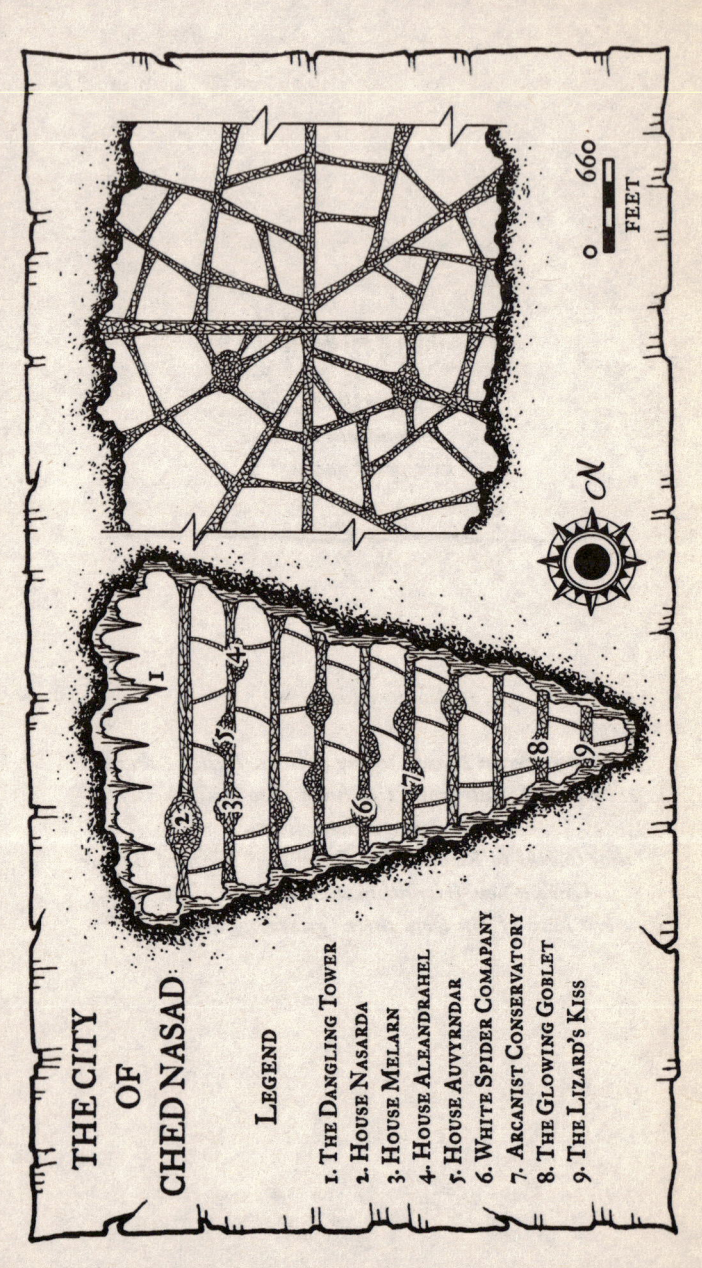

THE CITY
OF
CHED NASAD

LEGEND

1. THE DANGLING TOWER
2. HOUSE NASARDA
3. HOUSE MELARN
4. HOUSE ALEANDRAHEL
5. HOUSE AUVYRNDAR
6. WHITE SPIDER COMAPANY
7. ARCANIST CONSERVATORY
8. THE GLOWING GOBLET
9. THE LIZARD'S KISS

0   660
FEET

N

She felt as if a bit of herself was sliding from her womb, and for a moment she felt diminished, as if she were giving too much away.

The regret was fleeting.

For in chaos, the one would become many, and the many would travel along diverse roads and to goals that seemed equally diverse but were, in effect, one and the same. In the end there would be one again, and it would be as it had been. This was rebirth more than birth; this was growth more than diminishment or separation.

This was as it had been through the millennia and how it must be for her to persevere through the ages to come.

She was vulnerable now—she knew that—and so many enemies would strike at her, given the chance. So many of her own minions would deign to replace her, given the chance.

But they, all of them, held their weapons in defense, she knew, or in aspirations of conquests that seemed grand but were, in the vast scale of time and space, tiny and inconsequential.

More than anything else, it was the understanding and appreciation of time and space, the foresight to view events as they might be seen a hundred years hence, a thousand years hence, that truly separated the deities from the mortals, the gods from the chattel. A moment of weakness in exchange for a millennium of surging power. . . .

So, in spite of her vulnerability, in spite of her weakness (which she hated above all else), she was filled with joy as another egg slid from her arachnid torso.

For the growing essence in the egg was her.

Chapter

O N E

"And why should my aunt trust anyone who sends a male to do her work for her?" Eliss'pra said, staring disdainfully down her nose at Zammzt.

The drow priestess reclined imperiously upon an overstuffed couch that had been further padded with an assortment of plush fabrics, as much for decoration as comfort. Quorlana thought the slender dark elf should have looked oddly out of place in the richly appointed private lounge, dressed as she was in her finely crafted chain shirt and with her mace close at hand. Yet Eliss'pra somehow managed to appear as though she was counted among House Unnamed's most exclusive clientele. Quorlana wrinkled her nose in distaste; she knew well which House Eliss'pra represented, and she found that the haughty drow reclining opposite her exhibited a little bit too much of her aunt's superior affectations.

Zammzt inclined his head slightly, acknowledging the other dark elf's concern.

"My mistress has given me certain . . . gifts that she hopes express her complete and enthusiastic sincerity in this matter," he said. "She also wishes me to inform you that there will be many more of them once the agreement is sealed. Perhaps that will assuage your own fears, as well," he added with what he must have intended as a deferential smile, though Quorlana found it to be more feral than anything. Zammzt was not a handsome male at all.

"Your 'mistress,' " Eliss'pra replied, avoiding both appellations and names, as the five of them gathered there had agreed at the outset, "is asking for a great deal from my aunt, indeed from each of the Houses represented here. Gifts are not nearly a generous enough token of trust. You must do better than that."

"Yes," Nadal chimed in, sitting just to Quorlana's right. "My grandmother will not even consider this alliance without some serious proof that House—" The drow male, dressed in a rather plain *piwafwi*, snapped his mouth shut in mid-word. His insignia proclaimed him as wizard member of the Disciples of Phelthong. He caught his breath and continued, "I mean your mistress—that your mistress is actually committing these funds you speak of."

He seemed chagrinned that he had nearly divulged a name, but the male maintained his firm expression.

"He's right," Dylsinae added from Quorlana's other side, her smooth, beautiful skin nearly glowing from the scented oils that she habitually slathered on herself. Her gauzy, hugging dress contrasted sharply with Eliss'pra's armor, reflecting her propensity for partaking in hedonistic pleasures. Her sister, the matron mother, was perhaps even more decadent. "None of those whom we represent will lift a finger until you give us some evidence that we aren't all putting our own heads on pikes. There are far more . . . interesting . . . pastimes to indulge in than rebellion," Dylsinae finished, stretching languidly.

Quorlana wished she were not sitting quite so close to the harlot. The perfume of her oils was sickly sweet.

Despite her general distaste for the other four drow, Quorlana agreed with them on this matter, and she admitted as much to the group.

"If my mother were to ally our own House with you other four lesser Houses against our common enemies, she would need certain assurances that we would not be left by the rest of you to dangle as scapegoats the moment events turned difficult. I'm not at all certain such a thing exists."

"Believe me," Zammzt responded, circling to make eye contact with each of them in turn, "I understand your concerns and your reluctance. As I said, these gifts I have been ordered to bestow upon your Houses are but a small token of my mistress's commitment to this alliance."

He reached inside his *piwafwi* and produced a scroll tube, and a rather ornate one, at that. After slipping a fat roll of parchment from the tube, he unfurled the scroll. Quorlana sat forward in her own chair, suddenly curious as to what the dark elf male might have.

Scanning the contents of his stack of curled parchment, Zammzt sorted them and began to circle the gathering, removing a set of pages and handing them to each co-conspirator in turn. When he handed Quorlana her sheaf, she took it from him gingerly, uncertain what kind of magical trap might be inlaid in the pages. She eyed them carefully, but her suspicions were dispelled; they were spells, not curses. He was offering them scrolls as gifts!

Quorlana felt elation rise up into her. Such a treasure was priceless in days of such uncertainty and unease. The Dark Mother's absence had put a strain on every priestess who worshiped her. Quorlana herself had not been able to weave her own divine magic in four tendays, and she broke out into a sweat every time she thought on it. But with scrolls, the fear, the anxiety, the sense of hopelessness might be staved off, at least for a time.

It was only with the utmost effort that the drow priestess resisted the urge to read through the scrolls there and then. Forcing herself to remember whom she served, at least for the moment, she instead pocketed the parchment sheets inside her *piwafwi* and turned her attention back to the clandestine gathering in front of her.

"The only other proof strong enough to convince you of our sincerity would be moving forward with hiring the mercenaries," Zammzt said, though none of the other dark elves seemed to be paying the least bit of attention to him.

Eliss'pra and Dylsinae were both wide-eyed with the same excitement Quorlana felt. Nadal, though not as personally thrilled—the spells were worthless to him as a wizard—could still recognize the value of the gifts.

"It should be obvious to each of you," Zammzt continued, "that once our House approaches outsiders, there is no turning back. We would be completely committed, with or without your pledge of alliance. That, my charming companions, is putting the cart before the lizard."

"Nonetheless," Eliss'pra answered, still smiling as she gazed on the scrolls in her hands, "that is precisely what you must do if you wish to count my aunt among your allies."

"Yes," Dylsinae agreed.

Nadal nodded his concurrence.

"I think my mother would be willing to accept those terms. Especially after she sees these," Quorlana voiced her assent, then gestured at the scrolls tucked away in her *piwafwi*. "Most definitely if there are more where these came from."

How in the Underdark do they have precious scrolls to spare? she wondered.

Zammzt frowned and said, "I am not promising anything. I very much doubt that I can convince her to agree to this, but if she is willing, I will procure the services of the mercenaries and bring you the proof."

No one spoke. They were all one step away from the point of no return, and despite the fact that none of them were actually in a position to make the decision, they felt the weight of that decision just as heavily.

"Then we will meet again after you have hired the army," Eliss'pra said, rising from her couch. "Until then, I don't wish to see any of you near me, not even on the same web street."

Gripping her mace tightly, the drow priestess stalked out of the private lounge.

One by one, the others also departed, even Zammzt, until Quorlana was alone in the room.

Our time has come, the drow insisted silently. *Lolth has issued a challenge. The great Houses of Ched Nasad will fall, and ours will rise up to take their place. Our time has come at last.*

🕷   🕷   🕷

Aliisza was so used to the tanarukks' constant grunting, snarling, and slavering that she rarely heard it anymore, so the quiet that surrounded her as she strode alone along the dwarven thoroughfare was noticeable. Being out and about in ancient Ammarindar without an escort of the half-fiend, half-orc hordes was a refreshing change. Kaanyr rarely asked her to—she refused to say "let"—do anything without an armed escort anymore, so she had almost forgotten how pleasant solitude really was. Still, as much as she was enjoying her privacy, however brief it might be, she had a purpose, and it quickened her steps.

She moved to the end of a long and broad boulevard, which had been hewn by long-dead dwarves from the unmarred bedrock of

7

the Underdark itself eons ago. Though she barely noticed it, the craftsmanship of the wide passageway was exquisite. Every angle was perfect, every column and cornice was thick and finely decorated with runes and stylized images of the stout folk. At the terminus of the boulevard, Aliisza entered a large chamber, which itself was large enough to have engulfed a small surface town. She turned into a side tunnel that would allow her to cut across several main passages and reach the avenue that would take her directly to Kaanyr's palace, deep in the center of the old city. It still surprised her how empty the city could be, even with all of the Sceptered One's Scourged Legions roaming around. She crossed the avenues and found the path she wanted, then hurried toward the palace.

A pair of tanarukk guards flanked the doorway into the throne room. The stocky, gray-green humanoids were hunched over as usual, their prominent tusks jutting forward defiantly from overly large lower jaws as they peered at her with their squinty red eyes. To Aliisza, it almost appeared that the two beasts were preparing to charge forward and ram her with their low, sloping foreheads. Aliisza knew that with her magic the scalelike ridges protruding from atop those foreheads were no threat to her, but still the creatures seemed uncertain of who she was, for they kept their battle-axes crossed before the opening as she approached. Finally, just before it seemed that she was actually going to have to slow her pace and say something—which would have made her very cross—the two coarse-haired, nearly naked beasts stepped aside and allowed her to enter without breaking her stride. She smiled to herself, wondering how much fun it would have been to flay them alive.

Passing through several outer chambers, Aliisza crossed the threshold into the throne room itself and spied the marquis cambion lounging on his throne, a great, hideous chair constructed of the bones of his enemies. Every time she saw the thing, she was reminded of how crass it was. She knew too many fiends who considered sitting atop a pile of bones to be some sort of symbol of power and glory, but in her opinion, it exhibited no class, no subtlety. It was Kaanyr Vhok's single biggest lack of vision.

Kaanyr had thrown one leg over the armrest of the throne and sat with his chin resting in his cupped hand, elbow against his knee. He was staring off into the upper reaches of the chamber, obviously thinking and oblivious to her.

Aliisza almost unconsciously began to saunter provocatively as she closed the distance between them, and yet she found that she was admiring his form as much as she hoped he was appreciating hers. His graying hair was roguishly disheveled and, combined with his swept-back ears, gave him the appearance of a maturing, if somewhat devil-may-care, half-elf. Aliisza crooked her mouth in a sly smile, thinking of him engaging in the many subterfuges he was so fond of, passing himself off on the surface world as a member of that fair race.

Kaanyr finally heard his consort's footsteps and looked up at her, his features brightening, though whether it was simply for the sight of her or the news she bore, she was not sure. She reached the first steps of the dais and climbed to where he sat, allowing just a hint of a pout to creep into her visage.

"Ah, my delectable one, you've come, and with news, I hope?" Kaanyr asked, straightening himself and patting his thigh.

Aliisza stuck out her tongue at him and sashayed the remaining distance to plop herself down atop his lap.

"You never just ravish me anymore, Kaanyr," she pretended to complain, wriggling her backside as she settled. "You only love me for the work I do for you."

"Oh, that's not fair, little one," Vhok replied, running his hand lovingly down one of her black, shiny leather wings. "Nor is it particularly true."

With that, he reached up with his other hand, and placing it behind her lustrous black curls, crushed her to him, engaging her

9

mouth with his own in a deep, spine-tingling kiss. For the briefest of moments she considered resisting him, playing one of the infinite variations of the games the two of them seemed to love so much, but the thought was short-lived. His hand strayed down her throat to the hollow of her neck, and it continued lower still. She practically buzzed at his touch, and she knew that with the news she brought him, such flirtations would only break the spell.

As it was, Kaanyr still pulled away after a moment's heated embrace and said, "Enough. Tell me what you found out."

This time, Aliisza really did pout. His caresses on her wings and elsewhere left her panting slightly, and important news or not, she was not ready to be cast aside so quickly. She considered withholding the information for a time, sending a subtle message that she was not to be trifled with. He might rule this place, but she was not his servant. She was consort, she was advisor, and she was free to find another lover, should he cease to satisfy her. Satisfying an alu—the daughter of a succubus and a human mate—was a challenge few were up to. Kaanyr was one of those few. She decided to tell him her news.

"They haven't veered from their course, though it's apparent they know we're closing in. Their scouts have spotted our skirmishers and have continued to avoid contact. We will have them pinned against the Araumycos, soon."

"You're certain they're not here to spy or to wage war? No quick strikes before vanishing into the wilds?"

Kaanyr was absently stroking one of her wings as he asked this, and the alu-fiend shivered in delight. He seemed not to notice her reaction.

"Fairly certain. They are apparently headed southeast, toward Ched Nasad. Each time we cut off their route, they seek out another. They seem intent on keeping to that path."

"Yet, they are not a caravan," he said. "They don't have goods or pack animals. In fact, they travel unreasonably lightly armed for drow. They are definitely up to something. The question is, what?"

Aliisza shivered again, though this time it was as much from the anticipation of the next bit of news as from Kaanyr's absent-minded petting.

"Oh, definitely not a caravan," she told him. "It's the strangest drow entourage I think I've seen wandering around the wilds. They have a draegloth with them."

Kaanyr straightened, staring straight into Aliisza's eyes, and asked, "A draegloth? Are you sure?"

When the alu nodded, he pursed his lips.

"Interesting. This just gets more and more intriguing. First, we haven't seen a drow caravan of any sort in the last few tendays. Finally, when a party of drow *do* venture out, they come straight through here, something they would normally avoid like the stink on a dretch, and lastly, they have a draegloth accompanying them, which means drow noble Houses are somehow personally involved. What in the Nine Hells are they up to?"

Vhok resumed staring off into the dark distance, again absently caressing his consort, this time letting his fingers trail gently down her ribs, which were exposed through the lacing of her shiny black leather corset. She sighed in delight but forced herself to stay focused.

"There's more. I listened in on a conversation when they stopped to rest. One of them, definitely a mage of some sort, was taunting another, who looked like a priestess."

"One of the males giving lip to a female? That can't last long."

"Not just any female. He referred to her as 'the Mistress of the Academy.' "

Kaanyr sat upright, his stare deeply penetrating her own.

"Oh, really," he said in a tone so intrigued, he never noticed that his move nearly made Aliisza fall to the floor at his feet.

She managed to maintain her balance, but she was forced to stand to avoid looking silly. She glared at the cambion.

He went on, oblivious, "Oh, this is just too good. One of the highest drow priestesses in all of Menzoberranzan is trying to sneak incognito through my tiny little domain. And she's letting a wizard run his mouth at her. No caravans for more than a month, and now this. This is too much fun!"

Kaanyr turned to face Aliisza once more, and upon seeing her glare, he cocked his head in confusion.

"What? What's wrong?"

The alu fumed, "You have no idea, do you?"

Kaanyr spread his hands helplessly and shook his head.

"Well, then I'm not going to tell you!" she snapped, and turned away from him.

"Aliisza." Vhok's voice was deep and commanding, and it sent shivers down her spine. He was angry, just as she'd hoped. "Aliisza, look at me."

She glanced back at him over her shoulder, letting one arched eyebrow rise questioningly. He had risen from the throne and was standing with his hands on his hips.

"Aliisza, I don't have time for this. Look at me!"

She shivered in spite of herself and turned fully around to face her lover. His eyes smoldered and made her melt. She pouted just a little, to let him know that she didn't like being chastised, but she was finished playing the game.

Vhok nodded slightly in satisfaction.

His visage softened a bit, and he said, "Whatever I did, I'll make it up to you later. Right now, though, you have to get back over there and find out what's going on. See if you can get face to face with them and 'invite' them to pay us a visit. But be careful. I don't want this to explode in my face. If a high priestess and a draegloth are part of this group, then the rest of them are dangerous, too. Keep the

Scourged close, to hem them in, but don't waste too many bodies on an all-out attack. But also don't make it too obvious that you're holding them back. Also, don't—"

Aliisza rolled her eyes, feeling a little insulted.

"I've done this a time or two before, you know," she interrupted, her voice thick with sarcasm. "I think I know what to do. But . . ."

She stepped closer to Kaanyr—into him, really—rising up on her tiptoes and wrapping her arms around his waist and curling one smooth, bare leg around the back of his calf. She drew herself close, let her body press against his, and continued.

"When I'm done with this little task," she said, her voice smoky with desire, "you're going to tend to *my* needs for a while." She leaned up and nibbled on his ear, then whispered, "Your teasing is working too well, love."

🕷   🕷   🕷

Triel didn't like brooding, but she caught herself doing it frequently of late. This time, when she realized she was at it again, she was suddenly aware of the faces of the other seven matrons, looking at her expectantly. She blinked and stared back at them for a moment, trying to recall the words of the conversation that had droned in the background of her thoughts. She could remember voices but nothing more.

"I asked," Matron Miz'ri Mizzrym said, "what thoughts have you given to other courses of action, should your sister fail to return?"

When Triel still did not respond, the hard-faced matron mother added, "There *are* thoughts floating around somewhere in there today, aren't there, Mother?"

Triel blinked again, jolted fully back to the conversation at hand by the Mizzrym's biting words, focusing her attention where it ought to be instead of on the empty sensation she felt where the goddess's presence should have been. Other courses of action . . .

"Of course," she replied at last. "I've been giving that considerable thought, but before we delve too deeply into alternatives, I think we must exercise some patience."

Matron Mez'Barris Armgo snorted. "Have you been listening to a word we've said in the last five minutes, Mother? Patience is a luxury we no longer have. We exhausted so much of our reserves of magic quelling the uprising we might—*might*, I say—be able to withstand another major insurrection, should one occur. As much as I love a good battle, putting down another slave rebellion would be wasteful, when it's only a matter of time before Gracklstugh or the survivors of Blingdenstone determine that we are powerless, without . . ."

The hulking, brutish matron mother faltered, unwilling, even as forward and tactless as she usually was, to put words to the crisis they all faced.

"If they aren't already aware," Zeerith Q'Xorlarrin interjected, glossing over Mez'Barris's unfinished thought. "Even now, one or more of the other nations could be amassing an army to drive to our gates. New voices could be whispering poison into the ears of the lesser creatures down in the Braeryn or the Bazaar, voices belonging to those clever enough to mask their true identities, their true intent. It's something we must consider and discuss."

"Oh, yes," Yasraena Dyrr said contemptuously. "Yes, let's sit here and discuss; not act, never act. We are afraid to venture forth into our own city!"

"Bite your tongue!" Triel snapped, growing more and more incensed.

She was angry not only at the direction of the conversation—suggestions of cowardice from the High Council!—but also at the ridicule, the unusually open vitriolic nature, of the other matrons' words. Ridicule directed at her.

"If there is one among us afraid to walk our own streets, she need no longer sit on this Council. Are you one such, Yasraena?"

The matron mother from House Agrach Dyrr grimaced at the chastisement she was receiving, and Triel realized it was not merely because Yasraena knew she had overstepped herself. It was the matron of House Baenre, supposedly an ally to Yasraena's house, that was administering this stern lecture. Triel intended it as such. It was time to send a message, to remind the other matron mothers that she still sat at the top of the power structure and she would not tolerate such insubordination from any of those sitting around her, ally or not.

"Perhaps Matron Q'Xorlarrin is right," Miz'ri Mizzrym said quietly, in an obvious attempt to steer the conversation in a new direction. "Perhaps we should consider not just who knows, not just who moves against us—covertly or otherwise—but who might be allying together against us. If even two or three of the other nations come together as our enemies . . ."

She let the thought trail off, and the other drow in the chamber looked uncomfortable, considering its obvious conclusion.

"We need to know what's going on," she continued, "at the very least. Our spy network among the duergar, the illithids, and other deep races has not been best used of late or perhaps isn't as strong as we would like. But what's in place should be funneling more information back to us about the intentions of potential threats."

"Oh, it should be doing more than that," Byrtyn Fey said. Triel raised her eyebrow in slight surprise, for the voluptuous matron mother of House Fey-Branche did not often find interest in discussions so far removed from her own hedonistic pleasures.

"It should be looking for possible weaknesses among our enemies. It should be exploiting those weaknesses, setting potential allies against one another, and perhaps, it should be on the lookout for dissatisfied elements of those traditional enemies, elements that might even consider a new alliance."

"What, are you mad?" Mez'Barris snapped. "Allying with outsiders? Who is there to trust? No matter how we approach such an alliance, the moment we reveal that we cannot receive blessings from our own goddess, potential allies will either laugh uproariously or trip over themselves running to spread the news."

"Don't be dense," Byrtyn snapped right back. "I know how fond you are of the straightforward, brutal-truth method for everything, but there are better, more subtle ways of luring an ally into your bed. Potential suitors need not know about your shortcomings until after you have partaken of their charms."

"Not being able to defend our own city from attack would be too obvious a shortcoming to try to hide," Zeerith said, frowning. "Our own charms will have to be most convincing to blind such potential suitors from the truth. Still, the idea has merit."

"It is impossible," Matron Mez'Barris said, folding her thick arms and leaning back as though dismissing the discussion. "The risk of discovery by our enemies would only be magnified, and the rewards are certainly not worth it."

"Spoken like a hag with few to share her bed," Byrtyn said smugly, stretching languidly to make certain her own well-rounded figure was plainly visible through the sheer fabric of her shimmering dress. "And one who's always trying to convince herself that she's better off without them, anyway."

Several of the other high priestesses gasped at the insult, but Mez'Barris only narrowed her piercing red eyes, staring daggers at Byrtyn.

"Enough!" Triel said finally, interrupting the glaring contest between the two matron mothers. "This bickering is pointless, and it's beneath us all."

She looked pointedly at both Mez'Barris and Byrtyn until both of them ceased their glowering and turned their attention back to her.

If only Jeggred were here, the matron mother of House Baenre thought.

Triel wondered briefly if she should be disturbed that she was once again wishing for the draegloth's soothing presence in the face of such adversity. It was something else she had caught herself doing often of late, and she feared what it symbolized. Perhaps she had grown to rely too much on external protection rather than her own abilities. She feared that it was a weakness, and weakness was definitely something she could ill afford in the current climate.

No, she corrected herself, not just now, not ever.

But the need for allies, however brief and volatile such alliances tended to be, were a necessary part of her life.

Maybe Byrtyn is right, she thought. Maybe that's what Menzoberranzan needs: an ally. Another nation, a race from the Underdark, to aid the noble Houses until this crisis has passed.

Triel tightened her jaw and shook her head softly, determined to banish such silly notions from her mind.

Nonsense, she told herself firmly. Menzoberranzan is the strongest city in the Underdark. We need no one. We will prevail as we always have, through cunning, and guile, and the favor of the goddess. Wherever she is. . . .

"I know very well the state of things in Menzoberranzan," Triel said, looking eye to eye with each matron mother present. "The crisis we face tests us—tests us more severely than any ever confronted by the ruling Houses in all the city's history—but we cannot let it get in the way of resolute administration of the city. The moment we begin to squabble, the moment we do not show a united front to the other Houses, to Tier Breche or Bregan D'aerthe, is the moment we show it to the rest of the world, and by then all is already lost.

"For the time being, we continue to show patience. Discussion of ways to deal with the crisis is welcome—calm, respectful discussion—" and Triel once again inclined her head toward the two matron

17

mothers—"or suggestions for new ways to explore what has happened to Lolth, but there is to be no more of this talk of fear or cowardice, and no more of these insults. That is the behavior of foolish males or the lesser races. We conduct the business of our Houses and our council as we have always done."

Triel made certain to catch each and every matron mother with her own gaze this time, staring intently into each pair of red eyes in turn, wanting to ensure that everyone present got her message—that and to ensure that she was showing a strong face.

Slowly, one by one, the other matron mothers nodded, willing, at least for the time being, to acquiesce to the Baenre's demands.

Wielding power always requires such a delicate touch Triel reminded herself as the group broke apart and the other high priestesses went their separate ways, returning to their homes. Like a supple switch, if you swing it about too vigorously, you just end up breaking it on the slave you are trying to goad.

Chapter

TWO

"I told you coming this way was a mistake," Pharaun panted as he pulled up from his headlong run.

The passage before the drow wizard ended abruptly, blocked by a great gray mass of spongy material that completely filled the tunnel. Turning back to face the direction from which he'd come, the dark elf quickly sloughed off his finely crafted knapsack, lowered it to the rocky floor, and scooted it out of the way with his foot.

"Don't gloat, Mizzrym," Quenthel said, her scowl heavy, stumbling up beside him.

The five snake heads that dangled, writhing, from the whip at the Baenre high priestess's hip rose up and hissed their own displeasure at the wizard, duplicating their mistress's mood, as usual. Quenthel yanked the scourge free of her belt and took up a position beside Pharaun, waiting.

The draegloth was right on the haughty drow's heels. Jeggred bore not one but two heavy bundles, and when the four-armed fiend reached the pair of dark elves, he tossed the supplies to the floor, apparently not the least bit winded from bearing them. He flashed a savage, twisted smile that exposed his yellowish fangs and turned around, advancing a few steps to position himself between Quenthel and anything that might come from the other direction, a low growl rumbling deep in his demonic throat.

The Master of Sorcere was in no mood for putting up with the high priestess's foul temper, and he grimaced as he considered several spells. Settling on one, he fished around in his *piwafwi,* fetching from a pocket inside the extravagant cloak the reagents he would need to weave the chosen magic. Eventually, he produced a bit of squid tentacle. He had warned them they would be trapped if they came this way, and so had Valas, but Quenthel had insisted. As usual, it was up to Pharaun to extricate them all.

Faeryl Zauvirr was the next to stumble into view, her breathing labored. The ambassador from Ched Nasad spotted the blockage in the passage and groaned, sliding her pack from her back and tossing it with a thud to the rocky floor next to the others'. She wearily produced a small crossbow from her own *piwafwi* and placed herself on the wizard's other side.

"They're right behind us," Ryld Argith announced as he and the last member of the drow contingent, Valas Hune, sprinted from around the curve of the passage.

Past the burly warrior and the diminutive scout, Pharaun could see the red glow of multiple pairs of eyes advancing on the group's position. The creatures peered forward eagerly, and the wizard estimated nearly two dozen tanarukks.

Stooped forward as though afflicted with a hunched back, the creatures were reminiscent of orcs, though their features were decidedly more demonic, with their scaled, sloping foreheads and their prominent tusks. They wore little armor, for their hides were scaly and tough, but the battle-axes many of them brandished were heavy and vicious-looking.

Pharaun shook his head in resignation and prepared to weave a spell.

The tanarukks howled in delight and lunged forward, eager, it seemed, to take the battle to their cornered prey. Several swarmed at Jeggred, and the fiend bellowed his own war cry, crouching and slashing wildly. He tossed one of the tanarukks aside effortlessly, slamming it against the far wall, near Ryld's position.

Pharaun gaped for a moment at the unbridled might and ferocity the draegloth displayed, even as two more of the humanoid attackers went down before the precision slashing of Splitter, the enchanted greatsword wielded with greater skill by Ryld Argith. Faeryl fired her crossbow from beside Pharaun then stooped to reload it. Quenthel, in the meantime, seemed content to watch her subordinates at work. More of the tanarukks swarmed in, though, and the wizard almost didn't react in time to one that slipped through the line of defense that Jeggred and Ryld had formed.

The slavering, green-skinned tanarukk leaped toward the wizard, its axe cocked back for a savage blow. Pharaun was just able to backpedal enough to avoid the slashing blade as it swooshed through the air where his face had been a heartbeat before. He considered calling the magical rapier from the enchanted ring that held it, tiny and out of the way until needed, but he knew the effort would be futile. The thin blade would never withstand the force of the axe, and besides, he couldn't get enough room between himself and the beast to use the more nimble weapon effectively. He was quickly running out of space to maneuver.

When the tanarukk arched its back and howled in pain and fury, Pharaun saw that Quenthel was behind it, already drawing her arm back for another swipe with her dreaded whip. The tanarukk whirled around, still screaming in anger. It raised its axe high for a killing blow, but before either it or the high priestess could finish their attacks, a flash of shadow materialized at the edge of Pharaun's field of vision—and the shadow became Valas Hune.

The mercenary scout darted in low behind the green-skinned creature and pulled one of his kukris harshly across the tanarukk's hamstring, crippling it with the oddly curved knife. Black blood spurted everywhere from the deep wound as the beast sank to one knee, flailing feebly with its hands, trying to find the source of its torment. As quickly as Valas had appeared, he was gone, vanished again in the shadows.

Quenthel took the opportunity to bring the whip down on the tanarukk again, and Pharaun saw the fangs of the snake heads sink deeply into the flesh of the creature's face and neck. Already, it was beginning to cough and choke, its face and tongue bloating, poisoned by the lashes from the whip. It dropped its axe and crumpled to the floor, spasming and crying out in anguish.

Pharaun realized he was holding his breath and exhaled sharply, regaining his wits. Disgusted with himself for being so undisciplined, he remembered the tiny piece of squid tentacle that he had in his hand. Righting himself, he made a rapid inspection of the battlefield in order to determine where best to place the spell he had in mind.

A host of dead tanarukks had piled up around Jeggred and Ryld, but still the remaining creatures fought their way to get nearer the pair, snarling and leaping about, looking for an opening where they could use their axes. The wizard decided he could easily position the magic behind those few savage humanoids that remained, but then he paused, startled.

A face had caught the drow mage's eye at the far back of the passage. He blinked and peered more carefully, not trusting his assumption. Lurking in the darkness, watching the battle, was a beautiful woman. Pharaun found her attractive, despite the fact that she was not a drow but appeared human. Black curly hair framed her face, and she was dressed in a tight, shiny leather corset that hugged her curves like a second skin. She seemed to be saying something to the last rank of humanoids, giving them orders and gesturing, but when she noticed Pharaun staring at her, she smiled, her highly arched eyebrows raising even farther in a bemused grin. That was when the wizard also noticed the black, leathery wings sprouting from her back. She wasn't human after all.

Pharaun shook his head in wonder. Such a gorgeous creature commanding a company of foul-smelling, enraged half-fiends somehow didn't seem right to the wizard. But, beautiful or not, she was on the other side of the fight. Sooner or later, he supposed, she would have to be dealt with.

Not here, though; not now.

Snapping back to the task at hand, Pharaun finished casting the dweomer he had chosen, and a collection of black tentacles sprang up, situated between the contingent of drow and the remaining tanarukks. Each of the slimy, writhing things was as thick as his thigh and squirming around, trying to locate anything to entangle. Too late, Pharaun noticed that Ryld had felled the remaining enemies that had challenged him directly and was stepping forward, ready to confront the handful that hung back.

Pharaun opened his mouth to shout a warning to the weapons master, but before the words were out he saw Jeggred reach over and grasp the Master of Melee-Magthere by the collar of his breastplate and yank him back, out of harm's way. An instant later, one of the tentacles wrapped itself around the lifeless body of a tanarukk that had been at Ryld's feet and quickly coiled more tightly, constricting the corpse. If the weapons master had still been there, it would have been his leg instead.

Numerous other tentacles squirmed and lashed out, grasping the surprised tanarukks and coiling around them. The creatures bellowed and screamed, thrashing and biting as the tentacles began to crush the life out of them. The she-demon on the far side merely arched one eyebrow at the appearance of the spell, taking a single step back so that she was clearly beyond the reach of the writhing black appendages. She seemed oddly content to watch as one by one, her troops began to grow silent, their breath lost, their ribs cracked.

Pharaun didn't waste time waiting for the spell to end and allow either the beautiful fiend or any of her remaining minions to reach his team. Not wanting to reveal the extent of his magic any more than necessary, the wizard stooped quickly and slapped at the ground before him. He took one last look at the beautiful fiend opposite him as darkness welled up between them. The moment that spell was finished, he began another, producing a pinch of gem dust from another pocket and weaving a spell that placed an invisible wall between the drow and the tanarukks.

The magical barrier was impervious to any normal attack, would withstand most magical assaults, and would buy the expedition time to find another way out. The wall of energy would not hold indefinitely, but it would last long enough for them to figure out how to escape unseen. Pharaun dusted his hands as he stepped back from the casting.

"Well, a fine solution that is," Quenthel sniped, "sealing us in here. We'd be better off facing those filthy beasts on the other side than just sitting here."

Ryld hunched down nearby, breathing heavily, cleaning his blade with a piece of cloth. Faeryl slumped, exhausted, against the far wall, trying to catch her breath. Only Jeggred and Valas seemed unwinded, both of them standing easy. The scout moved to study the blockage, while the draegloth hovered near Quenthel.

"As I tried to tell you," Pharaun retorted, running his hand along the surface of the damp, gray substance that prevented their passing, "this is the Araumycos. It could go on for miles."

The drow wizard knew his scolding tone was unmistakable, but he didn't care. Quenthel let out an exasperated sigh as she leaned against the wall of the passage. A massive fungus, the Araumycos resembled nothing so much as the exterior of a brain. It completely filled the passage.

"At least we can stop running for a while," Quenthel said. "I'm sick of carrying this damned thing."

She growled, kicking at the knapsack at her feet. She began rubbing her shoulders.

Pharaun shook his head, amazed at the high priestess's stubbornness. The mage had tried to be as deferential as possible, to let her see the folly of heading in this direction, but despite his warnings—and Valas's—the Mistress of Arach-Tinilith had, with her usual haughty demeanor, browbeat them into obeying her wishes anyway. Now they were pinned against the bloated growth, just as he had predicted, and she was simply going to ignore that fact.

Pharaun pursed his lips in vexation as he watched her out of the corner of his eye. She labored to work the stiffness out of her shoulders. He could only imagine the discomfort she must be feeling, but he had no pity for her plight. Despite the fact that his own haversack was magically lightened, Pharaun's shoulders ached, too. They had gone far beyond sore and were, he was certain, chaffed raw.

"Ah, yes," he said, continuing to examine the spongy growth, "you've made it quite clear how far beneath a Baenre—the Mistress of the Academy no less—it is to . . . how did you say it? . . . 'demean herself like a common slave lugging rothé dung through the moss beds.' But, I would respectfully point out—*again*—that it was *your* masterful tactical decision to leave our thralls and pack lizards behind, tethered and bleeding, in order to facilitate our escape from those cloakers."

The wizard knew full well that his cutting remarks would further sour her already unpleasant mood, but he truly didn't care.

Getting under Quenthel's skin gave him no end of delight, even during trying circumstances such as these.

"You presume much, *boy*," the high priestess snapped as she stood straight again, glaring balefully at him. "Perhaps too much. . . ."

Still not looking at her, Pharaun rolled his eyes where she could not see.

"A thousand times a thousand pardons, Mistress," he said, sensing the time was ripe to change the subject. "So I suppose you no longer intend to bother with the goods you think are stored in the Black Claw Mercantile storehouses in Ched Nasad. Even if they do rightfully belong to House Baenre, how are we going to get them back to Menzoberranzan? *You* certainly won't carry them, and once word gets around that you like to use your pack animals and drovers as bait, no one else will, either."

Pharaun stole a sidelong glance at the high priestess, mostly for the simple pleasure of observing her disgruntled state. Quenthel's scowl was particularly severe, drawing out fully the vertical line that ran between her brows and giving her that pinched look that the mage was beginning to find unduly comical. The wizard stifled a chuckle.

That managed to get under her skin, he thought, grinning, but then he noticed Jeggred moving to stand between the two of them.

The beast loomed over the wizard, and Pharaun's grin vanished. He held his breath as the draegloth smiled balefully. The fiend's fetid panting cascaded over him, making his stomach turn.

The demon served Quenthel unswervingly, and at a word from her, he would gladly attempt to rip the wizard—or anyone else in the group, for that matter—limb from limb with malice-laden glee. Thus far, that word had not come, but Pharaun did not relish the possibility of having to defend himself from the fiend's assault, especially in such close quarters where he would have a hard time getting clear to exercise his own allotment of spells. He would prefer a large cavern to make his stand against

Jeggred, but unfortunately, there was only this cramped passage, with no room to stay clear of the brute's claws.

Despite her current foul humor and the very ungainly way she had recently been bearing the load on her back, Quenthel somehow managed to look regal as she pushed herself away from the wall and stalked across the corridor toward Pharaun, her *piwafwi* swishing about her. He understood that she wasn't merely ignoring his jibes. She had waited until her faithful servant had moved into position to back her up before confronting the mage.

"I know very well what I said and did, and I do not need you mimicking my words back to me like some idiot savant, displayed in a gilded cage for all to look upon and laugh at." She focused her stare on him and held it there. "We are on a *diplomatic* mission, wizard, but those goods do belong to my House, and they will be returned there. I'll see to that. If I can't hire a caravan to carry them back, then you'll do it for me. Jeggred will make certain of it."

She held his gaze imperiously for a moment as Jeggred smiled carnally beside her. Finally, she straightened, made a subtle motion to the draegloth, and the fiend moved off to lick the gore from his claws.

"Find us a way around this . . . thing," Quenthel said, jabbing her finger toward the massive growth before she turned and strode back to her own pack and sank down to the floor.

Pharaun sighed and rolled his eyes, knowing he had pushed the high priestess too far. He would suffer more later for his little jibes. He looked over at Faeryl to gauge her reaction to the confrontation. The ambassador from Ched Nasad merely shook her head at him, scorn plain on her mien.

"I would think you, of all people, would be more than a little disgruntled that she's planning to strip your mother's mercantile company bare," he said quietly to her.

Faeryl shrugged and said, "It's no concern of mine. My House merely works for her—for House Baenre and for House Melarn.

They own Black Claw together, so if she wants to steal from her partners, who am I to stop her? As long as I get home . . ."

Pharaun was surprised to actually see a wistful look on the ambassador's face.

The Master of Sorcere grunted at Faeryl's response and turned once more to inspect the material that blocked their way. He was both fascinated at seeing it in person for the first time and desperate to seek a possible way around it. He knew that the Araumycos filled countless miles of caverns in this part of the Underdark, but travelers had sometimes been able to find ways around or through it.

Valas was already climbing up the surface of the growth, pressed tightly against it, working his way toward the upper reaches. Pharaun could see that the passage they had followed opened into what must be a larger cavern, for the ceiling, like the passage itself, rose abruptly. He could see that the scout was making his way toward a narrow gap between the growth and the side of the cavern, perhaps hoping that there was a way to squeeze through, though to where, Pharaun had no idea.

Pharaun considered the diminutive mercenary from Bregan D'aerthe to be a bit uncouth, but nonetheless, he was glad the wiry guide was along for the trip.

"How long do we have before that gives out?" Faeryl asked, staring back the way they all had come, back toward the inky blackness.

Pharaun was surprised that she spoke to him. She was emboldened, the wizard supposed, from their earlier conversation. Not bothering to look at the ambassador, Pharaun continued his inspection, producing a tiny flame at the tip of his finger with which he began scorching the fungus. Where the fire touched the growth, it blackened and withered, but it did not burn a hole through to anywhere.

"Not long," he said.

He sensed rather than saw her discomfort at his offhand comment. The wizard smiled despite himself as he worked, bemused at the irony of Faeryl's situation. It had not been that long ago that she had been desperate to make this journey, to return to her home city. Desperate enough to try sneaking out of Menzoberranzan and crossing Triel Baenre, the most powerful matron mother in the city, in the process. Faeryl had failed, of course. She had been captured at the gates, and she had wound up as Jeggred's imprisoned plaything to boot. Pharaun could only imagine what the draegloth might have been doing to her in the name of sport, but somehow the Zauvirr had earned a reprieve from Triel and had been assigned to participate in this little excursion to Ched Nasad.

In the end, Faeryl had achieved what she wanted, but the wizard wondered if she was still glad of it, despite her previous remarks. Even if she did get home, she was faced with the prospect of informing her mother, the matron mother of House Zauvirr, that Quenthel was coming to take everything. Absolutely everything. Regardless of the feasibility of such a move and the contingent's ability to actually pull it off unmolested by House Melarn, Faeryl and her mother would be the ones caught in the middle. He did not envy her position.

Plus, every time Jeggred so much as turned his gaze in her direction, she flinched and moved away. The fiend seemed to enjoy this, taking every opportunity to enhance the ambassador's discomfort through a suggestive smile, a lick of his lips, or a studied examination of his razor-sharp claws. It was clear to Pharaun that Faeryl was close to fully losing her composure. If that happened, he supposed they might have to actually let the draegloth have her and be done with it.

Then, of course, there was the matter of the supplies. Faeryl, like the rest of the members of the small excursion, had been forced to carry her own belongings for the better part of a tenday, something no high-born dark elf was accustomed to. Sedan chairs borne by slaves and porters was more her style, as it was Quenthel's. Leaving those thralls behind to stave off pursuit had been regrettable but necessary, and even with Jeggred's ability to carry a substantial portion of the load, the rest of them still had sizable burdens. He could hardly blame Faeryl if she was wondering whether this journey was nothing more than a huge mistake.

From Quenthel's demeanor it seemed she already knew that, or perhaps didn't care if Lolth's silence extended as far as Ched Nasad at least and that their journey of exploration had become more akin to a raid. That was fine with Pharaun, but still he suspected there would be more to take from Ched Nasad than a store of magical trinkets.

Glancing at his pack once more and feeling the tension in his own shoulders, Pharaun wished for maybe the tenth time that day that he could summon a magical disk to bear their supplies. So many of the drow noble Houses made steady use of such a handy spell that the matron mothers generally insisted their House wizards learn it while attending Sorcere, the arcane branch of the Academy. Pharaun had never bothered to familiarize himself with it, though, since he had his haversack with its magically roomy interior. Even loaded up with all of his grimoires, scrolls, and more mundane supplies, it weighed a fraction of what a normal pack would. Besides, back at the Academy, if he had ever had cause to transport something with the magical disk, there was always a ready supply of students on hand who could have performed the task for him. Still . . .

Pharaun dismissed the notion, reminding himself for the tenth time that his magic was an all-too-precious commodity. With the goddess Lolth still strangely silent, none of her priestesses could gain the favor of her divine magic, leaving both Quenthel and Faeryl severely hampered and limited in power. The wilds of the Underdark were no place to be while vulnerable. Besides, there was no small amount of satisfaction in watching Quenthel, the High Priestess of Arach-Tinilith, the clerical branch of the Academy, labor with her burden.

Quenthel sniffed, startling Pharaun out of his reverie. The high priestess gestured toward where the scout was still climbing. Only his legs were still visible. The rest of him disappeared into the crevice formed between the wall of the cavern and the fungus.

She turned to Ryld and said, "Your friend is looking for a way through. Stop daydreaming and help him." Turning then to Pharaun, she added, "You, too."

Deciding that he had tormented her enough for the moment, especially with Jeggred so near, Pharaun smiled and bowed low, flourishing his *piwafwi*, then continued to examine the Araumycos.

As Ryld joined him, the wizard muttered, "It's times like these when I find her most charming, eh?"

"You shouldn't taunt her," Ryld murmured back, sliding along in front of the fungus and reaching for his short sword. "All you're going to do is cause us anguish later."

He took an experimental swipe and sliced a section of the growth away from the main body. It fell to the floor at his feet, and he bent to pick it up, but it was already beginning to blacken and decay.

"Oh, I think you mean 'me,' my stout friend," the wizard replied, removing a small vial of acid from a hidden pocket in his *piwafwi* and pouring the contents on the surface of the fungus. "I'll be inundated with enough anguish for the lot of us before we ever reach Ched Nasad, I fear."

Where the liquid coated the growth, the fungus began to sizzle and blacken.

Ryld paused and cast a glance over at his friend. The warrior looked taken aback. Despite their many years of friendship, Pharaun knew that even Ryld still occasionally found the wizard's behavior uncouth.

It's the price I pay for my winning personality and clever wit, Pharaun told himself wryly.

He watched as a reasonably sized hole was eaten through the fungus. There was only more fungus beyond it.

"We could try to hack or burn our way through this stuff forever," Ryld grumbled, moving farther along the face of the blockage to a point directly beneath where Valas had ascended. "There's no telling how deep or how thick it is."

"True, but it's fascinating, nonetheless. Thus far, I have discovered that it can be damaged by acid, fire, and physical cuts. Regardless, the pieces I remove simply dissolve into a dark, decayed mass. Remarkable! I wonder if—"

"I certainly hope you don't mean to tell me that you're exhausting all of your potent wizardly forces on this thing," Ryld asked, glancing back at the still-darkened curtain of magic behind them. "We may need your tricks far more desperately in a moment."

"Don't be dull-witted, my blade-wielding companion," Pharaun answered, tucking a piece of rosy stone back into a pocket. "With my talents, I have more than enough to go around for everyone, even our charming pursuers."

Ryld grunted, and at that point a large hunk of fungus hit the floor of the cavern at Ryld's feet, already in the process of blackening. Ryld took a single step back, out of the line of fire, as several more pieces plopped down where he had been standing.

"It would appear that Valas is cutting his way through to somewhere," Pharaun observed, peering up to where the scout had, until recently, been visible. "I wonder if he's just experimenting or if he has actually discovered a means of egress."

The wizard craned his neck, trying to get a clearer view.

"There's a way through up here," Valas said, reappearing in full. "Come on."

"Well, that answers that question. Time to go," Pharaun said, turning to the rest of the group. He directed Quenthel and Faeryl upward, pointing to where the scout was visible. "We only have a few more moments before my wall of force wears off."

The other drow and the draegloth began floating upward, able to ascend through the magic of their House insignias. One by one, they disappeared through some unseen hole until only Pharaun was left. He began to magically rise up himself, realizing for the first time just how glad he was that they were not turning back to fight more of the tanarukks.

Aliisza smiled as she watched the last of her tanarukk charges tremble and lie still. The black tentacles that had destroyed them still curled and flailed, looking for anything new to latch onto. The alu-fiend was careful to stay out of reach of the grasping black appendages, though she knew that she could have removed them magically, if necessary. In fact, she could have intervened and dismissed the wizard's spell, rescuing her charges, but she had decided against it, and it wasn't because she feared to waste the spell. She was more curious than anything.

Aliisza knew that the dark elves and their demon would be more than capable, as drow tended to be. She moved back along the passage through which she and her squad of tanarukks had followed the drow, knowing that at least two of them had seen her. Yet they continued to turn away, as though they were running. Aliisza doubted the drow were there for any reason related to Kaanyr Vhok.

The alu wasted no time returning to the point at which she had set out with only the single squad, rejoining the larger force of which they had been a part, the force she commanded.

"They have moved into higher halls," she announced to the milling tanarukks, directing them along a new route. "We will cut them off at Blacktooth Rock. Do not tarry. They move fast."

With barely more than a grumble, the horde of humanoids set off, and it didn't take them more than a few minutes to reach the great intersection known to the Scourged Legion as Blacktooth Rock. It was a large, multi-leveled chamber where many different passages connected, and Aliisza wasn't even sure what the dwarves who'd cut the chamber once used it for. Much of it had been filled with the fungus colony the stoutfolk called Araumycos. There were still enough open passages there, however, that patrols of the Scourged Legion passed through frequently, and she knew that unless they utilized some magic to change their course, the passage the drow had taken to escape would ultimately lead them there as well.

The alu-fiend was still considering what she would do upon confronting the drow when her small battalion of tanarukks intercepted a second contingent of the humanoids, one she had sent to cut off escape along another route.

"What are you doing here?" she asked the sergeant, though she was actually glad for the reinforcements. "I assigned you to the Columned Chamber to watch for anything coming from the north."

"Yes," the sergeant answered. He was a hulking specimen who stood a good head taller than any of his fellows, his speech thick due to his prominent tusks. "But we got word that a large force of gray dwarves was spotted moving through the south part of Ammarindar, and a second patrol, one that had been stationed farther to the north and east, has completely disappeared."

"By the Abyss," Aliisza whispered. "What is going on?"

She considered for a moment, then issued orders for a small squad of tanarukks to return to Vhok's palace to report the news, while she and the remainder of the force continued to pursue the drow.

They know something about all this, she told herself as they set out, and I'm going to find out what it is.

Pharaun no longer jumped whenever Ryld silently returned after skulking along the group's back trail, so he showed no reaction when the warrior suddenly materialized in the group's midst. Splitter was still sheathed across the master of Melee-Magthere's back, so Pharaun knew that they were in no immediate danger. Nonetheless, he paid careful attention as his old friend began to convey a report to Quenthel in the silent hand language of the drow.

Our pursuers are on our trail again, the burly warrior signaled. *Several squads, all closing the gap.*

The snake heads hissed, echoing their mistress's irritation at this news before Quenthel quieted them with a whispered word.

How long before we are overtaken? she responded.

In the darkness, Pharaun saw Ryld shrug. *Perhaps ten minutes, no more.*

Quenthel replied, *We must rest, at least for a few moments longer. Besides, Valas has not yet returned. Figure out which way he went.*

She gestured at the intersection. Ryld nodded and moved to examine the walls near the three-way tunnel. If Valas had left some sign of the direction he'd taken, Ryld would find it, and they could continue.

Pharaun sighed, regretting ever having suggested they come this way to reach Ched Nasad. Passing through the domain of Kaanyr Vhok had been a risky choice, but one that Quenthel had finally insisted on, preferring speed over safety. So, the group moved through the Ammarindar, the ancient holdings of an even more ancient dwarven nation, long since wiped out.

Pharaun knew that Kaanyr Vhok had laid claim to the area since the fall of Hellgate Keep, which stood somewhere overhead in the World Above. Vhok, a marquis cambion demon, was an intensely unpleasant host, as Pharaun recalled. Most caravans generally avoided his little patch of the Underdark, so the passages they traversed had been little traveled, which Pharaun had hoped would help maintain the group's secrecy.

Even moving as surreptitiously as possible, the team was unable to avoid attracting the attention of Vhok's minions, and several of the cambion's patrols were once again relentlessly pursuing them. Pharaun had hoped that sneaking through the Araumycos would have thrown the tanarukks off, but he realized that they—or rather, the she-fiend, he supposed—knew exactly where the expedition was headed, even if they themselves did not. He had no doubt that even more were moving to outflank them, cut them off before they could move out of the region and beyond Vhok's reach. The question was, could they stay ahead of the patrols this time?

The Menzoberranyr couldn't afford to have to deal with the demon lord. With the news they carried, avoiding drawing attention to themselves from any of the great races of the Underdark was paramount. And yet, Pharaun had the sinking feeling that was going to be no easy matter. No part of the journey to Ched Nasad was going to be easy, he was certain. There was risk in every move, just like on the *sava* board.

In its own way, Quenthel's decision to relieve the group of extra baggage—and baggage bearers—had been fortuitous. They could set a faster pace without all the extras the high priestesses had initially insisted they bring along. The mage glanced at Quenthel, knowing she struggled between the notion of setting a faster pace and being sick to death of carrying a load that made her shoulders slump when she thought no one was watching. Pharaun suspected they could have gotten by with even less, and Quenthel might yet lighten her load, discarding more unnecessary provisions, before they reached the City of Webs. If they found themselves in another running fight with Vhok's hordes, it might be sooner rather than later.

Almost as if he knew time was growing short, Valas appeared, followed by Ryld and Jeggred. The drow scout trotted into the intersection and hunkered down against one wall of the passage, absently fingering one of the many outlandish trinkets that adorned his vest.

As Pharaun and Quenthel moved closer, Valas began flashing hand signals.

Our route takes us into a large chamber ahead.

Valas gestured along the passage from which he had just returned.

What's there? Quenthel signaled impatiently.

The scout shrugged then signed, *More of the fungus, but it doesn't block our path this time. We're almost beyond Vhok's reach.*

Then let's go, Quenthel replied. *I'm sick of this place.*

Valas nodded, and the group set off again. The passages through which the scout led them were once again wide and smooth, cut from the rock of the Underdark by skilled dwarf hands. They seemed to be making headway in the direction they wanted to go, as Faeryl commented more than once that things were starting to look familiar to her. With any luck, they would be out of Kaanyr Vhok's domain and into the outskirts of Ched Nasad's patrolled regions in short order. Quenthel seemed content this time to let Valas and Ryld interpret the ancient Dethek runes inscribed on the thoroughfares of the long-abandoned dwarven city and go where they suggested, for which Pharaun was intensely grateful. The sooner they reached the comforts of Ched Nasad, the better he'd feel, at least physically.

The mage had been contemplating making a suggestion to Quenthel, proposing to her that they enter the city discreetly. He wouldn't put it past the high priestess to want to stroll in with banners unfurled and demand to see the most powerful representatives of the noble Houses, just so she could tell them all that she was taking what was hers, Ched Nasad be damned. He had to think of a way to convince her to swallow her pride and do the smart thing, instead. It would be so much better for all of them if they didn't attract a lot of attention to themselves, at least not in the city streets.

Besides, Pharaun thought, *why do I want to be the guests of a bunch more matron mothers? An inn, especially a particularly splendid inn, would be much more satisfying.*

The trick, he realized, was in how to go about convincing Quenthel. Trying to make it look like her idea seemed the best choice, but working out a good, subtle way to plant the seed was tricky where the high priestess was concerned. She'd already shown that she was difficult to maneuver.

Push a little too hard, and she'd slap you down just because you were a male. Don't push hard enough, and she'd be too busy being in a foul temper to see what you were dangling in front of her face. Pharaun could think of a number of arguments he could use just to convince her, rather than trying to trick her into doing it his way, but again, with Quenthel, he knew he could argue until he was out of breath, and she might still refuse.

Pharaun suddenly realized that the passageway had begun to ascend, and fairly steeply, too. He glanced up and saw the others laboring to reach the top of the rise. As they crested the ridge, they drew to a halt, and Faeryl said something softly as she pointed into the distance. The wizard wondered what they had spotted. He quickened his own step, and when he caught up with them he paused. The panorama of a large, softly lit chamber greeted him. At least he assumed it was a large chamber. Judging from the curvature of the walls, it was quite grand, but more than half of it was filled with the great fungus. He shook his head, more impressed with the Araumycos than ever. The entirety of the growth was a single living organism, as best as any wizard or sage could determine. That this was a different part of the same entity they'd encountered nearly an hour ago was astonishing, but knowing that what he had seen, at least to this point, was still only a tiny part of the whole thing made his head swim.

The chamber itself was natural, with a mammoth black stalactite that looked remarkably like a huge fang just beginning to bite into the fungus, being the most prominent feature. Evidence of dwarven stoneworking was also in abundance. The drow had entered at a point fairly high along the exposed wall of the cavern, the passage emptying onto a large, balconied ledge that overlooked the floor. A large ramp, wide enough to accommodate several wagons side by side, descended from this ledge on the left side, entering into a series of switchbacks that crisscrossed down the side of the cavern below the ledge until it reached the floor. There, a smooth, paved road led to intersections scattered along the floor where other roads shot off to more switchbacks, eventually rising to a number of tunnels. In many cases, the pathways simply disappeared beneath the massive, pasty-gray fungus.

To Pharaun's eye, the whole place could have been a tiny city, similar to a portion of Menzoberranzan, except for two notable differences. First, the architecture was obviously and repulsively dwarven, all thick and blocky and dull to the eye. Second was the dim but pervasive light, which seemed to glow from almost everywhere and gave the whole chamber, indeed the entire stone surface, a pale, sickly gray glow. In Menzoberranzan, the city's velvety was blackness was broken by rich, luxurious hues of violet, green, and amber scattered across the cavern floor and ceiling. Here, everything was visible, glowing from some soft magical light that illuminated everywhere, but nothing had any color.

The dark elf wizard missed his home, longed to sit atop the balconies of the Academy and look out over the city. He yearned for even the simple pleasure of observing Narbondel, its red glow tracking the hours of the day and night. In the wilds, Pharaun had discovered that without the familiarity of the great clock in the City of Spiders he was losing all track of time, even though he had other, magical, means of following its passage. For a brief moment, Pharaun wondered if he would ever see Menzoberranzan again, and he felt a touch of—of what? Sadness? Was that what sadness felt like? It was odd, and the mage determined to shake it off.

What you need is a nice, hot, oiled bath, Mizzrym, followed by a deepstroke performed by a master masseur, and you'll have a spring in your step in no time.

With that encouraging thought, the wizard straightened up and turned his attention to his companions.

Valas had moved down along the ramp and had reached the first switchback. From Pharaun's vantage point, the diminutive scout looked truly tiny, giving the master of Sorcere a better sense of the scale of the chamber. Quenthel, Faeryl, Jeggred, and Ryld, meanwhile, were descending through the air to the next section of the path and were about halfway down, dropping in a loose cluster. Pharaun chuckled, wondering how the Mistress of the Academy was faring, still laboring with her baggage.

Well, Pharaun thought, that oil bath is waiting for you.

He took two steps toward the edge of the balcony to follow the high priestess and the others, when he felt rather than heard a disturbance behind him.

Khorrl Xornbane could not help but tense slightly as the door to the private booth where he sat waiting slid partially open. His hand dropped instinctively to grip the doubleaxe at his side. Even when Zammzt slipped through the narrow opening on soft footsteps and settled onto the cushioned bench on the opposite side of the table, the duergar did not yet relax. He peered warily through the still-open partition into the hallway beyond, looking to see who might be lurking in a shadow, watching them meet. There were only three other individuals there, and none of them seemed to be paying Zammzt any attention at all. Two drow dressed as merchants, led by a third dark elf who was obviously a host of the Glowing Goblet, made their way to another booth and disappeared inside. Khorrl frowned as the host delayed a moment longer. The servant cocked his head slightly to one side, apparently listening to something that was said from inside the meeting cubicle, spoken too softly for the duergar to overhear.

He's just taking a drink order, the duergar thought. No need to get antsy.

Despite his self-admonition, Khorrl knew he would not rest easy for at least another minute or two. It would not be the first time some fool had allowed himself to be followed during a meeting with the duergar mercenary, and he never again wanted to be in such a position, caught unaware and forced to fight his way out of a corner. Not only had he barely escaped, but it had sullied his reputation to boot. That part had angered him most of all.

Finally, when he was certain no one was studying either of them on the sly, Khorrl relaxed, though he had to consciously release his grip on the doubleaxe to do so. He looked across the table at Zammzt, noting the lack of a House insignia anywhere on the plain-looking drow's clothing. For his part, Zammzt was reclining casually on the cushioned bench, the tiniest hint of a smile on his face. Though Khorrl didn't consider himself a great judge of attractiveness, especially in other species, it was plain enough to him that Zammzt's face was far from noteworthy. The drow was simply too ordinary looking. If he didn't already serve a noble House, he would have never amounted to much more than a common artisan, a step up from a slave but little more. Khorrl supposed the fact that he was such a shrewd negotiator was the dark elf's single biggest saving grace.

"I assure you, I was not followed," Zammzt said, interrupting the duergar's musings. "I would have known it, if someone tried, and there's no reason at all for anyone to do so."

"Why do you think I was concerned about that?" Khorrl asked, settling back himself. "I haven't accused you of anything yet."

"The sour look on your face and the furtive glances you keep casting out the door make it plain enough," the dark elf replied, "though I don't question your concern. You will no doubt be glad to know that I observed your arrival from a secure position, and I will tell you that no one followed you, either."

Khorrl stiffened slightly again, trying to decide if he should be insulted or impressed. Few creatures had managed to study him unnoticed, certainly not in recent years. For him not to notice Zammzt's observations was surprising, if what the drow claimed was true. The duergar narrowed his eyes, wondering if the dark elf was merely lying to impress him. He doubted it, but still . . .

"Then you must feel secure enough to speak freely, hmm?" Khorrl asked, baiting his boothmate to see what his reaction would be.

Zammzt's smile deepened the tiniest bit as he waved a hand in dismissal and turned his gaze on the table in front of him.

"Of course," he said. "Though I would think you'd prefer to wait until the host has brought us drinks first."

"I've already turned him down," Khorrl replied, giving his own wave of dismissal. "I don't care to partake while I'm doing business."

"As I'm well aware, Master Xornbane, from your reputation. I, however, have already requested that a refreshment be delivered to the booth. I believe I hear it coming now."

Khorrl turned his gaze for the merest of moments to the crack in the door, even as he opened his mouth to point out that he'd heard nothing. He started to turn back to Zammzt, but then did a double-take, for sure enough, the host from the other booth had appeared at the far end of the hall with a tray of drinks. Khorrl snapped his mouth shut again as he watched the servant first deliver a pair of beverages to the other booth, then proceed toward him and his companion. Apparently, in addition to his surprising ability to shadow someone, Zammzt also sported exceptional hearing. After delivering the drink and inquiring if the duergar had changed his mind and wanted something, the host departed. Zammzt reached over and pushed the partition shut the rest of the way.

"I think it's safe to discuss our business," the dark elf said, his red eyes glittering in satisfaction as he took a sip from his frosty mug.

After a long pull, he sighed in delight and said, "Everything is in place. You should be receiving delivery of the first payment in the next day."

Khorrl eyed the drow for a long moment before finally nodding.

"And the amount is satisfactory?" the duergar mercenary asked. "None of my people goes into the city until I know that we'll be paid what I said."

"Absolutely. My mistress has instructed me to inform you that your fee is more than satisfactory. For the services you will be providing, she considers it a small price to pay."

"*Hmph*," Khorrl grunted noncommittally. "That remains to be seen, doesn't it? If she leaves me hanging in the middle of the fight, it won't have been nearly enough, and you know it."

Zammzt smiled that knowing smile again and nodded in acquiescence.

"I can only assure you that she and her allies intend to see this through to the very end. Once they set foot down this path, there is no turning back for them, either. You should be well aware of that."

"Perhaps, but if things go sour for us," Khorrl said, running his hand across his bald gray head, "I will come looking for her personally."

"Please, please. There's no need for idle threats here. The initial payment is coming. Just be sure you have the first group ready to go when it arrives."

Khorrl nodded, more firmly this time. He had never reneged on a contract before, and he wasn't about to now. His clan was getting paid an exorbitant sum to fight, and his employer considered it money well spent precisely because of that reputation. Clan Xornbane might be merely a mercenary band in the greater scheme of the duergar hierarchy, but he had always made sure they honored their commitments. That wasn't going to change as long as he was the head of the clan.

"They will be there," he said finally.

"Excellent," Zammzt replied. "My mistress is counting on it. Despite your assistance, toppling the rival Houses will not be easy. That is why she and her allies are paying you such a generous retainer."

Khorrl frowned again, thinking of what work lay ahead. The drow was right; overthrowing one drow noble House, even when their clergy was hamstrung, was no small feat. He and his males were expected to help bring down several. The clan would suffer losses in this, no question about it, but they had been eager to accept this particular contract, anyway. The rich reward of helping the dark elves destroy themselves paled only slightly in comparison to the payment itself. Those among Clan Xornbane who survived would receive larger shares for this work than for their last four contracts combined. It was well worth the loss of troops, especially among the lesser races of the front ranks.

By the Abyss, Khorrl thought. *I might even consider retirement when we're through here.*

"We will do what we're paid to do. You know our reputation," the duergar said, affectionately running his hand along the handle of his doubleaxe. "Though I would feel a lot more confident if I knew for sure that your priestesses won't suddenly find themselves kissed by the spider queen in the middle of the fight. It would be our downfall, and yours too, most likely."

Zammzt spread his hands in a placating gesture.

"That is a risk, to be sure," he said, almost—*almost*—sounding apologetic. "But the opportunity for my mistress and her co-conspirators is worth it. Rest assured, you will not be forgotten in this. She looks forward to the moment when she can thank you from her new position as one of the highest-ranking matron mothers in the city."

Khorrl nodded one last time and prepared to depart.

"Very well, then," he said. "We will be waiting for the first payment. The schedule is set."

He rose, pulling his doubleaxe up beside him. Before he slid the partition open, he turned to look back at the dark elf, who seemed content to stay a while and finish his drink. Khorrl caught the drow's gaze and held it.

"We're committed now," the gray dwarf said. "There's no turning back. Blood will flow in Ched Nasad. Mark my words."

※　　※　　※

Spinning, Pharaun summoned his magical rapier from the ring into one hand, and clasped his *piwafwi* closed with the other, before he was completely turned around. As he pivoted into a defensive stance, releasing the rapier to dance in the air before him, he reached into the pockets of his *piwafwi,* selecting by memory and feel the components he needed to weave a certain incantation.

Perhaps a dozen steps from Pharaun, a shimmering blue doorway, similar to the extradimensional portal he was fond of using himself, was just closing, winking out of existence. The lovely creature he had spotted briefly during the rather one-sided battle with the tanarukks stood just in front of it, her smile accenting her arched eyebrows as she regarded him, arms folded casually beneath her prominent breasts. In particular, she seemed to find his floating, weaving rapier of interest.

"I'm sorry, did I startle you?" she purred, and Pharaun found her voice to be delightfully throaty.

"Oh, it's quite all right," the mage replied, eyeing the she-fiend from head to toe. She was dressed in tight, black, form-fitting leather, and while thigh-high boots and a corset seemed far from practical as travel-wear to the drow, he had to appreciate the effectiveness of the ensemble.

It compliments her wings so well, he decided.

"I wondered when you'd show up again," Pharaun said, noting with his second sweeping gaze the numerous daggers protruding from her belt and the tops of her boots. An enchanted ring he wore enabled him to determine that one of those daggers was obviously magical, as well as the long sword strapped to her right thigh. A ring adorning her left finger also caught his attention, for it radiated a strong protective dweomer.

"So you've been expecting me. How delightful!" she said, sauntering languidly over to a section of the balcony and sitting, leaning back and resting on her hands as she brought one long leg up to prop it on the railing. She appeared to ignore the fact that the rapier danced along as she relocated, keeping itself between her and the mage. "It ruins my grand entrance a bit, I suppose, but then again, I doubt you're terribly impressed with parlor tricks like mine."

"On the contrary," Pharaun replied, moving to take a seat a few paces away but maintaining the position of the rapier between the two of them. "I am always delighted to make the acquaintance of a fellow practitioner. You can't imagine how dull and dreary it can be, traveling with unimaginative companions who can't appreciate the difference between a divination and an evocation."

He swept his arm out over the side in the general direction of the other drow, who were far below him and well out of earshot.

Despite his casual manner, the mage was on edge and quite wary. He was sure the alu-fiend was sizing him up just as critically as he was her, and he considered everything carefully before opening his mouth. He certainly didn't want to reveal something that could get him into trouble with her later. Nonetheless, he was fairly sure she already knew where the rest of his companions were, and pointing out their positions lower in the cavern was not giving away too big a secret.

"Don't be too sure," she said, absently toying with the lacing that ran up the side of her corset, "I can imagine your predicament quite well. You forget the crowd I normally run with. They can't appreciate much beyond the next chance they'll get to eat or rut, much less the intricacies involved in spinning a good spell. What's a girl to do?"

When she finished, she gave Pharaun what he assumed must be one of her best pouts.

"Yes, I can see your point," the wizard said, chuckling. "It can't be much of a choice . . . rutting with the males, or seeking out a little more refined entertainment. I can't blame you for slipping away from them for a while."

"Oh, I never stray too far away from them," the demon said, looking at the wizard levelly. "One or the other of us might get into trouble."

Pharaun nodded slightly, acknowledging the hint. Still, he couldn't help but grin, delighted as he was to be able to engage in such clever innuendo. It was another thing he missed since taking his leave of Menzoberranzan. It wasn't just that most drow displayed a total absence of humor, his companions seemed even more staid than usual, though given the circumstances that wasn't totally unexpected. Still, they were a tight-lipped lot.

Quenthel was clinging too fiercely to the mantle of leadership to spend time mentally sparring with the wizard, Faeryl said very little at all, Valas was hardly in the same vicinity, and Jeggred's discussions had a marked singularity of topic to them. Pharaun had long since grown tired of hearing of the draegloth's desires to rend his foes in one messy way or another. Ryld had always been more willing to converse with him than most, but even the warrior had been pointedly taciturn for most of the journey. With the exception of a few brief discussions regarding Quenthel's heavy-handed methods, they had simply stopped the banter that had always marked the friendship between them.

It wasn't as though Ryld wouldn't talk to him, Pharaun admitted to himself, but things definitely weren't the same as before.

Before I left him to his death during the insurrection, the mage concluded, inwardly sighing.

Ryld had accepted the wizard's apologies afterward, claimed he understood the necessity of it, but in reality the pair's friendship had been damaged. It wasn't that Pharaun felt any real sense of guilt over the decision. He simply missed the benefits of the friendship.

"I said, you seem to be burdened with heavy thoughts."

Pharaun started, realizing that the she-fiend had been speaking to him during his ruminations. As he refocused his attention on her, he noticed that the rapier had sagged low from inattention and he snapped it back onto guard. Furious with himself for relaxing his vigilance, he summoned the weapon back to him and let it disappear back into the ring.

No reason to keep it out, he thought ruefully. If she'd wanted to get past it and at me, she already had the perfect chance.

The wizard bowed his head slightly, wordlessly apologizing for his lapse in manners. The alu-fiend only smiled.

"You certainly don't want to hear about my troubles," he said at last, his tone bright. "You obviously dropped in on this social visit for other reasons."

"Again, don't be so sure," the fiend replied, standing and stretching indolently. "It requires some fairly extraordinary circumstances to bring a band of dark elves through Ammarindar—"

"Oh, nothing of any real consequence," Pharaun interjected.

"—especially a mistress of the Academy and her retinue," she continued, ignoring the wizard's interruption. "Very extraordinary circumstances, indeed."

She was looking at Pharaun, perhaps gauging his reaction.

In fact, his reaction was the slightest straightening of his back and shoulders, but it was only the merest hint of his true surprise.

She knew.

A dozen thoughts floated through the mage's head in the next instant, considerations of who might have betrayed them, who back in Menzoberranzan had sent them off on this journey for the mere purpose of disposing of them in the clutches of Kaanyr Vhok and his minions, but the notions were dismissed again just as quickly. The risk of exposing the plight of the priestesses of Lolth was far too great to risk by such a method. The she-fiend had discovered their identity in some other way. Her broadening smile and sparkling green eyes told him that he had confirmed her suspicions.

"Oh, don't get too lathered up about it," she said, laughing. "Your secret's safe with us—at least, for the time being," she added, the smile gone. "But it brings me to my reason for being here. The Sceptered One, Kaanyr Vhok, Master of the Scourged Legions, lord of the portion of the Underdark through which you currently trespass, would delight in having an audience with you. I'm here to extend that invitation."

Almost as if on cue, there was a shout, dimly echoing, from far below. Without thinking, Pharaun turned and gazed over the edge of the precipice to the cavern floor below. There, Quenthel and the others had been in the process of crossing to a lower tunnel, one without switchbacks. Valas was rushing back from the mouth of the egress, apparently to join them. Behind him, a flood of tanarukks emerged from the passage and from others flanking it.

Observing the scene had taken but an instant, but it had been enough for the she-fiend to expend some sort of magical energy, which Pharaun could see radiating around her. He was on his guard, expecting an attack, but she did not move. Her green eyes, however, smoldered. Whether it was with lust or anger, he wasn't sure.

"I think you should accompany me back to the palace," the demon said, her voice husky. "You will like it there. Very much."

She began to saunter toward him as she spoke, and he could sense the energy flow over him. She was hoping to magically coerce him, somehow, the mage supposed. He backed up a step and put on his best apologetic smile.

"That, I'm afraid, is very much out of the question, at least for the moment. My companions need me."

The she-fiend's smile faded, and she pursed her lips in irritation.

"They are surrounded, you know," she said, pausing in her advance. "This is, at least for the moment, still an amicable offer. Go to them, convince them to return with me to Kaanyr's palace, and I promise you that the meeting will be cordial. My forces below have been instructed merely to hold their positions and prevent you and your friends from departing until I have a chance to make the offer to you. Will you do that?"

Pharaun smiled. "How well do you know Kaanyr Vhok?" he asked, his tone suggestive.

Her smile deepened, and her eyes glittered with what was definitely lust.

"Quite well," she answered, "but then again, he's terribly busy, so not as well as I would like. Come back to his palace with me."

Pharaun's own smile widened, and he asked. "What's your name?"

The she-fiend giggled once in amusement and said, "I almost forgot to tell you! I'm Aliisza. Now, will you come with me?"

"It's a delight to meet you, Aliisza, I'm Pharaun, and I'd love to accompany you, but for the moment, duty calls. Am I to assume that we will meet with resistance down there? Or has our discussion set your mind at ease to such an extent that we might pass out of Ammarindar unhindered today?"

Aliisza grinned and said, "I had my orders, dear. You were not to pass beyond the borders without a fight, but I tell you what . . . I'll give you a sporting chance, just because I like you." Her voice had turned husky again. "Just this once, I'll stay out of it. A few hundred tanarukks shouldn't cause you undue trouble, should they?"

Pharaun cocked his head to one side, as if considering that, then said, "Well, they will be a substantially greater difficulty than if we could move on unmolested, but as you say, it's a sporting chance. Until the next time we meet, then."

In answer, Aliisza nodded and smiled.

The mage leaned backward and dropped over the side of the precipice.

        ❦   ❦   ❦

At Valas's distant shout, Quenthel looked up from where she had been staring absently at Jeggred's back, following the draegloth through the massive chamber. She spied the scout hurrying back from where he'd ventured ahead, and the high priestess spotted the hordes of tanarukks behind him, emerging from the sculpted tunnel wall. She swore under her breath, and the five snakes on her whip writhed in mimicry of her displeasure.

"We are cut off again, Mistress!" K'Sothra hissed. "Perhaps there is another way?"

"No, let us destroy them; taste their flesh and be done with them," Zinda argued, her own long black body straining forward eagerly.

"That's enough," Quenthel snapped, starting forward again to join with Valas.

The vipers quieted somewhat, but they still strained to pay attention to their mistress's surroundings, trying to sense any other possible dangers.

The tanarukks did not follow the scout but instead fanned out into a defensive formation. It seemed they were content to wait until the drow came to them.

So much the better, Quenthel thought grimly. They can line themselves up so that the wizard can decimate them most efficiently.

"What are they about?" Faeryl asked, trotting beside Quenthel. "Why aren't they chasing the male?"

She gestured toward Valas, who was only perhaps fifty paces from them.

"Why should they?" Quenthel countered, letting her long strides quickly close the gap between herself and Valas. "They somehow know we must go that way. It seems they're content to wait until we come to them."

Faeryl sniffed at this but said nothing more.

"We should wade through them and slice them, let their blood stain our feet as we tread upon their corpses," Jeggred suggested, his own long strides easily matching Quenthel's quicker ones.

The Mistress of Tier Breche looked over at the draegloth and saw him lick his feral lips in anticipation.

"Nonsense," she said crisply. "There's no need to get messy when they seem willing to oblige us by standing over there and letting Pharaun dispatch them with a well-placed spell or two. Right, wizard?"

When there was no answer, Quenthel spun to face him—only to discover that he was not behind her. Only Ryld kept pace with the two females and the draegloth.

"Where in the Abyss is that damnable mage?" Quenthel growled at Ryld, who raised an eyebrow in surprise and turned to look back.

"He was right behind me," the warrior replied, letting his gaze sweep back and upward, toward the tunnel through which they had originally entered. "I don't know—there!"

The weapons master pointed high up the wall, and Quenthel had to stop in order to turn around sufficiently to see where Ryld was pointing. When she spotted Pharaun, she muttered an invective under her breath. He wasn't alone. There was someone, a woman, in conversation with him.

"Who is that with him? What is he doing?" the high priestess asked no one in particular.

Ryld shrugged and said, "I have no idea, Mistress. I never heard him stop."

"Well, get him down here, now! I need him," Quenthel ordered.

Ryld made as if to protest, then shrugged, turned back, and broke into a rapid jog back along the thoroughfare. When she turned back, Valas had reached their position.

"So?" she asked the scout.

Valas took one deep, calming breath and explained, "They've cut off our route again, and they've made sure this time that we won't go around their flank."

The scout pointed to several other exits from the large chamber.

Quenthel could see already that more of the tanarukks were there, each group similar in size to the one directly in front of them. They were gathering on the ledges and ramps, just on their side of the tunnel openings. It wasn't hard to see that they were intentionally halting the drow's progress, trying to force them to turn back.

"Obviously, they aren't here merely to attack us," she said, thinking aloud, "so they must want something else."

"Perhaps I can explain," Pharaun said, materializing out of a shimmering blue doorway that hung in the open air only a few feet away. The portal snapped out of existence as the wizard primped himself a bit, straightening his *piwafwi* and adjusting his pack. "We've been invited to join Kaanyr Vhok, the master of those fellows, for a discussion."

"What are you talking about? Who was that woman you were speaking with back there?" Quenthel demanded, seething at how Pharaun seemed so full of himself all the time.

The fact that he could still freely use his magic, while she could not, continually galled her. Though he might never say anything, she knew he loved flaunting the fact of it in front of her every chance he could. To add insult to injury, he seemed taken with showing unbridled politeness toward her. She narrowed her eyes suspiciously. He wanted something, she was sure.

"We thought you were in trouble. I sent Ryld back to look into it," Quenthel said. She jabbed a single finger outward, pointing at the distant figure of the weapons master. "Now I'll have to send Jeggred to catch up with him while you stay here and explain to me what this is all about."

Before the high priestess could direct the draegloth to do her bidding, though, Pharaun cut in. "Oh, that's not necessary. Allow me but a moment." The wizard turned and faced Ryld, pointed his finger, and began to whisper. "Ryld, my dear friend, I appreciate your concern for me, but I am quite fine and standing here among our esteemed companions. You can return from your quest to rescue me."

In the distance, Quenthel saw the warrior start and straighten. He turned around as Pharaun spoke. Ryld seemed to shake his head in consternation, and Quenthel thought she heard him sigh, though of course it was only a whisper. By the time the mage was finished, Ryld was already trudging back in their direction.

"Very clever, mage," Quenthel said, clenching her teeth. "Now why don't you be as useful in other ways and tell me what you were doing up there."

"Of course. That was Aliisza, a charming and somewhat gregarious representative of Master Vhok's. She was lurking in the shadows back when we ran into them—" he gestured into the distance at the tanarukks—"in the previous tunnel. They answer to her, and she answers to Vhok."

"Well, how interesting," Quenthel said, folding her arms. "And just what did you two have to talk about for so long? You weren't, perhaps, coming to some sort of an agreement with her, were you?"

Pharaun looked genuinely pained and said, "High Priestess, I only listened politely while she extended her offer. I could not, of course, give her any sort of proper answer without first conversing with you. I suspected what your answer would be before I even mentioned the invitation, but I would be remiss in my duties if I didn't at least deliver the message."

"Indeed," Quenthel said. She knew good and well that the flamboyant wizard before her wouldn't have given a second thought to betraying her and the rest of them if it presented him with some worthwhile benefit. "Interesting that she chose you to be her messenger boy."

Pharaun grimaced, but only slightly.

"We share a common, uh . . . appreciation for the arcane arts," he said at last. "We spent a few moments in idle conversation about the difficulties of traveling with those who don't share that appreciation."

Quenthel snorted. "I'm sure you were interested in more than her wizardly skills."

The mage's grin didn't change, but his eyes hardened the slightest bit. Good, she thought. Remind him that you see right through him.

"Very well," she said. "We're certainly not going to go back with the brutes to see Vhok, so the question is, how do we get through them and on our way?"

"There's no way to get around them," Valas said, "unless the ambassador knows this area and has a notion of another route we can take," he finished, looking at Faeryl.

The Zauvirr priestess shook her head.

"We're still too far away from the proper outskirts of Ched Nasad for me to recognize any features with certainty," she said.

"Then we must slay them," Jeggred announced. "Let me engage them and cut a path for you, Mistress."

"No, Jeggred, there's no need, however much fun you might think it would be. Pharaun, here, is going to get us through this. Aren't you?"

The mage grinned bemusedly and said, "I might have an incantation or two that will allow us to make our way through to the tunnel.

Aliisza has assured me that, in good sporting fashion, she will stay out of it. Slaying these creatures should be minimal trouble."

"I'm not concerned with that. Just clear a path for us," Quenthel commanded.

"Very well," he said as he began to move forward, weaving the beginnings of a spell as he did so.

Chapter

FOUR

Aliisza wasn't sure how Kaanyr would receive her latest news, but it didn't slow her steps. Tarrying to deliver it served no purpose. He would find out eventually, and she might as well pass it to him and get on to other, more interesting things. Besides, she wasn't really troubled by the prospect of the cambion's anger. He might fly off the handle from time to time, but he knew better than to direct it at her. Whether or not he flew into a rage this time, she had an idea that might just soothe his ruffled feathers and give her a bit of fun, besides.

Passing through the great doorway and into the throne room, Aliisza expected to find Vhok sitting on his throne, but he was not. He paced in front of it, which meant that he had serious things on his mind, serious in a bad way. The alu-fiend had a pretty good idea what those things were.

"Any more information on what that duergar horde is doing?" she asked as she approached him.

Vhok looked up from his contemplation, seemed to stare right through her for a moment, and at last said, "All I've been able to determine at the moment is that they don't seem to be headed in this direction, which is good."

"Good? Why?" Aliisza asked. She moved to sit on the top step of the dais. "I thought you liked the idea of a little sport for the Legions. You told me the other night that things were getting a bit staid around—"

"Because something big is definitely going on," Kaanyr interrupted, "and because they were responsible for wiping out the patrol to the northeast."

Aliisza had been about to stretch out, hoping to distract Kaanyr from all of this serious discussion for a few moments of romance, but she sat straight.

"That wasn't just a roving band of duergar," Vhok continued, "they were professional mercenaries. The Xornbane clan, if the evidence is correct. They don't go anywhere without major coin changing hands and big battles in the works."

Aliisza pursed her lips in thought.

"So if they aren't moving against us," she said, "then where?"

"Though I already have an idea, I was hoping you could tell me," Kaanyr said, looking down at the alu-fiend. "Where are my guests?"

Aliisza avoided meeting Vhok's gaze.

"I wasn't able to convince them to join us," she said carefully, "and after they defeated my little patrol as easily as they did, I thought it wise not to pursue the matter so directly."

"Defeated? Wiped out is more like it."

Kaanyr's tone was measured, and Aliisza could tell he was displeased.

So he already knew, did he? Is he spying on me, now?

She was glad she'd been up front with him on the subject. It had been tempting to fudge the truth a bit, to tell him that the tanarukks had not followed her instructions, but in the end, something had convinced her that she was going to have to start being a little more careful with Vhok.

"They are formidable," she answered at last. "The wizard with them is . . . interesting. He's the one I spoke with, and it was definitely he who plowed through the Legions. Drow are formidable to begin with, and it was a tactical error on my part to engage them in such a large chamber. They were able to easily evade the Scourged simply by getting up off the floor and out of range. Pharaun laid waste to the troops without much of a thought."

"I'm sure you did the best you could," Kaanyr said, waving her explanation away. Aliisza scowled at the insult but said nothing. "It's probably just as well. It seems that the gray dwarves are bound and determined to reach Ched Nasad, which is where our little visitors are headed, as well, I think. We weren't going to dissuade them from that without bringing the entire might of the Scourged Legions, as well as some of your sisters, to bear."

"I did find out a couple more things," Aliisza said, ready to spring her idea on Vhok. "They are all high-ranking nobles from Menzoberranzan, not just the priestess. The wizard is powerful enough to be a member, if not a master, of Sorcere, and some of the things he admitted to convinced me that most of the others are of similar rank."

"Well, that's all very interesting, but I probably would have inferred that from the fact that the Mistress of the Academy was out with such a small group to begin with. It still doesn't tell me what they're doing. It may help to answer the questions of why the grays are on the move."

"Well, I have an idea about that," Aliisza said, reaching the moment of truth. She wondered if Kaanyr would agree with her plan or choose to use someone else. "Whatever it is they're planning to do when they reach Ched Nasad, they all seem very concerned, very grim. Whatever it is, it's serious, and I bet they aren't the only drow in the city who are in the know about it. So why don't I sneak into Ched Nasad and snoop around a little?"

Kaanyr looked at Aliisza, pursing his lips. She wasn't sure if he was thinking about her idea or just studying her to see if she was up to something. Of course she intended to do just what she said, so he had no reason not to trust her on it, but if she had a little fun on the side, well then, what would be the harm in that? She needed a vacation from Ammarindar, from Vhok. Maybe a little time apart would do him some good, too, she thought.

"All right," he said at last, and the alu-fiend grinned broadly before she caught herself. "Go and see what you can find out. In fact, I want you to drop in on Aunrae. If there's something going on, the matron mothers will be in the know. I'd like to keep my relationship with her on good terms, at least for the moment, so be polite. And keep me updated. I don't want to have to come find you to see what you've learned."

Aliisza was nodding energetically as she stood up and headed out the door.

"I will," she promised, already contemplating the sort of disguise she'd like to use.

🕷   🕷   🕷

As Khorrl felt the wagon finally roll to a stop, he almost groaned aloud. His legs were cramping where he'd wedged himself into the hiding spot beneath the pile of supplies. He could barely stand to be there much longer, and he prayed to Laduguer that the trip was actually over. He couldn't imagine having to crouch there for even another few minutes.

The tarp over the top of the wagon was thrown back, and dim light shone down on the goods stacked beneath it. Of course, to anyone not properly prepared, that's all they would have seen—a

THOMAS M. REID

wagonload of supplies for the city. Khorrl waited as he listened, not daring to move, in case it was merely another checkpoint. He didn't even want to breathe, for fear of being heard by whomever—or whatever—might be inspecting the wagon.

"It's all right," he heard a drow voice say, and he recognized it as belonging to Zammzt. The dark elf was near enough that there was no mistaking who he was talking to. "You can show yourselves, now. We're inside the storehouse."

With a thankful groan, Khorrl rose up, feeling his knees complaining. Around him, fourteen other duergar did the same, winking back into visibility one by one. They looked at each other, as if to confirm that everyone was all right, and began to peer around at their surroundings. Khorrl himself hopped awkwardly down from the wagon, grabbing his axe as he did so. Nearby, more wagons were being uncovered, and more of his fighters appeared, clambering out from between crates, barrels, and bales of foodstuffs. He knew that there were over twenty wagons, so he had about three hundred troops. More would arrive, in waves, over the course of the next several hours.

As Zammzt had promised, they were set up inside a large, open room, obviously a storehouse of some sort, though there were no goods there other than what was on the wagons. Ostensibly, the contents of the wagons were for the benefit of the Houses, but in reality, it was his army's supplies. They were going to be camping there for a few days, resting and preparing while the other duergar units arrived, all of them waiting until it was time to do their job. Khorrl hoped the storehouses would be left undisturbed, as promised.

A handful of drow moved about, uncovering wagons in order to free their hidden occupants or unloading the supplies and stacking them out of the way. Khorrl could see Zammzt looking a couple of wagons over, giving some young drow male a few instructions. When the dark elf was finished, he turned back to the duergar clan leader.

"I hope you find everything in order here, Captain Xornbane," Zammzt said, smiling. "I know it's not quite like roughing it in the wilds of the Underdark, but it should accommodate you well enough."

"It's fine, as long as no one comes snooping around here before we're ready to begin. The last thing we need is the city catching wind of us before your mistress is ready to fly her true colors."

Khorrl paced about as he spoke, trying to get the feeling back in his legs as much as surveying his temporary home.

"I seriously doubt that's going to be a problem," Zammzt said, smiling. Khorrl wanted to tell him to stop it. The grin reminded the duergar of a pack lizard's visage. "I've got loyal drow troops on guard duty around the storehouse, and you're sequestered here in the far back chamber. No one will bother you."

"If you say so," Khorrl answered doubtfully. He had seen more battles take a turn for the worse through the most simple, straightforward aspect of the plan going awry. "Just remember, all that beautiful treasure you gave me is already long gone, shipped off to safer parts. If you're thinking of turning the tables, you won't be seeing it again. It'll be an expensive betrayal."

Zammzt looked genuinely hurt, but only for a moment.

"I'm not sure you realize the risks my mistress takes, simply harboring an army here," said the drow. "If you're discovered, she too suffers the consequences. It really isn't in her best interests to turn on you, you know."

"Hmm," Khorrl answered. "We'll see."

"So, I presume you brought everything you need," the drow said, changing the subject, "but if there's anything else you want while you wait here, now is the time to ask. Though, for what we're paying you . . ."

Khorrl barked a deep laugh despite himself. The idea that he would bring his troops into such an uncertain situation without arranging for every provision, every possible contingency, was funny.

"No, we're fine. Now, when are we going to find out just exactly who we're supposed to be killing?"

"Soon, my gray friend," Zammzt said, that toothy smile blossoming again. "Very soon."

🕷   🕷   🕷

In the end, the battle with the tanarukks wasn't much of a fight at all. Pharaun had devastated rank upon rank of the slavering humanoids from a distance, even going so far as to decimate the reserve forces lurking in the back. He honestly didn't even find it sporting, especially when he was able to hover overhead, out of their reach, and attack them at his leisure.

The Menzoberranyr were well beyond the halls of Ammarindar, and after a night's rest they were closing in on Ched Nasad.

"We should be running into patrols by now," Faeryl grumbled as they hiked along. "We're within a quarter mile of the city. Something's wrong."

"I think we knew that before we left Menzoberranzan," Quenthel snapped.

The group found itself on the main thoroughfare that led into the city from the north, wondering when they would actually reach the surrounding outskirts of the city proper, the area protected by patrols. Pharaun couldn't blame Faeryl for being apprehensive. Even after several tendays of concern for her home city, he imagined that she might have held out some hope that she would find everything in order upon finally arriving. Still, he doubted that some disaster had befallen the city. Though they hadn't yet encountered any patrols, they were no longer alone on the road to the city.

Traffic flowing to and from Ched Nasad was a trickle of its normal self, at least according to the ambassador. Pharaun didn't doubt it. The avenue they followed was broad, wide enough for numerous caravans to pass in either direction, but there were no such convoys out and about that day. Most of those who shared the road with the Menzoberranyr were other drow, though the occasional gray dwarf, kobold, or goblin passed them as well. Those lesser beings gave the drow a wide berth. Any pedestrians who were headed toward the city were scattered just as far apart as those leaving, and Pharaun and his companions neither passed nor were passed by anyone.

The mage made a tactful attempt to bring up the suggestion he had been contemplating. "Quenthel, if something has happened here, similar to what we've been experiencing back home, it might be prudent to consider a less obvious entrance into the city."

"What do you mean?" the high priestess queried, looking sharply at Pharaun.

"Only that should we boldly approach and announce our stature and intentions, we might not receive the warm welcome we should under more ordinary circumstances."

"Why shouldn't they be glad to see us? Even relieved?"

It sounded as though Quenthel was growing indignant, and Pharaun struggled to find a way to explain his point in a way that wouldn't sound insulting.

Faeryl saved him the effort.

"Because they might think we're here to spy on them," she said.

Pharaun had to suppress a mild chuckle. It was, after all, the exact reason Triel had claimed when she imprisoned the envoy back in Menzoberranzan. It was a reasonable argument.

"Not if we insist upon meeting with the matron mothers of the highest Houses—" Quenthel began.

"With all due respect, Mistress," Faeryl interjected, "do you think you would react well to a high-ranking noble arriving in Menzoberranzan and insisting upon seeing you? During this time of crisis?"

Quenthel scowled and said nothing. Pharaun was relieved that the high priestess was at least willing to contemplate the idea.

"Even if they didn't think we were spies, they certainly would consider our visit to be highly unusual and would strive to keep an eye on us," the mage said. "We might be given the most luxurious accommodations and want for nothing, but we would also be absolutely unable to find out anything. Once we determine the state of things here, if it's really your intention to lay claim to the goods stored in the Black Claw Mercantile storehouses and take them back to Menzoberranzan, why draw undue attention to yourself? Were you planning to ask the matron mothers for them, first?"

Quenthel scowled at Pharaun as if the very idea of asking permission to take what was rightfully hers was preposterous. It was exactly the reaction he wanted.

"Faeryl," the wizard persisted, "even though the goods are rightfully the property of House Baenre and House Melarn, do you foresee Matron Mother Melarn—indeed, any of the other Houses—letting them out of the city?"

Faeryl smirked.

"Absolutely not," she answered. "I'm not certain how happy my own mother will be to hear about your plan." She smiled wanly and added, "I agree with the mage. The less you tell, the better your chances are of succeeding."

"Your arguments may have merit," Quenthel said. "So what else do you suggest? How do we enter unnoticed?"

"As traders, Mistress," Faeryl suggested, "members of the Black Claw Mercantile company. Triel said herself that we were here to check on House Baenre's financial interests, as well as to discover how widespread the problem is, so it's the truth, from a certain point of view."

"We don't look very much like traders," Valas said, trotting a little in front of the rest of them. "Perhaps Pharaun should use a spell of illusion to mask our looks."

"No," Faeryl replied. "Ched Nasad's guards are equipped to watch for that. They employ detection spells and devices to notice if you're trying sneak past them invisibly or under the guise of illusion. It's not necessary, anyway. You'd be surprised at what kind of bodyguards a wealthy trader would hire to protect her. I am a member of a trading house. If I tell the city guards that you're escorting me, and they get a good look at my house insignia, we shouldn't have any trouble, but you must remove your own insignia. They're likely to be recognized."

"Would you hire the likes of him?" Quenthel asked, pointing to Jeggred.

Faeryl frowned and said, "He could be a problem."

"Leave that to me," Pharaun said. "I have a couple of tricks up my sleeve that should aid us nicely. I can use them to get the draegloth past the patrols and into the city without them noticing him. As long as he cooperates, anyway."

Quenthel looked at Jeggred and asked, "Can you stay quiet and not try to tear the throat out of anyone?"

Jeggred regarded the high priestess askance but nodded.

"I am capable of subtlety when it is necessary, Mistress," he rumbled.

Sure you are, Pharaun thought.

"Very well," Quenthel said after a moment's deliberation. "We will enter the city incognito. Remove your insignia and try to look . . . common."

Everyone except Faeryl doffed their House brooches and began to stow as many of their finer accoutrements as possible.

"Pharaun," Quenthel said, nodding at Jeggred, "do what you must."

"First, I'm going to reduce you slightly in size, so that you aren't so, um . . . obvious," the wizard said, looking up at the eight-foot-tall creature. "You don't mind, do you?"

Jeggred grunted and glowered at the mage, but at a subtle gesture from Quenthel, he nodded acquiescence.

"Good," Pharaun continued. "Then, I'll cloak you with a spell designed to misdirect those divinations the patrols are likely to be using, and if you will don your *piwafwi*, pull the hood up, and stay in the back, we should get past them just fine."

"Yes, that should do nicely," Faeryl agreed.

"All right, then, here we go," Pharaun said, pulling a pinch of powdered iron from one of his many pockets and gesturing.

The draegloth began to shrink until he was no taller than any of the drow.

"Good," the wizard said, beginning the second spell.

When he was finished, he stepped back and said, "Now, draw that *piwafwi* around you to hide as much of you as possible."

"Yes, and lean on Ryld as though you're injured," Quenthel commanded. "Keep your head down like you're tired."

"Yes, good idea," Pharaun agreed, genuinely impressed. "We're all just road-weary merchants, ready for a hot bath and comfortable bed."

"Not a moment too soon," Valas said, his voice low. "I see a patrol up ahead."

Pharaun peered ahead into the distance and saw a large contingent of drow, some on foot, others riding lizards, moving down the road in their direction. They were fanned out across the width of the road, so there would be no way to avoid them.

"Just remain calm, and allow me to speak to them," Faeryl whispered.

The group began walking toward the patrol, with Ryld in the back, pretending to support a limping Jeggred. Pharaun could only guess at how much the warrior hated the scheme.

No matter, he thought. *We should have little difficulty getting past these sentries. We're just drow, trying to reach a drow city. Why would we be any trouble to them?*

As the groups drew close to one another, the patrol loosened weapons and slowed down, obviously preparing for trouble. One, the leader, Pharaun presumed, stepped forward a few more paces and held his hand outstretched before him, palm forward.

"Hold," he said, gesturing for the group to slow down. "State your name and business here."

Faeryl moved forward, past Valas, to come to a stop a few paces from the leader.

"I am Faeryl Zauvirr of House Zauvirr, Executive Negotiator for the Black Claw Mercantile." She removed her insignia and held it out for the patrol leader to get a good look and take it, if he wanted. "These are my caravan guards."

The sergeant or whatever he was stepped forward and took the insignia, then passed it back to an underling while he scrutinized Faeryl and the others, in turn.

"Caravan? What caravan? No goods have entered or left the city in six tendays, at least."

Faeryl nodded and explained, "Yes, I know. We are just recently from Menzoberranzan, but we lost what few goods we had in an attack along the way." She tossed her head back toward Ryld and Jeggred as a way of indicating her wounded companions, but with the suggestion that they weren't really important. The drow soldier in front of her peered over her shoulder for a brief moment, then nodded and returned his attention to her. "We wish to give our report and enjoy some civilization for a few days," she concluded, letting weariness creep into her voice.

Good, Pharaun thought. Tell them just enough of the truth to sound reasonable, without admitting anything.

"Attacked by what?" the leader asked.

The second-in-command handed the insignia back to him with a curt nod. Apparently it had passed muster, for the patrolman handed it back to Faeryl.

"What business is it of yours?" asked Quenthel sourly. "Do you always make it a practice of interrogating caravans this way?"

"Tanarukks," Pharaun said, stepping forward and placing his hand on Quenthel's arm. "She hates tanarukks. She's been in a bad mood ever since. A good deepstroke will do her wonders."

The Master of Sorcere could feel her bristle, but at least she didn't pull away from him. Beside her, the snakes of her whip stirred, but they didn't flail about as Pharaun feared they would.

The patrol leader glared at Quenthel for a moment but finally nodded and said, "We make it a practice when the city is—" he stopped himself from revealing more, then turned back to Faeryl—"You may pass, but good luck finding any 'civilization' to enjoy."

With that last bitter comment, he turned and motioned the rest of the patrol to part, creating a gap so that the entourage could pass through.

Faeryl nodded her thanks and motioned for the rest of them to follow her, then they were past the patrol and alone on the thoroughfare once again. Pharaun could see that the envoy was troubled by the patrol leader's words. He had to admit it was not a good sign.

"Let go of me!" Quenthel hissed, jerking her arm free, and the wizard blinked in surprise, having forgotten that he still grasped her and was steering her along.

"My apologies, Mistress," Pharaun said, bowing slightly. "In light of the situation, I thought it prudent to try to smooth things over the best way possible. In a way, though, it was good. You drew attention away from the draegloth."

"Fine," she answered, still scowling. "We got through them, that's the important thing. Now, let's see just how bad it is inside the city."

It wasn't long before the group had reached the gates of the City of Shimmering Webs. Continuing their masquerade as bruised and battered merchants, they passed through the guards there and found themselves inside.

It was chaos.

Chapter

FIVE

"You're late," Drisinil Melarn snapped as Ssipriina Zauvirr strode into the audience chamber of House Melarn.

The matron mother of House Zauvirr forced herself to suppress the hot retort that she ached to unleash, contenting herself instead with pursed lips.

"I am sincerely apologetic," Ssipriina lied, bowing low to the other matron mother, knowing she mocked the other drow simply through the use of such formal comments and antics. "It could not be helped. I had urgent business matters to attend to, issues that keep your coffers full, Matron Mother."

Ssipriina liked the dangerous glitter she was creating in Drisinil's hot eyes. It would be hard for the head of House Melarn to chastise her minion for working so diligently to keep her wealthy, and Ssipriina knew that. That's what made these subtle jibes all the more fun.

"Still, I sped here with as much haste as dignity would permit," Ssipriina added, "for I have good news. They have entered the city."

"You're sure?" the matron mother asked. "Do you have any indication that they've changed their plans?"

"Yes, I am sure of it," Ssipriina replied. "My male made contact with Faeryl only a few hours ago, and she informed him that they were headed toward the Fracture Gate in the lowest quarters of the city. Apparently, Mistress Baenre is still bent on stealing your goods. My spies saw them enter the city just a few minutes ago."

Drisinil sat in thought for a few moments, leaving Ssipriina standing expectantly. Finally, the matron mother stirred.

"They don't suspect that we know, do they?"

"I don't believe so. I have instructed Faeryl to be as agreeable as she can to whatever Quenthel is planning, and I have my spies set to keep track of them, wherever they go. They won't know a thing until it's too late."

"And you want to let them go through with it?"

"Well, not exactly, Matron Mother. I am suggesting that we let them get to the storehouse and get inside. We'll be there to catch them in the act. We'll have the proof, then, and we can present it to the other matron mothers."

"Hmm, yes, I like that," Drisinil Melarn said, shifting her considerable weight atop her throne. Her face held a look of determination. "I very much want to see Quenthel Baenre's face when she realizes she's not getting a single scrap of my wealth. I want her to realize she's just crossed the wrong House."

Truer words were never spoken, Ssipriina thought.

"Yes, of course. I will make plans for us to be there before they arrive at the storehouse. I trust that you wish for me to utilize House Melarn guards?"

"Absolutely," Drisinil said. "She needs to see just who she is trifling with. I want a strong presence there, Ssipriina, and when this crisis is over and the council lifts the ban on exportations, I'll make sure you're rewarded for your patience and diligence."

"Of course," Ssipriina said, bowing. "I will see to this matter personally."

❦ ❦ ❦

Ched Nasad was a bustling city filled with drow, duergar, and even the occasional illithid during normal times, but Valas found it suffocating. The scout was certain three times as many creatures occupied the place than was usual. It was brimming with desperate, starving masses who pushed and shoved their way along the thoroughfares, raising a deafening rumble and a pungent odor.

The gate through which the Menzoberranyr had entered was near the bottom of the City of Shimmering Webs, a metropolis filling a huge, **V**-shaped trench in the Underdark. The entirety of the city was crisscrossed with massive calcified webs set aglow with magic, a hundred or more layers of pathways that ran every direction and supported the population. Thousands of rounded, amorphous structures clung to these huge webs like egg-sacs or cocooned prey, thrusting up or dangling below and housing the citizens, guests, slaves, and their businesses. Right now, it looked like a writhing colony of ants swarmed over the webs, for as far as Valas could see overhead, the streets literally vibrated with the masses of humanoids taking refuge there.

The scout would normally have been in the lead of the entourage, but it was nearly impossible to move, so crowded were the streets. Instead, Quenthel had ordered Jeggred to run point, and the towering fiend was pushing his way slowly through the throngs. Valas stayed close behind the draegloth, and the rest of the group pressed in close behind the scout, fearful of getting cut off in the madness and winding up lost. Valas noted that time and again sullen-looking faces glowered at Jeggred while he growled and rumbled at everyone to stand aside. They all did, intimidated by the formidable creature.

There were few drow low in the city, but just about every other race was present. Many of the slave races, as well as representatives of the other major Underdark nations, clamored with one another, shouting, pushing, bartering, or just milling about. The Menzoberranyr stood out, and it was plain that they were being sized up by the populace. Sooner or later, there was going to be a problem.

More than once, Valas felt the brush of a hand or finger as someone in the milling crowd deftly attempted to pilfer a trinket from one of his pockets. He had already snatched two hands away from the charms pinned to the front of his shirt, leaving each with a nasty gash across the palm from one of his kukris.

Valas turned and glanced over his shoulder. Faeryl and Quenthel were both right behind him, the Mistress of Arach-Tinilith threatening bystanders with her horrid whip. Behind the two priestesses, Pharaun held his *piwafwi* closed and kept his head bowed, protecting himself from the press of the crowd. Ryld brought up the rear, using his bulk to shield the wizard in front of him.

This is ridiculous, the scout thought, shaking his head. We've got to get out of this part of town.

He started to lean over and tell Quenthel when a disturbance in front of Jeggred interrupted him. Valas turned back in time to see the draegloth pounce on an ogre armed with a greatsword that was blocking the path. A second ogre stood beside him, hefting a spiked club and glaring.

Jeggred leaped forward like a coiled spring, raking one of his razor-sharp claws across the front of the first ogre. The attack was so sudden, the creature didn't even have time to react. It stared down at its stomach as blood sprayed. Several screams erupted from the crowd as some struggled to get out of the way and others pushed and shoved to get a better view—or a chance to scavenge the bodies.

The first ogre opened its mouth to scream, sinking down to one knee and holding its hands across its midsection, as Jeggred slashed again, ripping the humanoid's throat out. The ogre gurgled and flailed, wide-eyed with fear.

The second ogre snarled and swung its club at Jeggred, slamming the spiked weapon into the draegloth's shoulder. The fiend spun with the blow, his mane of white hair flowing behind him. The twist avoided the worst of the damage and brought Jeggred back to face his enemy from a crouched position.

At that moment, Valas was knocked sideways by a lunging goblin, teeth bared and daggers drawn. Before the scout could kick the wretch away from him, Quenthel lashed out with her whip. Several pairs of fangs sank into the goblin's flesh, and it fell to the ground, writhing and frothing at the mouth. Valas lurched back to his feet before more of the throng could surge over him. He put his back to Quenthel and openly brandished his kukris, holding back several shouting, cursing gray dwarves.

The entourage had formed a defensive circle, Valas realized. Ryld had Splitter out, and the wizard's magical rapier danced in the air before him, while Pharaun himself held a small wand of some sort, eyeing the increasingly angry crowd. Even Faeryl held her hammer in her hands, swinging it back and forth experimentally. Only Jeggred wasn't a part of the defensive formation, having moved a few feet off, finishing his bloody work with the two ogres. Out of the corner of his eye, Valas could see the fiend biting his foe, ripping chunks of the ogre's face off.

"We've got to get higher!" Valas yelled at Quenthel over his shoulder. When the high priestess didn't seem to hear him, he repeated himself. "Mistress Quenthel, we need to get to a higher section of the city. This is not working!"

Next to him, Pharaun jerked as a crossbow bolt snapped against his *piwafwi*. Someone was taking potshots from the crowd.

"What do you suggest?" Quenthel called back, extending her whip and flailing at an unfortunate kobold that had squeezed to the front of the gathering and was shoved forward from behind.

"Follow me!" Faeryl cried, and she began to lift from the ground, rising up into the air. "We must get to the mercantile district, and this is the fastest way."

"No," Valas groaned, eyes widening. "I can't—! I have no way to stay with you!"

But it was too late. The other drow had began to follow the ambassador's example and were lifting from the ground. Valas backed into the center of what had once been their circle, warily eyeing the crowd around him.

"Ryld!" he shouted. "Wait!"

Valas saw the warrior look down at him, but before the other drow could take action, Valas was grabbed from behind. He tried to spin around and slash out with his kukri, but the grip on him was powerful, and he couldn't get a clean swing in. A split-second later, he was glad, for Jeggred was the one who had a hold of him. Coated in blood that matted the fiend's fur, the draegloth held tightly to the scout as he left the ground. A couple of bold gray dwarves stormed forward, intent on getting in a parting swipe with their war axes at Valas's feet, but Jeggred still had a large, clawed hand free and slashed out at them, forcing the pair of duergar to leap back to safety.

Several more crossbow bolts whizzed by, and one sank into the draegloth's flank next to Valas, but Jeggred only grunted and spun away, levitating upward to where the other drow had gone. Valas looked back down where they had been standing only moments before. Even as the webbed street receded, the scout saw the mob swarm over the dead ogres, ripping items of value from the bodies.

Savages, he thought.

Above, Faeryl had stopped on a smaller side street several levels higher than where the drow had been previously, in a quiet space between rows of vendors. In the main thoroughfare, the crowds were less dense than below, but only slightly. Valas knew they were still relatively low in the city, for the glimmering glow of spectral light that emanated from the mesh of stone webs still dazzled his sight when he looked up, twinkling far into the distance overhead. He knew that the higher they got, the better the neighborhoods would be. Near the top of the cavern, where the trench-shaped chamber was at its widest, the nobles had constructed their sprawling Houses sufficiently beyond the stench and noise of the common folk far below. The Menzoberranyr had quite a ways to go before they would be in that vicinity.

"Is it always that . . . revolting down there?" Quenthel asked as the group settled to the stone avenue, huddling together and keeping their voices low. "Why do the matron mothers tolerate that rabble?"

Jeggred released Valas, who straightened and turned to look at the draegloth, wondering how much of the blood on the fiend was his enemies' and how much was his own. Much of Jeggred's fur was matted with the hot, sticky fluid, but other than the crossbow bolt in his hip, the beast didn't seem to bear any wounds. The scout examined his own clothing and noted sullenly that he was sticky with ogre blood, too.

"The lesser races are not permitted to wander so freely in the higher sections of the city without special permission," Faeryl explained. "It'll get better once we get a little higher."

"I doubt it," the high priestess said, sniffing. "I doubt the matron mothers would suffer such an embarrassment lightly. Likely they're dealing with more urgent problems, and I think we all know what those urgent problems are."

Over Quenthel's shoulder, Valas could see a trio of female drow who had stopped and were staring at Jeggred as the fiend yanked the crossbow bolt free with a grunt of pain. One of the dark elves whispered something to her companions, and the three of them scurried away.

Pharaun was making a point of dusting his *piwafwi* clean and straightening the garment so that he was looking stylish and well groomed again.

"You are most likely correct," the Master of Sorcere said, nodding in acquiescence. "Still, it would not hurt for us to find a place to stay for the night, gathering our wits and perhaps some more information, too. I'm sure that between the six of us, we can find out a little more about why the city is in this condition."

"Finding a place to stay may prove difficult," Ryld commented. "I wonder if there's a vacant room to be had in all of Ched Nasad."

Valas frowned, imagining the looks they would receive as they inquired after accommodations.

"If we can," the scout said, "your bodyguard will attract substantial attention. Even now, we are drawing looks. We should not stay out in the open for much longer."

Quenthel dug in her pack of supplies and produced a wand. Moving closer to Jeggred, she aimed the magical device at the draegloth's bleeding puncture wound and uttered a few words. The bleeding stopped, and the hole began to close.

"Be more careful," the high priestess admonished her nephew as she stored the wand once more. "Healing magic is limited."

"Even as overcrowded as the city is," Faeryl said, "the higher levels will not be that bad. I know of a place where we may be able to get rooms."

"Perhaps we need to rethink this," Quenthel countered. "It seems obvious to me that there are troubles here. I think it would be wiser to pay House Zauvirr and House Melarn a visit. We would be assured of accommodations there."

"No," Pharaun said, and Quenthel's eyes widened in surprise. The mage continued quickly, before the high priestess could lash out at him. "You may be right, but even so, you don't want to lose the opportunity to move about freely, do you? If we have any hope of staking a claim to the stock of goods and coin for your House, we must be able to avoid the matron mothers' notice."

"Well," Quenthel said, seeming to waver, "I'm uncomfortable with the idea of living like commoners in an inn, but your argument still makes sense."

Valas watched as the high priestess bit her lip, deep in thought.

Pharaun continued, trying to press home his advantage, "You know they will tell us nothing if there is a problem. They will keep that information to themselves at all costs. This way, we can explore a little bit, try to discover possible clues to Lolth's disappearance. It will allow us the chance to determine what has brought Ched Nasad to this condition." He leaned in close to avoid being overheard, as another pair of drow—males who had been strolling past this time—stopped and stared for a moment. "If nothing else, we can learn from this city's mistakes."

Ryld turned and gave the pair of males a level look, and they quickly averted their eyes and continued on their way.

"Whatever we do, we'd better do it now," the weapons master said over his shoulder. "Valas is right . . . we're attracting too much attention."

"Then shall I show us the way to the inn I know of?" Faeryl asked. "It's called the House Unnamed, and it's just—"

"You will do no such thing," Quenthel interrupted. "You seem far too eager to help us, and at the expense of your own House."

Faeryl gaped at the Baenre high priestess.

"Mistress Quenthel, I am merely—"

"Enough," Quenthel cut the ambassador off. "Until I decide to let the matron mothers know I'm here, you will not be warning them ahead of time. Jeggred, it will be your responsibility to make sure she doesn't try to sneak off."

The draegloth grinned, first at Quenthel, then at the ambassador. "With pleasure, Mistress," he said.

Faeryl grimaced at the fiend's attentions, and Valas wondered just what had happened between the two of them prior to the group's departure. She'd behaved in that manner during the entire trip. He made a mental note to ask Ryld when they had a moment alone.

"Now," Quenthel said, turning to the other three of them, "which of you knows this city best?"

"I have visited Ched Nasad a number of times, Mistress Quenthel," Valas answered, and the other two males nodded in agreement, giving the scout center stage.

"Good. Find us an inn, someplace other than this 'House Unnamed.' Make it a good one, mind you. I won't put up with the squalor you might be used to."

Valas raised an eyebrow but said nothing. He found it interesting that the high priestess had changed her mind, agreeing to Pharaun's plan without actually admitting to it. He wondered if they would have words about it later, but for the moment, he was happy enough to do as she had instructed.

"The quickest way to get where we want to go is going to be by floating there," the scout said. "As long as Jeggred is willing to bear me, that is."

Quenthel looked first at the draegloth, then at Faeryl, and said, "You're not going to give me reason to have Jeggred or Pharaun kill you by trying to run away, are you?"

Faeryl glowered but shook her head.

"Good, then lead on, Valas. I am weary and would like to enjoy the Reverie on a proper couch for a change."

Jeggred lifted the scout up in one arm, and soon they were all rising easily toward the higher parts of the city. Faeryl had been right. As the group reached higher and higher elevations, the crowds abated somewhat. It was still busier than Valas had ever remembered, but at the higher levels, it was at least tolerable. He led them toward an upscale business section of the city, a zone where many of the lesser Houses, those with only enough power to make fortunes in trade as opposed to actually being powerful enough to run the city, maintained commercial offices.

It was this section, Valas knew, that many of the wealthy merchants from other regions of the Underdark frequented while visiting the city. The inns were extravagant enough that they would support the creature comforts expected by the trading community's elite, and they wouldn't do more than bat an eye even at someone as unusual as Jeggred. Valas hoped that there the Menzoberranyr would find a room that would satisfy Quenthel's need for pampering and not draw undue attention to themselves. If they could find a room at all.

Pharaun insisted that he be the one to negotiate with the innkeepers. The first two establishments nearly laughed in the wizard's face, and the third one made biting comments concerning the "Wrath of Lolth" before suggesting that a payment of submission for ritual cleansing would buy them the opportunity to share one room together. The fourth place had nothing either, but the proprietor there, a half-orc blind in one eye, suggested a place that was near the edge of the city, two sections higher. He claimed that his cousin ran the place and catered to mercenaries who hired on with caravans—or at least, they used to, when caravans still ran. Valas wondered which side of the family the relation was on.

It took a bit of searching before the group finally found the Flame and Serpent, a sprawling hive of stacked cocoon-shapes nestled together where one lonely strand of calcified webbing was anchored to the wall of the cavern. It held promise, if only by virtue of its out-of-the-way location and its appearance.

Quenthel balked upon first seeing the inn, but Pharaun suggested that they at least inquire inside before dismissing any possibility, and the high priestess once again let the male convince her.

She really must be weary, Valas mused. She's letting him run the show today. Well, one good night's Reverie, and that'll all change.

For a pleasant surprise, the inside of the Flame and Serpent was substantially more inviting than the outside had been. While Pharaun approached the innkeeper, a fat orc with silver caps on his tusks and two ogre bouncers to back him up, Valas looked around. There were certainly plenty of folk sitting in the tap room, and though Jeggred drew more than one lingering stare as he crouched beneath a ceiling that wasn't quite the right height for him, most of the patrons ignored them. Valas recognized why. They really were mercenaries, independents in the business for gold and little else, and as long as no one interfered with them or their livelihoods, they would keep to themselves. They were Valas's kind of folk.

Quenthel's expression was one of distaste, but Pharaun returned with a gleam in his eye and the good news that they had actually managed to get the Flame and Serpent's last two rooms. When the wizard mentioned the price, Quenthel rolled her eyes, but Valas realized they had probably still gotten a bargain.

"Only two?" Quenthel said doubtfully. "Then the males will have to share one, while Faeryl and I take the other. Jeggred, you, of course, will remain with me."

Faeryl's face looked stricken at the prospect of sharing her quarters with the draegloth, but she said nothing.

The rooms were not in the same area of the inn. The larger of the two, the one Quenthel claimed for her own, was a round chamber with a separate bathing room. It was near the front of the structure, with several small windows that looked out over the city. From their vantage, the females could see the magnificent glowing web streets stretching off into the distance both above and below. The smaller chamber was at the rear of the Flame and Serpent, an elongated room with two beds and a divan for a third person. The lone window opened to the wall of the cavern, where rivulets of water ran down, leaking through from the World Above and trickling down to the bottom of the **V**-shaped city, where it fed beds of fungi.

It's not much of a view, Valas decided, but it might prove useful for leaving the inn unobserved.

"I want to rest for a while, so you three," Quenthel said, looking at the males, "stay out of trouble. We will convene at the end of the day and discuss what to do next over our meal. Until then, leave me alone!"

With that she stalked off to her chambers, dragging Faeryl and Jeggred along with her.

Valas agreed to rest on the couch, and as the three of them unpacked a bit, Pharaun stood and stretched, cracking his back.

"I don't know about you two," the wizard said after a bit, "but I'm too excited to flop around here. I fancy a drink somewhere and maybe a chance to hear more of the buzz around town. Are you two interested in accompanying me?"

Valas looked at Ryld, who gave the scout a nod.

"Sure," they both said in unison, and the three of them set out together.

🕷   🕷   🕷

Three drow males moving through the streets of Ched Nasad proved to be much more anonymous than five drow and a draegloth, though Pharaun supposed that a large part of it was due to the fact that he, Ryld, and Valas were sauntering along back web streets in a higher section of the city. As they strolled, listening to the din of business all around them, the mage couldn't help but be thrilled at the exploration of the city. Unlike Menzoberranzan, Ched Nasad was a cosmopolitan collection of sights, sounds, and smells that permeated the entire city. He could certainly detect subtle differences as the trio moved through various sections of town, but regardless of

Insurrection

where they found themselves, the wizard absorbed it all, noting that the air vibrated with a kind of clamor, the feel of wheeling and dealing, that was only present in the baser areas of Menzoberranzan.

It was certainly more lively than Tier Breche, where Pharaun spent far too much time cloistered in the towers of the Academy, hidden away in Sorcere. Back home, he had made a habit of only getting out into the main city when he needed supplies or the occasional drink and bit of fun. It had been that way for many years, at least while his sister Greyanna longed to kill him. With her no longer posing a problem, he made a note to himself to partake of the more colorful neighborhoods of home more often.

As they strolled, Valas and Ryld seemed to be looking everywhere at once, but Pharaun knew that their attentiveness to the cacophony around them was due to a different reason than his own. Certainly, he was wary of a pickpocket or thug, but for the weapons master and the scout, it was what they had trained themselves to do for years upon years. They had honed their skills of wariness and observation to keen levels, and their entire beings reverberated with it. Pharaun doubted seriously that anyone in the city would get the drop on him while his two companions were in tow. It was a comforting thought, if only because it allowed him to truly relax and enjoy the splendor of the City of Shimmering Webs.

The mage certainly understood why Ched Nasad had been dubbed such. The tangle of streets crisscrossed in purples, ambers, greens, and yellows for hundreds of feet in every direction, and it was a marvelous sight. Everywhere the three of them walked vendors hawked mushrooms, or jewelry, or potions. Pharaun noticed that the goods seemed of an inferior sort, though, and few people were buying—everyone had a hint of something in his eyes. Fear, he decided. Everyone looked afraid.

One filthy looking drow male had small cages, each one holding a small four-armed humanoid with multifaceted eyes, mandibles, and a spidery abdomen. They were no more than a foot tall. Peering closer, Pharaun could see that the creatures had web-spinning capabilities. They shrank back as he studied them.

"You wish to buy one, Master?" the male asked hopefully, jumping up from where he had been sitting cross-legged.

"Infant chitines," Valas said. "The adults are hunted for sport, and whenever a nest is found the babies are brought back here and sold as pets."

"Interesting," Pharaun replied and briefly contemplated purchasing one, though from the look of things, the drow male was having little luck drawing any interest in his wares. "I'd consider getting one—as a present for Quenthel, you know—but these seem over priced."

The male's hopeful stare faded to disappointment, and he sat down on the edge of the street again.

Ryld snorted, and Valas shook his head.

"They're not too expensive," the scout said as they walked on. "The market's probably just flooded with them right now."

"Why is that?" Pharaun asked.

"Because chitines and choldriths worship the goddess, too," Valas answered quietly.

"Choldriths?"

"Chitine priestesses. Same racial stock, larger and dark-skinned. No hair, human eyes. I suspect that they may be suffering the same calamity that has befallen our own clerics."

Pharaun's curiosity was piqued.

"Really," he said, musing. "It might prove useful if we could track down some of these choldriths and find out if they are suffering the same fate. It's obvious that Ched Nasad endures the goddess's silence, too, and once we get proof, Quenthel may be at a loss for what to do next. This would give us the means to explore further, find out if Lolth's reticence is universal or just limited to our own race."

"It's a nice idea in theory, mage," Ryld said, shooing a goblin vendor away who was trying to convince him to buy a bowl of slugs, "but you'd be hard-pressed to track any down, and struggle even more to elicit information from them. The drow hunt them for sport, so the chitines and choldriths have learned to flee or fight to the death."

"Hmm," Pharaun responded, spying a little shop selling something he wanted. "Perhaps, but my particular talents could come in handy in such an endeavor."

The mage's companions followed him to a cramped kiosk selling spirits, which was hanging at the corner of two fairly large web streets. To reach it, customers had to slide down a steep ramp of webbing to the front of the vending stand, then ascend a ladder of webbing to return to the street. Pharaun studied the small crowd of people gathered around, each in turn descending the slide and purchasing a flask or mushroom cap of beverage.

"You'd think they could have put steps in on both sides," the Master of Sorcere sniffed disdainfully.

"Oh, by the Dark Mother," Ryld said, shaking his head. "I'll get us something."

With that, the warrior moved through the crowd, very few of whom were actually buying, instead begging coin or a sip from the paying customers. Ryld ignored them and descended upon the vendor, while Pharaun and Valas stood out of the way of traffic and took the opportunity to absorb the sights again.

When Ryld returned, he had a bit of a strange look on his face.

"What is it?" Valas asked.

"That gray dwarf charged me ten times what this swill is worth and seemed to take a certain delight in it."

"Well, a bit of gouging is to be expected, when caravan traffic has dried up," Pharaun said.

"Yes, but when a goblin asked for the same thing right after me, I heard the proprietor sell it to him for half what he charged me."

"Maybe the little thrall is a regular," Valas offered.

"Possibly," Pharaun said, opening the flask that Ryld had procured and inhaling a waft. He jerked his head back and scrunched up his face a bit. "I suspect it has more to do with relishing the opportunity to earn a little payback against the drow." He took a sip of the brandy and passed the flask to Valas. "After all, who regulates the commerce in the city? Who gets first choice of all the best vending locations? Who runs the caravan system? Who acquires the best trade goods?"

"In other words, who sticks it to the other races with regularity?" Ryld finished.

"Exactly. The gray dwarves, the trogs, the kuo-toans, and everyone else in this city know that the ruling class has fallen on hard times, and despite the fact that they've been allowed to trade in a city of dark elves, they won't waste a chance to earn a spot of revenge. And Ryld," Pharaun added, gesturing to the flask that Valas was handing to the warrior, "you would have been had at one-tenth the price."

Ryld shrugged, took a sip, and said, "You're drinking it, aren't you?"

The three companions continued on, sharing the flask and discussing the prospects of acquiring some sort of tangible confirmation that Lolth was absent from Ched Nasad. Pharaun continued to be deeply intrigued by the idea of investigating other races known to worship the goddess, and even as he contributed to the conversation, he mulled the concept over. It would require some research. Given time and Quenthel's willingness, he had a good idea where he might go to perform the study.

The mage's musings were interrupted when the trio ascended a webbed staircase, turned a corner, and found themselves on a colonnade overlooking an open plaza. From the congestion in the mall, Pharaun thought it obvious that refugees had taken to using the place as a sort of campground. Still, there was enough room to move along the raised walkway around the perimeter without brushing shoulder to shoulder with the riffraff, and the three dark elves glided along, ignoring the pleas and demands for coin from the unwashed around them.

A shout from below drew the drow's attention, and when Pharaun peered toward the center of the plaza, he spotted the source of the disturbance. A priestess was standing in a fairly open area, three or four hobgoblins gathered around her. She seemed to be mumbling something, but from a distance Pharaun couldn't make out what it was. The female drow raised her arm back and tried to lash out at one of the hobgoblins with a scourge, but the creature easily stepped aside, and the priestess stumbled forward from the exertion. She was quite drunk, Pharaun realized.

"Filthy animals," the priestess barked, staggering back upright. "Stay away from me!"

Pharaun noticed her unkempt state. Her *piwafwi* was soiled and sloughed half off her shoulders, her lustrous white hair was disheveled, and she held a bottle of something the wizard presumed to be liquor in her other hand.

The hobgoblins merely laughed at the drow before them, casually circling, which caused the priestess to turn, trying to keep an eye on them all. The effort made her stumble again, and she nearly went down in a heap.

"I don't think I've ever seen such a thing," Valas breathed. "The gall those subcreatures have is truly bewildering."

"Let's put a stop to this," Ryld said, taking a step forward.

Suddenly, Pharaun was aware of magic around him, an effect that seemed to be centered on him and his two companions. He reached out and put a hand on the warrior's arm.

"Wait," he said. "Let's see what happens."

When Ryld looked at the wizard quizzically, he continued, "Drawing attention to ourselves is not the best way to investigate. Besides," the mage added, "We might see once and for all if our theory is correct. This might be the proof we need."

The wizard flashed in sign language, *I think someone is watching us, observing us magically.*

Both Ryld and Valas raised eyebrows in concern, but before they could turn and look around, Pharaun cautioned, *Don't draw attention to the fact that we know. Just pretend we're watching the spectacle.*

Pharaun briefly considered dispelling the magic, but he discounted the idea because he knew it would only give their spy notification that they were aware of his or her presence. Instead, he pretended to turn his attention back to the brewing fight below while in actuality scanning the plaza for signs of someone looking at him rather than at the hobgoblins. There were a great many magical auras radiating from many different individuals, but no one, as far as the wizard could observe, seemed to be staring in his direction.

The hobgoblins seemed content for the moment to keep their distance, though they were increasingly pressed from behind by a gathering crowd. For her part, the priestess seemed to have lost interest in her detractors and was standing relatively still, her eyes closed, swaying slightly. She was mumbling something, but Pharaun again could not make it out.

Well, spy or no spy, he thought, I want to know what she's saying.

He reached into one of his many pockets and produced a tiny brass horn, with which he cast a spell. When the magic was complete, the wizard could hear the priestess's mutterings as though he were standing right in front of her.

"—beseech thee, our Mistress Lolth, return to me. Give me your blessings. Do not abandon me when I am your loyal an— *aieee!*"

One of the hobgoblins had chosen that moment to prod the drow with a sharpened stick, and she shrieked as she jumped, losing her grip on the bottle of spirits. It fell to the calcified pavement and shattered, spilling only the trickle that remained.

"Damn you, thrall!" she screamed at the hobgoblin that had molested her, attempting to stalk forward, her hand outstretched as though she were going to throttle him.

A second hobgoblin casually reached out with his own short spear and tripped the priestess, who went sprawling.

She rose to her hands and knees and began shouting, "My goddess, come to me, aid me! Do not abandon me, your loyal servant, who will obey—"

"Your goddess is dead," the first hobgoblin snarled, kicking the drow.

She grunted from the impact and toppled to the side, clutching for her scourge.

"No!" she shrieked. "Lolth would not abandon us! She is mighty, and her faithful are mighty!"

The four hobgoblins advanced together, and the drow priestess tried to kick at them, but the creature in the lead easily sidestepped the attack and jabbed down at her with his spear. Pharaun saw the point draw blood from the dark elf priestess's thigh.

Ryld snarled and flashed, *This is not right. We should do something.*

Valas nodded in agreement and produced his two kukris, one curved dagger in each hand.

The mage laid a hand on each drow's shoulder to slow them.

You only put our mission in danger, he signed. *As you can see, no other drow move to help her.*

He gestured down into the crowd, where several other dark elves were in attendance, observing dispassionately.

She has lost her faith and deserves no less, Pharaun admonished his companions.

It is not the priestess I am worried about, Ryld replied, a sullen look on his face, *but to allow those vermin to believe they can so blatantly confront a superior being spells trouble for us all. They should be put in their place.*

Perhaps, Pharaun responded, *but we need anonymity if we are to finish our task. Confronting those beasts does nothing to further our own goals.*

The wizard is right, Valas motioned, sagging back from the edge of the colonnade. *If the matron mothers hear that three outsiders interfered in what may very well be one of their own plots, we will no longer be able to walk this city unhindered and unobserved.*

If they're not already watching us, Ryld flashed. *Are we still being observed?* When Pharaun nodded yes, the warrior continued, *We've got the proof we sought, anyway. Let's return to the inn. I no longer have the stomach for this city.*

Pharaun nodded, though he did not share his friend's sentiment. Together, they turned and strolled back the way they had come, ignoring the screams of the priestess as the hobgoblins opened her a hundred times with quick, controlled thrusts of their short spears. After a few steps, the magical scrying vanished, and Pharaun cast his gaze around once more, hoping to find the source. He did not, and the three of them departed the plaza.

Behind them, the crowd that had gathered around the confrontation stirred and grew rowdy. Several other drow in the throng found themselves pushed and prodded as they tried to extricate themselves from the roiling multitudes. The other races were growing bold after witnessing the murder of a dark elf. Shouts rose up, curses to drow and their missing goddess. Finally, the handful of dark elves scrambled free, either rising up above the aggressors around them, or pushing through to more open streets. The mood was turning ugly in Ched Nasad.

Chapter

S I X

Aliisza, disguised as a lovely drow female, perched on the roof of a quaint shop that stood along the side of a street leading to the plaza, and she watched the comings and goings of the citizens, slaves, and visitors of Ched Nasad. The store offered fashionable, decorative silk wraps and other clothing, but the fiend crouching on its rounded, cocoonlike roof was not interested in making a purchase. Instead, she watched intently as Pharaun and the other two drow males turned away from the slaughter of one of their own race and strolled calmly in the other direction. She observed them as they disappeared down one of the calcified webs that served as a street in the unusual city. When they were almost out of sight, she hopped down from her vantage point and strode off after them.

Aliisza was not terribly surprised that the three dark elves she was shadowing had not aided the drunken priestess. She had seen far too much nonchalance in the city since she had arrived for it to strike her as odd. Still, she got the distinct impression that the entire group from Menzoberranzan was making a great effort to avoid drawing attention to itself. She intended to find out why, but first things first.

The alu could not help but smile as she made her way along the streets, following the wizard and his companions while pretending to shop for trinkets in the bazaars and markets. She studied the myriad lines of calcified webs that stretched across from one side of the massive cavern to the other, glowing faintly with magical, flickering light as far as the eye could see. She half expected to see some great, lumbering spider making its way across the vast webbing.

They sure do love their spider motifs, she thought wryly. Everything they do revolves around the great Lolth, Queen of the Spiders. You'd think they would learn to diversify a little bit, try to become a little more well-rounded.

She grinned at her own little joke. Drow were such odd creatures, she decided. On the one hand so deceitful and chaotic, always turning on one another, but on the other hand trying to live their lives by some code or structure, based on the tenets of faith set down by a demon who was as unpredictable as could possibly be.

At least they universally agree on one thing, the alu concluded, they all think they're superior to every other species in the Underdark, and on the surface, too.

Aliisza watched as a gaggle of kobold slaves, pushed along by their hobgoblin slavemasters, scurried from one web street down a sloped ramp to the next web street below. All in all, she had seen more species of creature in Ched Nasad than she could imagine being gathered anywhere else. The "lesser races" outnumbered the drow by two to one, she figured, and included surface dwarves, orcs, quaggoths, bugbears, and others, almost all of them slaves. The one possible exception to this was the gray dwarves, who traded honestly enough with the drow that they were tolerated in the city as merchants. In addition, Aliisza had seen an aboleth with its host of caretakers, illithids, grell, and what she suspected must be a deep dragon, for though it too was disguised as a dark elf, she detected the unmistakable scent as it strolled by.

The one notable exception to the eclectic collection of visitors were the beholders, for which Aliisza was not in the least sorry.

There's a race that's even more fond of itself than the dark elves, if that's even possible, the alu thought.

Eye tyrants were nothing but trouble as far as Aliisza was concerned, but fortunately they were in a perpetual state of war with the drow, so none were ever seen in the vicinity. If she had caught even a glimpse of one inside the great V-shaped cavern, she would have turned and headed the opposite direction as quickly as was fiendishly possible.

The alu blinked, realizing that with all her daydreaming, she was letting her quarry slip away. Glancing around, she spotted the trio of drow heading along a segment of web street toward a wall, into an out-of-the-way part of the city. She realized that they were in the mercantile district, and she recognized quickly enough that Pharaun and the others were headed for an inn set along the end of the dead-end thoroughfare.

Good, she thought. Now I can keep an eye on them and still enjoy the sights and sounds for a few days. Maybe I can even get the wizard alone for a little while. . . .

🕷 🕷 🕷

Faeryl Zauvirr brooded on the plush bed while Quenthel stalked back and forth in the room they shared at the Flame and Serpent. The high priestess didn't like to be kept waiting during the best of times, and she certainly didn't like being kept waiting in the middle of a strange city, tendays away from her homeland, and by three males, no less.

That damnable Mizzrym and his infuriating smile, Quenthel thought. I should have Jeggred rend him the moment he returns.

But she knew she couldn't eliminate the wizard or even allow him to be injured. As much as she loathed the situation, Quenthel knew she was dependent on Pharaun as a resource.

But when we return to Menzoberranzan . . .

The unfinished thought hovered in her mind, not so much because she didn't know what was to be done with the irritating mage but because she didn't know when, or if, she would see her home again.

It had been so long since she'd last felt the presence of Lolth, had last bathed in the goddess's glory and favor, that she wondered if she even properly remembered what it felt like.

Will it ever return? Is she gone?

Stop it! Quenthel silently scolded herself. If you are being tested, fool, then right now, your score is not high. Not high at all. Even if she did send you back for a purpose.

Jeggred opened the door and entered, stooping as he did so to avoid the low jamb overhead.

"They are back," he growled, sliding the door shut behind him.

"Where in the Hells were they?" Quenthel asked, still pacing.

"They went for a walk," the draegloth answered, shrugging.

Quenthel looked over at the creature, who was leering at Faeryl. The ambassador looked miserable under the fiend's scrutiny, and Quenthel wanted to laugh, remembering some of the things Triel had told her about the Zauvirr's torture at the hands of Jeggred. Even so, this was not the time.

Quenthel snapped, "Are those worthless males coming, or must I send you to fetch them?"

"They will be here shortly," Jeggred replied, turning away from Faeryl to crouch in a corner. "The mage told me he had something he needed to look over before they joined us." Even down on his haunches, the draegloth was as tall as the high priestess. His white mane of hair cascaded out behind him as he examined the claw of one hand, picking some fleck of something from its surface with the hand of one of his smaller arms. "They have been drinking," he finished, not looking up.

Quenthel swore, drawing a look from Faeryl, but the high priestess didn't care.

Out carousing, like foolish boys! she seethed. *When we return, they shall be put to work in the rothé fields.*

There was a knock at the door, and Quenthel stopped pacing at last, planting her hands on her hips as Jeggred rose to answer it. When he swung the portal open, Pharaun, Valas, and Ryld filed in. Quenthel was surprised to see the grim looks on the faces of the three males.

Before anyone had a chance to speak, Pharaun flashed, *Someone was watching us today, with magic. No one say a word until I ward the room.*

With that, he produced a small mirror and a tiny brass horn and used them to cast a spell of some sort, though Quenthel could not see any visible difference. Not that she expected to, but the idea of the wizard performing spells of his own accord, like everything he did, made her uneasy.

"The city is about to boil over," Pharaun said when he was finished casting. He took a seat on the couch and avoided looking directly at Quenthel.

He knows he's about to catch it, the high priestess thought.

"What do you mean? Who's been watching you? And what were you doing out there, anyway? Didn't I instruct you to get some rest and meet back here before the evening meal?"

"Actually, you did not, Mistress," Pharaun answered as the other two found places to lean against the far wall. "You said that *you* were going to rest, and you specifically told us to leave you alone. Under such circumstances, I didn't see the wisdom in disturbing you with trivialities like a refreshing walk."

Quenthel sighed. Once again the wizard was twisting her words around, using them to his advantage.

"As for who was watching us, I can't say. It might have been nothing, just a curious mage checking out some unusual-looking characters as a matter of course and moving on. Then again, it could have been someone specifically worried about us. I didn't see who was scrying. When I returned, I pulled out my grimoires and studied a spell that would detect scrying, though not stop it from happening. If I give a signal, everyone must be silent."

Quenthel nodded once, curtly, knowing that the wizard was taking wise precautions.

"Very well," she said. "What did you discover while you were strolling through the city that makes you believe it is about to 'boil over'?"

"It's true," Valas said quietly from his corner. "The lesser races are growing restless. We witnessed an attack today."

"So what?" the high priestess responded. "They squabble among themselves all the time back home."

"Yes, but this was a gang of them, assaulting a priestess," Ryld said. He was glowering, though at whom, Quenthel was not sure. "They were bold enough to kill her in front of everyone in an open plaza."

"They would dare?" It was Faeryl, sitting on the edge of the bed, her red eyes glittering with anger. "And you did nothing?"

"Truth be told, she was quite inebriated," Pharaun said, reclining on the couch. "Still, she provided us with the proof we needed. Ched Nasad's clergy suffers the same, ah . . . challenges that you do, Mistress."

Quenthel had folded her arms beneath her breasts and moved to stand in front of the wizard.

"You did nothing to aid her?" she asked, turning her gaze toward the other two males, watching as they looked away, some notion of guilt on their faces.

Pharaun shrugged and said, "To have interfered would have only drawn attention to the fact that we were in the city, Mistress. If we are to continue to investigate, we must maintain our inconspicuousness. Besides," he added, leaning forward again, "she was pleading for Lolth to return to her, right there in the open courtyard. She had clearly lost her resolution and was not, in my most humble opinion, fit to serve the goddess."

"In your—!" Faeryl seethed. "The opinion of a mere male is counted upon for very little in most issues. In the matters of the sisterhood, it matters not at all!"

She stood, taking a step toward the wizard. With a gesture from Quenthel, Jeggred was instantly between them. The ambassador shrank back from her one-time tormentor.

"Faeryl, my dear, in this you are usually correct," Quenthel said in her most soothing voice. It was one she rarely used, but in this instance she believed it was warranted. For his part, Pharaun gaped at her, which made her smile. "But, my dear, think on it," the high priestess continued. "The wizard is actually correct, though he may have stumbled upon this conclusion accidentally, addled with brandy though his mind seems to be. I understand your fears, but you must not let them eat away at your logic. If a priestess loses her faith in such a public spectacle, does she do her sisterhood any service?"

Faeryl shook her head as she backed away from Jeggred, returning to her spot on the bed.

"No, of course not," she mumbled at last. "She shames us all with her cowardice."

"Precisely," Quenthel said, nodding sagely, "and as foolish as it was for them to be out and about in the first place, these three silly boys would have only caused more harm to our progress if they had made a spectacle of themselves as well."

"Forgive my impudence, Mistress Quenthel," Faeryl said, her tone dreary. "I have returned home to find my city on the brink of implosion, where thralls dare to assault priestesses in open markets. As you love Menzoberranzan, your city and homeland, so I love Ched Nasad and do not wish to see her come to this end. I forgot myself in a moment of emotion."

Quenthel dismissed the apology with a wave of her hand.

"Understandable, in this time of crisis," she said, "but you must learn to control that emotion if we are to move forward."

"Do I take it, then, that you believe there is still more to be uncovered?" Pharaun asked.

"Perhaps," the high priestess answered, pacing once more. "I am willing to hear what the rest of you think, before I make my decision."

It was Valas who spoke first.

"I think it's unsafe to remain in the city for long, Mistress," the diminutive scout said. "We have discovered what we came here to learn, and I think it would be wise to return to Menzoberranzan before riots fill the streets and we get caught up in another slave revolt, or worse."

"I agree with Valas," Ryld added. "It is clear to me that the clerics here have handled the vanishing of Lolth less well than you and yours back home. There is little they can do for us."

Quenthel looked to Pharaun, knowing he would have something completely different and unorthodox in mind.

Pharaun shifted a bit, eyeing the other two males before saying, "I think we might do better to investigate further. Valas opened my eyes to another possible avenue of study, one that I would like to take advantage of. There are other races who venerate the Dark Mother besides drow, and it would behoove us to discover whether or not they, too, suffer her loss."

Quenthel nodded and said, "An interesting idea, but not one of much practicality. We are not loved by many others, and I doubt that those who worship Lolth would too freely impart such secretive information to us. Notice how we haven't been too forthcoming ourselves, even to the dark elves of our sister city. However, as there is still business I consider unfinished here, we will not be going just yet."

"Yes, precisely," Pharaun replied. "While you're busy with all that, I plan to at least look into my theory. I think I might know of a way to confirm it by tomorrow."

"I have other work for you tomorrow," Quenthel said, giving the wizard a cold gaze. "Faeryl, Jeggred, and I shall pay a visit to the storehouses of Black Claw Mercantile and take what rightfully belongs to House Baenre while the three of you find a means to transport it back. I intend to get out of the city with those goods as quickly as possible. The caravans are long overdue in Menzoberranzan, and we are here to make sure due payment is made."

Pharaun scowled briefly, and Quenthel was expecting an argument, but the wizard merely stood, nodding again.

Pharaun was surprised when Quenthel asked him to remain behind for a moment after dismissing the rest of the group, along with specific instructions to Jeggred to keep an eye on Faeryl, instructions that made the ambassador actually tremble. The wizard stood silently as Quenthel closed the door, then he cocked an eyebrow at her when she asked him if his detection spells were still in place.

"Yes, as a matter of fact, they are," the mage responded. "The divination should remain in place for a full day."

"Good," the high priestess said, nodding in satisfaction. "You're pretty talented with divining information, are you not?"

Pharaun could not help but grin but sat on the couch as he spread his hands ingenuously, wondering why she, of all drow, would pay him a compliment.

"I manage to get by," he said.

"I want you to do something for me," Quenthel said, biting her lip.

Pharaun tipped his head to one side, surprised, for it was not at all like her, especially in recent tendays, to pay him a compliment, much less ask a favor of him.

We are indeed a long way from Menzoberranzan, he thought wryly.

It would give the wizard leverage if he could perform a genuine task for her, but of course the first notion that popped into his head was the prospect of being played. Shrugging, he motioned for her to speak further.

After a lengthy pause, the high priestess said, "I want you to determine the identity of someone."

" 'Someone?' " Pharaun asked. "Surely you have more for me to work with?"

"Yes . . ." Quenthel answered, biting her lip again, "someone who was trying to kill me."

Pharaun sat upright on the couch, looking directly at the female in front of him.

"Kill you?"

He was surprised, not because it was so inconceivable that Quenthel was the target of an attack—merely being the Mistress of Arach-Tinilith brought with it a host of enemies—but because she had decided to trust him enough with this confidence and the task. If that was indeed what she really wanted. Maybe she was just trying to occupy his time, keep him from something else. A hundred possibilities swirled in his head.

"Someone back in Menzoberranzan sent several demons after me," Quenthel said. "Sent them right into the Academy. Fortunately, my prowess was sufficient to fend off the attacks, but I would like to put a stop to them before we return. It is a waste of both the lives of my charges and the magic I have been forced to consume in the effort."

Pharaun nodded, thinking. Someone powerful enough to bend demons to his will had to come from Sorcere, he reasoned. Certainly, plenty of mages in the school of magic had the wherewithal, but how many of them were so interested in eliminating Quenthel Baenre?

"I will look into it," the Master of Sorcere said. "If I can determine who sent the fiends in your direction, you will be the first to know it."

"Good," Quenthel said. "You will tell no one of this, not even the other members of our expedition."

"Of course not, Mistress," Pharaun replied. "This issue is between the two of us, and the two of us only."

"Very well," the high priestess said, indicating that the meeting was at an end. "Ferret out my enemy, and when we return to Menzoberranzan in triumph, I will make certain you are duly honored for your part. Your future at Tier Breche will be as bright as Narbondel."

Pharaun bowed low as a gesture of thanks.

If by that you mean I will glow with the flame of a thousand of your killing spells, he thought, then we shall see.

"I look forward to the accolades, Mistress Quenthel," the mage said aloud, and with that he pulled the door open for her and followed her out to attend to the evening meal with the others.

🕷 🕷 🕷

Gromph sat at his bone desk, mulling over his inability to peer into the Demonweb where Lolth resided. None of his usual scrying spells had been successful, and he was growing irritated. He was considering ways to get around this dilemma when the message arrived. It was a mere whisper, but Gromph nonetheless recognized Pharaun Mizzrym's magically transmitted voice.

Reached Ched Nasad. City in chaos; matron mothers ruling in name only. Investigating new possibility, more information next communication. Quenthel to visit Black Claw tomorrow.

Gromph's mouth tightened at the mention of his sister.

Hopefully, she will not come back, he thought.

The archmage knew of the spell the other wizard was using to communicate, and he was aware that he could whisper an answer to his counterpart. Unfortunately, he had not prepared for this. Thinking quickly, he whispered a few instructions.

"Focus attention on gathering information to aid our own situation. Keep me apprised of all new possibilities. Report on success at Black Claw with next—

"—contact," Gromph finished, but he knew that the spell had winked out before he'd managed to utter the last word. He shook his head, disgruntled, but he knew the Mizzrym was clever enough to figure out what he meant, regardless. Whether he would follow those instructions or not was an entirely different matter.

The Baenre wizard sat back in his chair, contemplating for a moment, pondering what condition the expedition team was likely to be in. He especially wondered how his sister fared and if the strain of his own attacks, coupled with the journey, had taken their toll. He certainly hoped so.

He suspected that she and Pharaun were clashing on a regular basis. The wizard was too independent, too full of himself to know when to placate the high priestess, and she had been too long inside the Academy, too used to getting her own way, unwilling to listen to advice, no matter how reasonable.

That's my sister, the archmage thought, frowning.

It often seemed to Gromph as if both of his sisters made poor decisions for no other purpose than to spite others. Even if Quenthel did survive her journey, Gromph thought she might very well be ripe for the slaughter when she returned. *If* she returned. If Quenthel were to lead the expedition into disaster in Ched Nasad, it would certainly be to Gromph's advantage. He could be rid of both her and the Mizzrym fop in one very charming blow. Yet, the fate of Menzoberranzan might very well rest on their shoulders. Was sending them off together the wisest choice?

Still uncertain what his next step would be regarding his own investigations of Lolth's domain, but with a whole new set of issues to deal with, Gromph arose from behind his bone desk and hurried to find his sister.

🕷 🕷 🕷

Triel scowled slightly when she saw Gromph enter the audience chamber. It was not a time for public petitioning, and though her brother was hardly some common supplicant, she had hoped to avoid any visitations for a while. The matron mother straightened herself in the overly large throne as her brother approached. The archmage bowed low and stepped close, further irritating the matron mother. She liked everyone to keep a little distance.

Gromph kept his voice low, leaning in so as to nearly whisper, "Triel, I have news."

Triel doubted the guards outside, flanking the doors, were going to hear a normal conversation, but her brother had not become Archmage of Menzoberranzan through carelessness. She inclined her head to listen.

"Do tell," she said.

"Quenthel and the others have reached Ched Nasad," the archmage said. "Pharaun Mizzrym reports that the city is in an uproar. Apparently, Menzoberranzan is not the only city afflicted with Lolth's disfavor."

"We don't know that it is disfavor!" Triel snapped. "There may be another explanation."

105

Gromph inclined his head slightly in apology.

"Afflicted with her absence," he corrected himself. "But the matron mothers there have done a poor job of keeping the situation quiet."

"How bad is it?"

"I gathered that trouble could be brewing . . . major trouble."

Triel sighed. As much of a relief as it was to find out Menzoberranzan was not being singled out for some sort of punishment, the news didn't get them any closer to discovering why the Dark Mother had chosen to disappear. Triel was at a loss as to the next step.

"Did he say what they were planning to do?" she asked her brother.

"Quenthel seems intent on following through with your instructions to bring back goods from Black Claw," Gromph replied.

The idea of more magical supplies lifted Triel's spirits slightly, but only slightly.

"Then I suppose they'll be returning within a few tendays," she said. "We are really no closer to an answer than we were when they left. It is only a matter of time before Menzoberranzan is in the same difficulties as her sister city."

"Unfortunately, you may be more correct than you understand."

"What other dire news do you have to report?"

If this was the way her mornings were going to start out, Triel considered remaining in Reverie until the midday meal a preferable alternative to actually rising and dealing with the issues at hand.

"I have received reports that our patrols are encountering a lot more activity around the perimeter of the city."

"What kind of activity?"

"Exactly what you might expect," Gromph said. "Though nothing has actually happened, no skirmishes breaking out, our patrols have spotted what looks to be scouting parties surveying our situation.

Duergar, deep gnomes, and even kuo-toans have been spotted in greater-than-normal numbers."

"They know. They can tell that things aren't right."

"Perhaps. Or, they could simply be passing by . . . traveling to somewhere else, and we've simply grown more sensitive to their presence."

"I doubt it," she replied. "This can't last. We're going to have to confront the situation soon. I will bring this up at the next council meeting."

"Of course," Gromph said and made a move to withdraw.

Triel motioned that her brother was dismissed and told herself that it was time to get on with her day, but she continued to brood atop her throne for some time after that.

※ ※ ※

Quenthel was thankful she had Jeggred along for the trip from the Flame and Serpent to the storehouse district. The mood of the city had grown worse since even the previous day, and the drow received more than a few menacing looks and jostles as they moved through the streets. Fortunately, the trio didn't have to travel far to get to where they needed to go, and much of the journey was made by way of levitation. Faeryl was in a sullen mood, despite the fact that she seemed more than eager to aid the Menzoberranyr. Perhaps she was still displeased with Quenthel's lack of trust, or maybe she simply couldn't abide Jeggred's presence. The high priestess couldn't blame her. The draegloth took such delight in tormenting Faeryl, Quenthel almost felt sorry for the younger drow. Almost.

Quenthel had sent the males to procure transportation for the return trip to Menzoberranzan. She wasn't about to haul her own provisions on her back again, whether they managed to locate a stockpile of goods or not, and if they did they would need sufficient pack lizards and guards to ensure the materials arrived safely.

Valas had warned the high priestess that anyone worth his salt was going to command an exorbitant price, if he could be convinced to work at all, but Quenthel didn't care and told the scout so.

Why is it, Quenthel thought as they approached Black Claw's storehouses from a back street, where there were fewer folk milling about, that with males you always have to explain things to them in exacting detail? Why can't they just do as they're told and be done with it?

Pharaun was the worst, she decided. Quenthel had no doubt that the wizard was off doing his own little tasks, completely ignoring her instructions to him to help Valas and Ryld. He had an infuriating habit of ignoring her wishes, and she would have to do something about that—when they got back to Menzoberranzan, of course. She needed his talents too much until then.

"Now, remember," Quenthel warned Faeryl as they neared the office side of the storehouse. "Tell them only what I instructed you. If I'm not happy with this little encounter, Jeggred will make sure it's not a problem in the future."

The draegloth was strolling along behind the two priestesses, and Faeryl stole a quick glance over her shoulder at him. Quenthel noticed her faint shudder and smiled to herself. It turned out to be quite useful that Triel had set Jeggred upon the girl back in Menzoberranzan. It had made her so . . . compliant.

"Yes, Mistress Quenthel," Faeryl replied. "I understand."

The three of them were at the door to the storehouse, where a contingent of six House Zauvirr guards barred the entrance. Faeryl approached boldly, even as the males goggled at the sight of the towering draegloth behind her.

"We must inspect the stores," Faeryl said in what Quenthel thought was a surprisingly commanding voice. "Stand aside and let us enter."

The male who appeared to be the leader managed to pull his gaze away from Jeggred long enough to look at her quizzically.

"I don't know you," he said. "What is your business?"

Faeryl stepped closer, standing a little taller so that he was forced to peer up at her scowling face. She grasped the House insignia that was pinned to her *piwafwi* and thrust it into his view.

"You know this, don't you?" she snapped, shaking the insignia. "You're here to keep out the riffraff, stupid boy, not bother a personal envoy of Matron Mothers Zauvirr and Melarn."

Quenthel noted with satisfaction that the lad gulped, visibly shaken as he moved with haste to the side, allowing Faeryl access to the door. The ambassador stepped inside, with the high priestess and Jeggred right behind her. As Quenthel strolled past, she smiled sweetly at one of the males, who still gaped at the draegloth, his eyes wide.

Inside the storehouse, which appeared to have been spun from webbing and hardened to stone, Faeryl led the way through an office area, through a large door, and into a cavernous chamber that had been subdivided into storage areas by low walls. Her footsteps echoing in the vast storeroom, Faeryl walked across the stone floor, hurrying past row after row of shelves and bins. Quenthel followed her, figuring the ambassador knew the way to the most valuable hoards of magic.

Quenthel supposed there was a secure section of the storehouse, and she began to worry. Any magic of value would likely be warded.

I should have brought that fop Mizzrym along, after all, she chided herself.

"Mistress!" Yngoth hissed, rising up from the whip. "We are in danger!"

Quenthel spun around, looking for signs of a threat, but she could see nothing.

"What danger?" she demanded. "Where?"

"A force is here . . . drow," Zinda answered, and all five of the snakes were agitating against her hip.

"Drow and others," Zinda added.

Someone's hiding, the high priestess realized. *What have you done, insolent child?*

A heartbeat later, a small host of drow appeared from behind a low wall, soldiers with swords and hand crossbows at the ready, and a handful of House wizards, too. They were all from House Zauvirr. Quenthel recognized two of the dark elves as matron mothers. It was obvious simply by their demeanor and bearing. One bore the insignia of House Zauvirr, and she was smiling coldly. The other, a rather plump drow, was most definitely not smiling and in fact looked quite distressed.

"By the Dark Mother," one of the males standing near Faeryl breathed, raising his crossbow and sighting down it at the fiend.

"He's dangerous," Faeryl called out, but several of the House wizards were already in action, casting spells even as the draegloth sprang forward, his teeth bared and his claws out, ready to shred anyone and everyone to ribbons. Faeryl took an involuntary step back, shuddering. Jeggred remained still, crouching as though he would spring again, snarling in fury, but unmoving otherwise.

"That will hold him," one of the wizards claimed.

Quenthel gasped in surprise, looking back and forth between Jeggred and Faeryl.

"Yes, Quenthel," Faeryl called out. "He has been rendered helpless. He cannot extract you from this."

Quenthel returned her glare to Faeryl as the soldiers fanned out, moving to surround her but staying well back. Many of the males aimed crossbows at her, and the wizards and priestesses all seemed ready to invoke various spells, should the Mistress of the Academy decide to bolt or attack. The snakes of Quenthel's whip writhed in agitation, snapping at anyone who stepped too close.

"You insolent little whelp of a drow," Quenthel snarled, shaking in fury as she looked at Faeryl, who only smiled sweetly in return. "All that time being so agreeable, and it was a lie. I knew you were being too accommodating. I should have let Jeggred have his way with you back in the wilds. I will see you flayed for this."

"That might prove difficult, *Mistress* Quenthel," Faeryl said, putting as much sarcasm as possible into her tone when she came to the honorific. "If you give this situation just a moment's thought, you will see, I'm sure, that you are overmatched. It really would be better if you surrendered this foolish standoff."

Quenthel blinked, weighing the ambassador's words. Finally, reluctantly, she realized that she was overmatched and nodded.

"Excellent, Mistress," Faeryl said. "Now, I think it would be a wise idea for you to lay down your arms and all of those wonderful trinkets I know you carry about yourself."

Quenthel's glare deepened, but she carefully set the whip down at her feet.

"Come on, Quenthel," Faeryl admonished. "I've been traveling with you for several tendays now. I know about the ring and the rod and all the other things. Don't make this more difficult."

Sighing, Quenthel began to remove the various items, and when Faeryl seemed satisfied that the high priestess could no longer be a significant threat, she ordered her to step away from the pile of goods.

As others swooped in and gathered up Quenthel's possessions, Faeryl stepped closer to Quenthel, smiling again.

"I am sorry it had to be this way, Quenthel," she said, "but I'm sure you understand."

Quenthel, who had regained some of her composure, smiled right back.

"Oh, I quite understand, Ambassador. My sister will be highly disappointed when she learns what you have done, but I wouldn't worry too much about that. It's a shame though . . . if there's one thing Triel will miss more than her sister, it would have to be her beloved son."

Faeryl didn't let her smile falter, but Quenthel thought the ambassador might have swallowed just a little nervously at the thought of the Matron Mother of House Baenre hearing the news that her draegloth had been destroyed.

Faeryl shrugged and said, "That's a worry for another time, Mistress. Now, if you will be so kind as to walk with me, I'll introduce Matron Mother Drisinil Melarn and my own mother, Mistress Ssipriina Zauvirr. They are most interested in hearing more about how you planned to steal our provisions and take them back to Menzoberranzan with you."

"Those goods belong in Menzoberranzan. They are ours by right," Quenthel said, angry all over again.

In the back of her mind, a part of her told herself that she really did need to learn to control her anger better, but she didn't want to listen.

Faeryl laughed cynically. "You didn't actually think I was going to let you steal from my House, did you?" she said. "From my city? You are mad!" Taking a calming breath, the ambassador continued, ice dripping from her voice, "Look around you, Mistress Baenre. This is what's left of your precious stores of goods."

For the first time, Quenthel realized that the rows and rows of shelves and bins were mostly empty. There was nothing in there to take. She had been thoroughly tricked, from the beginning of the journey, perhaps, played for the fool that she was. The betrayal was not unexpected, and Quenthel knew that had the roles been reversed, House Baenre would have carried the situation to the same conclusion. What galled her was that whatever foolish Baenre whelp had been responsible for the logistics of the deal had never bothered to put enough troops loyal to the House in place to ensure that nothing like this ever happened. Quenthel suspected that whatever loyal forces had been here had been summarily rounded up and executed when the crisis grew. The fact that no one was there now was a testament to that.

"What have you done with it?" Quenthel demanded, half interested in the answer and half stalling for time so she could assess the situation better.

Though there were a number of drow troops there, there was still a chance she could escape—though it would require leaving Jeggred behind.

Faeryl laughed, "Oh, don't worry. Black Claw made a tidy profit recently. The stock has been put to a far better use than what you intended, Mistress."

The mockery in the girl's tone was unmistakable.

"That's enough, Faeryl," Ssipriina Zauvirr said, taking a couple of steps forward. "There's no need to ruin the surprise we have in store for our guests."

As Faeryl lowered her head slightly in deference to her mother, she made her face stony smooth, but Quenthel knew that behind that facade, the Zauvirr daughter was delighted to have thwarted her.

Matron Mother Melarn also stepped forward—or rather, two heavily armed drow stepped forward, escorting her between them. She still frowned deeply, but she said nothing.

Ssipriina Zauvirr strolled halfway toward Quenthel and stopped.

"When my son managed to get into private contact with Faeryl and she was able to tell us what you were planning, we of course wasted no time in preparing for your arrival. I have to say, I am more than a little surprised that you actually expected to slip a storehouse full of goods out of the city, out from under our noses, without us noticing, but that's really of no consequence. As my daughter indicated, House Zauvirr has put the profits to a far better use."

Quenthel blinked in confusion.

"House Zauvirr?" she asked. "You are merely the caretakers. This company belongs to Houses Melarn and Baenre." The high priestess turned to the other matron mother and said, "Are you permitting this? Are you content to let these deceitful, low-class *merchants* make the decisions for your investments? You are far more trusting than I."

Drisinil Melarn didn't say a word, though she grimaced slightly when Quenthel spoke to her. Ssipriina Zauvirr laughed, a quick, bitter sound.

"Oh, she is far from content, Quenthel Baenre, but she has little choice in the matter."

Quenthel realized just why Matron Mother Melarn seemed so unhappy. The two drow flanking her were not escorts but guards.

"You would dare?" Quenthel asked. "You have laid hands on the matron mother of a high House of your own city and hope to get away with it? How can you expect to survive, when . . . when—"

The high priestess clamped her mouth shut, unwilling to finish the thought.

When Lolth will not grant you spells.

"Oh, not to worry," Ssipriina said, smiling even more deeply than before. "With the funds I've made selling off your valuables, I have ensured that House Zauvirr will never again kneel before the likes of you two."

Her eyes glittered red as she finished, and Quenthel saw pure hatred burning in them.

"Captain Xornbane, if you please?" Ssipriina called.

All around the drow gathering, appearing from nowhere, a horde of gray dwarves stood in a large circle, brandishing wicked-looking axes and heavy crossbows. Clearly, they had been standing there for a few moments but had simply been invisible. The duergar looked confident, ready for anything.

Quenthel felt the pit of her stomach leap into her throat, but before she could take any action she felt an invisible force seize her and hold her motionless. She couldn't move a muscle and saw that Drisinil Melarn was in a similar condition.

"Shall we kill them now?" one of the duergar asked, stepping forward.

Chapter

SEVEN

It's fortunate that Valas has been here before and knows the lay of the land, Ryld thought as he pushed his way through the throngs behind his companion.

The streets were more crowded than the previous day, if that was possible, and the warrior was sure that they would have made even slower progress if they'd been negotiating the web streets without a clue as to where to go for the right kind of information or the right kind of folk.

Ryld and Valas had set off shortly after the morning meal, the scout leading the larger drow into the lower quarters of the City of Shimmering Webs. At Quenthel's instructions, they were trying to find someone, anyone, who had supplies, equipment, and bodies available to serve them on the return trip to Menzoberranzan. Ryld still doubted the likelihood of the priestess acquiring anything worthwhile in the Black Claw storehouses, but he wasn't one to quibble with the Mistress of Arach-Tinilith. He had seen the folly of that with Pharaun. Or rather, he had seen the difficulties. Pharaun seemed to be getting away with his insidious little remarks more and more frequently, and the warrior realized, too, that the mage had begun following his own agenda more consistently.

Ryld pushed past a cluster of illithids—illithids! Five of them standing on a street corner, and no one paying them any mind—and he followed the scout into a particularly squalid-looking taproom.

Ryld couldn't get Pharaun off his mind. The mage seemed to be able to talk anyone around to his way of thinking, and when that didn't work, he'd figure out a way to do what he wanted anyway and explain it all away later.

The warrior wondered how often his old friend had done the very same thing to him in order to get what he wanted.

Valas shouldered his way through the crowded bar, heading for the back of the place. It always seemed to be at the rear tables where information was brokered, and in this tavern it was no exception. Ryld took up a position to watch his companion's back while Valas sat down across from a surly looking drow whose *piwafwi* was tattered and stained. The drow was definitely no noble, though Ryld would never hold that against him. Growing up on the streets of Menzoberranzan, the weapons master knew as well as anyone what it was like to be born a commoner.

A *sava* board rested on the table, and a game was in progress. Ryld could see that whoever had been across from this drow had played himself into a bad position and left before the inevitable conclusion. He found himself wanting to sit down and push a piece or two about, trying to stave off the endgame, but he forced himself to turn away, watching the crowded room for signs of trouble.

"We're looking for pack lizards," Valas began, setting a few gold coins on the table as he reached out and made a play on the *sava* board, "some supplies, and a few sellswords who can guard all of the above."

The drow snaked a hand out from under his shredded *piwafwi* and scooped up the gold before Valas had even completed his move, one that was not really of much help to his position, Ryld noted.

Better to let the fellow continue winning, the weapons master surmised.

"You and just about everyone else in the city," the drow chuckled, flashing a crooked smile that revealed several missing teeth. "Those kinds of things require more gold than the two of you are bound to have," he added, giving Valas and Ryld an appraising look.

"Don't worry about the coin," the scout replied while Ryld returned his attention to the room. "Just point us in the right direction."

"Well, then," the informant said, "I know a gray dwarf who might still have a few lizards available—for the right price, mind you—that would serve you well enough. How about buying a round of drinks while I get someone who can take you to him?"

Ryld pursed his lips in consternation. He had hoped this would be a quick affair, but of course it was not to be.

The drow slid out from the table, clapped Ryld on the shoulder, and said, "My, you're a healthy one, aren't you?" before pushing through the crowd.

Ryld stole a glance down at Valas, who seemed to be studying the *sava* board. The scout made no move to lure a serving boy over.

"Are you going to order those drinks, or should I do it?" the weapons master asked his companion.

"Don't worry about it," Valas answered, looking up. "When the wretch returns, I'll tell him I couldn't get anyone's attention in so crowded a place."

Ryld nodded and turned back to wait.

It didn't take long for the filthy drow to return, and he had not one, but four big half-ogres in tow. Ryld's eyes narrowed at the sight of them clearing a path through the crowd none too gently.

"We may have trouble," he muttered at Valas, who craned his neck to peer past the warrior.

"Let me out," Valas insisted, pushing Ryld forward enough to slip out from behind the table.

The scout stood next to the warrior, and Ryld noticed that Valas had his kukris in his hands, though he kept them down at his sides where they weren't easily seen.

"These are the fellows I was telling you about," the drow informant said to the biggest of the half-ogres. "They're the ones that's got lots of coin."

Ryld groaned inwardly as the half-ogre, who stood a good head taller than the drow, grinned ominously.

"We were just about to go fetch a round of drinks, as you suggested," Valas said, making as if to step past the half-ogre, who was blocking their way. "I guess we'll need a couple extra. Ryld, why don't you come help me carry them all? Then we can talk business with you boys."

"I've got a better idea," the half-ogre said, his voice deep and rumbling. "Why don't you sit down and tell us just how much gold you actually have? Then we'll decide if you can leave or not."

"I don't think that's such a good idea," Valas said, his voice steely cold. "We'll just take our business elsewhere."

"I suppose a half-ogre would be stupid enough," Ryld said to the scout, "to think that just because Lolth has gone quiet, we've forgotten how to fight."

The half-ogre smiled and said, "That's a pretty good joke, dark elf."

Then the creature lunged.

🕷 🕷 🕷

In the end, it was the most straightforward approach, Pharaun decided, that would grant him entry into one of the wizardly institutes. He knew all too well from his working knowledge of Sorcere's defenses that most forms of arcane stealth would likely be detected, however careful he might be. It was the nature of mages to be distrustful of other mages, and he had discovered that with a handful of different academies, schools, and research organizations to choose from in Ched Nasad, the local spellcasters were even more wary of one another.

Apparently, competition between the associations for luring new talent inside their halls was fierce, and the prestige garnered from successful recruiting paramount. True to drow nature, the societies weren't above using any method, however violent and underhanded, to shift the balance of power. What better way to get inside, Pharaun reasoned, than to pose as a prospective new member? All that it required was doffing his House insignia and asking at the front gates for the opportunity to speak with someone who could give him a tour, expound upon the amenities and responsibilities, and so on. He could easily pass himself off as a wayward wizard in need of a home without revealing his true level of expertise or the means by which he had acquired it.

The first place Pharaun visited was the imposing halls of the Disciples of Phelthong, run by the Archmage of Ched Nasad himself, Ildibane Nasadra. Pharaun figured that being the largest and best endowed of the various schools, it would have what he sought. However, he was careful to explain to the minor official who was sent to escort him that his interest, his area of specialty, lay in the study of creatures. It would be paramount for the facility to have a vast menagerie on hand if he was to feel truly at home. When he discovered that the Disciples did not maintain such a zoo, he politely declined to take a tour.

The second place Pharaun chose to investigate was known as the Arcanist Conservatory. It was neither the most impressive nor the least, but he picked it on a hunch. The drow who met with him after he'd explained himself to the sentries at the front of the edifice was an enchanter by the name of Kraszmyl Claddath of House Claddath, a short, surprisingly stocky fellow with slightly yellowing hair and bad teeth. Pharaun feigned skills of a middling nature as he introduced himself, and Kraszmyl seemed genuinely delighted to escort his guest through the premises.

"Tell me, Master Claddath, does the conservatory maintain a collection of live specimens on site?"

"Well, if you mean the best menagerie of creatures from both the World Above and the Underdark, properly housed and cared for, then yes."

"Oh, how delightful!" Pharaun didn't have to fake his excitement. "This sounds like the right place for me."

"Tell me, Master Pharaun, what is your particular expertise with this area of study?"

"Well, my last assignment was for a merchant who wanted me to study various breeding effects on rothé herds," the mage lied, "but I have a special interest in a new field. I am most curious to learn more about chitines and choldriths."

"Really?" Kraszmyl seemed nonplussed at the idea as he led Pharaun deeper into the confines of the conservatory. "Why in the world would you find such base creatures of interest?"

"Oh, they are tremendously fascinating!" Pharaun gushed. "While we find them to be nothing more than simple hunting sport, they actually have a unique culture and religious focus that in several ways mirrors our own."

"Oh, I see," Master Claddath said woodenly. "I hope you're not one of those odd cretins who actually thinks we should cease our hunting."

Pharaun laughed. "Certainly not," he said, "but imagine the possibilities if I could make them more of a challenge?"

"Yes, I could see the value in that. Well, here we are," the guide said, ushering Pharaun into a wing of the facilities that contained countless cages, cells, and holding pens.

Pharaun had never seen such a collection of species before, and he was more than impressed.

"It is spectacular!" he said.

"Yes, it is, Master Pharaun, but I have concluded by your reaction that you have seen nothing of the sort before. Now, why don't you tell me the real reason for your visit to our little conservatory today?"

Pharaun carefully reached into a pocket of his *piwafwi,* extracted a fragment of glass, and turned to look at the other wizard, who was shielded by a number of protections. He held a wand in his hand that he pointed at the visiting wizard, and Pharaun knew that the drow had already used it. Some sort of enchantment magic, he guessed.

Trying to charm me into explaining myself.

"Is this the way you greet all of your prospective new members?" Pharaun asked, smiling.

Kraszmyl looked mildly surprised, then tucked the wand away.

"No, just those wizards who show up out of nowhere, claiming to want to join our ranks."

The other wizard produced a second wand and aimed it at Pharaun.

"Especially those foolish enough to claim—"

Kraszmyl Claddath's words hung in the air, unfinished, as he transformed into glass. Of course, his *piwafwi,* the wand, and several other trinkets that adorned his body remained intact, but the flesh itself was pure, clear crystal.

Sighing in satisfaction, Pharaun pocketed the fragment of glass.

"If you hadn't been so busy expounding on my foolishness, you might have heard the words to my spell," he said to the inert figure, moving closer.

Being made of glass, the short, stocky drow was heavy. Pharaun persevered though, moving the transformed dark elf into exactly the right position.

"Now, let's see if we can find what we're looking for."

The Master of Sorcere felt the urge to hurry, for he doubted the menagerie would remain unattended for long. It would require many first-year students to clean and feed all the imprisoned specimens.

Moving through the aisles of cages, he looked around, trying to find what he needed. Even in his haste, he was truly impressed with the collection before him. He caught sight of some rather large cages in the back, but he had no time to satisfy his curiosity.

A pity, he thought, rounding a corner and continuing his search. I would like to spend a few tendays here.

Finally, after several rows, he came across the object of his desire. Sitting sullenly, her four arms sealed in some sort of resin casts, a lone choldrith glared up at him with decidedly humanoid silvery-white eyes. He squatted down to examine her.

She had charcoal-gray skin and was completely hairless. A set of diminutive mandibles, so small that Pharaun doubted they were functional, flanked her more humanoid mouth. Her ears jutted up beyond the top of her head, similar to a drow's but even more pronounced. Pharaun thought they looked vaguely like horns. From what little he already knew and had managed to learn about the species, he understood the necessity for the casts, to keep the creature from casting spells and freeing herself.

"I have a proposition for you," he said in the common language of the Underdark. The choldrith stared back him, saying nothing. "I imagine you can understand me well enough, but just in case"—he fumbled in his pockets for a few items—"it's a good thing I came prepared, eh?"

He produced a tiny clay ziggurat and a pinch of soot. Quickly, Pharaun wove a pair of spells, one to speak her language and the other to understand it, then tried again.

"If you will answer my questions, I will free you," he said.

Her eyes widened with hope, then narrowed with suspicion.

"You lie," she said in a strange, clicking speech, like the sound of a spider. "All drow lie to us."

"Perhaps that is true most of the time, but in this, I do not. I have nothing to gain by keeping you here and everything to gain by getting some answers."

When she only stared at Pharaun again, he asked, "What have you got to lose? You're trapped in a cage in a drow city, and your arms are encased in resin to keep you from calling on the Dark Mother. Except that doesn't matter, because she, too, has forsaken you, hasn't she?"

The choldrith's eyes widened again, and Pharaun knew it was true.

"You know about the goddess?" the creature asked.

"Yes, and I'm trying to find out where she's gone."

The wizard wasn't sure, but he thought he might have detected what would pass for a smile on the face of the wretched being.

"Then she does not love the dark elves more," she said, apparently to herself. "She has not abandoned the spider people in favor of you."

"No, her absence has been spread generously about to all her worshipers, it would appear," Pharaun answered. "What I'm trying to find out now is why?"

"The Dark Mother weaves her own webs. The Dark Mother seals herself away, but she will return."

"What? How? What tells you this?"

"I will tell you no more, killer of spider people. Free me or not, I have answered your question."

"So you have," Pharaun acknowledged, "and I will let you out of the cage. How you find your way home is up to you."

The wizard unlocked the cage door and stepped back. The choldrith edged warily toward the opening, eyeing Pharaun, obviously expecting a trick. He gestured toward the exit, palm open and up, and took another step back. The creature darted out of the cage and was halfway down the hall before the wizard caught himself laughing. He wondered how she would get the resin from her hands, but it was no longer his concern.

"Now that I know, it's time to go," he said aloud to himself. "But first, I can't resist a little peek . . ." and he turned to stroll toward the larger cages he had seen earlier.

Many of the larger cells were empty. It was the ones that were occupied that made Pharaun gasp. A creature unlike any he had ever seen before floated in one of the magically sealed chambers, something horrible and fascinating all at the same time. Its body was gray and soft, like the brain matter of creatures Pharaun had dissected in his younger days, with multiple tentacles hanging down from beneath it. A beak of some sort protruded from the front of the creature, but the wizard could not see any discernable eyes. It hovered in the prison, its tentacles hanging limply. Pharaun gazed at it a moment, then moved on.

The next creature he encountered was very familiar to the mage. The eye tyrant was a small specimen, no more than two feet in diameter. An adolescent, he surmised. The creature's eyes were all milky-white and scarred, effectively blinded and disabled. Still, watching the creature, Pharaun felt a little sense of dread.

From the other side of the great chamber, there was a shout, followed closely by a great crash and the sound of tinkling glass. The wizard smiled. *That would be Master Claddath, warning me that people are coming. Thank you for the tour, Kraszmyl.*

The mage wondered what kind of magical alarms he was triggering as he created one of his blue extradimensional doorways and stepped through to the outside of the Arcanist Conservatory.

No matter, he thought, allowing the magical passage to wink out as he floated between two levels of web streets, near a wall of the great cavern. *They'll simply think my presence there was an attack from a rival institution. If anyone thinks to ask the sentries, I shall be famous.*

With that, Pharaun drifted down to the street below and started on his way back to the Serpent and Flame.

He would have accounted the stroll back to the inn pleasant, had the streets not been so busy. All along the way, he caught snatches of conversation that centered mainly on the growing discontent of the citizens, the imminence of an attack from beyond the gates by all manner of fiendish armies, and the conviction that Lolth had abandoned the city to its fate. More than once, he witnessed the beginnings of a confrontation, but each time he saw trouble was beginning to brew, he wisely took a different route, frequently levitating either up or down to a different level to avoid the brawl.

"Pharaun," a voice called to him as he was making his way through a lane filled with cheese shops, wishing the odors were a bit less . . . well, stale.

Surprised and perhaps a bit unnerved at being flagged, he stuck his hands in his *piwafwi,* contemplating what sort of spell he might use to extract himself from trouble.

The wizard turned to find himself gazing at a beautiful drow female, her silvery white hair in lustrous curls down to her shoulders. She arched one high eyebrow at him and smiled, and he felt as though he knew her. Her dress was a bit unusual, and it lacked any sort of identifying insignia. Most telling of all, though, were the several auras of magic that she radiated, and he knew that she was not revealing everything.

"I beg pardon . . . do I know you?" Pharaun asked.

In response, she merely winked and crooked her finger for him to follow. Wondering what dangerous game he might be embroiled in but fancying a bit of fun, the wizard turned and sauntered after her. The female led him along a few streets, mostly back ways, and up a number of sections, until they found themselves in a residential area. The drow ducked into a small abode and turned and looked at him expectantly.

Pharaun hesitated at the doorway, looking around the street for any signs that would clue him in.

"Come on," his companion said, sticking her head back out. "Come inside."

"Why would I want to do that?" the wizard asked. "You've very obviously cloaked yourself in some obscuring magic, so your efforts to deceive me are only partially successful. I think my well being and I will remain out here, thank you all the same."

She simply smiled, and before his eyes the cloaking aura faded as her hair grew from light to dark, and her ebony skin transformed to the color of purest alabaster. The clothing she had attired herself in was transformed as well, into a black leather corset.

Pharaun smiled back.

"Hello, Aliisza," he said.

"Now, come inside so we can talk," the alu-fiend said, motioning for the mage to follow her and disappearing inside.

The interior of the home was small, if tidy, but it had the look of being lived in for a long time. The entirety of the place glowed with a soft violet hue, enough to illuminate the time-worn couch and table in the front room.

"I daresay this is not your place," Pharaun asked as he watched Aliisza slink across the floor and settle provocatively on the couch.

"No, I'm just borrowing it for a while," the demon said, reclining and propping a leg up. "I won't be here that long. Unfortunately, a home, unlike everything else in this city, is a bad investment at the moment. I doubt I could find a buyer, even if it did belong to me."

Pharaun grinned wryly as he settled into a chair across the room from the winged woman.

"So you've noticed the unstable marketplace, have you?" he replied. "A shame, that, but then it's not your worry, since it's not your place. Where are the owners at the moment?"

The alu-fiend smiled again, but her green eyes sparkled dangerously as she answered, "Oh, I don't think they'll be coming back. We've got the place all to ourselves, you know."

She turned over onto her stomach, propping herself up on her elbows and letting her feet wave lazily in the air above the backs of her thighs.

"Well, then, that holds promise," Pharaun said, his smile widening as he leaned forward. "But a clever girl like you must have things to do, places to go, Kaanyr Vhoks to see."

Aliisza made a face. "Come now, wizard. You're not going to plead honor or some such nonsense to me, are you? Kaanyr is a long ways away."

"It's not so much the Sceptered One I worry about, you lovely creature. It's me. My mother always told me not to get involved with bad girls, especially if they had wings. I'm just a wandering wizard, far from home. You might take advantage of me."

The alu-fiend giggled.

"Contrary to what your mother might have told you, we 'bad girls' aren't always looking to take you home to the Abyss with us. Sometimes, we just like the look of a fellow."

Pharaun looked down at his hands as he said, "Sure. And you just want to have some fun, right? I'd love to stay and keep you company, but I really do need to—"

"Pharaun, I already know what's going on," Aliisza said, her tone serious. "Your Spider Queen has vanished without a trace, leaving no scraps of magic for the ladies, and you came all the way from Menzoberranzan to find out why. I really couldn't care less. Well, that's not entirely true. I can't wait to see Kaanyr's face when I tell him, but it can wait. I just thought that before I head back to him and you went on your merry way back to your home, we might enjoy a little conversation."

She sat up, swinging her legs over the side of the couch to face him.

"Besides," she added, reaching up and beginning to loosen the laces of her corset, "you and I didn't get to finish sharing magic tricks."

"No one's expecting me for a bit," Pharaun chuckled. "I suppose I could stay for a little while."

Ryld knew Splitter would be next to useless in such tight quarters, so he had already reached down and grasped his short sword. He slid the blade smoothly and easily from its sheath in one smooth motion, remembering the feel of it in his hand, the balance, even as he brought it up to defend against the onrushing half-ogre. He parried the blow from the creature's upraised mace, then made a neat slice across the beast's midsection.

The half-ogre jerked just the tiniest bit in surprise, and Valas was on the creature from nowhere, drawing one of his kukris across its hamstring. There was a burst of light and a crackle from the strangely curved blade as it struck home, and the beast howled and toppled as it clutched its gut and leg in pain.

Out of the corner of his eye, Ryld spotted sudden movement, and he ducked just in time to avoid a hurled mug. The cup passed over his shoulder and hit the wall near the table, shattering in a spray of pottery. Ryld didn't waste the moment evaluating the source of the attack. He slashed at another of the half-ogres, drawing a thin opening across its upper arm that welled with blood as the creature staggered back, then the warrior was spinning away and parrying a large cudgel that a third foe, off to his right, swung at him.

The confrontation was drawing the attention of other patrons in the taproom, and Ryld could hear more than a few of them cheering the half-ogres, cursing him and Valas, and perhaps eyeing a chance to get in on the action themselves.

This is about to get really ugly, the warrior thought, warily waving the blade between himself and the half-ogre that blocked his way out.

A crossbow bolt struck him in the ribs, but his *piwafwi* and breastplate prevented the missile from penetrating. Still, the force of the shot staggered him the slightest bit, and the cudgel crashed down on his left shoulder with a loud crunch. His entire arm went numb, and he nearly lost his footing when something hooked his leg from behind and tried to topple him.

This is madness, the warrior thought as he scrambled back against the wall, shoving the table between himself and the rest of the patrons. Valas was nowhere to be seen.

"Get him!" someone snarled from the crowd.

"Kill the dark elves!" another cried.

Yet no one seemed eager to approach him.

Ryld kept his short sword leveled at the threats in front of him as he scanned the room for his companion, wondering if the scout had abandoned him in favor of escape. It would hardly have been the first time Ryld found himself in such a position.

When a pair of quaggoths—huge, white-furred humanoids sometimes known as deepbears—lunged at the warrior, Ryld was forced to return his attention to the difficulties at hand. Slashing with his short sword, he parried the spear the first creature tried to thrust through his chest, then sidestepped the second one's attack, which came very near to gashing his throat. A second crossbow bolt thunked against the wall near him, shattering against the stone.

At the same moment, Valas flashed into view again, having been hiding somehow in the middle of the crowd. The scout plunged both kukris into the back of the first quaggoth. Ryld blinked in surprise but took advantage of the opportunity to spin and slash low, cutting the second deepbear across both knees. Both creatures collapsed in sprays of blood as Valas joined Ryld against the wall.

"That was impressive," Ryld said as he and the scout kept the shouting, cursing throng at bay with their weapons.

"When those two came for you, I saw a chance and took it."

"How do you want to get out of here?" Ryld asked, surveying the room for any signs of escape. "Just fight our way through?"

"I don't know about you, but I've already got a means of escape," Valas replied. "See you on the outside."

With that, the scout backed into a shimmering blue doorway that had suddenly appeared at his back. Ryld had no time to gape as the door vanished from sight, leaving him alone against the horde of angry tavern patrons. A hobgoblin was closing warily from the right, while an orc and a strange lizard creature closed from the center and left, respectively.

Typical, he thought. Everyone but me must be able to blink in and out with those damnable doorways.

Ryld lunged in and cut high at the orc before spinning to deflect a blow from the lizard creature's short blade. The warrior kicked out at the hobgoblin and slashed again at the orc, this time catching his foe right across the cheek. Blood spattered, and Ryld began to work his way through the crowd, knowing he couldn't remain against the wall and hope to survive.

As he got in among the crowd and his opponents swirled around him, Ryld had an idea. Dropping to one knee, he made a couple of defensive thrusts as he reached down with his other hand and slapped the floor, calling up magical darkness. Nearly the entire taproom was engulfed in the inky blackness, and the battle cries of the crowd changed to the noise of confusion and panic. The darkness didn't bother Ryld. He was used to fighting blind, feeling and hearing his foes as easily as he'd watched them before.

The reaction of the pressing throng was exactly what Ryld had hoped for. Not eager to attack a foe they couldn't see and unwilling to get hit themselves, the crowd edged away from the warrior, giving him ample room. Reaching up, he slid Splitter off his back. With Valas gone, he no longer had to worry about controlling or shortening his swing. With the greatsword, he would be able to cut his way out much more quickly.

Not waiting for the unruly patrons to regain their wits, Ryld began slashing and cutting with bold stokes, clearing a path toward the door. The screams emanating from around the weapons master were unnerving to the rest of the brawlers. Quickly enough, Ryld emerged from the darkness, finding himself near the exit of the establishment. A couple more onlookers stood by the doorway, but when they saw the burly warrior appear with his greatsword leveled at them, they quickly scattered. Bruised and bleeding from several small cuts, Ryld darted through the exit and out onto the street.

Valas was leaning against a wall on the opposite side of the street, watching for him.

When Ryld saw the scout, he pursed his lips in displeasure, but before he could voice his anger, Valas nodded and said, "A lot easier to cut your way out of there without worrying about hitting me, wasn't it?"

Ryld opened his mouth to retort, realized that Valas was right, and snapped it shut again.

Finally, after the two of them began making their way down the thoroughfare, the warrior said, "The next place we try, we're taking a table near the front door."

It was only after Ryld realized that they weren't having to push their way through the crowds on the street, who parted for them warily, did he realize that he was still carrying Splitter in his hand, the blade dripping with blood.

"Yes, Captain Xornbane, by all means, dispatch them," Faeryl's mother said as the gray dwarves closed in on both Drisinil and Quenthel.

The two drow and the draegloth, unable to flee, stared about themselves. While Jeggrcd merely seethed with rage, straining to break free of the magical hold over him, Quenthel and Drisinil looked wild, desperate. The duergar who had spoken motioned, and several of the other gray dwarves moved in, axes lifted.

"Wait!" Faeryl exclaimed, then leaned in close to whisper with Ssipriina privately for a moment. "Mother, let's not kill the two Menzoberranyr yet. I'd like to keep them for a while."

"I think that would be an extraordinarily bad idea," one of the males near her mother said, also leaning in.

Faeryl glared at the impertinent male, whom she seemed to recall was not of the family but had worked diligently as an aid for a number of years. Zammzt, she thought his name was. She wrinkled her nose slightly, for he was far from pretty.

"Do you always butt into conversations you were not meant to hear?" the ambassador asked.

Zammzt merely bowed in acquiescence and said, "Forgive me, but I am only looking after the House's best interests. If this plan of subversion and surprise is to succeed in overthrowing House Melarn, then no one who knows the truth can be allowed to live. If the drow or the fiend are able to relay to anyone—anyone at all—what transpired here today, you will lose your backing from the other Houses. No one will support your rise to the council, Matron Mother. It's an unnecessary risk."

Matron Mother Zauvirr studied her daughter carefully for a moment then said, "He does have a point."

"Mother, believe me," Faeryl replied, "they will never get the chance to talk to anyone. I will make sure of it."

Ssipriina finally nodded and said, "All right, you've earned the chance to extract a little revenge, I suppose, but you must make certain that they do not talk to anyone, especially not Halisstra. Do you understand?"

Zammzt clicked his tongue in consternation, but he apparently knew better than to argue further. He had made his case and had lost. He moved off to engage in conversation with some of the House wizards.

Faeryl, elated, said, "Of course, Mother. I understand all too well. If our plan is to succeed, everyone must think these two were plotting together."

"Precisely. Now, I must go and prepare. We still have a lot of work to do."

With that, Ssipriina Zauvirr departed, Zammzt falling in beside her, his head leaning in close to discuss issues privately.

The ambassador moved back over to Quenthel once more.

"You see, *Mistress* Baenre," she said, trying to emphasize the honorific to the point of sounding absurd, "we didn't really steal the Black Claw merchandise. You did. Or at least, that's how it will appear when we report finding members of two powerful Houses meeting in secret, having already smuggled desperately needed supplies out of Ched Nasad and preparing to steal even more.

"I'm sure they'll wonder why Matron Mother Melarn would have wanted to turn her back on her own city in favor of Menzoberranzan, but unfortunately, they won't be able to ask her, since she resisted us and had to be killed."

Faeryl signaled to the commanding duergar and watched with a warm feeling as three of the gray dwarves stepped close. At her nod, they raised their axes high and swung. Behind her, Faeryl heard Quenthel's muffled cry of protest, but she didn't bother turning around.

There was no more than a grunt from Drisinil as three axes slammed into her flesh, but the blades bit deeply and the fat drow's eyes widened in pain and terror, though she couldn't react in any other way. The three duergar yanked their axes free and prepared to strike again, but Faeryl motioned for them to hold. She wanted to watch as Drisinil died slowly.

"You'll never look down your nose at me again, you fat rothé."

Drisinil's red eyes blinked and widened, seeming to plead with Faeryl in some way, but the younger drow only smiled as she stood casually, hands on hips, and watched the matron mother's lifeblood drip into a puddle on the floor around her motionless body. Drisinil shuddered, and her eyes began to glaze over. Her breathing was rapid for a moment or two, then stopped. Her lifeless eyes stared at nothing.

Faeryl turned back to Quenthel, who had been able to see the murder. The high priestess seemed to look both terrified and furious, all at the same time. The ambassador stepped in close to the Baenre noble and smiled.

"Of course, they'll be told that you were caught while trying to flee the scene, though you and I will know better, at least for a time. You and Jeggred are going to receive a stay of execution, just as I did back in Menzoberranzan. Aren't you pleased? Instead of dying right away, you'll get some of House Zauvirr's hospitality, just as I was graciously entertained by your sister."

Faeryl spat the words at her captive, the smile gone from her face. All of the hatred, the fear, surged to the forefront of her thoughts.

"And as for you, you wretched, foul-smelling beast," Faeryl said, turning to Jeggred, "I will ensure that you learn what true pain is."

The draegloth's eyes bored into her balefully, but she forced herself to stare resolutely back at him for three long breaths before finally turning away.

"Gruherth," Faeryl called, looking for one of her brothers in the throng of drow still milling about, "I want those two moved—secretly, mind you—to the dungeons in House Melarn."

Gruherth appeared and said, "We'll need a safe way to transport them."

"I'll take care of that," another wizard said, stepping closer to the fiend.

Pulling a few items from his pockets, the mage cast a spell, and a large white bubble formed around the draegloth. At the instruction of the wizard, four guards lifted the sphere—with surprising ease, Faeryl noted—and began to carry it into another part of the storehouse.

Very quickly, the same spell was applied to Quenthel, and four other drow boys bore her milky white sphere away, too.

Faeryl turned and looked for the duergar leader.

"Captain . . . Xornbane, is it?"

The gray dwarf who had given the order to kill Drisinil nodded.

"As I understand it, the next step in our plan is to get your company inside House Melarn unnoticed."

"That's right," the duergar repeated, folding his arms across his chest impatiently.

"Have all the arrangements been made to deal with this?"

"They have," he said, then he turned and trudged off after Faeryl's mother, leaving the ambassador to fume at his rudeness.

Gruherth reappeared.

"We're ready to begin moving everything through to the interior of House Melarn," he said to his sister. "Mother wants you there at the front so that we can throw off suspicion in case there are Melarn troops in sight once we begin crossing through the portal."

Faeryl grimaced but nodded. She had forgotten how much at her mother's beck and call she had been when she was last in the city. Still, she decided, it was better than being at Quenthel's beck and call.

Much better.

❀　　❀　　❀

Aliisza wriggled her toes in delight as she stretched out on the bed next to the wizard. It had been quite a while since she had felt this good, and it wasn't merely the physical pleasures that delighted her. This Pharaun was quite the wit, she had decided, boisterous and clever for a drow.

"How come you're so unlike the rest of your race?" the alu asked him, rolling over beside him and walking her alabaster fingers up his slender, graceful black arm, enjoying the contrast in color. "Every other dark elf I've ever met and talked to has been so staid and boring. You, on the other hand, make me laugh."

Pharaun, with his head propped on his hands as he lay stretched out on his back, smiled.

"Just unlucky, I suppose."

Aliisza furrowed her brow in confusion and asked, "What?"

"Can you imagine how it must be for me, being around 'staid and boring' drow all the time?" he asked, sitting up and folding his legs beneath him. "No one ever appreciates my witticisms. I offer up clever remarks, and I either get funny looks, if I'm speaking with other males, or scowls, if I'm in the presence of the ladies. It's damned depressing. So I say it's just bad luck. I was born a drow, but I was given a much sharper intellect than most of my species."

Aliisza giggled and rested her chin on both hands, gazing at the dark elf's red eyes.

"Oh, come on," she said. "It can't be that bad. At least you get to talk to other drow. Look at me. I spend the entire day herding tanarukks around."

"Oh, yes, the tanarukks. A few grunts and an obscene gesture, and they've recited their clan history, right?"

Aliisza laughed outright.

"They're not so bad as all that, but they certainly aren't ones for clever humor. Not even Kaanyr likes to devote this much time to just . . . talking—" She paused, seeing the wizard's smile turn into a frown. "What now?"

"Why did you have to go and mention his name? I was doing just fine until you brought up your other lover. That's no kind of pillow talk, you know."

"Sorry. I won't do it again," Aliisza promised. "But tell me . . . how is it you manage to spar with this high priestess of yours? I thought the females of your species didn't put up with too much of that nonsense."

Pharaun groaned and fell back against the pillow.

"She goes from bad to worse," he moaned to no one in particular. "Why do you keep bringing up these most unpleasant subjects? You're torturing me! Was I that unsatisfying?"

Aliisza punched him on the arm, laughing.

"Just answer the question."

Pharaun eyed her for a moment. He seemed suddenly wary.

"Why are you so curious?"

Aliisza shook her head.

"No real reason. Just curiosity, I suppose."

Pharaun rolled away from her to the side of the bed and asked, "Why are you here? In Ched Nasad, I mean."

Aliisza pouted just a little. She really hadn't meant to put him on edge, and now she had to think of a way to calm the wizard down again. She decided the truth, or just enough of it, was the best medicine.

"Because Kaanyr Vhok wants me to find out what's going on."

"You told me you already knew. In fact, you explained to me what's going on. What else are you looking for?"

"Nothing," the alu replied, reaching a hand out to stroke the back of the drow's arm with her fingers. "I have all the information I'm supposed to get. Well, except for visiting one of the matron mothers to see if she wants Kaanyr's assistance. They have some old pact or something. I'm still here because you're here."

Pharaun eyed her a moment longer, then chuckled and shook his head.

"I knew this was a bad idea," he said at last. "The matron mothers of this city are the one big thing I'd like most to avoid, and here you are, preparing to drop in on one. Somehow, that just doesn't bode well for me."

"Oh, stop it," Aliisza said, arching one of her eyebrows at the mage. "I'm not about to tell any matron mother about you. I wouldn't want word getting back to—back to you-know-who"—she smiled again "—though I don't see how you can avoid the matron mothers, given the company you're traveling with."

"What, Quenthel? No, that's not a problem. She knows House Melarn won't be too agreeable to her plan to take the Black Claw goods back to Menzoberranzan, so—" The wizard stopped in mid-sentence. "I shouldn't be telling you this. I am a sex-addled idiot."

He stared at Aliisza intently, his red eyes glittering.

The alu-fiend stared back, but she couldn't help but smile.

"What are you doing, considering whether to try to kill me to keep your secret safe?" she asked. Arching one eyebrow she shimmied back away from the wizard, leaning back on her elbows provocatively. "I have a better idea," she said, feeling her voice grow husky with desire. "Teach me another magic trick instead."

Pharaun, feeling a combination of exhilaration and dread, left Aliisza in the little house. Exhilarated from the satisfying afternoon he'd spent with the alu, he was dreading all the things he'd let slip. Though he'd repeatedly told himself to be wary, he'd stumbled several times thus far. Being with the fiend had reduced his normally sharp instinct for caution to some half-remembered sense of danger that he knew he ought to be cognizant of but wasn't. It was just an accepted practice that a drow never opened himself up to a fiend, that he should keep his dealings strictly business, and yet here he was, sharing her bed and spilling his best-kept secrets. Still, if he had to pick a risky diversion, Aliisza was quite the prize.

Whatever his apprehensions, Pharaun found that his steps were light as he made his way back to the Serpent and Flame. He had useful information to share with the rest of the Menzoberranyr, and he also had a couple of divinations he wanted to attempt that he hoped would clarify a bit just exactly what was going on in the Abyss. Plus, he might still have time to fulfill that request of Quenthel's. All in all, it was turning out to be a truly memorable day.

Despite his own elation, Pharaun could still feel the tension of the city buzzing in the air, and he was careful to avoid the worst of the crowds. After the experience of the previous day, he didn't think it wise to get caught up in a chest-thumping competition with a congregation of disgruntled citizens. He made certain to spend most of his time floating from section to section, avoiding completely the calcified webbing ladders that connected different levels.

The mage stopped along the way at a dingy-looking shop called Gauralt's Spices, a place that purported to offer hard-to-find components for spellcasting. Valas had mentioned it to him that morning before they set out on their separate errands, and Pharaun found it exactly where the scout had said it would be. Of course, getting what he needed might prove to be another matter, but Gauralt, a drow male who ran the place, was able to supply him with the four strips of ivory and the particular incense he needed, and he was on his way again in no time.

Back at the inn, none of the rest of the mage's companions had returned. He supposed that Ryld and Valas might spend most of the day attempting to round up the needed supplies and mounts for the return journey, but he was somewhat surprised that Quenthel, Faeryl, and Jeggred had not come back from the storehouse. He couldn't imagine what would require them to spend that much time there, but then it was just as well.

If she was here, he told himself, she'd simply find something to snipe about, anyway.

He began to make a mental checklist of the spells he wanted to cast. First, he would use his new components to try to track down who was trying to kill Quenthel.

And probably offer to help, he added, grinning.

He also planned to try again to take a peek into the Demonweb Pits.

It was a spell he had tried more than once back in Menzoberranzan, with no luck whatsoever, but he hoped it would yield more satisfying results away from the City of Spiders. The Master of Sorcere had no basis for this supposition, but he thought it was still worth an attempt.

Pharaun retrieved the four strips of ivory he'd acquired, along with the incense, and sat down to perform the spell. Casting it would leave him weary and low on spells, but if the knowledge he gained from it was useful, he would count the cost worthwhile.

The mage arranged the four strips of ivory into a rectangle upon the carpeting, lit the incense, and closed his eyes. It was not a spell he cast often, and it required a careful application of chanting and specific questions. He couldn't stumble at any point, for he didn't know when the next opportunity to try it would arise.

With the incense burning and the spell begun, Pharaun asked his question, beseeching the elemental forces of magic and the planes of existence to grant him a meaningful answer.

"Reveal to me the enemy of Quenthel Baenre of House Baenre in Menzoberranzan, the enemy who seeks to destroy her, who calls forth demons to slay her in the very temple where she reigns."

The burning incense flared, and smoke filled the room. After a moment, a message formed in Pharaun's mind, words uttered by the wind, or perhaps the Weave itself. However it was delivered, the message that Pharaun received was clear.

The one who seeks the high priestess's death shares her blood and her ambition. Quenthel's enemy sprang from the same womb but is not of the womb.

Pharaun blinked, his red eyes taking in the darkened room as the last remnants of the incense burned out and turned to ash.

Sprang from the same womb but not of the womb. A sibling, but not a female. A male? A brother? Gromph! It had to be. . . .

Pharaun was surprised, not so much that the Archmage of Menzoberranzan would wish his sister dead but by the fact that he hadn't see it before then. Gromph had much to gain by eliminating the only real rival for Triel's ear. The archmage could not have designs on the throne of House Baenre itself, but he could be the puppet master, pulling the strings behind the scenes. Quenthel disagreed with everything her brother said, and vice versa, so she was an obvious and powerful impediment to any ambitions he might have.

Adding to that was the fact that Gromph had the knowledge of the Academy's defenses and had the capability to summon forth the fiends used in the attacks. It was a talent few others possessed, at least few others with the interest to do so. There were other powerful wizards within the halls of Sorcere, and Pharaun supposed that some of them would like to see someone replace Quenthel as the Mistress of the Academy, but Gromph was the one who stood to gain the most.

Though he knew the answer, Pharaun wasn't sure what to do with it.

On the one hand, he considered, I'm here with Quenthel. Does telling her aid me more? Or do I simply seal my fate upon returning to Sorcere? If I tell Gromph that Quenthel is trying to find out who's after her, even do him a favor by misleading her—or eliminating her, a small part of his mind suggested—does my standing at Sorcere improve, or will he be unable to protect me from Triel's wrath?

Of course, Pharaun knew that most of his decisions hinged on the eventuality of returning to Menzoberranzan, and he was planning to argue with Quenthel against that course of action. There were still too many variables, too many possible outcomes, before he would know which side of the siblings' conflict to join. He could stall Quenthel for a while. She wouldn't know what might be involved in his quest for her information. For all she knew, he could be working through a spell that actually took days to complete or negotiating with an elemental of some sort, making a bargain to exchange some commodity for a casting of a spell he himself did not know. There were a number of lies he could tell her to keep her waiting.

For the time being, then, he decided he would stay mute on his findings and see which way the rothé herd roamed. When the time was right, he would play it to his advantage. Either outcome, and he would improve his station within the Academy.

Pharaun rested a few moments longer on the floor, recovering from the exertions of the spell then began packing up his paraphernalia, stowing the strips of ivory away in a pocket of his *piwafwi*.

Next, Pharaun removed a small mirror from his haversack. He briefly wondered if using the same spell he had just employed to find Quenthel's enemy would work better in these circumstances, but he couldn't cast it again without resting for a few hours then studying his spellbooks. Firming his resolve, the wizard began chanting the words needed to activate the magical scrying.

The Master of Sorcere knew the spell was dangerous. Attempting to look in on a deity without permission could have disastrous ramifications. Still, he was intent on trying, if only to discern more of what was going on in the wake of the goddess's absence. Drawing on the memories he had of his strange visit to the Demonweb Pits those decades past, he finished the spell and peered into the mirror, which was reflecting a cloudy image of elsewhere rather than his own dark-skinned face.

Pharaun gazed into the magical window for several minutes, waiting and hoping that he might recognize something in its murky depths. There was nothing. He willed the spectral eye that he knew was on the other end of his spell to glide forward, remotely peering this way and that, trying to catch a glimpse of something, anything solid in the formless fog.

The mage felt a tingle, a warning in the back of his mind. He mentally scrambled to release the spell, to sever the connection with the eye at the far side of oblivion, and he almost succeeded, but not quite. A backlash of energy slammed into him, hurtled outward through the mirror like a punch, while at the same time Pharaun sensed a wall of force sliding down, cutting him off from his magical eye.

As his senses returned, Pharaun realized he was sprawled on his back, blinking as his eyes tried to focus on the ceiling. He groaned and sat up, seeing that he had been hurtled backward from the mirror more than ten feet. He rose onto wobbly legs and staggered back over to the mirror. It was cracked, its glass surface spider-webbed into hundreds of fissures. He stared at the ruined mirror for a moment, wondering if the pattern was representative of something or merely a coincidence.

Well, that answers that question, Pharaun thought. A mere mortal cannot penetrate the veil that has settled over the sixty-sixth layer of the Abyss, but perhaps a higher being can.

The Master of Sorcere shook his head and sighed as he gingerly gathered the fragmented remains of the mirror.

Why do I go through this trouble? he thought as he tried to figure out where he should discard the ruined thing. Everything I do for everyone, and all I get is grief in return. I'll bet other folk don't go through this much trouble to track down their deities, he thought wryly. I'm sure they just look them up anytime—

The wizard froze in the middle of the room, the beginnings of an idea forming. He almost smacked himself in the head.

Of course! he thought. I've been going about this all wrong. Why didn't I think of this before? We're asking the wrong . . .

Tossing the mirror down in a tinkle of glass, Pharaun began to pace, mulling his idea over more carefully. A plan was beginning to form, one that was getting him excited. The hardest part, he realized, would be figuring out how to convince Quenthel.

It was not long after that that Ryld and Valas returned from their own excursions.

The wizard took one look at the pair of them and quickly surmised that their endeavors had not only ended unsatisfactorily but violently. Both drow were glum as well as bloodied and bruised. Valas walked with a slight limp, and Ryld seemed unable to lift his left arm above his waist. Almost as one, they dropped their gear on the floor and dropped down onto their Reverie couches.

"I gather that things did not go well today," Pharaun commented. "No chance to haul Quenthel's supplies out of here?"

"Three places," Valas muttered. "We tried three places and got into two scuffles for our troubles."

"There just isn't a pack lizard to be had, it seems," Ryld added, rubbing his eyes with his good hand. "If there is, no one is ready to sell it to outsiders."

"I don't find that hard to believe," Pharaun replied, "considering that no caravans have entered or left the city in such a long while. Everyone is holding tight to what they have, riding the crisis out."

Pharaun busied himself straightening his own things while the other two males sat still.

"I'll wager with you for who has to tell her," Ryld said to Valas. "Rock, knife, and parchment?"

The scout shook his head.

"Let's just make the wizard tell her," he said, pointing to Pharaun. "He seems to delight so in tormenting her, anyway, so what's one more bit of bad news out of his mouth?"

Ryld nodded, and Pharaun found himself smiling.

"Well, we all have a reprieve, at least for the moment," the mage said. "She and the other two haven't returned from the storehouse."

"Really?" Valas asked, sitting up. "I would have thought they'd return before us for sure."

Pharaun shrugged and said, "As would I, but none of them are here."

"That's fine by me," Ryld said, leaning back against the wall and closing his eyes. "The less I have to see of that damned draegloth, the better off I am."

Pharaun pursed his lips, realizing that what he was going to suggest next might not set well with either the weapons master or the scout.

"I found out something today, too," he said quietly.

Ryld opened one eye and looked at the wizard.

"Oh?"

Valas leaned forward on the edge of the bed.

"Have you determined what has happened to the Dark Mother?"

Pharaun chuckled and said, "Not exactly, but I did learn that her disappearance has not been limited to our own race. Other species feel her loss, as well."

"I don't know whether to consider that good news or not," the scout said, sitting back again.

"Nor do I," Pharaun agreed, "but I have also learned that something is sealing us out from the Demonweb Pits. I have attempted to scry there in hopes of learning something of the goddess's condition— indeed, if she yet exists—and I could not penetrate inside. A barrier protects it and keeps me, and others, outside."

"A barrier? You're speaking now of things I have no experience with," Ryld said. "What kind of barrier?"

"A potent one. I was nearly blasted into powder for my troubles," Pharaun said, a wry smile on his face. "I have tried it before, even spoke with Archmage Gromph before we left Menzoberranzan. He has experienced similar problems."

"It sounds as though whatever the Spider Queen is doing, she does not wish to be disturbed," Valas said.

"If it's her who's doing it," Ryld countered. "Perhaps another god has erected the barrier to prevent us from seeing her."

"Exactly!" Pharaun said eagerly. "Surely someone knows—or can find out—what we cannot discover."

"I thought that's what our mission was . . . to discover Lolth's fate," Valas said. "That's why we've come here."

"Yes, you are correct," Pharaun said, nodding, "though this business with storehouses of magic items seems to have become a higher priority. In the interest of bringing us back to the more fascinating part of our little expedition, I have an idea. I want to enlist help from the outside."

"Help? From whom?" Ryld was sitting up, too.

The wizard began to pace again as he explained his plan to his companions.

"A mere mortal, even someone with my acumen, can't penetrate the veil that has settled over the Demonweb Pits. Something is obviously intent on keeping us out. We need to enlist someone else's help in finding out what's going on there. Someone not of our own ilk."

Both of the other drow were watching the wizard intently, doubt plain on their faces.

"You can't mean . . ." Ryld said.

"Another god."

The weapons master seemed aghast. Valas said nothing but might have been contemplating the possibilities of such an act—and the ramifications.

"Perhaps a higher being," Pharaun continued, "especially one in close proximity to the Demonweb Pits—from one of the other layers of the Abyss—could, or possibly even already has, discovered more than we can possibly hope to on our own. Maybe we can convince one of them to tell us what has transpired or is transpiring inside.

"Not directly, of course," Pharaun added hastily, "but through an intermediary . . . a follower."

"You play a dangerous and foolish game, Pharaun Mizzrym," Ryld said, shaking his head. "The Dark Mother may find such a course blasphemous, a betrayal to the faith."

"Or she may congratulate me on being so innovative, so willing to examine and explore, whatever the risk. The other choice is to admit defeat, return to Menzoberranzan, and sit on our hands as our way of life ends."

"Quenthel will not be happy with this plan," Valas cautioned. "She will most likely consider it a personal affront to her."

"Yes, well, Quenthel is too focused on lining House Baenre's coffers to appreciate the larger picture before us. I'm beginning to wonder how wise a choice she was to lead this expedition. Don't stare at me like that, Ryld. . . . You've questioned more than a few of her decisions since we departed."

"Never openly. Not to her face."

"She's not here now, is she? My friend, I play with fire, I know that, but if I don't act where my heart lies then I've failed our race far worse than she. I'm content to steer things from behind the scenes, letting her believe she controls our tempo, our course, but such a method requires patience, more than a little frustration, at times, and the possibility of being thwarted or exposed. It would stand a much greater chance of success if the three of us worked together to maneuver her. I could use your help."

Valas had his chin in his hand, thinking. Ryld shook his head, lines of worry creasing his brow.

"You fight against millennia of tradition and habit, Pharaun," the weapons master said. "I can't say that I welcome the idea of returning to Menzoberranzan no better off than when we left, but usurping the high priestess's authority might very well see our heads on the parapets of House Baenre."

"The wizard has already been at it for a couple of tendays. . . ." Valas said.

"Perhaps, but until now, it was simply him against her; he hadn't brought us into it."

Pharaun clicked his tongue in exasperation.

"Do you honestly think that she won't hold us all responsible, regardless of the relative levels of involvement?" the Master of Sorcere asked. "She will blame you simply because you are a male, Master Argith."

Slowly, Ryld nodded.

"I suppose you're right," he said. "It still doesn't make me feel any better."

"I'm not suggesting we bind her with cord and throw her in a box, Weapons Master. All I'm asking is that you support me when I make a suggestion, that you back me, however subtly, when she and I disagree. Help me convince her that moving forward, rather than back to Menzoberranzan, is the wiser course of action."

"You make sense," Ryld replied, "but right now, your idea is just that. We must find someone willing to serve as the conduit. Do you know of any such creature?"

"I do," Valas said quietly.

Pharaun crouched down in front of the scout and asked, "You do? Who?"

"There's a priest I know, a follower of Vhaeraun."

"Vhaeraun," Ryld said in a clipped tone. "I doubt we'll receive any aid from him."

"Perhaps, but Tzirik is actually an old associate of mine," Valas replied.

At Ryld's surprised look, the scout added, "When you wander the wilds of the Underdark as much as I have, you have to be decidedly more pragmatic than in the cozy confines of Menzoberranzan. Tzirik Jaelre owes me a favor. If we can get to him, I think he might help us."

Valas turned to Pharaun and added, "Assuming, of course, that you have a notion of what he should do once we get there."

Pharaun replied, "I will when we find this priest. In the meantime, you keep this Tzirik Jaelre to yourself until I have words with Quenthel. At the right moment, mention that you know him, and we'll show her the wisdom of seeing this through to the end."

"I only hope the end comes later, rather than sooner," Ryld said grimly.

NINE

Halisstra couldn't breathe. The blood pounded in her ears, making it difficult to hear what Matron Mother Zauvirr was saying. She didn't want to listen, anyway.

"I wish it wasn't true, Halisstra, I really do, but there's no getting around it. We caught her in the act, and when we confronted her, she wouldn't surrender. Your mother tried to flee, and the soldiers just did their jobs. By the time I got to her, I couldn't help her."

Halisstra shook her head, trying to rid her thoughts of the hated words. Her mother, dead. It wasn't true. It couldn't be!

"No!" Halisstra cried out, pushing Danifae away. Her battle captive, all flimsy silks, was reaching out to her, trying to comfort her. "You're lying!"

She struggled to spin free, to get out of the room, but she found all avenues of escape cut off. Matron Mother Zauvirr's troops seemed to be standing idly by, as though they were merely guests in someone else's home, but they were strategically placed about the room to guard the doors. She looked around for some of her own family's soldiers, but there were none to be found. Matron Mother Zauvirr had planned well, delivering her devastating news from a position of strength.

Wilting, Halisstra sank down to the floor, unsure what to do. Only Danifae settled down next to her, making soothing noises and trying to reach out to calm her. She didn't want to be calmed. She wanted to slap the other drow, smack her across the room, but she knew better. If she had any hope at all of surviving this horrid situation, she would need the battle captive's aid. She had to think.

It wasn't so much that her mother was dead. Of course that didn't bother her. In other circumstances, she would have delighted in it, but there weren't any other circumstances. Her mother had been caught in an act of open treason against the city, or so Ssipriina claimed, and Halisstra had no way to refute it, despite the fact that it was a ludicrous notion. Her mother would never risk herself so openly, especially not aiding foreigners, regardless of how good the relationship was between their Houses. Not to mention the fact that smuggling the goods from Black Claw Mercantile out of the city would ruin House Melarn. There was nothing to gain from it and so much to lose.

Of course, when Ssipriina arrived in House Melarn's audience chamber, sat right down in Drisinil's throne and made her revelation, the unspoken implication was there. Drisinil was not acting alone. When the rest of the council learned of it, they would likely find Halisstra just as guilty of the crimes as her mother. They would imprison or execute everyone in the family, dissolve House Melarn, and divvy up its assets. Unless she found a way to counter it.

She had no doubt that Ssipriina was behind it all, was somehow benefiting from the destruction of House Melarn, but in order to make it work, she would have to eliminate Halisstra, too. Halisstra had to move fast, but she knew that the other drow wasn't about to let the First Daughter of House Melarn out of her sight. Her only chance to get help was to send Danifae, and that would only happen if Ssipriina Zauvirr believed the battle captive was more interested in saving her own skin than in supporting her mistress.

Halisstra glanced over at Danifae, taking a deep breath to calm herself, then began to flash signs at her servant, working secretively so that only her companion could see.

You have to turn on me, she signaled. *Convince them that you'd just as soon see me dead. Then get help. Go to House Maerret.*

When Danifae gave an almost imperceptible nod, Halisstra reached out and slapped her. Hard. The blow sent the battle captive falling backward, skidding across the floor. Danifae's eyes widened as her hand flew up to her cheek, but before she could open her mouth to spoil the effect, Halisstra screamed at her.

"How dare you suggest such a thing! I would never consider it!"

Danifae's red eyes narrowed, and whether the venomous look was genuine or part of the ploy, Halisstra wasn't sure.

"Then rot in a cell until they put your head on a pike, Mistress." She stood, deliberately brushing her backside, straightening the flimsy silks that did little to conceal her curvaceous body. "If you won't, then I'll do it and save myself."

Danifae turned to Ssipriina and said, "Mistress Zauvirr, I humbly beg you to help me procure my release from *her.*" She sneered this last as she jerked a thumb down at Halisstra, who was still sitting on the floor. "I'm sure we can come to some sort of arrangement that you would find gratifying enough to release me from my servitude."

Ssipriina alternated between looking at the battle captive before her and the noble daughter on the floor, blinking in surprise at the outburst. She opened her mouth as if to say something, then snapped it shut again.

Danifae, taking advantage of the silence, continued, "I'm just now starting to recall conversations with Mistress Halisstra that I think might implicate her. Given a few moments alone in her chambers, I could recall even more evidence that proves her foreknowledge in these disgraceful, treasonous acts."

She looked down at Halisstra, a knowing smirk on her face.

Despite the fact that she knew her servant was playing the part— at least she hoped that's all it was—Halisstra shuddered at the look on Danifae's face. Not having to try very hard to look scared, Drisinil's daughter took another deep breath.

"Matron Mother," Halisstra said, "I assure you I had absolutely no previous awareness of any possible plots of my mother's. My battle captive is obviously lying to you, trying to save her own worthless hide in exchange for damning me with false accusations. You cannot possibly accept the word of a battle captive. She would tell you anything to see me come to a bad end."

Ssipriina looked down at Halisstra for another moment and laughed.

"Of course she would, silly girl, and how fortunate for me." The matron mother turned to Danifae, smiled, and said, "Perhaps we can come to some sort of an agreement. Go and see what you can uncover."

Danifae smiled and bowed deeply to Matron Mother Zauvirr, then turned to depart. As she spun on one heel, she looked down at Halisstra, sneering.

As Halisstra let her gaze follow the backside of her servant, she heard Ssipriina take a deep breath.

"Now, what to do with you . . ." the matron mother said in a most unpleasant tone.

🕷   🕷   🕷

Faeryl Zauvirr loomed over her prisoner, smiling in delight. The beads of dampness that glistened on Quenthel Baenre's forehead ran in rivulets into her eyes, making her blink and squint. Her mouth was frozen in a grimace of pain and misery, though it was difficult for her to effect any other expression, with the rothéhide-bound dowel wedged so deeply into her mouth. The bit was held tightly in place with braided cord tied tightly behind her neck. Her long white hair was matted limply around her head and spread across the top of the table upon which she lay.

Faeryl stepped back from the table where Quenthel was stretched tightly, her wrists and ankles locked into manacles at either end of the long, narrow rack. The high priestess's naked body was taut, like the string of an instrument, and coated in a sheen of sweat that glimmered in the light of the braziers, but still Faeryl was not satisfied.

"Perhaps we should try the needles again," the ambassador mused aloud. "They fit so easily beneath the toenails, and it is such fun."

Quenthel grunted and shook her head, her red eyes wide.

"No? Then maybe there's something in here that I can use to amuse myself," Faeryl said, turning to one of the braziers and sorting the tools resting in it. "Some of these are glowing nicely, now. I've heard that these blunt ones are especially good for the eyes."

The grunts increased in rhythm and went up an octave.

Faeryl put her face back down in front of Quenthel's again, but she was no longer smiling.

"We've only scratched the surface, *Mistress* Baenre," she spat, once again stringing the honorific out. The sarcastic tone was becoming second nature to her. "We've got endless hours to enjoy this, and I want to make sure you experience every last little 'pleasantry' Jeggred inflicted on me."

Quenthel closed her eyes as a muted groan passed the bit shoved in her mouth.

Faeryl supposed the high priestess might be trembling, or perhaps it was simply the quivering of muscles, strained from being stretched so long. She chuckled and turned to examine the other prisoner.

Jeggred had been bound tightly to a stout column, lengths of chain encircling him from ankles to chin. The bonds were so tight, the draegloth could move only his head, which he tossed from side to side as he strained to break free. He snarled as Faeryl looked at him.

"Oh, I know," she cooed, stepping closer. "You want to gut me, don't you? You want to spill my blood and dance in it."

"You will die a slow, painful death," the fiend rumbled. "I will see to it personally."

Faeryl waved her hand in front of her nose.

"Stop talking, you vile beast. Your breath is most foul."

Jeggred only growled.

Faeryl fixed him with her gaze and said, "Do you remember the things you did to me?" She almost shuddered but forced herself to remain still. "I am going to repay you for it . . . every bit of it. I'll send your carcass back to Triel when I'm through."

Jeggred smiled.

"You can't begin to understand the methods of meting out pain. My attentions were but a part of those methods, and there is nothing you can conceive of that I will notice at all."

"Oh, really?" Faeryl replied, her lips pursed. "We'll see. My advisors have told me what things you feel and don't feel. 'He resists the burn of acid and fire, and he will not suffer from cold and lightning,' they said. But we'll find something. Yes, we will. Maybe sound, hmm? There is something you don't like, and when I discover what it is, you'll enjoy it for endless hours. I promise you."

There was a soft step upon the stone floor near the doorway. Faeryl turned in irritation to see what the intrusion was all about. It was Zammzt.

"What do you want?" Faeryl demanded.

She knew the aide was there at her mother's behest and that she was undoubtedly being summoned to attend to the matron mother. It didn't make her very happy, and though she could not take her annoyance out on her own mother, she could easily do so on the ugly male. The dark elf bent his knee and dipped his head slightly.

"I beg pardon, Mistress Zauvirr, but your mother requires your immediate presence in the audience chamber."

"Of course she does," Faeryl snarled. "If she has the slightest notion that I am not indisposed, she finds something for me to do."

When Zammzt hesitated for the slightest of moments, Faeryl gave him a cold stare.

"Well," she asked, "what are you waiting for? Go tell her I'm on my way!"

Zammzt scurried out of the torture room and disappeared around the corner, his *piwafwi* flying behind him. Faeryl returned her attention to Quenthel.

"I'll come back and visit with you some more in a bit," she said, "and when I do, I really want to give those needles another try. Maybe the fingernails this time, hmm?"

The bound form on the rack emitted a whimper.

"Oh, good, I'm pleased that you like the idea, too."

Danifae Yauntyrr didn't really expect Matron Mother Zauvirr to grant her free run of the entire House, and her suspicions were correct. As she departed the audience chamber with a final sneer back in Halisstra's direction, she was also careful to note Ssipriina's slight nod at two of the guards standing near the door. As she stepped through the portal, the guards silently and unobtrusively fell in behind her. The battle captive pursed her lips in the slightest hint of frustration, but she wouldn't have expected anything else. It really didn't matter. She'd just have to put on a bit more of a show.

Ignoring the two House Zauvirr soldiers who followed her, Danifae made her way back to Halisstra's private chambers, where she also took Reverie so that she could attend to the noble drow's every need. She guessed that the guards would not be so invasive as to follow her in, and again, her intuition was right. She strode through the door and shut it behind her. Once she was alone, she began to pace, mulling possibilities over in her mind.

Halisstra had just provided her servant with a perfect opportunity to free herself from the other drow's subjugation. Danifae almost laughed at her mistress's gullibility, thinking that Danifae would run to try to save her. After ten years as Halisstra's battle captive, Danifae wanted nothing more than to be rid of the wretched drow and her domination. She wanted nothing more than to return to Eryndlyn. The problem was, with Halisstra's binding in effect, Danifae wasn't sure she could actually get free, even with Ssipriina Zauvirr's help. In fact, she suspected that once she actually did turn on Halisstra and provide the "proof" of Drisinil's daughter's guilt to the matron mother, Ssipriina would simply let her perish along with Halisstra.

Danifae knew she had to ensure her own freedom first and not depend on another for it. But how?

She hated the effect of the binding, for it was insidious in its effectiveness. Though Danifae didn't truly believe it, she sometimes wished that the compulsion of the binding fully controlled her mind, rather than merely restricting her ability to distance herself from Halisstra. She told herself that it would have been better to serve the Melarn daughter as a mindless zombie rather than of her own accord, attending willingly to avoid the consequences of straying too far from her mistress. It locked her to Halisstra as surely as a length of chain around their ankles.

In the early years, Danifae wanted desperately to throttle her mistress, but Halisstra's death would bring about her own, and Danifae would experience her own demise in a slow, excruciatingly painful manner. That was the nature of the binding. It sustained her somehow, kept her alive as long as Halisstra willed it. Distance was not a factor, but the moment Danifae disregarded Halisstra's wishes and went her own way, she had no doubt that the other drow would simply let her wither away like a mushroom with its roots hacked off. Displease the dark elf, and with a thought, Danifae would succumb. By the Dark Mother, she hated it.

The binding's magic was alien to Danifae. She didn't understand what was required to sever it or if it even could be severed by any hand other than Halisstra's. The risk of discovery was too great to allow her the chance to inquire, and besides, Halisstra rarely let her servant out of her sight. With Halisstra under arrest, Danifae had the perfect opportunity to follow through, to finally find out what could be done, and there was no time. Halisstra was going to die unless Danifae convinced Ssipriina Zauvirr to find a solution to her problem, and she doubted that the matron mother would lift a finger to help her, even with her promises of damning testimony against the daughter of Drisinil Melarn. That only left Danifae with the option of actually saving Halisstra.

Damn her! the battle captive silently screamed as she sat on her mistress's Reverie couch, pounding a pillow for good measure. She wanted to rip the stuffing out, but long years of the fear of punishment had trained her to resist letting her emotions get the better of her, and she stayed her hand. Taking a deep breath to calm herself, she considered the situation.

The next problem, she realized, was that even if she somehow managed to extricate Halisstra—and by extension, herself—from this mess, life as they both knew it might very well be over. They might survive the coup, but even then, where would they go? Without Lolth's blessings to aid them, it was an especially bleak outlook.

Making up her mind, Danifae decided the next thing to do was to figure out who in House Melarn was still Halisstra's ally. The first thing she considered were the House guards. They had disappeared, and she had a pretty good idea why. Ssipriina had likely already gotten to them and given them the standard offer: change allegiance to House Zauvirr, or find themselves unemployed or dead. She doubted there were any who would still rally to Halisstra, but she had to at least look.

Danifae opened the door to the hallway and was slightly surprised to find the two guards who had followed her no longer present. She supposed that they assumed she wouldn't try anything as long as the House was locked down and had decided to go find something more interesting to do.

Just makes it easier for me, she thought, smiling as she slipped out. She hurried on her way.

The audience chamber of House Melarn was pretty much as Faeryl expected to find it. Her mother was seated on the lofty over-sized chair atop the dais at the front of the room, surrounded by her advisors, while House Zauvirr soldiers were spread inconspicuously but generously throughout the chamber. Faeryl absently wondered how her mother had managed to usurp control of the audience chamber without an argument from the House Melarn guards. Whatever lies she told them must have worked.

"There you are," Ssipriina said impatiently. "Come here. I want to go over your story once more before the others get here."

Faeryl sighed but dutifully approached the throne.

"Mother, I have the details memorized. I think I can—"

"You will go over them with me and continue doing it until *I* am convinced, you ungrateful brat! You will not stop until then."

Her mother looked entirely too comfortable in the throne, which was certainly grander than anything they had in their own manor. That was the difference between a merchant House and a truly noble House.

Faeryl longed to return to the dungeons, where she could rule over her charges in peace. She hated having to attend to her mother's demands. Where Quenthel was concerned, even if it was a little pond, at least she was the big fish. It was always that way. At the storehouse, when she'd orchestrated the transport of the prisoners, she had been in charge, however briefly. Under the scrutiny of her mother, she was the petulant child once more.

Faeryl dreamed of holding the reins of power someday, but being the fourth daughter in her House, and having been sent to Menzo-berranzan to represent House Zauvirr and House Melarn, to boot, she recognized the limitations to her chance to rise to the top. Even were she to someday sit upon the throne Ssipriina Zauvirr was hoping to claim through her orchestration of the day's events, Faeryl would still answer to others.

"Now," Ssipriina said, ticking off points one by one on her hand, "you were forced to come with Quenthel and the others. You noti-fied me at the earliest opportunity what House Baenre was planning. We set up an ambush to catch them, and only then did we discover that Drisinil was in on it. Do you understand?"

"Yes, Mother," Faeryl responded sullenly.

"Good. When the matron mothers get here, stay out of sight until I call for you. Do you understand?"

"Yes, Mother."

"And stop that. It's childish and petulant."

Faeryl frowned, but she clamped her mouth shut.

"That's better," Ssipriina said. "Now I think we need to get those males summoned here as quickly as possible. Zammzt, I think that's a job for you."

$\spadesuit$ $\spadesuit$ $\spadesuit$

When a knock sounded at the door to their room, Pharaun ex-pected to see Quenthel standing there. It was late, and the Master of Sorcere was beginning to wonder if something untoward had befallen the high priestess and her two companions. As he opened the portal, though, the wizard was instead surprised to discover a strange and rather plain-looking drow in the livery of a noble House.

"I beg forgiveness for disturbing you," the male said, "but I am seeking the wizard Pharaun Mizzrym and the warriors Ryld Argith and Valas Hune."

Pharaun kept his body planted firmly between the visitor and the interior of the room, shielding the other dark elf's view of it. Behind him, he could hear Valas and Ryld unsheathing weapons.

"Who are you?" the wizard asked, considering which spells remaining in his repertoire would suffice to defend himself against an attack.

"My name is Zammzt. I come at the behest of Matron Mother Ssipriina Zauvirr of House Zauvirr, Matron Mother Melarn of House Melarn, and Quenthel Baenre of House Baenre. Are you one of the three?"

"Perhaps," Pharaun answered, gauging the fellow's potential as a threat. The drow was, at the very least, radiating a number of magical auras. "It would depend on why you're looking for them."

"Mistress Quenthel is a guest of Mistress Drisinil Melarn of House Melarn. I am here to extend an invitation to you to join them for a banquet in your honor."

"Oh, how delightful," Pharaun said. "I assume that you can escort us there, as well?"

"Indeed, Master, uh . . ."

The mage rolled his eyes and said, "Pharaun. I'm the wizard."

"Certainly, Master Mizzrym, I have been instructed to escort you to House Melarn."

"I see. Well, then can you give me a moment to clean up? I'd hate to attend a dinner in my honor looking like this," the wizard said, gesturing at his *piwafwi*.

"Certainly, Master Mizzrym. I am at your convenience. The dinner will not start without you."

"Excellent," Pharaun replied. "Give me just a moment, and we'll be right out. You can wait for us down in the common room."

With that, he shut the door and turned to his companions.

"Either she got caught or she decided she was not getting treated well enough by the inn staff," Valas said, frowning.

"Either way, it is no good for us," Ryld added. "And I was just beginning to enjoy not being under any matron mothers' thumbs."

"Well, then . . . which is it, good masters?" Pharaun asked them both. "Out the window or to a dinner party?"

Ryld and Valas looked at one another.

Finally, Valas sighed, "Dinner."

"Very good," Pharaun said, "but before we go, I want to spend a few moments in contemplation of my grimoires. I have a feeling I might be in need of some arcane fortitude before the night is over."

"Yes, I think that's wise," Valas agreed. "Ryld and I could stand a bit of healing magic, if there's any to be had."

"Why don't you two go search the priestesses' room and see what you can turn up?" Pharaun suggested. "I know Quenthel had that wand, but she's likely to have kept it with her. There might be a potion or two, though."

The scout nodded, and he and Ryld slipped out of the room.

Pharaun opened up his haversack and pulled out his spellbooks, which were conveniently on top. That was the thing he truly loved about his magical carry-all. Whatever he needed always seemed to be on top. He sat down to peruse the pages.

The wizard could not recoup all of the incantations he had cast during the course of the day, as he would need to spend several hours resting before his body had recovered sufficiently for that, but he had wisely decided to hold off on committing the full compliment of spells to memory that morning, so he had an opportunity to choose four or five that would best suit the occasion.

Now, Pharaun wondered, what sorts of magical wizardry would be particularly useful for a dinner party?

He settled on his choices and began to study.

Nearly an hour later, the Master of Sorcere looked up at the sound of the two other males reentering the room.

"Ah, perfect timing," he said. "I think I'm ready to go. Did you have any luck?"

Ryld answered, "It took a bit of rummaging, but we managed to confiscate two potions from Quenthel's belongings. That's one more thing we agreed that you get to tell her when we see her next."

Pharaun chuckled, "Well, I must say, the draughts did you a world of good. You're certainly much more presentable than you were a mere hour ago. Are we ready, then?"

"I believe so," Valas replied. "We did a quick surveillance of the inn, and it appears that our escort is alone. Nothing suspicious about him so far."

"Then I suggest we leave at once," the Master of Sorcere said. "I'm starved, and I fancy a taste of something better to drink than the swill we purchased last evening."

Ryld and Valas exchanged looks, and the three of them found their way to the common room. The drow who called himself Zammzt was there, waiting patiently, but the look on his face told Pharaun that he was beginning to get a little nervous.

Probably wondering if we gave him the slip, the wizard thought. Worried about what he'd tell the matron mother when he had to report back that we wouldn't cooperate.

The stroll to the House would have been pleasant, Pharaun decided, if the streets weren't plagued by the occasional angry mob. Twice, the four of them had to make a quick dash down a side street or float to an- other level to avoid being engulfed in a tide of troublemakers. At one point, Pharaun thought he'd have to blast a way through the throng with a bolt of lightning or a ball of fire, but it never came to that. In order to keep up with them, Valas was forced to transport himself by way of an extradimensional doorway. This from an item Pharaun had, until then, been unaware the scout carried.

"You know," he said as they moved into the highest levels of the city, where the most lavish of the nobles' manors were located, "I quite seriously doubt we should remain for the full evening."

"What, you think the city is growing too dangerous?" Valas asked wryly. "If we had given it any thought, we might have considered packing our supplies and bringing them with us."

Pharaun slowed a step, thinking, but then he proceeded, saying, "You're right, but if the situation warrants it, I can return for the goods myself later."

The four drow arrived at last at House Melarn, an impressive bulge in the upper reaches of the city. The whole of the thing was stacked above the level of the street and also hung below it, and it covered an area two or three blocks wide and just as deep. To Pharaun, it looked like a massive cyst of some sort, which, he supposed, had been the intent of the architects who'd fashioned it.

The food and spirits had better be worth it, the wizard thought, sighing as he followed the others inside. Right now, it just looks like a prison.

❈   ❈   ❈

Aliisza loathed the form she'd chosen for herself, finding it ugly and without civility. Oh, certainly any orc who spotted her would have thought her beautiful, but the alu-fiend considered the race repulsive as a whole. Still, it had its advantages.

At the moment, that advantage was that Pharaun would not recognize her. Following the wizard and his two drow companions through the web streets of Ched Nasad, being led by a fourth drow—whom she found to be rather unattractive—Aliisza didn't want her lover of earlier in the day to spot her. As well, she found it easier to avoid notice as one of the baser creatures rather than as one of the dark elves. The drow citizens might have outnumbered the rest of the other races combined, but they appeared to be fearful of being alone in public, and though Aliisza certainly didn't fear for her own well-being, she thought it best to draw as little attention to herself as possible.

Besides, she found that she could overhear more interesting conversations if she was not in dark elf form. The other beings tended to stall or whisper whenever they saw any drow about, but they were not so mindful of their words when it was just an orc, beautiful for her race or not. Aliisza could certainly understand why.

There was talk of rebellion or of invasion everywhere she went. Half the inhabitants seemed to think the crisis in the City of Shimmering Webs was an opportunity to end the drow reign once and for all, while the other half believed that someone else was already in the process of doing just that and that everyone already living there would pay the price for it. One thing was constant, whatever other opinions were revealed: Everyone blamed the dark elves for their problems.

It was the drow, she heard, who had angered Lolth. She had turned away from the city, leaving it to fend for itself. Others said that Lolth had grown weak and ineffectual from the complacency of her worshipers, and this had allowed other deities to overwhelm her when she wasn't expecting or prepared for it. The most intriguing rumor of all, of course, was the tale that seemed most recent. Spreading like wildfire, it claimed that the matron mothers had discovered a traitor in their midst, one of their own who had collaborated with a high priestess from beyond the city to bring Ched Nasad low.

There were a dozen variations on that story. The traitors consorted with demons, the traitors were actually demons in disguise, the traitors were stealing from the city, the traitors were preparing to attack the city. . . .

Aliisza had little doubt about the veracity of the story, for she suspected that the high priestess must be Quenthel. Somehow, the Menzoberranyr had been apprehended in the middle of her little scheme, the one Pharaun regretted mentioning. She was curious about Pharaun's role in the rumor, or the portion of the story that included a matron mother. The alu-fiend wondered if Pharaun had been swept up in the events or if spending the afternoon with her—she shivered with delight at the memory of it—had allowed him to stay clear.

Even if he hadn't gotten entangled in the matron mothers' schemes thus far, he was bound to eventually. She knew this with a certainty born of having seen the political machinations of her own kind drag even the most unwilling creatures into its webbing. Pharaun would have a part to play in the unfolding events, as much for his inquisitive, forceful nature as for his relationship with the priestess he so casually followed.

Regardless of what the wizard wanted, he was in the company of a stranger, someone obviously of a noble House by the insignia on his *piwafwi*, and he didn't seem to be under duress or coerced. Perhaps he didn't know what was going on. Aliisza would have to puzzle on that some more. One thing was certain, however: The effect the rumor was having on the populace was not good.

Aliisza knew she shouldn't care if Pharaun had been apprehended. Theirs had been a relationship of mutual satisfaction, no more, no less. He was a pleasant diversion from Kaanyr Vhok, and she knew she would return to the cambion, had always intended to do so. Pharaun knew this as well, and the fact that he wasn't bothered by the informal nature of their "chance meeting" in the streets was what had made him so delicious.

But the alu-fiend did care, at least enough to consider whether or not she should figure out if he needed her help. She supposed she simply wasn't quite ready to give him up.

She also knew that that wasn't the only reason she hadn't yet returned to Ammarindar to report to Kaanyr Vhok all she'd discovered thus far. Perhaps it was the multitude of sights and sounds in the city that attracted her still. Perhaps it was the exquisite feeling she got whenever creatures of the race she chose for her disguise—whether it be dark elf, orc, or yet some other species—admired her form. It had been too long since she'd experienced that. She also wanted to see events unfold in the city. She sensed the tension in the air, and she wanted to witness the violence, the chaos, should something come to pass. Ched Nasad was more than ripe for such a thing. The place was literally buzzing with energy, with anticipation.

The four drow she followed moved casually, yet they always seemed to be adjusting their course to avoid the largest crowds, and they never tarried near side web streets or alleyways. It was clear to Aliisza that they were moving warily. More than once, they magically bypassed the worst of the crowds, levitating or using the magical doorways that both she and Pharaun employed from time to time. They led her into the higher sections of the city, and soon it became apparent to Aliisza that she would have to either stop or change shape in order to continue unhindered. There were going to be few orcs that high in the cavern, and she would draw attention to herself in her present guise.

Changing back to the drow form she'd used earlier, she followed the four dark elves farther, until they arrived at a large noble House, which they entered.

Aliisza found a quiet spot atop a building on the opposite side of the street and settled down to wait.

Chapter

TEN

Khorrl Xornbane knew that his fidgeting was a bad sign, but he couldn't help it. He and his clan had been hiding and waiting for so long he could hardly stand it any longer. Hiding several thousand duergar was never easy, but trying to do it in the middle of a city full of drow was taking its toll on his nerves. He was thankful that the waiting was almost over.

Until then, the fighting had been relatively easy and pain-free. Ambushing the matron mother and her retinue in the storehouse had been almost too simple. She obviously trusted the other matron mother far too much, and it had cost her. He wondered if anyone had discovered the bodies of her soldiers and advisors. They would, soon, he knew. The smell would lead someone to them.

Khorrl and his duergar were inside the manor itself, out of sight in an unused wing of the place, in a barracks where no soldiers were currently quartered. It was driving Khorrl mad. His sentries had not reported anyone even coming near the halls where he and his boys waited, but if anyone found them, the plan was ruined.

"Captain." An all-too-familiar voice came from the shadows at the edges of the storehouse.

Khorrl felt his heart begin to race with anticipation. Zammzt stepped from the shadows, a wry smile on his face.

"So?" the duergar asked.

"We've gotten the word," Zammzt replied. "It's time for you to go to work."

Khorrl rubbed his hands together in delight. At last. He began going over the plan in his head once more as he issued orders, and Zammzt faded back into the shadow from which he'd emerged.

The real fighting was about to begin.

❀　❀　❀

Faeryl was fast growing bored with all of it. She wished the matron mothers would simply see things as her mother had laid them out so carefully, declare House Melarn treasonous and dissolved, and permit House Zauvirr to rise to a position of prominence so that Ssipriina could sit on the Council. But of course, there was the prerequisite squabbling that had to take place, first. Faeryl supposed she would care a whole lot more if she stood to gain more, but her mother would still be ordering her around—and getting ordered around in turn, even if it was by someone other than Drisinil Melarn.

There's always someone using you as their footstool, Faeryl thought, no matter how high you reach. Even Triel Baenre was forced to nod her head in subservience to the whims of Lolth, and it's possible that the Dark Mother herself has been forced to—

"Faeryl, stop wasting our time with your idle fancies, and pay attention," Ssipriina Zauvirr said, snapping Faeryl out of her thoughts.

"Sorry, Mother," the younger drow answered, chagrined.

She focused her attention on the conversation at hand, for at least the matron mothers were no longer talking as one.

"I *said*," Inidil Mylyl declared, emphasizing the word to make sure everyone in the room understood that she was put out at having to repeat herself, "that hearing the tale in its entirety once more would go a long way toward clarifying just exactly how this managed to happen right under our noses. Perhaps Faeryl can indulge us for a few moments more to explain this."

Faeryl groaned inwardly. She had already explained herself three times to the first matron mothers to arrive. They had not been happy with several parts of her story, so she was going to have to tell the whole thing once more for those matron mothers who had chosen, for whatever reason, to arrive late. Of course, they were the most powerful drow in Ched Nasad, used to keeping others waiting and daring anyone to question them on it. She felt queasy as she crossed to the center of the room.

"Yes, of course, Matron Mother Mylyl," she said as politely as she could.

Compared to the collection of nobility in the room, House Zauvirr was still inconsequential and could be held accountable for everything Faeryl had done and said up to that point. Embarrassing one's own mother in front of her superiors was no way to climb to a higher position within a House, and the ambassador knew that both her tone and her explanation had to be handled just right.

"For the sake of understanding," she continued, "let me start by saying that House Zauvirr represents House Melarn in certain business interests, and I represent House Zauvirr's efforts on behalf of House Melarn in Menzoberranzan. I serve—or did serve, rather—as the ambassador to Triel Baenre herself. When the difficulties arose, they were, as you now know, experienced in Menzoberranzan as well. Concerned about this and the lack of caravan traffic between the two cities, I petitioned Matron Mother Baenre to allow me to return here in the hopes of finding out what was wrong.

"Triel refused, and in fact, effectively placed me under house arrest, for what concerns I never found out. She eventually imprisoned me when I tried to leave on my own. While I did not wish to damage the relationship between our Houses and House Baenre, my loyalty and concern lay solely with my own family and those families we serve here in Ched Nasad. I was ordered put to death for treason, but thankfully, the execution never occurred.

"Triel changed her mind at some point, choosing instead to forgive me whatever sins I supposedly committed. She assigned me to journey with her sister, Quenthel Baenre, and several others here to Ched Nasad to reestablish trading and to determine if more information was available concerning the, uh . . ."

"Child, we all know that Lolth has vanished. You don't have to tread around the subject." It was Matron Mother Aunrae Nasadra, the uncrowned queen of Ched Nasad, leader of the most powerful House in the city. Faeryl swallowed as Aunrae added, "Get to the point."

The ambassador nodded and continued. "Menzoberranzan had suffered an uprising, a slave revolt supported by outside forces. Containing it consumed a substantial amount of the sisterhood's divine resources. Matron Mother Triel sent the group of us here to find out if Lolth's disappearance was limited to Menzoberranzan or felt across all tribes of drow, but she also wanted Quenthel to procure any divine magic she could lay her hands on here. Quenthel and Triel had apparently rationalized that since House Baenre held part ownership in Black Claw Mercantile, anything the storehouses stocked was her city's by right. Once I was able to covertly relay this to my mother via my brother and his magical contacts, we worked together to set a trap and catch the Menzoberranyr in the act. It was only when we all arrived at the storehouse that we discovered Matron Mother Melarn was actually aiding the visitors.

My mother confronted both of them together, and Matron Mother Melarn tried to escape."

When she finished, Faeryl realized she was out of breath from rushing through the rest of her explanation. Matron Mother Aunrae had that effect on everyone.

"Drisinil was killed, cut down trying to flee," Ssipriina added, drawing attention back to herself. "I would have done whatever I could to spare her if I could have reached her in time, but it was too late, and my own magic is too weakened to stave off the passing."

"So you conspired to allow them to sneak into the city, going so far as to mislead a city patrol?"

The matron mother who asked this question was Jyslin Aleanrahel. Her features were sharp, almost fierce, and her reputation as a malicious, greedy drow who found fault in every action was legendary. Faeryl had never liked her, but she was hardly in a position to show that sentiment.

"They have no doubt been sent to spy on us," Jyslin continued, "and their supposed story of reestablishing contact here was simply a falsehood meant to keep you off-balance. I daresay the males still loose in the city are sending sensitive information back to their superiors even now, especially if this wizard is as capable as you alleged before. I might have expected you to be a more clever girl and keep them out of the city, but I suppose that's too much to ask."

"This is foolish," Umrae D'Dgttu, matron mother of the second most powerful House in the city said. "We've heard the story, some of us several times now. It is clear to me that House Zauvirr acted with the best intentions of Ched Nasad in mind. I move that we dissolve House Melarn forthwith."

Umrae was one of Ssipriina's secret allies, Faeryl knew. This was it. They were beginning the process, giving her mother what she wanted. Dissolution of House Melarn was the first step in granting Ssipriina a seat on the Council.

"I concur," said Ulviirala Rilynt, another of the four her mother had bribed. "The treason of House Melarn seems clear enough to me."

Faeryl stole a glance at Ssipriina and saw that she was trying hard not to smile too broadly.

"I'm more concerned with the veracity of their story," Lirdnolu Maerret said. "So far, all we've had to go on is this fanciful tale Ssipriina and her daughter have woven, with no neutral observer able to substantiate it. House Zauvirr stands to gain quite a lot by seeing Drisinil and her ilk dead. I for one am unwilling to so quickly assume they're telling the truth simply for the good of the city."

"Quite true," Jyslin Aleanrahel agreed. "Let's hear Drisinil's daughter speak."

Faeryl opened her mouth to protest then snapped it shut again. The matron mothers knew well the propensity drow had for scheming, and this was the challenge Ssipriina had cautioned her would come. There were some who would want the whole truth and would look to try to trap House Zauvirr in a lie, or if they were allies of House Melarn, try to pin whatever blame they could on Ssipriina. Her mother had cautioned Faeryl for patience during this time. When their new enemies were exposed, or if the decision didn't favor Zauvirr, their secret mercenary army would step forward.

Halisstra Melarn was brought from the dungeons below to answer for her mother's crimes. She was almost forcibly led into the chamber, flanked by two large female guards. She had been stripped of her fine clothing and was dressed in only a thin shift. She cast her eyes about the room, searching faces, perhaps hoping to find some sympathy or support among those present.

It was rumored that Halisstra had a soft streak, that she never seemed to show the type of tenacious ambition her mother wanted to see in her daughters. She was more interested, those rumors suggested, in slumming with her battle captive, Danifae, using the other drow's good looks to attract males to carouse with. There were even some who whispered that Matron Mother Melarn would have cast her out of the family, given the right circumstances. Faeryl knew that the slumming part was true, and that gave her an idea.

She spread her hands helplessly, as if acknowledging that she had failed in some way. "I beg your forgiveness for whatever flaws you see in our plan, Matron Mothers," Faeryl said quietly. "I am as disappointed as you that a House of our own beloved city would conspire with foreigners at our expense. I now recall additional damning evidence that might put this debate to rest."

"What?" Ssipriina said, leaning forward, obviously loath to see her daughter possibly ruin her own carefully laid web of lies.

Faeryl studiously ignored her mother.

"What do you mean?" Jyslin said, her eyes narrowing.

Faeryl was sure she had the advantage. Though she had not mentioned it before—since it was a lie she had only conceived of on the spur of the moment—there was no way Jyslin could challenge her for leaving it out of her story the first time. Faeryl could pretend she'd simply forgotten it until then.

"It's just that, right after passing through the gates of the city, I had the good fortune to spy Mistress Halisstra and her consort, Danifae Yauntyrr. I was surprised to see them in such a sordid section of the city, but I considered it a stroke of good fortune, nonetheless. I made a specific effort to move into their line of sight so that they would see it was me and notice I was with strangers. I thought for certain they had spotted me, and I even flashed a quick message to Danifae, but she either didn't recognize me or didn't want anyone to know they'd been there. She turned Halisstra away, and the two of them melted into the crowd. At the time, I didn't think anything of it, but now I realize that she must have been there to signal Quenthel and the others."

Halisstra's eyes grew wide at hearing Faeryl's accusations. She sputtered to find the words to defend herself.

"I . . . we never . . . Matron Mothers, I assure you that we never saw the ambassador and her companions in the lower sections of the city. I am innocent of the charges leveled against me."

Faeryl smiled to herself. Halisstra had specifically avoided denying that she had been there. It had been a gamble, supposing that the two of them might have been in the vicinity in the last couple of days, but it had paid off. The unwanted attention was being focused on Halisstra.

"Perhaps I am mistaken," Faeryl quickly interjected. She smiled at Halisstra, who was staring daggers at her in return. "It was crowded there, with all of the refugees and the base-born males in their revelry, so it's easy to understand how I only thought Danifae had caught the eye of someone in my party. The two of you were obviously seeking someone else."

Faeryl wanted to grin at her own cleverness. By pulling back, admitting she had made a mistake, she doubly damned Halisstra. The seed of doubt had been planted in everyone's mind, and the less she tried to force them to accept her theory, the more likely they all would be to believe it; such was drow nature. For those who chose to believe Halisstra's innocence, that left only one other reason for her to be in such an improper part of the city. Either way, it shed an unpleasant light on the daughter of a traitor.

Ssipriina turned to Jyslin Aleanrahel and said, "Matron Mother, I am only a trader, unused to the machinations of the higher nobility. If I had foreseen how greatly this would have displeased you, I would have conceived of a better way to deal with the crisis at hand. As it was, I still hope you will consider that I was keeping only the best interests of Ched Nasad in mind, acting in all ways on its behalf."

There was a general murmur from the matron mothers as they put their heads together, no doubt discussing the additional implications of guilt Faeryl's little tale had just heaped upon House Melarn. At the very least, the suggestion that Halisstra had been carousing with the commoners of the city meant that her disgraceful behavior was of the worst sort and she was unfit to rule a noble House. That half of it happened to be true only made the whole incident sweeter to Faeryl, who was simply glad she was no longer the drow everyone else was looking down their noses at.

"Enough!" Aunrae Nasadra shouted, rapping her rune-covered staff upon the floor. Even in such an impromptu meeting, the eldest and most powerful matron mother commanded absolute respect, and the room fell silent. "This nonsense is the reason we face the bleak loss of our goddess's favor. How can we expect Lolth to grant us her attention when we waste so much time and energy on such ridiculous discussions as who's stepped in the most rothé muck?" The matriarch walked among the others, peering at them all. "Whether or not House Melarn's progeny chooses to whore around with low-born males in the seamiest underbelly of Ched Nasad is of no concern to me."

Faeryl stole a glance at Halisstra, whose face was down in humiliation. Matron Mother Nasadra paid neither of them any heed.

"The streets are not safe for most drow," she said. "We all know the extra precautions we had to take even to come here. Our city is on the verge of disaster, mothers, and yet we must stand here and discuss the fate of a noble House, one high enough to have a seat on the Council.

"Ssipriina has suggested that we dissolve House Melarn and offer up Halisstra and these remaining outsiders as sacrifices to appease the masses as much as the Dark Mother. While we know nothing about why our beloved Lolth is angry with us, that she *is* angry with us, we are certain. Will this help? Will it bring her blessings back to us?

"If we make an example of the traitors and let the whole city see us do it will it quiet the citizens for a time? Perhaps, but more importantly, will it satisfy all of you? Will you return to your Houses satisfied that a House has fallen and that the hierarchy has shuffled sufficiently? There are things more fragile than the peace of our city, but they are few in number. This backstabbing, while inherent in our nature, is misplaced during this time of difficulties."

"What if this Baenre priestess's companions know something?" Halisstra asked. "What if they have an inkling of what troubles the Dark Mother? If you simply kill me, then you get what you want—one less House to stand in your way—but if you kill them, whether as spies or as sacrifices, you might lose valuable information."

"Shut your mouth, child!" Ssipriina hissed. "You've shamed us enough for one lifetime. Do not think that you can escape justice merely by pretending to be loyal now. It's too late for that."

Halisstra would not be deterred. She proceeded, ignoring the dark stares the matron mothers gave her.

"What if this wizard has discovered something?" she asked. "Faeryl has already told us he is clever and was not above antagonizing Quenthel. I would not put it past him to know more than he's letting on. Why kill him, when he might be so inclined to parlay with us? Could he be willing to reveal his own secrets? Perhaps even for a price? There are those among you who do not wish to hear what he has to say. He might expose the lies you have told concerning my mother and me."

Aunrae smiled and said, "Tell me, child, do you think Lolth would grant such a vision to a male? Do you think she would allow a *boy*, however clever, to unlock the secrets of her silence?"

"These are desperate times, Matron Mother, you said so yourself. I would not close any possible avenue of redemption, however thickly cloaked in folly it may seem. Of course, I have few avenues of redemption for my life left. I have my own desperate times. Whether you wish to question him or not, I merely ask that you bring him as a witness into these proceedings. His words could prove my own innocence."

Faeryl frowned, not liking where this was leading. She was beginning to think it had been a mistake to put the full plan into motion until Pharaun and the others had also been brought into custody, or better yet, killed. Maybe she could get to him before the rest of them had a chance to speak with him, take care of it herself, one way or another. Perhaps then her mother would stop treating her like a child.

Aunrae nodded, her mouth pursed as though considering the younger drow's words.

"You argue for your life, Halisstra Melarn, but still your pleas have some merit. We will wait to pass sentence on you until we've had a chance to hear all sides. As for the 'clever boy,' when he comes to us, when we have him in our possession, we will extract whatever information he has, fully and without paying any price. Somehow, I do not think Quenthel Baenre had established the proper leashes on her wizard. I do not intend to make the same mistake."

"Matron Mother Nasadra," Zammzt called from the back of the room, where he had just entered. "They are here."

Pharaun, Ryld, and Valas had been led inside and shown to a waiting room, an all-too-familiar sight to each of them and one that did nothing to set their minds at ease. They were left alone, or rather with only sentries posted at each of the exits to keep them company. Pharaun occupied his time strolling through the chamber, admiring the frescos and statuary that were in abundance there, primarily exhibiting the motif of spiders, webbing, and the glory of the dark elves. There were a goodly number of musical instruments as well, some he didn't even recognize. The Master of Sorcere supposed a good many of the works related to the history of House Melarn, but to Pharaun it was all just so much pomp and circumstance. Ryld and Valas, meanwhile, had their heads together in consultation, most likely discussing tactics for extricating themselves in the event that things went bad.

When the double doors at the far end of the room were thrown open, Pharaun turned to see not one but several ostentatious drow females—matriarchs all, he was sure—waiting in the large audience chamber beyond. They were attended by a retinue of House wizards, soldiers, and younger females, all of them in House livery and many of them, Pharaun noted, radiating magical protections and other spells.

"Good evening, and welcome to House Melarn," one somewhat tall and slender drow said imperiously, waiting on the throne as the three males moved into the room. "I am Matron Mother Ssipriina Zauvirr."

Pharaun bowed slightly as he moved to a place in front of the throne, far enough back so as not to seem threatening. Ryld and Valas moved to join him as the other matron mothers gathered around the throne, and the assortment of wizards, priestesses, and soldiers flanked everyone else.

Pharaun knew the woman was Faeryl's mother, of course, but he couldn't guess what she was doing on the throne of House Melarn.

The mage looked around the chamber, trying to find Faeryl. She was there, though off in a corner of the room, as if she were trying to avoid notice.

If I didn't know better, Pharaun thought wryly, I would have to assume they're expecting some sort of trouble.

Neither Valas nor Ryld said anything, but the wizard could feel them on either side of him, tense and ready to spring.

"We are honored and delighted to be guests in your House, Matron Mother Zauvirr," Pharaun said. "To what do we owe this auspicious occasion?"

And where in the Abyss are Quenthel and Jeggred? he silently added.

Ssipriina Zauvirr sniffed and replied, "On the contrary, Pharaun Mizzrym, I should be the one thanking you and asking you why you have graced the City of Shimmering Webs with your august presence.

The reputation that preceded you, telling of a confident, self-possessed mage of no small skill, was only half the story, it seems."

Pharaun smiled in the most disarming way he could muster as he shifted his weight to one foot, letting the other turn out slightly.

"Everyone has her own opinions, as always, Matron Mother. That is not to say that anyone is in error, only that affectations and realities do not always mesh, and for good reason."

"Of course," another matron mother said, moving forward from Ssipriina's left, "and our opinion is that you and your companions, while affecting the appearance of simple travelers or even emissaries from our sister city of Menzoberranzan, are in reality spies, here to steal from us and expose whatever weaknesses you thought you might be able to find to the world at large."

So much for affectations, thought Pharaun, shifting his weight uneasily.

He felt, rather than saw Ryld, to his left, and Valas, to his right, both stiffen at the undisguised accusation.

"Easy," he muttered under his breath. "Save the foolish heroics for the 'all-else-fails' part of the program."

Smoothing his face as best he could, the mage spread his hands in gracious acquiescence and said, "I'm sorry, Mistress . . ."

"Matron Mother Jyslin Aleanrahel, of House Aleanrahel."

Pharaun swallowed then said, "Matron Mother Aleanrahel. While I'm sure our efforts at avoiding attention must seem terribly surreptitious, I can assure you that we meant nothing antagonistic. We only wished to—"

"To avoid being confronted like this?" Jyslin interjected. "How well did that serve you?"

Pharaun sighed and said, "Not well at all, it appears, but my companions and I still aren't completely sure we understand your concerns. I must profess, I am confused as to why we're meeting here, if none of you is Matron Mother Melarn."

Several of the matron mothers gave each other knowing glances. Pharaun was thoroughly confused. He continued to scan the room and saw something else quite odd: a drow, obviously nobly born but stripped to her underclothes and held prisoner between two stout guards, and it wasn't Quenthel.

"Oh, we have no concerns," Jyslin Aleanrahel replied. "Not anymore. Until you arrived, we were concerned that we would not be able to detain you, that you might try to slip out of the city. We were concerned that you would report your discoveries to your superiors back in the City of Spiders. We were more concerned that you would try something foolish, like concluding your high priestess's ill-conceived plan of theft and spying. You've cooperated nicely, though, so we feel we have the situation well in hand."

Ryld made an almost inaudible strangled noise, and the mage felt the warrior shift his weight. In response, several of the soldiers, who had unassumingly fanned out to more completely surround the trio, tensed as though expecting Ryld to lunge at them.

Pharaun frowned.

"I wasn't aware that our high priestess was planning anything of the sort," he said. "If something is amiss, we must all work to see that it is rectified. Just tell us where she is, and I'm sure we can resolve whatever—"

"Quenthel Baenre was caught committing treasonous acts against Ched Nasad," yet a third matron mother said, stepping out from behind the throne. Pharaun sensed that this one, with a graceful age about her face, might just be the most formidable drow he'd ever met. "There was no doubt about her guilt. She died trying to flee the scene of her crimes."

Pharaun blinked, reeling. Dead? Quenthel Baenre was dead? He wasn't sure whether to laugh or be worried. Behind him, he heard both of his companions' gasps of surprise.

"She was caught conspiring with House Melarn to illegally enter the city and steal valuable resources belonging to us," the older drow said, "and we believe she was also committing espionage on behalf of Menzoberranzan. We consider these to be crimes against the city, against all drow, and most especially against the Dark Mother herself."

Conspiracy? Pharaun thought. How ridiculous could they be?

He stared at the throne where Faeryl's mother sat, and he was beginning to understand who was behind it, and perhaps why.

No wonder Faeryl was so eager to help us, he thought. She was leading us by our noses the whole time.

"Furthermore," the matron mother continued, "you, by association with Quenthel, are accused of the same charges. You are under arrest, and you will be confined on the premises until such time as we can determine your guilt or innocence."

"Not today," Ryld said, taking a step forward and reaching for Splitter.

As one, a multitude of soldiers brandished hand crossbows, and at least half a dozen wizards and priestesses appeared to ready spells.

"Ryld, you fool, wait!" Pharaun growled, still trying to keep his voice low. "There are better ways . . ."

Valas reached a hand out and stopped the larger drow from finishing the act of unsheathing his greatsword.

"Not yet," the scout pleaded. "We've got no chance like this."

Ryld snarled, but he released the hilt of his weapon and stepped back again.

"Good," the third matron mother said. "You are not as foolhardy as Faeryl suggested. Though the bravado is misplaced here, I'm sure it's served you well in the past."

"Mistress . . . ?" Pharaun began.

"Aunrae Nasadra, of First House Nasadra," the drow finished for him.

Of course you are, the wizard thought.

"Mistress Nasadra," he said, "while I am shocked and saddened by the news of Quenthel's death, I implore you to hear me out. I have absolutely no knowledge of any conspiracy between her and anyone here in the city. There must have been a great misunderstanding."

"I doubt it," Aunrae replied, "but you may yet have a chance to prove it and spare your neck. Simply tell us the truth. Did you or did you not sneak into the city and meet in secret with Drisinil Melarn, matron mother of House Melarn, in order to steal goods out of Black Claw Mercantile's storehouses?"

Pharaun looked around at the myriad faces staring expectantly at him—and at the scores of weapons leveled at him and his two companions—and he did the only thing he could; he lied.

"Absolutely, Mistress Nasadra," he deadpanned, and everyone including Ryld and Valas gasped. Before the other two Menzoberranyr could refute his false admission, he continued, "Or rather, Quenthel must have. It all makes sense, now. You see, Mistress, she ordered my two companions and me to track down caravans that could help transport a large amount of goods, without telling us what they were for. Mistress Baenre told us males very little, you must realize.

"Right before we set out to follow her instructions, I overheard her speaking with Faeryl Zauvirr, the ambassador to Menzoberranzan who was accompanying us. I recall that she said something about meeting with her mother and one other, though of course at the time, I didn't know to whom she was referring. She asked Faeryl something to the effect of, 'and you're certain the meeting place is secure? We can't afford to be seen, you know.' "

"You pompous, smart-mouthed liar!" Faeryl screamed from across the room. "Kill them now and be done with it!"

Pharaun did all he could to avoid smiling. Around him, everyone began to talk at once, and though he heard more than a few snatches of conversation condemning him and his outlandish story, he knew that he had sown the seeds of doubt. Already, though, the troops who had surrounded them—troops wearing the insignia of House Zauvirr—began to advance uncertainly upon the three of them.

"All right, wizard," Ryld hissed, "we're out of time. What are we going to do?"

Pharaun opened his mouth to tell the warrior that he had absolutely no idea, when a sudden and violent shudder rocked the chamber, causing everyone to stumble and flail about, their center of balance disrupted. A split second later, a monumental thundercrash penetrated the walls, deep and loud, and reverberated through the entire room.

"By the Dark Mother," someone cried as everyone looked at everyone else in confusion and panic.

A servant ran into the chamber, a wild look of fear in his eyes.

"Mistresses! It's duergar! Hundreds of them, surrounding us . . . they're attacking!" Another sonic shock knocked the liveried boy to his knees, and he seemed to hug the floor in terror. "They burn the stones themselves, Mothers. The city is burning!"

Aliisza was more than a little surprised to see the horde of duergar seemingly appear out of thin air around the great manor Pharaun and his companions had entered. From the looks on their faces, though, she wasn't nearly as surprised as the drow who were guarding the place. The gray dwarves, whom she estimated numbered between two and three thousand, had formed a line along one side of the manor house before making themselves visible by firing off a volley of crossbows. They also lobbed several dozen small clay pots, which burst into orange balls of flame upon impacting the stonework wall that surrounded the manor.

The few drow who'd been lounging around near the palatial front gates scrambled for cover as the hail of bolts and incendiary bombs struck. The blast from the initial attack shook the entire web street, and Aliisza had to improve her grip to avoid slipping and falling from her roost on the roof of the building on the opposite side of the open plaza. When she could look again, she saw that few of the dark elves had survived the first attack.

An alarm was quickly sounded inside the courtyard of the cyst-like building, and more drow appeared from inside, a large contingent of them, in fact. Aliisza watched as they formed a line across the protective wall and returned fire with their hand crossbows. Several duergar dropped before the barrage, but the gray dwarves exhibited wise tactics, throwing up a shield wall with the front rank and firing a second volley from behind that protective barrier. In several places, the stone itself seemed to burn from the duergar fire bombs, and the fire was spreading.

In the plaza, citizens of Ched Nasad scrambled for cover, and in the distance, Aliisza could see a large column of troops marching, one web street over, in her direction. The duergar were about to have unwanted company . . . or so she thought.

That's when the second mass of gray dwarves appeared inside the courtyard, flanking the drow who had formed up to defend the front gates.

Oh, how clever, the alu-fiend thought. They look like they've done this a time or two.

🕸   🕸   🕸

Pharaun never hesitated.

"Scatter," he said sharply to the two drow with him.

He willed a spell into being. Ordinarily he would have needed at least a few seconds to speak the phrase and perform the gestures to bring the effect about, but he had enhanced this particular magic, and this conjuration simply happened as he thought it, with no gestures, words, or delays. A thick, roiling mist appeared, obscuring everything around the wizard. He knew that Ryld would know how to take care of himself, and he hoped that Valas would understand, too. He promptly dismissed them from his mind as he levitated upward.

Another concussive blast shook the House, though the wizard, hovering in the air, only heard it this time. He floated all the way to the ceiling, casting a spell of invisibility on himself. He knew it wouldn't completely obscure him from the more clever wizards and matron mothers, but it would at least prevent the common soldiery from spotting him. From below, he could hear the turmoil and confusion as a host of drow reacted to both the messenger's words and the rumbles in the foundation.

When he reached the ceiling, Pharaun reached inside his *piwafwi* and extracted a small pinch of diamond dust. He incanted once more, watching as the dust vanished in a sparkle of light. It would further conceal him, he hoped, this time from detection magic.

By then, someone had had the presence of mind to magically dissipate Pharaun's mist, and the floor below was clear once more. The Master of Sorcere surveyed the entire chamber, looking for signs of Ryld and Valas. The scout was nowhere to be found, which didn't surprise the wizard in the least, and Ryld had maneuvered himself off to one side of the room. The weapons master crouched behind some statuary, Splitter in hand, watching as the enemy ran here and there.

He won't stay hidden long, Pharaun reasoned, knowing the matron mothers still intended to mete out their own personal justice just as soon as they could restore some order.

Considering quickly, the wizard dug out a bit of fleece from one of his pockets. With it he manufactured another spell. This one he cast at Ryld, creating a little enhancement to the warrior's hiding place. When he was done, a new, illusory statue stood where Ryld was, further concealing him.

Pharaun turned his attention back to the center of the room, where several wizards were standing, some of them casting. Another was carefully turning, peering in every direction, and Pharaun could see that magic emanated from the drow.

They're looking for us, the Master of Sorcere realized.

Fumbling around in his pockets, Pharaun found what he was looking for: a tiny hammer and bell, both made of silver. Striking the hammer against the bell, the wizard produced another magical effect. This time, the results were flashy.

A horrid vibration beat through the floor beneath the wizards' feet, causing them to clap their hands over their ears and stumble about. Even the one who'd been scanning the room seemed startled, though he planted his feet and continued searching. As the vibration reached a crescendo, the stone of the floor itself could no longer stand the strain and began to fracture. A thousand spiderwebbing cracks shot through the floor, making footing unstable and knocking many of the wizards down. The floor continued to fracture until it was nothing but pulverized powder, half a foot deep. The downed wizards kicked up dust as they flailed about, trying to regain their footing. Several of them didn't move at all.

Excellent, Pharaun thought, but his elation was short-lived. Ryld had been discovered and was engaged in a fierce battle with several House Melarn soldiers and at least two priestesses. Though blood streamed from a gash across one arm, the warrior was otherwise holding his own, but Pharaun knew that it wouldn't last long if anyone was able to bring magic into play. Already, the mage could see a priestess unfurling a scroll. Before he could act, though, Valas stepped up behind her, seemingly from nowhere—How does he do that? Pharaun marveled—and plunged one of his two curved daggers into the small of her back. As the cleric dropped woodenly to the floor, the scout was turning away, and Pharaun lost sight of him again when the wizard turned his attention for a moment to the other side of the room.

There, several of the matron mothers had come together, protected by a significant portion of their entourage, and were huddled around something Pharaun couldn't see. He considered whether to strike at them while they were in such close proximity but dismissed the idea.

Don't want to draw any more attention to myself than necessary, he decided.

Pharaun felt the tingle of magic being cast at him, and he saw another wizard with his finger pointed in his direction. Somehow, they'd discovered his position. Pharaun realized he was glowing with a pale violet flame, despite his invisible state. Already, several other wizards were looking in his direction, and a handful of soldiers were arming crossbows.

Damnation! the mage thought.

He quickly pulled his *piwafwi* around himself and turned away as the first volley of bolts crashed into the ceiling around him. He felt a pair of the missiles strike his back, but the *piwafwi* did its job. There was no way he could eliminate the faerie fire around himself without also dismissing the invisibility, he knew, but if he simply let himself be a target, he would wind up a pincushion. Shaking his head in consternation, Pharaun quickly dropped from his position, pulling up just short of hitting the floor.

The contingent of wizards and soldiers had followed Pharaun's descent and were moving to close with him. Two soldiers brandishing long swords came at him from opposite sides, and though he was able to duck the first attack cleanly, the other one caught him flush across the arm, penetrating his *piwafwi*. Blood spurted from the gash as the mage cried out in pain. A heartbeat later, he and his two adversaries were engulfed in a torrent, as though they had danced their dance into the center of a waterfall—only it wasn't water. It burned like fire, and both of the sword wielders shrieked and thrashed as their skin blistered and reddened. Pharaun felt his own skin bubbling and boiling as he flung his *piwafwi* up to shield his face and threw himself clear, moving at an unnaturally rapid pace, thanks to the magic of his boots.

Rolling free of the downpour of acid, Pharaun summoned his rapier as he leaped to his feet, continuing his forward progress right at two more soldiers. He used the hovering, dancing rapier to hold the pair of drow at bay just enough so he could pass between them before they even knew he was coming. Once he was through, he headed in the direction of Ryld, while more crossbow bolts and a couple of streaking missiles of light and fire fizzled out as they reached his form.

Valas had hidden himself away again, but Ryld was hard at work, surrounded by no less than six opponents. With each swing of Splitter, the burly warrior parried several weapons at once. His chest was heaving, and he was covered in blood from a dozen small wounds. He didn't appear capable of going on the offensive with so many foes surrounding him.

As Pharaun closed with his companion, he had the magical rapier slash at the back of one of Ryld's adversaries. The blade jabbed into the drow soldier from behind, causing the poor fellow to arch his back in agony and crumple to the ground. Grimly, Pharaun ordered the rapier to return and protect him as he began to conjure another spell.

Backing himself into a defensive position near the same statues that Ryld had used to hide himself earlier, the Master of Sorcere extracted a second pinch of the powdered diamond. This time, though, the spell he wove created an invisible barrier between himself and the dozen or so soldiers and wizards who had been pursuing him. The location where Ryld had chosen to hide was more or less in a corner of the great audience chamber, and Pharaun took advantage of that by stretching his invisible wall at an angle, sealing himself and the Master of Melee-Magthere off from most of the rest of the chamber, with only the five drow who were still surrounding Ryld to contend with.

The Master of Sorcere turned his attention to aiding Ryld as the other soldiers painfully discovered his magical wall. He ignored the thumps they made as the first two or three slammed into the barrier, but he couldn't help but smile. Ryld had fatally wounded a second foe, a priestess who was writhing on the floor in a growing pool of blood. Pharaun drew out his own crossbow and loaded the weapon even as he brought his dancing rapier to bear on a drow male who was trying to get in behind Ryld.

The rapier slashed, grazing the guard's shoulder, and as the soldier turned to protect himself from this new threat, Pharaun fired his crossbow, striking true. The soldier grunted in surprise and pain as the bolt took him in the shoulder of his weapon arm. He dropped his long sword and staggered backward, eyeing the rapier as it flitted about in front of him. Pharaun reloaded the crossbow and was taking aim when Valas stepped from a shadow and finished the guard from behind. Eyes wide, the drow gasped and tried to say something, seemed confused that his words wouldn't form, then died, sliding to the floor as the scout freed his kukri from its victim.

"I assume that's you, wizard? What's the point of being invisible if you're going to glow all purple like that?"

"I'm glad to see you wound up on the right side of things," Pharaun said, then staggered as another rumble shook the building. "By the Dark Mother, what is going on out there?" he said, steadying himself from the aftershocks.

"Whatever it is, I don't know if it's better to be out there or in here," Valas replied, wiping his curved dagger clean on the dead drow's *piwafwi*. "We've got to get out of here."

Pharaun nodded, forgetting that the scout couldn't see him, then he said, "I agree" before turning to see how Ryld had fared.

The warrior was facing only a single opponent, stepping warily around the slick pools of blood as he feinted a few times. His ploys weren't terribly effective, and he was gasping for breath. His close-cropped white hair was matted red with blood.

Valas crept forward, ready to get in another attack from behind the moment an opportunity presented itself, so the mage turned his attention back to his magical wall, confident his two companions had the situation well in hand.

On the other side of the barrier, several of the drow wizards were levitating, testing to see if Pharaun had left any gaps along the ceiling. Another wizard was obviously casting, trying to find something that would dispel the effect. Soldiers stood at the ready, fingering their weapons and eyeing Pharaun and his two companions balefully. Pharaun knew by sense that the magical partition still held, but it would only be a matter of time before their enemies would find the right combination of magic to bring it down.

At that moment, Pharaun noted the smoke on the far side of the room. It was where the matron mothers had been, but they were no longer there.

Of course not, the mage thought sardonically. They're not going to come out until they know we're in custody again.

The smoke, however, was thick and black and seemed to be pouring into the room through a hole in the wall. He could see flames licking the stone, and he realized what was going on.

"We've definitcly got to get out of here," the mage said to Valas.

"That's what I said," Valas replied, "but you seem to have sealed us in here."

Ryld had dispatched his final adversary and sank down to one knee, trying to regain his breath.

"Hello, Pharaun. It's good to 'see' you. You two aren't going to walk through walls again, are you?" Ryld asked, heaving himself to his feet again.

On the other side of the barrier, some of the House Melarn delegation had lost interest in them, turning and pointing back at the smoke or running toward it. Whatever was happening in the obscured side of the audience chamber, they were very agitated.

"Alas," Pharaun answered the warrior, "I have exhausted my quota of wall-walking for the day. I'll have to rely on more conventional means of egress, I'm afraid. Still, we shouldn't tarry. That smoke is from the same stuff we had to deal with during the insurrection back in Menzoberranzan."

"The fire bombs that burned the very stone?" Valas asked.

"Then that means . . ." Ryld added.

"Precisely. We may be contending with associates of Syrzan, or others, who are inciting the populace to riot and arming them with the same tools of destruction."

"I thought you said the alhoon was operating alone, an outcast from its own kind," Ryld said, turning in circles and analyzing every nook and cranny of the corner of the room.

"I did," Pharaun admitted. "In my conversation with the thing during our captivity, it claimed that very thing. Perhaps whoever supplied it or its minions with the alchemical incendiary jugs is serving multiple fronts."

"Regardless of who's doing it, we know how grave the situation is," Valas said. "We need to get out of the city."

"Again, I agree," Pharaun said. "I suggest we make a run for it once I lower the barrier."

"Into that mob?" Ryld countered. "We should try to find another way out."

"But that's the quickest way to the streets. We don't know our way around in here, and House Melarn could be an inferno before long."

"Look," Ryld argued, "you may be feeling fine, but I can't take another stand-up fight right now." He gestured at his own bloody form. "There's got to be other ways out of this House. Let's go find one." The warrior gestured toward a door in the corner and added, "Leave your barrier up and let's go."

Valas nodded and said, "Ryld is right. We can't fight through all of them. Let's try another route."

"Very well," Pharaun sighed, "but if the House falls down around our ears, I will personally blame both of you."

He gestured toward the door, inviting Valas to lead the way.

❦ ❦ ❦

For the first few minutes, the halls of House Melarn were remarkably empty as Ryld, Pharaun, and Valas limped their way through them. Occasionally, the trio heard running footsteps in the twisting, winding passages that threaded their way through the massive structure, but they were able to avoid confrontations by either taking a detour or momentarily hiding. It appeared to the Master of Melee-Magthere that most of the inhabitants were focusing their attention outside, where the bulk of the fighting was taking place.

As they reached an intersection, Valas held up his hand for a halt, and the scout slunk off in one direction, investigating the route ahead. Ryld and Pharaun pressed themselves against the wall, trying to remain out of sight. The wizard was no longer invisible, nor was he glowing with that annoying, flickering purple hue. Ryld had taken care of that with a pass of his enchanted blade. The warrior could see that his companion's skin was blistered, and he imagined that Pharaun was in considerable pain. His own wounds troubled him only when he thought about them.

Don't you have some sort of magic that can help us locate an exit? Ryld flashed to the wizard as they waited.

Pharaun shook his head.

Such spells exist, but I don't know them, he silently replied. *Without knowing the way, we could be down here forever. This is a fool's errand, Ryld.*

Then perhaps we should just follow the soldiers. They can unwittingly lead us out of here.

Pharaun waved away the warrior's suggestion, though whether it

195

was in exasperation or acceptance, Ryld wasn't sure.

The risk of discovery or disaster is greater if we do that.

Ryld shrugged but gave no other reply. Instead, he turned to watch for Valas's return.

Why do I bother arguing? the weapons master thought as his listened for telltale sounds. He's already made up his mind.

Valas returned at that moment, gesturing for them to follow him. Together, they crept forward into a new corridor, and Valas pointed to a doorway on the opposite side.

That's a kitchen, he signaled, *and beyond it is a pantry. On the other side, here*—the scout pointed to a door near the trio—*is a mess hall. I think we're in the barracks section.*

Well, that's not a good place to be, Pharaun gestured. *We want to avoid the guards, not come bunk with them.*

Valas gave Pharaun a baleful look and motioned for the other two to follow him. *I think there's a stairwell leading up just past this area,* he flashed as he led the way through the passage.

Ryld thought they might actually get lucky and get through the guards' quarters unnoticed, but as they neared the opposite end of the passageway that bisected the barracks and the mess, they heard the approach of a large contingent from ahead of them. As one, the three drow turned to scamper back in the other direction, but at that moment several House Zauvirr soldiers appeared at the other end. They were pinned between the two forces.

"Damn!" Pharaun growled as he reached inside his *piwafwi.* "Hold them off while I see what I can do."

Nodding, Ryld slipped Splitter free and approached the group coming from where Valas had indicated stairs.

If we can cut through them, the warrior reasoned, at least we can continue the way we want to go.

The soldiers, numbering four, gave a shout of warning and unsheathed their weapons.

"Come on, you son of a drider," one of them snarled, stepping in with a long sword and a short sword together, one in each hand.

The other three fanned out, looking for a chance to flank the burly intruder. Ryld kept his blade level and loose, waiting and watching, shifting from foot to foot in hopes of preventing any of his foes from getting past him and to his back, or reaching Pharaun. He worried that his hands, still covered with drying blood, would be too slick to wield his blade properly.

The first opponent stepped in, slashing with his short sword up high, then bringing his long sword through in a sweep across Ryld's midsection. The weapons master ducked below the first slice and parried the lower blow with Splitter.

Try that again, and I'll have you down to two short swords, Ryld thought, watching to see if the other drow would fall into a pattern.

To his left, another of the soldiers was trying to scoot along the wall, obviously hoping he could squeeze past Ryld, but the Master of Melee-Magthere was keeping them all in his line of sight. He made a quick slash to the side, causing the soldier to flinch back. Ryld bounced back to the middle of the corridor, still watching the drow with two blades. The other two drow, both on Ryld's right, were waiting and watching.

Fine with me, Ryld thought, keeping his main attention on the one in front of him.

The drow changed tactics this time, stepping in with the long sword leading, and proceeded through a flurry of blows with only that weapon, watching how Ryld blocked them. When Ryld swung through a parry and counterattacked, the other warrior was ready, deflecting the stroke with the short sword. Unfortunately, the engagement allowed the drow on Ryld's left to finally shoot past him.

"Pharaun!" Ryld called, "watch out!"

He stepped away from the center of the hallway, angling backward to keep his opponents in his sight, and the weapons master could hear cries of pain and terror behind him. He hoped it was the other group of drow, and not his two companions. The male with two swords pressed in again, and this time Ryld was ready for him. When the first swipe from the short sword passed high, Ryld knew that the long sword would follow low. This time when the stroke approached Ryld cut sharply with his own blade, neatly slicing the long sword in half. The broken end skittered away with a clatter.

"Damn you, motherless rothé!" the other drow snarled, but he gasped in the next instant as Ryld's momentum spun the weapons master fully around in a circle and into him again.

His cut was quick and true, and the opponent dropped to the floor with a groan. Ryld didn't waste time watching him fall. He was already sidestepping the attack from the soldier who'd gotten behind him and who was trying to cut at him from the back. He took a short spear in the side of his leg for his troubles and growled in pain as he back-stepped from the attack, limping. He couldn't let himself get turned away from anyone, yet they were moving to do just that by surrounding him.

Appearing as if from nowhere, Valas caught the soldier with the long sword from behind, sliding an arm around his neck and planting one of his kukris into the fellow's back. Seeing the attack, Ryld quickly turned and parried several thrusts from the short spears. The final two drow had hoped to get in close and attack Ryld while his attention was focused on the opposite side, but they'd lost their chance.

Ryld stepped fully into the middle of the hallway again, wanting as much room as possible to use Splitter. When the two House Zauvirr soldiers saw that the odds were down to two to one and would quickly be even with Valas beside him, they faltered and began to back up.

A staccato series of glowing bluish-white missiles shot past Ryld, slamming into the two drow as they tried to turn and flee. A few of the magical streaks of light fizzled out as they reached their targets, but far more of them struck true, causing the two soldiers to shudder and convulse as they went sprawling to the floor. Ryld glanced back to see Pharaun holding a slender length of some darkly stained wood cut from a tree on the surface world.

The wizard nodded in satisfaction and tucked the wand away.

"We mustn't tarry," he said, "Everyone in the entire House probably heard that."

Curious, Ryld took another glance back past Pharaun to where the other contingent of drow had been. They were all dead, clutched in the grip of the black, shiny tentacles the mage sometimes summoned. The tentacles continued to squeeze and contract around the bodies of those unfortunate soldiers or flailed about blindly if they had nothing to grip.

Turning back, Ryld followed the other two past the dead drow and into the stairwell.

🕷 🕷 🕷

Halisstra stumbled and lost her balance as the deep rumble shook House Melarn. To either side of her, the guards who were "escorting" her into the audience chamber stumbled as well, losing their grips on the drow noble's arms as they flailed about, trying to regain their collective balance. All around Halisstra, shouts rose as drow began to mill about uncertainly in the confusion caused by the vibration, whatever it was. Stunned as much by the proceedings that had been taking place in her mother's House—her House now, Halisstra realized—as by the shock wave that tore through the place, Halisstra merely stood in place, dressed in only her underclothes and with her arms securely manacled behind her back, staring at the chaos around her.

When the liveried servant from House Nasadra ran into the room, announcing the fighting outside, Halisstra blinked in astonishment.

199

Duergar? Attacking House Melarn? Why in the Abyss would they—

A second blast rocked House Melarn and knocked Halisstra off her feet. Or rather, it would have if someone hadn't caught her from behind.

"On your feet . . . I've got to get you out of here."

It was Danifae, dressed for battle and looking remarkably like just another guard in a House Zauvirr *piwafwi*.

Halisstra struggled to right herself with Danifae's help, then turned to look at her battle captive. The servant was not normally permitted to arm and armor herself, but she was currently wearing her old chain shirt and buckler and had her morning star at her side. Halisstra wondered how Danifae had managed to get to her accoutrements, which had been locked away in Halisstra's rooms, but she wasn't going to take the time to complain just then.

Halisstra heard a shout from behind them, and she turned, expecting to see her original guards realizing she was free. Instead, she discovered that a thick mist had filled the room, and she could see very little beyond a couple of paces away.

"Come on," Halisstra hissed, scrambling through the mist toward the back of the room, to a doorway leading deeper into the House where her own chambers were located. "Back to my rooms, and you can get these—"she held her arms out away from her back to indicate the manacles—"off me."

"Of course, Mistress," Danifae said, steering her superior by one arm through the thick, obscuring mist, along the wall and toward the door. "We'll thank someone later for hiding our escape with this fog."

"You mean, that's not something you and Lirdnolu Maerret planned to help extricate me from Ssipriina Zauvirr?"

Danifae laughed once, a bitter chuckle.

"Hardly," she said. "Despite my convincing performance before Matron Mother Zauvirr, you didn't really expect her to let me wander free did you? I had no way to reach House Maerret. No, that commotion back there was someone else's doing."

Once the two of them were out of the audience chamber and into the hall, Halisstra could see better, and she set off regally toward her own chambers, despite the fact that she was half-naked and bound. She hadn't managed more than three or four steps before a third rumble staggered her. She gasped as she lost her balance and stumbled against one wall of the hallway, but Danifae was there, catching hold of her mistress and steadying her as the tremor quieted.

"What the blazes is going on?" Halisstra demanded as they righted themselves and hurried on their way.

"I don't know for sure, but I can hazard a guess," her subordinate replied as they turned a corner. "There are riots welling up in the streets."

"Perhaps," Halisstra said, "but why would duergar target House Melarn?"

"That, I can't say," Danifae replied, "but my guess is it has more to do with Ssipriina Zauvirr's attempt to overthrow House Melarn than anything else. Regardless, it served my purposes well enough. Perhaps we can find out more in a little bit, after we get you out of those restraints."

"Yes," Halisstra answered, thinking. "Let's start with finding out where in the Nine Hells all of our House guards are."

"I can tell you that right now," Danifae offered as the duo turned another corner and entered Halisstra's chambers. "They accepted an offer they couldn't refuse: serve House Zauvirr or die."

Halisstra sighed.

"Is there anyone still loyal to me?" she asked, though she feared she already knew the answer.

"Possibly your brother, if he's still alive, but he's at the Dangling Tower and can't do us much good here," Danifae said, turning Halisstra around so that she could take a look at the locking mechanism on the restraints. "As for inside the House right now? I doubt anyone would be willing to aid you, except maybe those three males in the audience chamber, the ones from Menzoberranzan, and only if you win their trust." The battle captive shook her head. "I can't get these off right now. Better to break the chain and worry about them later."

"Fine . . . but what do you mean, 'win their trust?' How could I do that?"

Halisstra began to pace, pondering her options. Though she had managed to escape the matron mothers for the moment, she was still trapped—inside her own House, of all places—and doubted it would take long for Ssipriina's guards to close in on the two of them.

Danifae didn't answer right away. Halisstra turned to repeat her question and saw the other dark elf grab the noble's mace from where it stood in the corner by her bed. She was momentarily startled when Danifae returned to her side and pushed her to her knees, but she quickly understood the battle captive's intent, and positioned her hands near the floor where Danifae could strike the chain while it was against the stone.

"You could start by telling them that their high priestess is still alive," Danifae finally answered, drawing the mace back for a hard blow against the chain joining the manacles.

"What?" Halisstra gasped, turning to look at her servant. "Quenthel Baenre is alive?"

For a brief moment she wondered if her mother had also survived.

Danifae held her downstroke at the last moment when her mistress moved.

"Hold still!" she commanded, repositioning Halisstra for another try. "And yes, the Baenre priestess is alive. I saw both her and her demon companion in the dungeons earlier. While I was prowling around, trying to figure out what to do, I saw that male Mistress Zauvirr called Zammzt hurrying from that direction."

Danifae smacked her morning star hard against the chain, but the links didn't break.

"A few moments later," she continued, "Faeryl Zauvirr appeared, also coming from the lower levels. Curious, I decided to see what she was doing down there. She has them both bound to within an inch of their lives, and Quenthel Baenre is stretched tight on the rack at the moment."

Danifae lined up another blow with the mace.

"Then Ssipriina is lying! I can free the high priestess and get her to prove my innocence."

Halisstra felt elation for the first time since the catastrophic day had begun.

"Possibly," the battle captive answered dryly, taking another whack at the restraints, "but I doubt many of the matron mothers will choose to believe her. She may still be guilty of her crimes, even if you are innocent of yours. Enough of the matron mothers have an agenda that precludes you walking free from this. More likely—*ah ha!*"

The link Danifae had been pounding on finally crimped enough to separate the manacles.

Helping Halisstra to her feet, the battle captive continued, "More likely, they'll simply accuse you of trying to help her escape and offering that as a cover story."

Halisstra eyed the steel restraints still on her wrists, already finding them annoying, but they would have to wait. Free, at least for the moment, Halisstra's fear melted away. She was furious, and she couldn't decide who bore the majority of her anger.

"Well, I'm not just going to sit here while everyone else brings down House Melarn around my ears. Help me get ready, and let's go find that Baenre."

"As you wish," Danifae said, moving rapidly with the decision having been made.

With her servant's help, Halisstra quickly began to dress, first attiring herself in a set of plain but functional clothes, then donning her armor, a fine suit of chain mail bearing the coat of arms of House Melarn and several enchantments. Once that was on, Danifae handed Halisstra her mace and shield and scurried about the room to gather up other things Halisstra normally had with her when out in the city or beyond.

When Halisstra was dressed, Danifae grabbed her morning star, each of them wrapped themselves in a *piwafwi* marked with the insignia of House Zauvirr, and they were ready.

Outside Halisstra's rooms, the halls were quiet. No one had yet been sent to hunt for her, it appeared, for which the priestess was silently thankful. Once away from her private quarters, Halisstra began to breathe a little easier. No one would question two House guards moving through the halls.

That's when the two of them came around a bend in the hallway and spied three strange drow, two of them bruised and bleeding, creeping through the gloom. They were definitely not members of the household, but it took Halisstra another moment or two before she realized they were the three Menzoberranyr.

"Damn," one of them said, reaching inside his *piwafwi* as the other two brandished weapons and advanced warily.

Matron Mother Zauvirr wasn't merely angry. Angry was for sub-ordinates who knew to hold their tongues in the presence of their superiors despite their feelings. Angry was for those times when you had to slap a child because it didn't know any better. No, angry wasn't nearly strong enough a word to describe what Ssipriina was feeling. Someone was going to pay for this foolishness. Someone was going to *die*.

She stormed through the hallways of her own House Zauvirr, having slipped out of Drisinil's manor during the confusion and magically transported herself back home. There was something she wanted to get, something she needed, though she hadn't expected to, when the day started. She almost hoped that someone would cross her path as she marched along, that someone would make the mis-take of accosting her, of interrupting her train of thought for some idiotic and perfectly pointless reason. She really hoped they would

. . . it would be fun, in a distracting sort of way, to watch some hapless male bleed out as she ripped him up. She was furious enough to do it with her bare hands.

A guard would do nicely, she thought. *Any foolish boy who even looks at me.*

All of her planning, wasted. All of the careful manipulation, the bribes, the theft, the smuggling of valuables and troops, even the fortuitous arrival of the damnable Menzoberranyr and her clever scheme to fit them into the plan was for naught. Someone had blundered, and she would have his head.

I had them in the palm of my hand, Ssipriina thought. *They were ready to anoint me. Even after that ridiculous story the wizard made up.*

That obvious attempt to derail her plans wouldn't have stopped her. No one would have believed him, even after her foolish daughter reacted. Ssipriina thought Faeryl had sounded like the petulant child that she still was.

I should never have brought her in on this.

Ssipriina realized her mind was wandering. It was the fury, keeping her from thinking straight.

Faeryl I can deal with later. There's nothing to be done except to fight and win, but it would have been so much easier if the gray dwarves had remained out of sight. Who told them to move out?

As the matron mother arrived at her rooms, she decided that ferreting out the guilty party would also have to wait until later. Her full attention was needed elsewhere. She was about to spring something on the entire city. Something very special. Ssipriina grinned when she imagined it.

🕷   🕷   🕷

Faeryl stumbled and fell against the corridor wall when House Melarn first began to shake.

The servants were screaming, and from somewhere she heard, "Mistresses! It's duergar! Hundreds of them, surrounding us . . . they're attacking!"

A second shock wave rumbled through the House.

"They burn the stones themselves, Mothers. The city is burning!"

With a sinking feeling, Faeryl knew it for the truth. She had lived through this experience before, though it had been in the bowels of House Baenre, chained to a column. Even so, she remembered the rumbles from above, felt the vibrations in the ground. When she had been freed by Triel Baenre and invited to join the mission to Ched Nasad, she had gotten all the details of the insurrection in the streets of Menzoberranzan from others. Their descriptions of the jugs of fire, the fire that burned stone itself, were vivid. She could only imagine what it would feel like on a web street of Ched Nasad.

Faeryl groaned. Her mother's plan was falling apart. The duergar weren't supposed to appear unless the negotiations with the other matron mothers went badly. Despite that idiot Pharaun's asinine claim of her involvement in the conspiracy, the situation was far from out of hand.

Mother pulled the trigger too soon, the ambassador decided. *She must have gotten cold feet and didn't bother to tell me. How typical.*

Shaking her head, Faeryl scrambled up to her feet again as the room was enveloped in a thick, murky fog. She knew who was most likely behind it. As much as she wanted to slice Pharaun into a thousand tiny pieces, there was too much confusion.

Besides, the ambassador grudgingly admitted, *he and his boys are not to be trifled with. I'll let mother's wizards take care of them. I've got to get rid of Quenthel and that loathsome beast.*

Faeryl felt her way along the wall, stumbling as yet another blast rocked House Melarn. The mist cleared, and she could hear the sounds of combat on the far side of the room. She resisted the temptation to look, as much as she hoped to catch a glimpse of the wizard's demise. Instead, she managed to make her way to a door just as several dozen House soldiers came in, jostling her aside in their efforts to defend the audience chamber.

"Fools!" Faeryl hissed at them.

Almost shaking with rage, she departed the audience chamber and hurried toward the lower levels. She passed few other drow in the corridors, all of them looking confused. None of them seemed to know the origin of the disturbances, and at one point the ambassador overheard at least three priestesses discussing an earthquake as they passed her, going the opposite direction.

Faeryl didn't care to explain to them what was really happening. It was not her House. Turning a final corner, the ambassador hurried into the torture chamber where she had left Quenthel and Jeggred. They were not there. The room was not empty, however. One of the House torturemasters was methodically straightening tools that had been upset with the booming thumps from outside.

"Where are they?" Faeryl demanded, gesturing to the rack where Quenthel had been restrained.

The torturemaster turned and looked at her vacantly, not understanding.

Growling in exasperation, the ambassador repeated herself.

The other drow looked at her, then comprehension lit his features.

"Oh, they're not here," he said.

Faeryl rolled her eyes and said, "I can see that, you foolish boy. Where *are* they?"

"That ugly drow, Zammzt, ordered them taken to a cell," the torturemaster replied. "I saw to it personally."

Another severe blast rocked the room, and tools were scattered everywhere. Faeryl managed to grab hold of the column where Jeggred had been chained for support, but the other drow was not so lucky. He went down in a pile—and even more unfortunately, one of the many braziers of hot coals tipped over onto him, showering him with burning cinders. Screaming, the drow scrambled away from the embers, but he was already a conflagration, his clothes ignited and smoking as he flailed helplessly about.

Faeryl bit her lip in irritation.

Now, why do you suppose he would have moved them, and to where? she thought, turning to leave.

She decided she'd have to ask someone to show her, and she departed.

🕷 🕷 🕷

Pharaun faltered for only a moment at the sight of the two drow priestesses before him. One, quite simply, was beautiful. The other, while lacking the graceful curves and fluid motion of the first, was obviously nobly born and not unpleasant to look at, either. Then, getting a closer look, the wizard recognized her. She was the drow who had been in chains in the audience chamber only moments before. In fact, he realized, she still wore the manacles she'd been shackled with, though the connecting chain between them had been severed. Neither of the females looked happy to see him, Ryld, or Valas.

"Damn," Pharaun muttered, returning to his senses.

He reached inside his *piwafwi*, fumbling quickly for the wand he'd used to dispatch the drow soldiers not too long before. In front of him, Ryld went on guard, raising Splitter into an aggressive position as he advanced warily. Valas slipped to the opposite side of the hallway, automatically fanning out with Ryld to come at the adversaries from either flank.

The lovely creature who'd first caught the mage's eye hissed in vexation and brought a morning star out in front of her. She had a buckler on her other arm held to the side where Valas was closing.

"It's them!" she snarled, taking up a position in front of the other drow as though to defend her.

Both dark elves seemed quite capable of taking care of themselves, and Pharaun noted the finely tooled chain mail each of them wore. The one to the rear actually sported the House Melarn insignia on hers, and the wizard guessed she must be one of the dead matron mother's daughters.

Pharaun had his wand out, but before he could invoke the trigger words to use the thing, Ryld stepped in and launched a short series of strikes at the dark elf in front of him, who managed with some difficulty to parry the attacks with both her weapon and her buckler. The Master of Sorcere knew that Ryld was not really pressing his attack yet. The weapons master was attempting to size up the skill of his competition with a few well-placed feints before closing in to finish the job efficiently.

Valas continued to creep in from her other side, and she back-stepped more than once to prevent the scout from getting behind her. Pharaun aimed the wand and prepared to recite the activation phrase, when the other drow, the daughter of House Melarn, spoke up, causing him to falter.

"Hold, Danifae."

The drow in front retreated another couple steps, but she did not drop her guard.

"We have no quarrel with you," the still-unnamed Melarn said. "I know you don't have reason to trust us, but we're not the enemy. . . . They are."

She gestured upward, to the floors above.

Ryld took a threatening step forward then he too stopped and held his guard. Valas was watching both sides with glittering eyes, kukris at the ready.

"How convenient," Pharaun said, smiling coldly. "The imperiled daughter, implicated in her mother's treason and with no friends, making a peace offering. At least until we let down our guard, right? Then you turn us over to Matron Mother Zauvirr, claim you captured us, and hope she lets you off the hook."

"I could easily say the same about you, but I won't," the Melarn daughter replied. Without taking her eyes off Pharaun, she added, "Danifae, I said stand down!"

Pharaun raised an eyebrow at her tone of command. Danifae nodded in acquiescence, stepping farther back until she was side by side with her mistress.

"Well, you're right about that," Pharaun said. "We don't have any reason to believe you. If you're on the outs with Mistress Zauvirr, what are you doing down here, all decked out in your finest armor?"

"We're trying to save our own skins," the daughter said, a bit more testily than Pharaun thought necessary, considering she was trying to broker some sort of truce, albeit temporary. "I think we both might have been played by Ssipriina Zauvirr. If you come with us, help us, we might be able to get you information that will help prove it."

"Lower your weapons to the ground," Ryld said, "and we'll consider listening to you."

"I think not," the daughter countered. "At least, not until we have some assurances that you won't attack us the moment we do. I don't know for sure that you *weren't* in league with my mother."

Ryld snarled, raising Splitter and advancing again. Valas was doing likewise, still looking to maneuver around to the priestesses' left side.

"Ryld, Valas, wait," Pharaun called out quietly.

He had no doubt that the two warriors could dispatch the drow females with relatively little difficulty, as long as the wizard was backing them up with a careful selection of spells, but he was intrigued. Ryld cast a quick glance back over his shoulder at the wizard then shrugged and held his ground.

"I can assure you that we have never met your mother and had no dealings with her, ever. That wild tale in the audience chamber above was merely a contrivance to stall for time—ruffle everyone's feathers, so to speak. You seem to know who we are," Pharaun said, addressing the daughter of House Melarn, "but we are at a disadvantage. Who are you, and what is this information you are planning to use to buy our trust?"

In a flash of bluish light, Valas was stepping through a dimensional doorway, and as the one named Danifae turned to face the point where the scout had been standing only a split-second earlier, the Bregan D'aerthe scout was behind her, one hand gripping her wrist tightly where she held her morning star, the other hand holding a kukri at the line where her jawbone faded into her graceful neck. Though she was several inches taller than the scout, Valas was easily able to keep her overbalanced by shifting his hip under hers and levering her up off her feet.

Danifae's eyes bulged wide as she realized she'd been outmaneuvered, and she flailed about helplessly for a second or two until she grasped that the blade was at her neck, at which point she froze.

"Lay them down," Ryld said to both drow females, gesturing to their weapons with his greatsword. "To the floor, nice and quietly."

The Melarn daughter gasped in surprise at Valas's maneuver, narrowed her eyes, and took half a step toward her companion. When she realized she was outmatched, she sighed and settled her mace to the floor at her feet. Danifae sagged a bit in Valas's grasp and relinquished her weapon to the other female, who set that down as well.

"Excellent!" Pharaun said as Ryld kicked the two weapons safely away. "That wasn't so bad, now was it?"

"You could have trusted us," the daughter spat. "We gave you no reason not to."

Pharaun laughed out loud. Ryld stifled a chuckle of his own, and Valas, who released Danifae but kept his kukri carefully placed in the small of her back, was grinning behind her.

"You are a dark elf," the wizard said finally, regaining his composure. "That alone is enough for me not to trust you, but beyond that, if you think we're going to trust anyone in this cursed city, you're the biggest fool I've met in a while. Yet, I am not completely uninterested in negotiating, so you may still get a chance to redeem yourself. You can start by answering my questions. Who are you, and what is the nature of this information?"

The Melarn daughter grimaced but finally answered, "I am Halisstra Melarn, as you have surmised by now, I'm sure. This is Danifae, my personal servant. What I meant was, your friend the high priestess and her demon companion aren't dead."

Pharaun felt his eyes bulge at this revelation. He heard both Ryld and Valas breathe in sharply.

"Really," the mage said, trying to sound offhand as he regained his composure, "and how would you know that?"

"Because I've seen them," Danifae, still locked in Valas's grip, answered.

"Apparently," Halisstra said, "Ssipriina Zauvirr simply told everyone that the priestess was dead so that there would be no demands for her side of the story. They probably *should* have killed them, but I guess Faeryl had other plans for her."

At the mention of the ambassador, Pharaun tilted his head.

"You know Faeryl Zauvirr?" he asked.

"Yes," Halisstra replied, "I know her. We grew up together. Since our Houses have—or rather, *had*—a business relationship, her mother and mine spent quite a bit of time together. She might very well be with the Baenre priestess right now. I suspect she's torturing them both."

"Is that so?" Pharaun asked.

Ryld, who still had his greatsword trained on the two females, snorted, "Why does that not surprise me?"

"I wonder how the esteemed high priestess managed to get herself caught in the first place?" Pharaun pondered aloud.

"It was an ambush," Halisstra said. "When they were at a Black Claw Mercantile storehouse. Faeryl was in on it, I guess. Her mother met them there with a host of guards who subdued the high priest-ess and the demon that was with them. They claim they had to kill my mother, who was trying to escape, though now I wonder if she truly is dead."

"Well now," Pharaun said, even more intrigued than before, "some things are beginning to make more sense. Now I know why Faeryl was being so agreeable during the trip here. She wanted Quenthel to go to the storehouse. It was their plan to take Quenthel all along."

"Not just Quenthel, but all of you," said Halisstra. "I'm guessing she intended to capture all of you at once, but when you didn't appear at the storehouse with the others she had to amend her plan. She'd be quite pleased, I'm sure, if you were all dead."

"Yes," the mage said wryly, "we were informed of that very fact not an hour ago. Needless to say, we weren't too keen on the idea, ourselves."

"So where's Mistress Baenre?" Ryld demanded. "We're going to find her and leave. You can help us or join everyone else who's gotten in our way thus far."

Halisstra looked appraisingly at the warrior.

"What is it you expect to accomplish by finding her?" she asked.

"We're going to get her out of here, and we're going to go find——"

"Weapons Master Argith," Pharaun interrupted, pulling the war-rior to the side where they could talk privately. "I'm not sure that's really the wisest course of action. We need to get out of here before the whole House falls down, don't you agree?"

"And leave the Mistress of the Academy here?" Ryld countered. "We should try to find her."

Pharaun looked questioningly at his companion and asked, "Why in the Underdark would we do that?"

Ryld's eyes flashed in anger.

"You may be eager to be rid of her, wizard," he said, "but I am not."

"Oh?" Pharaun replied, growing hot himself. "If I didn't know better, I would think you were sweet on the high priestess. Have you forgotten so soon her disdain for you?"

"Whatever your own ambitions are, I still serve the task I was given by Matron Mother Baenre and the rest of the High Council. Quenthel still plays a large part in that, and I have no desire to betray Menzoberranzan herself to suit my own personal vendettas."

Another shock wave tore through House Melarn, and Pharaun was forced to rise into the air to keep his balance.

"Can we argue about this later?" Valas interjected, still gripping Danifae as the two of them tried to maintain their balance. "I agree with Ryld, at least for the moment. We may yet need Quenthel, who is still our best connection to the Dark Mother, and the only one who can tell us if we're succeeding in reconnecting with Lolth. If we do find Tzirik, it may behoove us to have her there."

Pharaun sighed, chagrinned that he had raised his voice enough to be overheard.

"Very well," he said. "We will attempt to find her before we depart, but remember what I said. If the House falls down around our ears, I will personally blame both of you."

He smiled, hoping a little levity would ease the tensions. Ryld still scowled but nodded curtly once the decision was made.

Another rumbling shock wave rocked House Melarn and forced everyone to shift their feet in order to keep their balance. Halisstra looked around with no small level of concern in her eyes.

"If you want to find your high priestess, then let me take you to her," she said. "Danifae and I have no quarrel with you, as I admitted before, and everything I've told you thus far is the truth. We have no allies here, and neither do you. Joining together could be mutually beneficial."

"All right," Pharaun said. "We'll suppose for the moment that we're going to trust you to take us to her. It will make our chances of getting out of here in one piece markedly better, but just to make certain you don't consider trying anything, shall we say, troublesome, I think Danifae here will accompany us with her arms bound behind her. Valas and I will keep a good eye on her while you and Ryld keep to the front."

Danifae's eyes widened the slightest bit in protest at the suggestion, but Halisstra nodded after only a moment's consideration.

"Very well," she agreed. "We'll do it your way—for now. First, you must do something for me. You must answer a question, if you can. What is the state of things out on the streets? I have not had a chance to find out for myself since the shock waves began."

Pharaun shrugged helplessly.

"I fear I cannot tell you with any degree of accuracy," he said. "You were in the audience chamber when the attacks began and heard the warning cry. These duergar appear to be organized, though. My suspicion is that someone else, someone powerful, is behind them."

Halisstra looked sharply at the wizard and asked, "What gives you that impression?"

"The blasts we're feeling are due to incendiary alchemy. We encountered similar destruction back home recently. Whoever is supplying the duergar with them may be associated with the forces we dealt with in Menzoberranzan, and I will warn you now, the stone does indeed burn. We will be at risk as long as we remain inside your House."

Halisstra looked fearful, but she nodded in thanks.

"Then the sooner I can get you what you want, the sooner we can get outside and find out for sure. Danifae, I want you to comply with their instructions. Do you understand me?"

With a small sigh, the other drow female nodded.

"Yes, Mistress," she answered then moved over so that Valas could use a length of cord to bind her hands securely behind her back.

"Wonderful. It's nice to see how we're all getting along so well together," Pharaun said. "Now, Halisstra Melarn, why don't you lead the way?"

"Before I do, allow me to help you in a more immediate way. Let me heal your injuries."

Pharaun glanced over at Ryld, who subtly shook his head, frowning. Shrugging, the wizard decided to ignore his companion's concerns. His face hurt where the acid had burned him.

"All right," he answered, "you can tend to me. But if this is a trick, my two compatriots here will see to it that it never happens again."

"I understand," Halisstra said. "I'm just going to pull a wand out, so please don't get jumpy, all right?"

Pharaun nodded and waited as the daughter of Drisinil Melarn produced the wand and utilized it. The mage immediately felt the effects of the divine magic and breathed a sigh of relief.

"Thank you," he said.

Quickly enough, Halisstra similarly healed both Ryld and Valas.

"There . . . you see?" she said, tucking the wand away again. "We really are on your side."

"Indeed," Pharaun replied noncommittally. "We'll just develop the trust slowly, I think. If you please?" he said, gesturing down the hallway.

Halisstra eyed the wizard for a moment, as if assessing whether or not she was making a mistake, then turned and set off down the corridor. Ryld walked close by her side, Splitter hovering protectively close to her.

🦂 🦂 🦂

Aliisza was not certain exactly when the battle outside the noble House had gotten so out of hand, but it was clearly becoming a major engagement, drawing the attention of the entire city.

Sitting on the edge of a building that hung off the side of a web street several street levels above the raging combat, her feet dangling off into space, she watched anxiously as yet another wave of goblins and kobolds crashed into the ranks of duergar positioned around the spacious structure.

The alu wasn't sure why she felt worry over the outcome of the clash. Oh, she understood well enough that she actually felt concern for Pharaun's well-being. She just didn't understand why she did. She wouldn't have imagined that she would care at all for the drow, and indeed her feelings were nothing close to true affection. Still, she found him clever and amusing, and she had enjoyed her time with him earlier in the day.

I guess I'm just not through with him, she decided.

So she waited and watched, wondering if he was going to get out alive. She knew he might have managed to transport himself and his two companions someplace else by means of an extradimensional doorway or similar magic. That was the most likely possibility, actually, and she doubted he was still inside. For some reason, though, she felt compelled to stay and watch. Something in the back of her mind told her that the wizard was still there.

At least the battle is interesting, Aliisza mused.

The gray dwarves had soundly defeated the initial force of drow, pinning the dark elves between the two lines of attackers like steel caught between hammer and anvil. The dark elves were flattened and slaughtered in a matter of moments. Some lucky few had managed to get inside the front door of the manse, but the duergar were in the process of battering that down. Aliisza doubted the portal would hold much longer.

Beyond the walls of the estate, more drow marched to relieve the siege or perhaps to gain their fair share of the spoils. Arriving quickly, driving slave troops before them, the new force was larger than the duergar's, and the gray dwarves found their position reversed, defending the house rather than attacking it. Though the goblins and kobolds out-numbered the duergar by a substantial ratio, they were no match for the gray dwarves' battle tactics and incendiary pots. Three times, the drow had forced their army of lesser beings to assault the walls, and three times they had been repulsed, suffering heavy casualties.

Aliisza understood the tactic all too well, though. The duergar were forced to expend magic to defend themselves, and the drow were happy to sacrifice their shock troops in exchange for draining the gray dwarves' reserves of magic. They were only slaves, after all. A few more waves, and perhaps the duergar would begin to break.

The only problem, Aliisza realized, was that the duergar had uti-lized such a large quantity of the incendiary clay pots that most of the plaza was burning. The air was getting thick with smoke, and the drow were forced to stay back from the spreading conflagration. In several places, the palatial house was burning too, and Aliisza won-dered how much damage the building could sustain before it began to break apart. Though she knew the stone-shaping forces used to build the city had made the web streets and their attached structures as strong as steel, the abode was still precariously perched. If enough of the stone burned, the whole house might break away.

That would be a sight to see.

Aliisza spotted a commotion down a side street, not far from the plaza where the bulk of the fighting had been taking place. There were a handful of drow there, but little else. The alu supposed they might have been a scouting or screening force.

The fiend decided to move in for a closer look. She stepped over the side of the roof and dropped down to another, two levels below, magically slowing her descent. She crouched low as a half-giant passed, not wanting to distract the creature.

The half-giant strode along the wide street, its war axe held loosely in its hand. The blade of the weapon was slick with blood, dripping a trail behind it as it moved. The air was thick with smoke.

A gang of dark elves, soldiers led by priestesses and wizards, poured into the street in the distance, organized and grim, seeking to stop the half-giant. Before they could take three steps in the direction of their quarry, a huge chunk of something crashed to the street between them. The weight of it shook the street, and the sound it made was like a thousand blades striking a thousand shields. It made the half-giant nearly fall, and it had to drop to one knee before it completely lost its balance.

Aliisza peered through the smoke to see what had landed atop the web street. It was nothing but a smoking pile of rock, but the fiend could tell that it had been a part of the street overhead. Actually, it looked like part of the street and a couple of buildings. The whole pile of rubble was ablaze, thick plumes of smoke pouring off it. She looked up, wondering where the chunk of the city had come from.

Even through the smoky haze, Aliisza could see a thoroughfare above them, crossing at an angle, connecting to the besieged House. A large chunk of the road was missing, as if a huge bite had been taken out of the immense spiderweb strand. Flames still licked the stone of the causeway where it had broken off, bringing a small part of the House with it. The rest of the immense structure still sat where it had, but Aliisza realized that more of it could go at any moment. The alu saw how dangerous it was to be down there, below the burning stone.

The half-giant must have sensed this too, for it turned to move back along the street, retracing its steps. That's when a second drow patrol came into view. It was a small group, no more than five or six, but their leader was a wizard, and he had a wand in his hand. The wizard gestured with the wand and a crackling bolt of electricity shot out of the end of it, catching the half-giant square in the chest. The creature howled in pain as its hair burned away. It nearly dropped its war axe, and even after the attack was over, Aliisza saw that the beast couldn't work its fingers right for a moment. The dark elves swarmed toward it, crossbows and swords out and ready.

The half-giant wasn't so easily felled. Aliisza watched, fascinated, as the towering humanoid fumbled in its hip pouch and pulled out a handful of clay jugs. From one knee, it threw them in the direction of the charging drow. Miraculously, its aim was very good, and almost all of the containers flew toward the dark elves, who shied away when they saw what was coming. The jugs shattered on the street and burst into flame, sending a wall of fire and smoke skyward in a blast that Aliisza could feel on her face.

By the Abyss, Aliisza breathed, unable to tear her gaze away from this wonderful display of destruction.

Drow leaped clear of the attack and scrambled to get away from the conflagration, which charred the street in seconds. A couple of the dark elves managed to escape to the half-giant's side of the fire. Realizing they were pinned between the half-giant and the blaze, they looked for some avenue of escape, eyeing the huge beast warily.

Lumbering to its feet again, the half-giant began striding purposefully toward them, gripping its war axe with both hands. Almost as one, the drow turned and fled to the side of the street, leaping over the edge and drifting downward into the smoky vastness below.

At almost the same moment, the street shifted, tilting sideways, and the half-giant stumbled toward the edge. Aliisza watched as the massive humanoid looked around wildly, trying to find out why its footing had grown precarious so suddenly. She saw, too, that the fire it had started with its incendiary pots had already burned through a significant portion of the calcified webbing that was the street, and it was coming apart. The other end had already been weakened by the impact from the rubble, and a whole section of thoroughfare shifted and groaned. The alu knew it wouldn't remain together for much longer.

Amazingly, the half-giant ran toward the fire, taking great, lumbering strides that shook the crumbling roadway and caused chunks of it to fall away from the fiery crack. As the entire path shuddered and snapped free, tipping downward, hinged where the pile of slag had dropped on it earlier, the creature leaped, crossing the distance, passing through the roiling flames. Aliisza's mouth dropped in amazement. The half-giant cleared the flames, reaching the other side, landing with a mammoth *thump* that made the projecting end of the street that was still intact quiver and bounce.

Behind the half-giant, the falling piece of street went tumbling down into the darkness below, eventually landing somewhere with a thunderous boom. Ahead of the towering humanoid, three drow stood staring at the hulking creature, mouths agape. Even from her vantage point, Aliisza could see that the half-giant smiled as it advanced. It raised its war axe and plodded forward. The wizard panicked and turned to flee, leaving only two soldiers to face the creature. Surprisingly, they turned as one to meet the advancing half-giant. One of the two took a tentative step forward, measuring where and how he would attack, when he was shoved hard from behind by his companion, who turned and retreated.

The first drow stumbled, off-balance, right into the path of the half-giant. Aliisza smirked. The fleeing dark elf was sacrificing his partner so that he could escape.

Raising its war axe, the half-giant prepared to cleave the sprawled male in half. Desperately, the dark elf raised his long sword and rammed it into the half-giant's stomach.

The creature roared, arching its back, and its downward swing went awry, biting through the drow's arm instead of his torso. The dark elf screamed as the half-giant fell forward, collapsing on him and driving the sword deeper into itself.

The soldier had dealt the killing blow, Aliisza realized, as the half-giant lay on top of him, unmoving. The boy cried out in pain. He was trapped, pinned beneath the half-giant's weight and with only one good arm to try to free himself.

"Ilphrim! Ilphrim, help me!" the drow cried out, but Ilphrim was long gone, and the fire burned closer.

Aliisza sighed. The battle had been particularly entertaining, but it appeared to be over, though the wounded drow pinned beneath the half-giant still squirmed occasionally. She considered his companion's treachery, pushing him into the path of the rampaging half-giant, to be very clever. She laughed quietly.

The trapped and dying drow moved his arm again, futilely trying to shift the weight of the half-giant off himself so he could wriggle free, but Aliisza knew he would never do it, not with only one arm.

In a sudden and very uncharacteristic act of compassion, the alu-fiend leaped off her perch and floated down to where the dark elf lay feebly squirming. The drow spotted her and tensed, eyeing her warily. She only smiled and nudged a discarded dagger a bit closer to him, so that it was within reach of his free hand. Stepping back, she waited and watched to see if he would do the right thing.

The drow contemplated her for a moment, then he seemed to nod in understanding. He took hold of the dagger and saluted Aliisza with it before he started cutting pieces off the half-giant's corpse. It was going to take a while, and it was already messy, but he might just cut his way free before the web street collapsed.

Smiling in satisfaction, Aliisza turned away and headed back up to her original vantage point, worrying anew over Pharaun's fate.

The five drow worked their way into the bowels of House Melarn for what seemed like hours, though Pharaun was fairly certain they'd only been at it for about fifteen minutes. On several occasions, the group was forced to stop while a member of the House guard crossed paths with them, and once, Halisstra actually posed as a member of House Zauvirr, issuing orders to a group of sentries to head to the surface to help in the defense of the House.

"The lower levels are not usually very heavily occupied," Halisstra said at one point. "I suspect most of Ssipriina's servants and troops are above, aiding in the defense of the House. It's not much farther, now."

The mage nodded as the five of them continued on their way. More than once, Pharaun caught himself gazing in infatuation at the gorgeous creature beside him. She seemed to be considerably unhappy at the state of things, especially the fact that she was helpless to defend herself with her arms bound as they were, but she kept her gaze cast demurely down, and the wizard only found this to be even more endearing.

The group took one last stairwell down and found themselves in a dismal cell block. The hall was undecorated, unlike the posh elegance of the levels above, and the stale stench of unwashed bodies, faint though it was, gave a certain hint of what was to be found there. Halisstra led the five of them to a doorway at the end of a short hall. It was stout and obviously designed to withstand considerable force.

The drow priestess stepped up to the portal and waved her House Melarn brooch before it. There was an audible click as the magic of the insignia operated the locks set into the door. Halisstra pushed the door aside and moved through into the chamber beyond, which appeared to be a guard room, currently empty. At the far side of the chamber, a hallway stretched off into darkness.

Pharaun, spotting movement in the corridor there, put a finger to his lips and motioned for quiet.

Someone is there. Be alert—and no noise, he signed, pointing to both Halisstra and Danifae.

The two drow females nodded, and Pharaun gestured for Halisstra to proceed. As she entered the hallway, the others followed her in. The majority of the cells were empty, their doors standing open and the chambers within dark and silent. However, about halfway down, Pharaun could detect the low voice of someone speaking. It emanated from one of the cells on his right, and he could just see the door being swung shut from inside.

Moving as quietly as they could, the five of them closed the gap to the doorway. The portal was not completely sealed, and Pharaun was able to peer inside the cell. Quenthel was there, naked and crouched against the far wall. A heavy steel collar was around her neck, with a thick chain running from it to a bolt set into the stone of the wall. The high priestess was gagged with some sort of thick bit that was wedged tightly in her mouth, and her arms were obviously incapacitated, stuck together in some sort of thick, viscous black blob in front of her. She had been very effectively immobilized, and Pharaun understood all too well, completely prohibited from casting, should she still have a divine enchantment locked away after all this time without contact with Lolth.

To one side, against another wall of the cell, Jeggred stood glowering. He too was chained to the wall, thick bands of adamantine encasing his neck, arms, and legs. Pharaun could see that the restraints were magically strengthened, but even so, the draegloth strained against them, refusing to admit even for a moment that he was not going to break free. Again and again, Jeggred jerked on the chains, causing them to rattle against the wall as he tried to lunge at the object of his wrath.

Faeryl Zauvirr stood just a little way out of the draegloth's reach, her back to Pharaun and Halisstra. She was standing over Quenthel in the middle of a scathing taunt.

". . . know you would have loved to tell the matron mothers the truth, but it's too late for that now. I only regret that we didn't have more time spend together, Quenthel."

Her voice dripped with acid.

"Come a little closer, Faeryl," Jeggred said, his deep voice flat with malice. "Let me caress you like before, in the underhalls of the Great Mound. Don't you want to feel my kiss again?"

Faeryl shuddered but ignored the draegloth, instead pulling a dagger from her belt.

Halisstra tapped Pharaun softly on the arm.

Let me lure her out here, the Melarn daughter signed.

Pharaun nodded and stepped back, out of sight. Ryld pulled Danifae against the wall next to the wizard, while Valas took up a position on the opposite side of the door.

"Still, it's going to be fun watching you both die," the wizard heard Faeryl say.

"I'm afraid we have other plans for her, Faeryl," Halisstra said, pushing the door open.

The ambassador hissed in anger.

"What are you doing here?" she snarled. "You should be dead!"

Then, apparently realizing that Halisstra had discovered her secret, Faeryl's tone changed.

"You don't really think I'm going to let you walk out of here alive, do you? To run and tell the others what you found? I don't think so."

Halisstra's tone was equally cold.

"On the contrary. You don't think I came down here alone, did you? Danifae!" the Melarn daughter called out, back over her shoulder. "It's true. Run, and tell them what we found."

"I think not," Faeryl said, appearing in the hallway as though she had leaped past the priestess. "You're not going to tell . . ."

The words died in Faeryl's mouth as she spotted Pharaun, Ryld, and Danifae leaning against the wall.

"You!" she spat. "Halisstra, you cast your lot with *them?* You're a bigger fool than I thought."

The look in Faeryl's eyes was decidedly nervous, and her fear only grew as she felt Valas step in behind her and take hold of her arm. The point of the scout's kukri settled against the hollow of her throat.

Pharaun reached out and held out his hand, waiting for Faeryl to relinquish her dagger to him. Eyeing any possible avenue of escape, she appeared ready to bolt but realized she had no chance against so many. She relinquished the dagger, flipping the handle around and laying the weapon in the wizard's palm.

"Perhaps I am a fool," Halisstra said, "but at least I have them as allies, which is more than I can say for you. Did you enjoy your little game of lies? I hope it was worth it. I think it will be the last thing you enjoy. Ever."

"Watch her," the mage said to Valas as he stepped into the cell, Halisstra close behind.

It was obvious from the relieved look in Quenthel's eyes that she was glad to see him. Pharaun only smiled as he uttered a magical phrase. The collar around Quenthel's neck clicked open.

"Help her," he directed to Halisstra.

Pharaun then moved over to Jeggred, whose red, feral eyes glittered in anticipation.

"Your arrival was timely, wizard," the draegloth said, spreading his arms wide. "Free me so that I may rend the traitor and watch the life fade from her eyes."

"You will do no such thing," Quenthel said. Halisstra had helped the high priestess remove the gag. "Do not touch her, Jeggred. Do you understand me?"

Jeggred looked at Quenthel for a moment, but then the demon inclined his head in acquiescence.

"As you wish and command, Mistress."

Pharaun had but one more spell with which to unlock the restraints that held Jeggred, and he quickly utilized it to free one of the draegloth's arms. For the other bindings, the mage decided to cast a different spell, one that would suppress the magic that strengthened the adamantine. He quickly wove the dispelling magic and watched as the aura surrounding the metal faded from his sight.

"Try to break it, now," he said to Jeggred.

The draegloth jerked experimentally on the chains holding him to the walls, then he really leaned into the effort, but the adamantine links still would not yield.

Pharaun frowned.

"Perhaps a bit of cold, to make them brittle," he mused aloud, producing a small, clear crystal from his *piwafwi*. "Gather the lengths together in a group," he directed the draegloth. Jeggred did so, holding them in his free hand like a set of reins on a pack lizard.

Pointing the crystal at the sections of chain, the Master of Sorcere focused a cone of magically summoned arctic air along their lengths. When the incantation was completed, he gestured for Jeggred to try again.

This time, when the fiend began to work the restraints over, the frosty metal shattered, freeing him. He still had the collar and manacles around his neck and limbs, but that could be dealt with later.

"My thanks, wizard," the draegloth said, then strode over to where Quenthel was in the process of freeing herself from the last of the black, sticky, resinlike substance that her hands had been encased in.

Quenthel stood in the center of the cell, naked but seemingly oblivious to it.

"Do you make a habit of remaining maddeningly out of reach until the last possible moment, Mizzrym?" she said, scowling slightly. "You cut your arrival a bit close, didn't you?"

Pharaun sighed inwardly, realizing that whatever gratitude had been present before had been replaced by the high priestess's usual haughty demeanor.

"My pardon, please, Mistress Baenre," he said in as gracious a tone as possible. "We dallied with some of the local maidens as long as we could before rushing here at the last moment. I didn't think you would mind terribly much."

Ryld chuckled at the wizard's snide remark, while both Halisstra and Danifae gave him sharp looks, reminding him that the two members of House Melarn were unaccustomed to his disrespectful relationship with Quenthel. The Mistress of the Academy merely scowled at him then turned away to face Faeryl, who cringed, still under Valas's guard.

"Strip her and give her clothes to me," Quenthel commanded, eliciting a high-pitched squeak of protest from the ambassador.

Valas held the prisoner steady as Ryld stepped up to help him, and Halisstra jumped forward almost eagerly and began to disrobe Faeryl, who struggled to avoid the ignominious fate.

"Just who are these two?" Quenthel snapped, eyeing Danifae.

The battle captive cocked her head to one side, eyeing the high priestess in return, as though gauging how much she should defer to this new leader.

"I am Danifae Yauntyrr, Mistress Baenre, formerly of Eryndlyn. I am Halisstra Melarn's personal attendant."

"A battle captive?" Quenthel smirked, and Danifae merely bowed her head.

Quickly enough, Faeryl stood naked in the midst of the group, still held between Valas and Ryld, while Quenthel donned the ambassador's clothing. As the high priestess was dressing, she jerked her head in the direction of the collar, still chained to the wall where she'd been restrained only moments before.

"Lock her up," Quenthel commanded.

"No!" Faeryl protested, trying desperately to jerk free of her two captors. As Valas, Halisstra, and Ryld all corralled her, the ambassador shrieked and began to fight against her captors. "No! You can't leave me down here. . . ."

"Shut up!" Quenthel said, slapping Faeryl. "You sniveling, wretched creature, did you really believe you could get away with your betrayal? Did you honestly think you could defy me, a Baenre, and the Mistress of Arach-Tinilith? By the Dark Mother, child, the depths of your foolishness surprise me! Lock her up," she repeated, gesturing once more at the thick adamantine collar.

"No!" Faeryl protested again, struggling as she was hauled over to the wall.

The ambassador flailed and kicked, but the scout and warrior held her tightly as Halisstra fitted the collar around her neck. When the adamantine band clicked shut, the imprisoned drow sobbed once, and as soon as the two males relinquished their grip on her, she began frantically jerking on the restraint.

Quenthel started to turn away, then paused.

"You can redeem yourself, if you like," she said to Faeryl.

"How?" the frantic dark elf asked. "Anything! I will do whatever you want."

"Tell me where my things are," Quenthel replied. "Tell me where all of my possessions were stored when I was brought here."

Faeryl's face fell in despair.

"I don't know," she sobbed, dropping to her knees in supplication. "Please don't leave me here. I will find them for you."

"Don't bother with her," Halisstra said. "I know where your things are, Quenthel Baenre."

Quenthel turned and eyed the daughter of House Melarn.

"Why should I trust you?" she asked.

"That is for you to decide," Halisstra answered, "but consider this . . . I led your males down here to find you, I lured the traitor out into the hall before she could kill you, and I live here and can find my way around. While that would ordinarily be a strike against me, as I told the wizard, I have no quarrel with you, and I do not want to see you suffer the consequences for House Zauvirr's betrayal of my mother."

Quenthel's eyebrows raised as she listened to the other priestess's words, then she looked at Pharaun.

"She speaks the truth," the wizard admitted. "At least thus far. She has thrown herself in with us, though she has few alternatives. The other matron mothers, led by Ssipriina Zauvirr, are wresting control of her House away from her, after the death of her mother."

"Hmm," Quenthel mused. "Very well. We'll address your status later. If you know where my things are, lead on."

"Wait!" Faeryl cried out, lunging forward against the chain around her neck. "She will betray you, Mistress. All the noble

Houses despise you for your plans to steal from the city. You can't trust her."

"On the contrary," Quenthel laughed derisively, shaking her head. "She is a Melarn, a member of the only House in Ched Nasad I *can* trust. Let's go."

The high priestess turned to depart the cell, and Pharaun was stepping into the hall behind her as Faeryl wailed once more, "You can't leave me here!"

The ambassador began a chant, and Pharaun recognized the pattern of the words as a divine incantation, though he wasn't sure what sort of spell the dark elf might still have retained in her memory.

Before she could complete the invocation, though, Jeggred was in front of Faeryl. The draegloth flicked a hand out, across her face, slicing his long claws across one cheek and catching her by surprise so that she lost her concentration and the words of the spell died in her mouth, the magic lost.

Faeryl cried out, backing away and clasping her bloody cheek. She began to tremble, remembering all the terrible things Jeggred had done to her. She cowered from the towering fiend, folding herself into the corner, as the draegloth glared down at her. He did not raise a hand to strike her further.

Quenthel stepped up beside the demon, wrapped her hands lovingly around his arm, and smiled at the imprisoned drow.

"You know, Faeryl," the Mistress of the Academy purred, "You're actually right."

Faeryl only blinked at Quenthel, terror in her eyes.

"You said before that I couldn't leave you here. Sadly, it's true. There's no telling what other spells you might still have tucked away in that clever little mind of yours. Jeggred, my pet, repay her for the things she did to us. Take your time . . . enjoy the moment."

Quenthel strolled out of the room, along with Ryld, but Pharaun remained, as did Halisstra and Danifae.

Faeryl's first scream rang in Pharaun's ears, echoing in the small cell. The draegloth had not yet touched the ambassador, but as the wizard watched, smiling, Jeggred moved closer. Her screams rose in pitch, and they were suddenly silenced as Jeggred casually reached out with one large clawed hand and grasped her by the neck, just beneath the collar she wore, cutting off her air. Madly, Faeryl began to flail at the fiend, but he easily lifted her up and extended his arm out fully, so that the naked drow's feet rose off the floor, kicking at the air. She pummeled feebly at the draegloth's arms, and just as she was fading, Jeggred released her, watching as she crumpled to the floor, gasping for air. Before she could fully regain her breath, he reached down and poked a single claw up under her chin.

Pharaun saw that the talon penetrated deep into the soft tissue, probably through the dark elf's tongue, pinning her mouth shut. Faeryl squealed in pain, but it was a muffled cry. She reached up to try to pull the fiend's hand away, but he slowly, relentlessly began to lift her, forcing her to scrabble to her feet, clinging to his arm with both her hands to support her weight and keep the talon from plunging deeper, penetrating the roof of her mouth. Higher and higher the draegloth lifted, until at last Faeryl was on her tiptoes, frantically trying to lift herself off this impaling spike by her arms alone, tears streaming down her face.

Jeggred merely held her there, watching her squirm, using his two smaller hands to caress the ambassador. He brought his other hand up and flicked a claw across her exposed throat, slicing through her vocal chords.

With blood streaming from the gash in her neck, her red eyes wild with terror, Faeryl tried to scream, but all that issued from her was a muffled, wet gurgle. Jeggred laughed and let her dangle, unable to cry out at all.

Danifae and Halisstra turned away, but whether satisfied or disturbed at the fiend's display of ruthlessness, Pharaun was not sure.

He was the only one who remained in the cell, and he couldn't draw his eyes away from the scene before him.

Blood ran down Faeryl's neck and chest, and her struggles were growing more and more feeble. Finally, perhaps growing tired of this sport, Jeggred raked at her again, across the abdomen this time, slicing cleanly so that her entrails were freed. The fiend let her drop to the ground at last, and Faeryl crumpled at the draegloth's feet, though Pharaun could see that she was not yet dead.

The ambassador blinked in shock and occasionally thrashed weakly as Jeggred crouched down. When Pharaun realized the demon was preparing to feast, dining on Faeryl even as she lay there, still conscious but too weak to fight him, the wizard finally had to turn away. The wet sounds of the demon at his meal followed him out into the hallway.

Gromph Baenre did not relish the latest message he had to deliver, for several reasons. First and foremost, it was not good news, and however much he was removed from the source of the report, he was still the messenger. Ordinarily, he wouldn't mind for that reason alone, for there were few individuals in Menzoberranzan who could actually take out their displeasure on him, the most powerful mage in the city. Of those few, most held on to only a shell of their former power and were relying on him to conceive of a way to restore it. No, being the bearer of bad news this day would not be as risky as it might on other days, but then he didn't often have to deliver such unpleasant information to his sister.

That brought the Archmage of Menzoberranzan around to the other cause for his distress. Triel Baenre was at home, which meant that Gromph had to go visit her, rather than the other way around. He detested leaving Sorcere, detested having to go to the Great Mound even more, and certainly didn't like doing any of it under such circumstances. It was yet another reason for him to add to his list of reasons why he wanted the crisis resolved. He was tired of all the inconvenience it was causing him personally.

As he flew over the streets of Menzoberranzan on his way to the Great Mound, Gromph peered below in consternation. He had sent word to the appropriate individuals in charge that more troops were to be dispatched, but he had yet to see the results of his orders. The disquiet below was growing again, and if they weren't careful, the nobles of the city would find themselves right back in the middle of another uprising.

Well, Triel could put her foot down again, he supposed, insist that the other matron mothers respond promptly when the call came for more soldiers, but he doubted it would make them quicken their pace one whit. They were going to tend to their own Houses first, High Council be damned.

Approaching the edge of House Baenre, Gromph settled himself to the balcony outside his sister's audience chamber. The guards on duty there peered at him warily for a moment, but when they saw who it was, they stiffened in salute. Ignoring them, the archmage walked briskly past them into the council chambers themselves, hoping to find Triel there. She was not.

Clicking his tongue in exasperation, Gromph passed out of the large audience chamber and into the hallway beyond, which led to her personal quarters. Arriving at the door to her suite of rooms, the archmage was greeted by a pair of stoic females, robust specimens who were well armed and apparently trained equally as well in the art of combat as divine magic.

The pair of guards crossed their heavy maces before the door.

"She is not to be disturbed," one of them said, her stare flat, making it clear she would brook no argument, brother or not.

Gromph sighed, making another mental mark to the tally of reasons he hated doing this. No matter how many times he had to push his proverbial weight around to get to see Triel in her private rooms, the matron mother's personal guards never made it any easier on him the next time. He'd had enough of it.

"I'm not going to stand here and argue with you about this, today. You've got one minute to tell her it's me and let me through, or I will leave you as two piles of smoking ash on her doorstep. Do I make myself clear?"

The flat stares turned mildly baleful, but after some careful consideration, the one who spoke finally nodded curtly and slipped inside, shutting the door behind her and leaving her partner to stare icily at the archmage while he folded his arms and tapped his foot.

Just when Gromph was seriously considering whether or not to make good on his threat, the door opened and the guard appeared again, motioning him through. Arching his eyebrow as though to say, "what else did you expect?" he pushed past her impatiently and shoved the door shut behind him.

Triel was not in the front room, though that didn't really surprise the wizard. Usually, if she was going to bother to be presentable for guests, she would see them in the audience chamber. He figured his odds were about even as to whether he'd discover her in the bedroom or in the baths, most likely with a lover. He tried the bedroom first, with no luck.

Moving through into the bathroom, Gromph found his sister, alone except for a pair of attendants, eyes closed and soaking in an oddly scented oil bath. The odor permeated the room and made him cough.

Triel opened one eye and looked at the wizard, then closed it again, making no move to greet him.

"You really shouldn't threaten my guards like that," she said, a bit testily. "They're standing there to keep the likes of you out, you know."

"A thousand apologies, Matron Mother," Gromph answered. "I will be certain to avoid helping you in the future. Please do drop by sometime and I'll be sure to keep you waiting outside *my* offices."

This time, both of Triel's eyes opened, but instead of growing angry, she appeared worried.

"What is it?" she asked. "Your news must be particularly unpleasant for you to behave so boorishly."

Gromph had to chuckle, but it was a bitter laugh.

"You know me better than most, sister. I suppose I should give you more credit. You're correct, though, the news is bad, and it comes from several fronts. Our patrols are telling me that traffic is picking up on the outskirts of the city. Nothing definitive, but they're growing fearful that we're due for some sort of aggressive act from somewhere, and soon."

"What sort of traffic?" Triel asked, shifting in the bath so that an attendant could begin to scrub her back with a rough cloth.

"Hard to say. Enough species come and go as it is, but they have reported an inordinate number of troglodyte sightings the last few days."

Triel made a noise in her throat, and at first Gromph wondered if it was in response to the ministrations of the attendant, but he realized it was derisive when his sister said, "Troglodytes? They've never been able to muster any sizable threat against us. You came all the way over here and harassed my guards to tell me that? Please."

Gromph clicked his tongue in vexation and strode across the tiled floor to take a seat on a long bench along one wall.

"No, of course not, but don't be so quick to dismiss any potential threat. More than enough generals saw their last battle from underestimating the enemy. We're vulnerable to any attack right now, and you know it."

"Fine, I'll take it under advisement," Triel said. "So, what else do you have to tell me? I'd like to enjoy the rest of my bath, but if you insist on giving me more bad news, I don't think I shall be able to."

Gromph shook his head.

"Yes, there is more bad news," he said.

"Oh, wonderful."

"I'm hearing bad things from our expedition to Ched Nasad."

The matron mother rolled over and sat up, shooing away the attendant. She seemed unconcerned that her upper body was exposed to him, though Gromph ignored that fact.

"What kind of bad things?" she asked, her tone grave.

"The last communication I received reported that riots were beginning. I haven't heard anything since, and the next reports are overdue."

"How long?"

"Two days. I already relayed that information to you."

"Do you have a means of contacting him?" Triel asked.

"Yes, but not for a while, and not really for the kind of conversation I suspect you'd like for me to have with him. Even with what I *can* do, I'll have to make preparations to use the appropriate magic."

"Fine, do that. In the meantime, what are your thoughts?"

Gromph considered the question then said, "Do I believe they are alive? Let's give them some credit. They are an enterprising lot, and I have no doubt that they can take care of themselves. That's half the reason you sent them away, isn't it?"

Triel's eyes narrowed slightly as she stood and let the oil cascade from her body.

"I do want them to succeed," she said. "It aids us nothing for them to perish, regardless of whatever benefits we both receive for having a few specific ones out of the way."

She motioned for the attendant to bring her a towel and had it wrapped around herself.

Gromph's stare was carefully neutral.

"I want them to succeed, too," he said. "My issues aside, this crisis affects every aspect of my studies and pursuits. My point was, if they were ingenious enough to be considered a threat here, I think they can take care of themselves in Ched Nasad."

"Find them," the matron mother commanded, "and let me know when you do."

"Even if I have to threaten your guards again?"

"Even if you have to leave them as piles of ash on my doorstep."

Gromph nodded and turned away as Triel began to dress with help from the two attendants. The archmage stopped and turned back to face his sister.

"Oh, and one more thing."

Triel looked over at her brother and asked, "Yes?"

"Will you please remind the other matron mothers of the importance of timely response to threats inside the city? I asked for reinforcements for several specific sections three hours ago, and they were still not in place when I came to visit."

"Again?" Triel sighed. "Yes, of course I will speak to them again."

"You know," Gromph added, almost as an afterthought. "It would probably help if House Baenre spared some extra soldiers for the cause. A show of good faith and all that."

"Really? Do you think we can afford to spare them?"

"I know of two right outside this door who could be put to far better use," the archmage replied, giving his sister a last, meaningful stare.

🕷 🕷 🕷

"Explain to me again what you think I have to gain by trusting you," Quenthel said, gnawing at a strip of dried rothé meat.

The seven of them were hiding in a mess hall in an unused wing of House Melarn. Only Jeggred was no longer hungry, having sated himself back in the dungeon.

It certainly took Faeryl a long time to die, Pharaun thought, shuddering, as he sat watching the draegloth lick himself clean. The wizard was having a hard time blocking out the image of the drow, still moving, still watching, even as the fiend had begun to feast.

Ryld and Valas stood guard near the door, both of them obviously anxious to be on their way. The rumbles from beyond the walls had ceased for the moment, and Pharaun wasn't sure whether that boded well or ill for them. If the fighting had been quashed that quickly, it was only a matter of time before Ssipriina began searching for them again. He was eager to be away, too.

As Quenthel continued to inhale the food, Halisstra pursed her lips and tried again to defend her usefulness to the Menzoberranyr.

"I can get you out of the House without notice," she said. "I know the best routes to take. If we encounter any of Ssipriina's guards along the way, I might be able to dismiss them without incident. Until you're safely out of the city, having the two of us accompany you is to your benefit."

Quenthel nodded as she ate.

"Perhaps," she said, pausing to sip from a waterskin. "Or perhaps you would simply like to lead us into ruin in your own way, maybe by lulling us into trusting you so that you can betray us to Ssipriina. For all I know, you still hold me responsible for the death of your mother, or are at the very least angry about my intentions."

Halisstra rolled her eyes where Quenthel could not see, and Pharaun had to quell a bemused smirk.

At least I'm not the only one who finds her unbelievably irrational at times, he thought.

"Yes, all of that could be true, certainly," Halisstra said, "but then I wouldn't have had much to gain by helping to rescue you when Ssipriina already had you in her clutches, don't you think?"

"Hmm," Quenthel said doubtfully, another bite of food in her mouth. She finished chewing and looked over at Pharaun. "What's your opinion?"

The Master of Sorcere sat up straighter, surprised that she was seeking his counsel.

I suppose that when you're surrounded by the bigger enemy, he mused, the smaller enemy seems a friend.

"Well, thus far they've given us no reason to doubt them," he answered. "Except, of course, their heritage itself. Regardless of whether you're inclined to trust a dark elf you've never met—a dark elf of a House that you so recently intended to betray, at that—our options seem severely limited without their company. I don't suppose we'd be all that worse off, anyway, should they decide to turn on us at an inopportune time."

Quenthel made a face at the wizard.

"Are you thinking with the right part of your body?" she asked sarcastically, nodding in the direction of Danifae, who sat on a couch off to one side, listening to the discussion.

When she became a part of it, she lowered her eyes demurely and folded her hands into her lap.

Pharaun smirked.

"Oh, absolutely, Mistress Baenre," he said dryly. "Nothing would please me more than to have additional females along on this trip, all with a ready suggestion on how something should be handled or a friendly comment on ways I might improve my demeanor for the benefit of everyone around me."

Halisstra's eyebrows shot up in surprise, and the wizard remembered again that she was unaccustomed to his manner with Quenthel.

For that matter, he thought, noting the high priestess's scowl, Quenthel herself is unaccustomed to my manner.

Taking a slightly more conciliatory tone, Pharaun added, "With all due respect, regardless of which part of my body I'm currently using to contemplate this matter, it seems undeniable that we stand much to gain and little to lose by trusting them, at least for the moment. Ask me again in half an hour, and my answer might be markedly different."

Quenthel chewed her rothé thoughtfully, though whether she was mulling his point or whether she was considering whether or not to allow Jeggred to dismember him, Pharaun wasn't sure.

"In any event," he finished, "we can ensure ourselves some degree of protection by keeping them close, under our scrutiny. If they lead us into a trap, we might yet negotiate with Ssipriina Zauvirr . . . turn them over in exchange for our own freedom. Only if we don't tell the matron mother what happened to Faeryl, of course," he added with a grin.

Halisstra's flat stare told Pharaun that she found both his humor and his insurance plan distasteful, but Quenthel seemed convinced.

The Mistress of Arach-Tinilith nodded after tossing back the last bit of water in the skin.

"Very well," she said to Halisstra. "You will serve as our guide out of this accursed House, and if you serve us well, you will be rewarded with your lives. Do I make myself clear?"

Halisstra swallowed once, but she finally nodded.

"I think at least for the time being that your weapons and magical trinkets will stay safe and sound in our possession. If you behave yourselves, you may earn them back."

Both of the other drow nodded their acquiescence.

"Good, then let's be on our way," the high priestess announced, dusting off her hands after finishing the dried meat.

"Before we go," Pharaun said. "there is the matter of 'where' to discuss."

Quenthel looked at the mage.

"We are returning to Menzoberranzan," she said. "The expedition was a failure. Universally, Lolth speaks to no one, and the goods I had hoped to bring back with me to help us defend ourselves do not exist. We have nothing to show for the journey."

"Exactly," Pharaun countered. "We have nothing definitive to bring back with us—yet. I say we push ahead, continue to try to determine what is happening."

"But we have nothing to pursue," Quenthel argued. "We know little more about the Dark Mother's absence than we did before we left."

"That's not entirely true," Pharaun said. "As I mentioned before, the goddess's absence is not limited merely to our race. Regardless, I have an idea. While *we* may not be able to discern any more information directly, we could enlist the aid of someone who can."

"Who?"

"A priest of Vhaeraun."

Quenthel rose from the chair where she had been sitting, fury plain on her face.

"You speak blasphemous words, wizard. We will do no such thing."

Even Halisstra had recoiled at the suggestion, Pharaun noted.

He raised his hands in supplication and pleaded, "I know it's unconventional, but hear me out before you dismiss the idea."

Quenthel began to pace, and Pharaun knew she was at least intrigued, if not happy, with the notion. Her desire to claim the glory of discovery in this matter rivaled his own, he supposed.

"Just what is it you think a priest of Vhaeraun—" Quenthel formed the god's name with a grimace—"could do for us? And where would we find one who could—or even would—aid us?"

Pharaun leaned forward eagerly.

"We struggle to see inside the Demonweb Pits," he explained, "but perhaps another god would not suffer the same difficulty. In this instance, with the proper sacrifices and deferential behavior, we might just be able to ask for a little audience in order to find out."

"Few of his ilk would even consider helping us," Quenthel said, waving her hand in dismissal, "and we know of none to even ask."

As Quenthel turned her back on him during her pacing, Pharaun looked over at Valas and nodded in encouragement.

Tell her, he signed.

Taking a deep breath and nodding, Valas said, "I know one."

Quenthel turned to face the diminutive scout.

"What?"

"I know a priest of Vhaeraun," Valas replied. "An old acquaintance of mine, Tzirik Jaelre. I think he would be willing."

"Really," Quenthel said, eyeing Pharaun and Valas alike, as though suspecting that the two were collaborating. "What makes you think he would help us?"

The mage carefully studied the tabletop in front of him.

She is too clever for her own good, he thought, knowing that if he admitted his foreknowledge, Quenthel was as likely as not to dismiss the whole idea just to spite him.

"He owes me a favor," Valas replied. "At the very least, he owes me enough to hear us out, even if he refuses. I don't think he'll refuse."

"How convenient. Pharaun?"

The wizard looked up, pretending to be thinking about something else.

"Hmm? Oh, yes. Well, it is very convenient that Valas knows someone who fits the bill. I wish you'd said something earlier," he said to the scout, "but I guess we can't all conceive of these flashes of brilliance. If Valas vouches for his friend then I say, what do we have to lose?"

Quenthel opened her mouth, possibly to retort, by the look on her face, but she never got the words out. A shock wave far stronger than any they had felt previously coursed through the House, knocking them and most of the furniture over.

"By the Dark Mother!" Halisstra screamed, stumbling against a wall. "The whole House is coming down!"

F O U R T E E N

Ssipriina Zauvirr and several guests stood atop an observation tower overlooking House Zauvirr. Leaning against the balustrade, she stared out over Ched Nasad. Her abode was not far from House Melarn, but in that direction, the matron mothers could see very little but thick smoke. Despite the obscuring clouds, the fighting around House Melarn still raged, and the sound of it reached the matron mothers even high on the tower.

"This has gotten out of control," Umrae D'Dgttu said grimly, standing beside Ssipriina. "Your agent said nothing of this stone-burning fire when we agreed to this plan."

"Yes," Ulviirala Rilynt chimed in, pacing back and forth behind them, her numerous bracelets, rings, and necklaces clanking with each step. "I dislike the idea of so much destruction, especially right now."

"Nonsense," Nedylene Zinard scolded, also leaning against the railing very casually but with her back to the unfolding scene of ruin.

She seemed more interested in her lacquered fingernails than in the activity around her. "We knew going into this that we might have to be aggressive. If we are to remake this city to our liking, now is the time to act, and we can let nothing stand in our way. Not the other Houses and not our own misgivings. Sometimes you have to break a few lizard eggs to make an omelet. Sometimes you have to kill a few slaves to win the day."

"Perhaps," Umrae D'Dgttu said, her whip-thin frame belying her puissance as the most powerful cleric among them, "but this is unnecessary. You should not have summoned us to install you as a new member of the Council until you eliminated *all* of the Menzoberranyr. Allowing that wizard to weave his lies did not help your cause."

ShriNeerune Hlaund snorted. "The wizard's lies were inconsequential. Ssipriina was a fool to send her mercenaries out so prematurely."

"I did not do that!" Ssipriina retorted. "Someone else gave them the signal before it was time. I still held out hope that we could resolve the dissolution of House Melarn bloodlessly. These fire pots were not my idea either. The gray dwarves procured them from somewhere else without my knowledge."

"So you're saying that you don't even have control over your own House?" ShriNeerune sneered. "And you expect us to continue to back you? I should have known better than to support a merchant House."

Ssipriina's fists clenched, and she dearly wanted to strike the dark elf belittling her, but she held them at her sides.

"I'd be careful, if I were you," she snapped, staring coldly at the offending drow. "I'm still the one those grays answer to, and right now, we're winning. You could find yourself on the other side of the battle very quickly."

"Enough," Umrae said, stepping between the two of them. "What's done is done. Now is the time to fight, not argue. Ssipriina, did you bring it?"

Ssipriina kept her stare steadily on ShriNeerune's face for a moment longer, her eyes narrow in anger, but then she turned away.

"Yes, of course," she answered. "I have it right here."

"Then let's do this," the thin matron mother said, motioning for the five of them to gather together. "It's time to claim our legacy."

Ssipriina nodded and produced a small bundle wrapped in black silk. Undoing the covering, she revealed a crystalline statue of a spider, as black as darkness itself, broken into several pieces. The head and the abdomen were separated, as were two sets of four legs, one for each side of the figurine. The five matron mothers gathered around as Ssipriina held the cloth in the palms of her hands, the collection of parts sitting atop it, stretching her arms out for them to see.

"It has been many years," Nedylene said, reaching out with her lacquered nails and lifting one set of legs to examine them. "The city will tremble before our might. Let us begin."

"Hold them steady, Ssipriina," Umrae warned.

She took hold of the abdomen of the statue. One by one, the other three matron mothers each took up a part. They looked from one to another, and finally, when Umrae nodded, they fitted the pieces together, making the figurine whole.

"Quickly, now!" Umrae hissed, and Ssipriina wasted no time re-wrapping the completed statue in the cloth.

Already, the matron mothers could see that the bundle was squirming, growing larger.

"Hurry!" ShriNeerune hissed. "Throw it!"

Ssipriina did. She reached back and hurled the bundle out into the void, as hard as she could, and as one the five matron mothers watched the wiggling cloth tumble away from House Zauvirr.

The cloth fell away, and the assembled drow gasped as one. The statue had transformed into a living thing, a spider as black as the crystal it was born from, and it was growing rapidly in size. In the blink of an eye, it was the size of a rothé, and as it disappeared past the side of the web street it was still growing.

Ssipriina watched, awed, as the creature shot forth a string of webbing at the street, attaching a line to anchor itself as it fell. Then it was gone, vanished from their vantage point.

The five dark elves waited breathlessly, hoping to catch another glimpse of the thing they had created. The strand of webbing had jerked taut and visibly vibrated as it dropped straight down. Obviously, the spider was still attached to it. For a moment, there was nothing to see, though all five matron mothers strained to do so, anyway.

When the first black leg stabbed into view, feeling for a foothold on the web street, Ssipriina felt her heart skip a beat. The appendage was longer than she was tall. Slowly, delicately, the spider lifted itself into view, and all five matron mothers took an involuntary step back from the balustrade, even though their creation was dozens of yards away from them. It was as large as the street was wide.

"By the Dark Mother," someone breathed. "It's magnificent!"

The giant spider righted itself atop the street, and Ssipriina could hear the screams of those below, screams of terror as the spider was spotted. It began to scurry in the other direction, toward the masses of soldiers still fighting several streets away.

"By the Abyss," Umrae groaned.

"What? What is it?" Nedylene asked, worry in her voice.

"There is no link," Umrae replied, her eyes closed in concentration. "I can't control it."

❦   ❦   ❦

Halisstra could feel her sense of impending dread growing. While House Melarn had not collapsed all together, as she had so direly predicted back in her rooms, it had certainly shaken violently more than once, and to her senses, familiar with every hallway, chamber, and nuance of the dwelling, it seemed to lean very slightly to one side. As impossible to fathom as the idea was, Halisstra wondered if the place was still stable. She wanted desperately to get outside and see for herself just what was happening in the city. The drow couldn't imagine violence so potent as to be able to physically disturb House Melarn.

The dark elf priestess was leading the others toward her mother's chambers, where she was certain Quenthel's personal belongings had been taken after the Mistress of the Academy had been imprisoned. Though she would have some competition from Aunrae Nasadra, Ssipriina Zauvirr would certainly claim much of House Melarn's bounty for herself, including the high priestess's personal items, to keep as trophies of her affront to the city of Menzoberranzan, if nothing else. It remained to be seen if everything Quenthel Baenre had in her possession upon arrival in the city was still there.

The more she thought about the actions of Ssipriina and the other matron mothers, the more incensed Halisstra grew. Beyond the consequences of turning on House Melarn, they were potentially offending the most powerful House in Menzoberranzan. Plus, the course of action they had taken seemed to Halisstra to be a symbolic thumbing of the nose at the very idea of even *trying* to discover what was going on with Lolth.

At least Quenthel and the others are trying to figure something out, she'd told herself more than once since her entanglement with them. Lolth might value devotion, but Halisstra didn't believe the goddess expected her servants to sit back and wait for her to come save them, even if they showed overzealous dedication or sacrificed a thousand gray dwarves.

Truthfully, Halisstra had found herself wondering just what Lolth wanted.

Halisstra passed through a large intersection and turned down a new pathway, one even more lavishly decorated, if that were possible, with plush carpeting, murals, and images of House Melarn triumphs. They were entering Drisinil's personal quarters, and Halisstra was fearful that a large contingent of House Zauvirr guards would be posted to protect the chambers, insurrection outside or not. The dark elf's concerns were well founded, for as she rounded a corner, she spotted a squadron of troops milling about, blocking access to the door beyond, which led into Drisinil's private residence.

"What are you doing down here?" Halisstra demanded, hoping to throw the soldiers off-balance with her commanding tone. "You are needed on the parapets at once!"

"I don't think so," the sergeant said, eyeing the motley group following the First Daughter as he raised his sword and pointed it at her. "We received word that the traitor had escaped, and now you appear right here, conveniently for us. I'm afraid we have orders to kill you and anyone aiding you."

The soldiers fanned out, brandishing their weapons as they advanced.

Halisstra's first instinct was to bring her mace up to defend herself, but her hand was empty, for Quenthel had not yet permitted her to rearm herself. Danifae, who was at Halisstra's side, was no longer bound, but she had no weapon, either. Danifae did, however, carry a small knapsack with some of their other belongings. Quenthel had agreed to let them stop at Halisstra's chambers and pack a few things before departing, for if the House continued to thrash about like it had, there was no telling when they might have to evacuate, and there would be no better chance later.

Out of the corner of her eye, Halisstra saw her attendant falter a step, too, but before the soldiers could close the gap, a blur of yellowish-white fur flashed between the two drow, slamming into the front rank of troops with a deep, unsettling snarl and a whirl of arms and claws. There was a sickening sound of rending flesh before Halisstra realized that the draegloth, Quenthel's personal bodyguard, was the source of the carnage.

Halisstra's gasp of surprise came only after three of the soldiers, including the sergeant, went down screaming before the onslaught of the creature, their bodies horribly mangled and their blood splattered everywhere. Several other soldiers began to surround the draegloth, trying to stay clear of the fiend's savage claws, but at the same time looking for ways to press the attack. Jeggred crouched, watching his multiple foes as they swarmed around him, lashing out with their swords but unwilling to get in close enough to do any good. A handful were already backing out of the fray, producing hand crossbows.

Another figure darted past Halisstra, and a third, and she settled back against the wall as Ryld and Valas entered the fight. The larger of the two, whom she had found striking when they first came face to face, was wielding his greatsword in a manner she found comforting. The blade seemed light and easy in his hands as he carved half the face off of one soldier and spun to swipe through the midsection of a second enemy in the same motion. The diminutive one, on the other hand, seemed content to slink up behind one of the drow soldiers still trying to find an opening inside Jeggred's deadly reach. The guard never heard or felt Valas coming, and when the scout planted his kukri into the small of the soldier's back, a flash of energy accompanied the stroke. The soldier arched his back in agony and crumpled to the ground as Valas pulled his blade free and stepped aside, disappearing into the shadows again.

"Get out of the way, foolish girl, and let them do their work," Quenthel snapped at Halisstra from behind.

The daughter of House Melarn glanced back over her shoulder to where the high priestess was standing. She saw the wizard producing some odd ingredient or another, which she knew meant he was preparing to fling a spell. In front of him, a rapier seemed to dance of its own accord in the air, as though it was defending him from any foes who might try to get close to him. She pressed herself against the wall to allow him ample room then sidestepped her way back to where Quenthel waited. On the opposite side of the passage, Danifae was doing the same.

"No sense getting in the thick of things when they're more than capable of handling it themselves," Quenthel explained, scowling. "At least they're good for that, if nothing else."

Halisstra wanted desperately to ask the other drow how she tolerated such insubordination from the three of them, especially the wizard, Pharaun, but she thought it best to keep her mouth shut and stay in the high priestess's good graces. It might be a long while before Quenthel trusted her, and she didn't want to do anything to jeopardize that.

A hissing sound accompanied a long, thin sliver of ice that shot from Pharaun's fingertips and streaked straight at one of the soldiers, embedding itself in the back of the drow's shoulder like a deadly icicle. The soldier cried out in pain and stumbled backward, but too late. Jeggred, seeing his foe's attention diverted, darted in and slashed with his massive claws, ripping through the muscle wall of the guard's abdomen and smiling delightedly as entrails began to tumble out. The force of the blow was so strong that it spun the dark elf around. With a sickening *plop*, the soldier fell onto his back, gazing sightlessly toward Halisstra while the contents of his body leaked out around him.

"Hold!" a voice shouted from behind Quenthel. Halisstra turned, along with the high priestess, to see a whole new force of soldiers, who had approached from the direction Halisstra and the others had come.

"Wizard, do something!" Quenthel ordered, stepping back as the new soldiers slipped their weapons from sheaths and trotted forward.

Pharaun spun around, and seeing the new threat, he stabbed a hand inside his *piwafwi* and produced several small items. His dancing rapier swung around and darted forward, bobbing and weaving through the air in an attempt to hold the new squad, which was even larger in size than the first one, at bay. At the same time, Halisstra heard the wizard utter some word or phrase under his breath. Though she didn't understand his speech, the effect was immediate and impressive. A blinding streak of lightning shot forward from the wizard's fingertips and struck the closest soldier squarely in the chest. Immediately afterward, several fingers of the same bolt crackled again, fanning outward from its first victim to strike the rest of the dark elves.

Halisstra cried out in pain and flung her arm up to shield her eyes from the flaring light of the bolt, cowering against the wall and cursing the wizard for blinding her and making her vulnerable to the soldiers' attacks. Her vision swam for several moments with the afterimage as she groped along the wall, trying to listen for the sound of imminent attack, but nothing came. Ahead, she heard one last gasp as someone was wounded, and the sounds of battle faded.

When her vision finally cleared, she saw Danifae and Quenthel looking as dazed as she felt. Pharaun appeared proud of himself, and the entire host of House Zauvirr soldiers lay on the ground to either side of her.

"Damn you, Pharaun," Quenthel snarled, her hands on her hips as she glared at the wizard, who was a few inches shorter than the high priestess. "You warn me next time you intend to cast a spell like that!"

Pharaun bowed, and Halisstra wasn't sure if it was meant to be mocking or not, but he said, "My apologies. There wasn't time to warn anyone. They would have been upon us if I hadn't acted as swiftly as I did."

Quenthel sniffed, apparently not completely satisfied with his explanation, but she said nothing else. After a moment, Halisstra realized that the Mistress of the Academy was looking at her.

"Well?" Quenthel said. "Lead on. I don't want another horde of Ssipriina's lackeys finding us still standing around their comrades' corpses."

Halisstra nodded curtly and turned toward the door. She was careful not to stare overly long at any of the bodies of the soldiers Jeggred had dispatched. She reached the door and waved her brooch in front of it, allowing the magic to do its work and unlock the portal. The priestess stepped inside and beckoned the others to follow her.

The interior of her mother's chambers was gaudy and out of style for Halisstra's tastes, but she paid the decorations no mind. As the rest of the group filed inside, she gestured toward the rest of the room and the different doorways.

"Mistress Baenre's things are here somewhere," Halisstra said. "If we spread out, we can find them more quickly."

As if to punctuate the need for urgency, another rumbling vibration bounced through the House, and Halisstra thought she heard the fracturing of solid rock.

"Never mind that," Quenthel said brusquely. "They're in there."

She pointed through one of the doorways.

"That's the bedrooms," Halisstra said, slightly puzzled at how the high priestess would know they were in there. "Come on," she said, and the entire group followed her into the interior chamber.

The oversized bed sat to one side, a huge, round affair that could accommodate five or six drow and probably had on more than one occasion, Halisstra supposed. In addition to that, there were a number of couches, chests, dressers, and tables for furniture, and rich tapestries covered every square foot of the walls.

Quenthel trudged across the room to a point between two tall armoires, where a tapestry woven of black fabric glowed in phosphorescent hues of green, purple, and yellow with an image of a drow priestess. Halisstra knew it was supposed to be her grandmother, and she wondered why Drisinil had kept it. Halisstra certainly didn't intend to keep anything to remind her of her own mother.

"Here," Quenthel said. "Everything's behind here."

"Well don't touch it, yet," Pharaun admonished, striding up beside her.

He studied the tapestry for a moment then nodded to himself as though satisfied. He took hold of a corner of the weaving and yanked it off the wall. Behind it was only bare stone.

Quenthel's scowl deepened, but the wizard simply produced a wand from inside the folds of his *piwafwi*, waved it about, and uttered an arcane phrase. He pocketed the magical device and went back to studying the space as the others gathered around. Danifae stood near Halisstra, and the priestess felt her attendant press something against her hand. Looking down, Halisstra saw that the battle captive had procured a pair of daggers and was handing one to her, on the sly.

Oh, you clever girl, Halisstra thought. She quickly palmed the weapon and tucked it into the folds of her *piwafwi*, out of sight. Then she returned her attention to what the wizard was doing.

"Yes, of course," Pharaun said, as though he had recognized something that should have been obvious to him. "All right everyone, step back. I can disarm the protective wards and sigils that are here, but I cannot deal with the more mechanical trap that I suspect is also present."

"That's all right," Valas said. "If you can remove all of the magical protections, I might be able to manage the rest."

Pharaun nodded and began to gesture and mutter, finally pointing toward the space between the two tall armoires with a flourish. Halisstra supposed the wizard must have some ability to sense the presence of various spells, wards, and charms, for she could not see what he was working on and had never known of a secret portal anywhere in her mother's rooms. Pharaun gazed at the wall a moment longer after he was finished with his casting then nodded for the scout to give it a try.

Valas moved up closely to the wall and began to inspect it little by little, inch by inch. Halisstra wanted to get in close beside him, to see what he was looking at, but she dared not disturb his concentration. At that moment, yet another in the series of rumbles shook the room, and Halisstra nearly lost her footing.

"By the Abyss!" Valas yelled, waving his arms in an effort to avoid falling against the wall. "This is no good. I can't do this with all of the—"

The scout's words were cut off as the whole room suddenly lurched and began to tilt. Halisstra fell to the floor as the chamber was no longer level but instead tipped to one side, away from the wall they had been inspecting. She realized she was screaming as she rolled along the floor. The movement stopped, but all through the House she could hear the horrendous sound of fracturing rock, loud popping noises that sounded as if the whole world was snapping apart.

"We've no time! We've got to get out now!" Halisstra heard one of the males yell.

"Not without my possessions," Quenthel insisted, sitting up and trying to stand on the yawing floor. "Get that door open—*now!*"

Pharaun, who had actually begun to levitate to avoid falling down, nodded as the others left their feet—all except Valas, who seemed perfectly capable of maintaining his balance despite the tilt of the floor.

The wizard removed a soft glove from inside his piwafwi. He donned it and began casting again as the floor made several popping sounds and began to tilt even more. A massive, glowing fist appeared, twice as tall as Pharaun, floating in the air in front of the mage. Pharaun guided the magical conjuration with his own gloved hand, turning it so that the knuckles were aimed at the point on the wall.

"Get back!" Pharaun yelled. "I don't know what kind of backlash this will create."

There was more popping from the structure of the House—closer, the sounds deafening—and Halisstra found she had her hands over her ears. Her heart was pounding in her chest.

We're going to die in here, she thought. The whole house is falling apart, and we're going to be crushed.

The magical fist lurched forward and slammed into the wall between the armoires, smacking against the stone with a powerful crunch. The wall cracked in several places. Pharaun directed the fist to back up and go again.

Quenthel was beside Halisstra, grabbing her by the arm.

"When he gets that wall down," the Mistress of Arach-Tinilith said, "we will need to hurry. What's the fastest way out of here?"

Halisstra looked at the other drow helplessly.

"We're in the very heart of the House," she answered. "The most protected point. It'll take us forever to get out, no matter which way we go."

Quenthel scowled, but then she nodded and moved away.

The giant fist had slammed into the wall two or three more times, and the wall was about to collapse.

One more blow should do it, Halisstra thought as she felt the concussions of more cracking and breaking beyond the room. If it's not too late already, she added to herself.

Around Halisstra, the others were wide-eyed, trying to maintain their balance and eyeing the walls, ceiling, and floor warily.

The next slam of the fist finally did the section of wall in, and it collapsed in a pile of rubble. Behind it, a small chamber sat dark and dusty, filled with shelves containing a number of items Halisstra had never seen before. Quenthel pushed ahead of everyone else and strode—or rather hiked, for it was like walking up a hillside—into the chamber, snatching up a five-headed snake whip with a gleam in her eye.

"Yes!" was all she said as she held the weapon aloft, the five vipers hissing and writhing joyously.

Quickly, Quenthel gathered up several other items that obviously belonged to her then eyed the other things displayed on the shelves.

"No time," Pharaun insisted. "We leave now!" Turning to Halisstra, the wizard demanded, "Which way is out? Get us there, before the whole place falls!"

Halisstra shook her head miserably.

"We're as far away from the exits as we can be!" she shouted over the cacophony of popping, shattering stone. The room lurched again. "There's no close way out!"

"Then I'll make one," Pharaun shouted. "Which direction is closest to the outside?"

Part of the ceiling on the far side of the room collapsed, sending a shower of stone fragments and dust into Halisstra's face. She covered her nose and mouth with one hand as she flung her arm up to shield her eyes from the stinging shards of rock that pelted her. She couldn't think. She was going to die. There was no way out, no escape—and no Lolth.

Halisstra felt the wizard's hands grasp her arms.

"Tell me," he shouted, "which way is the closest way to the outside, regardless of walls?"

Halisstra shook her head, trying to focus despite the panic rising in her chest. She spied Danifae clinging to Quenthel as both of them held on to the edge of the broken wall leading into the secret room. Jeggred had his claws embedded in the rock of the floor and was clambering along it toward his mistress.

The closest outside wall . . . which way?

An image appeared in her head, a mental map, and she knew that her mother's chambers backed up nearly to an outside wall, which meant that the secret room Pharaun and Quenthel had discovered was very close to the outside.

Frantically, Halisstra pointed to the hidden room.

"That way!" she yelled.

Pharaun nodded. Scrambling on his hands and knees, the wizard headed in that direction, almost slipping and sliding back the other way as the room tilted again. Halisstra began to slide along the floor, herself and decided against trying to stop, instead bracing her feet against the far, lowest wall. She craned her neck around to watch the mage as he began yet another spell. He seemed to have an endless supply of them. He dug in his *piwafwi* and pulled out something too small for Halisstra to see, then he began to gesticulate wildly in the direction of the wall at the back of the secret closet. Before her eyes, a tunnel formed right into the rock itself, and after about fifteen feet, it broke through into space beyond.

"Come on!" Pharaun shouted to everyone as the whole House seemed to be one solid rumble.

The noise of the cracking stone was deafening, and Halisstra had barely been able to hear the wizard. The room tilted over even more sharply, and Halisstra realized that it was nearly sideways, with the new opening to the outside almost over her head. She began to float, lifting herself magically toward the impromptu exit, as the other members of the group did the same. As she reached the top and was about to pass through into the open air of the city beyond, she saw that Jeggred had a hold of Valas. The draegloth lifted effortlessly toward the hole, and it was at that moment that Halisstra remembered that Danifae could not levitate either.

The House Melarn daughter looked down desperately and saw her attendant, crouched in the low corner of the room, near the collapsed ceiling, scrambling to stay atop the shifting pile of rock as the room continued to tip over. Danifae's eyes were blazing with fury as she gazed angrily up toward where everyone else was escaping the collapsing dwelling. There was another excruciatingly loud snapping sound as more stone buckled and popped, and Danifae, still inside the destroyed remains of House Melarn, was falling away.

❂   ❂   ❂

Khorrl Xornbane was bloody and exhausted. His clan, gathered all around him, looked that way too. He had no idea how long they'd been fighting, but it was too long. They needed rest and water. They couldn't keep this up for much longer. Unfortunately, the captain of Clan Xornbane feared that the day would grow much worse before it got better. He hoped he was wrong.

Khorrl had already passed the word that his troops were to abandon their positions defending House Melarn. They had been besieged there for so long and had used up so many of their firepots that he feared the place was growing unstable.

I'm not going to lose my boys that way, he told himself.

The remains of his forces were reforming on the opposite side of the plaza from the House, and for the moment they were being left alone. It was hard to be sure how long that peace would last, though, because none of them could see very far in the thick smoke of the burning stone.

What Khorrl and his duergar could see told the tale clearly enough, though. The plaza was covered with the bodies of goblins and kobolds. Littered in between them were slightly fewer drow, though the number of dead dark elves surprised him. More dead gray dwarves than Khorrl would have liked were scattered here and there, too. It had been a hellish day, and it was far from over, the captain feared.

"Sir," one of his aides said, running up to Khorrl, "we've completely abandoned the estate. The last of the troops have formed a line from that corner—" the young gray dwarf pointed through the smoke toward the edge of a dwelling behind them—"across to the flank of our main position, there." He swung his arm across to the far right side of the plaza.

"Good," Khorrl replied, visualizing the battlefield in his mind, since he could no longer clearly see it with his eyes.

"Also," the aide continued, "there's another force of drow coming toward us, from that direction."

He pointed off to the left, where the plaza was joined by a large web street. It was, regrettably, the weakest point of Clan Xornbane's defenses.

"Friend or foe? Did you get a look at their House insignias?"

The aide shrugged and said, "Not in this smoke."

Khorrl sighed. He would have to send scouts out to reconnoiter the new troops. He said as much to the aide, who saluted him and started to turn away.

"Wait," the captain said, and the aide stopped attentively. "Get some boys up there—" Khorrl pointed toward the street one level above where they were currently positioned—"I don't want another swarm of those damned dark elves dropping in on us like they did earlier."

"Yes, sir," the aide replied, and hurried off to execute his captain's commands.

Khorrl sighed again and turned to call for water. From behind him there was a loud popping sound, a sound he knew too well—splintering stone. He spun back around and peered through the gloom of smoke in the direction from which it had come. All up and down the lines that protected the clan's position, the word was spreading, and it reached Khorrl quickly enough. House Melarn was burning to oblivion, and it was about to go over.

Khorrl shook his head, knowing what was about to happen. He hoped his aide was right and hoped that all his boys had gotten out of there. He lamented the ones who couldn't, for whatever reason.

The popping started again, and grew louder and more steady. He could feel the vibrations in the stone beneath his feet. He almost wished he could see it, but in a way, he didn't. It was going to be a deathtrap for anyone still inside.

The snapping, splintering sound of stone reached a crescendo, and there was one final explosion, a tremor that shook the entire street enough that Khorrl had to brace himself with his axe. There was a jerk, and the rumbling ceased. Khorrl knew the whole building had gone over the side, tumbling into the void.

A few seconds later, there was a horrendous crash from below. House Melarn had struck something. A heartbeat later, he felt the vibrations of the impact. It was subtle, but for that sort of vibration to travel through a web street and into the walls of the huge cavern, and back along the other web streets, the initial impact must have been devastating.

It might take out several more streets, the duergar mused grimly.

"Sir!"

It was the aide again, rushing up to his captain, his look wide-eyed.

"What is it?" Khorrl demanded, wondering what would so shake up the lad.

"A spider! A huge one, as big as a house! It's coming this way!"

Khorrl groaned, realizing just how much worse things had gotten. He hated being right.

FIFTEEN

As he floated up and out of the collapsing building that had at one time been House Melarn, Pharaun Mizzrym heard a cry of anguish below him. Looking downward, he spied Halisstra, still emerging from the gaping opening that led into the ruin of her mother's chambers. She was staring back down into the building.

For the rest of his days, the wizard wouldn't be sure what convinced him to do it, but sensing that someone was still inside, he made up his mind in the blink of an eye to cast a spell. Yanking off his *piwafwi* and tossing it to Ryld, he uttered a quick arcane phrase and began transforming himself into a loathsome and wretched creature. He had seen the horrid thing several times before and in fact had hunted them for sport a few times in his younger days. As he dropped back down toward the crumbling building, which was beginning to break away from the last of its moorings and drop into the space below, he changed from the handsome drow elf with the winning smile to a winged woman with scaly hindquarters. Though the form was repulsive, it did have one advantage over the wizard's natural shape: It could fly. Pharaun hoped his harpy shape would be strong enough to lift whoever was still trapped inside.

Halisstra seemed about to drop back down into the cavernous room, which was tilted completely on its side, but Pharaun grasped hold of her *piwafwi* and shoved her to the side. She looked up at him, startled, and gave a quick shriek of surprise and horror, even as she stumbled back. She fumbled for something tucked inside her own *piwafwi*, and the mage got the impression she had no clue it was him. She was about to attack him.

"Get up with the others!" he hissed, motioning with one of his clawed hands. "I'll go back."

He saw the flash of a dagger, and Halisstra relaxed the slightest bit, seeming to understand who the harpy really was. He filed away for later the fact that she'd secreted a weapon on her person.

Halisstra nodded and pushed herself up from the edge of the hole even as Pharaun folded his wings to his side and stepped over the opening so that he could drop through. Inside, he saw Danifae flailing madly atop a pile of rocks that had once been the ceiling, as the mound of rubble shifted beneath her. At that point, House Melarn was truly falling, and the two of them with it. He noticed that the rubble shifted and ground itself together as the building plummeted downward, grinding itself into oblivion. It almost seemed to be draining out of a hole below her, like some great hourglass. She was struggling to keep from getting sucked down with the stone, but her leg was wedged between two large blocks, and she could not gain a sufficient grip anywhere else in order to pull her limb free.

Pharaun sank quickly down to where the battle captive struggled, unfurling his wings at the last moment to slow his descent and come to hover beside the drow female. Danifae responded, reaching out to try to grab hold of the creature before her. Whether she realized it was Pharaun or not, she didn't seem to care. Pharaun extended his taloned feet in her direction and worked his way to within her reach. She was sinking ever deeper into the debris pit. It was up to her knee, and when it shifted, she arched her head back and screamed more in frustration than in agony.

The instant Danifae had a solid grip on him, Pharaun began to thrash with his wings, exerting himself to rise up and out, hoping it would be enough to remove her from her predicament. He felt the resistance—not just of her weight, but also of her trapped leg—but he tugged and flapped, working to free her. Finally, with one last heave, he felt the resistance give, and he was barreling upward, Danifae clinging tightly to his legs. He soared toward the opening as the room continued to drop, and there was a massive roaring crash and a blinding cloud of dust as he shot out through the widening hole.

Once free of the room, Pharaun realized he really wasn't flying upward at all but was hovering in place as the entire structure of House Melarn fell away beneath them. He saw it smash into a web street that stretched across beneath it, and when it struck the thoroughfare a glancing blow, the rubble tumbled around so that it was spinning as it fell. If they'd been a moment longer in freeing themselves, the wizard realized with a shudder, he never would have been able to navigate his way out of the hole. The room would have spun and tumbled with him and Danifae trapped inside.

Both of them watched for a moment, awed, as the massive stone structure plummeted downward toward the bottom of the city. Finally, with a sickening boom, it struck somewhere far below, and the concussive impact reverberated all the way up to where they hovered.

Pharaun was beginning to feel the strain of trying to fly while holding so much weight. Struggling to see through the thick, choking dust that had been stirred up, he eyed what was left of the web street where House Melarn had been, portions of it still aflame, and saw that chunks of it, too, were giving out. Instead of heading straight up toward that spot, he veered to the side, away from the worst of the damage. Where the calcified webbing broadened into a plaza it was still solid and firm. As he labored in that direction, another major section of the street fell away, following House Melarn to the bottom. What was left was just a ledge jutting out into space.

The mage pumped his wings, steering the two of them toward the firmer pavement, past the ledge, which extended perhaps ten feet from the plaza and was twice as wide. When he was over the plaza, he sank down quickly, flapping his wings to force himself to fall off to one side rather than directly on top of Danifae. The drow female dropped right where he'd set her down and sprawled there, drawing deep, ragged breaths. He settled down next to her, none too gently himself, and collapsed. Little points of light swam in his vision as he gasped for breath in the dust-choked air. His limbs were leaden, and he could do nothing but listen to Danifae's and his own panting.

"That was some rescue effort," Ryld said, floating down next to the wizard. "I don't know what sort of terror you're supposed to be, but please don't ever try to save me looking like that. I'm liable to kill you before I know it's you."

Pharaun opened one eye and looked at the warrior as he mentally ended the transformation spell and returned to his own form.

"Certainly not," he answered between gasps. "You, my friend, would just have to extract your worthless carcass from poor Danifae's predicament yourself, should you ever find it thusly trapped. You haven't the beauty to warrant rescuing."

The other members of the group were all settling upon the plaza now, and as Halisstra ascended next to her battle captive attendant, she seemed to crumple, covering her face in her hands. Pharaun supposed he could understand her anguish. After all, her home was sitting at the bottom of the chasm.

"I owe you a very large debt, wizard," Danifae said. "My thanks."

Pharaun, propped up on his elbows, inclined his head in acknowledgement, still wondering what had possessed him to try the stunt in the first place. He certainly would have felt no regret at seeing the female plunge to her death, but in the end, he supposed, it would have been an awful waste.

"I'm sure there are ways you and I can find for you to repay me," he deadpanned, his face smooth.

"Yes," Halisstra said, looking up. "We both owe you. I will make certain we find a suitable reward for you."

She attempted to offer a genuinely warm smile for Pharaun. The wizard nodded again, intrigued by the suggestiveness of the drow's offer. He eyed the battle captive again, wondering just how willing she was to serve as recompense for the fact that she was still breathing. The look in her eyes made it clear she was not pleased, but she didn't voice her displeasure as the Melarn daughter then leaned in to inspect her counterpart in what Pharaun thought was a decidedly affectionate manner. Danifae's leg looked badly cut and bruised but not too much the worse for wear.

Quenthel clicked her tongue in exasperation and said, "Now that everyone is back from the brink of death, I think it's time to leave this city. First, though, we must see if we can salvage our other supplies back at the inn."

The others nodded in agreement.

"Let's go quickly," Pharaun suggested, aware of the noise of fighting, invisible through the haze but definitely coming closer. "We don't want to remain here for any longer than we have to, I think."

Pharaun stood, dusting himself off and picking up and replacing his *piwafwi* from where Ryld had dropped it only moments before. He gazed out across the city, for the first time, really, and the scene took his breath away.

"We may already be too late," the wizard breathed, overawed by the devastation he could only partially see, as so much was obscured by a hazy glow, or cloaked with thick smoke. The section of Ched Nasad where House Melarn had been was alive with flames. Recalling that he and Danifae had just escaped perishing in the monumental occurrence, he glanced down to where Halisstra and the other dark elf sat huddled together. Halisstra looked stricken, staring off into the vastness of the city as her attendant huddled close to her and whispered soothing words.

"Yes," Quenthel concurred. "This will get worse, much worse. Everyone stay alert. Master Argith, give the two of them their weapons," she said, gesturing toward Halisstra and Danifae. "I think they've earned the right to bear them after getting us out of that deathtrap."

The weapons master pulled a black circle of cloth from a pocket of his *piwafwi*, unfolded it, and threw it down upon the stone paving of the plaza. It transformed into a perfectly round hole, large enough for him to reach into. He began rummaging around inside it.

"I think our return to the inn will have to wait for later," Valas said, pointing. "We're not in the clear yet."

When Pharaun turned his gaze toward where the scout indicated, he groaned. Scores of gray dwarves were advancing in a line toward them from out of the smoke, faces grim, crossbows and axes brandished. Their front rank had formed a shield wall, while the second row prepared to fire missile weapons. They were mere yards away.

"Look out!" Halisstra cried, pointing in the opposite direction with the mace Ryld had just handed to her.

A host of drow soldiers and priestesses appeared out of the thick smoke, surging forward to meet the duergar head on.

❀   ❀   ❀

When the fiery, smoke-choked estate finally ripped loose from the web street and tumbled into the vast depths of the city below, Aliisza looked on with a mixture of fascination and disappointment. She was certain the wizard was lost to her, yet she marveled at the capacity for destruction the drow displayed. They were tearing apart their own city, with the capable help of several other species. She wondered what any of them hoped to gain from it, but she didn't really care. She was just sorry she couldn't enjoy any more flings with the mage.

With her consort dead, the alu prepared to make her way out of the city. She had no more cause to be there, and delaying her departure any longer would only place her at risk, however slight. She would rather not have to confront a host of drow or duergar, and she certainly didn't relish the thought of large amounts of stonework falling on her.

Before she could follow through on her intentions to leave, though, Aliisza spied movement a little way down from where the palatial abode had been but moments before. She wasn't sure, for the air in the vicinity was choked with smoke and dust, but she thought—

There. Something was definitely hovering in the air, a wretched creature the fiend knew well enough—a bird-woman known as a harpy—and it had company, a second form gripped in its talons. The pair of them hovered in mid-air, struggling to stay aloft, and the harpy veered up and to the side, bearing its cargo with it.

As Aliisza followed the pair's progress, she caught more movement out of the corner of her eye and realized the harpy and the drow clinging to it were being followed. It was the wizard's companions.

The alu found herself laughing, realizing that Pharaun must be the harpy in a transmuted state, no doubt one of his many spells. He really was an impressive mage, she thought. Somehow, some way, the entire group had managed to free themselves from the building just before it collapsed and vanished into the bottom of the cavern, and along the way, they had picked up two additional members.

Aliisza moved cautiously closer, wanting to get a better look without being seen, and when she did, her eyes narrowed. That wretch Pharaun had rescued some tart, a beautiful drow who, despite her current disheveled look, was obviously a lovely catch for the wizard. Even as she watched, the mage transformed back into his natural form, collapsing beside the female, giving her the eye even as he caught his breath.

Aliisza was furious, watching the mage ogle the drow. She would tear that trollop's eyes out herself! She would—!

Shaking with anger, she prepared to swoop in and make good on her silent threats, but the rest of the group settled around the pair. Clenching her fists in fury, Aliisza restrained herself, but she wanted to know what was going on. Quickly, she cast a spell and began to magically eavesdrop on their conversation.

—must see if we can salvage our other supplies back at the inn.

Then let's go quickly, she heard Pharaun say. *We don't want to remain here for any longer than we have to, I think.*

Grinning, Aliisza ended the spell and flew off, still careful to avoid drawing attention. She had an idea forming, and she was pleased with herself for thinking of it.

❀　❀　❀

"Get off this street!" Ryld urged, pointing to a smaller thoroughfare that ran past a temple off to one side where they might avoid the worst of the clash. "Hurry!" the warrior commanded, sprinting toward the side street.

Pharaun heard the call of his friend and tried to turn and scramble toward the side street that Ryld had indicated, but the wizard wasn't quite fast enough to avoid the press of drow streaming past him. Instead, he was buffeted along for several feet in the opposite direction before he finally managed to slip off to the side, taking refuge against a set of large stone stairs leading up to some immense public building. A moment later, Danifae staggered alongside him, dropping to her knees and panting for breath.

"Where are the others?" the wizard asked her, admiring her curves even as the battle raged around them.

"Don't know," she gasped. "Were . . . right behind me."

"We can't stay here," Pharaun told her.

He began to look around for a better vantage point upon which to watch for his companions without being in the midst of the fighting.

The battle was raging in the plaza where Pharaun and the others had become separated. A duergar stepped up to the pair of them, smiled maliciously, and raised a spiked warhammer to strike at the mage. Danifae was too quick, though, jerking her morning star around and into the gray dwarf's midsection. The stout creature gasped as the wind was knocked out of him, and Pharaun took advantage of the delay to cast a spell. A wide but thin fan of flame sprang from the wizard's fingertips and caught the humanoid squarely across the face. The duergar shrieked and staggered backward, flailing at his burning beard. Others in the crowd shifted and moved to avoid coming into contact with the blazing creature, and finally the duergar fell off-balance and collapsed, unmoving, to the paved street.

"Come on," Pharaun insisted, taking Danifae by the hand and leading her, still limping from her ordeal back in the collapsing House, up the stairs to the top of the landing.

A pair of gray dwarves started to follow the two of them then stopped about halfway up, aiming loaded crossbows. Pharaun spun away and yanked his *piwafwi*'s hood around him, using the cloak to shield both himself and Danifae. Two bolts smacked into the center of his back, giving him a vicious sting.

He cried out from the pain, sinking down to one knee. Angrily freeing his magical rapier, Pharaun turned back to face the pair of duergar, mentally directing the dancing weapon toward them. The wizard managed to engage the first gray dwarf, but the second one scrambled past the enchanted weapon and clambered up the steps toward him.

A blur of fur and claws landed on the steps between the mage and his foe, and Jeggred sliced and gashed at the duergar, spraying gouts of blood in every direction. The humanoid staggered back from the draegloth's onslaught, his arms held up defensively as he was cut down. When the first gray dwarf saw the fate of his companion, he backed down the steps and fled into the swirling maelstrom of skirmishing below.

"Stay here," Jeggred said, bounding back down into the crowd. "I will get the others."

Pharaun considered whether to obey the draegloth or ignore the beast. He would be much happier, he decided, if he could get up on top of the building, but he knew that Danifae was unable to follow him, should he choose to levitate there. He decided to await the return of Quenthel's pet.

"Back in here," he said to Danifae, stepping into the deeper darkness of the entryway and pulling her in after him.

From there, they could watch the street below without being so exposed.

Danifae pressed against Pharaun, trying to remain out of sight, but the effect was very distracting. The mage found himself pressing right back, while at the same time wondering how he could be so easily diverted during such a time.

It's not like you've never enjoyed the feel of the flesh before, he chided himself.

Still, he was glad that she lingered there, though whether her contact with him was purely happenstance or calculated, he wasn't sure.

The two of them did not have to wait long. Jeggred reappeared after a couple of moments, with Quenthel right behind him. Jeggred cut a swath through the crowd with his oversized claws, while the drow protected the fiend's back. As the duo forced their way through the throngs, more than a few fell before the draegloth's fierce strikes. Finally, they reached the stairs and hurried up to the landing.

"We're here," Pharaun said, gesturing for Quenthel and Jeggred to join him. "We've got to get to the roof," he said, pointing over their heads. "We can see much better from up there, and stay out of the fray."

Jeggred nodded and grabbed Danifae. Together, they began to levitate upward, reaching a spot on the roof that overlooked the sea of clashing bodies below. Pharaun and Quenthel followed quickly. The four of them settled down atop the rounded surface and dropped low, wanting to avoid creating too large a profile against the backdrop of the city. Pharaun did a careful inspection of the city streets one level up, trying to ascertain whether or not they'd been noticed from there. It appeared that they had not.

"Do you see them?" Quenthel asked no one in particular, and Pharaun returned his attention to the scene below.

The battle still raged, but it was beginning to thin somewhat as the body count grew.

"Nothing," the Master of Sorcere replied, and Danifae also shook her head.

"The warrior went running that way," the battle captive said, pointing toward a side street on the opposite side of the square. "I think Halisstra followed him."

"Yes, I heard him," Pharaun replied. "I tried to get there, but the surge was too much. When the fighting dies down, we can try to reach them."

"What about Valas?" Quenthel said. "What happened to him?"

Pharaun replied, "I don't know, but he can disappear even when you're looking right at him, so I don't think he's in much danger. He'll show up when we need him most."

By this time, the duergar were beginning to overwhelm the force of dark elves, and when reinforcements for the gray dwarves arrived, what was left of the drow turned and fled. Pharaun watched, hoping the throng of duergar would give chase, but they seemed content to hold up and regroup.

That's when everything went wrong.

Five or six crossbow bolts snapped against the roof next to the wizard, and a couple of them actually struck him in the back. Only the enchantments of his *piwafwi* protected him, but he was getting damned tired of being hit. Danifae was not so lucky. One of the bolts speared her through the calf, and she growled in pain as Pharaun leaped up to shield her with his own body.

A burst of flame and light exploded only a few feet to the wizard's right. Fire swept over the surface of the roof where they crouched as a second and a third burst landed near the first. The wizard flinched, then turned to see where the new attack was coming from. What he saw made his heart sink. The attackers, whom Pharaun could see were more gray dwarves, were perched atop a web street one level above them and near the back line of the roof. They hurled more firepots in the drow's direction, and Jeggred roared in anger, hit by one of the incendiary pots.

"Damn it, Pharaun, you've led us into a crossfire!" Quenthel snarled at the mage. "We've got to get off this roof. Jeggred, shield me."

Quenthel turned to peer over the side, and Jeggred positioned himself to shield the three drow with his body as best he could. Part of his fur was smoking, but the draegloth didn't seem to notice.

"We can not stand here," he said.

"I know," Pharaun responded, examining the bolt wound in Danifae's leg more carefully.

It had struck the same leg that was already injured but didn't appear bad, having missed the bone and penetrated only the fleshy part of her calf. He snapped off what he could, and the battle captive gave a slight jerk.

Quenthel made a disgusted sound, pulling back from the edge.

"All of this commotion has attracted their attention below us," Quenthel said in a harsh tone. "We can't go that way."

"Then we'll go over the other side," the wizard replied.

He shoved what was left of the bolt through Danifae's leg and out. She hissed from the sudden pain, but bit her lip and stifled any more sounds. More crossbow bolts and firepots were smacking down against the stone around them.

"Is it poisoned?" Pharaun asked the high priestess.

In answer, one of the viper heads on Quenthel's whip rose up and hissed, "No."

More of the firepots slammed down nearby, adding to the roar of the fire, which was hot and spreading across the rock surface of the building.

"We'll be roasted rothé meat in a moment," the mage said. "Heal her so we can go!"

"Forget her," Quenthel replied. "Come on."

The Mistress of the Academy stood and moved toward the back of the building, still skulking behind the draegloth.

Pharaun looked back down at Danifae, shrugged, and began to stand. The female reached up and grabbed him by the *piwafwi*, a determined look on her face.

"Don't leave me here," she said. "I can walk. Just help me up."

Another pair of explosions erupted near her head, and she flinched forward as Pharaun took hold of her by the hand and hauled her to her feet.

"You won't regret it," she said, giving the wizard a brief but obvious look. "I'll be worth it."

Limping, blood flowing from the puncture, Danifae began to follow Quenthel and the draegloth.

"Jeggred!" she called. "Carry me!"

Pharaun realized his mouth was hanging open, and he snapped it shut. As he trotted after the battle captive, he saw Quenthel and the draegloth freeze, and he swept his gaze to where they were looking, at the back side of the building. Rising up from behind the roofline was an immense, chitinous leg of something all too familiar. The leg sought footing upon the rooftop, and two more appeared, followed by the head of a spider of massive size.

"Lolth preserve us," Quenthel breathed. "Where did that come from?"

The immense spider pulled itself into full view, scrambling ponderously over the back edge of the building, each step making the entire structure shake violently.

"Oh, no," Danifae said. "They didn't . . ."

"They, who?" Pharaun asked, involuntarily backing up a step.

Even Jeggred seemed anxious, watching the enormous arachnid, black and shiny, heave itself fully atop the building. Its mandibles clicked as it peered about, its multilensed eyes glistening in the firelight.

"And what did *they* do?" the wizard added.

"The matron mothers," Danifae replied. "They summoned a guardian spider. The fools."

Quenthel sucked in her breath.

"Indeed," the high priestess agreed. "We must flee."

Pharaun wanted to ask the two females what in the Abyss a guardian spider was, but at that moment, the arachnid spotted them, though they had remained quite still. It leaned forward eagerly, coming after them.

As one, they turned and fled over the side.

❀ ❀ ❀

As she reached the alley, following Ryld Argith, Halisstra turned to see who had caught up with her in the chaos of the swarming, fighting drow and duergar. Of the others, there was no sign.

"Come on!" Ryld shouted from up ahead, motioning frenetically for Halisstra to keep up with him.

Several duergar had followed them into the alley that ran alongside the temple and were closing in on her. She turned back for a moment, thinking to make a stand and drive them away, but a crossbow bolt snapped against the stone wall near the priestess, shattering and showering her with splinters. She turned again and ran, the gray dwarves pounding along after her.

As Halisstra caught up to Ryld, he fired his own crossbow once, to slow down the pursuit, and they sprinted along the alley together, weaving through the turns of the pathway, trying to lose their foes. The two of them turned one last corner and skidded to a stop. The alleyway ended at a solid wall, though one side was low, protecting some sort of covered porch.

"Damn," Ryld muttered, slipping his greatsword free. He turned back to prepare to face the oncoming gray dwarves. "Get ready," he told her, and Halisstra planted herself beside the warrior, her heavy mace feeling good in her hand.

"Why don't we just float up there?" she asked, pointing to the roofline as the first two duergar appeared.

The first of the gray dwarves wielded a wicked-looking, double-bladed axe, while the second had a heavy hammer that was easily twice the size of Halisstra's own mace. She readjusted the grip on her shield as the hammer-wielding dwarf advanced, hate gleaming in his eyes.

Ryld risked a quick glance upward before he stepped gracefully to the side, avoiding the first cut of the double-bladed axe and making a quick, neat cut of his own that the gray dwarf barely managed to parry.

"Only if we have to," the warrior replied. "No sense making ourselves a target for their crossbows."

Halisstra could see that though the duergar's weapon was larger, the creature was forced to put a lot behind each swing, while Ryld was able to sidestep and redirect his own weapon far more easily. Then the priestess was too busy thwarting her own attacker's strikes to watch the weapons master.

The first blow came low, aimed at her knees, and she dipped the shield down enough so that the hammer grazed it, scraping across as she spun back and out of the way to avoid taking the full brunt of the strike. The dwarf followed this with an uppercut swing, which Halisstra was forced to block with her weapon, again redirecting the hammer rather than trying to completely stop the swing. She brought her mace back around and waited, thinking to let her enemy tire himself by repeatedly over-swinging.

That was all good in theory, Halisstra realized, but when three more duergar appeared, she knew that she and Ryld had been cornered. This time, when the dwarf over-swung and she deflected the blow with her shield, she also kicked out, catching the gray dwarf with her boot in the side of his knee. The humanoid grunted and staggered backward a couple of steps, but another dwarf was there, ready to step into the fray. Halisstra moved to position herself next to Ryld again, working so that each of them could protect the other's flank, preventing the gray dwarves from getting inside their position.

Out of the corner of her eye, she saw Ryld, still battling with the gray dwarves. One of the humanoids lay dead at his feet, while another had a bloody gash across his thigh. Behind them, two more had appeared, and these had crossbows, which they brought to bear, waiting for openings to shoot at the two drow.

One of the duergar nudged his companion and pointed to the priestess. Together, they swung their crossbows around to put her in their sights, and Halisstra took refuge behind her shield. She felt one bolt strike her shield, but the other embedded itself in her shoulder. She grunted in pain and staggered backward, unable to keep her shield raised high enough for solid protection.

Another gray dwarf circled to Halisstra's shield side, seeing that her defenses were down, and brought his axe high for a new strike. She did her best to spin and face the duergar without exposing Ryld's flank, and she managed to parry the blow with her mace, but the crushing force of it made her stumble to one knee.

"Ryld! Help me!" she cried out, and as though sensing she was in trouble, the warrior was in front of her, battling all four of the foes at once.

The priestess risked a glance over at the gray dwarves who were reloading their crossbows. They were also pointing at her and grinning. Or rather, they were pointing over her head, Halisstra realized.

The priestess's heart sank as she took a peek above. More of the gray dwarves had already taken the roof, and these had thrown nets across the opening while she and Ryld had been engaged in the battle. They were trapped inside the alley, unable to escape. The duergar on the roofs also had crossbows, and as one of them fired at her, Halisstra flinched. The crossbow bolt whisked across her face, grazing her cheek. She felt wetness.

"Ryld!" she cried out as she stumbled to her feet again. "They're above us, too. We're trapped."

The warrior never acknowledged Halisstra's cry, so busy was he fending off four duergar. Slowly, he was being forced back, bloody gashes across his body, having to retreat a little at a time to keep the gray dwarves from surrounding him.

Gritting her teeth, Halisstra tested the end of the crossbow bolt that protruded from her arm and almost wretched from the pain that doing so produced. Her shield arm useless, the priestess rose to her feet anyway, gripping her mace and moving next to the warrior once more. She tried to stay beside him, to guard his flank and enjoy a similar protection.

One of the four gray dwarves was dead, but Ryld was breathing heavily. A duergar slipped around to Halisstra's side, trying to get inside her defenses. She swung her mace hard and caught the duergar closing in on her on the shoulder, feeling the satisfying crunch of metal on bone. The gray dwarf growled in anguish as he dropped his axe and fell back out of Ryld's reach.

Two more stepped in to take the wounded one's place, and Halisstra had to press in too closely to Ryld to avoid being struck down. Her movement hampered the weapons master's ability to fight, and he took a cut across his forearm as a result.

"By the Dark Mother," Ryld snarled, whipping Splitter around to cleave the offending gray dwarf's head completely off.

The body flopped to the ground as the head rolled away, past another duergar, who watched it pass him with a look of horror on his face.

Another crossbow bolt clacked against the stone of the street near Halisstra, and two more struck her armor, bouncing off. Ryld jerked as a bolt flew close to him, but he never turned his attention away from his adversaries, never deviated from his fluid motion and quick, precise strikes. Still, he and Halisstra were being backed into a corner, the priestess saw, and they would make easy prey for the snipers on the roof.

The first firepot exploded right behind Halisstra, making her jump and nearly get her head taken off by an axe. She scrambled away from the flames as she warded off another blow from the axe-wielding enemy in front of her with her mace, feeling the vibration of the blow all the way up her arm. Two more of the flaming contraptions smacked against the end of the street, the clay pots shattering and spilling fire everywhere. She risked a glance up and saw another one hurtling toward her. Somehow, her wounded shoulder screaming in agony, she managed to bring her shield up with both hands and deflected the pot so that it skipped off and hit the pavement between her and her opponent.

The gray dwarves fighting with them began backing up, and Halisstra saw that the duergar on the roof were creating a fire screen to seal her and Ryld off, trap them between the flames and the wall. She knew that they intended to pin the two drow down, and pick them off at their leisure. There was nowhere for the dark elves to go. They were going to die.

Chapter

SIXTEEN

The second time he got no reply from the distant wizard, Gromph slammed his fists down atop his bone desk in frustration. Two sendings, and nothing. What had happened to Pharaun? Why wouldn't he answer? The Archmage of Menzoberranzan rose up and began to pace.

Two different spies had already contacted him with reports of heavy fighting in Ched Nasad. The matron mothers were squabbling over something, it appeared, and like it or not, the team from Menzoberranzan appeared to be in the thick of it, but Gromph couldn't get any confirmation from the team itself. He considered whether or not he should try one last time.

Realizing he couldn't force the wizard to answer—Pharaun might be receiving the magical whispers and was simply unable to reply—Gromph decided against any further waste of magic. It was possible that Pharaun was unwilling to give himself away in the company of others who didn't know the full extent of what he was up to.

Or he's dead, Gromph thought.

It was a possibility, however unlikely that seemed. Pharaun Mizzrym had a knack for keeping himself out of the worst sorts of trouble, and coupled with Quenthel and the others, the archwizard had a difficult time imagining that they'd succumbed to whatever violence inundated the streets of the City of Shimmering Webs. Still, it wasn't impossible.

If the team was dead Gromph felt no remorse.

Gromph sighed and reached into one of the drawers of his desk, extracting a scroll tube. Pulling the bundle of rolled parchment free of the tube, he found the page he was looking for and tucked the others away again. Spreading his selected sheet out on the desktop, the archwizard took a deep breath and scanned through the spell once before preparing to cast it. He was just about to begin the incantation to try once more to reach the wizard when a thought struck him.

Just because he'd been communicating exclusively with Pharaun didn't mean he had to continue that way. Why not try some of the other members of the team? It was possible Pharaun was dead or incapacitated, but that didn't necessarily mean that all of them were. Quenthel was the most likely choice, but he didn't relish the thought of talking to her. Who would his next choice be? Ryld Argith.

Nodding to himself, Gromph read through the arcane words on the scroll, weaving the magic that would allow him to contact the warrior. He completed the phrases and felt the magic coalesce.

"Ryld, this is Gromph Baenre. No word from Pharaun. Give me an update on the situation. Whisper a reply at once."

Gromph sat back and waited for a response. It was deathly quiet in his secret chamber. If Ryld Argith answered, the archwizard would undoubtedly hear it. The silence seemed to stretch on, and Gromph was just about to throw up his hands in frustration and despair when the reply came. When he heard it, his blood actually ran cold.

I'm separated from Pharaun and the others, don't know where they are. Duergar are everywhere. The whole city is burning. We're cut off, no way—

Gromph slumped in his chair, sighing long and loudly, shaking his head in displeasure.

Triel is going to spit rocks when she hears this, he thought. How long can I hold off telling her? On the other hand, maybe Quenthel is dead.

The archmage caught himself smiling as he rose from his desk to go find his sister.

As Pharaun ended his descent at the steps of the building, he could see a sizable force of duergar, waiting and watching. Without hesitating, he took a couple steps forward then crouched and smacked his hand against the stone, summoning a sphere of darkness. Quickly, he retreated back up the steps just as Jeggred settled to the ground next to him, with Quenthel on his other side. A couple crossbow bolts whizzed by, but he ignored the missiles, motioning the other three to move into the protection of the porch where he and Danifae had taken refuge before. It was a small space, especially with the draegloth in attendance, but they all fit and when crouched down were at least partially shielded from the duergar on the street below. More importantly, they were out of sight of the spider.

Danifae sank to the stone floor, and the wizard could see that she was bleeding steadily from the wound in her leg. The battle captive opened her own pack and pulled out a strip of cloth. Wrapping the makeshift bandage around her leg, she held it there as Pharaun assisted her by tying it off. Quenthel looked on impassively.

Pharaun stole a glance at Quenthel and signed, where Danifae could not see, *If you heal her, we can move much faster.*

Quenthel shrugged and replied, *She is not a necessary part of this group. I will not waste the magic on her. There might not be any left later for you, if I did.*

Pharaun pursed his lips, wondering what it would take to convince Quenthel that the battle captive was an asset they could not do without. He turned his attention back to Danifae.

"Can you walk on it?" he asked her.

"Yes," she answered. "I can keep up."

"We will not wait for you, if you cannot," Quenthel said sharply, "and I will not permit Jeggred to be slowed down by carrying you. Do you understand?"

"Yes, Mistress," Danifae said.

Pharaun saw that her eyes narrowed a bit. He gestured with his palms down where Quenthel could not see, indicating for Danifae to be patient. He was not about to abandon her, even if he knew full well that she was playing upon his desires just to save her own hide.

At that moment, a single massive spider leg settled on the stone between the alcove and the shield of magical darkness that the mage had summoned, and a portion of the arachnid's body hove into view. It was the underside of the creature, Pharaun noted, holding his breath as he felt the tremor of it settling its weight on the web street. Beside him, the two females were wide-eyed, and Jeggred watched the scene warily, but none of them moved. As the spider glided down and away from their hiding place, the wizard sighed softly in relief. It had not noticed them.

Out beyond the protective blackness, Pharaun could hear the shouts of duergar—cries of terror—as the spider moved quickly away from the building where the mage and his companions were hiding. The vibrations of its steps grew ever softer as it departed.

Good, Pharaun thought. Chase them for a while.

"What in the Abyss is a guardian spider?" he asked aloud.

Danifae shrugged and said, "I don't know as much about them as Halisstra. You'll have to ask her if you want the details, but I can tell you that the matron mothers have, in the past, brought these creatures forth for various purposes. They must have conjured one today, maybe to turn the tide of the fighting."

Quenthel sighed and shook her head.

"Madness," she said quietly. "The matron mothers of this city pick the most foolish time to war with one another."

"I wouldn't limit the appellation of foolish solely to the matron mothers of *this* city," Pharaun muttered under his breath.

Quenthel glanced at him, but he simply smiled, and she turned her attention back to the unseen ruckus beyond the sphere of darkness, apparently not having clearly heard his remarks.

"Dispel the darkness," the high priestess ordered the wizard. "I want to see what's happening."

As I said, Pharaun thought, shaking his head.

Sighing, the mage gestured and the sphere of blackness vanished, revealing the street beyond. The spider was out of sight for the moment. In the street, nothing moved, though there were plenty of dead strewn about, duergar and drow alike.

"It seems to have wandered off," Quenthel observed, rising to her feet. "We should be going, too, before it comes back."

"Let's give it another couple of moments," Pharaun suggested, still unnerved at the appearance of the giant creature. "Just to make sure it's completely gone."

Quenthel scowled at the wizard then turned to the draegloth and said, "Go see."

Smiling, the fiend bounded out from their hiding place to peer in both directions.

At that moment the duergar chose to come out of hiding.

Scores of them poured out from around the corner and from the building across the street, as though they had been waiting for the drow to emerge from their hiding place.

"Get 'em!" one of the gray dwarves shouted.

The duergar formed up a semicircle, surrounding the dark elves' position, and Jeggred leaped back into the alcove as the first volley of crossbow bolts peppered the walls around them.

Cursing, Pharaun ducked low, using the elevation of the porch as a screen. He pointed his finger toward the street and spoke the arcane phrase that would trigger one of his spells. At once, a cloud of roiling smoke, shot through with white-hot embers, formed beneath him and began to flow away from the building and across the street. The duergar, many of whom had their crossbows loaded again and were aiming at the small group, eyed the fiery haze warily as it appeared and began to churn toward them. As it reached those in the front ranks and engulfed them, they began to scream and flail, scorched by the embers.

Gray dwarves fell back before the cloud as it burned their kin where they stood. The smoke was thick and black. It moved away from the building, and the screams of the duergar intensified as more and more of them succumbed to the scorching heat.

Pharaun crept out a little way to watch his handiwork. Jeggred stood beside him, unafraid of a stray missile, eyeing the cloud with delight.

"Can any of them survive?" the fiend asked.

"Not if you go dance among them," the Master of Sorcere replied. "The fire can't hurt you, right?"

"That is correct," the draegloth answered, and he bounded into the smoky fog.

The incendiary cloud had pushed across to the opposite side of the street. Bodies of duergar were scattered across its surface, charred and smoking. Several of them were openly burning. Jeggred emerged from within the roiling smoke, which Pharaun redirected to flow down the street, in the direction opposite they wished to go. It would continue of its own accord for some minutes before dissipating, ensuring that another horde of the enemy couldn't come up behind them. The draegloth was dripping with blood but had a very satisfied look on his face. He had an amputated arm in his hand and was chewing on it as he trotted back to where the three drow were crouched.

Pharaun studiously ignored the fiend's dining habits as Quenthel asked, "Are they all dead?"

"Either dead or running," the draegloth answered. "The street is clear."

"Then we should proceed. The spider could return at any moment, and we have no time to waste. Where did you say the others went?" the high priestess asked Pharaun.

The wizard pointed toward the alleyway where he had seen Ryld vanish moments before.

"The weapons master went in there," he said. "It's possible that one or both of the others joined him."

Before Pharaun could take more than a couple of steps, though, the street heaved and shook.

"Damnation!" he heard Quenthel cry out, and the mage risked a glance back.

The spider had spotted them and was skittering along the street, easily stepping over the roiling cloud of flame Pharaun had sent in that direction. The arachnid came toward them, and fast, its mandibles flexing eagerly.

Pharaun turned and fled from it.

❧   ❧   ❧

"I'm telling you, I want that thing killed, now!" Ssipriina Zauvirr screamed. "If you don't do it, we are all in a midden heap of trouble!"

She loomed over Khorrl Xornbane as the two stood on the steps of an upscale fashion shop, abandoned in the fighting, situated in the interior of the gray dwarves' position on the plaza. The shop was well back from the lines of battle, but Khorrl could plainly see the spider in the distance as the matron mother pointed at it. The massive creature clambered over a building near where Clan Xornbane was locked in a pitched battle with a force of antagonistic drow.

"And *I'm* telling *you*, I'm not sending my boys to fight that thing!" Khorrl snarled back, losing patience with this haughty dark elf. "You hired me to win you a seat on your blessed council by defeating your adversaries, not to clean up your mistakes. You and your cronies brought it here, so you and your cronies can figure out how to stop it. It's not my fault you can't control it!"

"*My* mistakes? Let's talk about mistakes, Captain. Let's talk about you and your mercenary rabble taking to the streets prematurely, ruining my well-laid plans for ascension to the Council in one foolish moment. Mistakes, indeed! We wouldn't even be in this position if you had followed simple orders."

Khorrl wanted to slice the offensive drow in half right then. If she hadn't brought a retinue of bodyguards with her, he would have, but he was outnumbered, and he knew that even if he got in the killing blow he would be taken down shortly thereafter. Instead, he squeezed his grip on his axe and sucked in a deep breath, trying to still the trembling rage that coursed through his body.

"Prematurely?" he said through clenched teeth. "I received direct orders from your boy Zammzt. If he didn't have the word from you, go talk to him. Either way, *stop wasting my time!*" he finished with a roar. "I am not sacrificing my lads needlessly to kill your spider. In fact, we're done, here.

"Forghel!" he called out, looking for his aide. "Forghel, sound the retreat. We're pulling out."

Khorrl knew he played a dangerous game, turning his back on the dark elf, but he wanted to bait her, see if she would lose her temper.

"Liar!" Ssipriina screamed once more. "Don't you blame your foolish gaffes on my House. You will not abandon your—Don't you walk away from me!

"To the Abyss with you. *Kill him!*" she screamed.

Smiling to himself, Khorrl gave a shrill whistle, and instantly, a host of his boys banished their invisibility and magically appeared, surrounding him, axes and crossbows ready. The captain turned back to face the advancing retinue of drow, looking specifically for Ssipriina.

The dark elf's bodyguards had begun to chase him down, but when the additional duergar materialized, the drow soldiers faltered a moment. That was all the Clan Xornbane troops needed. Charging forward, Khorrl's boys took the fight to the drow.

Of course, Ssipriina Zauvirr was not foolish enough to remain too close to the fighting, but she gave the captain one last baleful glare as she turned and retreated back down the steps in the opposite direction.

Grabbing up a crossbow from one of his gray dwarves who was standing close to him, Khorrl sighted down the weapon, taking aim at the withdrawing matron mother. He fired, but the bolt clacked loudly off a stone column at the corner of the building as Ssipriina rounded it and disappeared. She would be back, though, the captain knew, and she would bring more of her damnable soldiers with her.

"Sir, look," Forghel said, running up beside Khorrl.

The captain turned and looked back the way his aide was pointing, and his heart sank. The immense spider was positioned in the middle of the street, rearing up on its back legs, while its front appendages fluttered oddly in the air. A bluish line appeared in the air, as tall as the spider itself, and widened into an odd-shaped field of blue light.

A second spider stepped through the magical opening, equally as large as the first. It had somehow summoned a mate.

※ ※ ※

Ryld was growing tired. He didn't know how much longer he could defend himself and Halisstra from the crowd of gray dwarves that slowly, inexorably, pressed in at them from all sides. He knew he was running out of room to retreat. Soon, he would find his back against a wall, and there would be no more running.

Fire began to spill from above. The clay pots exploded all around him, and he knew it was only a matter of time before one of them found him.

Well, this is a fine way to go, the weapons master thought, ducking beneath a badly overswung hammer strike and cutting the duergar across his midsection. Backed into a corner in an alley, trapped like a rat in a cage, and burned to death. Well, you wanted to get out of Menzoberranzan and find a little excitement, fool. I guess this will have to do.

Surprisingly, the gray dwarves backed away from him, maintaining their guard as they retreated, and Ryld let them go. He was breathing heavily, his lungs feeling scorched from the acrid smoke that was all around him. A dozen or more insignificant gashes covered his arms and torso, burning like the stings of a viper.

If they don't want to fight, I'm not going to argue with them, he thought gratefully.

He kept his sword level as a threat but risked a quick glance up to the rooftops.

Sure enough, just as Halisstra had claimed, more of the foul dwarves had stretched netting across the way, preventing the two of them from escaping by that route. Ryld was certain he could pick them off with his crossbow but not if he had to dodge ground troops and firepots at the same time. He saw the duergar overhead hurl several more of the horrid things down, but instead of aiming at him, they threw wide, so that the bursts of flame erupted between Ryld and his foes on the ground.

They're trying to seal us in, the weapons master realized. Trap us and kill us without risk to themselves.

He was judging the width of the flames, trying to determine if he could leap across them without burning himself too much, when he realized that Halisstra was speaking to him.

"Ryld," the priestess was saying. "Ryld, I can get us out of here."

The warrior glanced over at her, ignoring the taunts and jeers from above as the duergar took their time, savoring the moment before dispatching the dark elves.

"How?" he asked.

"I can cast a spell," Halisstra replied. "A magical doorway that will get us out of here, but you've got to buy me some time!"

"Ah, Pharaun's favorite trick," Ryld replied. He eyed the low wall that was behind the two of them, and he pointed to it.

"Get over that," he said. "We'll be better protected from above and can decide what to do."

Without waiting for her to follow, Ryld levitated upward until he was at a height just above the top of the wall, which had originally been slightly over his head. He quickly stepped across it to the other side and lowered himself once again. Halisstra, her shield arm hanging limply at her side, was only a heartbeat behind him. She tumbled into the corner with a grunt of pain as Ryld watched for pursuit.

When the duergar saw where the two drow were going, they began yelling in rage. From above, they began to fling more of the firepots down, trying to target the two dark elves, but Ryld pulled Halisstra inside the protection of the covering that hung partially out over the enclosed area. There was a door in the wall to his back, but it appeared stout. He tried it, and as he suspected, it was locked. Several of the firepots had landed inside the little courtyard, but the warrior and the priestess were far enough back away from them that they were in no danger.

"Won't they ever run out of those things?" Halisstra complained as Ryld saw a hand grasp the top of the wall.

Pulling out his crossbow, he waited until a head appeared then fired, catching the gray dwarf directly in the face. The humanoid shrieked and toppled backward.

"Eventually," he replied, reloading, "but let's not stick around to see how long."

"Where should we go? We want to be able to find the others again, right?"

"Yes. We need to get to—"

Ryld cut his words off short as several screams erupted from the other side of the wall. It was only then that he realized that firepots were raining down on that side rather than on theirs.

"What the—?" he said, and scooted forward to the edge of the overhang.

Cautiously, he peered up to the roofline. It appeared that the duergar who had been there were gone. Then, in an instant, he spotted a drow form rise up just long enough to fling another firepot down before ducking out of sight again. Ryld began to laugh.

"What is it?" Halisstra asked, moving up beside the Master of Melee-Magthere. "What do you see?"

"It's Valas," Ryld replied, pointing. "He's taken care of our snipers for us."

Ryld placed his fingers in his mouth and gave a shrill whistle. A similar whistle emanated from above a moment later.

"He knows we know he's up there," Ryld said. "Let's save your spell for later and go join him."

Halisstra nodded.

"Before we go," the weapons master said, crouching beside the priestess, "let me see your arm."

He examined the bolt for a just a moment. It was sunk deep enough in her shoulder that he would have to force it out the other side.

"This will have to wait until Quenthel can heal it. However . . ."

Before she could protest, Ryld snapped the protruding end off.

"Goddess!" Halisstra grunted as she jerked from the pain, squinting her eyes shut.

She reached her other hand up, but Ryld grabbed her arm and held it away.

"Don't," the warrior said. "You'll only make it bleed."

Grimacing, Halisstra shook her head.

"No," she said. "I can heal it. Just let me—"

She pulled her arm free and reached inside her *piwafwi,* producing a wand.

"Push it out," she said, taking the broken end of the bolt and biting down on it.

Ryld complied, bracing her shoulder with one hand and preparing to shove the head of the bolt through with the other. In one clean, quick motion, the shaft was out. Before she could jerk away from him, Ryld pulled it completely free.

Halisstra sobbed once, then she spat out the splintered shaft, waved the wand, and uttered a trigger phrase. The bleeding stopped instantly and the wound closed. The priestess sagged back and closed her eyes in relief.

"Let's go," Ryld said, reaching out to help her to her feet, "before those fires burn out and the grays are over this wall."

"Wait," Halisstra said, and produced a second wand from inside her *piwafwi.* "Let's make it a little harder for them to shoot at us."

Ryld arched his brow at her, puzzled. Quickly, she invoked the power of the wand twice, and the two dark elves were completely invisible.

Ryld reached out and found the priestess. He took her hand.

"So we don't get separated," he explained.

Together, the two drow rose upward, watching as duergar alternated between scattering from the firepots that Valas was hurling down on them with deadly accuracy and firing ineffectually at the scout with their crossbows. As they neared the top, Ryld pulled out Splitter and sliced through the netting, parting the material easily with the enchanted greatsword. He and Halisstra passed through the hole and settled to the rooftop near where Valas knelt, peering over the edge.

"We owe you one," Ryld said to the scout as he moved away from the edge to avoid any stray crossbow bolts.

The roof was covered with the bodies of a good half dozen gray dwarves.

Valas glanced over to where the warrior's voice had come from but didn't react otherwise.

"I saw you come down here and figured I'd try to catch up by coming the long way around," he said, rising up to throw the last of his firepots. "When I saw these cretins here, laughing and throwing these things down, I knew you were in trouble."

"Let's get out of here," Ryld suggested. "Do you know where the others are?"

"I think they got up on the roofs on the other side of the square," the scout replied, dusting off his hands and backing away from the edge. "We'll find them. The wizard will be all flash and glory when they run into something, so we can track them that way."

Ryld turned to follow the scout.

"Too true," he said.

The three dark elves made their way across the rooftops until they came to another side street a little farther ahead of where they'd originally been separated. Valas climbed down the side of a gaudily decorated shop that had plenty of hand- and footholds, while Ryld and Halisstra descended by their customary levitating method. By the time they were on the ground, the invisibility magic had expired.

"Lead on," Ryld said to Valas, gesturing, and the scout took the fore as the three of them prowled through the street, making their way back toward the main thoroughfare.

The ground began to vibrate.

"What in the Underdark?" Ryld muttered, steadying himself as the street bounced beneath his feet. "What is that?"

"I don't know, but it's big," Valas replied. He looked over at Halisstra. "Do you have any clue?" he asked her.

Halisstra shook her head, but she had a worried look on her face.

"Let's not stay and find out," she said.

Valas nodded and proceeded out into the main street. Peering in both directions, he had to reach a hand out to stabilize himself, for the quivering had grown stronger.

"Oh, no," Halisstra said, her voice stricken.

Ryld looked over at her and asked, "What? What is it?"

"Oh, by the Dark Mother," the priestess said, putting a hand to her mouth in terror. "They summoned one."

"Summoned *what?*" Ryld demanded.

"One of those," Valas said from the warrior's other side, and when Ryld turned to look, he saw the scout pointing.

The weapons master turned to peer in the direction his companion indicated and saw a spider the size of the entire square clambering into view. He sucked in his breath, feeling his knees go weak.

"Oh, no."

🕷   🕷   🕷

Pharaun knew that with his magically enhanced boots he could easily outrun the other drow, and that's precisely what he did. The wizard sprinted ahead, careful to maintain his balance on the quivering web street as the colossal spider pursued them. He had but a handful of spells left, and there was little if anything left in his repertoire that might affect the huge arachnid. A far better bet, he decided, was to misdirect the creature, perhaps conjure an obscuring mist that would allow him and the others to hide and sneak away while the spider was distracted—but he didn't dare stop to weave the spell.

"Pharaun!" someone shouted from ahead, and the wizard glanced over in time to see Ryld, Valas, and Halisstra standing in the mouth of a side street, gawking slack-jawed at the massive spider behind him.

He veered in their direction and darted into the shadow of the alley. Only then did he stop to catch his breath.

"I've never . . . seen anything . . . like it," the wizard panted. "Danifae called it a . . . guardian spider."

"Yes," Halisstra said softly, still staring at it. "The matron mothers must have called i—Oh, by the Dark Mother . . . it's summoning another one!"

Pharaun turned to see what Halisstra was talking about, looking past Jeggred and Quenthel as they came into view, running for all they were worth, with Danifae limping behind them. The spider had stopped pursuing them, and was rearing up on its hind legs, flailing about with its front limbs in the air. The wizard gasped when an enormous gate opened up in front of the spider, as large as the creature itself. Through the hazy murk of the bluish-white portal, the wizard watched, aghast, as a second massive spider clambered through and onto the street. The portal shut quickly behind it.

"Oh, no," Quenthel murmured. "How many times can they do that?"

"I don't know," Halisstra said from somewhere behind the wizard.

"Once is too many," Pharaun said. "We've got to get out of here."

He spun away from the massive arachnids, ready to sprint in the opposite direction.

"Wait!" Halisstra cried, pointing.

The mage glanced back once more.

Danifae was still limping badly and had not been able to keep up. As the second spider passed through the portal, it appeared on the opposite side of the battle captive. She was trapped between the two creatures, and was sprawled in the middle of the street as well.

"She's hurt!" Halisstra cried.

She took a tentative step forward to go to the aid of her attendant.

"Don't be a fool," Ryld said, grabbing the priestess by the arm as Jeggred and Quenthel joined them. "You'll only get yourself killed, too."

Halisstra jerked herself free and took another step out into the open.

"I don't care," she said. "I'm going to help her."

With that, the First Daughter of House Melarn dashed across the open area to where her servant was struggling to regain her feet.

The spiders sensed the movement, and both of them began to close in.

Chapter

SEVENTEEN

Pharaun cursed and took a step after Halisstra, thinking he might have to magically cloak the two of them in order to save them.

"Don't," Quenthel ordered. "Danifae was unlucky enough to be wounded. I will not exhaust either resources or time saving her. Let's go while the spiders are distracted."

"But—" Pharaun began, but when he saw the look in the high priestess's eyes, he shook his head and stepped back into the alley. He regretted the idea of losing them—or at least, losing the beautiful Danifae. "Very well," he said.

"I'm not leaving," Ryld said, and he turned to sprint out into the street, following Halisstra.

"No!" Quenthel shouted at the Master of Melee-Magthere, but it was too late. Ryld was already ten steps away, removing Splitter from its sheath on his back as he charged toward the closest of the two spiders. "Damn you all to the Abyss!" Quenthel raged.

Shrugging, Pharaun turned and followed the weapons master.

"Go after them!" Quenthel growled from behind the wizard.

Pharaun could only assume she was talking to him, though why she was ordering him to do something he had already made up his mind to accomplish, he couldn't fathom. Soon enough, though, the draegloth flashed past him, sprinting down the street in the direction he also traveled.

The mage pulled up a few yards from the closest spider, watching as Halisstra reached her servant and knelt down. Somehow, along the way, she had fumbled a wand free from her cloak, and she quickly utilized it, causing both drow to disappear. The spider, looming over the spot where the pair had just been visible, snapped down once, clacking its mandibles together in obvious frustration. The beast began moving its head back and forth, trying to find its prey. In the distance, the second spider had turned its attention to something else. Fortunately, it was not coming their way—at least for the moment.

Pharaun, of course, could still see the two females, for he was aware of the magic they radiated. It appeared to him that Halisstra was dragging Danifae to the side, out of harm's way, but the spider somehow sensed where the two females were, and it dipped its head again, missing a direct bite but coming close enough with its attack that it grazed Halisstra, knocking her down. Shivering in delight at having felt its prey, the spider raised up for another attack.

Ryld had almost reached the creature, and his long legs covered the remaining distance quickly. He leaped through the air, Splitter raised high overhead. As the warrior sailed past the hindmost leg of the giant spider, he swung the greatsword around with all his might, cutting cleanly through the appendage. Black blood spurted everywhere, and the spider reared up, kicking with its ruined leg and barely missing the weapons master.

At nearly the same time, Jeggred launched himself into the air toward another leg, grabbing a hold of the spider and climbing upward. Pharaun could see the draegloth's claws extended, and the fiend used them to great effect as he quickly ascended the creature's limb. Fearlessly, Jeggred slashed and clawed his way to the spider's body and began to climb the slick black abdomen, working his way higher and higher.

The effect of the two attacks was instantaneous. The spider jerked away from its intended meal and spun around, looking to bite whatever tormented it. Its one ruined leg twitched erratically, but otherwise the arachnid lost none of its stability. Ryld had rolled into a crouch after his sweeping sword strike, and he had Splitter up, ready to fend off the spider as it maneuvered to face him.

Pharaun shook his head and considered what he could do to aid in the fight. There was really only one choice. Most of his spells were gone, and the few remaining to him were not offensive in nature. He reached inside his *piwafwi* and produced a wand, a single segment of iron that was about as long as his forearm. Extending it outward, he uttered a trigger phrase and activated the magic in the wand. Instantly, a sizzling bolt of electrical energy leaped forward from the end of the wand, arcing through the air and crackling across the surface of the spider's head. The discharge caused the spider to recoil, chattering and quivering, from Ryld's position. As the last remnants of the bolt dissipated, Pharaun could see that the spider's leathery hide and multifaceted eyes were smoldering.

Pharaun started when he heard the twang of a bowstring strumming, and he glanced down to his right. Valas was there, kneeling, firing off a short bow. The wizard had seen the diminutive scout carrying the weapon all along, but up until then, Valas had apparently had little cause to use it. The Bregan D'aerthe scout lined up and released four shots in the time it took Pharaun to assess the situation, and his aim was true. The arrows embedded themselves in the nearest eye of the spider, one after another, puncturing the many-sided orb like a massive pin cushion. The spider thrashed about in response.

At the same time, Ryld was on his feet again, running with the spider, looking to get in another strike. This time, however, the warrior was not so lucky. As the jerking, pain-crazed creature spasmed along the street, one of its legs swept the warrior off his feet, sending the burly drow tumbling. Ryld landed hard, losing his greatsword in the process.

The massive arachnid was skittering straight toward Pharaun and Valas, and the wizard could see Jeggred on top of it, sitting astride the thing's huge neck, slashing madly with his claws and flinging gobbets of flesh and black blood everywhere as the fiend sawed into the spider's head. The spider reared and jerked, trying to shake Jeggred from its body, but the draegloth clung tenaciously to it, sinking his claws deeply into the beast's flesh to maintain his hold.

The wizard took an involuntary step backward as the onrushing spider closed the distance quickly, its rapid steps making the web street buck and bounce. Raising his wand, the mage fired off a second lightning bolt, letting it crackle over the spider's head, knowing Jeggred would be resistant to its destructive power.

The electrical discharge obviously hurt the massive beast—Pharaun could clearly see scorch marks on its shiny black skin—but it didn't slow a whit. It ambled drunkenly toward the mage and the scout even as Valas pumped a dozen arrows into it.

Goddess! thought Pharaun, backing up another step.

He wanted to turn and run, but he couldn't make himself stop watching the charging creature. Valas was back-stepping too, still firing arrows, but they were both in the spider's sight and it was clearly targeting them as the cause of its woes.

Just as the spider reached the pair of drow and snapped downward, Ryld leaped into view, swinging Splitter in a huge arc and smashing the blade savagely across the creature's face. The lightning bolt had obviously bought the weapons master enough time to retrieve his greatsword.

The arachnid jerked backward, more blood dripping freely from the fresh wound, but it was not to be so easily deterred. It snapped at Ryld once, twice, and the warrior fended the attacks off with his greatsword, laboring to keep the twitching mandibles away from him.

Pharaun scrambled backward again, happy enough to let the broad-shouldered weapons master bear the brunt of the combat. Pharaun raised his wand for a third lightning strike, hoping that would fell the beast, but before he could activate the wand the spider snapped down at Ryld a third time, and the warrior's luck ran out.

The spider's mandibles closed tightly around the Master of Melee-Magthere, who grunted in pain and nearly lost his grip on Splitter. The creature hoisted him into the air, squeezing its captured prey tightly, trying to crush the life out him. Ryld arched his back in agony and began desperately hacking at the mandibles with his sword.

Pharaun hesitated to expend his magical bolts with Ryld in the way, and Valas likewise seemed at a loss, sighting down a drawn-back arrow but faltering. There was no clear shot. Even so, Jeggred continued to hew into the spider's flesh. The draegloth's arms were completely coated with sticky black fluid.

Why won't the blasted thing die? Pharaun thought in dismay.

He was tempted to jolt the creature despite the presence of his companions then he remembered his other wand. Reacting quickly, the wizard managed to fish the second item from inside his *piwafwi* just as the spider stumbled into both him and Valas. The scout went sprawling, rolling into a tumble several yards away, while Pharaun managed to avoid the worst of the blow by leaping out of the way at the last moment, aided by his magical boots.

Landing to one side, the wizard flicked the wand at the spider and uttered the trigger word, sending a host of glowing projectiles streaming from its tip directly at the spider's eyes. The five missiles swerved unerringly around Ryld and struck the creature's eyes in rapid succession. The great spider flinched away, opening its mandibles to chatter in pain, dropping Ryld in the process.

The weapons master fell limply toward the ground but somehow still retained consciousness enough to halt his own descent, drifting the last couple of feet to the pavement. The spider, meanwhile, reared up, its face a bloody mess, Jeggred still slashing at the top of its head.

There's no way it can withstand much more, the wizard thought.

"Finish it," Quenthel said, pointing past the spider. "Kill it and be done with it."

Pharaun could see the second spider coming their way, so he quickly discharged a second round of screaming projectiles from the wand. When they struck home, the spider finally collapsed in the middle of the street, nearly landing atop the still-prone Ryld. The creature didn't move, though its legs and mandibles spasmed awkwardly.

"Withdraw!" Quenthel demanded. "The other one is coming."

Pharaun ran to help Valas get Ryld to his feet, and the trio scurried as fast as they could back into the alley. Jeggred leaped down from his perch atop the dead arachnid and joined them. They all reached the protection of the side street simultaneously, and Pharaun turned back to see what had become of the pair from House Melarn. Farther up the street, the wizard could see the magical emanations of Halisstra and Danifae. They were walking toward him as quickly as the limping drow could move.

"They're almost here," Pharaun said, gesturing back to where he knew only he could see the two. "Keep still," the Master of Sorcere warned. "It might sense vibrations."

The two groups waited, apprehensive. Halisstra and Danifae stopped moving, pressing against the wall of the closest building as the second spider came closer. Pharaun slipped back into the shadows.

As the beast passed, Pharaun prepared to cast the spell he'd considered earlier, one that would bring about a heavy mist, should they need it, but they did not. As the giant arachnid moved off, the vibrations grew calmer. Pharaun stole another glance and saw that the two females were drawing closer.

"You would openly defy me?" Quenthel snarled, slapping a still-woozy Ryld across the cheek.

Jeggred rose up to his full height and moved to stand beside the high priestess, backing her while she meted out her discipline.

Ryld staggered back from the blow, and a trickle of blood dripped from the corner of his mouth, but he didn't flinch from the high priestess's gaze.

"They aren't so expendable as you might think," he said weakly but with his chin in the air. "Give them a chance to prove themselves before you abandon them. It might be you she's rushing back to aid next time."

Jeggred growled and took a step forward, but Quenthel held up her hand in a signal for him to be still. The draegloth glowered at Ryld but obeyed his mistress.

"Your days of questioning my authority are nigh ended," Quenthel said, turning to face both Ryld and Pharaun together. "When we get out of this city, there will be some changes. I am tired of this."

As if to mimic the Mistress of the Academy's foul mood, the snakes of her whip began to shimmy back and forth, hissing in vexation.

"All I say is that you are too quick to dismiss them," Ryld insisted. "They are more valuable than you give them credit for."

"He's right," Pharaun said, "Halisstra has demonstrated some resourcefulness. Don't discount them simply because they are not from Menzoberranzan."

Quenthel scowled at the two of them in turn then drew in Valas with her gaze for good measure. Halisstra and Danifae reached their position, still invisible.

"I am sorry," Halisstra said upon arriving, "but I could not abandon her. She still has a certain value to me."

Quenthel snorted but waved her hand in dismissal, as though minimizing the entire episode.

"You are aware of the conditions under which you will be permitted to stay with us. Keep up, or fall behind. We will not suffer you to slow us down."

She just doesn't want to let on how much we defy her, Pharaun realized. *She's pretending that remaining and waiting was her own act of generosity.* The wizard smirked to himself.

Halisstra let Danifae down and produced a wand from her belongings. She waved it over the battle captive's leg and murmured a phrase that the wizard didn't quite catch, but then he saw that the puncture wound had healed. The dark elf moved to Ryld to administer a similar healing effort to him, but Quenthel intervened.

"Where did you get that?" the high priestess demanded.

Halisstra started, not expecting such a venomous reaction to her charity.

"It's mine," she began to explain. "I brought it—"

"Not anymore, it isn't. Give it to me," Quenthel insisted.

Halisstra stared at the high priestess but made no move to hand over her magical trinket.

"If you don't want Jeggred to shred you to several pieces right now, hand that wand to me."

Slowly, her eyes burning with anger, Halisstra passed the wand to Quenthel.

The Mistress of Arach-Tinilith examined the wand carefully, nodding in satisfaction. She turned and used it on Ryld herself. As the divine power of the wand flowed into the warrior, his worst injuries closed, though several small scratches and bruises remained. When she was satisfied with the weapons master's condition, she tucked the wand away in her own belongings.

"Now," Quenthel said, turning her attention back on Halisstra, "we will have no more of this wasteful use of curing magic taking place. I will be the one who decides when and if a member of this group receives divine aid, is that clear?"

Halisstra nodded.

"Do you have any more magic secreted away that I should know about? Believe me, I will know if you do."

Drisinil's daughter sighed and nodded. She produced an additional wand and handed it over.

"You cannot use that, though," Halisstra mumbled. "It's arcane in nature. I also . . . dabble in that sort of magic."

"I see. Well, if it becomes necessary, you might get it back when you've proven your worth. Until then, I keep them both."

The high priestess turned and strolled a few feet away, completely ignoring the drow female who stared daggers at her back.

"Halisstra," Pharaun said, trying to change the subject and hoping to show Quenthel that the priestess was useful at the same time, "both you and Danifae seemed to know where these giant spiders came from. What can you tell us?"

"They're guardian spiders," the dark elf answered, her voice thick with anger, "summoned only in times of great need. Those two were so small . . . the matron mothers who conjured them must have had a rather minor one stored away."

"You mean they get bigger than that?" Valas asked incredulously.

"Certainly," Halisstra replied, warming to the subject. "How do you think the webs of the city first appeared here? Upon arriving in the cavern, the first high priestesses, along with their wizard counterparts, summoned spiders of immense size to spin the webs upon which the city would rest. It was with Lolth's blessing that these sacred creatures came to us, and they were magically stored, transformed into crystalline statues. From time to time they are brought forth again to repair sections of the city or to defend the chamber. Normally, though, they're controlled through a mental link to do our bidding and to gate in more of their kind only when we command it. I don't know exactly how. That is a secret reserved for the matron mothers."

"Blessed Dark Mother," Ryld said. "Do you think the other one will bring more?"

"I don't know," the priestess replied. "I hope not."

"Look," Pharaun said, glancing ahead, where the spider could still be seen scuttling along the web street.

A force of gray dwarves were on a pathway above it, peering over the side at the spider below them. A number of them had begun throwing more of the damnable firepots at the creature. As the little incendiary devices struck the arachnid, they burst into flame, and the colossal spider reared up as it began to burn, looking to eliminate the source of the pain.

More of the clay pots were cast down, several of them striking the spider on the head and abdomen. Rising up on its hind legs, the spider attempted to reach the duergar, but they were too high overhead. The spider spun in place, turning its back on its attackers, and fired a thick stream of fluid in their direction.

"Webbing," Pharaun noted aloud, impressed.

The stream of webbing sailed accurately, attaching to the underside of the web street, hardening as it did so. The spider turned and began to scamper up the strand of sticky filament, pursuing the gray dwarves, who were desperately clambering to get out of the way.

"The fools," Ryld said. "They just managed to get its attention focused on them. Fortunate for us, though."

"Enough," Quenthel said. "We still need to get our belongings from the inn and leave this wretched city."

Pharaun turned to gaze at the high priestess, knowing full well that his expression was one of dumbfounded amazement.

"You can't be serious! Look around," he said, gesturing out toward other parts of the city, where the distant glows of more and more fires were visible through the ever-thickening smoke. "The whole city is in turmoil.

"Use your ears," he continued, gesturing in a different direction, where the screams of the fighting and dying echoed off the walls of the huge cavern. "We're running out of time. I'm sure the whole city is choosing sides and taking the battle to the streets, and yet you want to tempt fate by trying to go after more of your trinkets? I think—"

"Listen to me, *boy*," Quenthel spat, her face livid. "We just went through this with your warrior friend. You will do as I say, or you will be left here to die. If you've forgotten who I am, allow me to remind you that I am High Priestess Quenthel Baenre, Mistress of Arach-Tinilith, Mistress of the Academy, Mistress of Tier Breche, First Sister of House Baenre of Menzoberranzan, and I will no longer tolerate your snide remarks and your haughty insubordination. Do you understand?"

As if to back up her words, Jeggred stepped forward and with a menacing growl took hold of the collar of Pharaun's *piwafwi*, bunching it up in his clawed fist.

The wizard glanced over to Ryld, who still looked weakened from his fight with the spider. Nonetheless, he had his hand on the hilt of Splitter and was stepping forward, ready to come between the draegloth and the mage. But Pharaun could tell by the warrior's expression that he was trying to determine just how badly he really wanted to choose sides at this juncture.

Jeggred whipped his head around and snarled, "Don't even think about it, weapons master. I will tear out your stomach and feast upon it if you interfere."

Ryld's expression tightened as he took offense at the draegloth's threats, but Pharaun gave a quick, subtle shake of his head to warn the warrior off.

"*Mistress* Quenthel, since you are so passionate about recovering your valuables," Pharaun said, trying to make his voice sound jovial, "then let's make haste, before the opportunity is wasted."

Quenthel smiled, obviously pleased at having successfully asserted herself and regained the upper hand.

"I knew you would appreciate the importance of my decision," she replied, turning away.

"So, wizard, how do you propose we cross over to the Flame and Serpent?" she asked, appraising the devastation alongside Pharaun. "What magic do you still have up your sleeve that can get us there quickly and safely?"

"None, Mistress Baenre," Pharaun replied in all seriousness. "I have consumed over half of my magic for the day, and I'm not even certain how we'll get out of the city."

"That's not good enough, Mizzrym."

"I have a counter-suggestion," the mage said, pursing his lips. "Let me go get the goods while you and the rest of the group wait here and rest. It's out of the way, fairly easily defended, and I can find you again when I come back. I have a spell to get me to the inn and back quickly, I just can't take all of you with me."

Quenthel scowled, thinking, and Pharaun wondered if, as often as she frowned so severely, the high priestess even realized she was making such a face.

"Very well," Quenthel said at last, nodding. "Do not dawdle."

"Oh, I don't intend to. The less chance there is of large chunks of this doomed city falling atop me, the better off I'll feel."

Quenthel turned and explained the plan to the rest of the group. Everyone nodded in agreement, ready for a respite.

Ryld pulled Pharaun aside and asked, "You *are* coming back, aren't you?"

Pharaun cocked an eyebrow and replied, "Besides having a fondness for you, my brooding weapons master, I still truly desire to get to the bottom of this mystery. My chances are better with you all than without."

Ryld looked at him for a long time before nodding.

"Be careful," he said, turning to find a seat against a wall of the alley, his crossbow out.

"How do you intend to cross the city?" Halisstra asked.

Her face was drawn and tired. Still, her eyes glittered red, as with some new determination.

"I have a spell of flying that I can use to get there and back again fairly quickly," Pharaun answered. "Unfortunately, I would be much better off if I were not visible, but I have already played that particular trick today."

"Maybe I can help," the daughter of what once was House Melarn said. "Mistress Quenthel, that wand you just confiscated from me would serve us well, with your approval."

"What is it?" the high priestess asked, seemingly pleased by the deference shown her.

"A spell that will render him invisible, even should he attack a foe," Halisstra replied. "I assure you, it will not harm him."

Quenthel scowled and looked at Pharaun for some sort of confirmation. The wizard nodded. He still believed the two females newly added to the group were trustworthy, and they certainly wouldn't be in much of a position to turn on the rest of them now.

"Very well," Quenthel said.

She produced the wand and passed it back to the other female. Halisstra took it, offering her thanks to the high priestess. She targeted her wand at Pharaun.

"Wait," the wizard said.

He produced a feather from inside his *piwafwi*. Using the feather as part of the casting, he enchanted himself with the ability to fly.

Tucking the feather back into its customary pocket, he turned to the priestess and said, "All right, go ahead. It's always easier to cast when you can see your own hands."

She smiled faintly and nodded, then summoned the magical energy from the wand. In but a moment, Pharaun was totally invisible. Halisstra offered the wand back to Quenthel.

"No," the high priestess said, shaking her head. "You can keep it. I think you learned your lesson."

"Yes, Mistress," Halisstra said with a smile that did not reach her eyes. She tucked the wand away and went to sit down once more, beside Danifae.

"I'll be back shortly," Pharaun said.

He rose into the air before anyone could think to reply.

❀   ❀   ❀

Danifae watched as the wizard disappeared, and she sensed when he departed the alley. Shaking her head, she sat back and watched the weapons master and the scout, both of whom paced, apparently eager to be away from there.

This is a strange lot I've wound up with, she decided. They are competent, and yet they bicker and argue unlike any group of dark elves I've ever seen.

The battle captive looked over at Quenthel, who was speaking quietly with the draegloth, Jeggred.

She's certainly an interesting one, Danifae decided.

It wasn't the first time she'd encountered a female like the high priestess—confident yet blustering at everything and everyone.

Still, Danifae thought, letting her eyes linger appreciatively over Quenthel's form, she's a fit leader.

Danifae turned her thoughts Halisstra. The First Daughter of House Melarn looked visibly shaken at the physical loss of her home, even though Ssipriina had already wrested possession of it from her. Danifae wondered how her mistress would hold up under that kind of duress. Certainly, there was no lamenting the destruction of House Melarn on her own part, but Danifae could imagine how it would feel if her own family had been wiped out in such a fashion. House Yauntyrr might well have been destroyed, for all she knew. It had been far too long since she'd last seen it. She didn't even know the fate of Eryndlyn itself in the current crisis, much less her own House.

"Let us come with you," Halisstra said to Quenthel. "Let us help you find the priest of Vhaeraun."

Danifae looked at her mistress sharply.

"What makes you think we're going to try to find the scout's friend?" Quenthel asked.

"I-I beg forgiveness, Mistress Baenre," Halisstra stammered. "I merely assumed—"

"Assumptions are best left to that miserable wretch, Pharaun," Quenthel warned.

Halisstra bowed her head.

"Of course, Mistress Baenre," she said. "Nonetheless, I would humbly ask that you permit me and my servant to accompany you. Our chances of survival are much greater if we stay together, and as you know, I have nothing left for me here."

The dark elf pursed her lips, obviously trying to control her emotions. Danifae thought it somewhat unbecoming, showing so much of her passion, but she would never say so, especially not in front of others.

Quenthel tapped her lips with her finger and nodded as though she understood the pain of Halisstra's plight, though Danifae seriously doubted the high priestess held any true compassion for Halisstra's situation.

"Yes, well, as long as you can continue to make yourself useful, and if you are willing to do what I say, then I see no reason why you cannot continue to travel with us."

Danifae cringed. No doubt this would take her farther away from Eryndlyn, not closer. She was going to have find a way to break the binding, and soon, and she thought perhaps the wizard had that capability. It would be easy enough for her to manipulate him into helping her, the way she caught him eyeing her all the time. Easy, indeed.

Halisstra bowed her head again in thanks and said, "If it is not too presumptuous, Mistress Baenre, may I ask what your intentions are?"

"Well, once we manage to get out of this city," Quenthel replied, emphasizing the words to show of what a daunting task that would be in and of itself, "I think we might actually pay a visit to this friend of the scout's. However infuriating the Mizzrym boy can be in so many other ways, he does occasionally have a good idea or two."

That's why you can't afford to alienate him or cause him bodily harm, Danifae surmised.

It wasn't difficult to see that Pharaun was really the most valuable member of the team. That raised the question of who was really the leader. Quenthel by default, but Pharaun by subtle necessity.

That will bear watching, Danifae thought with a smile.

❦   ❦   ❦

Ssipriina surveyed the troops she'd assembled in the courtyard of her estate and grimaced. So few remained of what she'd started the day with. Would they be enough? She let her gaze roam over them . . . soldiers, priestesses, wizards. How many had she lost in the destruction of House Melarn? How many more in the hours since, battling the rival Houses, her own duergar mercenaries, succumbing to the guardian spiders?

The matron mother shook her head, thinking of that debacle. It was certainly a blunder, but she refused to label it ill-conceived. Animating the creature to fight for her House had been clever, an idea her allies had all endorsed. Certainly, none of them had been able to foresee that the mental link used to control the spiders was in some way tied to their connection to Lolth. Without the goddess, there was no link, but once Ssipriina and the others had figured that out, it was too late. They had all missed that, and she refused to accept sole blame for it.

Still, the damage could have been contained, if only that double-crossing fool Khorrl had done his duty. She had paid him a matron mother's ransom. He should have jumped at her every beck and call, but instead he turned his back on her, gathered his mercenaries, and was preparing to pull out of Ched Nasad all together. The loss of his support was a tough blow, but what galled her more was how foolish he'd made her look—foolish in the eyes of her peers.

The other matron mothers, upon hearing that the duergar were no longer in House Zauvirr's service, had washed their hands of the alliance, immediately withdrawing their support for Ssipriina's claims. They had their own Houses to consider and couldn't afford to weaken themselves further in a lost cause.

Lost cause! Yes, she had been made to look foolish, and she would not have that. Ssipriina Zauvirr would show them what a lost cause was.

Let the rest of them distance themselves from her. Let them rot at the bottom of the chasm. She was not going to let these setbacks foil her plans. Half the city might burn, but when the smoke cleared, House Zauvirr would sit at the top of the heap.

Khorrl Xornbane was going to pay as well, but would her remaining troops be enough? Between her own House and those from House Melarn who had switched allegiance, she had assembled a potent army, but so many had been lost.

That was Clan Xornbane's fault, too. They'd let the battle around House Melarn get out of control. It was their horrible firepots that made the stone burn, that allowed the House to fall. It was needless destruction, brought about after needless fighting.

Ssipriina had no doubt that the gray dwarf captain had spoken the truth. Zammzt could very well have been behind the premature exposure of her mercenaries, but why? Which matron mother was he in league with? Which of them had something to gain by watching her plans build up, then teeter to disaster? There were so many, but she would have to determine that later.

Ssipriina would miss Zammzt. She needed his efficiency, his battle acumen. She didn't have enough strategists to put in charge of the forces she'd assembled. The ugly male would have served in that capacity nicely. Faeryl would be a suitable replacement, but she'd not been seen since the chaos at the end of the gathering of matron mothers. Ssipriina suspected that her daughter had perished when the estate crumbled into the bottom of the cavern.

Foolish girl, the matron mother thought. Good riddance.

Sighing, Ssipriina shook herself out of her musings and swept her gaze one last time over her undersized army. They would have to be enough. She would lead them herself, and they would be enough.

"Gather yourselves," the matron mother said, moving to a protected place in the middle of the milling mass of drow. "It's time to claim what's ours."

Chapter

EIGHTEEN

Pharaun tried to stay near the perimeter of the city as he made his way toward the Flame and Serpent. For one thing, he didn't relish the thought of being crushed at any moment by falling debris from above. Though it had only happened once, he'd been far too intimately involved with it than he cared to remember. He would avoid a repeat incident, if he could.

Secondly, the wizard knew that navigation would be easier if he followed the wall of the chasm, rather than trying to work his way through the central section of the city. Even then, the thick smoke caused him difficulty in flying. He was surprised at how haze-choked the cavern had become. More than once, he nearly careened off a trench wall, still intact web street, or building. Nonetheless, he still considered the challenge of navigating through that to be far safer than having to maneuver through the center of Ched Nasad, where the sound of fighting was constant.

Occasionally he heard explosions, loud pops, and howling winds in the distance as fierce magical battles raged. Arcane forces were being unleashed on gathering troops. There was no doubt about it— the entire city was engaged in a desperate struggle for control of the streets.

Mostly, the reverberations of conflict reached the mage's ears from his level or below. What had in all likelihood begun in the plaza outside of House Melarn had quickly spread, engulfing the citizens and visitors all across the city, on every level. The wizard wondered how many had actually managed to flee into the caverns surrounding the City of Shimmering Webs. Though the team from Menzoberranzan had been indisposed for much of the initial martial activity, he recalled that, since their escape from the collapse of House Melarn, they had seen surprisingly few ordinary folk in the streets. Of course, that was also because they'd spent most of their time high in the city, where only the nobles prowled. Farther down, in the lower sections, he imagined a much different scene. There, he supposed, the general rabble had gotten caught up in the fighting, much like the rebellion back home.

The uprising had taken a decidedly different twist than the insurrection in Menzoberranzan, though. The insurgents involved in the upheavals in Ched Nasad were the noble Houses themselves. Their own infighting was the flash point. Pharaun counted himself fortunate that the Houses of Menzoberranzan had proven less prone to petty backbiting. If they had, there might not be a city for him to return to. The mage grimaced, thinking of Gromph's attempts on Quenthel's life, and his own sister Greyanna's failed efforts to kill him.

There might not be anything left, he thought, before this is completely finished.

As he neared the section of the city where the inn was located, the wizard noticed that the damage was less severe there. In fact, the

Flame and Serpent was thus far unscathed. Immediately he saw the reason why. A horde of mismatched drow and other creatures, probably residents of the inn, self-reliant mercenaries, and whatnot had formed a perimeter defense around the place. It didn't appear that they were under fire at the moment, but an intense battle must have raged there earlier, judging by the number of bodies present.

Not wanting to be either attacked or drawn into the midst of the siege, Pharaun elected to circle around to the back side of the inn and enter it that way. He recalled the window of the room he shared with Valas and Ryld, the one that looked out on the wall of the massive cavern that Ched Nasad called home, and he made for that. He approached from the roof and settled down between the wall of the building and the wall of the trench. It was just wide enough for him to levitate down between the two, and he hovered there while he contemplated how best to get through the opening without attracting attention.

He had just the spell, the Master of Sorcere realized, a minor incantation that would open the window from the inside, so that he wouldn't have to break it to get through. Reaching into his *piwafwi*, he fumbled around in three or four pockets before he found what he was looking for. He pulled out a brass key and tapped it softly against the window as he uttered the words that would complete the spell. The window opened without resistance, and Pharaun squirmed inside the room.

The wizard, the weapons master, and the scout had taken all of their belongings when they'd left the inn upon being summoned to attend the "party" in their honor. That seems almost a lifetime ago, Pharaun mused as he made his way out the door and down the hall to Quenthel's chambers.

Upon reaching the door, the mage hesitated, wondering if the high priestess had placed some sort of protective enchantment on it before leaving, but then he remembered that Ryld and Valas had invaded the room when they came seeking healing magic. Chuckling, he tried the door and found it locked.

Of course, Pharaun silently muttered. *Leave it to Valas to put it back the way he found it.*

Shrugging, the wizard dug around in the pockets of his *piwafwi* yet again, drawing forth a pinch of clay and a small vial of water. Sprinkling the water over the clay, he invoked the Weave and completed the spell. A portion of the wall next to the door began to sag, transforming from solid stone to thick, viscous mud. The wall oozed down into a puddle, and Pharaun stepped back to avoid soiling his boots. When the opening was wide enough, the Master of Sorcere nimbly leaped through into the room beyond, avoiding the mess he'd made.

Pharaun spied Quenthel's backpack, filled with extra supplies, on a table near the Reverie couch. Some of Faeryl's things, including the ambassador's haversack, were on the other table. The wizard hefted the high priestess's pack and grunted.

So, the mage thought with a wry grin, *she finally figured out a way to make me carry her possessions.*

He slung the backpack over his shoulder, grabbed up the second one, Faeryl's, and turned to go.

A crossbow bolt smacked into Pharaun's chest, somehow managing to slip through the part in the *piwafwi*'s fabric, and embedded itself in his shoulder. The Master of Sorcere grunted and stumbled back into the room, spinning away so that his back was to his assailant and he was more completely protected by the *piwafwi*. He looked down to see that it was a drow bolt, and he realized his magical invisibility had worn off.

Pharaun staggered over to the opposite side of the room, dropping the two satchels as he scrambled to find cover. There were really only two good places he could go: behind the Reverie couch or into an armoire. As he rushed past the armoire, he grabbed the door and yanked it open, then shoved it shut again as he slumped behind the Reverie couch. The door to the oversized cabinet slammed shut just as two pairs of boots darted into the room, which Pharaun observed from beneath the couch. The mage stayed low, on his knees, watching under the couch as the two pairs of boots spread apart, both slowly headed toward the armoire, their owners presumably covering the room.

"He went into the cabinet," one of the creatures said in the language of the drow.

The crossbow bolt set his shoulder throbbing, but Pharaun quietly watched for his assailants to appear. He blinked, unable to focus clearly, and he suddenly began to feel lightheaded. He kept thinking that if he could just cast a spell, this would all be over, but a decision about which one or how to go about doing it eluded him. The crossbow bolt wound had begun to burn, and Pharaun realized that he was growing weak. The bolt had been coated with poison. He would have to hurry to get back to the others before it overwhelmed him, and he only hoped they had a means of treating the toxin.

As his foes both came into Pharaun's line of view, crossbows held up and ready, he could see why they'd attacked him on sight. They were both dark elves, and they wore the livery of House Zauvirr. Mentally kicking himself for not considering the possibility that Ssipriina might send someone to their inn on the expectation that he or others in the group might return, Pharaun tried to phrase the arcane words of a spell, but they wouldn't come. The two drow were grinning as they sighted down their crossbows at him.

Pharaun closed his eyes, wondering if it would hurt much to die, and pondered whether or not he could work his rapier free, when he heard a noise. The expected twang of crossbows being fired it was not. Instead, he heard a woman's voice—a familiar voice—uttering a quick phrase. The wizard squinted, his vision blurry, as a spray of intertwined, multicolored beams of light cascaded over his two foes.

Both drow reeled backward from the sudden, bright assault, crying out and flinging up their hands to cover their eyes. The first one spasmed as crackles of electricity raked over his body from the yellow ray of light, while the second drow was engulfed in flames upon coming into contact with the red beam.

Pharaun watched as the two soldiers crumpled to the ground. Whether either or both of them were dead or not, he didn't know, nor did he care. He was growing intolerably weak from the effects of the poison.

"Hello, Pharaun," the voice purred.

With an effort, Pharaun opened his eyes again and looked up, realizing who it was.

"Aliisza," he slurred, relaxing as the alu came around the couch toward him. "How did you find—"

The fiend's slap across Pharaun's face stung immensely and he jerked, alert, his eyes watering.

"What the—" the wizard grunted, rubbing his cheek as Aliisza squatted down beside him, her hand upraised. "What's the matter with you?"

He again wondered if he could produce the rapier.

"How dare you!" the alu growled, one eyebrow arched, but without the accompanying smile. "How could you be interested in that trollop after sharing *my* bed?"

Pharaun blinked, thoroughly confused. Trollop?

"Who in the blazes are you talking about?" he demanded, feebly raising his good arm to ward off the impending slap.

"Don't you play dumb with me, you wretched excuse for a dark elf. You know the one I mean. The pretty you pulled from that collapsing house. I should have gouged her eyes out!"

"Oh, by the Dark Mother," Pharaun muttered, understanding at last. "It's not what you think. . . ."

"Ooh! You males *always* say that. According to your gender, it never is. I don't want to hear it."

Aliisza reached down, grabbed the wizard by both lapels of his *piwafwi,* and drew him up to her. She crushed his mouth to hers in a rough kiss, biting his lip so hard he was sure she drew blood. In fact, he decided, it felt not so much like a kiss as like the fiend was marking her territory.

"That's so you won't forget me so easily. If you stray, I'll know it. I'll smell her on you, and I will not be happy. I'm not through with you yet, wizard," Aliisza warned, looking him in the eyes.

She blinked, and that sardonic smile was back.

"Well, I guess I'd better get you to some help," she said lightly, hefting Pharaun up and slinging him over her shoulder, careful of his chest, where the crossbow bolt still protruded.

The wizard felt the utter fool, being toted like a sack of mushrooms, but he could hardly protest. His entire body felt . . . well, "fuzzy" was the best word he could think of to describe it.

"The satchels," he mumbled into the alu's shoulder. "Don't forget the satchels."

Scooping up both Quenthel's and Faeryl's bags, Aliisza carried Pharaun across the room, out the hole he'd made in the wall, down the hallway, and back into his own room. She set the wizard down on the Reverie couch. Taking the satchels, she moved to the window and leaned out, bracing her feet against the rock wall of the chasm. Pharaun watched helplessly as she tossed the packs onto the roof.

The alu returned and scooped the wizard up once more and hauled him out into the gap between the building and the wall, shoving him upward above her. He felt the bolt in his shoulder ram against the side of the inn, but the pain was strangely diminished. Still, it was forceful enough to make him grunt.

"By the Abyss, can't you help at all?" she puffed, working the mage to the roof.

Pharaun didn't answer. His face was going numb, and everything was fading to black.

🕷 🕷 🕷

Ryld was sitting on the roof of a building that bordered the alley, with his legs dangling over the side, his crossbow in his hands, watching parts of Ched Nasad burn. Finally having a chance to really study the layout of the city, he could see what was happening with greater clarity. The fighting had diminished in the highest reaches, though he could still hear the sounds of combat from a couple of streets over. It was mostly the lower sections of the city that seemed to be receiving the worst of it, those areas where the lesser races were most numerous. He supposed that the violence down there took the form a general rioting, just a byproduct of the tensions of the city coupled with the more severe military maneuvers that had played out higher up. Of course, he supposed, having a large chunk of the city fall from above wasn't going to help calm things.

Halisstra sat down beside the weapons master and stared forlornly out at her homeland.

"Valas has gone to see what chance we have of getting out through any of the city gates," she told Ryld. "I told him about one or two places where we might be able to depart unseen, and he's going to see if they're secure."

Ryld only nodded. If anyone could sneak through the city unchallenged, it was the Bregan D'aerthe scout. He doubted seriously if any exits had been left unguarded, though.

"How could this have happened?" Halisstra muttered softly. "So much destruction."

"We have grown complacent," the Master of Melee-Magthere answered. "The drow race has been squabbling in a controlled manner for so long, we never expected that our own little games would get out of hand. And they—" the weapons master gestured downward, in the direction of the slums—"just feed off of it, now."

"But the fire. How is it possible to burn down a city made of stone?"

"Alchemy, I suppose. We saw the same thing in Menzoberranzan. It's more devastating here, because your whole city is suspended on stone webbing. They were very clever to bring the firepots here."

"Of course," the drow maiden breathed. "Set the webs on fire, and everything attached to them falls to its destruction. Including House Melarn."

Ryld glanced over at the dark elf beside him. Her face was one of sorrow, and her red eyes glistened with uncharacteristic tears. It was not often that he saw a drow cry. It was considered a sign of weakness. He found it refreshingly honest in the priestess.

"I am sorry for your loss. Perhaps we will learn from this. If we survive."

Something caught Ryld's eye, and he had his crossbow up and was sighting down the shaft in an instant. A winged figure, bobbing and weaving haphazardly, emerged from the smoke, coming for their position. It was a drow, possibly, though it had wings, and it bore a rather large bundle. The warrior could tell something was wrong by the erratic way it was flying. Suddenly, he recognized it— the demon from Ammarindar!

He had his finger on the trigger, ready to fire a bolt through her heart, before he realized she was carrying Pharaun.

As the demon closed in on the edge of the building, she seemed to lose her balance, and Ryld literally had to reach out and grab her as she went by. All three of them tumbled to the stone in a heap at Jeggred's feet. The draegloth stepped between the beautiful creature and the rest of the team.

"You!" Quenthel hissed, her scourge raised, ready to strike. "What are you doing here?"

The fiend, whom Pharaun referred to as Aliisza, Ryld remembered, eyed both Jeggred and the high priestess warily as she panted where she'd fallen. She made no move to defend herself.

"Bringing your precious wizard back to you, drow," she muttered. "I know how fond you are of him."

"He's hurt," Ryld said, turning the mage over.

Everyone but Jeggred gathered around as the weapons master began to examine Pharaun. It didn't take him long to find the puncture wound in the wizard's shoulder, a portion of a crossbow bolt still lodged in it. Most of the shaft had snapped off during his crash landing.

"The bolt is poisoned," Quenthel said, standing over Pharaun's prone body. "Healing him won't do a bit of good unless we get the poison out of his blood first. If we don't, he'll die."

"I could have told you that," Aliisza said, sitting up, though she was still breathing heavily from her ordeal. "Here . . . he insisted we bring these."

She tossed two backpacks at Quenthel's feet.

"So, how do we remove the poison?" Ryld asked Quenthel, looking up from where he was tending to the Master of Sorcere. "Do any of you have the magic to do so?"

Quenthel shook her head.

"Yngoth can sense it in his body," she said, patting the whip that was once again hanging from her hip, "but my spells are, of course, lost."

Ryld looked at both Halisstra and Danifae.

"How about either of you?"

Both females shook their heads.

"I dabble in a bit of arcane magic," Halisstra confessed, "but I am not yet powerful enough to eliminate poison."

Jeggred continued his vigil over Aliisza but said, "Perhaps our good friend the ambassador had some means of aiding him."

The draegloth nudged the satchel at his feet.

"You'd better hope she did," Ryld muttered at the unconscious Pharaun, sliding the pack over toward Quenthel. "There's nothing else we can do for you, my friend."

Pharaun was sweating profusely. Ryld knew the wizard might be their single best chance to escape the city. If they lost him, they might very well be trapped, unless Valas could find a way out.

Quenthel began rummaging through Faeryl's things, flinging clothing and personal items to the side. As she dug her way toward the bottom, Ryld thought he heard the high priestess mutter something disparaging about the ambassador and a comment about her being a waste of space then her face brightened as she pulled a thick tube free.

"Ah *ha!*" she said triumphantly. "Let's hope these are spells."

She opened the tube, slid out a handful of parchment pages and unfurled them, scanning their contents quickly.

"Oh, how delightful," she said. "Faeryl, you clever girl, where in the Underdark did you steal these from?"

Both Halisstra and Danifae crowded around the Mistress of Arach-Tinilith, each of them trying to get a glimpse of what was on the pages. The weapons master could see looks of elation on their faces.

"Is there anything helpful?" Ryld demanded. "Something to neutralize the poison?"

"I don't know, yet," Quenthel snapped. "Give me a moment."

She continued to scan the pages, leafing through them rapidly.

"Several of these could prove quite helpful," she said, "but I don't see—oh, wait. Yes! Pharaun Mizzrym, you are in luck. Give me some room," she said, motioning for Ryld to move out of the way.

The weapons master did so, sliding off to the side as Quenthel knelt beside the wizard. Laying one hand atop the wound, the high priestess began chanting, reading through the words on the scroll in her hand. There was a tiny flash of light as the handwritten text vanished from the page, and a soft glow passed through Pharaun's body, emanating from the point where Quenthel's hand touched him.

Almost immediately, the Master of Sorcere's breathing slowed, and he seemed more relaxed. His eyes were still closed, but he was smiling.

"My thanks, Mistress Quenthel," he said, and he sounded about as sincere as Ryld had ever heard him. "I ran into a spot of trouble at the inn, you see. A couple of fellows in the employ of Matron Mother Zauvirr were decidedly unhappy that I paid the place a visit. They caught me off guard."

"I find that terribly difficult to believe," Ryld said, eyeing Aliisza, who was still sitting on the opposite side of Jeggred.

"Yes, well, I'm sure you could have given them a lesson or two on how to more accurately find the most vulnerable point in a wizard's defenses."

"All right," the high priestess said, standing again. "Get that out of his shoulder, and I can heal him."

She went over to her own pack, where she tucked the scrolls, back in their protective tube, into a pocket. She began fishing around in another section of the container and produced a wand, which Ryld recognized from before.

The weapons master turned his attention back to the broken end of the bolt. He checked to see if it was lodged against any bone, and when he was satisfied that it was not, he gave a fierce shove, pushing the head through Pharaun's shoulder and out the back side.

Pharaun arched his back and cried out in pain.

"Damn it, Master Argith," he muttered finally, breathing fast. "You certainly know how to welcome a friend back."

The wizard closed his eyes, still grimacing.

"I think the greeting was entirely appropriate for someone who managed to get himself shot," Ryld replied, once more making room for Quenthel to work her own magic.

The high priestess waved her wand over the freshly bleeding puncture and muttered a trigger word. The flesh that was exposed began to knit itself together, closing the hole and forming a pale gray scar on his jet black flesh. Pharaun sighed as Quenthel stood up once more.

"There," she said, returning the wand to her pack. "Now, try to avoid crossbow bolts. There's only so much of that to go around."

Ryld threw a glance at Halisstra and saw the drow priestess looking jealous as she watched Quenthel store away the wand.

To the victor goes the spoils, he thought grimly. You bowed your head to her and named her your mistress . . . don't expect any generosity in return.

Pharaun was sitting up, helped by Danifae. He looked around. When he spotted Aliisza, still being guarded by the draegloth, he grimaced and pulled his hand free from the battle captive's. Ryld glanced over and saw that the dark-haired beauty was frowning severely.

Uh oh, Ryld thought. This smacks of a jealous lover. Surely the wizard isn't that big a fool, to lie with a demon. . . .

Pharaun managed to get to his feet and move over to where the demon sat.

"It's all right," he said to Jeggred as he passed. "You can stand down. She's not going to bite."

Jeggred studiously ignored the wizard and maintained his position.

"Look, I owe you for this," he said, speaking low but not so quietly that Ryld couldn't hear the conversation.

To his utter surprise, the demoness grabbed hold of Pharaun, her hands to either side of his head, and kissed him savagely. The wizard didn't do anything to resist, though the warrior could see his fists clenching and unclenching at his sides.

"Remember what I said," Aliisza said, pressing her mouth to the mage's ear, but speaking loudly enough that everyone could hear. "I will know."

Ryld saw that she was staring right at Danifae as she said this. The battle captive caught the steely stare and turned away, a smile of amused disbelief on her face. Quenthel gave a disgusted growl in the back of her throat and spun on her heel to ignore the ridiculous display.

"Now, I've been too long in this city," Aliisza said. "I'll leave you all to whatever silly dark elf games you intend to play while the place falls down around you."

With that, she opened a bluish-white doorway, stepping through as Jeggred snarled and made a leap for her, but she was gone.

"By the Dark Mother, Pharaun," Quenthel snapped. "All of your talk about not tempting fate, and you're off dallying with that . . . that *thing*? You are such a male."

Pharaun shrugged at the accusations.

"Nothing happened," he said, rubbing his mouth thoughtfully. "I went to get your things, I got jumped, and she saved my life. That's the end of it."

"See that it is," Quenthel snarled.

Pharaun looked around, scratching his head.

"Where's Valas?" he asked, and Danifae explained the situation to him.

The wizard nodded and said, "Yes, the sooner we can get out of the city, the more quickly we can figure out how to get to his friend, the priest."

The Master of Sorcere raised a single eyebrow and glanced over at Quenthel.

"Assuming we've settled on that as our next course of action?" he asked her.

The high priestess gave him a single curt nod.

"Yes, you've convinced me," she said. "Once we're clear of Ched Nasad, we'll need to decide the best way to reach this priest. I assume you have some means of getting us to where we'll want to go?"

Pharaun nodded as he got slowly to his feet.

"I may, depending on where Valas tells us the fellow is, but I won't be doing it today," he added. "I have nearly depleted my assortment of spells. Without some rest and a chance to review my grimoires, I'm severely hampered."

"Then let's just concentrate on getting out of Ched Nasad and worry about that later," Quenthel said. "As soon as Valas returns, we'll see what he's discovered and make appropriate plans."

"The news isn't good," the scout said, appearing is if on cue. He climbed up and over the wall against which they'd been sitting. "Every major gate seems to be either heavily guarded or under attack, and the other places Halisstra mentioned are inaccessible at the moment. There's no way out of the city."

"Nonsense," Quenthel said firmly. "Pharaun, do you have any means at all of transporting us? Some spell that would open a gate? Anything?"

The wizard shook his head.

"Then we'll just have to clear a path through one of the gates. I'm sure that with the seven of us we can accomplish this."

"There is only one way to find out," the mage answered. He studied their position for a moment then turned to Valas. "We need to get up higher, above those duergar, don't you think?"

Valas nodded and said, "The fighting is still heavy over in that direction. If we can avoid that, all the better."

"Let's not dawdle any longer," Pharaun agreed. "We go up."

Quenthel nodded her assent to the plan, and everyone prepared to depart.

As Ryld assembled his gear, he realized that he was exhausted. Between his exploits with Valas at the taverns, fighting their way into and out of House Melarn, and dealing with both the duergar and the spiders, the warrior hadn't rested in over a day.

It has to be almost morning, he realized, and we're not even close to being finished, yet. Let's hope we can find a relatively painless way to slip past the gate forces.

The team set out, but they had to move in shifts, for Jeggred had to carry both Valas and Danifae to higher ground, and the draegloth, despite his immense strength, could only transport one of the dark elves at a time. Thus, half the group rose to the next web street overhead as Jeggred conveyed one drow, while the remainder waited with the other for the fiend to return.

The first team, consisting of Pharaun, Quenthel, and Jeggred carrying Danifae, alit atop a web street and discovered that it was actually being defended by drow troops. Several of the dark elves leveled hand crossbows at the four of them, and when they saw the draegloth, they nearly panicked.

"What in the Nine Hells is that?" one of the soldiers, an older male with plenty of battle scars, called out, pointing to Jeggred with his crossbow.

The fiend growled low, turning to face his would-be assailants, but Pharaun stepped between the draegloth and the others.

"Easy, there," the wizard said, his hands out, palms up in a placating manner. "We're just passing through. No need to get jumpy."

Beside him, Quenthel sniffed, but when the drow soldiers saw that she seemed unconcerned by the fiend's presence, they quieted down, returning their attention below them, where the fighting was still taking place. Jeggred departed to retrieve Valas.

Pharaun found a spot to take a seat and did so, reclining against a wall to rest for a few moments.

"Might as well get comfortable," he said to the two females with him. "Rest when you can."

Quenthel scowled but consented to sit across from the wizard, and Danifae settled down, too.

The trio's rest was short-lived, though, for soon, shouts emerged from farther along the street. All the drow around them grew restless as word spread that dark elves from an enemy House were heading their way.

A priestess of middling rank came stalking down the street, accompanied by a pair of male wizards. They were cajoling the troops to form up.

"On your feet! It's time. Get up, you worthless rothé, and fight! Fight for House Maerret!"

When she reached Pharaun and the others, she stopped and stared at them.

"What are you three doing here? You're not part of this unit. Who are you?"

Pharaun gave the priestess that same placating motion that he'd used earlier and said, "We're just passersby, not here to cause any trouble."

"Well, you'll join ranks, then. Get forward and help the other wizards."

"We thought we'd better serve the cause by helping to watch this end of road," Pharaun replied, smiling broadly. "You never know when those pesky grays will try to circumnavigate our flank and surprise us."

"Get on your feet, wizard, and go join the other spellcasters. And you two! You can help me rally the troops and keep order. Up off your hind ends—*now!*"

Pharaun could see that Quenthel was about to lash out at the priestess, so before she could cause a scene, he pulled the drow commander to the side.

"Listen," he said quietly. "We're actually working on a special assignment for Matron Mother Drisinil Melarn. We've got permission to avoid the fighting while we take care of a very important mission."

"Oh, is that so?" one of the male wizards replied coldly. "Well, Drisinil Melarn was my mother, and I happen to know that she was murdered by traitors before this civil war even started. Since you don't wear a House insignia, I'm guessing you're the spies who were accused of collaborating with her. Maybe it's time you died."

The Melarn wizard stepped back, reaching into his *piwafwi*, but before Pharaun could react, a voice drifted from behind him.

"Hello, Q'arlynd," Halisstra said as she and the others floated up over the side of the web street.

The Melarn wizard stopped, peering at the priestess for a moment. Then he broke into a broad grin.

"Dear sister," he said. "I thought you were dead."

N I N E T E E N

"When the fighting got worse, several of the matron mothers, including Maerret, came to the Dangling Tower and asked us to aid them," Q'arlynd explained. "They said it was a full-scale civil war and the rebels were going to tear the city apart if we didn't stop them. Matron Mother Lirdnolu explained to me what had happened to House Melarn. I knew Mother was dead, and we'd heard that she was killed by Ssipriina Zauvirr with collaborators from the outside who wanted to see the downfall of Ched Nasad."

"And you thought I'd perished, too," Halisstra said, squatting down beside her brother.

"Yes, either at the same time Mother was murdered or in the fall of our House. Is it really gone?" the Melarn wizard asked.

Halisstra only nodded.

"By the Dark Mother," he breathed.

"Well, the family reunion is nice and all, but we still need to get out of this city," Pharaun said, standing. "What's the situation? Where's the closest way out that we can get through?"

Q'arlynd shook his head and said, "There are none, so I've heard. All the gates have either been commandeered by rebel forces or hordes of escaped slaves or they've collapsed outright because of the fighting. This alchemical fire that burns through stone is wreaking havoc on—"

"Believe me, we know," the Master of Sorcere interrupted, "but your report doesn't leave us with many options. We've got to find a way to get free of the city."

Quenthel had just opened her mouth, most likely to command Pharaun to figure out a method of escaping Ched Nasad, the wizard imagined, when a commotion broke out from farther down the boulevard. Pharaun turned and looked just in time to see a jumble of dark elves stumbling to their feet in disarray. Many of them fell again just as quickly, cut down by a growing horde of gray dwarves who were emerging through a magical doorway hovering in the air only a couple of feet above the street. The duergar were streaming through as fast as they could, firing off crossbows at any drow targets they could find before casting the missile weapons aside and pulling out axes, hammers, and the occasional mace.

"Attack! We're under attack!" the cry went up as more drow surged to their feet, moving to stop the advance of the gray dwarves.

"Come on, you flat-footed, sorry excuses for soldiers—get up there and fight before they split us down the middle!" the battle priestess yelled, returning from the far end of the street and shoving troops forward as fast as she could get to them. "Wizard! Throw a spell! Drive them back. If they reach the square, we're done for."

Pharaun sighed and nodded, grabbing the battle priestess and spinning her around to face him. His smile was gone.

"Tell your troops to fall back to this point," he said.

"What? And let them come at us unopposed? I think not."

"Do it, or they will be trapped. Set up three positions of missile fire, here—" he pointed to several positions in the street—"there, and there."

The battle priestess looked at the mage as though he were crazy but finally nodded and shouted for an organized retreat.

Pharaun rolled his eyes at the battle priestess's short-sightedness and began organizing the drow soldiers himself, sorting them into groups of crossbowmen, stationing them where he'd pointed earlier. As more and more of the dark elves dropped back from the duergar, they fell in with the others already positioned. As a unit, they began to fire into the mass of milling gray dwarves, who were slaughtering the few remaining stragglers.

They're lost to us, the wizard said to himself.

He cast, and a great mass of webs appeared, spanning the width of the street, anchored to the pavement and the buildings on either side. A handful of the dark elves were caught in the sticky strands, and perhaps a dozen or so were trapped on the other side, but the gray dwarves were effectively sealed off from advancing, at least until they penetrated the webs or the spell wore off.

"Come on," Q'arlynd said, motioning upward as he began to levitate.

Pharaun followed the other wizard upward to a position where they could see over the top of his webs, down into the field of battle where the gray dwarves had quickly killed the few remaining drow who had been trapped with them. The duergar were milling about, seemingly unsure what to do. Halisstra's brother had components out, ready to cast a spell, and one look at the lump of bat guano in his hand told Pharaun what the wizard planned.

"Hold on," Pharaun said, laying a hand on Q'arlynd's arm. "They're waiting," he explained, pointing down at the duergar. "They want a shaman or something to come try to dispel the webs. He's probably the same one who opened the dimensional doorway."

Sure enough, a duergar dressed in robes and wearing several totems and other magical trinkets stepped through the glowing doorway. One of the duergar addressed him—Pharaun couldn't hear what was being said—and pointed to the webs. The shaman nodded and began to cast.

"Do it," Pharaun said.

Q'arlynd went into action, letting loose with his spell, aiming it directly at the shaman. It was a direct hit, and that entire side of the street was engulfed in a white-hot ball of fire that blossomed outward and vaporized an instant later. Charred and burning gray dwarves lay everywhere. A few moved, having survived, but they were few and far between. Most importantly, the dimensional pathway had been banished, winking out when the shaman who created it died.

The two wizards settled back to the ground again, noting that Q'arlynd's fiery ball of magic had ignited the webs, which were quickly burning away. Already, though, another gateway was forming, this one at the opposite end of the street. The battle priestess rallied her troops to deal with the new threat.

"You know you only delayed the inevitable," Quenthel said as Pharaun and Q'arlynd returned. "We're wasting time, here. We have to get out of the city."

"I know," the Master of Sorcere replied, "but it was fun."

"Look!" Danifae shouted, pointing toward the new gateway.

Duergar were streaming out, and drow were arriving from above and below, levitating from the web streets on the two adjacent levels.

"It's House Zauvirr troops," the battle captive explained. "They've got us pinned."

"Fall back," the battle priestess commanded, turning to point back the way the duergar had come, but as she began to direct her soldiers, she took a crossbow bolt in the ear. The missile passed through and protruded from the other side of her head, and she was already dead, motionless, as she fell to the pavement.

"We're surrounded!" Q'arlynd cried out. "Stand and fight!"

He produced a wand and waved it, conjuring a sudden and violent tempest of ice fragments the size of Pharaun's head. The chunks of ice pelted down on the front ranks of gray dwarves, beating them down and slicing them to ribbons amid cries of anguish.

In reply, the duergar began throwing more of the firepots into the ever-tightening mass of House Maerret drow, who were bunched together and made easy targets. More and more of the gray dwarves appeared, forming ranks, establishing a shield wall in front so that the back ranks would have protection as they fired crossbows and hurled firepots and spells.

Pharaun had no idea where any of his companions were. Everyone had been scattered in the initial panic of the attack. He had no concerns that they couldn't take care of themselves, at least for the moment, but the longer they remained there, the less their chances became of escaping at all. He spun in place, looking for a sign of any of them in the thickening smoke, when a creature materialized in front of the wizard, its back to him.

Pharaun's ability to note magical emanations made it clear to him that this creature had been summoned from somewhere, most likely the lower planes. It was a huge thing, vaguely humanoid, covered with white fur and possessed of four arms. It had a sloping brow and a flattened nose, but the most terrifying aspect was its gaping mouth and fangs. The beast spun around, roaring in rage, and spotted the wizard. Its red eyes glittered in delight as it lunged forward, claws outstretched, ready to rend the Master of Sorcere.

Pharaun fumbled to free his rapier, but the fiendish creature was on him too fast, and he took a painful slash across the shoulder that knocked him sideways several feet. The wizard stumbled to the ground as the thing bounded forward again, pounding its chest with all four fists and roaring a challenge.

Goddess, Pharaun thought in a panic, scrambling backward and trying to activate his rapier.

From one side, a flash of movement caught the mage's eye, and Valas darted in behind the beast, raking both kukris along its hamstrings. The beast roared in pain but amazingly, it spun around before Valas could blend into the surroundings, slashing at the diminutive scout with outstretched claws.

Pharaun heard the other drow grunt and watched him go sprawling from the force of the blow, but it bought him the time he needed to get his rapier free. He mentally commanded the thin blade to attack, and when it jabbed at the beast, which was looming over Valas, the creature snarled and spun back to see what had hurt it. Valas scrambled to his feet and faded from sight.

The fiendish thing growled and roared, swiping at the dancing rapier, but the blade was too quick, darting and weaving and getting several pokes in. Already, the white fur of the monster was tainted red from multiple wounds. This only seemed to be enraging the beast further, and Pharaun had to suppress a grin.

With the blade now protecting him from attack, the wizard could cast a spell. He gestured and uttered a few syllables, and instantly, he was surrounded by more than half a dozen exact duplicates of himself that flickered and spun about.

At the same time, a clay pot shattered right at the feet of the summoned creature, engulfing it in flames. It screamed in pain and flailed about, and Pharaun was forced to back a few steps to avoid it as it went running to escape its torment. Blinded by fire and pain, the fiendish creature charged over the side of the web street, vanishing into the void below.

Pharaun turned to assay the battle, his rapier still bobbing and weaving, waiting for a target, and the wizard nearly got his head taken off by a series of whirling blades. This spell he knew well enough, for it was a favorite of the priestesses, but he doubted that any of the drow had cast it. Two of the spinning blades tore through his *piwafwi*, nipping at his arm and creating quick, thin lines of blood. Instinctively, he dropped to the ground, avoiding the full brunt of the spell, though several of his duplicates vanished after being struck. The mage rolled out from beneath the spinning range of the spell and regained his feet.

Quenthel was nearby, a wand in one hand and her whip in the other. She was slashing at a duergar with her whip, and at the same time, Pharaun noted, she was directing a glowing, floating apparition of a hammer about with the wand. She swiped at the gray dwarf with her whip, and as he backed up to avoid the attack, she brought the hammer in from behind, slamming it into the back of his skull. The duergar jerked once, his eyes rolled up into his head, and he crumpled to the ground.

Ryld maneuvered into view, swinging Splitter all around himself. Pharaun could see that the Master of Melee-Magthere was engaged with three drow, and the way they were handling their own weapons, it appeared that Ryld had matched up with fellow weapons masters. The three opponents stalked around him, feinting and jabbing, trying to get the warrior to over-commit on defense, but Ryld maintained his position, flowing from one stance to the next. Pharaun could see that, despite the exhaustion that was apparent in Ryld's heavy breathing, there was also a gleam in the weapons master's eye. It was taking every ounce of concentration Ryld had, but he actually seemed to be enjoying the challenge.

Black, waving tentacles appeared among Ryld and his three adversaries, and Pharaun watched as two of the writhing appendages latched on to the Master of Melee-Magthere, while several more slithered around the legs and ankles of his foes. All four of the combatants were trapped, and yet none of them was willing to lower his guard in order to try to free himself.

Reacting quickly, Pharaun yanked his wand free of his *piwafwi* and triggered it, sending five screaming points of light into the first of the two tentacles that held Ryld down. The tentacle spasmed and vanished. With a quick spin of his greatsword, Ryld cut through the second black, shiny appendage, then leaped into the air as more of the writhing things reached for him. He levitated upward, out of range of the three weapons masters, who were struggling to free themselves. Before they could, though, a handful of duergar closed in, firing crossbows at the helpless drow, and the dark elves went down quickly.

Pharaun could see that House Maerret's position had been completely overrun. Duergar had closed in on one side, and drow on the other. The fight was simply a mad, whirling jumble of perhaps three dozen combatants fighting for their lives. What few remaining forces of House Maerret still survived were dropping quickly. Opponents closed in from all sides, and soon enough, Pharaun was reunited with his companions as the circle that surrounded them drew tighter and tighter.

"We're out of time," Quenthel said, still swinging her whip and directing magical hammers at her foes. "Do something now, wizard!"

"You!" came an angry shout from behind Pharaun. He turned to see who was making the commotion, and standing there, facing Quenthel, was Ssipriina Zauvirr, glaring at all of them. "You are the reason for all of this!" she screamed, raising her mace and pointing at them. "You should never have come to Ched Nasad!"

"Zauvirr!" came a second angry shout, a much more gruff voice, from the other side. Pharaun turned back the way he had originally been watching and spotted a large, well-armored duergar, one obviously of rank. "Foolish drow, I will see you dead!" the gray dwarf called.

"Betrayer!" Ssipriina spat back. "I should have known better than to trust you, Khorrl Xornbane. You can die with the meddlers. Kill them," she cried to her few remaining soldiers, who were massing in a line. "Kill them all!"

"Death to all drow!" Khorrl Xornbane roared, and motioned his handful of troops forward.

Pharaun's shoulders sagged.

We're never going to get out of here, he thought, swinging his magical rapier around.

Thick black smoke from the burning stone was blinding Ryld, making it hard to see more than a few feet in any direction. The battlefield had suddenly grown quiet. There were no more explosions, no flashing bursts from the firepots. Only the sound of steel on steel, but even that was greatly diminished.

He stepped forward to meet an onrushing contingent of gray dwarves. To his left, Halisstra also entered the fray, her heavy mace and an impressive mithral shield held ready. Quenthel took up a position on the warrior's other side, swinging her whip back and forth experimentally as she advanced.

The duergar, dozens of them, fanned out to meet the eclectic group, bloodlust plain in their eyes. Two came directly at Ryld, battle-axes held high. The weapons master parried the first swing at his shoulder and sidestepped a cut to the knees from his second foe. He brought the greatsword down atop the axe, snapping the haft cleanly, but then had to shift his weight almost off-balance to avoid a punching dagger to the ribs. Spinning, he kicked out with one booted foot, catching the gray dwarf square on the wrist and sending the dagger flying.

A third duergar loomed up behind Ryld, holding a length of chain that he spun in a circle over his head. Ryld saw that the foe was eyeing his legs, so when the attack came, he managed to leap high enough that the metal links missed him and went skittering across the pavement. In mid-leap, Ryld managed to turn completely around, flicking his blade across the head of the first gray dwarf's axe, unable to knock it completely loose, but nonetheless managing to force the combatant off-balance. As he landed, Ryld swung Splitter back around again, swiping at the chain-wielder's throat. The duergar jerked back from the attack, reeling in his chain for another attempt then stiffened in pain as the head of Danifae's morning star came down squarely on his skull in an enchanted shower of sparks. The creature slumped over as Danifae spun away to attack another foe.

Ryld maneuvered back around to face his original foe, who had regained his balance and had his axe level again. His companion, holding his injured wrist limply at his side, had fumbled a smaller hand axe free and was circling around Ryld, still trying to maneuver behind the weapons master. Ryld stepped back as though he were trying to avoid being surrounded, even as he casually blocked a couple of strokes from the battle-axe. Finally, when he saw the gray dwarf rear back for another, even more powerful cut, he planted his toe inside the coils of chain that the downed duergar had been swinging and flipped it up with his leg. As the chain sprayed out, it caught the humanoid squarely in the face. The duergar flinched, ruining his attack.

The Master of Melee-Magthere saw the hand axe coming toward his shoulder and twisted himself so that the blade just missed him then flicked Splitter back and up, slicing cleanly through the gray dwarf's arm at the elbow. Howling in agony, the duergar stumbled away, letting the momentum of the blow bear him out of harm's way. Ryld let the sword swing spin him completely around so that he planted his feet facing once more in the direction of the original enemy, who had disentangled himself from the chain and had flung it away.

Ryld shifted his greatsword a couple times, circling with the gray dwarf, the two of them warily sizing one another up. The weapons master stepped into a handful of slices and thrusts, flinging half-hearted attacks toward the dwarf that never really threatened it but allowed Ryld to see just how eager his opponent was to engage with him. The gray dwarf shied away from every cut and parry, and the Master of Melee-Magthere knew the duergar would break off the fight soon, assuming its companions dwindled to sufficiently small numbers around it.

Ryld stepped into an attack again, keeping his blade low and squarely in front of him, and the duergar trod backward another step. Then, as if out of nowhere, Valas appeared from the shadows, swinging one of his kukris low across the gray dwarf's hamstring. The duergar's knee buckled, and the scout came over the top with his other blade, stabbing it into the creature's chest. The duergar made a gurgling sound as he shivered and fell over.

The Master of Melee-Magthere shifted his attention elsewhere as soon as he saw the threat eliminated. He spied Jeggred ripping a drow to shreds. Only two others were visible, looking for a way to get inside the draegloth's reach, but Ryld doubted that would be the case for long. Another dark elf was fighting to keep Pharaun's rapier away from him, but Quenthel was closing on his flank, and the high priestess lashed out with her scourge, allowing the snake heads to sink their teeth deeply into the creature's neck. Jerking from the sudden sting of the bites, the drow was unable to maintain his attention on the rapier, which ran through his eye.

Another foe was squared off with Halisstra, who warded off a pair of stout blows with her mithral shield. On the third stroke from the dark elf across from her, she used the shield to deflect the strike and throw her opponent off-balance, then swung the heavy mace in her other hand upward in a vicious stroke, right into his chin. There was a loud, drumlike boom, a magical concussion that was obviously much louder than the simple impact of metal on bone, and the drow sank to the ground, his jaw shattered.

Breathing heavily, Ryld surveyed the battlefield. In addition to his six companions and Halisstra's brother, the only ones still standing were a small circle of perhaps a dozen exhausted drow and duergar who had ceased fighting for the moment and were watching as the duergar commander squared off with Ssipriina Zauvirr. The gray dwarf and the matron mother circled one another warily, as smoke wafted about, obscuring everything beyond the circle of Menzoberranyr and the three remaining members of House Melarn.

"Now is our chance," Pharaun said from next to the weapons master. "Let's go."

"No," Quenthel and Halisstra said together.

"Not until she goes down," the daughter of Drisinil Melarn added.

The Mistress of Arach-Tinilith nodded in agreement and said, "If she kills him, we're finishing her."

Pharaun groaned. "This is hardly the time for revenge, Mistresses."

Ssipriina feinted with her mace, and as the gray dwarf twisted out of the way of the attack, the drow palmed a wand and aimed it at her enemy. A thin ray of grayish light shot forth from the tip of the magical device, striking the duergar squarely in the chest. The gray dwarf clutched at his chest and cried out. He dropped to one knee with a groan, and Ssipriina loomed over him.

The duergar disappeared.

Snarling in rage at this trickery, the matron mother slammed her mace down where her foe had been, but she struck nothing but the pavement. Spinning, she swung back and forth wildly, trying to gain a lucky hit, but she found nothing.

The gray dwarf commander appeared again, leaping forward from one side as Ssipriina had turned her back to him. His axe was high, but his war cry gave the drow time to roll away from the worst of the attack. Instead of taking the blade of his weapon full on her skull, it raked across the back of her shoulder with a spurt of crimson.

The matron mother cried out, tumbling prone. She rolled to one side as Khorrl lifted his axe for another stroke. As she came around to face him, she fired off another beam with the wand.

With a grunt, Khorrl Xornbane dropped his axe and clutched his stomach, then crumpled to the ground, letting out a gurgling death sigh.

Quenthel and Halisstra both came at Ssipriina, who was trying to get to her feet, clutching her wounded shoulder with her good hand. Quenthel stepped to one side of the matron mother and struck down with her whip. The fangs of the snakes bit into the drow's flesh and she screeched in pain, then tried to spin around and aim the wand at the high priestess. Halisstra was ready for that, though, and she swung her mace down hard on Ssipriina's hand. The crunch of bone was unmistakable.

Around them all, the duergar and the drow began to fight again, and Ryld had to duck to avoid a sword swung at him by one of the dark elves. He sank to one knee and reversed Splitter, driving the point of the blade into his opponent's midsection. The drow threw up blood and sank to his knees, staring down at the sword in his gut. Impassively, Ryld planted his boot on the other drow's chest and yanked his greatsword free, turning back to see what was happening between the females as the body of his foe collapsed.

Quenthel had a hold of Ssipriina's hair, holding her head up. Both of the matron mother's arms were injured, and she could barely lift them to protect herself—and the poison was starting to take effect.

"Stop it!" Quenthel cried, yelling at the combatants around her. "Stop fighting, *now!*"

Slowly, the duergar and the drow began to back away, turning to look at Quenthel.

"Enough!" the Mistress of Arach-Tinilith said, her voice echoing through the haze. "This is pointless. The city is burning, and we must get out. If you stay here now and try to kill your enemies, you simply bring about your own death. That is not the drow way, and I cannot imagine it is the duergar way, either."

There were murmurs all around as the dark elves and the gray dwarves eyed each other hatefully, but Ryld saw more than a few shake their heads, agreeing with what Quenthel was saying.

"If you want any chance of living, then go your separate ways and get out of here, before the whole—"

The web street shook violently, tossing everyone about. Ryld, already on one knee, managed to maintain his balance. He peered around uncertainly. The whole length of the calcified webbing was unstable, listing sharply to one side. Ryld knew their time was up, and he began to levitate. Then he spotted what had created the upheaval as a second shock wave made the crumbling pavement shift again.

A giant spider had descended from overhead and was scurrying toward them. Behind it, a second spider was also drifting downward, playing out a length of web as it glided down.

Damnation, Ryld thought. There's just no end to this.

He peered around, looking for a direction to go to get clear of the approaching beasts.

Pharaun appeared beside the weapons master, hovering in the air and eyeing the advancing spiders.

"I think I've had quite enough of this," the wizard commented dryly, allowing his dancing rapier to disappear into his ring.

Ryld saw Quenthel and Halisstra, still standing over the slowly dying Ssipriina. He pointed them out to Pharaun.

"They don't know, yet," he said, dropping back down. "We've got to warn them!"

Once on his feet, the weapons master carefully managed to hold his balance as he rushed across the intervening space.

"*Spiders!*" he shouted as he neared them, pointing.

Quenthel looked up and her eyes grew wide. Jeggred appeared out of the haze of smoke next to her, his fur matted with blackening blood.

"We still don't know where to go," Pharaun said, a tinge of despair in his voice as he joined Ryld. "The best choice for now is simply over the side."

"Use your magic," Quenthel commanded. "Get us out of here!"

Pharaun spread his hands helplessly.

"Believe me, Mistress," he said, "if I had the means I would be using it. I've got nothing left. I can't conjure a gate just by willing it."

The first spider loomed closer, and Jeggred advanced toward it, determined to keep himself between the giant arachnid and his mistress. Valas slunk into the group, pulling Danifae along by the hand. The battle captive had a large cut across her forehead, and blood was dripping down into her eyes, making it difficult for her to see.

"Wait!" Ssipriina said, gasping for air as the poison closed her throat. "I know . . . of a way out. Save me . . . from . . . poison . . ."

"What?" Pharaun demanded. "Where? Get us there!"

"Say it, wretch," Quenthel commanded.

"Dangling . . . Tower," the dying matron mother replied. "Old, unused . . . dormant portal. Poison . . . please . . ."

Ignoring Ssipriina's pleas, Quenthel turned to Pharaun and asked, "Could you activate it?"

"I'll damn well try," Pharaun said. "Which way?"

"There . . ." Ssipriina whispered, looking up.

Ryld followed her gaze to a see a large, stalactite-shaped building hanging above them, an inverted tower like many of the estates back in Menzoberranzan. He groaned.

"We don't have enough time to get there!" Pharaun cried.

"Why not?" Q'arlynd Melarn said, floating up into the air to demonstrate. "We just levitate!"

"We can't all do that," Pharaun replied desperately. "As I've pointed out a time or two today already, I am fresh out of transportive spells."

"The battle captive gets left behind," Quenthel said bluntly. "I'm sorry, but that's the way it has to be."

Danifae sank to her knees, her head bowed. She seemed to accept her fate, but Ryld actually felt sorry for the drow. As if to punctuate the lack of time, the stone beneath them shifted again. Ryld left his feet to keep from losing his balance, and everyone else did, too, all except Valas and Danifae.

Q'arlynd shook his head.

"I didn't know," he said, shrugging. "Let's go."

"Wait!" Halisstra said. "I can get us all there," the priestess volunteered.

Pharaun and Quenthel both turned and looked at her. "You can?" the wizard asked.

"Yes," Halisstra said, nodding. "I dabble a bit in magic, myself. Different from your style, but some things are the same. Ryld says you're fond of using those dimensional doorways. I can do that."

Pharaun motioned for her to hurry.

"Open it into the main gallery," Q'arlynd shouted to Halisstra, pointing upward. "Where I took you that time?"

Another shock wave reverberated through the web street, causing it to buck wildly. Danifae and Valas both went sprawling, nearly being tossed over the side. The first spider was upon them, and Jeggred engaged it in a fight, levitating up to strike at its head. Ryld peered around wildly as the spider reared up and snapped at the draegloth, causing the web street to buck again.

The biggest rumble yet whipped through the thoroughfare, and the stone began to shift and crack.

"It's going to collapse!" Ryld shouted.

"Priestess, open your doorway!" Pharaun yelled as another roiling tremor dislodged the side of the street only a few feet away from them. "We're going through now!"

"No!" screamed Ssipriina, holding the wand she'd used to defeat Khorrl in both of her hands, her feet splayed out beside her, trying to maintain her balance.

She mumbled something and aimed the beam at Halisstra. The gray sliver of light struck the priestess in the leg and she buckled over in agony.

"You're . . . going to . . . die with me," the crazed matron mother said, turning the wand toward Quenthel. "No one . . . gets out . . . alive!"

Quenthel couldn't flee, as she was hovering in the air. She eyed the enraged drow across from her, licking her lips in desperation.

"I think not!" Halisstra shouted, standing straight again.

Before Ssipriina could trigger the wand again, the priestess spun around, swinging her mace with both hands. She struck the matron mother squarely in the face. There was a loud thunderclap, and Ssipriina Zauvirr was driven back a dozen feet, her face a ruined mess of pulpy flesh and bone.

"To the Abyss with you!" Halisstra screamed at Ssipriina Zauvirr's lifeless body.

Groaning and clutching at her leg, Halisstra wove a spell as the web street tilted again. She was singing, her voice quavering over the roar of battle. Ryld had never heard such a sound. She held a single, perfect note, and a bluish-white doorway opened in the air before her.

"Jeggred! Let's go!" Quenthel called, moving toward the doorway.

The draegloth dropped his attacks on the spider and scampered backward. When he reached the rest of them, he caught hold of Valas, while Halisstra helped Q'arlynd get a hold of Danifae. Pharaun launched himself through the opening. Ryld followed the wizard to protect him from whatever might be on the other side, stepping through the magical frame just as the street gave way and tumbled into the darkness below him. He hoped the others were right behind him.

The moment the doorway opened, Pharaun dived through it, hoping he was doing the right thing by trusting the children of House Melarn with his life. For all the wizard knew, she could have picked that moment to exact her revenge upon the Menzoberranyr for all the injustices they'd inflicted upon her family, her home, and herself. She certainly had a right to.

But the pathway didn't deposit the wizard into some scorching furnace or pit of doom. It was a poshly decorated hall, but unfortunately the mage found himself facing a huge, slavering lizard with incredibly sharp teeth. The being spotted him and advanced eagerly, eyeing the wizard as if he were its next meal.

Reacting quickly, the mage flung himself backward, out of the way of the thing, and willed a spell into being that created a series of floating balls of lightning. As the lizard darted toward him, Pharaun directed the balls to engage the creature, sparking as they did so. The beast jerked and backed away, but Pharaun was relentless, slamming all of the spheres of lightning into it. After the fourth one, the creature sprawled to the ground. It twitched a couple of times and lay still.

"What in the Abyss is that?" Ryld asked, popping through the portal with Splitter up and ready. "Are we in the right place?"

"Fortunately, yes," Pharaun replied, jumping up. A shiver through the building caused him to stumble forward. "Unfortunately, Halisstra, having never been here before, must not have known about the guard animals inside. Or else Q'arlynd forgot to warn us."

"By the Dark Mother!" Danifae said, spying the beast as she leaped through into the cell. She had her morning star up in an instant. "Is it dead?"

"I certainly hope so," Valas said, following close behind.

The scout had his kukris in his hands, and he was looking at the dead lizard. The hall shook again, and part of a wall collapsed, exposing the room to the city outside. Everyone splayed their legs out to try and maintain their balance.

One by one, the rest of the team passed through the portal to join them. Jeggred was the last one to clear the gate.

"The whole city's falling," the draegloth announced. Halisstra let the doorway wink out once he was safely through. "The falling stonework must be making the entire cavern quake with its force."

The fiend sounded too matter-of-fact for the wizard's taste.

Halisstra's brother was casting a spell, one Pharaun didn't recognize. He began to radiate an aura of divination magic—Pharaun's ring told him that much—as he looked around, almost as if he was sniffing something out.

"The dormant portal is this way," Q'arlynd said, leading the group out into a hallway. "Follow me."

The entourage followed the Melarn wizard through several passages, up a couple of staircases, and into a hallway that obviously hadn't been used in a long time. Several times during the journey, the structure shook, but they were deeper rumbles, vibrating through the whole of the Underdark.

"If this doesn't work . . ." Quenthel began.

"It'll work," Pharaun cut her off. "I'll need a couple of moments to study it, but it will work."

"You'd better hope so, wizard," the high priestess muttered.

Q'arlynd led them all to the end of the passage and stopped before an open doorway at the end of it.

"It's in there," he said, "but it's magically sealed and warded with protective glyphs. I have no way of getting through."

Pharaun knelt to study the opening. The barrier between the hallway and the larger room beyond was invisible but solid. Pharaun could see that it radiated some sort of magic and reported such.

"If I had the proper type of magic at my disposal," the Master of Sorcere said, "I'd be able to bring it down in mere seconds, but as it is, I can't do so until I've had a chance to rest and regroup."

"Do you have another magical doorway at your disposal?" Quenthel asked Halisstra.

The priestess shook her head miserably, reaching out to steady herself against a wall as another rumble rocked the room and everyone in it.

"Well, then, wizard, what are we going to do?" the Mistress of Arach-Tinilith asked. "We can't sit in here while you recharge your magical energies."

"Quite true," the mage replied. "Give me a moment."

"Mizzrym, we don't have a moment!"

As Pharaun studied their predicament, the building shook again, even more roughly. Everyone was pitched to the floor, and behind them a large portion of the ceiling collapsed, with shards of stone showering down.

"That is getting tiresome," Quenthel complained, regaining her feet with a horrid scowl on her face. "I will *not* die trapped in a cage like some animal. Not after all I've been through."

Growling deeply, Jeggred bounded across to the door and began to attack the invisible opening, raking his claws ineffectually against the barrier. A crackle of electrical energy raked over his body, but it didn't stop him from throwing himself at it again and again. His efforts were fruitless.

"Jeggred, stop it!" Quenthel said at last. "You're not helping."

With another deep-throated growl, the draegloth backed off.

"If we don't get through there," Danifae said to Pharaun, measuring each word for emphasis, "we're all going to be pulverized. Do something!"

"All right, all right," the mage replied, holding up a hand. "The problem is, we have no way to open the door from the inside. The magic that seals us out here keeps me from using even a simple spell. If I was over there, I could simply remove the barrier manually, but that's easier said than done. That's all. Such a simple trick, and yet impossible . . ."

He looked at them all miserably.

"Wait," Ryld said, stepping over near the wizard. "Move back."

Raising Splitter high over his head, the weapons master swung the blade down hard against the barrier. The enchanted weapon sliced into it with a flash of light, and Pharaun saw the magical emanations from the seal fade from view. The blade had dissipated the magic.

"Thank the Dark Mother," someone said as the entire group rushed into the chamber beyond.

"All right, wizard, lead us out of here," Quenthel said, sounding desperate, "and hurry!"

"We'll be departed in a moment," Pharaun said, gesturing for Q'arlynd to show him the way.

The Melarn wizard led the group into the large chamber, which looked like a library, though all the shelves were empty. Several statues lined the walls. Q'arlynd headed toward a spot on one wall, near the back of the room. It was an archway, but it led nowhere at the moment, filled instead with worked stone blocks. It did, however, glow with faint dweomers of transference.

"Here," he said.

"Excellent!" Pharaun replied, grinning as he studied the spot more closely. "Now, I'll just need a moment to—"

The mage's words were cut off by yet another tremor in the floor. This was followed by another, and another, again definitely different than the previous rumbling. Turning to look over his shoulder, Pharaun groaned. A massive statue of iron was striding slowly but inexorably toward them, and with each step the floor trembled under its weight.

"Lolth preserve us," Ryld said, dropping into a defensive crouch. "What is that?"

"It's a magical construct," Pharaun answered. "A golem. I can't do anything about it."

Ryld leaped forward to slice at the huge thing. His blade struck against the side of the construct and skittered off.

Pharaun shouted, "If it exhales, don't breathe the vapors!"

Jeggred snarled and leaped at the golem, slashing at it. In response, the huge construct swung one massive fist around and caught the draegloth squarely in the ribs, sending him flying across the room with a painful grunt. Jeggred was down on his hands and knees, shaking his head.

Ryld moved in again, wary of the huge sword in the golem's other hand. When the weapons master found an opening, he lunged forward, swiping at the metallic hide of the construct. Sparks flew as Splitter cut a deep furrow across the golem's flank. Ryld spun and ducked down, trying to stay behind the thing.

Another tremor rocked the chamber, and part of the ceiling collapsed behind the golem, sending bookshelves flying as shards of wood.

Pharaun went down on one knee from the shaking, then looked up to see that part of the room on the far side had not just collapsed but had completely broken away and disappeared. The Dangling Tower was coming apart around them, just as House Melarn had done. Beyond the jagged edge of the room, Pharaun could see the smoky glow of the burning city. They were indeed running out of time.

"Forget the fight," Quenthel said, grabbing the wizard by the collar of his *piwafwi* and spinning him to face her. "Just get that portal open. *Now!*"

Pharaun nodded and turned away as Jeggred leaped back in beside Ryld. Valas, Halisstra, and Q'arlynd also circled the construct, each of them waiting until the thing turned its attention to another before sliding in to gain an attack. Ignoring the fight behind him, Pharaun concentrated on studying the magical glows from the portal. He needed a few moments to determine the key that would activate the thing.

"Hurry!" Quenthel said, watching him over his shoulder.

Pharaun gave the high priestess a very deliberate look.

"Don't rush me," he said flatly, and continued studying.

Behind the mage came a deep grunt, and Ryld slid up against the wall in a heap. The weapons master shook his head, apparently trying to clear the cobwebs, and regained his feet.

"Hurry," the weapons master hissed, "I don't know how long we can keep this thing off you."

Pharaun rolled his eyes and bent to his task once more. He tumbled onto his side as the floor bucked with another foundation-crumbling shudder.

"I've just about got it," the Master of Sorcere said, when half the wall next to the portal exploded in a shower of rock and dust.

Fragments of debris smacked into the wizard, knocking the breath from him as he went sprawling. He felt the floor shift, not just from buckling but because the whole building was tipping. He knew it was going to break away soon, and their chances for escaping the city would disappear with it.

The mage struggled up into a sitting position and looked around. What was left of the room was considerably smaller than before. The iron golem teetered near the edge of the floor, then took a step toward its nearest foe, causing the stone beneath its feet to groan. Everyone in the group lay sprawled, half buried in rubble and dust, and just beyond Valas, the floor was gone, replaced by the void of the city. The rock groaned and shifted again as the golem took a step toward the scout, and Valas rolled toward the opening.

"Jeggred," Pharaun yelled, "grab Valas!"

Even as the words left his mouth, Valas, who seemed considerably dazed, tumbled the rest of the way over and dropped over the edge, disappearing from sight.

The draegloth, who had been caught beneath a large section of collapsing rubble, let out a snarl of fury so unearthly that it chilled Pharaun's blood. Shoving his way out of the debris, the enraged fiend leaped across the distance and dived over the edge after the scout.

The golem swung its sword toward the demon, but it was too slow. With Jeggred out of sight, the golem focused its attention on its next victim. Q'arlynd Melarn lay facedown, unmoving, close to it. Nearby, Danifae was sprawled across the shattered remains of a bookcase, the wound on her forehead bleeding freely. The golem took another step, and Pharaun nearly fell as the stone floor popped and protested.

We're not going to make it, the mage thought, trying to figure out a way to distract the golem from killing the unconscious pair.

Out of the corner of his eye, Pharaun saw Ryld regain his feet.

"Help them!" the wizard shouted to his friend, pointing to Danifae and Q'arlynd.

The weapons master had a deep gash across his forehead, but his red eyes seemed clear, and when he spotted the forms of the battle captive and the Melarn mage, and the golem moving toward them, he nodded.

The room tilted over some more, and Pharaun slid across the floor a few feet. The blackness of the vast cavern of the city yawned before him. He ignored it and looked to Ryld.

The weapons master measured his distance from the golem, who had gotten close enough to Danifae that it raised its sword high, preparing to deliver a killing blow. Ryld sprang forward, charging as fast as he could, aided by the downhill slope of the floor. When he was within a few feet of the construct, he leaped into the air, extended both feet, and hit the golem with a pile-driving kick to its midsection. The force of the blow drove Ryld back up the slope of the floor, and the golem barely seemed to move.

But then Pharaun saw that it was teetering. The construct took a step back to steady itself, and had the floor been level, it probably would have worked, but the weight of the golem, coupled with the slope of the floor, caused it to overbalance. Another step backward brought the toppling construct near the edge of the floor, and the room shifted more, sinking and increasing the slope. Then, with one final off-balance step, the golem shifted forward again, falling up the slope rather than down. It dropped to one knee and reached out for Q'arlynd, who was shaking his head as he returned to consciousness.

The fractured stone could no longer hold the construct's weight, and it gave out beneath the golem. Even then, the construct latched on to the wizard, gripping him tightly. Q'arlynd screamed in agony. Ryld took two steps forward to save the wizard, but both Q'arlynd and the golem slowly, ponderously went over, slipping from sight.

Halisstra cried out, "*No!*" from the other side of the room.

She ran to the edge, but the weapons master grabbed her and held her back, shaking his head.

Disheartened, Pharaun turned back to the portal. He thought he'd it figured out and reached forward, ready to activate the magic of the portal, and stopped. Something felt . . . wrong. The room shifted over some more, and the wizard was forced to begin levitating to maintain his position. Behind him, he heard one of the females give a startled scream, but he ignored it. Peering at the magical emanations, he realized that he was seeing something illusory. He hadn't noticed it before, but understanding what to look for, it was much clearer.

"Pharaun," Quenthel yelled as everyone gathered around him, "if you can make that thing work, do it! The whole city is going down!"

Shaking his head at what he'd been about to do, the mage began to cast a spell, one that he'd not expected to need that day but was thankful for. He fished an ointment from one of his many pockets and dabbed a bit on each eyelid. Suddenly, everything about the archway became plain to his vision. He could see the runes that had been hidden from his view before, scribed into the stone around it. He cast a second spell, one to decipher the script, and found what he was looking for. The writing contained the trigger word.

"I've got it!" he shouted. "Get ready!"

Pharaun stepped back, uttered the triggering word aloud, and the portal shimmered to life, glowing with a deep purple hue. The whole thing took on a sense of depth, of distance. The stone in the center of the arch faded and was replaced by a shimmering curtain of light.

Pharaun turned back to his companions and shouted, "It's ready! Step through!"

Quenthel was the closest, but she hesitated.

"Where does it go?" she asked.

"I don't know," Pharaun admitted. "The script inscribed on the perimeter mentions something about a city, but I don't recognize the name. We'll find out on the other side."

Quenthel shook her head.

"No. Someone else must go through first."

Ryld, Halisstra, and Danifae were gathered around, with the weapons master helping to keep Danifae from sliding down the floor to her death. The rest of them were levitating.

Ryld pushed Danifae toward the opening and said, "I'm right behind you!"

The master of Melee-Magthere nudged the battle captive into the arch. Danifae cast one last, aggravated look over her shoulder, nodded, and leaned forward into the archway. In a flash, she was gone. Ryld lunged forward a heartbeat later, followed by Halisstra.

Pharaun looked at Quenthel.

"Well?" he said.

"You first," she replied, still gazing at the gate in trepidation.

"I can't," the Master of Sorcere explained. "I must go last. Because I opened it, the portal will shut behind me."

"What about Jeggred?"

"I will wait for them as long as I can," Pharaun said as another groan emanated from the stonework around them.

The remains of the building tilted some more, and Quenthel's eyes widened.

"There is no more time. Go through!" Pharaun said, and he pushed Quenthel toward the opening.

In a fury, the high priestess spun around, her hand reaching for the whip at her side. The five snakes were writhing madly, lashing at the mage even from where they hung, but the building lurched and tipped and Quenthel couldn't hold on. She stumbled against the wizard, and the snakes snapped ineffectually against his *piwafwi*.

Pharaun caught her and set her on her feet again.

"Please," he said to her. "We don't have time for this."

Quenthel's scowl faded slightly, and she looked at the wizard with a slight smirk.

"If I didn't know better, I would think you're getting soft, wizard."

With that, she backed into the archway and was gone.

Pharaun shook his head in wonder and turned to see if there was any sign of Jeggred and Valas. The floor was slanted at a fairly steep pitch, and the mage slid down its surface toward the edge to peer over the side. Below, he could see the two of them, rising as rapidly as Jeggred's levitation would allow. Chunks of stone and other debris was falling into the void beyond them, and Pharaun knocked a fragment loose from the edge of the crumbling floor. He cringed as he watched it tumble toward them, but it shot past, barely missing them.

Finally, almost excruciatingly slowly, the draegloth and his charge reached what was left of the structure. Together, the three of them worked their way toward the archway, which still glowed with an intense light.

"The others are waiting on the other side," Pharaun explained, motioning to the doorway. "I have to go last. Hurry!"

Without hesitating, Jeggred leaped through the archway and vanished. Valas scrambled to go after him just as there was one final, bone-rattling tremor, and the remains of the room began to free fall. Pharaun gave the scout a good shove and dived in after him.

The portal sealed up and its light faded. A heartbeat later, what was left of the Dangling Tower, including the wall where the portal had been anchored, shattered into a million fragments as it struck a web street below.

✿ ✿ ✿

Aliisza cringed when she saw the fury in Kaanyr Vhok's eyes. He was displeased that she had neglected to keep him apprised of the situation in the drow city, and even her explanation of her troubles, the difficulties she had encountered with the drow, did little to soften his mood.

"So you say the entire city is ruined?" the cambion growled, pacing. "Brought down by a horde of miserable gray dwarves?"

"Not just gray dwarves, darling, but the drow themselves. They squabbled among themselves so much that they lost control. It destroyed them."

"How could this have happened? Not that I bear any regret at the fall of the overly proud dark elves, but they do not seem to be the type who would allow such a travesty to occur to their great city. The forces of the Underdark are clearly out of balance."

"I know," the alu-fiend said, moving close to her mate, "but there is a reason."

"You know what it is?"

"Yes, love, but your pacing is putting me on edge. Sit down, and I will tell you."

Kaanyr Vhok sighed, but turned and plopped himself down in his throne.

"All right," he said, patting his lap. "Tell me."

Aliisza sashayed over to Vhok and settled herself into his lap. She had missed him, she realized, more than she'd thought she would. She leaned around and began to nuzzle his ear.

"Mmm," he said, "I missed you," echoing her own thoughts. "But before we get to the 'welcome homes,' tell me what you found out."

Aliisza giggled as his fingers stroked her arm.

"They've lost contact with their goddess," she whispered, blowing the words softly into his ear.

"What?" the cambion rumbled, sitting up straight and nearly dumping the demon on the floor. "Are you serious?"

The alu-fiend folded her arms beneath her breasts in a huff.

"Of course I'm serious," she sniped. "Lolth has vanished from their sight, and they're trying to figure out why, but of course, them being—what did you call them? Oh, yes—'overly proud dark elves.' Them being overly proud and set in their ways, they warred with one another to the point of bringing about their own extinction."

"I see. Well, with Lolth out of the picture, I suppose if you wanted to gain a little retribution for some wrongs inflicted upon you in the past, now would be the time to do it," the cambion said, staring absently into the distance.

"So, are you thinking of exacting a little revenge?" Aliisza said, nuzzling against her lover's neck again.

"Maybe," Vhok replied. "We'll have to see. I guess it won't be against Ched Nasad, hmm?"

"Mmm," Aliisza purred, squirming, as Kaanyr Vhok's fingers began to roam over her body again. "I guess not."

All thoughts of the ruined City of Shimmering Webs left her then, for a good, long while.

🕷   🕷   🕷

High above the ruined City of Shimmering Webs, a single dark elf sat upon a perch of stone near the roof of the great cavern and watched. The smoke was heavy there, thick and acrid, but it didn't bother him. He stared down at the destruction and smiled.

He was not attractive, not by drow standards, certainly, and few of any other species would look on him and think him handsome in the least, but he didn't mind that either. What he sought was much more substantial than beauty.

They will be pleased, Zammzt thought, watching as fires slowly burned away, as whole sections of the city crumbled and collapsed, dropping into the murky depths of the cavern below. It is a good first step. There is still much to be done, but it is a good first step.

Shaking himself out of his reverie, the drow stood and stretched. I must go, he thought, somewhat regretfully.

He was proud of what he'd wrought, and he wished to stay and observe it a bit longer, but the others would be waiting.

Sighing, he turned his sweeping gaze over the ruins of Ched Nasad one last time, then stepped into the darkest recesses of the shadows and vanished.

THOMAS M. REID

The author of *Insurrection* and The Scions of Arrabar Trilogy rescues Aliisza and Kaanyr Vhok from the tattered remnants of their assault on Menzoberranzan, and sends them off on a quest across the multiverse that will leave FORGOTTEN REALMS® fans reeling!

THE EMPYREAN ODYSSEY

BOOK I
THE GOSSAMER PLAIN

Kaanyr Vhok, fresh from his defeat against the drow, turns to hated Sundabar for the victory his demonic forces demand, but there's more to his ambitions than just one human city. In his quest for arcane power, he sends the alu-fiend Aliisza on a mission that will challenge her in ways she never dreamed of.

BOOK II
THE FRACTURED SKY

A demon surrounded by angels in a universe of righteousness? How did that become Aliisza's life?

November 2008

BOOK III
THE CRYSTAL MOUNTAIN

What Aliisza has witnessed has changed her forever, but that's nothing compared to what has happened to the multiverse itself. The startling climax will change the nature of the cosmos forever.

Mid-2009

"Reid is proving himself to be one of the best up and coming authors in the FORGOTTEN REALMS universe."
—fantasy-fan.org

LISA SMEDMAN

The New York Times best-selling author of *Extinction* follows up on the War of the Spider Queen with a new trilogy that brings the Chosen of Lolth out of the Demonweb Pits and on a bloody rampage across Faerûn.

THE LADY PENITENT

BOOK I
SACRIFICE OF THE WIDOW
Halisstra Melarn has been a priestess of Lolth, a repentant follower of Eilistraee, and a would-be killer of gods, but now she's been transformed into the monstrous Lady Penitent, and those she once called friends will feel the sting of her venom.

BOOK II
STORM OF THE DEAD
As the followers of Eilistraee fall one by one to Halisstra's wrath, Lolth turns her attention to the other gods.

September 2007

BOOK III
ASCENDANCY OF THE LAST
The dark elves of Faerûn must finally choose between a goddess that offers redemption and peace, or a goddess that demands sacrifice and blood. We know what a human would choose, but what about a drow?

June 2008

RICHARD LEE BYERS

The author of *Dissolution* and The Year of Rogue Dragons sets his
sights on the realm of Thay in a new trilogy that no
FORGOTTEN REALMS® fan can afford to miss.

THE HAUNTED LAND

BOOK I
UNCLEAN

Many powerful wizards hold Thay in their control, but when one of them
grows weary of being one of many, and goes to war, it will be at the head of
an army of undead.

BOOK II
UNDEAD

The dead walk in Thay, and as the rest of Faerûn looks on in stunned horror, the very
nature of this mysterious, dangerous realm begins to change.

March 2008

BOOK III
UNHOLY

Forces undreamed of even by Szass Tam have brought havoc and death to Thay, but
the lich's true intentions remain a mystery—a mystery that could spell doom for the
entire world.

Early 2009

ANTHOLOGY
REALMS OF THE DEAD

A collection of new short stories by some of the Realms' most popular authors sheds
new light on the horrible nature of the undead of Faerûn. Prepare yourself for the
terror of the *Realms of the Dead*.

Early 2010

PAUL S. KEMP

"I would rank Kemp among WotC's most talented authors, past and present, such as R. A. Salvatore, Elaine Cunningham, and Troy Denning."
—Fantasy Hotlist

The *New York Times* best-selling author of *Resurrection* and The Erevis Cale Trilogy plunges ever deeper into the shadows that surround the FORGOTTEN REALMS® world in this Realms-shaking new trilogy.

THE TWILIGHT WAR

BOOK I
SHADOWBRED
It takes a shade to know a shade, but will take more than a shade to stand against the Twelve Princes of Shade Enclave. All of the realm of Sembia may not be enough.

BOOK II
SHADOWSTORM
Civil war rends Sembia, and the ancient archwizards of Shade offer to help. But with friends like these . . .

September 2007

BOOK III
SHADOWREALM
No longer content to stay within the bounds of their magnificent floating city, the Shadovar promise a new era, and a new empire, for the future of Faerûn.

May 2008

anthology
REALMS OF WAR
A collection of all new stories by your favorite FORGOTTEN REALMS authors digs deep into the bloody history of Faerûn.

January 2008

THE KNIGHTS OF MYTH DRANNOR

A brand new trilogy by master storyteller

ED GREENWOOD

Join the creator of the FORGOTTEN REALMS® world as he explores the early adventures of his original and most celebrated characters from the moment they earn the name "Swords of Eveningstar" to the day they prove themselves worthy of it.

BOOK I
SWORDS OF EVENINGSTAR

Florin Falconhand has always dreamed of adventure. When he saves the life of the king of Cormyr, his dream comes true and he earns an adventuring charter for himself and his friends. Unfortunately for Florin, he has also earned the enmity of several nobles and the attention of some of Cormyr's most dangerous denizens.

Now available in paperback!

BOOK II
SWORDS OF DRAGONFIRE

Victory never comes without sacrifice. Florin Falconhand and the Swords of Eveningstar have lost friends in their adventures, but in true heroic fashion, they press on. Unfortunately, there are those who would see the Swords of Eveningstar pay for lives lost and damage wrecked, regardless of where the true blame lies.

August 2007

BOOK III
THE SWORD NEVER SLEEPS

Fame has found the Swords of Eveningstar, but with fame comes danger. Nefarious forces have dark designs on these adventurers who seem to overturn the most clever of plots. And if the Swords will not be made into their tools, they will be destroyed.

August 2008

During the Last War, Gaven was an adventurer, searching the darkest reaches of the underworld. But an encounter with a powerful artifact forever changed him, breaking his mind and landing him in the deepest cell of the darkest prison in all the world.

THE DRACONIC PROPHECIES

BOOK I

When war looms on the horizon, some see it as more than renewed hostilities between nations. Some see the fulfillment of an ancient prophecy—one that promises both the doom and salvation of the world. And Gaven may be the key to it all.

THE STORM DRAGON

The first EBERRON® hardcover by veteran game designer and the author of *In the Claws of the Tiger*:

James Wyatt

SEPTEMBER 2007

WELCOME TO THE

WORLD

Created by Keith Baker and developed by Bill Slavicsek and James Wyatt, EBERRON® is the latest setting designed for the DUNGEONS & DRAGONS® Roleplaying game, novels, comic books, and electronic games.

ANCIENT, WIDESPREAD MAGIC

Magic pervades the EBERRON world. Artificers create wonders of engineering and architecture. Wizards and sorcerers use their spells in war and peace. Magic also leaves its mark—the coveted dragonmark—on members of a gifted aristocracy. Some use their gifts to rule wisely and well, but too many rule with ruthless greed, seeking only to expand their own dominance.

INTRIGUE AND MYSTERY

A land ravaged by generations of war. Enemy nations that fought each other to a standstill over countless, bloody battlefields now turn to subtler methods of conflict. While nations scheme and merchants bicker, priceless secrets from the past lie buried and lost in the devastation, waiting to be tracked down by intrepid scholars and rediscovered by audacious adventurers.

SWASHBUCKLING ADVENTURE

The EBERRON setting is no place for the timid. Courage, strength, and quick thinking are needed to survive and prosper in this land of peril and high adventure.

RICHARD A. KNAAK

THE OGRE TITANS

The Grand Lord Golgren has been savagely crushing
all opposition to his control of the harsh ogre lands of
Kern and Blöde, first sweeping away rival chieftains, then
rebuilding the capital in his image. For this he has had to
deal with the ogre titans, dark, sorcerous giants who have
contempt for his leadership.

VOLUME ONE
THE BLACK TALON

Among the ogres, where every ritual demands blood and every ally can
become a deadly foe, Golgren seeks whatever advantage he can obtain,
even if it means a possible alliance with the Knights of Solamnia, a
questionable pact with a mysterious wizard, and trusting an elven slave
who might wish him dead.

December 2007

VOLUME TWO
THE FIRE ROSE

With his other enemies beginning to converge on him from all sides,
Golgren, now Grand Khan of all his kind, must battle with the
Ogre Titans for mastery of a mysterious artifact capable of ultimate
transformation and power.

December 2008

VOLUME THREE
THE GARGOYLE KING

Forced from the throne he has so long coveted, Golgren makes a final
stand for control of the ogre lands against the Titans . . . against an
enemy as ancient and powerful as a god.

December 2009

JEAN RABE

THE STONETELLERS

"Jean Rabe is adept at weaving a web of deceit and lies, mixed with adventure, magic, and mystery."
—sffworld.com on *Betrayal*

Jean Rabe returns to the DRAGONLANCE® world with a tale of slavery, rebellion, and the struggle for freedom.

VOLUME ONE
THE REBELLION

After decades of service, nature has dealt the goblins a stroke of luck. Earthquakes strike the Dark Knights' camp and mines, crippling the Knights and giving the goblins their best chance to escape. But their freedom will not be easy to win.

August 2007

VOLUME TWO
DEATH MARCH

The escaped slaves—led by the hobgoblin Direfang—embark on a journey fraught with danger as they leave Neraka to cross the ocean and enter the Qualinesti Forest, where they believe themselves free. . . .

August 2008

VOLUME THREE
GOBLIN NATION

A goblin nation rises in the old forest, building fortresses and fighting to hold onto their new homeland, while the sorcerers among them search for powerful magic cradled far beneath the trees.

August 2009

MARGARET WEIS
&
TRACY HICKMAN

The co-creators of the DRAGONLANCE® world return to the epic tale that introduced Krynn to a generation of fans!

THE LOST CHRONICLES

VOLUME ONE
DRAGONS OF THE DWARVEN DEPTHS

As Tanis and Flint bargain for refuge in Thorbardin, Raistlin and Caramon go to Neraka to search for one of the spellbooks of Fistandantilus. The refugees in Thorbardin are trapped when the draconian army marches, and Flint undertakes a quest to find the Hammer of Kharas to free them all, while Sturm becomes a key of a different sort.

Now Available in Paperback!

VOLUME TWO
DRAGONS OF THE HIGHLORD SKIES

Dragon Highlord Ariakas assigns the recovery of the dragon orb taken to Ice Wall to Kitiara Uth-Matar, who is rising up the ranks of both the dark forces and of Ariakas's esteem. Finding the orb proves easy, but getting it from Laurana proves more difficult. Difficult enough to attract the attention of Lord Soth.

Now Available in Hardcover!

VOLUME THREE
DRAGONS OF THE HOURGLASS MAGE

The wizard Raistlin Majere takes the black robes and travels to the capital city of the evil empire, Neraka, to serve the Queen of Darkness.

July 2008

R.A. Salvatore's
WAR OF THE SPIDER QUEEN BOOK III

Condemnation

RICHARD BAKER

R. A. SALVATORE'S

War of the Spider Queen Book III: Condemnation

Distributed to the hobby, toy, and comic trade in the United States and Canada by regional distributors.

Distributed worldwide by Wizards of the Coast, Inc. and regional distributors.

FORGOTTEN REALMS, WIZARDS OF THE COAST, and their logos are trademarks of Wizards of the Coast, Inc., in the USA and other countries.

All Wizards of the Coast characters, character names, and the distinctive likenesses thereof are trademarks of Wizards of the Coast, Inc.

Printed in the U.S.A.

Cover art by Brom
First Printing: May 2003
Library of Congress Catalog Card Number: 2003116417

9 8 7 6 5 4

US ISBN: 0-7869-3202-3
UK ISBN: 0-7869-3203-1
620-96541-001-EN

U.S., CANADA,
ASIA, PACIFIC, & LATIN AMERICA
Wizards of the Coast, Inc.
P.O. Box 707
Renton, WA 98057-0707
+1-800-324-6496

EUROPEAN HEADQUARTERS
Wizards of the Coast, Belgium
T Hosfveld 6d
1702 Groot-Bijgaarden
Belgium
+322 467 3360

Visit our website at **www.wizards.com**

FORGOTTEN REALMS

R.A. Salvatore's
WAR OF THE SPIDER QUEEN

BOOK I
Dissolution
RICHARD LEE BYERS

BOOK II
Insurrection
THOMAS M. REID

BOOK III
Condemnation
RICHARD BAKER

BOOK IV
Extinction
LISA SMEDMAN
JANUARY 2004

BOOK V
Annihilation
PHILIP ATHANS
JULY 2004

BOOK VI
Resurrection
PAUL S. KEMP
APRIL 2005

For Lynn R. Baker, Jr.

1942-2002

Godspeed, Dad.

Acknowledgments

Thanks to Phil Athans for thinking big and paying the price, to Bob Salvatore for sharing his sandbox, and to Ed Greenwood for sharing his world.
Oh, and special thanks to Kim for putting up with me, and to Alex and Hannah for teaching me something new every day.

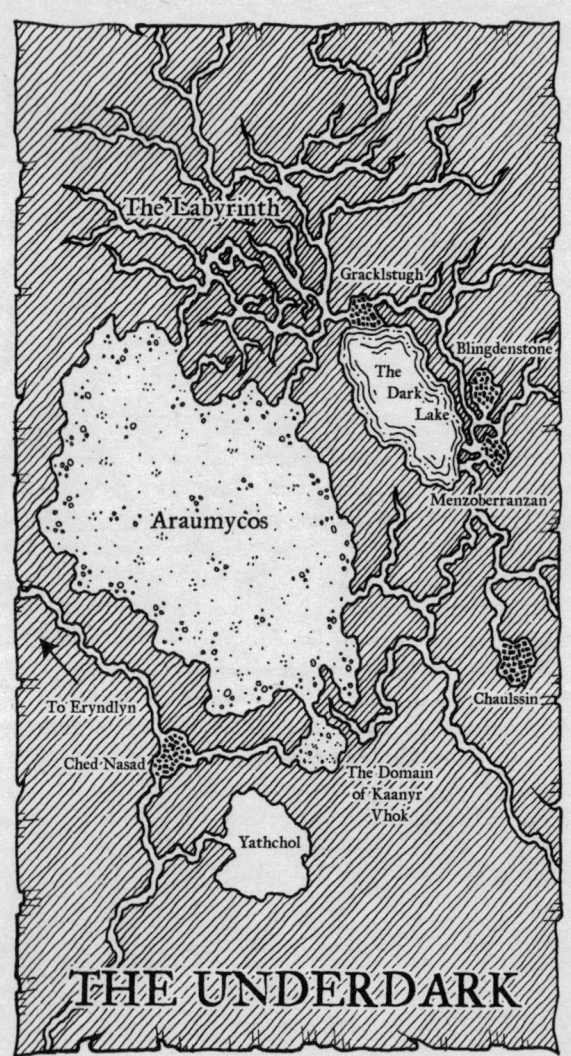

THE UNDERDARK

The food was gone and with it the warmth. All was hollow and empty, save the call to break free. That came most insistently, a subtle urging growing into desperation.

Eight tiny legs answered that imploring call. Eight tiny weapons struck at the concave wall. Battering and tearing, following the lighter shade of gray in this dark place.

A hole appeared in the leathery surface and the eight legs coordinated their attacks at that very spot, sensing weakness. Weakness could not be tolerated. Weakness had to be exploited, immediately and without mercy.

One by one, ten by ten, a thousand by a thousand, a million by a million, tiny legs waved in the misty space between universes for the first time, tearing free of their circular prisons. Driven by hunger and ambition, by fear and an instinctive vileness, the millions of arachnids fought their first battle against a pliable, leathery barrier. Hardly a worthy adversary, but they fought with an urgency wrought of knowing that the first to emerge would hold a great advantage, knowing that they—all of them—were hungry.

And knowing there was nothing to eat but each other.

The warmth of the egg sac was gone, devoured. The quiet moments of solitude, of awakening, of first sense of consciousness, were past. The walls that had served as shelter and protection became an impediment and nothing more. The soft shell was a barricade against food, against necessary battle, against satiation on so many levels.

Against power.

And that, most of all, could not be tolerated by these blessed and cursed offspring. So they fought and tore and scrabbled and scrambled to get out.

To eat.

To climb.

To dominate.

To kill.

To become. . . .

Streams of dust and sand hissed over old red stone. Halisstra Melarn drew her *piwafwi* close around her, and shivered in the bitter wind. The night was cold, colder than the deeps and caverns far below the world's surface, and the wind moaned mournfully through the weathered ruins, crouching dead and silent in arid hills. Once a great city stood there, but no more. Shattered domes and tottering colonnades whispered of a proud and skillful race, long gone. Vast ramparts still stood against the desert wind, and the broken stumps of towers reached for the heavens.

In different circumstances Halisstra might have spent days wandering the silent ways of the mighty ruins and pondering their long-lost tale, but at the moment a far greater and more terrifying mystery held her rapt with awe and horror. Above the black silhouettes of crumbling towers and crooked walls, a sea of stars glittered like cold hard ice in a black and limitless sky.

She'd heard of such things all her life, of course. Intellectually she understood the concept of an open sky in place of a cavern roof, and the ludicrously distant pinpricks of light overhead, but to sit out in the open beneath such a sight and gaze on it with her own eyes . . . that was something else indeed. In her two hundred years she had never ventured more than a few dozen miles from Ched Nasad, and she had certainly never come within miles of the surface. Very few dark elves from the City of Shimmering Webs had. Like most drow, they largely ignored the world outside the endless intrigues, scheming, and remorseless self-interest of life in Ched Nasad.

She stared at the glittering lights above and bitterly savored the irony. The pinprick diamonds and the vast night sky were real. They had existed for some unimaginably long time, long before she had happened to look up in that forlorn, freezing desert and notice them, and they would doubtless continue long after she was gone. But Ched Nasad, the city of her birth, the city whose rivalries and loyalties and fortunes had completely absorbed all of her intellectual abilities and attention for her entire life, was no more. Not a day ago she had stood on the high balconies of House Nasadra and stared down in horror at burning stone and falling castles, witness to her city's catastrophic destruction. Ched Nasad, with its wondrous webs of stone and darkly beautiful fairy-castles clinging to the chasm walls—Ched Nasad, with its awesome arrogance and hubris, its darkly beautiful noble houses and its ceaseless veneration of the Spider Queen herself—Ched Nasad, the center of Halisstra's existence, was no more.

With a sigh, Halisstra tore her gaze away from the sky overhead and stood. She was tall for a drow, almost five and a half feet in height, and slender as a rapier. While her features lacked the alluring, almost rapacious sensuality many highborn drow women possessed, she was beautiful in an austere and measured manner. Even after hours of furious fighting and desperate struggle to escape fire, foe, and calamity, Halisstra moved with cold, absentminded gracefulness, the calm self-possession of a woman born to be a queen.

Sand pelted against the jet-black steel of her armor, while the wind caught at her cloak and tried to tug it away from her. Halisstra knew well the damp, chill motions of air in vast spaces under the earth, but the desert city was scoured by a relentless, stinging blast that buffeted her from a different direction moment to moment. She put the wind, the stars, and the ruins out of her mind, and silently drifted back to the others. They huddled in the lee of a great wall in a small court studded with broken pillars. At one end of the plaza the empty remnants of a lordly palace stood. No furnishings had survived the centuries of sand and weathering that had scoured the city, but the colonnades and courts, high chambers and proud halls, indicated that the building had once been the residence of a family of some power in the city, perhaps even the rulers or lords of the place. Not far away within the sand-blasted walls stood a blank stone portal, an archway of strange black stone, that housed a magical gate leading back to Ched Nasad. Through that portal Halisstra and the others had made their escape from the sack of the drow city.

She paused and studied her six companions. Danifae, her lady-in-waiting, knelt gracefully at one side, her perfect face composed, eyes closed serenely. She might have been dozing lightly, or simply awaiting the next turn of events with equanimity. Fifteen years before, Danifae, a captive priestess from the city of Eryndlyn, had been gifted to Halisstra as a maidservant. Young, beautiful, and clever, Danifae had resigned herself to bondage with surprising grace. She had no choice, really—a silver locket over Danifae's heart enslaved the girl with a powerful enchantment. What passed behind those lustrous eyes and perfect features not even Halisstra could guess, but Danifae had served her as faithfully and as competently as her binding demanded, and perhaps even more than that. Halisstra found herself comforted to no small degree by the simple fact that Danifae was still with her.

Her remaining five companions did not comfort her in the least. The events of Ched Nasad's last days had thrown Halisstra in with a party of travelers from distant Menzoberranzan, a city that had in the course of time been Ched Nasad's enemy, rival, trading partner, and master. Quenthel Baenre sat wrapped in her own thoughts, her cloak pulled close against the chill. A sister priestess of the Spider

Queen, Quenthel was a scion of House Baenre, the leading clan of Menzoberranzan. Of course, Quenthel was no friend of Halisstra's simply because they both served as priestesses of Lolth; most drow noblewomen served the Spider Queen and spent their lives feuding for station and preeminence in her worship. That was the way of things for the drow, the pattern dictated by Lolth. If it pleased the Spider Queen to reward those who proved most ruthless, most ambitious in her service, then what else could a dark elf do?

Quenthel was in many ways the epitome of drow womanhood, a matriarch in the making who combined piety in Lolth's service with physical beauty, strength of character, and absolute ruthlessness. Of the five travelers from Menzoberranzan, she was by far the most dangerous to Halisstra. Halisstra, too, was the daughter of a matron mother and a priestess of Lolth, so she knew well that she would have to watch Quenthel closely. For the moment, they were allies, but it would not take much for Quenthel to decide that Halisstra was more useful as a follower, as a captive, or simply dead.

Quenthel commanded the loyalty of the hulking Jeggred, a draegloth of her own House Baenre. The draegloth was half-demon, half-drow, the son of Quenthel's elder sister and some unnamed denizen of the Abyss. Jeggred towered over the other drow, a four-armed creature of bestial aspect who held a murderous violence in check at all times. His face was drowlike, and he walked upright, but a gleaming silver pelt covered his dark skin at chest, shoulders, and loins, and his claws were as long and as sharp as daggers. Halisstra didn't fear Jeggred, as the draegloth was Quenthel's creature and would not lay a finger on her without his mistress's express command. He might be the instrument of Halisstra's death, if Quenthel chose to order it, but there was no point in regarding him as anything other than Quenthel's weapon.

The wizard Pharaun intrigued Halisstra greatly. The study of arcane lore was something that, like swordplay, was traditionally left to males. A powerful wizard merited a certain amount of respect despite the fact that he was male. In fact, Halisstra knew of more than one instance in which the matron mother of an important house ruled only with the consent of the powerful male wizards of the family, a situation that had always struck her as perverse and dangerous. Pharaun acted as if he commanded that kind of power and influence. Oh, he deferred to Quenthel quickly enough, but never without a sardonic smile or an insincere remark, and at times his disrespectful carriage verged on outright rebellion. That meant that he was either a complete fool—hardly likely, since he'd been handpicked in Menzoberranzan for the dangerous journey to Ched Nasad—or he was powerful enough to hold his own against the natural tyranny of a noble female like Quenthel. Pharaun struck Halisstra as a potentially critical ally against Quenthel, if it turned out that she and Quenthel could not reach an understanding.

It seemed to Halisstra that Ryld Argith was to Pharaun what Jeggred was to Quenthel. A powerfully built weapons master whose stature matched Halisstra's own, Ryld was a fighter of tremendous skill. Halisstra had seen that for herself in the escape from Ched Nasad. Like most males, he maintained a properly deferential demeanor in Quenthel's presence. That was a good sign to Halisstra. Ryld might easily transfer loyalties to another woman of high birth in a pinch. She couldn't count on Ryld turning against either Pharaun or Quenthel, but pure drow were less steadfast in their loyalties than the average draegloth. . . .

The last and the least of the party from Menzoberranzan was the scout, Valas Hune. A small, furtive male, he said little and observed much. Halisstra had seen his type before. Useful enough in the sort of tasks they excelled at, they wanted nothing to do with the machinations of priestesses and matriarchs and did all they could to stay well clear of the politics of the great Houses. At the moment, Valas was crouched over a small pile of dry brush, working to start a fire.

"Is there any chance we will be pursued?" Ryld said into the icy wind.

"I doubt it," Quenthel muttered. "The whole House fell after we used the portal. How could we be followed?"

"It is not impossible, dear Quenthel," Pharaun replied. "A competent wizard might be able to discern where the portal led to, even though it was destroyed. He might even be able to repair the portal sufficiently to make use of it. I suppose it depends on how badly we are missed in Ched Nasad." He glanced up at Halisstra and asked, "What about it, my lady? Don't you think it likely that your kinfolk will hold us to blame for the unfortunate events of the last few hours? Won't they go to great lengths to exact vengeance upon us?"

Halisstra looked at him. The question made no sense to her. Who could possibly be left to fix blame for the duergar attack on the party of Menzoberranyr? House Melarn had fallen, and House Nasadra as well. She became aware of a great weariness in her body, a leaden feeling in her heart and a fog in her mind, and she allowed herself to sink to the sand across from the others.

"Anyone still in Ched Nasad has greater things to concern herself with than your whereabouts," she managed.

"I think the lady has put you in your place, Pharaun," Ryld said, laughing. "The world and all within it do not revolve around you, you know."

Pharaun accepted the jibe with a sardonic grin and a gesture of self-deprecation.

"Just as well," he said lightly. He turned to Valas, who patiently struck sparks at his pile of brush. "Are you sure that's wise? That fire will be visible from quite a distance."

"It's not much later than midnight, unless I miss my guess," the scout replied without looking up from his task. "If you think it's cold now, wait until the hours before dawn. We need fire, regardless of the risk."

"How do you know how late it is," Quenthel asked, "or how cold it'll get?"

Valas struck a spark and quickly crouched to shelter it from the wind. In a few moments, the brush crackled and burned brightly. The scout fed it carefully with more brush.

"You see the pattern of stars to the south?" he said. "Six of them that look a little like a crown? Those are winter stars. They rise early and set late this time of year. You'll note that they're near the zenith."

"You've traveled on the surface before," Quenthel observed.

"Yes, Mistress," Valas said, but did not elaborate.

"If it's the middle of the night, what is that glow in the sky?" she asked. "Surely that must be the dawn."

"A late moonrise."

"It's not the sun coming up? It's so bright!"

Valas looked up, smiled coldly, and said, "If that was the sun, Mistress, the stars would be fading from half the sky. Trust me, it's the moon. If we stay here, you'll come to know the sun soon enough."

Quenthel fell silent, perhaps chagrined by her mistake. Halisstra didn't hold it against her—she had made the same mistake herself.

"That raises an excellent question," said Pharaun. "Presumably, we do not wish to stay here for very long. So, then, what shall we do?"

He looked deliberately at Quenthel Baenre, challenging her with his question.

Quenthel didn't rise to the bait. She gazed off at the silver glow in the east, as if she hadn't heard the question. Moon shadows faint as ghosts began to grow from weathered walls and crumbling columns, so dim that only the eyes of drow accustomed to the gloom of the Underdark could perceive them. Quenthel reached down to the sand beside her and let a handful run between her fingers, watching the way the wind swept away the silver stream. For the first time, it occurred to Halisstra that Quenthel and the other Menzoberranyr might feel something of the same weariness, the same desolation, that lay over her own heart, not because they felt her loss, but because they understood that they had witnessed *a* loss, a great and terrible one.

The silence stretched out for a long time, until Pharaun shifted and opened his mouth as if to speak again. Quenthel spoke before he could, her voice cold and scornful.

"What shall we do, Pharaun? We shall do whatever I *decide* we should do. We are exhausted and wounded, and I have no magic to restore our strength and heal our wounds." She grimaced, and let the rest of the sand slip through her fingers. "For now, rest. I will determine our course of action tomorrow."

Hundreds of miles from the desert ruins, another dark elf stood in another ruined city.

This was a drow city, a jutting bulwark of black stone that thrust out from the wall of a vast, lightless chasm. In arrangement it had once been something like a mighty fortress built upon a great rocky hilltop, only turned on its side to glower out over an empty space where foul winds from the unplumbed abyss below howled up into unseen caverns above. Though its turrets and spires leaned boldly out over a horrifying precipice, the place did not seem frail or precarious in any sense. Its massive pier of rock was one of the bones of the world, a thick spar rooted so securely in the chasm wall that nothing short of the unmaking of Toril would tear it loose.

Those few scholars who remembered the place knew it as Chaulssin, the City of Wyrmshadows, and even most of them forgot why the city was called that. In the lightless fortress on the edge of an abyss, the shadows themselves lived. Inky pools of midnight blacker than a drow's heart curled and flowed from tower to tower. Whispering darkness slithered like a gigantic, hungering dragon in and about the needle-like spires and the open-sided galleries of the dead city. From time to time the living shadows swallowed portions of the city for centuries, drawing a palace or a temple deep into a cold place beyond the circles of the world.

Nimor Imphraezl climbed deliberately through Chaulssin's deserted galleries, seemingly oblivious to the living black curtains that danced and writhed in the city's dark places. The maddening howl of the endless hurricane rising up past the city walls ripped at his cloak and sent his long silver hair streaming from his head, but he paid it no mind. This was his place, his refuge, and its perils and madness simply familiar features undeserving of his attention. Nimor wore the shape of a slim, almost boyish dark elf, which was to say that he was short of stature and slender as a reed. The top of his head would barely reach the nose of a typical female, and any female with a little height to her would tower over him head and shoulders.

Despite his graceful build, Nimor virtually radiated power. His small frame seemed to burst with a precise strength and lethal quickness far out of proportion to his body. His face was narrow but handsome, almost beautiful, and he carried himself with the supreme arrogance of a noble-born drow who feared nothing in his path. It was a part he played well, being a drow of a high House, a prince of his ruined city. If he was something else, something more, well . . . those few dark elves who lived there with him were much the same.

Nimor reached the end of the gallery and turned inward, climbing up a grand stairway cut through the heart of the monolithic spur to which Chaulssin clung. The cacophony of the winds outside faded quickly to a distant but deep whispering, sibilant and penetrating. There was no place one could go within Chaulssin to escape the sound. He set his hand on the hilt of his rapier and followed the spiraling black steps up into a great dark chamber, a vaulted cathedral of shadows in the heart of the city. Flickering torches of everburning fire in bronze sconces cast faint, ruddy pools of light along the ribbed walls, streaks of red that faded into the blackness of the vault overhead. Up there the shadows were close indeed, a roiling well of blackness that even Nimor's eyes could not penetrate.

"Nimor. You are late."

Standing in a circle in the center of the room, the seven Patron Fathers of the Jaezred Chaulssin turned as one to watch Nimor approach. On the far side of the circle stood Patron Grandfather Mauzzkyl, a hale old dark elf with broad shoulders and a deep chest, his hair thinning to a sharp widow's peak.

"The Patron Fathers do not wait on the pleasure of the Anointed Blade of the Jaezred Chaulssin," Mauzzkyl said.

"Revered Grandfather, my delay was unavoidable," Nimor replied.

He joined the circle in the place that had been left for him, offering no obeisance and expecting none from the others. As the

Anointed Blade he answered only to the Patron Grandfather, and in fact stood higher among the Jaezred Chaulssin than any of the Patron Fathers except Mauzzkyl.

"I am lately come from Menzoberranzan," he added, "and tarried as long as I could to observe events before departing."

"How stand matters there?" asked Patron Father Tomphael. He was slender and rakish, much like Nimor in appearance, but he preferred the robes of a wizard to the mail of a fighter, and he possessed a streak of caution that sometimes verged on cowardice. "How does our revolt fare?"

"Not as well as I might like, but about as well as I expected," admitted Nimor. Tomphael's divinations had no doubt revealed that much. Did the Patron Father hope to catch the Anointed Blade concealing a failure? Nimor almost smiled at the simplicity of it. "The slaves were crushed easily enough. Gromph Baenre took an interest in things, and his agents seem to have destroyed or driven off our illithilich friend. On the positive side, we did expose something of the spider-kissers' weakness to the common Menzoberranyr, which is promising, and the priestesses obliged us by using a significant amount of their hoarded magic to destroy their own rebellious slaves. The city is weakened thereby."

"You might have taken a more direct hand in the affair," said Patron Xorthaul, who wore the black mail of a priest. "If you had slain the archmage's lackeys—"

"The revolt we sponsored still would have been crushed, and I would have put them on their guard too soon," Nimor interrupted. "Remember, Patron Xorthaul, this was never intended to be anything other than a simple feint, easily deflected, by which we might assay the real strength of the matron mothers of Menzoberranzan. The next blow will be the one that beats down their guard and slices deep into flesh." He decided to turn the topic and set someone else on the defensive. "As I am the last to arrive, I have no news of how affairs proceed in the other cities. What of Eryndlyn? Or Ched Nasad?"

Cold smiles twisted cruel faces. Nimor blinked. It wasn't often that the patron fathers encountered an event in which they could collectively take pleasure. Grandfather Mauzzkyl himself broke the news.

"Eryndlyn proceeds much as we expected—Patron Father Tomphael brought tidings not dissimilar to your own—but Ched Nasad. . . . From Ched Nasad, Patron Father Zammzt returns in triumph."

"Really?" drawled Nimor, impressed despite himself.

He restrained a hot flash of jealousy and turned to face Zammzt, a dark elf of such unremarkable appearance he might have been a lowly armorer or swordsmith, a common artisan barely a step above a slave. Zammzt merely folded his arms across his chest and inclined his head in recognition of Grandfather Mauzzkyl's remark.

"What happened?" asked Nimor. "Ched Nasad should not have fallen so easily."

"As it happened, Anointed Blade, the stonefire bombs your duergar allies provided us had a devastating effect on the calcified webs upon which Ched Nasad was built," Zammzt said, doubtless feigning his humility. "Just as flame consumes a cobweb, the stonefire devoured the very structure of the city. With their castles and their palaces plummeting to the bottom of the cavern like burning sparks of paper, the Ched Nasadans could organize no real defense at all. No strong point of any significance survived the fires, and few of the House armies escaped from the conflagrations to contest the cavern."

"What is left of the city?"

"Very little, I'm afraid. A few isolated districts and outlying structures relegated to side caverns survived the fire. Of the city's people, I would guess that half perished in the fall and roughly one-third fled into the outer tunnels, where they will doubtless come to a variety of bad ends. Most of the survivors belong to those minor Houses allied with us, or minor Houses who were quick to appreciate the new order of things in the city."

Nimor stroked his chin and said, "So, from a city of twenty thousand, only three thousand remain?"

"A little less, after the slaves fled the city," Zammzt replied, allowing himself a fierce grin. "Of the spider-kissing females, nothing remains."

"Likely some number of Lolth priestesses escaped with those who fled into the Underdark," Nimor mused. "They won't all die in the tunnels. Still, that is great news, Patron Father. We have freed our first city from Lolth's dominion. Others are sure to follow."

Patron Father Xorthaul, the mail-clad priest, snorted in dissent.

"What's the point of removing the Lolth-worshipers from a city if you must level the city to do it?" he asked. "We may rule Ched Nasad now, but all we rule is a smoking chasm and a few dispossessed wretches."

Mauzzkyl shifted his weight and said sharply, "That does not matter, Xorthaul. We have spoken before of the costs of our efforts. Decades, even centuries of misery are nothing if we achieve our ends. Our master is patient." The revered grandfather offered a hard, cruel grin. "We have in two short months accomplished something our fathers among the Jaezred Chaulssin have worked toward for centuries. I would gladly repeat a dozen Ched Nasads all across the Underdark if it succeeded in breaking the Spider Queen's stranglehold over our race. Ched Nasad may be in ruins, but when the city rises again it will rise in our image, its society molded by our beliefs and guided by our secret hand. We are not mere assassins or anarchists, Xorthaul, we are the cold and deliberate hand that culls the weak, the blade that sculpts history."

The collected dark elves nodded assent. Mauzzkyl turned to face Nimor.

"Nimor, my Anointed Blade, Menzoberranzan cries out for the cleansing fire that has purged Ched Nasad. Do not fail in this."

"Revered Grandfather, I assure you that I will not," Nimor said. "I have already prepared my next move. I have reached an understanding with one of the great Houses. They will support us, but they require a demonstration of our resolve and competence. I am reasonably confident that I can oblige them. Within days, one House of Menzoberranzan will be lacking a matron mother and another will be ensnared in our net."

Mauzzkyl smiled in cold approval and said, "I wish you good hunting, then, Anointed Blade."

Nimor bowed once, and turned to leave the circle. Behind him, he could hear the patron fathers dispersing, each to return to his own hidden House in cities scattered over thousands of miles through the Underdark. Secret cabals of the Jaezred Chaulssin existed in at least one minor House of most drow cities. Each patron father ruled absolutely over a conspiracy of faith and gender that spanned generations, centuries, and the formidable hatred of one drow for another. The glaring exception was Menzoberranzan. There, the old Matron Baenre who had ruled absolutely for so long had never allowed the assassin House to gain a foothold. While eight patron fathers returned to cities where there were dozens of loyal killers and priests of Lolth-hating gods at their command, Nimor Imphraezl went alone to Menzoberranzan to resume the destruction of a city.

🕷 🕷 🕷

Sunrise was splendid and terrible. For an hour or more before dawn it had been growing lighter, as the stars paled in the rose-streaked sky and the frigid blast of desert wind slackened toward a fitful calm. Halisstra waited for it, watching from the top of a rambling, half-buried wall. Long before the sun broke over the horizon she was astounded by how far she could see, picking out dark jagged mountains that might have been ten miles or a hundred miles away. When the sun finally rose, it was like a fountain of liquid gold exploding across the barren landscape, in the space of a moment blinding Halisstra completely. She gasped and pressed the heels of her hands to her eyes, which ached from that single brief glimpse as if someone had shoved white daggers into her head.

"That was unwise, my lady," murmured Danifae from close by. "Our eyes were not meant to look on such a sight. You might do yourself an injury . . . and without Lolth's favor, it may prove difficult to heal such a thing."

"I wished to see a dawn," Halisstra said.

13

She turned away from the light of day and shaded her eyes, then dropped lightly to the sand in the shade of the great wall. In shadow she could tolerate the brilliance of the sun, but what would it be like in the middle of the day? Would they be able to see at all, or would they all be blinded completely?

"Once," she said, "our ancestors gazed on the daylit world without fear of the sun. They walked unafraid beneath the sky, beneath the fires of day, and the darkness was what they feared. Can you imagine such a thing?"

Danifae offered a demure smile that did not reach her eyes. Halisstra knew the look well. It was an expression the maid used to indulge her mistress, agreeing to a remark to which she had no response. Danifae indicated the ruined palace and its courts with a tilt of her head.

"Mistress Baenre has called Pharaun and the others to attend her," the battle captive said. "I believe she means to decide what to do next."

"She sent you for me?" Halisstra asked absently.

"No, Mistress."

Halisstra looked up sharply. Danifae offered a shy shrug.

"I thought you might wish to be present anyway."

"Indeed," replied Halisstra.

She smoothed her cloak and glanced around once more at the crumbling ruins that stretched as far as she could see. In the long shadows of sunrise, the wall tops glowed orange, and pools of blackness lay behind them. Since the wind had died, Halisstra became aware of a sense of watchfulness, of old hostility perhaps, waiting somewhere in the walls and broken domes.

The two women picked their way back to the party's camp in the stone-flagged courtyard and quietly joined the discussion. Quenthel glanced at them as they approached, but kept her attention on the others.

"We have learned that the priestesses of Ched Nasad have lost Lolth's favor, just as we have. We did not learn why. We learned that Houses allied to us through trade and blood had elected to appropriate our much-needed property for their own, turning their backs on us. We failed to restore the flow of trade to Menzoberranzan—"

"A failure for which we can hardly be held accountable," Pharaun interrupted. "The city is completely destroyed. The status of Baenre trade interests in Ched Nasad is now moot."

Quenthel continued as if the wizard had not spoken, "Finally, we find ourselves in some godsforsaken portion of the World Above, at some unknown distance from our home, low on provisions and stranded in a hostile desert. Have I accurately summed up events?"

Valas shifted uncomfortably and said, "All but the last, I think. I believe that we are somewhere in the desert known as Anauroch, in fact in its northwestern portions. If I am correct, Menzoberranzan lies perhaps five hundred miles west of us, and somewhat . . . down, of course."

"You have been here before?"

"No," the scout said, "but there are only a few deserts in Faerûn, especially at so northerly a latitude, so it is a very good bet that Anauroch is where we must be. There is a range of snow-capped mountains perhaps forty or fifty miles to our west, which you can see quite clearly in the daylight. Those I believe to be the Graypeak or Nether Mountains. They could be the Ice Mountains, but if we were so far north as to see them, I would think we would be in the High Ice, and not in this sandy and rocky stretch of the Great Desert."

"I've come to trust your sense of direction, but I can't say I relish the prospect of marching half a thousand miles across the surface lands to get home," Ryld Argith said, rubbing his hand over his short-cropped hair. He moved stiffly in his armor, bruised and battered beneath the mail from their desperate fight to escape Ched Nasad. "Citadel Adbar, Sundabar, and Silverymoon would all stand in our way, and they have very little love for our kind."

"Let them try to stop us," growled Jeggred. "We'll travel by night, when the humans and the light-elves are blind. Even if someone should stumble into us, well, the surface dwellers are soft. I don't fear them. Neither should you."

Ryld bridled at the draegloth's remark, but Quenthel silenced him with a raised hand.

"We will do what we have to do," she said. "If we have to spend the next two months creeping across the surface realms under cover of night, we will do exactly that."

She turned gracefully and paced away, gazing thoughtfully at the ruined court around them.

The party fell silent as each of the dark elves watched Quenthel's back. Pharaun pushed himself erect and wrapped his *piwafwi* closer around his lean torso. The black cloak flapped in the bitter wind.

"The question that vexes me," the mage said to no one in particular, "is whether we have accomplished what we set out to do. I do not relish the idea of crawling back to Menzoberranzan with nothing more to show for months of effort than news of Ched Nasad's fall."

"No priestess of the Spider Queen holds the answers we seek," said Quenthel. "We will return to Menzoberranzan. I can only trust that the goddess will make clear the meaning of her silence when it suits her."

Pharaun grimaced and said, "Blind faith is a poor substitute for a plan by which you might win the answers you seek."

"Faith in the goddess is the only thing we have," Halisstra snapped. She shifted half a step closer to the master of Sorcere. "You have forgotten your place if you address a high priestess of Lolth in such a manner. Do not forget it again."

Pharaun opened his mouth to frame what would no doubt have been an even more inflammatory retort, but Ryld, sitting next to him, simply cleared his throat and scratched at his chin. The wizard paused a moment under the eyes of his companions, and shrugged.

"All I meant was that it seems clear to me that the Spider Queen means for us to puzzle out her silence for ourselves."

"How do you suggest we should do that?" Quenthel asked. She folded her arms and pivoted to glare at Pharaun. "In case you have forgotten, we've toiled for months to discern the cause of the Silence."

"But we have not exhausted all avenues of investigation, have we?" Pharaun said. "In Ched Nasad, we spoke of seeking the assistance of a priest of Vhaeraun, possibly Master Hune's acquaintance Tzirik. We drow have other deities beside Lolth, after all. Is it so unreasonable to speculate that another god might be able to explain Lolth's unusual silence?"

The circle fell still. The wizard's words were not ones commonly heard in Menzoberranzan. Few dared utter such thoughts in the presence of the Spider Queen's clergy.

"I see no need to go begging favors of a male heretic worshiping a miserable whelp of a god," Quenthel said. "I doubt that Lolth has deigned to confide her purposes in any lesser powers."

"You are probably correct," said Pharaun. "She certainly hasn't confided them in you, after all."

Jeggred snarled at the wizard, and Pharaun raised his hands in a placating gesture, rolling his eyes.

Valas licked his lips nervously and offered, "Most of you have spent the great majority of your lives in Menzoberranzan, as is fit and proper for drow of your respective stations. I have traveled more widely, and I have visited places that secretly—even openly, in some cases—permit the worship of gods other than Lolth." He noticed the gathering thunder in Quenthel's face, mirrored in Halisstra's. The scout winced but pressed on. "Under the wise rule of the matron mothers, the worship of drow gods other than Lolth has hardly flourished in Menzoberranzan, and so you may not hold a high opinion of the practice, but I can attest to the fact that the priests of the lesser gods of our race can call upon spells and guidance from their deities, too."

"Where might we find Tzirik?" Ryld asked Valas.

"When last I met him, he lived among outcasts in a remote region known as the Labyrinth, south and west of the Darklake by perhaps a hundred miles. This was some time ago, of course."

"Outcasts," snorted Halisstra.

She was not the only one to express disgust. In the endless game played between the great Houses of the drow, of course there were losers. Most died, but some chose flight over death, taking up a hardscrabble and ignominious existence in the remote stretches of the Underdark. Others abandoned their home cities for different reasons—including, Halisstra supposed, the veneration of gods other than Lolth. She found it hard to believe that anyone so weak as to have been run out of her home city could offer much help at all.

"We'll solve our own problems," she said.

Pharaun glanced up at Halisstra, cold humor dancing in his eyes.

"I forgot that you now have some experience with the peculiar misfortune of being deprived of a home city," he remarked. "And I applaud your celerity in including yourself in 'our' discussions and 'our' problems. Your selflessness is laudable."

Halisstra shut her mouth, stung by the words. There would be many hundreds, even thousands of survivors from Ched Nasad scattered in as many tunnels and bolt-holes in the black caverns and passages around the city. Most of those would end their lives in the jaws of mindless monsters, or perhaps fall into wretched slavery as captives of drow from other cities, duergar, or even more horrible Underdark races like the mind flayers or the aboleths. And a few might hope to find some kind of life for themselves through their own wits and resourcefulness. It was not unknown for a House to take into its ranks a defeated enemy who had demonstrated her usefulness. House Melarn was dead. Wherever Halisstra journeyed next, she would be starting from square one. The advantages of her birth, the wealth and power of her city, all that meant nothing anymore.

She considered her reply carefully, conscious of the acute interest of the other drow around her, and said, "Spare me your pity." She spoke in a murderous hiss, putting iron in her voice that she did not feel. "Unless I miss my guess, Menzoberranzan doesn't stand so very far from Ched Nasad's fate, else you never would have come to seek our aid. Our difficulties are your difficulties, are they not?"

Her words had the desired effect. The wizard looked away, while the other Menzoberranyr shifted nervously, studying each other's reactions. Quenthel visibly flinched, her mouth tightening into a fierce scowl.

"Enough, both of you," she said, turning to Valas. "This outcast priest of Vhaeraun—why would he aid us in any way? He is not likely to entertain an especially charitable attitude toward our cause."

Valas replied, "I couldn't say, Mistress. All I can do is bring you to him. What happens after that depends on you."

The ruined courtyard fell silent. The sun was a double handspan into the sky, and blinding shafts of pure light sliced through the darkness of the ruined court from crumbling embrasures in the high walls. The ruins were apparently not as desolate as Halisstra had thought. She could hear the furtive sounds of small creatures scrabbling across sand and rubble, faint and small in the distance.

"The Labyrinth lies only a hundred miles from the Darklake?" Quenthel asked. The scout nodded once. The priestess folded her arms and thought. "Then it's not very far from our homeward course, in any event. Pharaun, do you command any magic that might speed our travel? Fighting our way home across the surface realms appeals to me no more than it does the weapons master."

The wizard leered and rose to his feet, preening under Quenthel's request for help.

"Teleportation is risky," he said. "First, the *faerzress* of the Underdark makes it dangerous to attempt transport spells. More to the point, I have never visited the Labyrinth, and so have no idea where I would be going. I would almost certainly fail. I know a spell to transform myself or others into different shapes more suited for travel, though. Perhaps if we were dragons or giant bats or something that would fly well by night. . . ." The wizard tapped his chin, considering the problem. "Whomever we press into service as a mount would have to stay in that shape until I changed him back, of course, and we'd still be looking at a couple of tendays of travel. Or . . . I know a spell of walking through shadows. It's dangerous, and I couldn't take us straight to the Labyrinth, as I have never been there and the spell is best employed to reach places you know well. I could take you to Mantol-Derith, though, which is hard by the shores of the Darklake. It would shorten our journey considerably."

"Why didn't you mention that before, when we were discussing months of marching across the surface?" said Jeggred, shaking his head in irritation.

"If you recall, we had not yet decided where we were going," Pharaun replied. "I intended to offer my services at the appropriate time."

Ryld said, "You could have transported us from Menzoberranzan to Ched Nasad in the first place. Why in the world did we walk?"

"Because I have good reason to fear the plane of shadow. As a younger and more impulsive mage I learned—the hard way—that shadow walking confers no special protection against the attentions of those creatures that dwell in the dark realm. In fact, I was very nearly devoured by something I would not care to meet again." The wizard offered a wry grin and added, "Naturally, I now regard shadow walking as an option of last resort. I only suggest it now because I deem it slightly less dangerous than tendays of travel across the surface world."

"We will exercise all due caution," Quenthel said. "Let's be about it, then."

"Not so fast. I must prepare the spell. I will require about an hour to make ready."

"Do so without delay," Quenthel said. She glanced around at the ruins, and shaded her eyes. "The sooner we are back below ground, the better."

While Pharaun retired to a dark, quiet chamber to study his grimoires and ready his spells, the rest of the party gathered their gear and prepared to leave. They were woefully unprepared for a long journey on the surface; Halisstra and Danifae had no packs or supplies of any kind. The Menzoberranyr had wisely recovered their packs before escaping Ched Nasad, but their long journey to the City of Shimmering Webs had depleted their stores.

While they waited for Pharaun, Halisstra studied the ruins in more detail. She had something of a scholarly inclination, and deliberately taking an interest in the ancient city was as good a way as any of keeping her mind from dwelling on the last awful hours of her home city. The others busied themselves with the small tasks of breaking camp, or waited patiently in the deepest shadows they could find. Halisstra gathered the few things she had brought and set out from the ruined court. Her eye fell on Danifae, who knelt quietly in the shade of a broken arch, calmly watching her leave.

Halisstra paused, and called, "Come, Danifae."

She didn't like the idea of leaving her servant alone with the Menzoberranyr. Danifae had served her well for years, but circumstances had changed.

The maidservant stood smoothly and followed. Halisstra led her through the crumbling shell of the palace surrounding the courtyard, and they emerged onto a wide boulevard arrowing through the heart of the old city. The air had warmed noticeably in the hour or more since sunrise, but it was still bitterly cold, and the brilliance of the day seemed almost enhanced by the crystal clarity of the skies. Both women stood blinded for several long moments in the sunshine.

"This is no good," muttered Halisstra. "I'm squinting so hard I can't see my hand in front of my face."

Even when she managed to open her eyes, she could see little more than bright, painful spots.

"Valas says it's possible to get used to daylight, with time," Danifae offered. "I find that hard to believe, now that I have experienced it myself. A good thing we mean to return to the Underdark soon." Halisstra heard a small tearing sound from beside her, and Danifae pressed a strip of cloth into her hand. "Tie this over your eyes, Mistress. Perhaps it will help."

Halisstra managed to arrange the dark cloth as a makeshift veil. It did indeed help to abate the fierce glare of the sun.

"That's better," Halisstra said.

Danifae tore another small strip and bound it around her own eyes as her mistress examined the ruins. It seemed to Halisstra that the palace they'd taken shelter in was one of the more prominent buildings, which only made sense. Magical portals were not easy to make, and were often found in well-hidden or vigilantly guarded locations. A colonnade stood along the front of the palace, and across the boulevard was another great building—a temple, or perhaps a court of some kind. There was something familiar about the architecture of the buildings.

"Netherese," she said. "See the square column bases, and the pointed arches in the windows?"

"I thought Netherese cities floated in the air, and were completely destroyed by some magical cataclysm," Danifae replied. "How could anything like this still stand?"

"It could have been one of the successor states," Halisstra said, "built after the great mythallars of the old Netherese cities failed. They would share many of the same architectural features, but would have been more mundane, less magical."

"There's writing up there," Danifae said, pointing at the facade of a crumbled building. "There . . . above the columns."

Halisstra followed Danifae's gesture. "Yes," she said. "That's Netherese."

"You can read it?" Danifae asked.

"I have studied several languages—the common tongue of the surface, High Netherese, Illuskan, even some of the speech of dragons," Halisstra replied. "Our libraries contain fascinating histories and potent lore recorded in languages other than drow. I developed the habit of studying such things over a century ago, when I believed I might find some forgotten spell or secret that might prove useful against my rivals. As it turned out, I found little of that sort of thing, but I did find that I enjoyed learning for its own sake."

"What does it say, then?"

"I'm not sure of some of the words, but I think it reads, 'High Hall of Justice, Hlaungadath—In Truth's Light No Lies Abide.' "

"What a simpleminded sentiment."

Halisstra indicated the ruins around them and said, "You can see how far it got them. I know that name, though, Hlaungadath. I have seen maps of the surface world. Valas's estimate of our location was accurate."

"Even a male can do something right from time to time," Danifae said.

Halisstra smiled and turned away to scan the ruins for any other sites of interest.

Something tawny and quick ducked swiftly out of sight. Halisstra froze on the instant, staring hard at the spot where she'd seen it, a gap in a masonry wall a short distance away. Nothing moved there, but from another direction came the sound of rubble shifting. Without looking away, she touched Danifae's arm.

We're not alone here, she signed. *Back to the others—quickly.*

Together, they backed away from the court of justice and out into the street again. As they turned to retrace their steps, something long and low, covered with sand-colored scales, slid out into the boulevard. Its stubby wings clearly could never support it in flight, but its powerful talons and gaping jaws were much more developed. The dragon paused and raised up its head for a better look at the two drow on the street before it, and it hissed in delight. It was easily fifty feet from nose to tail, a hulking, powerful creature whose eyes gleamed with cunning and malice.

"Lolth protect us!" Danifae gasped.

The two women backed away in a new direction, at a right angle to the palace where their companions waited. The dragon followed leisurely, sinuously winding from side to side as it paced after them.

"It's herding us away from the others," Halisstra snarled.

She sensed hard stone behind her, and risked a quick glance backward. They were pinned against a building, sliding alongside it as they tried to keep their distance from the monster. A dark alleyway gaped just a few feet away. Halisstra hesitated for a heartbeat, then grasped Danifae by the wrist and darted into the narrow opening at the best speed she could manage.

Something waited for them in the shadows of the alley. Before Halisstra could skid to a stop, a tall golden creature reared up before her, half lion, half woman, beautiful and graceful. With a cold, cruel smile, the lion-woman reached out her hand and caressed Halisstra's cheek. Her touch was cool, soothing, and in an instant Halisstra felt her fear, her determination, her very willpower drain softly away. Vaguely she reached up to push the creature's hand away from her face.

"Don't be afraid," the creature said in a lovely voice. "Lie down and rest here a while. You are among friends, and no harm will come to you."

Halisstra stood paralyzed, recognizing that the creature's words made no sense, but empty of the willpower she needed to resist. Danifae whirled her away by her arm and slapped her hard across the face.

"It's a lamia!" she snapped. "It seeks to beguile you!"

The lamia snarled in anger, its beautiful features suddenly hard and cruel.

"Do not resist," it said, its voice harsher.

Halisstra could feel the creature's spell drawing over her, sapping at her resolve, seeking to subjugate her will to its own. She knew that if she gave in she would go willingly to her death, even lie down helplessly while the lamia devoured her if it asked her to, but the sting of Danifae's slap had reawakened the wellsprings of her will, just enough to fight through the lamia's sweet words.

"We are drow," Halisstra managed to gasp. "Our wills may not be broken by such as you."

The lamia bared its teeth in fierce anger and drew a bronze dagger from its hip, but Halisstra and Danifae backed out of the shadowed alley into the sun.

The dragon's gone, signed Danifae.

Halisstra shook her head and replied, *An illusion. We were deceived.*

Something was still hovering in the center of the street, a faint flickering phantasm that might have been about the size of the thing they had seen before, and they could hear as if from very far away its hissing protests.

"Illusion," Danifae spat in disgust.

The dragon-wisp gnawed at the corners of their minds, joined by other, more insistent murmuring and shadows. Buildings seemed to shimmer and vanish, replaced by ruins of different appearance. Dark and horrible things slithered through the rubble, closing off retreat. Ghostly drow dressed in resplendent robes appeared, smiling and happy, calling for them to join them in their blissful revels if only they would surrender first.

The lamia padded softly out into the street after them, holding its dagger behind its back.

"You may resist our enticements for a time," she purred, "but eventually we will wear you down." She reached out with her hand again. "Won't you let me smooth away your cares? Won't you let me touch you again? It would be so much easier."

A swift, graceful movement caught Halisstra's eye, and she glanced quickly to her left. Another lamia, this one male, had leaped to a wall top overshadowing their retreat. He was bronzed and handsome, lithe and tawny, and he smiled cruelly down on them.

"Your journey must have been long and tiresome," he said in voice of gold. "Won't you tell me of your travels? I want to hear all about them."

From the dark doorway of the court of justice, a third lamia emerged.

"Yes, indeed, tell us, tell us," the monster crooned. "What finer way to pass the day, eh? Rest, rest, and let us care for you."

It leaned against a great spear and smiled beatifically at them.

Halisstra and Danifae exchanged a single glance, and fled for their lives.

Gromph Baenre, Archmage of Menzoberranzan, was dissatisfied. Though the slave revolt had been quelled without too much trouble, it disturbed him greatly that so many drow males had made common cause against the matron mothers. Not only that, they had made common cause with slave races to turn against the city. It bespoke desperate fear long suppressed, and something else beside—it suggested an unseen enemy who found a way to give that fear a voice and a mission. Drow simply did not cooperate so easily with each other that a coordinated rebellion could take shape secretly and spring full-grown to life.

The watchful lull that blanketed the city in the aftermath of the crushing of the revolt and the illithilich's demise struck Gromph as something malevolent and deceitful.

He stood up from his writing desk and paced across his chamber, thinking. Kyorli, the rat that served as his familiar, eyed him with cool disinterest as it munched on a slice of rothé cheese.

The sight of the rat somehow reminded the archmage that he hadn't heard from Pharaun in a while. The arrogant popinjay had reported that Ched Nasad was in a state of chaos. Perhaps it was time to check in on him.

Gromph stepped through an archway into an open shaft and levitated up to the room that served as his scrying chamber. Of necessity it was somewhat less well warded than other portions of his demesnes, since he required a certain amount of magical transparency in order to cast his mind out into the wide world around his palace. He reached the chamber and sat cross-legged in front of a low table on which rested a great crystal orb.

With a pass of his aged hands, he muttered the device's activating words and commanded, "Show me Pharaun Mizzrym, the impudent whelp who thinks he can replace me someday."

The last was not strictly necessary, but Gromph found it helpful to give voice to his frustrations before attempting to scry.

The orb grew gray and milky, swirling with fog, then it exploded with unheralded radiance. Gromph swore and averted his eyes. For a moment he believed that Pharaun had devised some new spell to discourage enemies from spying on him, but the Archmage soon recognized the peculiar quality of the brilliance.

Daylight.

Wondering what the Master of Sorcere could possibly be doing on the surface, Gromph shaded his eyes and peered again, looking closer. He saw Pharaun, sitting in the shadow of a crumbling wall as he studied his spellbooks. None of the other dark elves who had accompanied the wizard were in sight, though Gromph could see a nearby archway leading out into a hatefully brilliant courtyard beyond.

The tiny image of Pharaun looked up and frowned. The wizard had sensed Gromph's spying, as any skilled wielder of magic was likely to do. Pharaun made a few silent passes with his hands, and the picture faded. Pharaun had cast a spell to block the scrying, though chances were good he had no idea who might be watching him.

"So you think you will elude me so easily?" Gromph said, staring at the grayness.

He steepled his fingers before him and cast a spell of his own, a mental sending to dispatch a message straight to the errant wizard.

Where are you? What transpired in Ched Nasad? What do you intend to do next?

He composed himself to receive Pharaun's reply—the spell of sending conveyed the recipient's response within a few minutes. The moments crept by, as Gromph gazed out the high, narrow windows of his scrying chamber, awaiting the younger wizard's response.

He felt the feathery touch of Pharaun's words appearing in his mind: *Anauroch. Ched Nasad was destroyed by rebellion and stonefire. Lolth's silence did extend there. We now seek a priest of Vhaeraun in hope of answers.*

The contact faded after those twenty-five words. That particular spell didn't permit lengthy conversations, but Pharaun had answered Gromph's questions with uncharacteristic efficiency.

"Ched Nasad destroyed?" breathed Gromph.

That merited immediate investigation. He turned again to his crystal orb and commanded it to show him the City of Shimmering Webs. It took a moment for the mist to clear, and reveal to the Archmage a complete calamity.

Where Ched Nasad had stood, there was nothing but remnant strands of calcified webbing, dripping slowly into a black abyss like molten glass from a glazier's pipe. Of the city's sinister palaces and wall-climbing castles, virtually nothing remained.

"Lolth protect us," murmured Gromph, sickened at the sight.

He had no particular love for the City of Shimmering Webs, but whatever misfortune had befallen Ched Nasad might visit Menzoberranzan in time. Ched Nasad had been a city nearly as large and as powerful as Menzoberranzan itself, but Gromph could see with his own eyes the completeness of its ruin. If one building in twenty of the city remained, he would have been surprised.

Gromph shifted his orb's vision, searching as best he could for some sign of survivors, but the main cavern was largely deserted. He saw more than a few burned bodies among the smoldering debris, but any drow who'd lived through the burning of the city were clearly sheltering in the nearby caverns. Gromph was unable to bring them into the view of his scrying device, so after a time he decided that the effort was irrelevant and allowed the crystal orb to go dim again. He sat for a long time in silence, gazing absently at the darkened orb.

"Now, do I need to share this with dear Triel?" he asked himself when he finally stirred from his reverie.

He knew something that the matron mothers presumably did not, and that was always the sign of possibility. The trouble was, Gromph had no idea what possible advantage he could derive from hoarding the knowledge, and the risks of failing to communicate what he had learned were all too clear. Knowing that Lolth's silence extended beyond Menzoberranzan, he might mount a direct challenge to the priestesses—if he were inclined to do so—but even if he brought the full strength of Sorcere against the ruling Houses of the city, what would be left if he did succeed? The smoldering wreckage of Ched Nasad seemed a likely result. Most likely the House loyalties among the masters of the wizards' school would cripple any such nonsense from the start.

No, Gromph decided. I am no revolutionary anxious to sweep away the old order—not yet, anyway.

Besides, the most likely cause of all the trouble was some insidious new snare of Lolth's devising. Gromph wouldn't put it past the Spider Queen to fall completely and inexplicably silent, just to see who might slink out of the shadows in order to take advantage of her priestesses' temporary "weakness." That meant that sooner or later, Lolth would tire of her game and restore her favor to her clerics. When that happened, woe to anyone foolish enough to have shown the shallowness of his allegiance to the established order. No, the wisest thing to do was to pass along to Triel what he'd learned, and to make sure Matron Baenre didn't hoard the knowledge to herself. Pharaun's words indicated in a few quick brushstrokes a very grave danger to Menzoberranzan, and Gromph refused to be remembered as the archmage who allowed his city to be razed.

With a sigh, he stood and dropped silently back down the shaft. He rather hoped Triel was in the middle of something awkward, so that he could savor the petty pleasure of interrupting her with news that could not wait.

🕷 🕷 🕷

"The question is not where we should go next," observed Pharaun with a wry grimace. "The question is how we shall escape Hlaungadath alive." The Master of Sorcere was exhausted. Dust plastered the blood and sweat on his face, and he was so tired he could do no more than collapse into the shadow of a long, crumbling wall. Having long since exhausted any spells useful in battle, he wielded a wand of thin black iron from which he called forth bolts of lightning. Pharaun glanced up at the sky as if to gauge how much more daylight remained, and he quickly winced away. "Will the cursed sun never set?"

"Get up, wizard," said Quenthel. "If we rest, we die."

She, too, trembled with exhaustion, but she stayed on her feet. The long snake-headed whips she carried still coiled and hissed dangerously, covered with gore, but blood trickled from a nasty cut above her left eye, and two furrows of broken and twisted links in her mail shirt showed just how close she'd come to dying under the claws of some hulking monstrosity of gray skin and spiderlike eyes.

"You're more vulnerable to the lamias' powers of suggestion and illusion while you're fatigued," Halisstra said. "Better to die fighting than to fall under the dominion of such a creature."

She was in much the same condition as the others. Since she and Danifae had survived their initial encounter with the monsters, it had been an hours-long running battle through the streets and empty buildings of the ruins. First, a large pride of lamias had tried to overwhelm the party with their beguiling powers, but drow on guard for such magical tricks were no easy prey. Halisstra and the others steeled themselves for a fight against the lion-bodied monsters, but the lamias—deceitful and cowardly things that they

30

were—withdrew from the battle and instead hurled wave after wave of beguiled thralls at the drow party. Lamias might have lacked for physical courage, but the manticores, asabis, gargoyles, and other assorted creatures under their control certainly did not.

"Neither option appeals to me," Quenthel growled. She turned slowly, studying the walls and structures around them, seeking escape. "There. I can see the open desert just beyond those buildings. Maybe they'll abandon the chase if we leave the city."

"Unwise, Mistress," said Valas. He crouched by an archway leading into their temporary refuge, watching for the next assault. "Once we leave the shelter of the walls, they'll know exactly where we are. We'd be visible for miles out in the open, even with our *piwafwis*—they weren't made to hide us in bright daylight on an open plain. Concealment is our best defense."

Ryld nodded wearily. He stood by another doorway, his greatsword resting on his shoulder.

"They would surround us and drag us down out there," the Master of Melee-Magthere said. "Best to try to keep moving within the ruins, and hope the lamias—ah, damn. We've got more company."

Rubble shifted somewhere in the maze of crumbling walls beyond their refuge as something large padded closer.

"Watch out for illusions," Halisstra said.

She balanced her mace in her hand and tugged at her shield, making sure it was strapped securely to her arm. Behind her, Danifae crouched, a long dagger in her hand. Halisstra wasn't happy about arming her battle captive, but at the moment they needed all the help they could get, and it was plainly in Danifae's best interests to make sure they didn't all fall prey to the denizens of Hlaungadath.

The lamias tried something new. Against the gap in the wall that Jeggred guarded, the monsters hurled a wave of lizardlike asabis, savage creatures that hissed in anger as they threw themselves against the draegloth with scimitars and falchions clutched in their scaly hands. Three more challenged Valas while a pair of gargoyles streaked over the walls and dropped into the midst of the ruined building behind Ryld, their great black wings raising huge clouds of dust with every beat. The weapons master whirled to face the threat behind him, cursing.

Jeggred howled in rage and leaped to meet the rush of the asabis, batting aside flashing blades and snapping jaws while he tore at the lizard warriors with his great talons. The white-haired demon used his four arms to wreak terrible carnage, but even Jeggred was tiring. Blows he would have eluded with his freakish speed landed awkwardly. He blocked one slashing scimitar badly with his left outer arm, and suffered a long bloody cut halfway from elbow to wrist. Another blade scored his torso, starting a stream of red across his white-pelted chest. The draegloth roared in rage and redoubled his efforts.

Ryld slashed at the gargoyles while Halisstra and Quenthel ran to his side. Quenthel lashed at one with her whip. The snake heads wound around the creature's taloned legs and sank fangs into stony flesh, but the gargoyle beat furiously for height and dragged the priestess off her feet and across the dusty structure. Pharaun raised his wand to blast the monsters with deadly lightning, but spun in a half-circle and fell, a crossbow bolt transfixing his right forearm. The wand flew from his hands.

"The rooftops!" the wizard called.

Halisstra backed away from the gargoyles and squinted at the bright sky, searching for more attackers. Tawny blurs crouched atop a high wall perhaps forty or fifty yards distant, a handful of lamias who carried heavy crossbows and watched carefully for opportunities to shoot into the fray, their beautiful faces twisted into evil grins. Even as she watched, one took at shot at Ryld. The bolt whistled past the weapons master's head, smashing a divot from the soft stone wall nearby. Ryld flinched away.

"Someone take care of the snipers!" he snapped, while slashing at the gargoyles.

A second later, two more bolts flew at Ryld. One bounced from his breastplate, but the other caught him on the right side while his arms were raised to wield Splitter. The bolt lodged in the arm-opening of his armor. Ryld staggered back two steps and collapsed in the dust.

Halisstra reached down and snatched up Pharaun's wand.

"Aid Quenthel," she told Danifae.

She leveled the wizard's weapon at the lamias on the high wall. She knew something about using such devices—a talent she wouldn't normally have wished to reveal, but the fight was desperate. She spoke an arcane word, and a bolt of purple lightning shot out at the first lamia, blasting the creature from the wall in a spray of shattered stone. Thunder reverberated in the dusty ruin. She aimed at the next lamia, but the monsters weren't stupid. They abandoned their lofty perches at once, leaping back behind the wall to avoid more lightning.

From the shadow of the back wall, Pharaun returned to the battle, armed with another wand. This one produced a blazing bolt of fire, which he directed against the gargoyles overhead. With shrieks of pain, the monsters flapped off, though the one poisoned by Quenthel's whips didn't get far before its wings folded. It plummeted down among the rooftops some distance away.

Valas dispatched the last of his attackers with a double-handed slash that nearly cut the creature in two, and Jeggred stood amid a virtual heap of asabi bodies, his flanks heaving. The wizard glanced around once, and noticed Ryld on the ground.

"Damn," he muttered.

He knelt by the weapons master and turned him over. Ryld was dying. Blood streamed from the bolt in his chest, and he fought for each breath, bloody spittle streaking his gray lips. The wizard scowled, then looked up at Quenthel.

"Do something," he said. "We need him."

Quenthel folded her arms with a cold frown and said, "Unfortunately, Lolth does not choose to grant me spells of healing at the moment, and I have already expended almost all of the healing magic I brought on our journey. There is little I can do for him."

Halisstra narrowed her eyes, thinking. Again, she didn't like the thought of what she was about to do, but there was a benefit to revealing her secret. If she proved herself useful, the Menzoberranyr would be hesitant to discard her.

Besides, she thought, they likely already know.

"Move aside," she said quietly. "I can help him."

Quenthel and Pharaun looked up suspiciously.

"How?" Quenthel demanded. "Do you mean to say that Lolth has not withdrawn her favor from you?"

"No," Halisstra replied. She knelt by Ryld and examined him. She would have to move quickly. If he died, he would be beyond her assistance. "Lolth has denied me spells, just as she has Quenthel, and presumably every other priestess of our race. I have some ability to heal by a different means, though."

With that, she began to sing. Her song was a strange keening threnody, something dark and eerie that tugged at the drow admiration for beauty, ambition, and black deeds skillfully done. Halisstra molded the shape of her voice and the ancient words of the song, summoning the magic of her lament as she set her hand on the quarrel and drew it from the wound.

Ryld started, his eyes wide and staring, and blood spurted over Halisstra's hands—but the wound closed into a puckered scar, and the weapons master coughed himself awake.

"What happened?" he groaned.

"What happened, indeed?" Quenthel replied. She eyed Halisstra suspiciously. "Was that what I thought it was?"

Halisstra nodded and stood, wiping blood from her hands.

"It is a tradition in my House that those females who are suited for it may study the arts of the *bae'qeshel*, the dark minstrels. As you can see, there is power in song, something that few of our kind care to study. I have been trained in the minstrel's lore."

Ryld sat up, looking down at his breastplate and the bloody quarrel lying in the dust. He looked up at Halisstra.

"You healed me?" he asked.

Halisstra offered her hand and pulled him to his feet.

"As your friend Pharaun observed, we need you too much to allow you to inconvenience us with your death."

Ryld met her eyes, obviously considering some reply. Gratitude was not an emotion many drow bothered to act upon. The weapons master perhaps wondered what Halisstra might choose to do with his.

She spared him any more serious reflections by turning her attention to Pharaun, and handing the iron wand back to him.

"Here," she said. "You dropped this."

Pharaun inclined his head and replied, "I admit I was surprised to see you wield it, but I heard you sing in Ched Nasad. Shame on me for not adding two and two."

"Let me see your arm," Halisstra said.

She sang the song of healing again, and repaired Pharaun's injury.

She would have examined the others and aided them if she could, but Quenthel interrupted her.

"No one else is dying," the high priestess said. "We must move now or our enemies will surely descend on us again. Valas, you lead the way. Head toward the outer walls so that we may make for the open desert if we decide to flee."

"Very well, Mistress Baenre," the scout acquiesced. "It will be as you say."

THREE

Kaanyr Vhok, the half-demon prince known as the Sceptered One, stood on a high balcony over the old dwarven foundry and watched his armorers at work. The great smelter had once been the heart of the fallen realm of Ammarindar. The cavern was immense, and its roof rested upon dozens of towering pillars carved into the shapes of dragons, glowing red with angry firelight and the lurid radiance of molten metal. The clanging of hammers and roar of kilns at work filled the air. Dozens of hulking tanarukks, bestial fiends bred from orcs and demons, toiled on the foundry floor. They might have lacked the skill and enchantments of the dwarves who once worked there, but Kaanyr Vhok's soldiers possessed a cunning instinct for the making of deadly weapons infused with dark lore.

Kaanyr himself fit the infernal scene well. Tall and powerful, he had the stature of a strong-thewed human warrior and the strength of a stone giant. His skin was red and hot to the touch, and his flesh was hard enough to turn a blade. He was strikingly handsome, though his eyes danced with malice and his teeth were as black as coal. He wore a golden breastplate and carried a pair of wicked short swords made from some demonic black iron in rune-chased scabbards at his belt. He grinned fiercely with delight as he looked out over the gathering storm of his army.

"I now lead nearly two thousand tanarukk warriors," he said over his shoulder, "and I have just as many orcs, ogres, trolls, and giants at my command. I think the time has come to try my strength, my love."

Aliisza allowed herself a smile and moved closer, pressing herself to the demon prince's side. Like Kaanyr Vhok, she too possessed demonic blood. In her case, she was an alu-fiend, the spawn of a succubus and some mortal sorcerer. Wings as smooth as black leather sprouted from her shoulder blades, but other than that she was dusky and seductive, voluptuous and inviting, a half-demoness whose allure few mortal men could resist. She was also clever, capricious, and very skilled in magic, and therefore well-suited to be the consort of a demonspawned warlord such as Kaanyr.

"Menzoberranzan?" she purred, tracing the filigree of his armor with one fingertip.

"Of course. There seems to be nothing worth the taking in Ched Nasad, after all." Kaanyr frowned, and his gaze grew distant. "If the dark elves are without the protection of their spider goddess, and unable to govern their interminable feuds, I may have an opportunity to seize the greatness I have always coveted. Having mastered the ruins of Ammarindar, I find that I hunger for something more. Subjugating a city of drow appeals to me."

"Others have had that thought," Aliisza pointed out. "The Menzoberranyr I spoke with in Ched Nasad suggested that his own city had suffered a significant slave uprising, sponsored by some outside agency. I think the duergar mercenaries who fought in Ched Nasad would not have left the city to whatever House hired them, once they'd managed to take it. If the duergar firebombs hadn't worked so well, I suspect Clan Xornbane would rule Ched Nasad now."

"Or I would," Kaanyr said. He narrowed his eyes. "If you had reported the situation to me in a more timely manner, I might have been able to bring my army against Ched Nasad when the drow and duergar were exhausted from fighting each other."

Aliisza licked her lips.

"You would have lost whatever forces you brought into the city," she replied. "Your tanarukks could have endured the fires, of course, but the collapse of the city streets destroyed everything in the cavern. Trust me, you missed no opportunities in Ched Nasad."

Kaanyr did not reply. Instead, he disentangled himself from Aliisza and vaulted lightly over the balcony rail, descending to the foundry floor. The warlord had no wings, but his demonic heritage conferred the ability to fly through effort of will. Aliisza frowned, and followed behind him, spreading her black pinions wide to catch the blazing updrafts of the room. Kaanyr was still sore about Ched Nasad, and that was not good, she reflected. If the warlord ever tired of her, he was certainly capable of having her killed in some grisly manner, past intimacies notwithstanding. There was nothing of which he was not capable, if his temper got the better of him.

The half-demon alighted beside a sand mold filling with molten iron. A pair of tanarukks stood by, carefully watching over the pour. Kaanyr squatted down by the white-hot metal and absently stirred his fingers in it. It was hot enough to cause him discomfort, and after a moment he shook the molten iron from his fingers and brushed them against his thigh.

"Good iron," he said to the tanarukks. "Carry on, lads."

He straightened and continued on his way. Aliisza fluttered to the stone floor and fell into step behind him.

"The thing that troubles me is this," Kaanyr mused. "Why did the Xornbane duergar betray the House that employed them by burning the whole city? Was it simply a dispute over pay? Or did they intend from the start to bring ruin to Ched Nasad? If so, was Horgar Steelshadow behind it? Did the prince of Gracklstugh send his mercenaries to Ched Nasad to destroy the city, or did Clan Xornbane do that for someone else?"

"Does it matter?" Aliisza asked, sidling up beside him again.

"The city was destroyed, regardless of anyone's intentions. The great Houses of Ched Nasad are dead, and there aren't many Xornbane dwarves remaining, for that matter."

"It matters because I find myself wondering whether the duergar of Gracklstugh plan to attack Menzoberranzan next," Kaanyr said. "I have amassed no small strength here, but I do not believe I can take Menzoberranzan unless the dark elves are reduced to utter chaos and helplessness. If the duergar mean to march on the city too, my opportunities are limitless."

"Ah," Aliisza breathed. "You could sell your services to the dark elves, the gray dwarves, both, or neither. Hmm, that *is* interesting."

"And the price I command will increase with the number of warriors I bring, and my proximity to Menzoberranzan, but it depends on the intentions of the gray dwarves." The half-demon let out a bark of hard laughter. "I would not care to find myself on Menzoberranzan's doorstep, facing a strong and united dark elf city with no allies at hand."

"Why do I get the feeling that you're about to send me away again?" Aliisza pouted. She stretched her wings languorously around Kaanyr, halting him as she reached up to turn him toward her. "I've only just come back, you know."

"Clever girl," Vhok said with a smile. "Yes, I mean to dispatch you on another mission. This time, though, you won't have to creep about and stay out of sight. You will call on Horgar Steelshadow, the Crown Prince of Gracklstugh, as my personal envoy—a diplomat, if you like. Find out if the gray dwarves intend to attack Menzoberranzan. If they do, let them know that I would like to join them. If they don't . . . well, see if you can't persuade them that it's in their best interest to destroy Menzoberranzan while the dark elves are weak."

"The dwarves are not likely to confide in me."

"Of course they won't want to confide in you. However, if they do intend to attack, they will see the advantage of gaining me as an ally. If they don't plan on attacking, the fact that I am willing to ally with them may decide the issue for them. They wish Menzoberranzan no good, so you need not worry that they'll stand up for the drow."

"Envoy. . . ." Aliisza murmured. "It sounds better than spy, doesn't it? I suppose I can carry your message for you, my sweet, fierce Kaanyr, but maybe you should provide me with some special incentive to hurry home, hmm?"

Kaanyr Vhok circled her with his powerful arms and nuzzled the hollow of her neck.

"Very well, my pet," he rumbled. "Though I sometimes wonder if you are utterly insatiable."

＊　　＊　　＊

A desperate hour of flight from ruin to ruin saw the battered company to a hard-won refuge from the monsters who ruled Hlaungadath. Beneath the hulking shell of a square tower they found a sand-choked stair descending into cool, lightless catacombs beneath the city. Buoyed by their find, the dark elves slipped through a maze of buried shrines, subterranean wells, and echoing colonnades of brown stone, finally holing up in a deep, disused gallery that showed no signs of recent use. It was a cheerless and desolate spot, but it was free of blinding sunlight and mind-controlling monsters, and that was all they needed.

"Pharaun, prepare your spells quickly," Quenthel commanded after sizing up the chamber. "Halisstra, you and Ryld will stand watch here. Jeggred, you and Valas keep watch on the far archway, over there."

"Unfortunately, you must keep your watch for some time," the wizard said. He made a rueful gesture. "I was ready to study my spellbook earlier, when I'd had some time to rest in the courtyard of the palace above, but the poor hospitality of our lamia hosts has left me somewhat fatigued. I must rest for some time before I will be able to ready my spells."

"We're all tired," Quenthel snarled. "We have no time for you to rest. Prepare your spells at once!"

The snakes of her whip coiled and hissed in agitation.

"The exercise would be pointless, dear Quenthel. You must

keep our enemies away from me until I have recovered from my exertions."

"If he is so powerless," Jeggred rumbled, "now would be as good a time as any to punish him for his disrespectful attitude and many transgressions."

"Stupid creature," Pharaun snorted. "Slay me, and all of you will die in these light-blasted wastelands within a day. Or perhaps you have suddenly acquired a knack for the arcane arts?"

Jeggred bristled, but Quenthel silenced him with nothing more than a look. The draegloth stalked off to take up his watch at the far end of the long, dusty chamber, crouching in a jumble of fallen stones near the opposite entrance. Valas sighed and trotted off to join him.

"Ready your spells as fast as you can, wizard," the priestess said, deadly anger tightly contained in her voice. "I have little patience left for your wit. Give Halisstra your lightning wand in case we need spells of that sort to repel another attack."

It was a measure of his true exhaustion that Pharaun didn't even bother to seek the last word. He turned to Halisstra and dropped the black iron wand into her hand with a sour smile.

"I suppose you know how to use this already. I'll want it back, of course, so please try not to exhaust it completely. They're hard to make."

"I won't use it unless I have to," Halisstra said.

She watched as the wizard found a shadowed spot beside a large column and sat down cross-legged, leaning against the cold stone, and she tucked the wand into her belt. Quenthel composed herself against the opposite wall, watching Pharaun as if to make sure he was not feigning his need for rest. Ryld Argith pushed himself erect and set out for the passage leading back toward the monster-haunted surface, leaning on his massive greatsword as he did so.

Halisstra started to follow, but Danifae said, "Shall I keep watch here, Mistress Melarn?"

The girl knelt on the dusty floor between the wizard and the priestess, the dagger thrust through her belt. She looked up at Halisstra, her expression blank and perfect, the picture of an innocent question.

The Melarn priestess repressed a grimace. Arming a battle captive was tantamount to admitting one no longer had the strength to force her submission, and she suspected that Danifae would later exact a difficult price for continued compliance. Danifae watched serenely as her mistress considered the offer. Halisstra could feel Quenthel's eyes on her too, and she steeled herself against glancing at the Baenre priestess to measure her approval.

"You may keep the dagger to defend yourself—for now," Halisstra allowed. "Your vigilance is not required. Do not presume to suggest such a thing again."

"Of course, Mistress Melarn," Danifae replied.

The girl's face was devoid of emotion, but Halisstra didn't like the thoughtful look in Danifae's eye as she composed herself to wait.

Will her binding hold? Halisstra mused.

In the heart of House Melarn, surrounded by the full strength of her enemies, Danifae would not have dared to throw off the magical compulsion that enslaved her, even if she could do such a thing. Things had changed, though. Danifae's care in how she addressed her mistress in front of Quenthel did not escape Halisstra's notice. Without her House, her city, to invest Halisstra with absolute dominion over what she called her own—her life, her loyalties, and possessions such as Danifae—any or all of those things might be wrested away from her. The thought left her feeling as hollow and as brittle as a rotten piece of bone.

What happens when Danifae decides to test the bounds of her captivity in earnest? she wondered. Would Quenthel permit Halisstra to retain her mastery over the girl, or would the Baenre intercede simply to spite Halisstra and strip her of one more shred of her status? For that matter, was Quenthel capable of freeing Danifae and claiming Halisstra herself as a battle captive?

The girl studied Halisstra from her lowered eyes, demure and beautiful. Patient.

"Are you coming?" Ryld asked. He stood in the mouth of the passage, waiting.

"Yes, of course," Halisstra said, barely repressing a scowl.

Deliberately turning her back on the servant, Halisstra followed Ryld back out to the tunnels leading to their refuge. For the moment, she was safe enough. Danifae could not remove the silver locket from her neck with all of her will, strength, and effort. The moment she touched it, the enchantment would lock her muscles into rigidity until she abandoned the attempt. Nor could she ask someone else to remove it for her, since the moment she tried to speak of the locket, her tongue would freeze in her mouth. As long as the locket encircled her neck, Danifae was compelled to serve Halisstra, even to the point of giving her own life to save her mistress. Danifae had borne her bondage well, but Halisstra had no intention of removing the locket in the presence of the Menzoberranyr—if, in fact, she ever did.

She and Ryld took up positions in a small rotunda a short ways down the tunnel, a dark and open space from which they could keep the approach to their refuge under careful observation without being seen themselves. Folded in their *piwafwis*, they were virtually indistinguishable from the dark stone around them. Despite the capricious chaos and gnawing ambition that burned in every drow heart, any drow of accomplishment was capable of patience and iron discipline in the performance of an important task, and so Halisstra and Ryld set themselves to watch and wait in vigilant silence.

Halisstra tried to empty her mind of all but the input of her senses, to better stand her watch, but she found that her head was filled with thoughts that did not care to be dismissed. It occurred to Halisstra that whatever became of her from this day forward, she would rise or fall based on nothing more than her own strength, cunning, and ruthlessness. The displeasure of House Melarn meant nothing. If she desired respect, she would have to make the displeasure of Halisstra Melarn something to be feared in its place. All because Lolth had decided to test those most faithful to her. By the caprice of the goddess House Melarn of Ched Nasad, whose leading females for centuries beyond counting had poured out blood and treasure upon the Spider Queen's altars, had been cast down.

Why? Halisstra wondered. Why?

The answer was cold and empty, of course. Lolth's machinations were not for her priestesses to understand, and her tests could be cruel indeed. Halisstra ground her teeth softly and tried to thrust her weak questions out of her heart. If Lolth chose to test Halisstra's faith by stripping her of everything she held dear to see if the First Daughter of House Melarn could win it back, the Spider Queen would find her equal to the challenge.

Care to talk about it? Ryld's fingers flashed discretely in the sophisticated sign language of the dark elves.

Talk about what?

Whatever it is that troubles you. Something has you tied in a knot, priestess.

It is nothing to concern a male, she replied.

Of course. It never is.

Their eyes met across the small chamber. Halisstra was surprised to find Ryld's face twisted in a curious expression of bitter resignation and wry amusement at the same time. She studied him carefully, trying to ascertain what motive he might have had for striking up a conversation.

He was very tall and strongly built for a male—for any dark elf, really—just as tall as she was herself. His close-cropped hair was an exotic affectation in drow society, a strangely ascetic austerity for a race that delighted in things of beauty and personal refinement. Drow were ruthlessly pragmatic in their dealings with one another, but not in their grooming. Most males in Halisstra's experience preened themselves, affecting silken grace and deadly guile. Pharaun virtually epitomized the type. Ryld, she realized, was something very different.

You fight well, she offered—not an apology, not to a male, but still something. *You could have let me die in Ched Nasad, yet you risked yourself to save me. Why?*

We had an agreement. You led us to safety, and we helped you escape.

Yes, but I had discharged my end of the bargain by that time. There was no need to honor yours.

There was no need not to. Ryld offered a slight smile, and shifted to a soft whisper. "Besides, it seems that it was in my own interests to save you, as not an hour ago you saved my life in turn. We are indebted to each other."

Halisstra laughed at that, so quietly that no one more than ten feet away would have noticed.

We are not a race given to honoring our debts, she signed.

That has been made clear to me more than once, the weapons master replied. A brief flicker of pain crossed his face, and Halisstra wondered exactly whom the Master of Melee-Magthere had trusted, and why he'd done something so foolish. Before she could ask, he continued, *So tell me of the* bae'qeshel. *I do not know of them.*

"By tradition," she whispered, "our wizards, swordsmen, and clerics are trained in academies. This is true in most drow cities. The reason you do not know of the *bae'qeshel* is that the bardic training is not a public matter. We pass our secrets, one mistress to one student at a time."

I thought the noble Houses had little use for common minstrels.

"The *bae'qeshel* are not common minstrels, weapons master," Halisstra said in a low voice. "We are a proud and ancient sect, the *bae'qeshel telphraezzar,* the Whisperers of the Dark Queen. I am a priestess of Lolth, as are the other females of my House, but I was chosen to spend many long years as a girl studying the *bae'qeshel* lore. I revere the goddess not only with my service as her priestess, but with the gift of raising the ancient songs of our race, which are pleasing to her ears. House Melarn has always been proud to raise one *bae'qeshel* into the sisterhood of Lolth's service in each generation."

"If your songs are sacred to Lolth, why do they work while other spells fail?" Ryld asked.

"Because the songs possess a power in and of themselves, like a wizard's spells. We do not channel the divine power of the Queen of Spiders to wield our songs. Regrettably, my skill with such things is nothing compared to the divine might I could wield in Lolth's name, if she would restore her favor to me."

"An interesting talent, nonetheless," he murmured. Ryld glanced back down the passageway toward the chamber where the others waited. "It seems quiet enough. We may have some time to wait yet. If I know Pharaun, he will need hours to regain his strength. Tell me, do you play *sava*?"

🕷   🕷   🕷

Nimor clung to the shadows of a gigantic stalactite, one of many such stone fangs reaching down from the ceiling of Menzoberranzan's vast cavern. Old passages and precarious paths crisscrossed the city's roof, and many of the stalactites were in fact carved into darkly beautiful castles and aeries all the more spectacular for their bold arrogance. Only drow would make homes out of fragile stone spears a thousand feet above the cavern floor. Highborn dark elves frequently possessed innate magic or enchanted trinkets that freed them of concern over heights, and gave little thought to dizzying overlooks that would terrify bats. Their slaves and servants were not so fortunate, and must have found life in a ceiling spire something peculiarly nerve-racking.

The more important ceiling spires were of course magically reinforced against the inevitable fall, and would not fail unless magic itself gave out—but more than one proud old palace stood dusty and abandoned at the top of the city, the House that claimed it too weak in the Art to maintain the spells that made the place tenable. It was in just such an empty place that Nimor crouched, leaning out over a dark abyss to study his target below.

House Faen Tlabbar, Third House of Menzoberranzan, lay below him and a short distance to his left. The castle sprawled over several towering stalagmites and columns, its elegant balustrades and soaring buttresses belying the underlying strength of the rambling towers and mighty bulwarks of dark stone. Faen Tlabbar's compound was one of the largest and proudest of any in Menzoberranzan that did not sit on the high plateau of Qu'ellarz'orl, the most prestigious of the underground city's noble districts. Instead House Tlabbar's palace clambered up along the southern wall of

46

Menzoberranzan's great cavern, until its highest spires surmounted the plateau in whose shadow it sat, as if the matrons of the Third House wished to be able to peer over the plateau's edge and gaze enviously upon the manors fortunate enough to be located alongside the exalted House Baenre.

It was an apt analogy for Faen Tlabbar's political maneuverings. Only two Houses stood ahead of them in Menzoberranzan's dark hierarchy: Baenre, the First, and Barrison Del'Armgo, the Second. Nimor thought it likely that Matron Mother Tlabbar harbored great aspirations for her House. Del'Armgo, the Second House, was strong but with few allies. Baenre, the strongest, was as weak as it had been in centuries. Houses such as Faen Tlabbar gazed on the Baenre and remembered centuries of absolute arrogance, humiliating condescension, and they wondered whether the time had come for several lesser Houses to band together and end Baenre's dominance once and for all.

"That would be a merry game to watch," Nimor mused.

He suspected that in such a scenario Baenre might prove stronger than their resentful rivals guessed, but the bloodletting would be spectacular. Several great Houses would fall, for Baenre would not go alone into the gentle night. Of course, that would go a long way toward advancing the schemes of the Anointed Blade of the Jaezred Chaulssin.

That would be a play for another day, though. Nimor meant to strike a deep and grievous blow at Faen Tlabbar, not incite them against House Baenre. Ghenni Tlabbar, Matron of the Third House, would die beneath his blade. Her blood would purchase treason on a grand scale, and place into the assassin's hand the stiletto Nimor meant to drive into Menzoberranzan's heart.

A scrabbling sound and the clink of mail caught Nimor's notice. He withdrew softly into the shadows and waited patiently as a squad of Tlabbar warriors mounted on great riding lizards climbed along a small, unworked stalactite nearby. The pallid reptiles possessed large, sticky pads on their clawed feet that allowed them to cling to the sheerest of surfaces, and many of Menzoberranzan's noble

Houses used the creatures for patrolling the high places of the city's vast cavern. Faen Tlabbar was renowned for its squadrons of lizard cavalry. The assassin had studied the Tlabbar patrols from his precarious perch for more than an hour, carefully timing their sweeps.

Right on time, Nimor observed. *You've allowed yourselves to become predictable, lads.*

The riders carried crossbows and lances at the ready, scurrying along in single file as they looped around the smaller stalactite and scanned the cavern ceiling. As Nimor expected, the leader turned to the left and followed the curve of the stone pinnacle down and out of sight.

"You would do well to vary your routine, Captain," Nimor whispered to the departing squad. "An intrepid fellow such as myself might be deterred by the possibility of your unexpected return."

With a single silent spring, Nimor launched himself out into the vast darkness, plunging through the eternal night.

By an accident of cavern formation, House Tlabbar held little of the city's roof and overcaverns. One large column and a pair of small stalactites linked Tlabbar to the ceiling, which meant that Tlabbar had something of a blind spot directly over its palace roof. This was the weakness Nimor intended to exploit. His black cloak streamed behind him, and cold air rushed past his face. Nimor bared his teeth in a savage grin, delighting in the long seconds of his great leap. His body burned with the dark fires of his heritage, and he longed to shed his rakish guise, but this was not the time.

While he fell, he mouthed the words to a spell that made him invisible, and as the spearlike pinnacle of Faen Tlabbar's central palace rushed up at him, he quickly halted his fall by employing his power of levitation. Less than six heartbeats from the moment he'd leaped from the abandoned stalactite overhead, Nimor alighted on the knifelike ridge of a steep hall, invisible and undetected. He listened for any sign that he had been detected, then he glided toward the hall's juncture with the castle proper, his steps as silent as death.

The dark elves of Faen Tlabbar were not unaware of their vulnerability to assault from above, and vigilant sentries manned battlements and cupolas atop the palace, watching for intruders. Nimor avoided them carefully. Those who were able to see invisible foes—and there were more than a few—were not in the habit of watching for an invisible foe who also glided from shadow to shadow with the stealth of a master assassin. Nimor was more concerned with the various magical barriers shielding the house. He habitually protected himself with spells designed to counter and confuse various forms of magical detection, but they were not foolproof.

Green and gold radiance glimmered around him as he crept along the steep, tiled roof of a square tower. The Faen Tlabbar, like many other Houses, used magic to illuminate and decorate the baroque spires and balconies of their home. Nimor lowered himself to his belly and edged down even farther, headfirst, listening carefully. Below him he expected to find a guard post, and an entrance leading into the manor itself. Over the decades the Jaezred Chaulssin had used magic to scry what they could of the layout and defenses of many great Houses in more than one drow city, and the slender assassin had carefully studied his brotherhood's notes and drawings on House Tlabbar. The information was, of course, incomplete and out of date, as parts of the castle were blocked from all scrying, and the Jaezred Chaulssin had not studied the Houses of Menzoberranzan in a very long time. Nimor would have preferred to update his information through the bribery or capture of a Tlabbar guard, but he simply did not have the time to arrange such a thing and keep the rest of his timetable intact.

He heard the soft sounds of movement on the balcony below the eave of the roof he lay on. Two, he guessed, at least one wearing chain mail. He would have to be swift—a single outcry could spell the end of his single-handed assault on the castle. With calculating patience, Nimor edged out even more and found himself looking down on a curving gallery beneath the overhanging eave. To his left, the walkway became a walled stair leading down to the lower battlements, while to his right it simply ended at a black doorway. The door itself stood open. Directly beneath him stood a drow male in armor, gazing out over a lower courtyard.

Nimor studied the fellow for a full thirty heartbeats, planning his strike as he quietly slipped his dagger from its sheath. It was a blade of green-black enchanted steel that glistened wetly in the glimmering faerielight. Then, still invisible, he rolled himself off the roof and dropped down behind the Tlabbar guard.

The assassin's feet thudded softly to the flagstones. The guard started to turn and opened his mouth to cry out, but with one remorseless movement, Nimor clapped a hand over the fellow's face and punched his dagger deep into the base of the skull. The blade grated on bone, and the Tlabbar guard simply sagged into Nimor's arms, dead on his feet.

Nimor let the nerveless body slump to the floor and looked up at the other sentry in the guard post, a fellow in the black robes of a wizard. The Tlabbar mage glanced over at the rustle of sound, just in time to see his watch mate fold up and collapse for no apparent cause—for Nimor was still invisible.

"Zilzmaer?" he said sharply. "What is it?"

Nimor bounded forward and rammed his bloody knife up under the wizard's chin, nailing his jaws closed and transfixing the Tlabbar's brain. The mage jerked two or three times, violently, then shuddered and died.

"Shh," the assassin hissed. "It's nothing. Go to sleep."

He laid the wizard alongside his companion, and turned to the dark archway leading into the castle proper.

Knife in hand, he stalked through—only to be halted by an invisible, intangible barrier that blocked the archway as surely as a wall of masonry. Nimor frowned, summoned up his willpower, and tried the archway again, only to find his passage barred in mid-step.

"Damnation," he muttered. "A forbidding."

The Tlabbar castle, or its interior anyway, was warded by a great fixed spell that utterly prevented an enemy from setting foot within. Nimor could elude or undo some magical traps, but the forbidding was simply beyond his ability to penetrate.

That explains the open door, he thought. *The Tlabbars are confident in their magical defenses. Now what?*

Nimor sheathed his knife and studied the archway. A spell of forbidding could be crafted to defend a building or area in one of several ways, but if the Tlabbars wanted to move about their own castle, they would have had to make a forbidding through which one could pass without too much difficulty—perhaps with a token of some kind, or maybe with a password. Nimor quickly searched the bodies of the two Tlabbar guards he'd slain, but found nothing that seemed like it might serve as a token to pass the forbidding.

It might be anything, he thought. A cloak clasp, an enchanted coin in a purse, an earring or a necklace . . .

He decided he didn't have time to experiment. With one hand he picked up the dead wizard and tucked the fellow under his arm, then he strode back to the archway and steeled himself to step through. This time, he passed through without resistance, as if the ward was simply gone.

Something the Tlabbar guards wear, then, Nimor decided.

He briefly considered shouldering the dead wizard and carrying the fellow along in case he needed to pass another warding inside the castle, but decided against it. Stealth and speed were his best defenses, and lugging a corpse through the castle was not particularly subtle. Besides, the Tlabbars were not likely to have two forbiddings in their palace, or to use the same key for both if they did. He unceremoniously dumped the wizard on the other side of the doorway, and headed inside.

The archway opened into a long, high-ceilinged corridor that ran above one of the Tlabbar halls. Doors made of pale zurkhwood lined the hall, opening into studies, parlors, trophy rooms, and other such chambers if Nimor's old maps were correct. He ignored them all and darted swiftly down the hall, reaching a small staircase at the end that descended to the level below. Here he encountered a magical glyph barring passage on the stair, but he sensed the trap before stepping close enough to trigger it. He simply vaulted over the rail instead, dropping lightly to the stairs below. The stairs swept around in a grand curve and led him to another gleaming black corridor near the center of the Tlabbar castle, leading to the House shrine.

The floor was polished black marble that would have gleamed like a mirror had there been any light to see by. Not far ahead, a pair of House guards stood watch over a great double door leading into Lolth's sanctuary.

Nimor smiled invisibly and congratulated himself on his timing. The matron mother, and perhaps a daughter or two, would be within, performing some empty ritual to their mute goddess.

Carefully staying out of sight, Nimor took one more look around to make sure no one else was approaching. He studied the two guards outside the door. They seemed no more than young officers, proudly attired for their exalted duty as guards to the matron mother, but Nimor did not trust his eyes. The two were more than they seemed, he was certain of it. He decided to bypass them if he could.

Gathering himself, Nimor raised his left hand, on which gleamed a ring as black as jet. The ring of shadows was perhaps his most useful weapon, a device that conferred a number of useful magical powers. He called upon one of those powers, and melted into the shadows of the black corridor only to step out on the far side of the shrine's door, into House Tlabbar's most sacred sanctum.

The temple almost filled the central floor of the great palace, its graceful dome rising overhead, chased in silver and jet with Lolth's spider insignia. The shrine was lit with a sinister silvery radiance, the better to display the lavish wealth House Faen Tlabbar had expended in decorating the Spider Queen's chapel. Nimor spared no admiration on the gold baubles and gem-encrusted images, though.

Matron Mother Ghenni and two of her daughters abased themselves before the towering black idol of the silent goddess, groveling before Lolth, no doubt beseeching the Spider Queen to restore her favor to the House. No one else waited within. Apparently the matron mother felt that her guards and servants did not need to see her and her daughters prostrate themselves in their private adorations. Nimor's information on Faen Tlabbar had once again been proven accurate.

The assassin silently drew his rapier and advanced, eyeing his prey. Ghenni was a striking dark elf, a female with a voluptuous body and a sinuous grace that allowed her to carry her years better than many females a hundred years younger. He noted the dark glint of mail beneath her emerald robes, and smiled. Apparently even the matron mother of a strong House didn't feel entirely safe in her own home without the Spider Queen's protection.

The matron mother paused in her observances, warned by something—a small sound, the flicker of a shadow, possibly just intuition. She raised herself up to her knees and looked around, wariness plain on her face.

"Sil'zet, Vadalma," she hissed. "We are not alone."

The two girls halted at once, still stretched out on the cold stone floor. They glanced about warily. Ghenni stood carefully, reaching for a wand at her belt.

"Who are you?" she demanded. "Who dares intrude on our devotions?"

Nimor made no answer but glided closer. The matron mother didn't see him, he was certain of that, but just as he drew within sword reach, he felt a *presence* coalesce in the room. An unseen demonic force took shape in the air near the top of the dome.

"Beware, Matron," a cold voice hissed. "An assassin approaches you unseen."

To her credit, the Matron Mother of House Faen Tlabbar did not quail. As her daughters scrambled to their feet, Ghenni took two steps back and quickly gestured with her wand, snapping out a word of command. A sphere of roiling blackness hurled forth from the wand and burst behind Nimor in an inky blot of frigid shadows that lashed out like living things hungry for prey. The assassin ignored the spell, as he was already leaping forward. With a precise thrust, he ran the Faen Tlabbar through with his rapier. The blade was as black as night, a long stiletto of intangible shadowstuff that simply glided through the matron mother's mail shirt as if the armor wasn't even there. Its effect on the priestess was as lethal as one might expect. He twisted the blade in her heart and grinned, though she still could not see him.

"Greetings, Matron Mother," he hissed aloud. "Perhaps you will find the answers you were seeking when you reach Lolth's black hells."

Ghenni gasped once and coughed blood. She staggered back, clutching at the blade in her heart, and her eyes rolled up in her head and she toppled to the floor. Nimor withdrew his rapier and whirled on the daughter on the left, Sil'zet, while the demon took shape over Ghenni's body. It was a skeletal creature wrapped in green flames, armed with a black-glowing scimitar of pale bone.

The demon evidently could see him perfectly, for it set on Nimor at once. It aimed a ferocious cut at his head, which he simply ducked, but the creature reversed its blade with surprising speed and backhanded a second cut waist high. Nimor scowled and skipped back, momentarily thwarted. Behind the demon, he saw Sil'zet unrolling a scroll to read, while Vadalma held her ground, stooping to retrieve her mother's wand while guarding herself with a dagger.

"You will not escape this room with your life, assassin," Vadalma cried. "Guards! To me!"

Nimor heard the guards outside fumbling at the chapel door. He ducked and darted, keeping away from the bone demon, but unwilling to engage it. Slaying a guardian demon was pointless, after all. He had only a few moments more, and he wanted to make the most of them. The assassin took one quick step and rolled beneath the demon's guard, coming up beside Sil'zet as she declaimed the words of her scroll. He rammed his dagger into the small of her back while parrying the bone demon's scimitar with his own black rapier. Sil'zet shrieked in agony and wrenched away, but Nimor tripped her expertly. She sprawled to the ground and writhed. Nimor followed her and sank the point of his rapier into the notch of her collarbone.

This time, the demon made him pay for ignoring it. Screeching in rage, it flailed at him with its bone sword, cutting a long, burning gash across his shoulder blade as he tried to spin out of the way. Nimor gritted his teeth against the pain and rolled away before the creature could cut him in two.

Vadalma barked out the command word for her mother's wand and blasted blindly with the shadow sphere in Nimor's direction, flaying the assassin's flesh with ebon tendrils as cold and as sharp as razors.

The door guards burst in with blades bared, their faces cold and expressionless. They closed with uncanny swiftness, sword points weaving as they groped closer to Nimor, following him with quick jerks of their heads as if the scuffle of his boots and panting of his breath betrayed him.

I've done what I came for, Nimor decided.

Ghenni was dead, and Sil'zet clearly dying. Her heels drummed on the marble floor as she drowned in her own blood. He would have liked to have killed Vadalma as well, but the demon and the door guards—whatever they actually were—simply complicated matters beyond practical resolution.

With a grimace of resignation, Nimor backed off several steps and blinked away with the power of his ring, emerging an instant later near the balcony where he had first entered the castle. The forbidding kept him from escaping in a single dimensional leap, but the assassin simply seized the body of the Tlabbar wizard he'd left by the door and darted outside again. The cut across his shoulders burned abominably, and his legs ached where the icy tendrils of the sphere had lashed him, but Nimor drew in a deep breath and allowed himself a feral grin of triumph.

"Fortunate fellows," he said to the dead males at his feet. "When the Tlabbars determine that you guarded the door through which I came, you will be glad that you are dead."

The bodies made no response, of course. They never did.

He glanced out at the faerielight glimmering over the battlements of the castle, listening to the alarms and cries of dismay rising from within. He would have liked to savor the sounds for a long time, but pursuit could not be far behind. With a sigh, he clenched his fist around his black ring and willed himself away.

Halisstra and Ryld played two games, using a small travel-ing board the weapons master kept in a pouch at his belt. Ryld Argith won both games, though Halisstra pressed him hard in both. She'd always had a knack for *sava*, though she could tell early on that she was playing a master. Long, silent hours passed in the darkness, with no sign that the lamias had discovered their hiding place.

I can't believe they haven't followed us, Halisstra remarked at the end of the second game.

We slew many of their favorite thralls, I guess. The lamias were careless of the lives of their slaves, and perhaps do not have enough left to do a proper job of searching the city for us. Ryld smiled coldly. *For that matter, we slew a few lamias, too. Perhaps they're not very anxious to find us.*

As long as they leave us be, Halisstra replied.

With the *sava* game no longer holding her interest, she realized that she was dreadfully hungry. They'd eaten a thin breakfast before sunrise from the few supplies they'd brought from Ched Nasad, but Halisstra was certain that the day was drawing down. Drow could stand privation better than most, but hard combat followed by hours of vigilance had left her physically exhausted.

I'm starving, she flashed at Ryld. *Things seem quiet. I'm going to slip back to the camp and break out some stores. Stay alert.*

The weapons master nodded, and whispered, "Hurry back."

Halisstra rose and wrapped her *piwafwi* close around her. The hall was still and dark, as it had been for hours. She stole quietly back to the chamber where the others waited for Pharaun to ready his spells, using all the stealth she could muster. She could hear soft voices ahead, Quenthel and Danifae conversing quietly in the ruined gallery.

A dark shadow flitted across Halisstra's heart. When she thought about it, there were few things she wished Danifae and Quenthel to speak about.

I should not have left them alone, she chided herself. *I let Quenthel order me about like a male!*

Deliberately, she crept closer, a silent shadow in the darkness. She could see Pharaun sitting wrapped in a blanket, deep in Reverie as he leaned against the wall, his eyes heavy and half-lidded. Quenthel and Danifae sat close together, turned a little away from the wizard, which brought them close to the passage in which Halisstra stood.

"What do you think you will do when we return to Menzoberranzan, girl? Do you think some high station awaits your mistress there?" Quenthel said, her whispers scornful and acidic.

"I do not know, Mistress," Danifae said after a long time. "I have not thought that far ahead."

"Orcswill. You have been thinking hard from the moment I laid eyes on you in the audience hall of House Melarn. In fact, I'll even hazard a guess as to what must occupy your thoughts. You are wondering how you can bring about your return to House Yauntyrr in Eryndlyn, with Halisstra Melarn as your battle captive."

"I dare not entertain such a thought—"

Quenthel laughed cruelly and said, "Save your innocent protests for someone more gullible, girl. You still have not answered my question. Why should I take you and your mistress back to Menzoberranzan?"

"It would be my hope," Danifae said in a faltering voice, "that I might have an opportunity to demonstrate my usefulness to you, so that you might choose to give me the opportunity to serve."

"I see you do not presume to answer for your mistress this time," Quenthel snorted. "So I should reward your faithless insolence by shielding you in House Baenre, when I know that you are nothing more than an opportunistic viper who will abandon her mistress as soon as the mood strikes her?"

"You misjudge me," Danifae said. "The tradition of adopting the best and most useful nobles of a defeated house is a way of life among our people. My mistress and I—"

The vipers of Quenthel's whip hissed and cracked close by Danifae's face, silencing her.

"I think," said Quenthel, "that I misjudge nothing at all. You are a simpering fawn of a girl who lacked the strength to keep herself from being taken as another's slave. You are nothing more than a useless ornament to me—or you are a very patient and very clever little sycophant, in which case bringing you into my home is not very useful, either." She sat back, sneering at Danifae. "Perhaps I should simply advise Halisstra of this conversation. I doubt your mistress would be pleased to know how much you presume in her behalf. It is most unbecoming in a handmaiden, after all."

"It is your prerogative, Mistress," Danifae said, bowing her head. "You may do as you please with me. I can only place myself at your convenience." She looked up again from her submissive pose, and licked her lips. "In captivity I have come to understand something of the nature of power, what it means to hold absolute power over someone else. If I am not to wield that kind of power myself, then all that remains is to place myself into the care of a female who understands these things, too. Halisstra Melarn is my mistress, but only at your pleasure. When the time comes that you choose to consider the matter, I pray you will allow me to demonstrate my more useful qualities and earn the chance to live as your slave. You, more so than my mistress, understand the exercise of power."

"Cease your meaningless flattery, girl," Quenthel said. She stood smoothly and stepped close, looming menacingly above the kneeling girl with a smile on her lips. "I told you once that I can see past your pretty face. Besides, an appreciation for the uses of silence is only one of the virtues I find endearing in those I take under my gentle guidance."

"I beg you, Mistress," Danifae murmured. She leaned forward to nuzzle her face against Quenthel's thighs, eyes closed, entwining her arms around the Baenre's knees. "I would do anything to earn your favor. I beg you."

Quenthel's snake-headed scourge curled and teased Danifae's silver hair. The Mistress of the Academy stood in silence, the same cold smile on her face. When she reached down and gently raised Danifae's chin with one hand, she bent down to look closely into her eyes.

"Understand this," Quenthel said in a low voice. "I know exactly what you're doing, and you will not win this game. The women of House Baenre are made of sterner stuff than the weaklings of House Melarn. Savor every heartbeat, foolish girl, because in the instant you no longer amuse me, your life ends."

Quenthel disentangled herself and walked away, resuming her restless pacing across the dusty chamber. Danifae rose and moved to the same spot in which Halisstra had left her, kneeling gracefully and composing herself to wait.

Halisstra exhaled quietly in the shadowed passageway, forcing her knotted limbs to relax. She had not realized how tense she had become.

Now, what shall I make of that? she thought.

More than once in the girl's long years as her servant she had used Danifae's beauty to secure favors. If she called Danifae to account for presuming to address Quenthel in Halisstra's absence, she was certain that she knew how the girl would respond. Danifae would claim that she was simply exploring Quenthel's regard for Halisstra by feigning the attenuation of her loyalty to House Melarn, a plausible excuse to approach Quenthel under the circumstances. Under such a scenario, Danifae could claim that she was simply telling Quenthel what she wanted to hear, in order to measure whether there was a place for her and her mistress in the powerful priestess's House. She would most likely finish with submissive apologies, and ask Halisstra to take her life if her actions had somehow displeased her noble mistress.

On the other hand, did it not seem equally likely that Danifae's approach to Quenthel was unfeigned? If the maidservant found a way to escape the magical binding that held her captive, she would need Quenthel's approval, or else her freedom might come at the cost of her life. It was quite possible that nothing more than the deadly capriciousness of a highborn priestess prevented Danifae from seeking release from her bondage. After all, if Danifae claimed her freedom and looked to Quenthel to guarantee it, the Baenre might choose to destroy the girl for her presumption. Any drow would delight in encouraging the dreams of a slave, only to dash them to pieces for nothing more than an instant's dark pleasure.

Only a day before, Halisstra would have described Danifae as one of her most prized possessions. She was not only held to an unbreakable loyalty, but she served also as a confidante, perhaps even something of a friend—even if her faithfulness was magically compelled. They had shared many diversions and plotted many intrigues together. Danifae had been eager to follow her into her self-imposed exile, volunteering to share her trials and continue her servitude. Of course she would have paid a terrible price had she remained in House Melarn after Halisstra's flight, but had she been too eager, perhaps?

"Here I stand, afraid to confront or discipline my own handmaid," Halisstra breathed. "Lolth has cast me low, indeed."

With her coldness locked away in her heart, Halisstra carefully retraced her steps. She wasn't hungry anymore, but it was necessary to allay suspicions. She turned around, and advanced more openly toward the party's hiding place, allowing a slight scuff of her boot soles against the sand-covered stones to whisper through the dead, still air of the chamber. She would let Quenthel and Danifae believe she had heard nothing, but she would watch both of them closely from that point forward.

🕷   🕷   🕷

Nimor Imphraezl made his way among the grand palaces and jagged stalagmites of the Qu'ellarz'orl, draped in a hooded *piwafwi*. He wore a merchant's insignia, posing as a well-to-do commoner with business on the high plateau of Menzoberranzan's haughtiest noble Houses. It was a thin disguise, as anyone taking note of his confident step and rakish manner would not mistake him for anything other than a noble drow himself. The costume was not uncommon among highborn males who wished to move about incognito. Certain spells at his command might have sufficed to offer him almost any appearance he could think of, but Nimor had discovered long ago that the simplest disguises were often the best. Most drow houses were guarded by defenders who would note the approach of someone veiled in webs of illusion, but spotting a common disguise required a mundane vigilance that some dark elves had forgotten.

He passed a pair of Baenre armsmen, walking in the opposite direction. The noble lads eyed him with open curiosity and not a little suspicion. Nimor bowed deeply and offered an empty pleasantry. The young rakes glanced back over their shoulders at him once or twice, but continued on their business. Baenre boys had become hesitant to start trouble unless they were certain of themselves. Nimor took an extra turn or two on his way to his destination anyway, just to make sure they hadn't taken it into their heads to follow him. With one last double-back to clear his trail, he turned to a high walled palace near the center of the plateau and approached the fortresslike gate.

House Agrach Dyrr, the Fifth House of Menzoberranzan, clambered in and around nine needle-like towers of rock within the bounds of a great dry moat. Each fang of rock had been joined to its neighbor by a graceful wall of adamantine-reinforced stone, impossibly slender and strong. Flying buttresses, bladelike and beautiful, linked the natural towers to those wrought by drow, a narrow cluster of minarets and spires in the center of the compound that rose hundreds of feet above the plateau floor. A railless bridge spanned in a single elegant arch the sheer chasm surrounding the structure.

Nimor climbed the bridge and approached openly. Near the far end he was challenged by several swordsmen and a pair of competent-looking wizards.

"Hold," called the gate captain. "Who are you, and what is your business with Agrach Dyrr?"

The assassin halted with a smile. He could sense the myriad instruments of death trained upon him, as if he might suddenly take it into his head to utter some truly inappropriate answer.

"I am Reethk Vaszune, a purveyor of magical ingredients and reagents," he said, bowing and spreading his arms. "I have been summoned by the Old Dyrr to discuss the sale of my goods."

The gate captain relaxed and said, "The master told us to expect you, Reethk Vaszune. Come this way."

Nimor followed the captain through several grand reception halls and high, echoing chambers in the great heart of the Agrach Dyrr castle. The captain showed him to a small sitting room, elaborately furnished in exotic corals and limestone rendered in the motifs of the kuo-toa, the fish creatures who dwelled in some of the Underdark's subterranean seas. Exotic enough to bespeak the House's wealth and taste, the room radiated arrogance.

"I am informed that Master Dyrr will join us shortly," the guard captain said.

A moment later, a hidden door in the opposite wall slid smoothly open, and Old Dyrr appeared. The ancient wizard was decrepit indeed, a rare sight for any elf, let alone a drow. He leaned on a great staff of black wood, and his ebon skin seemed as thin and delicate as parchment. A bright, cold spark burned in the old wizard's eye, hinting at reserves of ambition and vitality that had not yet been tapped completely despite his great age.

"We are delighted to see you again so soon, Master Reethk," the ancient drow said with a dry, crackling voice. "Have you perchance obtained the things we discussed?"

"I believe you will be satisfied, Lord Dyrr," Nimor said.

He glanced at the guard captain, who looked to the old wizard to make sure that he was dismissed. Dyrr sent him along with a small wave of his hand, then the old wizard made another gesture and spoke an arcane word, encapsulating the chamber in a sphere of crawling blackness that hissed and moaned softly like a thing alive.

"I hope you'll forgive me, young one, if I take steps to ensure that our conversation remains private," the ancient drow wheezed. "Eavesdropping seems to be a way of life among our kind."

He shuffled to an ornately carved chair and lowered himself into the seat, seemingly careless of the fact that he bared the nape of his wattled neck to Nimor in so doing.

"A sensible precaution," Nimor said.

The old one reckons me no threat, the assassin noted. Either he is very trusting—unlikely—or very confident. If he has such confidence in isolating himself with me, then either he does not have the measure of my strength, or I do not have the measure of his.

"It *is* confidence, young one," the old wizard said, "and you do not have the measure of me, for we are both of us more than we appear." Dyrr laughed again, a wet and rasping sound. "Yes, your thoughts are known to me. I did not reach my advanced age through carelessness. Now, take a seat. We will dispense with this foolishness and discuss our business."

Nimor spread his hands in a gesture of acquiescence and took the chair opposite the old wizard. With some care he organized his thoughts, locking away his darker secrets in a place he would not examine while Dyrr sat by reading his thoughts. Instead he concentrated solely on the matter at hand.

"You have no doubt heard of the unfortunate demise of the Matron Mother of House Faen Tlabbar?" the assassin said. "And her daughter Sil'zet, as well?"

"It did not escape my notice. Count on the Tlabbars to go crying murder to the ruling council. What possible action did they hope to exhort from the other matron mothers, I wonder?"

"Perhaps they were overcome with grief," Nimor replied.

He reached slowly into a pouch at his side, allowing the wizard to note the deliberate nature of his motion. From the pouch he withdrew a platinum brooch, worked in the barred double-curve symbol of Faen Tlabbar and crowned by a dark ruby. Nimor placed it on the table.

"The matron mother's own House brooch, which I managed to pocket as a keepsake for you. I hope your scrying shield is good, Lord Dyrr. No doubt the Tlabbar wizards will be seeking that emblem with all the magic at their disposal."

"Half-witted children fumbling in the dark," Dyrr muttered. "Five hundred years ago I'd forgotten more about the Art than that whole house full of wizards had collectively deciphered in all their years of training."

He reached out one near-skeletal hand for the brooch and weighed it in his hand.

"I am sure you have a means to confirm the authenticity of the brooch," said Nimor.

"Oh, I believe you, assassin. I do not think you have cheated me, but I will examine the issue later, just to be certain."

The wizard left the brooch sitting on the table and leaned back into his chair. Nimor waited patiently while Dyrr settled back, tapping one long, thin finger on his staff, a satisfied smile on his face.

"Well," the old wizard said finally, "in our previous meeting I required that you demonstrate to me the reach and skill of your brotherhood by removing an enemy of my House, and I suppose that you have done exactly that. You have won my ear. So what is it that the Jaezred Chaulssin want of House Agrach Dyrr?"

Nimor shifted and shot a sharp glance at the wizard. Dyrr was very well informed indeed, to know of that name. Very few outside of Chaulssin did. In fact, Nimor had studiously avoided bringing it up when he had first approached the ancient lord. He wondered what clues he had left for the wizard to decipher, and whether Dyrr could be permitted that knowledge.

"Do not be hasty, boy," Dyrr cautioned him. "You gave away nothing that I did not already know. I have been aware of the House of Shadows for quite a long time."

"I am impressed," Nimor said.

"On the contrary, you believe that I am making empty boasts." Dyrr pointed at his own temple and smiled coldly. "I am not given to bluffing or making wild guesses. Long ago I discerned a pattern of activity that spanned a number of the great cities of our race and inferred the existence of a secret league between seemingly weak minor Houses, each renowned for the skill of its assassins, each reputed to be governed by its males, each a secret ally of the others. These families that otherwise would have been devoured by their ambitious matriarchal rivals instead survived through the convenient and violent deaths of any emergent enemies.

"Though I find it ironic that any particular House of the Jaezred Chaulssin must, by definition, be considered the blackest sort of traitors to the city unfortunate enough to host them. Placing loyalty to your House above loyalty to your city is not a particularly egregious sin, of course, but to acknowledge a tie of loyalty to a House in another city all together, that is something entirely different, is it not?"

Nimor kept his mind carefully empty and said, "You seem to know all our secrets."

He studied the wizard carefully, trying not to let the calculations he performed in his mind show.

"Not entirely true," Dyrr replied. "I would give much to know how your brotherhood orders its Houses, where your true strength is held, and who rules your society. You name yourselves after the city of Chaulssin, which fell into shadow many hundreds of years ago. I wonder about the significance of that appellation."

He knows more than we can permit, Nimor thought.

He glanced up sharply at the old wizard, realizing that Dyrr would have noted that thought. The ancient mage simply studied him with his weak gaze and inclined his head. The assassin regained the mastery of his thoughts and decided to change the subject.

"For the sake of our friendship, I respectfully submit that it would be best for all involved if you did not do anything with your knowledge that would draw it to anyone else's attention. We feel quite strongly that our secrets are best left that way."

"I will do as I wish. However, I do not wish to incur your enmity. I think it would be inconvenient to have the Jaezred Chaulssin as my enemy."

"It is not merely inconvenient, Lord Dyrr; it is invariably fatal."

"Perhaps. In any event, I will keep your secrets."

The old drow laughed softly, clutching his staff with his withered hands.

"Now, let's get to our business, young one. You and your fellows demonstrated no small amount of ability in the murder of Matron Mother Tlabbar, the enemy of my House. Very well, I am suitably impressed. What is it you want of Agrach Dyrr?"

"I need an ally in Menzoberranzan, Lord Dyrr, and I have a strong suspicion that you might be that ally." Nimor leaned forward, offering a sly grin. "Events now proceed in this city that will lead to the downfall of the Houses ahead of yours. If you choose to be a part of those events, you will find that House Agrach Dyrr is possessed of a great opportunity to order the city largely as you like. We believe you can help us to steer Menzoberranzan through the difficult times ahead."

"And if we refuse, we die?"

Nimor shrugged.

"Given the uncertainty of matters as they stand," said Dyrr, "I am hesitant to embrace a cause I know little about."

"Understandable. I will, of course, elaborate, but I hope you will recognize the wisdom, in these uncertain times, of taking aggressive and resolute steps to create the certainty you wish to see. Impose your vision on events, instead of allowing events to limit your imagination."

"Easy words to speak, young one, but more difficult to render into action," Dyrr said.

The ancient wizard fell silent for a long time, regarding the rakish assassin with a baleful, unblinking gaze. Nimor met his eyes without flinching, but he found himself wondering again what hidden strength the Agrach high mage must hold. Dyrr smiled again, doubtless reading Nimor's thoughts, and shifted in his seat.

"Very well, then, Prince of Chaulssin. You have awakened my curiosity. Explain exactly what you mean, and what you plan, and I will say if House Agrach Dyrr can stand by your bold actions or not."

§ § §

"Gather closely, dear friends," Pharaun said with a flourish, "and I will explain a few things it would be wise to remember while we walk within the shadows."

The wizard stood confidently in the center of the chamber, arms folded, showing no hint of the exhaustion or despair of the day's desperate flight. Stirring from his Reverie shortly before sunset, he had spent almost an hour preparing dozens of spells from his collection of traveling tomes.

While no one bothered to draw closer to the wizard, all focused their attention on him. Pharaun grinned in delight, pleased as ever by the attention. He knotted his fists behind his back as if lecturing to novices at Sorcere, and began.

"When we are ready, I will lead us along a path that skirts the Fringe—the borders of the Plane of Shadow. We will travel quite swiftly, and minor inconveniences such as icy mountains, hungry monsters, and thick-headed humans won't trouble us in the least. I expect a walk of ten to twelve hours to reach Mantol-Derith, provided that I do not become lost and lead you all into some grisly demise in an uncivilized plane far from Faerûn."

"You fail to reassure me, Pharaun," Ryld sighed.

"Oh, I haven't ever gotten myself lost in the Shadow Deep, nor do I know of a wizard who has. Of course, one would simply never hear from such an unfortunate fellow again, so perhaps a mishap in shadow walking might explain the disappearance of a young mage I knew—"

"Get to the point," Quenthel snapped.

"Oh, fine. There are two important things to remember, then, for those of you challenged by the effort. First, while we need fear no difficulties in this world while we walk, we gain no special protection from the hazards of the Plane of Shadow. There are things in that place that will object to our passage if they happen upon us—I encountered one such creature the last time I traveled this way, and it was very nearly the last of my marvelous adventures.

"Second, and most importantly, do *not* lose sight of me. Stay close by and follow me diligently. If you lose contact with me while we traverse the Plane of Shadow, you will likely wander its gloomy barrens for all eternity—or until something terrible devours you, which will probably happen rather soon. My attention must remain on maintaining the spell and navigating the Fringe, so don't make it easy for me to misplace you, unless of course I don't like you, in which case please feel free to amble the Shadow Deep at will."

"Will the lamias be able to follow us?" Ryld asked, his eye still on the passage leading back to the ruins above.

"No, not unless they have a wizard as learned and charming as I, and he knows a spell that permits one to track shadow walkers, which I do not." Pharaun smiled. "You will be able to shake the dust of the surface from your boots, friend Ryld. Concern yourself no more with the perils of this place, and save your worry for what we might meet on the Fringe." The wizard glanced around, and nodded to himself. "All right, then. Take each other's hands—there's a good fellow, Jeggred, you can get everybody at once, can't you?—and be still while I cast the spell."

Pharaun raised his hands and muttered a series of arcane syllables, working his spell.

Halisstra stood between Danifae and Valas, their hands linked. The great subterranean gallery grew somehow *darker*, if such a thing could be possible in an unlit room underground. Drow could see quite well even in the darkest places, but it seemed to Halisstra as if some kind of murk hung in the air. At first glance, it seemed that Pharaun had succeeded in little more than conjuring a gloom around the party, but as she studied her surroundings more closely, she realized that she was indeed no longer upon Faerûn. A preternatural chill gnawed at her exposed skin, radiating from the cold dust beneath her feet. The high, rune-carved columns that lined the space were twisted caricatures that loomed bizarrely out over the chamber's open floor.

"Strange," she murmured. "I expected something . . . different."

"This is the way of the shadow, dear lady," Pharaun said. His voice seemed flat and distant, despite the fact he stood no more than six feet from her. "This plane has no substance of its own. It is made up of echoes from our own world, and other, stranger places. We stand in the shadow of the ruins above, but they are not the same ruins we recently traversed. The lamias and their minions do not exist here. Now, remember, stay close, and do not lose sight of me."

The wizard set off along the passage leading back to the surface. Halisstra blinked in surprise. He took only one small step as he turned away from the party, but he was suddenly across the room, and a second step carried him perilously far down the corridor outside. She hurried to keep him in sight, only to find that a single step caused the chamber to blur into darkness. She stood so close to Pharaun that she had to restrain an impulse to back up a step, lest she throw herself even farther away.

The wizard smirked at her discomfiture and said, "I am flattered by your attention, dear lady, but you need not stay quite so close." He laughed softly. "Just step when I step, and you will pace me more easily."

He took several slow, measured strides, holding back a bit as the rest of the party caught the trick of it, and in a moment they all marched together along the dusty streets of Hlaungadath beneath a cold and starless sky. Each step seemed to catapult Halisstra forty, perhaps fifty feet across the dim terrain. The black shapes of ruined buildings leered and leaned from all sides, huddling down close over the streets as if to hem in the travelers, only to fade into dark blurs with each careful stride.

Outside the ruined walls, Pharaun paused a moment to check

on the party. He nodded toward the desert stretching to cold mountains in the west, and he began to march quickly, setting a rapid pace that belied his effete mannerisms and aversion to the toils of travel. Finally able to stretch out her legs, Halisstra began to gain a sense of just how quickly they were moving. In five minutes of walking they left the site of the Netherese city a league behind them, a dark blot on the dim breast of the sands. In thirty minutes the mountains, nothing more than a distant fence of snowcapped peaks from Hlaungadath's streets, towered up over them like a rampart of night. The shadow walk also made light of the most difficult terrain in their path. Without hesitation Pharaun stepped out over a sheer ravine as if it simply did not exist. The magic of his spell and the strange plane they traversed brought his foot down securely on the far side of the obstacle. Climbing the long, rugged slopes leading up into the mountains was no more work than stepping from stone to stone across a stream.

"Tell me, Pharaun," Quenthel said after a time, "why did we crawl through miles of dangerous Underdark passages to reach Ched Nasad, when you might have used this spell to shorten our journey?"

Halisstra could sense the ire hidden in the Baenre's voice, even through the murk and gloom of the Shadow Fringe.

"Three reasons, fair Quenthel," Pharaun replied, not taking his eyes from the unseen path he followed. "First, you did not ask me to do any such thing. Second, the wizards of Ched Nasad arranged certain defenses against intrusions of this sort. Finally, as I said before, the Fringe is a dangerous place. I only suggested this after we all agreed that marching for months across the sun-blasted surface world presented an even less appealing prospect."

Quenthel seemed to consider the wizard's words, while mountains reeled and gnarled black trees began to appear around them.

"In the future," the Mistress of Arach-Tinilith said, "I shall expect you to volunteer useful information or suggestions in a timely manner. Your reticence in advancing ideas may cost us all our lives.

Is that worth the meager pleasure you derive from knowing something we may not?"

The Master of Sorcere's teeth gleamed in his dark face, and he continued without making a reply. For some time he devoted his attention to navigating the Fringe. As Pharaun was under normal circumstances the most garrulous of the company, the effort of concentrating on his spell left the small party of dark elves unusually silent. They fell into a watchful march, winding quietly along in single file behind the wizard, as the immeasurable journey through the darkness stretched out into what might have been hours or even days. Halisstra found herself beginning to consider the very curious notion that this was the real world, the true substance of things, and the bland mundane rigidity of her own world was the illusion. She found that she did not care for that thought at all.

After a long time, Pharaun raised his hand and called a halt. They stood on a small gray stone bridge, arching over a deep gully through which trickled a dark, bubbling stream. Nearby the black ramparts of an abandoned city jutted into the lightless sky, a place that seemed more like a fortress than a town, its thick walls pierced by turret-guarded gates.

"We're about halfway to our destination," Pharaun said. "I suggest half an hour's rest, and maybe a meal from what stores we have. We should be able to replenish our supplies when we reach Mantol-Derith."

Ryld gestured at the empty castle nearby and said, "What is that place?"

"That?" Pharaun glanced over his shoulder. "Who knows? Maybe it's the echo of a surface city in our world, or maybe it's a reflection of some other reality all together. The Shadow is like that."

The company huddled by the low stone wall of the bridge and made a dreary repast from their dwindling provisions. The ever present chill of the place leeched away the warmth of Halisstra's body, as if the stones beneath her hungered for her very life. The gloom smothered their spirits, deadening any attempt at conversation, making it hard to even think with any degree of acuteness. When the time came to set off again, Halisstra was surprised by the sheer lethargy that had crept into her limbs. She had little desire to do anything except sink back down to the ground and lie still, wrapped in shadows. Only with a fierce and focused effort of will did she drive herself into motion again.

They set off into the unending night, and had gone on for some distance from the vicinity of the old bridge when Halisstra became aware of the fact that they were being followed. She was not sure of it, at first. Whatever trailed them was stealthy, and the deadening effects of the Shadow made her unsure if she had really heard something or not. It seemed to whisper and titter in the darkness, a presence that announced itself in a stirring of the motionless air, the faint rush of wind behind them. She turned and studied the path, searching for their pursuer, but she saw nothing save the weary faces of her companions.

Valas brought up the rear of the march, and he looked up at her as he drew close.

You sense it too? he signed.

"What is it?" Halisstra wondered aloud. "What manner of things live in a place like this?"

The scout shrugged wearily and said, "Something that Pharaun has reason to fear, which alarms me." He reached out and turned her back toward the rest of the party. Halisstra was shocked to see how far they'd moved away in the few short moments she had stood watching. "Come, we do not want to be left behind. Perhaps what hunts us will be content to follow."

They hurried to catch up to the others—and at that moment, their pursuer attacked. Striding up out of the shadows behind them loomed a tremendous figure composed of pure darkness, a black, faceless giant towering more than twenty feet in height. Despite its great size, the thing moved swiftly and silently toward them, strangely graceful. Two shining ovals of silver marked its eyes, and long, spidery talons reached for Halisstra and Valas. Its sibilant whispers filled their minds with awful things, like fat pale worms crawling through rotten meat.

"Pharaun, wait!" Halisstra cried.

She fumbled for her mace as the dark giant approached. Beside her, Valas swore and swept out his curved blades, crouching in a fighting stance. A nauseating, tangible chill radiated from the creature, like the cold that seeped through the entire plane but far more concentrated and malevolent in the presence of the monster. The dark giant shimmered, acquiring an almost oily appearance, and it sprang forward in a sudden burst of motion.

Before Halisstra could cry out another warning, one blow of its massive taloned fist knocked her sprawling to the ground. It turned to fix its pale and terrible gaze upon Valas. The Bregan D'aerthe scout screamed in terror and averted his eyes, dropping one kukri and allowing the second to droop limply from his hand.

Jeggred roared a challenge and bounded toward the monster, talons extended. The dark giant slammed the half-demon to the ground with one blow of its long black hand. The draegloth scrambled back to his feet and leaped up to rake deep, black furrows across the giant's thighs and abdomen, seeking to eviscerate the creature, but the wounds closed after the draegloth's claws passed through the thing's flesh. Jeggred howled in frustration and redoubled his futile assault.

"Stand back, you fool!" Pharaun cried from nearby. "It is a nightwalker. You need powerful magic to harm it."

The wizard chanted a dire spell, and a bright bolt of green lightning shot out to smite the creature high in its torso—but the pernicious energy just flowed away from the monster's featureless black hide, leaving it unharmed.

Your spells are useless, whispered a dark and terrible voice in Halisstra's mind. *Your weapons are useless. You are mine, foolish drow.*

"We will see about that," Halisstra snarled.

She picked herself up and dashed forward, raising her mace. The weapon was enchanted, and she hoped it would prove powerful enough to harm the creature. A long arm with deadly talons raked at her, but Halisstra tumbled beneath the monster's grasp and hammered at the nightwalker's knee. With a sharp crack of sound and a flash of actinic light, the weapon detonated with the force of a thunderclap. The nightwalker made no sound, but its knee buckled, and it staggered.

Quenthel's whip hissed through the air, flaying at the creature's face. The vipers tore and snapped through dark flesh, leaving great gory wounds, but the monster seemed unaffected by the deadly venom coursing through the weapon. Apparently even the most virulent poison did not discomfit its shadowstuff.

Ryld, wheeling and spinning, slashed at the monster with his gleaming greatsword. The nightwalker reached out to wrest away his weapon, but the Master of Melee-Magthere danced back and sheared off half the creature's hand with one savage blow. The nightwalker screamed soundlessly, its anguished cry stabbing through their very minds. Ignoring the others, the creature fastened its baleful gaze on Ryld, and conjured up from the black soil underfoot a dreadful, dark vapor that blotted out all sight.

Halisstra groped her way into the black mist, seeking the monster. The vapor seared her nose like vitriol and ate at her eyes, burning like fire. She persevered, and felt the giant looming over her. She raised her mace and struck again, hammering at the creature's legs. From beside her she heard the hiss of Quenthel's whip, tearing into dark flesh. Great black talons raked through the vapor, ripping at Halisstra's shield, driving her to the ground.

"It's here!" she called, hoping to lead someone else to the battle, but the acidic mists burned like fire in her throat.

She narrowed her eyes to nothing more than bare slits, and flailed back at the monster. The nightwalker's venomous will settled over her like a blanket of madness, seeking to rend away her reason, but she endured the new assault, lashing out again and again.

Ryld's sword lanced through the murk like a white razor, opening dreadful wounds in the shadow creature's body. Black fluid splattered like droplets of poison, and the mind-whispers of the nightwalker rose into a hellish mental shriek that dragged Halisstra to the very edge of madness—and there was silence.

She felt the thing abruptly discorporate around her, its body exploding into black, stinking mist that dissipated into the shadows.

Still gagging on the poisonous black vapors the creature had raised, Halisstra stumbled out of the dark cloud and fell to all fours, gasping for breath. Her chest burned as if she'd drunk molten sulfur. When at last she could open her eyes and take notice of her surroundings again, she found that most of the rest of the party had fared little better than she.

Ryld slumped against a stone, his greatsword point down before him. He was leaning on the blade, exhausted. Quenthel stood close by, her hands on her knees, coughing wretchedly.

When at last she could draw breath, the high priestess looked up at Pharaun and said, "That is what you encountered before?"

The wizard nodded and said, "Nightwalkers. They roam the Fringe. Creatures of undead darkness, evil personified. As you saw, they can be . . . formidable."

The Mistress of the Academy drew herself up and returned her whip to her belt.

"I think I understand why you hesitated to volunteer this method of travel until now," she said.

Despite his exhaustion, the wizard preened.

"Careful, Quenthel," he said in a mocking voice, "you almost acknowledged my usefulness."

The high priestess's eyes narrowed, and she straightened proudly. She obviously didn't care to be the subject of the wizard's humor. Seemingly ignorant of the smoldering glare Quenthel fixed on him, Pharaun made a grand gesture indicating the formless dark ahead of them.

"Our path leads now into the shadow of our own Underdark," he said. "I suggest we redouble our efforts and finish our march quickly, as there may be more nightwalkers about."

"That's a damned cheerful thought," grumbled Ryld. "How much farther now?"

"Not more than an hour, perhaps two," Pharaun answered.

The wizard waited while the dark elves stood and fell in behind him again. Ryld and Valas, the two who had borne the virulence of the nightwalker's dread gaze, seemed gray with weariness, hardly able to keep their feet.

"Come," said Pharaun. "Mantol-Derith is no Menzoberranzan, but it will be the most civilized place we've seen in days, and no one is likely to want to kill us.

"Not right away, at least."

F I V E

Nothing more troubled them for the rest of the shadow walk, and they emerged from the Fringe not long after the nightwalker's attack, returning to the mundane world on the floor of a narrow, subterranean gorge. The walls were marked with various trail signs and messages from previous travelers who had stopped there. It was obviously a commonly used campsite near the trade cavern. The company rested there for hours, warming up from the insidious chill of the Shadow Fringe. After resting, they left the gorge and found their way out into a long, smooth-sided tunnel that bored for miles through the dark, broken by occasional open caverns along the way.

Valas led the company, as he was familiar with their arrival point and the route they found themselves traveling. After the burning skies of the daylit surface and the miserable gloom of the Plane of Shadow, the routine perils of the Underdark felt like old friends. This was their world, the place where they belonged, even those of their number who had rarely journeyed outside their home cities.

After a march of about two miles, Valas called a brief halt and knelt down to sketch a crude map in the dust of the passage floor.

"Mantol-Derith lies not more than half a mile ahead. Remember, this is a place of trade and association with other races. We do not rule Mantol-Derith—no one does—and so it would be prudent to avoid giving offense to anyone you encounter there, unless you're looking for a fight that may waste our time and resources.

"Also, I have been considering how best to find our way from the trade cavern to the holdings of House Jaelre in the Labyrinth. From here our path must traverse the dominion of Gracklstugh, city of the gray dwarves."

"Under no circumstances will we approach Gracklstugh," Quenthel said at once. "The gray dwarves destroyed Ched Nasad. I see no reason to present myself at their doorstep for slaughter."

"We have few other options, Mistress," Valas said. "We are northeast of the duergar realm, and the Labyrinth lies several days southwest of the city. We cannot skirt the city to the south because the Darklake is in the way, and the duergar patrol its waters. Skirting the city to the north would take us at least two tendays of difficult travel through tunnels I do not know well at all."

"Why did we bother to come this way, then?" Jeggred muttered. "We might as well have returned to Menzoberranzan."

"Well, for one thing, Gracklstugh still lies between us and House Jaelre, whether we're in Mantol-Derith or Menzoberranzan," Pharaun replied. He tapped three points on Valas's crudely sketched map. "The gray dwarves must be addressed in either scenario. The question is simply whether we dare to pass through Gracklstugh, or not."

"Could you shadow walk us past the city?" Danifae asked.

Pharaun grimaced and said, "I have never traveled past Mantol-Derith in this direction, and shadow walking is best employed to reach a familiar destination. At any rate, it wouldn't surprise me to find that the duergar have defended their realm against the passage of travelers on nearby planes."

"Are we certain that the gray dwarves would object to our presence?" Ryld asked. "Merchants from Menzoberranzan journey to Gracklstugh often enough, and gray dwarf merchants bring their wares to Menzoberranzan's bazaar. It's possible that Gracklstugh had nothing to do with the duergar mercenaries who attacked Ched Nasad."

"I have heard nothing that suggests to me that we should risk entering Gracklstugh," Quenthel said. She made a curt gesture with her hand, silencing the debate. "I prefer not to gamble on the hospitality of the gray dwarves, not after the fall of Ched Nasad. We will go around the city to the north, and trust that Master Hune can find us a way through."

Halisstra glanced at Ryld and Valas. The scout chewed on his lip, worrying at the problem, while the weapons master simply lowered his eyes in resignation.

"We are only a mile or two from this cavern known as Mantol-Derith?" Halisstra asked, pointing at the sketch.

"Yes, my lady," Valas replied.

"And regardless of which course we choose, we must pass through the place?"

The Bregan D'aerthe scout simply nodded again.

"Then perhaps we should see what we can learn in the trade cavern before we make our decision," Halisstra offered. She could feel Quenthel's eyes on her, but she did not look at the Baenre. "There might be duergar merchants there who could shed some light on the question for us. If not, well, we'll have to provision ourselves there anyway before striking out into the wilds of the Underdark."

"A reasonable suggestion," Pharaun remarked. "There are a dozen mercenary companies based in the City of Blades. Is it not likely that the duergar we fought in Ched Nasad were hired by a drow House, and had no special allegiance to Gracklstugh?"

"They did Gracklstugh's work when they destroyed the city," Quenthel said darkly. She stood and set her hands on her hips, still staring at the sketch on the floor. She thought for a moment, then angrily swept it out with her foot. "We will see what we learn in

Mantol-Derith, then. I suspect that time is of the essence, and if we can avoid a detour of twenty or thirty days to skirt the city, we should do so, but if we hear anything to indicate that Gracklstugh may be closed to our kind, we strike out into the barrens."

Valas Hune nodded and said, "Very well, Mistress. I suspect we will be able to arrange passage unless the duergar are openly at war with Menzoberranzan. I've dealt with the gray dwarves before, and there is nothing they would not sell for the right price. I will seek out a duergar guide in Mantol-Derith and see what I can learn."

"Good enough," said Quenthel. "Take us to the duergar, and we will—"

"No, Mistress, not 'we'," the scout said. He stood and brushed off his hands. "Most duergar have little liking for drow under any circumstances, less so for noble-born drow, and even less for priestesses of the Spider Queen. Your presence would only complicate things. It might be best if I handled any negotiations myself."

Quenthel frowned.

Jeggred, standing close behind her, rumbled, "I could go along to keep an eye on him, Mistress."

Pharaun barked sharp laughter at the thought and said, "If a priestess of Lolth makes a gray dwarf nervous, *what do you think he'd make of you?*"

The draegloth bridled, but Quenthel shook her head.

"No," she said. "he's right. We will find a place to wait, and perhaps see what news there is to be had, while Valas takes care of the details."

They resumed their march, and soon came to Mantol-Derith. The place was much smaller than Halisstra expected, a cavern not more than sixty or seventy feet in height and perhaps twice that in width, though it twisted and snaked for many hundreds of yards. She was used to the immensity of Ched Nasad's great canyon, and the stories she'd heard of other places of civilization underground usually involved tremendous caverns miles across. Mantol-Derith would have been nothing more than a side cavern in a drow city.

It was also much less crowded than she would have expected. The marketplaces in her home city had always been busy places, thronged by common drow or the slaves of nobles engaged in their various errands. The market of a drow city usually hummed with industry, energy, and activity, even if those qualities were peculiarly distorted to match the aesthetic tastes of drow society. Mantol-Derith was comparatively silent and forbidding. Here and there throughout the cavern's winding length, small groups of merchants sat or squatted, their wares secured in coffers and casks behind them instead of rolled out on display. No one shouted, or haggled, or laughed. What business transpired there seemed best conducted in whispers and shadows.

Creatures from many different races gathered at Mantol-Derith. More than a few drow merchants held various corners of the cavern, most from Menzoberranzan if Halisstra read the blazons on their goods correctly. Mind flayers glided smoothly from place to place, mauve skin glistening damply, tentacles writhing beneath their cephalopod faces. A handful of sullen svirfneblin huddled together in one spot, eyeing the drow with unalloyed resentment. Of course the duergar were present in numbers, too. Short and broad-shouldered, the gaunt gray dwarves gathered together in secretive cabals, conversing with each softly in their guttural tongue.

Halisstra trailed close behind Pharaun, studying each group as they passed. She noticed that the wizard was trading discreet signs with Valas as they wound deeper into the marketplace.

Not many merchants here today, the wizard observed. *Where are they all?*

Valas glanced over his shoulder to make sure Quenthel wasn't looking, and answered, *Chaos in Menzoberranzan means few buyers. Few buyers means few sellers. Anarchy seems to be bad for business.*

The scout turned to eye a band of duergar nearby, and said over his shoulder to the rest of the company, "Go on ahead. You'll find an inn of sorts a little farther on. I will meet you there soon."

He quietly approached the gray dwarves, making a strange gesture of greeting with his hands folded before him, and engaged the duergar merchants in whispered conversation. The rest of the party moved on.

They found the "inn" to which the scout referred in a dank warren of caves near the southern end of Mantol-Derith. There, a surly duergar woman terrorized a handful of goblin slaves, driving them mercilessly from one task to another. Several small cookfires smoldered haphazardly in the area, warming iron pots of thick stew tended by the harried cooks. Other slaves scrambled to tap casks of mushroom ale or stolen surface lagers, serving silent customers who simply gathered around the fires, sitting on flat boulders arranged like chairs. Sturdy doors of petrified mushroom fiber or rusted iron plate sealed off crevices in the walls nearby. Halisstra presumed that these led to the guest rooms of the gray dwarf's inn. The chambers were most likely secure behind the strong doors, but she couldn't imagine that they were at all comfortable.

"How . . . rustic," Halisstra said.

She wondered for one terrible moment if it would be her fate to live out the rest of her expatriate existence crouched in some similar hovel.

"It's even more charming than the last time I was here," Pharaun said with a forced smile. "The dwarf there is Dinnka. You'll find that this nameless wayside inn of hers constitutes the finest lodgings available in Mantol-Derith. You'll get food, fire, and shelter—three things that are hard to come by in the wilds of the Underdark—and pay a small fortune for it."

"It will be better than resting in a monster-haunted surface ruin, I suppose," Quenthel said.

She led the way as the party approached one of the cookfires. A trio of bugbears occupied the seats there, apparently mercenaries of some skill, judging by the quality of the armor they wore. The hairy creatures brooded over big leather jacks of mushroom ale, and gnawed at haunches of rothé meat. One by one the hulking warriors looked up as the five drow and Jeggred approached. Quenthel folded her arms and looked at the creatures with contempt.

"Well?" she said.

The bugbears growled, setting down ale and meat as their great fists dropped down to rest on axe-hafts thrust through their belts. The motion caught Halisstra's eye. Bugbears with any lick of sense would have vacated their places immediately, almost anywhere in the Underdark. They might not have been drow slaves—clearly they weren't, if they were in Mantol-Derith—but she'd ventured out into similar places near Ched Nasad enough times to understand that creatures like bugbears learned quickly to give way to the truly dangerous denizens of the Lands Below, such as noble dark elves.

"Well, what?" snarled the largest of the three. "It'll take more'n a drow sneer t'make us give up our seats."

"Think y'can just push us aroun'?" the second bugbear added. "You elfies ain't as scary as y'was, y'know. Maybe yous'll have t'start showin' off why we's oughtta do what y'says."

Quenthel waited for a moment, then said one word: "Jeggred."

The draegloth bounded forward and seized the first bugbear. With his two smaller arms he clamped down over the bugbear's hands, preventing him from drawing any of the weapons at his side. He locked one fighting talon around the creature's head, holding him tightly, and with his other fighting hand he plunged his powerful talons into the bugbear's face. The mercenary screamed something in his uncouth language and struggled against the draegloth. Jeggred grinned, knotted his claws deep in the shrieking monster's head, and yanked back hard, ripping off the front of the bugbear's skull. Blood and brain matter splattered the bugbear's companions, who scrambled to their feet, drawing swords and axes.

Jeggred lowered the twitching body a bit and looked over it at the other two.

"Next?" he purred.

The two remaining bugbears stumbled back, and fled in abject terror. Jeggred shook his white-furred head and tossed the corpse aside, taking a seat at the fire. He helped himself to a hunk of roast dropped by a bugbear, and raised one of their jacks in another hand.

"Bugbears. . . ." he muttered.

"Hey, you!"

The surly duergar innkeeper—Dinnka—scuttled forward, anger plain on her face.

"Those three hadn't settled their tab yet," she complained. "Now how in all the screaming hells am I going to get my gold from them?"

Ryld stooped and removed the bugbear's belt pouch. He tossed it to Dinnka.

"Settle up with this," the weapons master said, "and start our tab with what's left. We'll want good wine, and more food."

The duergar woman caught the purse, but she did not move.

"I don't appreciate your scaring off paying customers, drow. Nor killing them, neither. Next time do your murdering at home, where it belongs."

She marched off, already barking orders at the goblin slaves underfoot.

Halisstra watched her go, then she looked back to the others and flashed, *That was odd. Did you hear what the bugbear said?*

"What he said about the drow not being as scary as they used to be?" Ryld said, then he switched to sign. *Has word of Ched Nasad's fall reached this place so quickly? It was only a couple of days ago, and Mantol-Derith is many days' travel from the City of Shimmering Webs.*

It's possible that magical scrying or spells of communication might have spread the word already, Halisstra said. *Or . . . perhaps he meant something else. Perhaps something of our unusual difficulties is known here.*

That, thought Halisstra, was a very disturbing scenario. Gray dwarves and mind flayers were competent foes, creatures who knew many secrets of sorcery. If they had discerned the drow's weakness, it would not be unduly surprising, but if common bugbear mercenaries were aware of matters in Ched Nasad or Menzoberranzan, it must be widely known indeed.

Goblin slaves returned to their fire, laden with somewhat better fare than the bugbears had enjoyed, and flagons of cool wine from some surface vineyard. The small slaves gathered up the hulking body of the fallen bugbear and dragged it off into the darkness. The dark elves paid them scant attention. Goblin slaves were so far beneath their notice that they might as well have not existed. The party ate and drank in silence, occupied with their own thoughts.

After a time, Valas joined them, accompanied by another gray dwarf. This one was a male, with a short beard of iron grey and not a single hair on his head above his eyebrows. The duergar wore a shirt of chain mail and carried a wicked hand axe at his side. His visage was maimed by a set of three great furrowed scars that had taken off one ear and twisted the right side of his face into a nightmarish map of old pain. He might have been a merchant, a mercenary, or a miner—his dour attire offered few hints as to his trade.

"This is Ghevel Coalhewer," the scout said. "He owns a boat moored nearby, on the Darklake. He will take us to Gracklstugh tomorrow."

"I'll want me payment in advance," the gray dwarf warned. "And I'll have ye know I've a contract o' redress with me guild back home. If ye think to slit me throat and dump me over the side out on the lake, ye'll be hunted down for it."

"A trusting soul," Pharaun said with a smile. "We've no interest in robbing you, Master Coalhewer."

"I'll take me precautions, just the same." The duergar looked at Valas and asked, "Ye know where the boat is. Pay me now, and ye can meet me there tomorrow early."

"How do we know you won't rob us, dwarf?" rumbled Jeggred.

"It's usually bad business to rob drow, not unless ye be sure to get away with it," the dwarf replied. " 'Course, that may be changing, but no' so fast that I'll chance it today."

Valas jingled a pouch in front of the duergar and dropped it into his hand. The dwarf immediately poured out its contents into his big, weathered palm, appraising the gemstones there before scooping them back into the pouch.

"Ye must be in a rush, or yer man here might've struck a better bargain. Ah, well, ye drow don't appreciate a good gemstone, anyway."

He turned and stumped away into the darkness.

"That's the last you'll see of him," Jeggred said. "You should have waited to pay him."

"He insisted on it," Valas said. "He said something about wanting to make sure we didn't kill him to recover the fare." The scout looked after the duergar, and shrugged. "I don't think he would cheat us. If he was that kind of duergar, well, he wouldn't last long in Mantol-Derith. People here don't take kindly to being cheated."

"He can secure safe passage through Gracklstugh?" Ryld asked.

Valas spread his hands and replied, "We'll have to carry some kind of documents or letters, which Coalhewer can arrange for us. I think it's some kind of mercantile license."

"We're carrying no goods," Pharaun observed dryly. "Doesn't that explanation seem a little thin?"

"I told him that Lady Quenthel's family has business holdings in Eryndlyn she wishes to check on, and that if she finds things in order, she might be interested in negotiating for the services of duergar teamsters to transport her goods across Gracklstugh's territory. I also implied that Coalhewer might do well to make himself a part of the arrangement."

Pharaun didn't have time to reply before the cavern echoed softly with the stealthy padding of numerous feet. The dark elves glanced up from the fire to see a large band of bugbear warriors approaching, led by the two mercenaries who had fled a few minutes before. At least a dozen of their fellows followed close behind them, axes and spiked flails dangling from hairy paws, murder in their eyes. The other patrons of Dinnka's inn began to slip away from their places, seeking safer environs. The hulking humanoids muttered and growled to each other in their own tongue.

"Tell me," said Valas, "did someone happen to kill, maim, or humiliate a bugbear when I was talking with Coalhewer?" The scout glanced back at the others, and at Jeggred, who shrugged. He sighed. "Was I unclear when I advised against starting fights here?"

"There was a misunderstanding over the seating arrangements," Quenthel explained.

Ryld stood, threw his cloak over his shoulder to clear his arms for fighting, and said, "Should've guessed there might be more of them nearby."

"Time to remind these stupid creatures of the order of things," Halisstra remarked.

Quenthel stood and drew her five-headed whip, eyeing the approaching warriors with a wry smile.

"Jeggred?" she said.

Gromph Baenre stood on a balcony high above Menzoberranzan, studying the dim faerielights of the drow city. He had been waiting for nearly an hour, and his patience was almost exhausted. Under most circumstances an hour here or an hour there would have meant nothing to a dark elf with centuries of life behind him, but this was different. The archmage waited in fear, dreading the arrival of the one who had summoned him to this clandestine encounter. It was not a sensation Gromph was accustomed to, and he found that he did not care for it at all. He had, of course, taken extreme steps to protect his person, girding himself with an array of formidable defensive spells and a carefully considered selection of protective magical devices. The archmage was not entirely confident that those precautions would deter the one who came to meet him in that lonely, windswept spot.

"Gromph Baenre," a voice, cold and rasping, greeted him. Before the archmage even began to turn, he felt the presence of the other, an icy chill that somehow managed to sink past his defenses, the smell of great and terrible magic. "How good of you to accept my invitation. It has been a long time, has it not?"

The ancient sorcerer Dyrr approached from the shadows at the back of the balcony, leaning on his great staff, his feet seeming not to move at all as he glided forward in a rustle of robes no quicker than an old man's shuffle.

Among the ambitious drow of his own House, it suited Dyrr

to wear the shape of a venerable old dark elf of fantastic age, but Gromph's arcane sight pierced the guise to the truth behind it. Dyrr was dead, dead these many centuries. Nothing remained of the ancient mage but dusty bones clothed in tattered shreds of mummified flesh. His hands were the claws of a skeleton, his robes were faded and threadbare, and his face was a hideous grinning skull, the black eye sockets alight with the bright green flame of his powerful spirit.

"I see that my poor guise does not deceive you," the lich rasped. "In truth, I would have been disappointed if you were so easily beguiled, Archmage."

"Lord Dyrr," said Gromph, a cautious greeting. He inclined his head without taking his eyes off the lichdrow. "In truth, I am surprised to find that you are still among us. I have heard whispers that you still lived—er, so to speak—secluded in your house. I thought from time to time that I detected an old and canny hand guiding the affairs of Agrach Dyrr, but I have not met anyone who claims to have seen you in almost two hundred years, and it's been almost twice that since last we spoke."

"I value my privacy, and encourage my descendants to value my privacy as well. It's best for all involved if my hand remains hidden. We wouldn't want to make the matron mothers nervous now, would we?"

"Indeed. In my experience they react poorly to surprises."

The lich laughed, a horrible sound that chilled the blood. He moved closer, gliding forward to stand by Gromph's side and look out over the city. The archmage found himself more than a little unsettled by the unnatural presence of the undead creature—again, a sensation he did not experience often at all.

What secrets does this walking ghost hold in its empty skull? Gromph wondered. What does he know about this city that no one else remembers? What lonely and terrible heights of lore has he scaled alone in the dreary centuries of his deathless existence?

The questions troubled Gromph, but he decided to put such speculation behind him for the moment.

"Well, Lord Dyrr, you requested this meeting. What shall we talk about?"

"You were always admirably direct, young Baenre," the lich said. "It's a refreshing quality among our kind. To get swiftly to the point, what do you think of the recent difficulties that have beset our fair city? More specifically, what do you think should be done about the powerlessness that has descended upon our ruling caste of priestesses?"

"What should be done?" Gromph replied. "That's hard to say, when the question would seem to be what can be done? It is hardly within my power to entreat the Queen of the Demonweb Pits to restore her favor to her priestesses. Lolth will do as she will."

"As ever. I do not mean to imply that you could do otherwise." The lich paused, the green fire of its gaze locked on the archmage. "What do you see when you look out over Menzoberranzan today, Gromph?"

"Disorder. Peril. Denial."

"And, perhaps, opportunity?"

Gromph hesitated a moment, then said, "Yes, of course."

"You hesitated. You do not agree with me?"

"No, it is not that."

The archmage frowned, and chose his words with care. He did not wish to give offense to the powerful apparition. Dyrr seemed civil enough, but the mind did not always stand up well to ages of undeath. He had to assume that there was nothing the lich was not capable of.

"Lord Dyrr," he said, "surely you have observed that there is no end to the wiles of the Spider Queen. The only certainty of our existence is that Lolth is a capricious and demanding deity, a goddess who delights in teaching very harsh lessons indeed. What if her silence is a ruse to test her faithful? Isn't it likely, even probable, that Lolth withholds her favor from her priestesses to see how they respond? Or—worse yet—to see whether the enemies of her clerics might be emboldened to creep out from the shadows and assault her minions directly? If that is the case, what then becomes of anyone foolish enough to defy the Queen of Spiders when she tires of her test and restores her full favor to her priestesses, just as abruptly as she withdrew it? I would not care to be caught out by such a ploy. Not at all."

"Your logic is sound enough, though I think you have perhaps allowed the habit of caution to hobble your thoughts," Dyrr said. "I could almost agree with you, dear boy, except for this one fact. In the more than two thousand years that I have walked this world, I have never seen this happen before. Oh, I can recall several occasions when Lolth denied her clerics spells for a few days, and many instances in which she arbitrarily decided to stop favoring this priestess or that House all together, casting them down to their enemies, but never has she abandoned our entire race for month after month." The lich glanced up in a reflective manner. "It seems a poor way to treat one's worshipers. Should I ever attain godhood, I think I will try to do a better job of it."

"What precisely do you propose, then, Lord Dyrr?"

"I propose nothing yet, but I do consider, young Baenre, whether powerless clerics should be trusted with the rule of this city for very much longer at all. You and I, we still command great and terrible powers, do we not? The mystic secrets of our Art have not abandoned us, nor are they likely to at any point in the future. Perhaps it is time to look to the security of our civilization, the defense of our city, by taking up the reins of governance the matron mothers are no longer strong enough to hold. Our city's peril grows with every hour. We have rivals outside the Dark Dominion, after all, other races and realms that threaten us."

"And that is precisely why I am hesitant to turn drow wizards against drow priestesses," Gromph replied. "The only thing that could possibly increase our current vulnerability would be to start a civil war. To spare ourselves the fate of Ched Nasad, we must shore up the existing order until the crisis has passed."

"And what thanks do you think you will earn, from the priestesses or from the Spider Queen herself, for that blind loyalty?" Dyrr turned back to Gromph and tapped one skeletal forefinger in the center of the archmage's chest. Gromph could not restrain a shudder. "You have potential, young Gromph. You are not without talent, and you see past House Baenre to Menzoberranzan itself. Put those qualities to work and consider carefully the course you choose in the next few days. Events are coming that will provide you with an opportunity for greatness, or failure. Do not make the wrong choice."

Gromph took a cautious step backward, moving out over the vast gulf of the cavern and hovering in the air.

"I am afraid I must tend Narbondel, Lord Dyrr. I will take my leave now . . . and I will think carefully on your words. You may have appreciated the situation more accurately than I."

The burning green gaze of the lichdrow followed Gromph down into the darkness as he fell softly toward the city below. He would indeed think long and hard about the lich's words. He might stall Dyrr once with civility and caution, but he would not be able to do so indefinitely. Gromph didn't doubt the lich would expect a different answer when next they spoke.

🕷 🕷 🕷

The Darklake was a strange and terrible place. A blackness greater than any Halisstra had ever known enveloped her and her companions, a space so vast that its unseen recesses gnawed at the mind. The great caverns of the drow were often miles across, tremendous places harboring cities of many thousands, but—if Coalhewer did not exaggerate—the Darklake occupied a cavern well over one hundred miles from side to side, and thousands of feet in height. Great island columns the size of mountains held up the mighty roof, creating fanglike archipelagos in the darkness. The waters of the lake virtually filled the immense space. As they sailed across its surface the ceiling was often less than a spearcast above them, leaving many hundreds, or even thousands of feet of black mystery below their feet. It was an unsettling sensation.

Coalhewer's boat was less than comforting itself. It was an asymmetrical vessel made mostly of planks sawn from the woody stems of a particular type of gigantic Underdark mushroom, and treated with lacquers for strength and rigidity. The zurkhwood formed a broad platform, which floated on a cluster of soft air bladders taken from some aquatic species of giant fungus. The whole thing was riveted together with the excellent metalwork of the gray dwarves.

Four hulking skeletons—ogres in life, perhaps, or maybe trolls—crouched in a well-like area in the boat's center, endlessly turning two large cranks that drove a pair of zurkhwood waterwheels. The mindless undead never tired, never complained, never even slowed their pace unless Coalhewer ordered them to, driving the boat onward with no sound but the soft rush of water over the wheels and the faint clicking and scraping of their bones in motion. The gray dwarf stood near the stern on a small, elevated bridge, high enough to see over the waterwheels. He peered ahead into the darkness, arms folded across his thick chest, keeping his thoughts to himself.

The passengers crouched on the cold, uncomfortable deck or paced back and forth, staying a little ways back from the railless edge of the platform. The journey from Mantol-Derith was not extremely swift, as the vessel was not quick, and Coalhewer had to carefully thread his way around places where the cavern roof dropped so low there wasn't enough room for the boat.

Valas spent most of his time standing on the bridge beside the dwarf, keeping a careful eye on the course he steered. Pharaun sat cross-legged at the base of the structure, deep in Reverie, while Ryld and Jeggred kept a sharp watch on the port and starboard sides respectively, making sure that none of the lake's denizens approached undetected. The priestesses kept to themselves, wrapped in Reveries of their own or staring out over the lightless waters, lost in thought.

They passed almost two full days in that manner, pausing only briefly for austere meals or to let the duergar captain rest. Coalhewer was extraordinarily cautious about showing any kind of light and made them build their cookfires in a small, secluded fire-box that shielded the flames from view.

"There's too many things as are drawn by the light," he muttered. "Even this much may be dangerous."

After their third such meal, late on their second day of travel, Halisstra retired to the bow of the boat so that she could look out over the waters and not find herself staring at one or another of her companions. In the furious battle to escape Hlaungadath, and the walk through the Plane of Shadow, she had had little time to embrace and understand her new circumstances. Empty hours of listening to the soft murmur of water and the insectlike clicking and scraping of the boat's skeletal engine had unfortunately failed to immerse her in activity, leaving her with the opportunity to replay the fall of Ched Nasad over and over again in her head.

What became of my House? she wondered. *Did any of our servants and soldiers survive by escaping Ched Nasad? Are they together, and who leads them? Or did they all die amid the flame and ruin?*

Matron Mother Melarn's death left Halisstra as the head of the House—presuming that none of her younger cousins had managed to claim leadership. If one of them had, Halisstra was certain she could wrest it away from her kinswoman. She had always been the most favored of the Melarn daughters, the oldest, the strongest, and she knew her cousins could not deny her her birthright.

But it seemed very likely indeed that her birthright was nothing more than ash and rubble at the floor of Ched Nasad's great chasm. Even if some part of her household had escaped, would she want to seek them out and join them in a miserable, squalid, and dangerous exile in the Underdark?

This was not how it was supposed to be, she thought. *I was to ascend to my mother's place in time, and wield the power that had been hers and her mother's before her. The thousand strands of Ched Nasad would have met at my feet. My least desire I might have fulfilled with a word, a look, a simple frown. Instead, I am a rootless wanderer.*

Why, Lolth? she cried out in her mind. *Why? What offense did we give you? What weakness did we show?*

Once Halisstra had heard the dark whispers of the Spider Queen in her heart, but that place was empty. Lolth chose not to answer. She did not even choose to punish Halisstra for the temerity of demanding an answer.

If Lolth had truly abandoned her, what would become of her if she followed her House down into death? All of her life, Halisstra had believed that her faithful service as a priestess and a *bae'qeshel* to the Queen of the Demonweb Pits would earn her a high place in Lolth's domain after her death, but what would become of her now? Would her rootless spirit be interred with the other unfortunate souls no god claimed in the afterlife, fated to dissipate and die the real and eternal death in the gray voids reserved for the faithless? Halisstra shivered in horror. Lolth's faith was hard, and weaklings had no place in it, but a priestess could expect that she would be rewarded in death for her service in life. If that was no longer true . . .

Danifae approached with sinuous grace and knelt beside her. She looked into Halisstra's face boldly, and did not lower her eyes.

"Grief is a sweet wine, Mistress Melarn. If you drink but a little, you are tempted to drink more, and things are never improved by overindulging in either."

Halisstra looked away to compose herself. She did not care to share her secret horror with Danifae.

"Grief is not enough of a word for what is in my heart," she said. "I have thought of little else since we began this interminable voyage. Ched Nasad was more than a city, Danifae. It was a dream, a dark and glorious dream of the Spider Queen. Graceful castles, soaring webs, Houses full of wealth and pride and ambition, all burned to ashes in a few short hours. The city, its matrons and daughters, the beautiful web-spun palaces, all lost now, and for what reason?" She closed her eyes and battled the hot ache in the hollow of her breast. "The dwarves did not destroy us. We destroyed ourselves."

"I will not mourn the passing of Ched Nasad," Danifae said. Halisstra looked up sharply, cut more by the girl's dispassionate tone than her words. "It was a city full of enemies, most of whom are dead, while others flee as paupers into the wilds of the Underdark.

No, I will not mourn Ched Nasad. Who, besides the few Ched Nasadans who survive, will?"

Halisstra did not choose to answer. No one would grieve for a city of drow, not even other dark elves. That was the way of the drow. The strong endured, and the weak fell by the wayside, as the Spider Queen demanded. Danifae waited for a long time before she spoke again.

"Have you given thought to what we will do next?"

Halisstra glanced at her and said, "Our lot is already cast with the Menzoberranyr, is it not?"

"For today, yes, but tomorrow will your purposes and theirs coincide? What will you do if Lolth's favor returns tomorrow? Where would you go?"

"Does it matter?" Halisstra said. "Return to Ched Nasad, I suppose, and gather together what survivors I can. It will be a hard task, more than I likely could hope to accomplish even in a lifetime, but with the Spider Queen's blessing House Melarn may yet rise again."

"Do you think Quenthel would permit such a thing?"

"Why should she care what I do with the rest of my life? Especially if I spend it raising a wretched fragment of a House over the smoking ruins of my city?" Halisstra said bitterly.

Danifae merely spread her hands. Halisstra understood. What reason would a Baenre need to do anything at all, really? The Menzoberranyr might have been their saviors from the wreck of Ched Nasad, but at a word from Quenthel they might become their captors, or their killers. The girl glanced back to where the others meditated or stood their watches, and changed to signs, carefully hidden from the rest of the company.

Perhaps it might be wise to consider exactly how we can make ourselves indispensable to the Menzoberranyr, she motioned. *The hour will come when we will no longer wish to rely on Quenthel Baenre's benevolence, such as it is.*

"Careful," Halisstra cautioned.

She sat up straight and deliberately controlled her own impulse to look over her shoulder. Danifae had an uncanny instinct for manipulation, but if Quenthel suspected that Halisstra and Danifae planned to undermine her authority—or even impose limits on her freedom of action—Halisstra didn't doubt that the Baenre would take quick and drastic steps to remove a perceived challenge.

It is a dangerous thing you suggest, Danifae. Quenthel would not hesitate to kill a challenger, and if I were killed—

I would not survive, Danifae finished for her. *I understand the conditions of my captivity quite well, Mistress Melarn. Still, inaction in the face of our danger is every bit as risky as what I am about to propose. Hear me out, and you can decide what you wish me to do.*

Halisstra measured the girl, studying her perfect features, her alluring figure. She thought of the conversation between Quenthel and Danifae she had overheard in the catacombs of Hlaungadath. She could put a halt to Danifae's scheming with a word, of course. She could even compel it through the magic of the locket—but then she wouldn't know what Danifae plotted, would she?

"Very well," she said. *Tell me what you have in mind.*

Gracklstugh, like Menzoberranzan, was a cavern city. Unlike the realm of the dark elves, the stalagmites harbored great stinking smelters and foundries, not the elegant castles of noble families. The air had an acrid reek, and the clamor of industry rang endlessly throughout the cavern—the roaring of fires, the metallic ringing of iron on iron, and the rush of polluted streams carrying away the wastes of the duergar forges. Unlike Menzoberranzan, lightless except for the delicate faerie fire applied to decorate drow palaces, Gracklstugh glowed with reflected firelight and the occasional harsh glare of white-hot metal splashing into molds. It was a singularly unlovely place, an affront to any highborn drow. Halisstra thought the place seemed like nothing less than the Hells' own foundry.

At its eastern end, the great cavern of the city sloped down sharply to join the immense gulf of the Darklake, so that Gracklstugh was a subterranean port—though few among the Underdark races used waterways such as the Darklake in their commerce. Consequently the wharves and lakeside warehouses of the duergar city constituted one of its poorest and most dangerous districts. Coalhewer moored his macabre vessel at the end of a crumbling stone quay occupied by a handful of ships of the same general design.

"Get yer things and step lively," the dwarf snapped. "The less ye're seen t'be about the streets, the better. Spider-kissers in the City of Blades be well-advised to step soft and quick, if ye take my meaning."

Valas shot the others a quick look and signed, *No killing! It will not be tolerated here.*

The scout shouldered his pack and followed the dwarf down the quay, wrapping his *piwafwi* around him to conceal the swords at his hip.

Pharaun glanced up at Jeggred and said, "You won't like it here, half-demon. How will you pass the time without something helpless to dismember?"

"I will simply while away the hours considering how I might kill you, wizard," the draegloth rumbled.

Still, Jeggred blew out his breath and drew his own long cloak over his white mane, doing the best he could to hunch over and make himself inconspicuous. The rest of the party followed after, threading their way through the dilapidated streets of the city's dock quarter to a fortresslike inn a few blocks from the wharves. A sign lettered in both Dwarvish and Undercommon named the place as the Cold Foundry. The building itself consisted of an encircling stone wall, guarding a number of small, free-standing blockhouses. The company halted just outside the inn's front gate, which stood beside a pen holding huge, foul-smelling pack lizards.

"Hardly an appealing prospect," muttered Pharaun. "Still, I suppose it's better than a rock on a cavern floor."

Valas conferred briefly with Coalhewer, then turned to the rest of the dark elves and said quietly, "Coalhewer and I will arrange safe passage out of the city and look into provisioning. It'll likely involve some bribes to obtain proper licenses and such, which will take time. We should plan on staying here for at least a full day, perhaps two."

"Can we spare the time?" Ryld asked.

"That would be up to Mistress Quenthel," Valas said, "but we may be many days on the next leg of our journey. We accomplish nothing by starving to death after a tenday or two in the wilds of the Underdark."

Quenthel studied the cheerless duergar inn, and made her decision.

"We will stay two nights, and leave early on the day after tomorrow," she said. "I would stay longer, but I am hesitant to trust our fortunes to the continued hospitality of the duergar. Events are moving too quickly for us to tarry long."

She looked at the scout, and at Coalhewer, who stood a short distance off, watching the street with arms folded and pointedly not listening in on the dark elves' conversation.

Is this place safe? she signed. *Will the dwarf betray us?*

Safe enough, the scout replied. *Keep Jeggred out of sight. The rest of you should be fine, as long as you avoid confrontations.* He flicked his eyes at Coalhewer and added, *The dwarf understands that we will pay well for his services, but if he should come to believe that we might kill him rather than pay him, he will undoubtedly find a way to have us all arrested. He knows we're something more than merchants, but he doesn't care what errand brings us here as long as he's paid.*

A loose end to be tied up? Ryld asked.

Too dangerous now, Valas signed. *I will keep a close eye on him as long as we're here.*

"Take Ryld with you, just in case," Quenthel said.

Ryld nodded and tugged at his pack, adjusting it to ride better between his shoulder blades.

"Ready when you are," he said.

"I can't say I won't welcome the company, if trouble comes," Valas replied. "Well, let's not keep Master Coalhewer waiting. If you don't hear back from us by midday tomorrow, presume the worst and get out of the city by the quickest means at hand."

The scout hurried off with Ryld striding along a step behind him.

They collected Coalhewer and made their way deeper into the city.

"It's that boundless good cheer we find endearing in you, Valas," Pharaun remarked to the scout's back. "Well, I too have errands to run. I must find what passes for a dealer in arcane reagents in this grim place, and replenish my spell components."

"Don't take too long," Quenthel said. She glanced over at Halisstra and Danifae. "Well, aren't you coming?"

"Not yet," Halisstra said. "As long as we're here, I think I will see to providing Danifae with weapons and armor. We'll be back when she is suitably equipped."

"I thought you didn't care to allow your battle captive to fight for you," Quenthel said, her eyes narrowing in calculation.

"I have decided that Danifae is something of a liability as long as she's unarmed and unarmored. I don't want my property damaged for no good reason."

Halisstra could almost feel the depth of Quenthel's suspicion, and the Baenre silently stroked the hilt of her whip as she studied the Ched Nasadan and her handmaid thoughtfully.

Good, thought Halisstra. Let her wonder what hold I have over Danifae that I feel confident arming her. A little uncertainty might improve her assessment of our usefulness.

"Don't wander far or get yourselves into trouble," Quenthel said. "I won't hesitate to set out without either of you if the circumstances so dictate."

She motioned to Jeggred and marched into the Cold Foundry, apparently dismissing both the Ched Nasadan and the Eryndlyrr from her thoughts.

Halisstra couldn't repress a smile of satisfaction as Quenthel disappeared from view, Jeggred slinking behind her. She exchanged looks with Danifae, and the two set off into the duergar city.

Though Coalhewer had insisted that the city was open to folk of all races, provided they brought gold, Halisstra could not convince herself that a pair of dark elves were truly safe in Gracklstugh. The short, stocky gray dwarves crowding the streets went about their business with a sullen purposefulness that Halisstra didn't like at all. They didn't laugh, or primp and preen, or even trade veiled threats with one another. Instead, they glared angrily at passersby of any race, including their own, and stomped along beneath heavy shirts of mail, fists gripped tightly on the hafts of axes and hammers thrust through their broad belts. Only after Halisstra and Danifae had passed half a dozen folk of other races in the streets did she begin to relax.

Halisstra paused in a spot between two towering smelters and looked around.

"There. I know little Dwarvish, but I think those signs advertise weaponsmiths."

They turned down the street, which was little more than a winding footpath rounding the castle-like stalagmites. Past the great stone pillars, they came to something resembling a town square of sorts, an open place surrounded by low, fortlike buildings of mortared stone. Here they found a large storefront displaying dozens of weapons and suits of armor beneath a merchant's sign.

"This seems promising," Halisstra said. She ducked through the low door and stepped inside, Danifae behind her.

The place was filled with martial accoutrements of all sorts, much of it dwarven, but a number of pieces from other races—heavy iron blades of orog-work, kuo-toan armor made from the scales of some great pale fish, and black mithral mail of drow-make. Two well-armed duergar busied themselves with assembling a suit of half-plate armor at a workbench to one side of the door. They fixed suspicious stares on Halisstra and Danifae when the dark elves walked in, and kept a wary eye on them as the priestess and her handmaid examined the merchandise.

"Mistress Melarn," Danifae called.

Halisstra turned to find the girl gazing up at a well-made suit of drow chain mail, worked with the emblem of a minor House she did not know. A matching buckler hung near the mail, with a morningstar of black steel alongside it. The head of the weapon was fashioned in the shape of a demonic face with twisting, spikelike horns. Halisstra carefully muttered the words of a spell of detection, and smiled at the result. The arms were magical—not overwhelmingly so, but certainly as good as or better than anything she'd hoped to find in the city.

"What can you tell us of these drow arms?" she asked of the shopkeepers.

The duergar halted their work. The two might have been twins; Halisstra could hardly tell them apart.

"Trophy," one of them rasped. "A captain in the service of Laird Thrazgad sold 'em a couple of months ago. Don't know where he got 'em."

"They're enchanted," said the other dwarf. "Won't be cheap. Not at all cheap."

Halisstra moved over to the counter, and fished a small pouch from inside her hauberk. She pored through its contents, and picked out several fine emeralds to set on the counter.

"Do we have a deal?"

The gray dwarf stood and approached to study the emeralds.

He scowled and said, "More than that. A lot more."

Halisstra met his gaze evenly. She hadn't managed to carry away much from her House before it fell, and she simply couldn't waste it on a gray dwarf's greed, not if she had other options open to her.

"Danifae, have another look at the mail," she said over her shoulder. "Make sure it's what you want."

Danifae read her intent perfectly. The girl picked up the morningstar and hefted it in her hand, feeling out its balance. As Halisstra had hoped, the second dwarf became nervous, watching a dark elf handle merchandise so valuable. He set down his work and moved over to keep a closer eye on her, making sure he stood between Danifae and the door. Danifae immediately began to offer a variety of comments about the arms, admiring the mail, questioning the strength of the enchantments, and generally engaging the fellow in conversation.

"It'll take five times that weight of gemstones," the duergar at the counter told Halisstra. "And they'll have to be good stones, too."

"Very well, then," Halisstra said.

She shrugged a leather case from her back and set it on the countertop. Unwrapping it carefully, she withdrew her lyre, a small, curved instrument of dragonbone, strung with mithral wire and chased with mithral filigree.

"As you can see, it's an exquisite piece of work," she said.

She picked it up and strummed it as if to show off its qualities—and quietly sang a *bae'qeshel* song. The dwarf gaped at her, then recoiled in horror when he realized she was casting a spell. Before he could call out a warning, the magic of the song ensnared him.

"What's going on there?" the duergar watching Danifae demanded.

"Tell your friend it's all right," Halisstra whispered across the counter. "You don't want the lyre."

"It's fine," the first dwarf said. "She's offering the lyre, but we don't want it."

"Of course not," the second muttered. "Do you see any instruments in here?"

He returned his attention to Danifae, who asked him about the best way to care for mail in damp places.

"Now," said Halisstra to the dwarf she'd beguiled, "we're a little far apart at the moment, but I'm certain we can strike a good bargain. You're going to sell us the arms my handmaid is looking over. Will you take the emeralds as a down payment? I will come back in a couple of days with a very handsome sum to square my account."

"The stones'll do as a down payment," the merchant allowed, "but my partner won't be happy with that. He'll think you don't mean to come back."

"Let him think I've paid in full, then, and he won't trouble you." Halisstra said.

She thought for a moment more, then leaned forward and held the fellow with her eye.

"You know," she said softly, "if something were to happen to your partner, the entire business would be yours to run as you see fit, wouldn't it? You could keep *all* of the profits, couldn't you?"

An avaricious gleam came to the merchant's eye.

"I think you're right," he said. "I don't know why it didn't occur to me before!"

"Patience," Halisstra advised. "Anytime today would be fine. Oh, and I would appreciate it if you didn't mention to anyone else that my friend and I had done business with you. Let's just keep this between the two of us."

❦   ❦   ❦

Nimor departed Menzoberranzan, carrying various payments and tokens to indicate that Reethk Vaszune had entered into an arrangement to provide the wizards of Agrach Dyrr with certain spell reagents and components on the small chance that he might be required to talk his way out of the city. The details of the true arrangement he had forged he carried in no place except his own mind. The Anointed Blade of the Jaezred Chaulssin was well satisfied with his work of the past few days. While he did not strictly need Agrach Dyrr for what he had in mind, the accommodation he'd reached with the ancient master of the House would make the task ahead of him much easier.

Nimor slipped from the Qu'ellarz'orl into a small side cavern leading out into the Dark Dominion. He had come to know the maze of dangerous passages surrounding the great city quite well in the past few months, and he quickly found a dark, quiet spot unobserved by any of the city's defenders. The Anointed Blade stretched out his hand toward the blank stone of the passage wall. The Ring of Shadows gleamed on his left hand, a small circle of inky darkness that seemed more like a tiny hole in the world than a piece of ornamentation. Among its other powers, the ring made available to him the ability to walk paths in the Plane of Shadow and so freed him from many of the constraints that travel on foot would otherwise place on him.

He stepped forward toward the wall, and vanished into the Shadow Fringe. His destination lay not much more than a hundred miles from Menzoberranzan. He'd made the trip several times before, and it rarely took more than an hour. No son of Chaulssin had much to fear walking among the shadows, so Nimor occupied himself during his journey by weighing the value of his alliance with Agrach Dyrr, and wondering whether the ancient sorcerer who secretly ruled the House could be trusted to do as he said he would.

Nimor followed the dark path the ring forged through the Shadow Fringe for a measureless span of time, and the road began to twist back toward the mundane world. It was nearly impossible to judge the passage of hours in the Fringe, but the magic of the spell was such that the path it created would, in its own time, emerge at the desired destination. The assassin set his hand to the hilt of his rapier and took the last step of his journey, stepping through a veil of gloom into a large, vaultlike chamber of carefully fitted stone blocks. Only one door led from the room, a great portal of iron reinforced by strengthening spells. Nimor drew from beneath his mail vest a large bronze key and fitted it to the looming portal. The door swung open with a squeal of rust.

Beyond the door stood a great, dark hall lit by red-glowing coals in iron braziers. Like the vault it was made of dressed stone, its ceiling supported by massive columns, but unlike similar chambers in drow palaces, the space was devoid of decoration or adornment. Nimor felt the presence of some number of guardians, though they chose not to reveal themselves.

"It is I, Nimor Imphraezl," he said. "Inform the crown prince that I am here."

From the air beside him several duergar guards appeared, shedding their invisibility. The gray dwarves stood a head shorter than the drow, but they were broad of shoulder and long of torso, their legs thick and short, their arms powerfully muscled. They wore black plate armor and carried battle-axes and shields emblazoned with the symbol of Gracklstugh. One duergar woman, her rank indicated only by a single strip of gold filigree on the brow of her helm, studied him carefully.

"The crown prince has left instructions to show you to a guest apartment in the palace. He will call on you shortly."

She made the courtesy sound like an order.

The assassin folded his arms and suffered himself to be marched off by a pair of the prince's own Stone Guards. The gray dwarves eyed him uneasily, as if they expected mischief from Nimor. In truth, there was little love lost between duergar and drow, despite the fact that Menzoberranzan and Gracklstugh had stood as neighbors for millennia. Gray dwarf and dark elf had fought more than one vicious war for control of the hundred-odd miles of cavern and chasm that lay between the two cities. The fact that no such war had been fought in a century or more simply indicated that both races had come to hold a grudging respect for their enemy's strength, and not any real lessening of the ill will between them.

The guards led him through the labyrinthine corridors of Gracklstugh's palace and showed him to a large suite in a disused portion of the fortress. The furnishings were simple and functional, as fitted duergar taste. Nimor settled down to wait, moving over to gaze out of a slitlike window at the gray dwarf city beyond the palace. The city was as unlovely as ever, a reeking cauldron of smoke and noise.

After a time, Nimor noted the approach of footsteps outside and turned as Horgar Steelshadow entered the suite, flanked by a pair of Stone Guards.

"Ah," the dark elf said, inclining his head. "A good day to you, my lord. How fares the City of Blades?"

"I doubt that you care," Horgar replied. For the ruler of such a powerful city, the crown prince was in many ways unremarkable. He looked very much like all the other duergar in the room, with a sullen cast to his eyes and a hairless skull. He carried a scepter of office and did not wear armor, which was all that differentiated him from his bodyguards. He motioned the guards to remain by the door, and strode over to speak quietly to Nimor. "Well? What news?"

"I believe I have found the allies I was seeking in Menzoberranzan, dear prince. A strong House eager to see the current order of things overthrown, but whose loyalty is not in question there. The hour of your victory approaches."

"Hmph. House Zauvirr was eager to hire our mercenaries in Ched Nasad, but damned few of Khorrl Xornbane's folk came back. I don't doubt that you or that Zammzt fellow whispered the same thing in Khorrl's ear when you hired his company."

"Xornbane's losses were regrettable, but in truth we did not expect the exceptional effectiveness of your stonefire bombs against Ched Nasad's calcified webs. Absent that unforeseeable chance, Khorrl Xornbane would have taken the city with House Zauvirr."

The duergar prince scowled, his beard jutting out like a bottle-brush.

"I warned Khorrl that dark elves have a habit of poorly rewarding mercenaries, especially dwarves. I won't let another of our mercenary companies march into peril like that again. Xornbane was an eighth of this city's strength."

"I have no need of a single company of mercenaries, Prince, no matter how large and fierce," Nimor assured him. "I have need of your whole army. March in your full strength, and you need not fear defeat in detail."

"It still smells like an insidious drow ruse to me."

Nimor frowned and said, "Prince Horgar, if you are hesitant to hazard any risks at all, you will rarely win a throw of the dice. You have an opportunity to achieve something great, but I cannot tell you that your success is guaranteed, or that there are no risks in our enterprise."

"We're not talking about a handful of coins riding on a stupid game," the duergar prince said. "We're talking about my throne riding on a war that could take a turn I don't care for in any number of ways. Don't try to shore up my resolve with empty observations about risk and reward."

"Very well, then, I shall not, but I will point out that when last we met you said you wanted only one thing before you would consent to lead your army against Menzoberranzan, and that was a substantial ally within the city itself. I have provided you that ally. When will it ever be better for you to strike out at the threat a strong Menzoberranzan poses to your kingdom? Their priestesses are powerless, they have already endured a costly slave rebellion, and now I bring to you a great House willing to assist you in your efforts. What more do we lack, Prince?"

The duergar scowled and turned away to stare out at Gracklstugh. He stood for a time, thinking hard. Nimor watched him waver, and decided it was time to set the hook.

Lowering his voice, he moved close and said, "What better way to secure your seat against the unruly lairds you fear, than by distracting them with a campaign beyond your borders? Even if you should fail to take Menzoberranzan, some diligent planning should ensure that the forces of the most dangerous lairds seem to find the deadliest part of any battle you fight. In truth I believe it is within your grasp to win a great victory over Menzoberranzan, and wreck the strength of your most rebellious nobles at the same time."

The duergar prince grunted and studied Nimor closely.

"You presume much, dark elf," said Horgar. "What is it you hope to gain by destroying Menzoberranzan, eh? Why do you seek to set me on this course of action?"

The assassin grinned and clapped the duergar on the shoulder. The Stone Guards in the chamber shifted nervously, disapproving of the contact.

"My dear Prince Horgar, the answer is simple," Nimor said. "Revenge. Your army is to be the instrument of my vengeance. Naturally I recognize that you will not raze Menzoberranzan simply because I ask it, so it is a necessary part of my design that you are provided with the suitable motivation to do what I wish done. I have worked long and hard to bring about the circumstances under which the army of Gracklstugh might be aimed at the city I hate—including, I might add, assisting you with the small problem of your father's thoughtless longevity. How can I make my purpose plainer?"

"I paid for your help in that case with hundreds of stonefire bombs," the duergar prince said, bridling. "Do not speak of my father's . . . death again. If I came to believe that you might seek to influence my actions with that story, I would have to make sure that whatever information you possessed never came to light. Do you understand me?"

"Oh, I did not mean anything by the remark, Horgar. I merely pointed out that I had been useful to you before, and that I may prove useful again. Now, can I count on the army of Gracklstugh, or not?"

Horgar Steelshadow, Crown Prince of Gracklstugh, reluctantly nodded assent.

"We will come," he said. "Now, explain to me who exactly will be aiding us inside Menzoberranzan, and how he'll be able to help."

Ryld could feel hateful eyes lingering on his broad back as he followed Valas and Coalhewer through the streets of the duergar city. He was all too conscious of the fact that he was out of his element. He towered a good twenty inches over any of the gray dwarves, and his coal-black skin and inky *piwafwi* didn't help him to blend in at all. The three travelers wound their way through a swordsmith's district, a narrow alleyway lined on both sides by open-air forges where duergar in leather aprons hammered endlessly on glowing metal. Ryld knew a thing or two about good steel, and he could see at a glance that the dwarves knew their work.

The weapons master quickened his step and drew alongside Valas.

"Where are we going?" he asked as quietly as possible over the ringing hammers. "I thought we needed to obtain some sort of official license or pass. Shouldn't we be heading for a courthouse, or something?"

"If ye wanted a royal license, ye would," Coalhewer answered, "but that would take ye months and cost ye a fortune in bribes. No, I'm takin' ye to call on the household of the clan laird Muzgardt. He'll give ye a writ o' passage that should get ye where ye want to go."

Ryld nodded. It was not so different from Menzoberranzan, after all.

"How far will Muzgardt's writ run?" Valas asked. "Will it get us out of Gracklstugh's dominions?"

"Muzgardt's clan be merchants. They deal in ale and liquors throughout the Deepkingdom, and sometimes bring outside brews into the city—drow wine, svirfneblin brandy, even some vintages from the surface, or so I hear. Ye'll find his folk all over the realm." Coalhewer laughed a nasty laugh and added, " 'Course, Muzgardt sells passage to those as want it, too. He likes his gold."

Ryld smiled. Coalhewer was a grasping, avaricious fellow by anyone's standards. Muzgardt's greed must be something noteworthy indeed for a dwarf like Coalhewer to comment on it.

They came to the end of the street of swordsmiths and found themselves back in the vicinity of the Darklake, though farther north along the shore. Before them stood a huge, ramshackle brewery made from loose stone stacked to make walls between the petrified stems of a small forest of gigantic mushrooms. Big copper vats steamed within, filling the air with a heavy, yeasty stink. Dozens of copper kegs stood nearby, and burly gray dwarves swarmed over the place, mashing fungus, mixing fermenting masses, and filling casks with freshly brewed ale.

"A dwarf's second love after gold," Coalhewer said with a crooked smile. "Ah, Muzgardt's lads do good work, I tell ye."

The dwarf led Ryld and Valas into the brewhouse and past the huge vats to a small shack or shelter in the back of the place. A pair of gray dwarves stood in heavy mail armor, wicked-looking axes resting close at hand. The guards glared angrily at the dark elves, and picked up their weapons.

"What d'ye want?" one growled.

"Thummud," Coalhewer replied. "Got a business proposition for him."

"Stay here," the first guard said.

He ducked through a ragged curtain in the doorway, and returned a moment later.

"Thummud'll see ye, but the drow'll have t'leave their weapons at the door. Don't trust 'em."

Ryld looked at Valas and signed, *Are we worried about an ambush?*

The scout replied, *Coalhewer knows there are five more in our party,*

110

including a capable wizard and a draegloth. I don't think he'd lead us into a trap—but watch your back anyway.

"Enough finger-talk," the guard snarled. "Talk so's we can understand ye, if ye've got anything to say."

"Always," Ryld said aloud to Valas.

He gave the duergar a hard look, but shrugged Splitter from his shoulder and set the greatsword against one wall. He unbuckled his short sword from its sheath at his hip and set it nearby.

"There's a curse on the big blade," he said. "You won't like what happens if you try to handle it."

Valas set down his shortbow and arrows, then dropped his kukris to the ground. The duergar guards checked the two dark elves for concealed weapons, then ushered them into the gloomy shelter. The place was an office of sorts, with ledgers and records scattered about. By a large standing clerk's desk stood one of the fattest gray dwarfs Ryld had ever seen, a round-bodied fellow with thick arms and heavy shoulders. Duergar tended to run toward a gaunt, broad-shouldered build despite their short, powerful stature, but the brewmaster Thummud was as round as one of his kegs.

"Coalhewer," he said by way of a greeting. "What can you do for me?"

"I've got a party of dark elves as need a writ o' business from Muzgardt," Coalhewer said. "They'd prefer not to wait on a royal permit."

"What sort of business?"

"We deal in gemstones, mostly," Valas said. "We're looking into setting up transport through the Deepkingdom. We need to be able to move around and talk to a lot of people, and as Coalhewer said, we don't want to wait for months to get a royal license."

"Ye're stupid or ye're lying, then. Ye'll pay ten times the cost of a royal license to get a writ from our clan laird. Most merchants I know wouldn't do such a thing."

Valas glanced up at Ryld, then looked back to Thummud and said, "All right, then. We've got some rivals from back home that are doing a fine business here, and we want to sound out their suppliers to see if they can't be encouraged to sell to us instead of the others.

A royal license wouldn't really extend that far, would it?"

Thummud snorted, "No, I suppose not."

"Can ye help me clients, or not?" Coalhewer asked. "Or do I have to go see Ironhead, or maybe Anvilthew?"

"Clan Muzgardt might be able to help ye," Thummud said after a long moment. "We'll want two hundred pieces of gold for each body on the writ, and ye can't have it today."

Coalhewer glanced up at the dark elves. Ryld nodded to him.

"They'll pay the laird's fee," the duergar sailor said, "but they want to get started right quick."

"Doesn't matter what yer clients want," Thummud replied with a shrug. "I'll have to take up the matter with the clan laird before I write you a pass."

"Ye never had to before!"

The fat dwarf folded his arms and set his jaw stubbornly. He glared at Coalhewer and the dark elves.

"Be that as it may, the crown prince's soldiers have been checking our writs and passes too closely of late. Horgar's let it be known that he wants to know who's in the Deepkingdom and why, and he's leaning on the clan lairds to withhold their writs. We'll be able to get yer clients theirs, I think, but I'll have to gain Muzgardt's blessing first. Come back tomorrow, or the day after."

Coalhewer muttered into his beard, but he didn't bother to argue the point any further. He jerked his head toward the curtain, and led Ryld and Valas outside. The dark elves picked up their arms, and in a few minutes they'd left the brewery behind them.

"Now, what should we make of that?" Valas wondered aloud. "Do you know another clan that might help out, Coalhewer?"

"Maybe, but if Horgar's cracking down on informal passes and such things, ye'll have trouble anywhere ye go." The dwarf scratched at his beard. "I'll have to ask some questions, and I don't think ye'd best be with me."

Ryld looked to Valas, who thought carefully before agreeing, and even then the weapons master didn't think his fellow Menzoberranyr looked sufficiently confident in their guide's loyalty.

When Halisstra and Danifae returned to the Cold Foundry, they found that Quenthel had rented one of the inn's larger wings, a freestanding structure with its own small common room and eight private chambers on two floors. The whole wing seemed to be built and decorated to a duergar's conception of drow comfort. Its furnishings were proportioned for drow-sized guests, not dwarves, it was richly appointed with tapestries and lavish rugs, and all the doors had locks. Dark elves didn't require endless hours of sleep in the same manner as lesser races, but few drow felt safe or comfortable in a deep, dreaming Reverie unless they were taking their ease behind a locked door.

The rest of the company, with the exception of Pharaun, reclined on the rugs or sat at the common room's table, partaking of a bountiful meal accompanied by silver ewers of wine. Armor and packs lay stacked against the walls, but weapons remained within easy reach.

Halisstra raised an eyebrow, eyeing the banquet spread out on the sideboard. A large roast of rothé, several wheels of finely molded cheeses, and steaming platters of braised mushrooms reminded her how long she'd been without a decent, hot meal.

"The food's safe?" she asked.

Quenthel snorted. "Do you think we're stupid? Of course we checked it. The innkeeper sent us a cask of drugged wine the first time around, but we complained to the management"—Jeggred looked up and smiled with a mouthful of fangs at that, and Halisstra guessed she knew what form that complaint had taken—"so the banquet is complimentary. Enjoy."

Halisstra performed her own examination of the table anyway, relying on a magic ring she wore for just that purpose. Poisons were too commonplace among highborn drow to take any meal for granted. Satisfied, she helped herself and sat down by the table. Danifae took some food as well, and took a place, reclining on a low lounge near Quenthel.

"I see the wizard has not yet returned. Have you had any luck?" Halisstra asked Valas as she ate.

The scout sat cross-legged beside the door, his knife belt loosened but still around his narrow hips. He sipped at a mug of mulled wine, and chewed thoughtfully on a piece of bread.

"After a fashion," he said. "The weapons master and I encountered no overt hostility, but we didn't get as far as I would have liked, despite our efforts to impress upon the duergar the importance of time." He jingled the pouch of coins at his belt. "I don't know if this is a sign that something unusual is happening, but Coalhewer didn't like it."

"Where is the dwarf?" asked Danifae.

"He wanted to see if he could obtain a writ through other channels."

"You trust him to do that?"

"Not entirely, but it's something we could not easily do ourselves." The scout grimaced and said, "It's one thing to deal with the duergar clans in a reasonably forthright fashion. If I was caught looking into forging our passes, I would look very much like a spy, wouldn't I? And so would all of you, by association."

"Real spies would approach Gracklstugh in much the same manner we have," Ryld said from one corner, where Splitter leaned against the wall, within easy reach.

"True, but remember that Coalhewer is something of a smuggler himself. He's hardly anxious to bring us to the attention of the crown prince," Valas replied. "Still, the weapons master and I settled for replenishing our provisions, so we're ready to leave whenever Coalhewer obtains our pass."

"It seems we've done all we can for now," Halisstra observed. "I, for one, am tired of blinding deserts, soul-bleaching shadowlands, and bare cavern floors. If we're soon to return to the bleak and comfortless wilds, I'll enjoy what civilization I can."

Halisstra held up her cup for Danifae to fill. The battle captive rose sinuously and refilled her mistress's goblet.

"Drink if you like, but don't let your wits become too sodden," Quenthel warned from her couch. "We're hardly among friends in this filthy city."

"When are any of us truly among friends?" Ryld asked with a snort.

Halisstra laughed softly and said, "Indeed, Ryld, but tonight we can rest in comfort, confident in the knowledge that we none of us trust each other and that not too far away lurk grim enemies who would destroy us if they could. Would we have it any other way?"

Danifae carried the ewer to Quenthel. Ignoring the subtle writhing of the priestess's serpent whip, she lowered her eyes and leaned forward to refill the high priestess's cup.

"We must seize what pleasures we can when the opportunity arises," Danifae added. "Is that not the purpose of power?"

Halisstra sipped her wine and watched the scene. Danifae had neglected to don an arming-coat beneath her mail, as she had found the black mithral shirt without its leather padding. Of course, Halisstra had already offered Danifae a spare coat of her own, and she had no doubt that in the morning Danifae would accept it. In the meantime, the girl's perfect dark skin gleamed through the metal mesh, and her full, round breasts swayed enticingly beneath the steel as she stooped to pour Quenthel's wine. The males in the room could not take their eyes from her, try as they might. Even Jeggred, four-armed hulking beast that he was, seemed entranced by the girl's grace and beauty. Valas frowned and busied himself with oiling his kukris, obviously sensing the peril of the moment and recoiling with his usual caution. Ryld, on the other hand. . . .

Ryld was looking at her. Halisstra carefully kept the surprise from her face as she met the weapons master's gaze. Their eyes locked. His expression seemed avid, intense, and Halisstra knew that Danifae's posturing could not have escaped his notice, but instead of gaping at the girl in her armor of metal mesh, the weapons master turned that gaze on her.

Ryld offered a slight smile and made a soft gesture with his hand: *An interesting play.*

I do not follow your meaning, Halisstra replied, though she could see easily enough that the weapons master knew perfectly well that she did.

She returned her attention to Danifae as the girl kneeled close beside Quenthel, sipping her own wine. The company grew quiet, and Ryld pulled out his traveling *sava* set to play a game against Valas while the others contented themselves with savoring a moment's respite from danger.

Pharaun returned eventually, a handful of scrolls tucked under one arm. He retired to his chamber after a couple of halfhearted jibes at the weapons master to break his concentration. Ryld won anyway, though the Bregan D'aerthe scout gave a good account of himself.

"It has been a long day," Quenthel said. "I shall retire to my chambers. Jeggred, Valas, split the watch tonight. Two others will watch tomorrow."

She stood and stretched, and turned her eyes on Danifae before gliding out of the room.

"I think I'll do the same," Danifae said.

The battle captive glanced at Halisstra, offered a coy smile, and went quickly after Quenthel. Ryld put away his *sava* board and headed up to his room, while Valas and Jeggred tossed a coin for first watch. Halisstra stood, gathered her *piwafwi* around her, and went up to her own room. She paused briefly by Quenthel's door and listened, just long enough to hear what might have been a soft gasp or a rustle of clothing, then she moved on. Quenthel's serpents would likely report an eavesdropper at her door.

Clever girl, Halisstra thought. Quenthel was an astute and daring move indeed.

In Ched Nasad Halisstra had sent Danifae to seduce a rival on more than one occasion. Even the most pragmatic priestess had her favorite pets, and sometimes an otherwise cold and calculating female might be manipulated through her secret pleasures. Halisstra doubted that Danifae could succeed in establishing any real influence over Quenthel, but at the worst, she was providing the Mistress of Arach-Tinilith with a reason not to abandon Halisstra and her handmaid on a whim. Of course, if Danifae's services proved *too* valuable to Quenthel, the Baenre might be inclined to claim the captive as her own, but that was a risk Halisstra was willing to take.

Even if Danifae continued to encourage the Baenre to do just that, Halisstra thought of the silver locket around the girl's neck, and allowed herself a smile. Unless Danifae managed to free herself of the binding spell, she couldn't take the smallest step in that direction, as Halisstra's death would precipitate her own. For the moment Halisstra felt she could rely on Danifae's loyalty.

Halisstra found her room and undressed for bed, setting her armor on a chest in the small room and leaving her mace where she could reach it quickly.

She drifted into Reverie thinking about Quenthel and Danifae together.

🕷   🕷   🕷

Aliisza rode in an iron palanquin through the streets of Gracklstugh, carried by four ogres and escorted by a dozen tanarukk warriors. The tanarukks wore armor of burnished iron and carried wickedly hooked greatswords. One fellow carried a yellow banner emblazoned with Kaanyr Vhok's assumed symbol—a scepter clasped in a gauntleted hand. Twice their number of gray dwarf warriors escorted the embassy along, suspicious glares fixed rigidly on the black palanquin and its occupant. The alu-fiend preened just a little beneath the attention. She would have moved much quicker on her own, of course, but making a grand entrance into the city of the gray dwarves might encourage the duergar to take her seriously. Besides, it was fun.

The journey from the halls of old Ammarindar had not been particularly swift or easy. Aliisza and her warriors had pressed hard at their best possible speed for five days along ancient dwarven highways to reach the shores of the Darklake, and it had taken three days more to obtain a duergar boat to cross it. She was growing tired of dashing this way and that through the Underdark at Kaanyr Vhok's command. On the other hand, it continued to demonstrate her usefulness to the demonspawned warlord, and perhaps it wasn't a bad thing that circumstances gave her reasons to leave his side from time to time. It whetted his appetite for her return, and sometimes gave her the opportunity to indulge her taste for . . . variety.

Gracklstugh seemed to be one great smithy, a city of roaring forges and reeking smoke. It struck Aliisza as not unlike the foundry hall in the ruins of Ammarindar, except Kaanyr Vhok's forge was only a fraction of the size of the gray dwarf realm.

What an ugly place, Aliisza thought. Still, the sheer scale of the work that went on around her was staggering. More than once, she spotted components of siege engines of enormous size being assembled in their workshops. Ched Nasad might have been far more graceful and insidious, but Gracklstugh was *strong*. Dwarven skill and single-mindedness seemed almost a match for drow magic and cruelty.

The gray dwarves turned her escort toward a great fortress delved into a mighty stalagmite. Ramparts of stone and turrets of iron guarded the sloping sides of the duergar castle. As the ogres carried her into the open gate of the king's palace, Aliisza could not check her impulse to glance up at the mighty portcullis and deadly devices poised to crush any attack. She had several ways to escape if she needed to, but none of her warriors would get out of the palace alive if the gray dwarves decided not to let them leave.

The procession came to a halt in a large, cheerless hall whose floor was made of polished stone slabs.

"It seems that I am here," Aliisza said to herself.

She tapped on the palanquin's side, and the ogres lowered the carriage carefully to the floor. The alu-fiend waited for the seat to settle, then let herself out, straightening and stretching her wings.

A duergar officer wearing a plain black surcoat over his armor approached her.

"You said you wished to see the crown prince," he stated.

"At his earliest convenience," Aliisza replied. She'd had the same conversation several times that day with various gray dwarf lieutenants and captains.

"Who are you, again?"

"I am Aliisza, an envoy from Kaanyr Vhok, the Sceptered One, Lord of Ammarindar and Master of Hellgate Keep. I believe your crown prince will find my lord's message worth listening to."

The officer scowled doubtfully.

"They stay here," he said, nodding at Aliisza's entourage. "Follow me."

Aliisza glanced at the leader of her escort, a battered old tanarukk champion with a missing tusk, and said, "You and your warriors wait here. I might be a while."

She followed the duergar captain deeper into the fortress, flanked by another half-dozen gray dwarf soldiers. She decided to think of them as an honor guard.

They climbed a wide, sweeping stairway that might have been impressive if the gray dwarves had taken a single step toward decorating the place, and finally came to a throne room with huge, stone columns supporting a vaulted ceiling high overhead.

At the far end of the chamber stood a knot of gray dwarves. By the way they moved, and the cold regard in their eyes, Aliisza guessed that they were the high advisors and nobles of the realm, but their garb displayed no such ostentation. In their midst stood the only gray dwarf she'd seen yet with any kind of ornamentation, a burly fellow who wore a hauberk of gleaming chain mail beneath an embroidered surcoat of black and gold. A circlet of gold rested atop his bare head, and rings of gold gathered the braids of his beard.

The captain escorting Aliisza motioned for her to halt and went closer to whisper in the ear of the crown prince. The gray dwarf ruler glared at Aliisza, then stepped forward, thick arms folded across his chest.

"Welcome to Gracklstugh," he said, though his hard eyes offered no welcome at all. "I am Horgar Steelshadow. What does Kaanyr Vhok want of me?"

Not long on the social graces, Aliisza noted.

Well, she'd never met a gray dwarf who was. She decided to speak plainly and not waste time on flattery or subtlety, as it was clear any such efforts would be lost on the ruler of Gracklstugh. She offered a small bow, and straightened.

"Kaanyr dispatched me to ask a few questions about what happened in Ched Nasad, and to perhaps explore some other issues," she said. She glanced at the other gray dwarves standing nearby. "Does everyone here enjoy your confidence?"

Horgar frowned, and muttered something in Dwarvish. Several of the advisors or nobles moved off, returning to whatever duties they had elsewhere. A pair of heavily armored guards in black surcoats remained behind, as well as another important-looking duergar, a scarred fellow in armor who wore a tabard marked with a red symbol.

"My Stone Guards stay," Horgar said, then indicated the scarred dwarf. "This is the clan laird Borwald Firehand, marshal of Gracklstugh's army."

Borwald returned Aliisza's nod of greeting with a sullen glare. She shrugged and got back to the point, deciding to match directness with directness.

"A duergar clan—Xornbane, wasn't it?—attacked the drow city

of Ched Nasad, and precipitated its destruction. Kaanyr Vhok wonders if you set them to it."

"Clan Xornbane are mercenaries," Borwald answered. The scar he carried creased the side of his bald head from cheekbone to three inches behind the ear, leaving a visible indentation. "Whatever job they took in Ched Nasad is an issue of commerce, not of Deepkingdom policy. You should take up the matter with them."

"I would, but survivors are hard to find," Aliisza said. "As near as we can tell, they trapped themselves in the city they burned." She returned her gaze to Horgar Steelshadow and asked, "So, did they destroy Ched Nasad with your blessing?"

"With my blessing?" The duergar prince thought for a moment, then said, "I am not unhappy that the City of Shimmering Webs fell, but I did not dispatch Clan Xornbane to do that piece of work. Khorrl Xornbane was hired by one of Ched Nasad's matron mothers to help her destroy those Houses ahead of hers. I did not choose to interfere with Xornbane's business."

"In that case, Xornbane's choice of tactics seems spectacularly unsound. They delivered their employer a smoking ruin, and sustained horrible losses in doing so," Aliisza observed.

"I am afraid that I was at least in part responsible for that," said a melodious voice to one side.

From the shadow of a pillar in the great hall a slim form emerged, a rakish drow of short stature and catlike grace. He was a handsome fellow, impeccably dressed in garments of black and gray, and he wore a matched rapier and dagger at his hip.

"On behalf of my fellows," the newcomer said, "I arranged for Khorrl's troops to be provided with the stonefire bombs that proved so effective in the slave uprising in Menzoberranzan. I did not imagine they would destroy Ched Nasad in its entirety, of course."

Aliisza raised an eyebrow and said, "I did not expect to find a dark elf in the confidence of the prince of the duergar."

"I am something of a sellsword," the fellow replied, "tasked with effecting certain changes in a handful of Houses in Ched Nasad and

Menzoberranzan." He offered her a slight smile that didn't reach his intense eyes. "Call me Nimor."

"Nimor," Aliisza replied. "Whatever your purpose, you certainly effected a change in Ched Nasad. What do you have in mind regarding Menzoberranzan?"

Horgar shifted uncomfortably and asked, "What interest is this to Kaanyr Vhok?"

"Well, had we known that someone meant to attack Ched Nasad, we might have offered our assistance," Aliisza replied. "My lord scents opportunity in the dark elves' difficulties. If someone were considering a similar effort to lay low Menzoberranzan, we might be willing to take on partners in our business."

Borwald sneered, "I doubt the Deepkingdom would have any need of a few hundred rabble squatting in fungus-grown ruins."

Aliisza suppressed her annoyance.

They're duergar, she told herself, abrasive and crass. This is how they are.

"Your intelligence is somewhat out of date," she said. "My lord commands over two thousand hardened tanarukk warriors, each of them as strong as an ogre and three times as smart. We have built forges and armories, perhaps not as grand as those of Gracklstugh, but sufficient to arm and armor our soldiers. We command auxiliary troops as well—bugbears, ogres, giants, and such—more numerous than our tanarukk legion." She leveled her gaze on Borwald and added, "We don't have the strength of the Deepkingdom, Firehand, but we could take on twice our number of gray dwarves and give them a fierce fight. You denigrate Kaanyr Vhok's Scoured Legion at your peril."

"I am not unaware of Kaanyr Vhok's growing strength," Horgar muttered, tugging at his beard. "Speak plainly. What does your lord want?"

No subtlety at all, Aliisza lamented. Kaanyr might as well have sent a dim-witted ogre to deliver this message.

"Kaanyr Vhok wants to know if you intend to march on Menzoberranzan. If you do, he wishes to join you. As I have just said,

I believe that the Scoured Legion could be a valuable ally."

"We might not want you for an ally, if we were thinking of any such thing," Horgar said. "We might think we have sufficient strength to get what we want without splitting the prize."

"You might think that," Aliisza conceded. "If you were correct, the dark elves of Menzoberranzan would be well-advised to seek allies against you. I wonder to whom they could turn for help?"

"I would crush Kaanyr Vhok if he did anything so foolish," Horgar growled. "Go back to your demonspawned master and tell him—"

"A moment, Prince Horgar," Nimor said, stepping between the duergar and the alu-fiend. "Let us not be hasty. We should give Lady Aliisza's message careful thought before we consider our reply."

Horgar snarled, "You do not tell me how to conduct my kingdom's affairs, drow!"

"Of course not, my lord prince, but I would very much like to confer with you at greater length on this question." Nimor turned back to Aliisza and said, "I presume you would be willing to remain as a guest of the crown prince while we discuss your master's offer?"

Aliisza merely smiled. She let her eyes linger on the slim figure of the dark elf. Given an opportunity, she felt sure that she could convince him to see the virtues of her proposal, though she also sensed that there was more to this Nimor than met the eye. Unfortunately, Horgar and his Marshal Firehand were less likely to succumb to her special talents. She could wait a day or two and see if Nimor succeeded in advancing her arguments for her.

The duergar prince measured her, mulling over Nimor's words. Finally, he relented.

"You may stay a short time, while I think about your offer. I'll have the captain set aside quarters in the palace for you. Your soldiers will have to stay in a barracks near my own guards. They will not be permitted in the castle."

"I will require some attendants."

"Fine, you can retain two, if you wish. The rest go."

Horgar looked toward the end of the hall and gestured. His captain came trotting up.

"We will speak again when I have made up my mind," he told her.

"In that event, I will be available at your convenience," she said to Horgar, but she let her eyes linger on Nimor as she spoke.

🕷 🕷 🕷

"It can't be done today," Thummud of Clan Muzgardt told Ryld, Valas, and Coalhewer. The fat duergar stood with a mallet in his hand, carefully sealing a fresh keg of mushroom ale. "Try again in a day or two, I guess."

Coalhewer swore under his breath, but the two drow exchanged wary looks. It hardly escaped Ryld's notice that over a dozen duergar brewers happened to be hard at work very close by the spot where Thummud stood, and that many of them had the unmistakable glint of metal beneath their smocks. The brewer wasn't in the habit of taking chances, it seemed.

"That's what you said yesterday," Ryld said. "Time is pressing."

"Not my problem," Thummud replied. He finished tapping down the lid, and set the mallet on top of the cask. "Ye'll have t'wait, like it or not."

Valas sighed and reached for the purse at his belt. He jingled it judiciously and set it down nearby.

"You'll find gemstones in there worth better than twice what we agreed on," the scout said. "They're yours if you get us that writ today."

Thummud's eyes narrowed. "Now I'm wondering what ye really be up to," he said slowly. "No honest purpose, of that I'm sure."

"Consider this a personal bonus," Ryld said quietly. "Your laird expects two hundred pieces of gold per head, and you'll see to it he gets that. What's left over, he doesn't need to know about, does he?"

"I can't say as ye wouldn't get what ye want some other time,"

Thummud admitted with a shrug, "but the laird was certain of his words to me on this matter. I'd be crossin' him to do this bit o' business with ye, and old Muzgardt would have me head for it." The brewer thought about things for a moment, and added, "Better make it three or four days, I think. The crown prince's lads are all over the city, and I don't need 'em to see ye coming here every damned day."

The stout dwarf heaved the keg up onto his shoulder and stomped off, leaving the two dark elves standing with Coalhewer in the middle of the sullen crowd of brewers.

"Now what?" Ryld asked Valas.

"Go back to the inn and wait, I'd say," Coalhewer muttered. "Ye'll have no luck standing here. Come back in a couple of days."

"Quenthel won't like that," Ryld said, still addressing the drow scout.

All Valas could do was shrug.

The two drow and their guide left the Muzgardt brewery, wrapped in their own thoughts. They marched along for a short distance, putting the brewery well behind them.

"I'm beginning to wonder whether we shouldn't just write our own letter of passage," Valas said softly. "We wouldn't need it for long, after all."

"That's a bad idea," Coalhewer said. "Ye might forge a letter that looks about right, but ye need Muzgardt's blessing. If ye get stopped, ye'll be held while they check to be sure that ye've got the blessing of the laird. That ye won't have until Muzgardt grants it to ye."

"Damn," Valas muttered.

Ryld examined the situation, trying to figure what to make of it. Either Coalhewer had purposely led them to a dead end, or the difficulty in obtaining the passes was unfeigned. For the first possibility, Ryld couldn't see any reason why Coalhewer would delay the company in Gracklstugh. Perhaps the dwarf meant to set them up in some way, but if that was the case, wouldn't he have had ample opportunity to spring whatever surprise he might have had in mind? On the other hand, if Coalhewer and Thummud weren't collaborating in some elaborate deception, why would the crown prince happen to choose the occasion of the company's visit to Gracklstugh to crack down on foreigners moving about the realm?

Because he's got something he doesn't want foreigners to see, of course, Ryld decided. What wouldn't he want outsiders to see?

Ryld halted dead in the street. Valas and Coalhewer turned a few steps farther on, looking back at him.

"What is it?" Valas asked.

"You and I have something we need to do," Ryld said to Valas, then he turned to their guide. "Come to the inn tomorrow morning."

Coalhewer frowned.

"Fine," he said. The duergar turned and headed down the street, muttering under his breath, "Don't blame me if ye get arrested for doing whatever it is ye have in mind. I won't speak up for ye. I'll be on me boat if ye need me."

What is it? Valas asked after the dwarf disappeared into the shadowed street.

The crown prince is limiting freedom of movement for foreign merchants and travelers, Ryld answered. *He doesn't want news from the city to get out. I think the army of Gracklstugh is going to march.*

Valas blinked and signed, *You think so?*

"It's what I would do," Ryld answered. "The question is, how to make sure of it."

He glanced around the street. As always, any gray dwarf in sight was staring at the two dark elves with undisguised hostility.

Investigating your suspicion makes us exactly the sort of fellows the crown prince's soldiers will be looking for, Valas signed. The wiry scout frowned, thinking. *What would you need to see to confirm your fear?*

A supply train, Ryld answered at once. *Wagons, pack lizards, that sort of thing. You wouldn't gather that together unless you meant to march, and it would take several days to do it. You'd need a lot of space.*

Agreed, Valas answered.

Valas thought, frowning as he tugged absently at the odd charms and tokens he carried on his clothing.

Feel like taking a chance? the scout signed.

Ryld glanced around the street. Thummud had pretty much told them outright that things wouldn't change for several more days at a minimum, and that was not going to please Quenthel. If Gracklstugh meant to attack Menzoberranzan, he wanted to know about it before the duergar army marched. They would want to find a way to send a warning back home. The duergar were no slave rabble to be crushed at the leisure of the great Houses. The army of the City of Blades would be large, strong, disciplined, and well armed for an assault on the drow, and Ryld didn't like the thought of what an army of that sort might do to his home city.

Let's go, he replied.

Valas nodded and set off at once. Instead of heading back to the lakeside district and the Cold Foundry, he turned deeper, toward the heart of the cavern. They weaved through the foul-smelling streets and dark alleyways for a fair distance, passing through business districts where duergar artisans and merchants kept their shops in cramped buildings of fieldstone. The hour was growing late, and traffic along the dwarf city's streets seemed to be diminishing. The two dark elves finally reached a street that ran along the edge of a deep cleft or chasm bisecting the city's higher, more inaccessible districts from its ramshackle lakeside neighborhoods. Numerous bridges of stone spanned the gap, leading to narrow streets that continued on the far side. A squad of vigilant duergar soldiers stood watch at the foot of each, barring passage across the chasm.

The scout drew Ryld into the shadow of an alleyway and nodded toward the rift and its bridges.

Laduguer's Furrow, he signed. *Also known as the Cleft. Everything on the west side is strictly off limits to foreigners. There are a couple of large side caverns on the far side that might serve as good marshalling grounds, and they'd be secure from any casual observation.*

Ryld studied the Bregan D'aerthe scout thoughtfully, wondering how he knew so much about a part of the city that was supposedly off limits.

I take it you've been there before? Ryld asked.

I've passed through Gracklstugh a couple of times.

I wonder if there's anyplace Valas *hasn't* been, Ryld thought. He shifted in the shadows to get a better look at the guarded bridges. He was a fair hand at staying out of sight when he needed to, but he didn't like the possibilities offered by the narrow, railless spans. There was no cover at all once one set foot on any of the bridges.

How do we cross? he asked.

Valas finished his knots and stepped close, setting his right foot in one bottom loop and crooking his right arm through the topmost.

"Stay close to this stalagmite as you ascend," he said. "We'll want the cover."

Ryld nodded and reached up absently to touch the insignia pinned to his breast. It identified him as a Master of Melee-Magthere, and like the clasps and brooches of many noble Houses, it was enchanted with the power of levitation. Valas didn't doubt that Ryld had fought long and hard to win the right to wear it.

As he'd hoped, the enchantment proved strong enough to support both Ryld's weight and the Bregan D'aerthe's. Effortlessly they glided up into the smoke and gloom of Gracklstugh's upper reaches, until the fumes obscured the streets below. From the top of the great cavern, the floor seemed shrouded in haze and smoke, glaring firelight making bright circles of glowing red mist in a hundred spots around them.

"This is better than I thought," Valas said. "The smoke and fumes give us some concealment."

"And they make my eyes water," Ryld said. He reached the ceiling and found that the cavern roof was rough and pitted. "Which way?"

"To your right. Yes, that's it."

Valas indicated the northern wall of the city with a jerk of his chin, keeping his foot and arm secure in the rope stirrups he'd fashioned. Carefully, Ryld turned to face the ceiling more evenly, and he pulled himself along hand over hand as if he were climbing a vertical wall of rock. The scout shifted to secure his grip, and kept his own eyes down at the cavern floor below, directing the weapons master in his progress.

"One gray dwarf wizard with a spell of cancellation would certainly ruin our day," Ryld remarked. "Aren't you a little nervous in that arrangement?"

"I've always had a good head for heights, but let's not talk about it anymore."

Ryld chuckled.

For days, the journey had been simply uneventful and dreary. The tactical challenge of spying in the heart of the duergar city, though, fully engaged them both.

"Head more to your left," Valas said, interrupting his own thoughts. "There's a bit of a ledge on the cavern wall that should run the way we want to go."

Ryld complied, and the two of them carefully leveled off and descended along the sloping roof of the cavern until they found the place where it dropped more or less straight down and became the wall. There, an old weathered seam circled the cavern like the eaves of an old tavern. The weapons master looked at it dubiously, but as they drew close Valas disentangled himself and leaped lightly down to crouch in the space like a skinny spider.

Ryld followed, somewhat more awkwardly. He could manage it, barely, but he was lucky to have the magic of his insignia to fall back on if his footing or grip failed him.

Valas moved confidently forward, following the seam as it descended sharply and disappeared around a sharp bend overlooking a side cavern.

Ryld scrambled down after him, cursing silently as his foot dislodged some loose rock and sent it clattering down the clifflike wall. The forges and hammers of Gracklstugh covered the sound fairly well, though, and they were still above Laduguer's Furrow. The rock skittered into the abyss and vanished.

Valas glanced back from his perch at the bend.

Carefully, he signed. *Come up here and see this.*

Ryld worked his way up beside the scout, finally stretching out on his belly to stay on the ledge. The seam ran down to a side cave and turned in sharply. From their vantage a hundred feet or more above the floor, they could see a good-sized cavern, perhaps three or four hundred yards long and about half that wide. The walls were hewn into barracks rooms, enough to house quite a large number of soldiers, but the floor of the place was level and open, a good drilling ground for bodies of troops.

From end to end, it was crowded with wagons and pack lizards. Hundreds of duergar swarmed over the scene, securing great panniers to the ugly reptiles, loading wagons, and preparing siege engines for travel. The noxious reek of the city's smelters didn't suffice to mask the heavy smell of animal dung in the large chamber, and the lizards' hisses and rasping croaks filled the air.

Valas began counting wagons and pack beasts, trying to estimate the size of the force that might be on the march. After a few minutes, he finally tore his eyes away.

Somewhere between two and three thousand? Ryld said.

The scout frowned and replied, *I think somewhat more, maybe four thousand all together, but there may be more trains gathering in other caverns nearby.*

Is there any reason to think they're not bound for Menzoberranzan? Ryld asked.

We're not their only enemies. Still, I don't like the timing.

"I don't believe in coincidences, either," Ryld whispered. He carefully began to worm his way back from the edge, taking great pains to dislodge no more rocks. "I would suggest checking the other caves for more soldiers, but I think we've seen more than the duergar would want already, and I don't feel like pressing my luck. We'd best get back and report this to the others."

C h a p t e r

E I G H T

"We should just leave," growled Jeggred. His white fur was streaked with red wine, and hot grease from a roast of rothé meat stained his muzzle. The draegloth didn't take well to long waits, and two days of confining himself to the Cold Foundry had been hard for him. "We could be out of the city before they knew we'd gone."

"I fear it wouldn't be as simple as you make it sound," Ryld said. He knelt by his pack, stuffing sacks with the least perishable items from the buffet. He dropped the sacks into a yawning black circle beside him—a magical hole that could be picked up and carried as if it was nothing but a piece of dark cloth. It could hold hundreds of pounds of gear and supplies, but weighed nothing at all. "You may not have noticed, but I'm sure I'm not the only one who marked the spies watching this inn. We wouldn't make a quarter mile before we were swarmed under duergar soldiers."

"So?" the draegloth demanded. "I fear no dwarf!"

"Duergar aren't goblins or gnolls, too stupid to use their numbers well, too clumsy and crude to stand a chance in a one-on-one duel. I've met duergar swordsmen nearly as good as I am. I have no doubt that a number of such formidable fellows would be banded together against us, and the duergar count skilled wizards and clerics among their ranks, too."

"We should have known better than to march into a duergar city," Halisstra said. "What a miserable piece of timing."

She hurried to don her armor, a suit of highly enchanted chain mail that carried the arms of House Melarn on its breast. She wondered if the best strategy would be to simply wait a few more days and allow the gray dwarves to relax their vigilant stance. On the other hand, if they delayed too long, there was always the chance that the merchant she'd charmed to part with Danifae's new arms would recover his wits and report the incident to the authorities. Had they simply murdered the merchants . . . but no, if they'd been caught at that, they would already have paid with their lives.

She tugged at the long hem of the mail hauberk and wriggled to settle it better on her shoulders.

"Master Argith, how long will it take the duergar army to march?" Halisstra asked.

"Soon," Ryld said. "They can't keep that many pack lizards in harness for long. The question is how long after the army sallies before they allow travel to resume. If we wait them out, we might be delayed for days."

"Delayed—or disposed of," Danifae warned.

"We will set out at once," Quenthel said, putting a halt to the debate.

The Mistress of the Academy dressed for battle, her face set in a black scowl, her whips writhing in agitation.

"That begs the question that was raised a moment ago—which way do we go?" asked Ryld.

The weapons master finished with his supplies and picked up the hole, rolling it tightly and slipping it into his pack.

"I can retrace our steps back to Mantol-Derith," Pharaun offered, "but it will be difficult to move forward from here. I don't know the way to the Labyrinth, so any stroll we took on the Plane of Shadow would doubtless lead us to a strange and cheerless end. There are too many of you for me to teleport us all together, so unless someone feels like answering to the gray dwarves for the rest of the company's sudden departure, I suppose that's out as well."

"What about a spell to conceal our identities?" Ryld asked.

"Regrettably," the wizard replied, "gray dwarves are notoriously resistant to illusions of any kind."

Halisstra added, "If only one saw through a disguise and saw a party of dark elves. . . ."

"Better to simply render us all invisible," the Master of Sorcere said. "Yes, that would be the most expedient solution to this little conundrum. It quite reminds me of a time when—"

"Enough." Quenthel shifted in her seat and asked Valas, "Do we need to set out for the Labyrinth from here, or could you find a way around Gracklstugh if we retraced our steps a bit?"

"It will take several more days to circle the city," the scout answered, "but I could guide you past Gracklstugh's borders."

"Fine," Quenthel said. "We will head back for the docks and make use of Coalhewer's boat. It's the most direct route out of the city from here, and unless I miss my guess, the lakeside will be less heavily guarded than the tunnels. Is everybody armed?" She looked around quickly. No one requested more time to prepare, so the Baenre priestess nodded with a small gesture of approval and turned to Pharaun. "What must we do for your spell to succeed?"

"Join hands and stay close to me," Pharaun said, "or wander off if you like, in which case you will find yourself inconveniently visible. I will not be held responsible for any difficulties that ensue."

Fully armed and armored, packs shouldered, all but Valas joined hands and waited. The Master of Sorcere, standing in their center, hissed out a sibilant string of arcane words and wove his hands in mystic passes. They all vanished from view. Halisstra could feel Danifae's hand on her left shoulder, and she clasped Ryld's cuirass with her own right hand, but as far as her eyes could tell, only the scout was in the room.

"Are you ready, Master Hune?" Pharaun asked, unseen.

Valas offered a small nod. He was dressed in what passed for his own finery, a simple vest of chain mail over a good shirt of spider silk and dark breeches, his *piwafwi* thrown over one shoulder in a rakish fashion. Odd badges and tokens pinned here and there to his clothing, the defenses and charms of half a dozen races, completed his ensemble.

"I'll dawdle in the courtyard a moment. Make sure you're all out swiftly; it will look less suspicious if I don't stand around for long. I'll join you at Coalhewer's boat in ten minutes."

"You'll be tailed," Ryld said.

Valas Hune seemed honestly offended.

"No one alive can follow me when I do not wish to be followed," he said.

Valas went out into the courtyard, throwing open the door to their room and taking a long moment to stretch. Halisstra felt Ryld shuffle forward, and she did likewise, crowding close behind him as Danifae pressed up behind her. The girl's breath was warm at her neck.

While the Bregan D'aerthe scout casually strolled out of the inn's gate and turned left toward the city's central district, Halisstra and the others bent around in an awkward circle and headed right, back to the docks. The streets were not deserted, but neither were they busy. Most duergar were back in their drab residences after a long day in the city's forges and foundries. Had the company been forced into flight at the beginning or the end of the workday, their deception might have been given away by the sheer accident of a busy gray dwarf bumping into their invisible chain as they skulked down the street.

Halisstra risked one more glance over her shoulder at Valas, who strolled quickly down the street in the opposite direction, looking a little furtive himself—a better disguise than complete nonchalance, which would have been jarring in a place like Gracklstugh. She also noted a gray dwarf porter who hefted a small cask of brandy to his shoulder as the scout passed and turned to follow, seemingly nothing more than a common laborer hired to carry goods from one part of the city to another. Valas could not have missed him, she decided. *The mercenary is too sharp to miss a straightforward tail like that.*

Though Halisstra expected a hue and a cry at any moment from hidden watchers, their progress was unimpeded until they reached the docks. As they hurried across the stone quays toward the strange vessels moored there, Ryld suddenly halted, surprising her. Halisstra walked into his back before she realized he'd stopped. Danifae bumped into her as well, as the whole column came to a halt.

"Trouble," whispered Pharaun. "A patrol of duergar soldiers in the crown prince's colors just came around the corner of the next street over. They're invisible, too, and there's a wizard-looking fellow leading them in our direction."

"They see us?" Jeggred rumbled. "What use are you, mage?"

"There are spells that allow one to see the invisible," Pharaun replied. "I'm using one right now, in fact, which is why I can see the guards, and you cannot. I suppose that begs the question, what use are y—"

"You there! Dismiss your spell, and lay down your weapons!" the leader of the duergar patrol called. A clatter of arms echoed across the silent street, though Halisstra still could not make out any of the gray dwarves. "You are under arrest!"

"Jeggred, Ryld, Pharaun—deal with them," Quenthel ordered. "Danifae, Halisstra, stay with me."

She dashed off down the pier, ghosting into visibility as she left Pharaun's magical influence behind. Jeggred and Ryld charged in the opposite direction, Splitter appearing in the weapons master's hand as if he had worked an enchantment of his own. Pharaun snarled out a short phrase of words that seemed to shiver the very air of the quay, and a moment later a ripple of light washed over the opposite side of the street, revealing the armored duergar where they stood. The wizard followed instantly with another spell, becoming visible himself as he pointed a black ray at the wizard among the gray dwarf soldiers. The purple lance struck the duergar mage in the center of his chest, and the enemy wizard collapsed like a puppet with its strings cut.

"Next time, strike first and issue challenges later," Pharaun remarked. He started to work another spell as the draegloth and the weapons master crashed into the ranks of the patrol, hewing and slashing with abandon.

Halisstra followed Quenthel as she ran down the pier and leaped onto Coalhewer's boat. The massive undead skeletons stood motionless in their well in the center of the hull, nothing more than inert machinery awaiting command. Beneath the bridge, the duergar smuggler stirred and sat up from a thin bedroll, snatching up a hand axe close by his sleeping place.

"Who goes there?" he roared, scrambling to his feet. "Why, ye—"

He was cut off by the impact of Quenthel's boot in the center of his chest, slamming him back down to the deck.

The Baenre raised her whip to finish the smuggler, but Halisstra called, "Wait! We may need him to run this thing."

"You believed that story of his?" Quenthel said, not taking her eyes from the dwarf. "Of course he wanted us to think we needed him to run the boat."

"True or not, now is not the time to gamble on our escape," Halisstra said. "We'd look damned foolish if we fought our way through a patrol of the prince's soldiers and couldn't leave the pier."

"Fell out of the crown prince's favor, did ye?" Coalhewer said. He stood slowly and offered a fierce grin. From the end of the pier a sudden bright glare of lightning and a booming thunderclap announced the arrival of duergar reinforcements. "If ye kill me, ye'll never escape. Now, what's a fair price fer taking you off this pier, I wonder?"

Quenthel bristled and doubtless would have struck him down then, but Halisstra stepped between them.

"If we get caught here," the Melarn priestess said, "we'll implicate you in whatever charges are brought against us, dwarf. Now get us underway."

Coalhewer stared up at the three dark elves, his face contorted with fury.

"I dealt fairly with ye, and this be my thanks?" he snarled. "I should've known better than to traffic with yer kind!"

He whirled to cast off the lines securing the macabre vessel to the quay, barking orders at the hulking skeletons in the center of the boat.

Quenthel looked at Halisstra with narrowed eyes and asked, "Why spare the dwarf? You know he's lying about commanding the boat."

Halisstra shrugged and said, "You can always kill him later, if you're so inclined."

As the wheels at the side of the vessel began to churn in the water, Ryld and Jeggred sprinted up, clambering aboard. Blood dripped from both the half-demon's talons and Splitter. Pharaun bounded up a moment later, after sealing the end of the pier with a wall of roaring flame to keep the soldiers at bay.

"That won't hold them for long, I'm sure," the wizard said. "There must be three or four mages back there, and they'll extinguish that wall quickly enough. Best we get well away from here before they can fling their spells against our humble conveyance."

Ryld studied the wall of fire at the pier's end and scowled.

"You realize you've also blocked Valas's escape with that spell," he grated. "We need him, Pharaun. We can't leave him here."

"I'm flattered, Master Argith."

From the shadows of the vessel's stern, Valas stood up and adjusted his *piwafwi*.

"Where in Lolth's dark hells did you come from?" the weapons master said, blinking and rubbing his eyes.

"I boarded just a few steps behind the three ladies," the scout said. He glanced around, savoring the open surprise on the faces of his companions, then made a small bow and a gesture of self-deprecation. "As I said, I am not easily followed or marked when I do not wish to be. Besides, it seemed that the three of you had the crown prince's soldiers in hand."

The Master of Melee-Magthere snorted, and returned Splitter to its sheath across his back. He turned to the city's waterfront, which was receding quickly into the darkness. Fire still glowed along the piers, illuminating the bizarre profiles of more duergar vessels whose crews swarmed the decks, shouting orders at each other and scurrying to obey the crown prince's soldiers.

"I hope our vessel is faster than theirs," Ryld said.

"Not to worry," Coalhewer called from his perch. "This be the fastest vessel on the Darklake. None of those scows can catch us."

He snapped out another order to the hulking skeletons driving the boat, and the undead monstrosities redoubled their efforts, driving their crankshafts faster and faster, until a froth of white foam boiled at the paddlewheels. The duergar city faded into the darkness behind them, marked by nothing more than a red glare on the cavern ceiling.

"A dire development all this," Quenthel mused. "Menzoberranzan hardly needs a war with the duergar now."

"Do we alter our course?" Ryld asked. "Menzoberranzan must be warned of the duergar army."

The Mistress of Arach-Tinilith stood in thought for a moment, then said, "No. What we're doing is more important, and if I am not mistaken Pharaun possesses the means to pass a warning to the archmage. Is that not so, wizard?"

The Master of Sorcere simply smiled and spread his hands.

🕷   🕷   🕷

Nimor's soft footfalls echoed in corridor after empty corridor as he made his way through the crown prince's fortress. At odd intervals he passed pairs of scowling guards in heavy armor, halberds held upright, and he wondered if they ever tired of looking at the blank stone walls in the course of their duties.

Most likely not, he decided. Duergar were simply insensitive to that sort of thing.

In his hand, Nimor idly flipped a small envelope from finger to finger. The Lady Aliisza of the Sceptered One's Court (an inventive title if Nimor had ever heard one) had invited him to join her for dinner

138

in her chambers, observing that the gray dwarves had so far failed to invite her to any kind of banquet or dinner. Nimor didn't expect that companionship for dinner was the only thing on her agenda.

Arriving at the rooms assigned to the Sceptered One's envoy, he tucked his invitation back into his breast pocket, and rapped twice at the door.

"Enter," called a soft voice.

Nimor let himself in. Aliisza waited by a table spread with quite an impressive meal, complete with a bottle of wine from the World Above and a pair of glasses already poured. She wore a flowing skirt of red silk with a tight-fitting corselet trimmed with black lace. The colors suited her, he noted, and even went well with her soft black wings.

"Lady Aliisza," he said, offering a bow. "I am flattered. I am certain the repast before me did not come from the crown prince's kitchens."

"There is a limit to how much smoked rothé cheese and black sporeflour bread one can stand," she said. She took the wine glasses in hand and moved close to extend him one. "I admit, I had my entourage scour the city to find inns and taverns willing to provide meals suited to an elf's palate."

Nimor took the glass and swirled it, bringing it to his nose to inhale the aroma. Not only did it allow him to appreciate the wine's bouquet, but he could sniff the vintage for any signs of the various subtle poisons with which he was familiar. He would have proved difficult to poison in any case, but he did not detect any strange scents.

"You have my thanks, dear lady. I have been traveling of late, and have been forced to live on very plain fare indeed."

Aliisza sipped at her own wine, and nodded at the table.

"In that case, why don't we eat while we talk?"

Nimor took the seat opposite the half-demon, and fell to his meal. One of the consequences of his true nature was a surprising ability to eat far more than one might expect for a dark elf of his slight build, and to go for quite a long time between meals. The rothé roast with mushroom gravy was cool and rare in the middle and quite excellent, the small blind fish were somewhat saltier than he would have cared for, and the wine was dry and strong, a good match for the roast.

"So, to what do I owe the pleasure of this occasion?" he asked between mouthfuls.

"You intrigue me, Nimor Imphraezl. I want to know more about who you are, and what interests you represent."

"Who I am? I have given you my true name," Nimor replied.

"That is not exactly the sort of answer I had in mind." Aliisza leaned forward, her eyes fixed on him. "What I meant was, whom do you serve? What are you doing here?"

Nimor felt a subtle flutter at the edges of his thoughts, as if he was trying to remember something he'd momentarily misplaced. He leaned back in his chair and grinned at the alu-fiend.

"I hope you'll forgive me, dear lady, but I recently found myself in an interview in which the other party could read my thoughts, and so I have taken steps to defend myself against such things this evening. You won't pick your answers from my mind."

Aliisza frowned and said, "Now I wonder what thoughts you have to guard so well, Nimor. Are you afraid that I wouldn't like what I found there?"

"We all have our secrets." Nimor teased his wine and admired the bouquet again. He would not give her the complete truth, of course, but what he would offer was truthful enough under the circumstances. "I belong to a minor House of Menzoberranzan with some unusual practices of which the matron mothers would not approve," he began. "Among other things, we do not subject ourselves to the tyranny of our Lolth-worshiping female relations, and we possess old and strong ties to minor Houses with similar practices in several other cities. We masquerade as low-ranking merchants, but we keep our true nature and capabilities quite secret."

"Capabilities?"

"We are assassins, dear lady, and we are very good at what we do."

Aliisza leaned forward, resting her delicate chin on her fingertips as she studied Nimor with her dark, mischievous gaze.

"So what is an assassin of Menzoberranzan doing in Gracklstugh, advising Horgar Steelshadow as he musters his army for war?" she asked. "Wouldn't that constitute the worst sort of treason?"

Nimor shrugged and replied, "We wish to see the order of things upset. We cannot defeat the great Houses of our city without an army, and Gracklstugh's is the strongest in this corner of the Underdark. As soon as it became evident that Lolth had abandoned her priestesses, we realized that we had a golden opportunity to strike a mortal blow against the great Houses. We have been doing all that we can to help Horgar see that our opportunity is his opportunity, too."

"Aren't you concerned that the duergar might prove unwilling to relinquish the drow city to your care once they've conquered it?"

"Of course," Nimor said, "but in all honesty, we view the fall of the Spider Queen's Houses as a goal desirable enough to outweigh the risks of duergar perfidy. Even if Gracklstugh turned on my House and occupied Menzoberranzan for a hundred years, we would still survive, and we would reclaim the city in time."

Aliisza stood gracefully and paced over to a narrow, slitlike window overlooking the city.

"Do you really think the Spider Queen will allow her city to fall? What becomes of the gray dwarves' assault if the priestesses of Lolth suddenly recover their powers?"

"We are a long-lived race, dear lady. My grandfather saw with his own eyes the events of a thousand years past. We do not forget the past the way other races do. In all our legends, our lore, we have never encountered a silence so complete and long-lasting. Even if it proves to be temporary, well, it represents a chance that comes along only once every couple of thousand years, doesn't it? How could we not choose this moment to strike?"

"Perhaps you're right. I've spoken to other drow who seem to feel these are extraordinary and unprecedented times." Aliisza glanced over her shoulder at him and added, "In fact, in Ched Nasad I encountered a mission of high-ranking Menzoberranyr who had come to the city in the hopes of discovering the causes of Lolth's silence. Quenthel Baenre, the Mistress of Arach-Tinilith, led the company."

"I've heard of Mistress Quenthel's mission. So they made it to Ched Nasad?"

"After passing through Kaanyr Vhok's territory, yes. They arrived just in time to witness the city's destruction."

"Did any of them survive?"

Aliisza shrugged and said, "I could not say for certain. They were a capable lot. If anyone could escape the city's fall, they would have."

Nimor tapped his finger on the table, thinking. Was Quenthel's mission of investigation significant, then? He'd simply figured that the matron mothers had decided to shuffle the Mistress of Arach-Tinilith out of the city for a time in the event that she was entertaining dangerous aspirations. Still, it represented a wild card, an unknown factor that the Jaezred Chaulssin might be wise to take note of. A party of powerful dark elves roaming the Underdark might find the opportunity to cause all sorts of trouble.

"Did they find any answers to their questions?" he asked.

"None that I know of," Aliisza said. She turned back from the window and glided over to the table again, then changed the subject. "You seemed very anxious to argue my case with the crown prince. Might I ask why?"

The assassin shifted in his seat and leaned back, allowing his gaze to rest on her.

"You touched on this already," he said. "Either Gracklstugh is strong enough to defeat Menzoberranzan, or it isn't. If it is not, then Kaanyr Vhok's Scoured Legion is likely to tip the scales in our favor. If Gracklstugh is strong enough, then the Scoured Legion might serve as a useful check on Horgar's aspirations. We wouldn't want the crown prince to forget the details of our arrangement."

"And why should the Scoured Legion serve as your army in the field?"

"Because Horgar won't have you for an ally unless I persuade him that he'd be better served with Kaanyr Vhok's tanarukks at his side than attacking his flank," Nimor answered. "Besides, your master doesn't want to sit at home while events unfold. He sent you here to urge the duergar to attack Menzoberranzan, did he not?"

Aliisza hid her smile with a sip of wine.

"Well, there is that," she admitted. "So, will you ask the duergar to accept our help, or not?"

The assassin studied the alu-fiend while he considered the question. Agrach Dyrr was a useful ally, but he doubted that the Fifth House of Menzoberranzan had the strength to counterbalance Horgar's army if push came to shove. Another force on the field would increase the chances of success for the Jaezred Chaulssin, and with three factions to work with, it should be possible to align two against the third in whatever combination was necessary to advance his goals. In extremis, the Jaezred Chaulssin could bring their own strength to bear, but they were not numerous, and it was always preferable to expend the resources of one's allies before tapping your own reserves.

"I think," he said at length, "that we won't give Horgar the chance to refuse your help. Do you know of a place called the Pillars of Woe?"

Aliisza frowned and shook her head.

"It's a gorge between Gracklstugh and Menzoberranzan," Nimor said, "a place I have great plans for. I am certain that some of Kaanyr Vhok's scouts will know the spot, and I'll make sure you know where to find it. Go back to Kaanyr Vhok and have him bring the Scoured Legion to the Pillars of Woe with all possible speed. You will have your chance to assist in the destruction of Menzoberranzan. If the crown prince proves completely unreasonable, you will have other opportunities available to you, but I believe that Horgar will accept your stake in events once he encounters your force in the field."

"That sounds risky."

"Risk is the cost of opportunity, dear lady. It cannot be avoided."

Aliisza measured him with her smoky gaze.

"All right," she said, "but I'll warn you that Kaanyr will be quite put out with me if he marches his army off into the wilds of the Underdark and misses all the fun."

"I will not disappoint you," Nimor promised. He allowed himself a deep draught of wine, and pushed his chair away from the table. "That would seem to conclude our business, Lady Aliisza. I thank you for the fine supper and the pleasant company."

"Leaving so soon?" Aliisza said, with just a hint of a pout.

She drifted closer, a mischievous fire springing up in her eyes, and Nimor found his gaze roving over the voluptuous curves of her body. She leaned forward to put her hands on the arms of his chair, and enfolded her wings around him. With sinuous grace she lowered herself closer to nibble at his ear, pressing her soft, hot flesh against him.

"If we've finished our business already, Nimor Imphraezl, it must be time for pleasure," she whispered into his ear.

Nimor inhaled the delicious odor of her perfume and found his hands roving to stroke her hips and bring her closer still.

"If you insist," he murmured, kissing the hollow of her neck.

She shivered in his arms as he reached up to unlace her corselet.

The crude paddlewheels at the sides of Coalhewer's boat clattered loudly in the darkness, churning the black water into furious, white, rushing foam. The hulking skeletons in their well-like space at the boat's center stooped and rose, stooped and rose, their bony hands clamped to the crankshafts driving the wheels. Relentlessly, tirelessly, they continued their mindless work, held to their labors by the necromantic magic that had animated them years, or perhaps decades past. Halisstra was no judge of waterborne travel, but it seemed to her that Coalhewer's boat was holding to a pace that would be difficult to match.

She risked a glance back over her shoulder to see if her companions had marked any signs of pursuit. Ryld, Jeggred, and Pharaun all stood in the rear of the boat, watching its wake. Quenthel sat on a large trunk just under the boat's scaffoldlike bridge, also gazing back toward Gracklstugh. Valas stood on the bridge alongside Coalhewer, making sure that the duergar captain kept the ungainly vehicle to the course he desired.

Halisstra and Danifae had taken up the posts of lookouts, peering ahead to make sure they didn't run headlong into trouble. Halisstra hadn't bothered to debate the arrangement. The males were best placed between the rest of the company and the most likely threats, and Pharaun was probably their best weapon against any pursuit out of Gracklstugh.

The city itself was no longer visible, except as a long, low red smudge. The firelight of the dwarves' forges could be seen for several miles across the vast black space of the Dark Lake's open waters, a sense of distance that reminded Halisstra of the unnatural vistas of the World Above. They'd churned their way east and south from Gracklstugh's waterfront for several hours, with no sign of anyone following, but Halisstra couldn't shake the impression that they were not clear of the duergar yet. Reluctantly she shifted her gaze back to the boundless dark in front of the boat, and checked her crossbow to make sure it was ready to fire.

Halisstra carefully scanned her half of the bow, starting with the water close to the boat and working her way farther out until even her drow sight could make out nothing more through the blackness, then she returned her gaze to the boat and started again. Great stalactites or columns—it was impossible to tell—descended from the ceiling and vanished into the inky water at odd intervals, creating titanic pillars of stone for the boat to navigate around. In other spots the jagged points of stalagmites jutted from the surface like spears. Coalhewer steered well clear of those, pointing out that there might be two submerged rocks for every one that broke the surface.

"I can't believe I'm crouching on the deck of a duergar boat, fleeing for my life from a city I'd never seen before three days ago," Halisstra murmured, breaking the long silence. "Two tendays ago I was the heir apparent of a great House in a noble city. One tenday ago I was a prisoner, betrayed by the petty malice of Faeryl Zauvirr, and now here I am, a rootless wanderer with nothing more to my name than the armor on my back and whatever odds and ends are stowed in my pack. I just cannot fathom why."

"I am not unfamiliar with changes in one's circumstances and fortunes," Danifae said. "What is the point of asking why? It is the will of the Spider Queen."

"Is it?" Halisstra asked. "House Melarn stood for twenty centuries or more, only to fall in the hour when Lolth withdrew her favor from our entire race. It was only in her absence that our enemies could overthrow us."

Danifae did not reply, nor did Halisstra expect her to. That thought was perilously close to heresy, after all. To suggest that something had occurred against Lolth's will was to doubt the power of the Spider Queen, and to question Lolth's power was to invite death and condemnation as a faithless weakling. The fate that awaited the faithless in the afterlife was too terrible to contemplate. Unless Lolth chose to take the soul of a follower to her divine abode in the Demonweb Pits, a drow's spirit would be condemned to anguish and oblivion in the barren wastelands where the dead of all kinds were judged. Only abject worship and perfect service could sway the Dark Queen to intercede on one's behalf and grant life beyond life, eternal existence as one of Lolth's divine host.

Of course, thought Halisstra, if Lolth is dead, then damnation and oblivion become unavoidable, don't they?

She blanched at the thought and shivered in horror, standing quickly and pacing away from the bridge to hide her face from the others.

I must not think such things, she told herself. Better to empty my mind of all thoughts than to entertain blasphemy.

She closed her eyes and took a deep breath, doing her best to banish her insidious doubts.

"We've got trouble," Ryld announced from the afterdeck. The weapons master knelt and peered through the darkness behind the boat. "Three boats, much like this one."

"I see them," Pharaun said. He glanced up at the bridge. "Master

Coalhewer, I thought you said this was the fastest vessel on the Dark-lake. Am I to gather that you exaggerated a bit?"

The dwarf scowled back into the darkness and replied, "I've never been overtaken before today, so how was I t'know any different?"

He muttered a foul string of curses and paced from one end of the bridge to the other, never taking his eyes off the following boats.

"They're not gaining on us by much," Quenthel observed after a long moment. "It's going to take them a while to catch us."

Halisstra turned and clambered past the bridge to gaze aft. She could see the pursuing boats, just barely. They trailed behind Coal-hewer's craft by a bowshot, black ghosts silhouetted faintly against the dying red smudge that marked the city behind them. A glimmer of white played at the bow of each boat where it parted the waters.

She looked up at the duergar and asked, "Can't you make this thing go any faster?"

Coalhewer growled and waved a hand at the skeletons driving the craft.

"They've been told to go as fast as they can," he said. "We might speed her up by throwing weight over the side, but there's no telling if it'd be help enough."

"How far are we from the southern wall of the cavern?" asked Quenthel.

"I don't know these waters well. Three miles, I'd guess."

"Then keep to your course," the Baenre decided. "Once we're ashore, we'll be able to outdistance any pursuit, or pick our ground to fight on if we decide not to run."

"But what of my boat?" Coalhewer demanded. "D'ye have any idea how much I paid for it?"

"I'm certain I hadn't invited you along, dwarf," Quenthel replied.

She turned her back on the duergar and settled down to wait, absently stroking her whip as she watched the pursuing boats draw closer.

The boat churned on, passing more stalagmites jutting up from the waters as the pursuing boats edged closer. Halisstra and Danifae watched carefully for obstacles ahead, but despite herself, Halisstra could not resist the impulse to glance over her shoulder every few minutes to check on their pursuers. Each time she did, the boats had closed a little more, until she could actually make out discrete individuals moving around on their decks. Fifteen minutes after they'd first come into view behind Coalhewer's boat, the duergar vessels began to fire missiles after them—heavy crossbow bolts that fell hissing into their wake, and clumsy catapult-shot of great flaming spheres that soared past the boat to smash against the dank columns littering the surrounding waters.

"Zigzag a bit," Quenthel told the dwarf. "We don't want to be hit by one of those."

"They'll gain faster on us if I do," Coalhewer protested, but he began to ease his wheel from one side to the other, trying to avoid keeping straight on any heading for too long.

"Ryld, Valas, return fire at the lead boat. Don't use more than half your arrows or bolts. We may need them later on." Quenthel glanced around, and nodded at Halisstra. "You too, Halisstra. Danifae, keep watch forward. Pharaun, answer those catapults."

Valas turned around on the bridge and braced himself against intersecting rails, fitting an arrow to his string. He aimed for the lead boat, and loosed an arrow. Ryld and Halisstra followed a moment later with bolts of their own. After a long heartbeat of flight time, the tiny figure of a gray dwarf threw up its arms and reeled over the side of the boat, vanishing beneath its flailing paddles. Other dwarves scurried for cover, raising large mantlets to cover themselves.

Pharaun stepped forward and gestured boldly at the leading boat, barking out the words of a spell. From his fingertips a small orange bead of flame streaked out, darting across the dark water with the speed of an arrow. It seemed to vanish into the blackness, swallowed by the bulk of the leading boat—and a brilliant blast of flame erupted right at the pursuer's prow, scouring the foredecks with a roar that echoed through the great cavern. Duergar wreathed in flames lurched and stumbled in the distance, with more of them falling or throwing themselves over the side.

"Well done!" Quenthel cried.

Even Jeggred roared in glee, but a moment later a buzzing globe of blue energy rose from the second ship and streaked back at them. Pharaun started a spell of deflection or warding, but he was unable to parry the blow, and glaring streaks of lightning enveloped Coalhewer's boat. The very air roared with dozens of thunderclaps and explosions as crawling arcs of electricity detonated barrels, casks, and fittings, or sizzled into flesh. Halisstra cried out and buckled to the deck as a bolt stabbed through her left hip, while Ryld collapsed jerking to the deck, his breastplate glowing blue-white with the lightning ball's energy.

The skeletal rowers kept at their toil, driving the boat onward.

Pharaun jerked out his wand and hurled a bolt back at the boat that had launched the lightning ball at them. A skipping meteor of blinding fire flew at them from the leading boat, bounding across the water with an almost animate hunger. By a stroke of good luck, the missile struck a low-lying rocky outcropping and detonated behind them, spreading a slick of burning fluid across the water's surface. The third boat fired its catapult again, sending a comet-like ball of flame whizzing clear over the bridge to explode a short distance ahead.

"Damnation," Coalhewer snarled. "They've got the range on us!"

"It seems that I am somewhat outnumbered," Pharaun called out between spells. "Perhaps we should redouble our efforts to escape?"

Arrows hissed past them, clattering against the boat or sticking into the zurkhwood decks with heavy *tchunks*!

"Halisstra," the wizard called, "would you take my wand—the one in my hand, I mean—and use it to discourage that fellow on the first boat?"

Halisstra ignored the hot ache in her hip and scrambled aft. She took the iron wand from the wizard's hand, aiming at the lead boat as she barked out its command word. The air crackled with sparks and ozone as the bolt blasted back at the pursuing boat, only to flare impotently against some kind of spell shield that had been raised by the duergar wizards behind them.

Pharaun chanted out the words of another spell, and a thick white mist arose in their wake, its billows spreading across the water with startling speed. Almost instantly, it sprawled across their stern like a wall of white, completely blocking the pursuing boats from view.

"There," said the wizard. "That should slow them a bit."

"It's fog. Won't they just sail right through it?" Ryld asked.

"That is no ordinary fog, my friend. That fog is thick enough to arrest an arrow in mid-flight. Best of all, it is highly acidic, so that anyone blundering about in there will be slowly eaten away." The wizard smiled and folded his arms. "Ah, *damn it,* I'm good."

Quenthel opened her mouth, most likely to take issue with the wizard's self-congratulations, when Danifae called from the bow, "Stop! Rocks ahead! Stop!"

"Bloody hell!" gasped Coalhewer. "All back full! All back full, ye great bony louts!"

The turning skeletons slowed their furious pumping, unable to arrest the heavy wheels all at once, and slowly began to spin the paddles back the other way. The dwarf did not wait on them, slamming his wheel hard over to veer away from the black line of fanglike rocks ahead. The lake seemed to come to an end, shoaling up quickly to meet the plunging ceiling. The shoreline extended left and right for as far as Halisstra could see. The boat slued to an awkward halt, its starboard bow rebounding from a thankfully rounded rock in their path. The impact staggered everyone on board, and nearly pitched Danifae headlong over the bow.

"Now what?" Ryld asked, picking himself up off the deck. "They've got us pinned against the cavern wall."

"How long will your fog delay the gray dwarves?" Quenthel snapped at Pharaun.

"No more than a couple of minutes," he answered. "They might choose to back out and go around, of course."

Pharaun stared intently at his handiwork. In the distance, duergar screamed in pain, their cries of agony oddly muffled by the insidious white mist.

"The spell is unlikely to kill or disable very many of them," the wizard added, "and I don't think it'll sink their boats."

"Then this is where we get off," Quenthel said. She pointed at the cavern wall. "We'll take cover in the rocks there, and stay out of sight. We'll send the boat that way—" she pointed toward the east—"and let the crown prince's men chase it away from us."

"I won't be yer decoy!" Coalhewer snapped. "Ye got me into this mess, and ye'll get me out of it!"

The dark elves ignored the dwarf as they hurriedly threw their packs to the wet rocks below the bow. Jeggred bounded down into the icy water and struggled up on shore, followed by Ryld and Pharaun. Valas swarmed down from the bridge and vaulted down as well.

"You're wasting my time," Quenthel said to the duergar captain. "Go on, now, and take your chances, or stay here and face the draegloth."

She leaped lightly to the boulders below, joined by Halisstra and Danifae a moment later.

"But if ye . . . ah, damn the lot of ye to Lolth's spidery hells!" Coalhewer swore.

He dashed back up to his bridge and began to bark orders at the skeletal rowers again. The boat slowly backed away from the rocks.

"If they catch me," he shouted back, "I'll tell them exactly where to find ye!"

Quenthel narrowed her eyes. She started to gesture to Jeggred, but Halisstra shook her head and started a low, droning *bae'qeshel* song. She gathered the force of her will and hurled it full upon the livid dwarf.

"Escape, Coalhewer," she hissed. "Flee as quickly as you may, and do not let yourself be caught. If you are caught, better to swim to safety than to let yourself be taken."

The invisible webs of the spell settled about the dwarf like a snowfall of deadly venom. He stared open-mouthed at Halisstra, then whirled to redouble his efforts to take his boat clear before the fog lifted. Quenthel glanced at Halisstra and raised an eyebrow.

"It seemed best to make sure he would flee as we wanted him to," Halisstra explained as she quickly gathered her things and hurried for the cover of the boulders and stalagmites above the waterline.

Quenthel followed a step behind her. They splashed ashore and settled behind a large rock just as the prow of the first duergar boat, still glowing red with embers left from the fireball Pharaun had hurled at it, nosed through the deadly mists. The dark elves drew their *piwafwis* close around them and held still, watching as the duergar stirred and broke from whatever shelters they'd managed to find from the acidic fog.

One of the gray dwarves pointed and shouted, and the others joined the clamor. Turning sharply in the water, they slewed around the ship's bow and set off after Coalhewer's vanishing boat.

Good, signed Pharaun. I was afraid they were using magic to follow us. It seems that Master Coalhewer will render us one last service after all.

What do you think will happen when they catch him? Ryld asked.

The duergar boats pulled out of earshot.

"I suppose it depends on whether or not he can swim," Halisstra said.

A long day's march later, pausing only long enough to allow Pharaun to finally craft a sending to pass news of Gracklstugh's army to Gromph, the company came to the Labyrinth. They emerged from winding, unexplored passageways into a series of miles-long natural tunnels interspersed with long, hewn ways and small, square chambers. Coalhewer, his boat, and the pursuit from Gracklstugh they'd left twenty miles or more behind them.

The tunnels were black basalt, cold and sharp, the frozen remnants of great fires from the beginning of the world. From time to time the party encountered great vertical rifts hundreds of feet high, where tunnels ended in blank walls with rough, perilous steps cut up or down to a different level where the path continued. Whole sheets of the world's crust had sunk or fractured in places, shearing off the old lava tunnels and leaving behind vast, lightless chasms deep in the earth. A few of these places were spanned by slender bridges of stone, or circled by crude paths hacked from the hard rock of the walls. Everywhere they turned, more square passages and twisting, smooth-floored tunnels branched from their line of march, so that in the space of an hour Halisstra was forced to concede that she'd become hopelessly lost.

"I see why they call this place the Labyrinth," she said softly, as the company threaded its way along a narrow ledge overlooking another of the chasms. "This place is truly a maze."

"It's worse than you think," Valas replied from the front of the party. He paused to examine the path ahead, and another of the ubiquitous openings on one side. "It's close to two hundred miles from north to south, and almost half that from east to west. Most of it is exactly like this, a confusion of lava tubes and hand-cut tunnels with thousands of branching turns and twists."

"How can you hope to find House Jaelre in all this?" Ryld asked. "Do you know this place so well that you've mastered it?"

"Mastered it? Hardly. You could spend a lifetime here and never see the whole thing, but I do know something of its ways. Several well-traveled caravan routes exist along some of the straighter paths, though we're not near any of those. Few travelers approach the Labyrinth from the east, as we have." The scout stepped a little ahead and brushed his hand against the wall, near the place where the other tunnel opened up. Old, strange symbols glowed with a greenish light beneath his fingertips. "Fortunately, the builders carved runes to identify their secret ways. It's a code of markings that holds true throughout the Labyrinth. I solved the puzzle when I last journeyed here. We're not in tunnels I traveled before, but I think I know how to reach them from here."

"You are a lad of many talents," Pharaun observed.

"Who carved these tunnels?" Halisstra asked. "If this place is as big as you say, it must have been a powerful realm in its day, but I can tell at a glance those marks aren't ours. Nor are they duergar, illithid, or aboleth."

"Minotaurs," Valas replied. "I don't know how long ago their realm rose or fell, but there was a great kingdom of them here at some point in the past."

"Minotaurs?" Quenthel sneered. "They're bestial savages. They could hardly have the wits or the patience to undertake work of this scope, let alone build a great realm."

Valas shrugged and said, "That may be true now, but a thousand years ago, who knows? I've found plenty of their artifacts and remains scattered through this region. The horned skulls are quite distinctive. My friends among House Jaelre told me that many minotaurs still roam the wild places and disused passages of the Labyrinth, including demonic beasts armed with powerful sorcery. Their patrols skirmished with the monsters regularly."

"One wonders whether we might at some point in our journey happen to pass through a realm filled with cheerful, civilized folk genuinely concerned for our well-being and eager to help us on our way," Pharaun muttered. "I am beginning to think our fair city lies at the bottom of a barrel of venomous snakes."

"If so, we're quicker, stronger, and more venomous than any other snake in the barrel," Quenthel said with a smile. "Come, let's continue. If there are any minotaurs about, they would be well-advised not to show themselves where the children of Menzoberranzan choose to walk."

The company continued on for several hours more through endless gloomy halls and contorted passages before calling a halt to rest and replenish their strength. The stretch of the Labyrinth they wandered seemed to be quite deserted. They found few signs that anything, even the mindless predatory creatures of the Underdark, had passed that way in many years. The air was preternaturally still and silent. Whenever their whispered conversation died away for a moment, the quiet of the place seemed to rush in upon them, pressing close with a strangely hostile quality, as if the very stone resented their presence.

After Valas and Ryld had been set to watch, the rest wrapped themselves in their *piwafwis* and made themselves as comfortable as possible on the cold stone floor of the cavern. Halisstra let her eyes fall half-closed and drifted off into a deep Reverie, dreaming about endless tunnels and strange old secrets buried in mold. In her dream she thought she could make out a faint, distant rustling or whisper in the quiet, as if she might hear something more if only she moved a little ways off from the others, out into the darkness alone. Despite the fact that the air was completely still and motionless, she discerned the distant deep sighing of wind far off in the tunnels, a low moaning sound that tickled at the edge of her awareness, like something important she had forgotten. Lolth's whispers sometimes came to one in that fashion, a sibilant sigh of wordless intent filling a priestess with knowledge of the demon queen's desires.

Hope and fear stirred in Halisstra's heart and she came closer to wakefulness.

What is your wish, Goddess? she cried out in her mind. *Tell me how House Melarn might win your favor again. Tell me how Ched Nasad might be made whole. I will do anything you command of me!*

Faithless daughter, the wind whispered back to her. *Foolish weakling.*

Horror jolted Halisstra from her Reyerie and she sat up straight, her heart pounding.

Only a dream, she told herself. I dreamed of what I wished to happen, and what I feared might come, but nothing more. The Spider Queen has not spoken. She has not condemned me.

Nearby, the others lay on the cold stone floor or sat wrapped deep in their own meditations, taking their rest, while a little distance away Ryld stood guard, a broad-shouldered shape motionless in the dark. The daughter of House Melarn lowered her eyes and listened to the curious sound of the wind, surrounded in the darkness her people had made theirs.

"Lolth does not speak," she whispered. "I heard only the wind, nothing else."

Why has the Goddess abandoned us? Why did she allow Ched Nasad to fall? How did we incur her wrath? Halisstra wondered. Her eyes stung with bitter tears. Were we unworthy of her?

The wind rose again, this time closer, louder. It was not a

whistling, or even a rushing sound. It reminded her of the call of a deep-voiced horn far off, perhaps many horns, and it was growing. Halisstra frowned, puzzled. Was this some strange phenomenon of the Labyrinth, a rush of air through pipelike tunnels in the dark? Such things were not unknown in other places of the Underdark. In some cases the winds could scour a tunnel bare of life, they were so sudden and powerful. This one muttered and babbled and thrummed as she listened, many great horns roaring at once—

Halisstra leaped to her feet. Ryld stood staring back the way they had come, Splitter gleaming in his hand.

"Do you hear them?" she called to Ryld. "The minotaurs are coming!"

"I thought it was the wind," the fighter growled. "Rouse the others."

He sprinted down the passageway toward the approaching host, shouting for Valas to join him from his post in the other direction. Halisstra snatched up her pack and shouldered it quickly, rousing the rest of the company with shouts of alarm and the occasional quick kick for those who were slow to shake off their deep trances.

She readied her crossbow, loading a quarrel as she peered down the tunnel behind them.

The floor quivered beneath her feet. Great footfalls as hard as rock came in a stamping rush, and deep bellows and snorts echoed and echoed again in a roiling cacophony that filled the passage. Hot animal stink assaulted her nostrils, and she saw them—an onrushing mob of dozens of the hulking brutes, huge bull-headed monsters with shaggy pelts and massive hooves, clutching mighty axes and flails in their thickly muscled fists.

Before that storm Ryld and Valas skipped and darted like sparrows blown before a gale, battling furiously for their lives against the bloodthirsty savages. Halisstra took aim quickly and shot one monster in the chest with her powerful crossbow, but the creature was so blood-maddened it simply ignored the bolt buried in its thick torso. She laid in another quarrel as the bow's magic cocked it again, only to have her shot spoiled by Jeggred's rush into the fray.

"Jeggred, you idiot, there are too many to fight!" she cried.

The draegloth ignored her and threw himself against the horde. For a moment the half-demon's size and fury held up the minotaurs' charge, but over Jeggred's white-furred shoulders and the flashing blades of Ryld and Valas, Halisstra could make out dozens more of the hirsute monsters, fanged mouths bellowing challenges, eyes glowing red with rage. Several had fallen before Splitter, Valas's curved knives, and Jeggred's talons, but battle-frenzied minotaurs shrugged off all but the most grievous of injuries, clawing over each other to get at the drow invaders.

Halisstra shifted to one side and shot again, while Danifae joined her with her own crossbow. Quenthel danced just behind Jeggred, flicking her deadly scourge at monsters threatening to swarm over the draegloth, and Pharaun shouted an arcane word that hurled a bright globe of crackling energy into the midst of the minotaur ranks. The sphere detonated with a clap of thunder and blasted bright arcs of lightning across the tunnel, charring some minotaurs into cinders, and burning great black wounds in others.

In the searing light of the lightning ball, Halisstra saw something taller and lankier than the minotaurs, behind the front ranks, a demonic presence—no, several demons—driving the angry monsters on. Huge black wings shrouded the things in shadow, and their dark horns glowed red with heat.

Roars and bellows filled the passage with rage, while the ring of steel on steel came so fast and hard that Halisstra could barely hear herself shout, "There are demons back there!"

"I see them," Quenthel replied. She fell back a couple of steps and seized Pharaun by the arm. "Can you dismiss them?"

"I have no such spell ready," the wizard replied. "Besides, getting rid of the demons isn't going to get us out of this little imbroglio. I think we—"

"I don't care what you think!" Quenthel screamed. "If you can't banish the demons, then bar the passage!"

Pharaun grimaced, but he complied by beginning another

spell. Halisstra reloaded and searched for another clear shot. Ryld crouched low and hamstrung a minotaur attacking him with an axe big enough to split an anvil, and gutted the creature with an upward draw cut across its belly. Valas was upended by a flailing chain that yanked his feet out from under him. The scout rolled away, narrowly escaping having his skull pulped.

One or more of the demons behind the battling minotaurs hurled a barrage of green, fiery bolts at the dark elves. One dissipated against Quenthel's inborn resistance to magic, while two others burned Pharaun and Danifae with vitriolic fire. Somehow the wizard managed to complete his spell.

What Halisstra assumed was some sort of invisible barrier forced most of the minotaurs and their demonic masters back, while a pair of the frontline fighters found themselves suddenly cut off from their allies. While the main host of the bull creatures hurled themselves against Pharaun's invisible wall and tried vainly to batter their way through with their crude, clumsy weapons, the dark elves quickly cut down the minotaurs unfortunate enough to have been caught on the drow's side.

In a few moments the screams and impacts of the fight had died away to the dull, attenuated bellowing of the minotaurs on the other side of the wall, milling about and shaking their weapons in anger at the drow. The minotaurs turned away all at once and darted back the way they'd come, running hard. A dozen or more hulking carcasses remained scattered on the floor.

Ryld backed away carefully, helping Valas to his feet. Jeggred stood panting, bleeding from a dozen small wounds.

"How long will that wall hold?" Quenthel asked.

"No more than a quarter of an hour," Pharaun answered. "The demons can probably get through it if they wish, but I suspect that they're leading those minotaurs around through other tunnels to come at us from the other side. May I suggest we remove ourselves from the vicinity before we find out how they mean to circumvent my barrier?"

Quenthel scowled, grabbed her pack, and said, "Fine. Let's go."

8　8　8

If it had been in his nature to show alarm by pacing back and forth across his sanctum, Gromph Baenre would have spent most of the previous hour doing so. Instead, he peered into the great crystal ball that rested in the center of his scrying sanctum, confirming Pharaun's report. How exactly had the Master of Sorcere worded it?

Felicitations, mighty Gromph. It may interest you to learn that the army of Gracklstugh now marches on Menzoberranzan. We continue on our course. Good luck!

"Arrogant popinjay," Gromph muttered to himself. The boy had no respect for his elders.

Before dashing off to the matron mothers in a panic, Gromph had of course decided to investigate Pharaun's report with his own careful scrying and study. The milky orb revealed a fine scene for the archmage's eyes, a long column of marching duergar warriors winding through the Underdark. Huge pack lizards carried heavy bundles of supplies and various infernal devices of war. Siege engines trundled along behind long lines of ogre slaves.

Gaining even that glimpse of the army on the move was difficult, as duergar wizards sought to conceal the movements of their prince's army from the scrying efforts of hostile mages. Gromph, however, was an extraordinarily capable diviner. It had taken him some time, but he had eventually pierced the duergar wizards' defenses.

Gromph examined the scene closely, seeking out the most minute details—the insignia of marching soldiers, the exact size and condition of the tunnels they passed through, the cadence of the Dwarvish marching chants. He wanted to be absolutely certain he understood the scope and immediacy of the threat before he brought his news to the attention of the Council, as the matron mothers would doubtless expect him to have already divined the answers to any questions they might think of. The most disturbing question, of course, was how long it might have taken him to learn of the marching army if

Pharaun Mizzrym hadn't been passing through Gracklstugh. The duergar might have covered half the distance between the cities before an outpost or a far-ranging patrol detected the army.

"Damnation," the archmage growled.

Whether or not Menzoberranzan was ready, the next challenge to the city gathered in the smoky pits of the duergar realm a hundred miles to the south. Gromph sighed and decided that he might as well deal with the unpleasant business of telling the Council what he'd seen sooner rather than later. He rose with one smooth motion, arranged his robes, and took up his favorite staff. It would not do to appear before the matron mothers in anything less than complete and total self-assurance, especially when bringing such dire news to them.

He was just about to step into the stone shaft at the rear of the chamber and descend to his apartments in Sorcere when he felt a familiar, crawling sensation. Someone was scrying upon him—an accomplishment of no small skill, considering the steps he took to prevent such occurrences. Gromph started to work a spell to sever the magical spying, but stopped himself. He was engaged in nothing he cared to conceal, and he was curious to discover whether a duergar wizard had managed to detect his own scrying.

"Do you have anything you wish to say to me," he asked the air, "or shall I simply strike you blind where you sit?"

Save your spell, came a cold, rasping voice in his head. *As I haven't had eyes in my skull in over a thousand years, I doubt you could do them much harm.*

"Lord Dyrr," Gromph said, frowning. "To what do I owe the honor of your attentions?"

And how did you find me? he wondered, though he was careful not to voice the question.

I wish to continue the conversation we began a few days past, young Gromph, the lich's voice replied. *I intend to expand upon my earlier offer by describing in greater detail some of the schemes I have in mind. After all, if I am to ask you to trust me, then I suppose I must extend you a token of trust first.*

"Indeed. Well, I would be happy to oblige you, but I have urgent business with the Council. Perhaps we could take up this conversation a little later?"

Gromph glanced around the room, and his eyes fell on the crystal orb in the chamber's oriel. The sphere swirled with pearly green opalescence.

Ah, of course, the archmage realized. He found me here, where my screens against hostile divinations are weakened by the transparency of my scrying place. I must investigate ways to guard against such occurrences without hampering my own efforts.

I fear I must speak with you now, Dyrr pressed. *I will not delay you for very long, and I believe you will be glad you listened to me before facing our scheming females. May I join you there?*

Gromph paused and gazed up at the unseen presence watching him, repressing an angry scowl. Inviting a creature like Dyrr into his conjuring chambers was not something he cared to do on a whim. Whether or not the ancient sorcerer had anything Gromph wished to hear, it was true that the matron mothers would not take kindly to waiting on his arrival. He tapped his finger on the great wooden staff at his side, considering carefully. He had no wish to give offense to Dyrr if it could be avoided, and after long centuries of undeath it was hard to say what the lich might or might not find offensive. Besides, Gromph stood in his own sanctum, where many potent magical defenses lay within his reach. . . .

"Very well, Lord Dyrr. Though I really must insist that we keep our conversation short, as my business with the Council is exceedingly urgent."

The air began to seethe and hum a few feet in front of the archmage, and with a sudden crack of sound, the ancient lichdrow stood before him. The creature leaned on a staff of his own, a mighty implement made from four adamantine rods twisted around each other and bound at head and heel. A small buckler of black metal in the shape of a demonic face twisted in an idiot's grin hovered in the air at his elbow. Dyrr did not bother with his living guise, and stood revealed as a horrid skeleton with eyes as black as death.

"Greetings, Archmage. I apologize for inconveniencing you," the lich said. He fixed his blank sockets on Gromph. "What is it that drives you to seek an audience with the matrons today, young Gromph?"

"With all due respect, Lord Dyrr, I believe that is a matter for their ears, not yours. Now, what offer do you have for me that cannot wait?"

"As you wish, then," Dyrr said. "An army marches against Menzoberranzan from the south—the gray dwarves have apparently heard of our troubles and have decided to take advantage of the opportunity this offers."

"Yes, I know," Gromph snapped. "It is for this very reason that I must leave at once. If you have nothing else . . . ?"

He started toward the plain stone shaft leading down into his apartments.

"I find that I am pleased that my news did not surprise you," the lich said. "If you had not known of the duergar army, I would have had to make sure that it did not come to your attention, if you take my meaning." Dyrr turned to face Gromph's back with a terrible scraping and clicking sound of bones rubbing together. "You may recall we spoke a few days past regarding a time when you must make a decision. The time has come to do so."

Gromph stopped in his tracks and turned around carefully. He'd hoped that wasn't the lich's motive in confronting him, but it seemed Dyrr intended to press the issue whether the archmage wished him to or not.

"A decision, Dyrr?"

"Do not play at misunderstanding me. I know you're far too intelligent for that. All you need do is withhold your report for a few more days, and you can rush over to panic the matrons with news of a duergar army on our doorstep. In fact, my plans will be well served if you do so at a time and in a manner convenient to me."

"That would place the city in peril," Gromph said.

"It is in peril already, young Gromph. I mean to impose some measure of order on the inevitable. You could be of great assistance to me in the coming days, or. . . ."

"I see," said Gromph.

He narrowed his eyes, considering his options. He could feign acceptance, and do as he wished anyway, but that would certainly invite the lich's wrath at the time and place of Dyrr's choosing. He could refuse outright, which would likely result in a deadly contest on the spot to determine whose will would prevail.

Or I could agree in earnest, he thought. *Who's to say that we might not channel the forces marshalling against the city into useful chaos, valuable progress? There will doubtless be tremendous damage, but the Menzoberranzan that emerged from such a crucible of blood and fire might be a better, stronger city in the end, a city purged of the ruthless tyranny of the sadistic priestesses and instead governed by the cold, passionless intelligence of pragmatic wizards. Every cruelty could be made to serve a rational purpose, every excess curbed to produce a city whose strength was not spent on its own internecine strife. Would not such a city be worthy of his loyalty?*

Would such a city have any place for a Baenre? he answered himself.

No revolution such as Dyrr dreamed of could possibly end with anything but complete annihilation for the First House of Menzoberranzan. While Gromph despised his sisters and loathed many of the simpering relations who populated Castle Baenre, he would be damned if he would allow some lesser House to unseat his high and ancient family as the supreme power of Menzoberranzan. There could be, really, only one response.

As quick as thought, Gromph raised his hand and unleashed a terrible, brilliant blast of colors at the lich, a spell whose energy he had prepared with such care and effort that it took only the merest act of will to unleash it. Colors never seen in the gloom of the cavern city lanced through his conjury, each carrying with it a different doom, blight, or energy. A quivering blue bolt of electricity passed so close to Dyrr that the lich's ancient robes crackled with tiny arcs, while a bright orange ray burned the ancient creature with acid powerful enough to melt stone. A third ray, a beam of insidious violet, was deflected by the lich's animated buckler. The device tittered like a wicked child as it intercepted the attack.

"I am the Archmage of Menzoberranzan," Gromph roared. "I am no one's errand boy!"

Dyrr recoiled with a wailing shriek of anger as the acid splattered and hissed, gnawing at his ancient flesh. The smell of burning bone filled the magnificent conjury with a horrid stench. Gromph followed up his first assault by raising an abjuration he hoped would turn Dyrr's spells back at him. The archmage fully expected that it would take every ruse, every defense, every subtle and deadly spell at his command to defeat a thing as powerful as the Lord of Agrach Dyrr.

Gromph concluded his turning spell just in time, as Dyrr recovered with impossible speed and lashed out with a dire black ray of invidious energy that would have ripped away great portions of the archmage's very life-force had it struck home. Instead, the ebon beam rebounded on Gromph's shield and struck Dyrr in the center of his torso. This, however, had an unforeseen effect. Instead of shredding the ancient lich's own life-force, the crackling black energy swelled the Lord of Agrach Dyrr with its horrible power. The lich laughed aloud.

"A clever move, Gromph, but I fear it miscarried. Living creatures are grievously harmed by that spell, but the undead are invigorated by it!"

The archmage muttered a curse and struck again, this time directing a vile green ray at the laughing lich. It burned a perfect round hole in Dyrr's breastbone, blasting undead flesh and bone to dust. The lich screeched again in whatever passed for pain in its undead state and leaped aside before Gromph could disintegrate him outright.

Even as the archmage commenced another casting, Dyrr snarled out the words of a dark and murderous spell that clawed horribly at Gromph's flesh, sucking greedily at the very fluids of his body and bleaching his skin with a thousand needles of agony. Gromph gasped aloud in pain and lost the spell he'd been preparing to cast, stumbling back over a marble bench and falling heavily to the floor.

Damn it all, he thought. I need to buy a moment's respite.

Fortunately, he was in his sanctum, surrounded by a dozen weapons he might employ.

Gromph rolled to his elbow and barked out, "*Szashune!* Destroy him!"

In one alcove of the room, a tall statue of a four-armed swordsman carved from perfect black obsidian stirred to life, striding out into the chamber as it hefted and clashed its ebon blades like a living warrior.

Dyrr skittered away several steps and spoke a word. The lich soared up out of the spiderstone golem's reach, but Gromph used the opportunity of the distraction to summon up the most destructive spell he knew and hurl it at the airborne lich. From his outstretched hands eight brilliant orbs of blinding white energy streaked out to blast through the lich's undead form, each detonating in a stone-shattering explosion that demolished great gaping pieces of the undead sorcerer. The exploding meteors caused no small damage to Gromph's sanctum, blasting a pair of old bookshelves to flinders and snapping an arm from the spiderstone golem as if the device was a toy damaged by a petulant child. Gromph cried out in triumph as pieces of Dyrr clattered to the floor.

Dust billowed from the hovering form of the lich, and his skull nodded down to his breastbone almost as if his animating magic was failing him, but the bony creature returned to itself with startling speed. Dyrr looked up again as wicked green light grew strong in his eye sockets, and he laughed.

"My old bones aren't the entirety of my being, Gromph," he rasped. "You abuse them to no great effect."

He started to intone another spell, but the archmage struck again, seeking to dispel any enchantments or abjurations protecting the lich. Dyrr's flying spell failed, and the lich sank down into blade-reach of the living statue waiting below.

The golem rushed forward. The massive construct pounded at the lich with terrific blows of its three remaining arms, its gleaming black face completely expressionless. The conjury rang with the mighty impact of the blows. Gromph bared his teeth in a savage grin.

"You might not be tied to your moldering corpse, lich, but you'll have a difficult time casting spells when you've been dismembered and buried in a dozen different graves," he called. "You were a fool to challenge me here!"

Gromph prowled closer, looking for an opening to strike again with a spell.

Dyrr endured two, then three tremendous blows from the towering statue, staggering in his steps as bone cracked and split. The demon-faced buckler darted and wheeled around him, laughing shrilly and blocking even more blows than that, parrying strike after strike from the stone construct. The sorcerer retreated a step, found his footing, and spread his arms wide. His gleaming black robes shimmered once, and exploded outward in a deadly spinning saw of razor-sharp blades that carved chunks of stone from Gromph's golem and diced tables, furnishings, and books with abandon.

Blades slashed through the archmage's own potent defensive enchantments, gashing him in a dozen places, though nowhere deep enough to kill. Gromph threw himself flat to duck beneath the disk of flying razors, blinking blood from his eyes as his golem crumbled into worthless black rock.

Dyrr shouted in triumph and leaped forward at the archmage, swinging his adamantine staff with startling speed and swiftness. Gromph yelped in surprise and rolled aside just in time to avoid a two-handed blow that split the marble flagstone right where he'd fallen.

"That does not befit mages of our station!" Gromph howled, scrambling to his feet.

Dyrr didn't answer. Instead the lich leaped after him, clearing off whole tabletops and bookshelves with great two-handed sweeps of his staff.

Gromph shouted a spell that ripped the lich's weapon from his grasp, hurling it across the room with such force that the adamantine rod stuck, quivering end first, in the chamber's wall like a javelin thrown by a giant.

As Dyrr floundered for balance, Gromph took a moment to craft a potent spell defense, a shimmering globe that would completely negate the effects of all but the most powerful of spells. So fortified, he hunted quickly through the various incantations locked in his mind, seeking the most efficacious to employ against the Lord of Agrach Dyrr.

"Ah," Dyrr remarked, studying the shimmering sphere. "An excellent defense, young Gromph, but not impervious to one of my skill."

The lich muttered a word of awful power and scuttled forward, his skeletal talons outstretched. Seemingly unconcerned by Gromph's defensive spell the lich plunged his hand through the dancing globe of color and grasped the archmage by one arm. Gromph shrieked in dismay as the power of the lich's spell struck full upon him, blasting his defensive globe to motes of winking light and locking his every muscle into an absolute rigidity.

"Gromph Baenre, thou art encysted," Dyrr intoned, his naked teeth gleamed against the great and terrible blackness within his skull.

The archmage had one long glimpse at the triumphant lich standing over him, then he started to fall. Gromph, unable to move, plummeted straight down through the floor, through the flickering rooms and chambers of Sorcere, through a vast distance into the yawning black rock below the tower, the city, the world. For one terrible instant Gromph felt himself at the bottom of a measureless well, staring up through uncounted miles of darkness at the pin-prick figure of his nemesis above. The darkness fell in upon him and smothered him in its embrace.

In the archmage's chambers in Sorcere, the lich Dyrr stood, looking down at the spot in the floor where he had condemned Gromph Baenre. Had he been a living mage Dyrr might have panted for breath, trembled with fatigue, or perhaps even collapsed from mortal wounds sustained in the fierce duel, but the dark magic binding his undead sinews and bones together was not subject to the weaknesses of the living.

"Bide there a time, young Gromph," he said to the empty place. "I may find a use for you yet, perhaps in a century or two."

He made a curt gesture and vanished from the conjury.

The great peals of a thunderclap echoed through the black stone passageways, a rumbling so deep and visceral that Halisstra could feel it more than hear it. She crouched in the shadow of a great stone arch and risked a quick glance across the great hall. On the far side, below the drow party, a handful of hulking monsters picked themselves up off the floor and sought cover. Several more lay still in the rubble and wreckage of the lower portion of the hall.

"That broke their rush," Halisstra called out to her companions. "They're regrouping, though."

"Determined bastards," Pharaun said.

The wizard sheltered behind a towering pillar of stone, grimacing with fatigue. Over the previous day and a half the company had marched at least thirty miles through the endless corridors of the Labyrinth, pursued at every turn by seemingly endless hordes of minotaurs and baphomet demons. On two occasions the dark elves had narrowly avoided fiendishly clever efforts to trap them by closing off the tunnels they were fleeing through.

"I have few spells of that sort left," Pharaun said. "We need to find a place where I can rest and ready more spells."

"You'll rest when we all do, wizard," Quenthel growled. The Baenre and her whip were splattered with gore, and her armor showed more than one ugly rent where a deadly blow had barely been turned.

"We're close to the Jaelre. We must be. Let's move again before the minotaurs organize another charge."

The other drow exchanged looks, but they pushed themselves to their feet and followed Quenthel and Valas into another passage. This ran for perhaps four hundred yards before opening into another great hall, this one featuring tall, fluted columns and a floor paved with well-fitted flagstones. Graceful, winding staircases rose up along the cavern walls to meet long, sheltered galleries where dim faerie fire burned, illuminating chambers that might once have been workshops, merchant houses, or simply the modest homes of soldiers and artisans.

"Drow work again," Ryld observed. "And again, abandoned. You're certain this is the place, Valas?"

The scout nodded wearily, his right hand clamped over a shallow but bloody wound on his left shoulder.

"I have been in this very cavern before," he replied. "These are Jaelre dwellings. Up there a number of armorers lived, and over on that wall was an inn I stayed at. The palace of the Jaelre nobles lies just through the next passage."

Quenthel leaped up a short, curving stairway and glanced into some kind of shop, its windows dark and empty. She swore and moved past several others, looking into each in turn before descending back to the floor of the main hall.

"If these are the Jaelre dwellings, then where in all the screaming hells are the Jaelre?" she demanded. "Did the accursed minotaurs slay them all?"

"I doubt it," Halisstra said. "No battle was fought here—we would have seen the signs. Even if the minotaurs had carried off all the bodies over the years, there would be scorch marks, broken flagstones, the remnants of ruined weapons. I think the Jaelre left this place of their own accord."

"How long ago was it that you were here, Valas?" asked Ryld.

"Almost fifty years," the scout said. "Not that long ago, really. The Jaelre skirmished frequently with the minotaurs back then, and these caverns were guarded by both physical and magical defenses."

He studied the great chamber carefully. "Let me proceed ahead a little ways. I will see if I can find anything in the palace that might illuminate this riddle."

"Should we all go?" Ryld asked.

"Best not. There is only one entrance to the palace, and we could be trapped inside if the minotaurs return in numbers. Remain outside, so that you can escape if you need to. I will return in a few minutes."

The scout slipped off into the darkness, leaving the company in the abandoned hall.

"I think I agree with Mistress Melarn," Ryld said. "It seems the Jaelre carried away everything of value and left this place."

"A great deal of trouble for nothing, then," Pharaun remarked. "If there's anything so disappointing as fruitless toil and hardship, I'm not sure what it is."

The company stood in silence a moment, each occupied with his own thoughts.

Halisstra ached with exhaustion, her legs as weak as water. She had avoided any serious injury, but on the other hand she had almost completely exhausted her reservoir of magical strength over the past few hours, wielding her *bae'qeshel* songs to confuse the attacking hordes, strengthen her companions, and staunch the worst of her companions' wounds.

Jeggred, lurking at the rear of the band near the tunnel leading back to the previous room, broke the silence.

"If the mercenary does not return soon, we will be fighting again," the draegloth said. "I do not hear the minotaurs behind us any longer, which means they're probably circling around to come at us from another direction."

"We've taught them not to come at us down long, straight tunnels, I suppose," Ryld observed. He studied the Jaelre cavern with a practiced eye. "Best not to let them catch us in the open like this. They might overwhelm us with sheer numbers."

Danifae asked quietly, "What if this is a dead end?"

"It can't be," Quenthel said. "Somewhere in these caverns we'll discover where it is the Jaelre have fled to, and we will follow. I have come too far to return to Menzoberranzan empty-handed."

"That's all very good," Pharaun said. "However, I feel constrained to point out that we are exhausted and have almost used up our magical strength. Blundering through these halls and corridors until the minotaurs manage to trap and kill us is sheer stupidity. Why don't we lie low in one of those artisan homes—say, in that gallery over there—and rest until we're ready to continue? I believe I can conceal our presence from our pursuers."

Quenthel's eyes flashed with fire as she said, "We will rest when I see fit. Until then, we keep moving."

"I do not believe you understand what I am saying—" Pharaun began, rising to his feet and speaking with short, clipped words.

"I do not believe you understand what I am commanding you to do!" Quenthel snapped. She whirled on the wizard and stepped close, her whips writhing in agitation. "You will cease your incessant questioning of my leadership."

"When you begin to lead intelligently, I will," Pharaun retorted, his calm demeanor finally cracking. "Now, listen—"

Jeggred rose with a feral snarl and grasped the wizard around the upper arms with his huge fighting claws, pulling him away from Quenthel and hurling him across the floor.

"Show some respect!" the draegloth thundered. "You address High Priestess Quenthel Baenre, Mistress of Arach-Tinilith, Mistress of the Academy, Mistress of Tier Breche, First Sister of House Baenre of Menzoberranzan . . . you insolent dog!"

Pharaun's eyes flashed as he leaped to his feet. The facade of good humor fell from his face, leaving nothing but cold, perfect malice.

"Never lay a hand on me again," he said in a deadly hiss.

His hands crooked at his sides, ready to shape awful spells against the draegloth, while Jeggred crouched and made ready to spring.

Quenthel shifted the grip on her scourge and paced closer as the serpent heads curled and darted, striking at the air in their agitation. Ryld set one hand on Splitter's hilt and watched all three, his face an expressionless mask.

"This is madness," Halisstra said as she backed away, pointing her crossbow at the floor. "We must cooperate if we want to get out of here alive."

Quenthel opened her mouth to speak, perhaps to issue the order that would send Jeggred charging at the wizard regardless of the consequences, but at that moment Valas returned, trotting up to the company. The scout came to a halt, taking in the situation with a glance.

"What is going on here?" he asked carefully.

When no one answered, the Bregan D'aerthe looked at each of the company in turn.

"I cannot believe this. Have you not had your fill of fighting in the last forty hours? How can you even consider spending the last of your strength, your magic, your blood, slaughtering each other, when we've already fought our way across half of the damned Labyrinth?"

"We are in no mood to be harangued by you, mercenary," said Quenthel. "Be silent." She glared at Pharaun, and thrust her whip through her belt. "It serves no purpose to fight each other here."

"Agreed," said Pharaun—perhaps the tersest statement the loquacious mage had uttered in the time Halisstra had known him. From some unsuspected well of discipline the wizard mastered his anger and straightened, relaxing his hands. "I will not be handled like a common goblin, though. That I will not bear."

"And I will not be taunted and baited at every turn," Quenthel replied. She turned to Valas. "Master Hune, did you find anything in the palace?"

The scout glanced nervously at Quenthel and Pharaun, as did Halisstra and Danifae.

"In fact, I did," he said. "In the main hall of the palace there is a large portal of some kind. Unless I misread the signs, a large number of people passed through it. I suspect House Jaelre lies somewhere on the other side, in some new abode."

"Where does the portal lead?" Ryld asked.

Valas shrugged and said, "I have no idea, but there is certainly one way to find out."

"Fine," said Quenthel. "We will put your portal to the test at once, before the minotaurs and their demons return. In a few minutes, anywhere will be better than here."

She let one long glare linger on Pharaun, who finally had the good sense to avert his eyes in what would have to suffice for a bow.

Halisstra let out a breath she didn't realize she'd been holding.

"Now this I did not expect," remarked Pharaun.

The wizard sighed and sat down on a rock, allowing his pack to drop to the moss-covered ground. The company stood in the mouth of a low cavern looking up at a daylit forest, somewhere on the surface. The Jaelre portal lay a few hundred yards behind them in a damp, winding cavern that led to a large, steep-sided sinkhole with lichen-covered boulders and trickling rills of cold water splashing down from the hillside above.

The day was heavily overcast—in fact, a light rain was falling—and the clouds, coupled with the gloom of the forest, helped to ameliorate the insufferable brightness of the sun. It was not so harshly brilliant a day as they had seen in the cloudless desert of Anauroch a tenday past, but to eyes long accustomed to the utter lightlessness of the Underdark, the diffuse sunlight still seemed as harsh as the glare of a lightning stroke.

"Should we keep moving?" Ryld asked. He'd returned Splitter to its sheath, angled across his broad back, but he held a crossbow at the ready and squinted into the towering green trees. "It won't take the minotaurs long to figure out where we went."

"It doesn't matter if they do," Pharaun said. "The portal was keyed to function for drow alone. It's nothing more than a wall of blank stone to our friends in the Labyrinth—a sensible precaution on the part of the Jaelre, I suppose, though had I been in their shoes I believe I would not have ruled out the possibility of attackers of my own race."

"You're certain of that?" Quenthel asked.

The wizard nodded and replied, "I was careful to examine the portal before we stepped through. Leaping blindly through portals is a bad habit, and should be reserved only for the gravest of situations, such as escaping imminent death in the destruction of a city. And, before anyone asks, we can still retrace our steps if we wish. The portal functions in both directions."

"I am not in a hurry to return to the Labyrinth. Better the sun-blasted surface than that," Halisstra murmured.

She picked her way across the floor of the sinkhole, studying the forest overhead. The air was cool, and she noted that the trees nearby were mostly needleleafs of some kind, trees that did not lose their foliage in the wintertime, if she remembered correctly. A number of barren trees of a different sort stood in and among the evergreens, trees with slender white trunks and only a handful of ragged red and brown leaves clinging in an odd clump near the crown. Dead? she wondered. Or merely bare of leaves for the winter months? She'd read many accounts of the World Above, its peoples, its green plants and animals, its changing seasons, but there was a great difference between reading about something and experiencing it firsthand.

"Where on the surface are we?" Quenthel asked.

Valas stared hard at the trees for a long time, and craned his head up to squint at the dimly glowing patch of clouds that hid the sun. He turned in a slow circle to examine the hillside nearby. Finally he knelt and ran his fingers over the soft green mat of mosses clinging to the boulders in the cavern mouth.

"Northern Faerûn," he said. "It's early winter, as it should be. You can't see the sun too well to judge its position in the sky, but I can certainly feel it, as I suspect we all do. We're in the same general latitude as the lands above Menzoberranzan—not more than a few hundred miles either north or south, I think."

"Somewhere in the High Forest, then?" Danifae asked.

"Possibly. I'm not sure the trees look right. I've traveled the surface lands near our city, and the foliage looks different from what I remember of the High Forest. We might be some ways distant from Menzoberranzan."

"Excellent," muttered Pharaun. "We trek through the Underdark to Ched Nasad, are forced through a portal to the surface hundreds of miles from home, then we trek back down into the Underdark through shadow and peril, only to pass through another portal that takes us back to the surface, perhaps even farther from home. One wonders if we might have simply marched here from Hlaungadath without our pleasant detour through the Plane of Shadow, the delightful hospitality of Gracklstugh, and our lovely little tour of the minotaur-infested Labyrinth."

"Your spirits must be rebounding, Pharaun," Ryld observed. "You've found your sarcasm again."

"A sharper weapon than your sword, my friend, and just as devastating when properly employed," the wizard said. He ran his hands over his torso and winced. "I feel half dead. Every time I turned around, some hulking bull-headed brute was trying to cleave me in two with an axe or pin me to the floor with a spear. Might I trouble you for one of your healing songs, dear lady?" he asked Halisstra.

"Do not repair his injuries," Quenthel snapped. She still stood with one hand clamped around her torso, blood trickling between her fingers. "No one is mortally injured. Conserve your magic."

"Now, that is precisely—" Pharaun began again, glaring at Quenthel and climbing to his feet.

"Stop it!" Halisstra snapped. "I have exhausted my songs of power, so it does not matter. When I have recovered my magical

177

strength I will heal all who need it, because it is foolish to press on in our state. Until then, we will have to rely on mundane methods to address your injuries. Danifae, help me dress these wounds."

The battle captive turned to Jeggred, who stood near, and motioned for him to sit down, shrugging her pack from her shoulders to search for bandages and ointments. The draegloth did not protest, a sign of how exhausted he was.

Halisstra glanced over the others and decided that the wizard was most in need of attention. After pushing him back down onto the boulder, she took out her own supply of bandages. She studied Pharaun's upper arm, where Jeggred's talons had scored the flesh, and she began to apply an ointment from among the supplies they'd purchased in Gracklstugh.

"This will sting," she said pleasantly.

Pharaun mouthed an awful curse and jumped as if he had been stabbed, yelping in pain.

"You did that on purpose!" he said.

"Of course," Halisstra replied.

While she and Danifae worked on the others, Valas scrambled up a narrow path hidden along the wall of the sinkhole. He studied the ground carefully, and paused to stare thoughtfully into the forest nearby.

Halisstra looked up at him and asked, "Did you find something of interest, Master Hune?"

"There is a path here that climbs up out of the cave mouth," the Bregan D'aerthe answered, "but I couldn't say where the Jaelre went. Several game trails converge here, but none seem to have been used by any number of folk."

"In the Jaelre palace in the Labyrinth you said you'd found clear signs that they had used the portal. How could there be no signs on this side?" Quenthel demanded.

"Dust and grit in the Underdark can hold signs of passage for many years, Mistress. On the surface, it is not so easy. It rains, it snows, the small plants quickly grow over disused paths. Had the Jaelre passed this way in great numbers within the last tenday or two,

I would probably see the signs, but if they came this way five or ten years ago, I would be left with nothing to read."

"They would not have marched far across the surface," Quenthel mused. "They can't be far away."

"You're probably correct, Mistress," Valas replied. "The Jaelre would doubtless have preferred to move by night, staying under the cover of the trees during the day. If this is a very large forest—the High Forest, or perhaps Cormanthor—they might be hundreds of miles away."

"There's a cheerful thought," Pharaun muttered. "What in the world brought the Jaelre up here, anyway? Didn't they consider the possibility that the surface dwellers would slaughter them as eagerly as the minotaurs did?"

"When I knew them years ago, Tzirik and his fellows spoke from time to time of returning to the surface," Valas said. He turned away from the forest and lightly dropped back down into the cave mouth. "Reclaiming the World Above is part of the doctrine of the Masked Lord, and the captains and rulers of House Jaelre wondered if the so-called Retreat of our light-blinded surface kin might not be an invitation to claim the lands the surface elves were abandoning."

"Did it not occur to you back in Ched Nasad that your heretical friends might have decided to act upon their wishful thinking and abandon that black, fiend-ravaged warren they called home?" Quenthel asked. "Did it not occur to you that you might have been leading us into a dead end in the Labyrinth?"

The Bregan D'aerthe scout shifted nervously under Quenthel's gaze, and said, "I didn't see any better alternatives, Mistress. Not if we truly want to get to the bottom of things."

"You were so eager to solve the mystery of the Spider Queen's silence that you chose to gamble that your friend Tzirik was still in the Labyrinth, even though you knew his House had been planning to flee the place for years?" Ryld asked. "We endured a great deal of peril in the city of the duergar and the domain of the minotaurs to satisfy your curiosity."

"Perhaps we were not meant to find this Tzirik at all," said

Quenthel. "Perhaps Master Hune has led us far away from our true mission over the last few tendays, and perhaps it was no accident that he did so."

"When we considered the question of whether we should return to Menzoberranzan," Jeggred said, "it was the Bregan D'aerthe who urged us to set off in search of this priest Tzirik—a heretic priest none of us have even heard of, except for Valas." His eyes narrowed, and the draegloth climbed to his feet, his four clawed hands balling into fists as he shouldered Danifae aside. "Things become clear, now. Our guide is a Vhaeraunite heretic, and he has served the Masked Lord well by leading us through useless perils for days on end."

"This is ludicrous," Valas protested. "I would hardly have led the Bregan D'aerthe to the defense of Menzoberranzan if I was an enemy of the city."

"Ah, but it is the classic ruse," Danifae purred. "Introduce your victims to the agent you have chosen for their destruction by giving them reason to trust her. In your case, the job seems to have been expertly done indeed."

"Even if that was the case," Valas said, "why did I not betray you to the duergar in Gracklstugh? Or leave you to the minotaurs in the Labyrinth? I could have arranged your deaths, not a mere delay. If I was your enemy, you can be certain that is what I would have done."

"Perhaps you would have placed yourself in peril by betraying us in either Gracklstugh or the Labyrinth," Pharaun observed. "Still, you raise a cogent point in your own defense."

"Nothing more than the glib lies of a traitor," Jeggred snarled. He glanced at Quenthel. "Command me, Mistress. Shall I rend him limb from limb for you?"

Valas lowered his hands to the hilts of his kukris, and licked his lips. He was gray with fear, but his eyes sparked with anger. Each of the others in the company turned their eyes to Quenthel, who still leaned against a boulder, her whips quiescent at her waist. She stayed silent, as rain splattered down in the forest and birds chirped and called in the distance.

"I withhold judgment for the moment," she said, looking at the scout. "If you are loyal, we shall need you to find Tzirik—if the Vhaeraunite priest exists, of course—but you would be well advised to produce the Jaelre and their high priest quickly, Master Hune."

"I have no idea where they might be," Valas said. "You might as well condemn me now, and prepare yourself for Bregan D'aerthe's response."

Quenthel exchanged a long look with Jeggred. The draegloth smiled, his needle-like fangs gleaming in his dark face.

Halisstra wasn't sure what to think, as she hadn't known the scout for more than a tenday, and couldn't say what might or might not have happened in Menzoberranzan before the Menzoberranyr came to Ched Nasad. She was, however, certain that they would all regret it if Quenthel had Valas killed and it turned out that the guide's services were still required, or that his powerful mercenary guild decided to seek vengeance for the death of their scout.

"What is the best means of locating the Jaelre from here?" Halisstra asked, hoping to deflect the conversation into a less dangerous course.

Valas hesitated, then said, "As Mistress Quenthel pointed out, they are unlikely to have moved far. We can search in an expanding spiral until we come across better information."

"A plan that sounds wearying and tedious," Pharaun commented. "Marching aimlessly through this blinding woodland does not appeal to me."

"Find a surface dweller and pry information from him," Ryld said. "Assuming, of course, that any are nearby, and that they know anything of the whereabouts of House Jaelre."

"Again, we would have to march off in order to locate a surface dweller, as none conveniently present themselves here," Pharaun observed. "Your plan differs in no significant respects from Master Hune's."

"Then what would you propose?" asked Quenthel, her voice icy.

"Allow me to rest and study my spellbooks. In the morning, I can prepare a spell that may reveal the location of our missing House of heretical outcasts." He raised his hand to forestall the Baenre's protests and added, "I know, I know, you would like to continue this very moment, but if I can successfully divine the goal of our search, it is likely to save us many hours of marching in the wrong direction. The delay will also give the lovely Lady Melarn a chance to regain her own magical strength, and perhaps heal us of the worst of our wounds."

"You may learn nothing from your spells," Quenthel said. "Magic of that sort is notoriously fickle."

Pharaun simply looked at her.

Quenthel looked up at the sky, blinking in the merciless gray light that permeated the clouds above. She sighed and looked back down at the others, her eyes lingering overlong on Danifae. The battle captive tilted her head down in a single, almost imperceptible nod that Halisstra wasn't even certain she saw.

"Very well," the Mistress of Arach-Tinilith said finally. "It would be wise for us to wait for the cover of darkness in any event, so we will set up camp in the cave below, where this accursed sunlight will not trouble us so much. Master Hune, you will stay close by me until we find this Tzirik of yours."

Nimor Imphraezl made his way swiftly along the wide ledge, passing a long line of marching duergar on his right hand while skirting the edge of a black abyss on his left. Moving an army of several thousand through the dark and lightless ways of the Underdark was a formidable challenge, and many of the smaller, more direct routes were simply impassable to a body of so many soldiers. That left only the most capacious caverns and tunnels, and those routes frequently passed through dangers that the stealthier ways avoided.

The road clung to the shoulder of a great subterranean canyon, winding in a northerly direction forty miles from Gracklstugh. The day's march was not more than two hours old, and the gray dwarf army had already lost a fully laden pack lizard—and five soldiers unlucky enough to be close to the beast—to a flight of hungry yrthaks, raking the high trail with their sonic blasts.

No tremendous loss, Nimor reflected, but every day brought its own mishap or accident, and so the army's attrition began. In all truthfulness, the Jaezred Chaulssin assassin had not really grasped the enormous effort required to move a large, well-equipped army a hundred miles through the Underdark. He was quite familiar with journeying the dark ways by himself or in the company of a small band of merchants or scouts, traveling light, making use of the secret byways and known refuges that lay hidden along the main routes of travel. Having marched several days alongside an army, with ample opportunity to observe minor setbacks, difficulties, and challenges he hadn't even imagined, Nimor appreciated the scope of the expedition. The duergar were anxious indeed to strike a mortal blow at a neighbor in distress, if they were willing to tolerate the vast expense in beasts, soldiers, and materiel required to put an army in the field.

The assassin rounded a precarious bend, and came upon the crown prince's diligence: a floating hull of iron, perhaps thirty feet long and ten wide, ensorcelled not only to levitate itself above the ground but also to move as directed by the gray dwarves controlling the thing. Its ugly black form bristled with spikes to repel attackers and armored slits through which the occupants could fire missiles or work deadly spells on anyone outside. The diligence was pierced with several large, shuttered windows that were propped open, and through these Nimor glimpsed the quiet and orderly bustle of the duergar leaders and their chief assistants. The whole construct functioned as command post, throne, and bedchamber for the crown prince while in the field with his army. It was the perfect embodiment of the dwarf approach to things, Nimor reflected, a device displaying skillful craftsmanship and powerful magic, but no grace or beauty.

With a light bound he hopped up onto the running board of the diligence and ducked through a thick iron door. Inside, dim lights gleamed from blue globes, illuminating a great table that held a representation of the tunnels and caverns between Gracklstugh and Menzoberranzan. There the lords and captains of the gray dwarves studied their army's march and planned for the battles to come. The assassin took in the various officers and servants with one quick glance then turned to the elevated center portion of the diligence. The lord of the City of Blades sat at a high table with his most important advisors and watched over the planning below.

"Good news, my lord prince," Nimor said, sweeping into the circle of captains and guards surrounding Horgar Steelshadow. "I have been advised that the Archmage of Menzoberranzan, old Gromph Baenre himself, has been removed from the *sava* board of our little game. The matron mothers do not yet suspect our advance into their territory."

"If you say so," the duergar lord replied gruffly. "In dealing with the dark elves I have found it prudent not to rule out the presence of an archmage until I see him dead under my own hammer."

The assembled gray dwarves around Horgar nodded, and glared at Nimor with undisguised suspicion. A drow turncoat might have been a useful ally in a war against Menzoberranzan, but that did not mean they considered Nimor a reliable partner.

Nimor spied a gold pitcher standing by the high table and poured himself a great goblet of dark wine.

"Gromph Baenre is not the only skilled wizard in Menzoberranzan," growled Borwald Firehand. Short and stocky even for a gray dwarf, the marshal gripped the table with his huge, powerful hands and leaned forward to glare at the assassin. "That cursed wizard school of theirs is full of talented mages. Your allies played their hand too quickly, drow. We're still fifteen days from Menzoberranzan, and Gromph's death will provoke alarm."

"A sensible notion, but not entirely correct," Nimor said. He drained off a large gulp from his goblet, savoring the moment. "Gromph will be missed soon, I'm sure, but instead of casting their arcane gaze out into the Underdark to search for approaching foes, every Master of Sorcere will be searching fruitlessly for the archmage and scheming against his colleagues. While the crown prince's army approaches, the most powerful wizards in the city will have their eyes firmly fixed on each other, and more than a few will seek to murder their colleagues to win the archmage's vacant seat."

"The Masters of Sorcere will surely set aside their ambitions once they come to realize their peril," the crown prince said. He cut off Nimor with a curt gesture and added, "Yes, I know you say they may not, but we would be wise to plan on meeting an organized and well-directed magical defense of the city. Still, that was a well-struck blow, well-struck indeed."

He rose, and shouldered his way past the clan lairds and guards to approach the map table, beckoning Nimor to follow. The assassin circled to the other side of the table to attend the duergar ruler's words. Horgar traced their route with one thick finger.

"If the wizards of Menzoberranzan do not note our approach," Horgar said, "then the question becomes, at what point will they perceive their danger?"

The clan laird Borwald thrust his way to the tableside and indicated a cavern intersection.

"Presuming we don't encounter any drow patrols, the first place we'll meet the enemy is here, at the cavern called Rhazzt's Dilemma. The Menzoberranyr have long maintained a small outpost there to watch this road, as it's one of the few large enough for an army to use. Our vanguard should reach it in five days' time. After that, our path forks and we must make our first hard decision. We can choose to go north, through the Pillars of Woe, or circle around to the west, which adds at least six days to our march. The Pillars are likely to be held against us, and so could delay us indefinitely."

"The Pillars of Woe . . ." Horgar said. The prince tugged at his iron-gray beard as he studied the map. "When the drow learn we're coming, they'll certainly move troops there and hold the pass against us. That way is no good, then. We'll want to follow the other branch to the west, and circle around to approach the city from that side. The time it adds to our march cannot be helped."

"On the contrary, I mean for you to take the straighter path," Nimor said. "Passing through the Pillars of Woe will save you six days, and once you're on the other side, you will be on Menzoberranzan's doorstep. If you go through the western passes, you'll find the terrain there much less favorable."

The duergar lord snorted and said, "Perhaps you have not traveled this way before, Nimor. It is a difficult road you've chosen, if you plan to force the Pillars of Woe. The canyon becomes narrow there and climbs steeply. Two mighty columns bar the upper end, with only a narrow way between them. Even a small force of drow can hold it indefinitely."

"You can beat the Menzoberranyr to the Pillars, Crown Prince," the assassin said. "I will deliver the outpost of Rhazzt's Dilemma to you. We shall allow the defenders of the post to report a duergar force on the march, but even as the message speeds back to the matron mothers, your forces will race ahead to lay a deadly trap at the Pillars of Woe. There, you will destroy the army the rulers of the city send to hold the gap."

"If you can give us the outpost, drow, why allow the soldiers there to send any warning at all?" growled Borwald. "Better to cling to our secrecy as long as possible."

"The pinnacle of deceit," said Nimor, "lies not in depriving your foe of information, but in showing your foe the thing that he expects to see. Even with the stroke we have engineered against the city's wizards, they cannot help but note our approach soon. Best for us to control the circumstances under which the crown prince's army is reported to Menzoberranzan's rulers, and perhaps anticipate their response."

"This intrigues me. Go on," Horgar said.

"The soldiers of Menzoberranzan expect that an army approaching along this road must be delayed by the effort to take Rhazzt's Dilemma, giving the city time to man the choke point at the Pillars of Woe in sufficient strength to defeat any further attack. I suggest you allow the outpost to make its report and alert the rulers of Menzoberranzan to the presence of your army. Before the matron mothers can muster an army to face you, we will take Rhazzt's Dilemma by storm. We will be waiting to intercept the drow march at the Pillars of Woe."

"Your plan has two fundamental flaws," said Borwald, sneering in contempt. "First, you presume that the outpost can be taken whenever we wish. Second, you seem to think that the matron mothers will choose to send out their army instead of standing fast to await a siege. I would give much to know how you intend to engineer these two feats."

"Easily done," the assassin replied. "The outpost will fall because much of its garrison has been withdrawn to keep order in the city. Of those soldiers that remain, many are Agrach Dyrr. That is why I urged you to choose this road for your attack. The outpost will be betrayed into your hands when the time is right."

"You knew this before we set out," Horgar said. "In the future, you will share such information in a more timely manner. What would we have done if you'd met some accident of the march? We must know exactly what kind of help you will lend us, and when you will be able to do so."

Nimor laughed coldly and said, "It would be good for our continued friendship, Prince Horgar, if you find yourself wondering from time to time exactly how helpful I might turn out to be."

Halisstra roused herself from her Reverie to find that she was cold and wet. During the night, a light dusting of wretched stuff that she guessed must be snow had fallen over the forest, bedecking every branch with a thin coating of brilliant white. The novelty of the experience had worn off quickly for her, particularly after she realized that it had soaked her clothing and *piwafwi* with frigid water. The reality of snow on the surface was far less appealing than any account of the phenomenon she'd read in the comfort of her House library.

Overhead, the sky was sullen and gray again, but brighter than the previous day—bright enough to cause no little discomfort to the drow travelers. Since Quenthel didn't choose to drive them out into the sunlight after Pharaun had rested and studied his spells, they passed most of the day's bright hours sheltering deep in the cavern away from the light. The company didn't prepare to break camp until late in the day, when the sun was already beginning to sink into the west.

"Remind me to conduct some research into methods by which that infernal orb might be extinguished," remarked Pharaun, squinting up into the snow-laden sky. "It's still up there behind all those blessed clouds, burning my eyes."

"You're not the first of our kind to find its light painful," Quenthel replied. "In fact, the more you complain about it, the more it troubles me, so keep your whimpering to yourself and get about the business of casting your spell."

"Of course, most impressive Mistress," Pharaun said in an acerbic voice.

He turned away and hurried off across the snow-covered rocks and boulders before Quenthel could make a proper retort. The Baenre muttered a black curse under her breath and turned away as well, busying herself with watching Danifae as the battle captive stuffed Quenthel's bedroll and blankets into her pack. The rest of the company kept to a studious silence and pretended not to notice the interplay, either between Quenthel and Pharaun, or Quenthel and Danifae. They gathered up their own belongings and broke camp.

Halisstra picked up her own pack and followed Pharaun across the floor of the sinkhole, scrambling up after him along the hidden path that ascended to the forest floor. Standing in the clearing surrounding the sunken spot where the cavern mouth had undermined the hillside, she found that the forest was very dense and pressed in close on all sides. Everywhere she looked, the wall of trees and brush was the same, a verdant barrier with no landmarks at all, no distant mountains by which she could orient herself, not even an orderly plan of sand-covered streets to follow. Even in the most twisted caverns of the Underdark, one usually was offered only a handful of choices at a time—forward or back, left or right, up or down. In the forest, she might simply walk off in any direction she liked and eventually arrive somewhere. It was an unsettling and unfamiliar feeling.

She finished her careful examination of the forested hillside, and faced Pharaun again. The rest of the company watched him as well, variously standing or squatting on their heels and shading their faces with their hands as they awaited the wizard's guidance.

"If I say anything," said Pharaun, staring into the trees and speaking over his shoulder, "anything at all, mark it carefully. I may or may not understand exactly what it is I see."

He extended his arms wide and closed his eyes, whispering harsh syllables of arcane power over and over again as he turned in a slow circle.

The eldritch sensation of magic at work tugged at Halisstra, a feeling that was almost palpable, yet maddeningly distant. A strange, cold breeze arose, sighing in the treetops as it bent them first one way, then another, growing stronger moment by moment. Boughfuls of snow shifted and fell as the weird wind increased to a wild, shrieking gale. Halisstra raised a hand to shield her eyes from flying dust and grit. Through it all, she heard Pharaun's voice growing deeper, more powerful, as the spell took on a life of its own and seemed to drag itself from his throat. She lost her footing and slid awkwardly to one knee, her hair whipping around her head like something alive.

The magic of Pharaun's divination bore him aloft. Arms still outstretched, he revolved in the air as the winds circled with him. His eyes were blank and silver, cast upward to the heavens. A nimbus of green energy began to coalesce around the wizard's body, and he gave out a great howl of anguish. Bolts of emerald fire exploded from his halo to scour and blast at the boulders nearby. Each green ray sliced into rock like a rapier into soft flesh, causing the stones to split and flake with deafening cracks. Where each green bolt played, a black rune or pattern formed in the damaged stone, appearing as if etched by acid in the exposed rock. The designs made Halisstra's eyes ache to look at them, and from the air in the center of the clearing, Pharaun began to mutter in a horrible voice that somehow carried through the wind and thunder.

"Five days west lies a small river," the wizard intoned. "Turn south and follow its dark swift waters upstream another day, to the gates of Minauthkeep. The Masked Lord's servant dwells there. He will aid you and betray you, though neither in the manner you expect. Each of you save one will commit betrayal before your quest is done."

The spell concluded. The wind died away, the green energy dissipated, and Pharaun came slumping down from his lofty perch as if he'd been dropped from a rooftop. The wizard struck the hard earth awkwardly and crumpled, huddling with his face in the cold slush covering the ground. As the reverberations of the spell's violence fell away in the snowy wood, the black-etched runes carved into rocks and boulders faded as well, flaking away in tiny bits of ebon dust that evaporated within the space of moments.

The rest of the company straightened and exchanged dark looks.

"I can see why he's slow to cast that spell," Ryld remarked.

He moved forward and caught Pharaun by one feebly waving arm, turning him over and checking for any obvious signs of injury. Pharaun looked up and managed a weak grin.

"Good news and bad, I suppose," he said. "Tzirik seems to be alive and well, at least."

"The directions are clear," Valas said with care. "I think I can keep us heading west easily enough."

"What did you mean by that last bit?" Jeggred said to Pharaun, ignoring Valas. "About the betrayal?"

The draegloth tightened his fists.

"About each of us betraying someone? Why, I couldn't begin to guess," the wizard said. He coughed and sat upright, waving away Ryld's help. "It's the nature of the magic to offer cryptic predictions like that, threatening little riddles that you have little hope of solving until it suddenly becomes obvious that the event you feared has come to pass." He offered a wry chuckle. "If only one of us doesn't have some shocking act of treachery to pull off in the near future, I must say I'd like to know who's sleeping on the job. He'll tarnish our reputation if he's not careful."

Halisstra studied the rest of the company, noting the impassive faces, the thoughtful eyes. Danifae met her gaze with a slight smile and the merest flicker of her gray eyes toward Quenthel, a gesture so small and secret that no one save Halisstra could note it.

Despite the wizard's easy dismissal of the exact words of the divination, she wasn't pleased to learn that every one of her companions would at some point in the future commit some kind of treacherous act or another. Or, more likely, all but one of her companions. Just because Halisstra planned no immediate act of betrayal didn't mean she might not choose to take advantage of an opportunity arising later. She had not held her rank as First Daughter of House Melarn without developing a certain ruthless instinct for such things. If ruin had not come to Ched Nasad, Halisstra didn't doubt that at some point in the fullness of time she would have seriously plotted against her own mother to claim leadership of the house. Matron Melarn had unseated Halisstra's grandmother in the same manner and for the same reasons many hundreds of years past. It was no more or less than the Spider Queen's way.

"Well," Pharaun said as he pushed himself to his feet, still shivering. The wizard accepted his pack from Ryld, moving gingerly. "It seems I have provided a destination. So which way is west, Master Hune?"

Valas nodded toward the near side of the clearing and said, "There are a couple of game trails leading more or less toward the setting sun."

"Come," said Quenthel. "The sooner we set out, the sooner we arrive. I have no wish to spend one hour more than we must in this light-seared land. Master Hune, you will take your customary place as our guide. Master Argith, you will accompany him. Halisstra, you will bring up the rear and keep an eye behind us."

Halisstra frowned and shifted uncomfortably. That struck her as a job suitable for a male. In their travels over the past few days Jeggred had customarily brought up the rear. It didn't escape Halisstra that changing the order of the march kept Jeggred close by Quenthel, where the draegloth could protect the Baenre priestess from any attack. She likewise noted that Quenthel had referred to both Valas and Ryld as "master," while calling her only Halisstra.

There was no point in protesting, of course, so she only waited as the rest of the company filed off into the woods, following Valas's path. She unslung her crossbow and made sure the weapon was ready for quick use. After allowing the rest of the company a lead of about fifty yards, Halisstra set off after them.

E L E V E N

The surface woodland proved to be a strange and disquieting place. As the party moved away from the clearing's edge, the tangled underbrush vanished, leaving only an endless green hall of round trunks rising to the forest roof above, like the pillars of some dark elven hall somewhere in the Lands Below. Old, fallen logs lay scattered here and there, covered in bright green moss. Some were so large that the company had to detour hundreds of feet around them, or scramble awkwardly over or under. A dusting of snow had filtered to the ground, and cold water dripped steadily from the branches above. Unlike the lifeless desolation of Anauroch, the forest was filled not only with mighty trees and twining brambles, but all manner of small birds and animals. After a dozen heart-stopping starts, Halisstra soon learned to identify a number of discrete birdcalls and animal sounds and relegate them to the realm of the insignificant.

She had at first feared that she would easily lose sight of the company ahead, but away from the crowded foliage by the infrequent clearings, the underbrush consisted of ferns and other green plants rarely more than waist high. As darkness fell over the forest floor, her vision improved, and Halisstra felt more and more comfortable.

The drow marched on through the night, halting a little before daybreak to set up camp in an old ruined tower whose broken white stones were covered by moss. Smooth and delicately veined, the place showed remarkable elegance of form, and the lintel of its long-vanished door was carved in a flowering vine design—clearly the work of surface elves. After Pharaun checked the place for lingering spells that could be dangerous to drow, the company made camp to pass the painful bright hours of the day. Quenthel ordered Jeggred and Pharaun to keep watch, and the others enjoyed the shade and safety provided by the partial floors and graceful walls of the ruined tower.

At sundown they ate, broke camp, and set off again, in the same order as before, marching again through the night. They passed the next two days and nights in much the same way, resting while the sun was out and traveling by night. Valas even managed to shoot a small, hoofed animal a little before dawn at the end of their third night of travel, and Halisstra was surprised to find that its meat was light and succulent, better than that of a young rothé.

Toward the end of the day the clouds returned, darker and thicker than before, and as the daylight failed and the dark elves made ready for their fourth march on the surface, a soft snow began to fall, wet and heavy. It was eerily silent, as if the entire forest held its breath to keep from intruding on the moment. Halisstra watched vigilantly behind the company, taking a dozen steps forward and turning to scan the trail behind them, sometimes walking backward for several minutes at a time, glancing to the front only to be sure of her footing. If Pharaun's divinations were accurate, they should reach the stream at the end of that night or perhaps the next, which meant that House Jaelre and the Vhaeraunite priest were only a day beyond.

With the objective of their long journey so close at hand, it occurred to Halisstra that she had no reason why the heretic would consider helping them. Valas might have been an old acquaintance, but no cleric of the Masked Lord would aid priestesses of Lolth simply out of the goodness of his heart. Some price would have to be met, of that Halisstra was certain. Wealth, perhaps? Quenthel and her comrades carried many valuable gemstones. It was the easiest and most compact way to transport wealth through the wilds of the Underdark. Halisstra had stuffed her own pockets too before fleeing Ched Nasad. She doubted that a powerful Vhaeraunite would be so easily purchased, though.

Coercion might be possible, or they might have to barter some kind of service to win his aid. Danifae was occasionally useful in such arrangements. Any drow had at least one enemy in need of a setback.

She realized she'd fallen a bit behind, so she picked up her pace to take up position closer behind the main body of the company. She trotted easily through the darkness, her boots gliding through the snow, until she caught sight of Jeggred's hulking form and the smaller shapes of her companions moving ahead of her. Halisstra settled back into her pace, and turned to glance back down the trail.

Someone was there.

From all sides she heard the whisper-quiet sounds of soft feet stealing through the woods, then the sounds were abruptly cut off by a perfect, impenetrable silence that could only be magical.

Halisstra hissed in alarm, but heard nothing. She brought up her crossbow. Directly up the path a lanky male elf with skin as white as the snow darted toward her, armed with a gracefully curved war axe in one hand and a shorter hand axe in the other. His eyes glittered like green death in the night.

"Watch out!" she cried, trying to warn her companions, but again nothing broke the perfect silence.

Without a moment's hesitation she whirled and fired her crossbow at Jeggred, perhaps fifty yards ahead. She skewed her aim a bit, so instead of taking him between the shoulder blades the quarrel struck quivering into a tree beside the half-demon's head. The draegloth leaped and shouted—or so she guessed, anyway, since she couldn't hear it—but, more importantly, he turned to see what was happening behind him, and spied the surface elves stealing up from behind them.

An instant later, the elf axeman was upon Halisstra, whirling his two matched crescent blades in a deadly pattern of gleaming steel. He was shouting something too, a war cry perhaps. Halisstra gave up her fine crossbow to deflect the first stroke of the long axe, leaped back out of the reach of the shorter one, and hastily drew her mace, slinging her shield from her shoulder. The pale elf leaped forward to engage again, and they circled, trading skillful blows that failed to find their mark.

Halisstra could see more green-armored shapes flitting through the woods toward her, swords and spears glittering in the darkness. She redoubled her efforts and put the two-axe fighter on the defensive, hoping to batter down his defenses before she was surrounded by foes.

A brilliant, searing light detonated along the trail behind her, filling the darkened forest with the painful glare of daylight. The last thing she saw before the spell blinded her completely was a company of surface elves and human warriors, dashing up to join the fray.

There was only one thing Halisstra could do. Raising her shield to buy a moment's time, she ducked down, grasped a handful of dirt and dried leaves from the ground at her feet, and imbued them with magical darkness, making good use of the power shared by all drow. A heavy blow fell on her shield, without a sound, and she quickly scuttled away from the axeman, staying low to the ground and feeling her way along. Some of her enemies would be waiting for her to emerge from the impenetrable blackness—at least, that was what Halisstra would have done in their place. The wisest thing to do was to remain within as long as possible in the hopes that the surface dwellers had no more magic suitable for canceling or dispelling her field of darkness.

As with any drow noble familiar with battle, Halisstra knew to an instant how long her own dome of darkness would persist. In her case, she could sustain the magical gloom for almost three hours. If she lay still and quiet for a long time, the surface dwellers might very well think she'd slipped away. At the very least, she was reasonably sure she could outwait the spell of silence that covered the area. Once her hearing returned, she might be able to form a better guess as to what to do next.

Mace in hand, she groped her way to a large tree, leaned against its trunk, and settled down to wait.

🕷 🕷 🕷

Nimor stood patiently in the hall outside the council chamber, studiously allowing his shoulders to slump and his face to sag. He was supposed to be tired, after all. Dressed in the arms of an officer of House Agrach Dyrr, he'd purportedly fought his way free of the battle at Rhazzt's Dilemma in order to carry word of the attack to the matron mothers. Of course, the Agrach Dyrr garrison had already delivered the outpost to the army of Gracklstugh, but the matron mothers didn't know that yet.

Feigning exhaustion, despair, and resolve in the proper quantities was difficult for him, especially when his heart raced with excitement and his body quivered in anticipation. Long-laid plans had found their moment and unfolded slowly toward a terrible fruition. Through his own labors and toils he had altered the course of two great cities. Both moved ponderously and yet inevitably toward a terrible collision he had imagined months before, and with each hour events gathered speed and required less and less of his guidance. Soon he could allow himself to vanish from the stage once more, his great toils done, and make ready to reap the rewards of his labors.

To divert himself while he awaited the summons to the council in the chamber beyond, Nimor studied the hall with care. One never knew, after all, when a half-remembered doorway or a choice of exits might spell the difference between life and death. The Hall of Petition, as the place was called, formed the entrance to the matron mothers' secretive council chamber. The high ladies themselves rarely passed through this room. They had various secret and magical ways to travel from their palaces and castles to their seats within. Instead, the Hall of Petition was the place where all who had business with the council awaited the matrons' pleasure. Naturally, it was nearly empty.

Any drow who needed something simply begged it of one of the matron mothers, and most carefully and respectfully at that. Only those drow commanded to appear before the council waited in the Hall of Petition, and again, anyone whose presence was commanded had probably already made his report to one of the matron mothers beforehand. The hall was most commonly employed as a convenient place for persons of interest to the council to wait until called within to deliver her report, present her request, or more often plead her case and hear judgment.

Sixteen proud male warriors and wizards stood in or around the hall, two from each of the Houses whose matron mothers sat on the council. They were ostensibly designated as a guard for the entire council, but in truth each male spent most of his time carefully watching the males of rival Houses to make sure that no secret attack was afoot that day.

The floor, all of polished black marble with veins of gold, gleamed in the dim light of faerie fire globes set high in the ceiling, and great friezes along the walls showed the story of Menzoberranzan's founding.

Several minor functionaries scurried about the hall, bowing and scraping to all who deserved such obsequiousness, and imperiously disregarding any who did not. Nimor, wearing the arms of a minor officer of House Agrach Dyrr, fell somewhere in between.

To Nimor's great surprise, he was kept waiting only forty minutes before one of the chamberlains approached and gestured toward the door.

"The Council expects your report, Captain," he said.

Nimor followed the official into the council chamber itself, bowing to the high seats of the eight matron mothers. Each was attended by one or two of her daughters, nieces, or favorites. A grand archway to one side of the chamber led off to a set of smaller shrines and halls adjacent to the council, to which the matrons' attendants and secretaries could be dismissed should the matron mothers decide to discuss their business in private.

"Matron Mothers, Captain Zhayemd of House Agrach Dyrr," the chamberlain announced.

Nimor bowed again, and held the pose as he surreptitiously studied the matron mothers.

Triel Baenre sat at the head of the Council, of course. Petite and pretty, she seemed too young for the place of honor, though she was of course hundreds of years in age. Mez'Barris Armgo of House Del'Armgo sat next to her, then came the place where the Matron Mother of House Faen Tlabbar formerly sat. Nimor studiously did not smile, but he allowed his gaze to linger a moment on a young female who occupied Ghenni's place—Vadalma, the fifth daughter of the House. Either the first four destroyed each other squabbling for their mother's place, he reflected, or young Vadalma was much more accomplished than she looked.

Opposite the new Faen Tlabbar matron sat Yasraena Dyrr, graceful and lissome, well at ease in the chair she had occupied since Auro'pol's demise.

"Ah, I see my captain has arrived," Yasraena said to her peers. "Welcome, Zhayemd. You have endured much today, but I am afraid I must subject you to one more ordeal before you can be allowed your well-deserved rest. Tell the Council the tidings you brought me earlier."

"As you wish, Honored Matron," Nimor said. He glanced around at the highborn females and affected a trace of nervousness. "Matron Mothers, I have come from the garrison at Rhazzt's Dilemma. We have come under attack from a great force of duergar and their allies, including derro, durzagons, giants, and many slave troops. We do not expect to delay them for more time than it takes the duergar to bring their siege engines into play."

"I know that place," Mez'Barris Armgo said. "It lies three or four days' travel south of the city. Is your news that old? Why did your spellcasters not warn us through magic instead of sending you to report in person?"

"Our wizard was slain in the first assault, Matron Del'Armgo. He had the misfortune to be leading a patrol outside our defenses and apparently fell victim to the approaching duergar. When Mistress Nafyrra Dyrr—the commander of our detachment—realized we had no means to signal a warning, she dispatched me at once to carry a message back to Menzoberranzan. This all occurred earlier this morning."

"You have only answered one of the questions I posed, Captain," the Matron Mother of House Barrison Del'Armgo observed. "Rhazzt's Dilemma came under attack this morning, but the outpost lies more than thirty miles south of here, a journey of several days."

Nimor affected a trace of hesitation, and glanced deliberately at Yasraena Dyrr as if seeking guidance. The Matron Mother of House Agrach Dyrr simply inclined her head in assent.

"I made use of a somewhat unreliable portal to shorten my journey from several days to a few hours, Matron Del'Armgo," he said. "It lies a mile or two from the outpost and is somewhat difficult to use, as it functions only intermittently. The other side lies in a disused cavern in the Dark Dominion. My House has known of it for some time, though we did not trust the portal's magic enough to employ it except in a dire emergency."

"I have no doubt that Barrison Del'Armgo knows of similar portals in and around the city," Yasraena Dyrr observed. "Forgive us if we neglected to mention the existence of this one until today."

"The portal is irrelevant," Triel Baenre said, making a dismissive gesture of her hand. "The captain is here to make his report, and that is sufficient. Tell me what you observed of this duergar army."

"I would guess it to number somewhere around three to four thousand gray dwarves, plus a number of slave soldiers—mostly orcs and ogres. We noted the banners of eight companies in the attack, and many more held back in reserve. There could be more, of course, or the duergar may have deliberately attempted to deceive us by carrying false banners into battle."

"A raid," muttered Prid'eesoth Tuin of House Tuin'Tarl. "Your outpost is simply being tested, Captain."

Nimor shifted his feet and did his best to look determined, serious, and dutifully subservient.

"Mistress Nafyrra does not believe so, Matron Tuin," Nimor said. "We have fought off duergar raids on numerous occasions, but nothing like the onslaught we encountered this morning. If we are not besieged by the whole army of Gracklstugh, it's certainly close enough."

"How strong is your garrison?" Yasraena Dyrr asked.

"Our garrison numbers almost eighty warriors, and we have an excellent defensive position, Honored Matron. We can hold out for several days, but the outpost will fall when the duergar bring up their siege engines, or employ the right sort of magic."

"It should not surprise me to learn that this duergar onslaught is little more than a particularly large and aggressive raid," Vadalma of Faen Tlabbar said. "I am sure Matron Dyrr has reported what her males believe to be the case, but perhaps the matter should be investigated before we react in blind panic. A simple confirmation of the report, at the least. After we have properly assessed the scope of the threat, the Council can deliberate over the best means to address it."

"Under most circumstances, our young sister would be wise to suggest a more thorough assessment of the situation," said Yasraena. She had been well coached. Nimor lowered his gaze to keep his smile from showing. "However, my officers tell me that, if we wish to meet the duergar army outside the city, the place to do it is at the Pillars of Woe, between here and Rhazzt's Dilemma. A strong army dispatched quickly can hold the pillars against any conceivable assault, but if we delay too long, the duergar will reach it before we do. We would throw away a very significant advantage of position. We should, of course, seek confirmation of the report with all due haste, but while we're investigating, our soldiers should be marching."

"Shouldn't we simply stand on the defensive here, in the city cavern?" asked Mez'Barris Armgo. "We can fortify the approaches easily enough, and the duergar army would have a difficult time surrounding the city in its entirety while the threat of our own intact army remains within."

"If we allow the gray dwarves to infest the city," one of the other matron mothers said, "we shall surely see illithid, aboleth, and humanoid armies at our doorstep in no time at all. We have many enemies. Look at what happened to Ched Nasad."

The eight high priestesses exchanged somber looks.

"Clearly, the Council must reach some decisions quickly," Triel Baenre said, breaking her thoughtful silence. "We don't have much time if we wish to meet the duergar outside the city, so I will order half of Baenre's troops to make ready to march. I advise the rest of you to do the same. If we decide to stand on the defensive in the city cavern, we can have our soldiers stand down, but if we decide to march, we will want to be able to march soon."

"I favor a vigorous and aggressive defense of the city," said Yasraena Dyrr. "Hard exertion now may serve to deter further attacks later. I will order half the strength of House Dyrr to make ready at once." She studied the other matrons carefully and added, "Provided, of course, that some other Houses agree to shoulder a share of the risk and assist us. Either we all make the same commitment, or none."

"House Baenre guarantees Agrach Dyrr until the return of the expedition," Triel said briskly.

Nimor nodded to himself. He'd expected that the leader of Menzoberranzan's strongest House would choose to lead by example in this instance. Among other things, it deflected any predatory designs of the other Houses into an external activity, where the Baenre could be seen to be taking strong and decisive action to secure the city. Triel was badly in need of such measures.

She looked up at the various guards, advisors, and guests in the council chamber and said, "The matron mothers must discuss how best to meet this treacherous attack in private. Leave us."

"Captain Zhayemd," Yasraena Dyrr said, "I would like it if you took command of the Agrach Dyrr contingent and began your preparations at once. I know you have fought your way through great peril already today, but you have intimate knowledge of the field of battle, and I have the utmost confidence in you."

"I will serve to the best of my abilities," Nimor said. "With the goddess's aid, I will scour our city's foes from our territory."

He offered another deep bow to the matron mothers, and quietly withdrew.

🕷   🕷   🕷

The forest sounds abruptly returned, signaling the end of the spell of silence. Wind sighed in the treetops, a small brook ran somewhere nearby, and tiny rustles and scuttling sounds whispered in the darkness as the small creatures of the woods—or larger ones who knew how to be stealthy—moved about nearby. Halisstra listened for a long time, hoping to hear some sort of positive evidence that the surface dwellers had gone or that her comrades battled on somewhere nearby, but no ringing swords or thunderous spells split the night. She heard nothing as convenient as an enemy conversation to help her decide if her foes had left, or were instead crouched silently outside the darkness, waiting for her to emerge. Halisstra could be quite patient when it suited her, and she was not unused to hardship and danger, but the sheer nervous tension of stretching out to identify and categorize every tiny sound that came to her ears soon left beads of sweat trickling down her face.

If Quenthel and the others were nearby, I would hear it, she decided. The fight must have carried them far ahead by now.

Her heart pounded at the thought of being lost in the endless woods alone, a reviled enemy to any creature who walked the surface world.

Better to die trying to rejoin the others, Halisstra decided. At least I know where they're going, if I can manage to keep my course.

First, she needed to escape from the darkness that sheltered her. She did not choose to dismiss the magical gloom, deciding to leave it to continue until it failed in an hour or two. There was a small chance that her enemies might be waiting quietly outside for the darkness to fail before moving in. Halisstra groped in her belt pouch and withdrew a slender ivory wand. She felt very carefully to determine if it was the wand she needed, and when she was convinced that she had the right one, she tapped it against her chest and whispered a word.

Though there was no way for her to verify it, sitting on the forest floor in the magical darkness, the wand's magic had made her invisible. She stood as quietly as she could, cringing at every soft rustle or clink of her mail, and began steadily moving away.

Halisstra broke out into the open night much sooner than she expected—it seemed she had been sitting no more than six or seven feet from the edge of the darkness. Confident in her invisibility, she stood up straight and looked around. The forest looked much as it had before, except there was no sign of her companions or the woodsmen and surface elves who had attacked them. The moon was rising, and its brilliant silver light flooded the forest floor. She set off in what she hoped was a westerly direction, moving as quickly and quietly as she could.

She soon came upon the scene of a furious battle, if she read the signs right. Several large, blackened circles in the forest still smoldered. In other places the bodies of perhaps half a dozen surface elves and green-garbed human warriors lay where they'd fallen, most bearing the marks of sword, mace, and talon. Of the drow, there was no sign.

Halisstra tried to remember what she'd seen of the pale elves and their human allies, deciding that there might have been as many as fifteen to twenty of the surface folk.

"Where are your comrades, I wonder?" she asked the fallen warriors before moving on.

Halisstra only managed another half mile through the moonlit forest before she stumbled into the ambush. One moment she was stealing along, quick and confident, eager to catch up to the rest of the company and the familiar perils of their association, the next she was surprised by the appearance of a surface elf wizard who simply stepped out of a tree and hurled a spell at her, barking words of arcane might as he gestured with his hands.

"Quick!" he shouted. "We have her!"

Halisstra's invisibility failed at once, undone by the surface wizard, and from the foliage and tree trunks all around her a dozen of the pale elves and the green-clad humans abruptly appeared, weapons at the ready. They leaped at her, murder in their eyes, filling the forest with their war cries and shouts of exultation.

Recognizing the hopelessness of her plight, Halisstra snarled in pure drow rage and charged to meet the surface warriors, determined not to sell her life cheaply.

The first foe in her path was a hulking human with a bristling black beard, fighting with a pair of short swords. He launched into a spinning attack, stabbing one blade at her eyes to raise her shield and slipping the other low to gut her while her guard was high. Halisstra simply dodged aside and hammered down at his extended left arm with her mace, striking a heavy blow that cracked bone and jarred the blade from his injured hand. The man grunted in pain but kept at her, giving ground grudgingly as he continued to hew and slash with his one remaining sword.

Three more of his comrades moved up to engage Halisstra from all sides, and she was forced on the defensive, batting spear and blade aside with her shield and delivering crushing parries with her magical mace. The forest echoed with the sounds of steel on steel.

"Take her alive if you can," called the wizard. "Lord Dessaer wants to find out who these newcomers are and where they came from."

"Easier said than done," grunted the first swordsman, still holding his ground despite the loss of his off-hand blade. "She does not seem interested in surrendering."

Halisstra growled in frustration and abruptly turned on the elf to her left, slipping inside the point of his spear and rushing him. The fellow backstepped and brought in his weapon as quickly as he could, but she had him.

With a snarl of cold glee she smashed her mace hard at the bridge of his nose. The weapon struck with a deadly crack of thunder and blew apart the skull of her victim, who fell in a nerveless heap.

She paid the price for her aggressive move a moment later when the elf swordsman behind her jammed the point of his weapon into her left shoulder blade despite her cat-quick effort to twist away from the attack. Steel grated on bone, and Halisstra cried out in pain as the strength fled from her shield arm. A moment later an arrow fired from an archer standing off a bit struck quivering in the back of her right calf, buckling her leg.

"Now we've got her, lads!" called the elf swordsman.

He raised his blade for another stroke, but Halisstra allowed herself to crumple completely to the ground and rolled up under his guard, destroying his left hip with another thundering blow of her mace. The elf screamed and reeled away to collapse thrashing in the snow.

Halisstra tried to regain her feet, but the wizard hammered her with a blinding bolt of lightning. The force of the spell literally picked her up and flung her through the air, depositing her in a small, icy creek nearby. Halisstra's whole body jerked and ached from the wizard's energy, and she became aware of the distinct, charred scent of her own burned flesh.

She pushed herself up on one arm and responded by hurling a *bae'qeshel* song at him, a deadly, sharp chord that flayed the bark from the trees and kicked up the dusting of snow into a stinging storm of white. The elf wizard swore and covered himself with his cloak, shielding his eyes and enduring the deadly song.

Halisstra began another song, but the warriors splashed up to her, and the burly human with the beard silenced her with a hard kick to the jaw that knocked her sprawling again. All went dark for an instant, and when she could see again, no less than four deadly blades were poised over her. The heavy swordsman glared down at her over the point of his sword.

"By all means, continue," he spat. "Our clerics can question your corpse as easily as they can question you."

Halisstra tried to clear her head of the roaring pain and the ringing in her ears. She looked around and saw nothing but death in the eyes of the surface dwellers.

I can feign surrender, she told herself. *Quenthel and the others must know I'm missing, and they will make efforts to find me.*

"I yield," she said in the human's brutish tongue.

Halisstra allowed her head to fall back against the stream bank and her eyes to close. She felt herself jerked upright, her mail stripped from her, and her hands bound roughly behind her back. The whole time she studiously ignored her captors, keeping her mind sequestered from her situation by focusing on the exhaustive catechisms to Lolth she had been obliged to learn as a novice.

"She must be someone important. Look at this armor. I don't think I've ever seen its equal."

"We've a lyre here, and a couple of wands," muttered the ranger with the broken hand as he pawed through her belongings. "Be careful, lads, she may be a bard. We ought to gag her to be safe."

"Bring me that healing potion, quickly. Fandar is dying."

Halisstra glanced over at the elf swordsman whose hip she had shattered. Several of his companions knelt by him in the snow and mud, trying to comfort him as he writhed weakly in agony. Bright blood flecked the snow nearby. She watched the scene absently, her mind a thousand miles distant.

"Cursed drow witch. Thank the gods they don't all fight like that."

The elf wizard appeared in front of her, his handsome face taut and angry.

"Hood her, fellows," he ordered the others. "No sense letting her know where she is."

"Where are you taking me?" Halisstra demanded.

"Our lord has some things he would like to know," the wizard replied. His smile had a distinctly cold and wintry cast to it, and his eyes were as sharp as knives. "In my experience, most drow are so venomous they'd rather choke on their own blood than do anything sensible and useful, and I expect you'll prove no different. Lord Dessaer will ask you a few questions, you'll call him something impolite, and we'll take you out back and gut you like a fish. That's a damned sight better than our captives fare in your hands, after all."

The hood came down over Halisstra's face and was jerked tight around her neck.

Ryld crouched in the shadows of a great tree with a trunk so thick and tall it might have been the forest's Narbondel. Splitter rode between his shoulders, virtually unused in the company's most recent battle. He leaned out a little and carefully peered into the dappled moonlight and shadow of the forest floor, searching for a target. With Pharaun he'd waited quietly to guard the party's backtrail, hoping to turn the tables on the elves and humans who'd harried them so long. After several valiant attempts to bring the drow to close combat, the surface elves and their human allies had learned to respect the dark elf party's skill and ferocity. They soon fought a slow and stealthy battle of arrows in the dark, punctuated with quick ambuscades and quicker retreats.

An arrow hissed in the dark. Ryld jerked back just in time to glimpse a white-feathered shaft fly past, so close to the tree trunk that its fletching kissed the bark. Had he relied on the tree for cover, the expertly aimed arrow would have skewered him through the eye.

"No point waiting any longer, now," Pharaun whispered.

The wizard had greeted Quenthel's order to lay an ambush with a distinct lack of enthusiasm, and he wasn't at all unhappy to call the effort a failure and rejoin the rest of the band. He muttered the harsh syllables of a spell and gestured in a peculiar fashion, concentrating.

In a moment the wizard straightened and motioned to Ryld, *Come. I've created an image that will make it seem that we still stand guard here, but you and I are invisible to our antagonists. Follow me quietly, and stay close.*

Ryld nodded and moved off stealthily just behind the wizard. He took one last glance at the desolate forest behind them, wondering if the wizard's trick would work.

Halisstra is back there somewhere, he thought. Most likely dead.

The surface dwellers had shown no interest in taking prisoners, and in the logical part of his mind Ryld simply wrote off her loss as another casualty of battle, just as he might account for the untimely fall of any useful comrade. He'd fought enough battles over the years to understand that warriors die, but despite that, he found Halisstra's loss strangely unsettling.

Pharaun paused, turning in a slow circle as he searched for some sign of the rest of the company or any foes still on their trail. Ryld held still and listened. A gentle wind moved the treetops and sighed in the branches overhead. Leaves rustled, and branches creaked. A small brook trickled nearby, but he could detect nothing that might signal danger—or Halisstra's return.

Stupid to hope for such a thing, he told himself.

Something troubles you? motioned Pharaun.

No, the weapons master replied.

The wizard studied him, the brilliant silver moonlight gleaming on his handsome face.

Tell me you're not worried about the female!

Of course not, Ryld replied. *I'm concerned only because she's been a valuable comrade, and I don't like the idea of proceeding without her skill at healing. But I am not concerned on any other account. I am no fool.*

I think perhaps you protest too much, Pharaun signed. *It does not matter, I suppose.*

He started to say more, but at that moment a soft rustle behind them cut off his words. Wizard and swordsman turned together, Ryld's hand stealing to Splitter's hilt as he aimed his crossbow with the other hand, but from the bright shadows Valas Hune suddenly appeared. Of all the company, the Bregan D'aerthe seemed almost as skilled as the surface dwellers in the patient cat-and-mouse game of forest hunting.

Did you catch sight of any of our foes? the scout asked.

No, but someone saw enough of Ryld to shoot an arrow, Pharaun replied. *Since they seemed to guess where we were, we left an illusion and came to rejoin you.*

Any sign of Halisstra? Ryld asked.

No. Nor you, then? Valas replied.

Perhaps half an hour ago we heard sounds of fighting from back down the trail. It went on for a couple of minutes. That might have been her, Pharaun signed.

"There it is, then," Valas muttered under his breath. "Well, come on then. The others are waiting, and if we can't ambush our pursuers, we might as well keep moving. The longer they keep us here, the more likely it is that more of them will show up and join the fight."

The scout led the way as he hurried through the trees and brush, moving swiftly and silently. Pharaun and Ryld could not match the softness of his steps, but the wizard's magic seemed an adequate ruse, since they encountered no more hidden archers or spearmen. In a few hundred yards they came to a small, steep ravine, well screened by thick brush and large boulders. There they found Quenthel, Danifae, and Jeggred lying low, watching vigilantly for any sign of a renewed attack.

"Did you surprise the archers?" Quenthel asked.

"No. They located us quickly, and avoided a fight," Ryld replied. He ran a hand over his stubbled scalp and sighed. "This is not a good battlefield for us. We can't bring the surface elves to grips, not with the advantage they have in this terrain, but if we don't do anything, they'll eventually surround us and cut us to pieces with arrows."

Valas nodded in agreement and added, "They're working to find and flank us now. We've got a few minutes here, but we're going to have to move or fight soon. Ten minutes or less, I think."

"Let them come," rumbled Jeggred. "We killed a dozen of them not an hour ago when they stole up on us from behind. Now that we know the day-walkers are out there, we'll slaughter them in heaps."

"The next assault will most likely consist of a rain of arrows from archers we won't even be able to see," Valas said. "I doubt that the surface dwellers will oblige us by lining up for us to kill. Worse yet, what if the rangers sent for help? The next attack might come at daybreak with two or three times the numbers we've seen so far. I don't relish the thought of being showered with arrows and spells after the sun comes up and our opponents suddenly begin to see much better than we do."

"Fine," Jeggred snarled. "So what would you do, then?"

"Withdraw," Ryld answered for the scout. "Make the best speed we can and keep moving. With luck we'll outdistance our pursuers before the sun comes up, and maybe we'll find a good place to hide."

"Or maybe we'll reach territory controlled by the Jaelre," Valas added.

"Which may, of course, prove to be even more dangerous than playing cat-and-mouse with our friends the surface dwellers," Pharaun said. "If the Jaelre aren't fond of visitors. . . ."

"It doesn't matter if they are or not," Quenthel said. "We came to speak to their priest, and we will do so, even if we have to cut our way through half their House to do it."

"Your suggestion is not very encouraging, Master Hune," Danifae said. She bled freely from a wound in her right arm, where a hard-driven arrow had actually punched through her mail and transfixed her upper arm. As she spoke she worked awkwardly with one hand to bind the wound. "What happens if we fail to outpace our enemies? They seem well able to keep up with us in these damnable woods."

"One moment," Ryld said. "What about Mistress Melarn? She's back there somewhere."

"Most likely dead already," Valas said with a shrug. "Or a prisoner."

"Shouldn't we make sure of that before we leave her?" the weapons master replied. "Her healing songs are the only magic of that sort we have left to us. Common sense dictates—"

"Common sense dictates that we don't waste time and blood on a corpse," Quenthel interrupted. "No one came after me when—"

She stopped herself, then stood and walked over to help Danifae cinch her bandage.

"Our mission lies ahead of us, not behind," the Mistress of Arach-Tinilith said. "The quest is more important than any one drow."

Ryld rubbed his hand over his face and glanced around the company. Valas looked away, busying himself with some unimportant fastening of his armor. Pharaun stared at Quenthel with an expression that made it clear the wizard noted the priestess's hypocrisy, if nothing else. She had, after all, spent more time in Ched Nasad hoping to empty Baenre storehouses of their goods than seeking the renewed attention of Lolth.

Danifae stared off into the woods behind them, her brow furrowed with concern, but obviously unwilling to argue the point on behalf of her mistress.

Finally Quenthel turned to Pharaun and said, "Perhaps our skilled wizard has some magic that might help us discourage these cursed day-walkers from following too closely?"

Pharaun stroked his chin, and thought.

"Our chief difficulty in these circumstances," the Master of Sorcere said at length, "lies in the fact that our antagonists are able to use this terrain to their advantage, and our *dis*advantage. Should a forest fire suddenly arise, the smoke and flames would—"

Valas laughed and interrupted, "I'm afraid you know little of surface forests, Master Mizzrym. These trees are far too wet to oblige you with a forest fire now. Try again in a few months, after summer has dried them out."

"Oh," the wizard replied, "I can see that's true for *mundane* fire."

"You won't be able to prevent fire from sweeping back on us," Ryld said, the idea giving him some anxiety.

"Well, I can't be certain they won't, but my fires will burn in the manner I choose," Pharaun said. "As Master Hune observed, the forest is damp enough that the trees won't catch unless directly affected by my spell. We will, of course, have the advantage of knowing how and when the fires begin."

Quenthel thought for a moment, then said, "Very well, you may proceed."

Ryld felt his throat tighten and he stepped away from the group, quickly regaining control of himself.

The Master of Sorcere stood and reached into a pouch at his belt to withdraw a tiny silk purse. He emptied it into his hand. Red dust glittered in the moonlight. Pharaun studied the forest, turned to sense the wind, and spoke his spell quickly, casting the powder into the air. Bright crimson sparks appeared amid the falling dust, growing brighter and more numerous moment by moment. With another gesture, Pharaun scattered the burning motes across a great, wide arc of the forest before him.

As each tiny mote settled to the ground, it flared into life, growing into a spiderlike shape fully as large as a man's head. Wreathed in crimson flame, the fire spiders scuttled across the ground, moving deeper into the trees. Whatever they touched smoldered at first, then burst into flame. The wood was indeed wet, and the flames were smoky and slow to spread—but Pharaun had conjured hundreds of the spider creatures. The living motes of fire seemed to set upon the moss-grown trunks with a peculiarly savage ferocity, almost as if the presence of so much timber had provoked them into a frenzy of fiery destruction.

"Good, good," Pharaun murmured. "They like trees . . . they truly do."

"The fire's too slow to burn our pursuers," Quenthel observed.

"I've never heard of a surface elf who'd allow a fire such as this to burn unchecked in his precious forest," Pharaun said with a smile. "They'll be busy chasing down my spiders and extinguishing the flames for some time.

Quenthel watched the blaze a moment longer, and smiled.

"It may serve, then," she said. "Master Hune, take the lead. I mean to reach House Jaelre before we're troubled by the surface dwellers again."

🕷 🕷 🕷

Kaanyr Vhok folded his well-muscled arms and frowned.

"How many this time?" he asked.

Kaanyr surveyed the aftermath of a battle between the tanarukks of his vanguard and a titanic purple worm, a carnivorous giant over a hundred feet in length. The worm was dead, hacked to death by dozens of the half-demon's soldiers, but a handful of the Sceptered One's troops lay torn and crushed by the monster they had killed.

"Seven, my lord, but we slew the beast, as you can see."

The tanarukk captain called Ruinfist leaned on his huge greataxe, spattered with the foul juices of the creature. The orc-demon's left hand had been mangled in some battle long before, and was encased in a locked battle-gauntlet that served as a better weapon than the damaged hand it covered.

"The warriors heard it moving in the rock," Ruinfist continued, "but it came through the ceiling and dropped on them."

"I didn't bring you here to slay mindless worms," Kaanyr said. "Nor did I bring warriors to this spot to feed whatever monster happens by. This was a battle best avoided, Ruinfist. These seven warriors won't be with us when we meet the dark elves, will they?"

"No, my lord," the tanarukk growled. He lowered his head. "I will tell the patrol leaders to do what they can to avoid needless battles."

"Good," said Kaanyr. He offered the tanarukk a hard grin and clapped the creature on the shoulder. "Save your axes for the drow, Ruinfist. We'll be on them soon enough."

A hungry light flared in the tanarukk's eyes, and the demon-orc raised his tusked jaw again. He growled in assent and trotted off to go find his fellow captains.

"You did not discipline him?" Aliisza asked, slinking out of the shadows. "Mercy is not a quality I am accustomed to in you, love."

The cambion lord turned at her approach.

"Sometimes," he replied, "one soft word serves the purpose of two hard ones. Knowing which to choose and when is the art of leadership." Kaanyr nudged one of his dead warriors with his toe, and smiled. "Besides, how can I take offense at a show of the very fighting spirit I've worked so hard to instill in my Scoured Legion? It's the nature of a tanarukk to throw himself into battle and bring down his foe or die trying."

Aliisza looked at the purple worm and shuddered.

"I think that's the biggest worm I've ever seen," she murmured.

The half-demon's seat of power in the ruins of ancient Ammarindar was the better part of two hundred and fifty miles southeast of Menzoberranzan, and the Darklake was an obstacle in their path. Fortunately, tanarukks were fast, hearty, and could endure swift marches with few supplies. The dwarves of ancient Ammarindar had carved great subterranean highways through their realm, broad, smooth-floored tunnels that ran for mile after mile through the endless gloom. Kaanyr was somewhat disconcerted to think that the tremendous cavern of the Darklake lay somewhere a mile or two beneath his feet, but the old dwarven road offered far and away their best route to the environs of Menzoberranzan. If the road happened to be plagued by hungry monsters, well, any other route would have problems of its own.

He shook himself from his reflections and started to walk back toward the long file of his warriors, streaming past the scene of the battle in a ragged double-column.

"So, tell me again about this Nimor," Kaanyr said. "I can easily understand Horgar Steelshadow's motive in mustering this attack. The gray dwarves and the dark elves have fought many wars over the centuries. What I don't understand is what's in it for a drow assassin?"

"As best I can tell," Aliisza replied, "he hates the great Houses of Menzoberranzan enough that he'll destroy the city in order to bring about their fall."

"Such a purity of intent is rare in a dark elf. You know he's lied to you, of course."

Kaanyr suspected, as always, that Aliisza was holding something of her encounter with Nimor to herself. After all, she was an alufiend, the daughter of a succubus, and her weapons and methods were obvious.

"Lied?" she quipped. "To me?"

"I merely point out that that one should beware of dark elves bearing gifts," Kaanyr replied. "He might have convinced you it was in my best interest to bring my army here, but I don't believe for a heartbeat that your mysterious assassin doesn't have more to gain from this alliance than I do."

"That goes without saying, doesn't it?" she said. "If you see that, why did you agree to bring your army to the Pillars of Woe?"

"Because something is going to happen there," Kaanyr said. "My ambitions have reached the borders of old Ammarindar, and I don't care to arrest them there."

The cambion watched his fierce warriors marching by, staring past them to the dark visions that enthralled him.

"We'll be approaching from above and to the east," Kaanyr said, "perfectly positioned to flank a force trying to hold the Pillars against the approach of Gracklstugh's army. On the surface, that is why Horgar Steelshadow and his drow assassin want us there. It might suit their purposes to sit in the gorge a few days and let the drow decimate my soldiers before they attempt to force the pass. Being on the same side of an obstacle as our enemies carries a liability, as well as an opportunity. I wouldn't put it past Horgar to manufacture some excuse for a delay in order to let my tanarukks handle the brunt of the fighting."

Aliisza cozied up beside him and purred, "Until the battle is joined, love, you haven't chosen sides. The dark elves might pay, and pay well, for your assistance at a critical juncture of the campaign. Even if that assistance takes the form of simply not doing anything to aid the gray dwarves in their attack."

Kaanyr Vhok bared his pointed teeth in a wry smile.

"There is that," he admitted. "All right, then. We'll see what happens when the Pillars of Woe stand before us."

☙   ☙   ☙

Halisstra was marched for several miles through the forest, gagged, hooded, her hands manacled behind her. The surface elves had healed the wound in her calf in order to keep her from slowing them down, but the rest of her injuries they didn't bother to tend. While they'd removed her mail and shield, they did permit her to keep her arming jacket against the cold night air—after searching carefully to make sure they didn't miss any hidden weapons or magical devices.

Eventually they reached a place where the forest floor underfoot gave way to stone, and she could hear the whispers and rustles of a number of people around her. The air grew warmer, and sullen firelight penetrated the hood over her eyes.

"Lord Dessaer," a voice close by said, "the captive Hurmaendyr spoke of."

"So I see. Remove her hood. I would look on her face," said a deep, thoughtful voice from somewhere ahead of her.

Her captors removed the hood, leaving Halisstra squinting in the bright light of an elegant hall made of gleaming silver-hued wood. Flowering vines wound along posts and beams, and a fire glowed to one side in a large hearth. Several pale elves watched her carefully—apparently guards of some kind, dressed in silver-hued scale mail with polearms and swords at their hips.

Lord Dessaer was a tall half-elf with golden hair and pale skin with a faint bronze hue to it. He was well-muscled for a male, nearly as big as Ryld, and he wore a breastplate of gleaming gold with noble accoutrements.

"Remove her gag, too," the elf lord said. "She'll have little to say otherwise."

"Careful, my lord," spoke the captor beside her, whom Halisstra saw was the black-bearded human she'd fought in the forest. "She knows something of the bard's arts, and may be able to speak a spell with her hands bound."

"I will exercise all due caution, Curnil." The lord of the hall moved closer, gazing thoughtfully into Halisstra's blood-red eyes, and said, "So, what shall we call you?"

Halisstra stood mute.

"Are you Auzkovyn or Jaelre?" Dessaer asked.

"I am not of House Jaelre," she said. "I do not know of the other House you name."

Lord Dessaer exchanged a worried glance with his advisors.

"You belong to a third faction, then?"

"I was traveling with a small company, on a trade mission," she replied. "We sought no trouble with surface dwellers."

"A drow's word is regarded with some skepticism in these lands," Dessaer replied. "If you're not Auzkovyn or Jaelre, then what was your business in Cormanthor?"

"As I said, it was a trade mission," Halisstra lied.

"Indeed," drawled Dessaer. "Cormanthor was not entirely abandoned during the Retreat, and my people object strongly to the drow effort to seize our old homeland. Now, I would like to know who exactly you and your companions are, and what you were doing in our forest."

"Our business is our own," Halisstra answered. "We intend no harm for any surface folk, and mean to be gone from this place as soon as our business is done."

"So I should simply allow you to go free, is that it?"

"You would do yourself no harm if you did so."

"My warriors engage in deadly battles every day against your kind," Dessaer said. "Even if you say you have nothing to do with the Jaelre or the Auzkovyn, that doesn't mean you're not our enemy. We do not ask quarter of the drow, nor do we extend it to them. Unless you succeed in explaining to my satisfaction why you should be spared, you will be executed."

The lord of the surface folk folded his arms before his breastplate, and fixed her with a fierce stare.

"Our business is with House Jaelre," Halisstra said. She drew herself up as best she could with her arms bound behind her. "It does not concern surface elves. As I said before, my company is not here to cause any trouble to you or your people."

Lord Dessaer sighed, then nodded to Halisstra's guards.

"Escort the lady to her cell," he said, "and let us see if she becomes more helpful with some time to fully consider her situation."

Halisstra's guards replaced her hood, covering her eyes again. She stood passively and allowed them to do so without protest. If her captors came to expect compliance from her, there was always the chance they might make a mistake and give her a chance to get out of her bonds.

Her guards led her out of the hall and back outdoors again. She could feel the deep chill of the air, and sensed the growing brightness in the sky even through her hood. Dawn was near, and the night was vanishing at the sun's approach. She wondered if her captors meant to lock her in some open cage, a place where the curious and malcontent could come by to jeer and torment her, but instead they led her into another building and down a short flight of stone steps.

Keys jangled, a heavy door creaked open, and she was led through. Her hands were unbound, only to be secured again in heavy iron manacles as rough hands maneuvered her into place.

"Listen well, drow," a voice said. "You will be unhooded and ungagged, at Lord Dessaer's command. However, the first time you attempt to work a spell, you will be fitted with a steel muzzle and hooded so closely you will labor for every breath. We don't go out of our way to mistreat prisoners, but we'll repay every trouble you cause us threefold. If we have to break your limbs and shatter your jaw to keep you docile, we will."

Her hood was removed. Halisstra blinked in the bright cell, illuminated by a hot beam of sunlight pouring in from a grate up in one corner. Several armed guards watched her carefully for any sign of trouble. She simply ignored them and allowed herself to slump against the wall. Her hands were chained together tightly, and the manacles were bound to a secure anchor in the ceiling, cleverly designed to take in any slack.

The guards left her half a loaf of some kind of crusty, gold-brown bread and a soft leather jack of cool water, and they exited the cell. The door was riveted iron plate, evidently locked and barred from outside.

So what now? she wondered, staring at the opposite wall.

From what little she'd seen of the surface town, Halisstra suspected that her comrades could break her out easily enough with a determined effort.

"Hardly likely," Halisstra muttered to herself.

She was a Houseless outcast whose usefulness did not overcome the simple fact that, as the eldest daughter of a high House, she stood as Quenthel's most dangerous rival in the band. The Mistress of the Academy would be only too happy to abandon Halisstra to whatever fate awaited her.

Who would argue against Quenthel on her behalf?

Danifae? Halisstra thought.

She allowed her head to drop to her chest and she laughed softly and bitterly.

I must be desperate indeed, to hope for Danifae's compassion, she thought.

Once dragged off as a battle captive herself, Danifae would find the situation deliciously, perfectly ironic. The binding spell wouldn't let Danifae raise a hand against her, but without specific instructions, the battle captive would not be compelled to seek her out.

With nothing else to do but stare at the wall, Halisstra decided to close her eyes and rest. She still ached in calf, torso, and jaw from the injuries she'd sustained in her desperate last stand. As much as she longed to use the *bae'qeshel* songs to heal herself, she dared not. The pain would have to be endured.

With a simple mental exercise she distanced her mind from her body's pain and fatigue, and slipped deep into Reverie.

In Dessaer's audience hall, the half-elf lord watched his soldiers lead the dark elf away while he stroked his beard thoughtfully.

"So, Seyll," he said, "What do you make of this?"

From behind a hidden screen a slender form in a skirt and jacket of embroidered green glided forward. She was a full-blooded elf, thin and graceful—and she was also a drow, her skin black as ink, the irises of her eyes a startling red. She moved close to Dessaer and gazed after the departing soldiers with their hooded captive.

"I think she's telling the truth," she said. "At least, she's not a Jaelre or an Auzkovyn."

"What shall I do with her?" the lord asked. "She killed Harvaldor, and she damned near killed Fandar as well."

"With Eilistraee's grace, I will restore Harvaldor to life and heal Fandar," the drow woman said. "Besides, is it not the case that Curnil's patrol attacked her and her companions on sight? She was simply defending herself."

Dessaer raised an eyebrow in surprise and glanced at Seyll.

"You intend to give her your goddess's message?"

"It is my sacred duty," Seyll replied. "After all, until it was given to me, I was very much like her."

She inclined her head to indicate the absent prisoner.

"She's a proud one from a high House," Dessaer said. "I doubt she'll care to hear Eilistraee's words." He rested a hand on the drow priestess's shoulder. "Be careful, Seyll. She'll say or do anything to get you to lower your guard, and if you do, she'll kill you if you stand between her and freedom."

"Be that as it may, my duty is clear," Seyll replied.

"I will delay my judgment for a tenday," the Lord of Elventree said, "but if she refuses to hear your message I must act to protect my people."

"I know," said Seyll. "I do not intend to fail."

THIRTEEN

The Houses of Menzoberranzan mustered for battle. From a dozen castles and palaces, caverns and strongholds, slender males in elegant black chain mail marched in proud columns or pranced along in the high saddles of riding lizards, pennons flying from their lances. Under normal circumstances each House might have sent hundreds more slave warriors, a rabble of kobolds, orcs, goblins, and ogres to drive into their foes before valuable drow troops were committed to battle, but armed slaves were something of a scarcity after the alhoon's uprising. Thousands of lesser humanoids had survived the revolt and its failure, as well as the dreadful reprisals that ensued, but the warriors among the slave races had naturally suffered the greatest losses. Even those who'd been allowed to surrender were certainly not to be trusted with weapons again.

Nimor sat in the saddle of an Agrach Dyrr war-lizard, and smiled in satisfaction as the forces of House Dyrr marched past before him. The companies gathered in a small, somewhat cramped plaza near the border between West Wall and Narbondellyn, ironically enough not very far at all from the compound of House Faen Tlabbar. Each drow swordsman carried a light kit in addition to his arms and armor, and a supply train of sorts was taking shape as each company brought its own pack lizards and attendants. Many of the common folk of the city had turned out to watch the mustering of the army, as it was easily the largest assemblage of soldiers the matron mothers had commanded since the ill-fated assault on Mithral Hall years before.

"I surmise that the Council meeting went well," said Dyrr, standing at Nimor's stirrup.

The undead sorcerer did not appear in his own shape, of course, nor even that of the aged male he affected within his own house. His current guise was that of a nondescript Agrach Dyrr wizard, young and hale, draped with the fine vestments of his House.

"Your matron mother was well coached," Nimor replied. He kept his voice low, even though no one stood close enough to eavesdrop. "We've got half the soldiers in the city mustering for battle."

"Yasraena has proven a useful front," the lich observed. "I have known a dozen or more Matron Mother Dyrrs, and from time to time I find that my female relations object to my . . . unique position within the House. Yasraena would kill me if she could, of course, but she knows that Agrach Dyrr would of necessity be destroyed should something unfortunate befall me. I have made her aware of certain long-standing arrangements in order to discourage her from surprising me."

Nimor chuckled dryly and said, "I suspect that you are rarely surprised, Lord Dyrr."

"Success follows preparation in equal measure, young Nimor. Consider that your lesson for the day." The lich affected a smile across his illusory features, and stepped away from Nimor's mount. "Good luck in your venture, Captain."

Nimor wheeled the war-lizard around as the last of the column passed by.

He turned back to the lich and said, "One more word. Narbondel was illuminated hours late a tenday ago, but every day since it has been illuminated on time, and it is whispered throughout the city that the Masters of Sorcere have misplaced their archmage."

Dyrr smiled and spread his hands.

"As Archmage Baenre may be unavailable for quite some time," the lich said, "it would please me to find the Masters of Sorcere determine on their own who among them should take Gromph's seat."

"Won't Matron Mother Baenre and the Council have something to say about that?"

"Not if the assembled masters realize the power they truly hold now," Dyrr said. "I am not a member of the Academy, of course, but a couple of young pups of my House are, and they keep me well-informed. The masters debate whether this is the time to break with tradition and name their own archmage, but half of them scheme to eliminate any fellow clever and bold enough to take the job, while the other half contemplate whether they might return to their own Houses and rule there. Breaking from the Council in such a way would mean civil war, and those few masters who don't realize the civil war is raging already are arguing to adhere to the status quo in fear of Lolth's return. Regardless, Sorcere is well and truly paralyzed by Gromph's absence."

The lich turned, leaning heavily on his tall staff, and ambled off with a dry, crackling laugh.

Nimor raised an eyebrow and watched the lich depart, considering his ally's words, then he trotted off after the column.

"Lieutenant Jazzt!" he called.

From alongside the marching column of House Agrach Dyrr's warriors, a small, scarred male detached himself and came trotting to Nimor's side. The soldiers marching in the expedition knew very well that "Captain Zhayemd" was no scion of their House, but it had been explained to them that the detachment's commander enjoyed Matron Mother Yasraena's complete confidence and had, in fact, been adopted into the leadership of their ancient clan—a common enough practice among the high Houses of the city. Nimor didn't doubt that Jazzt Dyrr, second cousin to the matron mother herself, had received some additional and specific orders concerning the circumstances under which he was to ignore Nimor's commands, but as Nimor intended to scrupulously honor his bargain with Agrach Dyrr, he was reasonably certain that the Dyrr officer would offer no trouble.

"Yes, Captain?" Jazzt said.

He was careful not to show any expression at all, simply regarding Nimor with the bland curiosity of a seasoned veteran.

"Form up the company there, beside the Baenre contingent. Tell the men to make ready for a long march. I hope to set out within the hour."

"Yes, Captain," Jazzt replied.

The lieutenant stepped back and saluted sharply, then turned and began to bark orders to the Agrach Dyrr soldiers. Nimor turned his mount aside and trotted across the plaza to a small tent bustling with activity. There, the highborn officers and commanders of each of the various House contingents had gathered, most with some number of sergeants and messengers in train. Several arguments on all manner of different topics—the order of march, the best place to halt at the end of the day, the fastest route to the Pillars of Woe—proceeded at the same time.

He dismounted, handed the reins of his war-lizard to a nearby slave, and strode into the midst of the confusion, pushing through to the partitioned area. He had to flash his insignia of House and rank to gain admittance. Inside, a knot of captains and officers from various Houses stood engaged in several different conversations at the same time. The occasion of raising an army and marching to war seemed to displace the normal rivalries and vendettas, at least for a time. Instead of dueling each other in the streets, the rakish fellows sought to outshine each other with deeds of valor and ruthlessness on the battlefield.

Nimor surveyed the commanders, noting the insignias of six out of eight great Houses, and another half dozen of the largest and strongest minor Houses. His eye fell on a male wearing the insignia of House Baenre, as the fellow held up his hands and raised his voice to capture the attention of the other officers.

"Go back to your companies and look to your supply trains," Andzrel Baenre, Weapons Master of House Baenre, said. "I want a list from each of you of the number of pack beasts and wagons in your train, and a general inventory of your stores. Return within the hour. Our female relations will doubtless debate many issues of high strategy, but it will fall to us to work out the details of supply trains and battle signals, and we still have much to discuss."

Andzrel was a tall, slender fellow who wore armor of blacked mithral plate and a dark cloak. His tabard proudly displayed the emblem of House Baenre, and his eyes held iron discipline, an expression of directness and purpose that was unusual in a drow of high birth, whether male or female.

The commanders broke up and strode from the tent, heading back to their detachments. Nimor allowed them to pass by. As he moved up to speak with the Baenre weapons master, the assassin muttered a spell.

"Master Baenre," Nimor asked, covering the last syllables of the enchantment.

"Yes," the weapons master said, blinking at Nimor. "I . . . uh . . ."

Nimor smiled, seeing the effect the enchantment had on the drow, and knowing that for quite some time, Andzrel Baenre and he would be very close friends.

"You are familiar to me, but I do not believe I know you," said Andzrel. "You wear the arms of Agrach Dyrr."

"I am Zhayemd Dyrr, and I command my House's company," Nimor replied. "Do you have any idea when the priestesses will deign to join us, or at least allow us to start on our way?"

"I believe the matron mothers are still deciding which of them will lead the expedition," Andzrel replied, seemingly recovered. "None of them trusts any of the others enough to voluntarily leave the city now, but they all think it's clear that someone had better be put in charge of the males."

Nimor laughed at that.

"You have a talent for plain speaking, sir." Nimor glanced around at the other captains and officers in the pavilion and added,

"I assume you've tallied which Houses are here, and how many troops—and of what type—each has brought? The priestesses will want to know that, and it will be helpful for us all to have an idea of who's marching next to whom."

He could think of other uses for the information, of course, but there was no need to mention that, was there?

"Of course," Andzrel replied. He pointed at a table in the outer portion of the tent, where several Baenre officers studied maps and reports. "I'll need you to give those fellows the strength of your complement, the number of infantry and cavalry, and some information on your supply train, as well. After which I would like to ask you some questions about the route of our march and the place we expect to meet the duergar army. I understand you're familiar with the region, as well as the composition and tactics of the duergar force."

Nimor straightened his cuirass and nodded earnestly.

"Certainly," he said. "I know them well."

⚜ ⚜ ⚜

Halisstra was roused from her dreams by the sound of her cell door opening. She glanced up, wondering if perhaps the time had come when the surface folk would simply put her to the blade.

"I have no more to say to your lord," she said, though the thought crossed her mind that selling out her comrades was preferable to death by torture, especially if she could gain her freedom in the exchange.

"Fine," a woman's voice replied. "I hope then that you will consent to speak with me."

A slender figure slipped through the open door, which was closed and locked behind her. Veiled in a long, dark cloak, the visitor paused to study Halisstra then she reached up with hands as black as coal and slipped back her hood to reveal a face of gleaming ebony, and eyes as red as blood.

"I am Seyll Auzkovyn," the drow said, "and I have come to give you my lady's message: 'A rightful place awaits you in the Realms

Above, in the Land of the Great Light. Come in peace and live beneath the sun again, where trees and flowers grow.' "

"A priestess of Eilistraee," Halisstra murmured. She had heard of the cult before, of course. The Spider Queen held nothing but scorn for the weak, idealistic faith of the Dark Maiden, whose worshipers dreamed of redemption and acceptance in the World Above. "Well, I did come in peace, and I do seem to have found my rightful place in this tidy little cell. I expect wonderful flowers bloom just beyond the bars of my window, and I am more than a little thankful that the thrice-cursed sun shines no deeper into my prison." She laughed bitterly. "Somehow the holy message of your silly little dancing goddess rings a little false today. Now go away, and let me get back to the important business of preparing myself for the inevitable tortures that await me when the so-called lord of this fetid dungheap of a village loses his patience with my intransigent ways."

"You sound like me, when I first heard Eilistraee's message," Seyll replied. She moved closer and sat on the floor beside Halisstra. "Like yourself, I was a priestess of the Spider Queen who found herself a captive of the surface folk. Though I've lived here for several years now, I still find the light of the sun overly harsh."

"Don't flatter yourself, apostate," snarled Halisstra. "I'm nothing like you."

"You might be surprised," Seyll continued calmly, her placid demeanor unchanged. "Have the Spider Queen's punishments ever struck you as needless or wasteful? Have you ever failed to nurture a friendship because you feared betrayal? Have you ever, perhaps, watched a child of your own body, your own heart, destroyed because she failed at a senseless test, only to tell yourself that she was too weak to live? Did you ever wonder if there was a point to the deliberate and calculated cruelty that poisons our entire race?"

"Of course there's a point," Halisstra replied. "We're surrounded on all sides by vicious enemies. If we didn't take steps to hone our people to their finest edge, we would become slaves—no, worse yet, we would become *rothé*."

"And have Lolth's judgments in fact made you stronger?"

"Of course."

"Prove it, then. Offer an example." Seyll watched her, then leaned forward and said, "You remember countless tests and battles, naturally, but you can't prove that you were made stronger by them. You don't know what might have happened if you hadn't been subjected to those tortures."

"Simple semantics. Naturally I can't prove that things are other than they are."

Halisstra glared at the heretic, profoundly annoyed. She would have found the conversation irritating and irrelevant under the best of circumstances, but with her hands and feet chained together, slumped against the cold, hard wall of a stone cell with a painful shaft of sunlight slanting in, it was positively infuriating. Still, she had very little to occupy her mind otherwise, and there was a small chance that a display of enthusiasm for Seyll's faith might win her a parole of sorts. Lolth was completely intolerant of apostates, but to feign acceptance of another faith in order to win the freedom to betray the trust of one's captors . . . that was the sort of cleverness the Spider Queen admired. The trick, of course, was not to appear too eager, yet just uncertain enough that Seyll and her friends might come to hope for a true change in Halisstra's heart.

"You are annoying me," she said to Seyll. "Leave me alone."

"As you wish," Seyll said. She stood gracefully, and offered Halisstra a smile. "Consider what I've said, and ask yourself if there might be some truth to it. If your faith in Lolth is as strong as you think, surely it can withstand a little examination. May Eilistraee bless you and warm your heart."

She pulled her hood back over her head, and silently withdrew. Halisstra turned her own face away so Seyll couldn't see the cruel smile that twisted her features.

Rear guard, mused Ryld, seems to be the spot Quenthel saves for the person she deems least useful at the moment.

He paused to listen to the forest around him, seeking for any sound that might indicate an approaching enemy. He heard nothing but the steady patter of cold rain. Pharaun's fire-spiders had managed to set a smoky blaze in the woods behind them, but the rain had likely prevented the fires from burning too much of the forest. The weapons master glanced up into the sky, allowing the cold drops to splash on his face and noting the sullen silver glow behind the clouds.

At least the rain is washing out our trail, he thought.

After a hard march the previous night and lying low in a thick tangle of brush through a long, sunny day, they had resumed their hike in the evening only to meet a deluge soon after setting out. The forest floor was nothing but mud and slush.

Taking a moment to adjust his hood, Ryld set out again, trying hard not to hurry his steps too much. He would not be much of a rear guard if he closed up right behind the others, but on the other hand, the last thing he wanted to do was fall so far behind that he missed an innocent turn of the trail and wandered off alone into the endless woods. If Halisstra wasn't worth going back for, he was under no delusions as to what would happen if he managed to become separated from the rest of the company. He tramped on for quite some time, pausing every few dozen yards to listen and scan the forest.

Soon he became aware of the louder, more insistent sound of water in motion—a swift forest stream, dark and wide, that sluiced through muddy banks covered in thorns and bracken. A large log had been felled to cross the stream, its upper surface sawn flat to form a reasonably secure bridge. Quenthel and the others waited there, silently watching their surroundings. Ryld noted the crossbows pointed in his direction, and the acute attentiveness of his companions. Clearly the running battle with the surface folk had taught his comrades to be wary of the woods.

"Hold your fire," he called softly. "It's Ryld."

"Master Argith," Quenthel said. "I was beginning to wonder if you'd lost the trail."

Ryld bowed to Quenthel and joined the others. He took a moment to sit on the stump of the log, fishing in the pockets of his cloak for a small flask of duergar brandy. Normally he wouldn't risk diluting his senses with alcohol, but hours of marching in cold rain had soaked his clothing and left him chilled to the bone. The liquor brought a hot glow to the middle of his body with one good mouthful.

"Is this your stream?" he asked Pharaun.

"Yes," the wizard said without hesitation. "Here, we cross and turn to the south, following the river upstream. House Jaelre is not more than a couple of miles away."

He pointed at Ryld with one finger and muttered a magical syllable. The flask rose up from the weapons master's hand and bobbed through the air to the wizard, who promptly helped himself to a healthy swallow.

"My thanks," said Pharaun. "The gray dwarves may be odious churls, but they distill a good brandy."

"Don't drink too much," Quenthel said. "The Jaelre are as likely to shoot us as look at us. I need you alert and sharp-witted, wizard. Master Argith, keep up close with the rest of us from this point on. I'm more worried about what lies before us now than behind."

"As you wish, Mistress," Ryld said.

He held out his hand to Pharaun, who took one more small swallow and tossed the flask back to Ryld. The weapons master stood, shouldered his pack, and led the way across the bridge. The surface of the log was slick and uneven, and doubtless would have been trouble for a clumsy dwarf or awkward human, but the dark elves negotiated the crossing with ease.

On the other side, they found the overgrown remnants of an old stone road, cracked and broken by the twisting roots of countless trees and hundreds of years of frosts and thaws. Smooth white stone, expertly joined, marked it as the work of the ancient surface elves who once inhabited the forest. Ryld was not so poorly educated that he had not heard of Cormanthor, the great forest empire of the surface elves, or the fallen glory of its legendary capital city of Myth Drannor. Other than the names, though, he knew very little of who the builders of the forest empire had been and what had befallen them.

Moving slowly and carefully, the company advanced in an open skirmish line, prepared to defend themselves against any attack. They followed the old road for more than a mile, just as Pharaun had said they would, and they came upon the wreckage of old walls and battlements ringing some ancient stronghold. Green vines wreathed the walls, thriving despite the winter season, but the wall was cracked and holed in a dozen places. A rusted iron gate lay across the road where it pierced the walls, a barrier that had long since fallen into uselessness. Beyond the walls, a small stony tor rose from the forest floor, crowned by a large pentagonal keep of white stone. At first Ryld thought the place was whole and intact, but as he studied it, he realized that the tower-tops were holed and that more than one of the flying buttresses linking the outlying towers to the main body of the keep had collapsed with the years. Green vines knotted their roots in the riven stone, covering the ruins in a living blanket.

"Ruins," Jeggred growled in disgust. "Your insipid spells have failed you, wizard—or you have deliberately led us astray. Are you in league with our treacherous scout, perhaps?"

"My spells do not fail," Pharaun replied. "This is the place. The Jaelre are here."

"Then where are they?" the draegloth snarled. "If you—"

"Silence, both of you!" Valas snapped. He moved a few steps away from the gate, his footfalls as soft as those of a stalking leopard, an arrow lying across his bow. "This place is not as abandoned as it looks."

Ryld moved over to take shelter by a tottering old column of masonry, setting one hand on Splitter's hilt. Danifae and Pharaun did the same on the other side of the road, staring hard at the ruined keep. Quenthel, however, chose not to move at all.

Instead she stood confidently in the center of the path and called out, "You of House Jaelre! We wish to speak with your leaders at once!"

From a dozen places of concealment, stealthy shapes in dark cloaks that deceived the eye by mimicking the wearer's surroundings slowly stood, bows and wands pointed at the Menzoberranyr. One of the figures, a female carrying a double-ended sword, pushed back her hood and eyed the company with cold contempt.

"You are miserable spider-kissers," she hissed. "What do you have that the lords of House Jaelre could possibly want, other than your corpses feathered with our arrows?"

Quenthel bridled and allowed one hand to fall to her whip. The weapon writhed slowly, the serpent heads snapping their fangs in agitation.

"I am Quenthel Baenre, Mistress of Arach-Tinilith, and I do not bicker on doorsteps with common gate guards. Announce our arrival to your masters, so that we can get in out of this damnable rain."

The Jaelre captain narrowed her eyes and motioned to her soldiers, who shifted position and made ready to fire. Valas shook his head and lowered his bow, stepping forward quickly with one hand in the air.

"Wait," he said. "If Tzirik the priest is still among you, tell him that Valas Hune is here. We have a proposition for him."

"I doubt our high priest will have much use for any proposal of yours," the guard captain said.

"If nothing else, he'll find out why we came a thousand miles from Menzoberranzan to speak to him," Valas replied.

The captain glared at Quenthel, then said, "Lower your weapons and wait there. Do not move, or my soldiers will fire, and there are more of us than you think."

Valas nodded once, and set his bow down on the ground. He glanced at the others, and took a seat on the edge of a crumbling old fountain. The rest followed suit, though Quenthel didn't demean herself by taking a seat. Instead she folded her arms and waited with imperious displeasure. Ryld glanced around the courtyard full of hostile warriors, and rubbed his head with a sigh.

Quenthel knows how to make an impression, eh? Pharaun gestured discretely.

Females, Ryld replied, just as discretely.

He carefully reached into his cloak and withdrew the brandy flask again.

The most doleful torment of incarceration, reflected Halisstra, was boredom, pure and simple. Like most of her extraordinarily long-lived kind, the priestess hardly noticed the passing of hours, days, even tendays when her mind was engaged. Yet, despite the wisdom and patience of her more than two hundred years, a few hours' confinement in a featureless stone cell seemed more onerous than months of the harsh discipline she endured in her youth.

The endless hours of the day crept by, a day in which her body longed to rest despite the painful glare of sunlight streaming in through that one cursed window. Meanwhile her thoughts veered wildly from praying for her comrades to return and rescue her to fomenting the most hideous and agonizing tortures she could imagine for each one for abandoning her to capture.

Eventually, she fell into Reverie, her mind empty of new schemes or old memories, and her awareness so dim and distant that she might have been sleeping in truth. Exhaustion had finally caught up with her, not just the sheer physical exhaustion of the long tendays of travel and peril through desert, shadow, Underdark, and forest, but a kind of mental fatigue rooted deeply in the grief she still carried for the loss of the House she was to one day rule. Halisstra might not have permitted herself to shed a tear for Ched Nasad, but the malignant truth of her plight had an odd way of surfacing in her thoughts, poisoning them with a cold, hopeless disbelief that was difficult to set aside. Long hours of imprisonment offered her the opportunity to exhume the hateful situation in its entirety and contemplate her loss of station, wealth, and security until her horrible fascination was in some way sated.

At dusk the guards brought her fresh food, a bowl of some bland but nourishing stew and another half loaf of bread. Halisstra found herself ravenously hungry, and she devoured the meal with little thought to the possibility of poison or drugs. Soon after she'd finished, the door to her cell was unlocked with a rusty scraping of iron, and Seyll Auzkovyn slipped inside again.

The priestess had shed her long, heavy cloak, and wore an elegant lady's riding outfit, an embroidered green jacket and knee-length skirt over a blouse of cream and high boots that matched the jacket. The sight of a drow priestess dressed as a noble surface elf struck Halisstra as jarringly incongruous.

"Did the surface lord dress you like that?" she sneered at the Eilistraee worshiper. "You seem almost a perfectly helpless gentlelady of the accursed sun elves in that outfit."

"How else should I dress?" Seyll replied. "I'm among friends here, and need not wear armor. Besides, I found that the skull and spider motifs of my previous wardrobe seemed to alarm the surface folk." She made a small gesture to the jailers outside, and the door was closed behind her. "Anyway," she added, "there are no sun elves here."

"They're all the same to me," Halisstra said.

"When you know them better, you'll be able to tell their kindred easily enough."

"I have no wish to know them better."

"Are you so certain of that? There is always advantage in knowing one's enemies . . . especially if they need not be your enemies."

Seyll knelt easily on the floor beside Halisstra and composed herself. She was young, not much more than a hundred, and pretty enough in her own way, but her carriage was . . . wrong. Her eyes lacked the hungering ambition or the cold appraisal Halisstra was accustomed to seeing mirrored in the faces around her. One could easily mistake Seyll's patient expression for a sort of submissiveness, the lack of the will necessary to achieve, and yet there was a calm assurance about her that hinted at strength held in check.

Halisstra's eyes fell to Seyll's hands, as the priestess smoothed her garments. They were strong, and callused like a weapons master's.

"I had the opportunity to examine the heraldry of your arms today, and study the devices. Melarn is a leading House of the city of Ched Nasad, is it not?"

"It was," Halisstra said.

She instantly regretted the slip. If the surface folk didn't know of Ched Nasad's fate, then she hardly needed to provide them with a gift of information. She had to set a price on anything she revealed.

"You were defeated in a House war?"

It was a reasonable guess on Seyll's part, as most drow Houses that vanished, lost status, or otherwise fell low usually did so because of the actions of other Houses.

"Not quite."

Seyll waited a long moment for Halisstra to elaborate, and when she did not, the Eilistraee priestess shifted tactics.

"Ched Nasad is a long way from Cormanthor. At least six or seven hundred miles, with the great desert of Anauroch and the phaerimm-haunted Buried Realms between here and there. Lord Dessaer is curious about the circumstances that would bring a high-ranking daughter of a powerful House of Ched Nasad into the lands of his people. To be honest, I am curious too."

"So this is to be the method of interrogation, then?" Halisstra said. "A sympathetic ear to garner the answers to questions asked in seeming friendship?"

"Some account of your purpose in Cormanthor must be made before Lord Dessaer will release you into my parole. If your business is as innocent as you say, you need not be imprisoned here."

"Release me?" Halisstra laughed long and quietly. "Ah, I see you have not lost your penchant for cruelty despite your apostasy, Auzkovyn. Did your surface friends ask you to play on a prisoner's hopes by offering freedom in exchange for cooperation, or did you suggest the tactic? Did you really think a single day in this accursed cell would reduce me to desperately grasping at phantom hopes?"

"The hopes I offer are not phantoms," Seyll said. "Tell us what you're doing here, show us that you're no enemy of the peaceful folk of Cormanthor, and you will have your liberty."

"You can't expect me to believe that."

"I am here, am I not?" Seyll answered. "Clearly some of our kind learn to live in peace with the surface folk."

"Of course you have nothing to fear among the surface folk," Halisstra retorted. "Your vapid, dancing goddess is too weak to threaten them."

"As I told you before, I was a priestess of Lolth when I was captured," Seyll said. She formed her hands into a gesture of supplication, a ceremonial pose Halisstra knew well. In the tongue of the abyssal planes where Lolth dwelt, Seyll mouthed the words of a high and secret prayer: " 'Great Goddess, Mother of the Dark, grant me the blood of my enemies for drink and their living hearts for meat. Grant me the screams of their young for song, grant me the helplessness of their males for my satiation, grant me the wealth of their houses for my bed. By this unworthy sacrifice I honor you, Queen of Spiders, and beseech of you the strength to destroy my foes.' "

The infernal words seemed to crackle with dark power, each harsh syllable charged with an evil potency that spread through the cell like a slick of poison. Seyll made a drawing motion of her hand, showing the manner in which the knife was to be wielded, and settled back on her heels.

Shifting back to Elvish, she closed her eyes and said, "Many hapless souls died beneath my knife, yet I found redemption and peace here. Whether the same awaits you is a question I cannot answer, but I offer myself as proof that you can walk these lands in peace if you wish."

Halisstra stared at Seyll, almost as if seeing her for the first time. She had been about to condemn the priestess once more as a weak failure, a traitor to the one true drow goddess, but the words died on her lips. No one but a priestess of high station would have been taught that rite, yet Seyll had decided to turn her back on Lolth. Not only that, but she still lived, and seemed to have found some amount of contentment in her decision. Halisstra had of course been indoctrinated over years of training to regard heresy, apostasy, as the vilest sort of crime imaginable. Yet in her years of sacrifice and abasement before the Spider Queen's altar she had never before encountered a true apostate. Oh, she'd slandered some of her rivals with false accusations of turning away from the Spider Queen, but actually sitting in the presence of someone who had committed the ultimate betrayal of the goddess, and—so far, at least—lived to tell the tale. . . .

"I want to challenge you to do something," Seyll said. "I believe you have the intelligence and the imagination for it, but we shall see. Imagine, for a moment, that you could live in a place where you can walk the streets without fearing an assassin's dagger in your back. Imagine that your friends—*real* friends—want nothing more from you than the pleasure of your company, that your sisters cherish your accomplishments instead of resenting your successes, and your children are not murdered for an accidental failing. Imagine that your lovers seek you out for who you are, and not your station or influence. Imagine that your goddess asks you to celebrate her with your joy, not your terror."

"There is no such—"

"You answer too quickly. I asked you to imagine it, if you can," Seyll said. She stood and moved away, turning her back on Halisstra. "I will wait."

"I can't imagine such nonsense. It's an empty fantasy, signifying nothing. We're not meant for such things; no one is, not dark elf, not light-elf, not even the insipid humans. Only a fool dwells on dreams."

238

"Yet, for the sake of argument at least, would it not seem a pleasant thing?" Seyll said over her shoulder. "You must entertain impossible dreams all the time. All thinking creatures do. Perhaps you've dreamed of having your enemies in your power, or of a lover you couldn't take, or of rising to the station you truly merit."

Halisstra snorted, truly irritated, and shook her hands in her manacles.

"If you can imagine the destruction of all your enemies at once," Seyll pressed, "you can certainly imagine the faithfulness of a friend or a goddess pleased by your loyalty, not your sacrifice."

"All gods demand sacrifice. You delude yourself if you think Eilistraee is any different. Perhaps you're simply too weak-minded to understand your bonds." Halisstra looked away and added, "You have succeeded in boring me again. You may leave now."

The priestess walked to the door. She rapped once on the rusty iron and waited, turning back to face Halisstra.

"What if I show you that you're wrong?" she said softly. "Tomorrow night we dance in the forest for Eilistraee's delight. I will bring you there, and you will see for yourself what our goddess demands of us."

"I will have no part of it," Halisstra snapped, finally irritated enough to forget her resolve to feign a grudging conversion to the surface dwellers' vapid beliefs.

"Your faith in your Spider Queen is so weak you can't bear to watch us dance?" Seyll asked. "Listen, watch, and judge for yourself. That's all I ask."

🕷   🕷   🕷

The endless black gale that shrieked up through the vertical streets of ruined Chaulssin welcomed Nimor's return with a barrage of gusts so powerful that even he was momentarily rocked on his feet. His white hair whipping around his head like a wild halo, the Anointed Blade paused a moment in his steps to allow the blast to die away.

He could not remain long in the City of Wyrmshadows, not while Menzoberranzan's army marched and the Agrach Dyrr contingent tramped along without him, but he wasn't in such a hurry that he couldn't tarry a moment in the hidden citadel of his secret House. Nimor Imphraezl was a prince of Chaulssin, after all, and the magnificent ruin, the hell-carved citadel, was his domain. He had not been born there, of course, nor had he spent his childhood years in the shadow-haunted city. The place was too perilous for the young, so the Jaezred Chaulssin fostered their princes in a dozen minor Houses in as many cities throughout the Underdark. From the time he reached adulthood and came into his ancient birthright, though, Nimor had regarded the windswept ruin as his own palace.

The gust passed, at least as much as any blast of wind ever did in the black chasm yawning around the city, and the assassin continued on his way. Menzoberranzan was little more than an hour distant through the Plane of Shadow, and so it was fairly easy for Nimor to manufacture an excuse to absent himself from the marching column to tend to some "personal matters." Even if Andzrel Baenre summoned the House captains to a sudden council of war during Nimor's absence, he took little risk in leaving for a short time. The army moved quickly, as armies go, but no one would find it overly suspicious for a noble to tarry in the city for a short time before riding out to catch up to the column.

He reached the great, spiraling stair cut through the heart of Chaulssin's stone mountain and ascended quickly, taking the steps two at a time. In the great hall at the top, he found the patron fathers assembled again, clustered together in twos and threes as they traded news and fomented plots to advance the House during their time of remarkable opportunity. Grandfather Mauzzkyl turned to level his fearsome glare upon Nimor as the assassin entered.

"Once again you keep us waiting," he said.

"I beg your forgiveness, Revered Grandfather," Nimor replied. He drew up into the circle with the others and made a small bow. The winds outside the chamber moaned eerily in the distance. "I was summoned to a council of war that I did not think it wise to miss."

"One might say the same of this gathering," observed Patron Father Tomphael.

Nimor forced a smile and replied, "I have been working for some time to cultivate a particular identity and level of responsibility among Menzoberranzan's defenders, Tomphael. That sort of effort is not to be lightly thrown aside. Until the revered grandfather instructs me otherwise, I will keep you waiting when it is necessary to protect our plots against the Spider Queen's favored—"

"Enough, Nimor," Mauzzkyl rumbled. "How do things proceed in Menzoberranzan?"

"Very well, Revered Grandfather. Crown Prince Horgar Steelshadow of Gracklstugh marches an army of nearly five thousand duergar on Menzoberranzan. The matron mothers have decided to meet the duergar in the field instead of awaiting a siege, since they fear the belligerence of other Underdark realms. I have, however, arranged for the crown prince's army to steal a march on the Menzoberranyr, and I also have command of a contingent of troops who can be turned at the right moment to help assure the outcome we desire. Finally, I have convinced the cambion warlord Kaanyr Vhok to bring his army of tanarukks against Menzoberranzan as well, though I am less certain of the Scoured Legion. Vhok may or may not show, and if he does, he has little allegiance to our cause."

"You intend to destroy the forces of Menzoberranzan in detail, then," Patron Xorthaul observed. The black-armored priest stroked his chin. "What if the Menzoberranyr prove more resilient than you expect, and defeat the duergar instead? Or Kaanyr Vhok proves unfaithful? It might have been better to lure a smaller force into your trap, Anointed Blade. Your first play is too risky."

"If I had presented the duergar as less of a threat, the matron mothers would have been sorely tempted to ignore them altogether. As matters stand, one of three results may come of the battle between Gracklstugh and Menzoberranzan. The duergar might win, it could be in effect a draw, or the drow could prevail. We're doing what we can to deliver Menzoberranzan's army into the crown prince's hands, but even if he fails to destroy the Lolthites outright, there is an excellent chance the duergar will badly maul the Menzoberranyr—in which case, the duergar may weaken our enemies so badly we can overthrow them ourselves. At the worst, if Gracklstugh is routed, well . . . other than the failure of our plan, we lose little."

"Remember, Patron Xorthaul, our strategy against Menzoberranzan is a strategy of attrition," Mauzzkyl said. "The city is too strong to take in one stroke, so we must bleed it to death with a dozen cuts."

"Menzoberranzan's wizards will certainly divine the existence of such a great army so close to their city," Patron Tomphael, himself a wizard, observed. "The matron mothers will recall their force, or reverse your ambush on the duergar instead."

"Our allies in Agrach Dyrr have helped us with this," said Nimor. "Gromph Baenre has vanished. The Masters of Sorcere are quite naturally testing each other's resolve and resources to determine who shall be the next archmage."

"There are many powerful wizards serving the city's Houses, Nimor," Tomphael replied. "They will not be distracted by an opportunity at Sorcere."

Nimor permitted himself a rueful nod and said, "True, but as we well know, House wizards tend to spend a lot of their time spying out the weaknesses of other Houses. So far, no one seems to have come forward to dispute the version of events I advanced to the Council."

"It would be no more than the better part of wisdom to set your plans with the assumption that your plots will be unmasked at the most inconvenient time possible," Patron Xorthaul said. "What will you do if some raw apprentice in some second-rate House happens to scry the approach of the crown prince's army, and the matron mothers recall theirs? They might stand a siege forever."

"Now you understand," Nimor said patiently, "why I went so far as to approach Agrach Dyrr with an open offer of alliance, and decided to risk bringing Kaanyr Vhok into the equation. We need the Fifth House against that very possibility, to admit Horgar's army—or the Scoured Legion—into the city, if it comes to that."

Mauzzkyl folded his arms and lowered his fiery gaze.

"In either case, we shall have them," the revered grandfather said, a smile of dark satisfaction twisting his features. "If Kaanyr Vhok betrays you, you still have Agrach Dyrr. If Agrach Dyrr betrays you, you have the cambion. I presume that Dyrr and Vhok know nothing of each other?"

Nimor said, "I thought it best to reserve at least one surprise against each of my ostensible allies, Revered Grandfather. It seemed wise to me to make certain that I would have as many options as possible, for as long as possible, in developing the attack on the city."

"Excellent. What assistance might we provide you?"

The Anointed Blade considered the question. He was sorely tempted to say none at all, and claim all the glory of the victory to come, but the time was coming when his ability to move from place to place would be limited by the role he played at the head of Menzoberranzan's army, and he needed help in handling Kaanyr Vhok. Besides, if the Sceptered One proved unfaithful, he could blame whomever had been sent to the warlord.

"We should gather our strength and be ready to strike when our allies play their part in reducing Menzoberranzan's defenses," he said.

"We do not have any great force at arms, Anointed Blade," Mauzzkyl said. "I will not commit the Jaezred Chaulssin to a pitched battle."

"I understand, Revered Grandfather." If they gathered all their strength in one place, the secret House would hardly amount to the numbers of a single minor House of Menzoberranzan—though the Jaezred Chaulssin could have an impact out of all proportion to their numbers. "I need one of my brothers to go to Kaanyr Vhok's Scoured Legion and steer the warlord in the right direction. My responsibilities in Menzoberranzan's army and my efforts to guide Horgar Steelshadow and the renegade Agrach Dyrr do not permit me sufficient time to look after Kaanyr Vhok as well as I would like."

Mauzzkyl nodded and said, "Very well. Zammzt, there is nothing left for you to do at Ched Nasad. I want you to go to Kaanyr Vhok and serve as our voice in his camp. Do whatever you must in order to keep his army aligned against Menzoberranzan, but you will answer to Nimor."

The plain-faced assassin replied, "Of course, Revered Grandfather."

He glanced over at Nimor, but did not allow his thoughts to show on his face.

"I approached the warlord through his consort, Aliisza," Nimor told Zammzt. "She is an alu-fiend and a sorceress of no small skill. She knows that I represent a society or order of some kind, so she should not be surprised to receive another of us."

Though I doubt she'll extend you the same welcome she gave to me, he told himself.

"When do you expect the Menzoberranyr to first encounter Horgar's army?" Mauzzkyl asked.

"Four days, I think."

"Do what you can to sow dissent and uncertainty, Anointed Blade," Mauzzkyl said. "The time for subterfuge and stealth is ending. The Jaezred Chaulssin leave the shadows and take the field. Destroy the matron mothers' army and bring your duergar allies to Menzoberranzan as quickly as possible. We will meet you there, and we will see if the Masked Lord favors us our not."

Nimor bowed again, then turned and strode away from the assembled patron fathers. Something would go amiss in his plan—something had to. One could not create such an elaborate collision of so many disparate forces without some of the components falling by the wayside. As best he could tell, though, the Jaezred Chaulssin were prepared. The longer he could keep secret the deadly maneuverings of his allies and his House, the better his chances for success.

Perhaps I will encourage Andzrel to appoint me chief of the expedition's scouts, Nimor thought. *No need to trouble the Baenre with irrelevant reports of armies on the move, after all.*

The dark elves of House Jaelre proved to be suspicious and ungracious hosts. Ryld had expected to be shown into an audience room of some kind, where they would meet a clan matriarch and bribe, threaten, or persuade her into allowing them to consult with the priest Tzirik. However, nothing like that occurred. Since they refused to surrender their weapons, the Jaelre drow ushered the company into a small, disused guardroom that had once warded the ruined castle's main gate.

"You will wait here until Tzirik chooses to receive you," the female commanding the watch told them. "If you attempt to leave this room, we will take that as a sign of hostile intent and fall on you at once."

"We are a high embassy from a powerful city," Quenthel said in response. "You mistreat us at your peril."

"You are slaves of the Spider Queen, and most likely spies and saboteurs," the captain replied. "Lolth holds no sway here, spider-kissing bitch."

She closed and locked the iron door before Quenthel could summon a suitable retort, though the fierce agitation of her snake-headed whip certainly hinted at the depths of her anger.

"Do we intend to remain confined here, like rabble locked up in a debtors' gaol?" Jeggred snarled. "I have half a mind to—"

"Not yet, Jeggred," Quenthel countered.

She paced back and forth angrily, her mouth working in silent fury. Pure ire fueled Quenthel with relentless energy. Confinement in a small room with her pent-up anger would be difficult for all of them.

Danifae watched her, then restrained Quenthel's agitated pacing with a gentle hand on the Baenre's arm.

"What is it, slave?" the priestess snapped.

"Your zeal is admirable, Mistress," Danifae said, "but, please, we must be patient now." She shielded her hands as best she could and added, *Remember, we may be watched.*

"She has a point, dear Quenthel," Pharaun said. "You don't want to start a fight against the very people we came to see. Your hard words and proud manner play better at Arach-Tinilith than on another god's doorstep."

Quenthel turned a look of such icy hatred on the wizard that Danifae put up a hand to steady her. Danifae herself shot Pharaun a venomous look, contempt twisting her beautiful features.

"Silence, Pharaun," the battle captive snapped. "Your smug arrogance and endless baiting play better at Sorcere. At least the Mistress has the strength of her convictions—all you have is cynicism."

Danifae studied Quenthel's face and offered her a shy smile.

"Save your anger for later, Mistress," the battle captive said softly. "Surely the goddess will be more pleased if you exact an accounting of the faithless after you've wrung the usefulness from them than if you destroy the tools required to serve her."

Quenthel allowed herself to relax. She drew a deep breath, and took a seat at a barren wood table on which a flagon of water stood.

"Fine, then," Quenthel breathed. "We will see what happens."

That, Ryld guessed, was about as close as Quenthel would ever come to admitting that she had been wrong about something. With little else to do, the company settled down to endure whatever wait the Jaelre chose to test them with.

Long hours passed. The night faded into an overcast morning, which then gave way to a gray, rain-soaked afternoon.

Studying what portions of the old castle he could see from the slitlike windows, Ryld came to the conclusion that Minauthkeep was not half so ruined as it first appeared. The Jaelre had cleverly repaired much of the ancient structure while leaving the outward appearance mostly unchanged.

Eventually, as the wait grew interminable, the weapons master settled back against the wall of the chamber and allowed himself to drift off into a light trance, Splitter bared across his lap in case he needed it quickly.

He was roused from Reverie near nightfall, when the iron door of the chamber abruptly boomed with three forceful knocks. The lock turned, and the watch captain of the previous night entered, with several more Jaelre guards behind her.

"You are summoned before High Priest Tzirik," she said. "You are to disarm yourselves here. The wizard must consent to have his thumbs bound together, and the draegloth will be manacled."

"I will not," Jeggred snapped. "We're not your prisoners, to be dragged before your master in chains. Why should we do for you what you lack the strength to make us do?"

"You came to us, half-breed," the captain said.

"Mistress?" Danifae whispered.

Without taking her eyes from the captain's face, Quenthel drew out her whip. Weighing it in one hand, she seemed to struggle with herself, then she tossed it to the corner of the chamber.

"Yngoth, watch over our arms," she said to one of the hissing vipers. "Strike dead any who would tamper with our belongings in our absence. Jeggred, you will permit yourself to be bound. Pharaun, you as well."

Ryld sighed and set Splitter on the floor, kicking the blade to within striking distance of Quenthel's vipers. Valas discarded his kukris as well. With a grimace of distaste, Pharaun stepped up and held out his hands. A Jaelre drow tied his thumbs together with stout cord, a measure that would make it very difficult for the mage to make the complex gestures and passes needed for many of his spells. Jeggred's large upper arms, the long ones with the wicked claws, were chained together, but his smaller humanoid arms were left free.

The draegloth rumbled.

"Be still, nephew," Quenthel said, then she turned to the Jaelre captain. "Take us to the priest."

The watch captain nodded to her soldiers, who formed up in a tight phalanx around the Menzoberranyr, swords drawn. They marched the company out of the guardroom and into the depths of the keep. The company was shown into a large hall or gallery appointed as a shrine to Vhaeraun, the Masked Lord. Ryld studied the temple with some interest. He'd never set foot in a place dedicated to any deity but Lolth. At the upper end of the hall, across from the entrance, a great half-mask the size of a tower shield hung from the wall, overlooking the shrine. The symbol was made of beaten copper, with two black disks to mark the eyes.

Two males waited for them. The first was young, dressed in black leather armor that showed off a well-muscled chest. A curved kukri was thrust through his belt, and a small green asp was coiled around his arm. His left leg was encased in an awkward harness of iron and leather, and he moved stiffly. The second was unusually short and stocky, with brawny shoulders and a bald pate, dressed in a breastplate of black mithral and masked with a ceremonial veil of black silk.

"The visitors, my lords," the watch captain said.

The veiled priest studied them. His expression was virtually unreadable behind the veil.

"Valas Hune, as I live and breathe," he said at last. "Well, this is a surprise. I haven't seen you in more than fifty years." He hesitated a moment longer, then strode forward boldly and clapped the Bregan D'aerthe scout on the shoulders. "It has been too long, old friend. How are things with you?"

"Tzirik," Valas said. He smiled back, his dour face stretching with unaccustomed enjoyment, and he took the priest's hand in a firm grip. He glanced around the chamber. "I see you have finally achieved the Return you were always talking about. As far as how things go with me, well, that will take some explaining."

Tzirik studied the company carefully.

"A Master of Sorcere," the priest said, "and another of Melee-Magthere."

"Master Pharaun Mizzrym, an accomplished wizard," Valas replied, "and Master Ryld Argith, a weapons master of no small skill."

"Gentlemen, if Valas vouches for you, you are welcome guests in Minauthkeep," the priest said. When he looked at the others, his face hardened, geniality fading into sharp appraisal.

"The draegloth is Jeggred," Valas said, "a scion of House Baenre. The lesser priestess is Danifae Yauntyrr, a highborn lady of Eryndlyn, late a battle captive. The leader of our company is—"

"High Priestess Quenthel Baenre," Quenthel interrupted, "Mistress of Arach-Tinilith, Mistress of the Academy, Mistress of Tier-Breche, First Sister of House Baenre of Menzoberranzan."

"Ah," Tzirik said. "We rarely have dealings with those of your persuasion, let alone a priestess possessed of so many impressive titles."

"You will find me possessed of more than titles, priest," Quenthel replied.

Tzirik's face went cold.

"Lolth may rule in your buried cities," he said, "but here in the night of the surface world, Vhaeraun is the master." He turned and gestured to the crippled male behind him. "In the interest of common courtesy, may I present my cousin, Jezz of House Jaelre."

The younger male limped forward.

"You are a long way from home, Menzoberranyr," he said in a rasping voice. "That, more than anything, spared you. The spider-kissers we feud with come up from Maerimydra, a few miles south of here, but we have not met folk from Menzoberranzan in quite some time."

He laughed softly, finding humor in some private joke. Tzirik smiled as well, but the smile did not reach his eyes.

"Jezz refers to the ironic fact that we are Menzoberranyr ourselves, or at least were, once upon a time. Almost five hundred years ago the wise and beneficent Matron Baenre ordered our House destroyed for the twin perversions of being governed by males and following the Masked Lord. Many of my kin died screaming in the dungeons of Castle Baenre. Of those who escaped, many more died in the long, hard years of exile in the lonely places of the Underdark. You must understand how ironic it is for a Baenre daughter to place herself in our power. If nothing else comes of whatever business you bring before me, Valas, you will have my gratitude for this." He moved closer and folded his powerful arms. "So, why do you seek me, Baenre?"

Quenthel kept her face impassive.

"We need you to commune with Vhaeraun," she said, "and ask your god a few questions on our behalf. We are willing to pay and pay well for your trouble."

Tzirik's eyebrows rose.

"Really? And why would Vhaeraun want me to do this for you?"

"You will, of course, discover what it is that brings us here, and what your god knows of it."

"I could torture you for a few years and discover as much," the priest said. "Or, for that matter, having agreed to ask the Masked Lord your questions, I might not see fit to share the answers."

"True, perhaps," Quenthel said, "though I think you might find that we are far from helpless, even with our weapons back in our chambers. Before we make a trial of that, let us see if we can reach an agreement of sorts."

"She's bluffing," Jezz remarked. "Why deal with these venomous creatures? Spare your friend if you like, but slay the priestesses at once."

"Patience, young Jezz. There is always time for that later," Tzirik said. He paced away, then looked back to Quenthel. "What is it you wish to learn?"

Quenthel squared her shoulders and met the priest's gaze evenly.

"We wish to know what has become of Lolth," she said. "The goddess refuses us our spells, and has done so for many months now. Since we do not have access to the magic she normally grants us, we have no way to ask her ourselves."

"Your fickle goddess is testing you," Tzirik said with a laugh. "She's withholding your spells simply to see how long you remain loyal."

"So we thought at first," Quenthel said, "but it has been nearly four months now, and we can only conclude that it is her will that we should seek the answer for ourselves."

"Why ask a priest of Vhaeraun?" Jezz asked. "Surely the priestesses of a neighboring city could be persuaded to intervene on your behalf."

"They have lost contact with the goddess, too," Danifae answered. "I came from Ched Nasad, where we had experienced the same silence as the priestesses of Menzoberranzan. We have reason to believe that all the drow cities throughout the Underdark are in the same situation. Lolth is speaking to no one, drow and lesser races alike."

"That would explain the retreat of Maerimydra," Jezz said quietly to Tzirik. "If their priestesses are powerless, they might be too busy with their own difficulties to cause any trouble for us."

"The facts would seem to fit," Tzirik replied. He turned his attention to Pharaun. "What of your vaunted wizards? Could they not summon up demons and devils aplenty and question them as to your goddess's mysterious silence, or use divination spells of their own?"

"We found that the infernal powers knew little more than we did," Pharaun said. "It seems as if Lolth has barred contact with the neighboring layers of the Abyss, sealing the borders of her realm against other powers." He raised his thumb-bound hands and made a small self-deprecatory gesture. "That is what I surmised from the reports of my colleagues investigating the matter, at any length. I did not do so personally, as the archmage has instructed me not to conjure such beings on pain of a particularly grotesque death."

Tzirik studied the Menzoberranyr, then paced over to consult with Jezz. The two Jaelre spoke together quietly, while the Menzoberranyr waited. Ryld surreptitiously studied the guards nearby, calculating which of them he could disarm in order to provide himself with a weapon if it came to that. He still wore his dwarven breastplate, and felt reasonably confident that he could wrest a halberd away from one of the guards before he was run through—though it might be a better move to use his belt knife to sever Pharaun's bonds as the first step in any kind of fight.

He was interrupted in his planning when Tzirik and Jezz returned to the company.

"I will intercede with Vhaeraun on your behalf," the high priest of the Jaelre said, "not least because I, too, would like to know what Lolth is up to. However, I think it is fair to expect a service for a service, and as you have approached me and not the other way around, I will seek Vhaeraun's guidance only after you have completed your task."

"Fine," grated Quenthel. "What do you wish us to do?"

"Three days west of here lie the ruins of Myth Drannor, once the capital of the old surface elf realm of Cormanthyr," Tzirik said. "During the course of our exploration of the ruins, we have come to suspect that a book containing secret and powerful lore—the Geildirion of Cimbar—is buried in the secret library of a ruined wizard's tower. We have need of the knowledge that is in the Geildirion, for it will help us to master the ancient magical wards our long-lost surface cousins raised about their realm. Unfortunately, demons, devils, and fiends of all kinds plague the city's ruins, and the tower itself is home to an unusually powerful beholder mage. We have sent two expeditions to the tower, but the beholder destroyed or drove off our scouts with ease. I have no wish to throw away the lives of more of my charges, but I would dearly like to possess that book. Since you seem to be the best Menzoberranzan has to offer, perhaps you can succeed where our warriors have so far failed. Bring me the Geildirion, and I will seek Vhaeraun's insight regarding Lolth's silence."

"Done," Quenthel replied. "Provide us a guide to this place, and we will get your book for you."

Jezz laughed softly and said, "You might not be so quick to agree, if you knew how dangerous the beholder really is. You will earn our aid, that is for certain."

At nightfall, Seyll, accompanied by a young drow woman and a pale elf maiden, came for Halisstra. The priestess of Eilistraee was armed and armored beneath her green cloak, a long sword at her hip. She wore high leather boots, and carried a bundle under one arm.

"It's raining," she said as she entered the cell, "but our senior priestesses say it will be clear later on, when the moon rises. Tonight we will go to honor our goddess."

Halisstra shifted in her chains and rose.

"I will not honor Eilistraee," she said.

"You need not participate. I am simply offering you the opportunity to observe and draw your own conclusions. You challenged me to demonstrate that my goddess is not a cruel or jealous one. I stand ready to offer proof."

"Doubtless you think to ensnare me with some beguiling enchantments," Halisstra said. "Do not think I will be duped so easily."

"No one will attempt to work any magic on you," Seyll replied.

She set down her bundle and unwrapped it. Inside was a large leather case, boots, and a cloak not unlike her own. "I have brought your lyre, in the hopes that you might honor us with a song if you feel so inclined."

"I doubt you will take much pleasure in the *bae'qeshel* songs," Halisstra said.

"We will see," the priestess said. "You've been manacled here for three days, and I'm offering you a chance to get out of your cell."

"Only to be returned here when you're done hectoring me about your goddess."

"As we discussed before, you need only offer Lord Dessaer an accounting of yourself to be free," Seyll said. She produced a set of keys and dangled them in front of Halisstra. "Xarra and Feliane are here to help me escort you safely to and from the spot of our ceremony tonight, and I'm afraid I must insist on keeping your hands bound."

Halisstra glanced at the other two women. They wore chain mail beneath their cloaks, too, and also carried swords at their hips. She had little wish to watch some meaningless drivel in Eilistraee's name, but Seyll offered her a chance to get out of her cell. At the very worst, Seyll's vigilance would not lapse, and no opportunities for escape would arise, leaving Halisstra no worse for wear. At best, Seyll and her fellow clerics might make a mistake that Halisstra could capitalize on.

In either case, she would at least have an opportunity to spy out some of the town and the surrounding forest, which might come in useful if a chance to escape came up later—and there was always the chance of that.

"Very well," she said.

Seyll unlocked Halisstra's manacles, and helped the Melarn priestess to don the winter clothing and cloak she'd brought. She knotted a strong silver cord around Halisstra's hands, and the small party left the palace dungeons and ascended into a cold, rain-spattered night.

Elventree was not really a town, nor an outpost, nor an encampment, but something in between. Ruined walls of white stone crisscrossed the place, hinting at the old ramparts and broad squares of a good-sized surface town, but most were crumbling with age. Many of the original buildings were nothing more than empty shells, but a number of them seemed to have been appropriated by the town's current residents, who had covered the old buildings with wooden latticework or permanent tents in order to turn the proud old structures into humble, semi-permanent woodsmen's homes. Great gnarled trees rose from the cracked pavement of ancient courtyards, and many structures actually stood well off the ground in their mighty branches, linked by swaying catwalks of silver rope and white planks. A handful of the town's original buildings still stood more or less intact.

Halisstra saw that she had been imprisoned beneath an old watch-tower. Across the square an elegant palace rose through the trees, illuminated by hundreds of soft lanterns. Lord Dessaer's palace, she surmised. The sound of distant song and laughter drifted through the air.

The priestesses of Eilistraee led Halisstra along an old boulevard that quickly carried them out of the town and into the dark, rainy forest. They marched for quite some time, the silence of the night broken only by soft footfalls on the forest floor and the constant pattering of the rain—which did indeed slacken noticeably as they went on, giving way to a partial overcast through which stars on occasion appeared.

Halisstra had had about all of the World Above that she cared to endure, but she occupied herself by quietly working at the knots of the rope binding her hands while keeping an eye on her captors, hoping they would relax their vigilance. Xarra, the drow, walked in front, while Feliane marched at the rear. Seyll stayed close by Halisstra at all times, either a little before her or a little behind.

"Where are you taking me?" Halisstra asked as the walk dragged on.

"A place we call the Dancing Stone," Seyll answered. "It is sacred to Eilistraee."

"The forest looks all alike to me," said Halisstra. "How can you tell one part of it from another?"

"We know this trail well," Seyll replied. "In fact, we're not all that far from where we first encountered you and your companions. They abandoned you, and haven't been seen since that night."

Halisstra took a sip from her own flask to hide the smile that flitted across her features. The apostate priestess had made a mistake, and she didn't even realize it. If they weren't far from where she'd been captured, it stood to reason that she could follow the directions of Pharaun's vision from there and have a reasonable chance of locating the Jaelre drow. Regardless of what else she accomplished that night, it had already been worth her while.

They came to a loud, rushing creek, its bed strewn with large boulders. Xarra crossed first, leaping lightly from rock to rock and continuing into the woods on the far side, keeping watch for any danger. Seyll followed, a few steps ahead of Halisstra, her eyes on the uncertain footing beneath her. Halisstra started to follow. The rushing water was loud, even though the creek was shallow and not at all wide. The moon slipped behind the clouds, momentarily darkening the forest floor.

Halisstra scented opportunity.

She quickly hopped two rocks into the stream and halted, as if studying her next step. Instead she pitched her voice low and began a *bae'qeshel* song, the sound covered by the noisy creek. Seyll continued to pick her way ahead, and behind Halisstra the surface elf Feliane stopped, waiting for her to cross.

It was difficult with her hands bound, even as loosely as they were, but the power of the enchantment was in Halisstra's voice, not her hands. Even as Feliane lost patience and hopped forward to aid her, Halisstra turned around and fixed her red eyes on the pale girl's face.

"Angardh xorr feleal," she hissed. "Dear Feliane, would you draw your sword and free me of these troublesome bonds? I am afraid I will fall."

The charm ensnared the young priestess easily. With a blank expression, she drew her blade.

"Of course," the elf murmured vacantly.

She drew the razor edge carefully through the cords on Halisstra's wrists. Halisstra glanced over her shoulder at Seyll and carefully moved to shield Feliane's work with her body.

"What's wrong?" Seyll called.

"Don't answer," Halisstra whispered to the girl. She kept her hands together and turned carefully to face the priestess. "A moment!" she called. "I'm not certain of this step with my hands bound. The next rock seems slippery."

Seyll glanced at the creek, then retraced her steps, leaping one rock to the next as she came back toward Halisstra and Feliane. Halisstra twisted to look back at Feliane, standing behind her with her sword drawn.

"Dear Feliane," she said sweetly, "may I borrow your sword for a moment?"

The girl frowned slightly, perhaps aware somewhere in the depths of her enchantment-fogged mind that something was not right, but she extended the sword's hilt to Halisstra. Again concealing the movement with her body, Halisstra took the blade in her hand.

"Here," said Seyll. The Eilistraee priestess reached the next boulder and set her feet carefully, extending a hand. "Take my arm, and I will steady you."

Halisstra spun with the quickness of a cat and buried Feliane's sword beneath Seyll's outstretched arm. The priestess gasped in cold shock and crumpled at once, slipping from her perch to fall awkwardly in the icy stream. She slumped down the moss-covered boulder and came to rest leaning against the stone, sitting waist deep in the rushing water.

Halisstra withdrew the sword and turned back to Feliane, who stared at her with dumb amazement.

"Seyll's been hurt, girl," Halisstra snapped. "Quick, run back to Elventree and fetch help! Go!"

The pale elf maiden managed only one jerky nod before she whirled and raced off. Halisstra leaped over Seyll's rock and dashed quickly over the path. Xarra, the younger drow priestess, emerged suddenly from the wooded banks ahead of her, returning to find out what had delayed the others. To her credit, Xarra took in the situation with a single glance. She raised her crossbow and took quick aim.

Halisstra threw herself aside, twisting in midair as she sprang. Xarra's quarrel hissed by her torso so closely she felt it tug at her coat as it flew past.

"You missed your shot, girl," Halisstra snarled.

Xarra dropped her crossbow and reached for her sword. She died before the blade had cleared her scabbard, spitted through the throat. Halisstra straightened and looked down at the body, her heart pounding. The stream sang loudly beside her, and the air smelled of rain and wet leaves.

What next? she wondered.

Her prized mail, mace, and crossbow were in Lord Dessaer's keeping in Elventree, and as much as she wanted to recover her possessions, it didn't seem likely that she would be able to without the assistance of the Menzoberranyr. Her best move would be to arm herself as well as she could, take what provisions she could from Seyll and Xarra, and strike out in search of the Jaelre. With luck she would find them before Dessaer's rangers found her.

Halisstra thrust the sword through her belt and ventured back out into the stream to see if Seyll was carrying anything of use. She splashed down into the cold stream beside the Eilistraee priestess, gathered her up beneath the arms, and hoisted her back onto the stone slab in order to get a better look at her gear. The armor was clearly magical, as was the shield slung over Seyll's shoulder and the sword at her belt. Halisstra began unfastening the mail, intending to strip it from Seyll's body.

Seyll's eyes fluttered, and she groaned, "Halisstra. . . ."

Halisstra recoiled, startled above all else, and somewhat repulsed to find that she was stripping the corpse of someone who was not quite dead yet. She glanced down at the stone and studied a coursing rivulet of blood streaming from Seyll's side to the foaming water of the creek. The priestess's breath sounded wet and shallow, and bright flecks of blood stained her lips.

"I hope you will forgive me, Seyll, but I have need of your arms and armor, and you will be dead in a very short time," Halisstra remarked. "I have decided to decline your gracious invitation to join your observances tonight, as I have pressing business elsewhere in the forest."

"The . . . others?" Seyll gasped.

"Xarra had the decency to die swiftly and without awkward conversation. The surface girl I charmed and sent running off into the forest."

Halisstra unbuckled Seyll's sword belt and dragged it loose, setting it well out of the dying drow's reach. She set to work on the armor fastenings.

"While I admire your determination to save me from myself, Seyll, I can't believe you didn't see this as a likely outcome of your attempt to convert me."

"A risk . . . we are all . . . prepared to take," Seyll managed. "No one is beyond redemption."

She mumbled something more and reached up to interfere with Halisstra's work, but the Melarn priestess simply batted her hands away.

"A foolish risk, then. Lolth has punished your faithlessness through my hand, apostate," Halisstra said. She pulled off Seyll's boots and undid the leggings of her mail. "Tell me, was it worth it, to follow the path that led you to a cold and pointless death here in this miserable forest?"

To Halisstra's surprise, Seyll smiled, finding some last reservoir of strength.

"Worth it? Upon . . . my soul, yes." She laid her head back and gazed up into Halisstra's face. "I . . . have hope for you still," she whispered. "Do not . . . concern yourself . . . with me. I . . . have been . . . redeemed."

Her eyes closed for the final time, and the wet sound of her breathing halted.

Halisstra paused in her work. She had expected anger, resentment, perhaps even fear or scorn, but forgiveness? What power did the Dark Maiden hold over her worshipers that they could die with a blessing for their enemies on their lips?

Seyll turned away from the Spider Queen, she told herself, and through me the Spider Queen exacted her vengeance. Yet Seyll died with calm assurance, as if she had escaped Lolth finally and completely with the ending of her life.

"The Spider Queen take your soul," she said to the dead priestess, but somehow she doubted that Lolth would.

🕷   🕷   🕷

"A swift march is our surest path to victory," Andzrel Baenre said, addressing the assembled priestesses.

Nimor stood to one side and watched the Baenre weapons master, one of only a handful of males invited to take counsel with the assembled females. All of the great Houses, and no less than sixteen of the minor ones, were represented in the hastily mustered Army of the Black Spider, named for the banners under which they marched. Nearly thirty high priestesses—at least one from almost every House, and in some cases, several high priestesses from the same House—filled the great command pavilion provided by the Baenre contingent, watching Andzrel like predatory cats while reclining, sitting, or standing as rank and opportunity dictated. Nimor and the other few males stood, of course. No mere male would be seated while a high priestess remained standing.

"We lead some four thousand drow soldiers and twenty-five hundred slave soldiers into battle. By all reports it would seem that we are evenly matched with the duergar army that marches up from the south, but we do not intend to meet the duergar in a fair fight, of course." The word "fair" sent a wave of chuckles echoing through the tent. Andzrel used a slender baton to direct their attention to a large map inked on rothé-vellum. "We can stop a force significantly stronger than our own by picking the right ground to fight for. The place we will halt the duergar advance is here, at the Pillars of Woe."

"If I decide that your plan has merit, you mean," drawled

Mez'Barris Armgo of House Barrison Del'Armgo. "Triel Baenre may trust in your judgment, but I intend to think for myself, boy."

A tall, powerful female, the matron mother of the Second House was the ranking priestess present and nominally in command of the entire expedition. Each of the Houses had contributed some number of its priestesses to command their contingents in battle, ranging from unblooded acolytes to first daughters and matron mothers. Weapons masters such as Andzrel and males—including Nimor in his role as Zhayemd Dyrr—commanded warbands, companies, and cavalry squadrons, attending to the endless details of organizing the army of Menzoberranzan.

"My cousin presents House Baenre's views, Matron Mez'Barris," Zal'therra Baenre rasped. "Matron Triel endorses the weapons master's battle plan."

Foremost of Triel Baenre's cousins, Zal'therra looked nothing like the petite Matron Mother of House Baenre. She was tall and broadly built in the shoulders, a strapping female with a remarkable amount of physical fortitude and a coarse, intimidating manner. She and Mez'Barris were two of a kind in physique, yet the Matron Mother of House Del'Armgo possessed a brilliant, vicious cunning that was nothing more than a sullen streak in the Baenre priestess. Mez'Barris fixed her red eyes on the younger woman, but did not respond.

Andzrel knew better than to speak while the two females sparred. He waited through a moment of silence before he continued the briefing.

"Here is Rhazzt's Dilemma," he said, "where Captain Zhayemd of Agrach Dyrr reported the duergar vanguard yesterday morning. It lies about twenty-five miles south of the Pillars of Woe, at the lower end of the canyon. Assuming the worst, we can expect the duergar to storm the outpost and force the entrance by sometime late today, perhaps tomorrow if we're lucky. Duergar are hearty soldiers and can march all day long, but they're slow, and their army will be burdened with a long supply train and heavy siege engines. Ascending the gorge will be difficult going. It seems that, in the worst case again, they should reach the Pillars in five days—more likely seven or eight."

"How do you know the gray dwarves haven't overrun the outpost already?" a priestess of Tuin'Tarl asked.

"We do not, Mistress Tuin'Tarl. The duergar wizards and clerics are preventing our efforts to scry the surroundings, a common tactic in warfare of this sort." Andzrel nodded to Nimor and added, "That is why it is essential to deploy a screen of capable scouts, to find out through mundane means what our wizards cannot see. Zhayemd of Agrach Dyrr is charged with the command of our reconnaissance."

Andzrel waited a moment to see if the priestess had any more questions, then went on, "In any event, our armies travel faster than the gray dwarves, and we have a much easier route. I would expect our vanguard to reach the Pillars of Woe three to four days from now. If we hold the upper exit from the gorge, the duergar will never break our defenses. As you can see, it is something of a race, and therefore we should make all possible speed."

"What plan do you have for battle, Zal'therra?" asked another priestess, the mistress of the House Xorlarrin contingent.

Nimor smiled at the remark. Zal'therra had certainly been instructed by Triel to rely on her House weapons master's advice in planning the battle, but the high priestesses naturally talked past Andzrel as if he wasn't even there.

"Andzrel will present it," the Baenre priestess replied, as if she'd just finished explaining it all to him and choose to allow him to show off her genius.

If the weapons master took note of the slight, he did not show it.

"We will build a strong, well-anchored line across the mouth of the gorge. A few hundred troops should suffice for this, but we will commit a thousand. The remainder of our soldiers will be held in reserve and secure various small passageways and flanking caverns in the vicinity." Andzrel set down his baton and faced the assembled priestesses, his face expressionless except for the keen glitter of determination in his eyes. "I mean to allow the duergar to come to us, and break them between the Pillars of Woe. When they have hurled their strength on us in vain, we will pursue them back down the gorge and slaughter them and their minions in heaps."

"And what if the duergar choose not to force the Pillars?" Mez'Barris asked, addressing Andzrel directly.

"The duergar are invading our lands, Matron Mother, so the burden of action is on them. If they decide not to try the Pillars, we will wait them out—our supply lines are much shorter than theirs. In a matter of days they will have to choose between going forward and going back."

Mez'Barris gazed at the map, considering Andzrel's answer.

"Very well," she said. "I want to see just how quickly we can reach the spot you have in mind. Extend the march by two hours a day. If we reach the Pillars of Woe in three days, we should have time to rest before battle is joined. I want our fastest forces to make a dash for the Pillars, just in case. There is no reason we couldn't have a couple of hundred scouts at the top of that gorge in a day and a half. Now, if you will excuse us, I wish to discuss with my sister priestesses the best use of our talents in the upcoming conflict."

Andzrel offered a shallow bow, and withdrew from the room. Nimor fell in beside the Baenre weapons master as they left the black pavilion, flanked by a handful of other officers. The tent stood in a large, round tunnel crowded with soldiers and pack lizards, banner after banner of various Houses stretching out of sight up and down the passage.

"Zhayemd," said Andzrel, "I want you to assume command of our vanguard, as Matron Mother Del'Armgo suggests. Take your Agrach Dyrr cavalry and make speed tomorrow and the next day. Our lack of information about the duergar army makes me nervous. I'll have some of the other riders join you, so that you'll have a strong company to hold the pass if worse comes to worst."

"I must consult with our high priestess," Nimor said, though he had no intention of doing any such thing. The weapons master, still under Nimor's powerful and lasting enchantment, would trust him anyway. "I believe she will support the suggestion, though."

"Good," Andzrel said as they reached the Baenre camp. He clapped Nimor on the shoulder. "If you find the duergar somewhere they're not supposed to be, report back at once. I want no foolishness out of you. You are the eyes of our army."

Nimor smiled and said, "Do not worry, Master Andzrel. I intend to leave nothing to chance."

Jezz the Lame crouched awkwardly in the shadow of a ruined wall, gazing across a small square at a large, round tower a stone's throw away.

"There," he said. "The beholder's tower. There's a flight of stairs leading up to the door, which we have previously found to be unlocked but guarded by deadly magical traps. You'll see several small windows in the upper levels, perhaps large enough for a small drow to slip through. We haven't tried those, though."

Ryld, who crouched just behind the Jaelre, leaned out to take a look for himself. The tower was much as Jezz had described it, surrounded by the sprawling ruins of Myth Drannor. After using Pharaun's magic to speed their travel to the old elven capital and resting a few hours to prepare, the company had spent most of the night fighting their way through the ruins.

Myth Drannor was little more than a great wreckage of white stone overgrown with trees and vines, but once it had been something more. The old surface elf city might not have been as large as Menzoberranzan or as infernally grand as Ched Nasad, but it possessed an elegance and beauty that equaled, if not exceeded, the best examples of drow architecture.

Ryld cast a careful glance to the rooftops.

"No sign of devils," he said. "Perhaps we've slain enough that they've decided not to trouble us anymore."

"Unlikely," Jezz said with a snort. "They've drawn back to organize another attack, and await the arrival of more powerful fiends before trying us again."

"In that event, we should take advantage of the respite to do what we came to do," Quenthel said. She too moved up to study the tower. "I see nothing that encourages me to change our plan. Pharaun, cast your spell."

"As you wish, dear Quenthel," the wizard began, "though I must say that I do not entirely agree with the stratagem of—"

Angry glares from every other member of the company silenced Pharaun before he finished his protest. He sighed and fluttered his hand.

"Oh, very well."

The wizard straightened and carefully spoke the words of his spell, the potent syllables ringing with magical power. An intangible wave seemed to roll over Ryld and the others. In its wake, Ryld felt strength and quickness drain from his limbs, and Splitter seemed to grow heavier in his hand, its gleaming blade suddenly dulled. Ryld was no wizard, but like any accomplished drow he had over the years armed himself with various magical devices and enchantments to increase his speed, his strength, the toughness of his armor, the deadliness of his weapons. Pharaun's spell temporarily abolished all magic in the vicinity, leaving Ryld without the benefit of a single enchantment, and the other drow were similarly affected. The strangest effect of all was the sudden inertness of Quenthel's fearsome whip. One moment the snakes hissed and writhed of their own accord, alert and vicious, and in the next they dangled like dead things from the weapon's haft.

"Stay close to me, if you wish to stay within the spell's effect," Pharaun said.

He licked his lips nervously. Within the zone of antimagic he'd just created, he could cast no spells, and his own formidable array of enchanted devices and protections were inert, too. The wizard readied his hand crossbow, and loosened his dagger in its sheath.

"I feel like I'm going up against a dragon with a dinner knife," he muttered.

Ryld clapped him on the shoulder and stood. He sheathed Splitter and drew his own crossbow.

"Yes, but your spell pulls the dragon's fangs," he said.

"Get moving," Quenthel said.

She looked more than a little uncomfortable herself. Evidently she didn't care for the unmoving silence of her weapon. Without waiting, she loped across the courtyard and bounded up the steps leading to the tower's door. The others followed, blinking in the light of the approaching dawn. Ryld made a point of keeping watch on the ruined streets and walls behind the party, watching for the return of any of Myth Drannor's monstrous denizens. The last thing they needed was a band of blood-maddened devils to descend on them while they'd suppressed their own magic.

At the door of the tower, Quenthel stepped aside for Jeggred. The hulking draegloth moved up and wrenched the door open, bounding inside. Masonry cracked and clattered to the stone steps. Quenthel followed hard on his heels, then Danifae and Valas. Ryld looked around one last time, and noticed Jezz hanging back.

"You're not coming?" he asked the Jaelre.

"I intend to observe only," Jezz replied. "Defeating the beholder is your task, not mine. If you survive, I'll join you in a few minutes."

Ryld scowled, but ducked inside. They were in a foyer of some kind, illuminated by slanting rays of dim light from holes in the ancient masonry. At the far end of the room, a second door stood. Once the foyer might have been a grand and impressive hall, but the tiles of the floor were cracked and split by deep green mold, and the proud banners and arrases that hung on the walls were little more than tattered rags. Pharaun stood close by, examining an intricate symbol clearly etched on one block of the floor. The whole emblem was a little larger than his hand, with a great complexity of curving lines and characters.

"A symbol of discord," the wizard observed. "If we were not protected by the antimagic field, it would have caused us to fall on each other with murderous fury . . . but we hardly need a symbol for that, do we?"

"The next room?" Ryld asked.

Jeggred was already by the door. The draegloth opened it and quickly bounded through, followed by the others, into a round chamber not unlike the bottom of a well. Several of the floors above had long since collapsed, burying the ground floor in rubble and wreckage, with great wooden beams protruding from the mess. Heaps of masonry taller than a drow impeded movement.

Ryld stared into the empty space above, searching for any sign of the monster that was supposed to lurk there. The others did as well, but all was still.

"I see no beholder," Jeggred said.

Ryld was about to reply when something above them responded in a horrible, croaking voice, "Of course not, fools. I do not wish to be seen!"

An instant later the creature lashed out at them. From somewhere high overhead, near the top of the ruined tower, several brilliant rays of magical energy—the deadly beams each of the monster's eyes could fire in order to wound, paralyze, charm, or even disintegrate its foes—lanced downward at the drow, followed by a great blue bolt of lightning conjured by the unseen monster. Ryld could not see the magic's source.

The rays and crackling bolt of electricity abruptly winked out just over the drow's heads, negated by Pharaun's zone of null magic. The creature tried again, bringing different rays to bear and incanting some horrible spell in its deep, droning voice, but those were no more successful.

Ryld aimed his crossbow up the shaft and guessed at the spot from which the rays had stabbed down at them, loosing his bolt with practiced skill. A squeal of pain overhead told him that he'd guessed his target well. Valas, Danifae, and Pharaun fired too, while Jeggred snatched up a good-sized brick in one fighting claw and hurled it up into the darkness with surprising swiftness. Not all of their barrage struck home, of course. Even if it had been visible, a beholder's thick chitinous hide could deflect many attacks, and scoring a square hit on the creature when it was garbed in invisibility was more than a little difficult. Still, a couple of quarrels struck home.

The beholder mage obviously comprehended the nature of the company's defense very quickly on its own. Instead of striking directly at the dark elves, it turned its deadly gaze on the wreckage of the upper floors. With one eye ray it burned through the base of a heavy wooden beam projecting from the tower's stone wall, and with another it seized the timber in a telekinetic grip and flung it down at

Valas, who was plying his shortbow to great effect. The scout threw himself aside just in time to avoid being crushed beneath the massive timber, but lost his balance and fell amid the rubble. Dust and the cracking of stone filled the air. The beholder instantly went to work on another wooden beam. In the meantime the creature changed its droning incantation and began another spell.

"We need to climb higher," Quenthel said. "The creature is above Pharaun's spell."

"Do you propose that I should jump?" Pharaun asked. He ducked a head-sized chunk of masonry clattering down from above, and took aim with his crossbow again. "The antimagic that protects us also prevents us from flying or levitating up to get at—"

"For Lolth's sake," Ryld exclaimed. *Sign!*

Valas slipped and scrambled over to one side, seeking a better vantage. The scout drew his shortbow carefully, and loosed another arrow. The beholder above let out a horrible screech. The eye rays winked out, and debris stopped falling from overhead.

The beholder retreated back above the next intact floor, Valas signed. *We'll have to go up and get it.*

Ryld studied the interior walls of the ruined towers carefully. Perhaps four of the lower floors were missing, leaving at least two or three intact above the ceiling of the highest floor they could see. At a guess, it was at least a sixty-foot climb, and the masonry was old and damaged. A skilled climber could make good use of the wreckage of the beams that formerly supported the lower floors, but it was nothing he cared to try.

I don't like the climb, he replied.

Nor do I, Danifae added. The creature knows we're protected by anti-magic. Will it expect us to abandon the spell in order to get to it?

"Possibly," said Pharaun. At a sharp look from Ryld he signed, *One wonders if perhaps we should have studied this situation at greater length before agreeing to the task the Jaelre set us.*

Pharaun, like the others, moved carefully across the floor of the chamber, peering upward.

The wizard craned back his head and called, "Ho! Beholder! As we are at something of an impasse, will you consent to parlay?"

Quenthel fumed.

"You speak for us, wizard?" she growled.

From the heights of the tower overhead the deep, rasping voice came again.

"Parlay? On what account? You have invaded my home, impudent fools."

"Pharaun—" Quenthel started.

"You have a book we want," the wizard replied, ignoring the high priestess. "I guess it's called the Geildirion of Cimbar. Give it to us, and we'll trouble you no more."

The beholder fell silent, evidently considering the offer. Quenthel stared daggers at the wizard, but like the others, she listened for the beholder's reply.

"The book is extremely valuable," the creature replied finally. "I will not yield it up because some whelp of a dark elf demands it of me. Retreat, and I will consent to spare your lives."

Quenthel snorted and said, "As if we expected anything different." She made a small wave of her hand to call the others' attention to her, and signed, *On the count of three, Pharaun will dismiss his spell. Danifae and Ryld—you will follow me up the shaft. Pharaun, when we reach the halfway point, you will then teleport yourself and Jeggred to the floor above and take the monster unawares while it focuses its attention on defending the shaft. Valas, you remain here and cover our ascent with your bow. Come up as quickly as you can once we reach the top.* The Baenre did not wait to entertain any refinements to her plan, beginning her countdown at once.

One, two . . . three!

Pharaun made a curt gesture and dismissed his spell of antimagic. Ryld felt the arcane power of his belt, his gauntlets, and his sword flood back into his limbs. He drew Splitter and ascended into the shaft, using the levitation charm with which his Melee-Magthere insignia was imbued. With luck, the sword's ability to disrupt enchantments would shield him from the worst of what the beholder mage could send their way.

Quenthel and Danifae rose alongside him, three black, graceful forms sliding smoothly up into the darkness. Pharaun moved up beside Jeggred and watched their progress, one hand on the draegloth's white-furred shoulder.

The ceiling of the shaft featured a circular opening at one side, cluttered somewhat by the remnants of the old stairwell that once climbed the tower. Ryld peered at the opening, expecting incandescent death at any moment.

The beholder mage did not disappoint him.

A brilliant green ray flashed into existence, lancing toward Ryld. He parried it with Splitter, and felt a tingle in the hilt as the greatsword destroyed the insidious ray. Beside him, Danifae yelped and swerved aside from another tremendous bolt of lightning that arced out to sear all three dark elves, leaving the odor of charred wood and ozone in the air.

Arrows hissed up from underneath, whistling past the weapons master as Valas fired at the unseen foe. Ryld snarled in defiance and willed himself upward with more haste. Another spell struck Quenthel—some kind of dispelling magic that snuffed out her levitation. She flailed her arms and plummeted to the floor below. Ryld reached out to catch her, but the Baenre was simply not close enough. She struck the floor at the bottom of the shaft after a fall of close to forty feet. Quenthel crashed into the rubble like a falling meteor, and vanished in dust and wreckage.

"Keep going!" shouted Danifae. "We're almost at the top!"

The beholder mage must have reached the same conclusion. A moment later, a barrier of solid ice appeared, walling off the top of the shaft and trapping the drow beneath it.

"Damn!" swore Ryld.

Danifae glowered at the barrier and said, "Maybe we can—"

At that moment, Jezz the Lame appeared on the floor of the chamber. He wheeled and hurled a spell back through the doorway, then slammed the door shut.

"Whatever it is you're doing, finish it," the Jaelre called. "The devils have returned in force!"

Ryld looked up at the sheet of ice covering the top of the shaft, then down again at the rubble-strewn floor. Quenthel lay half-buried in the shattered masonry, unmoving. Spells rumbled above the ice, sure signs that Pharaun and Jeggred had found their foe, but the creature's barrier had effectively cut the company in half. Abandoning the effort to get at the beholder mage might give the monster the chance to destroy the company in detail, but Quenthel was dead or injured below.

"Up," Ryld decided. "Going back is no good. Valas, Jezz, aid Quenthel!"

He came up beneath the gleaming white ceiling and struck at the icy wall with Splitter, using the sword's ability to rend enchantments. Razor-sharp shards of ice flew from the spot he struck, but the sword failed to undo the beholder's magic. Ryld cursed and tried again, with no more success.

Below them, the door to the tower boomed with a heavy blow. Valas quickly shouldered his bow and scuttled over the heaps of masonry and rubble filling the bottom of the shaft, heading toward the spot where Quenthel had fallen.

Jezz the Lame growled something and worked a spell, clogging the tower's foyer with a mass of sticky webbing. He mouthed the words of another spell and arrowed up into the air, leaving Valas and Quenthel on the floor of the shaft.

"Forget the priestess," he called to Valas. "Come, if you want to live!"

The scout grimaced in frustration.

"I can't climb and carry her!" he snapped as a second blow at the door splintered wood and bent iron.

The ancient door would not withstand another blow. Valas glanced up the shaft and down at Quenthel, and reached down and unfastened her House Baenre brooch from her shoulder. Her snake-headed whip stirred in agitation, and Yngoth actually struck at the scout, but Valas scrambled back and fixed the brooch to his tunic.

"I'm trying to save your mistress," he barked at the whip.

The scout moved close and grasped Quenthel under the arms, using the power of her own brooch to levitate away from the floor.

Meanwhile, Ryld measured the icy barrier in front of him.

"All right, then," he muttered.

He backed up, set his feet as best he could against the shaft's wall, and drew Splitter back for the mightiest blow he could muster. With a cry of rage, he struck the wall a tremendous blow, Splitter's blade shearing through the magical ice even as waves of excruciating cold washed over him. He ignored the pain and swung again, and again—and the sheet of ice cracked into a dozen pieces and fell away to the floor below. Without waiting for the others, Ryld hurled himself up into the beholder's lair.

Within a day of Seyll's murder, Halisstra began to wonder if she might have been better off going with the Eilistraee priestess and feigning conversion. It might have been a strategy unlikely to reunite her with her comrades, but it would have meant that she would have enjoyed shelter, food, and the opportunity to perhaps regain her equipment, instead of an interminable march through the freezing woods. As dawn approached, she could find no better shelter than a small, damp hollow surrounded by drow-high boulders and bare trees. Shivering, she shrugged off her stolen backpack and searched it thoroughly, hoping against hope that she had somehow overlooked some key implement or a scrap of food.

Seyll and her followers had not anticipated a wilderness sojourn of more than a few hours. They carried no more gear than Halisstra would have, had she decided to venture out to a well-known cavern a mile or two from Ched Nasad. They certainly hadn't equipped themselves for the convenience of their captive's escape.

With the crossbow she'd taken from Xarra and the *bae'qeshel* songs at her command, she had a fair chance of dropping any game she came across, but in her hours and hours of wandering she'd not seen anything larger than a bird. Even if she did succeed in killing something for her dinner, she had no means to cook it, and Halisstra was beginning to suspect that the forest itself conspired against her.

She was reasonably sure that she'd managed to keep heading west after her escape from the heretic. If Seyll hadn't been lying when she said they were near the spot where Halisstra had been captured, the Melarn priestess was no more than one or two nights' march from the small river Pharaun had described in his vision. Since the river ran south to north somewhere in front of her, it seemed a difficult target to miss as long as she kept moving west.

Halisstra tried to keep the sunset and moonset ahead of her, and a little to her left, since they'd be somewhat south of her at this time of year—or so she'd gathered from watching Valas navigate the woods over the past few days. Of course, she had no way of knowing whether to turn upstream or downstream when she did reach Pharaun's river, since she couldn't be sure that she'd struck the stream at the spot the wizard anticipated. For that matter, she was unlikely to know for certain whether she'd found the right stream at all. She'd already crossed a dozen small brooks in a day and a half, and while she didn't think any of them could properly be called a river, she simply didn't have enough experience of the surface world to be sure.

"Of course, that all presumes that I haven't been wandering in circles for hours," Halisstra muttered.

It could be that the most sensible thing to do would be to abandon the notion of searching for the Jaelre, and pick the straightest course out of the forest she could find. Sooner or later, she might find civilization again, and beg, borrow, or steal food and other supplies—or charm a guide who could lead her to the Jaelre.

She closed her eyes, trying to build a mental picture of Cormanthor and the lands around it. She was in the eastern part of the forest, she knew—so was her best course east, toward the rising sun? There was little on that side of the forest except for the human settlement of Harrowdale, if she recalled her geography. Or was she better off turning south? Several more dales lay in that direction, so her odds of reaching civilization seemed better that way, even if that meant she would have a longer trek to reach the eaves of the forest. North she ruled out at once, since she was fairly certain that Elventree lay in that direction. Any way she went, she would be turning her back on the Jaelre and her sacred mission, at least for a time.

"This would be easier if the goddess would consent to answer my prayers," she grumbled.

When she realized what she'd said, she couldn't help but glance around and put a hand to her mouth. Lolth did not look kindly on complainers.

She passed a cold, wet, and miserable day hunched down among the rocks of her small hiding place, drifting in and out of Reverie. More than once she wished she'd had the presence of mind to order Feliane to guide her to the Jaelre, or at least give up her cloak and pack before dashing off in a panic. Lord Dessaer's rangers were most likely on her trail, of course, and they would not show her much mercy if she fell into their hands again. Even so, Halisstra was beginning to feel that a quick execution by the surface elves might be preferable to a long and lonely death by starvation in the endless forest.

At nightfall she rose, gathered her belongings, and scrambled out of her hiding place. She stood on the forest floor, looking toward the direction she reckoned west, then south, and west again. South might offer a better chance of finding a human or surface elf settlement, but she couldn't bring herself to abandon the hope of rejoining her comrades. Better to try one more march west, and if she still hadn't found Pharaun's river by dawn, she'd think about giving up the effort.

"West, then," she said to herself.

She walked for a couple of hours, trying to keep the moon left of her, even though she felt it rather than saw it. The night was cold, and high thin clouds scudded by overhead, driven by a fierce blast of wind that didn't reach down to the shelter of the trees. The woods were cold and still, probably pitch black by a surface dweller's standards, but Halisstra found that the diffuse moonlight flooded the forest like a sea of gleaming silver shadow. She paused to study the sky, trying to gauge whether she was allowing the moon's passage to affect her course too much, when she heard the faint sound of rushing water.

Carefully she stole forward, trotting softly through the night, and she emerged at the bank of a wide, shallow brook that splashed over a pebbly bed. It was wider than any she'd seen yet, easily thirty to forty feet, and it ran from her left to her right.

"Is this it?" she breathed.

It seemed large enough, and it was about where she'd expected to find it—a march and a half from the place where she'd been captured. Halisstra crouched and studied the swift water, thinking. If she made the wrong decision, she might follow the stream into some desolate and unpopulated portion of the woods and die a lonely death of hunger and cold. Then again, her prospects weren't very bright no matter what she did. Halisstra snorted to herself, and followed the stream to her left. What did she have to lose?

She managed another mile or so before the night's walk and the cold air made her hunger too great to be borne any longer, and she resolved to stop and make a midnight meal of whatever supplies she had left. Halisstra shook her pack off her shoulder and started to look around when an odd whirring sound fluttered through the air. Without even thinking about it, Halisstra threw herself flat on the ground—she knew the sound too well.

Two small quarrels flew past her, one sinking into a nearby tree trunk, the other glancing from her armored sleeve. Halisstra rolled behind the tree and quickly sang a spell of invisibility, hoping to throw off her assailants' aim, when she happened to glance again at the bolt. It was small and black, with red fletching; the bolt of a drow hand crossbow.

Several stealthy attackers moved closer through the wood, their presence indicated only by the occasional rustle of leaves on the ground or a low signaling whistle. Halisstra carefully stood, still hiding behind the tree.

In a low voice she called, "Hold your fire. I killed the Eilistraeen priestess who carried these arms. I serve the Spider Queen."

Her voice carried the hint of a *bae'qeshel* song that gave her words an undeniable sincerity.

Several drow stalked closer, their feet rustling softly in the underbrush. Halisstra caught sight of them, furtive males in green and black who prowled through the moonlit forest like panthers. They peered into the darkness, searching for her, but her spell concealed her well enough.

She set her hand to the hilt of Seyll's sword and shifted slightly to ready her shield in case they found a way to defeat her invisibility.

One of the drow in front of her paused a moment and replied, "We've been looking for you."

"Looking for me?" Halisstra said. "I seek an audience with Tzirik. Can you take me to him?"

The Jaelre warriors halted. Their fingers flashed quickly, signing to each other. After a moment, the warrior who had spoken straightened and lowered his crossbow.

"Your company of spider-kissers came to Minauthkeep three days ago," he said. "You were separated from them?"

Hoping that Quenthel and the others had done nothing to make enemies of the Jaelre, Halisstra decided to answer honestly.

"Yes," she said.

"Very well, then," the stranger replied. "High Priest Tzirik ordered us to find you, so we'll take you back. Why, and what becomes of you there, is up to him."

Halisstra allowed her invisibility to fade, and nodded. The Jaelre drow fell in around her and set off at a quick pace toward the south, following the stream. She might have had no idea where she was, but the Jaelre seemed to know the woods well enough. In less than an hour, they came to a ruined keep, its white walls gleaming in the moonlight. The stream passed a stone's throw from the fortress.

I had the right stream, Halisstra noted with some surprise.

She'd kept her course for two nights and veered only a couple of miles too far to her right, it seemed. She thought about what would have happened if she'd crossed the stream and continued. The thought made her shiver.

The Jaelre scouts led Halisstra into the ruined keep, past watchful guards who crouched in hidden places and kept an eye on the forest all around. She discovered that the place was in much better repair than it seemed from outside. Her guards escorted her to a modest hall whose only furnishings were a large fire and an array of hunting trophies, mostly surface creatures Halisstra did not recognize. She waited for a long time, growing hungrier and thirstier, but eventually a short, solidly built male of middle years appeared, his face covered in a ceremonial black veil.

"Lucky me," he said in a rich voice. "Twice in three days servants of the Spider Queen have called upon my home and asked for me by name. I begin to wonder if Lolth wishes me to reconsider my devotion to the Masked Lord."

"You are Tzirik?" Halisstra asked.

"I am he," the priest said, folding his arms and studying her. "And you must be Halisstra."

"I am Halisstra Melarn, First Daughter of House Melarn, Second House of Ched Nasad. I understand that my companions are here."

"Indeed they are," Tzirik said. He offered a cold smile. "One thing at a time, though. I see you wear the arms of a priestess of Eilistraee. How did you come by them?"

"As I told your warriors, my company was attacked by surface elves some distance away from here five days ago. My companions escaped the attack, but I was captured and taken to a place called Elventree. There, a female who called herself Seyll Auzkovyn called on me in my cell, and sought to indoctrinate me in the ways of Eilistraee."

"A rather simpleminded notion," Tzirik observed. "Continue, please."

"I allowed her to believe I might be swayed," Halisstra said. "She offered to take me to a rite they were to hold two nights ago out in the forest. I found an opportunity to escape as we traveled to their ceremony."

She glanced down at the mail and weapons she wore. The naivete of the female still surprised Halisstra. Seyll had not seemed like a stupid drow, not by any stretch of the imagination, and yet she had fatally misjudged Halisstra.

"In any event," she finished, "I took the liberty of borrowing some things Seyll had no more use for, since the good people of Elventree confiscated my own weapons and armor."

"And now you would like to be reunited with your comrades?"

"Provided they're not dead or imprisoned, yes," she replied.

"Nothing like that," said the priest. "They asked me to provide an unusual service for them, so I thought of something they could do for me by way of compensation for my time and trouble. If they succeed, they should return in a day or two. The question is, will you be here to greet them?"

Halisstra narrowed her eyes and remained silent. The high priest paced over by the fire and took a poker from a stand by the hearth. He prodded at the crackling logs.

"The comrades who abandoned you to captivity among the surface folk told me a very unusual story," said the priest. "Doubtless you're thinking to yourself, 'How can I know how much they told Tzirik?' You can't, of course, so the wisest thing to do would be to tell me everything."

"My companions may not appreciate that when they return," Halisstra said.

"Your companions will never know you were here if you fail to satisfy my curiosity, Mistress Melarn," Tzirik said. He set down the poker, and lowered himself into a seat by the fire. "Now, why don't you start at the beginning?"

🕷   🕷   🕷

Ryld crouched in the thick embrace of a deadly, acidic fog, trying hard not to draw breath despite the fact that he panted for air. His skin burned as if liquid fire had been poured over his body, and ugly welts were already rising wherever his ebon skin was exposed to the air. To stay where he was invited nothing less than a slow, agonizing death, but the vapors clung to his limbs like soft white hands, impeding his every movement. The cursed beholder lurked somewhere in the chamber, but where?

A brilliant bolt of lightning illuminated the white murk, lashing out with a dozen crackling arcs as it plowed through the mist. The weapons master threw himself aside and fell slowly to the floor, cushioned by the clinging mists, as a mighty thunderclap shook the stones of the chamber and rattled his teeth in his head.

"Pharaun!" he shouted. "Where is the damned—?"

He instantly regretted speaking, as needles of hot pain filled his nose and throat.

"Against the east wall!" the wizard replied from some distance away.

The Master of Sorcere fell at once into another spell, rushing his words as he tried to cast as quickly as possible. Meanwhile the beholder mage droned its horrid spell-song, muttering the black words of half a dozen incantations at once. Lightning flashed again, followed by the whining shrieks of conjured missiles arrowing for their targets, and the cries, shouts, and curses of his companions.

Ryld finally reached the floor, where he found himself fetched up against one curving stone wall—the only landmark he could make out in the horrible mist. Without pausing for thought, he scrabbled forward at the best speed he could, hoping to emerge from the acidic fog before it burned the flesh from his face.

Goddess, what a mess! he thought, slashing and cleaving at the thick tendrils of fog with Splitter.

The beholder had been waiting for them to resort to magic to ascend the shaft, and it had scoured the company with every spell at its command.

"The devils are coming up after us!" Jezz shouted from somewhere beyond the burning fog. "Finish this thing quickly so that we can get what we came for and leave!"

Finish it quickly, Ryld thought with a grimace. That's a novel idea.

He surged forward and suddenly found himself free of the deadly, clinging fog. No one else stood nearby, though he could hear his companions battling in the mists behind him.

"Damnation!" he muttered.

Clear of the unnatural fog, it was apparent that the whole floor of the tower had once been a royally appointed suite of rooms. A thick red haze of dust on the floor might have once been a plush carpet, and the walls were finished in patterns of orange and gold tile to form the image of a surface forest with its normally green leaves for some reason rendered in reds, oranges, and yellows. Ryld coughed, his eyes streaming from contact with the noxious fumes. Evidently he'd blundered through an archway into a different chamber, but another doorway led out of the room on the far side.

"Where in all the screaming hells am I?"

Something screeched in rage ahead, and the room beyond the arch flared brightly with magical fire. Ryld hefted Splitter and dashed into the next room, right into the middle of a fierce skirmish.

Danifae and Jezz battled against a pair of lean, scaly devils almost ten feet tall, horrible fiends with huge wings who fought with razor-sharp scourges and barbed tails that dripped with green venom. Several lesser devils hissed and surged behind the two already in the room, pressing forward and looking for a chance to join the fight.

"The devils are upon us!" Jezz cried.

The Jaelre fought with a curved knife in one hand, and a deadly white spell-flame wreathing the other. One of the big devils sprang at Jezz and hammered its iron chains past the Jaelre's defenses, spinning the surface drow to the floor. The creature stooped over the dazed Jaelre and reached for his throat.

Ryld glided forward, feinted high to bring the devil's weapon up to guard its face, and crouched low to take off its leg at the knee. The huge fiend roared in pain and toppled, its wings fluttering awkwardly as black blood spurted from the horrible wound. Ryld moved in close and reversed his grip on Splitter to finish the monster on the ground, but it replied with a flurry of slashing claws and snapping teeth, while lashing its barbed tail at him so quickly that only the stoutness of his dwarven breastplate saved him from being spitted on the wounded devil's sting.

Ryld parried furiously, battling for his life, as yet more devils—a group composed of man-sized creatures who were armed with knife-like barbs jutting from their scaly bodies—swarmed closer, their fanged faces twisted in hellish glee.

"Dark elves to feast on!" they gloated. "Drow hearts to eat!"

"We've got to get out of here!" Danifae cried. "We can't hold them!"

She whirled her morningstar with skill and strength, dueling the other big devil and a pair of the smaller ones who snatched at her from her flanks.

"There's no place to go," Ryld snapped. "The beholder's behind us!"

He could feel deadly spells flying in the chamber behind him, the reverberations of thunderbolts and the soul-searing chill of slaying spells that made his flesh crawl.

This isn't working, he thought. We're split in two, fighting two dangerous enemies.

They needed to regroup and focus on one foe or the other, or abandon the field all together and try again later. Presuming, of course, that the denizens of Myth Drannor allowed them to retreat at all. More than likely, they'd all die here, surrounded and over-whelmed by endless hordes of bloodthirsty demons. Quenthel and Valas were likely dead already.

Enough, Ryld snarled to himself. We didn't come all this way to be defeated here!

He redoubled his attack, stepped inside the big devil's reach, and drove Splitter's point through the creature's scaly neck. It flailed violently at him, but it was dying, and its convulsions gouged stone and clawed at the air instead of mauling Ryld. The weapons master leaped over the creature's body to engage the smaller barbed devils already moving toward him.

Jezz rejoined the fray, pulling out a scroll from his belt and hur-riedly reading off an abjuration that blasted several of the lesser devils back to whatever infernal realm they had crawled out of.

Two more instantly replaced their banished comrades.

"We have to move!" the Jaelre cried. "The beholder is our enemy. The devils are just a distraction!"

Ryld grimaced again. If they tried to flee, they'd be pulled down from behind. Still, he started backing his way toward the door leading to the beholder, praying that the creature was not in a position to see them. He gave ground grudgingly, unwilling to blunder into another fight while one still raged.

To his surprise, one of the devils on the other side of the chamber dropped out of view, and another one shrieked as a serpent-headed scourge sank its fangs into the back of its neck. Struggling through the ranks of the devils, Valas and Quenthel limped into sight. The scout supported the badly injured priestess, warding her side with one of his kukris while she lashed and flailed with her deadly scourge.

Danifae and Ryld took advantage of the devils' momentary disadvantage to press home attacks against their immediate foes. Quenthel slumped to one wall, fumbling with Halisstra's healing wand at her side, while Valas drew his second knife and darted into the fray, slashing and stabbing the devils from behind.

"Hurry!" Quenthel gasped. "A pit fiend and a dozen more devils are just behind us."

Ryld cut down another of the barbed devils, while Danifae splattered the brains of a second across the chamber wall with a two-handed blow of her morningstar. In the space of a few moments, the dark elves cleared the room of devils. Jezz produced another scroll and quickly read off a spell, sealing the doorway behind Quenthel and Valas with a crackling sheet of sparking yellow energy.

"That will only hold the creature for a moment," he cautioned.

The Baenre looked around the chamber. The fall in the shaft must have hurt her badly. Blood caked the side of her head, and her eyes didn't seem to want to focus. One arm hung limp at her side, but she held herself upright.

"Where's the beholder," she asked, "Pharaun, and Jeggred?"

Ryld jerked his head at the archway behind him. Another spell rumbled through the air.

"Back there somewhere," he said. "The beholder—"

He was interrupted by the sudden, sickening awareness of an overwhelming presence approaching Jezz's barrier, something unseen that seemed to shake the very stones of the tower with its footfalls.

"The pit fiend comes," Danifae reported, panting for breath, her eyes wide with alarm.

"Go," Quenthel said, waving them forward with her good arm.

Without another word, the dark elves scrambled for the other exit, plunging into the next room heedless of the spells that thundered and crawled in the space beyond.

❁ ❁ ❁

Triel Baenre stood on a high bridge of House Baenre, gazing toward Narbondel. The creeping ring of radiance that slowly climbed the mighty stone column marked the passage of time in Menzoberranzan. The glow stood near the pillar's upper end, which meant that the day would soon be done. Not for the first time it struck her as ironic that a race that had been driven from the world of light almost ten thousand years in the past would have the slightest use for marking the passage of days and nights in the manner of the surface folk, when the night was eternal and changeless in the Underdark, but it had proven somewhat useful over the years to remember the endless march of unseen days in the world above. It helped in dealing with those who had more use for the custom, such as merchants who brought a few of the surface's more exotic and desirable goods down to the City of the Spider Queen.

Not that many of those had visited Menzoberranzan of late. War was hard on commerce.

The other question that came to Triel's mind as she looked out over Narbondel and the city below was somewhat less abstract: Who would be coming in an hour or two to cast the spells that renewed

Narbondel's fiery ring? The office of archmage still belonged to her brother Gromph, missing for more than a tenday, but the Masters of Sorcere would not permit the high seat to remain empty for much longer. She'd learned that several of the more ambitious masters already maneuvered for the post. Doubtless Pharaun Mizzrym would have been among them if he had remained in the city, but the errand to Ched Nasad had fortunately removed the hero of the hour from Menzoberranzan at the very moment that he might have put his fame to its best use. She turned her head slightly and spoke over her shoulder to the loyal Baenre guards who stood a respectful distance behind her.

"Send for Nauzhror," she said. "Tell him I desire his counsel on a matter of some importance. He may attend me in the chapel."

Triel made her way to the great temple of Lolth that lay in the center of House Baenre's Great Mound, her attention far from her surroundings as she contemplated the multiplicity of troubles that had descended over the city in the past few months. She was almost grateful to the duergar for providing her with a cause to which she could rally the Council, and through them the dozens of lesser Houses that comprised Menzoberranzan's strength. A victory in the tunnels south of the city would do much to restore House Baenre's preeminence.

On the other hand, another setback could be disastrous. Even if Baenre remained the wealthiest and most powerful House, the Council might see fit to remove House Baenre as the First House. None of them alone, perhaps not even any two of them together, could hope to defeat House Baenre, but what if all seven of the other Houses on the Council agreed that it was time to pull down the strongest among them?

"Lolth preserve us," Triel muttered, and shivered with true fear.

In terms of numbers of troops, magical might, and sheer wealth, the other Houses had always possessed the wherewithal to destroy House Baenre if they chose to unite against the First House. What they had never possessed was the blessing of the goddess for an act of such impropriety. If the Spider Queen returned her attention to

Menzoberranzan and destroyed the Second through the Eighth Houses for their presumption the day after they obliterated House Baenre, well, Baenre would hardly be helped by it. Without Lolth's wrath to deter the ambitions of the other great Houses, a unified attack against Baenre seemed more like an inevitability than a possibility.

The trick, mused Triel, is to keep the other Houses from settling thorny issues such as who would be First House after Baenre's fall, and tempt some of the smaller Houses with the places of the larger ones.

If Houses such as Xorlarrin or Agrach Dyrr could be convinced that they would advance with more certainty by supporting Baenre against a conspiracy of Barrison Del'Armgo and Faen Tlabbar than they would by turning against the First House, then House Baenre could withstand almost any threat from its lesser neighbors.

She paused at the door to the chapel, examining the notion with acute distaste. Could she really feel that House Baenre needed *allies*? The old Matron Baenre had not governed with anyone's consent. She had ruled the city because she was so strong no one could contemplate resisting her will.

Triel scowled and gestured at the chapel guards, who pulled open the doors and bowed before her.

Her sister Sos'Umptu awaited her in the chapel. Sos'Umptu had Quenthel's height, but took after Triel's thoughtful reserve as opposed to the willfulness of Quenthel or her unlamented sister Bladen'Kerst. Sos'Umptu possessed a calculated, deliberate maliciousness that she kept in careful check, never picking a feud she could not win. She briefly lowered her eyes, the minimal gesture of respect Triel's position demanded, then straightened.

"Any news from the army, eldest sister?" she asked in a soft voice.

"Not as yet. Zal'therra tells me that Mez'Barris has dispatched a small force to go ahead and seize a strategic pass in the path of the duergar army, which seems sensible enough. The rest of the Army of the Black Spider follows as fast as it may."

"It is a difficult situation. I wonder if perhaps you should have led the army in person."

Triel frowned. She was not accustomed to having her actions openly scrutinized by anyone, but if she couldn't survive the criticism of her family, how could she hope to cow the other matrons?

"Given the unusual situation," Triel replied, "I felt it wisest to remain close to the city."

"Perhaps. The problem is simple, of course—if the army is defeated, the blame will naturally attach to you. If the army triumphs, you have made a hero of Mez'Barris Del'Armgo."

"As well as Zal'therra and Andzrel," Triel pointed out. "I admit I have more to lose than to gain, but I will not second-guess myself now."

She studied the chapel, gazing up at the great magical image depicting the Queen of Spiders. While Sos'Umptu watched, Triel performed a perfunctory obeisance.

"You have not observed the goddess's rites as closely as you might over the last few tendays," Sos'Umptu said.

The goddess has not observed us for far longer, Triel found herself thinking.

She hurriedly thrust the blasphemous thought from her mind, horrified that something so irreverent could ferment in her head. She maintained her outward calm with the ease of long practice, returning her attention to her sister.

"We are confronted by yet another challenge," Triel said. "The Masters of Sorcere clamor for Gromph's replacement. House Baenre has placed archmages on Sorcere's throne as we liked for many hundreds of years, but this time, I am weighing the value of supporting the candidate of another House for the position. It might be . . . expedient."

Sos'Umptu's eyes widened by the thickness of a blade, and she said, "You seek my counsel?"

"As Gromph has absented himself, and Quenthel is far away, I find that the children of my formidable mother are in short supply. Very few females—and even fewer males—understand the lessons Mother taught us." Triel snorted in irritation. "Not even all our siblings, for that matter. Bladen'Kerst understood nothing but strength and cruelty, and Vendes was simply murderous. I have need of a sharp mind, a subtle mind, trained by my mother, and it occurs to me that I have allowed you to lurk in this chapel far too long." Triel moved a half-step closer and hardened her expression. "Understand that you advise me at my pleasure, and do not mistake consideration for indecision. I will brook no questioning of my right to rule."

Sos'Umptu nodded and said, "Very well. I think we should presume that Gromph has been killed. He would not have lightly abandoned his duties, and there are at least two reasons someone might have killed him. Either someone wanted to strike against the archmage himself, or someone wanted to strike against the leading wizard of House Baenre. If the former, well, whomever becomes archmage next will either be the culprit, or the next target. Why should we hurry to place a Baenre wizard weaker than Gromph into that position, when there is at least some chance we might lose whomever we promote?"

"I don't like the idea of surrendering such an important post to another family, but I like the idea of losing another skilled wizard even less," Triel mused. "Especially when we might forge a stronger tie with another House by allowing them to advance their candidate, who would then become the target of whatever power was strong enough to destroy Gromph."

"I don't understand," Sos'Umptu replied. "You seek *allies?*"

"It occurs to me that we might do well to ally ourselves with a great House of middle rank, perhaps two," said Triel. "It seems a sound precaution against any effort by the Second or Third Houses to rally the rest in common cause against us."

Sos'Umptu stroked her chin and said, "You believe matters have become as dangerous as that? Mother would never have agreed to such a thing."

"Mother lived in a different time," Triel said. "Do not compare me to her again."

Triel fixed her eyes on her sister until the priestess dropped her gaze. Sos'Umptu was clever, but not strong. If she joined forces with Quenthel, or maybe a cabal of the more capable cousins such as

Zal'therra, she would be a threat to Triel, but until then she could be trusted—within reason.

"What if Gromph's assassination was an attack on House Baenre," Triel asked, "and not simply a means to open the post of archmage?"

"In that case, we would be well advised to raise another Baenre wizard over Sorcere. Failing to do so would make us seem weak, and if the other Houses perceive us as vulnerable, they might be tempted to try the very thing you fear."

"Your advice does not provide me much comfort, Sos'Umptu," Triel grated. "And I am concerned, not afraid."

"There is another possibility," Sos'Umptu said. "Delay. Maintain that Gromph is still Archmage of Menzoberranzan for as long as possible. For that matter, spread the story that you have sent him off on a special mission and he will not be back for a while. The longer we delay, the more likely it is that events will make the circumstances of his disappearance clearer. If the Army of the Black Spider finds victory in the tunnels to the south, then your position might be strengthened enough that you can do as you will with the archmage's post."

Triel nodded. It was a sound piece of advice. Though she hated to admit that if Lolth continued to refuse her spells she might face a challenge for the leadership of the House, it didn't hurt her to begin strengthening her own ties to Sos'Umptu. She might need all the sisters she could get.

The door to the chapel creaked open, and a plump male dressed in elegant black robes entered. He resembled nothing so much as a housecat that had been fed too much, satisfied with his own superiority. Nauzhror Baenre was Triel's first cousin once removed, the son of one of her mother's nieces. His familiar, a hairy spider as well fed as the wizard himself, perched on Nauzhror's shoulder. He was accounted a Master of Sorcere, the only Baenre so recognized other than old Gromph himself, and was reputed to be an abjurer of some skill. Younger than Gromph, he had a habit of maintaining an insouciant smirk that made it hard to gauge what he was thinking.

Try as she might, Triel could not imagine him wearing the robes of the Archmage of Menzoberranzan.

"You sent for me, Matron Mother?"

"I am going to make it known," Triel said, "that my brother Gromph is engaged in a mission of great importance and secrecy, and will return to resume his duties as Archmage of Menzoberranzan in due time. In the meantime, I am going to allow the Masters of Sorcere to designate a substitute to attend to the responsibilities of the position. You will support the best candidate from either House Xorlarrin or Agrach Dyrr."

Nauzhror's smirk failed him.

"M-matron Mother," he stammered. "I . . . I had thought that perhaps I should assume the—"

"Are you Gromph's equal, Nauzhror?" Triel asked.

The abjurer might have been soft in appearance, but his eyes betrayed a hard and calculating mind—and a pragmatic one, as well.

"Were I the archmage's equal, Matron Mother, I would have challenged him for his title already." He thought for a moment, reaching up to stroke the spider that sat on his shoulder. "In time I expect to equal and perhaps surpass his skill, but I must study the Art for many years before I can call myself his peer."

"As I thought. Consider this, then," Triel said. "Whomever engineered Gromph's disappearance will most likely make short work of you if you presumed to call yourself Archmage of Menzoberranzan. The day may come when you realize your ambition, cousin, but that day is not today."

Nauzhror did not hesitate to incline his head and reply, "Yes, Matron Mother. I will do as you command."

"You are now acting House Wizard of House Baenre, Nauzhror. If it turns out that my brother is no more, you will hold the position in earnest, but for now I have need of your spells and counsel. Settle your affairs in Sorcere for the time being. I will have your personal effects brought here."

Nauzhror genuflected and said, "I thank you for your confidence in my abilities, Matron Mother."

"My confidence in your abilities extends exactly this far, cousin: Do not get killed," said Triel. "As of this moment, any male with the least aptitude for wizardry in House Baenre is yours to train. We need a cadre of skilled arcanists to equal those fielded by Del'Armgo or Xorlarrin."

"Such a collection of talent cannot be produced overnight, Matron Mother. It will be the work of years to match Xorlarrin's strength in wizardry."

"Then it is a work best begun immediately."

Triel studied the corpulent wizard and found herself hoping against hope that her House's future did not rest in his oily hands.

"There is one thing more, Nauzhror," she said as the wizard stepped away. "Consider it your first duty as House Wizard." Triel moved close and fixed her eyes on his, daring him to smile into her face. "You will find out what has happened to my brother."

🕷 🕷 🕷

Ryld barreled through a short, curving corridor, Jezz and Valas at his heels. Danifae helped Quenthel to stagger along behind them. The weapons master followed the corridor back to his right, and emerged into a large hall or ballroom of some kind. The beholder mage drifted there, a hulking monstrosity in the form of a chitin-covered orb six feet across, its ten eyestalks writhing as it hurled spell after spell at Pharaun and Jeggred. The wizard stood encased in a globe of magical energy, some kind of defensive spell that protected him while he dueled spell-for-spell with the monster. Jeggred stood immobile, his face locked into a needle-fanged grimace as he struggled to throw off the influence of some baneful spell or another.

"Persistent insects," the beholder snarled as it caught sight of Ryld and the others. "Leave me be!"

The creature floated back through an open archway, retreating to another portion of its lair.

Pharaun turned wearily to face the others. One side of his clothing was spattered with smoking holes, where some kind of acid had burned him, and he trembled with fatigue.

"Ah, I see my worthy companions have at last elected to join me," he observed. "Excellent! I was afraid you might miss the pleasure of hazarding life and limb against a murderous foe."

"What's wrong with Jeggred?" Quenthel managed.

"He's ensnared by a holding spell of some kind, and I expended all of my dispelling magic in my duel. If you can free him, please do so. I wouldn't want to be selfish, and keep the beholder all to myself."

"Shut up, Pharaun," Danifae rasped. "We have to finish the beholder, quick. There's a pit fiend and a dozen more devils just behind us, and we're about to be caught between the two."

The wizard grimaced. A dangerous light flickered in his eyes as he looked at Danifae, then at Jezz the Lame.

"If your magical tome is this much trouble, perhaps we should keep it for ourselves," the Master of Sorcere observed.

"Tzirik will not share the results of his divinations with you if you betray us," the Jaelre said simply. "Decide what is more important to you, spider-kisser, and do it quickly."

"Stop it, Pharaun," Ryld said.

He moved over to where Jeggred stood frozen, and laid Splitter alongside the draegloth to break the enchantment that held him. The half-demon blinked his eyes and scowled, slowly straightening.

"One problem at a time," Ryld continued. "Do you have any magic that can keep the devils off our backs long enough for us to defeat the beholder?"

The wizard answered, "No, they'd be among us in just a moment, and that would be a scene, wouldn't it? The—wait a moment, I have an idea. We won't keep out the devils. In fact, we'll let them in."

Infernal power crackled and snapped in the room behind them.

"That's the pit fiend destroying my wall," Jezz said. "Explain quickly, Menzoberranyr."

Pharaun began chanting a spell, and weaving his hands in the arcane gestures necessary to shape and control his magic.

"Do not resist," he told the others. "Ah, there we go. I've covered us all with a veil of illusion. We're all devils now."

Ryld glanced down at himself and noted nothing different, but when he looked back up, he saw that he was standing in the middle of a company of barbed devils. He recoiled momentarily, and noticed the other devils flinching too. Faintly, as though draped in a diaphanous gauze, he could see the natural forms of the other dark elves beneath their scaly exteriors.

"I can see through this," he warned.

"Yes, but you're expecting it," said the devil who stood where Pharaun had. "This should create no small amount of confusion for our foes, but we must move quickly. We want the devils to come upon us while we're dealing with the beholder."

The wizard glided across the chamber, following the beholder, and the rest of the company fell in behind him, hurrying after Pharaun as the howls of the pursuing devils rose in the corridor behind them. They climbed a spiraling stair and found the beholder waiting for them in what seemed to be a large throne room. The monster hesitated as the company burst in, cloaked in their devilish guises.

"The dark elves are not here," the beholder rasped. "Search the rest of the tower. They must be found!"

"I'm afraid you are mistaken," Pharaun laughed, and he hurled a blast of lightning at the creature that charred a dinner plate sized patch of its chitinous hide.

At the same time, Valas fired a pair of arrows that sank into its armored body, while Ryld, Jeggred, and Danifae broke into a charge.

The creature recovered from its surprise with incredible alacrity, whirling to flay the attacking drow with its deadly rays and spells. Jeggred was flung across the room with a telekinetic ray, while Danifae had to throw herself flat to avoid the incandescent green sweep of a disintegrating ray. Ryld got three steps farther before no less than three of the monster's thin eyestalks whipped around, spotting him at once and lashing out with more spells. A hail of incandescent bolts of energy streaked out to meet his charge, punching into his torso like the blows of a dwarven warhammer. Ryld grunted in pain, and stumbled to the hard floor.

At that moment, a flood of devils climbed up out of the staircase behind them, pouring into the room. In the space of half a dozen heartbeats, the scene descended into complete chaos, as the devils thronged the room, some turning angry glares on the beholder, others simply halting in confusion, surprised to find so many of their fellows already in the room.

From the floor Danifae pointed up at the beholder and screeched, "The beholder is in league with the dark elves! Slay it! Eat its eyes!"

The devils paused just long enough for the beholder to scour their front ranks with deadly spells, and they set upon it, flinging themselves at the monster. Rock-hard talons clawed and gouged at the beholder, while devils exploded under bolts of white fire or crumbled into lifeless stone beneath the beholder's eye rays.

Ryld had been about to leap up and engage the monster again, but he caught Pharaun's cautioning gesture, and feigned injury. The wizard's strategy was brilliant—let the beholder and the devils battle, and their foes might destroy each other.

"Weak-minded fools!" the beholder hissed. "The dark elves have deceived you!"

Still it wreaked terrible devastation with its spells and eye rays, trying to repel the devils' attack. The stink of charred flesh and the eldritch sensation of deadly magic filled the air.

A palpable sense of *wrong* flitted across Ryld's heart, and a hulking pit fiend climbed into the room. The mighty devil stood twice as tall as a drow, its torso rippling with muscle, its vast black wings mantling it like a cloak of ebon glory. It took in the scene with a malignant, measuring gaze, and Ryld's heart sank as he realized that the powerful fiend was not in the least deceived by Pharaun's illusion.

With one absent gesture the huge devil conjured up a great, seething orb of black fire in its claw, and hurled the sinister blast at Pharaun. The dark blot exploded in a tremendous explosion of evil flame that rocked the tower to its foundations, throwing Pharaun a dozen feet through the air and scorching him terribly as lesser devils and drow alike were sent flying like ninepins.

"They are right here!" the creature bellowed in a voice like a roaring forge. "Destroy the dark elves!"

The pit fiend started to call up another infernal blast, but Jeggred—still veiled in his devilish guise—hurled into the mighty fiend's flank, clawing and tearing with abandon. The great devil roared in rage, staggering under the draegloth's assault.

"Lolth's sweet chaos," Ryld muttered.

Which was more dangerous, the beholder mage or the pit fiend? The beholder still blasted any devil it saw, veiled drow or not, and most of the pit fiend's minions had fallen already. The pit fiend hammered and slashed at Jeggred, who stood toe-to-toe with the infernal lord, giving as good as he got.

The weapons master glanced between the two enemies, hesitated only a moment, and decided. Silently as an arrow whispering through the dark, Ryld scrambled up and leaped forward, aiming a tremendous cut at the beholder's round body. The beholder mage spotted him at once and blasted a bolt of lightning in his direction, but he tumbled aside and kept coming. Another eye fixed on him, and the beholder's drone took on a peculiarly horrid and deadly sound. Rather than wait to find out what spell the monster could cast with that eye, Ryld altered his path and bounded into the air, reaching out to sever the tentacle cleanly with Splitter's gleaming blade.

The beholder's drone broke in a piercing shriek of pain. The monster whirled to face Ryld with its jaws gaping, but the weapons master took careful aim and severed another waving eye before ducking down and scrambling beneath the bloated sphere of the hovering creature's body. None of the beholder's eyes could see directly beneath its own bulk.

Dropping to one knee, Ryld shortened his grip on Splitter, and thrust the greatsword up into the chitinous underside of the monster. Black, thick gore streamed down the blade, and the huge monster shuddered and shrieked again.

"Well done!" Jezz cried.

The Jaelre renegade commenced to bark out arcane words, his hands weaving in mystical patterns. He conjured up a seething missile of mystic acid that burned another eyestalk from the beholder's body as the monster rolled and twisted in agony.

Ryld yanked out his sword and rolled aside even as the beholder tried to crush him beneath its bulk, its jaws snapping at him. He found himself looking directly at the front of its body, where its great central eye had once gazed out from an armored carapace. The central eye was nothing but an empty socket. An old lesson came to the weapons master's mind: a beholder that wished to learn magic had to blind itself in order to do so.

The lesser eyes flailed and twisted on their tentacles, trying to focus on Ryld. The weapons master saw his opportunity and his target at the same moment. With one swift bound he drove Splitter like a lance straight through the empty central socket and deep into the creature's alien brain. With grim determination he sawed the greatsword in and out, side to side, while dark gore spurted and streamed from the awful wound.

The beholder gave one great shudder, its jaws snapped shut, and its waving eyestalks—those that remained—went limp. It sank slowly toward the floor.

Ryld glanced up and saw another devil closing on him, apparently having discerned his true form through the illusion, and he snatched out his short sword to gut the fiend as it threw itself on him. The devil knocked him to the floor, its foul blood pouring out all over him. Ryld gagged in revulsion and shouldered the jerking corpse aside, wrenching his sword out of the creature's midsection with his right hand while he dragged Splitter clear of the beholder mage's eye with the left. He shook his head to clear his eyes of the blood of his foes.

By the chamber's entrance, Jeggred sprawled to the ground beneath another terrible spell from the pit fiend, a roaring column of fire that blackened the draegloth's fur and might have incinerated him outright if not for the half-demon's native resistance to fire.

Jeggred screeched and rolled across the floor, trying to smother the burning embers, but as the pit fiend followed to strike at him again, Danifae appeared in front of it and dealt the monster a mighty blow that cracked its kneecap. The devil staggered and flared its wings for balance—and Valas buried three arrows in its back, sinking each shaft feather-deep between the fiend's shoulder blades.

Ryld started forward cautiously, preparing to engage the devil lord in his own turn, but Pharaun, blistered and smoking, rose from the spot where the devil's fireball had blasted him, and lashed out with a brilliant spray of iridescent colors that caught the pit fiend as it turned to confront the archer. A green ray carved a deep, black, boiling wound in the center of the pit fiend's torso, while a virulent yellow ray exploded with crackling arcs of electricity as it grazed the devil's hip. The monster staggered back two steps, and toppled, a smoking corpse. The chamber fell silent as the echoes of its thunderous fall died away.

Pharaun picked himself up gingerly, cradling one arm close to his body. One hand and part of his face were mottled and pink, abraded horribly by the fleeting touch of the beholder's disintegration ray, while his robes smoked with the fading effects of the dark fireball the pit fiend had conjured. The other dark elves slowly relaxed their guard, glancing around in some surprise to find no more foes on the field, and no life-threatening injuries among their number. Quenthel fumbled at her belt and produced Halisstra's healing wand, which she began to use to repair her own injuries, murmuring quiet prayers as she wielded the device.

"That," said Pharaun, "was not easy. We should have demanded something more from the Jaelre for our services."

"You came to us, spider-kisser," Jezz said.

He limped up to study the beholder's corpse where it sprawled on the steps of the ancient dais. Valas and Danifae followed, both keeping an eye on the stairwell behind them.

"Spread out and search for the book," said the Jaelre. "We must locate the Geildirion and withdraw before all the devils in Myth Drannor descend upon us."

Jezz followed his own advice at once, ransacking a set of dusty workbenches and cluttered scroll racks along the far side of the beholder's room.

Ryld sat down on a step and started to scrape the blood from Splitter's blade. He was exhausted. Jeggred, on the other hand, threw himself into the search, hurling heavy pieces of disused furniture aside and pulling down bookshelves. It occurred to Ryld that the draegloth was unlikely to find that the beholder had stashed a valuable book underneath the wreckage of a dusty old couch, but it seemed to keep the half-demon occupied. Ryld settled for staying out of the draegloth's way.

"Hold still, all of you!" Pharaun said sharply.

The wizard spoke a spell and commenced to turn slowly in a circle, studying the whole room intently. The rest of the company, including Jezz, halted their hurried ransacking and watched him impatiently. Pharaun continued past Jeggred, past Valas, and halted as he faced a blank wall. He smiled in a predatory fashion, evidently pleased with himself.

"I have defeated the defenses of our deceased adversary," he said. "That wall is an illusion covering an antechamber."

He gestured again, and part of the wall not far from Ryld abruptly vanished, revealing a large alcove or niche filled with ramshackle bookshelves cluttered with various old tomes and scrolls. Jezz hopped awkwardly to the bookshelf and started rifling through the titles, shoving each into a satchel at his hip.

"Ryld, Jeggred, keep watch," said Quenthel. She stood straighter, and the dazed look in her eyes was gone, but she frowned as she replaced the healing wand in her pack. "Valas, tidy up the beholder's gold and jewels. There's no point in leaving the loot here, and one never knows when it might be helpful." She looked over at the Jaelre sorcerer, who stood holding a great tome covered in green scales. "Well, Master Jezz, is that the book you wished to recover?"

Jezz blew dust from the cover and ran his slim fingers over the rough leather. He smiled, his handsome face twisting with glee.

"The Geildirion," he breathed. "Yes, this is the tome. I have what we came for."

"Good," said Quenthel. "Let's get out of here while we can. I think I've had all I can stand of this place."

Chapter

SEVENTEEN

Halisstra sat in a window bench, alone in the apartment set aside for her, and plucked idly at the strings of her dragonbone lyre. She'd been confined to the room for two days, and she found herself growing more than a little weary of incarceration.

Whatever I manage to find in this whole venture, she promised herself, *I will not be locked up again.*

She had expected torture, magical compulsion, or worse during her interrogation, but Tzirik seemed to have taken her at her word. More than a few drow would have indulged themselves in the opportunity to torture a prisoner regardless of whether she was being truthful or not, leading Halisstra to wonder if Tzirik was waiting for word of Quenthel and the others before doing something that might anger them. Halisstra didn't think the Mistress of Arach-Tinilith and her comrades had managed to cow the entire House, but it was entirely possible that their competence had persuaded Tzirik not to look for trouble without good cause.

She looked out the narrow, barred window. Dawn was fast approaching. The sky was already growing painfully bright in the east, though the sun had not yet risen. Halisstra could make out the endless green forest of Cormanthor, rolling away from her for mile after mile.

A knock at the door startled her, followed by the jingling of keys in the lock. She looked around and stood as Tzirik entered the room, dressed in a resplendent high-collared coat of red and black.

"Mistress Melarn," he said, offering an indulgent bow, "your comrades have returned. If you'll come with me, we shall see whether they had some good reason for abandoning you in the wilds of the World Above."

Halisstra set down her lyre and asked, "Were they successful?"

"In fact, they were, which is why I intend to set you at your liberty now. Had they failed, I'd planned to use you as a hostage to compel them to try again."

She snorted in amusement, and the priest escorted her from the room. He led her through the elegant pale halls and corridors of Minauthkeep. A pair of Jaelre warriors trailed them, dressed in cuirasses dyed a mottled green and brown, short swords at their hips. They came to a small chapel, decorated in the colors of Vhaeraun, and there they found Quenthel, Danifae, and the rest of the company waiting.

"I see you have survived the rigors of Myth Drannor and returned to tell the tale," Tzirik said by way of a greeting. "As you see, it seems I have found something of yours, just as you have found something of mine."

Halisstra studied the faces of her former companions as she appeared. Most showed some degree or another of surprise—a raised eyebrow, an exchange of glances. Ryld offered her a warm smile before dropping his gaze and shifting his feet nervously, while Danifae actually came forward to clasp her hand.

"Mistress Melarn," she said. "We thought you lost."

"I was," Halisstra replied.

She was surprised to find how relieved she was to be back among her former companions—though they were interlopers from a rival city—and her scheming battle captive. Danifae might not have been Halisstra's ornament anymore, but the binding spell was still there, making her the only ally Halisstra had left in the world.

"Where have you been?" Quenthel asked.

"I was subjected to several days worth of effort to convert me to the worship of Eilistraee, if you can believe such a thing," Halisstra answered. "Lolth granted me an opportunity to slay two of the Eilistraeen clerics and escape."

Though her heart glowed with dark pride at her accomplishment, Halisstra found herself feeling a bit disappointed by the results of her treachery. She was no stranger to the traitor's dark art, but it seemed as if she had only managed to do what was expected of her.

"Undoubtedly the surface folk set you free to see what you were up to," Quenthel said. "It's an old trick."

"So we thought, too," Tzirik said. "However, we investigated Mistress Melarn's story and found it to be true. It's almost comical, the naivete of our sisters in Eilistraee's worship." He paused and rubbed his hands together. "Be that as it may, Jezz informs me that you helped him recover the tome we needed."

"We *helped* him?" Jeggred growled.

"His task was to bring back the book," Tzirik replied, "not to battle the denizens of Myth Drannor."

"You have your book," Quenthel said. Ignoring Jeggred's snarl, she folded her arms and fixed her eyes on Tzirik. "Are you ready to fulfill your end of the bargain?"

"I have already done so," the priest replied. He glanced up at the bronze image high on the wall, and made a small genuflection. "Whether or not you returned alive, I intended to consult with the Masked Lord and find out for myself what takes Lolth from you. Your story made me quite curious."

Quenthel virtually ground her teeth in frustration.

"What did you learn, then?" she managed.

Tzirik savored his knowledge, responding with a deliberate smirk as he paced away from the company and took a seat on a small dais that stood to one side of the chapel.

He steepled his fingers together and said, "In all essentials your story is true. Lolth does not grant her priestesses spells, nor does she reply to any entreaties."

"We already knew as much," Pharaun observed.

"But I did not," the priest answered. "In any event, it seems that Lolth has, in some manner, barricaded herself within her infernal domain. She denies contact not only to her priestesses, but all other beings both mortal and divine, which would explain why the demons you conjured up to question about the Spider Queen's doings were unable to assist you."

The Menzoberranyr stood silent, considering Tzirik's answer. Halisstra was puzzled, as well.

"Why would the goddess do this?" she wondered aloud.

"In the spirit of candor, I will admit that Vhaeraun either does not know or does not wish for me to know," Tzirik said. He fixed his cold gaze on Halisstra. "For the moment, divine capriciousness seems as good an explanation as any."

"Is she . . . alive?" Ryld asked quietly. Quenthel and the other priestesses turned angry glares on the weapons master, but he ignored them and went on. "What I mean to say is, would we know if she had been slain by another god, or sickened, or imprisoned against her will?"

"If only we were so lucky," Tzirik said, laughing. "No, Lolth still lives, however you might define that for a goddess. As to whether she has sealed herself into the Demonweb Pits, or been sealed in by another power, Vhaeraun did not say."

"When will this condition end?" Halisstra asked.

"Again, Vhaeraun either does not know or does not wish for me to know," Tzirik said. "The better question might be, will it end? The answer to that is yes, it will end in time, but before you take too much comfort in that I must remind you that a goddess may have a very different sense of what we would consider to be a reasonable wait. The Masked Lord might have been referring to something that would happen tomorrow, next month, next year, or perhaps a hundred years from now."

"We can't wait that long," Quenthel murmured. Her expression was distant, fixed on events in faraway Menzoberranzan. "A resolution must be reached soon."

"Take up the worship of a more caring deity, then," Tzirik replied. "If you're interested, I would be happy to discourse at length on the virtues of the Masked Lord."

Quenthel bristled, but held her tongue—a feat of remarkable self-control for the Baenre priestess.

"I decline," she said. "Does the Masked Lord have any other advice for us, priest?"

"In fact, he does," Tzirik replied. He shifted in his seat, leaning forward to convey his point to Quenthel. "These were the exact words he spoke to me, so take note of them. 'The children of the Spider Queen should seek her for answers.'"

"But we have," Halisstra cried. "All of us, but she does not hear us."

"I don't think that's what he meant," Danifae said. "I think Vhaeraun is suggesting that we won't learn anything more unless we go to the Demonweb Pits ourselves, and beseech the goddess in person."

Tzirik remained silent and watched the Menzoberranyr. Quenthel paced in a small circle, considering the idea.

"The Spider Queen requires a certain amount of initiative and self-reliance in her priestesses," the Mistress of Arach-Tinilith said, "but she also demands obedience. To go before her in her divine abode in the expectation of answers . . . Lolth does not smile on such effrontery."

Halisstra fell silent, thinking furiously over what Tzirik suggested. Ventures into other planes of existence were not unknown, of course. Pharaun's spell had carried the company across the Plane of Shadow, after all, and there were many more universes that mortals armed with the right magic could reach, a multitude of heavens and hells, wonders and terrors beyond the confines of the physical world, but the notion of attempting such a journey without Lolth's explicit invitation terrified Halisstra.

"The penalties for failing to understand the goddess's will in this matter would be severe indeed," Halisstra said.

"Have we not just heard the goddess's will?" Danifae asked. "She led us to this place and this question through her silence, just as surely as if she had placed the commands directly in our hearts. She might be angered if we fail to do this."

Halisstra was accustomed to a feeling of certainty when it came to interpreting the Spider Queen's wishes. Before the divine silence had fallen over the priestesses of Lolth, she'd known the rare touch of the goddess's whispers in her mind. It didn't happen often, of course—she was only one priestess, and Lolth was served by uncounted thousands—but she knew what it felt like to understand to the depths of her soul what the Spider Queen wished, and how she could accomplish it. Halisstra felt nothing. Lolth's will, evidently, was that she should figure it out for herself.

Halisstra glanced up, where the bronze mask of Vhaeraun hung over a black altar. The foreignness of the place seemed palpable, a tangible expression of everything she had lost. Instead of standing before the ancient altar in the proud temple of House Melarn, Lolth's divine certitude thrumming in her very soul as she performed the rites of sacrifice and abasement the Spider Queen demanded, she stood alone, lost, an interloper in the temple of a pretender god, groping blindly for a hint of Lolth's intentions for her.

She imagined standing before Lolth, her soul naked to her goddess, her eyes blasted by the sight of Lolth's dark glory, her ears scoured by the sound of the Spider Queen's sibilant voice. Perhaps it was effrontery to think that Lolth would erase her doubts, supply answers for her questions and a balm for her wounded heart, but Halisstra discovered that she did not care. If Lolth chose to discard her, to punish her, then she would, but then why had she destroyed Ched Nasad and House Melarn if not to bring Halisstra before her and receive her plea?

"I agree with Danifae," she said at last. "I cannot see what the point of this has been, other than to summon us before the goddess's throne. We will find our answers in her presence."

Quenthel nodded slowly and said, "I read her will in the same way, sisters. We must go to the Demonweb Pits."

Ryld and Valas exchanged worried looks.

"A sojourn to the sixty-sixth layer of the Abyss," Pharaun observed. "Well, I have dreamed of the place. It would be interesting to see if the reality matches my dream from years ago, though I have to say, I do not relish the thought of meeting Lolth in person. She minced my soul to pieces when I had that vision. It took me months to recover."

"Perhaps we should return to Menzoberranzan and report what we have learned before we consider anything rash?" Ryld asked, clearly alarmed by the prospect of descending into the infernal realms.

"Now that I understand the goddess's will, I do not wish to delay in obeying it," Quenthel said. "Pharaun can use his sending spell to apprise Gromph of our intentions."

"More to the point," Valas said, "how exactly does one get to the Demonweb Pits?"

"Worship Lolth all your life," Quenthel replied, a dark look clouding her eyes, "then die."

Halisstra glanced at the high priestess, then looked at the scout and said, "Were the goddess granting us our spells, we could do it easily enough. Without them, it is not so easy. Pharaun?"

The wizard wrung his hands.

"I will learn the proper spells at the first opportunity," he said. "I suppose I will have to locate a wizard of some accomplishment who happens to know the right spells, and persuade him to share one with me."

"That will not be necessary, Master Pharaun," Tzirik said. He stood up from his seat and descended the dais, powerful and confident. "As it so happens, my god has not seen fit to deprive me of my spells. I have an interest in seeing for myself what transpires in Lolth's domain. We can leave as soon as tonight, if you like."

🕷   🕷   🕷

Company by company, the Army of the Black Spider marched proudly into the open cavern behind the Pillars of Woe. It was nothing compared to the vast cavern of Menzoberranzan, or the incomprehensible gulf of the Darklake, but the plain at the head of the gorge was still impressive, an asymmetrical space perhaps half a mile across, its ceiling rising a couple of hundred feet overhead. Innumerable columns supported its roof, and shelflike side caverns twisted away on all sides like highways beckoning in the dark.

Nimor surveyed the place from astride his war-lizard, watching as the great Houses of Menzoberranzan filed into the cavern, forming up in glittering squares beneath a dozen different banners. He'd had more than two days to reconnoiter the various crevices, caves, and passages leading to the open spot. The strategic value of the Pillars of Woe was obvious. Only one road lead south through a torturous canyon, yet several tunnels met where he'd led the drow, each leading into Menzoberranzan's Dark Dominion.

"A good place for a battle," he said, nodding to himself with satisfaction.

His mount, vicious and stupid beast that it was, still seemed to dully sense the impending conflict. It hissed and pawed at the pebble-strewn floor, its tail twitching in agitation.

Nimor waited near the center of the scout line holding the gap between the Pillars, at the head of a force of almost a hundred Agrach Dyrr riders. Those among his scout force who had any other House allegiance lay sprawled among the rocks and crevices of the gorge below, where Nimor and his men had slaughtered them soon after reaching the Pillars of Woe.

Nimor ached to go riding up to greet Mez'Barris Armgo, Andzrel Baenre, and the rest of the army's priestesses and commanders. He could see their pavilion, already rising in the center of the cavern.

The difficulty with a betrayal spanning a whole battlefield, he thought, is that one simply can't be everywhere at once to savor the moment in its entirety.

He noted a lean runner-lizard pelting from the command pavilion toward where his company waited.

"It seems I am wanted, lads," he called to the Agrach Dyrr soldiers waiting behind him. "You know what to do. Wait for the signal. When it comes, hold nothing back."

Nimor kicked his war-lizard into motion and rode back a short distance to meet the messenger. The rider was a young fellow in the livery of House Baenre—no doubt a favored nephew or cousin, given a relatively safe task in order to gain a blooding without too much risk. He wore no helmet, allowing his hair to stream out behind him like a mane. A bright red banner fluttered from a harness secured to his saddle.

"You are Captain Zhayemd?" he called, slowing his lizard to greet Nimor.

"I am."

"Your presence is requested at the command pavilion immediately, sir. Matron Del'Armgo wants to know where the gray dwarves are, and how best to dispose the troops."

"I see," Nimor replied. "Well, ride on back and tell her I'll be along presently."

"With respect, sir, I am to—"

Three great horn blasts, two short followed by one long, bellowed up from the space between the Pillars of Woe, echoing so loudly it seemed the rock itself had given voice to the cry. The messenger broke off and twisted his mount around, padding past Nimor to peer back toward the Pillars.

"Lolth's wrath, what was that?" he said.

"That," said Nimor, "would be the signal for the duergar attack."

From the depths of the gorge beneath the Pillars of Woe came the ground-shaking rumble of an army on the move. Below Nimor's line of scouts, hundreds of duergar lizard riders suddenly rose from beneath carefully arranged blankets of camouflage and pelted up and into the gap Nimor's scouts were supposed to hold. Behind the duergar cavalry, rank upon rank of duergar infantry ran forward, shouting their uncouth war cries, hammers and axes raised high. The Agrach Dyrr riders scrambled to their saddles, taking position to bottle up the charge between the mammoth columns of rock—and, as arranged, they wheeled in unison and dashed to one side, leaving the line unguarded.

"The Agrach Dyrr! They betray us!" the messenger shouted, horror and shock on his face.

He wrenched his mount around, but Nimor leaned out from his saddle and ran the boy through. The young Baenre clutched at his wound, swaying, and toppled from the saddle. Nimor slapped his sword against the lizard's rump and sent the beast bolting off back into the main cavern, the dead messenger dragging behind it with his feet tangled in the stirrups.

Nimor spurred his mount up onto an uneven shelf of rock about fifteen feet above the cavern floor, overlooking the Pillars. From that vantage he could see most of the cavern.

"A good view of the fray, my prince!" he called. "What a magnificent day for your triumph, eh?"

"I'll tell you in a quarter-hour if we have a victory or not."

From the shadows at the back of the ledge, Horgar Steelshadow emerged. He and his personal guards were warded by a well-crafted illusion, invisible to anyone below, unless one knew precisely where to find them.

"Do not come closer, Nimor," the crown prince said. "I do not wish someone below to notice you disappearing into a wall, and become overly curious about what might be up here."

"Surely you mean to join the battle, Prince Horgar? I know you are a dwarf of no small valor."

"I will venture into the fray when I'm certain I will not need to issue any more orders, Nimor. In another few moments you won't be able to hear a fellow shouting in your ear."

Nimor turned his attention back to the battle. The Agrach Dyrr riders, well clear of the Pillars, charged madly in a circle, skirting the perimeter of the cave and avoiding the main mass of the Menzoberranyr army. Their task was to get to the rear and aid the Agrach Dyrr infantry in sealing the tunnel through which the Army of the Black Spider had just come.

Duergar cavalry streamed up and through the gap, overrunning the positions that had been supposedly held against them and spilling out onto the cavern floor. Several of the House contingents in the van of the march milled about in evident disorder, surprised to find themselves suddenly faced with a thundering charge in an open field instead of siege-work and camp-building behind a stout line.

Other Houses responded to the sudden assault with adroitness and valor. The huge Baenre contingent raised a fierce war cry of their own, and dashed forward to seize the pass before any more duergar could flood through it.

"A bold move, Andzrel," Nimor said, not without admiration. "Unfortunately, I think it's too late to put the cork back in that bottle."

Nimor flicked his war-lizard's reins and positioned himself for a better view of the cavern center. He'd expected the mad rush of motion, the sight of armored ranks surging forward to crash and retreat like the bloody surf of an iron sea, but the sound of the battle was intolerable. Caught by rock above, below, and to all sides, the roars, screams, and clang of weapons on shields became completely indistinguishable, growing into a single great thundering sound that continued to build and build as more and more warriors became embroiled in the fighting.

"The noise will stand to our advantage," he cried over his shoulder to Horgar, though he could not hear his own words. "The commanders of the Army of the Black Spider must decide how to respond, and give the appropriate orders."

"Aye," the gray dwarf monarch answered. Nimor had to strain to understand him. "The middle of a fight is hardly the best time to draw up your plan of battle!"

A brilliant lightning bolt tore into the duergar ranks, followed by a thunderclap audible even over the din of the battle. Exploding balls of fire and scathing sheets of flame streaked across the battlefield, as wizards on each side began to make their presence felt.

Nimor frowned. A handful of powerful wizards could decide the issue, even in the teeth of the ferocious duergar assault and the duplicity of his allies in Agrach Dyrr, but there were wizards among the duergar troops, too, many of them disguised as common riders and infantrymen. As the drow mages struck at the attacking gray dwarves, they gave away their own positions. Duergar wizards answered each bolt of lightning, each blast of fire, in kind, and in moments the cavern was filled with flashes of painful light and ruddy fire, the air hot and acrid with the mighty magic thrown heedlessly from one side to the other.

Try as he might, Nimor couldn't tell whose magic would prevail, as the whole terrible scene descended into complete anarchy. In the space of a few dozen heartbeats, the sheer mass of Menzoberranyr troops in the middle of the cavern checked the initial rush of the duergar charge, the two armies tangling in a long line of contact that snaked across the cavern floor for hundreds of yards. Standards waved and fell, war-lizards reared and plunged, as the great charge bogged down into a thousand individual duels.

Rushing columns of heavily armored duergar pressed through the seams where dark elf Houses met, streaming in and around their desperately battling foes. Nimor smiled grimly. The dark elves had very little notion of how to weld their companies together to make an army into a single weapon, but each House contingent was a small army of deadly, seasoned veterans by itself. The duergar assault had smashed the Army of the Black Spider into twenty smaller forces that swarmed and stung back like a basket of scorpions that had been kicked over.

"Our victory is still in question, Nimor," Horgar called from above. "The cursed wizards have checked our first assault!"

"Yes, but you have forced the Pillars, have you not?" Nimor shouted back. "I'd thought the initial charge would break the Menzoberranyr outright, but it seems the House armies are not so easily swept away."

As he surveyed the battle, Nimor thought the gray dwarves, with advantage of surprise, would most likely be able to defeat the Houses of Menzoberranzan in detail, but it would be a long hard day of fighting to reduce the dark elf force. House Baenre, in particular, had managed to close the Pillars of Woe for the moment, and the longer Andzrel held the pass, the better the dark elves' chances were.

Fortunately, Nimor had taken steps against this very possibility. The Menzoberranyr seemed heavily engaged to the front with the gray dwarf assault. It was time to slip his knife between Menzoberranzan's ribs while their swords were locked.

"Now, Aliisza," he said into the raging air.

Nimor wheeled his mount around, drew his sword, and spurred his war-lizard down into the confused fray. Mez'Barris Armgo and Andzrel Baenre were somewhere near the center of the fight, and he intended to make sure they did not escape the destruction of their army.

🕷   🕷   🕷

A little less than half a mile away, crowded into a small tunnel that descended from the east toward the upper field at the head of the Pillars of Woe, Aliisza stood with her eyes closed, her mind focused on the spell that allowed her to observe Nimor. By virtue of the magic she used, she heard his every word as if he'd spoken clearly in a quiet room. She shook herself and allowed the spell to dissipate.

"It's time," she said to Kaanyr Vhok.

"Good," the warlord said. His pointed teeth were bared in a fierce smile, anticipating battle. He glanced at the assassin Zammzt, who stood nearby. "Well, renegade, I suppose this is your lucky day. I will throw my warriors against the dark elves, not your duergar allies."

Zammzt inclined his head and replied, "I assure you, you will not regret it, Warlord. Destroy this army, and Menzoberranzan will lie naked before you."

Kaanyr strode past the alu-fiend and the dark elf to the place where his standard-bearers stood.

"Sound the charge!" he cried.

Instantly, a dozen bugbear drummers struck their instruments, sounding a simple three-beat ruffle, repeating three times. Thronging the tunnel below, the tanarukks of Kaanyr Vhok's Scoured Legion howled in bloodlust and pressed forward, stamping their feet and clashing their axes as they poured down the tunnel. Kaanyr drew his own molten sword and joined his charging troops, as his guards and standard-bearers hurried to keep up. Aliisza caught her breath at the sight, and took to the air to wing after Kaanyr's standard. A battle like this didn't come along every day, after all.

Ahead of the charging tanarukks, one of the cavern walls on the flank of the Army of the Black Spider seemed to shimmer, and abruptly vanished, revealing a gaping tunnel mouth that had been concealed by a clever illusion. The screaming horde of slavering tanarukks poured from the hidden roadway, streaming out to take the drow army from behind while the great Houses were engaged by the duergar riders who had come up through the Pillars of Woe. Aliisza glimpsed Kaanyr's red banner flying proudly at the head of the force, and the Scoured Legion slammed into the battle.

Only a handful of minor Houses stood in the path of the onrushing horde. The wave of bloodthirsty orc-demons overran them, a spear of red-hot iron punching deep into the army's flank. Aliisza found herself whooping in exultation and terror, gripped by the terrible spectacle and helpless to express her excitement in any other way. The Army of the Black Spider was hopelessly entangled in the very battle it did not want to fight, a wild melee in open terrain against the combined armies of Gracklstugh and Kaanyr Vhok. Like islands in a swirling sea of foes, each House of Menzoberranzan stood alone against a tide of steel and spell, battling for its life.

The alu-fiend alighted atop a blunt stalagmite and stared down at the battle below her.

Ah, Nimor, she thought. What a great and terrible thing you have done!

🕷 🕷 🕷

Nimor Imphraezl, Anointed Blade of the Jaezred Chaulssin, waded through a scene such as all the devils in all the hells could hardly have imagined. The blood of dozens of highborn drow mingled on his rapier and splattered his black mail. His war-lizard was long gone, burned out from under him by a lightning bolt hurled by a Tuin'Tarl wizard, and his limbs ached with fatigue and a dozen minor wounds, but Nimor grinned savagely, giddy with the results of his deadly work.

"Who has accomplished something now, Revered Grandfather?"

he laughed aloud. "Zammzt may have delivered Ched Nasad into your hands, but I have brought low the favored city of the Spider Queen!"

The battle had raged for several hours. Instead of holding an impregnable line between the Pillars of Woe, the Army of the Black Spider had found itself beset on all sides by a foe who'd picked the terrain and the moment to strike. Of course, like a great dumb beast with a mortal wound in its belly, a broken army could take a long time to die, thrashing and convulsing for hours as its blood slowly ran out. In the battles of the World Above, perhaps the defeated drow would have thrown down their arms and hoped for good terms from the victors. In the ruthless calculus of warfare in the Underdark, quarter was neither given nor asked. The gray dwarves had no intention of allowing a single dark elf to survive the day. The warriors of Menzoberranzan knew that, and they fought to the death.

Some of the smaller Houses were smashed apart and scattered throughout the cavern, leaving drow in pairs or threes to sell their lives as dearly as they could. Bands of duergar, bugbears, ogres, and other soldiers loyal to the Crown Prince of Gracklstugh roamed the cavern, drunk on slaughter as they hunted the wretched drow whose companies had been scattered by the assault. Some Houses stood where they were in the great cavern, fighting furiously as the duergar tide rose higher and higher, assailing them from all sides, and some of the Houses held together and tried to cut their way out of the fray, hoping to snatch survival from the specter of a catastrophic defeat.

The soldiers of Barrison Del'Armgo had been driven into a narrow, twisting side-tunnel, and forced from the field. Retreating through a passage only twenty feet wide, the proud warriors of the Second House held off repeated duergar assaults. Mez'Barris was penned in and unable to join with any other Houses, while her supplies burned along with the rest of the train, fired by the Agrach Dyrr infantry who had brought up the rear of the day's march. Del'Armgo would have a long and hungry march home.

House Xorlarrin's company, well stocked with the potent wizards the House was famed for, was caught near the center of the cavern, far from any place of relative security. The Xorlarrin mages kept five times their number of duergar at arm's length for most of the day by raising walls of fire and ice, and lashing out with sweeping blasts of destructive energy—but their wizards were tiring, exhausting their spells. Hundreds of duergar lancers mounted on war-lizards waited for the chance to ride down the Xorlarrins when their arcane defenses failed.

The proud company of House Baenre, more than five hundred strong, stood like a rock as lesser Houses were shattered and pulled down around them. As Nimor had predicted, Andzrel Baenre had been forced to relinquish the Pillars of Woe soon after seizing them, and his forces had slowly battled their way across the cavern to the tunnel mouth through which the Army of the Black Spider had marched only hours before. The Baenre turned their full attention on the Agrach Dyrr who barred escape back down the path of the march. Quarrels, javelins, and deadly spells flew thick and fast as the two Houses battled furiously. While the Baenre outnumbered the treacherous Agrach Dyrr more than two to one, the warriors of the First House were obliged to defend themselves against attacks on all sides while they tried to cut their way through to escape.

Nimor stalked toward the thick of the fighting, picking his way past the dead and the dying. Fortunately, he'd readied several spells of invisibility for the day, otherwise he would have been waylaid time and time again by raging tanarukks or grim duergar anxious to slay any drow they encountered. Hundreds of Horgar's Stone Guards clashed with the Baenre footsoldiers ahead of him, while the Agrach Dyrr barricaded the mouth of the main tunnel on the opposite side. Nimor carefully skirted the fight, catching sight of Andzrel and Zal'therra beneath the Baenre banner.

The Baenre leaders led their soldiers into the thick of the battle against the Agrach Dyrr, slowly but surely cutting their way through the warriors of the treacherous House. A tight knot of bodyguards surrounded them.

The assassin grinned, seeing his opportunity. The Baenre leaders had committed themselves to the fray. If he could destroy them, he would decapitate the Baenre contingent, and if their force disintegrated, there was an excellent chance that nothing of the Army of the Black Spider would survive the day.

Nimor spotted Jazzt Dyrr, who stood back from the melee, directing the Agrach Dyrr soldiers. The nobleman held his hand to a bloody slash across his ribs. The assassin hurried over and released his invisibility.

"A job well done, my kinsman," he shouted to Jazzt. "Continue to hold the Baenre on this side, and the crown prince's guard will grind them to nothing."

Jazzt looked up. Fatigue and pain faded from his face as he surveyed the fight.

"Easier said than done," he said. "The Baenre fight like demons, and more than a few of our own lads won't be going home." He straightened, and offered Nimor his hand. "I had my misgivings about you, Zhayemd, but your plan seems to be unfolding well enough. I'd say we could use you here, but I take it from the blood all over you that you're keeping yourself busy."

"The great Houses still hold in the center of the cavern floor, but this is the spot of decision," Nimor replied. His eyes were fixed on the Baenre banner. "Lend me whatever lads you can. I mean to kill the Baenre commanders."

"Good, we need the help," Jazzt replied. He gestured sharply, and brought up a reserve of a dozen seasoned warriors. "You lads, you go with Zhayemd. Take the Baenre banner!"

Nimor readied his rapier and dagger while the fresh fighters gathered behind him. The melee edged closer, as the Baenre continued to claw their way toward escape. He could see the Baenre standard, waving above the center of the fight. Andzrel himself stood near the forefront, surrounded by the best House Baenre had to offer, while Zal'therra hobbled along a few steps back. The priestess was struggling with a bad wound in her hip, and she had her arm around another Baenre as the line advanced.

Nimor waited until the leading Baenre guardsmen were within a spearcast of his soldiers, and shouted, "Up and at them, lads!"

With a ragged cheer the warriors of Agrach Dyrr dashed forward from their hiding places, some firing crossbows into the Baenre before discarding the weapons and drawing blades. Quarrels hissed in the tunnel mouth. Some bounced from the armor of the Baenre guards and priestesses, but other quarrels struck home. The Baenre guards readied themselves for Agrach Dyrr's charge as best they could. Zal'therra hopped to one side of the tunnel and defended herself with a huge, black, two-headed flail, unwilling to trust her injured leg enough to press into the skirmish but still far from helpless—as an Agrach Dyrr soldier learned when she expertly tripped him and followed up with a blow that pulped the wretch's skull. In a moment the din of steel on steel and the awful sound of steel in flesh filled the corridor, accompanied by the screams, grunts, and curses of the fighters.

Andzrel, unlike his kinswoman, threw himself into the fight, wielding a double-ended sword with expert skill and lashing out with brutal spinning kicks to hammer his foes to the ground while they parried his flashing blades. Nimor watched in admiration as the furious assault swayed back and forth, then, the Agrach Dyrr making way, he approached the Baenre weapons master.

"Greetings, Andzrel," he called. "Your master of scouts must report that the duergar seem to have slipped past our line at the Pillars of Woe, and now pose a considerable danger to the Army of the Black Spider."

Andzrel Baenre fell still as the skirmish swept away from him. Hard anger seethed beneath his disciplined manner.

"Zhayemd," he spat. "You have made a grave mistake in confronting me. You would have been wiser to savor the fruits of your treachery from afar."

"We shall see," Nimor replied.

He leaped forward and aimed a murderous thrust straight for the center of the Baenre's torso, but Andzrel was not unprepared. The weapons master twisted aside and brought up his double-sword in a spinning parry that deflected Nimor's blade, and whirled in close to slam his armored elbow against the side of the assassin's head. Had

Nimor been the slight drow he appeared to be, the blow might have fractured his skull. Instead it merely jolted him, hard. He responded by spinning the other way and bringing up his off-hand dagger in a hidden slash that scored Andzrel beneath the breastplate. The weapons master took half a step back and leaped into the air, planting his boot in the assassin's ribs, but Nimor merely grunted and threw Andzrel back with contemptuous strength.

Andzrel rolled and came up with his sword high, his eyes wide.

"What in all the goddess's hells *are* you?" he muttered.

Before Nimor could compose a suitable answer, the weapons master's hand flashed down to his boot and he hurled a knife straight for Nimor's throat. The assassin threw his arm in front of his face and caught the blade in the meat of his left forearm. He snarled and pulled it out, blood spattering the dusty cavern floor.

Andzrel didn't wait for him, of course. The Baenre followed his thrown dagger by hurling himself forward and rolling under Nimor's guard, trying to run him through with a quick jab.

Nimor jumped clear over the weapons master, pulling his feet up close to his body, and landed on the other side. As Andzrel reversed his thrust and came back up, Nimor punched his rapier through the Baenre's breastplate and scored a deep wound in the weapons master's side. Andzrel grunted and stumbled, losing his balance. He sprawled to the ground at Nimor's feet, his two-ended sword flat on the ground below him.

"A good effort," Nimor said, drawing back his sword to finish off the Baenre.

Before he could strike, a globe of amber energy encased him. Magical force halted the thrust of his blade as surely as if he'd tried to skewer Narbondel, and resisted his knife as well.

"What in the Nine Hells?" Nimor demanded.

The assassin snarled in rage, even as he realized that the sounds of battle in the tunnel had increased threefold at the same instant. He glared out of the sphere, trying to determine where it had come from and what was happening.

Outside, dozens of fresh Baenre troops poured into the fight from the tunnel behind the Agrach Dyrr, catching Jazzt and his footsoldiers between hammer and anvil. The Agrach Dyrr blocking the tunnel were quickly driven away or killed, clearing the retreat for the House Baenre contingent. Nimor watched in cold wrath as the Baenre began to stream past his magical prison, reinforcing their embattled kin. In the space of a few moments, the battle rolled away from him and back into the main cavern.

Nimor glanced back down the tunnel, and found himself looking at a tall, round-bodied wizard in the colors of House Baenre, who studied the amber globe with a smirk of self-satisfaction. Zal'therra and Andzrel both stared at the newcomer as well.

"Nauzhror," said the priestess. Blood streamed from her injured hip. "Your timing is impeccable."

"A fortunate accident, really," the wizard purred. "The matron mother instructed me to obtain news from the field, and so I scried the army, found the battle underway, and noted your difficulties. I made use of a very valuable scroll to raise a gate and bring you some help." He turned and studied Nimor in the globe of energy. "Isn't this fierce fellow Captain Zhayemd of Agrach Dyrr?"

"So he says, anyway," Andzrel gritted. "Can you destroy him in that sphere?"

"Not right away. It simply captures someone for a time, encapsulating the victim in an impervious shield of magical force. It will fade in a short while, after which you may kill him at your leisure."

"Later, then," Andzrel said, dismissing the question of the trapped Nimor.

With one hand he groped for a small vial at his belt—a healing potion, Nimor guessed—and drank it down. He glanced back at the fighting, his face expressionless as he studied the savage melee.

Zal'therra limped up beside him and said, "Make ready to charge. With Nauzhror's reinforcements, we can turn the tables on these cursed dwarves and tanarukks." She looked over to the wizard. "How many soldiers did you bring?"

"Only a single company, I fear. The matron mother did not want to risk any more of our strength in a lost battle, if things go poorly."

Zal'therra began to protest, but Andzrel set a hand on her arm.

"No," he said, "the matron mother was right. Now that we've secured our line of retreat, we must withdraw any Houses we can from the fight. The duergar and their tanarukk allies have won the day."

Nauzhror's eyes widened and he asked, "Is it as bad as that?"

"If we move swiftly," Andzrel answered, "we will bring a good portion of our soldiers off the field yet. Once we've got the important Houses out of the fray, we can make a fighting retreat all the way to Menzoberranzan if we have to. There is no time to lose, if we want to save Xorlarrin and Tuin'Tarl. Fey-Branche is all but gone, I haven't the faintest idea what happened to Barrison Del'Armgo, and Duskryn and Kenafin were swept away by the tanarukks. Menzoberranzan can't lose any more drow here."

"Your retreat will only delay the inevitable," Nimor said. "You can't stop it now."

Andzrel leaned on his two-bladed sword and threw a dark look at Nimor.

"On second thought," the weapons master said, "I'll detail a few lads to wait for this sphere to fade. I see no reason to let him live a moment longer than I have to." He met Nimor's eyes with a cold expression. "Your House will rue the day you betrayed our city, traitor."

Nimor tried the force globe again, to no avail. Andzrel, Zal'therra, and the Baenre wizard turned away and followed their soldiers into the renewed battle, while several Baenre guards trotted back and took up stations surrounding the sphere of force.

"I'll see you in Menzoberranzan," Nimor promised the Baenre.

The Anointed Blade invoked the power of his ring, and disappeared from the force globe into the welcoming shadows.

E I G H T E E N

Four hours later, the company stood again beneath the bronze mask of Vhaeraun in the chapel of Minauthkeep. Battered, filthy mail had been laboriously cleaned, broken links mended, arming coats laundered. Those who had lost their packs, bedrolls, or other gear carried replacements purchased from Jaelre merchants. For the first time since leaving Gracklstugh Halisstra felt clean, rested, and reasonably well prepared for the next step in her journey. She sorely missed the mail she'd worn as First Daughter of House Melarn, and the thundering mace her mother had given her a century past, but she still had her lyre, and Seyll Auzkovyn's mail and sword were not entirely useless substitutes.

The sword in particular seemed a fine piece of work. It carried a potent virtue of holiness that made it tingle unpleasantly in the dark elf's grip, but Halisstra suspected its blade would be unbearable to any fell creature who felt its bite. Considering the fact that she intended to descend into the Abyss itself, where such creatures would likely set upon the company in numbers, she was willing to endure the sword's distasteful enchantment for a time.

Tzirik had donned a suit of black mithral plate armor decorated with grotesque demonic figures and chased with gold filigree. A wickedly spiked mace hung at his belt, and he wore a great masked helm in the shape of a demon's skull. He radiated confidence and energy, as if he'd waited a long time for the opportunity to serve his god with worthwhile stakes at hand.

"As you know," said the priest, "there is more than one way to leave this plane of existence and venture into the dimensions beyond. I have examined the issue at length, and I have decided that we shall travel in astral form. Now, if—"

"That would require us to leave our bodies comatose while our spirits journeyed to the Abyss," Quenthel interrupted. "Why would you even hope I might consent to that?"

"Betrayal," Jeggred rumbled. "He intends to have his comrades slit our throats while our bodies lie uninhabited."

The draegloth took a step forward, baring his fangs at the Vhae-raunite priest.

"I choose to travel in astral form for two reasons, Mistress Baenre," Tzirik replied, ignoring Jeggred. "First, it is marginally safer, in that if someone's roving spirit happened to be killed while visiting the Demonweb Pits, that person would not truly be dead—he would awaken here, unharmed. A spirit is a difficult thing to destroy, after all. Second, as far as I can tell, we have no real alternative. I have already attempted to plane shift bodily to the Demonweb Pits, and the spell failed outright. I believe the barrier or seal of which the Masked Lord spoke prevented the direct transference of a physical body into Lolth's demesnes."

"Yet you believe you'll be able to carry our astral forms there, when the realm is still sealed?" Halisstra asked.

"I know of only two ways to take you to the Demonweb Pits, and if one doesn't work, the other must," Tzirik said with a shrug. "The Masked Lord himself has instructed me to take you there, so there must be a way. Still, if you happen to know of any permanent gates or portals connecting our world with the Abyss, or the Demonweb Pits itself, I suppose you could make use of such a device."

"Show me that physical travel will not work," Quenthel said.

"Step close," Tzirik said from behind his mask, his voice carrying a certain dry amusement, "and join hands with me."

The drow shuffled close and joined hands in a circle with Tzirik, who took a place between Quenthel and Danifae, laying his left hand over their joined hands and leaving his right free to make the gestures necessary for the spell. He collected himself, then chanted out a rolling, powerful prayer whose unholy words filled the air with a nearly tangible darkness.

Halisstra watched carefully to make certain that the priest cast the spell correctly, and as far as she could tell, he did. For a moment she thought it would work, as the Jaelre chapel grew misty and faint around them, and her body seemed to somehow drop away from the world without moving an inch—but then she sensed through some preternatural perception an impediment, a barrier that prevented the company from materializing again in a new place and seemed to almost jolt them back to Minauthkeep. She reeled drunkenly as her senses whirled.

"That happened the last time I tried it," Tzirik said.

Thunder gathered in Quenthel's brow, but she managed to keep her calm as she detached her hand from Danifae's and steadied herself against Jeggred.

"Pharaun," the high priestess said, "what did you observe?"

The wizard raised an eyebrow, perhaps surprised to be consulted by the Baenre, and said, "It seems plausible enough. If we travel by projecting our spirits into the Astral Plane, we won't be going directly from this plane of existence to the Abyss. We'd actually traverse the astral sea and approach Lolth's domain as spirits. It may be that the mysterious barrier we encountered does not bar such an approach." The wizard smoothed his robes, considering. "And that might explain why our conjured demons couldn't manage the trick either. They do not travel between planes by astral projection, as they have no souls."

Quenthel muttered something to herself, folded her arms, and turned back to Tzirik.

"Fine," she said. "You have convinced me. Where do you intend to leave our bodies?"

Tzirik walked over to one wall of the chapel and depressed a hidden stud, revealing a secret chamber behind the bronze mask of Vhaeraun. It was not large, but eight elegant old divans—furnishings that might have dated back to the castle's days as a home to the surface elves of Cormanthyr—were arranged in a tight circle in the room, heads together, feet outward.

"Only a handful of my people know of this room's existence," said the priest, "and I have instructed them to make no intrusion for as long as may prove necessary. You need not fear any harm here."

Ryld, who stood a little behind Jeggred, turned away from Tzirik and gestured subtly to Pharaun and Halisstra, *So if our spirits are defeated while we are astral, we return to our bodies. What happens to our spirits if someone sticks a knife in our bodies?*

Death, the wizard replied. *A cautious fellow would make sure his body was someplace safe and guarded by trustworthy sorts before sending his spirit off to some other plane.*

Ryld grimaced, but made no other reply.

The company followed Tzirik into the small room. Halisstra stared with some trepidation at the old couch in front of her, knowing that she was doing so but unable to look away. She wasn't the only member of the company regarding the divans like a collection of coffins; Quenthel must have been having the same thoughts.

She looked up from the couch to Tzirik and said, "We will leave behind a guard. Someone I trust will be here to watch over our bodies until I return, just as someone you trust will be watching over you."

"Ah," Tzirik said. "You are a dark elf indeed. Do as you will."

"He might mean to have this whole castle descend upon whomever we leave behind," Jeggred snarled. "Best leave two, maybe three."

"Our sentry's only duty will be to cut Tzirik's throat before he's overwhelmed," Pharaun said. "The question is, who stays?"

Quenthel glanced at Ryld, then her eyes slid toward Halisstra. For

324

a moment Halisstra feared that Quenthel meant to leave her behind in order to deny her the audience she sought with Lolth, but even as her heart thudded in apprehension she realized that the last thing the Baenre would want—if she truly viewed Halisstra as a threat, anyway—would be a Melarn conscious and alone with her own helpless body. Quenthel's eyes narrowed as she weighed the same considerations, and she turned to Jeggred.

"You must stay here," she said to the draegloth.

Jeggred contorted himself in a spasm of anger.

"I am not going to sit here staring at your living corpses while you face the perils of the goddess's realm! Mother told me to guard you. How can I do that when you leave me behind?"

"You will be guarding me," Quenthel said. "No harm can come to me in astral form. It is here that I will be vulnerable, and I trust no one else with the task. It must be you, Jeggred."

The draegloth waved all four arms in protest and said, "You of all people know what awaits you in the Demonweb Pits, Mistress. You will need my strength there."

"Cease this at once," the Mistress of Arach-Tinilith commanded. Her eyes flashed, and her whip rippled and spat. "It is not for you to question me, nephew. You will discharge your obligation in the manner I direct."

Jeggred subsided into a sulking silence. In disgust he turned away and threw himself down on the stone floor, shucking his pack and bandoleer. Quenthel glanced at the others, and nodded at the couches.

"Come," she said. "The goddess awaits."

Tzirik waited while the Menzoberranyr chose divans and stretched out. He moved to the last one and sat down, then glanced over at Jeggred.

"If you will be staying here, half-demon, you should know that some of my kinfolk will be accompanying you on your vigil. Do not cause them any trouble, and I think you will find that they will be happy to leave you alone."

Jeggred sneered in answer, and Tzirik laid himself down awkwardly in his plate armor, arranging his mace so that it lay at his side.

Halisstra found that she was lying between Ryld and Danifae. She glanced over at the weapons master. Ryld's expression was taut and nervous. Clearly, astral travel was something beyond his experience too.

If our spirits are doing the traveling, why do we need all our weapons? he motioned to her.

They're part of you, she replied. *Your consciousness includes your belongings in your definition of yourself. Therefore, when your soul roams free from your body, your mind will imagine for you an astral copy of anything you have close at hand.*

"Reach out and take each other's hands," Tzirik said. "Make sure you have a good grasp. I do not want to leave anyone behind."

The priest started to chant again in his melodious voice. Halisstra stared at the ceiling and reached out to grasp Danifae with her right hand, and Ryld with her left.

Perhaps I should imagine for myself some good strong drink, Ryld observed.

He reached out and caught Halisstra's hand in his strong grip before she could reply.

Behind her, unseen on the other side of the circle, Tzirik continued his spell, speaking the harsh words of the magic with confidence and ease. Halisstra felt an electric jolt race through her body from hand to hand as the magic began to take life, joining her to Ryld and Danifae with a strange, tingling sensation. A sense of detachment swept through her, as if she'd all at once become weightless. She seemed to be floating up and out of herself, drawn by some irresistible force tugging on her in a direction she could not relate to up or down, left or right. The stone ceiling wavered and grew dim, pulling away from her faster and faster.

And she was gone.

Triel Baenre stalked gracefully past the ranks of her battered soldiers, her face held rigidly expressionless by nothing more than sheer iron determination. The exhausted troops stood at attention for her as best they could in the narrow tunnel. She'd had Nauzhror transport her immediately to the scene of the retreat to view with her own eyes the scope of Menzoberranzan's defeat, and she found that she did not like what she had seen. She did not like it all.

The passage was the better part of ten miles long, one of the main thoroughfares leading from the way-meeting at the Pillars of Woe to the shell of twisting passages and wild caverns known as Menzoberranzan's Dominion. It seemed that every second or third soldier she passed carried some obvious injury—a bandaged torso here, an arm in a sling there, a fellow using a broken spear shaft as a crutch against the other wall. The wounded did not bother her, though. What Triel found truly disconcerting was the fatigue and moroseness of the soldiers. She'd expected to find them tired, of course—Andzrel had marched the army for a day without halting to salvage something from the disaster of the Pillars of Woe—but she hadn't expected to find her soldiers so . . . *defeated*. They'd been beaten, and they knew it.

Andzrel trailed a respectful step behind the matron mother, not presuming to speak until addressed.

"How bad were the losses?" she finally asked, not looking at her weapons master.

"For the whole army, somewhere around a quarter to a third of our strength, Matron Mother. Some Houses fared much better or much worse than that, depending on the fortunes of battle."

"And House Baenre's contingent?"

"Ninety dead, forty-four seriously wounded," Andzrel replied. "About a quarter of our strength."

"We were fortunate to save that much, Matron Mother," Zal'therra added. "Some of the minor Houses were slaughtered to a male in—"

"I did not address you," Triel said.

She folded her arms and tried not to let the sick horror in her stomach show.

It will be a miracle if the Council doesn't rise in open revolt against me, the matron mother thought. Thank the goddess that Mez'Barris is lost somewhere, and Fey-Branche so badly weakened. Byrtyn Fey must guard her response with half her House army destroyed, and I will have some time to consider what must be done before I have to confront Mez'Barris, Lolth willing.

Then again, she thought, what was left of the Council, anyway? Faen Tlabbar, the Third House, was in the hands of an untried girl, and Yasraena Dyrr was not likely to present herself at the next meeting, was she? She and all her filthy House were barricaded in their castle, awaiting the arrival of their duergar allies, and apparently quite prepared to stand a siege.

That left Zeerith Q'Xorlarrin, Miz'ri Mizzrym, and Prid'eesoth Tuin as the only matron mothers she need concern herself with.

To distract herself from the unpleasant prospect ahead, Triel turned to face Andzrel and Zal'therra. More than anything, she longed to punish the weapons master and her cousin Zal'therra for leading her army into a disastrous ambush, but as far as she could tell, Andzrel's skill and Zal'therra's decisiveness had most likely extricated the Army of the Black Spider from a dreadful mauling. Menzoberranzan's army was battered, but intact.

"Where are the duergar now?" she asked.

"About three miles south of us," replied Andzrel. "House Mizzrym currently serves as rear guard, though I've sent almost a hundred of our own soldiers to stiffen the defense." Triel understood what Andzrel really meant—he'd put Baenre soldiers beside the Mizzrym to make sure that another betrayal of the sort Agrach Dyrr had engineered didn't take place. "The Scoured Legion advances through another passage to our east, circling around us. We don't dare try to make a stand in this tunnel, or the tanarukks will get by us."

"It would only take a hundred soldiers to hold this tunnel against almost any force, wouldn't it?" Triel asked.

"Yes, but the duergar have enough war wizards in their ranks, and siege engines in their train, that they wouldn't be halted for long by a rearguard action."

"Try it anyway," Triel grated. "Use slave troops, and leave enough officers behind to make sure they don't break and run. We need time, Weapons Master, and that's what rear guards are for."

Andzrel didn't argue the point, and Triel paced away to gather her thoughts. Drow rebels, slave revolts, duergar armies, dark treachery, a missing archmage, and tanarukk hordes—it was hard to see how matters could get much worse. Where could she even start to address any of these problems? Assault Agrach Dyrr, without the magical might of the city's assembled priestesses? Pick another spot to meet the duergar, and allow the tanarukks to sweep past?

"How did this happen?" she muttered aloud.

"Agrach Dyrr was in league with our city's enemies," Zal'therra replied. "They contrived to make up the vanguard of our army, and instead of holding the Pillars of Woe against the gray dwarves, they led us into a trap. They must be obliterated for their treachery."

"I was not speaking to you," Triel growled, and this time she could not restrain herself.

Though she knew Zal'therra was not to blame for the disastrous battle, she had to strike out at something. She slapped the girl, hard, rocking her to her heels despite the fact that Zal'therra towered almost a foot taller than her, and outweighed her by thirty pounds.

"You must come to expect treachery, you simpleminded fool!" Triel snarled. "Why were there no Baenre officers among our scouts? Why did you take no steps to verify the reports the Agrach Dyrr fed to you? If you had exercised even the most minimal amount of caution, our army would not be in tatters."

Zal'therra shrank back, saying, "Matron Mother, we all approved of Andzrel's plans—"

"Andzrel is a *weapon*, Zal'therra. Our House army is a *weapon*. Yours is the hand that must wield those weapons against our enemies. I sent you out to exercise your judgment and make decisions, to use your head and *think!*"

Triel whirled away to keep herself from striking Zal'therra again. If she did, she didn't think she'd be able to stop, and like it or not Zal'therra was probably the most promising of her cousins. Triel wouldn't be around forever, and she needed to give thought to leaving House Baenre with at least a few competent priestesses in the event that the day came when she would have to have her sisters murdered.

"Matron Mother," the girl managed, her eyes wide with fear, "I apologize for my failure."

"I never asked for an apology, girl, and a Baenre should never offer one," the matron mother rumbled, "but I will give you the opportunity to demonstrate that you have some redeeming portion of merit and resourcefulness. You will take command of the rearguard."

Triel gestured toward the south. There was an excellent chance that she was sending her cousin to her death, but she needed to know if Zal'therra had the wits and the resolve to become a leader of House Baenre, and if she found a way to survive the assignment and obtain any degree of success at all, Triel might consider permitting her to live.

"Make the duergar fight for every step they take toward Menzoberranzan," Triel added. "Your survival depends on your success. If you abandon this tunnel before three days pass, I will have you crucified."

Zal'therra bowed, and hurried off. Triel turned back to the weapons master.

"Understand that I do not hold you blameless, either," she said in a low voice. "You were the author of our grand strategy, and I committed the full weight of House Baenre's power and prestige to your battle plan, which has led us to a disaster the likes of which we have not seen since Mithral Hall. In any other circumstances, I would have you dumped into a pit of hungry centipedes with your tendons slashed for your failure, but . . . these are unusual times, and there exists the small possibility that your skill and grasp of strategy may prove useful in the days to come. Do not fail me again."

"Yes, Matron Mother," Andzrel said, bowing low.

"So," she continued, "where do we stop the duergar and their allies?"

Without hesitation, the weapons master replied, "We do not, Matron Mother. Given the losses we have already suffered, I advise withdrawing back to Menzoberranzan and preparing for a siege."

"I do not like that option," Triel snapped. "It reeks of defeat, and the longer an army sits on our doorstep, the more likely it is that they'll be reinforced by the arrival of some other enemy, such as the beholders or the mind flayers."

"That is possible, of course," Andzrel said, his voice carefully neutral, "but the gray dwarves will not find it easy to maintain a siege around Menzoberranzan, a hundred miles from their own city. I don't think the duergar can wait us out for more than a few months, and I doubt they have the numbers to take the city by storm. Our best course of action is to make the duergar set their siege, and see what kind of a threat we're really facing. It would provide us the opportunity to crush House Agrach Dyrr in the meantime."

"You're afraid to face the duergar in battle again?" Triel rasped.

"No, Matron Mother, but I will not advise a course of action that hazards the city on a battle for which we are not prepared, not unless we have no other choice. We are not yet at that point." He paused, then added, "We can always gather our strength within the city and sally in force in only a few days, if we see the need or the opportunity."

Triel weighed the weapons master's advice.

"I will return to Menzoberranzan and set the matter before the Council," she said at last, "but, until you're ordered otherwise, continue your withdrawal. I will have our captains in the city make ready to withstand a siege."

🕷 🕷 🕷

Halisstra opened her eyes and found herself drifting in an endless silver sea. Soft gray clouds moved slowly in the distance, while strange dark streaks twisted violently through the sky, anchored in ends so distant she couldn't perceive them, their middle parts revolving angrily like pieces of string rolled between a child's fingertips. She glanced down, wondering what supported her, and saw nothing but more of the strange pearly sky beneath her feet and all around her.

She drew in a sudden breath, surprised by the sight, and felt her lungs fill with something sweeter and perhaps a little more solid than air, but instead of gagging or drowning on the stuff she seemed perfectly acclimated to it. An electric thrill raced through her limbs as she found herself mesmerized by the simple act of respiration.

Halisstra raised her hand to her face in an unconscious desire to shield her eyes, and she noticed that her eyesight was preternaturally keen. Each link of her mailed gauntlet leaped out in perfect symmetry, its edges boldly defined, the leather of her gloves gleaming with discrete layers of oils and stains.

Words failed her.

"You have not ventured here before, Mistress Melarn?" said Tzirik from somewhere behind her.

Halisstra craned her neck back to look for him, but in response the entire vista seemed to revolve and spin in one quick, smooth motion, bringing into her view the floating forms of her companions. The Vhaeraunite priest stood—no, that was not right, *floated* was better—a dozen yards from her, his armor as sharp as the edge of a knife, his cloak rippling softly in a breeze Halisstra could not feel. He spoke softly, yet his voice carried with a marvelous clarity and precision that made it seem that he stood within arm's reach.

"I would have expected a priestess of your stature to be familiar with the astral realm," the priest added.

"I know something of what to expect, but I have never had the occasion to journey to other planes," she replied. "My knowledge of this place is only . . . theoretical."

She noted that each of her comrades seemed every bit as sharply defined, as tangible and real, as Tzirik himself. From some spot she could not easily perceive—somewhere in the middle of their backs, or perhaps the napes of their necks—sprang a slender, gleaming tendon of silver light.

Halisstra reached around behind her head and felt her own cord. The warm, pulsing artery vibrated with energy, and when her fingers brushed it, a powerful jolt quivered through her torso as if she'd just plucked the heartstring of her own soul. She jerked her hand back, and resolved not to try to touch her cord again.

"Your silver cord," Tzirik explained. "A nigh indestructible bond that ties your soul to its rightful home: your body, back in Minauth-keep." The priest offered a cruel smile. "You will want to be careful of it. There are few things that can part an astral traveler's cord, but if something did, that traveler would be destroyed in an instant."

Halisstra watched as Ryld felt for his own cord and touched it. His eyes widened and he snatched his hand back just as swiftly as she had withdrawn her own.

"How long do these things get?" the weapons master asked.

"They are infinite, Master Argith," Tzirik said. "Don't worry, they fade to intangibility within a foot or two of your skin, so you won't be tripping over your own cord. In fact, it has the habit of keeping itself out of your way, quite without a thought on your part."

Halisstra glanced around the company, watching as the Menzo-berranyr struggled to adjust themselves to their new environment. Ryld and Valas flailed their limbs slowly as if trying to tread water. Quenthel held herself as stiff as a blade, her limbs locked tight to her sides, while Danifae drifted languidly, her long white hair streaming behind her. Pharaun merely waited, his eyes sparkling with dark amusement as he watched the efforts of his companions. Tzirik glanced around, studying their surroundings, and nodded.

"This is something of a timeless place," he said, "but time does pass here, so I suppose we should begin our journey. Follow me, and stay close. You may think you can see forever from here, but things have a way of vanishing in the mists."

He glided off without moving, arms folded, his cloak whipping silently behind him.

Follow him how? Halisstra wondered, watching the priest go, but somehow in conceiving the desire to keep the priest close by, she found herself leaping forward with such alacrity that her next impulse was to yelp out loud, if only to herself, "Stop!"

And she did, so quickly and with so perfect an end to motion that her mind told her she *must* lurch forward, as if she had tried to stop too suddenly from a run. She managed to throw herself into a violent circle before she stopped completely. Fortunately, she was not the only one having trouble.

Danifae scowled prettily as she tried to make herself go anywhere at all, and Ryld and Valas had somehow collided with each other and clung together, unwilling to trust themselves to the void again.

"Oh, in the name of the goddess!" Quenthel growled, watching them. "Simply clear your minds and think of where you want to go."

"With all due respect, Mistress, where is it that we should desire to go?" Valas asked as he disentangled himself from Ryld.

"Concentrate on following the priest," the Baenre replied. "He cast the spell, so he will be able to find the portal leading into the Demonweb Pits. It may take many hours, but you will find that time passes strangely here."

With that, Quenthel moved off in pursuit of Tzirik.

Halisstra closed her eyes, took a deep breath, and concentrated on trailing the priest at a comfortable distance. She closed up quickly and smoothly, and this time she didn't allow herself to react in panic. Soon enough the rest of the company sailed along beside her, keeping together easily as they became more and more accustomed to the strangeness of the Astral Plane. Halisstra indulged herself by experimenting with her mode of locomotion, at first orienting herself horizontally so that she felt like she flew like a bird through the pearly void, then trying to face her direction of travel so that she felt as if she was walking swiftly without moving her legs.

As it turned out, it didn't really matter what she did with her body as long as her mind remained focused on staying near her companions, and the true immateriality of the astral sea began to seep into her understanding. She was only a spirit, weightless, perfect, yet she was in a place where spirits became tangible. Somewhere beyond the endless pearly expanse that met her eye lay the realms of the gods, a thousand infinite concepts of existence where the divine beings who ruled over the fate of all Faerûn—of all the worlds, for that matter—had their abodes. She could spend a hundred drow lifetimes exploring the domains that touched on the astral sea, and not even come close to seeing them all.

The thought made her feel small, almost insignificant, and she pushed it from her mind. Lolth had not called her to the Demonweb Pits for her to be overawed by the silver void of the Astral Plane. She had called Halisstra and the others to stand before her, capable and confident, to profess their faith and adoration. For what other purpose could the goddess have done all that she had done by withdrawing her power from her faithful, by permitting the fall of Ched Nasad, by causing the endless toils and tribulations that had assailed the First Daughter of House Melarn?

There is a purpose, Halisstra told herself, a purpose that will be made clear to me soon, if I keep my faith strong and do not falter.

The Queen of the Demonweb Pits has brought us this far. She will bring us a little farther.

NINETEEN

How long it took them to cross the Astral Plane, Halisstra could not begin to say. She'd never realized before the extent to which the routine processes of one's body measured the days. Her astral form didn't grow tired or hungry, and didn't know thirst or discomfort of any sort. Without the minor actions of looking after the body's needs—taking a sip from a waterskin when thirsty, halting to take a meal during their day's march, or even stopping to sink deep into Reverie and while away the bright hours of daylight—time simply lost its doleful count.

From time to time they caught glimpses of phenomena other than the endless pearly clouds and twisting gray vortices that streaked the surrounding sky. Strange bits of matter drifted through the astral sea. On several occasions they passed boulders or hillocks of rock and dirt that hovered in space like miniature worlds, some nearly the size of mountains, others only a few yards across. Weird, empty ruins graced the larger of them, the abodes of astral sojourners or long gone residents. The strangest things they came across were whirling pools of color slowly revolving in the astral medium. The hues ranged from bright, shining silver to blackest midnight shot with angry purple streaks.

"Don't stray too close to any of the color pools," Tzirik had said. "If you enter one you will be ejected into a different plane of existence, and I have no desire to wander into strange worlds looking for a careless traveling companion."

"How will we know which one will lead us to the Abyss?" Valas Hune asked.

"Do not worry, my friend, the spell Vhaeraun has granted me also confers a certain affinity for the destination I conceived when I shifted my spirit to this plane, and I am leading us more or less directly to the nearest color pool that will serve our purposes."

"How much longer must we travel?" Quenthel asked.

"We are drawing near," the priest answered. "It's hard to tell here, of course, but I would guess we are within four or five hours of our destination. We've already traveled for almost two days."

Two days? Halisstra thought. It seemed much less.

She found herself wondering what might have transpired back in Faerûn in two days. Did Jeggred still maintain his vigil over their inert bodies? He couldn't have been entirely remiss in his duties, as they were all still alive, but how many more days would pass before they reached their destination, beseeched the goddess for an audience, and managed to return to their native plane?

Absorbed in her own thoughts, Halisstra kept to herself for the balance of the journey, scarcely noticing that her companions did the same. It came as a surprise to her when Tzirik slowed his effortless flight and finally arrested his motion all together, facing a whirlpool of black with silver streaks that slowly churned in the astral medium a short distance from the travelers.

"The entrance to the Sixty-sixth Layer of the Abyss," the priest of Vhaeraun said. "So far our journey has been uneventful, but once we set foot within Lolth's domain that is bound to change. If you have any second thoughts about this quest, Mistress Baenre, this would be the time to express them."

"I have no reason to fear the Demonweb Pits," Quenthel sneered. "I intend to do what I came here to do."

Without waiting for the priest she arrowed forward and plunged herself into the whirling, inky blot. In the blink of an eye her gleaming astral form was lost to view, swallowed by the maelstrom.

"Impatient, isn't she?" Tzirik remarked.

He shrugged and moved into the color pool himself. Like Quenthel, Halisstra sensed a certainty in the moment, and she did not mean to let any quailing sway her from her intended course. She entered the pool of swirling night a heartbeat behind Tzirik, her teeth bared in a defiant snarl.

There was no sensation at first, though the pool swallowed her sight completely the moment she plunged within it. The medium seemed much the same as the rest of the Astral Plane—a weightless, cool, perfect nothingness—but the swirling current of the revolving pool caught her at once, tugging on her with some strange non-dimensional feeling of attraction or acceleration that dragged her psychic form in a direction she couldn't even begin to comprehend. It didn't hurt, but it felt so alien, so dislocating, that Halisstra gasped in shock and distress, shuddering violently in the grip of the astral maelstrom.

Goddess, help me! she pleaded in the silence of her own mind, as she flailed her arms and tried to extricate herself from the spinning mass. There was another long moment of indescribable motion, and—

She was through.

Halisstra swayed drunkenly with the return of gravity and struggled to catch her balance. She opened her eyes and found herself standing on something silver-gray, a steeply sloping ramp or wall top that dropped away an incredible distance before her. The rest of the party stood close by, looking around in silence as they rubbed their limbs nervously or fingered their weapons.

All around there was nothing but a black, smothering emptiness darker and more forbidding than the blackest chasm of the Underdark. Her nostrils filled with a foul, acrid scent, and a soft muttering updraft streamed constantly from below. Halisstra glanced into the abyss at her left hand and saw something gleaming there, a dull silver strand several miles away that sloped down through the darkness. Lesser strands intersected it at odd intervals, and as she followed some of them with her eyes she saw that they climbed back up slowly and met the very ramp or buttress on which she stood. The hot, stinking breeze grew momentarily stronger and actually managed to induce a great, gentle swaying in the monstrous strand.

"It's a spiderweb," Ryld muttered. "A gigantic spiderweb."

"This surprises you?" Pharaun said with a sardonic smirk.

Danifae took a couple of cautious steps down the surface of the strand. The whole thing was easily thirty or forty yards in diameter, yet because its surface was round, it was difficult to feel comfortable walking more than a dozen feet or so from the centerline of the strand. She knelt and brushed her fingers over the strand's surface, and grimaced.

"Sticky, but not dangerously so—and we appear to be completely physical again." She straightened, and stretched languidly. "Do I have two bodies now? One here, and one back in the Jaelre castle?"

"In fact, you do," Tzirik said. "When one leaves the astral sea and enters another plane, the traveling spirit constructs for itself the physical body it expects. You might say that your spirit must undergo a sort of condensation to resume a physical existence on another plane. When you leave this place, your spirit will return to the Astral Plane, while this shell you have created for yourself will simply fade away into nothingness."

"You seem well acquainted with the rigors of planar travel," Halisstra observed.

"Vhaeraun has called me to his service in the planes beyond Faerûn on several occasions," Tzirik admitted. "In fact, I have been in the Demonweb Pits before now. All the gods of our race reside here, each in their own domain within this great chasm of webbing. My previous business did not take me to Lolth's domain, though, and that was a good many years ago."

Quenthel scowled and said, "All of the Demonweb Pits are Lolth's domain, heretic. She is the queen of this entire layer of the Abyss, and the other so-called gods of our people exist here only at her sufferance."

"I am certain you have correctly parroted your faith's beliefs on the matter, and so I will not argue the point with you, priestess of Lolth. For our purposes, the exact relationship of our pantheon's deities is not very important."

Tzirik turned his back on Quenthel and surveyed the black gulf surrounding the party. He waved his hand in a sweeping gesture.

"Somewhere below us we will find some kind of gate or border marking the place where this entryway opens to Lolth's own domain—which, as I understand it, is much like the rest of the Demonweb Pits, except subject to her every whim and caprice."

"If the plane is infinite, then the spot we seek might be infinitely far away," Pharaun observed. "How are we to get from here to there?"

"If we had simply materialized at some random point in this reality, you would be correct, wizard," Tzirik replied. "However, the astral spell is not a random means of travel. We are not too far from what we seek—an hour's march, perhaps a day's, but not much farther. Since we know that Lolth's domain lies at the very nadir of this place, I would propose that we need only descend this strand and continue to descend each time we come to an intersection. In the meantime, be alert."

"There will be others," Quenthel added. "The souls of the recent dead. If you see anyone you recognize as a worshiper of the Spider Queen, we will follow them."

If Lolth is still calling them home, Halisstra thought.

The others seemed to be thinking the same thing.

The armored priest hefted his mace in his hand, adjusted the grip of his shield, and set off directly down the titanic gray strand, shoulders squared. The Menzoberranyr exchanged looks, but turned to follow, picking their way down the steeply pitched column of webbing behind the Jaelre priest.

The surface of the strand proved surprisingly easy to negotiate. Its surface was tacky, rather than truly adhesive, and it was composed of rough fibers that provided a sure footing. It was springy enough that it cushioned the jarring footfalls of the sharply descending walk.

At first Halisstra thought the place was as empty as the silvery seas of the Astral Plane, since the vast distances from strand to strand of the webbing gave the whole place a sense of immense vacancy. Yet the farther she went, the more she became conscious of an active malevolence in the very air of the place, as if the entire plane watched their intrusion and seethed with anger. Strange, rasping rustling and oddly insectile tittering sounds rode on the fetid updraft from below, a crawling sound of distant movement and activity that carried no small menace with it.

Sometimes Halisstra spied motion on neighboring strands, even though the sagging gray cables were miles away across the bottomless space. She could make out frenetic activity here and there, the creatures or objects responsible so far distant that it was impossible to guess what they might be. More than once she sensed presences in the airy voids around their strand, slow, foul things that glided on the noisome exhalations from below, wheeling and drifting closer to the drow travelers as if sizing up an easy meal.

They began to pass corpses at odd intervals, hulking forms of nightmare that combined the worst features of spiders and demons. Great rents had been torn in the chitinous shells of the monsters, limbs twisted off, hairy thoraxes crushed and oozing sour green paste. Winged vulture-demons lay in shabby piles of filthy feathers, their foul beaks agape in death. Bloated, froglike things hung suspended in the ropy fibers of the great strand, swaying slowly in the hot stench of the place. Some of the demons still clung to life, too horribly damaged to do more than quiver and rasp, or croak dire threats at the drow as the company carefully climbed down past them.

"This place is a charnel house of devils," Ryld muttered, holding one hand over his nose and mouth. "Is it always like this?"

"I saw nothing like this on my previous visit," Tzirik said. "What it means, I cannot say, but I would not care to meet that which tears apart demons."

"It is not like I recall, either," Quenthel said. Her face was set in a thoughtful frown, her voice quiet and strained. "Change is the essence of chaos, and chaos is an aspect of Lolth."

"Indeed," Pharaun said. The fastidious wizard held a handkerchief to his nose and picked his way around a huge spider corpse whose bulbous abdomen had burst entirely, strewing the strand with its horrid contents. "It seems not unlikely that they did this to themselves. Demons are violent creatures, after all. In the absence of a powerful, commanding presence, they often turn on each other."

"An absence . . ." Halisstra repeated. She frowned, studying the carnage. "There are no drow bodies here."

Having descended a goodly ways, the neighboring strands were closer, and the intersections more frequent. Halisstra could see more broken forms clinging to the tattered strands nearby. Whatever battle had raged there must have spanned dozens of strands and miles of gaping darkness.

"The Spider Queen . . ." said Halisstra. "She has abandoned the denizens of her own plane, just as she has abandoned us. Much as we have done in Ched Nasad, the demons of her realm have destroyed each other." She closed her eyes, trying to shut out the awful sight. The smell soured her stomach and left her light-headed with nausea. "Goddess, what is the *purpose?*" she murmured aloud.

"The Spider Queen will explain her purposes if she sees fit to do so," Quenthel answered. "We can only beseech the restoration of her favor, and trust that we will find approval in her eyes."

"We can also move along a little quicker, and stop gawking," Valas Hune called. He was at the rear of the band, an arrow laid across the string of his double-curved bow. The scout stood peering up the strand behind them, his face pinched in a worried frown. "Excuse the interruption, but we have company. Something is following us down the strand."

Halisstra followed the scout's gaze upward, swaying awkwardly as she lost her balance. She hadn't realized just how far they'd descended until she looked back up the massive strand, sloping upward steeper and steeper into the darkness overhead. Something was following them, a crawling horde of tiny, spiderlike figures that swarmed over the strand's entire circumference, heedless of whether they clung to the web's top, sides, or bottoms. They were still many hundreds of yards behind the company, but even at that distance Halisstra could tell that they were ogre-sized monstrosities, and the alacrity of their pursuit certainly didn't seem to be a good sign.

"I don't like the looks of that," Ryld said.

"Nor do I," Quenthel agreed. "Pharaun, do you have a spell prepared that can bar their passage?"

The Master of Sorcere shook his head and answered, "Not without risk of severing the strand, I fear, and I find myself strangely unwilling to chance that. I could instead confer a spell of flying on enough of us to perhaps abandon this strand and reach another, or we could simply descend to that strand below us by levitation."

He pointed at a slender, almost wispy web a long distance below them and a little to one side.

"Save your magic," Quenthel decided. "That strand will do. Master Argith, carry Valas and Danifae."

She slid down the side of the great strand they stood on, and pushed herself off into the darkness. One by one, the others followed. Halisstra risked one more glance at the scuttling terrors behind them, and hastened to follow the Baenre priestess. She scrambled down the curving side of the monstrous cable, and leaped out into the dark.

❈   ❈   ❈

Three days after his victory at the Pillars of Woe and twenty miles closer to Menzoberranzan, Nimor stood in the shadows at the mouth of the Lustrum, a wondrously rich mithral mine. Near the entrance, a wedge-shaped vault soared upward for hundreds of feet, widening as it climbed, but down on the cavern floor it was cramped and broken with the shattered remnants of huge boulders. The miners—slaves and soldiers of House Xorlarrin, or so he believed—had abandoned their tools and their homes in the face of the advancing duergar army, carrying off as much mithral ore as they could manage. Nimor gazed up at the narrow black rift above him.

The mithral mine was an interesting bit of decoration, but it was only one of the reasons he was there. The Lustrum stood between the army of Gracklstugh and the army of Kaanyr Vhok. The duergar stayed to the left and came up on Menzoberranzan's southwest side, while the tanarukks pushed right and approached the city from the southeast. The drow army retreated ahead of them, in full flight for the dubious safety of their home city. Menzoberranzan's Mantle—the great halo of twisting caverns and passageways ringing the city—offered the invading armies a thousand paths by which they might approach.

Of course, the matron mothers hadn't left their outer demesnes completely undefended. Nimor glanced down at the green shards of one of the city's infamous jade spiders, huge magical automatons of stone that guarded the city's approaches. The wreckage of the one at his feet still smoked with acrid black fumes from the stonefire bombs that had destroyed it a few hours before. They were clever and deadly devices, but without cadres of magic-wielding priestesses to hurl all sorts of awful dooms and blights on invaders, the jade spiders were not sufficient to the task of halting the two approaching armies.

How much longer until Menzoberranzan's great castles lie shattered like this device? Nimor mused.

The Anointed Blade was interrupted in his reflections by the tramp of dwarven boots and the angry scrape of iron on stone. The armored diligence of Crown Prince Horgar Steelshadow approached, escorted by a double file of the duergar lord's Stone Guards. Nimor winced at the resounding clangor of the duergar soldiers.

One would think they'd get their fill of hammer blows and noise back in their city, he thought.

He brushed off his tunic and went down to meet his ally.

"Well met, Crown Prince Horgar. I am pleased that you honored my request for a parley."

The duergar lord threw open the armored door in the side of his iron wagon, and stepped down to the cavern floor. Marshal

Borwald followed a step behind, his scarred face hidden by a great iron helm.

"I have been looking for you, Nimor Imphraezl," Horgar replied. "You vanished after guiding our vanguard to this maze of tunnels. What business did you have elsewhere that was more pressing than our assault on Menzoberranzan, I wonder?"

Victory had transformed the crown prince's dour pessimism into a kind of ferocious hunger for more victories, and Horgar's lairds echoed their ruler's attitude. Where before the sight of the assassin brought black scowls and dark mutterings, the lairds of Gracklstugh had come to acknowledge his presence with gruff nods and open envy of his successes.

"Why, Crown Prince, my business concerned the upcoming assault," Nimor said with a laugh. He kicked aside one of the jade shards from the ruined construct. "Once I'd shown your men how to disable these things it seemed to me that your army had matters well in hand, so I took the liberty of reporting to my superiors, and spying out how matters stand in the city."

The duergar prince frowned, his brows knitting in thought.

"You felt free to gamble with the tanarukk army," said Horgar. "They might have turned on us as easily as upon the Menzoberranyr, you know."

"Under normal circumstances, perhaps, but there is opportunity in the air. I can smell it, Kaanyr Vhok can smell it, and I think you can, too. We stand at a fulcrum on which many great events might be made to turn."

"Empty platitudes, Nimor," the gray dwarf growled.

He folded his thick arms and stared into the darkness, waiting. After a short time, a scuffling and snorting drifted through the darkness, followed by quick and heavy steps.

Bearing an iron palanquin the size of a small coach on their hairy shoulders, a score of tanarukks loped into the cavern, bestial eyes aglow with red hate, axes and maces gripped in their powerful fists. The gray dwarves and the orc-demons glared at each other, nervously muttering and fingering their weapons.

The door to the palanquin creaked open, and Kaanyr Vhok slowly straightened out of the chair. The half-demon warlord was resplendent in his armor of crimson and gold, and his fine-scaled skin and strong features bespoke presence and charisma in a way that Horgar's duergar churlishness and suspicious manner could never match. The alu-fiend Aliisza followed sinuously, stretching her wings as she emerged. Finally, Zammzt climbed out of the warlord's coach.

"Well, I have come," Kaanyr said in his powerful voice. He studied the assembled gray dwarves, and regarded Nimor as well. "We have driven the dark elves back to their city in disarray. Now how do we finish the job? And, more importantly, how shall we divide the spoils?"

· "Divide the spoils?" Horgar rasped. "I think not. You will not help yourself to part of my prize after my army shouldered the brunt of the hard work in defeating the drow at the Pillars of Woe. You will be paid fairly for your assistance, but do not presume to claim a share of my victory."

Kaanyr's handsome brow creased in an angry frown.

"I am not a beggar crying out for your largesse, dwarf," the cambion said. "Without my army's approach, you would still be fighting your way toward Menzoberranzan, one step at a time."

Horgar started to compose an angry retort, but Nimor quickly stepped between the gray dwarf and the half-demon and raised his arms.

"My lords!" he cried. "The only way the Menzoberranyr can defeat you is if the two of you turn on each other. If you cooperate, if you combine your efforts intelligently, the city will fall."

"Indeed," said Zammzt. The plain-faced assassin stood by Vhok's palanquin, shrouded in his dark cloak. "There is little point in dividing the spoils of a city that you have yet to capture. There is even less point in allowing the effort of dividing the spoils to prevent the city's fall in the first place."

"That may be true," Kaanyr said, folding his powerful arms across his broad chest, "but I will not be forgotten when the city is plundered. You brought me here, assassins."

"You brought me here, as well," Horgar rumbled, "and you brought the Agrach Dyrr. I suspect that your secret House will be hard-pressed to honor your promises to all three of your allies. Which of us do you mean to betray, I wonder?"

For the first time, Nimor found himself wondering if perhaps he had arrayed too many enemies against Menzoberranzan all at once. That was the nature of diplomacy in the Underdark, after all. No alliance outlived its usefulness, not even by a heartbeat.

To his surprise, he was rescued by Aliisza.

The alu-fiend draped herself at Kaanyr's side and said, "He will not honor his promises to either of you, as long as the city stands. How can he? We will all go home empty-handed if you cannot come to an agreement."

Nimor inclined his head in gratitude, making a very conscious effort not to allow his eyes to linger on Aliisza for too long when she stood next to Kaanyr Vhok. Somehow he doubted that she'd shared with her master the exact details of her visit to Gracklstugh, and he didn't want to give the half-demon any reason to become curious.

"Lady Aliisza's wisdom is as great as her beauty," he said. "For the sake of avoiding argument, I propose this: To Horgar, five-tenths of Menzoberranzan's wealth, populace, and territory; to Kaanyr Vhok, three-tenths; and for my own House, two-tenths, out of which I will come to terms with the Agrach Dyrr. All subject to final negotiation and adjustment when Menzoberranzan is ours, of course."

"My army outnumbers the cambion's by better than two to one, so why does he gain a share better than half of my own?" Horgar said.

"Because he is here," Nimor said. "Take your army and go home if you like, Horgar, but look around you before you depart. We stand at the Lustrum, the mithral mines of House Xorlarrin. Menzoberranzan controls dozens of treasures such as this, and its castles and vaults are filled with the wealth of five thousand years. If you do not fight, your share will be nothing."

That was the other reason Nimor had chosen the Lustrum as the place to hold his parley. It served as a tantalizing reminder of the true prize that waited.

Horgar's eyes darkened, but the duergar prince turned aside to study the chasm and the gaping adits nearby. Marshal Borwald leaned close and whispered something to the crown prince, and the other lairds muttered among themselves. After a moment, Horgar shifted his thick hands to his belt and cleared his throat.

"All right, then. Subject to final negotiation, we agree. So how do you intend to reduce the city?"

"You will crush Menzoberranzan between your two armies," Nimor said. "Given your victory at the Pillars of Woe, the Lolthites are committed to awaiting your assault in the city proper, but thanks to this maze of passages surrounding the city, they can't know where you'll make your attack. That means the Menzoberranyr will have to maintain a strong force in waiting somewhere near the city's center to respond to whatever point is threatened. The Scoured Legion will provide that threat, and when we force the Lolthites to commit to battle, the army of Gracklstugh will commence its attack and break into the city."

"It's not a bad plan," Kaanyr Vhok observed. "However, it is exactly what the Menzoberranyr must expect us to try, given the situation. They'll be very careful in committing their strength to any one threat."

"Aye," Horgar said. "How will you draw them out, now that you've taught them caution at the Pillars of Woe?"

Nimor smiled. It didn't escape him that Horgar and Kaanyr were examining the tactical problem of defeating Menzoberranzan, instead of quarreling over what they expected to gain from their efforts.

"My brothers and I expect to help in that regard," he said. "We're not numerous but we're well-placed, and, my lords, you have forgotten House Agrach Dyrr."

Horgar and Kaanyr exchanged a nod, even a smile.

Prepare well, Menzoberranzan, Nimor thought. I'm coming.

"I never imagined so many demons in my life," Ryld grunted. He leaned on Splitter, watching as a huge, bat-winged, bloated form spiraled feebly down into the darkness, vainly trying to fly with its wings savaged by blows of the weapons master's great-sword. He straightened and wiped the back of one hand across his brow. "It's getting hotter, too. I hope we're close to whatever we're looking for."

Halisstra and the rest of the company stood nearby, swaying with nausea or trembling with fatigue as the environment and their exertions warranted. For what seemed like hours, they'd continued to fight their way down strand after strand. Sometimes they descended for miles past strands that were empty or held nothing but corpses, but more and more frequently they encountered demons that were alive and hungry. Most of the infernal creatures threw themselves headlong into battle as if all reason had deserted them, but a few retained enough of their intelligence to employ their formidable magical abilities against the interlopers.

With fang, claw, sting, and unholy sorcery the denizens of the Demonweb Pits scoured and scored the drow company. It didn't help that Quenthel had commanded Pharaun to hoard his spells carefully so that the company met each new demonic threat with steel, not the wizard's magic.

"Save your breath, Master Argith," Quenthel said. She slowly straightened from her own fighting crouch, her whip splattered with the gore of a dozen demons. "We must press on."

The company hadn't gone more than another forty yards before their strand shuddered, and an enormous taloned hand appeared from beneath. Clawing its way around from the unseen bottom side of the web, a massive, bison-headed demon with foul, coarse fur sprouting from its shoulders and back hauled itself to the top of the strand and bellowed a vast challenge.

"A goristro!" Pharaun cried. "What in all the hells is that doing here?"

"Some pet of Lolth's that's gotten loose, I don't doubt," Tzirik replied.

The Vhaeraunite priest began to chant a spell, while the others leaped into action. Before the monster could clamber to its feet, Valas feathered it with at least three arrows, the black shafts sprouting from its shoulders and thick neck like pins in a cushion. The goristro snorted in pain and anger, and reached out one hulking hand to pick up the corpse of a small spider-demon nearby. It flung the corpse at Valas, catching the scout as he fished in his quiver for more arrows. The impact staggered Valas, who stumbled and slipped down the side of the strand, cursing in several languages.

Ryld ran forward with Splitter held high, Quenthel at his side, while Halisstra and Danifae carefully tried to circle the beast to one side as best they could on the narrow strand, hoping to surround it on all sides.

Tzirik finished his spell and shouted out a deep, rolling word of power, creating a great whirling disk of spinning razors across the goristro's torso. Blades bit and blood flew, but still the monster came on undeterred.

"What will it take to stop this thing?" Halisstra called. "Does it have any weaknesses?"

"It's stupid," Pharaun replied. "Barely sentient, really. Don't meet it blow for blow."

The wizard gestured and struck the monster with a gleaming green ray of energy that chewed into the goristro's chest, while Tzirik moved in behind Ryld and Quenthel to help them against the monster. The weapons master and the high priestess leaped and slashed at the creature's belly and torso, while dodging the ponderous blows of its enormous fists. One glancing blow spun Quenthel to her hands and knees, but she managed to scramble out of the way before the creature could finish her off.

"Noooot stuuuupiiiid!" roared the goristro.

It lifted one hoofed foot and stamped it down on the strand with such astonishing power that the whole miles-long cable thrummed like something alive. The shock wave threw all of the drow into the air, yet the goristro had failed to anticipate the consequences of its mighty stomp, for the shock threw it into the air as well. The monstrous demon landed awkwardly on its side and slid off the strand, catching itself by one arm dug into the upper surface. It scrambled and kicked, its struggles shaking the strand even more.

Quenthel picked herself up from the trembling surface, and weaved her way past the brute's arm to look down at its face. With a deliberate motion, she flicked her snake-headed whip at one of its beady eyes and destroyed the organ in a sickening burst of gore. The goristro howled in agony and recoiled, losing its grip on the strand and tumbling down into the abyss. Its bellows of rage continued for a long time, diminishing as it fell away from them. She didn't bother to watch it fall. Instead she turned to the rest of the company.

"Get up," she snarled. "We're wasting time."

Halisstra picked herself up from the web and glanced around. Valas scrambled back into view from his precarious position on the side of the strand. Danifae climbed to her feet as well. They followed after Quenthel as the Mistress of Arach-Tinilith set off again at once, moving at an impatient lope as she bounded down the strand. Halisstra was too tired to keep up the pace for long, but she had even less energy for an argument with the single-minded priestess, and so she merely set her jaw and endured.

They reached the bottom—almost.

For some time they'd noticed converging strands drawing closer to their own, and Halisstra could see the reason why. A great ring of webbing a dozen times thicker than any of the gray strands was suspended below them, binding the ends of the strands together. Its circumference was so great that Halisstra could hardly describe a curve at all in the ring's vast arc. In the center there was something—a titanic black structure or island of sorts hanging in the mighty web. The drow paused, surveying the scene, until Valas broke the silence.

"Is that it?" he said in a low voice.

"The entrance to Lolth's domain," Tzirik answered, "lies somewhere within that ring."

"Are you sure?" asked Ryld.

"I am," Quenthel replied for the priest.

She didn't look aside or hesitate, but simply set off again at the same hard pace.

As the strand approached the central ring its steep pitch gradually flattened and thickened somewhat, and for the first time in seemingly endless hours and miles the company found itself traversing something like level ground instead of picking their way down the sloping cable. More demonic and spidery corpses appeared, some half-buried in the strand as if they'd fallen from the limitless heights above—which they most likely had.

The travelers reached the thick ring and crossed one more stretch of twisted webbing only to find that the structure in the center was some kind of immense stone temple, a baroque building of gleaming black obsidian miles in diameter. Spiked stone buttresses soared across the bottomless space, linking the structure to the ring around it. Vast dark plazas of smooth stone large enough to swallow cities surrounded the temple's flanks. Without speaking, the company picked their way over to one of the colossal flying buttresses and advanced toward their goal.

Halisstra found herself trembling, not with exhaustion, but with a combination of terror and ecstasy as she realized that she must soon withstand Lolth's scrutiny in the flesh.

I am worthy, she told herself. *I must be.*

The demons that had plagued their progress through the webs didn't seem to care for the black temple. In any event, no more of the monsters pursued the company once they left the web behind them. For a long time the dark elves simply walked onward, crossing the huge outer plaza, as the walls of the temple came closer and closer, revealing their dark details.

Quenthel oriented their march on a sharp-edged break in the cyclopean wall, a huge cleft that must have been the temple's portico. From time to time they passed the strange, inanimate forms of large, spiderlike beings that seemed to be sculpted from fluid black stone. Oddly enough, the petrified forms grew smaller and smaller the closer they came to the cleft. Halisstra dismissed the mystery from her mind, concentrating only on the goal before her.

At last they reached the mouth of the temple, and looked upon its entrance. A vast face confronted them, the face of a cruelly beautiful dark elf, her features calm and still as if in contemplation. Perfect black stone barred the entrance from one side to the other, sculpted into the image of the Spider Queen's visage. Only her half-lidded eyes showed any animation at all. Gazing down blankly at the tiny supplicants below her, Lolth's eyes gleamed with a roiling, hellish glee focused entirely on whatever thoughts or processes lay behind them.

The company stood gazing up in wonder and terror, and Quenthel prostrated herself before the image of her goddess. Halisstra and Danifae joined her at once, groveling on the cold black stone. Even the males dropped to the ground, lying on their faces and averting their eyes. Tzirik, as a priest of Vhaeraun, settled for taking one knee and lowering his gaze respectfully. He didn't serve the Queen of the Demonweb Pits, but he and others of his faith certainly recognized her divinity.

"Great Queen!" called Quenthel. "We have come from Menzoberranzan to beseech you to restore your favor to your priestesses! Our enemies encroach on your holy city and threaten your faithful with destruction. We humbly beg you to instruct us in what we must do to find approval in your eyes. Arm us with your holy might once more, and we will hunt your enemies until their blood fills the Underdark and their souls fill your belly!"

The face did not respond.

Quenthel waited for a long time, still prostrate, then she licked her lips and uttered another prayer. Halisstra and Danifae joined their pleading to hers, and they begged and pleaded with every prayer, every invocation, every catechism they had ever been taught, scraping and groveling at the temple door. The males simply waited, still stretched out on the black stone. After a time, Tzirik moved off a short distance and sat down with his back to the face, communing with his own god. Halisstra ignored him and continued her supplications.

Still the face did not respond.

The three priestesses kept up their pleas for what must have been hours, but finally Quenthel pushed herself upright and gazed full on the visage of Lolth.

"Enough, sisters," said the Mistress of Arach-Tinilith. "The goddess plainly does not deign to answer us at this time."

"Perhaps we are in the wrong place," Pharaun suggested. "Perhaps we must go farther in order for you to offer your prayers."

"There is no place farther to go," Tzirik said, rejoining the party. "Vhaeraun informs me that this is the only point of approach to Lolth's domain through the Abyss. If she refuses to hear you at this spot, she will not hear you anywhere else in this plane."

"But why does she continue to ignore us?" Halisstra asked in a plaintive voice. She climbed to her feet, her heart sick with longing. After all that had happened—the fall of her House, the destruction of her city, the travails of the quest—to stand before Lolth's temple and be ignored was simply incomprehensible. "What more do we have to do?"

Tzirik shrugged and said, "I cannot answer that question."

"Apparently Lolth can't, either," Halisstra said.

She ignored the disapproval and fear that flickered across Quenthel's features, and strode up angrily to stand within arm's reach of the towering face.

"Hear me, Lolth!" she cried. "Answer me! What have we done to earn your displeasure? Where are you?"

"Speak with respect!" hissed Quenthel, her eyes wide with terror.

Ryld quailed, but managed to find the strength to take a couple of steps forward.

"Mistress Melarn . . ." he said, "Halisstra, come away from there. No good—"

"*Lolth!*" Halisstra screamed. "Answer me, damn you!"

She struck the cold stone of the face with her fists, flailing away in futility, in anger. Her mind went empty as animal fury rose up to overthrow her reason. She screamed curses upon her goddess, she battered at the uncaring face until her hands were bruised and bloody, and still no answer came. After a time she found herself

huddled against the cold stone, weeping, her hands broken and useless. Like a lost child, she cried with all the ache in her heart.

"Why? Why?" was all she could manage to say through her sobs.
"Why have you abandoned us? Why do you hate us?"

"You speak heresy," Quenthel said, her voice hard with disapproval. "Have you no faith left, Halisstra Melarn? The goddess will
speak in her own time."

"Do you really believe that still?" Halisstra muttered.

She turned her face away and gave herself up to her tears, no longer caring what Quenthel, or Danifae, or any of the others thought.
She'd had her answer from Lolth.

"Weak . . ." she heard Quenthel whisper.

Standing a short distance from the rest of the company, Tzirik
sighed and said, "Well, that's that, I suppose. Lolth hasn't chosen to
break her silence for you, so now I have something I must do."

He raised his arms and made a complex series of passes, while
muttering dire words of power. The air crackled with energy.
Quenthel's eyes widened as she recognized the spell the Vhaeraunite
spoke.

"Stop him!" she screeched, whirling to face the priest.

She started forward, raising her deadly whips, but Danifae caught
her arm as she rushed past.

"Carefully!" hissed Danifae. "Our bodies are still in Minauthkeep."

"He's creating a gate!" Quenthel snapped. "Here!"

"What are you doing, Tzirik?" Pharaun said with some alarm.

The wizard recoiled a step and prepared a defensive spell, but
Danifae's warning was just enough to cause him to hesitate before
interfering.

Ryld and Valas held their hands as well, uncertain of what would
happen if they harmed the cleric whose spell had brought them to
Lolth's door. The weapons master and the mercenary drew their
weapons but halted there.

"Pharaun, what should we do?" Ryld said.

Before the wizard could answer, Tzirik finished his spell. With an enormous tearing sound, a great black rift appeared in the air beside the Jaelre priest.

"I am here, my lord!" he cried into the rift. "I stand before the Face of Lolth!"

And from the depths of blackness within the rift, a voice of ineffable power, of terrible potency, answered, *"Good. I come."*

The blackness seemed to stir, and from the rift stepped something that had the size and shape of a lean, graceful drow male, but was obviously something more. Dressed in black leather, a purple mask draped over his face, the being radiated puissance and presence, his form almost quivering with the potentialities he contained. Even Halisstra, absorbed in her own misery with her back turned to the scene, whipped her head around as she sensed the being's arrival. With imperious ease, the being surveyed the plain of dark stone and the black temple.

"It is as I thought," he said to Tzirik, who had fallen prostrate at his feet. *"Rise, my son. You have done well, and brought me to a place from which I was barred."*

"I have only done as you commanded, Masked Lord," Tzirik said, standing slowly.

"Tzirik," Quenthel managed in a strangled voice, "what have you done?"

"He has opened a gate for me," the being who could only be a god said, with a cruel smile on his face. *"Do you not recognize the son of your own goddess, priestess of Lolth?"*

"Vhaeraun," Quenthel breathed.

The god folded his arms and drifted past the company of Menzoberranyr to confront the perfect stone visage, giving the mortals no further thought. He made a small shooing gesture with his left hand, and Halisstra, still huddled before the face, was violently hurled aside. She flew spinning through the air and landed badly at least thirty yards away, tumbling to a halt on the fluted ebon stone of the plaza.

"Dear Mother," Vhaeraun said, addressing the face, *"you were foolish to leave yourself in such a state."*

The god spontaneously began to grow, his radiance increasing as he soared to a height taller than a storm giant, scaling himself to the task at hand. He held out his hand, and from out of nowhere a black, gleaming sword made of shadows appeared in his grip, sized to his towering form.

A spearcast distant, Halisstra groaned and raised her eyes from the cold stone under her aching body. The Menzoberranyr stood paralyzed by indecision. Tzirik, on the other hand, watched smugly as Vhaeraun levitated upward to confront Lolth's gaze directly, blade in hand. With careful deliberation, the Masked Lord drew back his sword of shadows, his mask twisting into a rictus of hatred.

And Vhaeraun hewed at the Face of Lolth with all his godly might.

The sound of Vhaeraun's sword hammering at the great stone barrier shook the entire plane. Each blow set the great black fane at the web's center shuddering with the force of an earthquake, and from the center the reverberations pulsed through the immense gray cables that soared up into the endless night. Even though each stroke knocked her back down to the cold flagstones, Halisstra managed to stumble over to the company of Menzoberranyr, who, like her, staggered from side to side, trying to keep their balance in the face of Vhaeraun's assault.

Tzirik stood aside, still rapt with the glory of his god's presence, somehow able to ignore the damage the Masked Lord was wreaking as the shock waves passed through him with no effect. At each blow, a tiny network of glowing green cracks in the Face of Lolth seemed to spread just a little wider. Despite the incalculable force of each stroke of the god's blade, the visage of the Spider Queen seemed almost, but not quite, invulnerable to his assault.

The goddess does not respond, Halisstra thought in bleak amazement. She doesn't care.

She fell to her hands and knees amid the rest of the company, who ignored her, stupefied as they were by Vhaeraun's wrathful assault. Ryld knelt behind Splitter, averting his eyes and stoically enduring the punishing blows. Valas danced about in agitation, waving his arms, jerking his legs up and down like a spider on a pin. The scout didn't know whether to watch, run, or hide, and seemed to be trying to do all three at once. Pharaun levitated a foot or two above the ground to avoid the trembling impacts, shielding himself with some kind of spell as his eyes flicked from his companions to the god to Tzirik and back to Vhaeraun. Danifae, crouched nearby him, rolled with easy grace, keeping her feet beneath her as she watched each blow with a fierce, measuring gaze. Quenthel stood as stiffly as a statue, hammered by each tremor, her arms wrapped around her torso as if to hold in her distress. She watched the scene with a sick fascination, incapable of anything more.

Pharaun managed to break himself free of his indecision. He drifted close to Quenthel and seized her by the arm.

"What's happening here?" the wizard shouted in her ear. "What is he doing?"

The Baenre ground her teeth in frustration.

"I don't know," she admitted. "This is all wrong. It's not the same. There are no souls here."

"What souls?" the wizard asked. "Should we interfere?"

Both Ryld and Valas glanced up at that, their faces stricken.

"He's a *god*," Ryld managed to call out above the deafening clamor. "What do you propose we do?"

"Fine, then. Do we stay and watch, or do we leave? This doesn't seem to be a safe place to be," Pharaun replied.

Another shock wave lashed through the company, causing the wizard's spell shield to flare brightly.

"I'm not sure we can leave, even if we want to," Ryld said. He jerked his head at Tzirik, who watched the scene with an expression of dark joy behind his mask. "Don't we need him?"

"Should we leave, even to save ourselves?" Valas added. "We would seem to be culpable for—this." The scout shielded his eyes from the sight of Vhaeraun's efforts. "What happens when he breaches the temple? Mistress, what will happen? Is Lolth in there?"

Quenthel let out a shriek of despair.

Danifae fell at Quenthel's feet and asked, "Mistress, have you been here? Have you been here before?"

"I don't know!" the Mistress of Arach-Tinilith shouted.

She jerked her arm away from Pharaun and stormed over to Tzirik, weaving as the ground trembled underfoot. She spun him away from the facade of the temple, tearing him away from the dark adoration of his god, and gripped the breastplate of his armor with her hands.

"Why is he doing his?" she demanded. "What have you done, heretic?"

Tzirik blinked and shook his head, his eyes behind his mask still full of the glory of his epiphany.

"You do not know what you are witnessing, priestess of Lolth?" Tzirik said. He laughed deeply. "You have the rare good fortune to be present at the destruction of your goddess." He disentangled Quenthel's hands from his armor and took a step back, his voice rising in exultant glee. "You wish to know what is going on here, Lolthite? I will tell you. The Masked Lord is going to unseat your Spider Queen and overthrow her black tyranny forever! Our people will finally be freed of her venomous influence, and you and the rest of your parasitic kind will be swept away as well!"

Quenthel snarled in feral rage, "You will not live to see it!"

Her whip sprang into her hand, and she drew her arm back to flay the triumph from Tzirik's face. Before she'd even started her lash, Vhaeraun—a bowshot distant, his back to the company as he chiseled and bludgeoned at the growing crack in the stone visage—waved his left hand without turning around. From beneath Quenthel's feet a column of seething black magma exploded, hurling her dozens of feet into the air with bone-breaking force. Tzirik, standing almost within arm's length, was untouched, but the rest of the company scattered to avoid the hot, stone-shattering impacts of great round blobs of the molten rock.

The god didn't even break his hammerlike rhythm of blow after blow. He struck again and again, even as Quenthel plummeted back down to the flagstones of the plaza, screaming as gobs of the infernal rock clung to her flesh and burned. Valas and Ryld ran to her aid. Danifae cringed, but kept her eyes on the god engaged in his assault.

Pharaun studied the scene, and shook his head.

"This is insane," he muttered.

He made a curious gesture with his hand and disappeared, tele-porting away to some presumably safer locale. Halisstra saw him leave, and stood staring for one long moment before another impact of Vhaeraun's sword threw her to the ground. She lay there, defeated, while Quenthel thrashed and shrieked in agony nearby.

"Ah," breathed Vhaeraun. The god backed away from the face, which was split by a glowing green scar from the center of the fore-head straight down the bridge of the nose and across the lips to the cleft of the chin. *"Mother, have you nothing to say even now? Will you die in silence?"*

The face remained impassive, the roiling light in the introspec-tive eyes unchanged, but once again something seemed to tear the very fabric of the cosmos with a horrible ripping sound. A black gash appeared in the air near the face, and from it stepped another divine form.

Where Vhaeraun was lean and impossibly graceful, the newcomer was a thing of nightmare. Half spider and half drow, it clutched an armory of swords and maces in its six thickly muscled arms, and each of its chitinous legs ended in a vicious pincerlike claw. Its face, perversely enough, was that of a handsome drow male.

"Depart, Masked One," the spider-god commanded in a tortured, burbling voice. *"It is forbidden for you to intrude here."*

"Do not presume to stand between me and my destiny, Selvetarm," Vhaeraun snarled.

The monstrous spider-god Selvetarm waited no longer, but

darted forward with blinding speed, weaving his sextuple blades in an irresistible assault that might have dismembered a dozen giants in the space of two heartbeats.

Vhaeraun whirled aside, dancing through the storm of steel as if he chased Selvetarm's weapons instead of the other way around, parrying blows he found too inconvenient to elude and riposting with supernal grace. When the gods' weapons met, thunderclaps shook the ground.

Halisstra pushed herself upright, gaping in amazement. She might have stood transfixed at the scene indefinitely, but Ryld appeared at her elbow.

"We need your healing songs," he hissed. "Quenthel is badly burned."

What does it matter? Halisstra wondered.

Still, she climbed to her feet and made her way over to the fallen priestess. Quenthel writhed on the ground, hissing between her teeth as she strove unsuccessfully to master her pain. Ignoring the impossible duel that raged back and forth between the two deities, Halisstra focused on the Baenre's injuries and managed to begin the discordant threnody of a *bae'qeshel* song. She laid her hands on Quenthel's burns and wove as best she could, finding a momentary calm in the exercise of her talents for a tangible and immediate end. Quenthel's thrashings eased, and in a moment she opened her eyes. Her spells cast, Halisstra merely slumped down again and stared at the battling gods.

"What do we do?" she whispered. "What can we possibly do?"

"Endure," Ryld replied. He gripped her arm with one iron hand and met her eyes. "Wait and watch. Something will happen."

He looked back toward Vhaeraun and Selvetarm, too.

Valas rose from Quenthel's side and made his way over to Tzirik, crouching to keep his balance.

"Tzirik! What happens to this place, to us, if Vhaeraun defeats Selvetarm and destroys the face? Can you get us out of here?"

"What happens to us does not matter," answered the priest.

"Maybe not to you, but it matters greatly to me," Valas muttered. "Did you bring us here only to die, Tzirik?"

"I did not bring you here, mercenary, you brought me," the priest replied, giving Valas only a fraction of his attention. "None but the Spider Queen's priestesses could get this close to her temple, not even the Masked Lord. As to what happens when Vhaeraun defeats Selvetarm, well, we shall see."

He turned his full attention back to the dueling gods.

The Masked Lord and the Champion of Lolth fought on furiously. Ichor oozed from several black wounds in the half-spider's chitinous body, and dripping black shadow flowed from a handful of sword cuts that had kissed the graceful Vhaeraun. While the gods strove together in the realm of the physical, exchanging blows at a dizzying rate, they also confronted each other magically and psychically at the same time. Spells of terrible power blasted back and forth between them, deadlier even than Selvetarm's six weaving weapons. Their eyes locked on each other with a tangible contest whose potency tugged at what was left of Halisstra's reason, even from a hundred yards away. Missed blows and deflected spells caused terrible damage all around the two deities, gouging great craters in the walls of the temple and the flagstones of the plaza, and more than once coming perilously close to annihilating the mortal onlookers through sheer mischance.

"Treacherous jackal!" snarled Selvetarm. *"Your perfidy will not be rewarded!"*

"Simpleminded fool. Of course it shall," Vhaeraun retorted.

He leaped in among Selvetarm's flurrying blades and punched his shadow sword deep into the spider-god's bulbous abdomen. The Champion of Lolth shrieked and recoiled, but a moment later he seized Vhaeraun's ankle with one pincer and jerked the god to the ground. As quick as a cat he rained a torrent of deadly blows down on the Masked Lord.

Vhaeraun responded by invoking a colossal blast of burning shadowstuff that plunged straight down from some impossible height overhead and bathed both gods in black fire. Selvetarm roared in divine anguish, even as he hammered again and again at Vhaeraun.

With a horrible grinding sound that Halisstra and the other

onlookers felt in their very bones, the stone plaza disintegrated beneath them.

Still locked in their furious struggle, the two deities fell through the great temple island into the black abyss that waited below. Their roars of rage and the ground-shaking clamor of their weapons grew fainter and fainter as they fell away into the pit.

"They're gone," Ryld said numbly, stating the obvious. "Now what?"

No one had an answer for him, as the company gaped at the castle-sized shaft into nothingness the gods had left behind them. Distant flickers of light still danced from their battle, far below. For the space of several minutes the drow did nothing, climbing back to their feet, no one speaking at all. Tzirik merely folded his arms and waited.

"Did they destroy each other?" Valas ventured at last.

"I doubt it," Danifae said.

She looked thoughtfully at the glowing green crack that split Lolth's face, but said nothing more.

"If Lolth didn't care to respond to Vhaeraun's assault, I doubt she'll have anything to say to us," Ryld said. "We should get out of here."

The weapons master turned to speak to Tzirik, only to find that the Jaelre priest was locked in rapt attention, staring off into nothing, his expression alight with adoration.

"Yes, Lord," he whispered to no one. "Yes, I obey!"

Even as Ryld stepped forward to question the priest, the Jaelre priest gestured and spoke an unholy prayer. A whirling field of thousands of razor-sharp blades like that he'd used against the goristro sprang into existence a short distance around him, barricading Tzirik behind a cylindrical wall of tumbling metal.

Ryld yelped a curse and leaped backward, throwing himself out of the path of the murderous blades.

Tzirik ignored the weapons master, continuing with whatever task Vhaeraun had assigned him. With fumbling fingers the cleric drew a case from his belt and extracted a scroll, unrolled it, and began to read aloud from the parchment, beginning the words of another powerful spell while protected from the Menzoberranyr by his deadly barrier.

Halisstra looked up at him in dull surprise, trying to discern what spell the Jaelre priest was casting. It was difficult to bring herself to care any longer.

Even as Halisstra sank back down in apathy and despair, the fight rekindled in Quenthel. She surged up, groping for her whip.

"It's another gate!" she screamed. "Do not let him finish that spell!"

🕷 🕷 🕷

A few hundred yards distant, cloaked in darkness and drifting vapors, Pharaun sat cross-legged on the hard stone, hurrying to finish his spell. He'd watched the two gods battle to a standstill and plummet out of sight, but he was committed to his course and did not intend to stop. The spell of sending could not be cast quickly, and if he attempted to rush it, he would lose it all together. In the part of his mind that was not absorbed in the shaping of the magic, he wondered with no little trepidation whether the gods' omniscience might be complete enough to note his presence, note that he was casting a spell, and deduce why he was casting it—and whether the gods would deign to stop him. As best he could tell from his safe distance, though, Vhaeraun and Selvetarm were occupied with their fierce battle and were unlikely to be paying him much attention.

He completed the spell and whispered the message it would carry for him through the incalculable distances of dimensions and space, "Jeggred. We are in mortal peril. Slay Tzirik's physical body at once. We will return quickly, but guard us until we do. Quenthel commands it."

Pharaun sighed and stood, his expression thoughtful. The sending was reliable, but he didn't know for certain the effects of attempting it from another plane of existence. Nor did he know how long it would take his words to reach Jeggred back in Minauthkeep, or if the draegloth would choose to do as he asked even in Quenthel's name . . . or even if the cursed half-demon was still alive and free to kill the high priest.

The Master of Sorcere had a good sense of what to expect if all went as he hoped. It was only a matter of time, and not much at that.

"This would not be a good time to become obstinate, Jeggred," Pharaun muttered, even though his sending was gone already. "For once, do as I ask without question."

Warily, he began to creep back toward the distant cleft in the temple's massive wall.

Surrounded by his tumbling wall of blades, Tzirik stood aside from the rest of the company, quickly and expertly reading aloud from his scroll. He didn't bother explaining to the Menzoberranyr what Vhaeraun had told him to do, or why he was doing it. He simply proceeded as if they were not there at all, though he'd taken the precaution of raising a blade barrier to keep them from interfering.

Ryld and Valas stood close to the deadly, spinning razors, watching helplessly as the priest droned on. Danifae and Quenthel crouched a little father back, equally helpless, the determination to do something battling with their inability to discern what, exactly, they could do. Halisstra stood watching as well, but she merely waited to see what form her doom would take.

"Tzirik, stop!" cried Valas. "You have put us all in sufficient peril today. We will not allow you to continue."

"Kill him, Valas," Danifae said. "He will not listen, and he will not stop."

The scout stood paralyzed as the priest's chant approached the final, triumphant notes. His shoulders slumped, stricken with defeat. Without warning, Valas brought up his shortbow and fired.

The first arrow was deflected by a whirling blade in the magical barrier, but the second passed through cleanly and pierced Tzirik's gauntleted hand. The priest cried out in pain and dropped his scroll, which fluttered to the stone plaza, unexpended.

The Jaelre whirled on Valas, eyes afire with hate through his masked helm, and said, "Are you still the bitches' errand-boy, Valas? Don't you see that you're nothing but a well-heeled dog to them? Why do you persist in giving the Spider Queen your loyalty, when you could take the Masked Lord for your god and know true freedom?"

"Lolth will do as she will," Valas answered. "I, however, am loyal to Bregan D'aerthe, and to my city. We can't allow you, or even your god, to deflect us from our quest, Tzirik."

Tzirik's face clouded and he said, "You and your companions will not gainsay the will of Vhaeraun. I refuse to permit it."

He crouched and raised his shield, snarling out the words of another divine spell. Valas fired again, but his arrows only ricocheted from the priest's shield. Tzirik finished his spell and placed his wounded hand on the ground. A powerful tremor blasted through the stone and bludgeoned the Menzoberranyr, flinging them about like dolls and ripping open great cracks in the substance of the stone plain, crevices that led into absolute blackness below.

Valas staggered back and forth, trying to keep his balance as the stones cracked and buckled beneath him. Danifae steadied herself and snapped off a shot with her crossbow that passed through the blades and struck Tzirik a ringing hit on the breastplate, but the bolt shivered into pieces on the priest's armor.

Quenthel managed a desperate, off-balance leap to keep from toppling into a gaping crevice beneath her. She rolled awkwardly, and came up with a short iron rod in her hand. The high priestess barked a command word and discharged a white sphere of some magical, viscous substance at the priest, but Tzirik's seething blades ripped apart the viscid glob in a spray of gluey strands.

"Get up, Halisstra," Quenthel hissed. "Your sister priestesses need you!"

The powerful tremors took Halisstra's feet out from under her the first time she tried to stand. She shook her head and tried again.

My sisters need me? she thought. Strange, as our goddess apparently has no use for any of us who serve as her priestesses. If Lolth chooses to turn her back on me, to spurn my faithfulness and devotion, then the least I can do is return the favor.

Throughout Halisstra's life she had willingly joined ranks with her worst enemies, her most bitter rivals, when something rose to threaten the absolute dominion over dark elf society she and her sister priestesses shared. Staring off into the endless, empty expanse of the Demonweb Pits, she found that she would not take one single step in Lolth's name.

"Let him do as he will," she said to Quenthel. "Lolth has taught me not to care. If we managed to preserve Lolth's very existence today, do you think she would be grateful? If I tore my own heart out and laid it on the Spider Queen's altar, do you think she would be pleased by my sacrifice?"

Bitter laughter welled up in her throat and Halisstra gave herself over to it, even as Tzirik's tremors subsided. Her heart ached with a hurt that could rend the world in two, but she could not find a voice for it.

Quenthel stared at her in horror.

"Blasphemy," she managed to whisper.

The Mistress of Arach-Tinilith gathered up her whip and turned on Halisstra, but before she could strike, Tzirik struck with another spell, scouring the entire party with sheets of incandescent flames that raced back and forth across the stone plain like water sloshing on a plate. Halisstra threw herself flat and cried out in pain. The others cursed or cried out, scrabbling for cover that did not exist.

"Leave me!" Tzirik commanded from within his cage of whirling steel.

He stooped down and picked up his scroll, while the Menzoberranyr picked themselves up from the smoking stones.

Ryld rose slowly, his flesh seared at face and hands, and watched as the cleric started to cast his spell again. The weapons master eyed the spinning blades surrounding the priest, and with the quickness of a big cat, he gathered up his legs and sprang into the barrier, crouching low into the tightest ball possible. Droplets of blood splattered nearby as the whirling magical blades sparked and sliced against the weapons master's dwarven armor, drawing blood in a dozen places—but the Master of Melee-Magthere was through the barrier.

He staggered to his feet with an animal grunt of pain, Splitter gripped awkwardly in his slashed hands, but he managed to drive at Tzirik with the point of the greatsword. Once again the cleric was forced to drop his scroll. He parried the thrust with his shield and lashed back with his spiked mace.

Ryld avoided the blow only by leaping backward, so close to the whirling blades that sparks flew from his shoulders as the razors kissed his back. He recovered and glided forward again, spinning his deadly sword and slashing quickly at the Jaelre cleric.

Valas, standing outside the whirling blades, reached up to the nine-pointed star token on his breast and touched it. In the blink of an eye he vanished, reappearing inside the barrier behind Tzirik. He dropped his bow and drew his kukris, but Tzirik surprised him.

Turning his back on Ryld, the strong cleric took three power-ful strides and slammed his heavy shield into the Bregan D'aerthe even as Valas got his knives in hand. With a roar of anger the Jaelre shoved Valas back into the curtain of deadly razors and sent the scout stumbling through, spinning and screaming as the blades sliced his flesh.

Ryld made Tzirik pay by darting forward to strike out with a full double-handed slash across the torso that spun the priest half around, but the cleric's plate armor held against the blow. In re-sponse, Tzirik leaped in close to Ryld, inside the fighter's reach, and rained down a barrage of wicked blows with the spiked mace, driving the weapons master back.

Ryld gathered himself for another assault, but at that moment Quenthel hurled herself through the blades as well. One sliced her calf deeply and sent her stumbling when she passed through, and she went to one knee with a gasp of pain, blocking Ryld. Tzirik stepped back out of reach of the Baenre's whip, and quickly called out a spell.

Ryld froze in place as the cleric ensnared him, freezing his will and paralyzing his muscles.

Quick as a snake, Tzirik turned on Quenthel and hammered her to the ground even as she tried to stand on her injured leg. Avoiding the hissing serpent heads, Tzirik kicked her whip back outside the curtain of blades, and turned to crush Ryld's skull while the weapons master was helpless before him. The bronze mace drew back for the lethal blow—and Tzirik was sent reeling away from his intended victim, battered by a powerful blast of sound.

Halisstra, standing just on the other side of the blades, followed with a second *bae'qeshel* song and scoured the cleric again. She would not fight for Lolth again, but she would fight for her companions, Ryld in particular.

"Do not kill the priest," she called to her companions. "We need him to bring us home!"

"What do you suggest, then?" Danifae snapped from beside her. "He seems intent on destroying us!"

"Indeed," said Tzirik.

The Jaelre priest recovered from Halisstra's spells and lashed out with one of his own, calling down from the black skies above a column of crawling purple fire that blasted Halisstra and Danifae. The cleric wheeled to confront Quenthel, who was just gathering herself to leap at his back. He hefted his mace.

"I take great pleasure in slaying clerics of the Spider Queen," Tzirik said. "When you awake in Minauthkeep, I'll slay you again there."

He advanced on her, his cruel eyes alight as Quenthel hobbled awkwardly, seeking to dodge the inevitable blow.

Tzirik's breastplate simply vanished. The cleric halted in consternation, and glanced down. All other pieces of his full plate armor remained in place, but then—slowly—his arming coat vanished as well, revealing the smooth black flesh of his torso and chest.

"What in the Masked Lord's name?" he muttered, and glanced up just in time to turn away from Danifae, who shot a bolt at his heart that instead caught the cleric's shield. His mystification turned

I could think of no other options. I told Jeggred you ordered it, since I was not certain he would kill the cleric simply because I asked him to."

"Your cowardice ripped us away from the one place we had a hope of winning our answers," Quenthel growled.

"No," said Halisstra. "Pharaun's prudence engineered our escape from an impossible situation, in the one manner that had any hope of working."

"What is the point of escaping, when we failed to complete our quest?" the Baenre demanded.

"Answers? There were no answers to be had, Quenthel," Halisstra said. "We could have abased ourselves before her until the end of time, and the Spider Queen could not have cared less. The quest was pointless—and it was a quest you were never certain of anyway. Or were there storehouses to raid in the Abyss?"

"I let your blasphemy and pridefulness pass in the Demonweb Pits, girl, but I will not do so again," Quenthel said. "If you speak to me again in such a manner, I will have your tongue torn out at the roots. You will be punished for your lack of faith, Halisstra Melarn. The Spider Queen will visit unimaginable torments upon you for your lack of respect."

"At least that would be a sign that she lives," Halisstra replied.

She stood and began to gather her belongings. In the stone halls beyond their chamber, she could hear distant shouts of alarm and the clatter of many feet coming nearer. It seemed almost beneath her notice.

"The Jaelre are coming," Danifae said. "They might have something to say about the evisceration of their high priest."

"I would prefer not to have to cut my way out of this castle," Ryld offered. "I've had my fill of fighting today."

With a low growl, Quenthel tore her attention away from Halisstra and studied the small chamber. She chewed her lip in agitation, as if wrestling with an idea she didn't like, then she muttered a curse and turned to Pharaun.

"Do you have a spell that can get us out of here?"

Pharaun smirked, obviously pleased that Quenthel had been forced to resort to his powers so quickly after condemning his actions.

"It's a bit of a stretch, but I think I can teleport us all at once," he said. "Where do we wish to go? I can't bring us safely into the Underdark, but other than that. . . ."

"Anywhere but here," Quenthel replied. "We need time to consider what we've seen and learned, and what we must do next."

"The cave mouth the portal from the Labyrinth led to," Valas said. "It's several days' march from here, and not heavily traveled."

"Fine," Quenthel snapped. "Take us."

"Join hands, then," Pharaun said.

He placed his own hand over Ryld's and Halisstra's, and spoke a short phrase just as the first blows sounded on the panel of the secret door. In the blink of an eye they stood on the cold, mossy ground of the cave mouth in the forest clearing. It was close to dawn. The skies to the east were pearly gray, and cold dew lay heavy around their feet. The glen was as empty and cheerless as it had been the first time the company camped there, a little more than a tenday past. Most of the snow had melted off, and icy water trickled into the sinkhole and ran out of sight beneath the hill.

"Here we are," the wizard announced. "Now, if nobody minds too much, I believe I am going to find the most comfortable spot I can in the cavern below and sleep like a damned human."

He clambered down the slippery rocks without waiting for a response.

"Take your rest later, wizard," Quenthel called after him. "We must determine what we need to do next, the meaning of the things we saw—"

"What we saw has no meaning," Halisstra said, "and what we do next does not matter. I'm with Pharaun."

She summoned up the strength to leap lightly from boulder to boulder, descending back into the comforting and familiar darkness of the cavern below.

Behind her Quenthel fumed and Jeggred rumbled in displeasure, but Ryld and Valas shouldered their packs and followed Pharaun down into the cave. Danifae turned to the Baenre priestess and rested one hand on her shoulder.

"We are all troubled by what we've seen," the battle captive said, "but we're exhausted. We'll all think more clearly when we have had some rest, and perhaps then the goddess's will might be more plain to us."

Grudgingly, Quenthel nodded in assent, and the rest followed into the cave. Halisstra and Pharaun had already thrown themselves down on the pebbled floor of the cavern a few dozen yards from the entrance, shucking their packs and leaning back against the walls. The rest of the Menzoberranyr filed in slowly and picked out their own spots, collapsing wherever they happened to stop moving.

Seyll's bloodstained armor seemed unbearably heavy on Halisstra's shoulders, and the hilt of the Eilistraeean's sword jammed painfully into her ribs. She was too tired to find a better position.

"Will no one tell me what happened in the Demonweb Pits?" Jeggred railed. "I have waited in that empty stone room for days, guarding your sleeping bodies faithfully. I deserve to hear what happened."

"You will," Valas answered. "Later. I don't believe any of us rightly know what to make of it. Give us time to rest, and to reflect."

Rest? Halisstra thought.

She felt as if she could sleep—sleep in the unconscious and helpless manner of a human—for a tenday and not feel healed of the fatigue she carried. Her mind refused to reflect any longer on why Lolth had abandoned her, yet she had something in her heart that demanded examination, a grief that would not permit her the refuge of the Reverie until she had found some way to let it out.

With a sigh, she pulled her satchel close and opened it, taking out the leather case of her lyre. She carefully unsheathed the heirloom, running her fingers over the rune-carved dragonbone arms, touching the perfect mithral wire.

At least I still have this, she thought.

In the silence of the forest cave, Halisstra played the dark songs of the *bae'qeshel*, and softly gave voice to her unbearable grief.

THE CITY OF SPLENDORS
A WATERDEEP NOVEL
ED GREENWOOD AND ELAINE CUNNINGHAM

In the streets of Waterdeep, conspiracies run like water
through the gutters, bubbling beneath the seeming calm
of the city's life. As a band of young lords discovers there
is a dark side to the city they all love, a sinister mage and
his son seek to create perverted creatures to further their
twisted ends.

And across it all sprawls the great city itself: brawling,
drinking, laughing, living life to the fullest.

Even in the face of death.

Other titles available in The Cities series:

THE CITY OF RAVENS
RICHARD BAKER

TEMPLE HILL
DREW KARPYSHYN

THE JEWEL OF TURMISH
MEL ODOM

For more information visit **www.wizards.com**